THE
SHORT NOVELS
OF
DOSTOEVSKY

*Translated from the Russian
by Constance Garnett*

The Short Novels of

DOSTOEVSKY

With an Introduction
by THOMAS MANN

A PERMANENT LIBRARY BOOK

DIAL PRESS   **NEW YORK**

*These novels are published
by special arrangement with
The Macmillan Company*

Tenth Printing

Printed in the United States of America
by The Haddon Craftsmen, Scranton, Pa.

Contents

⟞⟝

Contents

PREFACE

DOSTOEVSKY — in Moderation

BY

THOMAS MANN

THERE was something very attractive to me about the invitation on the part of the Dial Press to write a preface to an edition of Dostoevsky's shorter novels, the six narratives included in this volume. The publisher's moderation which determined the character of this edition tended to put the commentator's mind at ease and to encourage him in a task from which he might otherwise have shrunk, not to say recoiled—the task of making the entire, tremendous cosmos of Dostoevsky's works the object of his consideration and discussion. Moreover this commentator would scarcely have had another chance in this life to render his critical tribute to the great Russian if it had not been for this opportunity to do it lightly, so to speak, in a limited space, for a specific purpose, and with the degree of self-restriction which the purpose charitably prescribes.

Strangely enough, my life as an author led me to write detailed studies on Tolstoy as well as on Goethe—several on each of them. But I have never formally written on two other cultural experiences of similar weight that moved me as deeply in my youth and that I never tired of renewing and intensifying in my mature years: I have never written on Nietzsche nor on Dostoevsky. I omitted writing the Nietzsche essay for which my friends often asked me, although it seemed to lie on my path. And the "profound, criminal, saintly face of Dostoevsky" (that was my characterization at one time) appears only fleetingly in my writings to vanish again quickly. Why this evasion, this shunning, this silence—in contrast with the inadequate, to be sure, but enthusiastic eloquence to which the greatness of the other two masters and stars inspired me? I know the answer. It was easy for me to render intimate and rapturous homage, tempered with tender irony, to the images of the divine and the fortunate, the children of nature in their exalted simplicity and their exuberant healthfulness: to the autobiographic aristocratism of the molder of a majestic personal culture, Goethe, and to the primitive epic force, the unrivaled naturalness, of the "great author of all the Russias," Tolstoy, with his clumsy, ever failing attempts at moralistic spiritualization of his pagan corporeality. But I am filled with awe, with a profound, mystic, silence-enjoining awe, in the presence of the religious greatness of the damned, in the presence of genius of disease and the disease of genius, of the type of the afflicted and the possessed, in whom saint and criminal are one. . . .

It is my feeling that the Daemonic is the poet's theme and not the writer's. It should speak from the depths of a work, if possible, in the garb of humor; to devote critical essays to it seems to me, mildly, an indiscretion. Possibly, even probably, this is only an extenuation of my indolence and cowardice. It is incomparably easier and more whole-some to write about divinely pagan healthfulness than about holy disease. We may amuse ourselves at the expense of the former, the fortunate children of nature and their artlessness; we cannot amuse ourselves at the expense of the children of the spirit, the great sinners and the damned, the sufferers of holy disease. I would find it utterly impossible to jest about Nietzsche and Dostoevsky as I have occasion-ally done in a novel about the egotistic child of a lucky star, Goethe, and in an essay about the colossal loutishness of Tolstoy's moralism. It follows that my reverence for the intimates of Hell, the devout and the diseased, is fundamentally much deeper—and only therefore less vocal —than my reverence for the sons of light. It is a good thing that this reverence of mine has now received an outward incentive to eloquence, though of a practically limited and restrained nature.

"The Pale Criminal"—whenever I read this chapter heading in *Zarathustra,* a morbidly inspired work of genius if ever there was one, the eerily grief-ridden features of Dostoevsky, as we know them from a number of good pictures, stand before me. Moreover, I suspect that they were in the mind of the drunken migrainist of Sils Maria when he wrote it. For Dostoevsky's work played a remarkable role in his life; he frequently mentions him in his letters as well as in his books (while I am not aware that he ever said a word about Tolstoy); he calls him the most profound psychologist in world literature and refers to him in a kind of unassuming enthusiasm as his "great teacher"— although in fact there is scarcely an indication of discipleship in his relation to his great Eastern brother-in-spirit. They were more nearly brothers in spirit, tragically grotesque companions in misfortune, in spite of fundamental differences in heredity and tradition—on the one hand the German professor, whose Luciferian genius, stimulated by disease, developed from the soil of classical learning, philological erudition, idealistic philosophy, and musical Romanticism; on the other, the Byzantine Christian, who was free from the humanistic inhibitions that limited the other, and who could occasionally be regarded as the "great teacher" simply because he was *not German* (for it was Nietzsche's most passionate desire to free himself of his Germanism), because he appeared as the liberator from bourgeois morality, and because he affirmed the will to psychological affront, to the crime of frank acknowledgment.

It seems impossible to speak of Dostoevsky's genius without being forced to think of the word "criminal." The eminent Russian critic Merezhkovsky uses it in various studies on the author of *The Karamazovs,* repeatedly and with a double meaning: referring, in the first place, to Dostoevsky himself and to "the criminal curiosity of his insight," and, in the second place, referring to the object of this insight, the human heart, whose most recondite and *most criminal* impulses he laid bare. "The reader," says this critic, "is aghast at his omniscience, his penetration into the conscience of a stranger. We are confronted by our own secret thoughts, which we would not reveal to a friend, not even to ourselves." Yet we are only apparently dealing with objective and quasi-medical scrutiny and diagnosis—it is in reality psychological lyricism in the widest sense of the word, admission and horrible confession, pitiless revelation of the criminal depths of the author's own conscience—and this accounts for the terrific moral force, the religious frightfulness of Dostoevsky's knowledge of the soul. A comparison with Proust, and with the psychological novelties, surprises, and knickknacks that abound in his works, at once exposes the difference in accent, in moral tone. The psychological curios and pertnesses of the Frenchman are simply amusing compared with the ghastly revelations of Dostoevsky, a man who had been in Hell. Could Proust have written *Crime and Punishment,* the greatest detective novel of all times? It was not the science that he lacked, but the conscience. . . . As far as Goethe is concerned, a psychologist of the first water from *Werther* to the *Elective Affinities,* Goethe declares frankly that he has never heard of a crime of which he did not feel capable himself. This is the word of a disciple of pietistic self-scrutiny but the element of Greek innocence predominates in it. It is a self-possessed word—a challenge to bourgeois morality, to be sure, but cool and haughty rather than filled with Christian contrition, bold rather than profound in a religious sense. Tolstoy was essentially his peer, in spite of all Christian velleity. "I have nothing to conceal from men," he used to say; "let them all know what I am doing!" Compare this with the confessions of the hero of *Notes from Underground* where he speaks of his secret dissipations. "Even at that time," he says, "I had a love for secrecy. I was terribly afraid that someone might see me, meet me, recognize me." His life, which could not bear ultimate frankness, ultimate exposure before the eyes of the world, was ruled by the secret of Hell.

Undoubtedly the subconsciousness and even the consciousness of this titanic creator was permanently burdened with a heavy sense of guilt, a sense of the criminal, and this feeling was by no means of purely hypochondriac nature. It was connected with his infirmity, the "sacred" disease, the pre-eminently mystic disease, epilepsy. He suffered from it from childhood, but the disease was fatally intensified by his trial when he was unjustly accused in the year 1849, at the age of twenty-eight, on a charge of political conspiracy and actually sentenced to death (he was already standing at the stake facing death when, at the last moment, his sentence was commuted to four years at hard labor in Siberia). It was his opinion that the disease would culminate in the exhaustion of his physical and intellectual powers, in death or insanity. The attacks occurred on the average of once a month, sometimes more frequently, at times even twice a week. He often described them: both in direct communication and by transferring the malady to psychologically favored characters in his novels: to the terrible Smerdyakov, to the hero of *The Idiot,* Prince Myshkin, to the nihilist and fanatic Kirilov in *The Possessed.* Two symptoms, according to his description, are characteristic of the falling sickness: the incomparable sense of rapture, of inner enlightenment, of harmony, of highest ecstasy, preceding by a few moments the spasm that begins with an inarticulate, no longer human scream—and the state of horrible depression and deep grief, of spiritual ruin and desolation, that follows it. This reaction seems to me even more symbolic of the nature of the disease than the exaltation that precedes the attack. Dostoevsky describes it as a rapture so strong and sweet "that one is ready to exchange ten years of life or even life itself for the bliss of these few seconds." The subsequent, terrific hangover, however, according to the confession of the great invalid, was marked by a "feeling of being a criminal," by the weight of unknown *guilt,* by the burden of an awful crime.

I don't know what neurologists think of the "sacred" disease, but in my opinion it is definitely rooted in the realm of the sexual, it is a wild and explosive manifestation of sex dynamics, a transferred and transfigured sexual act, a mystic dissipation. I repeat that I regard the subsequent state of contrition and misery, the mysterious feeling of guilt, as even more revealing than the preceding seconds of bliss for which "one is ready to exchange his life." No matter to what extent the malady menaced Dostoevsky's mental powers, it is certain that his genius is most intimately connected with it and colored by it, that his psychological insight, his understanding of crime and of what the Apocalypse calls "satanic depths," and most of all his ability to suggest secret *guilt* and to weave it into the background of his frequently horrible creatures—all these qualities are inseparably related to the disease. In the past of Svidrigailov *(Crime and Punishment),* for example, there is "a criminal affair of bestial, not to say fantastic, brutality, for which he would most certainly have been sent to Siberia." It is left to the more or less willing imagination of the reader to guess what this affair may be: in all probability it is a sex crime, possibly child rape —for this is also the secret or a part of the secret in the life of Stavrogin in *The Possessed,* that icy and contemptible masterful person before whom weaker creatures groveled in the dust, possibly one of the most weirdly attractive characters in world literature. There is an unpublished portion of this novel, "Stavrogin's Confession," in which he relates, among other things, the rape of a little girl. According to Merezhkovsky it is a powerful fragment, full of terrible realism transcending the bounds of art. Apparently this infamous crime constantly occupied the author's moral imagination. It is said that one day he confessed the commission of a sin of this sort to his famous colleague Turgenev, whom he hated and despised on account of his West European sympathies—undoubtedly a mendacious confession with which he merely wished to frighten and confuse the serene, humane, and quite unsatanic Turgenev. In St. Petersburg, when he was forty years old and had attained fame as the author of *The House of Death,* which had moved even the Czar to tears, in a family circle that included a number of very young girls, he once narrated the plot of a story he had planned in his youth, a novel in which a landed proprietor, a sedate and substantial man, suddenly remembers that two decades ago, after an all-night drinking bout with dissolute companions, he had raped a ten-year-old girl.

"Fyodor Mikhailovitch!" the mother of the household exclaimed, raising her hands in horror. "Have pity on us! The children are listening!"

Yes, he must have been a very remarkable citizen, this Fyodor Mikhailovitch.

Nietzsche's infirmity was not the falling sickness, although it is not difficult to picture the author of *Zarathustra* and *The Antichrist* as an epileptic. He shared the fate of many artists and particularly of a notable number of musicians (among whom he belongs after a fashion): he perished from progressive paralysis, a malady of unmistakably sexual origin, since medical science has long recognized it as the result of luetic infection. Viewed from the naturalistic-medical angle—a limited perspective, to be sure—Nietzsche's intellectual development is nothing but the case history of paralytic deterioration and degeneration—that is, he was propelled from a state of highly gifted normality upward into icy and grotesque spheres of fatal insight and moral isolation, a terrible and criminal degree of knowledge for which a delicate and kindhearted man, such as he was, in need of forbearance and indulgence, had never been born but for which, like Hamlet, he had only been called.

"Criminal"—I repeat the word in order to stress the psychological relationship of the cases of Nietzsche and Dostoevsky. It is no mere chance that the former was so strongly attracted to the latter that he called him his "great teacher." Excess is common to them both, the drunken unleashing of insight, coupled with a religious, i. e., satanistic moralism which in Nietzsche's case was called antimoralism. Nietzsche probably did not know the epileptic's mystic sense of guilt of which I spoke. But the fact that his personal conception of life made him familiar with that of the criminal is attested by one of his aphorisms, which I can't find at the moment but which I distinctly remember. In it he says that all intellectual isolation and alienation from the civil norm, all mental autonomy and ruthlessness, are related to the criminal's mode of life and afford an experiential insight into it. It seems to me that we can go even farther and say that all creative originality, all artistry in the widest sense of the word, does just that. The French painter and sculptor Degas once made the remark that the artist must approach his work in the same frame of mind in which the criminal commits his deed.

"Exceptional conditions make the artist," Nietzsche himself said: "all conditions that are profoundly related and interlaced with morbid phenomena; it seems impossible to be an artist and not to be sick." The German thinker probably did not know the nature of his disease, but he was well aware of his debt to it, and his letters and published works are full of heroic eulogies of disease as a means to knowledge. A typical symptom of paralysis, presumably due to hyperemia of the affected cerebral parts, is the surge of an intoxicating sense of bliss and power and an actual—though medically, of course, pathological—intensification of productive capacity. Before it clouds its victim's mind and kills him, the disease grants him illusory (in the sense of sane normality) experiences of power and sovereign facility, of enlightenment and blissful inspiration, so that he stands in awe of himself and is filled with the conviction that there has been no one like him in a thousand years; he regards himself as a divine mouthpiece, a vessel of grace, a god in his own right. We have descriptions of such euphoric affliction and of overwhelming inspiration in the letters of Hugo Wolf, in whose case they were invariably followed by periods of intellectual void and artistic impotence. But the most grandiose account of paralytic enlightenment, a stylistic masterpiece, is found in Nietzsche's *Ecce Homo,* in the third section of the chapter on *Zarathustra.* "Does anyone," he asks, "at the end of the nineteenth century have an idea of what poets of *powerful* eras called inspiration? If not, I shall describe it." It is clear that he regards his experience as something atavistic, something daemonically retrovertive, something belonging to another, more "powerful," more Godlike state of mankind, something foreign to the psychic capabilities of our faintly rationalistic epoch. And to think that what he is in truth describing— but what is truth: experience or medicine?—is a morbid state of irritation that mockingly precedes the paralytic collapse.

Possibly his concept of the "Eternal Return," to which he attaches great weight, is a product of euphoria, uncontrolled by reason, and a reminiscence rather than intellectual property. Merezhkovsky pointed out long ago that the idea of the "Superman" occurs in Dostoevsky, in the speeches of the aforementioned epileptic, Kirilov, in *The Possessed.* Dostoevsky's nihilistic seer says: "There will be a new man and everything will be new. History will be divided into two sections: from the gorilla to the annihilation of God, and from the annihilation of God to the physical transformation of the earth and of man"—in other words, to the appearance of the God-man, the superman. But no one seems to have noted that the idea of the Eternal Return is also to be found in *The Karamazovs,* in Ivan's dialogue with the Devil. "You're always thinking of our present earth!" says the Devil. "But our present earth has repeated itself, possibly *billions of times;* it would become senile, turned to ice, broke in two, fell apart, resolved itself into its elements, once more there was water 'over the firmament,' then the comet, next the sun, and finally, out of the sun, came the earth—this process has perhaps repeated itself times without number and each time *in the identical manner down to the last tiny detail* . . . isn't that the most unspeakably indecent boredom!"

Through the mouth of the Devil Dostoevsky designates as "indecent boredom" what Nietzsche hails with Dionysiac affirmation, adding "For I love you, Eternity!" But the idea is the same, and while I believe that the Superman is a case of coincidence based on intellectual fraternity, I am inclined to regard the "Eternal Return" as a result of reading, a subconscious, euphorically tinged memory of Dostoevsky.

I am aware that I may be making a mistake in chronology; it is a matter for the literary historians to examine. The important thing for me is a certain parallelism in the thinking of the two great invalids and then, moreover, the phenomenon of disease in the form of greatness or greatness in the form of disease—it is purely a matter of perspective in the evaluation of disease: as a diminution or an intensification of life. Considering disease as greatness and greatness as disease, the mere medical point of view proves pedantic and inadequate, at the very least one-sidedly naturalistic: the thing has an intellectual and cultural side, connected with life itself and with its enhancement and growth, a side which the biologist and physician never fully understand. Let us put it into words: a type of humanity matures, or is reconstructed from the forgotten past, which takes the concepts of life and health out of the hands of biology, in which the exclusive right to these concepts has been vested, and presumes to administer them in a freer, more pious, and certainly more truthful manner. For man is not a mere creature of biology.

Disease . . . First of all it is a question of who is sick, who is insane, who is epileptic or paralytic: an average dolt, whose disease, of course, lacks all intellectual and cultural aspects—or a Nietzsche, a Dostoevsky. In their cases the disease bears fruits that are more important and more beneficial to life and its development than any medically approved normality. The truth is that life has never been able to do without the morbid, and probably no adage is more inane than the one which says that "only disease can come from the diseased." Life is not prudish, and it is probably safe to say that life prefers creative, genius-bestowing disease a thousand times over to prosaic health; prefers disease, surmounting obstacles proudly on horseback, boldly leaping from peak to peak, to lounging, pedestrian healthfulness. Life is not finical and never thinks of making a moral distinction between health and infirmity. It seizes the bold product of disease, consumes and digests it, and as soon as it is assimilated, it is health. An entire horde, a generation of open-minded, healthy lads pounces upon the

work of diseased genius, genialized by disease, admires and praises it,
raises it to the skies, perpetuates it, transmutes it, and bequeathes it
to civilization, which does not live on the home-baked bread of health
alone. They all swear by the name of the great invalid, thanks to whose
madness they no longer need to be mad. Their healthfulness feeds
upon his madness and in them he will become healthy.

In other words, certain attainments of the soul and the intellect are
impossible without disease, without insanity, without spiritual crime,
and the great invalids are crucified victims, sacrificed to humanity and
its advancement, to the broadening of its feeling and knowledge—in
short, to its more sublime health. This is the reason for the aura of
devoutness that clearly surrounds the lives of these men and deeply
affects their self-consciousness. It is also the reason for the anticipatory
feelings which these victims have of power and of accomplishment and
of a vastly intensified life despite all suffering; feelings of triumph
that can be regarded as illusory only in a prosaic, medical sense: a
union of disease and power in their natures which scoffs at the ordinary
association of disease and weakness and by its paradoxy contributes
to the religious tinge of their existence. They force us to re-evaluate
the concepts of "disease" and "health," the relation of sickness and
life; they teach us to be cautious in our approach to the idea of "disease," for we are too prone always to give it a biological minus sign.
Nietzsche mentions this very point in a posthumous note to his *Will
to Power*. "Health and disease," he says "—be careful! The standard
must always be the efflorescence of the body, the resilience, courage,
and cheerfulness of the spirit—but naturally also *how much morbidity
it can absorb and conquer*—in other words, *make* healthy." (The
italics are Nietzsche's.) "That which would destroy more delicate men
is a stimulant for *great* healthfulness."

Nietzsche regarded himself as a sound person in the grand manner,
one who is stimulated by disease. But if in his case the relation of
disease and power is such that the greatest sense of power and its productive confirmation appear to be a consequence of disease (which lies
in the nature of paralysis), we are almost compelled in the case of
Dostoevsky the epileptic to regard his disease as a product of super-
abundant power, an explosion, an excess of tremendous health, and
we are confronted by the convincing fact that greatest vitality can at
times wear the mask of pale infirmity.

From the biological point of view the life of this man is most confusing: a quivering bundle of nerves, subject to spasms at a moment's

notice, "so sensitive as if he had been flayed and the mere contact with the air were painful" (quoted from *Notes from Underground*), he nevertheless managed to live a full sixty years (1821-1881), and in his four productive decades he erected a stupendous lifework of an unheard-of novelty and audacity, a surging wealth of passions and visions—a work which not only broadens our knowledge of man by its furor of "criminal" insight and confession, but also contains a surprising amount of mischievous humor, fantastic comedy, and "cheerfulness of the spirit." For, among other things, as the reader of the present edition will soon discover, this crucified man was also a really great humorist.

If Dostoevsky had written nothing else but the six short novels printed here, his name would no doubt still deserve a pre-eminent place in the history of the world's narrative literature. As a matter of fact they do not constitute one-tenth of his actual published writings, and his friends, who were familiar with the inside story of his work, assure us that of all the novels that Fyodor Mikhailovich carried with him in finished form, so to speak, and which he narrated enthusiastically and in detail, not one-tenth was ever put on paper. They say that he required practically no time at all for the elaboration of these countless outlines. And then we are expected to believe that disease represents an impoverishment of life!

The epic monuments which he erected—*Crime and Punishment, The Idiot, The Possessed, The Brothers Karamazov* (incidentally, they are not epics at all but colossal dramas, composed almost scenically, in which the soul-stirring action, often compressed into the period of a few days, unwinds in super-realistic and feverish dialogue)—were created not only under the scourge of disease but also under the blows of debt and degrading financial trouble that forced him to work at an unnatural rate of speed; he tells us that, in order to meet a deadline, he once wrote three and a half signatures—fifty-six pages—in two days and two nights. In foreign countries, in Baden-Baden and in Wiesbaden, where he had to flee from his creditors, he tried to ameliorate his impoverishment by gambling, only in most instances to complete his ruin. Then he would write begging letters in which he speaks the language of misery of the most depraved characters of his novels, of Marmeladov, for example. His passion for gambling was his second disease, possibly related to his first, a truly abnormal craving. To it we owe the wonderful novel *The Gambler,* who goes to a German resort, improbably and perversely named Roulettenburg; in this novel the psychology of morbid passion and of the demon Chance is exposed with unrivaled veracity.

This masterwork was written in 1867, between *Crime and Punishment* (1866) and *The Idiot* (1868-1869), and with all its greatness it represents a mere recreation. It is the latest of the stories in this volume, for the others were produced between 1846 and 1864. The earliest one is *The Double,* a pathological grotesque, which had appeared in the same year with Dostoevsky's first great novel, *Poor People* (1846), and it was a disappointment after the profound impression which the latter had made in Russia—probably with some justification; for in spite of brilliant details of the narrative, the young author was probably in error to believe that he had excelled Gogol, although *The Double* was strongly influenced by him. And he certainly did not surpass Edgar Allan Poe's *William Wilson,* where the same arch-romantic motif is treated in a morally profounder manner, resolving the clinical in the poetic

Be that as it may, our edition includes a number of wonderful "recreations" or perhaps preparations for masterworks to follow. *The Eternal Husband* dates from 1848, before the time of Dostoevsky's trial and deportation to Omsk in Siberia; its central figure is the embarrassingly ludicrous cuckold, from whose malicious anguish the eeriest effects are created. Then follows the period of confinement at hard labor, the horrible experience of the Katorga, which was to be movingly described later in St. Petersburg in *The House of Death,* the tale that stirred all Russia to tears. But the actual resumption of Dostoevsky's literary activity took place in Siberia with the writing (1859) of *The Friend of the Family,* also called *The Manor of Stepantchikovo,* justly famous for the incomparable character of the despotic hypocrite Foma Opiskin, a comic creation of the first rank, irresistible, rivaling Shakespeare and Molière. After this peak performance *Uncle's Dream,* which followed immediately, must frankly be regarded as a retrograde step. It is, if I may judge, too long-drawn-out for its content, a farce, whose tragic conclusion, the story of the tubercular young schoolmaster, is filled with unbearable sentimentalism derived from the early influence of Charles Dickens upon Dostoevsky's work. To make up for it, however, we find in *Uncle's Dream* the lovely Zinaida Afanasyevna, the type of the proud Russian girl, who enjoys the obvious and very suggestive love of an author whose Christian sympathy is ordinarily devoted to human misery, sin, vice, the depths of lust and crime, rather than to nobility of body and soul.

The chief item in our anthology, *Notes from Underground,* written in 1864, is an awe- and terror-inspiring example of this sympathy and this frightful insight. In its content it comes closest to Dostoevsky's great and completely characteristic products. In general it is regarded as a turning point in the poet's activity, as an awakening to a consciousness of himself. Today, when the painful and scornful conclusions, the radical frankness of this novel, ruthlessly transcending all novelistic and literary bounds, have long become part of our moral culture, today we can scarcely conceive the lurid sensation which this novel must have created at the time of its appearance—protest on the side of "idealistic" aestheticism and passionate agreement on the side of fanatical love for truth. I spoke of ruthlessness—Dostoevsky or the first-person hero or un-hero or anti-hero avoids that charge by the fiction that he is not writing for the public, not for publication, not even for a reader, but exclusively and secretly for himself alone. His train of thought is as follows: "In every man's memory there are things which he does not reveal to everyone, but only to his friends. There are also things which he does not reveal to his friends, but at best to himself and only under a pledge of secrecy. And finally there are things which man hesitates to reveal even to himself, and every decent person accumulates a considerable quantity of such things. In fact, you might say, the more decent a person is, the greater the number of such things that he carries around with him. I myself, at any rate, have only recently decided to recall a few of my earlier experiences; until now I have always avoided them, even with a certain uneasiness. . . ."

And so this "novel" consists of the unspeakably compromising record of these "earlier experiences," mingling the repulsive with the attractive in a hitherto unheard-of manner. The author, or the person whom he makes the author, is trying an experiment. "Is it possible," he inquires, "to be completely frank at least to oneself, and to tell the whole truth without reserve?" He is thinking of Heine, who made the statement that strictly truthful autobiographies were next to impossible; that everyone always told untruths about himself, like Rousseau, who slandered himself from pure vanity. The author concurs; but, he says, the difference between Rousseau and himself is that the former made his confession to the public, while he was writing for himself alone. And, he declares emphatically, if it appeared as if he were addressing a reader, this was a mere pretense, as he found it easier to write in that fashion. It is purely a matter of form, he says.

Of course, all that isn't true at all, for Dostoevsky was certainly writing for the public and for publication and for as many readers as possible, if only because he needed money badly. The artistic and almost facetious fiction of solitude and remoteness from literature is useful as an excuse for the radical cynicism of the frank confession. But the fiction within the fiction, the "appearance" of addressing himself to a reader, the constant haranguing of certain "gentlemen" with whom the speaker is arguing, that too is advantageous; for it brings an element of the discursive, the dialectic, the dramatic into the recital, an element in which Dostoevsky is very much at home and which makes even the most serious, the most wicked, the most debased things amusing in the highest sense.

I confess that I like the first part of *Notes from Underground* even better than the second, the stirring and shameful story of the prostitute Liza. I grant that the first part does not consist of action but of talk, and talk reminiscent in many respects of the depraved prating of certain religious personages in Dostoevsky's great novels. Granted also that it is hazardous talk in the strongest sense of the word, dangerously likely to confuse naïve minds, because it stresses skepticism against faith, and because it heretically attacks civilization and democracy and the humanitarians and the meliorists who believe that man strives for happiness and advancement while he is actually thirsting just as much for suffering, the only source of knowledge, that he really does not want the crystal palace and the anthill of social consummation, and that he will never renounce his predilection for destruction and chaos. All that sounds like reactionary wickedness and may worry well-meaning minds who believe that the most important thing today is the bridging of the chasm that yawns between intellectual realization and scandalously retarded social and economic reality. It *is* the most important thing—and yet those heresies are the truth: the dark side of truth, away from the sun, which no one dares to neglect who is interested in the truth, the whole truth, truth about man. The tortured paradoxes which Dostoevsky's "hero" hurls at his positivistic adversaries, antihuman as they sound, are spoken in the name of and out of love for humanity: on behalf of a new, deeper, and unrhetorical humanity that has passed through all the hells of suffering and of understanding.

As this edition of Dostoevsky compares with his complete work, and as his published work compares with that which he could and would have created if the limitations of human life had not prevented him— so the things I have said here about the titanic Russian compare to what could be said about him. Dostoevsky in moderation, Dostoevsky in reason, that was the watchword. When I told a friend of my intention to provide a preface for these volumes he said, laughing: "Be careful! You will write a book about him." I was careful.

THOMAS MANN, Pacific Palisades, California, July, 1945

The Gambler

FROM THE DIARY OF A YOUNG MAN

THE GAMBLER

Chapter 1

At LAST I have come back from my fortnight's absence. Our friends have already been two days in Roulettenburg. I imagined that they were expecting me with the greatest eagerness; I was mistaken, however. The General had an extremely independent air, he talked to me condescendingly and sent me away to his sister. I even fancied that the General was a little ashamed to look at me. Marya Filippovna was tremendously busy and scarcely spoke to me; she took the money, however, counted it, and listened to my whole report. They were expecting Mezentsov, the little Frenchman, and some Englishman; as usual, as soon as there was money there was a dinner-party; in the Moscow style. Polina Alexandrovna, seeing me, asked why I had been away so long, and without waiting for an answer went off somewhere. Of course, she did that on purpose. We must have an explanation, though. Things have accumulated.

They had assigned me a little room on the fourth storey of the hotel. They know here that I belong to the *General's suite.* It all looks as though they had managed to impress the people. The General is looked upon by every one here as a very rich Russian grandee. Even before dinner he commissioned me, among other things, to change two notes for a thousand francs each. I changed them at the office of the hotel. Now we shall be looked upon as millionaires for a whole week, at least. I wanted to take Misha and Nadya out for a walk, but on the stairs I was summoned back to the General; he had graciously bethought him to inquire where I was taking them. The man is absolutely unable to look me straight in the face; he would like to very much, but every time I meet his eyes with an intent, that is, disrespectful air, he seems overcome with embarrassment. In very bombastic language, piling one sentence on another, and at last losing his thread altogether, he gave me to understand that I was to take the children for a walk in the park, as far as possible from the Casino. At last he lost his temper completely, and added sharply: "Or else maybe you'll be taking

3

them into the gambling saloon. You must excuse me," he added, "but I know you are still rather thoughtless and capable, perhaps, of gambling. In any case, though, I am not your mentor and have no desire to be, yet I have the right, at any rate, to desire that you will not compromise me, so to speak. . . ."

"But I have no money," I said calmly; "one must have it before one can lose it."

"You shall have it at once," answered the General, flushing a little; he rummaged in his bureau, looked up in an account book, and it turned out that he had a hundred and twenty roubles owing me.

"How are we to settle up?" he said. "We must change it into thalers. Come, take a hundred thalers—the rest, of course, won't be lost."

I took the money without a word.

"Please don't be offended by my words, you are so ready to take offence. . . . If I did make an observation, it was only, so to speak, by way of warning, and, of course, I have some right to do so. . . ."

On my way home before dinner, with the children, I met a perfect cavalcade. Our party had driven out to look at some ruin. Two magnificent carriages, superb horses! In one carriage was Mlle. Blanche with Marya Filippovna and Polina; the Frenchman, the Englishman and our General were on horseback. The passers-by stopped and stared; a sensation was created; but the General will have a bad time, all the same. I calculated that with the four thousand francs I had brought, added to what they had evidently managed to get hold of, they had now seven or eight thousand francs; but that is not enough for Mlle. Blanche.

Mlle. Blanche, too, is staying at the hotel with her mother; our Frenchman is somewhere in the house, too. The footman calls him "Monsieur le Comte." Mlle. Blanche's mother is called "Madame la Comtesse"; well, who knows, they may be Comte and Comtesse.

I felt sure that M. le Comte would not recognize me when we assembled at dinner. The General, of course, would not have thought of introducing us or even saying a word to him on my behalf; and M. le Comte has been in Russia himself, and knows what is called an *outchitel* is very small fry. He knows me very well, however. But I must confess I made my appearance at dinner unbidden; I fancy the General forgot to give orders, or else he would certainly have sent me to dine at the *table d'hôte*. I came of my own accord, so that the General looked at me with astonishment. Kind-hearted Marya Filippovna immediately made a place for me; but my meeting with Mr. Astley saved the situation, and I could not help seeming to belong to the party.

I met this strange Englishman for the first time in the train in Prussia, where we sat opposite to one another, when I was travelling to join the family; then I came across him as I was going into France, and then again in Switzerland: in the course of that fortnight twice— and now I suddenly met him in Roulettenburg. I never met a man so shy in my life. He is stupidly shy and, of course, is aware of it himself, for he is by no means stupid. He is very sweet and gentle, however. I drew him into talk at our first meeting in Prussia. He told me that he had been that summer at North Cape, and that he was very anxious to visit the fair at Nizhni Novgorod. I don't know how he made acquaintance with the General; I believe that he is hopelessly in love with Polina. When she came in he glowed like a sunset. He was very glad that I was sitting beside him at the table and seemed already to look upon me as his bosom friend.

At dinner the Frenchman gave himself airs in an extraordinary way; he was nonchalant and majestic with every one. In Moscow, I remember, he used to blow soap bubbles. He talked a great deal about finance and Russian politics. The General sometimes ventured to contradict, but discreetly, and only so far as he could without too great loss of dignity.

I was in a strange mood; of course, before we were half through dinner I had asked myself my usual invariable question: "Why I went on dancing attendance on this General, and had not left them long ago?" From time to time I glanced at Polina Alexandrovna. She took no notice of me whatever. It ended by my flying into a rage and making up my mind to be rude.

I began by suddenly, apropos of nothing, breaking in on the conversation in a loud voice. What I longed to do above all things was to be abusive to the Frenchman. I turned round to the General and very loudly and distinctly, I believe, interrupted him. I observed that this summer it was utterly impossible for a Russian to dine at *table d'hôte*. The General turned upon me an astonished stare.

"If you are a self-respecting man," I went on, "you will certainly be inviting abuse and must put up with affronts to your dignity. In Paris, on the Rhine, even in Switzerland, there are so many little Poles, and French people who sympathize with them, that there's no chance for a Russian to utter a word."

I spoke in French. The General looked at me in amazement. I don't know whether he was angry or simply astonished at my so forgetting myself.

"It seems some one gave you a lesson," said the Frenchman, carelessly and contemptuously.

"I had a row for the first time with a Pole in Paris," I answered; "then with a French officer who took the Pole's part. And then some of the French came over to my side, when I told them how I tried to spit in Monseigneur's coffee."

"Spit?" asked the General, with dignified perplexity, and he even looked about him aghast.

The Frenchman scanned me mistrustfully.

"Just so," I answered. "After feeling convinced for two whole days that I might have to pay a brief visit to Rome about our business, I went to the office of the Papal Embassy to get my passport *viséed*. There I was met by a little abbé, a dried-up little man of about fifty, with a frost-bitten expression. After listening to me politely, but extremely drily, he asked me to wait a little. Though I was in a hurry, of course I sat down to wait, and took up *L'Opinion Nationale* and began reading a horribly abusive attack on Russia. Meanwhile, I heard some one in the next room ask to see Monseigneur; I saw my abbé bow to him. I addressed the same request to him again; he asked me to wait—more drily than ever. A little later some one else entered, a stranger, but on business, some Austrian; he was listened to and at once conducted upstairs. Then I felt very much vexed; I got up, went to the abbé and said resolutely, that as Monseigneur was receiving, he might settle my business, too. At once the abbé drew back in great surprise. It was beyond his comprehension that an insignificant Russian should dare to put himself on a level with Monseigneur's guests. As though delighted to have an opportunity of insulting me, he looked me up and down, and shouted in the most insolent tone: 'Can you really suppose that Monseigneur is going to leave his coffee on your account?' Then I shouted, too, but more loudly than he: 'Let me tell you I'm ready to spit in your Monseigneur's coffee! If you don't finish with my passport this minute, I'll go to him in person.'

" 'What! When the Cardinal is sitting with him!' cried the abbé, recoiling from me with horror, and, flinging wide his arms, he stood like a cross, with an air of being ready to die rather than let me pass.

"Then I answered him that 'I was a heretic and a barbarian, *que je suis hérétique et barbare*,' and that I cared nothing for all these Archbishops, Cardinals, Monseigneurs and all of them. In short, I showed I was not going to give way. The abbé looked at me with uneasy ill-humour, then snatched my passport and carried it upstairs. A minute later it had been *viséed*. Here, wouldn't you like to see it?" I took out the passport and showed the Roman *visé*.

"Well, I must say . . ." the General began.

"What saved you was saying that you were a heretic and barbarian," the Frenchman observed, with a smile. *"Cela n'était pas si bête."*

"Why, am I to model myself upon our Russians here? They sit, not daring to open their lips, and almost ready to deny they are Russians. In Paris, anyway in my hotel, they began to treat me much more attentively when I told every one about my passage-at-arms with the abbé. The fat Polish *pan,* the person most antagonistic to me at *table d'hôte,* sank into the background. The Frenchmen did not even resent it when I told them that I had, two years previously, seen a man at whom, in 1812, a French *chasseur* had shot simply in order to discharge his gun. The man was at that time a child of ten, and his family had not succeeded in leaving Moscow."

"That's impossible," the Frenchman boiled up; "a French soldier would not fire at a child!"

"Yet it happened," I answered. "I was told it by a most respectable captain on the retired list, and I saw the scar on his cheek from the bullet myself."

The Frenchman began talking rapidly and at great length. The General began to support him, but I recommended him to read, for instance, passages in the "Notes" of General Perovsky, who was a prisoner in the hands of the French in 1812. At last Marya Filippovna began talking of something else to change the conversation. The General was very much displeased with me, for the Frenchman and I had almost begun shouting at one another. But I fancy my dispute with the Frenchman pleased Mr. Astley very much. Getting up from the table, he asked me to have a glass of wine with him.

In the evening I duly succeeded in getting a quarter of an hour's talk with Polina Alexandrovna. Our conversation took place when we were all out for a walk. We all went into the park by the Casino. Polina sat down on a seat facing the fountain, and let Nadenka play with some children not far from her. I, too, let Misha run off to the fountain, and we were at last left alone.

We began, of course, at first with business. Polina simply flew into a rage when I gave her only seven hundred guldens. She had reckoned positively on my pawning her diamonds in Paris for two thousand guldens, if not more.

"I must have money, come what may," she said. "I must get it or I am lost."

I began asking her what had happened during my absence.

"Nothing, but the arrival of two pieces of news from Petersburg: first that Granny was very ill, and then, two days later, that she seemed to be dying. The news came from Timofey Petrovitch," added Polina, "and he's a trustworthy man. We are expecting every day to hear news of the end."

"So you are all in suspense here?" I asked.

"Of course, all of us, and all the time; we've been hoping for nothing else for the last six months."

"And are *you* hoping for it?" I asked.

"Why, I'm no relation. I am only the General's stepdaughter. But I am sure she will remember me in her will."

"I fancy you'll get a great deal," I said emphatically.

"Yes, she was fond of me; but what makes *you* think so?"

"Tell me," I answered with a question, "our *marquis* is initiated into all our secrets, it seems?"

"But why are you interested in that?" asked Polina, looking at me drily and austerely.

"I should think so; if I'm not mistaken, the General has already succeeded in borrowing from him."

"You guess very correctly."

"Well, would he have lent the money if he had not known about your 'granny'? Did you notice at dinner, three times speaking of her, he called her 'granny.' What intimate and friendly relations!"

"Yes, you are right. As soon as he knows that I have come into something by the will, he will pay his addresses to me at once. That is what you wanted to know, was it?"

"He will only begin to pay you his addresses? I thought he had been doing that a long time."

"You know perfectly well that he hasn't!" Polina said, with anger. "Where did you meet that Englishman?" she added, after a minute's silence.

"I knew you would ask about him directly."

I told her of my previous meetings with Mr. Astley on my journey.

"He is shy and given to falling in love, and, of course, he's fallen in love with you already."

"Yes, he's in love with me," answered Polina.

"And, of course, he's ten times as rich as the Frenchman. Why, is it certain that the Frenchman has anything? Isn't that open to doubt?"

"No, it is not. He has a château of some sort. The General has spoken of that positively. Well, are you satisfied?"

"If I were in your place I should certainly marry the Englishman."

"Why?" asked Polina.

"The Frenchman is better-looking, but he is nastier; and the Englishman, besides being honest, is ten times as rich," I snapped out.

"Yes, but on the other hand, the Frenchman is a *marquis* and clever," she answered, in the most composed manner.

"But is it true?" I went on, in the same way.

"It certainly is."

Polina greatly disliked my questions, and I saw that she was trying to make me angry by her tone and the strangeness of her answers. I said as much to her at once.

"Well, it really amuses me to see you in such a rage. You must pay for the very fact of my allowing you to ask such questions and make such suppositions."

"I certainly consider myself entitled to ask you any sort of question," I answered calmly, "just because I am prepared to pay any price you like for it, and I set no value at all on my life now."

Polina laughed.

"You told me last time at the Schlangenberg, that you were prepared, at a word from me, to throw yourself head foremost from the rock, and it is a thousand feet high, I believe. Some day I shall utter that word, solely in order to see how you will pay the price, and trust me, I won't give way. You are hateful to me, just because I've allowed you to take such liberties, and even more hateful because you are so necessary to me. But so long as you are necessary to me, I must take care of you."

She began getting up. She spoke with irritation. Of late she had always ended every conversation with me in anger and irritation, real anger.

"Allow me to ask you, what about Mlle. Blanche?" I asked, not liking to let her go without explanation.

"You know all about Mlle. Blanche. Nothing more has happened since. Mlle. Blanche will, no doubt, be Madame la Générale, that is, if the rumour of Granny's death is confirmed, of course, for Mlle. Blanche and her mother and her cousin twice removed, the *marquis*— all know very well that we are ruined."

"And is the General hopelessly in love?"

"That's not the point now. Listen and remember: take these seven hundred florins and go and play. Win me as much as you can at roulette; I must have money now, come what may."

Saying this, she called Nadenka and went into the Casino, where she joined the rest of the party. I turned into the first path to the left, wondering and reflecting. I felt as though I had had a blow on the head after the command to go and play roulette. Strange to say, I had plenty to think about, but I was completely absorbed in analyzing the essential nature of my feeling towards Polina. It was true I had been more at ease during that fortnight's absence than I was now on the day of my return, though on the journey I had been as melancholy and restless as a madman, and at moments had even seen her in my dreams. Once, waking up in the train (in Switzerland), I began talking aloud, I believe, with Polina, which amused all the passengers in the carriage with me. And once more now I asked myself the question: "Do I love her?" And again I could not answer it, or, rather, I answered for the hundredth time that I hated her. Yes, she was hateful to me. There were moments (on every occasion at the end of our talks) when I would have given my life to strangle her! I swear if it had been possible on the spot to plunge a sharp knife in her bosom, I believe I should have snatched it up with relish. And yet I swear by all that's sacred that if at the Schlangenberg, at the fashionable peak, she really had said to me, "Throw yourself down," I should have thrown myself down at once, also with positive relish. I knew that. In one way or another it must be settled. All this she understood wonderfully well, and the idea that I knew, positively and distinctly, how utterly beyond my reach she was, how utterly impossible my mad dreams were of fulfilment, that thought, I am convinced, afforded her extraordinary satisfaction; if not, how could she, cautious and intelligent as she was, have been on such intimate and open terms with me? I believe she had hitherto looked on me as that empress of ancient times looked on the slave before whom she did not mind undressing because she did not regard him as a human being. Yes, often she did not regard me as a human being!

I had her commission, however, to win at roulette, at all costs. I had no time to consider why must I play, and why such haste, and what new scheme was hatching in that ever-calculating brain. Moreover, it was evident that during that fortnight new facts had arisen of which I had no idea yet. I must discover all that and get to the bottom of it and as quickly as possible. But there was no time now; I must go to roulette.

Chapter 2

I CONFESS it was disagreeable to me. Though I had made up my mind that I would play, I had not proposed to play for other people. It rather threw me out of my reckoning, and I went into the gambling saloon with very disagreeable feelings. From the first glance I disliked everything in it. I cannot endure the flunkeyishness of the newspapers of the whole world, and especially our Russian papers, in which, almost every spring, the journalists write articles upon two things: first, on the extraordinary magnificence and luxury of the gambling saloons on the Rhine, and secondly, on the heaps of gold which are said to lie on the tables. They are not paid for it; it is simply done from disinterested obsequiousness. There was no sort of magnificence in these trashy rooms, and not only were there no piles of gold lying on the table, but there was hardly any gold at all. No doubt some time, in the course of the season, some eccentric person, either an Englishman or an Asiatic of some sort, a Turk, perhaps (as it was that summer), would suddenly turn up and lose or win immense sums; all the others play for paltry guldens, and on an average there is very little money lying on the tables.

As soon as I went into the gambling saloon (for the first time in my life), I could not for some time make up my mind to play. There was a crush besides. If I had been alone, even then, I believe I should soon have gone away and not have begun playing. I confess my heart was beating and I was not cool. I knew for certain, and had made up my mind long before, that I should not leave Roulettenburg unchanged, that some radical and fundamental change would take place in my destiny; so it must be and so it would be. Ridiculous as it may be that I should expect so much for myself from roulette, yet I consider even more ridiculous the conventional opinion accepted by all that it is stupid and absurd to expect anything from gambling. And why should gambling be worse than any other means of making money—for instance, commerce? It is true that only one out of a hundred wins, but what is that to me?

In any case I determined to look about me first and not to begin anything in earnest that evening. If anything did happen that evening it would happen by chance and be something slight, and I staked my money accordingly. Besides, I had to study the game; for, in spite of the thousand descriptions of roulette which I had read so eagerly, I understood absolutely nothing of its working until I saw it myself.

In the first place it all struck me as so dirty, somehow, morally horrid and dirty. I am not speaking at all of the greedy, uneasy faces which by dozens, even by hundreds, crowd round the gambling tables. I see absolutely nothing dirty in the wish to win as quickly and as much as possible. I always thought very stupid the answer of that fat and prosperous moralist, who replied to some one's excuse "that he played for a very small stake," "So much the worse, it is such petty covetousness." As though covetousness were not exactly the same, whether on a big scale or a petty one. It is a matter of proportion. What is paltry to Rothschild is wealth to me, and as for profits and winnings, people, not only at roulette, but everywhere, do nothing but try to gain or squeeze something out of one another. Whether profits or gains are nasty is a different question. But I am not solving that question here. Since I was myself possessed by an intense desire of winning, I felt as I went into the hall all this covetousness, and all this covetous filth if you like, in a sense congenial and convenient. It is most charming when people do not stand on ceremony with one another, but act openly and aboveboard. And, indeed, why deceive oneself? Gambling is a most foolish and imprudent pursuit! What was particularly ugly at first sight, in all the rabble round the roulette table, was the respect they paid to that pursuit, the solemnity and even reverence with which they all crowded round the tables. That is why a sharp distinction is drawn here between the kind of game that is *mauvais genre* and the kind that is permissible to well-bred people. There are two sorts of gambling: one the gentlemanly sort: the other the plebeian, mercenary sort, the game played by all sorts of riff-raff. The distinction is sternly observed here, and how contemptible this distinction really is! A gentleman may stake, for instance, five or ten louis d'or, rarely more; he may, however, stake as much as a thousand francs if he is very rich; but only for the sake of the play, simply for amusement, that is, simply to look on at the process of winning or of losing, but must on no account display an interest in winning. If he wins, he may laugh aloud, for instance; may make a remark to one of the bystanders; he may even put down another stake, and may even double it, but solely from curiosity, for the sake of watching and calculating the chances, and not from the plebeian desire to win. In fact, he must look on all gambling, roulette, *trente et quarante,* as nothing else than a pastime got up entirely for his amusement. He must not even suspect the greed for gain and the shifty dodges on which the bank depends.

It would be extremely good form, too, if he should imagine that all the other gamblers, all the rabble, trembling over a gulden, were rich men and gentlemen like himself and were playing simply for their diversion and amusement. This complete ignorance of reality and innocent view of people would be, of course, extremely aristocratic. I have seen many mammas push forward their daughters, innocent and elegant misses of fifteen and sixteen, and, giving them some gold coins, teach them how to play. The young lady wins or loses, invariably smiles and walks away, very well satisfied. Our General went up to the table with solid dignity; a flunkey rushed to hand him a chair, but he ignored the flunkey; he, very slowly and deliberately, took out his purse, very slowly and deliberately took three hundred francs in gold from his purse, staked them on the black, and won. He did not pick up his winnings, but left them on the table. Black turned up again; he didn't pick up his winnings that time either; and when, the third time, red turned up, he lost at once twelve hundred francs. He walked away with a smile and kept up his dignity. I am positive he was raging inwardly, and if the stake had been two or three times as much he would not have kept up his dignity but would have betrayed his feelings. A Frenchman did, however, before my eyes, win and lose as much as thirty thousand francs with perfect gaiety and no sign of emotion. A real gentleman should not show excitement even if he loses his whole fortune. Money ought to be so much below his gentlemanly dignity as to be scarcely worth noticing. Of course, it would have been extremely aristocratic not to notice the sordidness of all the rabble and all the surroundings. Sometimes, however, the opposite pose is no less aristocratic—to notice—that is, to look about one, even, perhaps, to stare through a lorgnette at the rabble; though always taking the rabble and the sordidness as nothing else but a diversion of a sort, as though it were a performance got up for the amusement of gentlemen. One may be jostled in that crowd, but one must look about one with complete conviction that one is oneself a spectator and that one is in no sense part of it. Though, again, to look very attentively is not quite the thing; that, again, would not be gentlemanly because, in any case, the spectacle does not deserve much, or close, attention. And, in fact, few spectacles do deserve a gentleman's close attention. And yet it seemed to me that all this was deserving of very close attention, especially for one who had come not only to observe it, but sincerely and genuinely reckoned himself as one of the rabble. As for my hidden moral convictions, there is no place for them, of course, in my present reasonings. Let that be enough for the present. I speak to relieve my conscience. But I notice one thing: that of late it has become horribly repugnant to me to test my thoughts and actions by any moral standard whatever. I was guided by something different. . . .

The rabble certainly did play very sordidly. I am ready to believe, indeed, that a great deal of the most ordinary thieving goes on at the gambling table. The croupiers who sit at each end of the table look at the stakes and reckon the winnings; they have a great deal to do. They are rabble, too! For the most part they are French. However, I was watching and observing, not with the object of describing roulette. I kept a sharp look-out for my own sake, so that I might know how to behave in the future. I noticed, for instance, that nothing was more common than for some one to stretch out his hand and snatch what one had won. A dispute would begin, often an uproar, and a nice job one would have to find witnesses and to prove that it was one's stake!

At first it was all an inexplicable puzzle to me. All I could guess and distinguish was that the stakes were on the numbers, on odd and even, and on the colours. I made up my mind to risk a hundred guldens of Polina Alexandrovna's money. The thought that I was not playing for myself seemed to throw me out of my reckoning. It was an extremely unpleasant feeling, and I wanted to be rid of it as soon as possible. I kept feeling that by beginning for Polina I should break my own luck. Is it impossible to approach the gambling table without becoming infected with superstition? I began by taking out five friedrichs d'or (fifty gulden) and putting them on the even. The wheel went round and thirteen turned up—I had lost. With a sickly feeling I staked another five friedrichs d'or on red, simply in order to settle the matter and go away. Red turned up. I staked all the ten friedrichs d'or—red turned up again. I staked all the money again on the same, and again red turned up. On receiving forty friedrichs d'or I staked twenty upon the twelve middle figures, not knowing what would come of it. I was paid three times my stake. In this way from ten friedrichs d'or I had all at once eighty. I was overcome by a strange, unusual feeling which was so unbearable that I made up my mind to go away. It seemed to me that I should not have been playing at all like that if I had been playing for myself. I staked the whole eighty friedrichs d'or, however, on even. This time four turned up; another eighty friedrichs d'or was poured out to me, and, gathering up the whole heap of a hundred and sixty friedrichs d'or, I set off to find Polina Alexandrovna.

They were all walking somewhere in the park and I only succeeded in seeing her after supper. This time the Frenchman was not of the party, and the General unbosomed himself. Among other things he thought fit to observe to me that he would not wish to see me at the gambling tables. It seemed to him that it would compromise him if I were to lose too much: "But even if you were to win a very large sum I should be compromised, too," he added significantly. "Of course, I have no right to dictate your actions, but you must admit yourself . . ." At this point he broke off, as his habit was. I answered, drily, that I had very little money, and so I could not lose very conspicuously, even if I did play. Going upstairs to my room I succeeded in handing Polina her winnings, and told her that I would not play for her another time.

"Why not?" she asked, in a tremor.

"Because I want to play on my own account," I answered, looking at her with surprise; "and it hinders me."

"Then you still continue in your conviction that roulette is your only escape and salvation?" she asked ironically.

I answered very earnestly, that I did; that as for my confidence that I should win, it might be absurd; I was ready to admit it, but that I wanted to be let alone.

Polina Alexandrovna began insisting I should go halves with her in to-day's winnings, and was giving me eighty friedrichs d'or, suggesting that I should go on playing on those terms. I refused the half, positively and finally, and told her that I could not play for other people, not because I didn't want to, but because I should certainly lose.

"Yet I, too," she said, pondering, "stupid as it seems, am building all my hopes on roulette. And so you must go on playing, sharing with me, and—of course—you will."

At this point she walked away, without listening to further objections.

Chapter 3

YET all yesterday she did not say a single word to me about playing, and avoided speaking to me altogether. Her manner to me remained unchanged: the same absolute carelessness on meeting me; there was even a shade of contempt and dislike. Altogether she did not care to conceal her aversion; I noticed that. In spite of that she did not conceal from me, either, that I was in some way necessary to her and that she was keeping me for some purpose. A strange relation had grown up between us, incomprehensible to me in many ways when I considered her pride and haughtiness with every one. She knew, for instance, that I loved her madly, even allowed me to speak of my passion; and, of course, she could not have shown greater contempt for me than by allowing me to speak of my passion without hindrance or restriction. It was as much as to say that she thought so little of my feelings that she did not care in the least what I talked about to her and what I felt for her. She had talked a great deal about her own affairs before, but had never been completely open. What is more, there was this peculiar refinement in her contempt for me: she would know, for instance, that I was aware of some circumstance in her life, or knew of some matter that greatly concerned her, or she would tell me herself something of her circumstances, if to forward her objects she had to make use of me in some way, as a slave or an errand-boy; but she would always tell me only so much as a man employed on her errands need know, and if I did not know the whole chain of events, if she saw herself how worried and anxious I was over her worries and anxieties, she never deigned to comfort me by giving me her full confidence as a friend; though she often made use of me for commissions that were not only troublesome, but dangerous, so that to my thinking she was bound to be open with me. Was it worth her while, indeed, to trouble herself about my feelings, about my being worried, and perhaps three times as much worried and tormented by her anxieties and failures as she was herself?

I knew of her intention to play roulette three weeks before. She had even warned me that I should have to play for her, and it would be improper for her to play herself. From the tone of her words, I noticed even then that she had serious anxieties, and was not actuated simply by a desire for money. What is money to her for its own sake? She must have some object, there must be some circumstance at which I can only guess, but of which so far I have no knowledge. Of course, the humiliation and the slavery in which she held me might have made it possible for me (it often does) to question her coarsely and bluntly. Seeing that in her eyes I was a slave and utterly insignificant, there was nothing for her to be offended at in my coarse curiosity. But the fact is, that though she allowed me to ask questions, she did not answer them, and sometimes did not notice them at all. That was the position between us.

A great deal was said yesterday about a telegram which had been sent off four days before, and to which no answer had been received. The General was evidently upset and preoccupied. It had, of course, something to do with Granny. The Frenchman was troubled, too. Yesterday, for instance, after dinner, they had a long, serious talk. The Frenchman's tone to all of us was unusually high and mighty, quite in the spirit of the saying: "Seat a pig at table and it will put its feet on it." Even with Polina he was casual to the point of rudeness; at the same time he gladly took part in the walks in the public gardens and in the rides and drives into the country. I had long known some of the circumstances that bound the Frenchman to the General: they had made plans for establishing a factory together in Russia; I don't know whether their project had fallen through, or whether it was being discussed. Moreover, I had by chance come to know part of a family secret. The Frenchman had actually, in the previous year, come to the General's rescue, and had given him thirty thousand roubles to make up a deficit of Government monies missing when he resigned his duties. And, of course, the General is in his grip; but now the principal person in the whole business is Mlle. Blanche; about that I am sure I'm not mistaken.

What is Mlle. Blanche? Here among us it is said that she is a distinguished Frenchwoman, with a colossal fortune and a mother accompanying her. It is known, too, that she is some sort of relation of our *marquis,* but a very distant one: a cousin, or something of the sort. I am told that before I went to Paris, the Frenchman and Mlle. Blanche were on much more ceremonious, were, so to speak, on a more delicate and refined footing; now their acquaintance, their friendship and relationship, was of a rather coarse and more intimate character. Perhaps our prospects seemed to them so poor that they did not think it very necessary to stand on ceremony and keep up appearances with us. I noticed even the day before yesterday how Mr. Astley looked at Mlle. Blanche and her mother. It seemed to me that he knew them. It even seemed to me that our Frenchman had met Mr. Astley before. Mr. Astley, however, is so shy, so reserved and silent, that one can be almost certain of him—he won't wash dirty linen in public. Anyway, the Frenchman barely bows to him and scarcely looks at him, so he is not afraid of him. One can understand that, perhaps, but why does Mlle. Blanche not look at him either? Especially when the *marquis* let slip yesterday in the course of conversation—I don't remember in what connection—that Mr. Astley had a colossal fortune and that he—the *marquis*—knew this for a fact; at that point Mlle. Blanche might well have looked at Mr. Astley. Altogether the General was uneasy. One can understand what a telegram announcing his aunt's death would mean!

Though I felt sure Polina was, apparently for some object, avoiding a conversation with me, I assumed a cold and indifferent air: I kept thinking that before long she would come to me of herself. But both to-day and yesterday I concentrated my attention principally on Mlle. Blanche. Poor General! He is completely done for! To fall in love at fifty-five with such a violent passion is a calamity, of course! When one takes into consideration the fact that he is a widower, his children, the ruin of his estate, his debts, and, finally, the woman it is his lot to fall in love with. Mlle. Blanche is handsome. But I don't know if I shall be understood if I say that she has a face of the type of which one might feel frightened. I, anyway, have always been afraid of women of that sort. She is probably five-and-twenty. She is well grown and broad, with sloping shoulders; she has a magnificent throat and bosom; her complexion is swarthy yellow. Her hair is as black as Indian ink, and she has a tremendous lot of it, enough to make two ordinary coiffures. Her eyes are black with yellowish whites; she has an insolent look in her eyes; her teeth are very white; her lips are always painted; she smells of musk. She dresses effectively, richly and with *chic,* but with much taste. Her hands and feet are exquisite. Her voice is a husky contralto. Sometimes she laughs, showing all her teeth, but her usual expression is a silent and impudent stare—before Polina and Marya Filippovna, anyway (there is a strange rumour that Marya Filippovna is going back to Russia). I fancy that Mlle. Blanche has had no sort of education. Possibly she is not even intelligent; but, on the other hand, she is striking and she is artful. I fancy her life has not passed without adventures. If one is to tell the whole truth, it is quite possible that the *marquis* is no relation of hers at all, and that her mother is not her mother. But there is evidence that in Berlin, where we went with them, her mother and she had some decent acquaintances. As for the *marquis* himself, though I still doubt his being a *marquis,* yet the fact that he is received in decent society—among Russians, for instance, in Moscow, and in some places in Germany—is not open to doubt. I don't know what he is in France. They say he has a château.

I thought that a great deal would have happened during this fortnight, and yet I don't know if anything decisive has been said between Mlle. Blanche and the General. Everything depends on our fortune, however; that is, whether the General can show them plenty of money. If, for instance, news were to come that Granny were not dead, I am convinced that Mlle. Blanche would vanish at once. It surprises and amuses me to see what a gossip I've become. Oh! how I loathe it all! How delighted I should be to drop it all, and them all! But can I leave Polina, can I give up spying round her? Spying, of course, is low, but what do I care about that?

I was interested in Mr. Astley, too, to-day and yesterday. Yes, I am convinced he's in love with Polina. It is curious and absurd how much may be expressed by the eyes of a modest and painfully chaste man, moved by love, at the very time when the man would gladly sink into the earth rather than express or betray anything by word or glance. Mr. Astley very often meets us on our walks. He takes off his hat and passes by, though, of course, he is dying to join us. If he is invited to do so, he immediately refuses. At places where we rest—at the Casino, by the bandstand, or before the fountain—he always stands somewhere not far from our seat; and wherever we may be—in the park, in the wood, or on the Schlangenberg—one has only to glance round, to look about one, and somewhere, either in the nearest path or behind the bushes, Mr. Astley's head appears. I fancy he is looking for an opportunity to have a conversation with me apart. This morning we met and exchanged a couple of words. He sometimes speaks very abruptly. Without saying "good-morning," he began by blurting out—

"Oh, Mlle. Blanche! . . . I have seen a great many women like Mlle. Blanche!"

He paused, looking at me significantly. What he meant to say by that I don't know. For on my asking what he meant, he shook his head with a sly smile, and added, "Oh, well, that's how it is. Is Mlle. Pauline very fond of flowers?"

"I don't know; I don't know at all," I answered.

"What? You don't even know that!" he cried, with the utmost amazement.

"I don't know; I haven't noticed at all," I repeated, laughing.

"H'm! That gives me a queer idea."

Then he shook his head and walked away. He looked pleased, though. We talked the most awful French together.

Chapter 4

TO-DAY has been an absurd, grotesque, ridiculous day. Now it is eleven o'clock at night. I am sitting in my little cupboard of a room, recalling it. It began with my having to go to roulette to play for Polina Alexandrovna. I took the hundred and sixty friedrichs d'or, but on two conditions: first, that I would not go halves—that is, if I won I would take nothing for myself; and secondly, that in the evening Polina should explain to me why she needed to win, and how much money. I can't, in any case, suppose that it is simply for the sake of money. Evidently the money is needed, and as quickly as possible, for some particular object. She promised to explain, and I set off. In the gambling hall the crowd was awful. How insolent and how greedy they all were! I forced my way into the middle and stood near the croupier; then I began timidly experimenting, staking two or three coins at a time. Meanwhile, I kept quiet and looked on; it seemed to me that calculation meant very little, and had by no means the importance attributed to it by some players. They sit with papers before them scrawled over in pencil, note the strokes, reckon, deduce the chances, calculate, finally stake and—lose exactly as we simple mortals who play without calculations. On the other hand, I drew one conclusion which I believe to be correct: that is, though there is no system, there really is a sort of order in the sequence of casual chances—and that, of course, is very strange. For instance, it happens that after the twelve middle numbers come the twelve later numbers; twice, for instance, it turns up on the twelve last numbers and passes to the twelve first numbers. After falling on the twelve first numbers, it passes again to numbers in the middle third, turns up three or four times in succession on numbers between thirteen and twenty-four, and again passes to numbers in the last third; then, after turning up two numbers between twenty-five and thirty-six, it passes to a number among the first twelve, turns up once again on a number among the first third, and again passes for three strokes in succession to the middle numbers; and in that way goes on for an hour and a half or two hours. One, three and two—one, three and two. It's very amusing. One day or one morning, for instance, red will be followed by black and back again almost without any order, shifting every minute, so that it never turns up red or black for more than two or three strokes in succession. Another day, or another evening, there will be nothing but red over and over again, turning up, for instance, more than twenty-two times in succession, and so for a whole day. A great deal of this was explained to me by Mr. Astley, who spent the whole morning at the tables, but did not once put down a stake.

As for me, I lost every farthing very quickly. I staked straight off twenty friedrichs d'or on even and won, staked again and again won, and went on like that two or three times. I imagine I must have had about four hundred friedrichs d'or in my hands in about five minutes.

At that point I ought to have gone away, but a strange sensation rose up in me, a sort of defiance of fate, a desire to challenge it, to put out my tongue at it. I laid down the largest stake allowed—four thousand gulden—and lost it. Then, getting hot, I pulled out all I had left, staked it on the same number, and lost again, after which I walked away from the table as though I were stunned. I could not even grasp what had happened to me, and did not tell Polina Alexandrovna of my losing till just before dinner. I spent the rest of the day sauntering in the park.

At dinner I was again in an excited state, just as I had been three days before. The Frenchman and Mlle. Blanche were dining with us again. It appeared that Mlle. Blanche had been in the gambling hall that morning and had witnessed my exploits. This time she addressed me, it seemed, somewhat attentively. The Frenchman set to work more directly, and asked me: Was it my own money I had lost? I fancy he suspects Polina. In fact, there is something behind it. I lied at once and said it was.

The General was extremely surprised. Where had I got such a sum? I explained that I had begun with ten friedrichs d'or, that after six or seven times staking successfully on equal chances I had five or six hundred gulden, and that afterwards I had lost it all in two turns.

All that, of course, sounded probable. As I explained this I looked at Polina, but I could distinguish nothing from her face. She let me lie, however, and did not set it right; from this I concluded that I had to lie and conceal that I was in collaboration with her. In any case, I thought to myself, she is bound to give me an explanation, and promised me this morning to reveal something.

I expected the General would have made some remark to me, but he remained mute; I noticed, however, signs of disturbance and uneasiness in his face. Possibly in his straitened circumstances it was simply painful to him to hear that such a pile of gold had come into, and within a quarter of an hour had passed out of, the hands of such a reckless fool as me.

I suspect that he had a rather hot encounter with the Frenchman yesterday. They were shut up together talking for a long time. The Frenchman went away seeming irritated, and came to see the General again early this morning—probably to continue the conversation of the previous day.

Hearing what I had lost, the Frenchman observed bitingly, even spitefully, that one ought to have more sense. He added—I don't know why—that though a great many Russians gamble, Russians were not, in his opinion, well qualified even for gambling.

"In my mind," said I, "roulette is simply made for Russians."

And when at my challenge the Frenchman laughed contemptuously, I observed that I was, of course, right, for to speak of the Russians as gamblers was abusing them far more than praising them, and so I might be believed.

"On what do you base your opinion?" asked the Frenchman.

"On the fact that the faculty of amassing capital has, with the progress of history, taken a place—and almost the foremost place—among the virtues and merits of the civilized man of the West. The Russian is not only incapable of amassing capital, but dissipates it in a reckless and unseemly way. Nevertheless we Russians need money, too," I added, "and consequently we are very glad and very eager to make use of such means as roulette, for instance, in which one can grow rich all at once, in two hours, without work. That's very fascinating to us; and since we play badly, recklessly, without taking trouble, we usually lose!"

"That's partly true," observed the Frenchman complacently.

"No, it is not true, and you ought to be ashamed to speak like that of your country," observed the General, sternly and impressively.

"Allow me," I answered. "I really don't know which is more disgusting: Russian unseemliness or the German faculty of accumulation by honest toil."

"What an unseemly idea!" exclaimed the General.

"What a Russian idea!" exclaimed the Frenchman.

I laughed; I had an intense desire to provoke them.

"Well, I should prefer to dwell all my life in a Kirgiz tent," I cried, "than bow down to the German idol."

"What idol?" cried the General, beginning to be angry in earnest.

"The German faculty for accumulating wealth. I've not been here long, but yet all I have been able to observe and verify revolts my Tatar blood. My God! I don't want any such virtue! I succeeded yesterday in making a round of eight miles, and it's all exactly as in the edifying German picture-books: there is here in every house a *vater* horribly virtuous and extraordinarily honest—so honest that you are afraid to go near him. I can't endure honest people whom one is afraid to go near. Every such German *vater* has a family, and in the evening they read improving books aloud. Elms and chestnut trees rustle over the house. The sun is setting; there is a stork on the roof, and everything is extraordinarily practical and touching. . . . Don't be angry, General; let me tell it in a touching style. I remember how my father used to read similar books to my mother and me under the lime-trees in the garden. . . . So I am in a position to judge. And in what complete bondage and submission every such family is here. They all work like oxen and all save money like Jews. Suppose the *vater* has saved up so many gulden and is reckoning on giving his son a trade or a bit of land; to do so, he gives his daughter no dowry, and she becomes an old maid. To do so, the youngest son is sold into bondage or into the army, and the money is added to the family capital. This is actually done here; I've been making inquiries. All this is done from nothing but honesty, from such intense honesty that the younger son who is sold believes that he is sold from nothing but honesty: and that is the ideal when the victim himself rejoices at being led to the sacrifice. What more? Why, the elder son is no better off: he has an Amalia and their hearts are united, but they can't be married because the pile of gulden is not large enough. They, too, wait with perfect morality and good faith, and go to the sacrifice with a smile. Amalia's cheeks grow thin and hollow. At last, in twenty years, their prosperity is increased; the gulden have been honestly and virtuously accumulating. The *vater* gives his blessing to the forty-year-old son and his Amalia of thirty-five, whose chest has grown hollow and whose nose has turned red. . . . With that he weeps, reads them a moral sermon, and dies. The eldest son becomes himself a virtuous *vater* and begins the same story over again. In that way, in fifty or seventy years, the grandson of the first *vater* really has a considerable capital, and he leaves it to his son, and he to his, and he to his, till in five or six generations one of them is a Baron Rothschild or goodness knows who. Come, isn't that a majestic spectacle? A hundred or two hundred years of continuous toil, patience, intelligence, honesty, character, determination, prudence, the stork on the roof! What more do you want? Why, there's nothing loftier than that; and from that standpoint they are beginning to judge the whole world and to punish the guilty; that is, any who are ever so little unlike them. Well, so that's the point: I would rather waste my substance in the Russian style or grow rich at roulette. I don't care to be Goppe and Co. in five generations. I want money for myself, and I don't look upon myself as something subordinate to capital and necessary to it. I know that I have been talking awful nonsense, but, never mind, such are my convictions."

"I don't know whether there is much truth in what you have been saying," said the General thoughtfully, "but I do know you begin to give yourself insufferable airs as soon as you are permitted to forget yourself in the least . . ."

As his habit was, he broke off without finishing. If our General began to speak of anything in the slightest degree more important than his ordinary everyday conversation, he never finished his sentences. The Frenchman listened carelessly with rather wide-open eyes; he had scarcely understood anything of what I had said. Polina gazed with haughty indifference. She seemed not to hear my words, or anything else that was said that day at table.

Chapter 5

SHE was unusually thoughtful, but directly we got up from table she bade me escort her for a walk. We took the children and went into the park towards the fountain.

As I felt particularly excited, I blurted out the crude and stupid question: why the Marquis de Grieux, our Frenchman, no longer escorted her when she went out anywhere, and did not even speak to her for days together.

"Because he is a rascal," she answered me strangely.

I had never heard her speak like that of De Grieux, and I received it in silence, afraid to interpret her irritability.

"Have you noticed that he is not on good terms with the General to-day?"

"You want to know what is the matter?" she answered drily and irritably. "You know that the General is completely mortgaged to him; all his property is his, and if Granny doesn't die, the Frenchman will come into possession of everything that is mortgaged to him."

"And is it true that everything is mortgaged? I had heard it, but I did not know that everything was."

"To be sure it is."

"Then farewell to Mlle. Blanche," said I. "She won't be the General's wife, then! Do you know, it strikes me the General is so much in love that he may shoot himself if Mlle. Blanche throws him over. It is dangerous to be so much in love at his age."

"I fancy that something will happen to him, too," Polina Alexandrovna observed musingly.

"And how splendid that would be!" I cried. "They couldn't have shown more coarsely that she was only marrying him for his money!

There's no regard for decency, even; there's no ceremony about it whatever. That's wonderful! And about Granny—could there be anything more comic and sordid than to be continually sending telegram after telegram: 'Is she dead, is she dead'? How do you like it, Polina Alexandrovna?"

"That's all nonsense," she said, interrupting me with an air of disgust. "I wonder at your being in such good spirits. What are you so pleased about? Surely not at having lost my money?"

"Why did you give it to me to lose? I told you I could not play for other people—especially for you! I obey you, whatever you order me to do, but I can't answer for the result. I warned you that nothing would come of it. Are you very much upset at losing so much money? What do you want so much for?"

"Why these questions?"

"Why, you promised to explain to me . . . Listen: I am absolutely convinced that when I begin playing for myself (and I've got twelve friedrichs d'or) I shall win. Then you can borrow as much from me as you like."

She made a contemptuous grimace.

"Don't be angry with me for such a suggestion," I went on. "I am so deeply conscious that I am nothing beside you—that is, in your eyes —that you may even borrow money from me. Presents from me cannot insult you. Besides, I lost yours."

She looked at me quickly, and seeing that I was speaking irritably and sarcastically, interrupted the conversation again.

"There's nothing of interest to you in my circumstances. If you want to know, I'm simply in debt. I've borrowed money and I wanted to repay it. I had the strange and mad idea that I should be sure to win here at the gambling table. Why I had the idea I can't understand, but I believed in it. Who knows, perhaps I believed it because no other alternative was left me."

"Or because it was quite *necessary* you should win. It's exactly like a drowning man clutching at a straw. You will admit that if he were not drowning he would not look at a straw as a branch of a tree."

Polina was surprised.

"Why," she said, "you were reckoning on the same thing yourself! A fortnight ago you said a great deal to me about your being absolutely convinced that you would win here at roulette, and tried to persuade me not to look upon you as mad; or were you joking then? But I remember you spoke so seriously that it was impossible to take it as a joke."

"That's true," I answered thoughtfully. "I am convinced to this moment that I shall win. I confess you have led me now to wonder why my senseless and unseemly failure to-day has not left the slightest doubt in me. I am still fully convinced that as soon as I begin playing for myself I shall be certain to win."

"Why are you so positive?"

"If you will have it—I don't know. I only know that I *must* win, that it is the only resource left me. Well, that's why, perhaps, I fancy I am bound to win."

"Then you, too, absolutely *must* have it, since you are so fanatically certain?"

"I wager you think I'm not capable of feeling that I *must* have anything?"

"That's nothing to me," Polina answered quietly and indifferently. "Yes, if you like. I doubt whether anything troubles you in earnest. You may be troubled, but not in earnest. You are an unstable person, not to be relied on. What do you want money for? I could see nothing serious in the reasons you brought forward the other day."

"By the way," I interrupted, "you said that you had to repay a debt. A fine debt it must be! To the Frenchman, I suppose?"

"What questions! You're particularly impertinent to-day. Are you drunk, perhaps?"

"You know that I consider myself at liberty to say anything to you, and sometimes ask you very candid questions. I repeat, I'm your slave, and one does not mind what one says to a slave, and cannot take offence at anything he says."

"And I can't endure that 'slave' theory of yours."

"Observe that I don't speak of my slavery because I want to be your slave. I simply speak of it as a fact which doesn't depend on me in the least."

"Tell me plainly, what do you want money for?"

"What do you want to know that for?"

"As you please," she replied, with a proud movement of her head.

"You can't endure the 'slave' theory, but insist on slavishness: 'Answer and don't argue.' So be it. Why do I want money? you ask. How can you ask? Money is everything!"

"I understand that, but not falling into such madness from wanting it! You, too, are growing frenzied, fatalistic. There must be something behind it, some special object. Speak without beating about the bush; I wish it."

She seemed beginning to get angry, and I was awfully pleased at her questioning me with such heat.

"Of course there is an object," I answered, "but I don't know how to explain what it is. Nothing else but that with money I should become to you a different man, not a slave."

"What? How will you manage that?"

"How shall I manage it? What, you don't even understand how I could manage to make you look at me as anything but a slave? Well, that's just what I don't care for, such surprise and incredulity!"

"You said this slavery was a pleasure to you. I thought it was myself."

"You thought so!" I cried, with a strange enjoyment. "Oh, how delightful such naïveté is from you! Oh, yes, yes, slavery to you is a pleasure. There is—there is a pleasure in the utmost limit of humiliation and insignificance!" I went on maundering. "Goodness knows, perhaps there is in the knout when the knout lies in the back and tears the flesh. . . . But I should perhaps like to enjoy another kind of enjoyment. Yesterday, in your presence, the General thought fit to read me a lecture for the seven hundred roubles a year which perhaps I may not receive from him after all. The Marquis de Grieux raises his eyebrows and stares at me without noticing me. And I, perhaps, have a passionate desire to pull the Marquis de Grieux by the nose in your presence!"

"That's the speech of a milksop. One can behave with dignity in any position. If there is a struggle, it is elevating, not humiliating."

"That's straight out of a copybook. You simply take for granted that I don't know how to behave with dignity; that is, that perhaps I am a man of moral dignity, but that I don't know how to behave with dignity. You understand that that perhaps may be so. Yes, all Russians are like that; and do you know why? Because Russians are too richly endowed and many-sided to be able readily to evolve a code of manners. It is a question of good form. For the most part we Russians are so richly endowed that we need genius to evolve our code of manners. And genius is most often absent, for, indeed, it is a rarity at all times. It's only among the French, and perhaps some other Europeans, that the code of manners is so well defined that one may have an air of the utmost dignity and yet be a man of no moral dignity whatever. That's why good form means so much with them. A Frenchman will put up with an insult, a real, moral insult, without blinking, but he wouldn't endure a flip on the nose for anything, because that is a breach of the received code, sanctified for ages. That's why our Russian young ladies have such a weakness for Frenchmen, that their manners are so good. Though, to my thinking, they have no manners at all; it's simply the cock in them, *le coq gaulois*. I can't understand it, though; I'm not a woman. Perhaps cocks are nice. And, in fact, I've been talking nonsense, and you don't stop me. You must stop me more often. When I talk to you I long to tell you everything, everything, everything. I am oblivious of all good manners. I'll even admit that I have no manners, no moral qualities either. I tell you that. I don't even worry my head about moral qualities of any sort; everything has come to a standstill in me now; you know why. I have not one human idea in my head. For a long time past I've known nothing that has gone on in the world, either in Russia or here. Here I've been through Dresden, and I don't remember what Dresden was like. You know what has swallowed me up. As I have no hope whatever and am nothing in your eyes, I speak openly: I see nothing but you everywhere, and all the rest is naught to me. Why and how I love you I don't know. Perhaps you are not at all nice really, you know. Fancy! I don't know whether you are good or not, even to look at. You certainly have not a good heart; your mind may very well be ignoble."

"Perhaps that's how it is you reckon on buying me with money," she said, "because you don't believe in my sense of honour."

"When did I reckon on buying you with money?" I cried.

"You have been talking till you don't know what you are saying. If you don't think of buying me, you think of buying my respect with your money."

"Oh no, that's not it at all. I told you it was difficult for me to explain. You are overwhelming me. Don't be angry with my chatter. You know why you can't be angry with me: I'm simply mad. Though I really don't care, even if you are angry. When I am upstairs in my little garret I have only to remember and imagine the rustle of your dress, and I am ready to bite off my hands. And what are you angry with me for? For calling myself your slave? Make use of my being your slave, make use of it, make use of it! Do you know that I shall kill you one day? I shall kill you not because I shall cease to love you or be jealous, I shall simply kill you because I have an impulse to devour you. You laugh. . . ."

"I'm not laughing," she answered wrathfully. "I order you to be silent."

She stood still, almost breathless with anger. Upon my word, I don't know whether she was handsome, but I always liked to look at her when she stood facing me like that, and so I often liked to provoke her anger. Perhaps she had noticed this and was angry on purpose. I said as much to her.

"How disgusting!" she said, with an air of repulsion.

"I don't care," I went on. "Do you know, too, that it is dangerous for us to walk together? I often have an irresistible longing to beat you, to disfigure you, to strangle you. And what do you think—won't it come to that? You are driving me into brain fever. Do you suppose I am afraid of a scandal? Your anger—why, what is your anger to me? I love you without hope, and I know that after this I shall love you a thousand times more than ever. If ever I do kill you I shall have to kill myself, too. Oh, well, I shall put off killing myself as long as possible, so as to go on feeling this insufferable pain of being without you. Do you know something incredible? I love you *more* every day, and yet that is almost impossible. And how can I help being a fatalist? Do you remember the day before yesterday, on the Schlangenberg, I whispered at your provocation, 'Say the word, and I will leap into that abyss?' If you had said that word I should have jumped in then. Don't you believe that I would have leapt down?"

"What stupid talk!" she cried.

"I don't care whether it is stupid or clever!" I cried. "I know that in your presence I must talk, and talk, and talk—and I do talk. I lose all self-respect in your presence, and I don't care."

"What use would it be for me to order you to jump off the Schlangenberg?" she said in a dry and peculiarly insulting manner. "It would be absolutely useless to me."

"Splendid," I cried; "you said that splendid 'useless' on purpose to overwhelm me. I see through you. Useless, you say? But pleasure is always of use, and savage, unbounded power—if only over a fly—is a pleasure in its way, too. Man is a despot by nature, and loves to be a torturer. You like it awfully."

I remember she looked at me with peculiar fixed attention. My face must have expressed my incoherent and absurd sensations. I remember to this moment that our conversation actually was almost word for word exactly as I have described it here. My eyes were bloodshot. There were flecks of foam on my lips. And as for the Schlangenberg, I swear on my word of honour even now, if she had told me to fling myself down I should have flung myself down! If only for a joke she had said it, with contempt, if with a jeer at me she had said it, I should even then have leapt down!

"No, why? I believe you," she pronounced, as only she knows

how to speak, with such contempt and venom, with such scorn that, by God, I could have killed her at the moment.

She risked it. I was not lying about that, too, in what I said to her.

"You are not a coward?" she asked me suddenly.

"Perhaps I am a coward. I don't know. . . . I have not thought about it for a long time."

"If I were to say to you, 'Kill this man,' would you kill him?"

"Whom?"

"Whom I choose."

"The Frenchman?"

"Don't ask questions, but answer. Whom I tell you. I want to know whether you spoke seriously just now?"

She waited for my answer so gravely and impatiently that it struck me as strange.

"Come, do tell me, what has been happening here?" I cried. "What are you afraid of—me, or what? I see all the muddle here for myself. You are the stepdaughter of a mad and ruined man possessed by a passion for that devil—Blanche. Then there is this Frenchman, with his mysterious influence over you, and—here you ask me now so gravely . . . such a question. At any rate let me know, or I shall go mad on the spot and do something. Are you ashamed to deign to be open with me? Surely you can't care what I think of you?"

"I am not speaking to you of that at all. I asked you a question and I'm waiting for the answer."

"Of course I will kill any one you tell me to," I cried. "But can you possibly . . . could you tell me to do it?"

"Do you suppose I should spare you? I shall tell you to, and stand aside and look on. Can you endure that? Why, no, as though you could! You would kill him, perhaps, if you were told, and then you would come and kill me for having dared to send you."

I felt as though I were stunned at these words. Of course, even then I looked upon her question as half a joke, a challenge; yet she had spoken very earnestly. I was struck, nevertheless, at her speaking out so frankly, at her maintaining such rights over me, at her accepting such power over me and saying so bluntly: "Go to ruin, and I'll stand aside and look on." In those words there was something so open and cynical that to my mind it was going too far. That, then, was how she looked at me. This was something more than slavery or insignificance. If one looks at a man like that, one exalts him to one's own level, and absurd and incredible as all our conversation was, yet there was a throb at my heart.

Suddenly she laughed. We were sitting on a bench, before the playing children, facing the place where the carriages used to stop and people used to get out in the avenue before the Casino.

"Do you see that stout baroness?" she cried. "That is Baroness Burmerhelm. She has only been here three days. Do you see her husband—a tall, lean Prussian with a stick? Do you remember how he looked at us the day before yesterday? Go up to the Baroness at once, take off your hat, and say something to her in French."

"Why?"

"You swore that you would jump down the Schlangenberg; you swear you are ready to kill any one if I tell you. Instead of these murders and tragedies I only want to laugh. Go without discussing it. I want to see the Baron thrash you with his stick."

"You challenge me; you think I won't do it?"

"Yes, I do challenge you. Go; I want you to!"

"By all means, I am going, though it's a wild freak. Only, I say, I hope it won't be unpleasant for the General, and through him for you. Upon my honour, I am not thinking of myself, but of you and the General. And what a mad idea to insult a woman!"

"Yes, you are only a chatterer, as I see," she said contemptuously. "Your eyes were fierce and bloodshot, but perhaps that was only because you had too much wine at dinner. Do you suppose that I don't understand that it is stupid and vulgar, and that the General would be angry? I simply want to laugh; I want to, and that's all about it! And what should you insult a woman for? Why, just to be thrashed."

I turned and went in silence to carry out her commission. Of course it was stupid, and of course I did not know how to get out of it, but as I began to get closer to the Baroness I remember, as it were, something within myself urging me on; it was an impulse of schoolboyish mischief. Besides, I was horribly overwrought, and felt just as though I were drunk.

Chapter 6

NOW two days have passed since that stupid day. And what a noise and fuss and talk and uproar there was! And how unseemly and disgraceful, how stupid and vulgar, it was! And I was the cause of it all. Yet at times it's laughable—to me, at any rate. I can't make up my mind what happened to me, whether I really was in a state of frenzy, or whether it was a momentary aberration and I behaved disgracefully till I was pulled up. At times it seemed to me that my mind was giving way. And at times it seems to me that I have not outgrown childhood and schoolboyishness, and that it was simply a crude schoolboy's prank.

It was Polina, it was all Polina! Perhaps I shouldn't have behaved like a schoolboy if it hadn't been for her. Who knows? perhaps I did it out of despair (stupid as it seems, though, to reason like that). And I don't understand, I don't understand what there is fine in her! She is fine, though; she is; I believe she's fine. She drives other men off their heads, too. She's tall and graceful, only very slender. It seems to me you could tie her in a knot or bend her double. Her foot is long and narrow—tormenting. Tormenting is just what it is. Her hair has a reddish tint. Her eyes are regular cat's eyes, but how proudly and disdainfully she can look with them. Four months ago, when I had only just come, she was talking hotly for a long while one evening with De Grieux in the drawing-room, and looked at him in such a way . . . that afterwards, when I went up to to my room to go to bed, I imagined that she must have just given him a slap in the face. She stood facing him and looked at him. It was from that evening that I loved her.

To come to the point, however.

I stepped off the path into the avenue, and stood waiting for the Baron and the Baroness. When they were five paces from me I took off my hat and bowed.

I remember the Baroness was wearing a light grey dress of immense circumference, with flounces, a crinoline, and a train. She was short and exceptionally stout, with such a fearful double chin that she seemed to have no neck. Her face was crimson. Her eyes were small, spiteful and insolent. She walked as though she were doing an honour to all beholders. The Baron was lean and tall. Like most Germans, he had a wry face covered with thousands of fine wrinkles, and wore spectacles; he was about forty-five. His legs seemed to start from his chest: that's a sign of race. He was as proud as a peacock. He was rather clumsy. There was something like a sheep in the expression of his face that would pass with them for profundity.

All this flashed upon my sight in three seconds.

My bow and the hat in my hand gradually arrested their attention. The Baron slightly knitted his brows. The Baroness simply sailed straight at me.

"*Madame la baronne,*" I articulated distinctly, emphasizing each word, "*j'ai l'honneur d'être votre esclave.*"

Then I bowed, replaced my hat, and walked past the Baron, turning my face towards him with a polite smile.

She had told me to take off my hat, but I had bowed and behaved like an impudent schoolboy on my own account. Goodness knows what impelled me to! I felt as though I were plunging into space.

"*Hein!*" cried, or rather croaked, the Baron, turning towards me with angry surprise.

I turned and remained in respectful expectation, still gazing at him with a smile. He was evidently perplexed, and raised his eyebrows as high as they would go. His face grew darker and darker. The Baroness, too, turned towards me, and she, too, stared in wrathful surprise. The passers-by began to look on. Some even stopped.

"*Hein!*" the Baron croaked again, with redoubled gutturalness and redoubled anger.

"*Ja wohl!*" I drawled, still looking him straight in the face.

"*Sind Sie rasend?*" he cried, waving his stick and beginning, I think, to be a little nervous. He was perhaps perplexed by my appearance. I was very well, even foppishly, dressed, like a man belonging to the best society.

"*Ja wo-o-ohl!*" I shouted suddenly at the top of my voice, drawling the *o* like the Berliners, who use the expression *Ja wohl* in every sentence, and drawl the letter *o* more or less according to the shade of their thought or feeling.

The Baron and Baroness turned away quickly and almost ran away from me in terror. Of the spectators, some were talking, others were gazing at me in amazement. I don't remember very clearly, though.

I turned and walked at my ordinary pace to Polina Alexandrovna. But when I was within a hundred paces of her seat, I saw her get up and walk with the children towards the hotel.

I overtook her at the door.

"I have performed . . . the foolery," I said, when I reached her.

"Well, what of it? Now you can get out of the scrape," she answered. She walked upstairs without even glancing at me.

I spent the whole evening walking about the park. I crossed the park and then the wood beyond and walked into another state. In a cottage I had an omelette and some wine; for that idyllic repast they extorted a whole thaler and a half.

It was eleven o'clock before I returned home. I was at once summoned before the General.

Our party occupied two suites in the hotel; they have four rooms. The first is a big room—a drawing-room with a piano in it. The next, also a large room, is the General's study. Here he was awaiting me, standing in the middle of the room in a majestic pose. De Grieux sat lolling on the sofa.

"Allow me to ask you, sir, what have you been about?" began the General, addressing me.

"I should be glad if you would go straight to the point, General," said I. "You probably mean to refer to my encounter with a German this morning?"

"A German? That German was Baron Burmerhelm, a very important personage! You insulted him and the Baroness."

"Not in the least."

"You alarmed them, sir!" cried the General.

"Not a bit of it. When I was in Berlin the sound was for ever in my ears of that *Ja wohl,* continually repeated at every word and disgustingly drawled out by them. When I met them in the avenue that *Ja wohl* suddenly came into my mind, I don't know why, and—well, it had an irritating effect on me. . . . Besides, the Baroness, who has met me three times, has the habit of walking straight at me as though I were a worm who might be trampled underfoot. You must admit that I, too, may have my proper pride. I took off my hat and said politely (I assure you I said it politely): *'Madame, j'ai l'honneur d'être votre esclave.'* When the Baron turned round and said, *'Hein!'* I felt an impulse to shout, *'Ja wohl!'* I shouted it twice: the first time in an ordinary tone, and the second—I drawled it as much as I could. That was all."

I must own I was intensely delighted at this extremely schoolboyish explanation. I had a strange desire to make the story as absurd as possible in the telling.

And as I went on, I got more and more to relish it.

"Are you laughing at me?" cried the General. He turned to the Frenchman and explained to him in French that I was positively going out of my way to provoke a scandal! De Grieux laughed contemptuously and shrugged his shoulders.

"Oh, don't imagine that; it was not so at all!" I cried. "My conduct was wrong, of course; I confess that with the utmost candour. My behaviour may even be called a stupid and improper schoolboy prank, but—nothing more. And do you know, General, I heartily regret it. But there is one circumstance which, to my mind at least, almost saves me from repentance. Lately, for the last fortnight, indeed, I've not been feeling well: I have felt ill, nervous, irritable, moody, and on some occasions I lose all control of myself. Really, I've sometimes had an intense impulse to attack the Marquis de Grieux and . . . However, there's no need to say, he might be offended. In short, it's the sign of illness. I don't know whether the Baroness Burmerhelm will take this fact into consideration when I beg her pardon (for I intend to apologize). I imagine she will not consider it, especially as that line of excuse has been somewhat abused in legal circles of late. Lawyers have taken to arguing in criminal cases that their clients were not responsible at the moment of their crime, and that it was a form of disease. 'He killed him,' they say, 'and has no memory of it.' And only imagine, General, the medical authorities support them—and actually maintain that there are illnesses, temporary aberrations, in which a man scarcely remembers anything, or has only a half or a quarter of his memory. But the Baron and Baroness are people of the older generation; besides, they are Prussian *junkers* and landowners, and so are probably unaware of this advance in the world of medical jurisprudence, and will not accept my explanation. What do you think, General?"

"Enough, sir," the General pronounced sharply, with surprised indignation; "enough! I will try once for all to rid myself of your mischievous pranks. You are not going to apologize to the Baron and Baroness. Any communication with you, even though it were to consist solely of your request for forgiveness, would be beneath their dignity. The Baron has learnt that you are a member of my household; he has already had an explanation with me at the Casino, and I assure you that he was within an ace of asking me to give him satisfaction. Do you understand what you have exposed me to—me, sir? I—I was forced to ask the Baron's pardon, and gave him my word that immediately, this very day, you would cease to be a member of my household."

"Allow me, allow me, General; then did he insist on that himself, that I should cease to belong to your household, as you were pleased to express it?"

"No, but I considered myself bound to give him that satisfaction, and, of course, the Baron was satisfied. We must part, sir. There is what is owing to you, four friedrichs d'or and three florins, according to the reckoning here. Here is the money, and here is the note of the account; you can verify it. Good-bye. From this time forth we are strangers. I've had nothing but trouble and unpleasantness from you. I will call the *kellner* and inform him from this day forth that I am not responsible for your hotel expenses. I have the honour to remain your obedient servant."

I took the money and the paper upon which the account was written in pencil, bowed to the General, and said to him very seriously—

"General, the matter cannot end like this. I am very sorry that you were put into an unpleasant position with the Baron, but, excuse me, you were to blame for it yourself. Why did you take it upon yourself to be responsible for me to the Baron? What is the meaning of the expression that I am a member of your household? I am simply a teacher in your house, that is all. I am neither your son nor your ward, and you cannot be responsible for my actions. I am a legally responsible person, I am twenty-five, I am a graduate of the university, I am a nobleman, I am not connected with you in any way. Nothing but my unbounded respect for your dignity prevents me now from demanding from you the fullest explanation and satisfaction for taking upon yourself the right to answer for me."

The General was so much amazed that he flung up his hands, then turned suddenly to the Frenchman and hurriedly informed him that I had just all but challenged him to a duel.

The Frenchman laughed aloud.

"But I am not going to let the Baron off," I said, with complete composure, not in the least embarrassed by M. de Grieux's laughter; "and as, General, you consented to listen to the Baron's complaint to-day and have taken up his cause, and have made yourself, as it were, a party in the whole affair, I have the honour to inform you that no later than to-morrow morning I shall ask the Baron on my own account for a formal explanation of the reasons which led him to apply to other persons—as though I were unable or unfit to answer for myself."

What I foresaw happened. The General, hearing of this new absurdity, became horribly nervous.

"What, do you mean to keep up this damnable business?" he shouted. "What a position you are putting me in—good heavens! Don't dare, don't dare, sir, or, I swear! . . . There are police here, too, and I . . . I . . . in fact, by my rank . . . and the Baron's, too . . . in fact, you shall be arrested and turned out of the state by the police, to teach you not to make a disturbance. Do you understand that, sir?" And although he was breathless with anger, he was also horribly frightened.

"General," I answered, with a composure that was insufferable to him, "you can't arrest any one for making a disturbance before they have made a disturbance. I have not yet begun to make my explanations to the Baron, and you don't know in the least in what form or on what grounds I intend to proceed. I only wish to have an explanation of a position insulting to me, *i. e.* that I am under the control of a person who has authority over my freedom of action. There is no need for you to be so anxious and uneasy."

"For goodness' sake, for goodness' sake, Alexey Ivanovitch, drop this insane intention!" muttered the General, suddenly changing his wrathful tone for one of entreaty, and even clutching me by the hand. "Fancy what it will lead to! Fresh unpleasantness! You must see for yourself that I must be particular here . . . particularly now! particularly now! . . . Oh, you don't know, you don't know all my circumstances! . . . When we leave this place I shall be willing to take you back again; I was only speaking of now, in fact—of course, you understand there are reasons!" he cried in despair. "Alexey Ivanovitch, Alexey Ivanovitch . . ."

Retreating to the door, I begged him more earnestly not to worry himself, promised him that everything should go off well and with propriety, and hastily withdrew.

The Russian abroad is sometimes too easily cowed, and is horribly afraid of what people will say, how they will look at him, and whether this or that will be the proper thing. In short, they behave as though they were in corsets, especially those who have pretensions to consequence. The thing that pleases them most is a certain established traditional etiquette, which they follow slavishly in hotels, on their walks, in assemblies, on a journey. . . . But the General had let slip that, apart from this, there was a particular circumstance, that he must be "particular." That was why he so weakly showed the white feather and changed his tone with me. I took this as evidence and made a note of it; and, of course, he might have brought my folly to the notice of the authorities, so that I really had to be careful.

I did not particularly want to anger the General, however; but I did want to anger Polina. Polina had treated me so badly, and had thrust me into such a stupid position, that I could not help wanting to force her to beg me to stop. My schoolboyish prank might compromise her, too. Moreover, another feeling and desire was taking shape in me: though I might be reduced to a nonentity in her presence, that did not prove that I could not hold my own before other people, or that the Baron could thrash me. I longed to have the laugh against them all, and to come off with flying colours. Let them see! She would be frightened by the scandal and call me back again, or, even if she didn't, at least she would see that I could hold my own.

(A wonderful piece of news! I have just heard from the nurse, whom I met on the stairs, that Marya Filippovna set off to-day, entirely alone, by the evening train to Karlsbad to see her cousin. What's the meaning of that? Nurse says that she has long been meaning to go; but how was it no one knew of it? Though perhaps I was the only one who did not know it. The nurse let slip that Marya Filippovna had words with the General the day before yesterday. I understand. No doubt that is Mlle. Blanche. Yes, something decisive is coming.)

Chapter 7

IN THE morning I called for the *kellner* and told him to make out a separate bill for me. My room was not such an expensive one as to make me feel alarmed and anxious to leave the hotel. I had sixteen friedrichs d'or, and there . . . there perhaps was wealth! Strange to say, I have not won yet, but I behave, I feel and think, like a rich man, and cannot imagine anything else.

In spite of the early hour I intended to go at once to see Mr. Astley at the Hôtel d'Angleterre, which was quite close by, when suddenly De Grieux came in to me. That had never happened before, and, what is more, that gentleman and I had for some time past been on very queer and strained terms. He openly displayed his contempt for me, even tried not to conceal it; and I—I had my own reasons for disliking him. In short, I hated him. His visit greatly surprised me. I at once detected that something special was brewing.

He came in very politely and complimented me on my room. Seeing that I had my hat in my hand, he inquired whether I could be going out for a walk so early. When he heard that I was going to see Mr. Astley on business, he pondered, he reflected, and his face assumed an exceedingly careworn expression.

De Grieux was like all Frenchmen; that is, gay and polite when necessary and profitable to be so, and insufferably tedious when the necessity to be gay and polite was over. A Frenchman is not often naturally polite. He is always polite, as it were, to order, with a motive. If he sees the necessity for being fantastic, original, a little out of the ordinary, then his freakishness is most stupid and unnatural, and is made up of accepted and long-vulgarized traditions. The natural Frenchman is composed of the most plebeian, petty, ordinary practical sense—in fact, he is one of the most wearisome creatures in the world. In my opinion, only the innocent and inexperienced—especially Russian young ladies—are fascinated by Frenchmen. To every decent person the conventionalism of the established traditions of drawing-room politeness, ease and gaiety are at once evident and intolerable.

"I have come to see you on business," he began, with marked directness, though with courtesy, "and I will not disguise that I have come as an ambassador, or rather as a mediator, from the General. As I know Russian very imperfectly I understood very little of what passed yesterday, but the General explained it to me in detail, and I confess . . ."

"But, listen, M. de Grieux," I interrupted; "here you have undertaken to be a mediator in this affair. I am, of course, an *outchitel,* and have never laid claim to the honour of being a great friend of this family, nor of being on particularly intimate terms with it, and so I don't know all the circumstances; but explain: are you now entirely a member of the family? You take such an interest in everything and are certain at once to be a mediator . . ."

This question did not please him. It was too transparent for him, and he did not want to speak out.

"I am connected with the General partly by business, partly by *certain special* circumstances," he said drily. "The General has sent me to ask you to abandon the intentions you expressed yesterday. All you thought of doing was no doubt very clever; but he begged me to represent to you that you would be utterly unsuccessful; what's more, the Baron will not receive you, and in any case is in a position to rid himself of any further unpleasantness on your part. You must see that yourself. Tell me, what is the object of going on with it? The General promises to take you back into his home at the first convenient opportunity, and until that time will continue your salary, *vos appointements.* That will be fairly profitable, won't it?"

I retorted very calmly that he was rather mistaken; that perhaps I shouldn't be kicked out at the Baron's, but, on the contrary, should be listened to; and I asked him to admit that he had probably come to find out what steps I was going to take in the matter.

"Oh, heavens! Since the General is so interested, he will, of course, be glad to know how you are going to behave, and what you are going to do."

I proceeded to explain, and he began listening, stretching himself at his ease and inclining his head on one side towards me, with an obvious, undisguised expression of irony on his face. Altogether he behaved very loftily. I tried with all my might to pretend that I took a very serious view of the matter. I explained that since the Baron had addressed a complaint of me to the General as though I were the latter's servant, he had, in the first place, deprived me thereby of my position; and secondly, had treated me as a person who was incapable of answering for himself and who was not worth speaking to. Of course, I said, I felt with justice that I had been insulted; however, considering the difference of age, position in society, and so on, and so on (I could scarcely restrain my laughter at this point), I did not want to rush into fresh indiscretion by directly insisting on satisfaction from the Baron, or even proposing a duel to him; nevertheless, I considered myself fully entitled to offer the Baron, and still more the Baroness, my apologies, especially since of late I had really felt ill, overwrought, and, so to say, fanciful, and so on, and so on. However, the Baron had, by his applying to the General, which was a slight to me, and by his insisting that the General should deprive me of my post, put me in such a position that now I could not offer him and the Baroness my apologies, because he and the Baroness and all the world would certainly suppose that I came to apologize because I was frightened and in order to be reinstated in my post. From all this it followed that I found myself now compelled to beg the Baron first of all to apologize to me in the most formal terms; for instance, to say that he had no desire to insult me. And when the Baron said this I should feel that my hands were set free, and with perfect candour and sincerity I should offer him my apologies. In brief, I concluded, I could only beg the Baron to untie my hands.

"Fie! how petty and how far-fetched! And why do you want to apologize? Come, admit, *monsieur ... monsieur ...* that you are doing all this on purpose to vex the General ... and perhaps you have some special object ... *mon cher monsieur ... pardon, j'ai oublié votre nom, M. Alexis? ... N'est-ce pas?*"

"But, excuse me, *mon cher marquis,* what has it to do with you?"

"*Mais le général ...*"

"But what about the General? He said something last night, that he had to be particularly careful ... and was so upset ... but I did not understand it."

"There is, there certainly is a particular circumstance," De Grieux caught me up in an insistent voice, in which a note of vexation was more and more marked. "You know Mlle. de Cominges ...?"

"That is, Mlle. Blanche?"

"Why, yes, Mlle. Blanche de Cominges . . . *et madame sa mère.* You see for yourself, the General . . . in short, the General is in love; in fact . . . in fact, the marriage may be celebrated here. And fancy, scandal, gossip . . ."

"I see no scandal or gossip connected with the marriage in this."

"But *le baron est si irascible, un caractère Prussien, vous savez, enfin il fera une querelle d'Allemand.*"

"With me, then, and not with you, for I no longer belong to the household. . . ." (I tried to be as irrational as possible on purpose.) "But, excuse me, is it settled, then, that Mlle. Blanche is to marry the General? What are they waiting for? I mean, why conceal this from us, at any rate from the members of the household?"

"I cannot . . . however, it is not quite . . . besides . . . you know, they are expecting news from Russia; the General has to make arrangements . . ."

"*Ah! ah! La baboulinka!*"

De Grieux looked at me with hatred.

"In short," he interrupted, "I fully rely on your innate courtesy, on your intelligence, on your tact. . . . You will certainly do this for the family in which you have been received like one of themselves, in which you have been liked and respected . . ."

"Excuse me, I've been dismissed! You maintain now that that is only in appearance; but you must admit, if you were told: 'I won't send you packing, but, for the look of the thing, kindly take yourself off' . . . You see, it comes almost to the same thing."

"Well, if that's how it is, if no request will have any influence on you," he began sternly and haughtily, "allow me to assure you that steps will be taken. There are authorities here; you'll be turned out to-day—*que diable! Un blanc-bec comme vous* wants to challenge a personage like the Baron! And do you think that you will not be interfered with? And, let me assure you, nobody is afraid of you here! I have approached you on my own account, because you have been worrying the General. And do you imagine that the Baron will not order his flunkeys to turn you out of the house?"

"But, you see, I'm not going myself," I answered, with the utmost composure. "You are mistaken, M. de Grieux; all this will be done much more decorously than you imagine. I am just setting off to Mr. Astley, and I am going to ask him to be my intermediary; in fact, to be my second. The man likes me, and certainly will not refuse. He will go to the Baron, and the Baron will receive him. Even if I am an *outchitel* and seem to be something subordinate and, well, defenceless, Mr. Astley is a nephew of a lord, of a real lord; every one knows that—Lord Pibroch—and that lord is here. Believe me, the Baron will be courteous to Mr. Astley and will listen to him. And if he won't listen, Mr. Astley will look upon it as a personal affront (you know how persistent Englishmen are), and will send a friend to call on the Baron; he has powerful friends. You may reckon, now, upon things not turning out quite as you expect."

The Frenchman was certainly scared; all this was really very much like the truth, and so it seemed that I really might be able to get up a scandal.

"Come, I beg you," he said in a voice of actual entreaty, "do drop the whole business! It seems to please you that it will cause a scandal! It is not satisfaction you want, but a scandal! As I have told you, it is very amusing and even witty—which is perhaps what you are aiming at. But, in short," he concluded, seeing that I had got up and was taking my hat, "I've come to give you these few lines from a certain person; read them; I was charged to wait for an answer."

Saying this, he took out of his pocket a little note, folded and sealed with a wafer, and handed it to me.

It was in Polina's handwriting.

"I fancy that you intend to go on with this affair, but there are special circumstances which I will explain to you perhaps later; please leave off and give way. It is all such silliness! I need you, and you promised yourself to obey me. Remember the Schlangenberg; I beg you to be obedient, and, if necessary, I command you.—Your P.

"P.S.—If you are angry with me for what happened yesterday, forgive me."

Everything seemed to be heaving before my eyes when I read these lines. My lips turned white and I began to tremble. The accursed Frenchman watched me with an exaggerated air of discretion, with his eyes turned away as though to avoid noticing my confusion. He had better have laughed at me outright.

"Very good," I answered; "tell Mademoiselle that she may set her mind at rest. Allow me to ask you," I added sharply, "why you have been so long giving me this letter. Instead of chattering about all sorts of nonsense, I think you ought to have begun with that . . . if you came expressly with that object."

"Oh, I wanted . . . all this is so strange that you must excuse my natural impatience. I was in haste to learn from you in person what you intended to do. Besides, I don't know what is in that note, and I thought there was no hurry for me to give it you."

"I understand: the long and the short of it is you were told only to give me the letter in case of the utmost necessity, and if you could settle it by word of mouth you were not to give it to me. Is that right? Tell me plainly, M. de Grieux."

"*Peut-être*," he said, assuming an air of peculiar reserve, and looking at me with a peculiar glance.

I took off my hat; he took off his hat and went out. It seemed to me that there was an ironical smile on his lips. And, indeed, what else could one expect?

"We'll be quits yet, Frenchy; we'll settle our accounts," I muttered as I went down the stairs. I could not think clearly; I felt as though I had had a blow on my head. The air revived me a little.

Two minutes later, as soon as ever I was able to reflect clearly, two thoughts stood out vividly before me: the *first* was that such trivial incidents, that a few mischievous and far-fetched threats from a mere boy, had caused such *universal* consternation! The *second* thought was: what sort of influence had this Frenchman over Polina? A mere word from him and she does anything he wants—writes a note and even *begs* me. Of course, their relations have always been a mystery to me from the very beginning, ever since I began to know them; but of late I have noticed in her a positive aversion and even contempt for him, while he did not even look at her, was absolutely rude to her. I had noticed it. Polina herself had spoken of him to me with aversion; she had dropped some extremely significant admissions . . . so he simply had her in his power. She was in some sort of bondage to him.

Chapter 8

ON THE promenade, as it is called here, that is, in the chestnut avenue, I met my Englishman.

"Oh, oh!" he began, as soon as he saw me. "I was coming to see you, and you are on your way to me. So you have parted from your people?"

"Tell me, first, how it is that you know all this?" I asked in amazement. "Is it possible that everybody knows of it?"

"Oh, no, every one doesn't; and, indeed, it's not worth their knowing. No one is talking about it."

"Then how do you know it?"

"I know, that is, I chanced to learn it. Now, where are you going when you leave here? I like you and that is why I was coming to see you."

"You are a splendid man, Mr. Astley," said I (I was very much interested, however, to know where he could have learnt it), "and since I have not yet had my coffee, and most likely you have not had a good cup, come to the café in the Casino. Let us sit down and have a smoke there, and I will tell you all about it, and . . . you tell me, too . . ."

The café was a hundred steps away. They brought us some coffee. We sat down and I lighted a cigarette. Mr. Astley did not light one and, gazing at me, prepared to listen.

"I am not going anywhere. I am staying here," I began.

"And I was sure you would," observed Mr. Astley approvingly.

On my way to Mr. Astley I had not meant to tell him anything of my love for Polina, and, in fact, I expressly intended to say nothing to him about it. All that time I had hardly said one word to him about it. He was, besides, very reserved. From the first I noticed that Polina had made a great impression upon him, but he never uttered her name. But, strange to say, now no sooner had he sat down and turned upon me his fixed, pewtery eyes, I felt, I don't know why, a desire to tell him everything, that is, all about my love in all its aspects. I was talking to him for half an hour and it was very pleasant to me; it was the first time I had talked of it! Noticing that at certain ardent sentences he was embarrassed, I purposely exaggerated my ardour. Only one thing I regret: I said, perhaps, more than I should about the Frenchman. . . .

Mr. Astley listened, sitting facing me without moving, looking straight into my eyes, not uttering a word, a sound; but when I spoke of the Frenchman, he suddenly pulled me up and asked me, severely, whether I had the right to refer to this circumstance which did not concern me? Mr. Astley always asked questions very strangely.

"You are right. I am afraid not," I answered.

"You can say nothing definite, nothing that is not supposition about that *marquis* and Miss Polina?"

I was surprised again at such a point-blank question from a man so reserved as Mr. Astley.

"No, nothing definite," I answered; "of course not."

"If so, you have done wrong, not only in speaking of it to me, but even in thinking of it yourself."

"Very good, very good; I admit it, but that is not the point now," I interrupted, wondering at myself. At this point I told him the whole of yesterday's story in full detail: Polina's prank, my adventure with the Baron, my dismissal, the General's extraordinary dismay, and, finally, I described in detail De Grieux's visit that morning. Lastly I showed him the note.

"What do you deduce from all this?" I asked. "I came on purpose to find out what you think. For my part, I could kill that Frenchman, and perhaps I shall."

"So could I," said Mr. Astley. "As regards Miss Polina, you know ... we may enter into relations even with people who are detestable to us if we are compelled by necessity. There may be relations of which you know nothing, dependent upon outside circumstances. I think you may set your mind at rest—to some extent, of course. As for her action yesterday, it was strange, of course; not that she wanted to get rid of you and expose you to the Baron's walking-stick (I don't understand why he did not use it, since he had it in his hand), but because such a prank is improper ... for such an ... exquisite young lady. Of course, she couldn't have expected that you would carry out her jesting wish so literally ..."

"Do you know what?" I cried suddenly, looking intently at Mr. Astley. "It strikes me that you have heard about this already—do you know from whom? From Miss Polina herself!"

Mr. Astley looked at me with surprise.

"Your eyes are sparkling and I can read your suspicion in them," he said, regaining his former composure; "but you have no right whatever to express your suspicions. I cannot recognize the right, and I absolutely refuse to answer your question."

"Enough! There's no need," I cried, strangely perturbed, and not knowing why it had come into my head. And when, where and how could Mr. Astley have been chosen by Polina to confide in? Though, of late, indeed, I had, to some extent, lost sight of Mr. Astley, and Polina was always an enigma to me, such an enigma that now, for instance, after launching into an account of my passion to Mr. Astley, I was suddenly struck while I was speaking by the fact that there was scarcely anything positive and definite I could say about our relations. Everything was, on the contrary, strange, unstable, and, in fact, quite unique.

"Oh, very well, very well. I am utterly perplexed and there is a great deal I can't understand at present," I answered, gasping as though I were breathless. "You are a good man, though. And now, another matter, and I ask not your advice, but your opinion."

After a brief pause I began.

"What do you think? Why was the General so scared? Why did he make such a to-do over my stupid practical joke? Such a fuss that even De Grieux thought it necessary to interfere (and he interferes only in the most important matters); visited me (think of that!), begged and besought me—he, De Grieux—begged and besought me! Note, finally, he came at nine o'clock, and by that time Miss Polina's letter was in his hands. One wonders when it was written. Perhaps they waked Miss Polina up on purpose! Apart from what I see clearly from this, that Miss Polina is his slave (for she even begs my forgiveness!)—apart from that, how is she concerned in all this, she personally; why is she so much interested? Why are they frightened of some Baron? And what if the General is marrying Mlle. Blanche de Cominges? They say that, owing to that circumstance, they must be *particular,* but you must admit that this is somewhat too particular! What do you think? I am sure from your eyes you know more about it than I do!"

Mr. Astley laughed and nodded.

"Certainly. I believe I know much more about it than you," he said. "Mlle. Blanche is the only person concerned, and I am sure that is the absolute truth."

"Well, what about Mlle. Blanche?" I cried impatiently. (I suddenly had a hope that something would be disclosed about Mlle. Polina.)

"I fancy that Mlle. Blanche has at the moment special reasons for avoiding a meeting with the Baron and Baroness, even more an unpleasant meeting, worse still, a scandalous one."

"Well, well . . ."

"Two years ago Mlle. Blanche was here at Roulettenburg in the season. I was here, too. Mlle. Blanche was not called Mlle. de Cominges then, and her mother, Madame *la maman* Cominges, was non-existent then. Anyway, she was never mentioned. De Grieux—De Grieux was not here either. I cherish the conviction that, far from being relations, they have only very recently become acquainted. He—De Grieux—has only become a marquis very recently, too—I am sure of that from one circumstance. One may assume, in fact, that his name has not been De Grieux very long either. I know a man here who has met him passing under another name."

"But he really has a very respectable circle of acquaintances."

"That may be. Even Mlle. Blanche may have. But two years ago, at the request of that very Baroness, Mlle. Blanche was invited by the police to leave the town, and she did leave it."

"How was that?"

"She made her appearance here first with an Italian, a prince of

some sort, with an historical name—Barberini, or something like it—
a man covered with rings and diamonds, not false ones either. They
used to drive about in a magnificent carriage. Mlle. Blanche used to
play *trente et quarante,* at first winning, though her luck changed later
on, as far as I remember. I remember one evening she lost a considerable sum. But, worse still, *un beau matin* her prince vanished; the horses
and the carriage vanished too, everything vanished. The bills owing at
the hotels were immense. Mlle. Selma (she suddenly ceased to be
Barberini, and became Mlle. Selma) was in the utmost despair. She
was shrieking and wailing all over the hotel, and rent her clothes in
her fury. There was a Polish count staying here at the hotel (all Polish
travellers are counts), and Mlle. Selma, rending her garments and
scratching her face like a cat with her beautiful perfumed fingers, made
some impression on him. They talked things over, and by dinner-time
she was consoled. In the evening he made his appearance at the Casino
with the lady on his arm. As usual, Mlle. Selma laughed very loudly,
and her manner was somewhat more free and easy than before. She
definitely showed that she belonged to the class of ladies who, when
they go up to the roulette table, shoulder the other players aside to clear
a space for themselves. That's particularly *chic* among such ladies. You
must have noticed it?"

"Oh, yes."

"It's not worth noticing. To the annoyance of the decent public they
are not moved on here—at least, not those of them who can change a
thousand-rouble note every day, at the roulette table. As soon as they
cease to produce a note to change they are asked to withdraw, however.
Mlle. Selma still went on changing notes, but her play became more
unlucky than ever. Note that such ladies are very often lucky in their
play; they have a wonderful self-control. However, my story is finished.
One day the count vanished just as the prince had done. However,
Mlle. Selma made her appearance at the roulette table alone; this time
no one came forward to offer her his arm. In two days she had lost
everything. After laying down her last louis d'or and losing it, she
looked round, and saw, close by her, Baron Burmerhelm, who was
scrutinizing her intently and with profound indignation. But Mlle.
Selma, not noticing his indignation, accosted the Baron with that smile
we all know so well, and asked him to put down ten louis d'or on the
red for her. In consequence of a complaint from the Baroness she received that evening an invitation not to show herself at the Casino
again. If you are surprised at my knowing all these petty and extremely
improper details, it is because I have heard them from Mr. Fider, one

of my relations, who carried off Mlle. Selma in his carriage from Roulettenburg to Spa that very evening. Now, remember, Mlle. Blanche wishes to become the General's wife; probably in order in future not to receive such invitations as that one from the police at the Casino, the year before last. Now she does not play; but that is because, as it seems, she has capital of her own which she lends out at a percentage to gamblers here. That's a much safer speculation. I even suspect that the luckless General is in debt to her. Perhaps De Grieux is, too. Perhaps De Grieux is associated with her. You will admit that, till the wedding, at any rate, she can hardly be anxious to attract the attention of the Baron and Baroness in any way. In short, in her position, nothing could be more disadvantageous than a scandal. You are connected with their party and your conduct might cause a scandal, especially as she appears in public every day either arm-in-arm with the General or in company with Miss Polina. Now do you understand?"

"No, I don't!" I cried, thumping the table so violently that the garçon ran up in alarm.

"Tell me, Mr. Astley," I said furiously. "If you knew all this story and, therefore, know positively what Mlle. Blanche de Cominges is, why didn't you warn me at least, the General, or, most of all, most of all, Miss Polina, who has shown herself here at the Casino in public, arm-in-arm with Mlle. Blanche? Can such a thing be allowed?"

"I had no reason to warn you, for you could have done nothing," Mr. Astley answered calmly. "Besides, warn them of what? The General knows about Mlle. Blanche perhaps more than I do, yet he still goes about with her and Miss Polina. The General is an unlucky man. I saw Mlle. Blanche yesterday, galloping on a splendid horse with M. de Grieux and that little Russian Prince, and the General was galloping after them on a chestnut. He told me in the morning that his legs ached, but he sat his horse well. And it struck me at that moment that he was an utterly ruined man. Besides, all this is no business of mine, and I have only lately had the honour of making Miss Polina's acquaintance. However" (Mr. Astley caught himself up), "I've told you already that I do not recognize your right to ask certain questions, though I have a genuine liking for you . . ."

"Enough," I said, getting up. "It is clear as daylight to me now, that Miss Polina knows all about Mlle. Blanche, but that she cannot part from her Frenchman, and so she brings herself to going about with Mlle. Blanche. Believe me, no other influence would compel her to go about with Mlle. Blanche and to beg me in her letter not to interfere with the Baron! Damn it all, there's no understanding it!"

"You forget, in the first place, that Mlle. de Cominges is the General's *fiancée,* and in the second place that Miss Polina is the General's stepdaughter, that she has a little brother and sister, the General's own children, who are utterly neglected by that insane man and have, I believe, been robbed by him."

"Yes, yes, that is so! To leave the children would mean abandoning them altogether; to remain means protecting their interests and, perhaps, saving some fragments of their property. Yes, yes, all that is true. But still, still! . . . Ah, now I understand why they are all so concerned about Granny!"

"About whom?" asked Mr. Astley.

"That old witch in Moscow who won't die, and about whom they are expecting a telegram that she is dying."

"Yes, of course, all interest is concentrated on her. Everything depends on what she leaves them! If he comes in for a fortune the General will marry, Miss Polina will be set free, and De Grieux . . ."

"Well, and De Grieux?"

"And De Grieux will be paid; that is all he is waiting for here."

"Is that all, do you think that is all he's waiting for?"

"I know nothing more." Mr. Astley was obstinately silent.

"But I do, I do!" I repeated fiercely. "He's waiting for the inheritance too, because Polina will get a dowry, and as soon as she gets the money will throw herself on his neck. All women are like that! Even the proudest of them turn into the meanest slaves! Polina is only capable of loving passionately: nothing else. That's my opinion of her! Look at her, particularly when she is sitting alone, thinking; it's something predestined, doomed, fated! She is capable of all the horrors of life, and passion . . . she . . . she . . . but who is that calling me?" I exclaimed suddenly. "Who is shouting? I heard some one shout in Russian: Alexey Ivanovitch! A woman's voice. Listen, listen!"

At this moment we were approaching the hotel. We had left the café long ago, almost without noticing it.

"I did hear a woman calling, but I don't know who was being called; it is Russian. Now I see where the shouts come from," said Mr. Astley. "It is that woman sitting in a big armchair who has just been carried up the steps by so many flunkeys. They are carrying trunks after her, so the train must have just come in."

"But why is she calling me? She is shouting again; look, she is waving to us."

"I see she is waving," said Mr. Astley.

"Alexey Ivanovitch! Alexey Ivanovitch! Mercy on us, what a dolt he is!" came desperate shouts from the hotel steps.

We almost ran to the entrance. I ran up the steps and . . . my hands dropped at my sides with amazement and my feet seemed rooted to the ground.

Chapter 9

A̲T THE top of the broad steps at the hotel entrance, surrounded by footmen and maids and the many obsequious servants of the hotel, in the presence of the *ober-kellner* himself, eager to receive the exalted visitor, who had arrived with her own servants and with so many trunks and boxes, and had been carried up the steps in an invalid-chair, was seated—*Granny!* Yes, it was she herself, the terrible old Moscow lady and wealthy landowner, Antonida Vassilyevna Tarasyevitchev, the *Granny* about whom telegrams had been sent and received, who had been dying and was not dead, and who had suddenly dropped upon us in person, like snow on our heads. Though she was seventy-five and had for the last five years lost the use of her legs and had to be carried about everywhere in a chair, yet she had arrived and was, as always, alert, captious, self-satisfied, sitting upright in her chair, shouting in a loud, peremptory voice and scolding every one. In fact, she was exactly the same as she had been on the only two occasions that I had the honour of seeing her during the time I had been tutor in the General's family. Naturally I stood rooted to the spot with amazement. As she was being carried up the steps, she had detected me a hundred paces away, with her lynx-like eyes, had recognized me and called me by my name, which she had made a note of, once for all, as she always did. And this was the woman they had expected to be in her coffin, buried, and leaving them her property. That was the thought that flashed into my mind. "Why, she will outlive all of us and every one in the hotel! But, my goodness! what will our friends do now, what will the General do? She will turn the whole hotel upside down!"

"Well, my good man, why are you standing with your eyes starting out of your head?" Granny went on shouting to me. "Can't you welcome me? Can't you say 'How do you do'? Or have you grown proud and won't? Or, perhaps, you don't recognize me? Potapitch, do you hear?" She turned to her butler, an old man with grey hair and a pink bald patch on his head, wearing a dress-coat and white tie. "Do you hear? he doesn't recognize me. They had buried me! They sent telegram upon telegram to ask whether I was dead or not! You see, I know all about it! Here, you see, I am quite alive."

"Upon my word, Antonida Vassilyevna, why should I wish you harm?" I answered gaily, recovering myself. "I was only surprised. . . . And how could I help being surprised at such an unexpected . . ."

"What is there to surprise you? I just got into the train and came. The train was comfortable and not jolting. Have you been for a walk?"

"Yes, I've been a walk to the Casino."

"It's pleasant here," said Granny, looking about her. "It's warm and the trees are magnificent. I like that! Are the family at home? The General?"

"Oh, yes, at this time they are sure to be all at home."

"So they have fixed hours here, and everything in style? They set the tone. I am told they keep their carriage, *les seigneurs russes!* They spend all their money and then they go abroad. And is Praskovya with them?"

"Yes, Polina Alexandrovna, too."

"And the Frenchy? Oh, well, I shall see them all for myself. Alexey Ivanovitch, show me the way straight to him. Are you comfortable here?"

"Fairly so, Antonida Vassilyevna."

"Potapitch, tell that dolt, the *kellner,* to give me a nice convenient set of rooms, not too high up, and take my things there at once. Why are they all so eager to carry me? Why do they put themselves forward? Ech, the slavish creatures! Who is this with you?" she asked, addressing me again.

"This is Mr. Astley," I answered.

"What Mr. Astley?"

"A traveller, a good friend of mine; an acquaintance of the General's, too."

"An Englishman. To be sure he stares at me and keeps his mouth shut. I like Englishmen, though. Well, carry me upstairs, straight to their rooms. Where are they?"

They carried Granny up; I walked up the broad staircase in front. Our procession was very striking. Every one we met stopped and stared. Our hotel is considered the best, the most expensive, and the most aristocratic in the place. Magnificent ladies and dignified Englishmen were always to be met on the staircase and in the corridors. Many people were making inquiries below of the *ober-kellner,* who was greatly impressed. He answered, of course, that this was a distinguished foreign lady, *une russe, une comtesse, grande dame,* and that she was taking the very apartments that had been occupied the week before by *la grande duchesse de* N. Granny's commanding and authoritative appearance as she was carried up in the chair was chiefly responsible for the sensation she caused. Whenever she met any one fresh she scrutinized him inquisitively and questioned me about him in a loud voice. Granny was powerfully built, and though she did not get up from her chair, it could be seen that she was very tall. Her back was as straight as a board and she did not lean back in her chair. Her big grey head with its large, bold features was held erect; she had a positively haughty and defiant expression; and it was evident that her air and gestures were perfectly natural. In spite of her seventy-five years there was still a certain vigour in her face: and even her teeth were almost perfect. She was wearing a black silk dress and a white cap.

"She interests me very much," Mr. Astley, who was going up beside me, whispered to me.

"She knows about the telegrams," I thought. "She knows about De Grieux, too, but I fancy she does not know much about Mlle. Blanche as yet." I communicated this thought to Mr. Astley.

Sinful man that I was, after the first surprise was over, I was immensely delighted at the thunderbolt that we were launching at the General. I was elated; and I walked in front feeling very gay.

Our apartments were on the third floor. Without announcing her arrival or even knocking at the door, I simply flung it wide-open and Granny was carried in, in triumph. All of them were, as by design, assembled in the General's study. It was twelve o'clock and, I believe, some excursion was being planned for the whole party. Some were to drive, others were to ride on horseback, some acquaintances had been asked to join the party. Besides the General and Polina, with the children and their nurse, there were sitting in the study De Grieux, Mlle. Blanche, again wearing her riding-habit, her mother, the little Prince, and a learned German traveller whom I had not seen before.

Granny's chair was set down in the middle of the room, three paces from the General. My goodness! I shall never forget the sensation! As we went in the General was describing something, while De Grieux was correcting him. I must observe that Mlle. Blanche and De Grieux had for the last few days been particularly attentive to the little Prince, *à la barbe du pauvre général,* and the tone of the party was extremely gay and genially intimate, though, perhaps, it was artificial. Seeing Granny, the General was struck dumb. His mouth dropped open and ħe broke off in the middle of a word. He gazed at her open-eyed, as though spellbound by the eye of a basilisk. Granny looked at him in silence, too, immovably, but what a triumphant, challenging and ironical look it was! They gazed at each other for ten full seconds in the midst of profound silence on the part of all around them. For the first moment De Grieux was petrified, but immediately afterwards a look of extreme uneasiness flitted over his face. Mlle. Blanche raised her eyebrows, opened her mouth and gazed wildly at Granny. The Prince and the learned German stared at the whole scene in great astonishment. Polina's eyes expressed the utmost wonder and perplexity, and she suddenly turned white as a handkerchief; a minute later the blood rushed rapidly into her face, flushing her cheeks. Yes, this was a catastrophe for all of them! I kept turning my eyes from Granny to all surrounding her and back again. Mr. Astley stood on one side, calm and polite as usual.

"Well, here I am! Instead of a telegram!" Granny broke the silence by going off into a peal of laughter. "Well, you didn't expect me?"

"Antonida Vassilyevna . . . Auntie . . . But how on earth . . ." muttered the unhappy General.

If Granny had remained silent for a few seconds longer, he would, perhaps, have had a stroke.

"How on earth what? I got into the train and came. What's the railway for? You all thought that I had been laid out, and had left you a fortune? You see, I know how you sent telegrams from here. What a lot of money you must have wasted on them! They cost a good bit from here. I simply threw my legs over my shoulders and came off here. Is this the Frenchman? M. de Grieux, I fancy?"

"*Oui, madame,*" De Grieux responded; "*et croyez, je suis si enchanté . . . votre santé . . . c'est un miracle . . . vous voir ici . . . une surprise charmante. . . .*"

"*Charmante,* I daresay; I know you, you mummer. I haven't this much faith in you," and she pointed her little finger at him. "Who is this?" she asked, indicating Mlle. Blanche. The striking-looking Frenchwoman, in a riding-habit with a whip in her hand, evidently impressed her. "Some one living here?"

"This is Mlle. Blanche de Cominges, and this is her mamma, Madame de Cominges; they are staying in this hotel," I explained.

"Is the daughter married?" Granny questioned me without ceremony.

"Mlle. de Cominges is an unmarried lady," I answered, purposely speaking in a low voice and as respectfully as possible.

"Lively?"

"I do not understand the question."

"You are not dull with her? Does she understand Russian? De Grieux picked it up in Moscow. He had a smattering of it."

I explained that Mlle. de Cominges had never been in Russia.

"Bonjour," said Granny, turning abruptly to Mlle. Blanche.

"Bonjour, madame." Mlle. Blanche made an elegant and ceremonious curtsey, hastening, under the cover of modesty and politeness, to express by her whole face and figure her extreme astonishment at such a strange question and manner of address.

"Oh, she casts down her eyes, she is giving herself airs and graces; you can see the sort she is at once; an actress of some kind. I'm stopping here below in the hotel," she said, turning suddenly to the General. "I shall be your neighbour. Are you glad or sorry?"

"Oh, Auntie! do believe in my sincere feelings . . . of pleasure," the General responded. He had by now recovered himself to some extent, and as, upon occasion, he could speak appropriately and with dignity, and even with some pretension to effectiveness, he began displaying his gifts now. "We have been so alarmed and upset by the news of your illness. . . . We received such despairing telegrams, and all at once . . ."

"Come, you are lying, you are lying," Granny interrupted at once.

"But how could you"—the General, too, made haste to interrupt, raising his voice and trying not to notice the word "lying"—"how could you bring yourself to undertake such a journey? You must admit that at your age and in your state of health . . . at any rate it is all so unexpected that our surprise is very natural. But I am so pleased . . . and we all" (he began smiling with an ingratiating and delighted air) "will try our utmost that you shall spend your season here as agreeably as possible. . . ."

"Come, that's enough; that's idle chatter; you are talking nonsense, as usual. I can dispose of my time for myself. Though I've nothing against you, I don't bear a grudge. You ask how I could come? What is there surprising about it? It was the simplest thing. And why are you so surprised? How are you, Praskovya? What do you do here?"

"How do you do, Granny?" said Polina, going up to her. "Have you been long on the journey?"

"Well, she's asked a sensible question—the others could say nothing but oh and ah! Why, you see, I lay in bed and lay in bed and was doctored and doctored, so I sent the doctors away and called in the sexton from St. Nicolas. He had cured a peasant woman of the same disease by means of hayseed. And he did me good, too. On the third day I was in a perspiration all day and I got up. Then my Germans gathered round again, put on their spectacles and began to argue. 'If you were to go abroad now,' said they, 'and take a course of the waters, all your symptoms would disappear.' And why shouldn't I? I thought. The fools of Zazhigins began sighing and moaning: 'Where are you off to?' they said. Well, so here I am! It took me a day to get ready, and the following week, on a Friday, I took a maid, and Potapitch, and the footman, Fyodor, but I sent Fyodor back from Berlin, because I saw he was not wanted, and I could have come quite alone. I took a special compartment and there are porters at all the stations, and for twenty kopecks they will carry you wherever you like. I say, what rooms he has taken!" she said in conclusion, looking about her. "How do you get the money, my good man? Why, everything you've got is mortgaged. What a lot of money you must owe to this Frenchman alone! I know all about it; you see, I know all about it!"

"Oh, Auntie . . ." said the General, all confusion. "I am surprised, Auntie . . . I imagine that I am free to act . . . Besides, my expenses are not beyond my means, and we are here . . ."

"They are not? You say so! Then you must have robbed your children of their last farthing—you, their trustee!"

"After that, after such words," began the General, indignant, "I really don't know . . ."

"To be sure you don't! I'll be bound you are always at roulette here? Have you whistled it all away?"

The General was so overwhelmed that he almost spluttered in the rush of his feelings.

"Roulette! I? In my position . . . I? Think what you are saying, Auntie; you must still be unwell . . ."

"Come, you are lying, you are lying. I'll be bound they can't tear you away; it's all lies! I'll have a look to-day what this roulette is like. You, Praskovya, tell me where to go and what to see, and Alexey Ivanovitch here will show me, and you, Potapitch, make a note of all the places to go to. What is there to see here?" she said, addressing Polina again.

"Close by are the ruins of the castle; then there is the Schlangenberg."

"What is it, the Schlangenberg? A wood or what?"

"No, not a wood, it's a mountain; there is a peak there . . ."

"What do you mean by a peak?"

"The very highest point on the mountain. It is an enclosed place—the view from it is unique."

"What about carrying my chair up the mountain? They wouldn't be able to drag it up, would they?"

"Oh, we can find porters," I answered.

At this moment, Fedosya, the nurse, came up to greet Granny and brought the General's children to her.

"Come, there's no need for kissing! I cannot bear kissing children, they always have dirty noses. Well, how do you get on here, Fedosya?"

"It's very, very nice here, Antonida Vassilyevna," answered Fedosya. "How have you been, ma'am? We've been so worried about you."

"I know, you are a good soul. Do you always have visitors?"—she turned to Polina again. "Who is that wretched little rascal in spectacles?"

"Prince Nilsky," Polina whispered.

"Ah, a Russian. And I thought he wouldn't understand! Perhaps he didn't hear. I have seen Mr. Astley already. Here he is again," said Granny, catching sight of him. "How do you do?"—she turned to him suddenly.

Mr. Astley bowed to her in silence.

"Have you no good news to tell me? Say something! Translate that to him, Polina."

Polina translated it.

"Yes. That with great pleasure and delight I am looking at you, and very glad that you are in good health," Mr. Astley answered seriously, but with perfect readiness. It was translated to Granny and it was evident she was pleased.

"How well Englishmen always answer," she observed. "That's why I always like Englishmen. There's no comparison between them and Frenchmen! Come and see me," she said, addressing Mr. Astley again. "I'll try not to worry you too much. Translate that to him, and tell him that I am here below—here below—do you hear? Below, below," she repeated to Mr. Astley, pointing downwards.

Mr. Astley was extremely pleased at the invitation.

Granny looked Polina up and down attentively and with a satisfied air.

"I was fond of you, Praskovya," she said suddenly. "You're a fine wench, the best of the lot, and as for will—my goodness! Well, I have will too; turn round. That's not a false chignon, is it?"

"No, Granny, it's my own."

"To be sure. I don't care for the silly fashion of the day. You look very nice. I should fall in love with you if I were a young gentleman. Why don't you get married? But it is time for me to go. And I want to

go out, for I've had nothing but the train and the train . . . Well, are
you still cross?" she added, turning to the General.

"Upon my word, Auntie, what nonsense!" cried the General, delighted. "I understand at your age . . ."

"Cette vieille est tombée en enfance," De Grieux whispered to me.

"I want to see everything here. Will you let me have Alexey Ivanovitch?" Granny went on to the General.

"Oh, as much as you like, but I will myself . . . and Polina, M. de
Grieux . . . we shall all think it a pleasure to accompany you."

"Mais, madame, cela sera un plaisir" . . . De Grieux addressed her
with a bewitching smile.

"A *plaisir,* to be sure; you are absurd, my good sir. I am not going
to give you any money, though," she added suddenly. "But now to my
rooms; I must have a look at them, and then we'll go the round of
everything. Come, lift me up." Granny was lifted up again and we all
flocked downstairs behind her chair. The General walked as though
stunned by a blow on the head. De Grieux was considering something.
Mlle. Blanche seemed about to remain, but for some reason she made
up her mind to come with the rest. The Prince followed her at once,
and no one was left in the General's study but Madame de Cominges
and the German.

Chapter 10

AT WATERING-PLACES and, I believe, in Europe generally,
hotelkeepers and *ober-kellners,* in assigning rooms to their visitors, are
guided not so much by the demands and desires of the latter as by
their own personal opinion of them, and, one must add, they are rarely
mistaken. But for some reason I cannot explain, they had assigned
Granny such a splendid suite that they had quite overshot the mark.
It consisted of four splendidly furnished rooms with a bathroom, quarters for the servants and a special room for the maid, and so on. Some
grande duchesse really had been staying in those rooms the week before, a fact of which the new occupant was informed at once, in order
to enhance the value of the apartments. Granny was carried, or rather
wheeled, through all the rooms, and she looked at them attentively
and severely. The *ober-kellner,* an elderly man with a bald head, followed her respectfully at this first survey.

I don't know what they all took Granny to be, but apparently for a very important and, above all, wealthy lady. They put down in the book at once: *"Madame la générale princesse de Tarasyevitchev,"* though Granny had never been a princess. Her servants, her special compartment in the train, the mass of useless bags, portmanteaus, and even chests that had come with Granny, probably laid the foundation of her prestige; while her invalid-chair, her abrupt tone and voice, her eccentric questions, which were made with the most unconstrained air that would tolerate no contradiction—in short, Granny's whole figure, erect, brisk, imperious—increased the awe in which she was held by all. As she looked at the rooms, Granny sometimes told them to stop her chair, pointed to some object in the furniture and addressed unexpected questions to the *ober-kellner,* who still smiled respectfully, though he was beginning to feel nervous. Granny put her questions in French, which she spoke, however, rather badly, so that I usually translated. The *ober-kellner's* answers for the most part did not please her and seemed unsatisfactory. And, indeed, she kept asking about all sorts of things quite irrelevant. Suddenly, for instance, stopping before a picture, a rather feeble copy of some well-known picture of a mythological subject, she would ask—

"Whose portrait is that?"

The *ober-kellner* replied that no doubt it was some countess.

"How is it you don't know? You live here and don't know. Why is it here? Why is she squinting?"

The *ober-kellner* could not answer these questions satisfactorily, and positively lost his head.

"Oh, what a blockhead!" commented Granny, in Russian.

She was wheeled on. The same performance was repeated with a Dresden statuette, which Granny looked at for a long time, and then ordered them to remove, no one knew why. Finally, she worried the *ober-kellner* about what the carpets in the bedroom cost, and where they had been woven! The *ober-kellner* promised to make inquiries.

"What asses," Granny grumbled, and concentrated her whole attention on the bed. "What a gorgeous canopy! Open the bed."

They opened the bed.

"More, more, turn it all over. Take off the pillows, the pillows, lift up the feather-bed."

Everything was turned over. Granny examined it attentively.

"It's a good thing there are no bugs. Take away all the linen! Make it up with my linen and my pillows. But all this is too gorgeous. Such rooms are not for an old woman like me. I shall be dreary all alone.

Alexey Ivanovitch, you must come and see me very often when your lessons with the children are over."

"I left the General's service yesterday," I answered, "and am living in the hotel quite independently."

"How is that?"

"A German of high rank, a Baron, with his Baroness, came here from Berlin the other day. I addressed him yesterday in German without keeping to the Berlin accent."

"Well, what then?"

"He thought it an impertinence and complained to the General, and yesterday the General discharged me."

"Why, did you swear at the Baron, or what? (though if you had it wouldn't have mattered!)"

"Oh, no. On the contrary, the Baron raised his stick to thrash me."

"And did you, sniveller, allow your tutor to be treated like that?" she said suddenly, addressing the General; "and turned him out of his place too! Noodles! you're all a set of noodles, as I see."

"Don't disturb yourself, Auntie," said the General, with a shade of condescending familiarity; "I can manage my own business. Besides, Alexey Ivanovitch has not given you quite a correct account of it."

"And you just put up with it?"—she turned to me.

"I meant to challenge the Baron to a duel," I answered, as calmly and as modestly as I could, "but the General opposed it."

"Why did you oppose it?"—Granny turned to the General again. ("And you can go, my good man; you can come when you are called," she said, addressing the *ober-kellner;* "no need to stand about gaping. I can't endure this Nürnberg rabble!")

The man bowed and went out, not, of course, understanding Granny's compliments.

"Upon my word, Auntie, surely a duel was out of the question."

"Why out of the question? Men are all cocks; so they should fight. You are all noodles, I see, you don't know how to stand up for your country. Come, take me up, Potapitch; see that there are always two porters: engage them. I don't want more than two. I shall only want them to carry me up and down stairs, and to wheel me on the levels in the street. Explain that to them; and pay them beforehand—they will be more respectful. You will always be with me yourself, and you, Alexey Ivanovitch, point out that Baron to me when we are out: that I may have a look at the von Baron. Well, where is the roulette?"

I explained that the roulette tables were in rooms in the Casino. Then followed questions: Were there many of them? Did many people play? Did they play all day long? How was it arranged? I answered at last, that she had much better see all this with her own eyes, and that it was rather difficult to describe it.

"Well, then, take me straight there! You go first, Alexey Ivanovitch!"

"Why, Auntie, don't you really mean to rest after your journey?" the General asked anxiously. He seemed rather flurried and, indeed, they all seemed embarrassed and were exchanging glances. Probably they all felt it rather risky and, indeed, humiliating to accompany Granny to the Casino, where, of course, she might do something eccentric, and in public; at the same time they all proposed to accompany her.

"Why should I rest? I am not tired and, besides, I've been sitting still for three days. And then we will go and see the springs and medicinal waters; where are they? And then . . . we'll go and see, what was it you said, Praskovya?—peak, wasn't it?"

"Yes, Granny."

"Well, peak, then, if it is a peak. And what else is there here?"

"There are a great many objects of interest, Granny," Polina exerted herself to say.

"Why don't you know them! Marfa, you shall come with me, too," she said, addressing her maid.

"But why should she come?" the General said fussily; "and in fact it's out of the question, and I doubt whether Potapitch will be admitted into the Casino."

"What nonsense! Am I to abandon her because she is a servant? She's a human being, too; here we have been on our travels for a week; she wants to have a look at things, too. With whom could she go except me? She wouldn't dare show her nose in the street by herself."

"But, Granny . . ."

"Why, are you ashamed to be with me? Then stay at home; you are not asked. Why, what a General! I am a General's widow myself. And why should you all come trailing after me? I can look at it all with Alexey Ivanovitch."

But De Grieux insisted that we should all accompany her, and launched out into the most polite phrases about the pleasure of accompanying her, and so on. We all started.

"*Elle est tombée en enfance,*" De Grieux repeated to the General; "*seule, elle fera des bêtises . . .*" I heard nothing more, but he evidently had some design, and, possibly, his hopes had revived.

It was half a mile to the Casino. The way was through an avenue of chestnuts to a square, going round which, they came out straight on the Casino. The General was to some extent reassured, for our procession, though somewhat eccentric, was, nevertheless, decorous and presentable. And there was nothing surprising in the fact of an invalid who could not walk putting in an appearance at the Casino; but, anyway, the General was afraid of the Casino; why should an invalid unable to walk, and an old lady, too, go into the gambling saloon? Polina and Mlle. Blanche walked on each side of the bath-chair. Mlle. Blanche laughed, was modestly animated and even sometimes jested very politely with Granny, so much so that the latter spoke of her approvingly at last. Polina, on the other side, was obliged to be continually answering Granny's innumerable questions, such as: "Who was that passed? Who was that woman driving past? Is it a big town? Is it a big garden? What are those trees? What's that hill? Do eagles fly here? What is that absurd-looking roof?" Mr. Astley walked beside me and whispered that he expected a great deal from that morning. Potapitch and Marfa walked in the background close behind the bath-chair, Potapitch in his swallow-tailed coat and white tie, but with a cap on his head, and Marfa (a red-faced maidservant, forty years old and beginning to turn grey) in a cap, cotton gown, and creaking goatskin slippers. Granny turned to them very often and addressed remarks to them. De Grieux was talking with an air of determination. Probably he was reassuring the General, evidently he was giving him some advice. But Granny had already pronounced the fatal phrase: "I am not going to give you money." Perhaps to De Grieux this announcement sounded incredible, but the General knew his aunt. I noticed that De Grieux and Mlle. Blanche were continually exchanging glances. I could distinguish the Prince and the German traveller at the further end of the avenue; they had stopped, and were walking away from us.

Our visit to the Casino was a triumph. The porters and attendants displayed the same deference as in the hotel. They looked at us, however, with curiosity. Granny began by giving orders that she should be wheeled through all the rooms. Some she admired, others made no impression on her; she asked questions about them all. At last we came to the roulette room. The lackeys, who stood like sentinels at closed doors, flung the doors wide open as though they were impressed.

Granny's appearance at the roulette table made a profound impression on the public. At the roulette tables and at the other end of the room, where there was a table with *trente et quarante,* there was a crowd of a hundred and fifty or two hundred players, several rows deep. Those who had succeeded in squeezing their way right up to the table, held fast, as they always do, and would not give up their places to any one until they had lost; for simple spectators were not allowed to stand at the tables and occupy the space. Though there were chairs set round the table, few of the players sat down, especially when there was a great crowd, because standing one could get closer and consequently pick out one's place and put down one's stake more conveniently. The second and the third rows pressed up upon the first, waiting and watching for their turn; but sometimes a hand would be impatiently thrust forward through the first row to put down a stake. Even from the third row people managed to seize chances of poking forward their stakes; consequently every ten or even five minutes there was some "scene" over disputed stakes at one end of the hall or another. The police of the Casino were, however, fairly good. It was, of course, impossible to prevent crowding; on the contrary, the owners were glad of the rush of people because it was profitable, but eight croupiers sitting round the table kept a vigilant watch on the stakes: they even kept count of them, and when disputes arose they could settle them. In extreme cases they called in the police, and the trouble was over in an instant. There were police officers in plain clothes stationed here and there among the players, so that they could not be recognized. They were especially on the look-out for thieves and professional pickpockets, who are very numerous at the roulette tables, as it affords them excellent opportunity for exercising their skill. The fact is, elsewhere thieves must pick pockets or break locks, and such enterprises, when unsuccessful, have a very troublesome ending. But in this case the thief has only to go up to the roulette table, begin playing, and all at once, openly and publicly, take another person's winnings and put them in his pocket. If a dispute arises, the cheat insists loudly that the stake was his. If the trick is played cleverly and the witnesses hesitate, the thief may often succeed in carrying off the money, if the sum is not a very large one, of course. In that case the croupiers or some one of the other players are almost certain to have been keeping an eye on it. But if the sum is not a large one, the real owner sometimes actually declines to keep up the dispute, and goes away shrinking from the scandal. But if they succeed in detecting a thief, they turn him out at once with contumely.

All this Granny watched from a distance with wild curiosity. She was much delighted at a thief's being turned out. *Trente et quarante* did not interest her very much; she was more pleased at roulette and the rolling of the little ball. She evinced a desire at last to get a closer view of the game. I don't know how it happened, but the attendants and other officious persons (principally Poles who had lost, and who

pressed their services on lucky players and foreigners of all sorts) at
once, and in spite of the crowd, cleared a place for Granny in the
very middle of the table beside the chief croupier, and wheeled her
chair to it. A number of visitors who were not playing, but watching
the play (chiefly Englishmen with their families), at once crowded
round the table to watch Granny from behind the players. Numbers
of lorgnettes were turned in her direction. The croupiers' expectations
rose. Such an eccentric person certainly seemed to promise something
out of the ordinary. An old woman of over seventy, who could not
walk, yet wished to play, was, of course, not a sight to be seen every day.
I squeezed my way up to the table too, and took my stand beside
Granny. Potapitch and Marfa were left somewhere in the distance
among the crowd. The General, Polina, De Grieux, and Mlle. Blanche
stood aside, too, among the spectators.

At first Granny began looking about at the players. She began in a
half whisper asking me abrupt, jerky questions. Who was that man and
who was this woman? She was particularly delighted by a young man
at the end of the table, who was playing for very high stakes, putting
down thousands and had, as people whispered around, already won
as much as forty thousand francs, which lay before him in heaps of
gold and banknotes. He was pale; his eyes glittered and his hands were
shaking; he was staking now without counting, by handfuls, and yet
he kept on winning and winning, kept raking in and raking in the
money. The attendants hung about him solicitously, set a chair for him,
cleared a place round him that he might have more room, that he
might not be crowded—all this in expectation of a liberal tip. Some
players, after they have won, tip the attendants without counting a
handful of coins in their joy. A Pole had already established himself
at his side, and was deferentially but continually whispering to him,
probably telling him what to stake on, advising and directing his play
—of course, he, too, expecting a tip later on! But the player scarcely
looked at him. He staked at random and kept winning. He evidently
did not know what he was doing.

Granny watched him for some minutes.

"Tell him," Granny said suddenly, growing excited and giving me
a poke, "tell him to give it up, to take his money quickly and go away.
He'll lose it all directly, he'll lose it all!" she urged, almost breathless
with agitation. "Where's Potapitch? Send Potapitch to him. Come,
tell him, tell him," she went on, poking me. "Where is Potapitch?
Sortez! Sortez!"—she began herself shouting to the young man.

I bent down to her and whispered resolutely that she must not shout like this here, that even talking aloud was forbidden, because it hindered counting and that we should be turned out directly.

"How vexatious! The man's lost! I suppose it's his own doing. . . . I can't look at him, it quite upsets me. What a dolt!" and Granny made haste to turn in another direction.

On the left, on the other side of the table, there was conspicuous among the players a young lady, and beside her a sort of dwarf. Who this dwarf was, and whether he was a relation or brought by her for the sake of effect, I don't know. I had noticed the lady before; she made her appearance at the gambling table every day, at one o'clock in the afternoon, and went away exactly at two; she always played for an hour. She was already known, and a chair was set for her at once. She took out of her pocket some gold, some thousand-franc notes, and began staking quietly, coolly, prudently, making pencil notes on a bit of paper of the numbers about which the chances grouped themselves, and trying to work out a system. She staked considerable sums. She used to win every day—one, two, or at the most three thousand francs —not more, and instantly went away. Granny scrutinized her for a long time.

"Well, that one won't lose! That one there won't lose! Of what class is she! Do you know? Who is she?"

"She must be a Frenchwoman, of a certain class, you know," I whispered.

"Ah, one can tell the bird by its flight. One can see she has a sharp claw. Explain to me now what every turn means and how one has to bet!"

I explained as far as I could to Granny all the various points on which one could stake: *rouge et noir, pair et impair, manque et passe,* and finally the various subtleties in the system of the numbers. Granny listened attentively, remembered, asked questions, and began to master it. One could point to examples of every kind, so that she very quickly and readily picked up a great deal.

"But what is *zéro?* You see that croupier, the curly-headed one, the chief one, showed *zéro* just now? And why did he scoop up everything that was on the table? Such a heap, he took it all for himself. What is the meaning of it?"

"*Zéro,* Granny, means that the bank wins all. If the little ball falls on *zéro,* everything on the table goes to the bank. It is true you can stake your money so as to keep it, but the bank pays nothing."

"You don't say so! And shall I get nothing?"

"No, Granny, if before this you had staked on *zéro* you would have got thirty-five times what you staked."

"What! thirty-five times, and does it often turn up? Why don't they stake on it, the fools."

"There are thirty-six chances against it, Granny."

"What nonsense. Potapitch! Potapitch! Stay, I've money with me— here." She took out of her pocket a tightly packed purse, and picked out of it a friedrich d'or. "Stake it on the *zéro* at once."

"Granny, *zéro* has only just turned up," I said; "so now it won't turn up for a long time. You will lose a great deal; wait a little, anyway."

"Oh, nonsense; put it down!"

"As you please, but it may not turn up again till the evening. You may go on staking thousands; it has happened."

"Oh, nonsense, nonsense. If you are afraid of the wolf you shouldn't go into the forest. What? Have I lost? Stake again!"

A second friedrich d'or was lost: she staked a third. Granny could scarcely sit still in her seat. She stared with feverish eyes at the little ball dancing on the spokes of the turning wheel. She lost a third, too. Granny was beside herself, she could not sit still, she even thumped on the table with her fist when the croupier announced, *"trente-six"* instead of the *zéro* she was expecting.

"There, look at it," said Granny angrily; "isn't that cursed little *zéro* coming soon? As sure as I'm alive, I'll sit here till *zéro* does come! It's that cursed curly-headed croupier's doing; he'll never let it come! Alexey Ivanovitch, stake two gold pieces at once! Staking as much as you do, even if *zéro* does come you'll get nothing by it."

"Granny!"

"Stake, stake! it is not your money."

I staked two friedrichs d'or. The ball flew about the wheel for a long time, at last it began dancing about the spokes. Granny was numb with excitement, and squeezed my fingers, and all at once—

"Zero!" boomed the croupier.

"You see, you see!"—Granny turned to me quickly, beaming and delighted. "I told you so. The Lord Himself put it into my head to stake those two gold pieces! Well, how much do I get now? Why don't they give it me? Potapitch, Marfa, where are they? Where have all our people got to? Potapitch, Potapitch!"

"Granny, afterwards," I whispered; "Potapitch is at the door, they won't let him in. Look, Granny, they are giving you the money, take it!" A heavy roll of printed blue notes, worth fifty friedrichs d'or, was thrust towards Granny and twenty friedrichs d'or were counted out to her. I scooped it all up in a shovel and handed it to Granny.

"Faites le jeu, messieurs! Faites le jeu, messieurs! Rien ne va plus?" called the croupier, inviting the public to stake, and preparing to turn the wheel.

"Heavens! we are too late. They're just going to turn it. Put it down, put it down!" Granny urged me in a flurry. "Don't dawdle, make haste!" She was beside herself and poked me with all her might.

"What am I to stake it on, Granny?"

"On *zéro*, on *zéro!* On *zéro* again! Stake as much as possible! How much have we got altogether? Seventy friedrichs d'or. There's no need to spare it. Stake twenty friedrichs d'or at once."

"Think what you are doing, Granny! Sometimes it does not turn up for two hundred times running! I assure you, you may go on staking your whole fortune."

"Oh, nonsense, nonsense! Put it down! How your tongue does wag! I know what I'm about." Granny was positively quivering with excitement.

"By the regulations it's not allowed to stake more than twelve roubles on *zéro* at once, Granny; here I have staked that."

"Why is it not allowed? Aren't you lying? Monsieur! Monsieur!"— she nudged the croupier, who was sitting near her on the left, and was about to set the wheel turning. *"Combien zéro? Douze? Douze?"*

I immediately interpreted the question in French.

"Oui, madame," the croupier confirmed politely; "as the winnings from no single stake must exceed four thousand florins by the regulations," he added in explanation.

"Well, there's no help for it, stake twelve."

"Le jeu est fait," cried the croupier. The wheel rotated, and thirty turned up. She had lost.

"Again, again, again! Stake again!" cried Granny. I no longer resisted, and, shrugging my shoulders, staked another twelve friedrichs d'or. The wheel turned a long time. Granny was simply quivering as she watched the wheel. "Can she really imagine that *zéro* will win again?" I thought, looking at her with wonder. Her face was beaming with a firm conviction of winning, an unhesitating expectation that in another minute they would shout *"Zéro!"* The ball jumped into the cage.

"Zéro!" cried the croupier.

"What!!!" Granny turned to me with intense triumph.

I was a gambler myself, I felt that at the moment my arms and legs were trembling, there was a throbbing in my head. Of course, this was a rare chance that *zéro* should have come up three times in some dozen turns; but there was nothing particularly wonderful about it. I had myself seen *zéro* turn up three times *running* two days before, and a gambler who had been zealously noting down the lucky numbers, observed aloud that, only the day before, *zéro* had turned up only once in twenty-four hours.

Granny's winnings were counted out to her with particular attention and deference as she had won such a large sum. She received four hundred and twenty friedrichs d'or, that is, four thousand florins and seventy friedrichs d'or. She was given twenty friedrichs d'or in gold, and four thousand florins in banknotes.

This time Granny did not call Potapitch; she had other preoccupations. She did not even babble or quiver outwardly! She was, if one may so express it, quivering inwardly. She was entirely concentrated on something, absorbed in one aim.

"Alexey Ivanovitch, he said that one could only stake four thousand florins at once, didn't he? Come, take it, stake the whole four thousand on the red," Granny commanded.

It was useless to protest; the wheel began rotating.

"*Rouge*," the croupier proclaimed.

Again she had won four thousand florins, making eight in all.

"Give me four, and stake four again on red," Granny commanded.

Again I staked four thousand.

"*Rouge*," the croupier pronounced again.

"Twelve thousand altogether! Give it me all here. Pour the gold here into the purse and put away the notes. That's enough! Home! Wheel my chair out."

Chapter 11

THE chair was wheeled to the door at the other end of the room. Granny was radiant. All our party immediately thronged round her with congratulations. However eccentric Granny's behaviour might be, her triumph covered a multitude of sins, and the General was no longer afraid of compromising himself in public by his relationship with such a strange woman. With a condescending and familiarly good-humoured smile, as though humouring a child, he congratulated Granny. He was, however, evidently impressed, like all the other spectators. People talked all round and pointed at Granny. Many passed by to get a closer view of her! Mr. Astley was talking of her aside, with two English acquaintances. Some majestic ladies gazed at her with majestic amazement, as though at a marvel. . . . De Grieux positively showered congratulations and smiles upon her.

"*Quelle victoire!*" he said.

"*Mais, madame, c'était du feu,*" Mlle. Blanche commented, with an ingratiating smile.

"Yes, I just went and won twelve thousand florins! Twelve, indeed; what about the gold? With the gold it makes almost thirteen. What is that in our money? Will it be six thousand?"

I explained that it made more than seven, and in the present state of exchange might even amount to eight.

"Well, that's something worth having, eight thousand! And you stay here, you noodles, and do nothing! Potapitch, Marfa, did you see?"

"My goodness! how did you do it, ma'am? Eight thousand!" exclaimed Marfa, wriggling.

"There! there's five gold pieces for you, here!"

Potapitch and Marfa flew to kiss her hand.

"And give the porters, too, a friedrich d'or each. Give it them in gold, Alexey Ivanovitch. Why is that flunkey bowing and the other one too? Are they congratulating me? Give them a friedrich d'or too."

"*Madame la princesse . . . un pauvre expatrié . . . malheur continuel . . . les princes russes sont si généreux . . .*" A person with moustaches and an obsequious smile, in a threadbare coat and gay-coloured waistcoat, came cringing about Granny's chair, waving his hat in his hand.

"Give him a friedrich d'or too. . . . No, give him two; that's enough, or there will be no end to them. Lift me up and carry me out. Praskovya"—she turned to Polina Alexandrovna—"I'll buy you a dress to-morrow, and I'll buy Mlle. . . . what's her name, Mlle. Blanche, isn't it? I'll buy her a dress too. Translate that to her, Praskovya!"

"*Merci, madame.*" Mlle. Blanche made a grateful curtsey while she exchanged an ironical smile with De Grieux and the General. The General was rather embarrassed and was greatly relieved when we reached the avenue.

"Fedosya—won't Fedosya be surprised," said Granny, thinking of the General's nurse. "I must make her a present of a dress. Hey, Alexey Ivanovitch, Alexey Ivanovitch, give this to the poor man."

A man in rags, with bent back, passed us on the road, and looked at us.

"And perhaps he is not a poor man, but a rogue, Granny."

"Give him a gulden, give it him!"

I went up to the man and gave it him. He looked at me in wild amazement, but took the gulden, however. He smelt of spirits.

"And you, Alexey Ivanovitch. Have you not tried your luck yet?"

"No, Granny."

"But your eyes were burning, I saw them."

"I shall try, Granny, I certainly shall later."

"And stake on *zéro* straight away. You will see! How much have you in hand?"

"Only twenty friedrichs d'or, Granny."

"That's not much. I will give you fifty friedrichs d'or. I will lend it if you like. Here, take this roll—but don't you expect anything, all the same, my good man, I am not going to give you anything," she said, suddenly addressing the General.

The latter winced, but he said nothing. De Grieux frowned.

"Que diable, c'est une terrible vieille!" he muttered to the General through his teeth.

"A beggar, a beggar, another beggar!" cried Granny. "Give him a gulden, too, Alexey Ivanovitch."

This time it was a grey-headed old man with a wooden leg, in a long-skirted blue coat and with a long stick in his hand. He looked like an old soldier. But when I held out a gulden to him he stepped back and looked at me angrily.

"Was ist's der Teufel," he shouted, following up with a dozen oaths.

"Oh, he's a fool," cried Granny, dismissing him with a wave of her hand. "Go on! I'm hungry! Now we'll have dinner directly; then I'll rest a little, and back here again."

"You want to play again, Granny!" I cried.

"What do you expect? That you should all sit here and sulk while I watch you?"

"Mais, madame—" De Grieux drew near—*"les chances peuvent tourner, une seule mauvaise chance et vous perdrez tout . . . surtout avec votre jeu . . . C'est terrible!"*

"Vous perdrez absolument," chirped Mlle. Blanche.

"But what is it to do with all of you? I shouldn't lose your money, but my own! And where is that Mr. Astley?" she asked me.

"He stayed in the Casino, Granny."

"I'm sorry, he's such a nice man."

On reaching home Granny met the *ober-kellner* on the stairs, called him and began bragging of her winnings; then she sent for Fedosya, made her a present of three friedrichs d'or and ordered dinner to be served. Fedosya and Marfa hovered over her at dinner.

"I watched you, ma'am," Marfa cackled, "and said to Potapitch, 'What does our lady want to do?' And the money on the table—saints alive! the money! I haven't seen so much money in the whole of my life, and all round were gentlefolk—nothing but gentlefolk sitting. 'And wherever do all these gentlefolk come from, Potapitch?' said I. May our Lady Herself help her, I thought. I was praying for you, ma'am, and my heart was simply sinking, simply sinking; I was all of a tremble. Lord help her, I thought, and here the Lord has sent you luck. I've been trembling ever since, ma'am. I'm all of a tremble now."

"Alexey Ivanovitch, after dinner, at four o'clock, get ready and we'll go. Now good-bye for a time; don't forget to send for a doctor for me. I must drink the waters, too. Go, or maybe you'll forget."

As I left Granny I was in a sort of stupor. I tried to imagine what would happen now to all our people and what turn things would take. I saw clearly that they (especially the General) had not yet succeeded in recovering from the first shock. The fact of Granny's arrival instead of the telegram which they were expecting from hour to hour to announce her death (and consequently the inheritance of her fortune) had so completely shattered the whole fabric of their plans and intentions that Granny's further exploits at roulette threw them into positive bewilderment and a sort of stupefaction seemed to have come over all of them.

Meanwhile this second fact was almost more important than the first; for though Granny had repeated twice that she would not give the General any money, yet, who knows?—there was no need to give up all hope yet. De Grieux, who was involved in all the General's affairs, had not lost hope. I am convinced that Mlle. Blanche, also much involved in the General's affairs (I should think so: to marry a General and with a considerable fortune!), would not have given up hope, and would have tried all her fascinating arts upon Granny—in contrast with the proud and incomprehensible Polina, who did not know how to curry favour with any one. But now, now that Granny had had such success at roulette, now that Granny's personality had shown itself so clearly and so typically (a refractory and imperious old lady, *et tombée en enfance*), now, perhaps, all was lost. Why, she was as pleased as a child, so pleased that she would go on till she was ruined and had lost everything. Heavens! I thought (and, God forgive me, with a malignant laugh), why, every friedrich d'or Granny staked just now must have been a fresh sore in the General's heart, must have maddened. De Grieux and infuriated Mlle. de Cominges, who saw the cup slipping from her lips. Another fact: even in her triumph and joy of winning, when Granny was giving money away to every one, and taking every passer-by for a beggar, even then she had let fall to the General, "I'm not going to give you anything, though!" That meant that she had fastened upon that idea, was sticking to it, had made up her mind about it. There was danger! danger!

All these reflections were revolving in my mind as I mounted the front stairs from Granny's apartments to my garret in the very top storey. All this interested me strongly. Though, of course, I could before have divined the strongest leading motives prompting the actors before me, yet I did not know for certain all the mysteries and intrigues of the drama. Polina had never been fully open with me. Though it did happen at times that she revealed her feelings to me, yet I noticed that almost always after such confidences she would make fun of all she had said, or would try to obscure the matter and put it in a different light. Oh, she had hidden a great deal! In any case, I foresaw that the *dénouement* of this mysterious and constrained position was at hand. One more shock—and everything would be ended and revealed. About my fortunes, which were also involved in all this, I scarcely troubled. I was in a strange mood: I had only twenty friedrichs d'or in my pocket; I was in a foreign land without a job or means of livelihood, without hope, without prospects, and—I did not trouble my head about it! If it had not been for the thought of Polina, I should have abandoned myself to the comic interest of the approaching catastrophe, and should have been shouting with laughter. But I was troubled about Polina; her fate was being decided, I divined that; but I regret to say that it was not altogether her fate that troubled me. I wanted to fathom her secrets; I wanted her to come to me and say: "I love you," and if not that, if that was senseless insanity, then . . . well, what was there to care about? Did I know what I wanted? I was like one demented: all I wanted was to be near her, in the halo of her glory, in her radiance, always, for ever, all my life. I knew nothing more! And could I leave her?

In their passage on the third storey I felt as though something nudged me. I turned round and, twenty paces or more from me, I saw coming out of a door Polina. She seemed waiting: and as soon as she saw me beckoned to me.

"Polina Alexandrovna . . ."

"Hush!" she said.

"Imagine," I whispered to her, "I felt as though some one had nudged me just now; I looked round—you! It seems as though there were a sort of electricity from you!"

"Take this letter," Polina articulated anxiously with a frown, probably not hearing what I had said, "and give it into Mr. Astley's own hands at once. Make haste, I beg you. There is no need of an answer. He will . . ."

She did not finish.

"Mr. Astley?" I repeated in surprise.

But Polina had already disappeared behind the door.

"Aha, so they are in correspondence!" I ran at once, of course, to Mr. Astley; first to his hotel, where I did not find him, then to the Casino, where I hurried through all the rooms: and at last, as I was returning home in vexation, almost in despair, I met him by chance, with a party of Englishmen and Englishwomen on horseback. I beckoned to him, stopped him and gave him the letter: we had not time even to exchange a glance. But I suspect that Mr. Astley purposely gave rein to his horse.

Was I tortured by jealousy? Anyway, I was in an utterly shattered condition. I did not even want to find out what they were writing to one another about. And so he was trusted by her! "Her friend, her friend," I thought, "and that is clear (and when has he had time to become her friend), but is there love in the case? Of course not," common-sense whispered to me. But common-sense alone counts for little in such cases; anyway, this, too, had to be cleared up. Things were growing unpleasantly complicated.

Before I had time to go into the hotel, first the porter and then the *ober-kellner,* coming out of his room, informed me that I was wanted, that I had been asked for, three times they had sent to ask: where was I?—that I was asked to go as quickly as possible to the General's rooms. I was in the most disagreeable frame of mind. In the General's room I found, besides the General himself, De Grieux and Mlle. Blanche—alone, without her mother. The mother was evidently an official one, only used for show. But when it came to real *business* she acted for herself. And probably the woman knew little of her so-called daughter's affairs.

They were, however, consulting warmly about something, and the doors of the study were actually locked—which had never happened before. Coming to the door, I heard loud voices—De Grieux's insolent and malignant voice, Blanche's shrill fury, and the General's pitiful tones, evidently defending himself about something. Upon my entrance they all, as it were, pulled themselves up and restrained them-- selves. De Grieux smoothed his hair and forced a smile into his angry face—that horrid official French smile which I so detest. The crushed and desperate General tried to assume an air of dignity, but it was a mechanical effort. Only Mlle. Blanche's countenance, blazing with anger, scarcely changed. She only ceased speaking while she fixed her eyes upon me in impatient expectation. I may mention that hitherto she had treated me with extraordinary casualness, had even refused to respond to my bows, and had simply declined to see me.

"Alexey Ivanovitch," the General began in a soft mollifying tone, "allow me to tell you that it is strange, exceedingly strange . . . in fact, your conduct in regard to me and my family . . . in fact, it is exceedingly strange . . ."

"*Eh! ce n'est pas ça,*" De Grieux interposed, with vexation and contempt. (There's no doubt he was the leading spirit.) "*Mon cher monsieur, notre cher général se trompe,* in taking up this tone" (I translate the rest of his speech in Russian), "but he meant to say . . . that is to warn you, or rather to beg you most earnestly not to ruin him— yes, indeed, not to ruin him! I make use of that expression."

"But how, how?" I interrupted.

"Why, you are undertaking to be the guide (or how shall I express it?) of this old woman, *cette pauvre terrible vieille*"—De Grieux himself hesitated—"but you know she'll lose everything; she will gamble away her whole fortune! You know yourself, you have seen yourself, how she plays! If she begins to lose, she will never leave off from obstinacy, from anger, and will lose everything, she will gamble away everything, and in such cases one can never regain one's losses and then . . . then . . ."

"And then," the General put in, "then you will ruin the whole family! I and my family are her heirs, she has no nearer relations. I tell you openly: my affairs are in a bad way, a very bad way. You know my position to some extent. . . . If she loses a considerable sum or even (Lord help us!) her whole fortune, what will become of me, of my children!" (The General looked round at De Grieux.) "Of me." (He looked round at Mlle. Blanche, who turned away from him with contempt.) "Alexey Ivanovitch, save us, save us! . . ."

"But how, General, how, how can I? . . . What influence have I in the matter?"

"Refuse, refuse, give her up! . . ."

"Then some one else will turn up," I said.

"*Ce n'est pas ça, ce n'est pas ça,*" De Grieux interrupted again, "*que diable!* No, don't desert her, but at least advise her, dissuade her, draw her away . . . don't let her play too much, distract her in some way."

"But how can I do that? If you would undertake the task yourself, M. de Grieux," I added, as naïvely as I could.

Here I caught a rapid, fiery, questioning glance from Mlle. Blanche at M. de Grieux. And in De Grieux's own face there was something peculiar, something he could not himself disguise.

"The point is, she won't accept me now!" De Grieux cried, with a wave of his hand. "If only . . . later on . . ."

De Grieux looked rapidly and meaningly at Mlle. Blanche.

"*O, mon cher M. Alexis, soyez si bon.*" Mlle. Blanche herself took a step towards me with a most fascinating smile, she seized me by both hands and pressed them warmly. Damn it all! That diabolical face knew how to change completely in one moment. At that instant her face was so imploring, so sweet, it was such a child-like and even mischievous smile; at the end of the phrase she gave me such a sly wink, unseen by all the rest; she meant to do for me completely, and it was successfully done; only it was horribly coarse.

Then the General leapt up, positively leapt up. "Alexey Ivanovitch, forgive me for beginning as I did just now. I did not mean that at all. . . . I beg you, I beseech you, I bow down before you in Russian style—you alone, you alone can save us. Mlle. de Cominges and I implore you—you understand, you understand, of course." He besought me, indicating Mlle. Blanche with his eyes. He was a very pitiful figure.

At that instant there came three subdued and respectful knocks at the door; it was opened—the corridor attendant was knocking and a few steps behind him stood Potapitch. They came with messages from Granny; they were charged to find and bring me at once. "She is angry," Potapitch informed me.

"But it is only half-past three."

"She could not get to sleep; she kept tossing about, and then at last she got up, sent for her chair and for you. She's at the front door now."

"*Quelle mégère,*" cried De Grieux.

I did, in fact, find Granny on the steps, out of all patience at my not being there. She could not wait till four o'clock.

"Come," she cried, and we set off again to roulette.

Chapter 12

GRANNY was in an impatient and irritable mood; it was evident that roulette had made a deep impression on her mind. She took no notice of anything else and was altogether absent-minded. For instance, she asked me no questions on the road as she had done before. Seeing a luxurious carriage whirling by, she was on the point of raising her hand and asking: What is it? Whose is it?—but I believe she did not hear what I answered: her absorption was continually interrupted by abrupt and impatient gesticulations. When I pointed out to her Baron and Baroness Burmerhelm, who were approaching the Casino, she looked absent-mindedly at them and said, quite indifferently, "Ah!" and, turning round quickly to Potapitch and Marfa, who were walking behind her, snapped out to them—

"Why are you hanging upon us? We can't take you every time! Go home! You and I are enough," she added, when they had hurriedly turned and gone home.

They were already expecting Granny at the Casino. They immediately made room for her in the same place, next to the croupier. I fancy that these croupiers, who are always so strictly decorous and appear to be ordinary officials who are absolutely indifferent as to whether the bank wins or loses, are by no means so unconcerned at the bank's losses and, of course, receive instructions for attracting players and for augmenting the profits—for which they doubtless receive prizes and bonuses. They looked upon Granny, anyway, as their prey.

Then just what we had expected happened.

This was how it was.

Granny pounced at once on *zéro* and immediately ordered me to stake twelve friedrichs d'or. She staked once, twice, three times—*zéro* never turned up.

"Put it down! Put it down!" Granny nudged me, impatiently. I obeyed.

"How many times have we staked?" she asked at last, grinding her teeth with impatience.

"I have staked twelve times, Granny. I have put down a hundred and forty-four friedrichs d'or. I tell you, Granny, very likely till evening . . ."

"Hold your tongue!" Granny interrupted. "Stake on *zéro,* and stake at once a thousand gulden on red. Here, take the note."

Red won, and *zéro* failed once more; a thousand gulden was gained.

"You see, you see!" whispered Granny, "we have gained almost all that we have lost. Stake again on *zéro;* we'll stake ten times more and then give it up."

But the fifth time Granny was thoroughly sick of it.

"The devil take that filthy *zéro.* Come, stake the whole four thousand gulden on the red," she commanded me.

"Granny! it will be so much; why, what if red does not turn up?" I besought her; but Granny almost beat me. (Indeed, she nudged me so violently that she might almost be said to have attacked me.) There was no help for it, I staked on red the whole four thousand won that morning. The wheel turned. Granny sat calmly and proudly erect, never doubting that she would certainly win.

"*Zéro!*" boomed the croupier.

At first Granny did not understand, but when she saw the croupier scoop up her four thousand gulden together with everything on the table, and learned that *zéro,* which had not turned up for so long and on which we had staked in vain almost two hundred friedrichs d'or, had, as though to spite her, turned up just as Granny was abusing it, she groaned and flung up her hands in view of the whole hall. People around actually laughed.

"Holy saints! The cursed thing has turned up!" Granny wailed, "the hateful, hateful thing! That's your doing! It's all your doing"— she pounced upon me furiously, pushing me. "It was you persuaded me."

"Granny, I talked sense to you; how can I answer for chance?"

"I'll chance you," she whispered angrily. "Go away."

"Good-bye, Granny." I turned to go away.

"Alexey Ivanovitch, Alexey Ivanovitch! stop. Where are you off to? Come, what's the matter, what's the matter? Ach, he's in a rage! Stupid, come, stay, stay; come, don't be angry; I am a fool myself! Come, tell me what are we to do now!"

"I won't undertake to tell you, Granny, because you will blame me. Play for yourself, tell me and I'll put down the stakes."

"Well, well! Come, stake another four thousand gulden on red! Here, take my pocket-book." She took it out of her pocket and gave it me. "Come, make haste and take it, there's twenty thousand roubles sterling in it."

"Granny," I murmured, "such stakes . . ."

"As sure as I am alive, I'll win it back. . . . Stake."

We staked and lost.

"Stake, stake the whole eight!"

"You can't, Granny, four is the highest stake! . . ."

"Well, stake four!"

This time we won. Granny cheered up.

"You see, you see," she nudged me; "stake four again!"

She staked—she lost; then we lost again and again.

"Granny, the whole twelve thousand is gone," I told her.

"I see it's all gone," she answered with the calm of fury, if I may
so express it. "I see, my good friend, I see," she muttered, with a
fixed, as it were, absent-minded stare. "Ech, as sure I am alive, stake
another four thousand gulden!"

"But there's no money, Granny; there are some of our Russian five
per cents. and some bills of exchange of some sort, but no money."

"And in the purse?"

"There's some small change, Granny."

"Are there any money-changers here? I was told one could change
any of our notes," Granny inquired resolutely.

"Oh, as much as you like, but what you'll lose on the exchange . . .
would horrify a Jew!"

"Nonsense! I'll win it all back. Take me! Call those blockheads!"

I wheeled away the chair; the porters appeared and we went out
of the Casino.

"Make haste, make haste, make haste," Granny commanded. "Show
us the way, Alexey Ivanovitch, and take us the nearest . . . Is it far?"

"Two steps, Granny."

But at the turning from the square into the avenue we were met
by our whole party: the General, De Grieux, Mlle. Blanche and her
mamma. Polina Alexandrovna was not with them, nor Mr. Astley
either.

"Well! Don't stop us!" cried Granny. "Well, what do you want?
I have no time to spare for you now!"

I walked behind; De Grieux ran up to me.

"She's lost all she gained this morning and twelve thousand gulden
as well. We are going to change some five per cents.," I whispered
to him quickly.

De Grieux stamped and ran to tell the General. We went on wheel-
ing Granny.

"Stop, stop!" the General whispered to me frantically.

"You try stopping her," I whispered.

"Auntie!" said the General, approaching, "Auntie . . . we are just . . . we are just . . ." his voice quivered and failed him, "hiring a horse and driving into the country . . . a most exquisite view . . . the peak . . . We were coming to invite you."

"Oh, bother you and your peak." Granny waved him off irritably.

"There are trees there . . . we will have tea . . ." the General went on, utterly desperate.

"Nous boirons du lait, sur l'herbe fraîche," added De Grieux, with ferocious fury.

Du lait, de l'herbe fraîche, that is the Paris bourgeois notion of the ideally idyllic; that is, as we all know, his conception of *nature et la vérité!*

"Oh, go on with you and your milk! Lap it up yourself; it gives me the bellyache. And why do you pester me?" cried Granny. "I tell you I've no time to waste."

"It's here, Granny," I said; "it's here!"

We had reached the house where the bank was. I went in to change the notes; Granny was left waiting at the entrance; De Grieux, the General and Blanche stood apart waiting, not knowing what to do. Granny looked wrathfully at them, and they walked away in the direction of the Casino.

They offered me such ruinous terms that I did not accept them, and went back to Granny for instructions.

"Ah, the brigands!" she cried, flinging up her hands. "Well, never mind! Change it," she cried resolutely; "stay, call the banker out to me!"

"One of the clerks, Granny, do you mean?"

"Yes, a clerk, it's all the same. Ach, the brigands!"

The clerk consented to come when he learned that it was an invalid and aged countess, unable to come in, who was asking for him. Granny spent a long time loudly and angrily reproaching him for swindling her, and haggled with him in a mixture of Russian, French and German, while I came to the rescue in translating. The grave clerk listened to us in silence and shook his head. He looked at Granny with an intent stare that was hardly respectful; at last he began smiling.

"Well, get along with you," cried Granny. "Choke yourself with the money! Change it with him, Alexey Ivanovitch; there's no time to waste, or we would go elsewhere. . . ."

"The clerk says that other banks give even less."

I don't remember the sums exactly, but the banker's charges were terrible. I received close upon twelve thousand florins in gold and notes, took the account and carried it to Granny.

"Well, well, well, it's no use counting it," she said, with a wave of her hand. "Make haste, make haste, make haste!

"I'll never stake again on that damned *zéro* nor on the red either," she pronounced, as she was wheeled up to the Casino.

This time I did my very utmost to impress upon her the necessity of staking smaller sums, trying to persuade her that with the change of luck she would always be able to increase her stake. But she was so impatient that, though she agreed at first, it was impossible to restrain her when the play had begun; as soon as she had won a stake of ten, of twenty friedrichs d'or——

"There, you see, there, you see," she would begin nudging me; "there, you see, we've won; if only we had staked four thousand instead of ten, we should have won four thousand, but as it is what's the good? It's all your doing, all your doing!"

And, vexed as I felt, watching her play, I made up my mind at last to keep quiet and to give no more advice.

Suddenly De Grieux skipped up.

The other two were close by; I noticed Mlle. Blanche standing on one side with her mother, exchanging amenities with the Prince. The General was obviously out of favour, almost banished. Blanche would not even look at him, though he was doing his utmost to cajole her! The poor General! He flushed and grew pale by turns, trembled and could not even follow Granny's play. Blanche and the Prince finally went away; the General ran after them.

"Madame, madame," De Grieux whispered in a honeyed voice to Granny, squeezing his way close up to her ear. "Madame, such stakes do not answer. . . . No, no, it's impossible . . ." he said, in broken Russian. "No!"

"How, then? Come, show me!" said Granny, turning to him.

De Grieux babbled something rapidly in French, began excitedly advising, said she must wait for a chance, began reckoning some numbers. . . . Granny did not understand a word. He kept turning to me, for me to translate; tapped the table with his fingers, pointed; finally took a pencil and was about to reckon something on paper. At last Granny lost patience.

"Come, get away, get away! You keep talking nonsense! 'Madame, madame,' he doesn't understand it himself; go away."

"*Mais, madame,*" De Grieux murmured, and he began once more showing and explaining.

"Well, stake once as he says," Granny said to me; "let us see: perhaps it really will answer."

All De Grieux wanted was to dissuade her from staking large sums; he suggested that she should stake on numbers, either individually or collectively. I staked as he directed, a friedrich d'or on each of the odd numbers in the first twelve and five friedrichs d'or respectively on the groups of numbers from twelve to eighteen and from eighteen to twenty-four, staking in all sixteen friedrichs d'or.

The wheel turned.

"*Zéro!*" cried the croupier.

We had lost everything.

"You blockhead!" cried Granny, addressing De Grieux. "You scoundrelly Frenchman! So this is how he advises, the monster. Go away, go away! He knows nothing about it and comes fussing round!"

Fearfully offended, De Grieux shrugged his shoulders, looked contemptuously at Granny, and walked away. He felt ashamed of having interfered; he had been in too great a hurry.

An hour later, in spite of all our efforts, we had lost everything.

"Home," cried Granny.

She did not utter a single word till we got into the avenue. In the avenue and approaching the hotel she began to break into exclamations—

"What a fool! What a silly fool! You're an old fool, you are!"

As soon as we got to her apartments—

"Tea!" cried Granny. "And pack up at once! We are going!"

"Where does your honour mean to go?" Marfa was beginning.

"What has it to do with you? Mind your own business! Potapitch, pack up everything: all the luggage. We are going back to Moscow. I have thrown away fifteen thousand roubles!"

"Fifteen thousand, madame! My God!" Potapitch cried, flinging up his hands with deep feeling, probably meaning to humour her.

"Come, come, you fool! He is beginning to whimper! Hold your tongue! Pack up! The bill, make haste, make haste!"

"The next train goes at half-past nine, Granny," I said, to check her furore.

"And what is it now?"

"Half-past seven."

"How annoying! Well, it doesn't matter! Alexey Ivanovitch, I haven't a farthing. Here are two more notes. Run there and change these for me too. Or I have nothing for the journey."

I set off. Returning to the hotel half an hour later, I found our whole party at Granny's. Learning that Granny was going off to Moscow, they seemed to be even more upset than by her losses. Even though her going might save her property, what was to become of the General? Who would pay De Grieux? Mlle. Blanche would, of course, decline to wait for Granny to die and would certainly now make up to the Prince or to somebody else. They were all standing before Granny, trying to console her and persuade her. Again Polina was not there. Granny was shouting at them furiously.

"Let me alone, you devils! What business is it of yours? Why does that goat's beard come forcing himself upon me?" she cried at De Grieux; "and you, my fine bird?" she cried, addressing Mlle. Blanche, "what are you after?"

"*Diantre!*" whispered Mlle. Blanche, with an angry flash of her eyes, but suddenly she burst out laughing and went out of the room.

"*Elle vivra cent ans!*" she called to the General, as she went out of the door.

"Ah, so you are reckoning on my death?" Granny yelled to the General. "Get away! Turn them all out, Alexey Ivanovitch! What business is it of yours? I've fooled away my own money, not yours!"

The General shrugged his shoulders, bowed and went out. De Grieux followed him.

"Call Praskovya," Granny told Marfa.

Five minutes later Marfa returned with Polina. All this time Polina had been sitting in her own room with the children, and I fancy had purposely made up her mind not to go out all day. Her face was serious, sad and anxious.

"Praskovya," began Granny, "is it true, as I learned by accident just now, that that fool, your stepfather, means to marry that silly feather-head of a Frenchwoman—an actress is she, or, something worse? Tell me, is it true?"

"I don't know anything about it for certain, Granny," answered Polina, "but from the words of Mlle. Blanche herself, who does not feel it necessary to conceal anything, I conclude . . ."

"Enough," Granny broke in vigorously, "I understand! I always reckoned that he was capable of it and I have always thought him a most foolish and feather-headed man. He thinks no end of himself, because he is a General (he was promoted from a Colonel on retiring), and he gives himself airs. I know, my good girl, how you kept sending telegram after telegram to Moscow, to ask if your old Granny would soon be laid out. They were on the look-out for my money;

without money that nasty hussy, what's her name—De Cominges—
wouldn't take him for her footman, especially with his false teeth. She
has a lot of money herself, they say, lends at interest, has made a
lot. I am not blaming you, Praskovya, it wasn't you who sent the
telegrams; and I don't want to remember the past, either. I know
you've got a bad temper—a wasp! You can sting to hurt; but I'm sorry
for you because I was fond of your mother, Katerina. Well, you throw
up everything here and come with me. You've nowhere to go, you
know; and it's not fitting for you to be with them now. Stop!" cried
Granny, as Polina was about to speak; "I've not finished. I ask nothing of you. As you know, I have in Moscow a palace; you can have
a whole storey to yourself and not come and see me for weeks at a
time if my temper does not suit you! Well, will you or not?"

"Let me ask you first: do you really mean to set off at once?"

"Do you suppose I'm joking, my good girl! I've said I'm going and
I'm going. I've wasted fifteen thousand roubles to-day over your
damned roulette. Five years ago I promised to rebuild a wooden church
with stone on my estate near Moscow, and instead of that I've thrown
away my money here. Now, my girl, I'm going home to build the
church."

"And the waters, Granny? You came to drink the waters?"

"Bother you and the waters, too. Don't irritate me, Praskovya; are
you doing it on purpose? Tell me, will you come or not?"

"I thank you very, very much," Polina began, with feeling, "for
the home you offer me. You have guessed my position to some extent.
I am so grateful to you that I shall perhaps come to you soon; but
now there are reasons . . . important reasons . . . and I can't decide
at once, on the spur of the moment. If you were staying only a fortnight . . ."

"You mean you won't?"

"I mean I can't. Besides, in any case I can't leave my brother and
sister, as . . . as . . . as it may actually happen that they may be left
abandoned, so . . . if you would take me with the children, Granny,
I certainly would come, and, believe me, I would repay you for it!"
she added warmly; "but without the children I can't come, Granny."

"Well, don't whimper." (Polina had no intention of whimpering—
indeed, I had never seen her cry.) "Some place will be found for the
chickens, my henhouse is big enough. Besides, it is time they were at
school. Well, so you are not coming now! Well, Praskovya, mind! I
wished for your good, but I know why you won't come! I know all
about it, Praskovya. That Frenchman will bring you no good."

Polina flushed crimson. I positively shuddered. (Every one knows all about it. I am the only one to know nothing!)

"Come, come, don't frown. I am not going to say anything more. Only take care no harm comes of it, understand. You are a clever wench; I shall be sorry for you. Well, that's enough. I should not like to look on you as on the others! Go along, good-bye!"

"I'll come to see you off," said Polina.

"There's no need, don't you interfere; I am sick of you all."

Polina was kissing Granny's hand, but the latter pulled it away and kissed her on the cheek.

As she passed me, Polina looked at me quickly and immediately turned away her eyes.

"Well, good-bye to you, too, Alexey Ivanovitch, there's only an hour before the train starts, and I think you must be tired out with me. Here, take these fifty pieces of gold."

"I thank you very much, Granny; I'm ashamed . . ."

"Come, come!" cried Granny, but so vigorously and angrily that I dared say no more and took it.

"When you are running about Moscow without a job come to me: I will give you some introductions. Now, get along with you!"

I went to my room and lay down on my bed. I lay there for half an hour on my back, with my hands clasped behind my head. The catastrophe had come at last, I had something to think about. I made up my mind to talk earnestly to Polina. The nasty Frenchman! So it was true then! But what could there be at the bottom of it? Polina and De Grieux! Heavens! what a pair!

It was all simply incredible. I suddenly jumped up, beside myself, to look for Mr. Astley, and at all costs to make him speak out. No doubt in this matter, too, he knew more than I did. Mr. Astley? He was another riddle to me!

But suddenly there was a tap at my door. I looked up. It was Potapitch.

"Alexy Ivanovitch, you are wanted to come to my lady!"

"What's the matter? Is she setting off? The train does not start for twenty minutes."

"She's uneasy, she can't sit still. 'Make haste, make haste!' she says, meaning to fetch you, sir. For Christ's sake, don't delay."

I ran downstairs at once. Granny was being wheeled out into the passage, her pocket-book was in her hand.

"Alexey Ivanovitch, go on ahead; we're coming."

"Where, Granny?"

"As sure as I'm alive, I'll win it back. Come, march, don't ask questions! Does the play go on there till midnight?"

I was thunderstruck. I thought a moment, but at once made up my mind.

"Do as you please, Antonida Vassilyevna, I'm not coming."

"What's that for? What now? Have you all eaten too many pancakes, or what?"

"Do as you please, I should blame myself for it afterwards; I won't. I won't take part in it or look on at it; spare me, Antonida Vassilyevna. Here are your fifty friedrichs d'or back; good-bye!" And, laying the fifty friedrichs d'or on the little table near which Granny's chair was standing, I bowed and went out.

"What nonsense!" Granny shouted after me. "Don't come if you don't want to, I can find the way by myself! Potapitch, come with me! Come, lift me up, carry me!"

I did not find Mr. Astley and returned home. It was late, after midnight, when I learned from Potapitch how Granny's day ended. She lost all that I had changed for her that evening—that is, in Russian money, another ten thousand roubles. The little Pole, to whom she had given two friedrichs d'or the day before, had attached himself to her and had directed her play the whole time. At first, before the Pole came, she had made Potapitch put down the stakes, but soon she dismissed him; it was at that moment the Pole turned up. As ill-luck would have it, he understood Russian and babbled away in a mixture of three languages, so that they understood each other after a fashion. Granny abused him mercilessly the whole time; and though he incessantly "laid himself at his lady's feet," "yet he couldn't be compared with you, Alexey Ivanovitch," said Potapitch. "She treated you *like a gentleman,* while the other—I saw it with my own eyes, God strike me dead—stole her money off the table. She caught him at it herself twice. She did give it to him with all sorts of names, sir, even pulled his hair once, upon my word she did, so that folks were laughing round about. She's lost everything, sir, everything, all you changed for her; we brought her back here—she only asked for a drink of water, crossed herself and went to bed. She's worn out, to be sure; she fell asleep at once. God send her heavenly dreams. Och! these foreign parts!" Potapitch wound up. "I said it would lead to no good. If only we could soon be back in Moscow! We'd everything we wanted at home in Moscow: a garden, flowers such as you don't have here, fragrance, the apples are swelling, plenty of room everywhere. No, we had to come abroad. Oh, oh, oh . . ."

Chapter 13

Now almost a whole month has passed since I touched these notes of mine, which were begun under the influence of confused but intense impressions. The catastrophe which I felt to be approaching has actually come, but in a form a hundred times more violent and startling than I had expected. It has all been something strange, grotesque and even tragic—at least for me. Several things have happened to me that were almost miraculous; that is, at least, how I look upon them to this day—though from another point of view, particularly in the whirl of events in which I was involved at that time, they were only somewhat out of the common. But what is most marvellous to me is my own attitude to all these events. To this day I cannot understand myself, and it has all floated by like a dream—even my passion—it was violent and sincere, but . . . what has become of it now? It is true that sometimes the thought flashes through my brain: "Wasn't I out of my mind then, and wasn't I all that time somewhere in a madhouse and perhaps I'm there now, so that was all my fancy and still is my fancy . . ." I put my notes together and read them over. (Who knows—perhaps to convince myself that I did not write them in a madhouse.) Now I am entirely alone. Autumn is coming on and the leaves are turning yellow. I'm still in this dismal little town (oh! how dismal the little German towns are!), and instead of considering what to do next, I go on living under the influence of the sensations I have just passed through, under the influence of memories still fresh, under the influence of the whirl of events which caught me up and flung me aside again. At times I fancy that I am still caught up in that whirlwind, that that storm is still raging, carrying me along with it, and again I lose sight of all order and measure and I whirl round and round again. . . .

However, I may, perhaps, leave off whirling and settle down in a way if, so far as I can, I put clearly before my mind all the incidents of the past month. I feel drawn to my pen again. Besides, I have sometimes nothing at all to do in the evenings. I am so hard up for something to do that, odd as it seems, I even take from the scurvy lending library here the novels of Paul de Kock (in a German translation), though I can't endure them; yet I read them and wonder at myself. It is as though I were afraid of breaking the spell of the recent past by a serious book or any serious occupation. It is as though that grotesque dream, with all the impressions left by it, was so precious to me that I am afraid to let anything new touch upon it for fear it should all vanish in smoke. Is it all so precious to me? Yes, of course it is precious. Perhaps I shall remember it for forty years. . . .

And so I take up my writing again. I can give a brief account of it to some extent now: the impressions are not at all the same.

In the first place, to finish with Granny. The following day she lost everything. It was what was bound to happen. When once any one is started upon that road, it is like a man in a sledge flying down a snow mountain more and more swiftly. She played all day till eight o'clock in the evening; I was not present and only know what happened from what I was told.

Potapitch was in attendance on her at the Casino all day. Several Poles in succession guided Granny's operations in the course of the day. She began by dismissing the Pole whose hair she had pulled the day before and taking on another, but he turned out almost worse. After dismissing the second, and accepting again the first, who had never left her side, but had been squeezing himself in behind her chair and continually poking his head in during the whole period of his disgrace, she sank at last into complete despair. The second Pole also refused to move away; one stationed himself on her right and the other on her left. They were abusing one another the whole time and quarrelling over the stakes and the game, calling each other *"laidak"* and other Polish civilities, making it up again, putting down money recklessly and playing at random. When they quarrelled they put the money down regardless of each other—one, for instance, on the red and the other on the black. It ended in their completely bewildering and overwhelming Granny, so that at last, almost in tears, she appealed to the old croupier, begging him to protect her and to send them away. They were, in fact, immediately turned out in spite of their outcries and protests; they both shouted out at once and tried to prove that Granny owed them something, that she had deceived them about something and had treated them basely and dishonourably. The luckless Potapitch told me all this the same evening almost with tears, and complained that they stuffed their pockets with money, that he himself had seen them shamelessly steal and continually thrust the money in their pockets. One, for instance, would beg five friedrichs d'or for his trouble and begin putting them down on the spot side by side with Granny's stakes. Granny won, but the man shouted that his stake was the winning one and that Granny's had lost. When they were dismissed Potapitch came forward and said that their pockets were full of gold. Granny at once bade the croupier to look into it and, in spite of the outcries of the Poles (they cackled like two cocks caught in the hand), the police came forward and their pockets were immediately emptied for Granny's benefit. Granny enjoyed unmistakable prestige among the croupiers and the whole staff of the Casino all that day, until she had lost everything. By degrees her fame spread all over the town. All the visitors at the watering-place, of all nations, small and great, streamed to look on at *"une vieille comtesse russe tombée en enfance,"* who had already lost "some millions."

But Granny gained very, very little by being rescued from the two Poles. They were at once replaced by a third, who spoke perfectly pure Russian and was dressed like a gentleman, though he did look like a flunkey with a huge moustache and a sense of his own importance. He, too "laid himself at his lady's feet and kissed them," but behaved haughtily to those about him, was despotic over the play; in fact, immediately behaved like Granny's master rather than her servant. Every minute, at every turn in the game, he turned to her and swore with awful oaths that he was himself a *"pan* of good position," and that he wouldn't take a kopeck of Granny's money. He repeated this oath so many times that Granny was completely intimidated. But as this *pan* certainly seemed at first to improve her luck, Granny was not willing to abandon him on her own account. An hour later the two Poles who had been turned out of the Casino turned up behind Granny's chair again, and again proffered their services if only to run errands for her. Potapitch swore that the *"pan* of good position" winked at them and even put something in their hands. As Granny had no dinner and could not leave her chair, one of the Poles certainly was of use: he ran off once to the dining-room of the Casino and brought her a cup of broth and afterwards some tea. They both ran about, however. But towards the end of the day, when it became evident to every one that she would stake her last banknote, there were behind her chair as many as six Poles who had never been seen or heard of before. When Granny was playing her last coin, they not only ceased to obey her, but took no notice of her whatever, squeezed their way up to the table in front of her, snatched the money themselves, put down the stakes and made their own play, shouted and quarrelled, talked to the *"pan* of good position" as to one of themselves, while the *"pan* of good position" himself seemed almost oblivious of Granny's existence. Even when Granny, after losing everything, was returning after eight o'clock to the hotel, three or four Poles ran at the side of her bath-chair, still unable to bring themselves to leave her; they kept shouting at the top of their voices, declaring in a hurried gabble that Granny had cheated them in some way and must give them something. They followed her in this way right up to the hotel, from which they were at last driven away with blows.

By Potapitch's reckoning Granny had lost in all ninety thousand roubles that day, apart from what she had lost the day before. All her notes, her exchequer bonds, all the shares she had with her, she had changed, one after another. I marvelled how she could have stood those seven or eight hours sitting there in her chair and scarcely leaving the table, but Potapitch told me that three or four times she had begun winning considerably; and, carried on by fresh hope, she could not tear herself away. But gamblers know how a man can sit for almost twenty-four hours at cards, without looking to right or to left.

Meanwhile, very critical events were taking place all that day at the hotel. In the morning, before eleven o'clock, when Granny was still at home, our people—that is, the General and De Grieux—made up their minds to take the final step. Learning that Granny had given up all idea of setting off, but was going back to the Casino, they went in full conclave (all but Polina) to talk things over with her finally and even *openly*. The General, trembling and with a sinking heart in view of the awful possibilities for himself, overdid it. After spending half an hour in prayers and entreaties and making a clean breast of everything—that is, of all his debts and even his passion for Mlle. Blanche (he quite lost his head), the General suddenly adopted a menacing tone and even began shouting and stamping at Granny; cried that she was disgracing their name, had become a scandal to the whole town, and finally . . . finally: "You are shaming the Russian name," cried the General, and he told her that the police would be called in! Granny finally drove him from her with a stick (an actual stick). The General and De Grieux consulted once or twice that morning, and the question that agitated them was whether it were not possible in some way to bring in the police, on the plea that an unfortunate but venerable old lady, sinking into her dotage, was gambling away her whole fortune, and so on; whether, in fact, it would be possible to put her under any sort of supervision or restraint. . . . But De Grieux only shrugged his shoulders and laughed in the General's face, as the latter pranced up and down his study talking excitedly. Finally, De Grieux went off with a wave of his hand. In the evening we learned that he had left the hotel altogether, after having been in very earnest and mysterious confabulation with Mlle. Blanche. As for Mlle. Blanche, she had taken her measures early in the morning: she threw the General over completely and would not even admit him to her presence. When the General ran to the Casino in search of her and met her arm-in-arm with the Prince, neither she nor Madame de Cominges deigned to notice him. The Prince did not bow to him either. Mlle. Blanche spent that whole day hard at work upon the Prince, trying to force from him a definite declaration. But alas! she was cruelly deceived in her reckoning! This little catastrophe took place in the evening. It suddenly came out that he was as poor as a church mouse, and, what is more, was himself reckoning on borrowing from her on an I O U to try his luck at roulette. Blanche turned him out indignantly and locked herself up in her room.

On the morning of that day I went to Mr. Astley—or, to be more exact, I went in search of Mr. Astley, but could find him nowhere. He was not at home, or in the park, or in the Casino. He was not dining at his hotel that day. It was past four o'clock when I suddenly saw him walking from the railway station towards the Hôtel d'Angleterre. He was in a hurry and was very much preoccupied, though it was hard to trace any anxiety or any perturbation whatever in his face. He held out his hand to me cordially, with his habitual exclamation "Ah!" but without stopping walked on with rather a rapid step. I attached myself to him, but he managed to answer me in such a way that I did not succeed in even asking him about anything. Moreover, I felt, for some reason, ashamed to begin speaking of Polina; he did not ask a word about her. I told him about Granny. He listened attentively and seriously and shrugged his shoulders.

"She will gamble away everything," I observed.

"Oh, yes," he answered; "she went in to play just as I was going away, and afterwards I learnt for a fact that she had lost everything. If there were time I would look in at the Casino, for it is curious."

"Where have you been?" I cried, wondering that I had not asked before.

"I've been in Frankfurt."

"On business?"

"Yes, on business."

Well, what more was there for me to ask? I did, however, continue walking beside him, but he suddenly turned into the Hôtel des Quatre Saisons, nodded to me and vanished. As I walked home I gradually realized that if I had talked to him for a couple of hours I should have learnt absolutely nothing, because . . . I had nothing to ask him! Yes, that was so, of course! I could not possibly formulate my question.

All that day Polina spent walking with the children and their nurse in the park, or sitting at home. She had for a long time past avoided the General, and scarcely spoke to him about anything—about anything serious, at any rate. I had noticed that for a long time past. But knowing what a position the General was in to-day, I imagined that he could hardly pass her over—that is, there could not but be an important conversation about family affairs between them. When, however, I returned to the hotel, after my conversation with Mr. Astley, I met Polina with the children. There was an expression of the most unruffled calm on her face, as though she alone had remained untouched by the family tempest. She nodded in response to my bow. I returned home feeling quite malignant.

I had, of course, avoided seeing her and had seen nothing of her since the incident with the Burmerhelms. There was some affectation and pose in this; but as time went on, I felt more and more genuinely indignant. Even if she did not care for me in the least, she should not, I thought, have trampled on my feelings like that and have received my declarations so contemptuously. She knew that I really loved her; she admitted me, she allowed me to speak like that! It is true that it had begun rather strangely. Some time before, long ago, in fact, two months before, I began to notice that she wanted to make me her friend, her *confidant,* and indeed was in a way testing me. But somehow this did not come off then; instead of that there remained the strange relations that existed between us; that is how it was I began to speak to her like that. But if my love repelled her, why did she not directly forbid me to speak of it?

She did not forbid me; indeed she sometimes provoked me to talk of it and . . . and, of course, she did this for fun. I know for certain. I noticed it unmistakably—it was agreeable to her to listen and to work me up to a state of misery, to wound me by some display of the utmost contempt and disregard. And, of course, she knew that I could not exist without her. It was three days since the affair with the Baron and I could not endure our separation any longer. When I met her just now near the Casino, my heart throbbed so that I turned pale. But she could not get on without me, either! She needed me and—surely, surely not as a buffoon, a clown?

She had a secret—that was clear! Her conversation with Granny had stabbed my heart. Why, I had urged her a thousand times to be open with me, and she knew that I was ready to give my life for her.

But she always put me off, almost with contempt, or had asked of me, instead of the sacrifice of my life, such pranks as the one with the Baron!

Was not that enough to make one indignant? Could that Frenchman be all the world to her? And Mr. Astley? But at that point the position became utterly incomprehensible—and meanwhile, my God! what agonies I went through!

On getting home, in an access of fury I snatched up my pen and scribbled the following letter to her—

"Polina Alexandrovna, I see clearly that the *dénouement* is at hand which will affect you also. I repeat for the last time: do you need my life or not? If I can be of use in *any way whatever,* dispose of me as you think fit, and I will meanwhile remain in my room and not go out at all. If you need me, write to me or send for me."

I sealed up this note and sent it off by the corridor attendant, instructing him to give it into her hands. I expected no answer, but three minutes later the attendant returned with the message that "she sent her greetings."

It was past six when I was summoned to the General.

He was in his study, dressed as though he were on the point of going out. His hat and coat were lying on the sofa. It seemed to me as I went in that he was standing in the middle of the room with his legs wide apart and his head hanging, talking aloud to himself. But as soon as he saw me, he rushed at me almost crying out, so that I involuntarily stepped back and was almost running away, but he seized me by both hands and drew me to the sofa; sat down on the sofa himself, made me sit down in an armchair just opposite himself, and, keeping tight hold of my hand, with trembling lips and with tears suddenly glistening on his eyelashes, began speaking in an imploring voice.

"Alexey Ivanovitch, save, save me, spare me."

It was a long while before I could understand. He kept talking and talking and talking, continually repeating, "Spare me, spare me!" At last I guessed that he expected something in the way of advice from me; or, rather, abandoned by all in his misery and anxiety, he had thought of me and had sent for me, simply to talk and talk and talk to me.

He was mad, or at any rate utterly distraught. He clasped his hands and was on the point of dropping on his knees before me to implore me (what do you suppose?) to go at once to Mlle. Blanche and to beseech, to urge her to return to him and marry him.

"Upon my word, General," I cried; "why, Mlle. Blanche is perhaps scarcely aware of my existence. What can I do?"

But it was vain to protest; he didn't understand what was said to him. He fell to talking about Granny, too, but with terrible incoherence; he was still harping on the idea of sending for the police.

"Among us, among us," he began, suddenly boiling over with indignation; "among us, in a well-ordered state, in fact, where there is a Government in control of things, such old women would have been put under guardianship at once! Yes, my dear sir, yes," he went on, suddenly dropping into a scolding tone, jumping up from his chair and pacing about the room; "you may not be aware of the fact, honoured sir," he said, addressing some imaginary "honoured sir" in the corner, "so let me tell you . . . yes . . . among us such old women are kept in order, kept in order; yes, indeed. . . . Oh, damn it all!"

And he flung himself on the sofa again, and a minute later, almost sobbing, gasping for breath, hastened to tell me that Mlle. Blanche would not marry him because Granny had come instead of the telegram, and that now it was clear he would not come into the inheritance. He imagined that I knew nothing of this till then. I began to speak of De Grieux; he waved his hand: "He has gone away! Everything of mine he has in pawn; I'm stripped of everything! That money you brought . . . that money—I don't know how much there is, I think seven hundred francs are left and that's enough, that's all and what's to come—I don't know, I don't know! . . ."

"How will you pay your hotel bill?" I cried in alarm; "and . . . afterwards what will you do?"

He looked at me pensively, but I fancy he did not understand and perhaps did not hear what I said. I tried to speak of Polina Alexandrovna, of the children; he hurriedly answered: "Yes! yes!" but at once fell to talking of the Prince again, saying that Blanche would go away with him now and "then . . . then, what am I to do, Alexey Ivanovitch?" he asked, addressing me suddenly. "I vow, by God! I don't know what to do; tell me, isn't this ingratitude? Isn't this ingratitude?"

Finally he dissolved into floods of tears.

There was no doing anything with such a man; it would be dangerous to leave him alone, too—something might happen to him. I got rid of him somehow, but let nurse know she must look in upon him pretty frequently, and also spoke to the corridor attendant, a very sensible fellow; he, too, promised me to keep an eye on the General.

I had hardly left the General when Potapitch came to summon me to Granny. It was eight o'clock and she had only just come back from the Casino after losing everything. I went to her; the old lady was sitting in an armchair, utterly worn out and evidently ill. Marfa was giving her a cup of tea and almost forcing her to drink it. And Granny's tone and voice were utterly changed.

"Good-day, Alexey Ivanovitch, my good sir," she said, bending her head slowly, and with dignity; "excuse me for troubling you once more, you must excuse an old woman. I have left everything behind there, my friend, nearly a hundred thousand roubles. You did well not to come with me yesterday. Now I have no money, not a farthing. I don't want to delay a moment, at half-past nine I'm setting off. I have sent to that Englishman of yours—what's his name, Astley—I want to ask him to lend me three thousand francs for a week. So you must persuade him not to take it amiss and refuse. I am still fairly well off, my friend. I have still three villages and two houses. And there is still some money. I didn't bring it all with me. I tell you this that he may not feel any doubts . . . Ah, here he is! One can see he is a nice man."

Mr. Astley had hastened to come at Granny's first summons. With no hesitation and without wasting words he promptly counted out three thousand francs for an I O U which Granny signed. When this business was settled he made haste to take his leave and go away.

"And now you can go, too, Alexey Ivanovitch. I have only a little over an hour left. I want to lie down: my bones ache. Don't be hard on an old fool like me. Henceforward I won't blame young people for being flighty, and it would be a sin for me now to blame that luckless fellow, your General, either. I won't give him any money, though, as he wants me to, because—to my thinking he is utterly silly; only, old fool as I am, I've no more sense than he. Verily God seeks out and punishes pride, even in old age. Well, good-bye. Marfa, lift me up!"

I wanted to see Granny off, however. What's more, I was in a state of suspense; I kept expecting that in another minute something would happen. I could not sit quietly in my room. I went out into the corridor, even for a moment went for a saunter along the avenue. My letter to her had been clear and decisive and the present catastrophe was, of course, a final one. I heard in the hotel that De Grieux had left. If she rejected me as a friend, perhaps she would not reject me as a servant. I was necessary to her, I was of use to her, if only to run her errands, it was bound to be so!

When the train was due to start I ran to the station and saw Granny into the train. Her whole party were together, in a special reserved compartment. "Thank you, my good friend, for your disinterested sympathy," she said, at parting from me; "and tell Praskovya, in reference to what we were discussing yesterday, I shall expect her."

I went home. Passing the General's rooms I met the old nurse and inquired after the General. "Oh, he's all right, sir," she answered me dolefully. I went in, however, but stood still in positive amazement. Mlle. Blanche and the General were both laughing heartily. Madame de Cominges was sitting on the sofa close by. The General was evidently beside himself with delight. He was murmuring incoherently and going off into prolonged fits of nervous laughter, during which his face was puckered with innumerable wrinkles and his eyes disappeared from sight. Afterwards I learnt from Blanche herself that, having dismissed the Prince and having heard how the General was weeping, she had taken it into her head to comfort him by going to see him for a minute. But the poor General did not know that at that time his fate was decided, and that Mlle. Blanche had already packed to set off for Paris by the first train next morning.

Stopping in the doorway of the General's study, I changed my mind and went away unnoticed. Going up to my own room and opening the door, I suddenly noticed a figure in the half-darkness sitting on a chair in the corner by the window. She did not get up when I went in. I went up quickly, looked, and—my heart stood still: it was Polina.

Chapter 14

I POSITIVELY cried out aloud.

"What is it? What is it?" she asked me strangely. She was pale and looked gloomy.

"You ask what is it? You? Here in my room!"

"If I come, then I come *altogether*. That's my way. You'll see that directly; light the candle."

I lighted a candle. She got up, went up to the table, and put before me an open letter.

"Read it," she ordered me.

"It's—it's De Grieux's handwriting," I cried, taking the letter. My hands trembled and the lines danced before my eyes. I have forgotten the exact wording of the letter, but here is the main drift of it, if not the actual words:

"Mademoiselle," wrote De Grieux, "an unfortunate circumstance compels me to go away at once. You have, no doubt, observed that I have purposely avoided a final explanation with you until such time as the whole position might be cleared up. The arrival of your old relation *(de la vieille dame)* and her absurd behaviour have put an end to my doubts. The unsettled state of my own affairs forbids me to cherish further the sweet hopes which I permitted myself to indulge for some time. I regret the past, but I trust that you will not detect in my behaviour anything unworthy of a gentleman and an honest man *(gentilhomme et honnête homme)*. Having lost almost all my money in loans to your stepfather, I find myself compelled to make the utmost use of what is left to me; I have already sent word to my friend in Petersburg to arrange at once for the sale of the estates he has mortgaged to me; knowing, however, that your frivolous stepfather has squandered your private fortune I have determined to forgive him fifty thousand francs, and I am returning him part of my claims on his property equivalent to that sum, so that you are now put in a position to regain all that you have lost by demanding the property from him by legal process. I hope, Mademoiselle, that in the present position of affairs my action will be very advantageous to you. I hope, too, that by this action I am fully performing the duty of a man and a gentleman. Rest assured that your memory is imprinted upon my heart for ever."

"Well, that's all clear," I said, turning to Polina; "surely you could have expected nothing else," I added, with indignation.

"I expected nothing," she answered, with apparent composure, though there was a tremor in her voice. "I had made up my mind long ago; I read his mind and knew what he was thinking. He thought that I was trying—that I should insist . . ." (She broke off without finishing her sentence, bit her lips and was silent.) "I purposely doubled my scorn towards him," she began again. "I waited to see what was coming from him. If a telegram had come telling of the inheritance I'd have flung him the money borrowed from that idiot, my stepfather, and would have sent him about his business. He has been hateful to me for ages and ages. Oh! he was not the same man! a thousand times over, I tell you, he was different! but now, now . . . Oh, with what happiness I could fling that fifty thousand in his nasty face and spit and stamp . . ."

"But the security, the I O U for that fifty thousand, is in the General's hands. Take it and return it to De Grieux."

"Oh, that's not the same thing, that's not the same thing . . ."

"Yes, that's true, it's not the same thing. Besides, what is the General capable of now? And Granny!" I cried suddenly.

Polina looked at me, as it were absent-mindedly and impatiently.

"Why Granny?" asked Polina, with vexation. "I can't go to her . . . And I don't want to ask any one's pardon," she added irritably.

"What's to be done!" I cried, "and how, oh, how could you love De Grieux! Oh, the scoundrel, the scoundrel! If you like I will kill him in a duel! Where is he now?"

"He's at Frankfurt, and will be there three days."

"One word from you and I'll set off to-morrow by the first train," I said, with stupid enthusiasm.

She laughed.

"Why, he'll say, maybe: 'Give me back the fifty thousand francs first.' Besides, what should you fight him for? . . . What nonsense it is!"

"But where, where is one to get that fifty thousand francs?" I repeated, grinding my teeth as though it had been possible to pick them up from the floor. "I say—Mr. Astley," I suggested, turning to her with a strange idea dawning upon me.

Her eyes flashed.

"What, do you mean to say *you yourself* want me to turn from you to that Englishman!" she said, looking in my face with a searching glance and smiling bitterly. For the first time in her life she addressed me in the second person singular.

I believe she was giddy with emotion at the moment, and all at once she sat down on the sofa as though she were exhausted.

It was as though I had been struck by a flash of lightning. I stood up and could not believe my eyes, could not believe my ears! Why, then she loved me! She had come to me and not to Mr. Astley!

She, she, a young girl, had come to my room in a hotel, so she had utterly compromised herself by her own act, and I, I was standing before her and still did not understand.

One wild idea flashed through my mind.

"Polina, give me only one hour. Stay here only one hour and . . . I'll come back. That's . . . that's essential! You shall see! Be here, be here!"

And I ran out of the room, not responding to her amazed and questioning look; she called something after me but I did not turn back.

Sometimes the wildest idea, the most apparently impossible thought, takes possession of one's mind so strongly that one accepts it at last as something substantial . . . more than that, if the idea is associated with a strong passionate desire, then sometimes one will accept it at last as something fated, inevitable, predestined—as something bound to be, and bound to happen. Perhaps there is something else in it, some combination of presentiments, some extraordinary effort of will, self-poisoning by one's own fancy—or something else—I don't know what, but on that evening (which I shall never in my life forget) something marvellous happened to me. Though it is quite justified by the laws of arithmetic, nevertheless it is a marvel to me to this day. And why, why had that conviction so long before taken such firm and deep root in my mind? I had certainly thought about it—I repeat—not as a chance among others which might or might not come to pass, but as something which was absolutely bound to happen!

It was a quarter past ten. I went into the Casino with a confident expectation and at the same time with an excitement I had never experienced before. There were still a good many people in the gambling hall, though not half as many as in the morning.

Between ten and eleven there are still to be found in the gambling halls the genuine desperate gamblers for whom nothing exists at a spa but roulette, who have come for that alone, who scarcely notice what is going on around them and take no interest in anything during the whole season, but play from morning till night and would be ready perhaps to play all night till dawn, too, if it were possible. And they always disperse with annoyance when at twelve o'clock the roulette hall is closed. And when the senior croupier announces, just before midnight. *"Les trois derniers coups, messieurs,"* they are ready to stake on those last three strokes all they have in their pockets— and do, in fact, lose most at that time. I went up to the very table where Granny had sat that day. It was not crowded, and so I soon took my place at the table standing. Exactly before me was the word *Passe* scrawled on the green cloth.

Passe is the series of numbers from nineteen inclusive to thirty-six.

The first series of numbers from one to eighteen inclusive is called *manque;* but what was that to me? I was not calculating, I had not even heard what had been the winning number last, and I did not ask about it when I began to play—as every player of any prudence would do. I pulled out all my twenty friedrichs d'or and staked them on *passe,* the word which lay before me.

"Vingt-deux," cried the croupier.

I had won and again staked all: including my winnings.

"Trente-et-un," cried the croupier.

I had won again. I had in all eighty friedrichs d'or. I staked the whole of that sum on the twelve middle numbers (my winnings would be three to one, but the chances were two to one against me). The wheel rotated and stopped at twenty-four. I was passed three rolls each of fifty friedrichs d'or in paper and ten gold coins; I had now two hundred friedrichs d'or.

I was as though in delirium and I moved the whole heap of gold to red—and suddenly thought better of it. And for the only time that whole evening, all the time I was playing, I felt chilled with terror and a shudder made my arms and legs tremble, I felt with horror and instantly realized what losing would mean for me now! My whole life was at stake.

"Rouge," cried the croupier, and I drew a breath; fiery pins and needles were tingling all over my body. I was paid in banknotes. It came to four thousand florins and eighty friedrichs d'or (I could still keep count at that stage).

Then, I remember, I staked two thousand florins on the twelve middle numbers, and lost: I staked my gold, the eighty friedrichs d'or, and lost. I was seized with fury: I snatched up the two hundred florins I had left and staked them on the first twelve numbers—haphazard, at random, without thinking! There was, however, an instant of suspense, like, perhaps, the feeling experienced by Madame Blanchard when she flew from a balloon in Paris to the earth.

"Quatre!" cried the croupier.

Now with my stake I had six thousand florins. I looked triumphant already. I was afraid of nothing—nothing, and staked four thousand florins on black. Nine people followed my example and staged on black. The croupiers exchanged glances and said something to one another. People were talking all round in suspense.

Black won. I don't remember my winnings after, nor what I staked on. I only remember as though in a dream that I won, I believe, sixteen thousand florins; suddenly three unlucky turns took twelve thousand from it; then I staked the last four thousand on *passe* (but I scarcely felt anything as I did so; I simply waited in a mechanical, senseless way)—and again I won; then I won four times running. I only remember that I gathered up money in thousands; I remember, too, that the middle twelve won most often and I kept to it. It turned up with a sort of regularity, certainly three or four times in succession, then it did not turn up twice running and then it followed three or four times in succession. Such astonishing regularity is sometimes met with in streaks, and that is what throws inveterate gamblers who calculate with a pencil in their hands out of their reckoning. And what horrible ironies of fate happen sometimes in such cases!

I believe not more than half an hour had passed since I came into the room, when suddenly the croupier informed me that I had won thirty thousand florins, and as the bank did not meet claims for a larger sum at one time the roulette would be closed till next morning. I snatched up all my gold, dropped it into my pockets, snatched up all my notes, and at once went into the other room where there was another roulette table; the whole crowd streamed after me; there at once a place was cleared for me and I fell to staking again haphazard without reckoning. I don't understand what saved me!

At times, however, a glimmer of prudence began to dawn upon my mind. I clung to certain numbers and combinations, but soon abandoned them and staked almost unconsciously. I must have been very absent-minded; I remember the croupiers several times corrected me. I made several gross mistakes. My temples were soaked with sweat and my hands were shaking. The Poles ran up, too, with offers of their services, but I listened to no one. My luck was unbroken! Suddenly there were sounds of loud talk and laughter, and every one cried "Bravo, bravo!" some even clapped their hands. Here, too, I collected three hundred thousand florins, and the bank closed till next day.

"Go away, go away," a voice whispered on my right.

It was a Frankfurt Jew; he was standing beside me all the time, and I believe sometimes helped me in my play.

"For goodness' sake go," another voice whispered in my left ear.

I took a hurried glance. It was a lady about thirty, very soberly and quietly dressed, with a tired, pale, sickly face which yet bore traces of having once been beautiful. At that moment I was stuffing my pockets with the notes, which I crumpled up anyhow, and gathering up the gold that lay on the table. Snatching up the last roll of notes, I succeeded in putting it into the pale lady's hands quite without attracting notice; I had an intense desire to do so at the time, and I remember her pale slim fingers pressed my hand warmly in token of gratitude. All that took place in one instant.

Having collected quickly all my winnings I went quickly to the *trente et quarante*.

Trente et quarante is frequented by the aristocratic public. Unlike roulette, it is a game of cards. Here the bank will pay up to a hundred thousand thalers at once. The largest stake is here also four thousand florins. I knew nothing of the game, and scarcely knew how to bet on it, except the red and the black upon which one can bet in this game too. And I stuck to red and black. The whole Casino crowded round. I don't remember whether I once thought of Polina all this time. I was experiencing an overwhelming enjoyment in scooping up and taking away the notes which grew up in a heap before me.

It seemed as though fate were urging me on. This time, as luck would have it, a circumstance occurred which, however, is fairly frequent in the game. Chance favours red, for instance, ten or even fifteen times in succession. I had heard two days before that in the previous week red had turned up twenty-two times in succession; it was something which had never been remembered in roulette, and it was talked of with amazement. Every one, of course, abandoned red at once, and after the tenth time, for instance, scarcely any one dared to stake on it. But none of the experienced players staked on black either. The experienced gambler knows what is meant by this "freak of chance." It would mean that after red had won sixteen times, at the seventeenth time the luck would infalliby fall on black. Novices at play rush to this conclusion in crowds, double and treble their stakes, and lose terribly.

But, noticing that red had turned up seven times running, by strange perversity I staked on it. I am convinced that vanity was half responsible for it; I wanted to impress the spectators by taking a mad risk, and—oh, the strange sensation—I remember distinctly that, quite apart from the promptings of vanity, I was possessed by an intense craving for risk. Perhaps passing through so many sensations my soul was not satisfied but only irritated by them and craved still more sensation— and stronger and stronger ones—till utterly exhausted. And, truly I am not lying, if the regulations had allowed me to stake fifty thousand florins at once, I should certainly have staked them. People around shouted that it was madness—that red had won fourteen times already!

"Monsieur a gagné déjá cent mille florins," I heard a voice say near me.

I suddenly came to myself. What? I had won during that evening a hundred thousand florins! And what more did I want? I fell on my banknotes, crumpled them up in my pockets without counting them, scooped up all my gold, all my rolls of notes, and ran out of the Casino. Every one was laughing as I went through the room, looking at my bulging pockets and at the way I staggered under the weight of gold. I think it weighed over twenty pounds. Several hands were held out to me; I gave it away in handfuls as I snatched it up. Two Jews stopped me at the outer door.

"You are bold—you are very bold," they said to me, "but be sure to go away to-morrow as soon as possible, or else you will lose it all—you will lose it all. . . ."

I didn't listen to them. The avenue was so dark that I could not see my hand before my face. It was half a mile to the hotel. I had never been afraid of thieves or robbers even as a small boy; I did not think of them now either. I don't remember what I thought of on the road; I had no thoughts. I was only aware of an immense enjoyment—success, victory, power—I don't know how to express it. Polina's image hovered before my mind too; I remembered her and was conscious I was going to her; I should be with her in a moment, should be telling her and showing her . . . But I hardly remembered what she had said to me earlier, and why I had gone, and all the sensations I had felt, not more than an hour and a half before, seemed to me something long past, transformed, grown old—something of which we should say no more because everything now would begin anew. Almost at the end of the avenue a sudden panic came upon me. What if I were robbed and murdered at this instant? At every step my panic grew greater. I almost ran. Suddenly, at the end of the avenue there was the glare of our hotel with its many windows lighted up—thank God, home!

I ran up to my storey and rapidly opened the door. Polina was there, sitting on the sofa with her arms crossed, with a lighted candle before her. She looked at me with amazement, and no doubt at that moment I must have looked rather strange. I stood before her and began flinging down all my piles of money on the table.

Chapter 15

I REMEMBER she fixed a very intent look on my face, but without even moving from her seat or changing her position.

"I've won two hundred thousand francs!" I cried, as I flung down the last roll of notes.

The huge bundles of notes and piles of gold filled up the whole table; I could not take my eyes off it. At moments I completely forgot Polina. At one moment I began arranging the heap of banknotes, folding them up together, at the next I began undoing the rolls of gold and heaping them up in one pile; then I abandoned it all and strode rapidly up and down the room, lost in thought, then went up to the table, counting the money again. Suddenly, as though coming to myself, I ran to the door and locked it with two turns of the key. Then I stood pondering before my little portmanteau.

"Shall I put it in the portmanteau till to-morrow?" I said, suddenly remembering Polina and turning towards her.

She was still sitting in the same place without stirring, but watching me attentively. Her expression was somehow strange; I did not like that expression. I am not mistaken if I say that there was hatred in it.

I went up to her quickly.

"Polina, here are twenty-five thousand florins—that's fifty thousand francs—more, in fact. Take it, throw it in his face to-morrow."

She did not answer me.

"If you like I will take you away early in the morning. Shall I?"

She suddenly burst out laughing. She laughed for a long time.

I looked at her with wonder and a mortified feeling. That laugh was very much like sarcastic laughter at my expense, which had always been so frequent at the times of my most passionate declarations.

At last she ceased laughing and frowned; she looked at me sternly from under her brows.

"I won't take your money," she declared contemptuously.

"How? What's this?" I cried. "Polina, why?"

"I won't take money for nothing."

"I offer it you as a friend; I offer you my life."

She looked at me with a long, penetrating look, as though she would pierce me through with it.

"You give too much," she said, with a laugh; "De Grieux's mistress is not worth fifty thousand francs."

"Polina, how can you talk to me like that!" I cried, reproachfully. "Am I a De Grieux?"

"I hate you! Yes . . . yes! . . . I love you no more than De Grieux," she cried, her eyes suddenly flashing.

Then she suddenly covered her face with her hands and went into hysterics. I rushed to her.

I realized that something had happened to her while I was away. She seemed quite out of her mind.

"Buy me! Do you want to? Do you want to? For fifty thousand francs, like De Grieux?" broke from her with convulsive sobs.

I held her in my arms, kissed her hands, her feet, fell on my knees before her.

Her hysterics passed off. She put both hands on my shoulders, and looked at me intently; she seemed trying to read something in my face. She listened to me, but evidently did not hear what I was saying to her. Some doubt and anxiety betrayed itself in her face. I was anxious about her; it seemed to me that her brain was giving way. Then she began softly drawing me to her; a trustful smile began straying over her face; but she suddenly pushed me away, and again fell to scanning me with a darkened look.

Suddenly she fell to embracing me.

"You love me, you love me, don't you?" she said. "Why, you . . . why, you . . . wanted to fight the Baron for my sake!"

And suddenly she burst out laughing—as though she had recalled something sweet and funny. She cried and laughed all at once. Well, what was I to do? I was in a fever myself. I remember she began saying something to me—but I could scarcely understand anything. It was a sort of delirium—a sort of babble—as though she wanted to tell me something as rapidly as possible—a delirium which was interrupted from time to time with the merriest laughter, which at last frightened me. "No, no; you are sweet, sweet," she repeated. "You are my faithful one!" And again she put her hand on my shoulders, again she looked at me and repeated, "You love me . . . love me . . . will love me?" I could not take my eyes off her; I had never seen her before in such a mood of love and tenderness; it is true this, of course, was delirium, but . . . noticing my passionate expression, she suddenly began smiling slyly; apropos of nothing she began suddenly talking of Mr. Astley.

She talked incessantly of Mr. Astley, however (she talked of him particularly when she had been trying to tell me of something that evening), but what she meant exactly I could not quite grasp; she seemed to be actually laughing at him. She repeated continually that he was waiting and that, did I know, he was certainly standing under the window?

"Yes, yes, under the window; come open it: look out: look out: he certainly is here! She pushed me to the window, but as soon as I made a movement to go she went off into peals of laughter and I remained with her, and she fell to embracing me.

"Shall we go away? shall we go away to-morrow?" The question suddenly came into her mind uneasily. "Well . . ." (and she sank into thought.) "Well, shall we overtake Granny; what do you think? I think we might overtake her at Berlin. What do you think she will say when she sees us? And Mr. Astley? . . . Well, he won't leap off the Schlangenberg—what do you think?" (She burst out laughing.) "Come, listen, do you know where he is going next summer? He wants to go to the North Pole for scientific investigations, and he has asked me to go with him, ha-ha-ha! He says that we Russians can do nothing without Europeans and are incapable of anything. . . . But he is good-natured, too! Do you know he makes excuses for the General? He says that Blanche . . . that passion—oh, I don't know, I don't know," she repeated, as though she didn't know what she was talking about. "They are poor—how sorry I am for them, and Granny . . . Come, listen, listen, how could you kill De Grieux? And did you really imagine you could kill him? Oh, silly fellow! Can you really think I would let you fight with De Grieux? Why, you did not even kill the Baron," she added, suddenly laughing. "Oh, how funny you were then with the Baron. I looked at you both from the seat; and how unwilling you were to go then, when I sent you. How I laughed then, how I laughed," she added, laughing.

And suddenly she kissed and embraced me again. Again she pressed her face to mine passionately and tenderly. I heard nothing and thought of nothing more. My head was in a whirl. . . .

I think it was about seven o'clock in the morning when I woke up. The sun was shining into the room. Polina was sitting beside me and looking about her strangely, as though she were waking from some darkness and trying to collect her thoughts. She, too, had only just woken up and was gazing at the table and the money. My head ached and was heavy. I tried to take Polina by the hand: she pushed me away and jumped up from the sofa. The dawning day was overcast. Rain had fallen before sunrise. She went to the window, she opened it, put out her head and shoulders and with her face in her hands and her elbows on the window-sill, stayed for three minutes looking out without turning to me or hearing what I said to her. I wondered with dread what would happen now and how it would end. All at once she got up from the window, went up to the table and, looking at me with infinite hatred, with lips trembling with anger, she said to me—

"Well, give me my fifty thousand francs now?"

"Polina, again, again?" I was beginning.

"Or have you changed your mind? Ha-ha-ha! Perhaps you regret it now."

Twenty-five thousand florins, counted out the evening before, were lying on the table; I took the money and gave it to her.

"It's mine now, isn't it? That's so, isn't it? Isn't it?" she asked me, spitefully holding the money in her hand.

"Yes, it was always yours," I answered.

"Well, there are your fifty thousand francs for you!"

With a swing of her arm she flung the money at me. It hit me a stinging blow in the face and the coins flew all over the table. After doing this Polina ran out of the room.

I know that at that moment she was certainly not in her right mind, though I don't understand such temporary insanity. It is true that she is still ill, even now, a month later. What was the cause of her condition, and, above all, of this whim? Was it wounded pride? Despair at having brought herself to come to me? Had I shown any sign of priding myself on my happiness, and did I, like De Grieux, want to get rid of her by giving her fifty thousand francs? But that was not so; I know that, on my conscience. I believe that her vanity was partly responsible; her vanity prompted her to distrust and insult me, although all that perhaps was not clear, even to herself. In that case, of course, I was punished for De Grieux and was made responsible, though I was not much to blame. It is true that all this was almost only delirium; it is true, too, that I knew she was in delirium and . . . did not take that fact into consideration; perhaps she cannot forgive me for that now. Yes, but that is now; but then, then? Why, she was not in such a delirium and so ill then as to be utterly oblivious of what she was doing; when she came to me with De Grieux's letter she knew what she was doing.

I made haste to thrust all my notes and my heap of gold into the bed, covered it over and went out ten minutes after Polina. I made sure she would run home, and I thought I would slip in to them on the sly, and in the hall ask the nurse how the young lady was. What was my astonishment when I learnt from Nurse, whom I met on the stairs, that Polina had not yet returned home and that Nurse was coming to me for her.

"She only just left my room about ten minutes ago; where can she have gone?"

Nurse looked at me reproachfully.

And meanwhile it had caused a regular scandal, which by now was all over the hotel. In the porter's room and at the *ober-kellner's* it was whispered that Fräulein had run out of the hotel in the rain at six o'clock in the morning in the direction of the Hôtel d'Angleterre. From what they said and hinted, I noticed that they all knew already that she had spent the night in my room. However, stories were being told of the whole family: it had become known all through the hotel that the General had gone out of his mind and was crying. The story was that Granny was his mother, who had come expressly from Russia to prevent her son's marriage with Mlle. de Cominges, and was going to cut him out of her will if he disobeyed her, and, as he certainly would disobey her, the Countess had purposely thrown away all her money at roulette before his eyes, so that he should get nothing. *"Diese Russen!"* repeated the *ober-kellner*, shaking his head indignantly. The others laughed. The *ober-kellner* was making out his bill. My winning was known about already. Karl, my corridor attendant, was the first to congratulate me. But I had no thought for any of them. I rushed to the Hôtel d'Angleterre.

It was early; Mr. Astley was seeing no one; learning that it was I, he came out into the corridor to me and stopped before me, turning his pewtery eyes upon me in silence, waiting to hear what I should say. I inquired about Polina.

"She is ill," answered Mr. Astley, looking at me as fixedly as before.

"Then she really is with you?"

"Yes, she is."

"Then, what do you . . . do you mean to keep her?"

"Yes."

"Mr. Astley, it will make a scandal; it's impossible. Besides, she is quite ill; perhaps you don't see it?"

"Oh, yes, I notice it, and I've just told you she is ill. If she had not been ill she would not have spent the night with you."

"Then you know that?"

"Yes, I know it. She came here yesterday and I would have taken her to a relation of mine, but as she was ill, she made a mistake and went to you."

"Fancy that! Well, I congratulate you, Mr. Astley. By the way, you've given me an idea: weren't you standing all night under our window? Miss Polina was making me open the window and look out all night to see whether you were standing under the window; she kept laughing about it."

"Really? No, I didn't stand under the window; but I was waiting in the corridor and walking round."

"But she must be looked after, Mr. Astley."

"Oh, yes, I've sent for the doctor, and, if she dies, you will answer to me for her death."

I was amazed.

"Upon my word, Mr. Astley, what do you want?"

"And is it true that you won two hundred thousand thalers yesterday?"

"Only a hundred thousand florins."

"Well, do you see, you had better go off to Paris this morning!"

"What for?"

"All Russians who have money go to Paris," Mr. Astley explained, in a tone of voice as though he had read this in a book.

"What could I do now in Paris, in the summer? I love her, Mr. Astley, you know it yourself."

"Really? I am convinced you don't. If you remain here you will certainly lose all you have won and you will have nothing left to go to Paris with. But, good-bye, I am perfectly certain you will go to Paris to-day."

"Very well, good-bye, only I shan't go to Paris. Think, Mr. Astley, what will be happening here? The General . . . and now this adventure with Miss Polina—why, that will be all over the town."

"Yes, all over the town; I believe the General is not thinking about that: he has no thoughts to spare for that. Besides, Miss Polina has a perfect right to live where she likes. In regard to that family, one may say quite correctly that the family no longer exists."

I walked away laughing at this Englishman's strange conviction that I was going to Paris. "He wants to shoot me in a duel, though," I thought, "if Mlle. Polina dies—what a complication!" I swear I was sorry for Polina, but, strange to say, from the very moment when I reached the gambling tables the previous evening and began winning a pile of money, my love had retreated, so to speak, into the background. I say this now; but at the time I did not realize all this clearly. Can I really be a gambler? Can I really . . . have loved Polina so strangely? No, I love her to this day. God is my witness! And then, when I left Mr. Astley and went home, I was genuinely miserable and blaming myself. But . . . at this point a very strange and silly thing happened to me.

I was hurrying to see the General, when suddenly not far from his rooms, a door was opened and some one called me. It was Madame *la veuve* Cominges, and she called me at the bidding of Mlle. Blanche. I went in to see Mlle. Blanche.

They had a small suite of apartments, consisting of two rooms. I could hear Mlle. Blanche laugh and call out from the bedroom.

She was getting up.

"*Ah, c'est lui! Viens donc, bête!* Is it true, *que tu as gagné une montagne d'or et d'argent? J'aimerais mieux l'or.*"

"Yes, I did win," I answered, laughing.

"How much?"

"A hundred thousand florins."

"*Bibi, comme tu es bête.* Why, come in here. I can't hear anything. *Nous ferons bombance, n'est-ce pas?*"

I went in to her. She was lying under a pink satin quilt, above which her robust, swarthy, wonderfully swarthy, shoulders were visible, shoulders such as one only sees in one's dreams, covered to some extent by a batiste nightgown bordered with white lace which was wonderfully becoming to her dark skin.

"*Mon fils, as-tu du cœur?*" she cried, seeing me, and burst out laughing. She laughed very good-humouredly, and sometimes quite genuinely.

"*Tout autre,*" I began, paraphrasing Corneille.

"Here you see, *vois-tu,*" she began babbling; "to begin with, find my stockings, help me to put them on; and then, *si tu n'es pas trop bête, je te prends à Paris.* You know I am just going."

"Just going?"

"In half an hour."

All her things were indeed packed. All her portmanteaus and things were ready. Coffee had been served some time before.

"*Eh bien,* if you like, *tu verras Paris. Dis donc qu'est-ce que c'est qu'un outchitel? Tu étais bien bête, quand tu étais outchitel.* Where are my stockings? Put them on for me?"

She thrust out some positively fascinating feet, little dark-skinned feet, not in the least misshapen, as feet that look so small in shoes always are. I laughed and began drawing her silk stockings on for her. Meanwhile Mlle. Blanche sat up in bed, prattling away.

"*Eh bien, que feras-tu, si je te prends avec?* To begin with, I want fifty thousand francs. You'll give them to me at Frankfurt. *Nous allons à Paris:* there we'll play together: *et je te ferai voir des étoiles en plein jour.* You will see women such as you have never seen before. Listen . . ."

"Wait a minute, so if I give you fifty thousand francs, what will be left for me?"

"*Et cent cinquante mille francs,* you have forgotten: and what's more, I consent to live with you a month, two months: *que sais-je!* In those two months we shall certainly get through that hundred and fifty thousand francs, you see, *je suis bonne enfant,* and I tell you beforehand, *mais tu verras des étoiles.*"

"What! all in two months!"

"Why! does that horrify you? *Ah, vil esclave!* But, do you know? **one** month of such a life is worth your whole existence. One month—

et après, le déluge! Mais tu ne peux comprendre; va! Go along, go along, you are not worth it! *Aie, que fais-tu?"*

At that moment I was putting a stocking on the other leg, but could not resist kissing it. She pulled it away and began hitting me on the head with the tip of her foot. At last, she turned me out altogether.

"Eh bien! mon outchitel, je t'attends, si tu veux; I am starting in a quarter of an hour!" she called after me.

On returning home I felt as though my head were going round. Well, it was not my fault that Mlle. Polina had thrown the whole pile of money in my face, and had even yesterday preferred Mr. Astley to me. Some of the banknotes that had been scattered about were still lying on the floor; I picked them up. At that moment the door opened and the *ober-kellner* himself made his appearance (he had never deigned to look into my room before) with a suggestion that I might like to move downstairs to a magnificent suite of apartments which had just been vacated by Count V.

I stood still and thought a little.

"My bill—I am just leaving, in ten minutes," I cried. "If it's to be Paris, let it be Paris," I thought to myself; "it seems it was fated at my birth!"

A quarter of an hour later we were actually sitting in a reserved compartment, Mlle. Blanche, Madame *la veuve* Cominges and I. Mlle. Blanche, looking at me, laughed till she was almost hysterical. Madame de Cominges followed suit; I cannot say that I felt cheerful. My life had broken in two, but since the previous day I had grown used to staking everything on a card. Perhaps it is really the truth that my sudden wealth was too much for me and had turned my head. *Peut-être, je ne demandais pas mieux.* It seemed to me for a time—but only for a time, the scenes were shifted. "But in a month I shall be here, and then . . . and then we will try our strength, Mr. Astley!" No, as I recall it now, I was awfully sad then, though I did laugh as loudly as that idiot, Blanche.

"But what is the matter with you? How silly you are! Oh! how silly you are!" Blanche kept exclaiming, interrupting her laughter to scold me in earnest. "Oh well, oh well, we'll spend your two hundred thousand francs: but in exchange *mais tu seras heureux comme un petit roi;* I will tie your cravat myself and introduce you to Hortense. And when we have spent all our money, you will come back here and break the bank again. What did the Jews tell you? The great thing is—boldness, and you have it, and you will bring me money to Paris more than once again. *Quant à moi je veux cinquante mille francs de rentes et alors . . ."*

"And the General?" I asked her.

"Why, the General, as you know, comes to see me every day with a bouquet. This time I purposely asked him to get me some very rare flowers. The poor fellow will come back and will find the bird has flown. He'll fly after us, you will see. Ha-ha-ha! I shall be awfully pleased to see him. He'll be of use to me in Paris; Mr. Astley will pay his bill here. . . ."

And so that was the way in which I went to Paris.

Chapter 16

WHAT shall I say about Paris? It was madness, of course, and foolery. I only spent a little over three weeks in Paris, and by the end of that time my hundred thousand francs was finished. I speak only of a hundred thousand. The other hundred thousand I gave to Mlle. Blanche in hard cash—fifty thousand at Frankfurt and three days later in Paris I gave her an I O U for another fifty thousand francs, though a week later she exchanged this for cash from me. *"Et les cent mille francs, qui nous restent, tu les mangeras avec moi, mon outchitel."* She always called me an *outchitel, i.e.,* a tutor. It is difficult to imagine anything in the world meaner, stingier and more niggardly than the class of creatures to which Mlle. Blanche belonged. But that was in the spending of her own money. As regards my hundred thousand francs, she openly informed me, later on, that she needed them to establish herself in Paris, "as now I am going to settle in decent style once for all, and now no one shall turn me aside for a long time; at least, that is my plan," she added. I hardly saw that hundred thousand, however; she kept the money the whole time, and in my purse, into which she looked every day, there was never more than a hundred francs, and always less and less.

"What do you want money for?" she would say, sometimes, in the simplest way, and I did not dispute with her. But she furnished and decorated her flat very nicely with that money, and afterwards, when she took me to her new abode, as she showed me the rooms, she said: "You see what care and taste can do even with the scantiest means." These "scanty means" amounted to fifty thousand francs, however. With the second fifty thousand she provided herself with a carriage and horses. Moreover, we gave two balls, that is, two evening parties at which were present Hortense, Lizette and Cléopatra, women remarkable in very many respects and even quite good-looking. At those two evenings I had to play the very foolish part of host, to receive and entertain the stupidest rich tradesmen, incredibly ignorant and shameless, various army lieutenants and miserable little authors and journalistic insects, who appeared in the most fashionable swallow-tails and straw-coloured gloves, and displayed a vanity and affectation whose proportions were beyond anything conceivable in Petersburg— and that is saying a great deal. Many of them thought fit to jeer at me; but I got drunk with champagne and lolled at full length in a back room. To me it was all loathsome to the last degree. *"C'est un outchitel,"* Blanche kept saying about me, *"il a gagné deux cent mille francs.* Without me he wouldn't have known how to spend it. And afterwards he will be an *outchitel* again; don't you know of a place for one? we ought to do something for him."

I had recourse to champagne very often, because I was often sad and dreadfully bored. I lived in the most bourgeois, in the most mercenary surroundings in which every *sou* was reckoned and accounted for. Blanche disliked me for the first fortnight: I noticed that; it is true, she dressed me like a dandy, and tied my cravat for me every day, but in her soul she genuinely despised me. I did not pay the slightest attention to that. Bored and dispirited, I used to go usually to the Château de Fleurs, where regularly every evening I got drunk and practised the *cancan* (which they dance so disgustingly there), and acquired in the end a kind of celebrity.

At last Blanche gauged my true character. She had for some reason conceived the idea that I should spend all the time we were together walking after her with a pencil and paper in my hand, and should always be reckoning how much she had spent, how much she had stolen, how much she would spend and how much more she would steal. And she was, of course, convinced that we should have a regular battle over every ten-franc piece. She had an answer in readiness for every attack that she anticipated from me; but when she found I did not attack her, she could not at first refrain from defending herself, unprovoked. Sometimes she would begin with great heat, but seeing that I remained silent as a rule, lying on a sofa gazing at the ceiling— at last, she was surprised. At first she thought I was simply stupid, *"un outchitel,"* and merely cut short her explanations, probably thinking to herself: "Why, he's a fool. There's no need to lay it on for him, since he doesn't understand." She would go away but come back again ten minutes later (this happened at a time when she was spending most ferociously, spending on a scale quite out of proportion to our means: she had, for instance, got rid of the horses first bought and bought another pair for sixteen thousand francs).

"Well, so you are not cross, *bibi?*" she said, coming up to me.

"N—n—n—no! You weary me!" I said, removing her hands from me, but this seemed to her so curious, that she immediately sat down beside me.

"You see, I only decided to pay so much because they could be sold later on if need be. They can be sold again for twenty thousand francs."

"No doubt, no doubt; they are splendid horses, and you have a fine turnout now; it suits you; well, that's enough."

"Then you are not cross?"

"Why should I be? You are sensible to provide yourself with things that are necessary to you. All that will be of use to you afterwards. I see that it is quite necessary for you to establish yourself in such a style; otherwise you will never save up your million. Our hundred thousand francs is only a beginning; a drop in the ocean."

Blanche had expected from me anything but such reflections (instead of outcries and reproaches). She seemed to drop from the clouds.

"So that's what you are like! *Mais tu as l'esprit pour comprendre. Sais-tu, mon garçon,* though you are an *outchitel* you ought to have been born a prince. So you don't grudge the money's going so quickly?"

"Bother the money! The quicker the better!"

"*Mais sais-tu . . . mais dis donc,* are you rich? *Mais sais-tu,* you really despise money too much. *Qu'est ce que tu feras après, dis donc?*"

"*Après,* I shall go to Homburg and win another hundred thousand francs."

"*Oui, oui, c'est ça, c'est magnifique!* And I know you will certainly win it and bring it here. *Dis donc,* why you will make me really love you. *Eh bien,* I will love you all the time for being like that, and won't once be unfaithful to you. You see, I have not loved you all this time, *parceque je croyais que tu n'étais qu'un outchitel (quelque chose comme un laquais, n'est-ce pas?),* but I have been faithful to you all the same, *parceque je suis bonne fille.*"

"Come, you are lying! How about Albert, that swarthy-faced little officer; do you suppose I didn't see last time?"

"Oh, oh, *mais tu es . . .*"

"Come, you are lying, you are lying; why, do you suppose I should be angry? Why, it's no matter; *il faut que la jeunesse se passe.* And there's no need for you to send him away if you had him before me and are fond of him. Only don't give him money, do you hear?"

"So you are not angry about it? *Mais tu es un vrai philosophe, sais-tu? Un vrai philosophe!*" she cried enthusiastically.

"*Eh bien! je t'aimerai, je t'aimerai—tu verras, tu seras content!*"

And from that time she really did seem to be attached to me, to be really affectionate; and so our last ten days passed. The "stars" promised me I did not see. But in some respects she really did keep her word. What is more, she introduced me to Hortense, who really was a remarkable woman in her own way, and in our circle was called *Thérèse philosophe.* . . .

However, there is no need to enlarge upon that; all that might make a separate story, in a different tone, which I do not want to introduce into this story. The fact is, I longed above everything for all this episode to be over. But our hundred thousand francs lasted, as I have mentioned already, almost a month—at which I was genuinely surprised; eighty thousand of that, at least, Blanche spent on things for herself, and we lived on no more than twenty thousand francs, and—yet it was enough. Blanche, who was in the end almost open with me (or, at any rate, did not lie to me about some things), declared that, anyway, the debts she had been obliged to make would not fall upon me: "I have never given you bills or I O U's to sign," she said, "because I was sorry for you; but any other girl would have certainly done it and got you into prison. You see, you see how I loved you and how good I am! Think of what that devil of a wedding alone is going to cost me!"

We really were going to have a wedding. It took place at the very end of my month, and it may be assumed that the last remains of my hundred thousand francs went upon it; that was how the thing ended; that is, my month ended with that, and after it I received my formal dismissal.

This was how it happened: a week after our arrival in Paris the General suddenly turned up. He came straight to Blanche, and from his first call almost lived with us. He had a lodging of his own, it is true. Blanche received him joyfully, with shrieks of laughter, and even flew to embrace him; as things had turned out, she was unwilling to let him go: and he had to follow her about everywhere, on the boulevards, and to the theatres, and to call on her acquaintances, and to take her for drives. The General was still of use for such purposes; he was of rather imposing and decorous appearance—he was above the average in height, with dyed whiskers and moustaches (he had once served in the Cuirassiers); he was still presentable-looking, though his face was puffy. His manners were superb; he looked well in evening dress. In Paris he began wearing his decorations. The promenade on the boulevard with a man like this was not only possible, but *advantageous*. The good-natured and senseless General was immensely delighted with all this; he had not reckoned upon it at all when he came to see us on arriving in Paris. He had come, then, almost trembling with terror; he was afraid that Blanche would make an uproar and order him to be turned out; and so he was highly delighted at the changed aspect of the position, and spent the whole month in a sort of senseless rapture: and he was in the same state when I left him. I learnt that on the morning of our sudden departure from Roulettenburg he had had some sort of a fit. He had fallen insensible, and had been all that week almost like a madman, talking incessantly. He was being nursed and doctored, but he suddenly threw up everything, got into the train and flew off to Paris. Of course, Blanche's reception was the best cure for him; but the traces of his illness remained long after, in spite of his joy and his enthusiastic condition. He was utterly incapable of reflection or even of carrying on a conversation on any serious subject; when any such topic was brought forward, he confined himself to nodding his head and ejaculating, "H'm!" at every word. He often laughed, but it was a nervous, sickly laugh, as though he were giggling; another time he would sit for hours looking as black as night, knitting his bushy brows. Of many things he had no recollection whatever; he had become absent-minded to an unseemly degree, and had acquired the habit of talking to himself. Blanche was the only person who could rouse him; and, indeed, his attacks of gloom and depression, when he hid himself in a corner, meant nothing but that he hadn't seen Blanche for a long time, or that Blanche had gone off somewhere without taking him, or had not been nice to him before going. At the same time he could not say what he wanted, and did not know why he was depressed and miserable. After sitting for two or three hours (I noticed this on two or three occasions when Blanche had gone out for the whole day, probably to see Albert), he would suddenly begin to look about him in a nervous fluster, to stare round, to recollect himself, and seem to be looking for something; but seeing no one and not remembering the question he meant to ask, he sank into forgetfulness again till Blanche reappeared, gay, frisky, gorgeously dressed, with her ringing laugh; she would run up to him, begin teasing him, and even kissing him—a favour which she did not often, however, bestow upon him. Once the General was so delighted to see her that he even burst into tears—I really marvelled at him.

From the very first, Blanche began to plead his cause before me. Indeed, she waxed eloquent in his behalf; reminded me that she had betrayed the General for my sake, that she was almost engaged to him, had given him her word; that he had abandoned his family on her account, and, lastly, that I had been in his service and ought to remember that, and that I ought to be ashamed. . . . I said nothing while she rattled away at a terrific pace. At last I laughed: and with that the matter ended, that is, at first, she thought I was a fool: and at last came to the conclusion that I was a very nice and accommodating man. In fact, I had the good fortune to win in the end the complete approval of that excellent young woman. (Blanche really was, though, a very good-natured girl—in her own way, of course; I had not such a high opinion of her at first.) "You're a kind and clever man," she used to say to me towards the end, "and . . . and . . . it's only a pity you are such a fool! You never, never, save anything!"

"*Un vrai russe, un calmouk!*" Several times she sent me to take the General for a walk about the streets, exactly as she might send her lapdog out with her footman. I took him, however, to the theatre, and to the Bal-Mabille, and to the restaurants. Blanche gave me the money for this, though the General had some of his own, and he was very fond of taking out his pocket-book before people. But I had almost to use force to prevent him from buying a brooch for seven hundred francs, by which he was fascinated in the Palais Royal and of which he wanted, at all costs, to make Blanche a present. But what was a brooch of seven hundred francs to her? The General hadn't more than a thousand francs altogether. I could never find out where he had got that money from. I imagine it was from Mr. Astley, especially as the latter had paid their bill at the hotel. As for the General's attitude to me all this time, I believe that he did not even guess at my relations with Blanche. Though he had heard vaguely that I had won a fortune, yet he probably supposed that I was with Blanche in the capacity of a private secretary or even a servant. Anyway, he always, as before, spoke to me condescendingly, authoritatively, and even sometimes fell to scolding me. One morning he amused Blanche and me immensely at breakfast. He was not at all ready to take offence, but suddenly he was huffy with me—why?—I don't know to this day. No doubt he did not know himself. In fact, he made a speech without a beginning or an end, *à bâtons rompus,* shouted that I was an impudent boy, that he would give me a lesson . . . that he would let me know it . . . and so on. But no one could make out anything from it. Blanche went off into peals of laughter. At last he was somehow appeased and taken out for a walk. I noticed sometimes, however, that he grew sad, that he was regretting some one and something, he was missing something, in spite of Blanche's presence. On two such occasions he began talking to me of himself, but could not express himself clearly, alluded to his times in the army, to his deceased wife, to his family affairs, to his property. He would stumble upon some phrase—and was delighted with it and would repeat it a hundred times a day, though perhaps it expressed neither his feelings nor his thoughts. I tried to talk to him about his children: but he turned off the subject with incoherent babble, and passed hurriedly to another topic: "Yes, yes, my children, you are right, my children!" Only once he grew sentimental—we were with him at the theatre: "Those unhappy children!" he began suddenly. "Yes, sir, those un—happy children!" And several times afterwards that evening he repeated the same words: "unhappy children!" Once, when I began to speak of Polina, he flew into a frenzy. "She's an ungrateful girl," he cried. "She's wicked and ungrateful! She has disgraced her family. If there were laws here I would make her mind her p's and q's. Yes, indeed, yes, indeed!" As for De Grieux, he could not bear even to hear his name: "He has been the ruin of me," he would say, "he has robbed me, he has destroyed me! He has been my nightmare for the last two years! He has haunted my dreams for whole months! It's, it's, it's . . . Oh, never speak to me of him!"

I saw there was an understanding between them, but, as usual, I said nothing. Blanche announced the news to me, first—it was just a week before we parted: *"Il a du chance,"* she babbled. "Granny really is ill this time, and certainly will die. Mr. Astley has sent a telegram. You must admit that the General is her heir, anyway, and even if he were not, he would not interfere with me in anything. In the first place, he has his pension, and in the second place, he will live in a back room and will be perfectly happy. I shall be 'Madame la Générale.' I shall get into a good set" (Blanche was continually dreaming of this), "in the end I shall be a Russian landowner, *j'aurai un château, des moujiks, et puis j'aurai toujours mon million."*

"Well, what if he begins to be jealous, begins to insist . . . on goodness knows what—do you understand?"

"Oh, no, *non, non, non!* How dare he! I have taken precautions, you needn't be afraid. I have even made him sign some I O U's for Albert. The least thing—and he will be arrested; and he won't dare!"

"Well, marry him. . . ."

The marriage was celebrated without any great pomp; it was a quiet family affair. Albert was invited and a few other intimate friends. Hortense, Cléopatra and company were studiously excluded. The bridegroom was extremely interested in his position. Blanche herself tied his cravat with her own hands, and pomaded his head: and in his swallow-tailed coat with his white tie he looked *très comme il faut.*

"Il est pourtant très comme il faut," Blanche herself observed to me, coming out of the General's room, as though the idea that the General was *très comme il faut* was a surprise even to her. Though I assisted at the whole affair as an idle spectator, yet I took so little interest in the details that I have to a great extent forgotten the course of events. I only remember that Blanche turned out not to be called "De Cominges," and her mamma not to be *la veuve* "Cominges," but "Du Placet." Why they had been both "De Cominges" till then, I don't know. But the General remained very much pleased with that, and "Du Placet" pleased him, in fact, better than "De Cominges." On the morning of the wedding, fully dressed for the part, he kept walking to and fro in the drawing-room, repeating to himself with a grave and important air, "Mlle. Blanche du Placet! Blanche du Placet, du Placet!" . . . and his countenance beamed with a certain complacency. At church, before the *maire,* and at the wedding breakfast at home, he was not only joyful but proud. There was a change in both of them. Blanche, too, had an air of peculiar dignity.

"I shall have to behave myself quite differently now," she said to me, perfectly seriously: *"mais vois-tu,* I never thought of one very horrid thing: I even fancy, to this day, I can't learn my surname. Zagoryansky, Zagozyansky, Madame la Générale de Sago—Sago, *ces diables de noms russes, enfin madame la générale a quatorze consonnes! Comme c'est agréable, n'est-ce pas?"*

At last we parted, and Blanche, that silly Blanche, positively shed tears when she said good-bye to me. *"Tu étais bon enfant,"* she said, whimpering. *"Je te croyais bête et tu en avais l'air,* but it suits you." And, pressing my hand at parting, she suddenly cried, *"Attends!"* rushed to her boudoir and, two minutes later, brought me a banknote for two thousand francs. That I should never have believed possible! "It may be of use to you. You may be a very learned *outchitel,* but you are an awfully stupid man. I am not going to give you more than two thousand, for you'll lose it gambling, anyway. Well, good-bye! *Nous serons toujours bon amis,* and if you win, be sure to come to me again, *et tu seras heureux!"*

I had five hundred francs left of my own. I had besides a splendid watch that cost a thousand francs, some diamond studs, and so on, so that I could go on a good time longer without anxiety. I am staying in this little town on purpose to collect myself, and, above all, I am waiting for Mr. Astley. I have learnt for a fact that he will pass through the town and stay here for twenty-four hours on business. I shall find out about everything; and then—then I shall go straight to Homburg. I am not going to Roulettenburg; not till next year anyway. They say it is a bad omen to try your luck twice running at the same tables; and Homburg is the real place for play.

Chapter 17

I T IS a year and eight months since I looked at these notes, and only now in sadness and dejection it has occurred to me to read them through. So I stopped then at my going to Homburg. My God! With what a light heart, comparatively speaking, I wrote those last lines! Though not with a light heart exactly, but with a sort of self-confidence, with undaunted hopes! Had I any doubt of myself? And now more than a year and a half has passed, and I am, to my own mind, far worse than a beggar! Yes, what is being a beggar? A beggar is nothing! I have simply ruined myself! However, there is nothing I can compare myself with, and there is no need to give myself a moral lecture! Nothing could be stupider than moral reflections at this date! Oh, self-satisfied people, with what proud satisfaction these prattlers prepare to deliver their lectures! If only they knew how thoroughly I understand the loathsomeness of my present position, they would not be able to bring their tongues to reprimand me. Why, what, what can they tell me that I do not know? And is that the point? The point is that—one turn of the wheel, and all will be changed, and those very moralists will be the first (I am convinced of that) to come up to congratulate me with friendly jests. And they will not all turn away from me as they do now. But, hang them all! What am I now? Zero. What may I be to-morrow? To-morrow I may rise from the dead and begin to live again! There are still the makings of a man in me.

I did, in fact, go to Homburg then, but . . . afterwards I went to Roulettenburg again, and to Spa. I have even been in Baden, where I went as valet to the councillor Gintse, a scoundrel, who was my master here. Yes, I was a lackey for five whole months! I got a place immediately after coming out of prison. (I was sent to prison in Roulettenburg for a debt I made here.) Some one, I don't know who, paid my debt—who was it? Was it Mr. Astley? Polina? I don't know, but the debt was paid; two hundred thalers in all, and I was set free. What could I do? I entered the service of this Gintse. He is a young man and frivolous, he liked to be idle, and I could read and write in three languages. At first I went into his service as a sort of secretary at thirty guldens a month; but I ended by becoming a regular valet: he had not the means to keep a secretary; and he lowered my wages; I had nowhere to go, I remained—and in that way became a lackey by my own doing. I had not enough to eat or to drink in his service, but on the other hand, in five months I saved up seventy gulden. One evening in Baden, however, I announced to him that I intended parting from him; the same evening I went to roulette. Oh, how my heart beat! No, it was not money that I wanted. All that I wanted then was that next day all these Gintses, all these *ober-kellners,* all these magnificent Baden ladies—that they might be all talking about me, repeating my story, wondering at me, admiring me, praising me, and doing homage to my new success. All these are childish dreams and desires, but . . . who knows, perhaps I should meet Polina again, too, I should tell her, and she would see that I was above all these stupid ups and downs of fate. . . . Oh, it was not money that was dear to me! I knew I should fling it away to some Blanche again and should drive in Paris again for three weeks with a pair of my own horses, costing sixteen thousand francs. I know for certain that I am not mean; I believe that I am not even a spendthrift—and yet with what a tremor, with what a thrill at my heart, I hear the croupier's cry: *trente-et-un, rouge, impair et passe,* or: *quatre, noir, pair et manque!* With what avidity I look at the gambling table on which louis d'or, friedrichs d'or and thalers lie scattered: on the piles of gold when they are scattered from the croupier's shovel like glowing embers, or at the piles of silver a yard high that lie round the wheel. Even on my way to the gambling hall, as soon as I hear, two rooms away, the clink of the scattered money I almost go into convulsions.

Oh! that evening, when I took my seventy gulden to the gambling table, was remarkable too. I began with ten gulden, staking them again on *passe.* I have a prejudice in favour of *passe.* I lost. I had sixty gulden left in silver money; I thought a little and chose *zéro.* I began staking five gulden at a time on *zéro;* at the third turn the wheel stopped at *zéro;* I almost died of joy when I received one hundred and seventy-five gulden; I had not been so delighted when I won a hundred thousand gulden. I immediately staked a hundred gulden on *rouge—*

it won; the two hundred on *rouge*—it won; the whole of the four
hundred on *noir*—it won; the whole eight hundred on *manque*—it
won; altogether with what I had before it made one thousand seven
hundred gulden and that—in less than five minutes! Yes, at moments
like that one forgets all one's former failures! Why, I had gained this
by risking more than life itself, I dared to risk it, and—there I was
again, a man among men.

I took a room at the hotel, locked myself in and sat till three o'clock
counting over my money. In the morning I woke up, no longer a
lackey. I determined the same day to go to Homburg: I had not been
a lackey or been in prison there. Half an hour before my train left, I
set off to stake on two hazards, no more, and lost fifteen hundred
florins. Yet I went to Homburg all the same, and I have been here
for a month. . . .

I am living, of course, in continual anxiety. I play for the tiniest
stakes, and I keep waiting for something, calculating, standing for
whole days at the gambling table and watching the play; I even dream
of playing—but I feel that in all this, I have, as it were, grown stiff
and wooden, as though I had sunk into a muddy swamp. I gather this
from my feeling when I met Mr. Astley. We had not seen each other
since that time, and we met by accident. This was how it happened:
I was walking in the gardens and reckoning that now I was almost
without money, but that I had fifty gulden—and that I had, moreover,
three days before paid all I owed at the hotel. And so it was possible
for me to go once more to roulette—if I were to win anything, I might
be able to go on playing; if I lost I should have to get a lackey's place
again, if I did not come across Russians in want of a tutor. Absorbed
in these thoughts, I went my daily walk, across the park and the forest
in the adjoining principality.

Sometimes I used to walk like this for four hours at a time, and go
back to Homburg hungry and tired. I had scarcely gone out of the
gardens into the park, when suddenly I saw on one of the seats Mr.
Astley. He saw me before I saw him, and called to me. I sat down
beside him. Detecting in him a certain dignity of manner, I instantly
moderated my delight; though I was awfully delighted to see him.

"And so you are here! I thought I should meet you," he said to me.
"Don't trouble yourself to tell me your story; I know, I know all about
it; I know every detail of your life during this last year and eight
months."

"Bah! What a watch you keep on your old friends!" I answered.
"It is very creditable in you not to forget. . . . Stay, though, you have

given me an idea. Wasn't it you bought me out of prison at Roulettenburg where I was imprisoned for debt for two hundred gulden? Some unknown person paid it for me."

"No, oh, no; it was not I who bought you out when you were in prison at Roulettenburg for a debt of two hundred gulden. But I knew that you were imprisoned for a debt of two hundred gulden."

"Then you know who did pay my debt?"

"Oh, no, I can't say that I know who bought you out."

"Strange; I don't know any of our Russians; besides, the Russians here, I imagine, would not do it; at home in Russia the Orthodox may buy out other Orthodox Christians. I thought it must have been some eccentric Englishman who did it as a freak."

Mr. Astley listened to me with some surprise. I believe he had expected to find me dejected and crushed.

"I am very glad, however, to find that you have quite maintained your independence of spirit and even your cheerfulness," he pronounced, with a rather disagreeable air.

"That is, you are chafing inwardly with vexation at my not being crushed and humiliated," I said, laughing.

He did not at once understand, but when he understood, he smiled.

"I like your observations: I recognize in those words my clever, enthusiastic and, at the same time, cynical old friend; only Russians can combine in themselves so many opposites at the same time. It is true, a man likes to see even his best friend humiliated; a great part of friendship rests on humiliation. But in the present case I assure you that I am genuinely glad that you are not dejected. Tell me, do you intend to give up gambling?"

"Oh, damn! I shall give it up at once as soon as I . . ."

"As soon as you have won back what you have lost! Just what I thought; you needn't say any more—I know—you have spoken unawares, and so you have spoken the truth. Tell me, have you any occupation except gambling?"

"No, none. . . ."

He began cross-examining me. I knew nothing. I scarcely looked into the newspapers, and had literally not opened a single book all that time.

"You've grown rusty," he observed. "You have not only given up life, all your interests, private and public, the duties of a man and a citizen, your friends (and you really had friends)—you have not only given up your objects, such as they were, all but gambling—you have even given up your memories. I remember you at an intense and ardent moment of your life; but I am sure you have forgotten all the best feelings you had then; your dreams, your most genuine desires now do not rise above *pair, impair, rouge, noir,* the twelve middle numbers, and so on, I am sure!"

"Enough, Mr. Astley, please, please don't remind me," I cried with vexation, almost with anger, "let me tell you, I've forgotten absolutely nothing; but I've only for a time put everything out of my mind, even my memories, until I can make a radical improvement in my circumstances; then . . . then you will see, I shall rise again from the dead!"

"You will be here still in ten years' time," he said. "I bet you I shall remind you of this on this very seat, if I'm alive."

"Well, that's enough," I interrupted impatiently; "and to prove to you that I am not so forgetful of the past, let me ask: where is Miss Polina now? If it was not you who got me out of prison, it must have been her doing. I have had no news of her of any sort since that time."

"No, oh no, I don't believe she did buy you out. She's in Switzerland now, and you'll do me a great favour if you leave off asking about Miss Polina," he said resolutely, and even with some anger.

"That means that she has wounded you very much!" I laughed with displeasure.

"Miss Polina is of all people deserving of respect the very best, but I repeat—you will do me a great favour if you cease questioning me concerning Miss Polina. You never knew her: and her name on your lips I regard as an insult to my moral feelings."

"You don't say so! you are wrong, however; besides, what have I to talk to you about except that, tell me that? Why, all our memories really amount to that! Don't be uneasy, though; I don't want to know your private secret affairs. . . . I am only interested, so to say, in Miss Polina's external affairs. That you could tell me in a couple of words."

"Certainly, on condition that with those two words all is over. Miss Polina was ill for a long time; she's ill even now. For some time she stayed with my mother and sister in the north of England. Six months ago, her grandmother—you remember that madwoman?—died and left her, personally, a fortune of seven thousand pounds. At the present time Miss Polina is travelling with the family of my married sister. Her little brother and sister, too, were provided for by their grandmother's will, and are at school in London. The General, her stepfather, died a month ago in Paris of a stroke. Mlle. Blanche treated him well, but succeeded in getting possession of all he received from the grandmother. . . . I believe that's all."

"And De Grieux? Is not he travelling in Switzerland, too?"

"No, De Grieux is not travelling in Switzerland: and I don't know where De Grieux is; besides, once for all, I warn you to avoid such insinuations and ungentlemanly coupling of names, or you will certainly have to answer for it to me."

"What! in spite of our friendly relations in the past?"

"Yes, in spite of our friendly relations in the past."

"I beg a thousand pardons, Mr. Astley. But allow me, though: there is nothing insulting or ungentlemanly about it; I am not blaming Miss Polina for anything. Besides—a Frenchman and a Russian young lady, speaking generally—it's a combination, Mr. Astley, which is beyond your or my explaining or fully comprehending."

"If you will not mention the name of De Grieux in company with another name, I should like you to explain what you mean by the expression of 'the Frenchman and the Russian young lady.' What do you mean by that 'combination'? Why the Frenchman exactly and why the Russian young lady?"

"You see you are interested. But that's a long story, Mr. Astley. You need to understand many things first. But it is an important question, however absurd it may seem at first sight. The Frenchman, Mr. Astley, is the product of a finished beautiful tradition. You, as a Briton, may not agree with this; I, as a Russian, do not either, from envy maybe; but our young ladies may be of a different opinion. You may think Racine artificial, affected and perfumed; probably you won't even read him. I, too, think him artificial, affected and perfumed—from one point of view even absurd; but he is charming, Mr. Astley, and, what is more, he is a great poet, whether we like it or not. The national type of Frenchman, or, rather, of Parisian, had been moulded into elegant forms while we were still bears. The revolution inherited the traditions of the aristocracy. Now even the vulgarest Frenchman has manners, modes of address, expressions and even thoughts, of perfectly elegant form, though his own initiative, his own soul and heart, have had no part in the creation of that form; it has all come to him through inheritance. Well, Mr. Astley, I must inform you now that there is not a creature on the earth more confiding, and more candid, than a good, clean and not too sophisticated Russian girl. De Grieux, appearing in a peculiar rôle, masquerading, can conquer her heart with extraordinary ease; he has elegance of form, Mr. Astley, and the young lady takes this form for his individual soul, as the natural form of his soul and his heart, and not as an external garment, which has come to him by inheritance. Though it will greatly displease you, I must tell you that Englishmen are for the most part awkward and inelegant, and Russians are rather quick to detect beauty, and are eager for it. But to detect beauty of soul and originality of character needs incomparably more independence and freedom than is to be found in our women, above all in our young ladies—and of course ever so much more experience. Miss Polina—forgive me, the word is spoken and one can't take it back—needs a long, long time to bring herself to prefer you to the scoundrel De Grieux. She thinks highly of you, becomes your friend, opens all her heart to you; but yet the hateful scoundrel, the base and petty money-grubber, De Grieux, will still dominate her heart. Mere obstinacy and vanity, so to say, will maintain his supremacy, because at one time this De Grieux appeared to her with the halo of an elegant marquis, a disillusioned liberal, who is supposed to have ruined himself to help her family and her frivolous stepfather. All these shams have been discovered later on. But the fact that they have been discovered makes no difference: anyway, what she wants is the original De Grieux—that's what she wants! And the more she hates the present De Grieux the more she pines for the original one, though he existed only in her imagination. You are a sugar-boiler, Mr. Astley."

"Yes, I am a partner in the well-known firm, Lovel & Co."

"Well, you see, Mr. Astley, on one side—a sugar-boiler, and on the other—Apollo Belvedere; it is somewhat incongruous. And I am not even a sugar-boiler; I am simply a paltry gambler at roulette, and have even been a lackey, which I think Miss Polina knows very well, as I fancy she has good detectives."

"You are exasperated, and that is why you talk all this nonsense," Mr. Astley said coolly, after a moment's thought. "Besides, there is nothing original in what you say."

"I admit that! But the awful thing is, my noble friend, that however stale, however hackneyed, however farcical my statements may be— they are nevertheless true! Anyway, you and I have made no way at all!"

"That's disgusting nonsense . . . because, because . . . let me tell you!" Mr. Astley, with flashing eyes, pronounced in a quivering voice, "let me tell you, you ungrateful, unworthy, shallow and unhappy man, that I am come to Homburg expressly at her wish, to see you, to have a long and open conversation with you and to tell her everything—what you are feeling, thinking, hoping, and . . . what you remember!"

"Is it possible? Is it possible?" I cried, and tears rushed in streams from my eyes.

I could not restrain them. I believe it was the first time it happened in my life.

"Yes, unhappy man, she loved you, and I can tell you that, because you are—a lost man! What is more, if I were to tell you that she loves you to this day—you would stay here just the same! Yes, you have destroyed yourself. You had some abilities, a lively disposition, and were not a bad fellow; you might have even been of service to your country, which is in such need of men, but—you will remain here, and your life is over. I don't blame you. To my mind all Russians are like that, or disposed to be like that. If it is not roulette it is something similar. The exceptions are very rare. You are not the first who does not understand the meaning of work (I am not talking of your peasantry). Roulette is a game pre-eminently for the Russians. So far you've been honest and preferred serving as a lackey to stealing. . . . But I dread to think what may come in the future. Enough, good-bye! No doubt you are in want of money? Here are ten louis d'or from me. I won't give you more, for you'll gamble it away in any case. Take it and good-bye! Take it!"

"No, Mr. Astley, after all you have said."

"Ta—ake it!" he cried. "I believe that you are still an honourable man, and I give it as a true friend gives to another friend. If I were sure that you would throw up gambling, leave Homburg and would return to your own country, I would be ready to give you at once a thousand pounds to begin a new career. But I don't give you a thousand pounds: I give you only ten louis d'or just because a thousand pounds and ten louis d'or are just the same to you now; it's all the same—you'll gamble it away. Take it and good-bye."

"I will take it if you will let me embrace you at parting."

"Oh, with pleasure!"

We embraced with sincere feeling, and Mr. Astley went away.

No, he is wrong! If I was crude and silly about Polina and De Grieux, he was crude and hasty about Russians. I say nothing of myself. However . . . however, all that is not the point for the time: that is all words, words, and words, deeds are what are wanted! Switzerland is the great thing now! To-morrow . . . Oh, if only it were possible to set off to-morrow! To begin anew, to rise again. I must show them. . . . Let Polina know that I still can be a man. I have only to . . . But now it's too late—but to-morrow . . . oh, I have a presentiment and it cannot fail to be! I have now fifteen louis d'or, and I have begun with fifteen gulden! If one begins carefully . . . and can I, can I be such a baby! Can I fail to understand that I am a lost man, but—can I not rise again! Yes! I have only for once in my life to be prudent and patient and—that is all! I have only for once to show will power and in one hour I can transform my destiny! The great thing is will power. Only remember what happened to me seven months ago at Roulettenburg just before my final failure. Oh! it was a remarkable instance of determination: I had lost everything then, everything. ... I was going out of the Casino, I looked, there was still one gulden in my waistcoat pocket: "Then I shall have something for dinner," I thought. But after I had gone a hundred paces I changed my mind and went back. I staked that gulden on *manque* (that time it was on *manque*), and there really is something peculiar in the feeling when, alone in a strange land, far from home and from friends, not knowing whether you will have anything to eat that day—you stake your last gulden, your very last! I won, and twenty minutes later I went out of the Casino, having a hundred and seventy gulden in my pocket. That's a fact! That's what the last gulden can sometimes do! And what if I had lost heart then? What if I had not dared to risk it? ...

To-morrow, to-morrow it will all be over!

Notes from
Underground

NOTES FROM UNDERGROUND[1]

Part 1

UNDERGROUND

[1]

I AM a sick man. . . . I am a spiteful man. I am an unattractive man. I believe my liver is diseased. However, I know nothing at all about my disease, and do not know for certain what ails me. I don't consult a doctor for it, and never have, though I have a respect for medicine and doctors. Besides, I am extremely superstitious, sufficiently so to respect medicine, anyway (I am well-educated enough not to be superstitious, but I am superstitious). No, I refuse to consult a doctor from spite. That you probably will not understand. Well, I understand it, though. Of course, I can't explain who it is precisely that I am mortifying in this case by my spite: I am perfectly well aware that I cannot "pay out" the doctors by not consulting them; I know better than any one that by all this I am only injuring myself and no one else. But still, if I don't consult a doctor it is from spite. My liver is bad, well —let it get worse!

I have been going on like that for a long time—twenty years. Now I am forty. I used to be in the government service, but am no longer. I was a spiteful official. I was rude and took pleasure in being so. I did

[1] The author of the diary and the diary itself are, of course, imaginary. Nevertheless it is clear that such persons as the writer of these notes not only may, but positively must, exist in our society, when we consider the circumstances in the midst of which our society is formed. I have tried to expose to the view of the public more distinctly than is commonly done one of the characters of the recent past. He is one of the representatives of a generation still living. In this fragment, entitled "Underground," this person introduces himself and his views, and, as it were, tries to explain the causes owing to which he has made his appearance and was bound to make his appearance in our midst. In the second fragment there are added the actual notes of this person concerning certain events in his life.— AUTHOR'S NOTE

not take bribes, you see, so I was bound to find a recompense in that, at least. (A poor jest, but I will not scratch it out. I wrote it thinking it would sound very witty; but now that I have seen myself that I only wanted to show off in a despicable way, I will not scratch it out on purpose!)

When petitioners used to come for information to the table at which I sat, I used to grind my teeth at them, and felt intense enjoyment when I succeeded in making anybody unhappy. I almost always did succeed. For the most part they were all timid people—of course, they were petitioners. But of the uppish ones there was one officer in particular I could not endure. He simply would not be humble, and clanked his sword in a disgusting way. I carried on a feud with him for eighteen months over that sword. At last I got the better of him. He left off clanking it. That happened in my youth, though.

But do you know, gentlemen, what was the chief point about my spite? Why, the whole point, the real sting of it lay in the fact that continually, even in the moment of the acutest spleen, I was inwardly conscious with shame that I was not only not a spiteful but not even an embittered man, that I was simply scaring sparrows at random and amusing myself by it. I might foam at the mouth, but bring me a doll to play with, give me a cup of tea with sugar in it, and maybe I should be appeased. I might even be genuinely touched, though probably I should grind my teeth at myself afterwards and lie awake at night with shame for months after. That was my way.

I was lying when I said just now that I was a spiteful official. I was lying from spite. I was simply amusing myself with the petitioners and with the officer, and in reality I never could become spiteful. I was conscious every moment in myself of many, very many elements absolutely opposite to that. I felt them positively swarming in me, these opposite elements. I knew that they had been swarming in me all my life and craving some outlet from me, but I would not let them, would not let them, purposely would not let them come out. They tormented me till I was ashamed: they drove me to convulsions and—sickened me, at last, how they sickened me! Now, are not you fancying, gentlemen, that I am expressing remorse for something now, that I am asking your forgiveness for something? I am sure you are fancying that. . . . However, I assure you I do not care if you are. . . .

It was not only that I could not become spiteful, I did not know how to become anything: neither spiteful nor kind, neither a rascal nor an honest man, neither a hero nor an insect. Now, I am living out my life in my corner, taunting myself with the spiteful and useless consolation that an intelligent man cannot become anything seriously, and it is only the fool who becomes anything. Yes, a man in the nineteenth century must and morally ought to be pre-eminently a characterless creature; a man of character, an active man, is pre-eminently a limited creature. That is my conviction of forty years. I am forty years old now, and you know forty years is a whole lifetime; you know it is extreme old age. To live longer than forty years is bad manners, is vulgar, immoral. Who does live beyond forty? Answer that, sincerely and honestly. I will tell you who do: fools and worthless fellows. I tell all old men that to their face, all these venerable old men, all these silver-haired and reverend seniors! I tell the whole world that to its face. I have a right to say so, for I shall go on living to sixty myself. To seventy! To eighty! . . . Stay, let me take breath. . . .

You imagine no doubt, gentlemen, that I want to amuse you. You are mistaken in that, too. I am by no means such a mirthful person as you imagine, or as you may imagine; however, irritated by all this babble (and I feel that you are irritated) you think fit to ask me who am I—then my answer is, I am a collegiate assessor. I was in the service that I might have something to eat (and solely for that reason), and when last year a distant relation left me six thousand roubles in his will I immediately retired from the service and settled down in my corner. I used to live in this corner before, but now I have settled down in it. My room is a wretched, horrid one in the outskirts of the town. My servant is an old country-woman, ill-natured from stupidity, and, moreover, there is always a nasty smell about her. I am told that the Petersburg climate is bad for me, and that with my small means it is very expensive to live in Petersburg. I know all that better than all these sage and experienced counsellors and monitors. . . . But I am remaining in Petersburg; I am not going away from Petersburg! I am not going away because . . . ech! Why, it is absolutely no matter whether I am going away or not going away.

But what can a decent man speak of with most pleasure?

Answer: Of himself.

Well, so I will talk about myself.

[II]

I want now to tell you, gentlemen, whether you care to hear it or not, why I could not even become an insect. I tell you solemnly, that I have many times tried to become an insect. But I was not equal even to that. I swear, gentlemen, that to be too conscious is an illness—a real thoroughgoing illness. For man's everyday needs, it would have been quite enough to have the ordinary human consciousness, that is, half or a quarter of the amount which falls to the lot of a cultivated man of our unhappy nineteenth century, especially one who has the fatal ill-luck to inhabit Petersburg, the most theoretical and intentional town on the whole terrestrial globe. (There are intentional and unintentional towns.) It would have been quite enough, for instance, to have the consciousness by which all so-called direct persons and men of action live. I bet you think I am writing all this from affectation, to be witty at the expense of men of action; and what is more, that from ill-bred affectation, I am clanking a sword like my officer. But, gentlemen, whoever can pride himself on his diseases and even swagger over them?

Though, after all, every one does do that; people do pride themselves on their diseases, and I do, may be, more than any one. We will not dispute it; my contention was absurd. But yet I am firmly persuaded that a great deal of consciousness, every sort of consciousness, in fact, is a disease. I stick to that. Let us leave that, too, for a minute. Tell me this: why does it happen that at the very, yes, at the very moments when I am most capable of feeling every refinement of all that is "good and beautiful," as they used to say at one time, it would, as though of design, happen to me not only to feel but to do such ugly things, such that . . . Well, in short, actions that all, perhaps, commit; but which, as though purposely, occurred to me at the very time when I was most conscious that they ought not to be committed. The more conscious I was of goodness and of all that was "good and beautiful," the more deeply I sank into my mire and the more ready I was to sink in it altogether. But the chief point was that all this was, as it were, not accidental in me, but as though it were bound to be so. It was as though it were my most normal condition, and not in the least disease or depravity, so that at last all desire in me to struggle against this depravity passed. It ended by my almost believing (perhaps actually believing) that this was perhaps my normal condition. But at first, in the beginning, what agonies I endured in that struggle! I did not believe it was the same with other people, and all my life I hid this fact about myself as a secret. I was ashamed (even now, perhaps, I am ashamed): I got to the point of feeling a sort of secret abnormal, despicable enjoyment in returning home to my corner on some disgusting Petersburg night, acutely conscious that that day I had committed a loathsome action again, that what was done could never be undone, and secretly, inwardly gnawing, gnawing at myself for it, tearing and consuming myself till at last the bitterness turned into a sort of shameful accursed sweetness, and at last—into positive real enjoyment! Yes, into enjoyment, into enjoyment! I insist upon that. I have spoken of this because I keep wanting to know for a fact whether other people feel such enjoyment. I will explain: the enjoyment was just from the too intense consciousness of one's own degradation; it was from feeling oneself that one had reached the last barrier, that it was horrible, but that it could not be otherwise; that there was no escape for you; that you never could become a different man; that even if time and faith were still left you to change into something different you would most likely not wish to change; or if you did wish to, even then you would do nothing; because perhaps in reality there was nothing for you to change into.

And the worst of it was, and the root of it all, that it was all in accord with the normal fundamental laws of over-acute consciousness, and with the inertia that was the direct result of those laws, and that consequently one was not only unable to change but could do absolutely nothing. Thus it would follow, as the result of acute consciousness, that one is not to blame in being a scoundrel; as though that were any consolation to the scoundrel once he has come to realize that he actually is a scoundrel. But enough. . . . Ech, I have talked a lot of nonsense, but what have I explained? How is enjoyment in this to be explained? But I will explain it. I will get to the bottom of it! That is why I have taken up my pen. . . .

I, for instance, have a great deal of *amour propre.* I am as suspicious and prone to take offence as a humpback or a dwarf. But upon my word I sometimes have had moments when if I had happened to be slapped in the face I should, perhaps, have been positively glad of it. I say, in earnest, that I should probably have been able to discover even in that a peculiar sort of enjoyment—the enjoyment, of course, of despair; but in despair there are the most intense enjoyments, especially when one is very acutely conscious of the hopelessness of one's position. And when one is slapped in the face—why then the consciousness of being rubbed into a pulp would positively overwhelm one. The worst of it is, look at it which way one will, it still turns out that I was always the most to blame in everything. And what is most humiliating of all, to blame for no fault of my own but, so to say, through the laws of nature. In the first place, to blame because I am cleverer than any of the people surrounding me. (I have always considered myself cleverer than any of the people surrounding me, and sometimes, would you believe it, have been positively ashamed of it. At any rate, I have all my life, as it were, turned my eyes away and never could look people straight in the face.) To blame, finally, because even if I had had magnanimity, I should only have had more suffering from the sense of its uselessness. I should certainly have never been able to do anything from being magnanimous—neither to forgive, for my assailant would perhaps have slapped me from the laws of nature, and one cannot forgive the laws of nature; nor to forget, for even if it were owing to the laws of nature, it is insulting all the same. Finally, even if I had wanted to be anything but magnanimous, had desired on the contrary to revenge myself on my assailant, I could not have revenged myself on any one for anything because I should certainly never have made up my mind to do anything, even if I had been able to. Why should I not have made up my mind? About that in particular I want to say a few words.

[III]

With people who know how to revenge themselves and to stand up for themselves in general, how is it done? Why, when they are possessed, let us suppose, by the feeling of revenge, then for the time there is nothing else but that feeling left in their whole being. Such a gentleman simply dashes straight for his object like an infuriated bull with its horns down, and nothing but a wall will stop him. (By the way: facing the wall, such gentlemen—that is, the "direct" persons and men of action—are genuinely nonplussed. For them a wall is not an evasion, as for us people who think and consequently do nothing; it is not an excuse for turning aside, an excuse for which we are always very glad, though we scarcely believe in it ourselves, as a rule. No, they are nonplussed in all sincerity. The wall has for them something tranquillizing, morally soothing, final—maybe even something mysterious . . . but of the wall later.)

Well, such a direct person I regard as the real normal man, as his tender mother Nature wished to see him when she graciously brought him into being on the earth. I envy such a man till I am green in the face. He is stupid. I am not disputing that, but perhaps the normal man should be stupid, how do you know? Perhaps it is very beautiful, in fact. And I am the more persuaded of that suspicion, if one can call it so, by the fact that if you take, for instance, the antithesis of the normal man, that is, the man of acute consciousness, who has come, of course, not out of the lap of Nature but out of a retort (this is almost mysticism, gentlemen, but I suspect this, too), this retort-made man is sometimes so nonplussed in the presence of his antithesis that with all his exaggerated consciousness he genuinely thinks of himself as a mouse and not a man. It may be an acutely conscious mouse, yet it is a mouse, while the other is a man, and therefore, et caetera, et caetera. And the worst of it is, he himself, his very own self, looks on himself as a mouse; no one asks him to do so; and that is an important point. Now let us look at this mouse in action. Let us suppose, for instance, that it feels insulted, too (and it almost always does feel insulted), and wants to revenge itself, too. There may even be a greater accumulation of spite in it than in *l'homme de la nature et de la vérité*. The base and nasty desire to vent that spite on its assailant rankles perhaps even more nastily in it than in *l'homme de la nature et de la vérité*. For through his innate stupidity the latter looks upon his revenge as justice pure and simple; while in consequence of his acute consciousness the mouse does not believe in the justice of it. To come at last to the deed itself, to the very act of revenge. Apart from the one fundamental nastiness the luckless mouse succeeds in creating around it so many other nastinesses in the form of doubts and questions, adds to the one question so many unsettled questions, that there inevitably works up around it a sort of fatal brew, a stinking mess, made up of its doubts, emotions, and of the contempt spat upon it by the direct men of action who stand solemnly about it as judges and arbitrators, laughing at it till their healthy sides ache. Of course the only thing left for it is to dismiss all that with a wave of its paw, and, with a smile of assumed contempt in which it does not even itself believe, creep ignominiously into its mouse-hole. There in its nasty, stinking, underground home our insulted, crushed and ridiculed mouse promptly becomes absorbed in cold, malignant and, above all, everlasting spite. For forty years together it will remember its injury down to the smallest, most ignominious details, and every time will add, of itself, details still more ignominious, spitefully teasing and tormenting itself with its own imagination. It will itself be ashamed of its imaginings, but yet it will recall it all, it will go over and over every detail, it will invent unheard-of things against itself, pretending that those things might happen, and will forgive nothing. Maybe it will begin to revenge itself, too, but, as it were, piecemeal, in trivial ways, from behind the stove, incognito, without believing either in its own right to vengeance, or in the success of its revenge, knowing that from all its efforts at revenge it will suffer a hundred times more than he on whom it revenges itself, while he, I daresay, will not even scratch himself. On its death-bed it will recall it all over again, with interest accumulated over all the years and . . .

But it is just in that cold, abominable half despair, half belief, in that conscious burying oneself alive for grief in the underworld for forty years, in that acutely recognized and yet partly doubtful hopelessness of one's position, in that hell of unsatisfied desires turned inward, in that fever of oscillations, of resolutions determined for ever and repented of again a minute later—that the savour of that strange enjoyment of which I have spoken lies. It is so subtle, so difficult of analysis, that persons who are a little limited, or even simply persons of strong nerves, will not understand a single atom of it. "Possibly," you will add on your own account with a grin, "people will not understand it either who have never received a slap in the face," and in that way you will politely hint to me that I too, perhaps, have had the experience of a slap in the face in my life, and so I speak as one who knows. I bet that you are thinking that. But set your minds at rest, gentlemen, I have not received a slap in the face, though it is absolutely a matter of indifference to me what you may think about it. Possibly, I even regret myself that I have given so few slaps in the face during my life. But enough . . . not another word on that subject of such extreme interest to you.

I will continue calmly concerning persons with strong nerves who do not understand a certain refinement of enjoyment. Though in certain circumstances these gentlemen bellow their loudest like bulls, though this, let us suppose, does them the greatest credit, yet, as I have said already, confronted with the impossible they subside at once. The impossible means the stone wall! What stone wall? Why, of course, the laws of nature, the deductions of natural science, mathematics. As soon as they prove to you, for instance, that you are descended from a monkey, then it is no use scowling, accept it for a fact. When they prove to you that in reality one drop of your own fat must be dearer to you than a hundred thousand of your fellow creatures, and that this conclusion is the final solution of all so-called virtues and duties and all such prejudices and fancies, then you have just to accept it, there is no help for it, for twice two is a law of mathematics. Just try refuting it.

"Upon my word," they will shout at you, "it is no use protesting: it is a case of twice two makes four! Nature does not ask your permission, she has nothing to do with your wishes, and whether you like her laws or dislike them, you are bound to accept her as she is, and consequently all her conclusions. A wall, you see, is a wall . . . and so on, and so on."

Merciful heavens! but what do I care for the laws of nature and arithmetic, when, for some reason, I dislike those laws and the fact that twice two makes four? Of course I cannot break through the wall by battering my head against it if I really have not the strength to knock it down, but I am not going to be reconciled to it simply because it is a stone wall and I have not the strength.

As though such a stone wall really were a consolation, and really did contain some word of conciliation, simply because it is as true as twice two makes four. Oh, absurdity of absurdities! How much better it is to understand it all, to recognize it all, all the impossibilities and the stone wall; not to be reconciled to one of those impossibilities and stone walls if it disgusts you to be reconciled to it; by the way of the most inevitable, logical combinations to reach the most revolting conclusions on the everlasting theme, that even for the stone wall you are yourself somehow to blame, though again it is as clear as day you are not to blame in the least, and therefore grinding your teeth in silent impotence to sink into luxurious inertia, brooding on the fact that there is no one even for you to feel vindictive against, that you have not, and perhaps never will have, an object for your spite, that it is a sleight-of-hand, a bit of juggling, a card-sharper's trick, that it is simply a mess, no knowing what and no knowing who, but in spite of all these uncertainties and jugglings, still there is an ache in you, and the more you do not know, the worse the ache.

[IV]

"Ha, ha, ha! You will be finding enjoyment in toothache next," you cry, with a laugh.

"Well? Even in toothache there is enjoyment," I answer. I had toothache for a whole month and I know there is. In that case, of course, people are not spiteful in silence, but moan; but they are not candid moans, they are malignant moans, and the malignancy is the whole point. The enjoyment of the sufferer finds expression in those moans; if he did not feel enjoyment in them he would not moan. It is a good example, gentlemen, and I will develop it. Those moans express in the first place all the aimlessness of your pain, which is so humiliating to your consciousness; the whole legal system of Nature on which you spit disdainfully, of course, but from which you suffer all the same while she does not. They express the consciousness that you have no enemy to punish, but that you have pain; the consciousness that in spite of all possible Vagenheims you are in complete slavery to your teeth; that if some one wishes it, your teeth will leave off aching, and if he does not, they will go on aching another three months; and that finally

if you are still contumacious and still protest, all that is left you for
your own gratification is to thrash yourself or beat your wall with your
fist as hard as you can, and absolutely nothing more. Well, these mortal
insults, these jeers on the part of some one unknown, end at last in an
enjoyment which sometimes reaches the highest degree of voluptuous-
ness. I ask you, gentlemen, listen sometimes to the moans of an educated man of the nineteenth century suffering from toothache, on the
second or third day of the attack, when he is beginning to moan, not
as he moaned on the first day, that is, not simply because he has toothache, not just as any coarse peasant, but as a man affected by progress
and European civilization, a man who is "divorced from the soil and
the national elements," as they express it nowadays. His moans become nasty, disgustingly malignant, and go on for whole days and
nights. And of course he knows himself that he is doing himself
no sort of good with his moans; he knows better than any one
that he is only lacerating and harassing himself and others for nothing;
he knows that even the audience before whom he is making his efforts,
and his whole family, listen to him with loathing, do not put a ha'porth
of faith in him, and inwardly understand that he might moan differently, more simply, without trills and flourishes, and that he is only
amusing himself like that from ill-humour, from malignancy. Well, in
all these recognitions and disgraces it is that there lies a voluptuous
pleasure. As though he would say: "I am worrying you, I am lacerating
your hearts, I am keeping every one in the house awake. Well, stay
awake then, you, too, feel every minute that I have toothache. I am
not a hero to you now, as I tried to seem before, but simply a nasty
person, an impostor. Well, so be it, then! I am very glad that you see
through me. It is nasty for you to hear my despicable moans: well, let
it be nasty; here I will let you have a nastier flourish in a minute. . . ."
You do not understand even now, gentlemen? No, it seems our development and our consciousness must go further to understand all the
intricacies of this pleasure. You laugh? Delighted. My jests, gentlemen,
are of course in bad taste, jerky, involved, lacking self-confidence. But
of course that is because I do not respect myself. Can a man of perception respect himself at all?

[v]

Come, can a man who attempts to find enjoyment in the very feeling
of his own degradation possibly have a spark of respect for himself?
I am not saying this now from any mawkish kind of remorse. And,

indeed, I could never endure saying, "Forgive me, Papa, I won't do it again," not because I am incapable of saying that—on the contrary, perhaps just because I have been too capable of it, and in what a way, too! As though of design I used to get into trouble in cases when I was not to blame in any way. That was the nastiest part of it. At the same time I was genuinely touched and penitent, I used to shed tears and, of course, deceived myself, though I was not acting in the least and there was a sick feeling in my heart at the time. . . . For that one could not blame even the laws of nature, though the laws of nature have continually all my life offended me more than anything. It is loathsome to remember it all, but it was loathsome even then. Of course, a minute or so later I would realize wrathfully that it was all a lie, a revolting lie, an affected lie, that is, all this penitence, this emotion, these vows of reform. You will ask why did I worry myself with such antics: answer, because it was very dull to sit with one's hands folded, and so one began cutting capers. That is really it. Observe yourselves more carefully, gentlemen, then you will understand that it is so. I invented adventures for myself and made up a life, so as at least to live in some way. How many times it has happened to me—well, for instance, to take offence simply on purpose, for nothing; and one knows oneself, of course, that one is offended at nothing, that one is putting it on, but yet one brings oneself, at last, to the point of being really offended. All my life I have had an impulse to play such pranks, so that in the end I could not control it in myself. Another time, twice, in fact, I tried hard to be in love. I suffered, too, gentlemen, I assure you. In the depth of my heart there was no faith in my suffering, only a faint stir of mockery, but yet I did suffer, and in the real, orthodox way; I was jealous, beside myself . . . and it was all from *ennui,* gentlemen, all from *ennui;* inertia overcame me. You know the direct, legitimate fruit of consciousness is inertia, that is, conscious sitting-with-the-hands-folded. I have referred to this already. I repeat, I repeat with emphasis: all "direct" persons and men of action are active just because they are stupid and limited. How explain that? I will tell you: in consequence of their limitation they take immediate and secondary causes for primary ones, and in that way persuade themselves more quickly and easily than other people do that they have found an infallible foundation for their activity, and their minds are at ease and you know that is the chief thing. To begin to act, you know, you must first have your mind completely at ease and no trace of doubt left in it. Why, how am I, for example, to set my mind at rest? Where are the primary causes on which I am to build? Where are my foundations? Where am I to get them from? I exercise myself in reflection, and consequently with me every primary cause at once draws after itself another still more primary, and so on to infinity. That is just the essence of every sort of consciousness and reflection. It must be a case of the laws of nature again. What is the result of it in the end? Why, just the same. Remember I spoke just now of vengeance. (I am sure you did not take it in.) I said that a man revenges himself because he sees justice in it. Therefore he has found a primary cause, that is, justice. And so he is at rest on all sides, and consequently he carries out his revenge calmly and successfully, being persuaded that he is doing a just and honest thing. But I see no justice in it, I find no sort of virtue in it either, and consequently if I attempt to revenge myself, it is only out of spite. Spite, of course, might overcome everything, all my doubts, and so might serve quite successfully in place of a primary cause, precisely because it is not a cause. But what is to be done if I have not even spite (I began with that just now, you know)? In consequence again of those accursed laws of consciousness, anger in me is subject to chemical disintegration. You look into it, the object flies off into air, your reasons evaporate, the criminal is not to be found, the wrong becomes not a wrong but a phantom, something like the toothache, for which no one is to blame, and consequently there is only the same outlet left again—that is, to beat the wall as hard as you can. So you give it up with a wave of the hand because you have not found a fundamental cause. And try letting yourself be carried away by your feelings, blindly, without reflection, without a primary cause, repelling consciousness at least for a time; hate or love, if only not to sit with your hands folded. The day after to-morrow, at the latest, you will begin despising yourself for having knowingly deceived yourself. Result: a soap-bubble and inertia. Oh, gentlemen, do you know, perhaps I consider myself an intelligent man only because all my life I have been able neither to begin nor to finish anything. Granted I am a babbler, a harmless vexatious babbler, like all of us. But what is to be done if the direct and sole vocation of every intelligent man is babble, that is, the intentional pouring of water through a sieve?

[VI]

Oh, if I had done nothing simply from laziness! Heavens, how I should have respected myself then. I should have respected myself because I should at least have been capable of being lazy; there would at least have been one quality, as it were, positive in me, in which I could have believed myself. Question: What is he? Answer: A sluggard; how very pleasant it would have been to hear that of oneself! It would mean that I was positively defined, it would mean that there was something to say about me. "Sluggard"—why, it is a calling and vocation, it is a career. Do not jest, it is so. I should then be a member of the best club by right, and should find my occupation in continually respecting myself. I knew a gentlemen who prided himself all his life on being a connoisseur of Lafitte. He considered this as his positive virtue, and never doubted himself. He died, not simply with a tranquil, but with a triumphant, conscience, and he was quite right, too. Then I should have chosen a career for myself, I should have been a sluggard and a glutton, not a simple one, but, for instance, one with sympathies for everything good and beautiful. How do you like that? I have long had visions of it. That "good and beautiful" weighs heavily on my mind at forty. But that is at forty; then—oh, then it would have been different! I should have found for myself a form of activity in keeping with it, to be precise, drinking to the health of everything "good and beautiful." I should have snatched at every opportunity to drop a tear into my glass and then to drain it to all that is "good and beautiful." I should then have turned everything into the good and the beautiful; in the nastiest, unquestionable trash, I should have sought out the good and the beautiful. I should have exuded tears like a wet sponge. An artist, for instance, paints a picture worthy of Gay. At once I drink to the health of the artist who painted the picture worthy of Gay, because I love all that is "good and beautiful." An author has written *As you will:* at once I drink to the health of "any one you will" because I love all that is "good and beautiful."

I should claim respect for doing so. I should persecute any one who would not show me respect. I should live at ease, I should die with dignity, why, it is charming, perfectly charming! And what a good round belly I should have grown, what a treble chin I should have established, what a ruby nose I should have coloured for myself, so that every one would have said, looking at me: "Here is an asset! Here is something real and solid!" And, say what you like, it is very agreeable to hear such remarks about oneself in this negative age.

[VII]

But these are all golden dreams. Oh, tell me, who was it first announced, who was it first proclaimed, that man only does nasty things because he does not know his own interests; and that if he were enlightened, if his eyes were opened to his real normal interests, man would at once cease to do nasty things, would at once become good and noble because, being enlightened and understanding his real advantage, he would see his own advantage in the good and nothing else, and we all know that not one man can, consciously, act against his own interests, consequently, so to say, through necessity, he would begin doing good? Oh, the babe! Oh, the pure, innocent child! Why, in the first place, when in all these thousands of years has there been a time when man has acted only from his own interest? What is to be done with the millions of facts that bear witness that men, *consciously,* that is, fully understanding their real interests, have left them in the background and have rushed headlong on another path, to meet peril and danger, compelled to this course by nobody and by nothing, but, as it were, simply disliking the beaten track, and have obstinately, wilfully, struck out another difficult, absurd way, seeking it almost in the darkness. So, I suppose, this obstinacy and perversity were pleasanter to them than any advantage. . . . Advantage! What is advantage?

And will you take it upon yourself to define with perfect accuracy in what the advantage of man consists? And what if it so happens that a man's advantage, *sometimes,* not only may, but even must, consist in his desiring in certain cases what is harmful to himself and not advantageous. And if so, there can be such a case, the whole principle falls into dust. What do you think—are there such cases? You laugh; laugh away, gentlemen, but only answer me: have man's advantages been reckoned up with perfect certainty? Are there not some which not only have not been included but cannot possibly be included under any classification? You see, you gentlemen have, to the best of my knowledge, taken your whole register of human advantages from the averages of statistical figures and politico-economical formulas. Your advantages are prosperity, wealth, freedom, peace—and so on, and so on. So that the man who should, for instance, go openly and knowingly in opposition to all that list would, to your thinking, and indeed mine too, of course, be an obscurantist or an absolute madman: would not he? But, you know, this is what is surprising: why does it so happen that all these statisticians, sages and lovers of humanity, when they reckon up human advantages invariably leave out one? They don't even take it into their reckoning in the form in which it should be taken, and the whole reckoning depends upon that. It would be no great matter, they would simply have to take it, this advantage, and add it to the list. But the trouble is, that this strange advantage does not fall under any classification and is not in place in any list. I have a friend for instance ... Ech! gentlemen, but of course he is your friend, too; and indeed there is no one, no one, to whom he is not a friend!

When he prepares for any undertaking this gentleman immediately explains to you, elegantly and clearly, exactly how he must act in accordance with the laws of reason and truth. What is more, he will talk to you with excitement and passion of the true normal interests of man; with irony he will upbraid the short-sighted fools who do not understand their own interests, nor the true significance of virtue; and, within a quarter of an hour, without any sudden outside provocation, but simply through something inside him which is stronger than all his interests, he will go off on quite a different tack—that is, act in direct opposition to what he has just been saying about himself, in opposition to the laws of reason, in opposition to his own advantage— in fact, in opposition to everything. ... I warn you that my friend is a compound personality, and therefore it is difficult to blame him as an individual. The fact is, gentlemen, it seems there must really exist something that is dearer to almost every man than his greatest advantages, or (not to be illogical) there is a most advantageous advantage (the very one omitted of which we spoke just now) which is more important and more advantageous than all other advantages, for the sake of which a man if necessary is ready to act in opposition to all laws; that is, in opposition to reason, honour, peace, prosperity—in fact, in opposition to all those excellent and useful things if only he can attain that fundamental, most advantageous advantage which is dearer to him than all. "Yes, but it's advantage all the same" you will retort. But excuse me, I'll make the point clear, and it is not a case of playing upon words. What matters is, that this advantage is remarkable from the very fact that it breaks down all our classifications, and continually shatters every system constructed by lovers of mankind for the benefit of mankind. In fact, it upsets everything. But before I mention this advantage to you, I want to compromise myself personally, and therefore I boldly declare that all these fine systems—all these theories for explaining to mankind their real normal interests, in order that inevitably striving to pursue these interests they may at once become good and noble—are, in my opinion, so far, mere logical exercises! Yes, logical exercises. Why, to maintain this theory of the regeneration of mankind by means of the pursuit of his own advantage is to my mind almost the same thing as ... as to affirm, for instance, following Buckle, that through civilization mankind becomes softer, and consequently less bloodthirsty, and less fitted for warfare. Logically it does seem to follow from his arguments. But man has such a predilection for systems and abstract deductions that he is ready to distort the truth intentionally, he is ready to deny the evidence of his senses only to justify his logic. I take this example because it is the most glaring instance of it. Only look about you: blood is being spilt in streams, and in the merriest way, as though it were champagne. Take the whole of the nineteenth century in which Buckle lived. Take Napoleon—the Great and also the present one. Take North America—the eternal union. Take the farce of Schleswig-Holstein. . . . And what is it that civilization softens in us? The only gain of civilization for mankind is the greater capacity for variety of sensations—and absolutely nothing more. And through the development of this many-sidedness man may come to finding enjoyment in bloodshed. In fact, this has already happened to him. Have you noticed that it is the most civilized gentlemen who have been the subtlest slaughterers, to whom the Attilas and Stenka Razins could not hold a candle, and if they are not so conspicuous as the Attilas and Stenka Razins it is simply because they are so often met with, are so ordinary and have become so familiar to us. In any case civilization has made mankind if not more blood-thirsty, at least more vilely, more loathsomely blood-thirsty. In old days he saw justice in bloodshed and with his conscience at peace exterminated those he thought proper. Now we do think bloodshed abominable and yet we engage in this abomination, and with more energy than ever. Which is worse? Decide that for yourselves.

They say that Cleopatra (excuse an instance from Roman history) was fond of sticking gold pins into her slave-girls' breasts and derived gratification from their screams and writhings. You will say that that was in the comparatively barbarous times; that these are barbarous times too, because also, comparatively speaking, pins are stuck in even now; that though man has now learned to see more clearly than in barbarous ages, he is still far from having learnt to act as reason and science would dictate. But yet you are fully convinced that he will be sure to learn when he gets rid of certain old bad habits, and when common sense and science have completely re-educated human nature and turned it in a normal direction. You are confident that then man will cease from *intentional* error and will, so to say, be compelled not to want to set his will against his normal interests. That is not all; then, you say, science itself will teach man (though to my mind it's a superfluous luxury) that he never has really had any caprice or will of his own, and that he himself is something of the nature of a piano-key or the stop of an organ, and that there are, besides, things called the laws of nature; so that everything he does is not done by his willing it, but is done of itself, by the laws of nature. Consequently we have only to discover these laws of nature, and man will no longer have to answer for his actions and life will become exceedingly easy for him. All human actions will then, of course, be tabulated according to these laws, mathematically, like tables of logarithms up to 108,000, and entered in an index; or, better still, there would be published certain edifying works of the nature of encyclopaedic lexicons, in which everything will be so clearly calculated and explained that there will be no more incidents or adventures in the world.

Then—this is all what you say—new economic relations will be established, all ready-made and worked out with mathematical exactitude, so that every possible question will vanish in the twinkling of an eye, simply because every possible answer to it will be provided. Then the "Palace of Crystal" will be built. Then . . . In fact, those will be halcyon days. Of course there is no guaranteeing (this is my comment) that it will not be, for instance, frightfully dull then (for what will one have to do when everything will be calculated and tabulated?), but on the other hand everything will be extraordinarily rational. Of course boredom may lead you to anything. It is boredom sets one sticking golden pins into people, but all that would not matter. What is bad (this is my comment again) is that I dare say people will be thankful for the gold pins then. Man is stupid, you know, phenomenally stupid; or rather he is not at all stupid, but he is so ungrateful that you could not find another like him in all creation. I, for instance, would not be in the least surprised if all of a sudden, apropos of nothing, in the midst of general prosperity a gentleman with an ignoble, or rather with a reactionary and ironical, countenance were to arise and, putting his arms akimbo, say to us all: "I say, gentlemen, hadn't we better kick over the whole show and scatter rationalism to the winds, simply to send these logarithms to the devil, and to enable us to live once more at our own sweet foolish will!" That again would not matter; but what is annoying is that he would be sure to find followers—such is the nature of man. And all that for the most foolish reason, which, one would think, was hardly worth mentioning: that is, that man everywhere and at all times, whoever he may be, has preferred to act as he chose and not in the least as his reason and advantage dictated. And one may choose what is contrary to one's own interests, and sometimes one *positively ought* (that is my idea). One's own free unfettered choice, one's own caprice—however wild it may be, one's own fancy worked up at times to frenzy—is that very "most advantageous advantage" which we have overlooked, which comes under no classification and against which all systems and theories are continually being shattered to atoms. And how do these wiseacres know that man wants a normal, a virtuous choice? What has made them conceive that man must want a rationally advantageous choice? What man wants is simply *independent* choice, whatever that independence may cost and wherever it may lead. And choice, of course, the devil only knows what choice. . . .

[viii]

"Ha! ha! ha! But you know there is no such thing as choice in reality, say what you like," you will interpose with a chuckle. "Science has succeeded in so far analyzing man that we know already that choice and what is called freedom of will is nothing else than——"

Stay, gentlemen, I meant to begin with that myself. I confess, I was rather frightened. I was just going to say that the devil only knows what choice depends on, and that perhaps that was a very good thing, but I remembered the teaching of science . . . and pulled myself up. And here you have begun upon it. Indeed, if there really is some day discovered a formula for all our desires and caprices—that is, an explanation of what they depend upon, by what laws they arise, how they develop, what they are aiming at in one case and in another and so on, that is, a real mathematical formula—then, most likely, man will at once cease to feel desire, indeed, he will be certain to. For who would want to choose by rule? Besides, he will at once be transformed from a human being into an organ-stop or something of the sort; for what is a man without desires, without free will and without choice, if not a stop in an organ? What do you think? Let us reckon the chances —can such a thing happen or not?

"H'm!" you decide. "Our choice is usually mistaken from a false view of our advantage. We sometimes choose absolute nonsense because in our foolishness we see in that nonsense the easiest means for attaining a supposed advantage. But when all that is explained and worked out on paper (which is perfectly possible, for it is contemptible and senseless to suppose that some laws of nature man will never understand), then certainly so-called desires will no longer exist. For if a desire should come into conflict with reason we shall then reason and not desire, because it will be impossible retaining our reason to be *senseless* in our desires, and in that way knowingly act against reason and desire to injure ourselves. And as all choice and reasoning can be really calculated—because there will some day be discovered the laws of our so-called free will—so, joking apart, there may one day be something like a table constructed of them, so that we really shall choose in accordance with it. If, for instance, some day they calculate and prove to me that I made a long nose at some one because I could not help making a long nose at him and that I had to do it in that particular way, what *freedom* is left me, especially if I am a learned man and have taken my degree somewhere? Then I should be able to calculate my whole life for thirty years beforehand. In short, if this could be arranged there would be nothing left for us to do; anyway, we should have to understand that. And, in fact, we ought unwearyingly to repeat to ourselves that at such and such a time and in such and such circumstances Nature does not ask our leave; that we have got to take her as she is and not fashion her to suit our fancy, and if we really aspire to formulas and tables of rules, and well, even . . . to the chemical retort, there's no help for it, we must accept the retort too, or else it will be accepted without our consent. . . ."

Yes, but here I come to a stop! Gentlemen, you must excuse me for being over-philosophical; it's the result of forty years underground! Allow me to indulge my fancy. You see, gentlemen, reason is an excellent thing, there's no disputing that, but reason is nothing but reason and satisfies only the rational side of man's nature, while will is a manifestation of the whole life, that is, of the whole human life including reason and all the impulses. And although our life, in this manifestation of it, is often worthless, yet it is life and not simply extracting square roots. Here I, for instance, quite naturally want to live, in order to satisfy all my capacities for life, and not simply my capacity for reasoning, that is, not simply one-twentieth of my capacity for life. What does reason know? Reason only knows what it has succeeded in learning (some things, perhaps, it will never learn; this is a poor comfort, but why not say so frankly?) and human nature acts as a whole, with everything that is in it, consciously or unconsciously, and, even if it goes wrong, it lives. I suspect, gentlemen, that you are looking at me with compassion; you tell me again that an enlightened and developed man, such, in short, as the future man will be, cannot consciously desire anything disadvantageous to himself, that that can be proved mathematically. I thoroughly agree, it can—by mathematics.

But I repeat for the hundredth time, there is one case, one only, when man may consciously, purposely, desire what is injurious to himself, what is stupid, very stupid—simply in order to have the right to desire for himself even what is very stupid and not to be bound by an obligation to desire only what is sensible. Of course, this very stupid thing, this caprice of ours, may be in reality, gentlemen, more advantageous for us than anything else on earth, especially in certain cases. And in particular it may be more advantageous than any advantage even when it does us obvious harm, and contradicts the soundest conclusions of our reason concerning our advantage—for in any circumstances it preserves for us what is most precious and most important—that is, our personality, our individuality. Some, you see, maintain that this really is the most precious thing for mankind; choice can, of course, if it chooses, be in agreement with reason; and especially if this be not abused but kept within bounds. It is profitable and sometimes even praiseworthy. But very often, and even most often, choice is utterly and stubbornly opposed to reason . . . and . . . and . . . do you know that that, too, is profitable, sometimes even praiseworthy? Gentlemen, let us suppose that man is not stupid. (Indeed one cannot refuse to suppose that, if only from the one consideration, that, if man is stupid, then who is wise?) But if he is not stupid, he is monstrously ungrateful! Phenomenally ungrateful. In fact, I believe that the best definition of man is the ungrateful biped. But that is not all, that is not his worst defect; his worst defect is his perpetual moral obliquity, perpetual—from the days of the Flood to the Schleswig-Holstein period.

Moral obliquity and consequently lack of good sense; for it has long been accepted that lack of good sense is due to no other cause than moral obliquity. Put it to the test and cast your eyes upon the history of mankind. What will you see? Is it a grand spectacle? Grand, if you like. Take the Colossus of Rhodes, for instance, that's worth something. With good reason Mr. Anaevsky testifies of it that some say that it is the work of man's hands, while others maintain that it has been created by Nature herself. Is it many-coloured? It may be it is many-coloured, too: if one takes the dress uniforms, military and civilian, of all peoples in all ages—that alone is worth something, and if you take the undress uniforms you will never get to the end of it; no historian would be equal to the job. Is it monotonous? It may be it's monotonous too: it's fighting and fighting; they are fighting now, they fought first and they fought last—you will admit that it is almost too monotonous. In short, one may say anything about the history of the world—anything that might enter the most disordered imagination. The only thing one can't say is that it's rational. The very word sticks in one's throat. And, indeed, this is the odd thing that is continually happening: there are continually turning up in life moral and rational persons, sages and lovers of humanity, who make it their object to live all their lives as morally and rationally as possible, to be, so to speak, a light to their neighbours simply in order to show them that it is possible to live morally and rationally in this world. And yet we all know that those very people sooner or later have been false to themselves, playing some queer trick, often a most unseemly one. Now I ask you: what can be expected of man since he is a being endowed with such strange qualities? Shower upon him every earthly blessing, drown him in a sea of happiness, so that nothing but bubbles of bliss can be seen on the surface; give him economic prosperity, such that he should have nothing else to do but sleep, eat cakes and busy himself with the continuation of his species, and even then out of sheer ingratitude, sheer spite, man would play you some nasty trick. He would even risk his cakes and would deliberately desire the most fatal rubbish, the most uneconomical absurdity, simply to introduce into all this positive good sense his fatal fantastic element. It is just his fantastic dreams, his vulgar folly, that he will desire to retain, simply in order to prove to himself—as though that were so necessary—that men still are men and not the keys of a piano, which the laws of nature threaten to control so completely that soon one will be able to desire nothing but by the calendar. And that is not all: even if man really were nothing but a piano-key, even if this were proved to him by natural science and mathematics, even then he would not become reasonable, but would purposely do something perverse out of simple ingratitude, simply to gain his point. And if he does not find means he will contrive destruction and chaos, will contrive sufferings of all sorts, only to gain his point! He will launch a curse upon the world, and as only man can curse (it is his privilege, the primary distinction between him and other animals) it may be by his curse alone he will attain his object—that is, convince himself that he is a man and not a piano-key! If you say that all this, too, can be calculated and tabulated —chaos and darkness and curses, so that the mere possibility of calculating it all beforehand would stop it all, and reason would reassert itself—then man would purposely go mad in order to be rid of reason and gain his point! I believe in it, I answer for it, for the whole work of man really seems to consist in nothing but proving to himself every minute that he is a man and not a piano-key! It may be at the cost of his skin, it may be by cannibalism! And this being so, can one help being tempted to rejoice that it has not yet come off, and that desire still depends on something we don't know?

You will scream at me (that is, if you condescend to do so) that no one is touching my free will, that all they are concerned with is that my will should of itself, of its own free will, coincide with my own normal interests, with the laws of nature and arithmetic.

Good heavens, gentlemen, what sort of free will is left when we come to tabulation and arithmetic, when it will all be a case of twice two makes four? Twice two makes four without my will. As if free will meant that!

[IX]

Gentlemen, I am joking, and I know myself that my jokes are not brilliant, but you know one can't take everything as a joke. I am, perhaps, jesting against the grain. Gentlemen, I am tormented by questions; answer them for me. You, for instance, want to cure men of their old habits and reform their will in accordance with science and good sense. But how do you know, not only that it is possible, but also that it is *desirable*, to reform man in that way? And what leads you to the conclusion that man's inclinations *need* reforming? In short, how do you know that such a reformation will be a benefit to man? And to go to the root of the matter, **why** are you so positively convinced that not to act against his real normal interests guaranteed by the conclusions of reason and arithmetic is certainly always advantageous for man and must always be a law for mankind? So far, you know, this is only your supposition. It may be the law of logic, but not the law of humanity. You think, gentlemen, perhaps that I am mad? Allow me to defend myself. I agree that man is pre-eminently a creative animal, predestined to strive consciously for an object and to engage in engineering—that is, incessantly and eternally to make new roads, *wherever they may lead*. But the reason why he wants sometimes to go off at a tangent may just be that he is *predestined* to make the road, and perhaps, too, that however stupid the "direct" practical man may be, the thought sometimes will occur to him that the road almost always does lead *somewhere,* and that the destination it leads to is less important than the process of making it, and that the chief thing is to save the well-conducted child from despising engineering, and so giving way to the fatal idleness, which, as we all know, is the mother of all the vices. Man likes to make roads and to create, that is a fact beyond dispute. But why has he such a passionate love for destruction and chaos also? Tell me that! But on that point I want to say a couple of words myself. May it not be that he loves chaos and destruction (there can be no disputing that he does sometimes love it) because he is instinctively afraid of attaining his object and completing the edifice he is constructing? Who knows, perhaps he only loves that edifice from a distance, and is by no means in love with it at close quarters; perhaps he only loves building it and does not want to live in it, but will leave it, when completed, for the use of *les animaux domestiques*—such as the ants, the sheep, and so on. Now the ants have quite a different taste. They have a marvellous edifice of that pattern which endures for ever—the ant-heap.

With the ant-heap the respectable race of ants began and with the ant-heap they will probably end, which does the greatest credit to their perseverance and good sense. But man is a frivolous and incongruous creature, and perhaps, like a chess-player, loves the process of the game, not the end of it. And who knows (there is no saying with certainty), perhaps the only goal on earth to which mankind is striving lies in this incessant process of attaining in other words, in life itself, and not in the thing to be attained, which must always be expressed as a formula, as positive as twice two makes four, and such positiveness is not life, gentlemen, but is the beginning of death. Anyway, man has always been afraid of this mathematical certainty, and I am afraid of it now. Granted that man does nothing but seek that mathematical certainty, he traverses oceans, sacrifices his life in the quest, but to succeed, really to find it, he dreads, I assure you. He feels that when he has found it there will be nothing for him to look for. When workmen have finished their work they do at least receive their pay, they go to the tavern, then they are taken to the police-station—and there is occupation for a week. But where can man go? Anyway, one can observe a certain awkwardness about him when he has attained such objects. He loves the process of attaining, but does not quite like to have attained, and that, of course, is very absurd. In fact, man is a comical creature; there seems to be a kind of jest in it all. But yet mathematical certainty is, after all, something insufferable. Twice two makes four seems to me simply a piece of insolence. Twice two makes four is a pert coxcomb who stands with arms akimbo barring your path and spitting. I admit that twice two makes four is an excellent thing, but if we are to give everything its due, twice two makes five is sometimes a very charming thing too.

And why are you so firmly, so triumphantly, convinced that only the normal and the positive—in other words, only what is conducive to welfare—is for the advantage of man? Is not reason in error as regards advantage? Does not man, perhaps, love something besides well-being? Perhaps he is just as fond of suffering? Perhaps suffering is just as great a benefit to him as well-being? Man is sometimes extraordinarily, passionately, in love with suffering, and that is a fact. There is no need to appeal to universal history to prove that; only ask yourself, if you are a man and have lived at all. As far as my personal opinion is concerned, to care only for well-being seems to me positively ill-bred. Whether it's good or bad, it is sometimes very pleasant, too, to smash things. I hold no brief for suffering nor for well-being either. I am standing for . . . my caprice, and for its being guaranteed to me when necessary. Suffering would be out of place in vaudevilles, for instance; I know that. In the "Palace of Crystal" it is unthinkable; suffering means doubt, negation, and what would be the good of a "palace of crystal" if there could be any doubt about it? And yet I think man will never renounce real suffering, that is, destruction and chaos. Why, suffering is the sole origin of consciousness. Though I did lay it down at the beginning that consciousness is the greatest misfortune for man, yet I know man prizes it and would not give it up for any satisfaction. Consciousness, for instance, is infinitely superior to twice two makes four. Once you have mathematical certainty there is nothing left to do or to understand. There will be nothing left but to bottle up your five senses and plunge into contemplation. While if you stick to consciousness, even though the same result is attained, you can at least flog yourself at times, and that will, at any rate, liven you up. Reactionary as it is, corporal punishment is better than nothing.

[x]

You believe in a palace of crystal that can never be destroyed—a palace at which one will not be able to put out one's tongue or make a long nose on the sly. And perhaps that is just why I am afraid of this edifice that it is of crystal and can never be destroyed and that one cannot put one's tongue out at it even on the sly.

You see, if it were not a palace, but a hen-house, I might creep into it to avoid getting wet, and yet I would not call the hen-house a palace out of gratitude to it for keeping me dry. You laugh and say that in such circumstances a hen-house is as good as a mansion. Yes, I answer, if one had to live simply to keep out of the rain.

But what is to be done if I have taken it into my head that that is not the only object in life, and that if one must live one had better live in a mansion. That is my choice, my desire. You will only eradicate it when you have changed my preference. Well, do change it, allure me with something else, give me another ideal. But meanwhile

I will not take a hen-house for a mansion. The palace of crystal may be an idle dream, it may be that it is inconsistent with the laws of nature and that I have invented it only through my own stupidity, through the old-fashioned irrational habits of my generation. But what does it matter to me that it is inconsistent? That makes no difference since it exists in my desires, or rather exists as long as my desires exist. Perhaps you are laughing again? Laugh away; I will put up with any mockery rather than pretend that I am satisfied when I am hungry. I know, anyway, that I will not be put off with a compromise, with a recurring zero, simply because it is consistent with the laws of nature and actually exists. I will not accept as the crown of my desires a block of buildings with tenements for the poor on a lease of a thousand years, and perhaps with a sign-board of a dentist hanging out. Destroy my desires, eradicate my ideals, show me something better, and I will follow you. You will say, perhaps, that is not worth your trouble; but in that case I can give you the same answer. We are discussing things seriously; but if you won't deign to give me your attention, I will drop your acquaintance. I can retreat into my underground hole.

But while I am alive and have desires I would rather my hand were withered off than bring one brick to such a building! Don't remind me that I have just rejected the palace of crystal for the sole reason that one cannot put out one's tongue at it. I did not say because I am so fond of putting my tongue out. Perhaps the thing I resented was, that of all your edifices there has not been one at which one could not put out one's tongue. On the contrary, I would let my tongue be cut off out of gratitude if things could be so arranged that I should lose all desire to put it out. It is not my fault that things cannot be so arranged, and that one must be satisfied with model flats. Then why am I made with such desires? Can I have been constructed simply in order to come to the conclusion that all my construction is a cheat? Can this be my whole purpose? I do not believe it.

But do you know what: I am convinced that we underground folk ought to be kept on a curb. Though we may sit forty years underground without speaking, when we do come out into the light of day and break out we talk and talk and talk. . . .

[XI]

The long and the short of it is, gentlemen, that it is better to do nothing! Better conscious inertia! And so hurrah for underground!

Though I have said that I envy the normal man to the last drop of my bile, yet I should not care to be in his place such as he is now (though I shall not cease envying him). No, no; anyway the underground life is more advantageous. There, at any rate, one can . . . Oh, but even now I am lying! I am lying because I know myself that it is not underground that is better, but something different, quite different, for which I am thirsting, but which I cannot find! Damn underground!

I will tell you another thing that would be better, and that is, if I myself believed in anything of what I have just written. I swear to you, gentlemen, there is not one thing, not one word of what I have written, that I really believe. That is, I believe it, perhaps, but at the same time I feel and suspect that I am lying like a cobbler.

"Then why have you written all this?" you will say to me.

"I ought to put you underground for forty years without anything to do and then come to you in your cellar, to find out what stage you have reached! How can a man be left with nothing to do for forty years?

"Isn't that shameful, isn't that humiliating?" you will say, perhaps, wagging your heads contemptuously. "You thirst for life and try to settle the problems of life by a logical tangle. And how persistent, how insolent are your sallies, and at the same time what a scare you are in! You talk nonsense and are pleased with it; you say impudent things and are in continual alarm and apologizing for them. You declare that you are afraid of nothing and at the same time try to ingratiate yourself in our good opinion. You declare that you are gnashing your teeth and at the same time you try to be witty so as to amuse us. You know that your witticisms are not witty, but you are evidently well satisfied with their literary value. You may, perhaps, have really suffered, but you have no respect for your own suffering. You may have sincerity, but you have no modesty; out of the pettiest vanity you expose your sincerity to publicity and ignominy. You doubtlessly mean to say something, but hide your last word through fear, because you have not the resolution to utter it, and only have a cowardly impudence. You boast of consciousness, but you are not sure of your ground, for though your mind works, yet your heart is darkened and corrupt, and you cannot have a full, genuine consciousness without a pure heart. And how intrusive you are, how you insist and grimace! Lies, lies, lies!"

Of course I have myself made up all the things you say. That, too, is from underground. I have been for forty years listening to you through a crack under the floor. I have invented them myself, there was nothing else I could invent. It is no wonder that I have learned it by heart and it has taken a literary form. . . .

But can you really be so credulous as to think that I will print all this and give it to you to read too? And another problem: why do I call you "gentlemen," why do I address you as though you really were my readers? Such confessions as I intend to make are never printed nor given to other people to read. Anyway, I am not strong-minded enough for that, and I don't see why I should be. But you see a fancy has occurred to me and I want to realize it at all costs. Let me explain.

Every man has reminiscences which he would not tell to every one, but only to his friends. He has other matters in his mind which he would not reveal even to his friends, but only to himself, and that in secret. But there are other things which a man is afraid to tell even to himself, and every decent man has a number of such things stored away in his mind. The more decent he is, the greater the number of such things in his mind. Anyway, I have only lately determined to remember some of my early adventures. Till now I have always avoided them, even with a certain uneasiness. Now, when I am not only recalling them, but have actually decided to write an account of them, I want to try the experiment whether one can, even with oneself, be perfectly open and not take fright at the whole truth. I will observe, in parenthesis, that Heine says that a true autobiography is almost an impossibility, and that man is bound to lie about himself. He considers that Rousseau certainly told lies about himself in his confessions, and even intentionally lied, out of vanity. I am convinced that Heine is right; I quite understand how sometimes one may, out of sheer vanity, attribute regular crimes to oneself, and indeed I can very well conceive that kind of vanity. But Heine judged of people who made their confessions to the public. I write only for myself, and I wish to declare once and for all that if I write as though I were addressing readers, that is simply because it is easier for me to write in that form. It is a form, an empty form—I shall never have readers. I have made this plain already. . . .

I don't wish to be hampered by any restrictions in the compilation of my notes. I shall not attempt any system or method. I will jot things down as I remember them.

But here, perhaps, some one will catch at the word and ask me: if you really don't reckon on readers, why do you make such compacts with yourself—and on paper too—that is, that you won't attempt any system or method, that you jot things down as you remember them, and so on, and so on? Why are you explaining? Why do you apologize?

Well, there it is, I answer.

There is a whole psychology in all this, though. Perhaps it is simply that I am a coward. And perhaps that I purposely imagine an audience before me in order that I may be more dignified while I write. There are perhaps thousands of reasons. Again, what is my object precisely in writing? If it is not for the benefit of the public why should I not simply recall these incidents in my own mind without putting them on paper?

Quite so; but yet it is more imposing on paper. There is something more impressive in it; I shall be better able to criticize myself and improve my style. Besides, I shall perhaps obtain actual relief from writing. To-day, for instance, I am particularly oppressed by one memory of a distant past. It came back vividly to my mind a few days ago, and has remained haunting me like an annoying tune that one cannot get rid of. And yet I must get rid of it somehow. I have hundreds of such reminiscences; but at times some one stands out from the hundred and oppresses me. For some reason I believe that if I write it down I should get rid of it. Why not try?

Besides, I am bored, and I never have anything to do. Writing will be a sort of work. They say work makes man kind-hearted and honest. Well, here is a chance for me, anyway.

Snow is falling to-day, yellow and dingy. It fell yesterday, too, and a few days ago. I fancy it is the wet snow that has reminded me of that incident which I cannot shake off now. And so let it be a story apropos of the falling snow.

Part 2

APROPOS OF THE WET SNOW

When from dark error's subjugation
My words of passionate exhortation
   Had wrenched thy fainting spirit free;
And writhing prone in thine affliction
Thou didst recall with malediction
   The vice that had encompassed thee:
And when thy slumbering conscience, fretting
   By recollection's torturing flame,
Thou didst reveal the hideous setting
   Of thy life's current ere I came:
When suddenly I saw thee sicken,
   And weeping, hide thine anguished face,
Revolted, maddened, horror-stricken,
   At memories of foul disgrace.
                                                NEKRASSOV (*translated by Juliet Soskice*)

[1]

AT THAT time I was only twenty-four. My life was even then gloomy, ill-regulated, and as solitary as that of a savage. I made friends with no one and positively avoided talking, and buried myself more and more in my hole. At work in the office I never looked at any one, and I was perfectly well aware that my companions looked upon me, not only as a queer fellow, but even looked upon me—I always fancied this—with a sort of loathing. I sometimes wondered why it was that nobody except me fancied that he was looked upon with aversion. One of the clerks had a most repulsive, pock-marked face, which looked positively villainous. I believe I should not have dared to look at any one with such an unsightly countenance. Another had such a very dirty old uniform that there was an unpleasant odour in his proximity. Yet not one of these gentlemen showed the slightest self-consciousness—either about their clothes or their countenance or their character in any way. Neither of them ever imagined that they were looked at with repulsion; if they had imagined it they would not have minded—so long as their superiors did not look at them in that way. It is clear to me now that, owing to my unbounded vanity and to the high standard I set for myself, I often looked at myself with furious discontent, which verged on loathing, and so I inwardly attributed the same feeling to every one. I hated my face, for instance: I thought it disgusting, and even suspected that there was something base in my expression, and so every day when I turned up at the office I tried to behave as independently as possible, and to assume a lofty expression, so that I might not be suspected of being abject. "My face may be ugly," I thought, "but let it be lofty, expressive, and, above all, *extremely* intelligent." But I was positively and painfully certain that it was impossible for my countenance ever to express those qualities. And what was worst of all, I thought it actually stupid-looking, and I would have been quite satisfied if I could have looked intelligent. In fact, I would even have put up with looking base if, at the same time, my face could have been thought strikingly intelligent.

Of course, I hated my fellow-clerks one and all, and I despised them all, yet at the same time I was, as it were, afraid of them. In fact, it happened at times that I thought more highly of them than of myself. It somehow happened quite suddenly that I alternated between despising them and thinking them superior to myself. A cultivated and decent man cannot be vain without setting a fearfully high standard for himself, and without despising and almost hating himself at certain moments. But whether I despised them or thought them superior I dropped my eyes almost every time I met any one. I even made experiments whether I could face So-and-So's looking at me, and I was always the first to drop my eyes. This worried me to distraction. I had a sickly dread, too, of being ridiculous, and so had a slavish passion for the conventional in everything external. I loved to fall into the common rut, and had a whole-hearted terror of any kind of eccentricity in myself. But how could I live up to it? I was morbidly sensitive, as a man of our age should be. They were all stupid, and as like one another as so many sheep. Perhaps I was the only one in the office who fancied that I was a coward and a slave, and I fancied it just because I was more highly developed. But it was not only that I fancied it, it really was so. I was a coward and a slave. I say this without the slightest embarrassment. Every decent man of our age must be a coward and a slave. That is his normal condition. Of that I am firmly persuaded. He is made and constructed to that very end. And not only at the present time owing to some casual circumstances, but always, at all times, a decent man is bound to be a coward and a slave. It is the law of nature for all decent people all over the earth. If any one of them happens to be valiant about something, he need not be comforted nor carried away by that; he would show the white feather just the same before something else. That is how it invariably and inevitably ends. Only donkeys and mules are valiant, and they only till they are pushed up to the wall. It is not worth while to pay attention to them, for they really are of no consequence.

Another circumstance, too, worried me in those days: that there was no one like me and I was unlike any one else. "I am alone and they are *every one*," I thought—and pondered.

From that it is evident that I was still a youngster.

The very opposite sometimes happened. It was loathsome sometimes to go to the office; things reached such a point that I often came home ill. But all at once, apropos of nothing, there would come a phase of skepticism and indifference (everything happened in phases to me), and I would laugh myself at my intolerance and fastidiousness, I would reproach myself with being *romantic*. At one time I was unwilling to speak to any one, while at other times I would not only talk, but go to the length of contemplating making friends with them. All my fastidiousness would suddenly, for no rhyme or reason, vanish. Who knows, perhaps I never had really had it, and it had simply been affected, and got out of books. I have not decided that question even now. Once I quite made friends with them, visited their homes, played preference, drank vodka, talked of promotions. . . . But here let me make a digression.

We Russians, speaking generally, have never had those foolish transcendental "romantics"—German, and still more French—on whom nothing produces any effect; if there were an earthquake, if all France perished at the barricades, they would still be the same, they would not even have the decency to affect a change, but would still go on singing their transcendental songs to the hour of their death, because they are fools. We, in Russia, have no fools; that is well known. That is what distinguishes us from foreign lands. Consequently these transcendental natures are not found amongst us in their pure form. The idea that they are is due to our "realistic" journalists and critics of that day, always on the lookout for Kostanzhoglos and Uncle Pyotr Ivanitches and foolishly accepting them as our ideal; they have slandered our romantics, taking them for the same transcendental sort as in Germany or France. On the contrary, the characteristics of our "romantics" are absolutely and directly opposed to the transcendental European type, and no European standard can be applied to them. (Allow me to make use of this word "romantic"—an old-fashioned and much respected word which has done good service and is familiar to all.) The characteristics of our romantics are to understand every-thing, *to see everything and to see it often incomparably more clearly than our most realistic minds see it;* to refuse to accept anyone or any-thing, but at the same time not to despise anything; to give way, to yield, from policy; never to lose sight of a useful practical object (such as rent-free quarters at the government expense, pensions, decora-tions), to keep their eye on that object through all the enthusiasms and volumes of lyrical poems, and at the same time to preserve "the good and the beautiful" inviolate within them to the hour of their death, and to preserve themselves also, incidentally, like some precious jewel wrapped in cotton wool if only for the benefit of "the good and the beautiful." Our "romantic" is a man of great breadth and the greatest rogue of all our rogues, I assure you. . . . I can assure you from experience, indeed. Of course, that is, if he is intelligent. But what am I saying! The romantic is always intelligent, and I only meant to observe that although we have had foolish romantics they don't count, and they were only so because in the flower of their youth they degen-erated into Germans, and to preserve their precious jewel more com-fortably, settled somewhere out there—by preference in Weimar or the Black Forest.

I, for instance, genuinely despised my official work and did not openly abuse it simply because I was in it myself and got a salary for it. Anyway, take note, I did not openly abuse it. Our romantic would rather go out of his mind—a thing, however, which very rarely happens—than take to open abuse, unless he had some other career in view; and he is never kicked out. At most, they would take him to the lunatic asylum as "the King of Spain" if he should go very mad. But it is only the thin, fair people who go out of their minds in Russia. Innumerable "romantics" attain later in life to considerable rank in the service. Their many-sidedness is remarkable! And what a faculty they have for the most contradictory sensations! I was comforted by this thought even in those days, and I am of the same opinion now. That is why there are so many "broad natures" among us who never lose their ideal even in the depths of degradation; and though they never stir a finger for their ideal, though they are arrant thieves and knaves, yet they tearfully cherish their first ideal and are extraordinarily honest at heart. Yes, it is only among us that the most incorrigible rogue can be absolutely and loftily honest at heart without in the least ceasing to be a rogue. I repeat, our romantics, frequently, become such accom-plished rascals (I use the term "rascals" affectionately), suddenly dis-play such a sense of reality and practical knowledge, that their bewildered superiors and the public generally can only ejaculate in amazement.

Their many-sidedness is really amazing, and goodness knows what it may develop into later on, and what the future has in store for us. It is not a poor material! I do not say this from any foolish or boastful patriotism. But I feel sure that you are again imagining that I am joking. Or perhaps it's just the contrary, and you are convinced that I really think so. Anyway, gentlemen, I shall welcome both views as an honour and a special favour. And do forgive my digression.

I did not, of course, maintain friendly relations with my comrades and soon was at loggerheads with them, and in my youth and inexperience I even gave up bowing to them, as though I had cut off all relations. That, however, only happened to me once. As a rule, I was always alone.

In the first place I spent most of my time at home, reading. I tried to stifle all that was continually seething within me by means of external impressions. And the only external means I had was reading. Reading, of course, was a great help—exciting me, giving me pleasure and pain. But at times it bored me fearfully. One longed for movement in spite of everything, and I plunged all at once into dark, underground, loathsome vice of the pettiest kind. My wretched passions were acute, smarting, from my continual, sickly irritability. I had hysterical impulses, with tears and convulsions. I had no resource except reading—that is, there was nothing in my surroundings which I could respect and which attracted me. I was overwhelmed with depression, too; I had an hysterical craving for incongruity and for contrast, and so I took to vice. I have not said all this to justify myself. . . . But, no! I am lying. I did want to justify myself. I make that little observation for my own benefit, gentlemen. I don't want to lie. I vowed to myself I would not.

And so, furtively, timidly, in solitude, at night, I indulged in filthy vice, with a feeling of shame which never deserted me, even at the most loathsome moments, and which at such moments nearly made me curse. Already even then I had my underground world in my soul. I was fearfully afraid of being seen, of being met, of being recognized. I visited various obscure haunts.

One night as I was passing a tavern I saw through a lighted window some gentlemen fighting with billiard cues, and saw one of them thrown out of the window. At other times I should have felt very much disgusted, but I was in such a mood at the time, that I actually envied the gentleman thrown out of the window—and I envied him so much that I even went into the tavern and into the billiard-room. "Perhaps," I thought, "I'll have a fight, too, and they'll throw me out of the window."

I was not drunk—but what is one to do—depression will drive a man to such a pitch of hysteria? But nothing happened. It seemed that I was not even equal to being thrown out of the window and I went away without having my fight.

An officer put me in my place from the first moment.

I was standing by the billiard-table and in my ignorance blocking up the way, and he wanted to pass; he took me by the shoulders and without a word—without a warning or an explanation—moved me from where I was standing to another spot and passed by as though he had not noticed me. I could have forgiven blows, but I could not forgive his having moved me without noticing me.

Devil knows what I would have given for a real regular quarrel —a more decent, a more *literary* one, so to speak. I had been treated like a fly. This officer was over six foot, while I was a spindly little fellow. But the quarrel was in my hands. I had only to protest and I certainly would have been thrown out of the window. But I changed my mind and preferred to beat a resentful retreat.

I went out of the tavern straight home, confused and troubled, and the next night I went out again with the same lewd intentions, still more furtively, abjectly and miserably than before, as it were, with tears in my eyes—but still I did go out again. Don't imagine, though, it was cowardice made me slink away from the officer: I never have been a coward at heart, though I have always been a coward in action. Don't be in a hurry to laugh—I assure you I can explain it all.

Oh, if only that officer had been one of the sort who would consent to fight a duel! But no, he was one of those gentlemen (alas, long extinct!) who preferred fighting with cues, or, like Gogol's Lieutenant Pirogov, appealing to the police. They did not fight duels and would have thought a duel with a civilian like me an utterly unseemly procedure in any case—and they looked upon the duel altogether as something impossible, something free-thinking and French. But they were quite ready to bully, especially when they were over six foot.

I did not slink away through cowardice, but through an unbounded vanity. I was afraid not of his six foot, not of getting a sound thrashing and being thrown out of the window; I should have had physical courage enough, I assure you; but I had not the moral courage. What I was afraid of was that every one present, from the insolent marker down to the lowest little stinking, pimply clerk in a greasy collar, would jeer at me and fail to understand when I began to protest and to address them in literary language. For of the point of honour—not of honour, but of the point of honour *(point d'honneur)*—one cannot speak among us except in literary language. You can't allude to the "point of honour" in ordinary language. I was fully convinced (the sense of reality, in spite of all my romanticism!) that they would all simply split their sides with laughter, and that the officer would not simply beat me, that is, without insulting me, but would certainly prod me in the back with his knee, kick me round the billiard-table, and only then perhaps have pity and drop me out of the window.

Of course, this trivial incident could not with me end in that. I often met that officer afterwards in the street and noticed him very carefully. I am not quite sure whether he recognized me, I imagine not; I judge from certain signs. But I—I stared at him with spite and hatred and so it went on . . . for several years! My resentment grew even deeper with years. At first I began making stealthy inquiries about this officer. It was difficult for me to do so, for I knew no one. But one day I heard some one shout his surname in the street as I was following him at a distance, as though I were tied to him—and so I learnt his surname. Another time I followed him to his flat, and for ten kopecks learnt from the porter where he lived, on which storey, whether he lived alone or with others, and so on—in fact, everything one could learn from a porter. One morning, though I had never tried my hand with the pen, it suddenly occurred to me to write a satire on this officer in the form of a novel which would unmask his villainy. I wrote the novel with relish. I did unmask his villainy, I even exaggerated it; at first I so altered his surname that it could easily be recognized, but on second thoughts I changed it, and sent the story to the *Otetchestvenniya Zapiski*. But at that time such attacks were not the fashion and my story was not printed. That was a great vexation to me.

Sometimes I was positively choked with resentment. At last I determined to challenge my enemy to a duel. I composed a splendid, charming letter to him, imploring him to apologize to me, and hinting rather plainly at a duel in case of refusal. The letter was so composed that if the officer had had the least understanding of the good and the beautiful he would certainly have flung himself on my neck and have offered me his friendship. And how fine that would have been! How we should have got on together! "He could have shielded me with his higher rank, while I could have improved his mind with my culture, and, well . . . my ideas, and all sorts of things might have happened."

Only fancy, this was two years after his insult to me, and my challenge would have been a ridiculous anachronism, in spite of all the ingenuity of my letter in disguising and explaining away the anachronism. But, thank God (to this day I thank the Almighty with tears in my eyes) I did not send the letter to him. Cold shivers run down my back when I think of what might have happened if I had sent it.

And all at once I revenged myself in the simplest way, by a stroke of genius! A brilliant thought suddenly dawned upon me. Sometimes on holidays I used to stroll along the sunny side of the Nevsky about four o'clock in the afternoon. Though it was hardly a stroll so much as a series of innumerable miseries, humiliations and resentments; but no doubt that was just what I wanted. I used to wriggle along in a most unseemly fashion, like an eel, continually moving aside to make way for generals, for officers of the Guards and the Hussars, or for ladies. At such minutes there used to be a convulsive twinge at my heart, and I used to feel hot all down my back at the mere thought of the wretchedness of my attire, of the wretchedness and abjectness of my little scurrying figure. This was a regular martyrdom, a continual, intolerable humiliation at the thought, which passed into an incessant and direct sensation, that I was a mere fly in the eyes of all this world, a nasty, disgusting fly—more intelligent, more highly developed, more refined in feeling than any of them, of course, but a fly that was continually making way for every one, insulted and injured by every one. Why I inflicted this torture upon myself, why I went to the Nevsky, I don't know. I felt simply drawn there at every possible opportunity.

Already then I began to experience a rush of the enjoyment of which I spoke in the first chapter. After my affair with the officer I felt even more drawn there than before: it was on the Nevsky that I met him most frequently, there I could admire him. He, too, went there chiefly on holidays. He, too, turned out of his path for generals and persons of high rank, and he, too, wriggled between them like an eel; but people like me, or even better dressed like me, he simply walked over; he made straight for them as though there was nothing but empty space before him, and never, under any circumstances, turned aside. I gloated over my resentment watching him and . . . always resentfully made way for him. It exasperated me that even in the street I could not be on an even footing with him.

"Why must you invariably be the first to move aside?" I kept asking myself in hysterical rage, waking up sometimes at three o'clock in the morning. "Why is it you and not he? There's no regulation about it;

there's no written law. Let the making way be equal as it usually is when refined people meet: he moves half-way and you move half-way; you pass with mutual respect."

But that never happened, and I always moved aside, while he did not even notice my making way for him. And lo and behold a bright idea dawned upon me! "What," I thought, "if I meet him and don't move on one side? What if I don't move aside on purpose, even if I knock up against him? How would that be?" This audacious idea took such a hold on me that it gave me no peace. I was dreaming of it continually, horribly, and I purposely went more frequently to the Nevsky in order to picture more vividly how I should do it when I did do it. I was delighted. This intention seemed to me more and more practical and possible.

"Of course I shall not really push him," I thought, already more good-natured in my joy. "I will simply not turn aside, will run up against him, not very violently, but just shouldering each other—just as much as decency permits. I will push against him just as much as he pushes against me." At last I made up my mind completely. But my preparations took a great deal of time. To begin with, when I carried out my plan I should need to be looking rather more decent, and so I had to think of my get-up. "In case of emergency, if, for instance, there were any sort of public scandal (and the public there is of the most *recherché:* the Countess walks there; Prince D. walks there; all the literary world is there), I must be well dressed; that inspires respect and of itself puts us on an equal footing in the eyes of society."

With this object I asked for some of my salary in advance, and bought at Tchurkin's a pair of black gloves and a decent hat. Black gloves seemed to me both more dignified and *bon ton* than the lemon-coloured ones which I had contemplated at first. "The colour is too gaudy, it looks as though one were trying to be conspicuous," and I did not take the lemon-coloured ones. I had got ready long beforehand a good shirt, with white bone studs; my overcoat was the only thing that held me back. The coat in itself was a very good one, it kept me warm; but it was wadded and it had a raccoon collar which was the height of vulgarity. I had to change the collar at any sacrifice, and to have a beaver one like an officer's. For this purpose I began visiting the Gostiny Dvor and after several attempts I pitched upon a piece of cheap German beaver. Though these German beavers soon grow shabby and look wretched, yet at first they look exceedingly well, and I only needed it for one occasion. I asked the price; even so, it was too expensive. After thinking it over thoroughly I decided to sell my raccoon collar. The rest of the money—a considerable sum for me, I decided to borrow from Anton Antonitch Syetotchkin, my immediate superior, an unassuming person, though grave and judicious. He never lent money to any one, but I had, on entering the service, been specially recommended to him by an important personage who had got me my berth. I was horribly worried. To borrow from Anton Antonitch seemed to me monstrous and shameful. I did not sleep for two or three nights. Indeed, I did not sleep well at that time, I was in a fever; I had a vague sinking at my heart or else a sudden throbbing, throbbing, throbbing! Anton Antonitch was surprised at first, then he frowned, then he reflected, and did after all lend me the money, receiving from me a written authorization to take from my salary a fortnight later the sum that he had lent me.

In this way everything was at last ready. The handsome beaver replaced the mean-looking raccoon, and I began by degrees to get to work. It would never have done to act off-hand, at random; the plan had to be carried out skilfully, by degrees. But I must confess that after many efforts I began to despair: we simply could not run into each other. I made every preparation, I was quite determined—it seemed as though we should run into one another directly—and before I knew what I was doing I had stepped aside for him again and he had passed without noticing me. I even prayed as I approached him that God would grant me determination. One time I had made up my mind thoroughly, but it ended in my stumbling and falling at his feet because at the very last instant when I was six inches from him my courage failed me. He very calmly stepped over me, while I flew on one side like a ball. That night I was ill again, feverish and delirious.

And suddenly it ended most happily. The night before I had made up my mind not to carry out my fatal plan and to abandon it all, and with that object I went to the Nevsky for the last time, just to see how I would abandon it all. Suddenly, three paces from my enemy, I unexpectedly made up my mind—I closed my eyes, and we ran full tilt, shoulder to shoulder, against one another! I did not budge an inch and passed him on a perfectly equal footing! He did not even look round and pretended not to notice it; but he was only pretending, I am convinced of that. I am convinced of that to this day! Of course, I got the worst of it—he was stronger, but that was not the point. The point was that I had attained my object, I had kept up my dignity, I had not yielded a step, and had put myself publicly on an equal social footing with him. I returned home feeling that I was fully avenged for everything. I was delighted. I was triumphant and sang Italian arias. Of course, I will not describe to you what happened to me three days later; if you have read my first chapter you can guess that for yourself. The officer was afterwards transferred; I have not seen him now for fourteen years. What is the dear fellow doing now? Whom is he walking over?

[II]

But the period of my dissipation would end and I always felt very sick afterwards. It was followed by remorse—I tried to drive it away: I felt too sick. By degrees, however, I grew used to that too. I grew used to everything, or rather I voluntarily resigned myself to enduring it. But I had a means of escape that reconciled everything—that was to find refuge in "the good and the beautiful," in dreams, of course. I was a terrible dreamer, I would dream for three months on end, tucked away in my corner, and you may believe me that at those moments I had no resemblance to the gentleman who, in the perturbation of his chicken heart, put a collar of German beaver on his greatcoat. I suddenly became a hero. I would not have admitted my six-foot lieutenant even if he had called on me. I could not even picture him before me then. What were my dreams and how I could satisfy myself with them, it is hard to say now, but at the time I was satisfied with them. Though, indeed, even now I am to some extent satisfied with them. Dreams were particularly sweet and vivid after a spell of dissipation; they came with remorse and with tears, with curses and transports. There were moments of such positive intoxication, of such happiness, that there was not the faintest trace of irony within me, on my honour. I had faith, hope, love. I believed blindly at such times that by some miracle, by some external circumstance, all this would suddenly open out, expand; that suddenly a vista of suitable activity—beneficent, good, and, above all, *ready-made* (what sort of activity I had no idea, but the great thing was that it should be all ready for me)—would rise up before me, and I should come out into the light of day, almost riding a white horse and crowned with laurel. Anything but the foremost place I could not conceive for myself, and for that very reason I quite contentedly occupied the lowest in reality. Either to be a hero or to grovel in the mud—there was nothing between. That was my ruin, for when I was in the mud I comforted myself with the thought that at other times I was a hero, and the hero was a cloak for the mud: for an ordinary man it was shameful to defile himself, but a hero was too lofty to be utterly defiled, and so he might defile himself.

It is worth noting that these attacks of "the good and the beautiful" visited me even during the period of dissipation and just at the times when I was touching the bottom. They came in separate spurts, as though reminding me of themselves, but did not banish the dissipation by their appearance. On the contrary, they seemed to add a zest to it by contrast, and were only sufficiently present to serve as an appetizing sauce. That sauce was made up of contradictions and sufferings, of agonizing inward analysis, and all these pangs and pin-pricks gave a certain piquancy, even a significance to my dissipation—in fact, completely answered the purpose of an appetizing sauce. There was a certain depth of meaning in it. And I could hardly have resigned myself to the simple, vulgar, direct debauchery of a clerk and have endured all the filthiness of it. What could have allured me about it then and have drawn me at night into the street? No, I had a lofty way of getting out of it all.

And what loving-kindness, oh Lord, what loving-kindness I felt at times in those dreams of mine! in those "flights into the good and the beautiful"; though it was fantastic love, though it was never applied to anything human in reality, yet there was so much of this love that one did not feel afterwards even the impulse to apply it in reality; that would have been superfluous. Everything, however, passed satisfactorily by a lazy and fascinating transition into the sphere of art, that is, into the beautiful forms of life, lying ready, largely stolen from the poets and novelists and adapted to all sorts of needs and uses. I, for instance, was triumphant over every one; every one, of course, was in dust and ashes, and was forced spontaneously to recognize my superiority, and I forgave them all. I was a poet and a grand gentleman, I fell in love; I came in for countless millions and immediately devoted them to humanity, and at the same time I confessed before all the people my shameful deeds, which, of course, were not merely shameful, but had in them much that was "good and beautiful," something in the Manfred style. Every one would kiss me and weep (what idiots they would be if they did not), while I should go barefoot and hungry preaching new ideas and fighting a victorious Austerlitz against the obscurantists. Then the band would play a march, an amnesty would be declared, the Pope would agree to retire from Rome to Brazil; then there would be a ball for the whole of Italy at the Villa Borghese on the shores of Lake Como, Lake Como being for that purpose transferred to the neighbourhood of Rome; then would come a scene in the bushes, and so on, and so on—as though you did not know all about it! You will say that it is vulgar and contemptible to drag all this into public after all the tears and transports which I have myself confessed. But why is it contemptible? Can you imagine that I am ashamed of it all, and that it was stupider than anything in your life, gentlemen? And I can assure you that some of these fancies were by no means badly composed. . . . It did not all happen on the shores of Lake Como. And yet you are right—it really is vulgar and contemptible. And most contemptible of all it is that now I am attempting to justify myself to you. And even more contemptible than that is my making this remark now. But that's enough, or there will be no end to it: each step will be more contemptible than the last. . . .

I could never stand more than three months of dreaming at a time without feeling an irresistible desire to plunge into society. To plunge into society meant to visit my superior at the office, Anton Antonitch Syetotchkin. He was the only permanent acquaintance I have had in my life, and I wonder at the fact myself now. But I only went to see him when that phase came over me, and when my dreams had reached such a point of bliss that it became essential at once to embrace my fellows and all mankind; and for that purpose I needed at least one human being, actually existing. I had to call on Anton Antonitch, however, on Tuesday—his at-home day; so I had always to time my passionate desire to embrace humanity so that it might fall on a Tuesday.

This Anton Antonitch lived on the fourth storey in a house in Five Corners, in four low-pitched rooms, one smaller than the other, of a particularly frugal and sallow appearance. He had two daughters and their aunt, who used to pour out the tea. Of the daughters one was thirteen and another fourteen, they both had snub noses, and I was awfully shy of them because they were always whispering and giggling together. The master of the house usually sat in his study on a leather couch in front of the table with some grey-headed gentleman, usually a colleague from our office or some other department. I never saw more than two or three visitors there, always the same. They talked about the excise duty, about business in the senate, about salaries, about promotions, about His Excellency, and the best means of pleasing him, and so on. I had the patience to sit like a fool beside these people for four hours at a stretch, listening to them without knowing what to say to them or venturing to say a word. I became stupefied, several times I felt myself perspiring, I was overcome by a sort of paralysis; but this was pleasant and good for me. On returning home I deferred for a time my desire to embrace all mankind.

I had, however, one other acquaintance of a sort, Simonov, who was an old schoolfellow. I had a number of schoolfellows indeed in Petersburg, but I did not associate with them and had even given up nodding to them in the street. I believe I had transferred into the depaitment I was in simply to avoid their company and to cut off all connection with my hateful childhood. Curses on that school and all those terrible years of penal servitude! In short, I parted from my schoolfellows as soon as I got out into the world. There were two or three left to whom I nodded in the street. One of them was Simonov, who had been in no way distinguished at school, was of a quiet and equable disposition; but I discovered in him a certain independence of character and even honesty. I don't even suppose that he was particularly stupid. I had at one time spent some rather soulful moments with him, but these had not lasted long and had somehow been suddenly clouded over. He was evidently uncomfortable at these reminiscences, and was, I fancy, always afraid that I might take up the same tone again. I suspected that he had an aversion for me, but still I went on going to see him, not being quite certain of it.

And so on one occasion, unable to endure my solitude and knowing that as it was Thursday Anton Antonitch's door would be closed, I thought of Simonov. Climbing up to his fourth storey I was thinking that the man disliked me and that it was a mistake to go and see him. But as it always happened that such reflections impelled me, as though purposely, to put myself into a false position, I went in. It was almost a year since I had last seen Simonov.

[III]

I found two of my old schoolfellows with him. They seemed to be discussing an important matter. All of them took scarcely any notice of my entrance, which was strange, for I had not met them for years. Evidently they looked upon me as something on the level of a common fly. I had not been treated like that even at school, though they all hated me. I knew, of course, that they must despise me now for my lack of success in the service, and for my having let myself sink so low, going about badly dressed and so on—which seemed to them a sign of my incapacity and insignificance. But I had not expected such contempt. Simonov was positively surprised at my turning up. Even in the old days he had always seemed surprised at my coming. All this disconcerted me: I sat down, feeling rather miserable, and began listening to what they were saying.

They were engaged in warm and earnest conversation about a farewell dinner which they wanted to arrange for the next day to a comrade of theirs called Zverkov, an officer in the army, who was going away to a distant province. This Zverkov had been all the time at school with me too. I had begun to hate him particularly in the upper forms. In the lower forms he had simply been a pretty, playful boy whom everybody liked. I had hated him, however, even in the lower forms, just because he was a pretty and playful boy. He was always bad at his lessons and got worse and worse as he went on; however, he left with a good certificate, as he had powerful interest. During his last year at school he came in for an estate of two hundred serfs, and as almost all of us were poor he took up a swaggering tone among us. He was vulgar in the extreme, but at the same time he was a good-natured fellow, even in his swaggering. In spite of superficial, fantastic and sham notions of honour and dignity, all but very few of us positively grovelled before Zverkov, and the more so the more he swaggered. And it was not from any interested motive that they grovelled, but simply because he had been favoured by the gifts of nature. Moreover, it was, as it were, an accepted idea among us that Zverkov was a specialist in regard to tact and the social graces. This last fact particularly infuriated me. I hated the abrupt self-confident tone of his voice, his admiration of his own witticisms, which were often frightfully stupid, though he was bold in his language; I hated his handsome but stupid face (for which I would, however, have gladly exchanged my intelligent one), and the free-and-easy military manners in fashion in the "forties." I hated the way in which he used to talk of his future conquests of women (he did not venture to begin his attack upon women until he had the epaulettes of an officer, and was looking forward to them with impatience), and boasted of the duels he would constantly be fighting. I remember how I, invariably so taciturn, suddenly fastened upon Zverkov, when one day talking at a leisure moment with his schoolfellows of his future relations with the fair sex, and growing as sportive as a puppy in the sun, he all at once declared that he would not leave a single village girl on his estate unnoticed, that that was his *droit de seigneur,* and that if the peasants dared to protest he would have them all flogged and double the tax on them, the bearded rascals. Our servile rabble applauded, but I attacked him, not from compassion for the girls and their fathers, but simply because they were applauding such an insect. I got the better of him on that occasion, but though Zverkov was stupid he was lively and impudent, and so laughed it off, and in such a way that my victory was not really complete: the laugh was on his side. He got the better of me on several occasions afterwards, but without malice, jestingly, casually. I remained angrily and contemptuously silent and would not answer him. When we left school he made advances to me; I did not rebuff them, for I was flattered, but we soon parted and quite naturally. Afterwards I heard of his barrack-room success as a lieutenant, and of the fast life he was leading. Then there came other rumours—of his successes in the service. By then he had taken to cutting me in the street, and I suspected that he was afraid of compromising himself by greeting a personage as insignificant as I. I saw him once in the theatre, in the third tier of boxes. By then he was wearing shoulder-straps. He was twisting and twirling about, ingratiating himself with the daughters of an ancient general. In three years he had gone off considerably, though he was still rather handsome and adroit. One could see that by the time he was thirty he would be corpulent. So it was to this Zverkov that my schoolfellows were going to give a dinner on his departure. They had kept up with him for those three years, though privately they did not consider themselves on an equal footing with him, I am convinced of that.

Of Simonov's two visitors, one was Ferfitchkin, a Russianized German—a little fellow with the face of a monkey, a blockhead who was always deriding every one, a very bitter enemy of mine from our days in the lower forms—a vulgar, impudent, swaggering fellow, who affected a most sensitive feeling of personal honour, though, of course, he was a wretched little coward at heart. He was one of those worshippers of Zverkov who made up to the latter from interested motives, and often borrowed money from him. Simonov's other visitor, Trudolyubov, was a person in no way remarkable—a tall young fellow, in the army, with a cold face, fairly honest, though he worshipped success of every sort, and was only capable of thinking of promotion. He was some sort of distant relation of Zverkov's, and this, foolish as it seems, gave him a certain importance among us. He always thought me of no consequence whatever; his behaviour to me, though not quite courteous, was tolerable.

"Well, with seven roubles each," said Trudolyubov, "twenty-one roubles between the three of us, we ought to be able to get a good dinner. Zverkov, of course, won't pay."

"Of course not, since we are inviting him," Simonov decided.

"Can you imagine," Ferfitchkin interrupted hotly and conceitedly, like some insolent flunkey boasting of his master the general's decorations, "can you imagine that Zverkov will let us pay alone? He will accept from delicacy, but he will order half a dozen bottles of champagne."

"Do we want half a dozen for the four of us?" observed Trudolyubov, taking notice only of the half-dozen.

"So the three of us, with Zverkov for the fourth, twenty-one roubles, at the Hôtel de Paris at five o'clock to-morrow," Simonov, who had been asked to make the arrangements, concluded finally.

"How twenty-one roubles?" I asked in some agitation, with a show of being offended; "if you count me it will not be twenty-one, but twenty-eight roubles."

It seemed to me that to invite myself so suddenly and unexpectedly would be positively graceful, and that they would all be conquered at once and would look at me with respect.

"Do you want to join, too?" Simonov observed, with no appearance of pleasure, seeming to avoid looking at me. He knew me through and through.

It infuriated me that he knew me so thoroughly.

"Why not? I am an old schoolfellow of his too, I believe, and I must own I feel hurt that you have left me out," I said, boiling over again.

"And where were we to find you?" Ferfitchkin put in roughly.

"You never were on good terms with Zverkov," Trudolyubov added, frowning.

But I had already clutched at the idea and would not give it up.

"It seems to me that no one has a right to form an opinion upon that," I retorted in a shaking voice, as though something tremendous had happened. "Perhaps that is just my reason for wishing it now, that I have not always been on good terms with him."

"Oh, there's no making you out . . . with these refinements," Trudolyubov jeered.

"We'll put your name down," Simonov decided, addressing me. "To-morrow at five o'clock at the Hôtel de Paris."

"What about the money?" Ferfitchkin began in an undertone, indicating me to Simonov, but he broke off, for even Simonov was embarrassed.

"That will do," said Trudolyubov, getting up. "If he wants to come so much, let him."

"But it's a private thing, between us friends," Ferfitchkin said crossly, as he too picked up his hat. "It's not an official gathering."

"We do not want at all, perhaps . . ."

They went away. Ferfitchkin did not greet me in any way as he went out, Trudolyubov barely nodded. Simonov, with whom I was left *tête-à-tête,* was in a state of vexation and perplexity, and looked at me queerly. He did not sit down and did not ask me to.

"H'm . . . yes . . . to-morrow, then. Will you pay your subscription now? I just ask so as to know," he muttered in embarrassment.

I flushed crimson, and as I did so I remembered that I had owed Simonov fifteen roubles for ages—which I had, indeed, never forgotten, though I had not paid it.

"You will understand, Simonov, that I could have no idea when I came here . . . I am very much vexed that I have forgotten. . . ."

"All right, all right, that doesn't matter. You can pay to-morrow after the dinner. I simply wanted to know. . . . Please don't . . ."

He broke off and began pacing the room still more vexed. As he walked he began to stamp with his heels.

"Am I keeping you?" I asked, after two minutes of silence.

"Oh!" he said, starting, "that is—to be truthful—yes. I have to go and see some one . . . not far from here," he added in an apologetic voice, somewhat abashed.

"My goodness, why didn't you say so?" I cried, seizing my cap with an astonishingly free-and-easy air, which was the last thing I should have expected of myself.

"It's close by . . . not two paces away," Simonov repeated, accompanying me to the front door with a fussy air which did not suit him at all. "So five o'clock, punctually, to-morrow," he called down the stairs after me. He was very glad to get rid of me. I was in a fury.

"What possessed me, what possessed me to force myself upon them?" I wondered, grinding my teeth as I strode along the street. "For a scoundrel, a pig like that Zverkov! Of course, I had better not go; of course, I must just snap my fingers at them. I am not bound in any way. I'll send Simonov a note by to-morrow's post. . . ."

But what made me furious was that I knew for certain that I should go, that I should make a point of going; and the more tactless, the more unseemly my going would be, the more certainly I would go.

And there was a positive obstacle to my going: I had no money. All I had was nine roubles, I had to give seven of that to my servant, Apollon, for his monthly wages. That was all I paid him—he had to keep himself.

Not to pay him was impossible, considering his character. But I will talk about that fellow, about that plague of mine, another time.

However, I knew I should go and should not pay him his wages.

That night I had the most hideous dreams. No wonder; all the evening I had been oppressed by memories of my miserable days at

school, and I could not shake them off. I was sent to the school by
distant relations, upon whom I was dependent and of whom I have
heard nothing since—they sent me there a forlorn, silent boy, already
crushed by their reproaches, already troubled by doubt, and looking
with savage distrust at every one. My schoolfellows met me with spiteful and merciless jibes because I was not like any of them. But I could
not endure their taunts; I could not give in to them with the ignoble
readiness with which they gave in to one another. I hated them from
the first, and shut myself away from every one in timid, wounded and
disproportionate pride. Their coarseness revolted me. They laughed
cynically at my face, at my clumsy figure; and yet what stupid faces
they had themselves. In our school the boys' faces seemed in a special
way to degenerate and grow stupider. How many fine-looking boys
came to us! In a few years they became repulsive. Even at sixteen I
wondered at them morosely; even when I was struck by the pettiness
of their thoughts, the stupidity of their pursuits, their games, their
conversations. They had no understanding of such essential things,
they took no interest in such striking, impressive subjects, that I could
not help considering them inferior to myself. It was not wounded
vanity that drove me to it, and for God's sake do not thrust upon me
your hackneyed remarks, repeated to nausea, that "I was only a
dreamer," while they even then had an understanding of life. They
understood nothing, they had no idea of real life, and I swear that
that was what made me most indignant with them. On the contrary,
the most obvious, striking reality they accepted with fantastic stupidity
and even at that time were accustomed to respect success. Everything
that was just, but oppressed and looked down upon, they laughed at
heartlessly and shamefully. They took rank for intelligence; even at
sixteen they were already talking about a snug berth. Of course a
great deal of it was due to their stupidity, to the bad examples with
which they had always been surrounded in their childhood and boyhood. They were monstrously depraved. Of course a great deal of that,
too, was superficial and an assumption of cynicism; of course there
were glimpses of youth and freshness even in their depravity; but even
that freshness was not attractive, and showed itself in a certain rakish-
ness. I hated them horribly, though perhaps I was worse than any of
them. They repaid me in the same way, and did not conceal their
aversion for me. But by then I did not desire their affection: on the
contrary I continually longed for their humiliation. To escape from
their derision I purposely began to make all the progress I could with
my studies and forced my way to the very top. This impressed them.

Moreover, they all began by degrees to grasp that I had already read books none of them could read, and understood things (not forming part of our school curriculum) of which they had not even heard. They took a savage and sarcastic view of it, but were morally impressed, especially as the teachers began to notice me on those grounds. The mockery ceased, but the hostility remained, and cold and strained relations became permanent between us. In the end I could not put up with it: with years a craving for society, for friends, developed in me. I attempted to get on friendly terms with some of my schoolfellows; but somehow or other my intimacy with them was always strained and soon ended of itself. Once, indeed, I did have a friend. But I was already a tyrant at heart; I wanted to exercise unbounded sway over him; I tried to instil into him a contempt for his surroundings; I required of him a disdainful and complete break with those surroundings. I frightened him with my passionate affection; I reduced him to tears, to hysterics. He was a simple and devoted soul; but when he devoted himself to me entirely I began to hate him immediately and repulsed him—as though all I needed him for was to win a victory over him, to subjugate him and nothing else. But I could not subjugate all of them; my friend was not at all like them either, he was, in fact, a rare exception. The first thing I did on leaving school was to give up the special job for which I had been destined so as to break all ties, to curse my past and shake the dust from off my feet. . . . And goodness knows why, after all that, I should go trudging off to Simonov's!

Early next morning I roused myself and jumped out of bed with excitement, as though it were all about to happen at once. But I believed that some radical change in my life was coming, and would inevitably come that day. Owing to its rarity, perhaps, any external event, however trivial, always made me feel as though some radical change in my life were at hand. I went to the office, however, as usual, but sneaked away home two hours earlier to get ready. The great thing, I thought, is not to be the first to arrive, or they will think I am overjoyed at coming. But there were thousands of such great points to consider, and they all agitated and overwhelmed me. I polished my boots a second time with my own hands; nothing in the world would have induced Apollon to clean them twice a day, as he considered that it was more than his duties required of him. I stole the brushes to clean them from the passage, being careful he should not detect it, for fear of his contempt. Then I minutely examined my clothes and thought that everything looked old, worn and threadbare. I had let myself get too slovenly. My uniform, perhaps, was tidy, but I could not go out to dinner in my uniform. The worst of it was that on the knee of my trousers was a big yellow stain. I had a foreboding that that stain would deprive me of nine-tenths of my personal dignity. I knew, too, that it was very poor to think so. "But this is no time for thinking: now I am in for the real thing," I thought, and my heart sank. I knew, too, perfectly well even then, that I was monstrously exaggerating the facts. But how could I help it? I could not control myself and was already shaking with fever. With despair I pictured to myself how coldly and disdainfully that "scoundrel" Zverkov would meet me; with what dull-witted, invincible contempt the blockhead Trudolyubov would look at me; with what impudent rudeness the insect Ferfitchkin would snigger at me in order to curry favour with Zverkov; how completely Simonov would take it all in, and how he would despise me for the abjectness of my vanity and lack of spirit— and, worst of all, how paltry, *unliterary,* commonplace it would all be.

Of course, the best thing would be not to go at all. But that was most impossible of all: if I feel impelled to do anything, I seem to be pitch-forked into it. I should have jeered at myself ever afterwards: "So you funked it, you funked it, you funked the *real thing!"* On the contrary, I passionately longed to show all that "rabble" that I was by no means such a spiritless creature as I seemed to myself. What is more, even in the acutest paroxysm of this cowardly fever, I dreamed of getting the upper hand, of dominating them, carrying them away, making them like me—if only for my "elevation of thought and unmistakable wit." They would abandon Zverkov, he would sit on one side, silent and ashamed, while I should crush him. Then, perhaps, we would be reconciled and drink to our everlasting friendship; but what was most bitter and most humiliating for me was that I knew even then, knew fully and for certain, that I needed nothing of all this really, that I did not really want to crush, to subdue, to attract them, and that I did not care a straw really for the result, even if I did achieve it. Oh, how I prayed for the day to pass quickly! In unutterable anguish I went to the window, opened the movable pane and looked out into the troubled darkness of the thickly falling wet snow. At last my wretched little clock hissed out five. I seized my hat and trying not to look at Apollon, who had been all day expecting his month's wages, but in his foolishness was unwilling to be the first to speak about it, I slipt between him and the door and jumping into a high-class sledge, on which I spent my last half-rouble, I drove up in grand style to the Hôtel de Paris.

[IV]

I had been certain the day before that I should be the first to arrive. But it was not a question of being the first to arrive. Not only were they not there, but I had difficulty in finding our room. The table was not laid even. What did it mean? After a good many questions I elicited from the waiters that the dinner had been ordered not for five, but for six o'clock. This was confirmed at the buffet too. I felt really ashamed to go on questioning them. It was only twenty-five minutes past five. If they changed the dinner hour they ought at least to have let me know—that is what the post is for, and not to have put me in an absurd position in my own eyes and . . . and even before the waiters. I sat down; the servant began laying the table; I felt even more humiliated when he was present. Towards six o'clock they brought in candles, though there were lamps burning in the room. It had not occurred to the waiter, however, to bring them in at once when I arrived. In the next room two gloomy, angry-looking persons were eating their dinners in silence at two different tables. There was a great deal of noise, even shouting, in a room further away; one could hear the laughter of a crowd of people, and nasty little shrieks in French: there were ladies at the dinner. It was sickening, in fact. I rarely passed more unpleasant moments, so much so that when they did arrive all together punctually at six I was overjoyed to see them, as though they were my deliverers, and even forgot that it was incumbent upon me to show resentment.

Zverkov walked in at the head of them; evidently he was the leading spirit. He and all of them were laughing; but, seeing me, Zverkov drew himself up a little, walked up to me deliberately with a slight, rather jaunty bend from the waist. He shook hands with me in a friendly, but not over-friendly, fashion, with a sort of circumspect courtesy like that of a general, as though in giving me his hand he were warding off something. I had imagined, on the contrary, that on coming in he would at once break into his habitual thin, shrill laugh and fall to making his insipid jokes and witticisms. I had been preparing for them ever since the previous day, but I had not expected such condescension, such high-official courtesy. So, then, he felt himself ineffably superior to me in every respect! If he only meant to insult me by that high-official tone, it would not matter, I thought—I could pay him back for it one way or another. But what if, in reality, without the least desire to be offensive, that sheep's-head had a notion in earnest that he was superior to me and could only look at me in a patronizing way? The very supposition made me gasp.

"I was surprised to hear of your desire to join us," he began, lisping and drawling, which was something new. "You and I seem to have seen nothing of one another. You fight shy of us. You shouldn't. We are not such terrible people as you think. Well, anyway, I am glad to renew our acquaintance."

And he turned carelessly to put down his hat on the window sill.

"Have you been waiting long?" Trudolyubov inquired.

"I arrived at five o'clock as you told me yesterday," I answered aloud, with an irritability that threatened an explosion.

"Didn't you let him know that we had changed the hour?" said Trudolyubov to Simonov.

"No, I didn't. I forgot," the latter replied, with no sign of regret, and without even apologizing to me he went off to order the *hors d'œuvres*.

"So you've been here a whole hour? Oh, poor fellow!" Zverkov cried ironically, for to his notions this was bound to be extremely funny. That rascal Ferfitchkin followed with his nasty little snigger like a puppy yapping. My position struck him, too, as exquisitely ludicrous and embarrassing.

"It isn't funny at all!" I cried to Ferfitchkin, more and more irritated. "It wasn't my fault, but other people's. They neglected to let me know. It was . . . it was . . . it was simply absurd."

"It's not only absurd, but something else as well," muttered Trudolyubov, naïvely taking my part. "You are not hard enough upon it. It was simply rudeness—unintentional, of course. And how could Simonov . . . h'm!"

"If a trick like that had been played on me," observed Ferfitchkin, "I should . . ."

"But you should have ordered something for yourself," Zverkov interrupted, "or simply asked for dinner without waiting for us."

"You will allow that I might have done that without your permission," I rapped out. "If I waited, it was . . ."

"Let us sit down, gentlemen," cried Simonov, coming in. "Everything is ready; I can answer for the champagne; it is capitally frozen. . . . You see, I did not know your address, where was I to look for you?" he suddenly turned to me, but again he seemed to avoid looking at me. Evidently he had something against me. It must have been what happened yesterday.

All sat down; I did the same. It was a round table. Trudolyubov was on my left, Simonov on my right. Zverkov was sitting opposite, Ferfitchkin next to him, between him and Trudolyubov.

"Tell me, are you . . . in a government office?" Zverkov went on attending to me. Seeing that I was embarrassed, he seriously thought that he ought to be friendly to me, and, so to speak, cheer me up.

"Does he want me to throw a bottle at his head?" I thought, in a fury. In my novel surroundings I was unnaturally ready to be irritated.

"In the N—— office," I answered jerkily, with my eyes on my plate.

"And ha-ave you a go-od berth? I say, what ma-a-de you leave your original job?"

"What ma-a-de me was that I wanted to leave my original job," I drawled more than he, hardly able to control myself. Ferfitchkin went off into a guffaw. Simonov looked at me ironically. Trudolyubov left off eating and began looking at me with curiosity.

Zverkov winced, but he tried not to notice it.

"And the remuneration?"

"What remuneration?"

"I mean, your sa-a-lary?"

"Why are you cross-examining me?" However, I told him at once what my salary was. I turned horribly red.

"It is not very handsome," Zverkov observed majestically.

"Yes, you can't afford to dine at cafés on that," Ferfitchkin added insolently.

"To my thinking it's very poor," Trudolyubov observed gravely.

"And how thin you have grown! How you have changed!" added Zverkov, with a shade of venom in his voice, scanning me and my attire with a sort of insolent compassion.

"Oh, spare his blushes," cried Ferfitchkin, sniggering.

"My dear sir, allow me to tell you I am not blushing," I broke out at last; "do you hear? I am dining here, at this café, at my own expense, not at other people's—note that, Mr. Ferfitchkin."

"Wha-at? Isn't every one here dining at his own expense? You would seem to be . . ." Ferfitchkin flew out at me, turning as red as a lobster, and looking me in the face with fury.

"Tha-at," I answered, feeling I had gone too far, "and I imagine it would be better to talk of something more intelligent."

"You intend to show off your intelligence, I suppose?"

"Don't disturb yourself, that would be quite out of place here."

"Why are you clacking away like that, my good sir, eh? Have you gone out of your wits in your office?"

"Enough, gentlemen, enough!" Zverkov cried, authoritatively.

"How stupid it is!" muttered Simonov.

"It really is stupid. We have met here, a company of friends, for a farewell dinner to a comrade and you carry on an altercation," said Trudolyubov, rudely addressing himself to me alone. "You invited yourself to join us, so don't disturb the general harmony."

"Enough, enough!" cried Zverkov. "Give over, gentlemen, it's out of place. Better let me tell you how I nearly got married the day before yesterday. . . ."

And then followed a burlesque narrative of how this gentleman had almost been married two days before. There was not a word about the marriage, however, but the story was adorned with generals, colonels and kammer-junkers, while Zverkov almost took the lead among them. It was greeted with approving laughter; Ferfitchkin positively squealed.

No one paid any attention to me, and I sat crushed and humiliated.

"Good heavens, these are not the people for me!" I thought. "And what a fool I have made of myself before them! I let Ferfitchkin go too far, though. The brutes imagine they are doing me an honour in letting me sit down with them. They don't understand that it's an honour to them and not to me! I've grown thinner! My clothes! Oh, damn my trousers! Zverkov noticed the yellow stain on the knee as soon as he came in. . . . But what's the use! I must get up at once, this very minute, take my hat and simply go without a word . . . with contempt! And to-morrow I can send a challenge. The scoundrels! As though I cared about the seven roubles. They may think . . . Damn it! I don't care about the seven roubles. I'll go this minute!"

Of course I remained. I drank sherry and Lafitte by the glassful in my discomfiture. Being unaccustomed to it, I was quickly affected. My annoyance increased as the wine went to my head. I longed all at once to insult them all in a most flagrant manner and then go away. To seize the moment and show what I could do, so that they would say, "He's clever, though he is absurd," and . . . and . . . in fact, damn them all!

I scanned them all insolently with my drowsy eyes. But they seemed to have forgotten me altogether. They were noisy, vociferous, cheerful. Zverkov was talking all the time. I began listening. Zverkov was talking of some exuberant lady whom he had at last led on to declaring her love (of course, he was lying like a horse), and how he had been helped in this affair by an intimate friend of his, a Prince Kolya, an officer in the Hussars, who had three thousand serfs.

"And yet this Kolya, who has three thousand serfs, has not put in an appearance here to-night to see you off," I cut in suddenly.

For a minute every one was silent. "You are drunk already." Trudolyubov deigned to notice me at last, glancing contemptuously in my direction. Zverkov, without a word, examined me as though I were an insect. I dropped my eyes. Simonov made haste to fill up the glasses with champagne.

Trudolyubov raised his glass, as did every one else but me.

"Your health and good luck on the journey!" he cried to Zverkov. "To old times, to our future, hurrah!"

They all tossed off their glasses, and crowded round Zverkov to kiss him. I did not move; my full glass stood untouched before me.

"Why, aren't you going to drink it?" roared Trudolyubov, losing patience and turning menacingly to me.

"I want to make a speech separately, on my own account . . . and then I'll drink it, Mr. Trudolyubov."

"Spiteful brute!" muttered Simonov. I drew myself up in my chair and feverishly seized my glass, prepared for something extraordinary, though I did not know myself precisely what I was going to say.

"Silence!" cried Ferfitchkin. "Now for a display of wit!"

Zverkov waited very gravely, knowing what was coming.

"Mr. Lieutenant Zverkov," I began, "let me tell you that I hate phrases, phrasemongers and men in corsets . . . that's the first point, and there is a second one to follow it."

There was a general stir.

"The second point is: I hate ribaldry and ribald talkers. Especially ribald talkers! The third point: I love justice, truth and honesty." I went on almost mechanically, for I was beginning to shiver with horror myself and had no idea how I came to be talking like this. "I love thought, Monsieur Zverkov; I love true comradeship, on an equal footing and not . . . H'm . . . I love . . . But, however, why not? I will drink your health, too, Mr. Zverkov. Seduce the Circassian girls, shoot the enemies of the fatherland and . . . and . . . to your health, Monsieur Zverkov!"

Zverkov got up from his seat, bowed to me and said:

"I am very much obliged to you." He was frightfully offended and turned pale.

"Damn the fellow!" roared Trudolyubov, bringing his fist down on the table.

"Well, he wants a punch in the face for that," squealed Ferfitchkin.

"We ought to turn him out." muttered Simonov.

"Not a word, gentlemen, not a movement!" cried Zverkov solemnly, checking the general indignation. "I thank you all, but I can show him for myself how much value I attach to his words."

"Mr. Ferfitchkin, you will give me satisfaction to-morrow for your words just now!" I said aloud, turning with dignity to Ferfitchkin.

"A duel, you mean? Certainly," he answered. But probably I was so ridiculous as I challenged him and it was so out of keeping with my appearance that everyone, including Ferfitchkin, was prostrate with laughter.

"Yes, let him alone, of course! He is quite drunk," Trudolyubov said with disgust.

"I shall never forgive myself for letting him join us," Simonov muttered again.

"Now is the time to throw a bottle at their heads," I thought to myself. I picked up the bottle . . . and filled my glass. . . . "No, I'd better sit on to the end," I went on thinking; "you would be pleased, my friends, if I went away. Nothing will induce me to go. I'll go on sitting here and drinking to the end, on purpose, as a sign that I don't think you of the slightest consequence. I will go on sitting and drinking, because this is a public-house and I paid my entrance money. I'll sit here and drink, for I look upon you as so many pawns, as inanimate pawns. I'll sit here and drink . . . and sing if I want to, yes, sing, for I have the right to . . . to sing . . . H'm!"

But I did not sing. I simply tried not to look at any of them. I assumed most unconcerned attitudes and waited with impatience for them to speak *first*. But alas, they did not address me! And oh, how I wished, how I wished at that moment to be reconciled to them! It struck eight, at last nine. They moved from the table to the sofa. Zverkov stretched himself on a lounge and put one foot on a round table. Wine was brought there. He did, as a fact, order three bottles on his own account. I, of course, was not invited to join them. They all sat round him on the sofa. They listened to him, almost with reverence. It was evident that they were fond of him. "What for? What for?" I wondered. From time to time they were moved to drunken enthusiasm and kissed each other. They talked of the Caucasus, of the nature of true passion, of snug berths in the service, of the income of an hussar called Podharzhevsky, whom none of them knew personally, and rejoiced in the largeness of it, of the extraordinary grace and beauty of a Princess D., whom none of them had ever seen; then it came to Shakespeare's being immortal.

I smiled contemptuously and walked up and down the other side of

the room, opposite the sofa, from the table to the stove and back again.
I tried my very utmost to show them that I could do without them, and
yet I purposely made a noise with my boots, thumping with my heels.
But it was all in vain. They paid no attention. I had the patience to
walk up and down in front of them from eight o'clock till eleven, in
the same place, from the table to the stove and back again. "I walk up
and down to please myself and no one can prevent me." The waiter
who came into the room stopped, from time to time, to look at me. I
was somewhat giddy from turning round so often; at moments it
seemed to me that I was in delirium. During those three hours I was
three times soaked with sweat and dry again. At times, with an
intense, acute pang I was stabbed to the heart by the thought that ten
years, twenty years, forty years would pass, and that even in forty
years I would remember with loathing and humiliation those filthiest,
most ludicrous, and most awful moments of my life. No one could
have gone out of his way to degrade himself more shamelessly, and
I fully realized it, fully, and yet I went on pacing up and down from
the table to the stove. "Oh, if you only knew what thoughts and
feelings I am capable of, how cultured I am!" I thought at moments,
mentally addressing the sofa on which my enemies were sitting. But
my enemies behaved as though I were not in the room. Once—only
once—they turned towards me, just when Zverkov was talking about
Shakespeare, and I suddenly gave a contemptuous laugh. I laughed in
such an affected and disgusting way that they all at once broke off
their conversation, and silently and gravely for two minutes watched
me walking up and down from the table to the stove, *taking no notice
of them.* But nothing came of it: they said nothing, and two minutes
later they ceased to notice me again. It struck eleven.

"Friends," cried Zverkov getting up from the sofa, "let us all be off
now, *there!*"

"Of course, of course," the others assented. I turned sharply to
Zverkov. I was so harassed, so exhausted, that I would have cut my
throat to put an end to it. I was in a fever; my hair, soaked with
perspiration, stuck to my forehead and temples.

"Zverkov, I beg your pardon," I said abruptly and resolutely.
"Ferfitchkin, yours too, and every one's, every one's: I have insulted
you all!"

"Aha! A duel is not in your line, old man," Ferfitchkin hissed
venomously.

It sent a sharp pang to my heart.

"No, it's not the duel I am afraid of, Ferfitchkin! I am ready to fight you to-morrow, after we are reconciled. I insist upon it, in fact, and you cannot refuse. I want to show you that I am not afraid of a duel. You shall fire first and I shall fire into the air."

"He is comforting himself," said Simonov.

"He's simply raving," said Trudolyubov.

"But let us pass. Why are you barring our way? What do you want?" Zverkov answered disdainfully.

They were all flushed; their eyes were bright: they had been drinking heavily.

"I ask for your friendship, Zverkov; I insulted you, but . . ."

"Insulted? *You* insulted *me?* Understand, sir, that you never, under any circumstances, could possibly insult *me.*"

"And that's enough for you. Out of the way!" concluded Trudolyubov.

"Olympia is mine, friends, that's agreed!" cried Zverkov.

"We won't dispute your right, we won't dispute your right," the others answered, laughing.

I stood as though spat upon. The party went noisily out of the room. Trudolyubov struck up some stupid song. Simonov remained behind for a moment to tip the waiters. I suddenly went up to him.

"Simonov! give me six roubles!" I said, with desperate resolution.

He looked at me in extreme amazement, with vacant eyes. He, too, was drunk.

"You don't mean you are coming with us?"

"Yes."

"I've no money," he snapped out, and with a scornful laugh he went out of the room.

I clutched at his overcoat. It was a nightmare.

"Simonov, I saw you had money. Why do you refuse me? Am I a scoundrel? Beware of refusing me: if you knew, if you knew why I am asking! My whole future, my whole plans depend upon it!"

Simonov pulled out the money and almost flung it at me.

"Take it, if you have no sense of shame!" he pronounced pitilessly, and ran to overtake them.

I was left for a moment alone. Disorder, the remains of dinner, a broken wine-glass on the floor, spilt wine, cigarette ends, fumes of drink and delirium in my brain, an agonizing misery in my heart and finally the waiter, who had seen and heard all and was looking inquisitively into my face.

"I am going there!" I cried. "Either they shall all go down on their knees to beg for my friendship, or I will give Zverkov a slap in the face!"

[v]

"So this is it, this is it at last—contact with real life," I muttered as I ran headlong downstairs. "This is very different from the Pope's leaving Rome and going to Brazil, very different from the ball on the shores of Lake Como!"

"You are a scoundrel," a thought flashed through my mind, "if you laugh at this now."

"No matter!" I cried, answering myself. "Now everything is lost!"

There was no trace to be seen of them, but that made no difference— I knew where they had gone.

At the steps was standing a solitary night sledge-driver in a rough peasant coat, powdered over with the still falling, wet, and as it were warm, snow. It was hot and steamy. The little shaggy piebald horse was also covered with snow and coughing, I remember that very well. I made a rush for the roughly made sledge; but as soon as I raised my foot to get into it, the recollection of how Simonov had just given me six roubles seemed to double me up and I tumbled into the sledge like a sack.

"No, I must do a great deal to make up for all that," I cried. "But I will make up for it or perish on the spot this very night. Start!"

We set off. There was a perfect whirl in my head.

"They won't go down on their knees to beg for my friendship. That is a mirage, cheap mirage, revolting, romantic and fantastical—that's another ball at Lake Como. And so I am bound to slap Zverkov's face! It is my duty to. And so it is settled; I am flying to give him a slap in the face. Hurry up!"

The driver tugged at the reins.

"As soon as I go in I'll give it him. Ought I before giving him the slap to say a few words by way of preface? No. I'll simply go in and give it him. They will all be sitting in the drawing-room, and he with Olympia on the sofa. That damned Olympia! She laughed at my looks on one occasion and refused me. I'll pull Olympia's hair, pull Zverkov's ears! No, better one ear, and pull him by it round the room. Maybe they will all begin beating me and will kick me out. That's most likely, indeed. No matter! Anyway, I shall first slap him; the initiative will be mine; and by the laws of honour that is everything: he will be branded and cannot wipe off the slap by any blows, by nothing but a duel. He will be forced to fight. And let them beat me now. Let them, the ungrateful wretches! Trudolyubov will beat me hardest, he is so strong; Ferfitchkin will be sure to catch hold sideways and tug at my hair. But no matter, no matter! That's what I am going for. The blockheads will be forced at last to see the tragedy of it all! When they drag me to the door I shall call out to them that in reality they are not worth my little finger. Get on, driver, get on!" I cried to the driver. He started and flicked his whip, I shouted so savagely.

"We shall fight at daybreak, that's a settled thing. I've done with the office. Ferfitchkin made a joke about it just now. But where can I get pistols? Nonsense! I'll get my salary in advance and buy them. And powder, and bullets? That's the second's business. And how can it all be done by daybreak? And where am I to get a second? I have no friends. Nonsense!" I cried, lashing myself up more and more. "It's of no consequence! the first person I meet in the street is bound to be my second, just as he would be bound to pull a drowning man out of water. The most eccentric things may happen. Even if I were to ask the Director himself to be my second to-morrow, he would be bound to consent, if only from a feeling of chivalry, and to keep the secret! Anton Antonitch. . . ."

The fact is, that at that very minute the disgusting absurdity of my plan and the other side of the question was clearer and more vivid to my imagination than it could be to any one on earth. But . . .

"Get on, driver, get on, you rascal, get on!"

"Ugh, sir!" said the son of toil.

Cold shivers suddenly ran down me. Wouldn't it be better . . . to go straight home? My God, my God! Why did I invite myself to this dinner yesterday? But no, it's impossible. And my walking up and down for three hours from the table to the stove? No, they, they and no one else must pay for my walking up and down! They must wipe out this dishonour! Drive on!

And what if they give me into custody? They won't dare! They'll be afraid of the scandal. And what if Zverkov is so contemptuous that he refuses to fight a duel? He is sure to; but in that case I'll show them . . . I will turn up at the posting station when he is setting off to-morrow, I'll catch him by the leg, I'll pull off his coat when he gets into the carriage. I'll get my teeth into his hand, I'll bite him. "See what lengths you can drive a desperate man to!" He may hit me on the head and they may belabour me from behind. I will shout to the assembled multitude: "Look at this young puppy who is driving off to captivate the Circassian girls after letting me spit in his face!"

Of course, after that everything will be over! The office will have vanished off the face of the earth. I shall be arrested, I shall be tried, I shall be dismissed from the service, thrown in prison, sent to Siberia. Never mind! In fifteen years when they let me out of prison I will trudge off to him, a beggar, in rags. I shall find him in some provincial town. He will be married and happy. He will have a grown-up daughter. . . . I shall say to him: "Look, monster, at my hollow cheeks and my rags! I've lost everything—my career, my happiness, art, science, *the woman I loved,* and all through you. Here are pistols. I have come to discharge my pistol and . . . and I . . . forgive you. Then I shall fire into the air and he will hear nothing more of me. . . .

I was actually on the point of tears, though I knew perfectly well at that moment that all this was out of Pushkin's *Silvio* and Lermontov's *Masquerade.* And all at once I felt horribly ashamed, so ashamed that I stopped the horse, got out of the sledge, and stood still in the snow in the middle of the street. The driver gazed at me, sighing and astonished.

What was I to do? I could not go on there—it was evidently stupid, and I could not leave things as they were, because that would seem as though . . . Heavens, how could I leave things! And after such insults! "No!" I cried, throwing myself into the sledge again. "It is ordained! It is fate! Drive on, drive on!"

And in my impatience I punched the sledge-driver on the back of the neck.

"What are you up to? What are you hitting me for?" the peasant shouted, but he whipped up his nag so that it began kicking.

The wet snow was falling in big flakes; I unbuttoned myself, regardless of it. I forgot everything else, for I had finally decided on the slap, and felt with horror that it was going to happen *now, at once,* and that *no force could stop it.* The deserted street lamps gleamed sullenly in the snowy darkness like torches at a funeral. The snow drifted under my greatcoat, under my coat, under my cravat, and melted there. I did not wrap myself up—all was lost, anyway.

At last we arrived. I jumped out, almost unconscious, ran up the steps and began knocking and kicking at the door. I felt fearfully weak, particularly in my legs and my knees. The door was opened quickly as though they knew I was coming. As a fact, Simonov had warned them that perhaps another gentleman would arrive, and this was a place in which one had to give notice and to observe certain precautions. It was one of those "millinery establishments" which were abolished by the police a good time ago. By day it really was a shop;

but at night, if one had an introduction, one might visit it for other purposes.

I walked rapidly through the dark shop into the familiar drawing-room, where there was only one candle burning, and stood still in amazement: there was no one there. "Where are they?" I asked somebody. But by now, of course, they had separated. Before me was standing a person with a stupid smile, the "madam" herself, who had seen me before. A minute later a door opened and another person came in.

Taking no notice of anything, I strode about the room, and, I believe, I talked to myself. I felt as though I had been saved from death and was conscious of this, joyfully, all over: I should have given that slap, I should certainly, certainly have given it! But now they were not here and . . . everything had vanished and changed! I looked round. I could not realize my condition yet. I looked mechanically at the girl who had come in: and had a glimpse of a fresh, young, rather pale face, with straight, dark eyebrows, and with grave, as it were wondering, eyes that attracted me at once; I should have hated her if she had been smiling. I began looking at her more intently and, as it were, with effort. I had not fully collected my thoughts. There was something simple and good-natured in her face, but something strangely grave. I am sure that this stood in her way here, and no one of those fools had noticed her. She could not, however, have been called a beauty, though she was tall, strong-looking, and well built. She was very simply dressed. Something loathsome stirred within me. I went straight up to her.

I chanced to look into the glass. My harassed face struck me as revolting in the extreme, pale, angry, abject, with dishevelled hair. "No matter, I am glad of it," I thought; "I am glad that I shall seem repulsive to her; I like that."

[VI]

. . . Somewhere behind a screen a clock began wheezing, as though oppressed by something, as though some one were strangling it. After an unnaturally prolonged wheezing there followed a shrill, nasty, and as it were unexpectedly rapid, chime—as though some one were suddenly jumping forward. It struck two. I woke up, though I had indeed not been asleep but lying half-conscious.

It was almost completely dark in the narrow, cramped, low-pitched room, cumbered up with an enormous wardrobe and piles of cardboard boxes and all sorts of frippery and litter. The candle end that had been burning on the table was going out and gave a faint flicker from time to time. In a few minutes there would be complete darkness.

I was not long in coming to myself; everything came back to my mind at once, without an effort, as though it had been in ambush to pounce upon me again. And, indeed, even while I was unconscious a point seemed continually to remain in my memory unforgotten, and round it my dreams moved drearily. But strange to say, everything that had happened to me in that day seemed to me now, on waking, to be in the far, far away past, as though I had long, long ago lived all that down.

My head was full of fumes. Something seemed to be hovering over me, rousing me, exciting me, and making me restless. Misery and spite seemed surging up in me again and seeking an outlet. Suddenly I saw beside me two wide-open eyes scrutinizing me curiously and persistently. The look in those eyes was coldly detached, sullen, as it were utterly remote; it weighed upon me.

A grim idea came into my brain and passed all over my body, as a horrible sensation, such as one feels when one goes into a damp and mouldy cellar. There was something unnatural in those two eyes, beginning to look at me only now. I recalled, too, that during those two hours I had not said a single word to this creature, and had, in fact, considered it utterly superfluous; in fact, the silence had for some reason gratified me. Now I suddenly realized vividly the hideous idea —revolting as a spider—of vice, which, without love, grossly and shamelessly begins with that in which true love finds its consummation. For a long time we gazed at each other like that, but she did not drop her eyes before mine and her expression did not change, so that at last I felt uncomfortable.

"What is your name?" I asked abruptly, to put an end to it.

"Liza," she answered almost in a whisper, but somehow far from graciously, and she turned her eyes away.

I was silent.

"What weather! The snow . . . it's disgusting!" I said, almost to myself, putting my arm under my head despondently, and gazing at the ceiling.

She made no answer. This was horrible.

"Have you always lived in Petersburg?" I asked a minute later, almost angrily, turning my head slightly towards her.

"No."

"Where do you come from?"

"From Riga," she answered reluctantly.

"Are you a German?"

"No, Russian."

"Have you been here long?"

"Where?"

"In this house?"

"A fortnight."

She spoke more and more jerkily. The candle went out; I could no longer distinguish her face.

"Have you a father and mother?"

"Yes . . . no . . . I have."

"Where are they?"

"There . . . in Riga."

"What are they?"

"Oh, nothing."

"Nothing? Why, what class are they?"

"Tradespeople."

"Have you always lived with them?"

"Yes."

"How old are you?"

"Twenty."

"Why did you leave them?"

"Oh, for no reason."

That answer meant "Let me alone; I feel sick, sad."

We were silent.

God knows why I did not go away. I felt myself more and more sick and dreary. The images of the previous day began of themselves, apart from my will, flitting through my memory in confusion. I suddenly recalled something I had seen that morning when, full of anxious thoughts, I was hurrying to the office.

"I saw them carrying a coffin out yesterday and they nearly dropped it," I suddenly said aloud, not that I desired to open the conversation, but as it were by accident.

"A coffin?"

"Yes, in the Haymarket; they were bringing it up out of a cellar."

"From a cellar?"

"Not from a cellar, but from a basement. Oh, you know . . . down below . . . from a house of ill-fame. It was filthy all round . . . Eggshells, litter . . . a stench. It was loathsome."

Silence.

"A nasty day to be buried," I began, simply to avoid being silent.

"Nasty, in what way?"

"The snow, the wet." (I yawned.)

"It makes no difference," she said suddenly, after a brief silence.

"No, it's horrid." (I yawned again.) "The grave-diggers must have sworn at getting drenched by the snow. And there must have been water in the grave."

"Why water in the grave?" she asked, with a sort of curiosity, but speaking even more harshly and abruptly than before.

I suddenly began to feel provoked.

"Why, there must have been water at the bottom a foot deep. You can't dig a dry grave in Volkovo Cemetery."

"Why?"

"Why? Why, the place is waterlogged. It's a regular marsh. So they bury them in water. I've seen it myself . . . many times."

(I had never seen it once, indeed I had never been in Volkovo, and had only heard stories of it.)

"Do you mean to say you don't mind how you die?"

"But why should I die?" she answered, as though defending herself.

"Why, some day you will die, and you will die just the same as that dead woman. She was . . . a girl like you. She died of consumption."

"A wench would have died in a hospital. . . ." (She knows all about it already: she said "wench," not "girl.")

"She was in debt to her madam," I retorted, more and more provoked by the discussion; "and went on earning money for her up to the end, though she was in consumption. Some sledge-drivers standing by were talking about her to some soldiers and telling them so. No doubt they knew her. They were laughing. They were going to meet in a pot-house to drink to her memory."

A great deal of this was my invention. Silence followed, profound silence. She did not stir.

"And is it better to die in a hospital?"

"Isn't it just the same? Besides, why should I die?" she added irritably.

"If not now, a little later."

"Why a little later?"

"Why, indeed? Now you are young, pretty, fresh, you fetch a high price. But after another year of this life you will be very different—you will go off."

"In a year?"

"Anyway, in a year you will be worth less," I continued malignantly. "You will go from here to something lower, another house; a year later —to a third, lower and lower, and in seven years you will come to a basement in the Haymarket. That will be if you were lucky. But it would be much worse if you got some disease, consumption, say . . . and caught a chill, or something or other. It's not easy to get over an illness in your way of life. If you catch anything you may not get rid of it. And so you would die."

"Oh, well, then I shall die," she answered, quite vindictively, and she made a quick movement.

"But one is sorry."

"Sorry for whom?"

"Sorry for life."

Silence.

"Have you been engaged to be married? Eh?"

"What's that to you?"

"Oh, I am not cross-examining you. It's nothing to me. Why are you so cross? Of course you may have had your own troubles. What is it to me? It's simply that I felt sorry."

"Sorry for whom?"

"Sorry for you."

"No need," she whispered hardly audibly, and again made a faint movement.

That incensed me at once. What! I was so gentle with her, and she . . .

"Why, do you think that you are on the right path?"

"I don't think anything."

"That's what's wrong, that you don't think. Realize it while there is still time. There still is time. You are still young, good-looking; you might love, be married, be happy. . . ."

"Not all married women are happy," she snapped out in the rude ⌐brupt tone she had used at first.

"Not all, of course, but anyway it is much better than the life here. Infinitely better. Besides, with love one can live even without happiness. Even in sorrow life is sweet; life is sweet, however one lives. But here what is there but . . . foulness. Phew!"

I turned away with disgust; I was no longer reasoning coldly. I began to feel myself what I was saying and warmed to the subject. I was already longing to expound the cherished ideas I had brooded over in my corner. Something suddenly flared up in me. An object had appeared before me.

"Never mind my being here, I am not an example for you. I am, perhaps, worse than you are. I was drunk when I came here, though," I hastened, however, to say in self-defence. "Besides, a man is no example for a woman. It's a different thing. I may degrade and defile myself, but I am not any one's slave. I come and go, and that's an end of it. I shake it off, and I am a different man. But you are a slave from the start. Yes, a slave! You give up everything, your whole freedom. If you want to break your chains afterwards, you won't be able to: you will be more and more fast in the snares. It is an accursed bondage. I know it. I won't speak of anything else, maybe you won't understand, but tell me: no doubt you are in debt to your madam? There, you see," I added, though she made no answer, but only listened in silence, entirely absorbed, "that's a bondage for you! You will never buy your freedom. They will see to that. It's like selling your soul to the Devil. . . . And besides . . . perhaps I, too, am just as unlucky— how do you know—and wallow in the mud on purpose, out of misery? You know, men take to drink from grief; well, maybe I am here from grief. Come, tell me, what is there good here? Here you and I . . . came together . . . just now and did not say one word to one another all the time, and it was only afterwards you began staring at me like a wild creature, and I at you. Is that loving? Is that how one human being should meet another? It's hideous, that's what it is!"

"Yes!" she assented sharply and hurriedly.

I was positively astounded by the promptitude of this "Yes." So the same thought may have been straying through her mind when she was staring at me just before. So she, too, was capable of certain thoughts? "Damn it all, this was interesting, this was a point of likeness!" I thought, almost rubbing my hands. And indeed it's easy to turn a young soul like that!

It was the exercise of my power that attracted me most.

She turned her head nearer to me, and it seemed to me in the darkness that she propped herself on her arm. Perhaps she was scrutinizing me. How I regretted that I could not see her eyes. I heard her deep breathing.

"Why have you come here?" I asked her, with a note of authority already in my voice.

"Oh, I don't know."

"But how nice it would be to be living in your father's house! It's warm and free; you have a home of your own."

"But what if it's worse than this?"

"I must take the right tone," flashed through my mind. "I may not get far with sentimentality." But it was only a momentary thought. I swear she really did interest me. Besides, I was exhausted and moody. And cunning so easily goes hand in hand with feeling.

"Who denies it!" I hastened to answer. "Anything may happen. I am convinced that some one has wronged you, and that you are more sinned against than sinning. Of course, I know nothing of your story, but it's not likely a girl like you has come here of her own inclination. . . ."

"A girl like me?" she whispered, hardly audibly; but I heard it.

Damn it all, I was flattering her. That was horrid. But perhaps it was a good thing. . . . She was silent.

"See, Liza, I will tell you about myself. If I had had a home from childhood, I shouldn't be what I am now. I often think that. However bad it may be at home, anyway they are your father and mother, and not enemies, strangers. Once a year at least, they'll show their love of you. Anyway, you know you are at home. I grew up without a home; and perhaps that's why I've turned so . . . unfeeling."

I waited again. "Perhaps she doesn't understand," I thought, "and, indeed, it is absurd—it's moralizing."

"If I were a father and had a daughter, I believe I should love my daughter more than my sons, really," I began indirectly, as though talking of something else, to distract her attention. I must confess I blushed.

"Why so?" she asked.

Ah! so she was listening!

"I don't know, Liza. I knew a father who was a stern, austere man, but used to go down on his knees to his daughter, used to kiss her hands, her feet, he couldn't make enough of her, really. When she danced at parties he used to stand for five hours at a stretch, gazing at her. He was mad over her: I understand that! She would fall asleep tired at night, and he would wake to kiss her in her sleep and make the sign of the cross over her. He would go about in a dirty old coat, he was stingy to every one else, but would spend his last penny for her, giving her expensive presents, and it was his greatest delight when she was pleased with what he gave her. Fathers always love their daughters more than the mothers do. Some girls live happily at home! And I believe I should never let my daughters marry."

"What next?" she said, with a faint smile.

"I should be jealous, I really should. To think that she should kiss any one else! That she should love a stranger more than her father! It's painful to imagine it. Of course, that's all nonsense, of course every father would be reasonable at last. But I believe before I should let her marry, I should worry myself to death; I should find fault with all her suitors. But I should end by letting her marry whom she herself loved. The one whom the daughter loves always seems the worst to the father, you know. That is always so. So many family troubles come from that."

"Some are glad to sell their daughters, rather than marrying them honourably."

Ah, so that was it!

"Such a thing, Liza, happens in those accursed families in which there is neither love nor God," I retorted warmly, "and where there is no love, there is no sense either. There are such families, it's true, but I am not speaking of them. You must have seen wickedness in your own family, if you talk like that. Truly, you must have been unlucky. H'm! . . . that sort of thing mostly comes about through poverty."

"And is it any better with the gentry? Even among the poor, honest people live happily."

"H'm . . . yes. Perhaps. Another thing, Liza, man is fond of reckoning up his troubles, but does not count his joys. If he counted them up as he ought, he would see that every lot has enough happiness provided for it. And what if all goes well with the family, if the blessing of God is upon it, if the husband is a good one, loves you, cherishes you, never leaves you! There is happiness in such a family! Even sometimes there is happiness in the midst of sorrow; and indeed sorrow is everywhere. If you marry *you will find out for yourself.* But think of the first years of married life with one you love: what happiness, what happiness there sometimes is in it! And indeed it's the ordinary thing. In those early days even quarrels with one's husband end happily. Some women get up quarrels with their husbands just because they love them. Indeed, I knew a woman like that: she seemed to say that because she loved him, she would torment him and make him feel it. You know that you may torment a man on purpose through love. Women are particularly given to that, thinking to themselves 'I will love him so, I will make so much of him afterwards, that it's no sin to torment him a little now.' And all in the house rejoice in the sight of you, and you are happy and gay and peaceful and honourable. . . . Then there are some women who are jealous. If he went off anywhere—I knew one such woman, she couldn't restrain herself, but would jump up at night and run off on the sly to find out where he was, whether he was with some other woman. That's a pity.

"And the woman knows herself it's wrong, and her heart fails her and she suffers, but she loves—it's all through love. And how sweet it is to make it up after quarrels, to own herself in the wrong or to forgive him! And they are both so happy all at once—as though they had met anew, been married over again; as though their love had begun afresh. And no one, no one should know what passes between husband and wife if they love one another. And whatever quarrels there may be between them they ought not to call in their own mothers to judge between them and tell tales of one another. They are their own judges.

"Love is a holy mystery and ought to be hidden from all other eyes, whatever happens. That makes it holier and better. They respect one another more, and much is built on respect. And if once there has been love, if they have been married for love, why should love pass away? Surely one can keep it! It is rare that one cannot keep it. And if the husband is kind and straightforward, why should not love last? The first phase of married love will pass, it is true, but then there will come a love that is better still. Then there will be the union of souls, they will have everything in common, there will be no secrets between them.

"And once they have children, the most difficult times will seem to them happy, so long as there is love and courage. Even toil will be a joy, you may deny yourself bread for your children and even that will be a joy. They will love you for it afterwards; so you are laying by for your future. As the children grow up you feel that you are an example, a support for them; that even after you die your children will always keep your thoughts and feelings, because they have received them from you, they will take on your semblance and likeness. So you see this is a great duty. How can it fail to draw the father and mother nearer? People say it's a trial to have children. Who says that? It is heavenly happiness! Are you fond of little children, Liza? I am awfully fond of them. You know—a little rosy baby boy at your bosom, and what husband's heart is not touched, seeing his wife nursing his child! A plump little rosy baby, sprawling and snuggling, chubby little hands and feet, clean tiny little nails, so tiny that it makes one laugh to look at them; eyes that look as if they understand everything. And while it sucks it clutches at your bosom with its little hand, plays. When its father comes up, the child tears itself away from the bosom, flings itself back, looks at its father, laughs, as though it were fearfully funny, and falls to sucking again. Or it will bite its mother's breast when its little teeth are coming, while it looks sideways at her with its little eyes as though to say, 'Look, I am biting!' Is not all that happiness when they are the three together, husband, wife and child? One can forgive a great deal for the sake of such moments. Yes, Liza, one must first learn to live oneself before one blames others!"

"It's by pictures, pictures like that one must get at you," I thought to myself, though I did speak with real feeling, and all at once I

198 The Short Novels of Dostoevsky

flushed crimson. "What if she were suddenly to burst out laughing, what should I do then?" That idea drove me to fury. Towards the end of my speech I really was excited, and now my vanity was somehow wounded. The silence continued. I almost nudged her.

"Why are you . . ." she began and stopped. But I understood: there was a quiver of something different in her voice, not abrupt, harsh and unyielding as before, but something soft and shamefaced, so shamefaced that I suddenly felt ashamed and guilty.

"What?" I asked, with tender curiosity.

"Why, you . . ."

"What?"

"Why, you . . . speak somehow like a book," she said, and again there was a note of irony in her voice.

That remark sent a pang to my heart. It was not what I was expecting.

I did not understand that she was hiding her feelings under irony, that this is usually the last refuge of modest and chaste-souled people when the privacy of their soul is coarsely and intrusively invaded, and that their pride makes them refuse to surrender till the last moment and shrink from giving expression to their feelings before you. I ought to have guessed the truth from the timidity with which she had repeatedly approached her sarcasm, only bringing herself to utter it at last with an effort. But I did not guess, and an evil feeling took possession of me.

"Wait a bit!" I thought.

[VII]

"Oh, hush, Liza! How can you talk about being like a book when it makes even me, an outsider, feel sick? Though I don't look at it as an outsider, for, indeed, it touches me to the heart. . . . Is it possible, is it possible that you do not feel sick at being here yourself? Evidently habit does wonders! God knows what habit can do with any one. Can you seriously think that you will never grow old, that you will always be good-looking, and that they will keep you here for ever and ever? I say nothing of the loathsomeness of the life here. . . . Though let me tell you this about it—about your present life, I mean; here though you are young now, attractive, nice, with soul and feeling, yet you know as soon as I came to myself just now I felt at once sick at being here with you! One can only come here when one is drunk. But if you were anywhere else, living as good people live, I should perhaps be more than attracted by you, should fall in love with you, should be glad of a look from you, let alone a word; I should hang about your door, should go down on my knees to you, should look upon you as my betrothed and think it an honour to be allowed to. I should not dare to have an impure thought about you. But here, you see, I know that I have only to whistle and you have to come with me whether you like it or not. I don't consult your wishes, but you mine. The lowest labourer hires himself as a workman but he doesn't make a slave of himself altogether; besides, he knows that he will be free again presently. But when are you free? Only think what you are giving up here! What is it you are making a slave of? It is your soul, together with your body; you are selling your soul which you have no right to dispose of! You give your love to be outraged by every drunkard! Love! But that's everything, you know, it's a priceless diamond, it's a maiden's treasure, love—why, a man would be ready to give his soul, to face death to gain that love. But how much is your love worth now? You are sold, all of you, body and soul, and there is no need to strive for love when you can have everything without love. And you know there is no greater insult to a girl than that, do you understand? To be sure, I have heard that they comfort you, poor fools, they let you have lovers of your own here. But you know that's simply a farce, that's simply a sham, it's just laughing at you, and you are taken in by it!

"Why, do you suppose he really loves you, that lover of yours? I don't believe it. How can he love you when he knows you may be called away from him any minute? He would be a low fellow if he did! Will he have a grain of respect for you? What have you in common with him? He laughs at you and robs you—that is all his love amounts to! You are lucky if he does not beat you. Very likely he does beat you, too. Ask him, if you have got one, whether he will marry you. He will laugh in your face, if he doesn't spit in it or give you a blow— though maybe he is not worth a bad halfpenny himself. And for what have you ruined your life, if you come to think of it? For the coffee they give you to drink and the plentiful meals? But with what object are they feeding you up? An honest girl couldn't swallow the food, for she would know what she was being fed for. You are in debt here, and, of course, you will always be in debt, and you will go on in debt to the end, till the visitors here begin to scorn you. And that will soon happen, don't rely upon your youth—all that flies by express train here, you know. You will be kicked out. And not simply kicked out; long before that she'll begin nagging at you, scolding you, abusing you, as though you had not sacrificed your health for her, had not thrown away your youth and your soul for her benefit, but as though you had ruined her, beggared her, robbed her. And don't expect any one to take your part: the others, your companions, will attack you, too, to win her favour, for all are in slavery here, and have lost all conscience and pity here long ago. They have become utterly vile, and nothing on earth is viler, more loathsome, and more insulting than their abuse.

"And you are laying down everything here, unconditionally, youth and health and beauty and hope, and at twenty-two you will look like a woman of five-and-thirty, and you will be lucky if you are not diseased, pray to God for that! No doubt you are thinking now that you have a gay time and no work to do! Yet there is no work harder or more dreadful in the world or ever has been. One would think that the heart alone would be worn out with tears. And you won't dare to say a word, not half a word when they drive you away from here; you will go away as though you were to blame. You will change to another house, then to a third, then somewhere else, till you come down at last to the Haymarket. There you will be beaten at every turn; that is good manners there, the visitors don't know how to be friendly without beating you. You don't believe that it is so hateful there? Go and look for yourself some time, you can see with your own eyes. Once, one New Year's Day, I saw a woman at a door. They had turned her out as a joke, to give her a taste of the frost because she had been crying so much, and they shut the door behind her. At nine o'clock in the morning she was already quite drunk, dishevelled, half-naked, covered with bruises, her face was powdered, but she had a black eye, blood was trickling from her nose and her teeth; some cabman had just given her a drubbing. She was sitting on the stone steps, a salt fish of some sort was in her hand; she was crying, wailing something about her luck and beating with the fish on the steps, and cabmen and drunken soldiers were crowding in the doorway taunting her. You don't believe that you will ever be like that? I should be sorry to believe it, too, but how do you know; maybe ten years, eight years ago that very woman with the salt fish came here fresh as a cherub, innocent, pure, knowing no evil, blushing at every word. Perhaps she was like you, proud, ready to take offence, not like the others; perhaps she looked like a queen, and knew what happiness was in store for the man who should love her and whom she should love. Do you see how it ended? And what if at that very minute when she was beating on the filthy steps with that fish, drunken and dishevelled—what if at that very minute she recalled the pure early days in her father's house, when she used to go to school and the neighbour's son watched for her on the way, declaring that he would love her as long as he lived, that he would devote his life to her, and when they vowed to love one another for ever and be married as soon as they were grown up!

"No, Liza, it would be happy for you if you were to die soon of consumption in some corner, in some cellar like that woman just now. In the hospital, do you say? You will be lucky if they take you, but what if you are still of use to the madam here? Consumption is a queer disease, it is not like fever. The patient goes on hoping till the last minute and says he is all right. He deludes himself. And that just suits your madam. Don't doubt it, that's how it is; you have sold your soul, and what is more you owe money, so you daren't say a word. But when you are dying, all will abandon you, all will turn away from you, for then there will be nothing to get from you. What's more, they will reproach you for cumbering the place, for being so long over dying. However you beg you won't get a drink of water without abuse: 'Whenever are you going off, you nasty hussy, you won't let us sleep with your moaning, you make the gentlemen sick.' That's true, I have heard such things said myself. They will thrust you dying into the filthiest corner in the cellar—in the damp and darkness; what will your thoughts be, lying there alone? When you die, strange hands will lay you out, with grumbling and impatience; no one will bless you, no one will sigh for you, they only want to get rid of you as soon as may be; they will buy a coffin, take you to the grave as they did that poor woman to-day, and celebrate your memory at the tavern. In the grave sleet, filth, wet snow—no need to put themselves out for you—'Let her down, Vanuha; it's just like her luck—even here, she is head-foremost, the hussy. Shorten the cord, you rascal.' 'It's all right as it is.' 'All right, is it? Why, she's on her side! She was a fellow-creature, after all! But never mind, throw the earth on her.' And they won't care to waste much time quarrelling over you. They will scatter the wet blue clay as quick as they can and go off to the tavern . . . and there your memory on earth will end; other women have children to go to their graves, fathers, husbands. While for you neither tear, nor sigh, nor remembrance; no one in the whole world will ever come to you, your name will vanish from the face of the earth—as though you had never existed, never been born at all! Nothing but filth and mud, however you knock at your coffin lid at night, when the dead arise, however you cry: 'Let me out, kind people, to live in the light of day! My life was no life at all; my life has been thrown away like a dishclout; it was drunk away in the tavern at the Haymarket; let me out, kind people, to live in the world again.' "

And I worked myself up to such a pitch that I began to have a lump in my throat myself, and . . . and all at once I stopped, sat up in dismay, and bending over apprehensively, began to listen with a beating heart. I had reason to be troubled.

I had felt for some time that I was turning her soul upside down and rending her heart, and—and the more I was convinced of it, the more eagerly I desired to gain my object as quickly and as effectually as possible. It was the exercise of my skill that carried me away; yet it was not merely sport. . . .

I knew I was speaking stiffly, artificially, even bookishly, in fact, I could not speak except "like a book." But that did not trouble me: I knew, I felt that I should be understood and that this very bookishness might be an assistance. But now, having attained my effect, I was suddenly panic-stricken. Never before had I witnessed such despair! She was lying on her face, thrusting her face into the pillow and clutching it in both hands. Her heart was being torn. Her youthful body was shuddering all over as though in convulsions. Suppressed sobs rent her bosom and suddenly burst out in weeping and wailing, then she pressed closer into the pillow: she did not want any one here, not a living soul, to know of her anguish and her tears. She bit the pillow, bit her hand till it bled (I saw that afterwards), or, thrusting her fingers into her dishevelled hair, seemed rigid with the effort of restraint, holding her breath and clenching her teeth. I began saying something, begging her to calm herself, but felt that I did not dare; and all at once, in a sort of cold shiver, almost in terror, began fumbling in the dark, trying hurriedly to get dressed to go. It was dark: though I tried my best I could not finish dressing quickly. Suddenly I felt a box of matches and a candlestick with a whole candle in it. As soon as the room was lighted up, Liza sprang up, sat up in bed, and with a contorted face, with a half-insane smile, looked at me almost senselessly. I sat down beside her and took her hands; she came to herself, made an impulsive movement towards me, would have caught hold of me, but did not dare, and slowly bowed her head before me.

"Liza, my dear, I was wrong . . . forgive me, my dear," I began, but she squeezed my hand in her fingers so tightly that I felt I was saying the wrong thing and stopped.

"This is my address, Liza, come to me."

"I will come," she answered resolutely, her head still bowed.

"But now I am going, good-bye . . . till we meet again."

I got up; she, too, stood up and suddenly flushed all over, gave a shudder, snatched up a shawl that was lying on a chair and muffled herself in it to her chin. As she did this she gave another sickly smile, blushed and looked at me strangely. I felt wretched; I was in haste to get away—to disappear.

"Wait a minute," she said suddenly, in the passage just at the doorway, stopping me with her hand on my overcoat. She put down the candle in hot haste and ran off; evidently she had thought of something or wanted to show me something. As she ran away she flushed, her eyes shone, and there was a smile on her lips—what was the meaning of it? Against my will I waited: she came back a minute later with an expression that seemed to ask forgiveness for something. In fact, it was not the same face, not the same look as the evening before: sullen, mistrustful and obstinate. Her eyes now were imploring, soft, and at the same time trustful, caressing, timid. The expression with which children look at people they are very fond of, of whom they are asking a favour. Her eyes were a light hazel, they were lovely eyes, full of life, and capable of expressing love as well as sullen hatred.

Making no explanation, as though I, as a sort of higher being, must understand everything without explanations, she held out a piece of paper to me. Her whole face was positively beaming at that instant with naïve, almost childish, triumph. I unfolded it. It was a letter to her from a medical student or some one of that sort—a very high-flown and flowery, but extremely respectful, love-letter. I don't recall the words now, but I remember well that through the high-flown phrases there was apparent a genuine feeling, which cannot be feigned. When I had finished reading it I met her glowing, questioning, and childishly impatient eyes fixed upon me. She fastened her eyes upon my face and waited impatiently for what I should say. In a few words, hurriedly, but with a sort of joy and pride, she explained to me that she had been to a dance somewhere in a private house, a family of "very nice people, *who knew nothing,* absolutely nothing, for she had only come here so lately and it had all happened . . . and she hadn't made up her mind to stay and was certainly going away as soon as she had paid her debt . . ." and at that party there had been the student who had danced with her all the evening. He had talked to her, and it turned out that he had known her in old days at Riga when he was a child, they had played together, but a very long time ago—and he knew her parents, but *about this* he knew nothing, nothing whatever, and had no suspicion! And the day after the dance (three days ago) he had sent her that letter through the friend with whom she had gone to the party . . . and . . . "well, that was all."

She dropped her shining eyes with a sort of bashfulness as she finished.

The poor girl was keeping that student's letter as a precious treasure, and had run to fetch it, her only treasure, because she did not want me to go away without knowing that she, too, was honestly and genuinely loved; that she, too, was addressed respectfully. No doubt that letter was destined to lie in her box and lead to nothing. But none the less, I am certain that she would keep it all her life as a precious treasure, as her pride and justification, and now at such a minute she had thought of that letter and brought it with naïve pride to raise herself in my eyes that I might see, that I, too, might think well of her. I said nothing, pressed her hand and went out. I so longed to get away. . . . I walked all the way home, in spite of the fact that the melting snow was still falling in heavy flakes. I was exhausted, shattered, in bewilderment. But behind the bewilderment the truth was already gleaming. The loathsome truth.

[VIII]

It was some time, however, before I consented to recognize that truth. Waking up in the morning after some hours of heavy, leaden sleep, and immediately realizing all that had happened on the previous day, I was positively amazed at my last night's *sentimentality* with Liza, at all those "outcries of horror and pity." "To think of having such an attack of womanish hysteria, pah!" I concluded. And what did I thrust my address upon her for? What if she comes? Let her come, though; it doesn't matter. . . . But *obviously* that was not now the chief and the most important matter: I had to make haste and at all costs save my reputation in the eyes of Zverkov and Simonov as quickly as possible; that was the chief business. And I was so taken up that morning that I actually forgot all about Liza.

First of all I had at once to repay what I had borrowed the day before from Simonov. I resolved on a desperate measure: to borrow fifteen roubles straight off from Anton Antonitch. As luck would have it he was in the best of humours that morning, and gave it to me at once, on the first asking. I was so delighted at this that, as I signed the I O U with a swaggering air, I told him casually that the night before "I had been keeping it up with some friends at the Hôtel de Paris; we were giving a farewell party to a comrade, in fact, I might say a friend of my childhood, and you know—a desperate rake, fearfully spoilt—of course, he belongs to a good family, and has considerable means, a brilliant career; he is witty, charming, a regular Lovelace, you understand; we drank an extra 'half-dozen' and . . ."

And it went off all right; all this was uttered very easily, unconstrainedly and complacently.

On reaching home I promptly wrote to Simonov.

To this hour I am lost in admiration when I recall the truly gentlemanly, good-humoured, candid tone of my letter. With tact and good breeding, and, above all, entirely without superfluous words, I blamed myself for all that had happened. I defended myself, "if I really may be allowed to defend myself," by alleging that being utterly unaccustomed to wine, I had been intoxicated with the first glass, which I said I had drunk before they arrived, while I was waiting for them at the Hôtel de Paris between five and six o'clock. I begged Simonov's pardon especially; I asked him to convey my explanations to all the others, especially to Zverkov, whom "I seemed to remember as though in a dream" I had insulted. I added that I would have called upon all of them myself, but my head ached, and besides I had not the face to. I was particularly pleased with a certain lightness, almost carelessness (strictly within the bounds of politeness, however), which was apparent in my style, and better than any possible arguments, gave them at once to understand that I took rather an independent view of "all that unpleasantness last night"; that I was by no means so utterly crushed as you, my friends, probably imagine; but on the contrary, looked upon it as a gentleman serenely respecting himself should look upon it. "On a young hero's past no censure is cast!"

"There is actually an aristocratic playfulness about it!" I thought admiringly, as I read over the letter. "And it's all because I am an intellectual and cultivated man! Another man in my place would not have known how to extricate himself, but here I have got out of it and am as jolly as ever again, and all because I am a cultivated and educated man of our day." And, indeed, perhaps, everything was due to the wine yesterday. H'm! . . . no, it was not the wine. I did not drink anything at all between five and six when I was waiting for them. I had lied to Simonov; I had lied shamelessly; and indeed I wasn't ashamed now. . . . Hang it all, though, the great thing was that I was rid of it.

I put six roubles in the letter, sealed it up, and asked Apollon to take it to Simonov. When he learned that there was money in the letter, Apollon became more respectful and agreed to take it. Towards evening I went out for a walk. My head was still aching and giddy after yesterday. But as evening came on and the twilight grew denser, my impressions and, following them, my thoughts grew more and more different and confused. Something was not dead within me, in the depths of my heart and conscience it would not die, and it showed itself in acute depression. For the most part I jostled my way through the most crowded business streets, along Myeshtchansky Street, along Sadovy Street and in Yusupov Garden. I always liked particularly sauntering along these streets in the dusk, just when there were crowds of working people of all sorts going home from their daily work, with faces looking cross with anxiety. What I liked was just that cheap bustle, that bare prose. On this occasion the jostling of the streets irritated me more than ever. I could not make out what was wrong with me, I could not find the clue, something seemed rising up continually in my soul, painfully, and refusing to be appeased. I returned home completely upset; it was just as though some crime were lying on my conscience.

The thought that Liza was coming worried me continually. It seemed queer to me that of all my recollections of yesterday this tormented me, as it were, especially, as it were, quite separately. Everything else I had quite succeeded in forgetting by the evening; I dismissed it all and was still perfectly satisfied with my letter to Simonov. But on this point I was not satisfied at all. It was as though I were worried only by Liza. "What if she comes," I thought incessantly, "well, it doesn't matter, let her come! H'm! it's horrid that she should see, for instance, how I live. Yesterday I seemed such a hero to her, while now, h'm! It's horrid, though, that I have let myself go so, the room looks like a beggar's. And I brought myself to go out to dinner in such a suit! And my American leather sofa with the stuffing sticking out. And my dressing-gown, which will not cover me, such tatters, and she will see all this and she will see Apollon. That beast is certain to insult her. He will fasten upon her in order to be rude to me. And I, of course, shall be panic-stricken as usual, I shall begin bowing and scraping before her and pulling my dressing-gown round me, I shall begin smiling, telling lies. Oh, the beastliness! And it isn't the beastliness of it that matters most! There is something more important, more loathsome, viler! Yes, viler! And to put on that dishonest lying mask again!" . . .

When I reached that thought I fired up all at once.

"Why dishonest? How dishonest? I was speaking sincerely last night. I remember there was real feeling in me, too. What I wanted was to excite an honourable feeling in her. . . . Her crying was a good thing, it will have a good effect."

Yet I could not feel at ease. All that evening, even when I had come back home, even after nine o'clock, when I calculated that Liza could not possibly come, she still haunted me, and what was worse, she came back to my mind always in the same position. One moment out of all that had happened last night stood vividly before my imagination; the moment when I struck a match and saw her pale, distorted face, with its look of torture. And what a pitiful, what an unnatural, what a distorted smile she had at that moment! But I did not know then that fifteen years later I should still in my imagination see Liza, always with the pitiful, distorted, inappropriate smile which was on her face at that minute.

Next day I was ready again to look upon it all as nonsense, due to over-excited nerves, and, above all, as *exaggerated*. I was always conscious of that weak point of mine, and sometimes very much afraid of it. "I exaggerate everything, that is where I go wrong," I repeated to myself every hour. But, however, "Liza will very likely come all the same" was the refrain with which all my reflections ended. I was so uneasy that I sometimes flew into a fury: "She'll come, she is certain to come!" I cried, running about the room, "if not to-day, she will come to-morrow; she'll find me out! The damnable romanticism of these pure hearts! Oh, the vileness—oh, the silliness—oh, the stupidity of these 'wretched sentimental souls'! Why, how fail to understand? How could one fail to understand?" . . .

But at this point I stopped short, and in great confusion, indeed.

And how few, how few words, I thought, in passing, were needed; how little of the idyllic (and affectedly, bookishly, artificially idyllic too) had sufficed to turn a whole human life at once according to my will. That's virginity, to be sure! Freshness of soil!

At times a thought occurred to me, to go to her, "to tell her all," and beg her not to come to me. But this thought stirred such wrath in me that I believed I should have crushed that "damned" Liza if she had chanced to be near me at the time. I should have insulted her, have spat at her, have turned her out, have struck her!

One day passed, however, another and another; she did not come and I began to grow calmer. I felt particularly bold and cheerful after nine o'clock, I even sometimes began dreaming, and rather sweetly: I, for instance, became the salvation of Liza, simply through her coming to me and my talking to her. . . . I develop her, educate her. Finally, I notice that she loves me, loves me passionately. I pretend not to understand (I don't know, however, why I pretend, just for effect, perhaps). At last all confusion, transfigured, trembling and sobbing, she flings herself at my feet and says that I am her saviour, and that she loves me better than anything in the world. I am amazed, but . . .

"Liza," I say, "can you imagine that I have not noticed your love? I saw it all, I divined it, but I did not dare to approach you first, because I had an influence over you and was afraid that you would force yourself, from gratitude, to respond to my love, would try to rouse in your heart a feeling which was perhaps absent, and I did not wish that . . . because it would be tyranny . . . it would be indelicate (in short, I launch off at that point into European, inexplicably lofty subtleties à la George Sand), but now, now you are mine, you are my creation, you are pure, you are good, you are my noble wife.

"'Into my house come bold and free,
   Its rightful mistress there to be.'"

Then we begin living together, go abroad and so on, and so on. In fact, in the end it seemed vulgar to me myself, and I began putting out my tongue at myself.

Besides, they won't let her out, "the hussy!" I thought. They don't let them go out very readily, especially in the evening (for some reason I fancied she would come in the evening, and at seven o'clock precisely). Though she did say she was not altogether a slave there yet, and had certain rights; so, h'm! Damn it all, she will come, she is sure to come!

It was a good thing, in fact, that Apollon distracted my attention at that time by his rudeness. He drove me beyond all patience! He was the bane of my life, the curse laid upon me by Providence. We had been squabbling continually for years, and I hated him. My God, how I hated him! I believe I had never hated anyone in my life as I hated him, especially at some moments. He was an elderly, dignified man, who worked part of his time as a tailor. But for some unknown reason he despised me beyond all measure, and looked down upon me insufferably. Though, indeed, he looked down upon every one. Simply to glance at that flaxen, smoothly brushed head, at the tuft of hair he combed up on his forehead and oiled with sunflower oil, at that dignified mouth, compressed into the shape of the letter V, made one feel one was confronting a man who never doubted of himself. He was a pedant, to the most extreme point, the greatest pedant I had met on earth, and with that had a vanity only befitting Alexander of Macedon. He was in love with every button on his coat, every nail on his fingers—absolutely in love with them, and he looked it! In his behaviour to me he was a perfect tyrant, he spoke very little to me, and if he chanced to glance at me he gave me a firm, majestically self-confident and invariably ironical look that drove me sometimes to fury. He did his work with the air of doing me the greatest favour. Though he did scarcely anything for me, and did not, indeed, consider himself bound to do anything. There could be no doubt that he looked upon me as the greatest fool on earth, and that he did not "get rid of me" was simply that he could get wages from me every month. He consented to do nothing for me for seven roubles a month. Many sins should be forgiven me for what I suffered from him. My hatred reached such a point that sometimes his very step almost threw me into convulsions. What I loathed particularly was his lisp. His tongue must have been a little too long or something of that sort, for he continually lisped, and seemed to be very proud of it, imagining that it greatly added to his dignity. He spoke in a slow, measured tone, with his hands behind his back and his eyes fixed on the ground. He maddened me particularly when he read aloud the Psalms to himself behind his partition. Many a battle I waged over that reading! But he was awfully fond of reading aloud in the evenings, in a slow, even, sing-song voice, as though over the dead. It is interesting that that is how he has ended: he hires himself out to read the Psalms over the dead, and at the same time he kills rats and makes blacking. But at that time I could not get rid of him, it was as though he were chemically combined with my existence. Besides, nothing would have induced him to consent to leave me. I could not live in furnished lodgings: my lodging was my private solitude, my shell, my cave, in which I concealed myself from all mankind, and Apollon seemed to me, for some reason, an integral part of that flat, and for seven years I could not turn him away.

To be two or three days behind with his wages, for instance, was impossible. He would have made such a fuss, I should not have known where to hide my head. But I was so exasperated with every one during those days, that I made up my mind for some reason and with some object to *punish* Apollon and not to pay him for a fortnight the wages that were owing him. I had for a long time—for the last two years—been intending to do this, simply in order to teach him not to give himself airs with me, and to show him that if I liked I could withhold his wages. I purposed to say nothing to him about it, and was purposely silent indeed, in order to score off his pride and force him to be the first to speak of his wages. Then I would take the seven roubles out of a drawer, show him I have the money put aside on purpose, but that I won't, I won't, I simply won't pay him his wages, I won't just because that is "what I wish," because "I am master, and it is for me to decide," because he has been disrespectful, because he has been rude; but if he were to ask respectfully I might be softened and give it to him, otherwise he might wait another fortnight, another three weeks, a whole month. . . .

But angry as I was, yet he got the better of me. I could not hold out for four days. He began as he always did begin in such cases, for there had been such cases already, there had been attempts (and it may be observed I knew all this beforehand, I knew his nasty tactics by heart). He would begin by fixing upon me an exceedingly severe stare, keeping it up for several minutes at a time, particularly on meeting me or seeing me out of the house. If I held out and pretended not to notice these stares, he would, still in silence, proceed to further tortures. All at once, apropos of nothing, he would walk softly and smoothly into my room, when I was pacing up and down or reading, stand at the door, one hand behind his back and one foot behind the other, and fix upon me a stare more than severe, utterly contemptuous. If I suddenly asked him what he wanted, he would make me no answer, but continue staring at me persistently for some seconds, then, with a peculiar compression of his lips and a most significant air, deliberately turn round and deliberately go back to his room. Two hours later he would come out again and again present himself before me in the same way. It had happened that in my fury I did not even ask him what he wanted, but simply raised my head sharply and imperiously and began staring back at him. So we stared at one another for two minutes; at last he turned with deliberation and dignity and went back again for two hours.

If I were still not brought to reason by all this, but persisted in my revolt, he would suddenly begin sighing while he looked at me, long, deep sighs as though measuring by them the depths of my moral degradation, and, of course, it ended at last by his triumphing completely: I raged and shouted, but still was forced to do what he wanted.

This time the usual staring manoeuvres had scarcely begun when I lost my temper and flew at him in a fury. I was irritated beyond endurance apart from him.

"Stay," I cried, in a frenzy, as he was slowly and silently turning, with one hand behind his back, to go to his room, "stay! Come back, come back, I tell you!" and I must have bawled so unnaturally, that he turned round and even looked at me with some wonder. However, he persisted in saying nothing, and that infuriated me.

"How dare you come and look at me like that without being sent for? Answer!"

After looking at me calmly for half a minute, he began turning round again.

"Stay!" I roared, running up to him, "don't stir! There. Answer, now: what did you come in to look at?"

"If you have any order to give me it's my duty to carry it out," he answered, after another silent pause, with a slow, measured lisp, raising his eyebrows and calmly twisting his head from one side to another, all this with exasperating composure.

"That's not what I am asking you about, you torturer!" I shouted, turning crimson with anger. "I'll tell you why you came here myself: you see, I don't give you your wages, you are so proud you don't want to bow down and ask for it, and so you come to punish me with your stupid stares, to worry me and you have no sus-pic-ion how stupid it is—stupid, stupid, stupid, stupid!" . . .

He would have turned round again without a word, but I seized him.

"Listen," I shouted to him. "Here's the money, do you see, here it is" (I took it out of the table drawer); "here's the seven roubles complete, but you are not going to have it, you . . . are . . . not . . . going . . . to . . . have it until you come respectfully with bowed head to beg my pardon. Do you hear?"

"That cannot be," he answered, with the most unnatural self-confidence.

"It shall be so," I said, "I give you my word of honour, it shall be!"

"And there's nothing for me to beg your pardon for," he went on, as though he had not noticed my exclamations at all. "Why, besides, you called me a 'torturer,' for which I can summon you at the police-station at any time for insulting behaviour."

"Go, summon me," I roared, "go at once, this very minute, this very second! You are a torturer all the same! a torturer!"

But he merely looked at me, then turned, and regardless of my loud calls to him, he walked to his room with an even step and without looking round.

"If it had not been for Liza nothing of this would have happened," I decidedly inwardly. Then, after waiting a minute, I went myself behind his screen with a dignified and solemn air, though my heart was beating slowly and violently.

"Apollon," I said quietly and emphatically, though I was breathless, "go at once without a minute's delay and fetch the police-officer."

He had meanwhile settled himself at his table, put on his spectacles and taken up some sewing. But, hearing my order, he burst into a guffaw.

"At once, go this minute! Go on, or else you can't imagine what will happen."

"You are certainly out of your mind," he observed, without even raising his head, lisping as deliberately as ever and threading his needle. "Whoever heard of a man sending for the police against himself? And as for being frightened—you are upsetting yourself about nothing, for nothing will come of it."

"Go!" I shrieked, clutching him by the shoulder. I felt I should strike him in a minute.

But I did not notice the door from the passage softly and slowly open at that instant and a figure come in, stop short, and begin staring at us in perplexity. I glanced, nearly swooned with shame, and rushed back to my room. There, clutching at my hair with both hands, I leaned my head against the wall and stood motionless in that position.

Two minutes later I heard Apollon's deliberate footsteps. "There is some woman asking for you," he said, looking at me with peculiar severity. Then he stood aside and let in Liza. He would not go away, but stared at us sarcastically.

"Go away, go away," I commanded in desperation. At that moment my clock began whirring and wheezing and struck seven.

[IX]

"Into my house come bold and free,
    Its rightful mistress there to be."

I stood before her crushed, crestfallen, revoltingly confused, and I believe I smiled as I did my utmost to wrap myself in the skirts of my ragged wadded dressing-gown—exactly as I had imagined the scene not long before in a fit of depression. After standing over us for a couple of minutes Apollon went away, but that did not make me more at ease. What made it worse was that she, too, was overwhelmed with confusion, more so, in fact, than I should have expected. At the sight of me, of course.

"Sit down," I said mechanically, moving a chair up to the table, and I sat down on the sofa. She obediently sat down at once and gazed at me open-eyed, evidently expecting something from me at once. This naïveté of expectation drove me to fury, but I restrained myself.

She ought to have tried not to notice, as though everything had been as usual, while instead of that, she . . . and I dimly felt that I should make her pay dearly for *all this*.

"You have found me in a strange position, Liza," I began, stammering and knowing that this was the wrong way to begin. "No, no, don't imagine anything," I cried, seeing that she had suddenly flushed. "I am not ashamed of my poverty. . . . On the contrary I look with pride on my poverty. I am poor but honourable. . . . One can be poor and honourable," I muttered. "However . . . would you like tea?" . . .

"No," she was beginning.

"Wait a minute."

I leapt up and ran to Apollon. I had to get out of the room somehow.

"Apollon," I whispered in feverish haste, flinging down before him the seven roubles which had remained all the time in my clenched fist, "here are your wages, you see I give them to you; but for that you must come to my rescue: bring me tea and a dozen rusks from the restaurant. If you won't go, you'll make me a miserable man! You don't know what this woman is. . . . This is—everything! You may be imagining something. . . . But you don't know what that woman is!" . . .

Apollon, who had already sat down to his work and put on his spectacles again, at first glanced askance at the money without speaking or putting down his needle; then, without paying the slightest attention to me or making any answer he went on busying himself with his needle, which he had not yet threaded. I waited before him for three minutes with my arms crossed *à la Napoléon*. My temples were moist with sweat. I was pale, I felt it. But, thank God, he must have been moved to pity, looking at me. Having threaded his needle, he deliberately got up from his seat, deliberately moved back his chair, deliberately took off his spectacles, deliberately counted the money, and finally asking me over his shoulder: "Shall I get a whole portion?" deliberately walked out of the room. As I was going back to Liza, the thought occurred to me on the way: shouldn't I run away just as I was in my dressing-gown, no matter where, and then let happen what would?

I sat down again. She looked at me uneasily. For some minutes we were silent.

"I will kill him," I shouted suddenly, striking the table with my fist so that the ink spurted out of the inkstand.

"What are you saying!" she cried, starting.

"I will kill him! kill him!" I shrieked, suddenly striking the table in absolute frenzy, and at the same time fully understanding how stupid it was to be in such a frenzy. "You don't know, Liza, what that torturer is to me. He is my torturer. . . . He has gone now to fetch some rusks; he . . ."

And suddenly I burst into tears. It was an hysterical attack. How ashamed I felt in the midst of my sobs; but still I could not restrain them.

She was frightened.

"What is the matter? What is wrong?" she cried, fussing about me.

"Water, give me water, over there!" I muttered in a faint voice, though I was inwardly conscious that I could have got on very well without water and without muttering in a faint voice. But I was what is called *putting it on,* to save appearances, though the attack was a genuine one.

She gave me water, looking at me in bewilderment. At that moment Apollon brought in the tea. It suddenly seemed to me that this commonplace, prosaic tea was horribly undignified and paltry after all that had happened, and I blushed crimson. Liza looked at Apollon with positive alarm. He went out without a glance at either of us.

"Liza, do you despise me?" I asked, looking at her fixedly, trembling with impatience to know what she was thinking.

She was confused, and did not know what to answer.

"Drink your tea," I said to her angrily. I was angry with myself, but, of course, it was she who would have to pay for it. A horrible spite against her suddenly surged up in my heart; I believe I could have killed her. To revenge myself on her I swore inwardly not to say a word to her all the time. "She is the cause of it all," I thought.

Our silence lasted for five minutes. The tea stood on the table; we did not touch it. I had got to the point of purposely refraining from beginning in order to embarrass her further; it was awkward for her to begin alone. Several times she glanced at me with mournful perplexity. I was obstinately silent. I was, of course, myself the chief sufferer, because I was fully conscious of the disgusting meanness of my spiteful stupidity, and yet at the same time I could not restrain myself.

"I want to . . . get away . . . from there altogether," she began, to break the silence in some way, but, poor girl, that was just what she ought not to have spoken about at such a stupid moment to a man so stupid as I was. My heart positively ached with pity for her tactless and unnecessary straightforwardness. But something hideous at once stifled all compassion in me; it even provoked me to greater venom. I did not care what happened. Another five minutes passed.

"Perhaps I am in your way," she began timidly, hardly audibly, and was getting up.

But as soon as I saw this first impulse of wounded dignity I positively trembled with spite, and at once burst out.

"Why have you come to me, tell me that, please?" I began, gasping for breath and regardless of logical connection in my words. I longed to have it all out at once, at one burst; I did not even trouble how to begin. "Why have you come? Answer, answer," I cried, hardly knowing what I was doing. "I'll tell you, my good girl, why you have come. You've come because I talked sentimental stuff to you then. So now you are soft as butter and longing for fine sentiments again. So you may as well know that I was laughing at you then. And I am laughing at you now. Why are you shuddering? Yes, I was laughing at you! I had been insulted just before, at dinner, by the fellows who came that evening before me. I came to you, meaning to thrash one of them, an officer; but I didn't succeed, I didn't find him; I had to avenge the insult on some one to get back my own again; you turned up, I vented my spleen on you and laughed at you. I had been humiliated, so I wanted to humiliate; I had been treated like a rag, so I wanted to show my power. . . . That's what it was, and you imagined I had come there on purpose to save you. Yes? You imagined that? You imagined that?"

I knew that she would perhaps be muddled and not take it all in exactly, but I knew, too, that she would grasp the gist of it, very well indeed. And so, indeed, she did. She turned white as a handkerchief, tried to say something, and her lips worked painfully; but she sank on a chair as though she had been felled by an axe. And all the time afterwards she listened to me with her lips parted and her eyes wide-open, shuddering with awful terror. The cynicism, the cynicism of my words overwhelmed her.

"Save you!" I went on, jumping up from my chair and running up and down the room before her. "Save you from what? But perhaps I am worse than you myself. Why didn't you throw it in my teeth when I was giving you that sermon: 'But what did you come here yourself for? Was it to read us a sermon?' Power, power was what I wanted then, sport was what I wanted, I wanted to wring out your tears, your humiliation, your hysteria—that was what I wanted then! Of course, I couldn't keep it up then, because I am a wretched creature, I was frightened, and, the devil knows why, gave you my address in my folly. Afterwards, before I got home, I was cursing and swearing at you because of that address, I hated you already because of the lies I had told you. Because I only like playing with words, only dreaming, but, do you know, what I really want is that you should all go to hell. That is what I want. I want peace; yes, I'd sell the whole world for a farthing, straight off, so long as I was left in peace. Is the world to go to pot, or am I to go without my tea? I say that the world may go to pot for me so long as I always get my tea. Did you know that, or not? Well, anyway, I know that I am a blackguard, a scoundrel, an egoist, a sluggard. Here I have been shuddering for the last three days at the thought of your coming. And do you know what has worried me particularly for these three days? That I posed as such a hero to you, and now you would see me in a wretched torn dressing-gown, beggarly, loathsome. I told you just now that I was not ashamed of my poverty; so you may as well know that I am ashamed of it; I am more ashamed of it than of anything, more afraid of it than of being found out if I were a thief, because I am as vain as though I had been skinned and the very air blowing on me hurt. Surely by now you must realize that I shall never forgive you for having found me in this wretched dressing-gown, just as I was flying at Apollon like a spiteful cur. The saviour, the former hero, was flying like a mangy, unkempt sheep-dog at his lackey, and the lackey was jeering at him! And I shall never forgive you for the tears I could not help shedding before you just now, like some silly woman put to shame! And for what I am confessing to you now, I shall never forgive *you* either! Yes—you must answer for it all because you turned up like this, because I am a blackguard, because I am the nastiest, stupidest, absurdest and most envious of all the worms on earth, who are not a bit better than I am, but, the devil knows why, are never put to confusion; while I shall always be insulted by every louse, that is my doom! And what is it to me that you don't understand a word of this! And what do I care, what do I care about you, and whether you go to ruin there or not? Do you understand? How I shall hate you now after saying this, for having been here and listening. Why, it's not once in a lifetime a man speaks out like this, and then it is in hysterics! . . . What more do you want? Why do you still stand confronting me, after all this? Why are you worrying me? Why don't you go?"

But at this point a strange thing happened: I was so accustomed to think and imagine everything from books, and to picture everything in the world to myself just as I had made it up in my dreams beforehand, that I could not all at once take in this strange circumstance.

What happened was this: Liza, insulted and crushed by me, understood a great deal more than I imagined. She understood from all this
what a woman understands first of all, if she feels genuine love, that is,
that I was myself unhappy.

The frightened and wounded expression on her face was followed
first by a look of sorrowful perplexity. When I began calling myself a
scoundrel and a blackguard and my tears flowed (the tirade was
accompanied throughout by tears) her whole face worked convulsively.
She was on the point of getting up and stopping me; when I finished
she took no notice of my shouting: "Why are you here, why don't you
go away?" but realized only that it must have been very bitter to me to
say all this. Besides, she was so crushed, poor girl; she considered herself infinitely beneath me; how could she feel anger or resentment?
She suddenly leapt up from her chair with an irresistible impulse and
held out her hands, yearning towards me, though still timid and not
daring to stir. . . . At this point there was a revulsion in my heart, too.
Then she suddenly rushed to me, threw her arms round me and burst
into tears. I, too, could not restrain myself, and sobbed as I never had
before.

"They won't let me . . . I can't be good!" I managed to articulate;
then I went to the sofa, fell on it face downwards, and sobbed on it
for a quarter of an hour in genuine hysterics. She came close to me,
put her arms round me and stayed motionless in that position. But
the trouble was that the hysterics could not go on for ever, and (I
am writing the loathsome truth) lying face downwards on the sofa
with my face thrust into my nasty leather pillow, I began by degrees
to be aware of a far-away, involuntary but irresistible feeling that it
would be awkward now for me to raise my head and look Liza straight
in the face. Why was I ashamed? I don't know, but I was ashamed.
The thought, too, came into my overwrought brain that our parts now
were completely changed, that she was now the heroine, while I was
just such a crushed and humiliated creature as she had been before
me that night—four days before. . . . And all this came into my
mind during the minutes I was lying on my face on the sofa.

My God! surely I was not envious of her then.

I don't know, to this day I cannot decide, and at the time, of course,
I was still less able to understand what I was feeling than now. I
cannot get on without domineering and tyrannizing over some one,
but . . . there is no explaining anything by reasoning and so it is
useless to reason.

I conquered myself, however, and raised my head; I had to do so sooner or later . . . and I am convinced to this day that it was just because I was ashamed to look at her that another feeling was suddenly kindled and flamed up in my heart . . . a feeling of mastery and possession. My eyes gleamed with passion, and I gripped her hands tightly. How I hated her and how I was drawn to her at that minute! The one feeling intensified the other. It was almost like an act of vengeance. At first there was a look of amazement, even of terror, on her face, but only for one instant. She warmly and rapturously embraced me.

[x]

A quarter of an hour later I was rushing up and down the room in frenzied impatience, from minute to minute I went up to the screen and peeped through the crack at Liza. She was sitting on the ground with her head leaning against the bed, and must have been crying. But she did not go away, and that irritated me. This time she understood it all. I had insulted her finally, but . . . there's no need to describe it. She realized that my outburst of passion had been simply revenge, a fresh humiliation, and that to my earlier, almost causeless hatred was added now a *personal hatred,* born of envy. . . . Though I do not maintain positively that she understood all this distinctly; but she certainly did fully understand that I was a despicable man, and what was worse, incapable of loving her.

I know I shall be told that this is incredible—but it is incredible to be as spiteful and stupid as I was; it may be added that it was strange I should not love her, or at any rate, appreciate her love. Why is it strange? In the first place, by then I was incapable of love, for, I repeat, with me loving meant tyrannizing and showing my moral superiority. I have never in my life been able to imagine any other sort of love, and have nowadays come to the point of sometimes thinking that love really consists in the right—freely given by the beloved object—to tyrannize over her.

Even in my underground dreams I did not imagine love except as a struggle. I began it always with hatred and ended it with moral subjugation, and afterwards I never knew what to do with the subjugated object. And what is there to wonder at in that, since I had succeeded in so corrupting myself, since I was so out of touch with "real life," as to have actually thought of reproaching her, and putting her to shame for having come to me to hear "fine sentiments"; and did not even guess that she had come not to hear fine sentiments, but to love me, because to a woman all reformation—all salvation from any sort of ruin, and all moral renewal—is included in love and can only show itself in that form.

I did not hate her so much, however, when I was running about the room and peeping through the crack in the screen. I was only insufferably oppressed by her being here. I wanted her to disappear. I wanted "peace," to be left alone in my underground world. Real life oppressed me with its novelty so much that I could hardly breathe.

But several minutes passed and she still remained without stirring, as though she were unconscious. I had the shamelessness to tap softly at the screen as though to remind her. . . . She started, sprang up, and flew to seek her kerchief, her hat, her coat, as though making her escape from me. . . . Two minutes later she came from behind the screen and looked with heavy eyes at me. I gave a spiteful grin, which was forced, however, to *keep up appearances,* and I turned away from her eyes.

"Good-bye," she said, going towards the door.

I ran up to her, seized her hand, opened it, thrust something in it and closed it again. Then I turned at once and dashed away in haste to the other corner of the room to avoid seeing, anyway. . . .

I did mean a moment since to tell a lie—to write that I did this accidentally, not knowing what I was doing through foolishness, through losing my head. But I don't want to lie, and so I will say straight out that I opened her hand and put the money in it . . . from spite. It came into my head to do this while I was running up and down the room and she was sitting behind the screen. But this I can say for certain: though I did that cruel thing purposely, it was not an impulse from the heart, but came from my evil brain. This cruelty was so affected, so purposely made up, so completely a product of the brain, of books, that I could not even keep it up a minute—first I dashed away to avoid seeing her, and then in shame and despair rushed after Liza. I opened the door in the passage and began listening.

"Liza! Liza!" I cried on the stairs, but in a low voice, not boldly.

There was no answer, but I fancied I heard her footsteps, lower down on the stairs.

"Liza!" I cried, more loudly.

No answer. But at that minute I heard the stiff outer glass door open heavily with a creak and slam violently, the sound echoed up the stairs.

She had gone. I went back to my room in hesitation. I felt horribly oppressed.

I stood still at the table beside the chair on which she had sat and looked aimlessly before me. A minute passed, suddenly I started; straight before me on the table I saw. . . . In short, I saw a crumpled blue five-rouble note, the one I had thrust into her hand a minute before. It was the same note; it could be no other, there was no other in the flat. So she had managed to fling it from her hand on the table at the moment when I had dashed into the further corner.

Well! I might have expected that she would do that. Might I have expected it? No, I was such an egoist, I was so lacking in respect for my fellow-creatures that I could not even imagine she would do so. I could not endure it. A minute later I flew like a madman to dress, flinging on what I could at random and ran headlong after her. She could not have got two hundred paces away when I ran out into the street.

It was a still night and the snow was coming down in masses and falling almost perpendicularly, covering the pavement and the empty street as though with a pillow. There was no one in the street, no sound was to be heard. The street lamps gave a disconsolate and useless glimmer. I ran two hundred paces to the cross-roads and stopped short.

Where had she gone? And why was I running after her?

Why? To fall down before her, to sob with remorse, to kiss her feet, to entreat her forgiveness! I longed for that, my whole breast was being rent to pieces, and never, never shall I recall that minute with indifference. But—what for? I thought. Should I not begin to hate her, perhaps, even to-morrow, just because I had kissed her feet to-day? Should I give her happiness? Had I not recognized that day, for the hundredth time, what I was worth? Should I not torture her?

I stood in the snow, gazing into the troubled darkness and pondered this.

"And will it not be better?" I mused fantastically, afterwards at home, stifling the living pang of my heart with fantastic dreams. "Will it not be better that she should keep the resentment of the insult for ever? Resentment—why, it is purification; it is a most stinging and painful consciousness! To-morrow I should have defiled her soul and have exhausted her heart, while now the feeling of insult will never die in her heart, and however loathsome the filth awaiting her— the feeling of insult will elevate and purify her . . . by hatred . . . h'm! . . . perhaps too, by forgiveness. . . . Will all that make things easier for her, though? . . ."

And, indeed, I will ask on my own account here an idle question:

which is better—cheap happiness or exalted sufferings? Well, which is better?

So I dreamed as I sat at home that evening, almost dead with the pain in my soul. Never had I endured such suffering and remorse, yet could there have been the faintest doubt when I ran out from my lodging that I should turn back half-way? I never met Liza again and I have heard nothing of her. I will add, too, that I remained for a long time afterwards pleased with the phrase about the benefit from resentment and hatred, in spite of the fact that I almost fell ill from misery.

Even now, so many years later, all this is somehow a very evil memory. I have many evil memories now, but . . . hadn't I better end my "Notes" here? I believe I made a mistake in beginning to write them, anyway I have felt ashamed all the time I've been writing this story; so it's hardly literature so much as a corrective punishment. Why, to tell long stories, showing how I have spoiled my life through morally rotting in my corner, through lack of fitting environment, through divorce from real life, and rankling spite in my underground world, would certainly not be interesting; a novel needs a hero, and all the traits for an anti-hero are *expressly* gathered together here, and what matters most, it all produces an unpleasant impression, for we are all divorced from life, we are all cripples, every one of us, more or less. We are so divorced from it that we feel at once a sort of loathing for real life, and so cannot bear to be reminded of it. Why, we have come almost to looking upon real life as an effort, almost as hard work, and we are all privately agreed that it is better in books. And why do we fuss and fume sometimes? Why are we perverse and ask for something else? We don't know what ourselves. It would be the worse for us if our petulant prayers were answered. Come, try, give any one of us, for instance, a little more independence, untie our hands, widen the spheres of our activity, relax the control and we . . . yes, I assure you . . . we should be begging to be under control again at once. I know that you will very likely be angry with me for that, and will begin shouting and stamping. Speak for yourself, you will say, and for your miseries in your underground holes, and don't dare to say all of us—excuse me, gentlemen, I am not justifying myself with that "all of us." As for what concerns me in particular I have only in my life carried to an extreme what you have not dared to carry half-way, and what's more, you have taken your cowardice for good sense, and have found comfort in deceiving yourselves. So that perhaps, after all, there is more life in me than in you. Look into it more carefully! Why, we don't even know what living means now, what it is, and what it is called! Leave us alone without books and we shall be lost and in confusion at once. We shall not know what to join on to, what to cling to, what to love and what to hate, what to respect and what to despise. We are oppressed at being men—men with a real individual body and blood, we are ashamed of it, we think it a disgrace and try to contrive to be some sort of impossible generalized man. We are still-born, and for generations past have been begotten, not by living fathers, and that suits us better and better. We are developing a taste for it. Soon we shall contrive to be born somehow from an idea. But enough; I don't want to write more from "Underground."

[*The notes of this paradoxalist do not end here, however. He could not refrain from going on with them, but it seems to us that we may stop here.*]

Uncle's Dream

FROM THE ANNALS OF MORDASOV

UNCLE'S DREAM

(FROM THE ANNALS OF MORDASOV)

Chapter 1

MARYA ALEXANDROVNA MOSKALEV is the leading lady in Mordasov, and of that there can be no possible question. She behaves as though she were independent of every one and every one else were dependent on her. It is true that scarcely any one likes her and, indeed, very many people sincerely hate her; but on the other hand every one is afraid of her, and that is just what she wants. Such a desire betokens a high degree of diplomacy. How is it, for instance, that Marya Alexandrovna, who is desperately fond of gossip, and cannot sleep all night if she has not heard something new the day before, how is it that with all that she knows how to deport herself so that it would never occur to any one looking at her that this majestic lady was the greatest gossip in the world, or at any rate in Mordasov? One would suppose, on the contrary, that gossip would die away in her presence, that backbiters would blush and tremble like schoolboys confronting their teacher, and that the conversation would not deal with any but the loftiest subjects. She knows about some of the Mordasov people facts so scandalous and so important that if she were to tell them on a suitable occasion and to make them public, as she so well knows how to do, there would be a regular earthquake of Lisbon in Mordasov. And at the same time she is very reserved over these secrets and will only tell them in extreme cases, and then only to her most intimate female friends. She confines herself to frightening people with hints at what she knows, and likes better to keep a man or a lady in continual apprehension than to deal them a final blow. That is intelligence, that is diplomacy! Marya Alexandrovna was always distinguished among us by her irreproachable *comme il faut,* upon which we all model ourselves. As regards *comme il faut* she is without a rival in Mordasov. She can, for instance, kill, tear to pieces, annihilate a rival with a single word, a performance we have witnessed; and at the same time she will have the air of not observing

225

that she has uttered that word. And we all know that this ability is characteristic of the very highest society. In fact, at all such tricks she is a match for Pinetti. Her connections are immense. Many persons who have visited Mordasov have been delighted with her hospitality, and have even kept up a correspondence with her after their departure. Some one even wrote her a poem, and Marya Alexandrovna showed it to us all with pride. One literary visitor dedicated to her his novel, which he read aloud to her in the evenings, and this made an extremely agreeable impression. A learned German, who came from Carlsruhe expressly to study some kind of worm with horns, which is found in our province, and who wrote four quarto volumes on the creature in question, was so enchanted by Marya Alexandrovna's hospitality and politeness that to this day he keeps up with her a correspondence of the most respectful and highly moral tone, from Carlsruhe. Marya Alexandrovna has even been compared in one respect with Napoleon. This comparison was of course made in jest by her enemies, more by way of sarcasm than truth. But while fully admitting the oddity of the comparison I make bold to ask one innocent question: why was Napoleon's head turned at last when he was too greatly exalted? The champions of the old dynasty used to ascribe this to the fact that Napoleon was not only not of royal blood, but was not even a *gentilhomme* of good family, and so was naturally alarmed at last by his own exalted state and was conscious of his real position. In spite of the obvious cleverness of this surmise, which recalls the most brilliant period of the old French court, I venture to add in my turn: how was it that Marya Alexandrovna's head was never under any circumstances turned, how was it that she always remained the leading lady in Mordasov? There were occasions when everybody asked: "How will Marya Alexandrovna act now in such difficult circumstances?" But the circumstances arrived and passed and—all went well! Everything remained satisfactory, as before; even better than before. Every one remembers, for instance, how her husband, Afanasy Matveyitch, was deprived of his post owing to his incompetence and feeble-mindedness, which excited the wrath of an inspector from the capital. Every one thought that Marya Alexandrovna would be depressed, would be humbled, would entreat and petition, would, in short, be crestfallen. Nothing of the sort: Marya Alexandrovna grasped that nothing could be gained by petitioning, and played her cards so well that she lost nothing of her influence in society, and her house is still looked upon as the house of most consequence in Mordasov. Anna Nikolaevna Antipov, the Public Prosecutor's wife, a sworn foe of Marya Alexandrovna's, though externally her friend, was already trumpeting her victory; but when we saw that Marya Alexandrovna could not be easily put to confusion, we realized that she had sent her roots far more deeply down than we had supposed.

By the way, since we have mentioned him we will say a few words about Afanasy Matveyitch, Marya Alexandrovna's husband. In the first place he was a man of very presentable exterior, and indeed of very correct principles, only on critical occasions he somehow lost his head, and looked like a sheep facing a new gate. He was extraordinarily dignified, especially in his white tie at name-day dinners, but his dignified air and presentability only lasted till the minute when he began to speak. Then there was nothing for it, if I may say so, but cotton wool in one's ears. He certainly was not worthy to belong to Marya Alexandrovna; that was the universal opinion, he had only kept his position through the genius of his wife; in my private judgment he ought long ago to have been in the kitchen garden scaring sparrows. There and only there he might have been of real unquestionable service to his fellow-countrymen. And so Marya Alexandrovna acted admirably in sending Afanasy Matveyitch to their country place, two and a half miles from Mordasov, where she had a hundred and twenty serfs—in parenthesis I may say, the whole property, the whole fortune upon which she so worthily maintained the dignity of her household. Everybody knew that she had kept Afanasy Matveyitch about her solely because he was in the government service and in receipt of a salary and . . . of other sums. As soon as he ceased to receive a salary and other sums, she immediately removed him to a distance on account of his incompetence and absolute uselessness. And every one commended Marya Alexandrovna's clear-sightedness and decision of character. In the country Afanasy Matveyitch is in clover. I went to see him and spent a whole hour with him fairly pleasantly. He tries on his white cravats, cleans his boots with his own hands, not from necessity but simply for love of the art, because he likes his boots to shine; he drinks tea three times a day, is exceedingly fond of going to the bathhouse, and—is contented. Do you remember the horrid scandal that was concocted among us a year and a half ago concerning Zinaida Afanasyevna, the only daughter of Marya Alexandrovna and Afanasy Matveyitch? Zinaida Afanasyevna is unquestionably beautiful, and is extremely well educated, yet she is three-and-twenty and is still unmarried. Among the reasons people give for Zina's being unmarried, one of the chief is considered to be the sinister rumour of some strange intimacy a year and a half ago with a wretched district schoolmaster—

a rumour which has persisted to this day. Even now there is talk of some love-letter written by Zina and said to have been passed from hand to hand in Mordasov; but I should like to know if any one has seen that letter. If it has passed from hand to hand, what has become of it? Every one has heard about it, but nobody has seen it. I, at any rate, have never come across any one who has seen this letter with his own eyes. If you drop a hint about it to Marya Alexandrovna she simply fails to understand you. Now let us assume that there really was something, and Zina did write the love-letter (I fancy, indeed, that it must have been so), how skilful it all was on Marya Alexandrovna's part! How adroitly was this awkward, scandalous affair suppressed and stifled! Not a trace, not a hint! Marya Alexandrovna takes no notice now of this ignoble slander, and at the same time, God knows how she may have worked to save the honour of her only daughter from the slightest slur. And as for Zina's not being married, that's very natural: there are no eligible young men here. The only fitting match for Zina would be a reigning prince. Have you ever seen a beauty like her? It is true that she is proud—too proud. They say that Mozglyakov is paying her his addresses, but it is hardly likely to come to a marriage. What is Mozglyakov? It is true that he is young, not bad-looking, a dandy, has a hundred and fifty serfs not mort-gaged, and comes from Petersburg. But in the first place, you know he is not quite sound in the upper storey. He is feather-headed, a chatterbox, and has some very new-fangled ideas. And after all what is an estate of a hundred and fifty serfs, especially with new-fangled ideas! That marriage won't come off.

All that the kind reader has read so far was written by me five months ago entirely from excess of feeling. I may as well confess betimes I have rather a partiality for Marya Alexandrovna. I wanted to write something like a eulogy on that magnificent lady, and to put it in the shape of a playful letter to a friend, on the model of the letters which used, at one time, in the old golden days that, thank God, will never return, to be published in the *Northern Bee* and other periodi-cals. But as I have no friend, and have, moreover, a certain innate literary timidity, my work has remained in my table drawer as my first literary effort and a memento of peaceful recreation in hours of leisure and comfort.

Five months have passed, and all at once a wonderful event has occurred in Mordasov: early one morning Prince K. arrived in the town and stopped at Marya Alexandrovna's house. The consequences of this arrival have been innumerable. The Prince spent only three days in Mordasov, but those three days have left behind them momentous memories that will never be effaced. I will say more: Prince K. produced, in a certain sense, a revolution in our town. The story of that revolution is, of course, one of the most significant pages in the annals of Mordasov. That page I have made up my mind at last, after some hesitation, to put into literary shape and lay before the criticism of the honoured public. My story will contain the full and remarkable history of the exaltation, glory and solemn downfall of Marya Alexandrovna and all her family: a worthy and alluring theme for an author. First of all, of course, I must explain what there was wonderful in Prince K.'s arriving in our town and staying at Marya Alexandrovna's—and to do that I must, of course, say a few words about Prince K. himself. And that I will do. Besides, the biography of that personage is absolutely essential for all the further development of our story. And so I will begin.

Chapter 2

I WILL begin by saying that Prince K. was not so extraordinarily aged, but yet he was so decrepit, so worn-out, that as one looked at him the thought instinctively occurred to one that in another minute he might drop to pieces. Extremely queer stories of the most fantastic kind were repeated in Mordasov about this prince. People even said that the old man was off his head. Every one thought it very strange that the owner of an estate of four thousand serfs, a man of distinguished family, who might, if he had chosen, have had a great influence in the province, should live in solitude on his magnificent estate, a complete hermit. Many had known Prince K. when he was staying in Mordasov six or seven years before, and they declared that in those days he could not endure solitude and had not the faintest resemblance to a hermit.

All that I could ascertain about him, on good authority, however, was this:

In his young days, which were, however, long ago, the Prince had made a brilliant début, he had led a gay life, flirted, had made several tours abroad, sang songs, made puns, and had at no period been distinguished by the brilliance of his intellectual gifts. Of course he had squandered all his fortune, and found himself in his old age without a farthing. Some one advised him to visit his estate, which was beginning to be sold by auction. He set off and arrived at Mordasov, where he stayed six months. He liked provincial life extremely. During those six months he dissipated all he had left, to the last halfpenny, spending his whole time in gambling and getting up various intrigues with the ladies of the province. He was, moreover, extremely good-natured, though of course not without certain princely airs, which were, however, regarded in Mordasov as characteristic of the highest society, and so, instead of annoying people, they positively impressed them favourably. The ladies especially were in perpetual ecstasy over their charming visitor. A number of curious reminiscences of him were preserved. People said among other things that the Prince spent more than half the day over his toilet, and was, it appeared, entirely made up of different little bits. No one knew when and where he had managed to become so dilapidated. He wore a wig, moustaches, whiskers, and even a little "imperial"—all, every hair of it, false, and of a magnificent black colour; he rouged and powdered every day. It was said that he had little springs to smooth away the wrinkles on his face, and these springs were in some peculiar way concealed in his hair. It was asserted, too, that he wore corsets, because he had lost a rib jumping somewhat clumsily out of a window on one of his amorous adventures in Italy. He limped with the left leg; it was maintained that the leg in question was an artificial one, and that the real one had been broken in the course of another similar adventure in Paris, and that he had been provided with a new cork leg of a special pattern. But what will not people say? It certainly was true that his right eye was a glass one, though it was a most skilful imitation. His teeth, too, were false. He spent whole days washing in various patent waters, scenting and pomading himself. It was recalled, however, that even then the Prince was perceptibly beginning to grow feeble, and that he had become insufferably garrulous. It seemed as though his career were drawing to its close. Every one knew that he had not a farthing. And all of a sudden, quite unexpectedly, one of his nearest relations, a very aged lady who had lived for many years in Paris and from whom he could have had no expectations, died, just a month after the funeral of her legal heir. The Prince found himself quite unexpectedly the heir to her fortune. A magnificent estate of four thousand serfs, about forty miles from Mordasov, all came to him. He at once prepared to go to Petersburg to settle his affairs. Our ladies got up a magnificent subscription dinner in his honour. It is recalled that the Prince was enchantingly gay at this farewell banquet, he made puns, made every one laugh, told the most extraordinary anecdotes, vowed that he would return as quickly as possible to Duhanovo (his new property), and promised that on his return there would be a continual round of fêtes, picnics, balls, and fireworks. For a whole year after his departure the ladies talked of this promise, and awaited their charming old friend with immense impatience. While awaiting his return they even made up parties to Duhanovo, where there was an old-world manor house and garden, with acacias lopped into the shape of lions, with artificial mounds, with lakes, upon which boats sailed up and down, with wooden images of Turks playing a pipe for figureheads, with arbours, with pavilions, with pleasure grounds, and other attractions.

At last the Prince returned, but to the general surprise and disappointment he did not even call at Mordasov on his way, but settled at Duhanovo and lived like a hermit. Strange rumours began to circulate, and altogether from that period the Prince's history became obscure and fantastic. To begin with, it was asserted that he had not been altogether successful in Petersburg, that some of his relations and future heirs tried to take advantage of the Prince's mental feebleness in order to get him put under some sort of supervision, fearing that he would squander everything again. What was more, some people declared that they had tried to put him in a lunatic asylum, but that one of his relations, a gentleman of consequence, had taken his part, explaining frankly to the others that the poor Prince, half-dead and half a dummy already, would probably soon die together, and then the property would come to them without the help of a lunatic asylum. I repeat again: what will not people say? especially in our town, Mordasov. All this, so it was said, scared the Prince terribly, so much so that he became a transformed character and turned into a hermit. Some of the Mordasov gentry went from curiosity to call upon him, but were either not received or met with a very strange reception. The Prince did not even recognize his old acquaintances. It was asserted that he did not want to recognize them. The Governor, too, paid him a visit.

He returned with the news that in his opinion the Prince really was a little off his head, and ever afterwards he made a wry face at any allusion to his visit to Duhanovo. The ladies were loud in their indignation. At last a fact of prime importance was discovered, namely, that the Prince was entirely in the power of one Stepanida Matveyevna, a woman no one knew anything about, who had come with him from Petersburg, was stout and elderly, and went about in cotton dresses with the keys in her hands; that the Prince obeyed her in everything like a child and did not dare to take a step without her permission, that she even washed him with her own hands, that she spoilt him, dandled him and comforted him like a child, and that finally she kept away from him all visitors, and especially the relations, who had been gradually beginning to visit Duhanovo to see how things were going. People in Mordasov discussed this incomprehensible relationship a great deal, especially the ladies. It was added that Stepanida Matveyevna had unchecked and independent control of the Prince's whole estate; that she dismissed the stewards, the bailiffs and the servants, and collected the revenues; but that she ruled it well, so that the peasants blessed their fate. As regards the Prince himself, it was learned that his days were spent almost entirely on his toilet, in trying on wigs and dress-coats; that he spent the rest of his time with Stepanida Matveyevna, that he played his game of cards with her, tried his fortune with the cards, only now and then going for a ride on a quiet English mare, on which occasions Stepanida Matveyevna invariably accompanied him in a closed chaise in case of mishap, for the Prince rode on horseback chiefly for effect, and could hardly keep in the saddle. He was sometimes seen also on foot, wearing an overcoat and wide-brimmed straw hat; with a lady's pink neckerchief round his neck, with an eyeglass in his eye and a wicker basket for mushrooms, cornflowers and other wild flowers; Stepanida Matveyevna always accompanied him, while behind them walked two tall footmen, and the carriage followed to be ready in case of need. When he was met by a peasant, who stepped aside, took off his hat, bowed low and said: "Good-day, Prince, your Excellency, our sunshine," the Prince promptly turned his lorgnette upon him, nodded graciously and said to him affably: *"Bonjour, mon ami, bonjour!"* Many such rumours were current in Mordasov; they could not forget the Prince: he was such a near neighbour! What was the general amazement when one fine day there was a report that the Prince, the eccentric hermit, had arrived in Mordasov in person and was staying at Marya Alexandrovna's! All was bustle and excitement. Every one was eager for an explanation, all asked one another what it meant? Some prepared to call on Marya Alexandrovna. The Prince's arrival struck every one as a wonder. The ladies sent one another notes, prepared to call on one another, sent their maids and their husbands to make inquiries. It seemed particularly strange and hard to understand why the Prince should stay at Marya Alexandrovna's rather than at any one else's. Anna Nikolaevna Antipov was particularly annoyed, because the Prince was a very distant relation of hers. But to solve all these questions it is absolutely necessary to call on Marya Alexandrovna herself, and we cordially invite the kind reader to do so. It is true that it is only ten o'clock in the morning, but I don't think she will refuse to receive an intimate friend. Us, at any rate, she will certainly admit.

Chapter 3

TEN o'clock in the morning. We are in Marya Alexandrovna's house in the main street, in the very room which the lady of the house on solemn occasions calls her *salon*. Marya Alexandrovna has also a boudoir. In this *salon* there are well-painted floors, and rather nice wall-papers that were ordered expressly for the walls. In the rather clumsy furniture red is the predominating colour. There is an open fireplace, over the mantelpiece a mirror, before the looking-glass a bronze clock with a Cupid on it in very bad taste. In the space between the windows there are two looking-glasses from which they have already removed the covers. On little tables in front of the looking-glass there are two more clocks. Against the wall at the further end is a magnificent piano, which was procured for Zina. Zina is musical. Round the glowing fire arm-chairs are set, as far as possible in picturesque confusion; among them a little table. At the other end of the room another table covered with a cloth of dazzling whiteness; on it a silver samovar is boiling and a pretty tea-service is set out. The samovar and the tea are presided over by Nastasya Petrovna Zyablov, a lady who lives with Marya Alexandrovna in the capacity of a distant relation. Two words about this lady. She is a widow, she is over thirty, a brunette with a fresh complexion, and with lively dark-brown eyes. Altogether she is good-looking. She is of a gay disposition and much given to laughter, rather sly, of course a scandalmonger, and very capable of managing any little affair of her own. She has two children, they are somewhere at school. She would very much like to get married again. She is rather independent in her behaviour. Her husband was an officer in the army. Marya Alexandrovna herself is sitting by the fire, in the very best of spirits, and in a becoming light green dress. She is highly delighted at the arrival of the Prince, who is at this moment upstairs, engaged in his toilet. She is so delighted that she does not even think it necessary to conceal her joy. Before her stands a young man, telling her something with animation. It is evident from his eyes that he is anxious to please his listeners. He is five-and-twenty. His manners would not be bad, but he frequently flies into raptures, and he has, besides, pretensions to wit and humour. He is very well dressed, fair, and rather nice-looking. But we have spoken of him already; he is Mr. Mozglyakov, of whom great things are expected. Marya Alexandrovna privately thinks that he is rather empty-headed, but gives him a warm welcome. He is a suitor for the hand of her daughter Zina, with whom, in his own words, he is madly in love. He turns every moment to Zina, trying to extract a smile from her lips by his wit and gaiety. But she is perceptibly cold and careless in her manner to him. At this instant she is standing apart, at the piano, and turning over a calendar with her fingers. She is one of those women who excite general enthusiasm and wonder whenever they appear in society. She is incredibly beautiful; tall, a brunette with exquisite, almost black eyes, a graceful figure and a superb bust. Her shoulders and arms are antique, her foot is fascinating, she has the step of a queen. She is a little pale to-day; but her full, crimson, exquisitely chiselled lips, between which gleam even, little teeth like threaded pearls, will haunt your dreams for the next three days if once you glance at them. Her expression is grave and severe. Monsieur Mozglyakov seems to fear her intent gaze, at least he winces when he ventures to glance at her. Her movements are disdainfully careless. She is dressed in simple white muslin, which suits her exquisitely, but then everything suits her. On her finger is a ring woven of hair, and from the colour, not her mamma's. Mozglyakov has never dared to ask her whose hair it is. That morning Zina is particularly silent and over-melancholy, as though preoccupied. Marya Alexandrovna, on the other hand, is ready to talk without stopping, though she, too, glances at her daughter from time to time with a peculiar, suspicious look; she does so, however, stealthily, as though she, too, were afraid of her.

"I am so delighted, so delighted, Pavel Alexandrovitch!" she prattles, "that I am ready to cry aloud my joy out of the window to every passer-by. To say nothing of the charming surprise you have given Zina and me by returning a fortnight earlier than you promised; that goes without saying! I am awfully glad that you have brought the dear Prince with you. You know how fond I am of the fascinating old darling! But no, no! You won't understand me. You young people can't understand my enthusiasm, however much I might assure you of it! You don't know what he was to me in the past, six years ago. Do you remember, Zina? I forget, though, you were staying with your aunt at that time. . . . You would not believe it, Pavel Alexandrovitch, I was his mentor, sister, mother! He did what I told him like a child! There was something naïve, tender and ennobling in our relations; something even, as it were, Arcadian. . . . I really don't know what to call it! That is why he thinks of my house alone with gratitude, *ce pauvre prince!* Do you know, Pavel Alexandrovitch, you may perhaps have saved him by bringing him to me! I have thought of him with a pang at my heart these last six years. You wouldn't believe it, he positively haunted my dreams. They say that monstrous woman has bewitched him, ruined him. But at last you have torn him out of her clutches! Yes, we must take advantage of the opportunity and save him altogether! But tell me once more, how did you succeed in doing it? Describe your whole meeting as fully as possible. Just now I was in such excitement that I only attended to the central fact, though all the little details, so to speak, make up the real flavour of it! I am awfully fond of trifling details, even on most important occasions what I notice first is the small points . . . and . . . while he is still engaged in his toilet . . ."

"But it is all just what I have told you already, Marya Alexandrovna," Mozglyakov responds with readiness, perfectly willing to tell his story for the tenth time, it is a pleasure to him. "I was travelling all night, of course I did not sleep all night, you can imagine what haste I was in," he adds, turning to Zina; "in short, I swore, I shouted, I demanded horses. I even made a row at the posting stations over getting horses; if it were printed it would make quite a poem in the latest fashion! But that is off the point! At six o'clock in the morning I reached the last station, Igishevo. I was all of a shiver, but I did not want to warm myself; I called for horses! I frightened the overseer's wife, who had a baby at the breast, I think I must have upset her milk. . . . The sunrise was enchanting. The hoar frost, you know, all crimson and silver! I took no notice of anything; in short, I was in desperate haste! I took the horses by storm; I snatched them from a collegiate councillor, and almost challenged him to a duel. I was told that a quarter of an hour before some prince had set off from the station travelling with his own horses; he had spent the night there. I scarcely listened. I got into my sledge, flew off, as though I were let off the chain. There is something like it in Fet, in some elegy of his. Just six miles from the town, at the cross-road leading to the Svyetozersky Monastery, I saw that something surprising had happened. A huge travelling coach was lying on its side, a coachman and two footmen were standing beside it in perplexity, and heart-rending shrieks and wails were coming from the carriage, that lay on its side. I was thinking of driving by: 'Let it lie on its side; it is no business of mine.' But I was overcome by a feeling of humanity, which, as Heine expresses it, pokes its nose into everything. I stopped. I, my Semyon and the driver—another true Russian heart—hastened to their assistance, and so the six of us together hoisted up the coach at last and set it on its legs, though indeed it had none, for it was on runners. Some peasants on their way to the town with wood helped too. I gave them a trifle. I thought, no doubt this is the same prince! I looked. My goodness! It was he, Prince Gavrila! 'What a meeting!' I cried out to him. 'Prince! Uncle!' Of course he scarcely recognized me at first sight; however, he almost knew me . . . at a second look. I must confess, however, that he hardly understands who I am now, and I believe he takes me for some one else and not a relation. I saw him seven years ago in Petersburg; but of course I was a boy then. I remembered him; he impressed me—but how should he remember me! I introduced myself; he was enchanted, embraced me, and at the same time he was trembling all over with fright and crying—he really was crying, I saw that with my own eyes! One thing and another— I persuaded him at last to get into my sledge and to come for at least one day to Mordasov, to rest and recover. He agreed without any ado. . . . He told me he was going to the Svyetozersky Monastery to visit the monk Misail, whom he honours and reveres; that Stepanida Matveyevna—and which of us relations has not heard of Stepanida Matveyevna? she drove me off with a broom from Duhanovo last year—that this Stepanida Matveyevna had received a letter telling her that some one of her folks in Moscow was at the last gasp; her father, or her daughter, I don't remember which exactly, and I am not interested to know, possibly father and daughter both together, with, maybe, the addition of a nephew, a potman in some public-house. . . . In short, she was so upset that she made up her mind to part from her prince for ten days, and flew off to adorn the capital with her presence. The Prince stayed quiet for one day, for another, tried on his wigs, pomaded, and painted himself; he tried to tell his fortune with the cards (maybe with beans too), but could not put up with it without Stepanida Matveyevna. He ordered his horses and set off to the Svyetozersky Monastery. Some one of his household, fearing the absent Stepanida Matveyevna, ventured to protest, but the Prince persisted. He set off yesterday, after dinner, stayed the night at Igishevo. He left the station at daybreak, and just at the turning that leads to

Father Misail's, went flying with his carriage almost into a ravine. I rescued him, persuaded him to visit our common and deeply respected friend, Marya Alexandrovna; he said that you were the most fascinating lady he had ever known—and here we are, and at this moment the Prince is upstairs adjusting his toilet with the assistance of his valet, whom he has not forgotten to bring with him, and whom he never will, under any circumstances, forget to take with him, for he would sooner die than consent to appear before ladies without certain preliminary preparations, or rather, adjustments. . . . That's the whole story! *Eine allerliebste Geschichte!"*

"But what a humorist he is, Zina!" cries Marya Alexandrovna, after hearing his story. "How charmingly he tells it. But listen, *Paul,* one question: explain to me exactly what relation you are to the Prince! You call him uncle?"

"Upon my word, Marya Alexandrovna, I do not know how or in what way I am related to him; it's seven times removed, I believe, maybe even seventy times seven. It's not a bit my fault; it's all Aunt Aglaya Mihalovna. Aunt Aglaya Mihalovna does nothing but count over the relations on her fingers, though; it was she forced me to go to see him last summer at Duhanovo. She should have gone herself! I simply call him uncle, he answers to that name. That's all our relationship for to-day, anyway. . . ."

"All the same, I repeat that it must have been a prompting from on High that led you to bring him straight to me! I tremble to think what would have happened to him, poor darling, if he had got into any one else's hands instead of mine. They would have pounced upon him, torn him to pieces, devoured him! They would have fallen upon him as though he were a gold mine—I dare say they would have robbed him! You cannot imagine what low, greedy, artful people there are here, Pavel Alexandrovitch! . . ."

"Upon my soul, to whom should he have been taken if not to you? What are you saying, Marya Alexandrovna?" puts in the widow, Nastasya Petrovna, as she pours out the tea. "You don't suppose he might have been taken to Anna Nikolaevna's?"

"But why is he so long coming? It's really strange," says Marya Alexandrovna, getting up from her seat impatiently.

"Uncle, do you mean? Why, I expect he will be another five hours up there dressing! Besides, as he had quite lost his memory, he has perhaps forgotten that he is on a visit to you. You know he is a most extraordinary person, Marya Alexandrovna!"

"Oh, come, come! What nonsense."

"Not nonsense at all, Marya Alexandrovna! He is half a made-up dummy, not a man! You saw him six years ago, but it is only an hour since I have seen him. He is half a corpse. He is only a reminiscence of a man; they have forgotten to bury him, you know! His eyes are artificial, his legs are made of cork, he is all worked by springs, he even talks by machinery."

"My goodness, what a giddy fellow you are, to listen to you!" exclaims Marya Alexandrovna, assuming a stern air. "Aren't you ashamed, a young man, and a relation, to talk like that about that venerable old man? To say nothing of his boundless kindliness"—and her voice takes a touching note—"remember that he is a relic, a scion, so to speak, of our aristocracy. My friend, *mon ami!* I understand that you are led into this frivolity by those modern ideas of which you are always talking. But, my goodness! I share those new ideas myself. I realize that what is at the root of your views is generous and creditable, I realize that there is, indeed, something lofty in those new ideas; but all that does not prevent my seeing the direct, so to speak, practical side of things. I have seen something of the world, I have seen more than you have, and, last of all, I am a mother, and you are still young. He is an old man, and so in our eyes he is absurd! What is more, last time you said that you would certainly emancipate your serfs, and that you must do something for the public weal, and all that comes from poring so much over your Shakespeare or somebody! Believe me, Pavel Alexandrovitch, your Shakespeare has had his day, and if he were to rise again he would not with all his cleverness understand anything about our life. If there is anything chivalrous and sublime in our contemporary society it is to be found only in the highest rank. A prince in a sack is still a prince; a prince in a hovel is as good as a prince in a palace! Here Natalya Dmitryevna's husband has built himself something like a palace—and yet he is Natalya Dmitryevna's husband and no more! And if Natalya Dmitryevna were to stick on fifty crinolines she would still remain the same Natalya Dmitryevna, and would add nothing to herself by it. You, too, represent the highest rank to some extent because you are descended from it. I consider myself not far removed from it, and it's an ill bird that fouls its own nest! But you will find out all this of yourself, *mon cher Paul,* better than I can tell you, and will forget your Shakespeare. I predict it. I am persuaded that you are not in earnest even now, but are talking like that because it is *chic.* But I have been chattering too long. You stay here, *mon cher Paul,* I will go upstairs and find out about the Prince. Perhaps he wants something, and with my stupid servants . . ."

And Marya Alexandrovna goes hurriedly out of the room at the thought of her stupid servants.

"Marya Alexandrovna seems very much pleased that that dressed-up creature, Anna Nikolaevna, has not got hold of the Prince. And you know she keeps declaring that she is related to him. She must be bursting with spite now!" remarked Nastasya Petrovna; but observing that she received no answer and glancing at Zina and Pavel Alexandrovitch, she grasped the situation at once and went out of the room as though on some errand. But to reward herself for her discretion she stopped just outside and listened at the door.

Pavel Alexandrovitch turned at once to Zina. He was in great agitation, his voice was quivering.

"Zinaida Afanasyevna, you are not angry with me?" he asked, with a timid and imploring air.

"With you! What for?" said Zina, raising her wonderful eyes and looking at him with a faint flush.

"For coming back so soon, Zinaida Afanasyevna! I could not resist it, I could not wait another fortnight. . . . I positively dreamed of you. I flew back to hear my fate. . . . But you frown, you are angry! Surely you will not refuse to let me hear something decisive?"

Zinaida certainly did frown.

"I expected you would talk of that," she answered, dropping her eyes again, in a firm and severe voice in which there was a note of vexation. "And as that expectation was very painful to me, the sooner it is over the better. Again you insist, that is, beg for an answer. Very well, I will repeat it to you again, for my answer is still the same as before: wait! I tell you again—I have not made up my mind yet, and cannot promise to be your wife. That is not exacted by force, Pavel Alexandrovitch. But to comfort you, I will add I do not definitely refuse you. Note, too, in giving you hope now of a favourable decision, I do this entirely out of consideration for your impatience and anxiety. I repeat that I wish to remain perfectly free in my decision, and if I tell you in the end that I do not consent, you must not blame me for having given you hope. And so realize that!"

"And so what does that amount to?" cried Mozglyakov in a plaintive voice. "Is that hope? Can I extract any hope at all from your words, Zinaida Afanasyevna?"

"Remember all I have told you and extract what you choose. It is for you to decide, but I will add nothing more. I do not refuse you yet, but only tell you, wait. I tell you again I reserve a perfect right to refuse you if I think fit. There is another thing I must tell you, Pavel Alexandrovitch: if you have returned before the time fixed for my answer in order to work upon me in indirect ways, relying on outside support, on the influence of Mamma, for instance, you have made a great mistake in your calculations. Then I shall refuse you straight out. Do you hear? And now—that's enough, and please, until the right time, do not utter one word more on this subject."

All this speech was pronounced drily, firmly, and without hesitation, as though it had been studied beforehand. Monsieur Paul felt that he had been made a fool of. At that moment Marya Alexandrovna returned. And almost immediately after her Madame Zyablov.

"He will be down directly, I fancy, Zina! Nastasya Petrovna, be quick, make some fresh tea!" Marya Alexandrovna was positively a little excited.

"Anna Nikolaevna has already sent to inquire. Her Anyutka has come flying to the kitchen to ask questions. I bet she's cross now!" Nastasya Petrovna announced, rushing up to the samovar.

"What is that to me!" Marya Alexandrovna said over her shoulder to Madame Zyablov. "As though I were interested to know what your Anna Nikolaevna is thinking. You may be sure I shan't send any one to her kitchen. And I wonder, I really wonder why you persist in regarding me as an enemy to poor Anna Nikolaevna, and not you only, but everybody in the town. I appeal to you, Pavel Alexandrovitch! You know us both. Come, what reason have I to be her enemy? Over precedence? But I don't care in the least about precedence. Let her be first, let her. I am ready to be the first to go and congratulate her on being first. And, after all, it's quite unfair. I will take her part —I am bound to take her part! She is maligned. Why do you all attack her? She is young and fond of fine clothes—is that a reason, pray? To my thinking fine clothes are better than something else— like Natalya Dmitryevna, who is fond—of what one really can't talk about. Is it because Anna Nikolaevna is always gadding about and can't stay at home? But my goodness! She has had no education, and of course she finds it tedious to open a book or occupy herself with anything for two minutes together. She flirts and makes eyes out of the window at any one who passes in the street. But why do people assure her she is so pretty when she has nothing but a white face? She is ridiculous at dances, I admit. But why assure her she dances the polka so splendidly? She wears impossible hats and head-dresses; but is it her fault that God has given her no taste, but has made her so easily

taken in? Assure her that it looks nice to pin a bit of coloured paper
in her hair, and she would stick it in her hair. She is a scandalmonger
—but that's the way here: there is no one in the town who does not
talk scandal. Sushilov, with his whiskers, is always there, morning,
noon, and almost night. But, dear me! No wonder, when her husband
plays cards till five in the morning. Besides, there are so many bad
examples here! Moreover, it *may be* only scandal. In short, I shall
always stand up for her, always. But, good gracious, here is the Prince!
It is he, it is he! I should know him among a thousand! At last I see
you, *mon prince!*" cried Marya Alexandrovna, and she flew to meet
the Prince as he entered.

Chapter 4

AT THE first casual glance you would not have taken the Prince
for an old man at all, it was only on a closer and more attentive
inspection that you discerned that he was a sort of corpse worked by
mechanism. All the resources of art were utilized to disguise this
mummy as a young man. A marvellous wig, whiskers, moustaches,
and a little imperial, all of a superb black, covered half his face. His
face was whitened and rouged with extraordinary skill, and there was
not a trace of wrinkles upon it. What had become of them? There is
no knowing. He was dressed in the height of fashion, as though he
had stepped out of a fashion-plate. He had on a visiting jacket or
something of the sort, upon my word I don't know what exactly, but
it was something extremely fashionable and up-to-date, created especially for morning calls. His gloves, his cravat, his waistcoat, his linen,
and so on, were all of dazzling freshness and artistic taste. The Prince
limped a little, but limped so elegantly that it seemed as though it
were prescribed by fashion. He had an eyeglass in his eye, the very
eyes that was itself of glass. The prince was saturated with scent. In
talking he drawled certain words in a peculiar way, perhaps from the
weakness of old age, perhaps because all his teeth were false, perhaps
for the sake of greater dignity. Certain syllables he pronounced with
extraordinary sweetness, with a special stress on certain vowels. *Yes*
with him was turned into *ye-es*. In all his manners there was a certain
carelessness, acquired in the course of his life as a dandy. But if anything of his old fashionable life was still preserved, it was preserved
as it were unconsciously in the form of some vague reminiscence, in

the form of some outlived buried past, which, alas! no cosmetics, corsets, perfumers or barbers could bring to life again. And so we shall do well to begin by confessing that if the man had not lost his wits he had long ago lost his memory, and was now constantly muddled, repeating himself, and even babbling at random. One needed a special knack to talk to him. But Marya Alexandrovna could rely upon herself, and at the sight of the Prince she flew into unutterable ecstasy.

"But you have not changed, not changed in the least!" she exclaimed, seizing her visitor by both hands and making him sit down in a comfortable arm-chair. "Sit down, Prince, sit down! It's six years, six whole years since we have met, and not a single letter, not one line all that time! Oh, how badly you have treated me, Prince! How angry I have been with you, *mon cher prince!* But—tea, tea! Oh, my goodness, Nastasya Petrovna, tea!"

"Thank you, tha-ank you, I am sor-ry," the Prince lisped (we forgot to say that he lisped a little, but that, too, he did as though it were the fashion). "I am so-or-ry! And only fancy, last year I qui-ite meant to come here," he added, looking round the room through his lorgnette. "But they scared me: you had chol-er-a here, I was told. . . ."

"No, Prince, we haven't had cholera here," said Marya Alexandrovna.

"There was the cattle plague here, Uncle!" Mozglyakov put in, anxious to distinguish himself. Marya Alexandrovna looked him up and down with a stern expression.

"To be sure, cattle pla-ague or something of the sort. . . . So I stayed at home. But how is your husband, my dear Anna Nikolaevna? Still at his pros-e-cuting duties?"

"N-no, Prince," said Marya Alexandrovna, a little disconcerted; "my husband is not prosecutor . . ."

"I'll bet Uncle has got mixed up and takes you for Anna Nikolaevna Antipov!" cried the sharp-witted Mozglyakov, but he pulled himself up at once, observing that Marya Alexandrovna seemed to be wincing apart from these explanations.

"Oh, ye-es, ye-es Anna Nikolaevna, and . . . and . . . (I keep forgetting!). Oh, ye-es, Antipov, An-ti-pov it is," the Prince acquiesced.

"N-no, Prince, you are very much mistaken," said Marya Alexandrovna, with a bitter smile. "I am not Anna Nikolaevna, and I must say I didn't at all expect that you wouldn't know me. You have surprised me, Prince. I am your old friend, Marya Alexandrovna Moskalev. Do you remember, Prince, Marya Alexandrovna? . . ."

"Marya A-lex-and-rovna, only fancy! And I actually supposed that you were (what's her name)—oh, ye-es, Anna Vassilyevna. . . . *C'est délicieux!* So I have come to the wrong place. And I thought, my dear fellow, that you were taking me to Anna Matveyevna. *C'est charmant!* It often happens like that with me, though. . . . I often go to the wrong place! I am satisfied, always satisfied, whatever happens. So you are not Nastasya Vassilyevna? That's interesting. . . ."

"Marya Alexandrovna, Prince, Marya Alexandrovna! Oh, how badly you have treated me! To forget your best, best friend!"

"Oh, ye-es, my be-est friend . . . *pardon, pardon!*" the Prince lisped, gazing at Zina.

"That is my daughter, Zina. You don't know her, Prince, she was away when you were here last, in the year 18—, do you remember?"

"Is that your daughter? *Charmante, charmante!*" muttered the Prince, eyeing Zina with avidity through his lorgnette. *"Mais quelle beauté!"* he murmured, evidently struck by her.

"Tea, Prince," said Marya Alexandrovna, calling the Prince's attention to the page standing before him with a tray in his hands. The Prince took the cup and looked attentively at the boy, who had pink and chubby cheeks.

"A-ah, is this your boy?" he said. "What a pret-ty boy! A-and I am sure he behaves ni-icely. . . ."

"But, Prince," Marya Alexandrovna interposed hurriedly, "I have heard of your terrible adventure! I must confess I was frightened out of my wits. . . . Weren't you hurt? Make sure! It is not a thing to neglect."

"He upset me! He upset me! The coachman upset me!" the Prince exclaimed, with extraordinary animation. "I thought the end of the world was coming or something of the sort, and so I must own I was so frightened that—holy saints forgive me!—I didn't know whether I was on my head or my feet! I hadn't expected it, I hadn't expected it! I did not ex-pect it at all. And it's all the fault of my coachman, Fe-o-fil. I rely upon you now entirely, my dear fellow: do what is necessary and investigate the matter thoroughly. I am per-suaded that it was an at-tempt on my life."

"All right, Uncle; all right," answered Pavel Alexandrovitch. "I will investigate it thoroughly. Only listen, Uncle! Forgive him this once, won't you? What do you say?"

"I won't forgive him on any account. I am persuaded that he was trying to ta-ake my life. He, together with Lavrenty, whom I left at home. Only fancy, he has got hold of some new ideas, you know!

There is a sort of scepticism in him . . . in short, he is a communist in the fullest sense of the word! I am positively afraid to meet him."

"Ah, what you say is so true, Prince!" exclaimed Marya Alexandrovna. "You wouldn't believe what I suffer from these good-for-nothing servants myself! Imagine, I have two new servants, and I must say they are so stupid that I am simply struggling with them from morning till night. You wouldn't believe how stupid they are, Prince!"

"Oh, ye-es; oh, ye-es. But I must say, I really prefer to have a footman rather stupid," observed the Prince, who like all old men was delighted when people listened to his chatter with obsequious attention; "it somehow suits a footman, and really is a vir-tue in him if he is simple-hearted and stupid. Only in certain cases, of course. It makes him more im-pos-ing, it gives a solem-nity to his countenance; it gives him a greater air of good breeding, and what I insist on most is a servant's good bre-ed-ing. Here I have my Te-ren-ty. You remember my Te-ren-ty, my dear fellow, don't you? As soon as I looked at him I predicted that he was destined to be a hall-porter! Stupid—phe-nom-enally. He stares like a sheep looking at water. But what imposing dignity! What solemnity! Such a pale pink double chin! You know, with a white cravat in full get-up, it does produce an effect. I took the greatest fancy to him. Sometimes I look at him and feel quite fascinated; he might be writing a dissertation—such a solemn air! In fact, he is a regular German philosopher Kant, or perhaps more truly, a fat, overfed turkey-cock. Perfectly *comme il faut* for a manservant."

Marya Alexandrovna laughed with enthusiasm, and even clapped her hands. Pavel Alexandrovitch seconded her with all his heart; he was extremely entertained by his "uncle." Nastasya Petrovna laughed too—even Zina gave a smile.

"But what humour, what gaiety, what wit you have, Prince!" exclaimed Marya Alexandrovna. "What a precious gift for noting the most subtle, the most amusing point! . . . And to vanish from society, to shut yourself up for five whole years! With such a talent! But you might write, Prince! You might be another Von Vizin, another Griboyedov, another Gogol! . . ."

"Oh, ye-es; oh, ye-es!" said the Prince, highly delighted; "I might, and do you know I used to be remarkably witty in the old days. I actually wrote a vau-de-ville for the stage. There were several ex-qui-site lines in it! It was never acted, though. . . ."

"Ah, how charming it would be to read it, and, do you know, Zina, it would be apropos now! They are getting up theatricals here—for a patriotic object, Prince—for the benefit of the wounded. . . . Your vaudeville would be the thing!"

"Of course! I am ready to write it again, indeed . . . though I have completely forgotten it. But I remember there were two or three puns, such that . . ." (and the Prince kissed his finger-tips) "and altogether when I was abro-ad I made a reg-u-lar fu-rore. I remember Lord Byron. We were on friendly terms. He danced the Cracoviana enchantingly at the Vienna Congress."

"Lord Byron, Uncle! Upon my word, Uncle, what do you mean?"

"Oh, ye-es, Lord Byron. Though perhaps it wasn't Lord Byron, but some one else. Quite so; not Lord Byron, but a Pole, I remember perfectly now. And that Pole was ve-ry ori-gi-nal, he gave himself out for a count, and it afterwards turned out that he was some sort of head cook, but he did dance the Cracoviana most en-chant-ing-ly, and at last he broke his leg. I wrote some verses on that occasion to:

> " 'Our dear little Pole
> To dance was his rôle.'

And what came then, I can't remember.

> " 'When he broke his limb
> No more capers for him.' "

"Oh, that must be how it went, Uncle," exclaimed Mozglyakov, entering more and more into the spirit of the thing.

"I think that is what it was, my dear fellow," answered the old man, "or something like it. But perhaps it wasn't it, but anyway, the verses turned out very successfully. . . . The fact is I've forgotten some things that have happened. It comes from being so busy."

"But tell us, Prince, what have you been doing all this time in your solitude?" Marya Alexandrovna inquired with interest. "I have so often thought of you, *mon cher prince,* that I must confess I am burning now with impatience to have a full account of it all."

"What have I been doing? Well, altogether, you know, I have a great de-al to do. Sometimes—one rests; and sometimes, you know, I go for walks and imagine all sorts of things. . . ."

"You must have a very powerful imagination, Uncle!"

"Extremely powerful, my dear boy. I sometimes imagine such things that I won-der at myself afterwards. When I was in Kaduev . . . Apropos! I believe you used to be Deputy Governor at Kaduev?"

"I, Uncle? Upon my soul, what do you mean?" exclaimed Pavel Alexandrovitch.

"Fancy, my dear fellow, and I have been taking you all the while for the Deputy Governor, and I was wondering to myself how is it that all of a sudden you had got quite a different face. . . . He had such a dig-ni-fied face—intelligent, you know. He was an exceptionally intelligent man, and he was always com-pos-ing verses, on all sorts of occasions. He was a bit like the king of diamonds in profile. . . ."

"No, Prince," Marya Alexandrovna interposed, "I vow you will ruin yourself by living like that! To shut yourself up in solitude for five years, to see no one, to hear nothing! But you are a doomed man, Prince. Ask any one among those who are devoted to you, and every one will tell you that you are a doomed man!"

"Really!" exclaimed the Prince.

"I assure you it is so; I am speaking to you as a friend, as a sister. I am speaking to you because you are dear to me, because the memory of the past is sacred to me! What have I to gain by pretending? No, you must reform your life fundamentally, or you will fall sick, you will waste away, you will die. . . ."

"Oh, dear me! Am I really going to die so soon?" exclaimed the Prince, panic-stricken. "And do you know, you have guessed right! I am frightfully troubled by haemorrhoids, especially at certain times. . . . And when I have attacks of it I generally have the most re-mark-able symptoms (I will tell you all about them). . . . To begin with . . ."

"Uncle, you will tell about that another time," Pavel Alexandrovitch interposed, "but now . . . isn't it time for us to start?"

"Oh, ye-es! Another time if you like. Possibly it is not so very interesting to listen to now I come to think of it. . . . At the same time it is a very curious complaint. It has several stages. . . . Remind me, my dear boy, I will describe this evening in de-tail one thing that happened. . . ."

"But listen, Prince, you ought to try a cure abroad," Marya Alexandrovna intervened again.

"Abroad? Oh, ye-es; oh, ye-es! I certainly shall go abroad. I remember when I was abroad in the twenties, it was won-der-fully gay. I almost got married to a French *vicomtesse*. I was tremendously in love with her at the time, and wanted to devote my life to her. I did not marry her, though; somebody else did. And such a strange thing happened, I was absent only two hours and the other man won the day, a German baron, he was; he was put into a madhouse for a time afterwards."

"But *cher prince,* what I meant was, that you must think seriously about your health. There are such doctors abroad . . . and besides, a

change of life does so much! You really must abandon your Duhanovo,
if only for a time."

"Ce-er-tain-ly! I have made up my mind to do so long ago, and, do
you know, I mean to try hy-drop-athy."

"Hydropathy?"

"Hydropathy. I have tried hy-drop-athy once already. I was at the
waters then. There was a Moscow lady there, I have forgotten her surname, only she was a very poetical lady, about seventy; she had a
daughter too, about fifty, a widow with cataract in her eye. She, too,
almost talked in verse. Afterwards she had a very unfortunate mishap:
she killed one of her serf girls in a rage and was tried for it. And, do
you know, they took it into their heads to make me try the water cure.
I must say I had nothing the matter with me; but they kept in-sisting:
'Try the cure, try the cure!' Simply from delicacy I began to drink
the waters; I thought I really should be better for it; I drank and drank
and drank and drank. I drank up a perfect waterfall, and, do you know,
hydropathy is really a very good thing and did me a very great deal of
good, so that if I had not fallen ill, I assure you I should have been
perfectly well. . . ."

"That is a very just conclusion, Uncle. Tell me, Uncle, have you
studied logic?"

"Upon my word, what questions you ask," Marya Alexandrovna
observed sternly, much scandalized.

"I did study it, my dear boy, but very long ago. I studied philosophy,
too, in Germany! I went through a whole course, but even at the time
I couldn't remember it. But . . . I must own . . . you have so frightened
me about this illness that I feel quite upset. I'll come back directly,
though. . . ."

"But where are you going, Prince?" cried Marya Alexandrovna in
amazement.

"I will be back directly, directly . . . I simply want to note down a
new idea. . . . *Au revoir.* . . ."

"What a specimen!" cried Pavel Alexandrovitch, and he went off
into a fit of laughter.

Marya Alexandrovna lost patience.

"I don't understand, I don't understand in the least what you are
laughing at," she began with heat. "To laugh at a venerable old man,
at a relation, to take advantage of his angelic kindness and to turn
every word he utters into ridicule! I blushed for you, Pavel Alexandrovitch! Tell me, please, what do you find absurd in him? I saw
nothing to laugh at in him."

"When he does not know people, when he sometimes talks nonsense?"

"But that is the effect of the awful life he is leading, of his horrible imprisonment for the last five years under the eye of that fiendish woman. One ought to pity him and not to laugh at him. He did not even know me, you were a witness of that yourself. That was, so to speak, a flagrant example! He absolutely must be saved! I suggested to him to go abroad simply in the hope that he might get rid of that . . . market-woman!"

"Do you know what? We ought to find him a wife, Marya Alexandrovna," cried Pavel Alexandrovitch.

"Again! You are incorrigible, Monsieur Mozglyakov!"

"No, Marya Alexandrovna, no! This time I am speaking seriously! Why shouldn't we marry him? It's an idea. *C'est une idée comme une autre*. What harm could it do him, kindly tell me that? On the contrary, he is in such a position that only such a step could save him! He is still legally able to marry. To begin with, he would be rescued from that trollop (excuse the expression). Secondly and chiefly—imagine that he picks out a girl or, better still, a widow—sweet, kind, sensible, tender and, above all, poor, who will look after him like a daughter and realize that he has been a benefactor to her in giving her the title of his wife. And what could be better for him than a noble and upright creature who would belong to him and would be continually at his side, instead of that . . . female. Of course she ought to be pretty, for even to this day Uncle loves a pretty face. Did you notice how he kept looking at Zinaida Afanasyevna?"

"But where will you find such a bride?" asked Nastasya Petrovna, listening attentively.

"Ah, there it is: why, you, for instance, if you were willing! Allow me to ask: aren't you perfectly suitable as a match for the Prince? In the first place you are pretty, secondly you are a widow, thirdly you are a lady, fourthly poor (for you really are not very well off), fifthly you are a very sensible woman and consequently will love him, keep him in cotton wool, send that person about her business, take him abroad, will feed him on semolina pudding and sweetmeats, all that up to the time when he leaves this transitory world, which will happen within a year and possibly within two or three months. Then you will be a princess, a wealthy widow, and as a reward for your pluck you can marry a marquis or a general! *C'est joli*, isn't it?"

"Why, my gracious! I believe I should fall in love with him, poor dear gentleman, out of mere gratitude if only he made me an offer!"

exclaimed Madame Zyablov, and her dark expressive eyes gleamed. "But that's—all nonsense."

"Nonsense? If you like, it needn't be nonsense! Ask me nicely and then you may cut off my finger if you are not engaged to him to-day! Why, there is nothing easier than to persuade or tempt Uncle into anything! He always says, 'Oh, yes; oh, yes!' You have heard him yourself. We will marry him so that he will hardly notice it. We will deceive him and marry him, perhaps: why, it is for his benefit, mercy upon us! ... You might dress up in your best to be ready for anything, Nastasya Petrovna."

Monsieur Mozglyakov's enthusiasm knew no bounds. Sensible though she might be, Madame Zyablov's mouth watered.

"I know I look a perfect slut to-day without your telling me," she replied. "I have grown shockingly careless, I have no ambition. That's how it is I go about such a grub. Why, do I really look like a cook?"

All this time Marya Alexandrovna was sitting with a strange look on her face. I am not mistaken if I say that she heard Pavel Alexandrovitch's strange proposition with a sort of dismay, as though disconcerted by it. ...

At last she recovered herself.

"All that is very nice, no doubt, but it is all nonsense and absurdity, and what is more—quite out of place," she interrupted Mozglyakov sharply.

"But why, my dear Marya Alexandrovna, why is it nonsense and out of place?"

"For many reasons, and first of all because you are in my house and the Prince is my guest, and I allow no one to show a lack of respect for my house. I look upon your words as nothing but a jest, Pavel Alexandrovitch. But, thank goodness, here is the Prince!"

"Here I am," cried the Prince, walking into the room. "It's wonderful, *cher ami,* how many different ideas I've had to-day. And at other times, perhaps you wouldn't believe it, I seem to have none at all. Nothing all day."

"That's probably from your tumble to-day, Uncle. It has upset your nerves, and that is how it is ..."

"I put it down to that myself, my dear fellow, and I think that the accident has been really ben-e-fi-cial. So that I have made up my mind to forgive my Fe-o-fil. Do you know what, I believe he was not trying to take my life after all, what do you think? Besides, he has been punished only lately by having his beard shaved off."

"His beard shaved off, Uncle! Why, he has a beard as big as the German Empire."

"Oh, ye-es, as big as the German Empire. You are generally very correct in your con-clu-sions, my dear boy. But it is a false one. And only fancy how it happened; I was sent a price list. The superbest beards for coachmen and gentlemen newly imported from abroad, also whiskers, imperials, moustaches, and so on, and all of the best qual-i-ty and at the most moderate prices. I thought I would send for a beard just to see what it was like. So I wrote for a coachman's beard, it really was a beard worth seeing! But it turned out that Fe-o-fil had a beard of his own almost twice as big. Of course we were puzzled what to do: to shave his off, or to send back the one they had sent us and let him wear his natural one? I thought and thought about it, and came to the conclusion that it was better for him to have the artificial one."

"Probably because art is better than nature, Uncle!"

"That was just it. And what distress it caused him when his beard was shaved off! As though he had parted with his whole career together with his beard. But isn't it time for us to start, my dear boy?"

"I am ready, Uncle."

"But I hope, Prince, that you are only going to the Governor's," Marya Alexandrovna exclaimed in excitement. "You are mine now, Prince, and belong to my family for the whole day. I am not going to tell you anything about the society here, of course. Perhaps you want to go to Anna Nikolaevna's, and I have not the right to disillusion you; besides, I am fully persuaded that time will tell its own story. But remember that I am your hostess, sister, nurse for the whole of to-day, and I must own that I tremble for you, Prince! You don't know these people, you don't yet know them."

"Rely on me, Marya Alexandrovna. Everything shall be as I promised you," said Mozglyakov.

"Oh, you feather-head! Rely on you! I expect you to dinner, Prince. We dine early. And how I regret that on this occasion my husband is in the country. How delighted he would have been to see you. He has such a respect for you, he has such a genuine affection for you."

"Your husband? So you have a husband too?" the Prince queried.

"Oh, my goodness, how forgetful you are, Prince! Why, you have utterly, utterly forgotten all the past! My husband, Afanasy Matveyitch, surely you have not forgotten him? He is in the country now, but you have seen him a thousand times in old days. Do you remember, Prince, Afanasy Matveyitch?"

"Afanasy Matveyitch! In the country, only fancy! *Mais c'est déli-*

cieux! So you have a husband too? What a strange thing, though? That's exactly like some vaudeville: 'The husband's on the stair, but the wife has gone to . . .' Excuse me, I have forgotten! Only the wife had gone off somewhere also, to Tula or to Yaroslav, anyway it's very funny."

" 'The husband is on the stair, but the wife has gone to Tver,' Uncle," Mozglyakov prompted him.

"Oh, ye-es! Oh, ye-es! Thank you, my dear boy, Tver it was. *Charmant, charmant!* So that it rhymes also. You always drop into rhyme, my dear boy. I didn't remember whether it was to Yaroslav or to Kostroma, but only that his wife had gone off somewhere too. *Charmant, charmant!* I have a little forgotten what I was beginning to speak about, though. . . . Ah, ye-es, so we are starting, my dear fellow. *Au revoir, madame. Adieu, ma charmante demoiselle,"* added the Prince, turning to Zina and kissing his finger-tips.

"To dinner, to dinner, Prince! Don't forget to make haste back," Marya Alexandrovna called after him.

Chapter 5

Y OU might just glance into the kitchen, Nastasya Petrovna," she said, after seeing the Prince out. "I have a presentiment that that monster Nikita will be sure to spoil the dinner! I am convinced that he is drunk by now. . . ."

Nastasya Petrovna obeyed. As she went out she looked suspiciously at Marya Alexandrovna and observed in her signs of exceptional agitation. Instead of going to look after the monster Nikita, Nastasya Petrovna went into the bigger drawing-room, from there through the corridor to her own room, from there into a little dark apartment, something like a lumber-room, where there were trunks standing, garments of some sort hanging, and the dirty linen of the whole family stored in bags. She went on tiptoe to the closed door, held her breath, stooped down, looked through the keyhole and listened. This door was one of the three doors of the very room in which Marya Alexandrovna and Zina had remained, and was always kept shut and locked.

Marya Alexandrovna considered Nastasya Petrovna a sly but exceedingly frivolous woman. No doubt the idea did at times occur to her that Nastasya Petrovna had no scruples and was given to eavesdropping. But at the present moment Marya Alexandrovna was so much engrossed and excited that she quite forgot to take certain precautions. She sat down in an easy chair and looked significantly at Zina. Zina was conscious of that gaze fixed upon her, and a feeling of uneasy depression began to weigh upon her heart.

"Zina!"

Zina slowly turned her pale face towards her, and lifted her dreamy black eyes.

"Zina, I intend to speak to you about an extremely important matter."

Zina turned completely round to her mother, folded her hands, and stood waiting. There was a look in her face of vexation and sarcasm, which she tried, however, to conceal.

"I want to ask you, Zina, what you thought to-day of *that* Mozglyakov?"

"You have known what I think of him for ever so long," answered Zina reluctantly.

"Yes, *mon enfant;* but it seems to me that he is becoming too persistent with his . . . attentions."

"He says he is in love with me, and his persistency is excusable."

"Strange; you used not to be so . . . ready to excuse him. On the contrary, you invariably attacked him whenever I spoke of him."

"It is strange, too, that you always defended him and were so set on my marrying him, and now you attack him."

"That is almost so. I don't deny it, Zina; I did desire to see you married to Mozglyakov. It was painful for me to see your continual depression, your unhappiness, which I am quite capable of understanding (whatever you may think of me) and which poisons my sleep at night. I felt sure at last that nothing but a complete change of life could save you! And that change must be—marriage. We are not well off and cannot, for instance, go abroad. The asses here are surprised that you are three-and-twenty and not yet married, and concoct a regular legend to explain it. But is it likely I should make a match for you with a local councillor, or with Ivan Ivanitch, our attorney here? Is there a husband here for you? Mozglyakov is empty-headed, of course, but he is the best of the lot. He is of a decent family, he has connections, he has a hundred and fifty serfs; that is better anyway than living by tricks and bribes, and God knows what shifts; that's why I turned my eyes upon him. But I swear I never had a real liking for him. I am persuaded that it was the hand of the Almighty that forewarned me. And if God were to send you even now something better—oh! what a good thing it will be that you have not pledged your word! You have not said anything positive to him to-day, have you, Zina?"

"Why all this pretence, Mamma, when the whole thing could be said in two words?" Zina brought out irritably.

"Pretence, Zina, pretence! And you can use a word like that to your mother? But what am I saying? For a long while past you have put no faith in your mother! For a long while past you have looked on me as your enemy and not your mother."

"Oh, do leave off, Mamma! Surely you and I need not dispute about words! Don't we understand each other? I should have thought it was high time we did."

"You wound me, my child! You do not believe that I am ready to do absolutely anything, anything, anything to secure your future."

Zina looked at her mother sarcastically and with annoyance.

"You don't want to marry me to that Prince to *secure* my future, do you?" she asked, with a queer smile.

"I have not said a word of that, but since you have mentioned it, I will say that if it were your lot to marry the Prince, it would be a great happiness for you and not at all senseless."

"And I consider that's simply nonsense!" cried Zina passionately. "Nonsense, nonsense! I also think, Mamma, that you have too much romantic inspiration, you are a poetess, in the fullest sense of the word; that's what they call you here. You are continually having projects. Their impossibility and absurdity do not deter you. I had a foreboding while the Prince was sitting here that you had this in your mind. When Mozglyakov began playing the fool, and declaring that we ought to find a wife for the old man, I read all you were thinking in your face. I am ready to bet that you are thinking of that, and that is what you are leading up to with me. But as your incessant scheming on my behalf is beginning to bore me to death, is beginning to torture me, I beg you not to say one word about it to me; do you hear, Mamma? not one word, and I should be glad if you would remember that!" She was breathless with anger.

"You are a child, Zina, a sick, irritable child," answered Marya Alexandrovna in a tearful voice full of emotion. "You speak disrespectfully to me and hurt my feelings. No mother would put up with what I endure from you every day! But you are nervous, you are ill, you are suffering, and I am a mother and, above all, a Christian. I must bear it and forgive. But one word, Zina: if I really were dreaming of that union—why do you look upon it as nonsense? To my mind Mozglyakov never spoke more sensibly than just now when he pointed out that it was essential for the Prince to marry—of course not that slut Nastasya. He was talking wildly about that."

"Listen, Mamma! Tell me straight out: are you questioning me like this out of curiosity, or with a motive?"

"I ask you only, why does it seem to you such nonsense?"

"Oh, how annoying! What a life!" exclaimed Zina, stamping with impatience. "I'll tell you why, if you still don't know: to say nothing of all the other absurdities—to take advantage of a wretched old man's having fallen into dotage, to deceive him, to marry him, a wreck, in order to get hold of his money and then every day, every hour, to long for his death, to my mind is not simply nonsense, but so base, so base, that I can't congratulate you on such ideas, Mamma!"

The silence lasted for a minute.

"Zina, do you remember what happened two years ago?" Marya Alexandrovna asked suddenly.

Zina started.

"Mamma," she said in a severe voice, "you promised me solemnly never to speak of that again."

"And now I solemnly beg you, my child, to allow me only once to break that promise which I have never broken till now, Zina! The time has come for a full explanation between us. These two years of silence have been awful! It can't go on like this! . . . I am ready to beg you on my knees to let me speak. Listen, Zina, your own mother begs you on her knees! At the same time I give you my solemn promise—the promise of an unhappy mother who adores her daughter —that I will never under any circumstances whatever, even if it were a question of my life, I will never speak of it again. This shall be the last time, but now—it is essential!"

Marya Alexandrovna was calculating on her words having their full effect.

"Speak," said Zina, turning perceptibly pale.

"Thank you, Zina. Two years ago poor dear Mitya, your little brother, had a tutor . . ."

"But why do you begin in this solemn way, Mamma! Why all this fine speaking, all these details, which are utterly unnecessary, which are painful, which are only too well known to both of us?" Zina cut her short with a kind of angry repulsion.

"Because, my child, I, your mother, am compelled to justify myself before you! Because I want to put it all before you from an absolutely different point of view, and not from the mistaken point of view from which you are in the habit of looking at it. In fact, that you might understand better the conclusion I am meaning to draw from all this. Do not imagine, my child, that I want to play with your feelings. No, Zina, you will find in me a true mother, and perhaps shedding tears at my feet, the feet of the *base woman* you have just called me, you will yourself implore the reconciliation you have so long, so haughtily rejected; that is why I wish to speak out the whole truth, Zina, the whole from the very beginning; otherwise I will be silent!"

"Speak," Zina repeated, cursing her mother's love of fine speeches from the bottom of her heart.

"I will continue, Zina: how this district school-teacher, hardly more than a boy, made an impression upon you, I could never understand. I put too much confidence in your good sense, in your honourable pride, and above all, in his utter insignificance (for one must tell the whole truth), to suspect there could be anything between you. And all of a sudden you come to me and announce that you intend to marry him! Zina! It was a dagger in my heart! I uttered a shriek and fell into a swoon. But . . . you remember all that? I need not say, I thought it needful to use all my authority, which you call tyranny. Only think, a boy, the son of a sacristan hired for twelve roubles a month, a scribbler of wretched doggerel, published out of kindness in the 'Library of Good Reading,' a fellow who could talk of nothing but that cursed Shakespeare—that boy, your husband, the husband of Zinaida Moskalev! Why, it is worthy of Florian and his shepherdesses! Forgive me, Zina, but the mere remembrance moves me to frenzy! I refused him, but no authority could keep you in check. Your father could do nothing but blink his eyes, and did not even understand when I tried to explain to him. You maintained your relations with that boy, even had interviews with him, and most awful of all, you even ventured to correspond with him. Rumours were spreading all over the town. Our neighbours began stabbing me with hints: they were already in high glee, they were already blowing their trumpets, and suddenly all my predictions were fulfilled in the most flagrant way. You quarrelled over something; he showed himself utterly unworthy of you . . . the wretched boy (I cannot call him a man), and threatened to show your letters about the town. At that threat, full of indignation, you were wild with anger and gave him a slap in the face. Yes, Zina, that circumstance, too, is known to me! I know all about it, all. That very day the miserable boy showed one of your letters to that scoundrel Zaushin, and within an hour that letter was already in the hands of Natalya Dmitryevna, my

deadly enemy. The same evening that madman, overcome with remorse, made an absurd attempt to poison himself. In a word, there
was a most appalling scandal! That slut Nastasya ran to me in alarm
with the terrible intelligence: the letter had been for a full hour in
Natalya Dmitryevna's hands; within two hours the whole town would
know of your disgrace! I controlled myself, I did not swoon—but
with what blows you struck at my heart, Zina! That shameless hussy,
that monster, Nastasya, demanded two hundred roubles, and for that
sum swore to get that letter back. I myself ran through the snow in
my thin slippers to the Jew Bumstein and pawned my jewel-case—a
keepsake from my sainted mother! Within two hours the letter was
in my hands: Nastasya had stolen it. She broke open a box and your
reputation was saved—there was nothing to prove the story! But in
what anxiety you made me pass that awful day! The next day I
noticed, for the first time in my life, some grey hairs in my head,
Zina! You have formed your own judgment now of that boy's conduct. You will agree now yourself, and perhaps with a bitter smile,
that it would have been the acme of folly to entrust your future to
his keeping. But from that time you have been fretting, you have
been tormenting yourself, my child; you cannot forget him, or rather
not him, he was always unworthy of you, but the phantom of your
past happiness. That unhappy youth is lying on his death-bed now,
I am told he is in consumption, and you—angel of goodness!—you
will not marry during his lifetime that you may not lacerate his feelings; for to this day he is tortured by jealousy, though I am persuaded that he never loved you with true exalted love! I know that
when he heard of Mozglyakov's attentions, he spied on you, sent to
find out, made inquiries. You are sparing him, my child; I have
guessed your secret, and God knows with what bitter tears I have
wetted my pillow!"

"Oh, do drop all that, Mamma!" Zina interrupted in unspeakable
misery. "I think you might have left your pillow out," she added
bitingly. "You can't speak without all this declamation and flourish!"

"You do not believe me, Zina! Do not look upon me with antagonism, my child! My eyes have not been dry for these two years, but
I hid my tears from you, and I swear that I, too, have greatly changed
during that time! I have long understood your feelings and, I regret to
say, that it is only now that I have realized all the depth of your
grief. Can you blame me, my dear, for looking on this attachment as
a romantic folly inspired by that cursed Shakespeare who will poke
his nose where he is not wanted? What mother will blame me for my

terror, for the steps I took, for the sternness of my decision? But now, now after seeing your suffering for these two years, I understand and appreciate your feelings. Believe me that I understand you, perhaps far better than you understand yourself. I am persuaded you love not him, that unnatural boy, but your golden dreams, your lost happiness, your exalted ideals. I, too, have loved, and perhaps more ardently than you. I have suffered myself; I, too, have had my exalted ideals. And so who can blame me now; and above all, can you blame me for regarding a match with the Prince as the thing best fitted to save you, most essential for you in your present position?"

Zina had been listening with wonder to this long tirade, knowing perfectly well that her mother would not take up this tone without some object. But the unexpected conclusion in her mother's last words utterly amazed her.

"Can you really propose to marry me to that Prince?" she cried, looking at her mother in astonishment and almost alarm. "Then it is not a mere dream, not a project, but your firm intention. So I guessed right? And . . . and . . . and in what way will such a marriage save me and be essential in my position? And . . . and . . . and in what way is all this worked in with what you have been saying just now—with all this story? . . . I really don't understand you, Mamma!"

"And I wonder how any one can fail to understand, *mon ange!*" exclaimed Marya Alexandrovna, growing excited in her turn. "In the first place the mere fact that you will move into a different society, a different world! You will leave for ever this detestable little town, full of terrible memories for you; where you have no friend, no welcome; where you have been slandered; where all these magpies hate you for your beauty. You may even go abroad this spring, to Italy, to Switzerland, to Spain; to Spain, Zina, to Spain, where there is the Alhambra and the Guadalquivir, not this wretched, miserable river here with its unseemly name. . . ."

"But excuse me, Mamma, you are talking as if I were already married, or at least as though the Prince had made me an offer."

"Don't trouble about that, my angel; I know what I am talking about. But—allow me to proceed. I have already mentioned the *first* point, now for the *second:* I understand, my child, with what repugnance you would give your hand to that Mozglyakov."

"I know without your telling me that I never shall be his wife!" Zina answered with heat, and her eyes flashed.

"And if you knew how well I understand your repugnance, my dear! It is an awful thing to swear before the altar of God to love one for whom you can feel no love! It is awful to belong to one whom you cannot even respect! And he will have your love; it is for that he will marry you. I can tell that by the look in his eyes when you turn away from him. How awful to keep up the pretence! I have endured that trial for twenty-five years. Your father has wrecked my life. He has, so to speak, sapped my youth, and how often you have seen my tears!"

"Papa is in the country, please let him alone," answered Zina.

"I know you always take his part. Ah, Zina! My heart ached, when from motives of prudence I desired your marriage with Mozglyakov. But there would be no need to dissemble with the Prince. Of course I need not say that you cannot care for him . . . with love, and indeed he is not capable of requiring such love. . . ."

"My goodness, what nonsense! But I assure you that you are mistaken from the very beginning upon the most essential point. Let me tell you that I don't want to sacrifice myself for no reason that I know of. Let me tell you that I don't want to be married to anybody, and that I shall remain single. For the last two years you have been nagging at me for not getting married. Well, you will have to make up your mind to accept it. I don't want to, and that is all! And so it shall be."

"But Zinotchka darling, for goodness' sake don't fly into a passion before you have heard what I have to say! What a hot-headed child you are, to be sure. Allow me to look at it from my point of view, and you will agree with me at once. The Prince will live for a year or two at the utmost, and to my mind it is better to be a young widow than an old maid, to say nothing of your being at his death a princess, free, wealthy, and independent! My dear, you may look with contempt on these calculations—calculations on his death! But I am a mother, and what mother would condemn me for my far-sightedness? Finally, if like an angel of goodness you still feel compassion for that boy, such compassion that you are unwilling to be married so long as he lives (as I conjecture is the case), reflect that you will give him fresh courage and relieve his mind by marrying the Prince! If he has a spark of common sense, he will understand, of course, that jealousy of the Prince would be misplaced, absurd; he will understand that you have married from motives of prudence, from necessity. He will understand, indeed, that is—I merely mean to say, you can marry any one you like when the Prince is dead."

"To put it plainly, it comes to this: marry the Prince, plunder him, reckoning on his death to marry a lover afterwards. You balance your accounts cleverly. You try to tempt me, offering me . . . I understand you, Mamma, I quite understand you! You never can resist a display of noble sentiments, even in the nastiest action. You had better have said simply and straightforwardly: 'Zina, it is base, but it is profitable, and so consent to do it!' that would be more candid, anyway."

"But why, my child, persist in looking at it from that point of view —from the point of view of deception, artfulness, self-interest? You regard my calculation as base, deceitful. But by all that is holy, what deceit is there about it, where is the baseness? Look at yourself in the glass; you are so lovely that one might give up a kingdom for your sake! And you, you a beauty, sacrifice your best years to an old man! Like a lovely star you will shed light on his declining hours; you, like the green ivy, will twine about his age; you, and not that nettle, that abominable woman, who has cast a spell on him, and from greed is sapping his existence. Do you think that his money, his princely rank, is more precious than you? Where is the deceit, where is the baseness in that? You don't know what you are saying, Zina!"

"They evidently are more precious, since I have to marry a decrepit wreck. Deceit is always deceit, Mamma, whatever the object may be."

"On the contrary, my dear, on the contrary! You may look at it from a lofty, indeed from a Christian point of view, my child! You said yourself on one occasion, in a moment of frenzy, that you would like to be a Sister of Mercy. Your heart had suffered, had grown hard. You said (I know this) that it could not love now. If you do not believe in love, turn your feelings to another loftier subject, turn it genuinely, like a child with all faith and reverence—and God will bless you. This old man has suffered too, he is unhappy, he is persecuted; I have known him for some years and have always cherished for him an incomprehensible sympathy, akin to love, as though I had a presentiment. Be his friend, be his daughter, be perhaps even his plaything—if one is to speak plainly. But warm his heart, and you will be doing an act godly and virtuous! He is ridiculous—don't think of that. He is half a man—have compassion on him; you are a Christian! Master yourself; such deeds are done by self-mastery. To our minds it is hard to bandage wounds in a hospital; it is revolting to breathe the infected air of the sick-room. But there are angels of mercy who do that and thank God for their vocation. Here is balm for your wounded heart, occupation, self-sacrifice—and you will heal your own wounds. Where is the egoism in it, where is the baseness? But you don't believe me. You imagine, perhaps, that I am dissimulating when I talk of duty, of self-sacrifice. You can't conceive that I, a frivolous, worldly woman, can have a heart feelings, principles. Well, refuse to believe, insult your mother, but admit that what she says is reasonable and helpful. Imagine that it is not I who am speaking but some one else; shut your eyes, turn round to the corner, imagine that some unseen voice is speaking to you. . . . What troubles you most is that it is all for the sake of money, as though it were some sale or purchase. Well, renounce the money if money is so hateful to you. Keep only what is barely necessary for yourself, and give away the rest to the poor. Help him, for instance, that luckless boy lying now on his death-bed."

"He will take no help," Zina said softly, as though to herself.

"He will not take it, but his mother will take it," Marya Alexandrovna answered triumphantly. "She will take it without his knowing. You sold your earrings, your aunt's present, and helped her six months ago; I know that. I know the old woman takes in washing to keep her unhappy son."

"He will soon have no need of help."

"I know what you are hinting at, too," Marya Alexandrovna caught her up; and an inspiration, a genuine inspiration, dawned upon her. "I know what you are alluding to. They say he is in consumption and will not live long. But who says that? The other day I purposely questioned Kalist Stanislavitch; I was anxious about him, because I have a heart, Zina. Kalist Stanislavitch answered me, that the illness was, of course, serious, but that he was convinced that, so far, the poor boy was not in consumption, but that it was only a rather severe affection of the chest. Question him yourself. He told me, as a fact, that under different circumstances, especially with a change of climate and surroundings, the patient might recover. He told me that in Spain— and I had heard it before and even read it—that in Spain there is some extraordinary island, I believe it is called Malaga—like some wine, in fact—where not only persons with weak lungs, but even consumptives recover simply from the climate, and that people go there on purpose to be treated, people of rank and consequence, of course; or commercial people too, if only they are rich. But the magical Alhambra, the myrtles, the lemons, the Spaniards on their mules! That alone would make an extraordinary impression on a poetical nature. You think he will not take your help, your money for the journey? Well, deceive him, then, if you are sorry for him! Deception is pardonable when it is to save a man's life. Give him hope, even promise him your love; tell him you will marry him when you are left a widow. Anything in the world can be said in an honourable way. Your mother will not teach you anything dishonourable, Zina; you will do this to save his life, so anything is permissible! You will restore him to life through hope; he will begin to take trouble over his health, to try and cure himself, to obey the doctors. He will try to regain his health for the sake of happiness. If he recovers, even though you do not marry him, anyway he will be well again, and anyway you will have saved him, you will have brought him back to life. And indeed one may even look at him with sympathy; perhaps fate has taught him a lesson and changed him for the better, and if only he is worthy of you—marry him, if you like, when you are left a widow. You will be wealthy and independent. If you restore him to health, you can give him a position in the world—a career. Your marriage will be more excusable then than now, when it is out of the question. What would be in store for you both if you were to venture on such madness now? Universal contempt, beggary, the task of pulling the nasty urchins' ears, for that is part of his duties, the reading of Shakespeare together, staying on for ever in Mordasov; and lastly, his speedy and inevitable death. While if you restore him to health you will be restoring him for a useful, virtuous life; if you forgive him, you will make him adore you. He is fretting over his abominable action, and opening a new life to him, forgiving him, you will give him hope and reconcile him to himself. He may enter the service, may rise to a good grade; and indeed, even if he does not recover, he will die happy, at peace with himself, in your arms—for you will be able to be with him at that moment—trusting in your love, forgiven by you, in the shade of the myrtles and lemons, under the azure exotic sky! Oh, Zina! all that is in your power! There is every advantage for you in it—and all that through marriage with the Prince."

Marya Alexandrovna had finished. Rather a prolonged silence followed. Zina's agitation was inexpressible.

We will not undertake to describe Zina's feelings; we cannot even conjecture them. But it seemed that Marya Alexandrovna had found the way to her heart. Not knowing what was the present state of her daughter's feelings, she had gone over every mood in which she might possibly be, and guessed that she had at last hit on the true path. She coarsely touched upon the sorest spot in Zina's heart. And, from old habit, she could not refrain from the exhibition of noble sentiments, which of course did not hoodwink Zina. "What does it matter if she does not believe me," thought Marya Alexandrovna. "If only J have made her think things over! If only I have clearly hinted at what I could not say outright!" So she argued, and she attained her object. The effect was produced. Zina listened greedily. Her cheeks glowed, her bosom heaved.

"Listen, Mamma," she said resolutely at last, though the sudden pallor of her face betrayed what that resolution cost her. "Listen, Mamma."

But at that moment a sudden noise in the entrance hall, and a harsh, shrill voice asking for Marya Alexandrovna, made Zina pause. Marya Alexandrovna jumped from her seat.

"Oh, my goodness!" she cried, "the devil has sent that magpie, the Colonel's wife; why, I all but turned her out of the house a fortnight ago!" she added, almost in despair. "But . . . but it is impossible not to receive her now! Impossible! She most likely has news, or she would not have dared to come. It is important, Zina! I must know. . . . We must neglect nothing now!—Oh, how grateful I am for your visit!" she cried, hastening to meet her guest. "How did you come to think of me, my precious Sofya Petrovna? What an en-chant-ing surprise."

Zina ran out of the room.

Chapter 6

THE Colonel's wife, Sofya Petrovna Karpuhin, had only a moral resemblance to a magpie. Physically she was more like a sparrow. She was a little lady, about fifty, with sharp little eyes, with freckles and yellow patches all over her face. On her little dried-up body, perched on strong, thin, sparrow-like little legs, was a dark silk dress which was always rustling, for the Colonel's lady could not keep still for two seconds. She was a spiteful and malignant gossip. She was mad on the fact of being a colonel's wife. She very often fought with her husband, the retired Colonel, and used to scratch his face. Moreover, she used to drink four glasses of vodka in the morning, and as many in the evening, and had an insane hatred for Anna Nikolaevna Antipov, who had turned her out of her house the week before, as well as for Natalya Dmitryevna Paskudin, who had assisted in the operation.

"I have only looked in for a minute, *mon ange,*" she twittered. "I really ought not to have sat down. I have only come to tell you what marvellous things are going on among us. The whole town has gone off its head about that Prince! Our wily ones—*vous comprenez*—are chasing him, hunting him down, snatching him from one another, regaling him with champagne—you wouldn't believe it! You wouldn't believe it! How could you bring yourself to let him go? Do you know that he is at Natalya Dmitryevna's now?"

"At Natalya Dmitryevna's!" cried Marya Alexandrovna, jumping up from her seat. "Why, he was only going to see the Governor, and afterwards, perhaps, to Anna Nikolaevna's, and was not going to stay long even there!"

"Not for long, I dare say; catch him now if you can! He did not find the Governor at home, then he went to Anna Nikolaevna's, promised to dine with her, and Natalya Dmitryevna, who is always with her nowadays, has carried him off to her house for lunch. There's your Prince!"

"And what . . . about Mozglyakov? Why, he promised . . ."

"Yes, your Mozglyakov, indeed! You think a lot of him, don't you? . . . Why, he has gone with him. You see if they don't get up a game of cards there, and he loses all his money as he did last year! Yes, and they'll make the Prince take a hand too, and strip him like bark. And the things she is spreading about, that Natalya! She is crying aloud that you are trying to ensnare the Prince, you know, with certain objects—*vous comprenez?* She is talking to him about it. Of course he doesn't understand; he sits like a wet cat and says, 'Oh, ye-es! oh, ye-es!' at every word. And she, she brought out her Sonka—only fancy! fifteen, and she still keeps her in short skirts, only down to the knee, so you can imagine. . . . They sent for that little orphan Mashka; she is in short skirts too, only above the knee—I looked through my lorgnette . . . they put some sort of red caps with feathers on their heads—I really don't know what it was meant for! And they made the two little magpies dance the Cossack dance to the piano before the Prince! Well, you know his weakness; he was melting with ecstasy. 'Contours! contours!' He looked at them through his lorgnette, and they did distinguish themselves, the magpies! They got red in the face, they twirled their legs, and it was such an exhibition that I was shocked, and that was all about it. Tfoo! Call that a dance! I've danced myself, the shawl dance, at the breaking-up party at Madame Jarnis's select boarding school—and it really was a distinguished performance. I was applauded by senators! The daughters of princes and counts were educated there! But this was simply a *cancan!* I grew hot with shame, I grew hot, hot! I simply could not sit it out! . . ."

"But . . . surely you have not been at Natalya Dmitryevna's yourself? Why, you . . ."

"Why, yes, she did insult me last week. I say that straight out to every one. *Mais, ma chère,* I wanted to have a peep at that Prince, if it was only through a crack in the door. I did go. For where else could I have seen him? I shouldn't have been to see her, if it hadn't been for that horrid old Prince! Only fancy, chocolate was handed round to every one, but not offered to me, and they did not say a word to me all the time. She did that on purpose, you know. The tub of a woman, I'll pay her out! But good-bye, *mon ange.* I am in a hurry now, a great hurry . . . I must find Akulina Panfilovna, and tell her . . . only you may as well say good-bye to the Prince now, he won't come back to you. You know he has no memory, so Anna Nikolaevna will certainly carry him off! They are all afraid that you . . . do you understand? on Zina's account."

"Quelle horreur!"

"I assure you the whole town is talking of it! Anna Nikolaevna is set on keeping him to dinner, and then to stay altogether. She is doing that to spite you, *mon ange.* I peeped into the servants' quarters; such a bustle going on there; they are preparing the dinner, such a clatter of knives. . . . They have sent for champagne. Make haste, make haste, and catch him on the road when he is on his way to her. Why, he promised to dine with you first! He is your visitor, and not hers! To think of her having the laugh of you, the sly jade, the marplot, the filthy slut! Why, she is not worth the sole of my shoe, though she is the prosecutor's wife! I am a colonel's wife myself! I was brought up at Madame Jarnis's select establishment . . . Tfoo! *Mais adieu, mon ange!* I have my own sledge waiting, or I would have gone with you. . . ."

The walking newspaper vanished. Marya Alexandrovna was all of a tremble with excitement, but her visitor's advice was extremely clear and practical. There was no reason to delay, and indeed no time to be lost. But the chief difficulty still remained. Marya Alexandrovna flew to Zina's room.

Zina, pale and troubled, was walking up and down the room, with her arms crossed and her head bowed. There were tears in her eyes, but there was a gleam of determination in the look she cast upon her mother. She made haste to hide her tears, and a sarcastic smile came on to her lips.

"Mamma," she said, before her mother could speak, "you wasted a great deal of your eloquence on me just now, far too much. But you did not blind me—I am not a child. To persuade myself that I am sacrificing myself like a Sister of Mercy, though I have no vocation for such a life, to justify the base deeds one commits from simple egoism, with the pretence of honourable motives—all that is casuistry which cannot deceive me. Do you hear? That could not deceive me, and I want you to know that!"

"But, *mon ange*," cried Marya Alexandrovna, crestfallen.

"Do not speak, Mamma. Have the patience to hear me to the end. Though I fully recognize that it is jesuitical casuistry, though I fully realize the utter baseness of such a proceeding, I fully accept your proposition—do you hear?—*fully;* and I tell you I am ready to marry the Prince, and even ready to second all your efforts to induce him to marry me. With what object I do so there is no need for you to know. It is enough that I have made up my mind. I have made up my mind to everything: I will put on his boots for him; I will be his servant; I will dance to please him, to make up for my baseness to him; I will do anything in the world that he may not regret having married me! But in return for my decision, I insist that you tell me openly by what means you are going to arrange it all. Since you have begun speaking so insistently about it, you could not—I know you—have done so without having some definite plan in your head. Be open for once in your life at least. Openness is the indispensable condition! I cannot decide without knowing exactly how you intend to do it all."

Marya Alexandrovna was so much taken aback by Zina's unexpected conclusion that for some time she stood facing her, dumb and motionless with amazement, and stared at her open-eyed. She had prepared herself to combat the obstinate romanticism of her daughter, of whose severe rectitude she stood in constant dread, and now she suddenly heard that her daughter agreed with her, and was ready to do anything, even in opposition to her principles! The whole affair was, in consequence, immensely simplified; and there was a gleam of joy in her eyes.

"Zinotchka!" she cried enthusiastically. "Zinotchka, you are my own flesh and blood!"

She could say no more, but flew to embrace her daughter.

"Oh, my goodness! I did not ask for your endearments, Mamma," cried Zina, with impatient repulsion. "I don't want your raptures! I ask you for an answer to my question, and nothing more."

"But, Zina, I love you! I adore you, and you repulse me. . . . You know I am doing my best for your happiness. . . ."

And unfeigned tears glistened in her eyes. Marya Alexandrovna really did love Zina in *her own way,* and on this occasion, in her success and her excitement, she was brimming over with sentimental emotion; in spite of a certain narrowness in her outlook, Zina understood that her mother loved her and—that love was burdensome to her. She would have been more at ease, indeed, if her mother had hated her. . . .

"Well, don't be angry, Mamma; I am so agitated," she said, to soothe her.

"I am not angry, I am not angry, my angel," Marya Alexandrovna twittered, reviving instantly. "Of course I know that you are agitated. Well, my dear, you insist on openness . . . certainly I will be open, entirely open, I assure you! If only you would trust me! And to begin with, I must tell you that I have not yet a definite plan—that is, in full detail, Zinotchka; and indeed I could not have; a clever girl like you will see why. I foresee some obstacles, in fact. . . . That magpie just now babbled all sorts of nonsense . . . (oh, my goodness, I must make haste). You see, I am entirely open! But I swear I will attain my object," she added, with enthusiasm. "My confidence is not romancing, as you called it just now, my angel; it rests on a basis of reality. It is founded on the absolute feeble-mindedness of the Prince, that is the canvas on which I can embroider what I like. The great thing is that they should not prevent me! As though those fools could outwit me!" she cried, bringing her hand down on the table, with a gleam in her eye. "That is my affair! And what is most necessary is to begin as quickly as we can, so as to settle what is most important to-day, if only it is possible."

"Very good, Mamma; only listen to one more . . . piece of openness: do you know why I am so interested to know your plan and have no faith in it? Because I cannot rely upon myself. I have said already that I have made up my mind to this base action; but if the details of your plan are really too revolting, too dirty, I warn you that I shan't be able to endure it, and I shall fling it all up. I know that that is only an added baseness; to resolve upon vileness, and to be afraid of the filth in which it is swimming; but there is no help for it. It will inevitably be so! . . ."

"But, Zinotchka, what is there particularly vile in it, *mon ange?*" Marya Alexandrovna was protesting timidly. "It is nothing but making an advantageous marriage, and everybody does that, you know! You have only to look at it from that point of view, and it all seems perfectly honourable. . . ."

"Ah, Mamma, for God's sake, don't try to deceive me! You see, I agree to anything, anything! What more do you want? Please don't be alarmed if I call things by their names. That is perhaps my only comfort now."

And a bitter smile came upon her lips.

"Well, well! that's all right, my angel; we can differ in our opinions and yet mutually respect each other. Only if you are anxious about the details and are afraid they will be nasty, leave all that business to me; I assure you that not a speck of dirt shall fall on you. Should I be willing to compromise you in people's eyes? Only rely on me and everything shall be settled capitally with the utmost decorum, above all, with the utmost decorum! There shall not be the slightest scandal, and if there should be the tiniest, unavoidable, little bit of scandal— well, what of it? Why, we shall be far away then! We shan't stay here, you know! They can talk as much as they like, we can despise them! They will be envious. And they are not worth worrying about! I wonder at you, Zinotchka—but don't be angry with me—how can you, with your pride, be afraid of them?"

"Oh, Mamma, I am not in the least afraid of them! You don't understand me a bit," Zina answered irritably.

"Well, well, my love, don't be angry. All I mean is that they are contriving some nasty plots every day of their lives, and here, just for once in your life . . . But how silly I am! What am I saying? It is not nasty at all! What is there nasty about it? On the contrary, it is perfectly honourable! I will prove that to you conclusively, Zina. I repeat, it all depends on how you look at it. . . ."

"Oh, do leave off, Mamma, with your arguments," Zina cried wrathfully, and she stamped impatiently.

"Well, my love, I'll say no more, I'll say no more! I have said something foolish again. . . ."

A brief silence followed. Marya Alexandrovna meekly waited for Zina to speak, and looked uneasily into her eyes, as a little dog who has done wrong watches its mistress.

"I don't understand how you are going to set to work," Zina continued, with repugnance. "I feel sure that you will only meet with ignominy. I despise their opinion, but for you it will mean disgrace."

"Oh, if that's all that is worrying you, my angel, please don't worry yourself! I beg you, I entreat you. If only we are agreed, you need not be anxious about me. Oh, if only you knew the storms I have weathered unharmed! The scrapes I have had to get out of! Well, only let me have a try. In any case we must lose no time in getting the Prince *tête-à-tête*. That is the very first thing. And all the rest will depend on it! But I can foresee the rest. They will all be up in arms, but ... that does not matter. I'll settle their business! I am frightened of Mozglyakov, too. ..."

"Mozglyakov!" Zina pronounced with contempt.

"Why, yes, Mozglyakov; only don't you be frightened, Zinotchka! I declare I'll bring him to such a pass that he will help us of himself! You don't know me, Zinotchka! You don't know what I am equal to in an emergency! Ah, Zinotchka, darling! When I heard about the Prince a little while ago, the thought flashed upon my brain even then. My whole mind seemed full of light at once. And who, who could expect that he would come to us? Why, such an opportunity might not occur once in a thousand years! Zinotchka, my angel, there is no dishonour in your marrying an old man and a broken-down cripple, but there would be in your marrying a man you could not endure, though you would *really* be his wife. And you won't be a real wife to the Prince, you know. Why, it is not marriage. It is only a domestic contract! Why, of course it will be a benefit to him, the fool! Why, it is bestowing priceless happiness on an old fool like that! Ah, how beautiful you are to-day, Zinotchka! Not beautiful, but a queen of beauty! Why, if I were a man I would win you half a kingdom, if you wanted it! They are all asses! How resist kissing this hand!" And Marya Alexandrovna kissed her daughter's hand warmly. "Why, this is my flesh and blood! We will marry him by force, if need be, the old fool! And how we will arrange life, you and I, Zinotchka! You won't drive away your old mother, when you are in luck, will you? Though we do quarrel, my angel, you have never had another friend like me, anyway ..."

"Mamma! If you have decided, perhaps it is time ... you were doing something. You are simply wasting time here!" said Zina impatiently.

"It is time, Zina, it is. Oh, I have been letting myself chatter too long!" cried Marya Alexandrovna, catching herself up. "They are trying to entice the Prince away altogether. I'll get into the sledge and set off at once. I'll drive round, call Mozglyakov out, and then ... Yes, I'll bring him away by force, if need be! Good-bye, Zinotchka, good-bye, darling; don't grieve, have no doubts, don't be sad—above all, don't be sad. Everything will turn out splendidly; everything shall be done with dignity and decorum! It makes all the difference how you look at it. .... Well, good-bye, good-bye."

Marya Alexandrovna made the sign of the cross over Zina, whisked out of the room, twisted and turned before the looking-glass in her own room for a brief instant, and two minutes later was being whirled along the streets of Mordasov in her sledge, which was always at the door at that hour in readiness for paying calls. Marya Alexandrovna lived *en grand*.

"No, you won't outwit me," she thought, as she sat in her sledge. "Zina consents, and that means half my task is done. And break down now! Nonsense! Ah, that Zina! She has agreed, anyway, at last! So some considerations do affect even her darling brain! I drew a tempting prospect for her! I touched her! But it is terrific how beautiful she is to-day! With her beauty I would have had Europe upside down to suit me. Oh, well, we'll wait and see. . . . Shakespeare will fade away when she becomes a princess and gets to know a thing or two. What does she know? Mordasov and her schoolmaster . . . H'm! . . . But what a princess she will be! I love in her that pride, that boldness. She is so unapproachable! She glances at you—it is the look of a queen. Why, how could she, how could she fail to see her advantage? She saw it at last! She'll see the rest. . . . I shall be with her, of course! In the end she will agree with me on every point! And she won't be able to get on without me. I shall be a princess myself. I shall be known in Petersburg. Farewell, horrid little town! The Prince will die and that boy will die, and then I will marry her to a reigning prince. Only one thing I am afraid of: didn't I confide too much in her? Wasn't I too open? Didn't I let myself be carried away by my feelings? She frightens me; oh, she frightens me!"

And Marya Alexandrovna became engrossed in her meditations; needless to say that they were of an active nature. But as the proverb has it: "A good will does more than compulsion."

Left alone, Zina spent a long time walking up and down the room, with her arms crossed. She pondered over many things. Often, and almost unconsciously, she repeated, "It's time, it's time, it's high time!" What did that fragmentary exclamation mean? More than once tears glistened on her long, silky eyelashes. She did not think of checking them or wiping them away. But there was no need for her mother to be anxious, and to try to penetrate into her daughter's thoughts. Zina had fully made up her mind, and was prepared for all the consequences.

"Wait a bit," thought Nastasya Petrovna, threading her way out of the lumber-room on the departure of the Colonel's wife. "And I was meaning to put on a pink ribbon for the benefit of that wretched Prince, and was fool enough to believe that he would marry me! Ah, Marya Alexandrovna, I am a slut, I am a beggar, I take bribes of two hundred roubles, do I? I dare say I ought to have let you off and taken nothing from a swell like you. I took the money honourably; I took it for the expenses connected with the job. . . . I might have had to give a bribe myself. What do you care that I demeaned myself to break the lock with my own hands? I did the dirty work for your benefit, while you sit with your hands in your lap! You have only to embroider on the canvas; wait a bit, I'll show you the canvas! I'll show you both whether I am a slut! You will appreciate Nastasya Petrovna and her kindness."

Chapter 7

BUT Marya Alexandrovna was led by her good genius. The project she was planning was a grand and daring one. To marry her daughter to a wealthy man, to a prince and to a wreck, to marry her without any one's knowing it, taking advantage of the feeble-mindedness and defencelessness of her guest, to do this by stealth like a thief, as Marya Alexandrovna's enemies would say, was not only bold but audacious. It was of course a profitable scheme, but in case of failure the schemers would be covered with disgrace. Marya Alexandrovna knew this, but she did not despair. "You don't know what storms I have weathered unharmed," she had said to Zina, and she had spoken truly. Otherwise she would not have been much of a heroine.

There is no disputing that all this was something like highway robbery; but Marya Alexandrovna did not take much notice of that. On that score she had one wonderful and unfailing reflection: "Once married, you can't be unmarried." A simple thought, but alluring the imagination with such extraordinary advantages that the mere conception of them sent thrills and shudders all over her. Altogether she was in great excitement, and sat in her sledge as though she were on thorns. Like a woman of inspiration with an unmistakable creative gift, she had already formed a plan of action. But this plan was still a rough sketch, altogether *en grand,* and still loomed somewhat dimly before her. A mass of details and unforeseen possibilities of all sorts awaited her. But Marya Alexandrovna had confidence in herself; she was agitated, not by fear of failure—no! she longed only to begin the fray as soon as possible. Impatience, a laudable impatience, fired her at the thought of delays and obstacles. But as we are speaking of obstacles we will ask leave to explain our meaning more fully. The chief trouble Marya Alexandrovna foresaw and expected was from her excellent fellow-citizens, and especially from the highly respectable

ladies of Mordasov. She knew by experience their implacable hatred
for herself. She was perfectly certain, for instance, that at that moment
every one in the town probably knew of her designs, although no
one had been told anything about them. She knew from bitter experience on more than one occasion, that no incident, even of the most
private nature, happened in her house in the morning without being
known by the evening to the humblest market-woman, the humblest
individual sitting behind a counter. Of course Marya Alexandrovna,
so far, had only a presentiment of trouble. But such presentiments
had never deceived her. She was not deceived now. This was what
had actually happened, though she knew nothing positive about it.
About midday, that is just three hours after the Prince's arrival in
Mordasov, strange rumours were circulating about the town. No one
knew where they had begun, but they spread instantly. All began
assuring one another that Marya Alexandrovna had already made
a match between the Prince and her Zina, her portionless, twenty-
three-year-old Zina; that Mozglyakov had been dismissed, and that
it was all signed and settled. What was the cause of these rumours?
Could it be that every one knew Marya Alexandrovna so well that
they instantly hit on the very centre of her secret thoughts and ideals?
Neither the incongruity of such a rumour with the usual order of
things, for such affairs can very rarely be settled in an hour, nor the
obvious lack of any foundation for the story, for no one could discover whence it had arisen, could shake the conviction of the people
of Mordasov. The rumours grew and took root with extraordinary
obstinacy. What is most remarkable is that they began to circulate
at the very time when Marya Alexandrovna was beginning her conversation with Zina on that very subject. So sharp are the noses of the
provincials! The instinct of provincial newsmongers sometimes approaches the miraculous, and of course there is some reason for it.
It is founded on the closest and most interested study of one another,
pursued through many years. Every provincial lives, as it were, under
a glass case. There is no possibility of concealing anything from your
excellent fellow-citizens. They know you by heart, they know even
what you don't know about yourself. The provincial ought, one would
think, by his very nature to be a psychologist and a specialist on human
nature. That is why I have been sometimes genuinely amazed at meeting in the provinces not psychologists and specialists on human nature,
but a very great number of asses. But that is aside; that is a superfluous reflection.

The news was like a thunderclap. A marriage with the Prince

appeared to every one so advantageous, so dazzling, that even the strangeness of the affair did not occur to any one. We will observe one other circumstance: Zina was almost more hated than Marya Alexandrovna—why?—I cannot tell. Possibly Zina's beauty may have been partly the reason. Perhaps the fact, too, that Marya Alexandrovna was anyway recognized as one of themselves by all the ladies of Mordasov, she was a berry off the same bush. If she had vanished from the town—who knows?—they might have regretted her. She enlivened their society by her goings-on. It would have been dull without her. Zina, on the contrary, behaved as if she were living in the clouds and not in Mordasov. She was somehow not on a level with these people, not their equal, and, possibly without being aware of it, behaved with insufferable haughtiness in their company! And now all of a sudden, that Zina, concerning whom there was a scandalous story, that proud, that haughty Zina was becoming a millionaire and a princess, was rising to rank and distinction. In a couple of years, when she would be a widow, she would marry a duke or maybe a general, who knows, perhaps a governor (and the Governor of Mordasov was, as luck would have it, a widower with a great weakness for the fair sex). Then she would be the lady of the greatest consequence in the province, and of course the mere thought of that was insufferable, and no news could ever have aroused more indignation in Mordasov than the news of Zina's marrying the Prince. Instantly a furious outcry rose on all sides. People declared that it was wicked, positively vile; that the Prince was out of his mind; that the old man was being deceived, that they were taking advantage of his feeble-mindedness to deceive him, to dupe him, to cheat him; that the old man must be saved from their bloodthirsty claws; that it was robbery and immorality, and finally that other girls were just as good as Zina; and other girls might just as well marry the Prince. All these objections and opinions, Marya Alexandrovna, so far, only surmised, but that was enough for her. She knew for certain that every one, absolutely every one, was ready to do everything possible, and even impossible, to frustrate her designs. Here they were trying to kidnap the Prince so that she would have to get him back by force. Besides, if she did succeed in catching the Prince and luring him back, she could not keep him for ever on the lead. Besides, who could guarantee that that day, within a couple of hours, the whole solemn conclave of Mordasov ladies would not be sitting in her drawing-room, would not call on her on some pretext which would make it impossible to refuse to see them. If they were refused admittance at the door, they would climb in at the window—

a feat almost impossible, though it did happen in Mordasov. In short, there was not an hour, not a second, to be lost, and meanwhile nothing had yet been begun. All at once an idea that was a stroke of genius flashed upon Marya Alexandrovna's brain, and was instantly matured there. Of that new idea we shall not neglect to speak in its proper place. Here we will only say that at that moment, our heroine was dashing along the streets of Mordasov full of menace and inspiration, resolving even upon actual violence should it prove necessary in order to get the Prince back. She did not yet know how it would be done and where she would meet him, but she did know positively that Mordasov would sink into the earth sooner than one jot of her present plans should fail of accomplishment.

Her first step could not have been more successful. She succeeded in waylaying the Prince in the street and taking him back to dinner. If I am asked how, in spite of all her enemies' devices, she managed to insist on getting her own way, so making Anna Nikolaevna look rather a fool—I am bound to say that I regard such a question as insulting to Marya Alexandrovna. Could she fail to triumph over any Anna Nikolaevna Antipov? She simply stopped the Prince on his way to her rival's house, and in spite of everything (including the protests of Mozglyakov, who was afraid of a scandal) transferred the old gentleman to her sledge. It was this that distinguished Marya Alexandrovna from her rivals, that on critical occasions she did not hesitate for fear of a scandal, taking as her motto that success justifies everything. The Prince, of course, made no great resistance, and, as usual, quickly forgot all about it, and was highly delighted. At dinner he babbled away without ceasing, was exceedingly lively, made jokes and puns, began telling anecdotes which he did not finish, or jumped from one story to another without being aware of it. At Natalya Dmitryevna's he had drunk three glasses of champagne; at dinner he drank more, and was completely fuddled. Marya Alexandrovna herself kept filling up his glass. The dinner was a very good one. The monster Nikita had not spoilt it. The lady of the house enlivened the party with the most fascinating graciousness. But the others, as though of design, seemed extraordinarily depressed. Zina maintained a sort of solemn silence. Mozglyakov was evidently put out and ate little. He was absorbed in thought, and as that was very exceptional with him, Marya Alexandrovna felt very uneasy. Nastasya Petrovna sat glum, and actually made signs to Mozglyakov which the latter entirely failed to observe. Had it not been for the enchanting suavity and vivacity of the hostess, the dinner would have been like a funeral.

Yet Marya Alexandrovna was inexpressibly excited. Zina alarmed her dreadfully with her mournful air and tear-stained eyes. And another difficulty was that there was need of haste, of prompt action; and that "accursed Mozglyakov" sitting on like a blockhead, troubling about nothing, and simply in the way! It was, of course, impossible to begin on such a subject before him. Marya Alexandrovna rose from the table in terrible uneasiness. What was her amazement, her delighted horror, if one may use such an expression, when, as soon as they arose from the table, Mozglyakov came up to her and suddenly, quite unexpectedly, announced that—to his great regret, of course—he was absolutely forced to take leave of them at once.

"Where are you going?" Marya Alexandrovna asked, with a note of extreme regret.

"Well, you see, Marya Alexandrovna," Mozglyakov began, with some uneasiness and even hesitation, "a very queer thing has happened to me. I really don't know how to tell you. . . . For goodness' sake give me advice."

"Why, what is it?"

"My godfather Boroduev, the merchant, you know, met me to-day. The old fellow was quite huffy, he scolded me and said I had grown proud. This is the third time I have been in Mordasov without his having a glimpse of me. 'Come to tea to-day,' he said. It is four o'clock now, and he drinks tea in the old-fashioned way—when he wakes up. What am I to do? It is a bore of course, Marya Alexandrovna, but think. He saved my poor father from hanging, you know, when he gambled away the government money. It was owing to that that he stood godfather to me. If I am so happy as to marry Zinaida Afanasyevna I have only a hundred and fifty serfs, while he has a million, people say, even more. He is childless. Seventy, think of it! If one pleases him he may leave one a hundred thousand in his will."

"Oh, my goodness! What are you about! Why are you delaying?" cried Marya Alexandrovna, scarcely concealing her relief. "Go to him, go to him! You must not let it slip. To be sure, I was noticing at dinner—you seemed so dull! Go, *mon ami,* go. Why, you ought to have paid a call in the morning to show that you appreciate, that you value, his kindness. Ah, you young people, you young people!"

"Why, Marya Alexandrovna," cried Mozglyakov in amazement, "you yourself attacked me for that acquaintance. Why, you said that he was a peasant with a great beard, connected with innkeepers, low-class people and attorneys."

"Oh! *mon ami!* We say a great many thoughtless things. I may make mistakes like any one else—I am not a saint. I don't remember, but I may have easily been in that mood. . . . Besides, you were not at that time paying your addresses to Zina. . . . Of course it is egoism on my part, but now I am forced to look at it from a different point of view, and what mother could blame me in the circumstances? Go, do not delay for a minute! Spend the evening with him too . . . and, listen! Say something to him about me. Tell him that I have a great regard, a great liking, a respect for him; and do it tactfully, nicely! Oh, my goodness, why, it quite went out of my head! I ought to have thought to suggest it to you!"

"You have quite reassured me, Marya Alexandrovna," Mozglyakov cried, enchanted. "I swear I will obey you in everything now! Why, I was simply afraid to tell you! . . . Well, good-bye, I am off. Make my apologies to Zinaida Afanasyevna. Though I shall certainly . . ."

"I give you my blessing, *mon ami*. Be sure you speak of me to him! He certainly is a very dear old man. I changed my opinion of him long ago. Though, indeed, I have always liked in him all those old-fashioned truly Russian ways of his. . . . *Au revoir, mon ami, au revoir!*"

"Oh, what a blessing that the devil has taken him off! No, it was the hand of God helping us!" she thought, breathless with joy.

Pavel Alexandrovitch went out into the hall, and was putting on his fur coat when Nastasya Petrovna seemed suddenly to spring from nowhere. She was lying in wait for him.

"Where are you going?" she said, holding him by the arm.

"To see Boroduev, my godfather, Nastasya Petrovna, who graciously stood sponsor at my christening. . . . He's a wealthy old man, he will leave me something, I must make up to him."

Pavel Alexandrovitch was in the best of spirits.

"To see Boroduev! Very well then, say good-bye to your bride," Nastasya Petrovna said, abruptly.

"How do you mean good-bye?"

"Why, what I say! You imagine she is yours already! While they are trying to marry her to the Prince. I have heard it myself."

"To the Prince? Mercy on us, Nastasya Petrovna!"

"Mercy on us, to be sure! Now wouldn't you like to look on and overhear? Put down your coat and come this way."

Pavel Alexandrovitch, petrified, put down his fur coat and followed Nastasya Petrovna on tiptoe; she led him to the same little lumber-room in which she had listened that morning.

"But upon my word, Nastasya Petrovna, I really don't understand."

"Oh, well, you'll understand when you bend down and listen. The farce will begin at once, no doubt."

"What farce?"

"Sh! don't speak so loud! The farce is that they are simply hoaxing you. This morning, when you had gone away with the Prince, Marya Alexandrovna was a whole hour persuading Zina to consent to marry this Prince; she said that nothing would be easier than to get round him and force him to get married, and she pitched such a fine tale that I felt quite sick. I overheard it all from here. Zina consented. How flattering they both were to you! They look upon you simply as a fool, and Zina said straight out that nothing would induce her to marry you. I am a fool, too! I meant to pin on a pink ribbon! Listen, now, listen!"

"But I say, it's the most unholy treachery, if so!" whispered Pavel Alexandrovitch, looking into Nastasya Petrovna's face in the most foolish way.

"Well, you only listen, and that's not all you'll hear."

"But listen where?"

"Why, stoop down here—to this keyhole. . . ."

"But Nastasya Petrovna . . . I . . . I am really not capable of listening at keyholes."

"Pooh, it's a bit late to think of that. It's a case of putting your honour in your pocket; since you've come you had better listen!"

"But really . . ."

"If you are incapable of it, then be made a fool of! One takes pity on you and you give yourself airs. What is it to me? I am not doing it for my own sake. I shall be gone from here before evening!"

Pavel Alexandrovitch, overcoming his scruples, stooped down to the keyhole. His heart was beating, there was a throbbing in his temples. He scarcely understood what was happening to him.

Chapter 8

So YOU had a very gay time at Natalya Dmitryevna's, Prince?" queried Marya Alexandrovna, surveying the field of the approaching conflict with a predatory eye, and desiring to begin the conversation as innocently as possible. Her heart was beating with excitement and anticipation.

After dinner they had taken the Prince at once to the *salon,* in which he had been received that morning. All solemn functions and receptions at Marya Alexandrovna's took place in this *salon*. She was proud of the room. The old man seemed rather limp after his six glasses of wine, and could hardly keep on his legs. But he chattered away without ceasing. His garrulousness was only intensified. Marya Alexandrovna realized that this spurt of excitement was only momentary, and that her guest, heavy from his potations, would soon be drowsy. She must seize the moment. Scanning the field of battle, she noticed with satisfaction that the lascivious old man was fixing upon Zina glances of peculiar avidity, and her maternal heart fluttered with joy.

"Ex-ceed-ing-ly gay," answered the Prince, "and you know Natalya Dmitryevna is an absolutely in-com-parable woman—in-com-parable!"

Though Marya Alexandrovna was so absorbed in her great plans, yet such ringing praise of her rival stabbed her to the heart.

"Upon my word, Prince," she cried, with flashing eyes. "I really don't know what to think if your Natalya Dmitryevna is an incomparable woman! You say that because you don't know our society, you don't know it at all! Why, it is a mere exhibition of fictitious qualities, of noble sentiments, a farce, an outer husk of gold. Remove that husk and you will find a perfect hell under the flowers; a perfect wasp's nest, where you will be devoured to the last bone!"

"Is it possible!" exclaimed the Prince; "you surprise me!"

"But I vow that it is so! Ah, *mon prince*. Do you know, Zina, I really ought to tell the Prince that absurd and undignified incident with Natalya Dmitryevna last week—do you remember? Yes, Prince —it is about your vaunted Natalya Dmitryevna, with whom you are so fascinated. Oh, my dearest Prince! I vow I am not a scandalmonger! But I certainly must tell you this, simply to amuse you, to show you in a living instance, in a magnifying glass, so to speak, what people here are like. A fortnight ago Natalya Dmitryevna came to see me. Coffee was served, and I went out of the room for something. I remember perfectly well how much sugar there was in my silver sugar-basin: it was quite full. I came back and looked: there were only three lumps lying at the bottom of the basin. No one had been left in the room but Natalya Dmitryevna. What do you say to that! She has a brick house of her own and heaps of money! It's an absurd, comical incident, but you can judge from that of the lofty tone of our society."

"Is it pos-si-ble!" exclaimed the Prince, genuinely surprised. "What unnatural greediness! Did she eat it all up alone?"

"So you see what an *incomparable* woman she is, Prince! How do you like that disgraceful incident? I believe I should have died on the ˉpot if I had brought myself to commit such a revolting action."

"To be sure; to be sure. . . . But, you know, she really is such a *belle femme.*"

"Natalya Dmitryevna! Upon my word, Prince, she is a perfect tub! Oh, Prince, Prince! What are you saying? I did expect better taste from you. . . ."

"To be sure, a tub . . . only, you know, she is such a fine figure . . . and that girl who da-anced, she is . . . such a good figure too. . . ."

"Sonitchka? But she is quite a child! She is only fourteen!"

"To be sure . . . only, you know, she is so agile and she has . . . such contours . . . too . . . they are developing, such a cha-arm-ing girl! And the other who da-anced with her, she is developing too. . . ."

"Ah, that is a luckless orphan, Prince! She often stays with them."

"An orph-an! She is a dirty girl, though, she might wash her hands, anyway. . . . Though she was at-tra-active, too. . . ."

As he said this the Prince scrutinized Zina through his lorgnette with a sort of growing avidity.

"Mais quelle charmante personne!" he muttered in an undertone melting with gratification.

"Zina, play us something, or, better still, sing! How she sings, Prince! She is equal to a professional, a professional! And if you only knew, Prince," Marya Alexandrovna went on in a low voice, when Zina had moved away to the piano with her soft swimming gait, which sent a thrill through the poor old man. "If only you knew what a daughter she is! What a loving nature she has, how tender she is with me! What feeling, what heart!"

"To be sure . . . feeling . . . and do you know, I have only known one woman in my life who could be compared with her for beau-uty," the Prince interrupted, with his mouth watering. "That was Countess Nainsky, she died thirty years ago. A most fas-ci-nating woman she was, an indescribable beauty, afterwards she married her cook. . . ."

"Her cook, prince!"

"To be sure, her cook . . . a Frenchman, abroad. She got a count's title for him abroad. He was a good-looking man, extremely well educated, with little mous-taches like this."

"And . . . and . . . how did they get on together, Prince?"

"To be sure, they got on very well together. Though they separated soon afterwards. He robbed her and went off. They quarrelled about some sauce. . . ."

"Mamma, what shall I play?" asked Zina

"You had better sing us something, Zina. How she sings, Prince! Are you fond of music?"

"Oh, ye-es! *Charmant, charmant!* I am very fond of music. I used to know Beethoven when I was abroad."

"Beethoven! Only fancy, Zina, the Prince used to know Beethoven," Marya Alexandrovna cried rapturously. "Oh, Prince, did you really know Beethoven?"

"To be sure . . . we were quite fri-ends, and he always had his nose in the snuff-box. Such a funny fellow."

"Beethoven!"

"To be sure, Beethoven, but perhaps it was not Beet-hoven, though, but some other Ger-man. There are such a lot of Germans out there . . . I believe I have mix-ed them up."

"What am I to sing, Mamma?" asked Zina.

"Oh, Zina! Sing that song in which there is so much chivalry, the one in which there is the lady of the castle and her troubadour. . . . Oh, Prince! How I love all that age of chivalry! Those castles, those castles! That mediaeval life. Those troubadours, heralds, tournaments. . . . I will accompany you, Zina. Come here closer, Prince! Ah, those castles, those castles!"

"To be sure . . . those castles. I love castles too," muttered the Prince rapturously, transfixing Zina with his solitary eye. "But . . . my goodness!" he exclaimed, "that so-ong, why, I know that so-ong! I heard that song long ago. . . . It brings back such memories. . . . Ah, my goodness!"

I will not undertake to describe what happened to the Prince while Zina was singing. She sang an old French song, which had once been in fashion. Zina sang it beautifully. Her pure resonant contralto went straight to the heart. Her lovely face, her wonderful eyes, the wonderful delicately moulded fingers with which she turned the music, her thick brilliant black hair, her heaving bosom, her whole figure, proud, lovely, noble, all this bewitched the poor old man completely. He did not take his eyes off her while she was singing, he gasped with emotion. His aged heart, warmed by the champagne, the music, and rising memories (what man has not favourite memories?), was throbbing faster and faster, as it had not beat for ages. . . . He was ready to fall on his knees before Zina, and was almost weeping when she finished.

"O, ma charmante enfant!" he cried, kissing her fingers, "*vous me ravissez!* Only just now, just now I remembered . . . But . . . but . . . O, ma charmante enfant. . . ."

And the Prince could not go on.

Marya Alexandrovna felt that her moment had come.

"Why are you wasting your life, Prince?" she exclaimed solemnly. "What feeling, what vital energy, what spiritual riches, and to bury yourself for your whole life in solitude! To run away from people, from your friends! But it is unpardonable! Think better of it, Prince! Look at life, so to speak, with a fresh eye! Evoke from your heart your memories of the past—the memories of your golden youth, of those golden days free from care; bring them back to life, restore yourself to life! Begin to live again in society among your fellows! Go abroad, go to Italy, to Spain—to Spain, Prince! . . . You want some one to guide you, a heart that would love you, that would honour you and feel with you. But you have friends! Summon them, call them to you and they will flock in crowds to your side! I would be the first to throw up everything and fly at your summons. I remember our friendship, Prince; I would abandon my husband and follow you . . . and, indeed, if I were younger, if I were as good and as lovely as my daughter, I would be your travelling companion, your friend, your wife, if that was your wish."

"And I am sure you were *une charmante personne* in your da-ay," said the Prince, blowing his nose. His eyes were moist with tears.

"We live again in our children, Prince," Marya Alexandrovna answered, with lofty feeling. "I, too, have my guardian angel! And that is my daughter, the friend of my heart, the partner of my thoughts, Prince. She has already refused seven offers, unwilling to part from me."

"So she would come with you when you ac-com-pan-y me abroad? In that case I will certainly go abroad," cried the Prince, growing more animated. "I will cer-er-tain-ly go! And if I might flatter myself with the ho-ope. . . . But she is a fascinating, fas-ci-na-ting child! *O, ma charmante enfant!* . . ." and the Prince began kissing her hand again. The poor man would have liked to drop on his knees before her.

"But . . . but, Prince, you say: can you flatter yourself with hope?" Marya Alexandrovna caught him up, conscious of a fresh rush of eloquence. "But you are strange, Prince. Can you consider yourself unworthy of a woman's devotion? It is not youth that makes a man handsome. Remember, that you, so to speak, are a scion of the old aristocracy. You are the embodiment of the most refined, the most chivalrous sentiments and . . . manners! Did not Maria love Mazeppa in his old age? I remember, I have read that Lauzun, that enchanting marquis at the court of Louis the . . . I have forgotten which, in his declining years, when he was an old man, won the heart of one of the leading court beauties! . . . And who has told you that you are old? Who has instilled that idea into you? Men like you do not grow old! You, with such wealth of feeling, of gaiety, of wit, of vital energy, of brilliant manners! Only show yourself at some spa abroad with a young wife, as beautiful as my Zina, for instance—I am not speaking of her, I only mention her for example—and you will see what a colossal sensation it will make! You a scion of the aristocracy, she— a queen of beauty! You will walk with her on your arm in triumph; she will sing in brilliant society, you, for your part, will scintillate with wit—and all the visitors at the spa will flock to look at you! All Europe will be ringing with your name, for all the newspapers, all the *feuille-tons* at the watering-places, will tell the same story. . . ."

"The *feuilletons*. . . . Oh, ye-es; oh, ye-es. That's in the newspapers. . . ." muttered the Prince, not understanding half Marya Alexandrovna's babble, and growing more and more limp every moment. "But . . . my chi-ild, if you are not ti-ired, sing that song you sang just now, once more."

"Oh, Prince! But she has other songs better still. . . . Do you remember *L'Hirondelle*, Prince? No doubt you have heard it?"

"Yes, I remember, or, rather, I have forgotten it. No, no; the same so-ong as be-fore, the same that she sang just now! I don't want *L'Hirondelle!* I want the same song. . . ." said the Prince, entreating like a child.

Zina sang it over again. The Prince could not restrain himself, and sank on his knees before her.

"*O, ma belle châtelaine!*" he cried, in a voice quavering with age and excitement. "*O, ma charmante châtelaine!* Oh, my sweet child! You have re-min-ded me of so much . . . of what was in the distant past. . . . I thought then that everything would be better than it was after-wards. In those days I used to sing duets . . . with the *vicomtesse* . . . that very song . . . and now . . . I don't know what now. . . ."

All this speech the Prince uttered breathless and gasping. His tongue was perceptibly faltering. Some words were almost impossible to understand. It could only be seen that he was in an extremely maudlin state; Marya Alexandrovna promptly threw oil on the flames.

"Prince! But perhaps you are falling in love with my Zina!" she cried, feeling that it was a solemn moment.

The Prince's answer surpassed her highest expectations.

"I am madly in love with her," cried the old man, suddenly reviving, still on his knees and trembling all over with excitement. "I am ready to devote my life to her, and if I could only ho-ope. . . . But lift me up, I feel ra-ather we-eak. . . . I . . . if I could only hope to offer her my heart, then . . . I . . . she would sing me so-ongs eve-ry day, and I could always look at her . . . always look at her. . . . Oh, my goodness!"

"Prince, Prince! You offer her your hand! You want to rob me of my Zina, my darling, my angel, Zina! But I will not let you go, Zina! You will have to tear her from my arms, from the arms of her mother!" Marya Alexandrovna rushed at her daughter and folded her tightly in her arms, though she was conscious of being somewhat violently repulsed. . . . The mamma was rather overdoing it. Zina felt that in every fibre of her being, and looked on at the farce with indescribable disgust. She was silent, however, and that was all Marya Alexandrovna wanted.

"She has refused nine offers, simply to avoid being parted from her mother!" she cried. "But now, my heart forebodes separation! This morning I noticed how she looked at you. . . . You impressed her with your aristocratic ways, Prince, with that refinement! . . . Oh! you are parting us; I have a presentiment of it."

"I ado-ore her!" muttered the Prince, still quivering like an aspen leaf.

"And so you will forsake your mother?" exclaimed Marya Alexan-urovna, dashing at her daughter once again.

Zina was in haste to put an end to the painful scene. She held out her lovely hand to the Prince, and even forced herself to smile. The Prince took the hand with reverence and covered it with kisses.

"Only now, I be-gin to live," he muttered, gasping with ecstasy.

"Zina," Marya Alexandrovna pronounced solemnly. "Look at this man! He is the noblest, the most honourable of all the men I know! He is a mediaeval knight! But she knows that, Prince; she knows it to my sorrow. . . . Oh, why did you come! I am giving you my treasure, my angel. Take care of her, Prince! That is the earnest prayer of a mother, and what mother will censure me for my sorrow!"

"Mamma, that is enough!" whispered Zina.

"You will protect her from insult, Prince. Your sword will flash in the face of any slanderer or backbiter who dare malign my Zina!"

"That is enough, Mamma, or I'll . . ."

"Ye-es, ye-es, it will flash. . . ." muttered the Prince. "Only now I begin to live. . . . I want the wedding to be at once, this minute . . . I . . . I want to send to Du-ha-no-vo at once. I have di-a-monds there. I want to lay them at her feet."

"What fire, what fervour! What nobility of feeling!" exclaimed Marya Alexandrovna. "And you could waste yourself, waste yourself,

withdrawing from the world! I shall say that a thousand times over!
I am beside myself when I think of that diabolical . . ."

"How co-ould I help it, I was so fri-ightened!" muttered the Prince,
whimpering and growing maudlin. "They wa-an-ted to put me in a
ma-adhouse. . . . I was frightened."

"In a madhouse! Oh, the monsters! Oh, the inhuman creatures! Oh,
the base treachery! Prince, I had heard that. But that was insanity on
the part of those people! What for, whatever for?"

"I don't know myself, what for!" answered the old man, feeling
weak, and sitting down in an easy chair. "I was at a ba-all, you know,
and I to-old some anecdote; and they did not li-ike it. And so there
was a fuss."

"Really only for that, Prince?"

"No. I played cards afterwards with Prince Pyotr Dementi-itch. I
couldn't make any tricks. I had two ki-ings and three queens . . . or,
rather, three queens and two ki-ings. . . . No; one ki-ing! And afterwards I had the queens . . ."

"And for that! For that! Oh, the fiendish inhumanity! You are
weeping, Prince! But now that will not happen again! Now I shall be
at your side, my Prince; I shall not part from Zina, and we shall see
if they dare to say a word! . . . And indeed you know, Prince, your
marriage will impress them. It will put them to shame! They will see
that you are still quite competent . . . that is, they will realize that such
a beauty would not have married a madman! Now you can hold up
your head proudly. You can look them straight in the face. . . ."

"Oh, ye-es; I will look them stra-aight in the face," muttered the
Prince, closing his eyes.

"He's nearly asleep, though," thought Marya Alexandrovna; "it is
merely wasting words."

"Prince, you are agitated, I see that; you absolutely must be quiet;
rest after your emotion," she said, bending over him maternally.

"Oh, ye-es; I should like to li-ie down a little," he said.

"Yes, yes! Calm yourself, Prince! This agitation. . . . Stay, I will
accompany you myself. . . . I will put you to bed myself, if need be.
Why are you looking at that portrait, Prince? It is the portrait of my
mother, an angel, not a woman! Oh, why is she not with us now!
She was a saintly woman, Prince, a saintly woman! I can call her
nothing else."

"A sa-aintly woman? *C'est joli.* . . . I had a mother too . . . *princesse*
. . . and only fancy, she was an ex-tra-or-din-arily fat woman. . . . But
that wasn't what I meant to say. . . . I am a lit-tle tired. *Adieu, ma*

charmante enfant! ... I ... de-ligh-ted ... to-day ... to-morrow ...
But no ma-atter! *au revoir, au revoir!*" At this point he tried to wave
a kiss, but slipped and almost fell down in the doorway.

"Take care, Prince! Lean on my arm," cried Marya Alexandrovna.

"*Charmant, charmant!*" he muttered as he went out. "Only now I
am be-gin-ning to live!"

Zina was left alone; unutterable bitterness weighed upon her heart.
She felt sick with repulsion. She was ready to despise herself. Her
cheeks were burning. Clenching her fists and setting her teeth, she
stood motionless with bowed head. Tears of shame gushed from her
eyes. . . . At that moment the door opened and Mozglyakov ran into
the room.

Chapter 9

H E HAD heard all, all!

He did not walk into the room, but actually ran in, pale with emotion and with fury. Zina gazed at him in amazement.

"So that's how it is," he shouted, panting. "At last I have found out
what you are!"

"What I am!" repeated Zina, staring at him as though he were mad;
and all at once her eyes flashed with anger. "How dare you speak like
that to me?" she cried, going up to him.

"I have heard it all!" Mozglyakov repeated solemnly, though he
involuntarily drew back a step.

"You heard? You've been listening," said Zina, looking at him
disdainfully.

"Yes! I've been listening. Yes, I brought myself to do a low thing,
but I learned what you are, the most . . . I don't know what words
to use to tell you . . . what you have shown yourself to be!" he answered, quailing more and more before Zina's eyes.

"If you have heard, what can you blame me for? What right have
you to blame me? What right have you to speak so rudely to me?"

"I? What right have I? And you can ask that? You are going to
marry the Prince, and I have no right! . . . Why, you gave me your
word!"

"When?"

"How can you ask when?"

"Why, only this morning, when you were pestering me, I told you straight out that I could say nothing positive."

"But you did not drive me away, you did not refuse me altogether. So you were keeping me in reserve! So you were drawing me on!"

A look of suffering as though from an acute, piercing, internal pain came into Zina's irritated face; but she mastered her feeling.

"That I did not drive you away," she said, clearly and emphatically, though there was a scarcely perceptible quiver in her voice, "was solely through pity. You implored me yourself to take time, not to say 'no,' but to get to know you better, and 'then,' you said, 'then, when you are convinced that I am an honourable man, perhaps you will not refuse me.' Those were your own words when first you pressed your suit. You cannot draw back from them. You had the insolence to say just now that I drew you on. But you saw yourself my aversion when I met you to-day, a fortnight earlier than you promised. That aversion I did not conceal from you; on the contrary, I displayed it. You noticed it yourself, for you asked me whether I was angry with you for coming back sooner. You know one is not drawing a man on if one cannot and does *not care* to conceal one's aversion. You have had the insolence to say that I was keeping you in reserve. To that I will answer, that what I thought about you was, 'though he is not endowed with very much intelligence, he may yet be a good man, and so one might marry him.' But now I am convinced, to my relief, that you are a fool, and what's more, an ill-natured fool. I have only now to wish you every happiness and *bon voyage.* Good-bye!"

Saying this, Zina turned from him and walked slowly towards the door.

Mozglyakov, guessing that all was lost, boiled with rage.

"Ah, so I am a fool," he cried, "so now I am a fool! Very well! Good-bye. But before I go away I'll tell the whole town how you and your mamma have tricked the old Prince, after making him drunk! I'll tell every one! I'll show you what Mozglyakov can do!"

Zina shuddered, and was stopping to answer; but after a moment's thought, she merely shrugged her shoulders contemptuously, and slammed the door after her.

At that moment Marya Alexandrovna appeared in the doorway. She had heard Mozglyakov's exclamation, in an instant guessed what it meant and shuddered with alarm. Mozglyakov had not gone yet, Mozglyakov near the Prince, Mozglyakov would spread it all over the town, and secrecy for a short time at least was essential! Marya Alexandrovna had her own calculations. She instantly grasped the situation, and the plan for subduing Mozglyakov was already formed.

"What is the matter, *mon ami?*" she said, going up to him and holding out her hand affectionately.

"What? *mon ami!*" he cried furiously. "After what you have been plotting, you call me *mon ami!* You don't catch me, honoured madame! And do you suppose you can deceive me again?"

"I am grieved, very much grieved to see you in such a *strange* state of mind, Pavel Alexandrovitch. What an expression to use! You do not even curb your language before a lady."

"Before a lady! You . . . you may be anything you like, but not a lady!" cried Mozglyakov.

I don't know what he meant to express by this exclamation, but probably something very tremendous.

Marya Alexandrovna looked blandly into his face.

"Sit down," she said mournfully, motioning him to the chair on which a quarter of an hour before the Prince had been reposing.

"But, do listen, Marya Alexandrovna!" cried Mozglyakov in perplexity. "You look at me as though you were not to blame in any way, but as though I had treated you badly! You can't go on like that, you know! . . . Such a tone! . . . Why, it is beyond all human endurance. . . . Do you know that?"

"My friend!" answered Marya Alexandrovna, "you must still allow me to call you that, for you have no better friend than I; my friend! You are unhappy, you are distressed, you are wounded to the heart— and so it is not to be wondered at that you speak to me in such a tone. But I am resolved to reveal to you everything, to open my whole heart, the more readily as I feel myself somewhat to blame in regard to you. Sit down, let us talk."

There was a sickly softness in Marya Alexandrovna's voice. There was a look of suffering in her face. Mozglyakov, astounded, sat down in an easy chair beside her.

"You have been listening?" she said, looking reproachfully into his face.

"Yes, I have been listening! If I hadn't listened I should have been a duffer. Anyway, I have found out all that you were plotting against me," Mozglyakov answered rudely, growing bolder and working himself into a passion.

"And you, you, with your breeding, with your principles, could bring yourself to such an action? Oh, good heavens!"

Mozglyakov positively jumped up from his chair.

"But, Marya Alexandrovna!" he cried, "it is insufferable to listen

to this! Think what you have brought yourself to do with your principles, and then you judge other people!"

"Another question," she said, without answering him. "Who put
you up to listening, who told you, who is the spy here? That's what
I want to know."

"Excuse me, but I won't tell you that."

"Very well, I shall find out for myself. I said, *Paul,* that I had treated
you badly. But if you go into it all, into all the circumstances, you will
see that, even if I am to blame, it is solely through a desire for your
good."

"Mine? My good? That is beyond everything! I warn you, you won't
delude me again! I am not such a child as that."

And he writhed in the arm-chair with such violence that it creaked.

"Please, my dear boy, keep cool, if you can. Listen to me attentively,
and you will agree with everything yourself. To begin with, I intended
to tell you about it at once, everything, everything, and you would
have heard the whole business from me in the fullest details, without
demeaning yourself to listen. That I did not explain it to you before
was simply because it was only a project. It might not have come off.
You see, I am being perfectly open with you. Secondly, do not blame
my daughter. She loves you madly, and it cost me incredible effort to
draw her away from you, and to induce her to consent to accept the
Prince."

"I have just had the happiness to receive the fullest proof of that *mad*
love," Mozglyakov pronounced ironically.

"Very good. But how were you speaking to her? Was that the way
that a lover should speak? Was that the way, indeed, for a well-bred
man to speak? You wounded and irritated her!"

"It is not a question of breeding now, Marya Alexandrovna. And
this morning, after you had both treated me to such honeyed looks, I
went off with the Prince and you blackguarded me behind my back!
You called me names—let me tell you that. I know all about it, I
know!"

"And no doubt from the same foul source?" said Marya Alexandrovna, with a contemptuous smile. "Yes, Pavel Alexandrovitch, I did
disparage you, I did talk against you, and I must confess I had a hard
struggle. But the very fact that I had to abuse you to her, even to
slander you, that very fact proves how hard it was for me to extort
her consent to abandon you! You short-sighted man! If she did not
care for you, would there have been any need for me to blacken your
character, to put you in an undignified and ridiculous light, to resort

to such extreme measures? But you do not know everything yet! I had to use my maternal authority to eradicate you from her heart, and after incredible efforts I wrung from her only the appearance of agreement. If you were listening just now you must have noticed that she did not support me with the Prince, by one word, one gesture. Throughout the whole scene she scarcely uttered a single word: she sang like an automaton. Her whole soul was aching with despondency, and it was from pity for her that, at last, I got the Prince away. I am sure that she wept as soon as she was alone. When you came in here you must have noticed her tears."

Mozglyakov did, in fact, remember that when he ran into the room he had noticed that Zina was in tears.

"But you, you, why were you against me, Marya Alexandrovna?" he cried. "Why did you blacken my character? Why did you slander me, as you yourself confess you did!"

"Ah, that is a different matter. If you had asked that question sensibly in the beginning, you would have had an answer to it long ago. Yes, you are right! It has all been my doing, and only mine. Don't mix Zina up in it. What was my object? I answer, in the first place, it was for Zina's sake. The Prince is a man of rank and fortune, he has connections, and marrying him, Zina would make a splendid match. Besides, if he dies, perhaps before long, indeed, for we are all more or less mortal, then Zina will be a young widow, a princess, in the highest society, and perhaps very wealthy. Then she can marry any one she likes; she would be able to make a still wealthier match. But of course she will marry the man she loves, the man she loved before, whose heart she wounded by marrying the Prince. Remorse alone would force her to atone for her treatment of the man she loved before."

"Hm!" mumbled Mozglyakov, looking thoughtfully at his boots.

"And the second thing is, and I will only mention it briefly," Marya Alexandrovna went on, "for perhaps you will not understand it. You read your Shakespeare, and draw all your lofty sentiments from him, but in real life, though you are *very good,* you are too young and I am a *mother,* Pavel Alexandrovitch. Listen: I am giving Zina to the Prince partly for his sake, to save him by this marriage. I loved that noble, most kindly, chivalrously honourable old man in the past. We were friends. He is unhappy in the claws of that hellish woman. She will bring him to his grave. God is my witness that I only persuaded Zina to consent to marry the Prince by putting before her all the greatness of her heroic self-sacrifice. She was carried away by the nobility of her feelings, by the fascination of an act of sacrifice. There is something chivalrous in her, too. I put before her what a lofty Christian act it was to be the prop, the comfort, the friend, the child, the lovely idol of one who has perhaps but one year yet to live. No hateful woman, no terror, no despondency should be about him in the last days of his life, but brightness, affection, love. These last declining days would seem like Paradise to him! Where is the egoism in that? Tell me, pray. It is more like the noble deed of a Sister of Mercy than egoism!"

"So you are doing this simply for the sake of the old Prince, simply as the sacrifice of a Sister of Mercy?" muttered Mozglyakov in an ironical voice.

"I understand that question, Pavel Alexandrovitch, it is clear enough. You imagine, perhaps, that the interests of the Prince are jesuitically intertwined with our own advantage? Well? Possibly those considerations were present in my brain, only they were not jesuitical, but unconscious. I know that you will be amazed at so open a confession, but one thing I do beg of you, Pavel Alexandrovitch: don't mix Zina up in that! She is pure as a dove; she is not calculating; she is capable of nothing but love, my sweet child! If any one has been calculating, it is I, and I alone! But in the first place, search your own conscience sternly, and tell me: who would not calculate in my position, in a case like this? We consider our interests even in the most magnanimous, even in the most disinterested of our actions, inevitably, involuntarily we consider them. No doubt we all deceive ourselves when we assure ourselves that we are acting solely from noble motives. I don't want to deceive myself; I admit that for all the purity of my motives I was calculating. But ask yourself, am I interested on my own behalf? I want nothing, Pavel Alexandrovitch, I have lived my life. I am calculating for her sake, for the sake of my angel, for my child, and—what mother can blame me for it?"

Tears glistened in Marya Alexandrovna's eyes. Pavel Alexandrovitch listened in astonishment to this candid confession, and blinked incredulously.

"Well, yes, what mother would?" he said at last. "You pitch a fine tale, Marya Alexandrovna, but . . . but, you know, you gave me your word! You gave me hopes. . . . How about me? Only think! You've made me look a pretty fool, haven't you?"

"But surely you don't imagine that I haven't thought of you, *mon cher Paul;* the advantage for you in all this was so immense, that it was that, indeed, that chiefly impelled me to undertake it all."

"Advantage for me!" cried Mozglyakov, completely dumbfounded this time. "How so?"

"My goodness! Can any one be so simple and short-sighted!" cried Marya Alexandrovna, turning up her eyes to the ceiling. "Oh, youth! youth! That is what comes of burying oneself in that Shakespeare, of dreaming, and of imagining that one is thinking for oneself when one is following the thoughts and the mind of others! You ask, my *good* Pavel Alexandrovitch, where your advantage is to be found in it. Allow me, for the sake of clearness, to make a digression. Zina loves you—that is beyond doubt! But I have noticed that, in spite of her obvious feeling for you, she has a secret lack of confidence in you, in your good feelings, in your propensities. I have noticed that at times she behaves to you, as it were intentionally, with coldness, the result of uncertainty and lack of confidence. Have you noticed that yourself, Pavel Alexandrovitch?"

"I have noticed it, and to-day indeed. . . . But what do you mean to say, Marya Alexandrovna?"

"There, you see you have noticed it yourself. So I was not mistaken, then. She has a strange lack of confidence in the stability of your character. I am a mother—and is it not for me to divine the secrets of my child's heart? Imagine now that instead of rushing into the room with reproaches, and even with abuse, irritating her, wounding and insulting her in her purity, her goodness and her pride, and so unwittingly confirming her suspicions of your evil propensities—imagine that you had accepted it all mildly, with tears of regret, perhaps, even, of despair, but with lofty nobility of feeling . . ."

"Hm! . . ."

"No, do not interrupt me, Pavel Alexandrovitch. I want to paint the whole picture which will strike your imagination. Imagine that you had gone to her and said: 'Zinaida! I love you more than life itself, but family reasons divide us. I understand those reasons. They are for your happiness, and I do not venture to rebel against them, Zinaida! I forgive you. Be happy if you can!' And at that point you would fix your gaze upon her, the gaze of a lamb at the sacrifice, if I may so express myself—imagine all that and only think what effect such words would have had on her heart!"

"Yes, Marya Alexandrovna, let us suppose all that; I understand all that. . . . But after all, if I had said all that I should have gained nothing by it."

"No, no, no, my dear! Don't interrupt me. I want to picture the scene in every detail that it may make the right impression on you.

Imagine that you meet her again a little later in the highest society; meet her at some ball, in a brilliantly lighted room, to the intoxicating strains of music, in the midst of magnificent women, and in the midst of this gay festival you alone mournful, melancholy, pale, leaning somewhere against a column (but so that you can be seen), watch her in the whirl of the ball. She dances. Around you flow the intoxicating strains of Strauss and the scintillating wit of the highest society— while you stand alone, pale and crushed by your passion. What will Zinaida feel then, do you suppose? With what eyes will she look at you. 'And I,' she will think, 'I doubted of that man who has sacrificed for me all—all, and has rent his heart for my sake.' Her old love would, of course, rise up again with irresistible force."

Marya Alexandrovna stopped to take breath. Mozglyakov wriggled in his easy-chair with such violence that it creaked again. Marya Alexandrovna went on:

"For the prince's health Zina will go abroad, to Italy, to Spain—to Spain where there are myrtles, lemons, where the sky is blue, where there is the Guadalquivir; the land of love, where one cannot live without loving: the land of roses, where kisses, so to speak, float in the air. You will follow her there; you will sacrifice your past in the service, your connections, everything. There your love will begin with irresistible force; love, youth! Spain—my God! Your love of course is untainted, holy; though you will languish gazing at one another. You understand me, *mon ami!* Of course there will be base, treacherous people, monsters who will declare that you have not been tempted abroad by family feeling for a suffering old relation. I have purposely called your love untainted, because such people will perhaps give it a very different significance. But I am a mother, Pavel Alexandrovitch, and am I likely to lead you astray! . . . Of course the Prince will not be in a condition to look after you both, but—what of that? Could such an abominable calumny be based on that? At last he will die, blessing his fate. Tell me: whom would Zina marry if not you? You are such a distant relation of the Prince's that that can be no hindrance to your marriage. You will wed her, young, wealthy, distinguished, and, only think!—when the grandest of our noblemen would be proud to marry her. Through her you will gain a footing in the highest circles of society, through her you will gain the highest rank and position. Now you have a hundred and fifty serfs, but then you will be rich; the Prince will arrange everything in his will. I will see to that. And, lastly and most important, she will have gained complete confidence in you, in your heart, in your feelings, and you will become in her eyes a hero of goodness and self-sacrifice! . . . And after that you ask where your advantage comes in? Why, you must be blind not to reflect, not to consider that advantage, when it stands not two steps from you, staring you in the face, smiling at you and crying out to you: 'Here I am, your advantage!' Pavel Alexandrovitch, upon my word!"

"Marya Alexandrovna!" cried Mozglyakov in extraordinary excitement, "now I understand it all. I have behaved coarsely, basely and caddishly!"

He leapt up from his seat and clutched his hair.

"And unreflectingly," added Marya Alexandrovna. "Above all, unreflectingly!"

"I am an ass, Marya Alexandrovna!" he cried, almost in despair. "Now all is lost, because I loved her so madly."

"Perhaps all is not lost," said Madame Moskalev softly, as though pondering something.

"Oh, if that were possible! Help me! Teach me! Save me!"

And Mozglyakov burst into tears.

"My dear!" said Marya Alexandrovna with commiseration, giving him her hand, "you have acted from excess of ardour, from the fervour of your passion, that is, from love for her! You were in despair, you did not know what you were doing! She ought to understand all that. . . ."

"I love her to madness, and am ready to sacrifice anything to her!" cried Mozglyakov.

"I tell you what, I will set you right with her. . . ."

"Marya Alexandrovna?"

"Yes, I will undertake to do that! I will bring you together. You must tell her everything—everything as I have told it you, just now."

"Oh, God! How kind you are, Marya Alexandrovna! But . . . would it be impossible to do it at once?"

"God forbid! Oh, how inexperienced you are, my dear! She is so proud. She will take this as a fresh insult, as insolence! To-morrow I will arrange it all; but now go away, to see that merchant, for instance . . . come in the evening, perhaps, but I would not advise you to."

"I will go away, I will! My God! You bring me back to life! But one more question. What if the Prince doesn't die so soon?"

"Oh, my God! how naïve you are, *mon cher Paul*. On the contrary, you must pray for his health. We must, with all our hearts, hope for length of days for that dear, kind, chivalrously honourable old man. I shall be the first to pray, night and day, with tears in my eyes, for my daughter's happiness. But, alas! I fear the Prince's health is hopeless. Moreover, he will have now to visit Petersburg, to take Zina into society. I fear, oh, I fear that this may be too much for him! But we will pray for the best, *cher Paul,* and the rest is—in God's Hands! . . . You are going now? I bless you, *mon ami!* Hope, be patient, be manly above all things, be manly! I never doubted the nobility of your sentiments. . . ."

She pressed his hand warmly, and Mozglyakov walked out of the room on tiptoe.

"Well, I have got rid of one fool!" she said triumphantly. "There are others left. . . ."

The door opened and Zina came in. She was paler than usual. Her eyes were flashing.

"Mamma," she said, "finish it quickly or I can't endure it! It's all so vile and nasty that I am ready to run out of the house. Don't torture me, don't irritate me! I feel sick—do you hear?—sick of all this filth!"

"Zina! What is the matter with you, my angel? You . . . you have been listening!" cried Marya Alexandrovna, looking intently and uneasily at Zina.

"Yes, I have been listening. Do you want to put me to shame as you did that fool? Listen, I swear that if you go on torturing me like this, and assign to me all sorts of low parts in this low farce, I will throw it all up and make an end of it at one blow. It is enough that I have brought myself to do the vile thing that is most important. But . . . I did not know myself! I shall be stifled in this filth."

And she went out, slamming the door.

Marya Alexandrovna gazed after her and pondered.

"Haste! haste!" she cried, starting. "She is the chief trouble, the chief danger, and if all these scoundrels won't let us alone, if they spread it all over the town—as they probably have done by now— all is lost! She will never endure the hubbub and will refuse. At all costs we must take the Prince into the country, and promptly too! I will fly off first myself, will haul along my blockhead and bring him here, he must make himself useful at last; meanwhile the old man will have had his sleep out, and we will set off."

She rang the bell.

"The horses?" she asked the servant who came in.

"They have been ready a long while," answered the footman.

The horses had been ordered at the moment when Marya Alexandrovna was taking the Prince upstairs.

She dressed, but first ran into Zina to tell her in rough outline her decision and to give her some instructions. But Zina could not listen to her. She was lying on her bed, with her face in her pillow, and her white arms bare to the elbows; she was shedding tears and tearing her long, exquisite hair. At moments she shuddered all over as though a cold shiver were running over her limbs. Marya Alexandrovna began talking, but Zina did not even lift her head.

After standing for some time beside her, Marya Alexandrovna went out in confusion, and to vent her feelings, got into the carriage and told her coachman to drive as fast as he could.

"It's a nuisance that Zina overheard it," she thought as she got into the carriage. "I brought Mozglyakov round with the same words that I used with her. She is proud, and perhaps was wounded. . . . Hm! But the great thing, the great thing is to make haste and settle it all before they have got wind of it! It's a pity! Well, and what if by ill luck the fool is not at home!"

And at the mere thought of that she was overcome with a fury that boded nothing pleasant to Afanasy Matveyitch; she could hardly sit still for impatience. The horses whirled her along full speed.

Chapter 10

THE carriage flew along. We mentioned before that an idea that was a stroke of genius had flashed into Marya Alexandrovna's brain that morning when she was hunting over the town for the Prince. We promised to refer to that idea in its proper place. But the reader knows it already. The idea was to kidnap the Prince in her turn, and to carry him off as quickly as possible to their estate in the neighbourhood, where the blissful Afanasy Matveyitch flourished in tranquility. There is no disguising the fact that Marya Alexandrovna was more and more overcome by an inexplicable uneasiness. This does happen at times to real heroes at the very moment when they are attaining their object. Some instinct suggested to her that it was dangerous to remain at Mordasov. "But once we are in the country," she thought, "the whole town may be upside down for all I care!" Of course, no time was to be lost even in the country. Anything might happen—anything, absolutely anything; though, of course, we put no faith in the rumours, circulated later about my heroine by her enemies, that at this juncture she was actually afraid of the police. In short, she saw that she must get the marriage of Zina and the Prince solemnized as quickly as possible. She had the means for doing so at hand. The village priest could celebrate the nuptials in their own home. The ceremony might actually be performed the day after to-morrow; in the last resort, even to-morrow. There were cases of weddings within two hours of the betrothal! They could present the haste, the absence of festivities, of betrothal, of bridesmaids, to the Prince as essentially *comme il faut;* they could impress upon him that it would be more in keeping with decorum and aristocratic style. In fact, it might all be made to appear as a romantic adventure, and so the most susceptible chord in the Prince's heart would be struck. If all else failed, they could always make him drunk, or, still better, keep him in a state of perpetual drunkenness. And afterwards, come what may, Zina would anyway be a princess! Even if they did not get off afterwards without a scandal—in Petersburg or Moscow, for instance, where the Prince had relations—even that had its consolations. In the first place, all that was in the future; and in the second, Marya Alexandrovna believed that in the best society scarcely anything ever happened without a scandal, especially in the matrimonial line; that this was, in fact, *chic,* though the scandals of the best society were, she imagined, necessarily all of a special stamp—on a grand scale, something after the style of *Monte Cristo* or *Les Mémoires du Diable.* That, in fact, Zina need only show herself in the best society, and her mamma need only be there to support her, and every one—absolutely every one—would instantly be conquered, and that not one of all those countesses and princesses would be capable of withstanding the sousing which Marya Alexandrovna alone was capable of giving them, collectively or individually, in true Mordasov style. In consequence of these reflections, Marya Alexandrovna was now flying to her country seat to fetch Afanasy Matveyitch, whose presence, she calculated, was now indispensable. Indeed, to take the Prince to the country would mean taking him to see Afanasy Matveyitch, whose acquaintance the Prince might not be anxious to make. If Afanasy Matveyitch were to give the invitation it would put quite a different complexion upon it. Moreover, the arrival of an elderly and dignified paterfamilias in a white cravat and a dress-coat, with a hat in his hand, who had come from distant parts at once on hearing about the Prince, might produce a very agreeable effect, might even flatter the *amour-propre* of the latter. It would be difficult to refuse an invitation so pressing and so ceremonious, thought Marya Alexandrovna. At last the carriage had driven the two and a half miles, and Sofron, the coachman, pulled up his horses at the front door of a rambling wooden building of one storey, somewhat dilapidated and blackened by age, with a long row of windows, and old lime-trees standing round it on all sides. This was the country house and summer residence of Marya Alexandrovna. Lights were already burning in the house.

"Where is the blockhead?" cried Marya Alexandrovna, bursting into the rooms like a hurricane. "What is that towel here for? Ah! he has been drying himself! Have you been to the baths again? And he is for ever swilling his tea! Well, why are you staring at me like that, you perfect fool? Why hasn't his hair been cut? Grishka! Grishka! Grishka! Why haven't you cut your master's hair, as I told you to last week?"

As she went into the room Marya Alexandrovna intended to greet her spouse far more gently, but seeing that he had just come from the bath-house and was sipping his tea with great enjoyment, she could not refrain from the bitterest indignation. And, indeed, her cares and anxieties were only equalled by the blissful quietism of the useless and incompetent Afanasy Matveyitch; the contrast instantly stung her to the heart. Meanwhile the blockhead, or to speak more respectfully, he who was called the blockhead, sat behind the samovar, and in senseless panic gazed at his better half with open mouth and round eyes, almost petrified by her appearance. The drowsy and clumsy figure of Grishka blinking at this scene was thrust in from the entry.

"He wouldn't let me, that is why I didn't cut it," he said in a grumbling and husky voice. "A dozen times I went up to him with the scissors, and said, 'The mistress will be coming directly, and then we shall both catch it; and what shall we do then?' 'No,' he said; 'wait a little. I am going to curl it on Sunday, so I must have my hair long.'"

"What? So he curls his hair. So you have begun curling your hair while I am away? What new fashion is this? Why, does it suit you— does it suit your wooden head? My goodness, how untidy it is here! What is this smell? I am asking you, you monster, what is this horrid smell here?" shouted his wife, scolding her innocent and completely flabbergasted husband more and more angrily.

"Mo . . . mother!" muttered her panic-stricken spouse, gazing with imploring eyes at his domineering tyrant, and not getting up from his seat. "Mo . . . Mother! . . ."

"How often have I knocked into your ass's head that I am not to be called 'Mother'? Mother, indeed, to you, a pigmy! How dare you use such a mode of address to a refined lady, whose proper place is in the best society, instead of beside an ass like you!"

"But . . . but you know, Marya Alexandrovna, you are my lawful wedded wife, and so I speak to you . . . as to my wife," Afanasy Matveyitch protested, and at the same moment put up both hands to his head to protect his hair.

"Oh, you ugly creature! Oh, you aspen post! Was anything ever more stupid than your answer? Lawful wedded wife? Lawful wedded wife, indeed, nowadays! Does anybody in good society make use of that stupid, clerical, that revoltingly vulgar expression, *'lawful wedded'*? And how dare you remind me that I am your wife, when I am doing my best, my very utmost, to forget it! Why are you putting your hands over your head? Look what his hair is like! Sopping, absolutely sopping! It won't be dry for another three hours! How can I take him now—how can I let people see him! What's to be done now?"

And Marya Alexandrovna wrung her hands in fury, running backwards and forwards in the room. The trouble, of course, was a small one, and could easily be set right; but the fact was that Marya Alexandrovna could not control her all-conquering and masterful spirit. She felt an irresistible craving to be constantly venting her wrath upon Afanasy Matveyitch, for tyranny is a habit which becomes an irresistible craving. And we all know what a contrast some refined ladies of a certain position are capable of at home behind the scenes; and it is just that contrast I wish to reproduce. Afanasy Matveyitch watched his wife's evolution with a tremor, and positively broke into a perspiration as he looked at her.

"Grishka," she cried at last, "dress your master at once: his dress-coat, his trousers, his white tie, his waistcoat. Look sharp! But where is his hair-brush? Where is the brush?"

"Mother! Why, I have just come from the bath; I shall catch cold if I drive to the town. . . ."

"You won't catch cold!"

"But my hair is wet. . . ."

"Well, we will dry it directly. Grishka, take the hair-brush; brush him till he is dry. Harder, harder, harder! That's it! that's it!"

At this command the zealous and devoted Grishka began brushing his master's hair with all his might, clutching him by the shoulder to get a more convenient grip, and pressing him down to the sofa. Afanasy Matveyitch frowned and almost wept.

"Now come here! Lift him up, Grishka! Where is the pomatum? Bend down, bend down, you good-for-nothing; bend down, you sluggard!"

And Marya Alexandrovna set to work to pomade her husband's head with her own hands, ruthlessly tugging at his thick, grizzled locks, which, to his sorrow, he had not had cut. Afanasy Matveyitch cleared his throat, gasped, but did not scream, and endured the whole operation submissively.

"You have sucked the life-blood out of me, you sloven!" said Marya Alexandrovna. "Bend down more, bend down!"

"How have I sucked your life-blood, Mother?" mumbled her husband, bending his head as far as he could.

"Blockhead! He doesn't understand allegory! Now comb your hair; and you, dress him, and look sharp!"

Our heroine sat down in an easy-chair and kept an inquisitorial watch on the whole ceremony of arraying Afanasy Matveyitch. Meanwhile he succeeded in getting his breath and recovering himself a little, and when the tying of his cravat was reached he even ventured to express an opinion of his own on the style and beauty of the knot. Finally, putting on his dress-coat, the worthy man was restored to cheerfulness, and looked at himself in the glass with some respect.

"Where are you taking me, Marya Alexandrovna?" he said, prinking before the looking-glass.

Marya Alexandrovna could not believe her ears. "Hear him! Oh, you dummy! How dare you ask me where I am taking you!"

"Mother, but, you know, one must know. . . ."

"Hold your tongue! Only I tell you if you call me 'Mother' once more, especially where we are going now, you shall be cut off tea for a month!"

The panic-stricken husband held his tongue.

"Ugh! Not a single decoration has he gained, the sloven!" she went on, looking at Afanasy Matveyitch's black coat contemptuously.

At last her husband was offended.

"It's the Government gives decorations, Mother; and I am a councillor and not a sloven," he said, with honourable indignation.

"What, what, what? So you have learnt to argue out here! Ah, you peasant! Ah, you sniveller! It's a pity I haven't time to see to you, or I'd . . . But I shan't forget it later on. Give him his hat, Grishka! Give him his overcoat! While I'm away get these three rooms ready; get the green corner room ready, too. Fetch your brooms instantly! Take the covers off the looking-glasses, off the clocks, too, and within an hour let everything be ready; and put on your swallow-tail yourself and give the servants gloves! Do you hear, Grishka, do you hear?"

They got into the carriage. Afanasy Matveyitch was puzzled and wondering. Meanwhile Marya Alexandrovna was deliberating how she could most intelligibly knock into her husband's brain certain admonitions indispensable in his present position. But her husband anticipated her.

"Do you know, Marya Alexandrovna, I had a most original dream this morning," he informed her quite unexpectedly, in the midst of silence on both sides.

"Phoo! you confounded dummy! Goodness knows what I thought you were going to say! Some stupid dream! How dare you interrupt me with your loutish dreams! Original! Do you understand what original means? Listen: I tell you for the last time, if you dare to say one word to-day about your dream or anything else, I'll . . . I don't know what I'll do to you! Listen attentively. Prince K. has come to stay with me. Do you remember Prince K.?"

"I remember him, mother, I remember him. What has he come for?"

"Be quiet; that is not your business. You must, as master of the house, invite him, with special politeness, to stay with us in the country. That is what I am taking you for. We shall set off and drive back to-day. But if you dare to utter one single word the whole evening, or to-morrow, or the day after to-morrow, or at any time, I'll set you to herd the geese for a whole year! Don't say anything, not a single word. That's the whole of your duty. Do you understand?"

"But if I am asked a question?"

"Never mind, hold your tongue."

"But you know it's impossible to hold one's tongue all the while, Marya Alexandrovna."

"In that case, answer in monosyllables; something, for instance, such as 'H'm!' or something of that kind, to show you are a sensible man and think before you speak."

"H'm!"

"Understand me: I am taking you because you have heard about the Prince and, delighted at his visit, have hastened to pay your respects to him and to ask him to visit you in the country. Do you understand?"

"H'm!"

"None of your h'mming now, you idiot! You answer me."

"Very good, Mother, it shall all be as you say. Only why am I to invite the Prince?"

"What, what? Arguing again! What business is it of yours what for? And how dare you ask questions about it?"

"But I keep wondering, Mother, how I am to invite him if I hold my tongue, as you tell me."

"I will speak for you, and you've simply got to bow—do you hear? to bow—and hold your hat in your hand. Do you understand?"

"I understand, Moth . . . Marya Alexandrovna."

"The Prince is extremely witty. If he says anything, even though it is not to you, you must respond to everything with a bright and good-humoured smile. Do you understand?"

"H'm!"

"H'mming again! Don't say 'H'm!' to me. Answer simply and directly. Do you hear?"

"I hear, Marya Alexandrovna; of course I hear. And I am saying 'H'm!' to practise saying it, as you told me. Only I keep wondering about the same thing, Mother: how it is to be. If the Prince says anything, you tell me to look at him and smile. Well, but if he asks me something?"

"You slow-witted dolt! I have told you already: hold your tongue. I will answer for you; you simply look at him and smile."

"Why, but he'll think I am dumb," grumbled Afanasy Matveyitch.

"As though that mattered! Let him think it; you'll conceal the fact that you are a fool, anyway."

"H'm! . . . But what if other people ask me some question?"

"Nobody will ask you; no one will be there. But in case—which God forbid!—somebody does come in, and if anybody does ask you a question, or say anything to you, you must answer at once by a sarcastic smile. Do you know what is meant by a sarcastic smile?"

"It means witty, doesn't it, Mother?"

"I'll teach you to be witty, you blockhead! And who would ask a fool like you to be witty? A mocking smile—don't you understand?—mocking and contemptuous."

"H'm!"

"Oh, I do feel uneasy about this blockhead!" Marya Alexandrovna murmured to herself. "He certainly has taken a vow to be the death of me! It really would have been better not to have brought him at all."

Absorbed in such reflections, in regret and anxiety, Marya Alexandrovna was continually popping her head out of the window and urging on the coachman. The horses raced along, but still it seemed too slow for her. Afanasy Matveyitch sat silently in his corner, inwardly repeating his lesson. At last the carriage drove into the town and stopped at Marya Alexandrovna's house. But our heroine had hardly had time to alight at the front door, when all at once she saw driving up to the house a two-seated sledge with a hood—the very sledge in which Anna Nikolaevna Antipov usually drove about. In the sledge were sitting two ladies. One of them was, of course, Anna Nikolaevna herself, the other Natalya Dmitryevna, who had of late been her devoted friend and follower. Marya Alexandrovna's heart sank. But before she had time to cry out, another carriage drove up— a sledge, in which there was evidently another visitor. There was a sound of joyful exclamations:

"Marya Alexandrovna! And with Afanasy Matveyitch, too! You have just arrived? Where from? How lucky! And we have come to spend the whole evening! What a surprise!"

The visitors sprang out at the front door, and chattered like swallows. Marya Alexandrovna could not believe her eyes or her ears.

"I'll see you further," she thought to herself. "It looks like a plot! I must inquire into it. But . . . you won't outwit me, you magpies. . . . You wait a bit. . . ."

Chapter 11

As MOZGLYAKOV left Marya Alexandrovna, he was apparently quite comforted. She had completely inflamed his imagination. He did not go to see Boroduev, feeling that he wanted to be alone. A perfect flood of heroic and romantic dreams would not let him rest. He dreamed of a solemn explanation with Zina, then of generous tears of forgiveness on his part, pallor and despair at the gorgeous ball in Petersburg, Spain, the Guadalquivir, love and the dying Prince joining their hands on his death-bed. Then his lovely wife devoted to him and for ever lost in admiration of his heroism and lofty feelings; incidentally, on the quiet, the attentions of some countess belonging to the best society into which he would certainly be brought by his marriage with Zina, the widow of Prince K.; a post as vice-governor, money— in fact, everything so eloquently described by Marya Alexandrovna passed once more through his gratified soul, caressing and attracting it, and, above all, flattering his vanity. But—and I really don't know how to explain it—as he began to be wearied by these raptures, the extremely vexatious reflection occurred to him: that all this was, in any case, in the future, while now anyway he had been made a fool of.

When this thought came into his mind, he noticed that he had wandered a long way into some solitary and unfamiliar suburb of Mordasov. It had grown dark. In the streets, with their rows of little houses sunk into the earth, there was a savage barking of the dogs which abound in provincial towns in alarming numbers, precisely in those quarters where there is nothing to guard and nothing to steal. Snow was beginning to fall and melting as it fell. From time to time he met a belated workman or a peasant woman in a sheepskin and high boots. All this, for some unknown reason, began to irritate Pavel Alexandrovitch—a very bad sign, for when things are going well everything strikes us in a charming and attractive light. Pavel Alexandrovitch could not help remembering that hitherto he had always been a leading figure in Mordasov. He had been highly gratified when in every house he had heard it hinted that he was an eligible *parti* and had been congratulated on that distinction. He was actually proud of being an eligible young man. And now he would appear before every one as on the shelf! There would be laughter at his expense. Of course he could not enlighten them, he could not talk to them about Petersburg ball-rooms with columns, and about the Guadalquivir! Thinking of all this, full of dejection and regret, he stumbled at last upon a thought which had for a long while been rankling unnoticed in his heart: "Was it all true? Would it all come to pass as Marya Alexandrovna had described it?" At that point he remembered very opportunely that Marya Alexandrovna was a very designing woman, that however worthy of general respect she might be, she was gossiping and lying from morning till night; that in getting rid of him now, she probably had her own reasons, and that drawing fancy pictures of the future was a thing that anybody could do. He thought of Zina, too, recalled her parting look at him, which expressed anything rather than concealed passion; and therewith appropriately remembered that an hour before she had called him a fool. At that recollection Pavel Alexandrovitch stopped short as though rooted to the spot, and flushed with shame till the tears came into his eyes. As ill-luck would have it, the next minute he had an unpleasant adventure: he stepped back and went flying from the wooden pavement into a heap of snow.

While he was floundering in the snow a pack of dogs, which had been pursuing him with their barking for some time, flew at him on all sides. One of them, the smallest and most aggressive, hung on to him, fastening its teeth into his fur coat. Fighting off the dogs, swearing aloud, and even cursing his fate, Pavel Alexandrovitch, with a torn coat and insufferable despondency in his heart, reached the corner of the street and only then realized that he had lost his way. We all know that a man who has lost his way in an unknown part of the town, especially at night, can never walk straight along the streets. Some unknown force seems at every moment to impel him to turn down every side street he comes to on his way. Following this system, Pavel Alexandrovitch was soon hopelessly lost. "Deuce take all these exalted notions!" he said to himself, spitting with anger. "And the devil himself take you with your lofty feelings and your Guadal-quivirs!" I cannot say that Mozglyakov was attractive at that moment.

After wandering about for a couple of hours, he arrived exhausted and harassed at Marya Alexandrovna's front door. He was surprised at seeing a number of carriages. "Can there be visitors, can it be an evening party?" he thought. "What's the object of it?" Questioning a servant he met, and learning that Marya Alexandrovna had been to their country house and had brought back with her Afanasy Mat-veyitch in a white cravat, and that the Prince was awake but had not yet come downstairs to join the visitors, Pavel Alexandrovitch went upstairs to his "uncle" without saying a word to any one. He was at the moment in that state of mind when a man of weak character is capable of committing some horrible, malignant and nasty action from revenge, without considering that he may have to regret it all his life afterwards.

Going upstairs, he saw the Prince sitting in an easy-chair before his travelling dressing-case, with an absolutely bald head, though he had his "imperial" and whiskers on. The wig was in the hands of his grey-haired old valet and favourite, Ivan Pahomitch. Pahomitch was combing it with an air of deep reflection and respect. As for the Prince, he presented a very sorry spectacle, having hardly recovered from his recent potations. He was sitting as it were, all of a heap, blinking, crumpled and out of sorts, and he looked at Mozglyakov as though he did not recognize him.

"How are you feeling, Uncle?" asked Mozglyakov.

"What! . . . That's you," said his "uncle" at last. "I've had a little nap, my boy. Oh, my goodness!" he cried, suddenly reviving, "why, I . . . haven't got my wi-ig on."

"Don't disturb yourself, Uncle. I . . . I will help you, if you like."

"But now you've learnt my secret! I said we ought to lo-ock the door. Come, my dear, you must give me your wo-ord of honour at once that you won't give away my secret and won't tell any one that my hair is fa-alse."

"Upon my word, Uncle! Can you think me capable of anything so base!" cried Mozglyakov, anxious to please the old gentleman, with . . . ulterior aims.

"Oh, ye-es; oh, ye-es! And as I see you are an honourable man, so be it, I will surprise you . . . and will tell you all my secrets. How do you like my mous-taches, my dear?"

"They are superb, Uncle! Marvellous! How can you have preserved them so long?"

"Don't deceive yourself, my dear, they are ar-ti-fi-cial," said the Prince, looking with triumph at Pavel Alexandrovitch.

"Is it possible? I can hardly believe it. And the whiskers? Confess, Uncle, you must darken them?"

"Darken them? They are not dyed, they are ar-ti-fi-cial."

"Artificial? No, Uncle, you may say what you like, but I don't believe it. You are laughing at me!"

"Parole d'honneur, mon ami!" the Prince cried triumphantly; "and only fan-cy, every one is de-ceived, like you. Even Stepanida Matveyevna cannot believe it, though she sometimes fix-es them on herself. But, I am sure, my boy, you will keep my secret. Give me your word of honour. . . ."

"On my word of honour, Uncle, I will keep it. I ask you again, can you think me capable of anything so base?"

"Oh, my dear, what a fall I have had while you were away to-day. Fe-o-fil upset me out of the carriage again."

"Upset you again! When?"

"We were on our way to the mon-as-tery. . . ."

"I know, uncle, this morning."

"No, no, two hours ago, not more. I set off to the monastery and he upset me. How frigh-tened I was, even now my heart isn't right."

"But you've been asleep, Uncle," said Mozglyakov, wondering.

"Oh, ye-es, I've been asleep . . . and afterwards I drove out, though indeed . . . though perhaps I . . . oh, how strange it is!"

"I assure you, Uncle, that you have been dreaming it! You have been quietly dozing ever since dinner."

"Really?" and the Prince pondered. "Oh, ye-es, perhaps I really did dream it, though I remember everything I dreamed. At first I dreamt of a very dreadful bull with horns; and then I dreamt of some pub-lic pro-se-cu-tor who seemed to have ho-orns, too. . . ."

"I suppose that was Nikolay Vassilitch Antipov, uncle?"

"Oh, yes, perhaps it was he; and then I dreamt of Napoleon Bonaparte. Do you know, my dear, they all tell me that I am like Napoleon Bonaparte . . . and in profile I am strikingly like some pope of old days! What do you think, my dear, am I like a pope?"

"I think you are more like Napoleon, Uncle."

"Oh, ye-es, full face. I think so myself, too, my dear. And I dreamt about him, when he was on the island, and you know he was so talkative, so sprightly, such a jo-olly fel-low that he quite amused me."

"Are you speaking of Napoleon, Uncle?" said Pavel Alexandrovitch, looking at the old man reflectively. A strange idea was beginning to dawn upon his mind, an idea which he could not yet define clearly to himself.

"Oh, ye-es, of Na-po-leon. We were discussing philosophy to-gether. And do you know, my dear, that I am really sorry the En-glish treated him so harshly. Of course, if he had not been kept on the chain he would have been attacking people again. He was a desperate man, but still I am sorry for him. I wouldn't have treated him so. I would have put him upon an un-in-habited island. . . ."

"Why on an uninhabited one?" asked Mozglyakov absent-mindedly.

"Well, perhaps, on an in-habited one; but inhabited only by sensible people. And I would have got up entertainments of all sorts for him: a theatre, concerts, ballets, and all at the government expense. I would have let him go for walks under supervision, of course, or else he would have slipped away at once. He was very fond of little pies. Well, I would have made him little pies every day. I would have looked after him like a father, so to speak. He would have re-pen-ted in my care. . . ."

Mozglyakov listened abent-mindedly to the babble of the old man not yet fully awake, and bit his nails with impatience. He wanted to turn the conversation upon marriage, though he scarcely yet knew why; an unbounded anger was surging in his heart. All at once the old man cried out in surprise:

"Oh, *mon ami!* Why, I forgot to tell you. Only fancy, I made a pro-po-sal to-day."

"A proposal, Uncle!" cried Mozglyakov, waking up.

"Why, ye-es, a pro-po-sal. Pahomitch, are you going? Very good. *C'est une charmante personne.* . . . But . . . I confess, my dear boy, I acted thought-less-ly. I only se-ee that now. Oh, dear me!"

"But excuse me, Uncle, when did you make this proposal?"

"I own, my dear boy, that I really don't quite know when it was. Didn't I dream it, perhaps? Ah, how queer it is, though!"

Mozglakov shuddered with delight. A new idea flashed upon his mind.

"But who was it you made an offer to, and when did you make it, Uncle?" he repeated impatiently.

"The daughter of the house, *mon ami . . . cette belle personne.* . . . I have for-got-ten her name, though. Only you see, my dear, I really can't get ma-arried. What am I to do now?"

"Yes, it will certainly be your ruin if you get married. But allow me to ask you one other question, Uncle. You seem to be convinced that you really have made an offer?"

"Oh, yes. . . . I am sure of it."

"But what if you have dreamed it all, just as you dreamed you had been upset out of your carriage a second time?"

"Oh, my goodness! Perhaps this really was a dream, too! So that I really don't know how to behave with them. How is one to find out for certain, my dear boy, whether I did make a proposal or not? But now fancy what a position I am in!"

"Do you know Uncle, I fancy there is no need to find out."

"How so?"

"I feel sure that you dreamed it."

"I think so, too, my dear, especially as I often have dreams of that sort."

"There you see, Uncle. Remember that you had a little wine at lunch, and then again at dinner, and in the end . . ."

"Oh, ye-es, my dear; it very like-ly was due to that."

"Besides, Uncle, however exhilarated you may have been, you couldn't possibly under any circumstances have made such a non-sensical proposal in reality. As far as I know you, Uncle, you are a man of the greatest good sense, and . . ."

"Oh, ye-es; oh, ye-es."

"Only consider one point: if your relations, who have nothing but ill-will for you in any case, were to hear of it, what would happen then?"

"Oh, my goodness!" cried the Prince in alarm, "what would happen then?"

"Upon my word! Why, they would all cry out in chorus that you were out of your mind when you did it, that you had gone mad, that you must be put under restraint, that you had been taken advantage of, and perhaps they would put you somewhere under supervision."

Mozglyakov knew what would frighten the Prince most.

"Oh, my God!" cried the Prince, trembling like a leaf. "Could they possibly shut me up?"

"And then only think, Uncle, could you possibly have made such an imprudent offer when you were awake? You undestand your own interests. I assure you solemnly that it was all a dream."

"It cer-tain-ly must have been a dream, it cer-tain-ly must!" the Prince repeated in a panic. "Oh, how sensibly you've thought it out, my de-ear boy! I am sincerely grateful to you for setting me right."

"I am awfully glad, Uncle, that I have met you to-day. Only fancy, if I had not been here you might really have been muddled, have thought that you were engaged, and have gone down to them as though you were. Think how dangerous!"

"Oh, ye-es . . . ye-es, dangerous."

"Remember that young lady is three-and-twenty; nobody wants to marry her, and all at once you, a man of wealth and rank, appear as a suitor! Why, they would snatch at the idea at once, would assure you you were engaged, and would force you perhaps into marriage. And they would calculate on the possibility of your dying before long."

"Really?"

"And remember, Uncle, a man of your qualities . . ."

"Oh, ye-es, with my qualities . . ."

"With your intelligence, with your politeness . . ."

"Oh, ye-es, with my intelligence, ye-es! . . ."

"And last, but not least, you are a prince. What a splendid match you might make if, for some reason, you really did want to marry! Only think what your relations would say!"

"Oh, my dear, why they would be the death of me! I have endured such treachery, such ill-treatment at their hands. . . . Would you believe it, I suspect they wanted to put me into a lu-na-tic asylum. Upon my word, my dear, wasn't that absurd? Why, what could I have done there . . . in a lu-na-tic asylum?"

"Quite so, Uncle, and so I won't leave your side when you go downstairs. There are visitors there now."

"Visitors? Oh, my goodness!"

"Don't be uneasy, Uncle, I will keep with you."

"But how grate-ful I am to you, my dear, you are simply my saviour! But do you know, I think I had better go away."

"To-morrow morning, Uncle, at seven o'clock to-morrow morning. But to-day you can take leave of every one and tell them you are going away."

"I will certainly go away . . . to Father Misail. . . . But my dear boy—what if they do make a match of it?"

"Don't be afraid, Uncle, I shall be with you, and whatever they say to you, whatever they hint at, you say straight out that it was all a dream, as it certainly was. . . ."

"Oh, ye-es, it cer-tain-ly must have been a dream. Only do you know, my dear, it was a most en-chan-ting dream! She is wonderfully good-looking, and do you know, such a figure. . . ."

"Well, farewell, Uncle. I am going downstairs, and you . . ."

"What! Are you going to leave me alone?" cried the Prince in alarm.

"No, Uncle, we'll both go down but separately; I'll go first, and then you. That will be better."

"Oh, ve-ry well, And by the way, I must jot down an idea."

"Quite so, Uncle, jot down your idea and then come down, don't delay. To-morrow morning . . ."

"And to-morrow morning to Father Misail, cer-tain-ly to Father Misail! *Charmant, charmant!* But do you know, my dear, she is won-der-ful-ly good-looking . . . such contours . . . and if I really had to be married . . ."

"God preserve you, Uncle."

"Oh, ye-es, God preserve me! . . . Well, good-bye, my dear, I'll come directly . . . only I will just jot down. *À propos,* I have been meaning to ask you for a long time. Have you read the memoirs of Casanova?"

"Yes, I have, Uncle. Why?"

"Oh, well . . . I have forgotten now what I meant to say. . . ."

"You will think of it later, Uncle. Good-bye for the present!"

"Good-bye, my dear, good-bye. Though it really was a fascinating dream, a fa-as-ci-na-ting dream! . . ."

Chapter 12

WE'VE all come to see you, all of us! and Praskovya Ilyinitchna is coming too, and Luiza Karlovna meant to come too," twittered Anna Nikolaevna, walking into the *salon* and looking about her greedily.

She was a rather pretty little lady, dressed expensively but in gaudy colours, and very well aware that she was pretty. She fancied that the Prince was hidden somewhere in a corner with Zina.

"And Katerina Petrovna is coming, and Felisata Mihalovna meant to be here too," added Natalya Dmitryevna, the lady of colossal proportions, remarkably like a grenadier, whose appearance had so delighted the Prince.

She had on an extraordinarily small pink hat perched on the back of her head. For the last three weeks she had been the devoted friend of Anna Nikolaevna, whose good graces she had long been trying to win, and whom, to judge by appearances, she could have swallowed up at one gulp, bones and all.

"I won't speak of the delight, I may call it, of seeing you both here and in the evening too," Marya Alexandrovna chanted, recovering from her first stupefaction. "But tell me, please, what miracle has brought you to me to-night, when I quite despaired of such an honour."

"Oh, my goodness, Marya Alexandrovna, what a forgetful lady you are!" said Natalya Dmitryevna in honeyed accents, mincing and speaking in a bashful and squeaky voice which was a very curious contrast to her appearance.

"*Mais ma charmante,*" twittered Anna Nikolaevna, "we must, you know, we really must complete our arrangements for these theatricals. Only to-day Pyotr Mihalovitch said to Kalist Stanislavitch that he was very much disappointed that it was not coming off well, and that we did nothing but fall out over it. So we met together this evening and thought: let us go to Marya Alexandrovna's and settle it all right away. Natalya Dmitryevna let the others know. They are all coming. So we will talk it all over together and all will go well. We won't let them say that we do nothing but quarrel, will we, *mon ange?*" she added playfully, kissing Marya Alexandrovna. "Oh, my goodness! Zinaida Afanasyevna! Why, you grow prettier every day!"

Anna Nikolaevna flew to shower kisses on Zina.

"Indeed, she has nothing else to do but grow prettier," Natalya Dmitryevna added in sugary accents, rubbing her huge hands.

"The devil take them! I did not think about those theatricals! They have been sharp, the magpies!" Marya Alexandrovna murmured, beside herself with fury.

"Especially, my angel, since that darling Prince is staying with you. You know there used to be a theatre at Duhanovo in the time of the late owners. We have made inquiries already and know that all the old scenery, the curtain, and even the costumes are put away somewhere. The Prince called on me to-day, and I was so surprised at seeing him that I quite forgot to speak of it. Now we will introduce the subject of the theatre, you must help us, and the Prince will order all the old trappings to be sent us. For who is there here you can trust to make anything like scenery? And what is more, we want to interest the Prince in our theatricals. He must subscribe, you see it is for charity. Perhaps he will even take a part—he is so sweet and obliging. Then it will be a wonderful success."

"Of course he will take a part. Why, he can be made to play any part," Natalya Dmitryevna added with vast significance.

Anna Nikolaevna had not misinformed Marya Alexandrovna: ladies kept arriving every minute. Marya Alexandrovna hardly had time to receive them and utter the exclamations demanded on such occasions by propriety and the rules of *comme il faut*.

I will not undertake to describe all the visitors. I will only mention that each one wore a look of extraordinary wiliness. Anticipation and a sort of wild impatience was expressed on every face. Some of the ladies had come with the express object of witnessing an extraordinary and scandalous scene, and would have been exceedingly wroth if they had had to drive home again without having seen it. On the surface they behaved with the utmost amiability, but Marya Alexandrovna resolutely prepared herself for the attack. There was a shover of questions about the Prince; they sounded most natural; yet each seemed to contain an allusion or innuendo. Tea was brought in; every one sat down. One group took possession of the piano. On being asked to play and sing, Zina answered that she did not feel quite well. The paleness of her face confirmed her words. Sympathetic inquiries were showered upon her, and the ladies even seized the opportunity to ask questions and drop hints. They inquired about Mozglyakov, too, and addressed these inquiries to Zina. Marya Alexandrovna displayed ten times her usual energy at that moment;

she saw everything that was going on in every corner of the room, heard what was said by each one of her visitors, though there were nearly a dozen of them, and answered every question immediately, without hesitating for a word. She was trembling for Zina and was surprised that she did not go away, as she had always done before on such occasions. She kept her eye, too, on Afanasy Matveyitch. Everybody always made fun of him in order to pique Marya Alexandrovna through her husband. On this occasion it might be possible to learn something from the simple-minded and open-hearted Afanasy Matveyitch. Marya Alexandrovna looked with anxiety at the way in which her husband was being besieged. Moreover, to every question he answered "H'm," with an expression so unhappy and unnatural that it might well have driven her to fury.

"Marya Alexandrovna, Afanasy Matveyitch won't talk to us at all!" cried one bold, sharp-eyed little lady, who was afraid of nobody and never embarrassed by anything. "Do tell him to be more polite with ladies."

"I really don't know what has come over him to-day," answered Marya Alexandrovna, interrupting her conversation with Anna Nikolaevna and Natalya Dmitryevna, with a gay smile. "He certainly is uncommunicative! He has scarcely said a word to me. Why don't you answer Felisata Mihalovna, *Athanase?* What did you ask him?"

"But . . . but . . . you know, Mother, you told me yourself . . ." Afanasy Matveyitch began muttering in his surprise and confusion. At that moment he was standing by the lighted fire, with his hands thrust into his waistcoat in a picturesque attitude which he had chosen for himself. He was sipping tea. The ladies' questions so embarrassed him that he blushed like a girl. When he began justifying himself, he caught such a terrible glance from his infuriated wife that he almost lost consciousness from terror. Not knowing what to do, anxious to put himself right and regain respect, he took a gulp at his tea; but the tea was too hot. Having taken it so hastily, he burnt himself terribly, dropped the cup, spluttered and choked so violently that he had to go out of the room, to the surprise of all present. In fact, everything was clear. Marya Alexandrovna realized that her visitors knew all about it and had met together with the worst intentions. The position was dangerous. They might talk to the feeble-minded old man and turn him from his purpose even in her presence. They might even take the Prince away from her, set him against her that very evening, and entice him away with them.

She might expect anything. But fate had another ordeal in store for her; the door opened and she beheld Mozglyakov, whom she had believed to be at Boroduev's and did not in the least expect that evening. She started as though something had stabbed her.

Mozglyakov stopped in the doorway and looked round at every one a little confused. He was not able to control his emotion, which was clearly apparent in his face.

"Oh, my goodness, Pavel Alexandrovitch!" cried several voices.

"Oh, my goodness! Why, it is Pavel Alexandrovitch. How was it you told us he had gone to Boroduev's, Marya Alexandrovna? We were told you were hiding at Boroduev's, Pavel Alexandrovitch!" Natalya Dmitryevna piped.

"Hiding?" repeated Mozglyakov, with a rather wry smile. "It is a strange expression! Excuse me, Natalya Dmitryevna! I don't conceal myself from any one, and I don't want to conceal anybody else, either," he added, looking significantly at Marya Alexandrovna.

Marya Alexandrovna was in a tremor.

"Can the blockhead be mutinous?" she wondered, looking searchingly at Mozglyakov. "No, that will be worse than anything. . . ."

"Is it true, Pavel Alexandrovitch, that they have given you the sack . . . at your office, I mean, of course?" the impudent Felisata Mihalovna asked pertly, sarcastically looking him straight in the face.

"The sack? What sack? I am simply transferring from one branch to another. I have a post in Petersburg," Mozglyakov answered coldly.

"Oh, I congratulate you, then," Felisata Mihalovna went on. "We were positively scared when we heard you were trying to get a post in Mordasov. The posts here can't be relied upon, Pavel Alexandrovitch, there is no keeping them."

"It is only as a teacher in the district school that you might find a vacancy," observed Natalya Dmitryevna.

The hint was so obvious and so crude that Anna Nikolaevna, confused, gently nudged her malicious friend with her foot.

"Do you imagine that Pavel Alexandrovitch would be willing to take the place of a wretched teacher?" put in Felisata Mihalovna.

But Pavel Alexandrovitch could not find an answer. He turned round and jostled against Afanasy Matveyitch, who held out his hand to him. Mozglyakov very stupidly did not take his hand, but gave him a low and ironical bow. Exceedingly irritated, he went up to Zina, and looking angrily into her face, muttered:

"This is all thanks to you. Wait a bit, I'll show you this very evening whether I am a fool."

"Why put it off? One can see that now," Zina answered aloud, looking her former suitor up and down with an air of aversion.

Mozglyakov turned away hurriedly, frightened by her loud voice.

"Have you been to see Boroduev?" Marya Alexandrovna ventured to inquire at last.

"No, I have been seeing Uncle."

"Uncle? So you have just been with the Prince, then?"

"Oh, my goodness! Then the Prince is awake? And we were told that he was still resting," added Natalya Dmitryevna, with a malignant look at Marya Alexandrovna.

"Don't trouble about the Prince, Natalya Dmitryevna," answered Mozglyakov; "he is awake, and now, thank God, he has all his senses about him. This morning he was given too much wine; first when he was with you, and afterwards here, till his head, never over-strong, was completely muddled. But now, thank God, we have had a little talk, and he has recovered his common-sense. He will be here directly to take leave of you, Marya Alexandrovna, and thank you for all your hospitality. To-morrow at daybreak we are setting off together to the monastery, and then I shall certainly escort him back to Duhanovo myself, to avoid a second accident like that of to-day; and then I shall hand him over to Stepanida Matveyevna, who by that time will certainly be back from Moscow and will not let him go on his travels a second time—I can answer for that."

As he said this, Mozglyakov looked spitefully at Marya Alexandrovna. She was sitting as though petrified with amazement. I admit with grief that my heroine was, perhaps for the first time in her life, cowed.

"So he is going away at daybreak to-morrow! How's that?" said Natalya Dmitryevna, addressing Marya Alexandrovna.

"How is that?" the visitors were heard saying naïvely. "Why, we heard that . . . why, that's very odd."

But their hostess did not know what answer to make. Suddenly the general attention was diverted in the most strange and eccentric way. In the adjoining room a strange noise was heard, and abrupt exclamations, and all at once, utterly unexpectedly, Sofya Petrovna Karpuhin dashed into Marya Alexandrovna's *salon*. Sofya Petrovna was unquestionably the most eccentric lady in Mordasov, so eccentric that it had even been decided of late not to receive her in society. It must be observed, too, that regularly every evening at seven o'clock it was her habit to take a nip of something—for the sake of her stomach, as she explained—and after it, she was as a rule in an emancipated state of mind, to put it mildly. She was in that state of mind now at the moment when she so unexpectedly burst in upon Marya Alexandrovna.

"So this is the way, Marya Alexandrovna," she shouted to be heard all over the room. "So this is the way you treat me! Don't disturb yourself, I have only come for a minute, I won't sit down. I've come on purpose to find out whether it is true what I am told! So you have balls, banquets, a betrothal party, but Sofya Petrovna must sit at home and knit a stocking! You've asked the whole town, but not me! Though this morning I was your friend and *mon ange* when I came to tell you what they were doing with the Prince at Natalya Dmitryevna's. And now here's Natalya Dmitryevna, whom you were abusing like a pickpocket, and who was abusing you, paying you a visit. Don't disturb yourself, Natalya Dmitryevna. I don't want your chocolate *à la santé,* at twopence a stick. I have better to drink at home! Tfoo!"

"One can see you have," observed Natalya Dmitryevna.

"But upon my word, Sofya Petrovna," cried Marya Alexandrovna, flushing with vexation, "what is the matter with you? Do control yourself at least."

"Don't trouble about me, Marya Alexandrovna, I know all about it, all about it!" cried Sofya Petrovna in her harsh, shrill voice. She was surrounded by the other visitors, who seemed to be enjoying this unexpected scene. "I have found out all about it. Your Nastasya ran round and told me the whole story. You pounced on this wretched Prince, made him drunk, and made him propose to your daughter whom nobody wants to marry now, and you imagine that you've become a fine bird now yourself—a duchess in lace! Tfoo! Don't disturb yourself. I am a Colonel's wife myself. I don't care if you don't invite me to your betrothal party. I have mixed with better people than you. I have dined with Countess Zalihvatsky. The head commissary, Kurotchkin, paid me his addresses. As though I wanted your invitation! Tfoo!"

"Come, Sofya Petrovna," answered Marya Alexandrovna, losing patience, "I must tell you, this is not the way to burst into a lady's house, especially in *such a condition,* and if you do not relieve me of your presence and your eloquent remarks, I shall promptly take steps to get rid of you."

"I know you will tell your nasty servants to turn me out! Don't excite yourself, I can find the way for myself. Good-bye; make any marriage you like. And you, Natalya Dmitryevna, don't laugh at me, if you please; I don't care a damn about your chocolate! Though I am not invited here. I don't go dancing jigs to amuse princes. What are you laughing at, Anna Nikolaevna? Sushilov has broken his leg; they've just carried him home! And you, Felisata Mihalovna, if you don't tell your bare-legged Matryoshka to drive your cow home in good time so she's not mooing under my window every day, I will break her legs. Good-bye, Marya Alexandrovna, good luck to you! Tfoo!"

Sofya Petrovna vanished. The visitors laughed. Marya Alexandrovna was thrown into extreme embarrassment.

"I think the lady has had a little too much," Natalya Dmitryevna brought out in her sugary voice.

"But what insolence!"

"Quelle abominable femme!"

"How funny she was, though!"

"Ah, what shocking things she said!"

"But what was it she said about a betrothal party? What betrothal party?" Felisata Mihalovna asked sarcastically.

"But this is awful!" Marya Alexandrovna burst out at last. "It is these monsters who scatter these absurd rumours by handfuls! It is not so strange, Felisata Mihalovna, that such ladies are to be found in our midst, no; what is more surprising is that these ladies are sought after, are listened to, are encouraged, are believed, are . . ."

"The Prince! the Prince!" all voices cried suddenly at once.

"Oh, my goodness! *Le cher prince!"*

"Oh, thank goodness! Now we shall find out all the details," Felisata Mihalovna whispered to her neighbour.

Chapter 13

THE Prince came in with a honeyed smile on his lips. The alarm which Mozglyakov had inspired in his chicken heart entirely disappeared at the sight of the ladies. He melted at once like a sweetmeat. The ladies greeted him with shrill cries of delight. Ladies always made a great deal of our old friend, and were very familiar with him. He was able to afford them incredible entertainment. Felisata Mihalovna had declared that morning (not in earnest, of course) that she was ready to sit on his knee, if that would give him any pleasure, "because he was a darling, darling old man, sweet beyond all bounds!" Marya Alexandrovna transfixed him with her eyes, trying to read something from his face and to divine from it the way out of her critical position. It was evident that Mozglyakov had said horrible things about her, and that her plans were in jeopardy. But nothing could be read from the Prince's face. He was the same as he had been that morning and as he always was.

"Ah, my goodness, here is the Prince! We have been waiting and waiting for you," cried several of the ladies.

"With impatience, Prince, with impatience!" piped others.

"That's extremely flat-ter-ing," lisped the Prince, sitting down at the table on which the samovar was boiling. The ladies immediately surrounded him. Anna Nikolaevna and Natalya Dmitryevna were the only ones left by the side of Marya Alexandrovna. Afanasy Matveyitch smiled respectfully. Mozglyakov smiled too, and with a defiant air looked at Zina, who, without taking the slightest notice of him, went and sat down by her father near the fire.

"Oh, Prince, is it true what they say, that you are leaving us?" piped Felisata Mihalovna.

"Oh, ye-es, *mesdames,* I am going away, I want to go abro-oad im-med-iately."

"Abroad, Prince, abroad!" they all cried in chorus. "What an idea!"

"Abro-oad," repeated the Prince, prinking. "And do you know, I want to go abroad particularly for the sake of the new ideas."

"How do you mean for the sake of the new ideas? New ideas about what?" said the ladies, exchanging glances with one another.

"Oh, ye-es, for the sake of the new ideas," repeated the Prince, with an air of the deepest conviction. "Every one now goes abroad for the sake of the new i-deas, and so I, too, want to gain ne-ew i-ideas."

"Don't you want, perhaps, to enter a masonic lodge, Uncle?" put in Mozglyakov, who evidently wished to impress the ladies by his wit and his ease.

"Oh, ye-es, my dear, you are quite right," the old man answered unexpectedly. "In old days I real-ly did belong to a masonic lodge abroad, and I, too, had a number of noble ideas. I intended, indeed, at that time to do a great deal for the en-light-en-ment of the peo-ple, and I quite decided at Frankfurt to set free my man Sidor whom I had brought with me from Russia. But to my surprise he ran away from me himself. He was an ex-treme-ly odd man. Afterwards I met him in Pa-ris, such a swell, with whiskers, he was walking along the boulevard with a mamselle. He looked at me, gave me a nod, and the mamselle with him was such a brisk, sharp-eyed, alluring creature . . ."

"Come, Uncle! Why, you'll be setting all your peasants free next, if you go abroad this time," cried Mozglyakov, laughing loudly.

"You have gu-essed perfectly right, my dear boy, what I desire to do," the Prince answered without hesitation. "I do want to set them all fre-ee."

"But upon my word, Prince, they will all run away from you directly, and then where will you get your money?" cried Felisata Mihalovna.

"Of course they would all run away," Anna Nikolaevna echoed, with a note of alarm.

"Oh, dear me, do you really think they would run away?" cried the Prince in astonishment.

"They would run away, they would all run away at once and would leave you alone," Natalya Dmitryevna confirmed.

"Oh, dear me! Well, then I shall not se-et them free. But of course I did not mean it."

"So much the better, Uncle," Mozglyakov said approvingly.

Till then, Marya Alexandrovna had been listening and watching in silence. It seemed to her that the Prince had entirely forgotten her, and that that was not natural.

"Allow me, Prince," she began in a loud and dignified voice, "to introduce my husband, Afanasy Matveyitch. He came expressly from our country house as soon as he heard you were staying with us."

Afanasy Matveyitch smiled and looked dignified. It seemed to him as though he were being praised.

"Ah, I am delighted," said the Prince, "A-fa-nasy Matveyitch! To be sure, I believe I remember something. A-fa-nasy Mat-ve-yitch. To be sure, that is the gentleman in the country. *Charmant, charmant,* delighted. My dear!" cried the Prince, turning to Mozglyakov. "Why, that's the very man, do you remember, who was in that rhyme this morning. How did it go? 'The husband's on the stair, and the wife has gone . . .' Oh, ye-es, the wife has gone away to some town."

"Oh, Prince, why that's true; 'The husband's on the stair, while the wife has gone to Tver,' the very vaudeville the actors played here last year,' Felisata Mihalovna put in.

"Oh, ye-es, precisely: to Tver; I always forget. *Charmant, charmant!* So you are that very man? Extremely glad to make your ac-quaintance," said the Prince, holding out his hand to the smiling Afanasy Matveyitch without getting up from his chair. "Well, I hope you are well?"

"H'm. . . ."

"He is quite well, Prince, quite well," Marya Alexandrovna answered hurriedly.

"Oh, ye-es, one can see he is quite well. And are you always in the country? Well, I am delighted. Why, what red che-eks he has and how he keeps laughing!"

Afanasy Matveyitch continued smiling, bowing, and even scraping with his foot. But at the Prince's last observation he could not restrain himself, and all of a sudden, apropos of nothing, in the most foolish way burst into a loud laugh. Everybody laughed. The ladies squealed with delight. Zina flushed and with flashing eyes looked at Marya Alexandrovna, who in her turn was bursting with anger. It was high time to change the conversation.

"How did you sleep, Prince?" she asked in a honeyed voice, at the same time turning a menacing look upon Afanasy Matveyitch to indicate that he should take himself off as quickly as possible.

"Oh, I had a very good sleep," answered the Prince; "and do you know, I had a most en-chan-ting dream, an en-chan-ting dream!"

"A dream! I love to hear people tell their dreams," cried Felisata Mihalovna.

"And I, too, I love it!" added Natalya Dmitryevna.

"An en-chan-ting dream!" repeated the Prince, with a mawkish smile; "but the dream is a dead secret!"

"How so, Prince, do you really mean you can't tell it us? It must have been a wonderful dream!" observed Anna Nikolaevna.

"A dead secret," repeated the Prince, gleefully tantalizing the ladies' curiosity.

"Oh, then it must be very interesting!" cried the ladies.

"I bet that the Prince dreamed that he fell on his knees before some beautiful young lady and made her an offer of marriage!" cried Felisata Mihalovna. "Come, Prince, own up that that's right! Darling Prince, confess!"

"Confess, Prince, confess," the others chimed in on all sides.

The Prince listened triumphantly and ecstatically to all their outcries. The ladies' supposition flattered his vanity extremely, and he almost licked his lips.

"Though I said that my dream was a dead secret," he answered at last, "yet I must admit, madame, that to my great surprise, you have guessed al-most per-fect-ly right."

"Guessed right!" cried Felisata Mihalovna rapturously. "Well, Prince! Well, now you absolutely must tell us who the beautiful young lady was!"

"You must tell us!"

"Does she live in these parts?"

"Darling Prince, do tell us! You must tell us, whatever happens!" they cried on all sides.

"*Mesdames, mesdames!* . . . If you are so very in-sis-tent to know, I can only tell you one thing, that it was the most fas-ci-na-ting and, I may say, the most vir-tu-ous young lady I know," mumbled the Prince, melting like wax.

"Most fascinating and . . . some one living here! Who could it be?" the ladies kept asking, exchanging significant glances and winking at one another.

"Of course, the one who is considered the chief belle here," said Natalya Dmitryevna, rubbing her huge red hands and looking with her cat-like eyes at Zina. All the others looked at Zina with her.

"Well, Prince, if you have such dreams, why don't you get married in reality?" asked Felisata Mihalovna, with a significant look at the others.

"What a splendid match we would make for you!" another lady put in.

"Prince, darling! do get married!" piped a third.

"Get married, get married!" they cried on all sides. "Why shouldn't you get married?"

"Oh, ye-es, why not get married?" the Prince assented, completely confused by these outcries.

"Uncle!" cried Mozglyakov.

"Oh, ye-es, my dear, I un-der-stand. I meant to tell you, *mesdames,* that I am not able to get married, and that when I have spent a delightful evening with our fascinating hostess, I shall set off to-mor-row to Father Misail at the monastery, and then I am going straight abroad so as to keep up with the progress of European en-light-en-ment."

Zina turned pale and looked at her mother with inexpressible misery. But Marya Alexandrovna had already made up her mind. Hitherto she had only been waiting, testing things, though she did realize that her project was ruined and that her enemies had circum-vented her successfully. At last she grasped the whole position, she made up her mind at one blow to crush the many-headed hydra. She got up from her easy-chair majestically and with resolute steps approached the table, scanning with haughty eyes her pigmy foes. There was the light of inspiration in that look. She determined to impress, to disconcert, all these venomous scandalmongers, to squash Mozglyakov as though he were a beetle, and by one bold resolute stroke to recapture all her lost influence over the imbecile Prince. Exceptional audacity was of course needed; but Marya Alexandrovna had no lack of audacity!

"*Mesdames,*" she began solemnly and with dignity (Marya Alexandrovna was particularly fond of a solemn manner), "*mesdames,* I have been listening for some time to your conversation, to your gay and witty jests, and I think it is time for me to put in my word. You know we have met together this evening—quite by chance (and I am so glad, so glad of it) . . . I should never have brought myself of my own accord to announce to you an important family secret and to publish it abroad sooner than the most ordinary feeling of decorum would dictate. Especially I must beg the forgiveness of my dear guest; but I fancied that he himself, by indirect hints at the very circumstance, gives me to understand that a formal and ceremonious announcement of our family secret will not be disagreeable, that, in fact, he desires this announcement. . . . Is it not so, Prince, I am not mistaken?"

"Oh, ye-es, you are not mistaken . . . and I am delighted!" said the Prince, without the faintest idea of what she was talking about.

For the sake of greater effect, Marya Alexandrovna stopped to take breath, and looked round at the whole company. All the visitors were listening to her words with spiteful and uneasy curiosity. Mozglyakov started. Zina flushed crimson and got up from her chair. Afanasy Matveyitch, in anticipation of something extraordinary, blew his nose to be ready for anything.

"Yes, *mesdames,* I am ready joyfully to confide to you my family secret. After dinner to-day the Prince, captivated by the beauty and . . . virtues of my daughter, did her the honour of offering her his hand. Prince!" she concluded in a voice quivering with tears and emotion, "dear Prince, you must not, you cannot be angry with me for my indiscretion! Nothing but my great joy as a mother could have torn from my heart this precious secret before the fitting time, and . . . what mother could blame me in this case?"

I cannot find words to describe the effect produced by Marya Alexandrovna's unexpected outburst. Every one seemed as though petrified with amazement. The treacherous visitors, who had thought they would frighten Marya Alexandrovna by their knowledge of her secret, had expected to crush her by the premature disclosure of that secret, who had expected to torment her, at first simply by allusions, were dumbfounded by such audacious candour. Such fearless audacity was a sure sign of power. "Then was the Prince really going to marry Zina of his own free will? Then had they not allured him, made him drunk, deceived him? Then he was not being forced into marriage in an underhand, dishonest way? Then Marya Alexandrovna was not afraid of anybody? Then it would be impossible to prevent the marriage, since the Prince was not being forced into it?" For a moment there was a sound of whispering which turned at once into shrill cries of delight. Natalya Dmitryevna was the first to embrace Marya Alexandrovna; Anna Nikolaevna followed her example, and after her Felisata Mihalovna. They all jumped up from their seats, they were all thrown into confusion, some of the ladies were pale from spite. They began to congratulate the embarrassed Zina; they even fastened on Afanasy Matveyitch. Marya Alexandrovna held out her arms in a picturesque attitude, and almost by force enfolded her daughter in her embrace. The Prince alone looked on at the scene with strange surprise, though he went on smiling as before. The scene pleased him in a way, however. At the sight of the mother embracing the daughter, he took out his handkerchief and wiped his eyes in which there gleamed a tear. Of course people rushed to congratulate him too.

"We congratulate you, Prince! We congratulate you!" the ladies cried on all sides.

"So you are going to get married?"

"So you are really going to get married!"

"Darling Prince, so you are going to get married?"

"Oh, ye-es; oh, ye-es," answered the Prince, extremely delighted with their raptures and their congratulations. "And I must say, that nothing gives me more pleasure than your kind sympathy, which I shall ne-ever forget, ne-ever forget. *Charmant! charmant!* You've brought tears into my eyes."

"Kiss me, Prince," Felisata Mihalovna cried, louder than all the rest.

"And I must say," the Prince went on, interrupted on all sides, "I am most of all surprised that Marya I-van-ov-na, our honoured hostess, has guessed my dream with such ex-tra-or-di-nary insight. It is as though she had dreamed it instead of me. Ex-tra-or-di-nary insight! Ex-tra-or-di-nary insight!"

"Oh, Prince, the dream again?"

"Come, confess, Prince, confess!" they all cried, surrounding him.

"Yes, Prince, there is no need for concealment, the time has come to reveal our secret!" Marya Alexandrovna said sternly and resolutely. "I understand your subtle allegory, the enchanting delicacy with which you tried to hint to me your desire to make public your engagement. Yes, *mesdames,* it is true: this afternoon the Prince went down on his knees to my daughter, and not in a dream but reality, and made her a formal offer."

"Exactly as though it were real and actually with the very same circumstances," repeated the Prince, *"Mademoiselle,"* he said, turning with marked courtesy to Zina, who had not yet recovered from her amazement, *"mademoiselle,* I swear that I would never have made so bold as to pronounce your name if others had not ut-tered it before me. It was fascinating dream, a fas-ci-na-ting dream, and I am doubly happy that I am now permitted to tell it to you. *Charmant, charmant! . . ."*

"But upon my word how is this? He is still talking about a dream," whispered Anna Nikolaevna to Marya Alexandrovna, who was somewhat flustered and had turned a little pale.

Alas! There was an ache and a tremor in Marya Alexandrovna's heart already, apart from those warning words.

"How is this?" whispered the ladies, looking at one another.

"Why, Prince," began Marya Alexandrovna, with a wry and sickly smile. "I protest, you surprise me! What is this strange idea about a dream? I confess I thought till now that you were jesting, but . . . if it is a joke, it is rather an inappropriate one. . . . I should desire, I should wish to put it down to your absent-mindedness, but . . ."

"Perhaps it really is the result of his absent-mindedness," hissed Natalya Dmitryevna.

"Oh, yes, perhaps it is absent-mindedness," the Prince assented, still not fully grasping what they were trying to get out of him. "And only fancy, I must tell you an a-nec-dote. In Petersburg I was invited to a fu-ne-ral to some people, *maison bourgeoise, mais honnête,* and I muddled it up and thought it was a name-day party. The name-day party had been the week before. I got ready a bouquet of camellias for the lady whose name day it was. I go in and what do I see, a respectable, dignified man lying on the table, so that I was quite surprised. I simply did not know what to do with myself and the bou-quet."

"Come, Prince, this is not a time for anecdotes!" Marya Alexandrovna interrupted with vexation. "Of course my daughter has no need to run after suitors, but this afternoon, beside that piano, you made her a proposal. I did not invite you to do so. . . . I was, I may say, astounded. . . . I was, of course, struck by one idea at the time, and I put it all off till you should wake. But I am a mother . . . she is my daughter. . . . You spoke yourself just now of a dream, and I thought that you wished, under the guise of allegory, to tell us of your engagement. I know very well that you will be dissuaded . . . and I suspect who it is . . . but . . . explain yourself, Prince, make haste and explain satisfactorily. You cannot jest like this with a respectable family."

"Oh, no, one cannot jest like this with a respectable family," the Prince assented mechanically, though he was beginning to be a little uneasy.

"But that is no answer, Prince, to my question. I beg you to give a definite answer; repeat at once, repeat before every one that you did make my daughter an offer this afternoon."

"Oh, ye-es, I am ready to repeat it, though I have already told the whole story, and Felisata Yakovlevna guessed my dream exactly."

"It was not a dream, it was not a dream!" cried Marya Alexandrovna in exasperation. "It was not a dream, it was reality, Prince; reality—do you hear?—reality!"

"Reality!" cried the Prince, getting up from his chair in his surprise. "Well, my dear, it is just as you foretold upstairs!" he added, turning to Mozglyakov. "But I assure you, honoured Marya Stepanovna, that you are in error! I am quite persuaded that I only dreamed it."

"Lord have mercy upon us!" cried Marya Alexandrovna.

"Don't upset yourself, Marya Alexandrovna," Natalya Dmitryevna put in. "Perhaps the Prince has forgotten. . . . He will remember."

"I wonder at you, Natalya Dmitryevna," retorted Marya Alexandrovna indignantly. "Can such things be forgotten? Can one forget it? Upon my word, Prince, are you laughing at us? Or you are, perhaps, playing the part of a profligate beau of the days of the Regency depicted by Dumas? Some Faire-la-cour or Lauzun? But apart from that not being in keeping with your years, I assure you that you will not succeed in it. My daughter is not a *vicomtesse*. Here, this afternoon, on this spot she sang to you, and carried away by her singing you dropped on your knees and made her an offer! Can I be dreaming? Can I be sleeping? Speak, Prince: am I awake or sleeping?"

"Oh, ye-es. . . . or rather, perhaps, no . . ." answered the bewildered Prince. "I mean, that I believe I am not dreaming now. You see, I was asleep this afternoon, and so I had a dream that in my sleep . . ."

"Tfoo, my goodness, what does it mean? Not asleep—asleep, dreaming—not dreaming! Why, goodness knows what it means. Are you raving, Prince?"

"Oh, ye-es, goodness knows . . . though I believe I'm utterly at sea now," said the Prince, turning uneasy glances around him.

"But how could you have dreamed it?" Marya Alexandrovna insisted in distress, "when I tell you your own dream in such detail, though you had not yet told any one of us about it!"

"But perhaps the Prince did tell somebody," said Natalya Dmitryevna.

"Oh, ye-es, perhaps I did tell somebody," the Prince repeated, utterly bewildered.

"Here's a farce," whispered Felisata Mihalovna to her neighbour.

"Good heavens, this is past all endurance!" cried Marya Alexandrovna, wringing her hands in a frenzy. "She sang to you, she sang a ballad! Did you dream that too?"

"Oh, ye-es; ye-es, indeed, I fancy she did sing a ballad," the Prince muttered meditatively.

And his face lightened up at some sudden recollection.

"My dear," he cried, addressing Mozglyakov, "I forget to tell you just now that there really was a ballad, and there were continually castles in that ballad, so that it seemed as if there were a great many castles; and then there was a troubadour! Oh, ye-es, I remember it all. . . . So that I even shed tears. . . . And now I am puzzled, it seems as if that really did happen and was not a dream."

"I must say, Uncle," answered Mozglyakov, speaking as calmly as he could, though his voice quivered from some emotion, "I must say it seems to me that it is very easy to account for that and make it fit in. I believe you really did listen to singing. Zinaida Afanasyevna sings beautifully. After dinner you were brought in here and Zinaida Afanasyevna sang the ballad to you. I was not there at the time, but you were probably touched by its recalling old days; perhaps remembering that very *vicomtesse* with whom you used once to sing ballads, and about whom you told us this morning. And then afterwards when you went to bed, in consequence of your pleasant impressions, you dreamed that you were in love and had made an offer."

Marya Alexandrovna was positively petrified by this audacity.

"Ah, my dear, that is just as it really was!" cried the Prince, delighted.

"It was just in consequence of those pleasant impressions. I certainly remember the ballad being sung to me, and it was because of that, that in my dream I wanted to get married. And it is true about the *vicomtesse* too. . . . Oh, how clever of you, my dear, to see it all! Well, now I am quite convinced that I dreamed all that! Marya Vassilyevna! I assure you that you are mistaken! It was a dream. Otherwise I should not be playing with your estimable feelings. . . ."

"Ah, now I see clearly who has been at work in this!" cried Marya Alexandrovna, beside herself with fury, addressing Mozglyakov. "It is you, you, sir; you dishonourable man, it is all your doing. You have muddled this unhappy imbecile, because you were refused! But you shall pay for this insult, you blackguard! You shall pay for it. You shall pay for it!"

"Marya Alexandrovna!" cried Mozglyakov, turning as red as a crab. "Your words are so . . . I really don't know what to say of your words. . . . No well-bred lady would allow herself . . . I am defending my kinsman, anyway. You must admit that to ensnare him like this . . ."

"Oh, ye-es, to ensnare like this . . ." the Prince chimed in, trying to hide behind Mozglyakov.

"Afanasy Matveyitch!" shrieked Marya Alexandrovna, in an unnatural voice. "Don't you hear how we are being outraged and dishonoured? Or have you lost all sense of your duties? Are you not the head of your family, but a repulsive wooden post? Why do you keep blinking? Any other husband would long ago have washed out such an insult to his family in blood! . . ."

"Wife," Afanasy Matveyitch began with dignity, proud that he was needed at last. "Wife! Didn't you perhaps dream it all, and afterwards when you woke up, you muddled it all to suit yourself! . . ."

But Afanasy Matveyitch was not destined to give full expression to his witty surmise. To that point the visitors had restrained themselves and had treacherously assumed an air of demure dignity. But at this point a loud burst of laughter that could not be restrained resounded through the room. Marya Alexandrovna, forgetting all propriety, rushed at her husband, probably with the intention of immediately scratching his eyes out. But she was restrained by force. Natalya Dmitryevna took advantage of the occasion to add just one drop more of venom.

"Oh, Marya Alexandrovna, perhaps that is just how it was, and you are upsetting yourself," she said, in a most honeyed voice.

"What was? How was it?" cried Marya Alexandrovna, not yet fully understanding it.

"Oh, Marya Alexandrovna, you know it sometimes does happen."

"What happens? Do you want to drive me crazy?"

"Perhaps you really did dream it?"

"Dream it, I? Dream it! And you dare to tell me that to my face?"

"Well, perhaps that is really how it was," responded Felisata Mihalovna.

"Oh, ye-es, perhaps that is how it really was," the Prince, too, muttered.

"He too, he too! Lord have mercy on us!" cried Marya Alexandrovna, clasping her hands.

"How you do upset yourself, Marya Alexandrovna! Remember that dreams are sent us from on high. If it is God's will, there is none can oppose Him, and we are all in His Hands. It's no use being angry about it."

"Oh, ye-es, it's no good being angry about it," the Prince chimed in.

"Do you take me for a lunatic!" Marya Alexandrovna articulated faintly, gasping from wrath. This was beyond human endurance. She hastily sought a chair and sank into a swoon. A hubbub followed.

"It was to do the correct thing that she fainted," Natalya Dmitryevna whispered to Anna Nikolaevna.

But at that instant, at the moment when the general bewilderment was greatest and the position was at its tensest, a person who had hitherto remained silent suddenly stepped forward—and immediately the whole character of the scene was changed. . . .

Chapter 14

ZINAIDA AFANASYEVNA was, speaking generally, of an extremely romantic disposition. I don't know whether this was, as Marya Alexandrovna maintained, due to too much reading of "that fool Shakespeare" with "her wretched little schoolmaster." But never in the course of her life at Mordasov had Zina permitted herself such an extraordinarily romantic or rather heroic action as the one which we are just about to describe.

Pale, with a look of determination in her eyes, but almost shaking with excitement, wonderfully lovely in her indignation, she stepped forward. Scanning the whole company with a slow, challenging look in the midst of the sudden silence, she turned to her mother, who at her first movement had promptly recovered from her swoon and opened her eyes.

"Mamma," said Zina, "why keep up deception? Why defile ourselves further by lying? It has all been made so foul that it is not worth taking degrading pains to cover up that foulness!"

"Zina, Zina! What is the matter with you? Think what you are doing!" cried Marya Alexandrovna, leaping up from her chair.

"I told you, I told you beforehand, Mamma, that I could not bear all this disgrace," Zina went on. "Is it necessary to degrade oneself even more, to defile oneself still further? But do you know, Mamma, that I take it all upon myself, for I am more to blame than any one. I, I by consenting, set this vile . . . intrigue . . . going! You are a mother; you love me, you meant to secure my happiness in your own way, according to your own ideas. You may be forgiven; but I, I, never."

"Zina, surely you don't mean to speak? . . . Oh, my God! I foresaw that that dagger would stab me to the heart!"

"Yes, Mamma, I shall speak out. I am disgraced, you . . . we are all disgraced! . . ."

"You are exaggerating, Zina! You are not yourself, and don't understand what you are saying! And what is the use of telling it? There is no sense in it. . . . The disgrace is not ours. I will show at once that the disgrace is not ours."

"No, Mamma," cried Zina, with an angry quiver in her voice, "I will not remain silent longer before these people, whose opinion I despise and who have come to jeer at us. I will not endure insult from them; not one of them has the right to throw dirt at me. They are all ready any minute to do thirty times worse than you or I! Dare they, can they be our judges? . . ."

"That's a nice thing! Do you hear what she says? What does it mean? It's insulting us!" was heard on all sides.

"The young lady simply does not know what she is saying," said Natalya Dmitryevna.

We may observe in parenthesis that Natalya Dmitryevna's remark was a true one. If Zina did not consider those ladies worthy to judge her, what was the object of rushing into such publicity, into such confessions before them? Zinaida Afanasyevna was, in fact, extremely hasty, such was the opinion of the best heads in Mordasov later on. Everything could have been set right, everything could have been smoothed over. It is true that Marya Alexandrovna, too, had damaged their position that evening by her hastiness and presumption. They need only have derided the imbecile old gentleman and have sent him about his business. But as though of design Zina, contrary to all good sense and Mordasov prudence, addressed herself to the Prince.

"Prince," she said to the old man, who was so impressed by her at that moment that he got up from his chair as a sign of respect. "Prince, forgive me, forgive us. We deceived you! We drew you on . . ."

"Oh, will you be silent, unhappy girl!" Marya Alexandrovna cried in a frenzy.

"Madame, madame! *Ma charmante enfant . . .*" muttered the Prince, much impressed.

But Zina's proud, impulsive and extremely idealistic character carried her at that instant far away from every propriety demanded by the reality of the position. She even forgot her mother, who was writhing in agony at her confession.

"Yes, we both deceived you, Prince; Mamma, by determining to make you marry me, and I, by consenting to it. You were given too much wine, I consented to sing and play a part before you. We, as Pavel Alexandrovitch has expressed it, have tricked you when you were weak and helpless, tricked you for the sake of your fortune, for the sake of your rank. All this was horribly base and I repent of it. But I swear to you, Prince, that it was from no base impulse that I brought myself to that base act. I meant . . . but what am I saying, it is twice as base to justify oneself for a thing like that! But I assure you, Prince, that if I had taken anything from you, I would have paid for it by being your plaything, your handmaid, your dancing girl, your slave. . . . I had vowed it, and would have kept my vow!"

A lump in her throat prevented her from going on. All the visitors seemed petrified and listened with their eyes starting out of their heads. Zina's strange and, to them, utterly unintelligible outbreak completely perplexed them; only the Prince was touched to tears, though he did not understand half of what Zina was saying.

"But I will marry you, *ma belle enfant,* if you wi-ish it so much," he muttered, "and it will be a gre-at honour to me! Only, I assure you that it real-ly was like a dream. . . . Why, I dream all sorts of things. Why are you so tro-oubled? I really don't understand it at all, *mon ami,*" he went on, addressing Mozglyakov. "You explain to me, please. . . ."

"And you, Pavel Alexandrovitch," said Zina, turning too to Mozglyakov, "you, on whom I once brought myself to look as my future husband, you who have now so cruelly revenged yourself on me, can you really have joined with these people to torture me and cover me with ignominy? And you told me you loved me! But it is not for me to preach to you, I am more to blame than you. . . . I have injured you, for I really did lure you on with promises, and my statements were lies and a tissue of falsehoods! I never loved you, and if I had brought myself to marry you it would simply have been to get away from here, from this accursed town, and to escape from all this corruption. . . . But, I swear to you, that if I had married you I would have made you a good and faithful wife. . . . You have cruelly revenged yourself on me, and if that flatters your pride . . ."

"Zinaida Afanasyevna!" cried Mozglyakov.

"If you still harbour a feeling of hatred for me . . ."

"Zinaida Afanasyevna! !"

"If you ever," said Zina, stifling her tears, "if you ever did love me! ! !"

"Zinaida Afanasyevna! ! !"

"Zina, Zina, my daughter," wailed Marya Alexandrovna.

"I am a scoundrel, Zinaida Afanasyevna, I am a scoundrel and nothing else," declared Mozglyakov, and general excitement followed. Cries of surprise and indignation were raised, but Mozglyakov stood as though rooted to the spot, incapable of thought or speech.

For weak and shallow characters accustomed to habitual subordination who have dared at last to be moved to wrath and to protest, in short, to be resolute and consistent, there is always a line—a limit—to their resolution and consistency, which is soon reached. Their protest is apt at first to be most vigorous. Their energy even approaches frenzy. They fling themselves against obstacles as though with closed eyes, and always take upon themselves burdens beyond their strength. But reaching a certain point, the frenzied man, as though frightened at himself, stops short, dumbfounded with the awful question, "What is this that I have done?" Then at once he grows limp, whimpers, asks for explanations, drops on his knees, begs forgiveness, implores that all shall be as before, only quickly, as quickly as possible. . . . This is almost exactly what happened now with Mozglyakov. After having been beside himself with fury, having invited trouble which now he ascribed entirely to himself alone, having satisfied his vanity and indignation and beginning to hate himself for it, he stopped short, conscience-stricken, before Zina's unexpected outbreak. Her last words crushed him completely. To rush from one extreme to another was the work of a minute.

"I am an ass, Zinaida Afanasyevna!" he cried, in a rush of frantic penitence. "No! What's an ass? An ass would be nothing. I am incomparably worse than an ass! But I will show you, Zinaida Afanasyevna, I will show you that even an ass may be an honourable man! . . . Uncle! I deceived you. It was I, I deceived you! You were not asleep; you really did make an offer, and I, I, like a scoundrel, out of revenge for having been refused, persuaded you that it had all been a dream."

"Wonderfully interesting things are coming out," whispered Natalya Dmitryevna in Anna Nikolaevna's ear.

"My dear," answered the Prince, "ple-ease calm yourself; you really frighten me with your shouting. I assure you that you are mis-ta-ken. . . . I am ready to be married by all means if it is necessary; but, you know, you assured me yourself that it was only a dream. . . ."

"Oh, how can I convince you! Tell me how to convince him! Uncle, Uncle! You know it's an important matter, most important, affecting family honour. Reflect! Consider!"

"My dear, certainly I will re-flect. Stay, let me recall it all in order. At first I dreamed of my coachman, Fe-o-fil . . ."

"Oh! it is not a question of Feofil now, Uncle."

"Oh, well, I suppose it is not a question of him now. Then there was Na-po-le-on, and then we seemed to be drinking tea and a lady came and ate up all the sugar."

"But, Uncle"—Mozglyakov bawled in the confusion of his mind—"why, it was Marya Alexandrovna herself told us that this morning about Natalya Dmitryevna! Why, I was here and heard it myself! I was hiding and looking at you through the keyhole. . . ."

"What, Marya Alexandrovna," Natalya Dmitryevna broke in; "so you told the Prince too that I stole the sugar out of your sugar-basin! So I come to steal your sugar, do I!"

"Get away with you!" cried Marya Alexandrovna, reduced to despair.

"No, I won't go away, Marya Alexandrovna. Don't dare to speak to me like that! . . . So I stole your sugar, did I? I have been hearing for a long time that you tell such nasty stories about me. Sofya Petrovna gave me an exact account of it. . . . So I steal your sugar, do I?"

"But, *mesdames*," cried the Prince, "it was only a dream, you know. Why, I dream all sorts of things. . . ."

"Cursed tub," Marya Alexandrovna muttered in an undertone.

"So I am a tub, am I!" shrieked Natalya Dmitryevna. "And who are you? I have known for ever so long that you called me a tub. I have got a husband, anyway, while you've got a fool. . . ."

"Oh, ye-es, I remember there was a tub too," muttered the Prince, unconsciously recalling his conversation with Marya Alexandrovna that morning.

"So you're insulting a lady too? How dare you, Prince, insult a lady? If I am a tub, you have no legs . . ."

"Who? I have no legs?"

"Yes, indeed, no legs and no teeth either, so that's what you are."

"Yes, and only one eye, too," shouted Marya Alexandrovna.

"You have stays instead of ribs," said Natalya Dmitryevna.

"Your face is worked by springs."

"You've no hair! . . ."

"And the idiot has a false moustache," cried Marya Alexandrovna.

"Do at least leave me my nose, Marya Stepanovna," cried the Prince, overwhelmed by such sudden candour. "My dear! Was it you gave me away? Did you tell them that my hair was false?"

"Uncle!"

"No, my dear, I really can't stay here any longer. Take me away . . . *quelle société!* What have you brought me to, my goodness?"

"Imbecile, scoundrel!" cried Marya Alexandrovna.

"Oh, dear!" said the poor Prince. "I've forgotten for the minute why I came here, but I shall re-mem-ber di-rect-ly. Take me away, dear boy, or they will te-ar me to pieces! Meanwhile . . . I must at once no-ote down a new idea. . . ."

"Let us go, Uncle, it is not too late; I will take you at once to an hotel and I will go with you. . . ."

"Oh, ye-es, to an ho-tel. *Adieu, ma charmante enfant.* . . . You alone . . . you alone . . . are good and vir-tu-ous. You are an hon-ou-rable girl. Come along, my dear boy. Oh, dear; oh, dear!"

But I will not describe the conclusion of the unpleasant scene which took place on the Prince's departure. The visitors dispersed with shrill scoldings and abuse. Marya Alexandrovna was left at last alone in the midst of the ruins of her former glory. Alas! Power, glory, consequence—all had vanished in that one evening. Marya Alexandrovna realized that she could never rise to her former height. Her despotic rule over local society which had lasted long years was annihilated for ever. What was left her now? To be philosophical? But she was not philosophical. She was in a paroxysm of rage all night. Zina was dishonoured, there would be endless gossip and scandal! Horrors!

As a faithful historian I ought to mention that from this frenzy the chief sufferer was Afanasy Matveyitch, who took refuge at last in the lumber-room, and stayed there freezing till morning; at last the morning came, but it brought nothing good. Misfortunes never come singly.

Chapter 15

IF DESTINY once begins to pursue some one with misfortune there is no end to its blows. That has been noticed long ago. Was the shame and disgrace of the previous day not enough for Marya Alexandrovna? No! Fate was preparing something more, something better.

Before ten o'clock in the morning a strange and almost incredible rumour was suddenly all over the town, welcomed by all with the most spiteful and venomous glee—as we generally do welcome any extraordinary scandal connected with any of our neighbours. "To be so lost to all shame and conscience!" people cried on all sides; "to demean herself to such a degree, to disregard all decorum, so utterly to cast off all restraint!" and so on, and so on.

This was what had happened, however. Early in the morning, a little before six o'clock, a poor and pitiful-looking old woman in tears and despair ran up to Marya Alexandrovna's house and besought the maidservant to wake the young lady immediately, only the young lady, and in secret, so that Marya Alexandrovna should in no way hear of it: Zina, pale and shattered, ran out to the old woman at once. The latter fell at her feet, kissed them, bathed them with her tears, and besought her to come with her to her sick Vasya, who had been so bad, so bad all night that he might perhaps not last through the day. The old woman, sobbing, told Zina that Vasya himself begged her to go for a last farewell before he died, implored her by all the holy angels, by all that had been in the past, and said that if she did not come he would die in despair. Zina at once resolved to go, though yielding to this entreaty would obviously confirm all the old malicious gossip about the intercepted letter, about her scandalous behaviour, and so on. Saying nothing to her mother, she threw on a cloak and at once hastened with the old woman right across the town to one of the poorest quarters of Mordasov, to the most out-of-the-way street, in which there was a little dilapidated house, with little slits for windows, fallen aslant, as it were sunken into the ground and almost buried under huge drifts of snow.

In this little house, in a little, low-pitched, musty room in which the huge stove filled up half the floor space, a young man was lying covered with an old greatcoat, on an unpainted wooden bed with a mattress as thin as a pancake. His face was pale and exhausted, his eyes glittered with a feverish glow, his hands were thin and dry as sticks, his breathing was laboured and husky. It could be seen that he had once been handsome; but disease had disfigured the delicate features of his handsome face, which was terrible and pitiful to look at, as the face of a consumptive, or rather of a dying man, always is. His old mother, who had been for a whole year, almost to the last hour, hoping for her Vasya's recovery, saw at last that he was not long for this world. She stood over him now crushed with grief, but tearless, clasping her hands and gazing at him as though she could never look at him enough; and though she knew it, she could not grasp that in a few days her Vasya, the apple of her eye, would be covered by the frozen earth out yonder under the snowdrifts in the wretched graveyard. But Vasya was not looking at her at that moment. His whole face, wasted and marked by suffering, was full of bliss. He saw before him, at last, her of whom he had been dreaming, asleep and awake, for the last year and a half in the long, dreary nights of his sickness. He saw that she had forgiven him, coming to him like the angel of the Lord as he lay at death's door. She was pressing his hands, was weeping over him, smiling at him, looking at him again with her wonderful eyes and—and all the past never to return, rose up in the dying man's soul. Life glowed again in his heart, and seemed at parting from him as though it would make the sufferer feel how hard it was to part.

"Zina," he said, "Zinotchka! Don't weep over me, don't mourn, don't grieve, don't remind me that I shall soon die. I shall look at you—yes, as I am looking at you now—I shall feel that our souls are together again, that you have forgiven me; I shall kiss your hands again as in old days, and die, perhaps, without noticing death! You have grown thin, Zinotchka! My angel, with what kindness you are looking at me now. And do you remember how you used to laugh in old days? Do you remember? ... Ah, Zina, I will not ask your forgiveness, I do not want to remember what happened, because, Zina, because though you have forgiven me I shall never forgive myself. There have been long nights, Zina, long, sleepless nights, awful nights, and in those nights on this bed I thought for long hours over many things, and made up my mind long ago that it is better for me to die; yes, by God, it is better! ... I am not fit for life, Zinotchka!"

Zina was weeping and mutely pressing his hands as though she would check his words.

"Why are you crying, my angel?" the sick man went on; "because I am dying—only for that? But you know all the past has been dead and buried long ago! You are cleverer than I, you are more pure-hearted, and so you have known a long time that I am a bad man. Can you still love me? And what it has cost me to endure the thought that you know I am a bad and shallow man. And how much pride there was in that, perhaps honourable pride ... I don't know. Oh, my dear, all my life has been a dream. I was always dreaming, for ever dreaming, but did not live. I was proud, I despised the herd; and in what was I superior to other people? I don't know. Purity of heart, generosity of feeling? But all that was dreaming, Zina, when we read Shakespeare together; but when it came to action I showed my purity and generosity of feeling."

"Hush!" said Zina, "hush! ... All that is not so, it is useless ... you are killing yourself."

"Why do you stop me, Zina? I know you have forgiven me, and perhaps you forgave me long ago; but you judged me—and understood the sort of man I am; that is what torments me. I am unworthy of your love, Zina! You were honest and great-souled in action too; you went to your mother and said that you would marry me and no one else, and you would have kept your word because with you words were not apart from action. While I, I! when it came to action ... Do you know, Zina, I did not understand then what you would be sacrificing in marrying me! I did not even understand that marrying me you might die of starvation. I never even thought of it; I only thought that you would marry me, a great poet (a future one, that is). I would not understand the reasons you brought forward begging me to put off our marriage; I tormented you, bullied you, reproached you, despised you, and it came at last to my threatening you with that letter. I was not even a scoundrel at that moment. I was simply a worm! Oh, how you must have despised me! Yes, it is well that I am dying! It is well that you did not marry me! I should have understood nothing of your sacrifice, I should have tormented you, I should have worried you over our poverty; the years would have passed, and who knows!—Perhaps I should have grown to hate you, as a hindrance in my life. Now it is better. Now at least my bitter tears have purified my heart. Ah, Zinotchka! love me a little as you used to love me once ... in this last hour at least. ... I know, of course, that I do not deserve your love, but ... but ... Oh, my angel!"

Several times in the course of this speech Zina, sobbing herself, tried to stop him. But he did not listen to her; he was tormented by a longing to express himself, and he went on speaking, though with difficulty, gasping in a hoarse and choking voice.

"If you hadn't met me, if you hadn't loved me, you would have lived!" said Zina. "Oh, why, why did we meet!"

"No, my darling, do not reproach yourself with my dying," the sick man went on. "I am the only person to blame for everything! How much vanity there was in it! Romantic foolishness! Have they told you my foolish history, Zina? You see, two years ago there was a convict here, a criminal and murderer; but when it came to punishment, he turned out to be the most cowardly creature. Knowing that they would not flog a sick man, he got hold of some spirit, put tobacco in it and drank it. He was attacked with such violent sickness, vomiting blood, and it lasted so long, that it affected his lungs. He was moved to the hospital, and within a few months he died of rapid consumption. Well, my angel, I thought of that convict that very day . . . you know, after that note . . . and made up my mind to destroy myself in the same way; but why do you think I chose consumption? Why didn't I strangle myself or drown myself? Was I afraid of immediate death? Perhaps it was that; but I keep fancying, Zinotchka, that even in this I could not lay aside romantic foolishness! Anyway, I had in my mind at the time the thought: how picturesque it would be, here I should lie in bed dying of consumption, while you would be distressed and unhappy at having sent me into consumption; you would come to me confessing yourself guilty, would fall on your knees before me. . . . I should forgive you, should die in your arms. It was silly, Zinotchka, silly, wasn't it?"

"Don't speak of it!" said Zina; "don't say that! You are not like that. Let us rather remember something else, that was good and happy in our past!"

"It is bitter to me, my darling, that is why I talk of it. I haven't seen you for a year and a half. I should like to open my heart to you now. You know ever since then I have been utterly alone, and I think there has not been one moment when I have not thought of you, my precious one. And do you know what, Zinotchka? How I longed to do something, to deserve that you should change your opinion of me! Until lately I did not believe that I should die. You know I was not laid up at first, for a long time I was walking about after my lungs were affected. And what absurd projects I had! I dreamed, for instance, of becoming all at once a great poet and publishing in the *Notes of the Fatherland* a poem unlike anything in the world. I thought of pouring into it all my feelings, all my soul, so that wherever you might be, I should be with you, always reminding you of me with my poem, and the very best of my dreams was that you would think at last and say,

'No! he is not such a bad man as I thought!' It was stupid, Zinotchka, wasn't it?"

"No, no, Vasya, no!" said Zina.

She fell on his breast and kissed his hands.

"And how jealous I was of you all this time! I believe I should have died if I had heard of your marriage. I sent, I kept watch on you, I spied. . . . She was constantly going" (and he nodded towards his mother). "You did not love Mozglyakov, did you, Zinotchka? Oh, my angel! Will you remember me when I am dead? I know you will remember; but years will pass, the heart will grow harder, you will grow cold, there will be winter in your soul, and you will forget me, Zinotchka! . . ."

"No, no, never! I shall not marry. . . . You are my first . . . and mine for ever. . . ."

"Everything dies, Zinotchka, even memories. . . . And our noble feelings die. Common-sense takes their place. What is the use of repining? Make use of life, Zina. Live long, live happily. Love some one else, if you can love; there is no loving the dead! Only think of me from time to time; do not remember what was bad, forgive the bad; but you know there was good, too, in our love, Zinotchka. Oh, golden days that never can return! . . . Listen, my angel, I always loved the evening hour of sunset. Think of me sometimes at that hour! Oh, no, no! Why die? Oh, how I long to come back to life again! Remember, my dear, remember, remember that time. It was spring then, the sun was shining so brightly, the flowers were in blossom, it was like a holiday all round us; and now look, look!"

And with a wasted hand the poor fellow pointed to the dingy, frozen window. Then he clutched Zina's hands, pressed them to his eyes and sobbed bitterly, bitterly. His sobs almost lacerated his racked breast.

And the whole day he was sobbing in anguish and misery. Zina did her best to comfort him, but she was half dead with misery. She told him that she would never forget him, and that she would never love another man as she loved him. He believed her, smiled, kissed her hands, but memories of the past only kindled fresh suffering in his soul. So passed the whole day. Meanwhile Marya Alexandrovna in alarm sent a dozen times to Zina entreating her to return home and not to ruin herself completely in public opinion. At last, when it was getting dark, almost beside herself with horror, she made up her mind to go to Zina herself. Calling her daughter out into the other room, she besought her almost on her knees "to turn aside this last worst dagger from her heart." Zina went out to her feeling ill, her head was burning. She listened and did not understand her mother. Marya Alexandrovna went away at last in despair, for Zina was determined to stay the night in the dying man's house. She did not leave his bedside all night. But the sick man grew worse and worse. The day came at last, but there was no hope that the sufferer would live through it. The old mother seemed frantic, she walked about as though she could not take it in, giving her son medicines which he would not take. His agony lasted a long time. He could not speak, and only incoherent, husky sounds broke from his throat. Up to the very last moment he gazed at Zina, still sought her with his eyes, and when the light in his eyes was beginning to grow dim, he still, with a straying, uncertain hand, felt for her hand to press it in his. Meanwhile the short winter day was passing. And when the last farewell gleam of sunshine gilded the solitary frozen window of the little room, the soul of the sufferer parted from his exhausted body and floated after that last ray. The old mother, seeing her adored boy lying dead before her, clasped her hands, uttered a shriek, and threw herself upon his breast.

"It is you, you snake in the grass, have been his ruin! You, accursed girl, with your ill deeds have parted us and been his undoing."

But Zina did not hear her. She stood over the dead man as though she had lost all comprehension. At last she bent down, made the sign of the cross over him, kissed him, and walked mechanically out of the room. Her eyes were burning, her head was going round. Her agonizing experiences, her two nights without sleep, almost deprived her of reason. She vaguely felt that all her past had been, as it were, torn out of her heart, and that a new life was beginning, gloomy and menacing. But before she had gone ten paces, Mozglyakov seemed to spring out of the earth before her; he seemed to be purposely lying in wait for her at that spot.

"Zinaida Afanasyevna," he began in a timorous whisper, looking nervously around him, for it was hardly dark yet, "Zinaida Afanasyevna, of course I am an ass. That is, if you like I am not an ass now, for you see, anyway, I have behaved honourably. But still I am sorry for having been an ass. . . . I am afraid I am muddled, Zinaida Afanasyevna, but that is due to all sorts of reasons . . ."

Zina gazed at him almost unconsciously, and went on her way in silence. As it was difficult for two to go abreast on the raised wooden pavement, and as Zina did not move aside. Pavel Alexandrovitch jumped off the pavement and ran by her side below, peeping up continually into her face.

"Zinaida Afanasyevna," he went on, "I have reflected, and if you are willing, I am prepared to renew my offer. I am ready to forget everything, Zinaida Afanasyevna, the whole disgrace, and to forgive it, but only on one condition: so long as we are here—let it all be kept secret. You will go away from here as soon as possible; I shall follow you secretly; we will be married in some remote place so that no one shall see it, and then at once we will go to Petersburg, travelling with posting horses, so you should only take a little portmanteau. Eh? Do you agree, Zinaida, Afanasyevna? Tell me quickly! I can't wait about, we might be seen together."

Zina made no answer, she only looked at Mozglyakov; but the look was such that he understood at once, took off his hat, bowed himself off, and vanished at the first turning into a side street.

"What is the meaning of it?" he thought. "That evening, the day before yesterday, she was all softness and sentiment, and took all the blame on herself? She changes from day to day, it seems!"

And meanwhile one event was following another in Mordasov. A tragic circumstance had occurred. After being driven to the hotel by Mozglyakov, the old Prince was taken ill the same night, and dangerously ill. The people of Mordasov heard the news next morning. Kalist Stanislavitch scarcely left his bedside. In the evening there was a consultation of all the Mordasov doctors. The invitations to request their attendance were written in Latin. But in spite of the Latin the Prince had already lost consciousness, was delirious, kept asking Kalist Stanislavitch to sing him a ballad, and talking about wigs; at times he seemed frightened and cried out. The doctors decided that the hospitality of Mordasov had set up inflammation of the stomach, which had somehow passed (probably on the journey) to the brain. They admitted the possibility also of some moral shock. They summed up in conclusion by saying that the Prince had been for a long time past predisposed to death, and so would certainly die. On the last point they were not mistaken, for three days later the poor old man died at the hotel.

This was a great shock to the people of Mordasov. No one had expected the affair to take such a serious turn. They flocked in crowds to the hotel where the dead body was lying; they discussed and debated, nodded their heads, and ended by severely censuring "the luckless Prince's murderers," understanding, of course, by that term, Marya Alexandrovna and her daughter. Every one felt that this affair from its extremely scandalous character might easily gain an unpleasant publicity, would perhaps reach faraway parts, and all sorts of possibilities were talked over and discussed. All this time Mozglyakov was in the greatest fuss and flurry, and at last his head was in a perfect whirl. He was in that state of mind when he saw Zina. His position was certainly difficult. He had brought the Prince into the town, he had moved him to the hotel, and now he did not know what to do with the dead man, where to bury him, whom to inform of his death! Should the body be taken to Duhanovo? Besides, he considered himself a nephew. He trembled with apprehension that he might be blamed for the venerable old man's death. "Very likely there will be talk of it in Petersburg in the best society!" he thought with a shudder.

He could not extract advice of any sort from his Mordasov acquaintances; they were all overcome by sudden consternation, they rushed away from the dead body and left Mozglyakov in gloomy isolation. But all at once the scene was completely transformed. Early the next morning a new visitor arrived in the town. Of this visitor all Mordasov instantly began talking, but they spoke of him mysteriously in a whisper, staring at him out of every chink and every window when he drove along the High Street on his way to the Governor's. Even Pyotr Mihalovitch seemed overawed, and did not know what tone to take with his visitor. The visitor was no other than the renowned Prince Shtchepetilov, a relative of the old Prince's, a man still youngish, about thirty-five, with shoulder-knots and the epaulettes of a colonel. The sight of those shoulder-knots struck awe into the hearts of all subordinate officials. The police-master, for instance, completely lost his head—in a moral sense, of course; physically he put in an appearance, though it was a very stiff and constrained appearance. It was at last learned that Prince Shtchepetilov had come from Petersburg, calling on the way at Duhanovo. Finding no one at Duhanovo, he flew off in pursuit of his uncle to Mordasov, where he had been thunderstruck by the news of the old man's death and the rumours concerning the circumstances attending it. Pyotr Mihalovitch was actually a little nervous as he gave the necessary explanations; and indeed every one in Mordasov had a guilty air. Moreover, the visitor had such a stern, such a dissatisfied face, though one would have thought it impossible to be dissatisfied with the fortune he was inheriting. He at once took everything into his own hands; Mozglyakov promptly and with shame effaced himself before the real, not self-styled, nephew and vanished—no one knew where. It was decided to move the dead body at once to the monastery, where a requiem service was arranged.

All the directions were given by the old Prince's kinsman briefly, drily, and sternly, but with tact and decorum. Next day all the town assembled at the monastery to hear the requiem service. An absurd rumour was current among the ladies that Marya Alexandrovna would appear at the church in person, and on her knees before the coffin would pray aloud for forgiveness, and that this all had to be in accordance with the law. All this, of course, proved to be nonsense, and Marya Alexandrovna did not come to the church. We forgot to say that immediately after Zina's return to the house, her mother decided that very evening to move to their country house, considering it impossible to remain longer in the town. There she listened anxiously from her seclusion to the rumours from the town, sent to find out about the new arrival, and was all the time in a state of fever. The road from the monastery to Duhanovo passed less than three-quarters of a mile from her windows, and so Marya Alexandrovna could command a convenient view of the long procession which stretched from the monastery to Duhanovo after the service. The coffin was upon a high hearse; and after it stretched a long string of carriages escorting it to the point where the road turns off to the town. And that gloomy hearse could be seen a long way further, a black patch against the white snow-covered plain, moving slowly with becoming dignity. But Marya Alexandrovna could not look at it long, she walked away from the window.

A week later she moved to Moscow with her daughter and Afanasy Matveyitch, and a month later the news reached Mordasov that Marya Alexandrovna's country house as well as her town house were for sale. And so this *comme-il-faut* lady was lost to Mordasov for ever! Even this could not pass without ill-natured jibes. It was asserted, for instance, that Afanasy Matveyitch was being sold with their country place. . . . One year passed and then a second, and Marya Alexandrovna was almost forgotten. Alas! that is how it always is in life! It was said, however, that she had bought another country place, and had moved to another provincial town, where, of course, she had already taken control of everything; that Zina was still unmarried, that Afanasy Matveyitch . . . However, it is hardly worth while to repeat these rumours, they were all very untrustworthy.

Three years have passed since I wrote the last line of the first part of my Mordasov chronicle, and who would have supposed that I should have occasion to open my manuscript again and to add another piece of news to my story? Well, here it is! I will begin with Pavel Alexandrovitch Mozglyakov. When he disappeared from Mordasov he went straight to Petersburg, where he successfully obtained the post in the service that had long been promised him. He soon forgot all the incidents at Mordasov, threw himself into the vortex of social life on

Vassilyevsky Island and had a gay time of it, flirted, kept up with the times, fell in love, made an offer, swallowed another refusal, and before he had digested it, was led by idleness and the frivolity of his character to get for himself a post on an expedition which was being sent to one of the remotest borders of our boundless fatherland, for inspection or for some other object, I don't know for certain what. The party successfully traversed all the forest and deserts, and at last, after long peregrinations, arrived in the chief town of that remote region to call on the Governor-General. He was a tall, lean, stern general, an old military man, who had been often wounded in battle, and had two stars and a white cross on his breast. He received the expedition with dignity and decorum, and invited all the officials to a ball which was to be given that very evening on the occasion of the name day of the governor's wife. Pavel Alexandrovitch was very much pleased. Attiring himself in his Petersburg suit in which he intended to produce an effect, he walked with a free and easy air into the big reception hall, but he was at once somewhat taken aback at the sight of the numbers of thick and plaited epaulettes and civilian uniforms with stars on their breasts. He had to pay his respects to the governor's wife, of whom he had heard that she was young and very good-looking. He went up to her, indeed, with aplomb, but was suddenly petrified with amazement. Before him stood Zina in a resplendent ball-dress and diamonds, looking proud and haughty. She completely failed to recognize Pavel Alexandrovitch. Her eyes glided over his face and at once turned to some one else. Astounded, Pavel Alexandrovitch moved to one side, and in the crowd came into collision with a timid young official who seemed to be frightened at finding himself at the governor's ball. Pavel Alexandrovitch immediately began to question him, and learned the most interesting facts. He learned that the governor had married two years ago, when he had visited Moscow, and that he had married a very wealthy young lady of a distinguished family; that the governor's wife "was awfully good-looking, even one might say a beauty of the first order, but that she behaved extremely proudly, and only danced with generals"; that at the present ball there were in all nine generals, their own and visitors, including the actual civil councillors; "that the governor's wife had a mamma who lived with her, and that this mamma belonged to the highest society, and was very clever," but that the mamma herself was completely dominated by the daughter, while the general himself simply doted on his spouse. Mozglyakov faltered a question about Afanasy Matveyitch, but they had no conception of his existence in "the remote region." Regaining his confidence a little, Mozglyakov walked about the rooms and soon saw Marya Alexandrovna, gorgeously attired, brandishing a costly fan and talking with animation to a personage of the fourth class. Round her clustered several ladies evidently anxious to propitiate her, and Marya Alexandrovna was apparently very gracious to all of them. Mozglyakov ventured to introduce himself. Marya Alexandrovna seemed a little startled, but almost instantly recovered herself. She graciously condescended to recognize Pavel Alexandrovitch, questioned him about Petersburg acquaintances, asked him why he was not abroad. To Mordasov she made no allusion whatever, as though such a place had no existence on earth. At last, after mentioning the name of a distinguished Petersburg prince and inquiring after his health, though Mozglyakov had no acquaintance whatever with the prince in question, she turned imperceptibly to a grand personage who was approaching, whose grey locks were fragrant with scent, and a minute later had completely forgotten Pavel Alexandrovitch, though he remained standing before her. With his hat in his hand and a sarcastic smile on his face, Mozglyakov returned to the great hall. Considering for some unknown reasons that he was insulted and even wounded, he resolved not to dance. A morose and absent expression and a biting Mephistophelean smile never left his face the whole evening. He leaned in a picturesque attitude against a column (as luck would have it, there were columns in the hall), and during the whole ball, that is for several hours together, he remained standing at the same place watching Zina. But alas! all his antics, all his striking attitudes, his disillusioned air and all the rest of it were thrown away. Zina completely failed to observe him. At last, enraged and with legs aching from long standing, hungry because as an unhappy lover he could not remain to supper, he returned to his lodgings quite worn out and feeling as though he had been beaten by some one. For a long while he did not go to bed, recalling the past which he had so long forgotten. Next morning new instructions arrived, and with relief Mozglyakov succeeded in being entrusted with the execution of them. He felt positively lighter-hearted as he drove out of the town. Snow was lying like a dazzling shroud over the boundless, deserted plain. In the distance on the very horizon stretched dark forests.

The mettlesome horses dashed along, flinging the powdery snow with their hoofs. The sledge bell tinkled, Pavel Alexandrovitch sank into thought, and then into dreams, and then into a sweet sleep. He woke at the third posting station, feeling fresh and well, with quite different thoughts in his mind.

The Eternal
Husband

THE ETERNAL HUSBAND

Chapter 1

VELCHANINOV

THE summer had come and, contrary to expectations, Velchaninov remained in Petersburg. The trip he had planned to the south of Russia had fallen through, and the end of his case was not in sight. This case—a lawsuit concerning an estate—had taken a very unfortunate turn. Three months earlier it had appeared to be quite straightforward, almost impossible to contest; but suddenly everything was changed. "And, in fact, everything has changed for the worse!" Velchaninov began frequently and resentfully repeating that phrase to himself. He was employing an adroit, expensive, and distinguished lawyer, and was not sparing money; but through impatience and lack of confidence he had been tempted to meddle in the case himself too. He read documents and wrote statements which the lawyer rejected point-blank, ran from one court to another, collected evidence, and probably hindered everything; the lawyer complained, at any rate, and tried to pack him off to a summer villa. But Velchaninov could not even make up his mind to go away. The dust, the stifling heat, the white nights of Petersburg, that always fret the nerves were what he was enjoying in town. His flat was near the Grand Theatre; he had only recently taken it, and it, too, was a failure. "Everything is a failure!" he thought. His nervousness increased every day; but he had for a long time past been subject to nervousness and hypochondria.

He was a man whose life had been full and varied, he was by no means young, thirty-eight or even thirty-nine, and his "old age," as he expressed it himself, had come upon him "quite unexpectedly"; but he realized himself that he had grown older less by the number than by the quality, so to say, of his years, and that if he had begun to be aware of waning powers, the change was rather from within than from without. In appearance he was still strong and hearty. He was a tall, sturdily-built fellow, with thick flaxen hair without a sign of greyness and a long fair beard almost half-way down his chest; at first sight he seemed somewhat slack and clumsy, but if you looked more attentively, you would detect at once that he was a man of excellent breeding, who had at some time received the education of an aristocrat. Velchaninov's manners were still free, assured and even gracious, in spite of his acquired grumpiness and slackness. And he was still, even now, full of the most unhesitating, the most snobbishly insolent self-confidence, the depth of which he did not himself suspect, although he was a man not merely intelligent, but even sometimes sensible, almost cultured and unmistakably gifted. His open and ruddy face had been in old days marked by a feminine softness of complexion which attracted the notice of women; and even now some people, looking at him, would say: "What a picture of health! What a complexion!" And yet this picture of health was cruelly subject to nervous depression. His eyes were large and blue, ten years earlier they had possessed great fascination; they were so bright, so gay, so careless that they could not but attract every one who came in contact with him. Now that he was verging on the forties, the brightness and good-humour were almost extinguished. Those eyes, which were already surrounded by tiny wrinkles, had begun to betray the cynicism of a worn-out man of doubtful morals, a duplicity, an ever-increasing irony and another shade of feeling, which was new: a shade of sadness and of pain— a sort of absent-minded sadness as though about nothing in particular and yet acute. This sadness was especially marked when he was alone. And, strange to say, this man who had been only a couple of years before fond of noisy gaiety, careless and good-humoured, who had been so capital a teller of funny stories, liked nothing now so well as being absolutely alone. He purposely gave up a great number of acquaintances whom he need not have given up even now, in spite of his financial difficulties. It is true that his vanity counted for something in this. With his vanity and mistrustfulness he could not have endured the society of his old acquaintances. But, by degrees, in solitude even his vanity began to change its character. It grew no less, quite the contrary, indeed; but it began to develop into a special sort of vanity which was new in him; it began at times to suffer from different causes—from unexpected causes which would have formerly been quite inconceivable, from causes of a "higher order" than ever before— "if one may use such an expression, if there really are higher or lower causes. . . ." This he added on his own account.

Yes, he had even come to that; he was worrying about some sort of *higher* ideas of which he would never have thought twice in earlier days. In his own mind and in his conscience he called "higher" all "ideas" at which (he found to his surprise) he could not laugh in his heart—there had never been such hitherto—in his secret heart only, of course; oh, in company it was a different matter! He knew very well, indeed, that—if only the occasion were to arise—he would the very next day, in spite of all the mysterious and reverent resolutions of his conscience, with perfect composure disavow all these "higher ideas" and be the first to turn them into ridicule, without, of course, admitting anything. And this was really the case, in spite of a certain and, indeed, considerable independence of thought, which he had of late gained at the expense of the "lower ideas" that had mastered him till then. And how often, when he got up in the morning, he began to be ashamed of the thoughts and feelings he had passed through during a sleepless night! And he had suffered continually of late from sleeplessness. He had noticed for some time past that he had become excessively sensitive about everything, trifles as well as matters of importance, and so he made up his mind to trust his feelings as little as possible. But he could not overlook some facts, the reality of which he was forced to admit. Of late his thoughts and sensations were sometimes at night completely transformed, and for the most part utterly unlike those which came to him in the early part of the day. This struck him—and he even consulted a distinguished doctor who was, however, an acquaintance; he spoke to him about it jocosely, of course. The answer he received was that the transformation of ideas and sensations, and even the possession of two distinct sets of thoughts and sensations, was a universal fact among persons "who think and feel," that the convictions of a whole lifetime were sometimes transformed under the melancholy influences of night and sleeplessness; without rhyme or reason most momentous decisions were taken; but all this, of course, was only true up to a certain point—and, in fact, if the subject were too conscious of the double nature of his feelings, so that it began to be a source of suffering to him, it was certainly a symptom of approaching illness; and then steps must be taken at once. The best thing of all was to make a radical change in the mode of life, to alter one's diet, or even to travel. Relaxing medicine was beneficial, of course.

Velchaninov did not care to hear more; but to his mind it was conclusively shown to be illness.

"And so all this is only illness, all these 'higher ideas' are mere illness and nothing more!" he sometimes exclaimed to himself resentfully. He was very loth to admit this.

Soon, however, what had happened exclusively in the hours of the night began to be repeated in the morning, only with more bitterness than at night, with anger instead of remorse, with irony instead of emotion. What really happened was that certain incidents in his past, even in his distant past, began suddenly, and God knows why, to come more and more frequently back to his mind, but they came back in quite a peculiar way. Velchaninov had, for instance, complained for a long time past of loss of memory: he would forget the faces of acquaintances, who were offended by his cutting them when they met; he sometimes completely forgot a book he had read months before; and yet in spite of this loss of memory, evident every day (and a source of great uneasiness to him), everything concerning the remote past, things that had been quite forgotten for ten or fifteen years, would sometimes come suddenly into his mind now with such amazing exactitude of details and impressions that he felt as though he were living through them again. Some of the facts he remembered had been so completely forgotten that it seemed to him a miracle that they could be recalled. But this was not all, and, indeed, what man of wide experience has not some memory of a peculiar sort? But the point was that all that was recalled came back now with a quite fresh, surprising and, till then, inconceivable point of view, and seemed as though some one were leading up to it on purpose. Why did some things he remembered strike him now as positive crimes? And it was not a question of the judgments of his mind only: he would have put little faith in his gloomy, solitary and sick mind; but it reached the point of curses and almost of tears, of inward tears. Why, two years before, he would not have believed it if he had been told that he would ever shed tears! At first, however, what he remembered was rather of a mortifying than of a sentimental character: he recalled certain failures and humiliations in society; he remembered, for instance, how he had been slandered by an intriguing fellow, and in consequence refused admittance to a certain house; how, for instance, and not so long ago, he had been publicly and unmistakably insulted, and had not challenged the offender to a duel; how in a circle of very pretty women he had been made the subject of an extremely witty epigram and had found no suitable answer. He even recollected one or two unpaid debts—trifling ones, it is true, but debts of honour—owing to people whom he had given up visiting and even spoke ill of. He was also worried (but only in his worst moments) by the thought of the two fortunes, both considerable ones, which he had squandered in the

stupidest way possible. But soon he began to remember things of a
"higher order."

Suddenly, for instance, apropos of nothing, he remembered the
forgotten, utterly forgotten, figure of a harmless, grey-headed and
absurd old clerk, whom he had once, long, long ago, and with absolute impunity, insulted in public simply to gratify his own conceit,
simply for the sake of an amusing and successful jest, which was repeated and increased his prestige. The incident had been so completely
forgotten that he could not even recall the old man's surname, though
all the surroundings of the incident rose before his mind with incredible clearness. He distinctly remembered that the old man was defending his daughter, who was unmarried, though no longer quite young,
and had become the subject of gossip in the town. The old man had
begun to answer angrily, but he suddenly burst out crying before the
whole company, which made some sensation. They had ended by
making him drunk with champagne as a joke and getting a hearty
laugh out of it. And now when, apropos of nothing, Velchaninov remembered how the poor old man had sobbed and hidden his face in
his hands like a child, it suddenly seemed to him as though he had
never forgotten it. And, strange to say, it had all seemed to him very
amusing at the time, especially some of the details, such as the way
he had covered his face with his hands; but now it was quite the
contrary.

Later, he recalled how, simply as a joke, he had slandered the very
pretty wife of a schoolmaster, and how the slander had reached the
husband's ears. Velchaninov had left the town soon after and never
knew what the final consequences of his slander had been, but now he
began to imagine how all might have ended—and there is no knowing
to what lengths his imagination might not have gone if this memory
had not suddenly been succeeded by a much more recent reminiscence
of a young girl of the working-class, to whom he had not even felt
attracted, and of whom, it must be admitted, he was actually ashamed.
Yet, though he could not have said what had induced him, he had got
her into trouble and had simply abandoned her and his child without
even saying good-bye (it was true, he had no time to spare), when
he left Petersburg. He had tried to find that girl for a whole year
afterwards, but he had not succeeded in tracing her. He had, it seemed,
hundreds of such reminiscences—and each one of them seemed to
bring dozens of others in its train. By degrees his vanity, too, began to
suffer.

We have said already that his vanity had degenerated into something peculiar. That was true. At moments (rare moments, however), he even forgot himself to such a degree that he ceased to be ashamed of not keeping his own carriage, that he trudged on foot from one court to another, that he began to be somewhat negligent in his dress. And if some one of his own acquaintance had scanned him with a sarcastic stare in the street or had simply refused to recognize him, he might really have had pride enough to pass him by without a frown. His indifference would have been genuine, not assumed for effect. Of course, this was only at times: these were only the moments of forgetfulness and nervous irritation, yet his vanity had by degrees grown less concerned with the subjects that had once affected it, and was becoming concentrated on one question, which haunted him continually.

"Why, one would think," he began reflecting satirically sometimes (and he almost always began by being satirical when he thought about himself), "why, one would think some one up aloft were anxious for the reformation of my morals, and were sending me these cursed reminiscences and 'tears of repentance'! So be it, but it's all useless! It is all shooting with blank cartridge! As though I did not know for certain, more certainly than certainty, that in spite of these fits of tearful remorse and self-reproach, I haven't a grain of independence for all my foolish middle age! Why, if the same temptation were to turn up to-morrow, if circumstances, for instance, were to make it to my interest to spread a rumour that the schoolmaster's wife had taken presents from me, I should certainly spread it, I shouldn't hesitate— and it would be even worse, more loathsome than the first time, just because it would be the second time and not the first time. Yes, if I were insulted again this minute by that little prince whose leg I shot off eleven years ago, though he was the only son of his mother, I should challenge him at once and condemn him to crutches again. So they are no better than blank cartridges, and there's no sense in them! And what's the good of remembering the past when I've not the slightest power of escaping from myself?"

And though the adventure with the schoolmaster's wife was not repeated, though he did not condemn any one else to crutches, the very idea that it inevitably would be the same, if the same circumstances arose, almost killed him . . . at times. One cannot, in reality, suffer from memories all the time; one can rest and enjoy oneself in the intervals.

So, indeed, Velchaninov did: he was ready to enjoy himself in the intervals; yet his sojourn in Petersburg grew more and more unpleasant as time went on. July was approaching. Intermittently he had flashes of determination to give up everything, the lawsuit and all, and to go away somewhere without looking back, to go suddenly, on the spur of the moment, to the Crimea, for instance. But, as a rule, an hour later he had scorned the idea and had laughed at it: "These hateful thoughts won't stop short at sending me to the south, if once they've begun and if I've any sense of decency, and so it's useless to run away from them, and, indeed, there's no reason to.

"And what's the object of running away?" he went on brooding in his despondency; "it's so dusty here, so stifling, everything in the house is so messy. In those law-courts where I hang about among those busy people, there is such a scurrying to and fro like mice, such a mass of sordid cares! All the people left in town, all the faces that flit by from morning till night so naïvely and openly betray their self-love, their guileless insolence, the cowardice of their little souls, the chicken-heartedness of their little natures—why, it's a paradise for a melancholy man, seriously speaking! Everything is open, everything is clear, no one thinks it necessary to hide anything as they do among our gentry in our summer villas or at watering-places abroad—and so it's more deserving of respect, if only for its openness and simplicity! . . . I won't go away! I'll stay here if I burst!"

Chapter 2

THE GENTLEMAN WITH CRAPE ON HIS HAT

IT WAS the third of July. The heat and stuffiness were insufferable. The day had been a very busy one for Velchaninov; he had had to spend the whole morning in walking and driving from place to place, and he had before him the prospect of an unavoidable visit that evening to a gentleman—a lawyer and a civil councillor—whom he hoped to catch unawares at his villa out of town. At six o'clock Velchaninov went at last into a restaurant (the fare was not beyond criticism, though the cooking was French) on the Nevsky Prospect, near the Police Bridge. He sat down at the little table in his usual corner and asked for the dinner of the day.

He used to eat the dinner that was provided for a rouble and paid extra for the wine, and he regarded this as a sacrifice to the unsettled state of his finances and an act of prudence on his part. Though he wondered how he could possibly eat such stuff, he nevertheless used to devour it to the last crumb—and every time with as much appetite as though he had not eaten for three days before. "There's something morbid about it," he would mutter to himself sometimes, noticing his appetite. But on this occasion he took his seat at his little table in a very bad humour, tossed his hat down angrily, put his elbows on the table, and sank into thought.

Though he could be so polite and, on occasion, so loftily imperturbable, he would probably now, if some one dining near him had been noisy, or the boy waiting on him had failed to understand at the first word, have been as blustering as a *junker* and would perhaps have made a scene.

The soup was put before him. He took up the ladle, but before he had time to help himself, he dropped it, and almost jumped up from the table. A surprising idea suddenly dawned upon him: at that instant—and God knows by what process—he suddenly realized the cause of his depression, of the special extra depression which had tormented him of late for several days together, had for some unknown reason fastened upon him and for some unknown cause refused to be shaken off; now he suddenly saw it all and it was as plain as a pikestaff.

"It's all that hat," he muttered as though inspired. "It's nothing but that cursed bowler hat with that beastly mourning crape that is the cause of it all!"

He began pondering—and the more he pondered the more morose he grew, and the more extraordinary "the whole adventure" seemed to him.

"But . . . it is not an adventure, though," he protested, distrustful of himself. "As though there were anything in the least like an adventure about it!"

All that had happened was this. Nearly a fortnight before (he did not really remember, but he fancied it was about a fortnight), he had first met somewhere in the street, near the corner of Podyatchesky Street and Myestchansky Street, a gentleman with crape on his hat. The gentleman was like any one else, there was nothing peculiar about him, he passed quickly, but he stared somewhat too fixedly at Velchaninov, and for some reason at once attracted his attention in a marked degree. His countenance struck Velchaninov as familiar. He had certainly at some time met it somewhere. "But I must have seen thousands of faces in my life, I can't remember them all!"

Before he had gone twenty paces further he seemed to have forgotten the encounter, in spite of the impression made at first. But the impression persisted the whole day—and it was somewhat singular, it took the form of a peculiar undefined annoyance. Now, a fortnight later, he remembered all that distinctly; he remembered, too, what he had failed to grasp at the time—that is, what his annoyance was due to; and he had so utterly failed to grasp it that he had not even connected his ill-humour all that evening with the meeting that morning.

But the gentleman had lost no time in recalling himself to Velchaninov's mind, and next day had come across the latter in the Nevsky Prospect again, and again stared at him rather strangely. Velchaninov dismissed him with a curse and immediately afterwards wondered why he cursed. It is true that there are faces that at once arouse an undefined and aimless aversion.

"Yes, I certainly have met him somewhere," he muttered thoughtfully, an hour after the meeting. And he remained in a very bad humour the whole evening afterwards; he even had a bad dream at night, and yet it never entered his head that the whole cause of this new fit of despondency was nothing but that gentleman in mourning, although he did not once think of him that evening! He had even been wrathful at the moment that such a "wretched object" could occupy his attention as long as it did and would certainly have thought it degrading to ascribe his agitation to him, if it had ever occurred to his mind to do so. Two days later they met again in a crowd coming off one of the Nevsky steamers. On this third occasion Velchaninov was ready to swear that the gentleman with the crape on his hat recognized him and made a dash for him, but was borne away in the crush; he fancied he had even had the "effrontery" to hold out his hand to him; perhaps he had even cried out and shouted his name. That, however, Velchaninov had not heard distinctly, but . . . "Who is the low fellow, though, and why does he not come up to me, if he really does know me, and if he is so anxious to?" he thought angrily, as he got into a cab and drove towards Smolny monastery. Half-an-hour later he was noisily arguing with his lawyer, but in the evening and the night he was suffering again from the most abominable and most fantastic attack of acute depression. "Am I in for a bilious attack?" he wondered uneasily, looking at himself in the looking-glass.

This was the third meeting. Afterwards, for five days in succession, he met "no one," and not a sign was seen of the low fellow. And yet the gentleman with the crape on his hat was continually in his mind. With some surprise Velchaninov caught himself wondering: "What's the matter with me—am I sick on his account, or what? H'm! . . .

and he must have a lot to do in Petersburg, too—and for whom is he wearing crape? He evidently recognized me, but I don't recognize him. And why do these people put on crape? It's out of keeping with him somehow. . . . I fancy if I look at him closer, I shall recognize him. . . ."

And something seemed faintly stirring in his memory, like some familiar but momentarily forgotten word, which one tries with all one's might to recall; one knows it very well and knows that one knows it; one knows exactly what it means, one is close upon it and yet it refuses to be remembered, in spite of one's efforts.

"It was . . . It was long ago . . . and it was somewhere . . . There was . . . there was . . . but, damn the fellow, whatever there was or wasn't. . . ." he cried angrily all at once; "it is not worth while to demean and degrade myself over that wretched fellow. . . ."

He grew horribly angry, but in the evening, when he suddenly remembered that he had been angry that morning, and "horribly" angry, it was extremely disagreeable to him; he felt as though some one had caught him in something shameful. He was bewildered and surprised.

"Then there must be reasons for my being so angry . . . apropos of nothing . . . at a mere reminiscence . . ." He left the thought unfinished.

And next day he felt angrier than ever, but this time he fancied he had grounds for it, and that he was quite right in feeling so; "It was unheard-of insolence," he thought. What had happened was the fourth meeting. The gentleman with crape on his hat had suddenly made his appearance again, as though he had sprung out of the earth. Velchaninov had just caught in the street the indispensable civil councillor before mentioned, of whom he was still in pursuit, meaning to pounce on him unawares at his summer villa, for the gentleman, whom Velchaninov scarcely knew, though it was so necessary to see him about his business, on that occasion as on this eluded him, and was evidently keeping out of sight and extremely reluctant to meet him. Delighted at coming across him at last, Velchaninov walked hurriedly beside him, glancing into his face and straining every effort to bring the wily old fellow to the discussion of a certain subject, in which the latter might be indiscreet enough to let slip the facts of which he had so long been on the track; but the crafty old man had his own views, and kept putting him off with laughter or silence—and it was just at this extremely absorbing moment that Velchaninov descried on the opposite pavement the gentleman with crape on his hat. He was standing staring at them both—he was watching them, that was evident, and seemed to be jeering at them.

"Damnation!" cried Velchaninov in a fury, as he left the civil councillor at his destination and ascribed his failure with him to the sudden appearance of that "impudent fellow." "Damnation! is he spying on me? He's evidently following me. Hired by some one, perhaps, and . . . and . . . and, by Jove! he was jeering at me! By Jove! I'll thrash him. . . . I'm sorry I've no stick with me! I'll buy a stick! I won't let it pass. Who is he? I insist on knowing who he is."

It was three days after this fourth meeting that Velchaninov was at his restaurant, as we have described him, agitated in earnest and even somewhat overwhelmed. He could not help being conscious of it himself, in spite of his pride. He was forced at last, putting all the circumstances together, to suspect that all his depression—all this *peculiar* despondency and the agitation that had persisted for the last fortnight—was caused by no other than this gentleman in mourning, "nonentity as he was."

"I may be a hypochondriac," thought Velchaninov, "and so I am ready to make a mountain out of a mole-hill, but does it make it any better for me that all this is *perhaps* only fancy! Why, if every rogue like that is going to be able to upset one in this way, why . . . it's . . . why? . . ."

Certainly in the meeting of that day (the fifth), which had so agitated Velchaninov, the mountain had proved to be little more than a mole-hill: the gentleman had as before darted by him, but this time without scrutinizing Velchaninov, and without, as before, betraying that he recognized him; on the contrary, he dropped his eyes and seemed to be very anxious to escape being noticed. Velchaninov turned round and shouted at the top of his voice—

"Hi! you with the crape on your hat! Hiding now! Stop! Who are you?"

The question (and his shouting altogether) was very irrational, but Velchaninov only realized that after he had uttered it. The gentleman turned round at the shout, stood still for a minute disconcerted, smiled, seemed on the point of doing or saying something, was obviously for a minute in a state of the utmost indecision, then he suddenly turned and rushed away without looking back. Velchaninov looked after him with astonishment.

"And what if it's a case of my forcing myself on him, not his forcing himself on me?" he thought. "And that's all it amounts to?"

When he had finished dinner he made haste to set off to the summer villa to see the civil councillor. He did not find him; he was informed that "his honour had not returned that day, and probably would not come back till three or four o'clock in the morning, as he was staying in town to a birthday party." This was so mortifying that, in his first fury, Velchaninov decided himself to go to the birthday party, and even set off to do so; but reflecting on the road that it was a long way to go, he dismissed the cab and trudged home on foot to his flat near the Grand Theatre. He felt that he wanted exercise. He must, at all costs, overcome his usual sleeplessness, and sleep sound that night, to soothe his excited nerves; and in order to sleep he must anyway be tired. And, as it was a long walk, it was half-past ten before he reached home, and he certainly was very tired.

Though he so criticized the flat that he had taken the previous March, and abused it so malignantly—excusing himself to himself on the plea that he was only "camping there temporarily," and stranded in Petersburg through that "damned lawsuit"—the flat was by no means so bad and so unsuitable as he made out. The approach was certainly rather dark and "grubby" under the gateway, but the flat itself, on the second storey, consisted of two big, lofty and bright rooms, separated from one another by a dark entry, and looking one into the street, the other into the courtyard. Adjoining the room the windows of which looked into the courtyard was a small study, which had been designed for a bedroom; but Velchaninov kept it littered with books and papers; he slept in one of the larger rooms, the one that looked into the street. He had a bed made up on the sofa. The furniture was quite decent, though second-hand, and he had besides a few articles of value—the relics of his former prosperity: bronze and china, and big, genuine Bokhara rugs; even two good pictures had been preserved; but everything had been unmistakably untidy and even dusty and nothing had been put in its place ever since his servant, Pelagea, had gone home to Novgorod for a holiday and left him alone. The oddity of having a solitary female servant for a bachelor and man of the world who was still anxious to keep up the style of a gentleman almost made Velchaninov blush, though he was very well satisfied with his Pelagea. The girl had come to him when he was taking the flat in the spring, from a family of his acquaintance who were going abroad, and she had put the flat to rights. But when she went away he could not bring himself to engage another woman; to engage a manservant was not worth while for a short time; besides, he did not like menservants. And so it was arranged that the sister of the porter's wife should come in every morning to clear up and that Velchaninov should leave the key at the porter's lodge when he went out. She did absolutely nothing, merely pocketed her wages; and he suspected her of pilfering. Yet he dismissed everything with a shrug and was positively glad that he was left quite alone in the flat. But there are limits to everything; and at some jaundiced moments the "filth" was absolutely insufferable to his nerves, and he almost always went into his rooms with a feeling of repugnance on returning home.

But this time he barely gave himself time to undress; flinging himself on the bed, he irritably resolved to think of nothing, but to go to sleep "this minute," whatever might happen; and, strange to say, he did fall asleep as soon as his head touched the pillow; such a thing had not happened to him for almost a month.

He slept for nearly three hours, but his sleep was uneasy, and he had strange dreams such as one has in fever. He dreamed of some crime which he had committed and concealed and of which he was accused by people who kept coming up to him. An immense crowd collected, but more people still came, so that the door was not shut but remained open. But his whole interest was centered on a strange person, once an intimate friend of his, who was dead, but now somehow suddenly came to see him. What made it most worrying was that Velchaninov did not know the man, had forgotten his name and could not recall it. All he knew was that he had once liked him very much. All the other people who had come up seemed expecting from this man a final word that would decide Velchaninov's guilt or innocence, and all were waiting impatiently. But he sat at the table without moving, was mute and would not speak. The noise did not cease for a moment, the general irritation grew more intense, and suddenly in a fury Velchaninov struck the man for refusing to speak, and felt a strange enjoyment in doing it. His heart thrilled with horror and misery at what he had done, but there was enjoyment in that thrill. Utterly exasperated, he struck him a second time and a third, and, drunk with rage and terror, which reached the pitch of madness, but in which there was an intense enjoyment, he lost count of his blows, and went on beating him without stopping. He wanted to demolish *it* all, all. Suddenly something happened: they all shrieked horribly and turned round to the door, as though expecting something, and at that instant there came the sound of a ring at the bell, repeated three times, with violence enough to pull the bell off. Velchaninov woke up and was wide-awake in an instant. He leapt headlong out of bed and rushed to the door; he was absolutely convinced that the ring at the bell was not a dream and that some one really had rung at his bell that moment. "It would be too unnatural for such a distinct, such a real, palpable ring to be only a dream!"

But to his surprise the ring at the bell turned out to be a dream, too. He opened the door, went out on the landing, even peeped down the stairs—there was absolutely no one there. The bell hung motionless. Surprised, but relieved, he went back into his room. When he had lighted a candle he remembered that he had left the door closed but not locked or bolted. He had sometimes in the past forgotten when he came home to lock the door for the night, not thinking it of much importance.

Pelagea had often given him a talking-to about it. He went back into the passage, shut the door, opened it once more and looked out on the landing, but only fastened the door on the inside with the hook, without taking the trouble to turn the key. The clock struck half-past two; so he must have slept three hours.

His dream had so disturbed him that he did not want to go to bed again at once, and made up his mind to walk up and down his room for half an hour or—"Time enough to smoke a cigar"—he thought. Hastily dressing, he went to the window and lifted the thick stuff curtain and the white blind behind it. It was already daylight in the street. The light summer nights of Petersburg always worked on his nerves and of late had intensified his insomnia, so that it was expressly on this account that he had, a fortnight previously, put up thick stuff curtains which completely excluded the light when they were fully drawn. Letting in the daylight and forgetting the lighted candle on the table, he fell to pacing up and down the room, still oppressed by a sort of sick and heavy feeling. The impression of the dream was still upon him. A real feeling of distress that he should have been capable of raising his hand against that man and beating him still persisted.

"That man doesn't exist, and never has existed; it's all a dream. Why am I worrying about it?"

He began thinking with exasperation, as though all his troubles were concentrated on this, that he was certainly beginning to be ill—"a sick man."

It was always painful to him to think that he was getting old and growing feebler, and in his bad moments he exaggerated his age and failing powers on purpose to irritate himself.

"Old age," he muttered; "I'm getting quite old, I'm losing my memory, I see apparitions, I dream dreams, bells ring. . . . Damn it all, I know from experience that such dreams are always a sign of fever with me. . . . I am convinced that all this business with the crape gentleman is a dream too. I was certainly right yesterday: it's I, I, who am pestering him, not he me. I've woven a romance about him, and I am hiding under the table in my fright at it. And why do I call him a low fellow? He may be a very decent person. His face is not attractive, certainly, though there is nothing particularly ugly about it; he's dressed like any one else. Only in his eyes there's something. . . . Here I'm at it again! I'm thinking about him again! ! What the devil does the look in his eyes matter to me? Can't I get on without that? . . ."

Among the thoughts that kept starting up in his mind, one rankled painfully: he felt suddenly convinced that this gentleman with the crape on his hat had once been an acquaintance on friendly terms with him, and now sneered at him when he met him because he knew some great secret about him in the past and saw him now in such a humiliating position. He went mechanically to the window, meaning to open it and get a breath of the night air, and—and he suddenly shuddered all over: it seemed to him that something incredible and unheard-of was suddenly happening before his eyes.

He had not yet opened the window but he made haste to slip behind the corner of the window and hide himself: on the deserted pavement opposite he had suddenly seen directly facing the house the man with the crape on his hat. The gentleman was standing on the pavement looking towards his windows, but evidently not noticing him, stared inquisitively at the house as though considering something. He seemed to be deliberating and unable to decide: he lifted his hand and seemed to put his finger to his forehead. At last he made up his mind: he took a cursory glance round, and began stealthily on tiptoe crossing the street. Yes: he had gone in at the gateway by the little gate (which sometimes in summer was left unbolted till three o'clock).

"He's coming to me," flashed on Velchaninov's mind, and, also on tiptoe, he ran headlong to the door and stood before it silent and numb with suspense, softly laying his trembling right hand on the hook of the door he had just fastened, listening intently for the sound of footsteps on the stairs.

His heart beat so violently that he was afraid he might not hear the stranger come up on tiptoe. He did not understand what it meant, but he felt it all with tenfold intensity. His dream seemed to have melted into reality. Velchaninov was by temperament bold. He sometimes liked to display fearlessness in the face of danger even if he were only admiring himself with no one else to look at him. But now there was something else as well. The man who had so lately been given up to hypochondria and nervous depression was completely transformed; he was not the same man. A nervous, noiseless laugh broke from him. From behind the closed door he divined every movement of the stranger.

"Ah! now he's coming in, he has come in, he's looking about him; he's listening downstairs; he's holding his breath, stealing up . . . ah! He has taken hold of the handle, he's pulling it, trying it! He reckoned on its not being locked! So he knows I sometimes forget to lock it! He's pulling at the handle again; why, does he imagine that the hook will come out? It's a pity to part! Isn't it a pity to let him go like this?"

And indeed everything must have happened just as he pictured it; some one really was standing on the other side of the door, and was softly and noiselessly trying the lock, and was pulling at the handle and—"Of course, he had his object in doing so." But by now Velchaninov had resolved to settle the question, and with a sort of glee got ready for the moment. He had an irresistible longing to unfasten the hook, suddenly to fling open the door, and to confront the "bugbear" face to face. "What may you be doing here, pray, honoured sir?"

And so he did: seizing the moment, he suddenly lifted the hook, pushed the door and—almost fell over the gentleman with crape on his hat.

Chapter 3

PAVEL PAVLOVITCH TRUSOTSKY

THE latter stood speechless, rooted to the spot. They stood facing one another in the doorway, and stared fixedly into each other's faces. Some moments passed and suddenly—Velchaninov recognized his visitor!

At the same time the visitor evidently realized that Velchaninov recognized him fully. There was a gleam in his eye that betrayed it. In one instant his whole face melted into a sugary smile.

"I have the pleasure, I believe, of addressing Alexey Ivanovitch?" he almost chanted in a voice of deep feeling, ludicrously incongruous with the circumstances.

"Surely you are not Pavel Pavlovitch Trusotsky?" Velchaninov brought out with an air of perplexity.

"We were acquainted nine years ago at T——, and if you will allow me to remind you—we were intimately acquainted."

"Yes . . . to be sure, but now it's three o'clock, and for the last ten minutes you've been trying whether my door was locked or not."

"Three o'clock!" cried the visitor, taking out his watch and seeming positively grieved and surprised; "why, so it is. Three! I beg your pardon, Alexey Ivanovitch, I ought to have considered before coming up: I'm quite ashamed. I'll come again and explain, in a day or two, but now . . ."

"No! If there's to be an explanation will you kindly give it me this minute!" Velchaninov caught him up. "Please walk inside, into this room—no doubt you intended to come into the room yourself, and have not turned up in the middle of the night simply to try the lock."

He was excited and at the same time disconcerted, and felt that he could not grasp the position. He was even somewhat ashamed—there proved to be neither mystery nor danger. The whole phantasmagoria had proved to be nothing; all that had turned up was the foolish figure of some Pavel Pavlovitch. And yet he did not believe that it was all so simple; he had a vague presentiment and dread of something. Making his visitor sit down in an arm-chair, he seated himself impatiently on his bed, not a yard away, bent forward with his hands on his knees and waited irritably for him to speak. He scanned him greedily and remembered him. But, strange to say, the man was silent, quite silent, and seemed not to realize that he was "in duty bound" to speak at once; on the contrary, he, too, gazed at Velchaninov with a look of expectation. It was possible that he was simply timid, feeling at first a certain awkwardness like a mouse in a trap; but Velchaninov flew into a rage.

"What do you mean by it!" he cried; "you are not a phantom or a dream, I suppose! You've not come to play at being dead, surely? Explain yourself, my good man!"

The visitor fidgeted, smiled, and began warily—

"So far as I see, what strikes you most of all is my coming at such an hour and under such peculiar circumstances. . . . So that, remembering all the past, and how we parted—it's really strange to me now. . . . Though, indeed, I had no intention of calling, and it has only happened by accident. . . ."

"How by accident? Why, I saw you through the window run across the street on tiptoe!"

"Ah, you saw me! So perhaps you know more about it all than I do! But I'm only irritating you. . . . You see, I arrived here three weeks ago on business of my own. . . . I am Pavel Pavlovitch Trusotsky, you know; you recognized me yourself. I am here to try to get transferred to another province, and to a post in another department considerably superior. . . . But all that's neither here nor there, though . . . The point is, if you must know, that I have been hanging about here for the last three weeks, and I seem to be spinning out my business on purpose—that is, the business of my transfer—and really, if it comes off I do believe I shan't notice that it has come off and shall stay on in your Petersburg, feeling as I do now. I hang about as though I had lost sight of my object and, as it were, pleased to have lost sight of it— feeling as I do! . . ."

"Feeling how?" Velchaninov asked, frowning.

The visitor raised his eyes to him, lifted his hat and pointed to the crape on it.

"Why, look; that's how I'm feeling."

Velchaninov gazed blankly first at the crape and then at the countenance of his visitor. Suddenly the colour rushed into his cheeks and he grew terribly agitated.

"Surely not Natalya Vassilyevna?"

"Yes! Natalya Vassilyevna! Last March . . . consumption, and almost suddenly, after two or three months' illness! And I am left—as you see!"

As he said this the visitor, in deep emotion, put out his hands on each side, the hat with the crape on it flapping in his left one, while he made a low bow that displayed his bald head for ten seconds at least.

His air and his gesture seemed to revive Velchaninov; an ironical and even provocative smile hovered on his lips—but only for a moment: the news of the death of this lady (whom he had known so long ago and had long ago succeeded in forgetting) gave him a shock which was a complete surprise to him.

"Is it possible?"—he muttered the first words that came to his tongue— "and why didn't you come straight and tell me?"

"I thank you for your sympathy. I see it and appreciate it, in spite of . . ."

"In spite of?"

"In spite of so many years of separation, you have just shown such sympathy for my sorrow and even for me that I am, of course, sensible of gratitude. That was all I wanted to express. It's not that I had doubts of my friends: I can find here the truest friends at once— Stepan Mihalovitch Bagautov, for instance. But you know, Alexey Ivanovitch, our acquaintance with you—friendship rather, as I gratefully recall it—was over nine years ago, you never came back to us; there was no interchange of letters. . . ."

The visitor chanted his phrases as though to music, but all the while that he was holding forth he looked at the floor, though, no doubt, all the time he saw everything. But Velchaninov had by now regained his composure.

With a very strange impression, which grew stronger and stronger, he listened to Pavel Pavlovitch and watched him, and when the latter suddenly paused, the most incongruous and surprising ideas rushed in a sudden flash into his mind.

"But how was it I didn't recognize you till now?" he cried, growing more animated. "Why, we've stumbled across each other five times in the street!"

"Yes; I remember that, too; you were constantly crossing my path—twice, or perhaps three times. . . ."

"That is, *you* were constantly coming upon me, not I upon you."

Velchaninov stood up and suddenly, quite unexpectedly, he began laughing. Pavel Pavlovitch paused, looked at him attentively, but at once continued—

"And as for your not recognizing me, you might well have forgotten me, and, besides, I've had smallpox and it has left some traces on my face."

"Smallpox? To be sure, he has had smallpox! However did you——"

"Manage that? Anything may happen. One never can tell, Alexey Ivanovitch; one does have such misfortunes."

"Only it's awfully funny all the same. But continue, continue, my dear friend!"

"Though I met you, too . . ."

"Stay! Why did you say 'manage that' just now? I meant to use a much more polite expression. But go on, go on!"

For some reason he felt more and more good-humoured. The feeling of shock was completely effaced by other emotions. He walked up and down the room with rapid steps.

"Even though I met you, and though when I set out for Petersburg I intended to seek you out, yet now, I repeat, I have been feeling so broken in spirit . . . and mentally shattered ever since March . . ."

"Oh, yes! shattered since March. . . . Stop a minute. Don't you smoke?"

"As you know, in old days when Natalya Vassilyevna was living I . . ."

"To be sure, to be sure; and since March?"

"Just a cigarette, perhaps."

"Here is a cigarette. Light it—and go on! Go on, it's awfully——"

And, lighting a cigar, Velchaninov quickly settled himself on the bed again.

Pavel Pavlovitch paused.

"But how excited you are yourself. Are you quite in good health?"

"Oh, damn my health!" Velchaninov was suddenly exasperated. "Continue!"

The visitor, for his part, looking at his companion's agitation, seemed better pleased and grew more self-confident.

"But what is there to continue?" he began again. "Imagine, Alexey Ivanovitch, in the first place, a man destroyed—that is, not simply destroyed, but fundamentally, so to say; a man whose existence is transformed after twenty years of married life, wandering about the streets with no consistent object, as though in a wilderness, almost in a state of oblivion, and finding a certain fascination in that oblivion. It is natural that sometimes when I meet an acquaintance, even a real friend, I purposely go out of my way to avoid approaching him, at such a moment of oblivion, I mean. And at another moment one remembers everything so, and so longs to see any one who has witnessed that recent past, gone now never to return, and has taken part in it, and one's heart beats so violently that one is ready to risk throwing oneself upon a friend by night as well as by day, even though one might have to wake him up at four o'clock in the morning on purpose. . . . I have made a mistake about the time only, not about our friendship; for this moment more than makes up for it. And as for the time, I really thought it was only twelve, feeling as I do. One drinks the cup of one's sorrow till one is drunk with it. And it's not sorrow, indeed, but the novelty of my state that crushes me. . . ."

"How strangely you express yourself!" Velchaninov observed gloomily, becoming extremely grave again.

"Yes, I do express myself strangely. . . ."

"And you're . . . not joking?"

"Joking!" exclaimed Pavel Pavlovitch in pained surprise, "and at the moment when I am announcing the sad . . ."

"Ach, don't speak of that, I entreat you!"

Velchaninov got up and began pacing the room again.

So passed five minutes. The visitor seemed about to get up too, but Velchaninov shouted: "Sit still, sit still!" and Pavel Pavlovitch obediently sank back into his arm-chair at once.

"But, how you have changed though," Velchaninov began again, suddenly stopping before him as though all at once struck by the thought. "You're dreadfully changed! Extraordinarily! Quite a different person."

"That's not strange: nine years."

"No, no, no, it's not a question of years! It's incredible how you've changed in appearance; you've become a different man!"

"That, too, may well be, in nine years."

"Or is it since March!"

"He—he!" Pavel Pavlovitch sniggered slily. "That's a funny idea of yours. . . . But if I may venture—what is the change exactly?"

"You ask what! The Pavel Pavlovitch I used to know was such a solid, decorous person, that Pavel Pavlovitch was such a clever chap, and now—this Pavel Pavlovitch is a regular *vaurien!*"

He was at that stage of irritability in which even reserved people say more than they ought.

"*Vaurien!* You think so? And not a clever chap now—not clever?" Pavel Pavlovitch chuckled with relish.

"Clever chap be damned! Now I daresay you really are too clever."

"I'm insolent, but this low fellow's more so and . . . and what is his object?" Velchaninov was thinking all the while.

"Ach, dearest, most precious friend!" cried the visitor suddenly, growing extremely agitated and turning round in his chair. "What are we saying? We are not in the world now, we're not in the society of the great and the worldly! We're two old friends, very old friends! And we've come together in the fullest sincerity to recall to one another the priceless bond of friendship of which the dear departed was the precious link!"

And he was so carried away by the ecstasy of his feeling that he bowed his head as before, hiding his face in his hat. Velchaninov watched him with aversion and uneasiness.

"What if he's simply a buffoon," flashed through his mind; "but n-no, n-no! I don't think he's drunk—he may be drunk, though: his face is red. Even if he were drunk—it comes to the same thing. What's he driving at? What does the low fellow want?"

"Do you remember, do you remember," cried Pavel Pavlovitch, removing the hat a little and seeming more and more carried away by his reminiscences, "do you remember our expeditions into the country, our evenings and little parties with dancing and innocent games at the house of His Excellency, our most hospitable Semyon Semyonovitch? And how we used to read together, the three of us, in the evening! And our first acquaintance with you, when you called on me that morning to make inquiries about your business, and even began to speak rather warmly, and suddenly Natalya Vassilyevna came in, and within ten minutes you had become a real friend of the family and so you were for a whole year, exactly as in Turgenev's play *A Provincial Lady*."

Velchaninov paced slowly up and down, looked at the floor, listened with impatience and repulsion, but—listened intently.

"The thought of *A Provincial Lady* never entered my head," he interrupted, somewhat confused, "and you never used to talk in such a shrill voice and such . . . unnatural language. What is that for?"

"I certainly used to be more silent—that is, I was more reserved," Pavel Pavlovitch interposed hurriedly. "You know I used to prefer listening while the dear departed talked. You remember how she used to talk, how wittily. . . . And in regard to *A Provincial Lady* and Stupendyev particularly, you are quite right, for I remember it was we ourselves, the precious departed and I, used to speak of that at quiet moments after you'd gone away—comparing our first meeting with that drama, for there really was a resemblance. About Stupendyev especially."

"What Stupendyev? Damn him!" cried Velchaninov, and he actually stamped, utterly disconcerted at the mention of "Stupendyev," owing to a disturbing recollection that was evoked by the name.

"Stupendyev is a character, a character in a play, the husband in *A Provincial Lady*," Pavel Pavlovitch piped in a voice of honeyed sweetness; "but it belonged to a different series of our precious and happy memories, when after your departure Stepan Mihalovitch Bagautov bestowed his friendship on us, exactly as you did, for five whole years."

"Bagautov? What do you mean? What Bagautov?" Velchaninov stood still as though petrified.

"Bagautov, Stepan Mihalovitch, who bestowed his friendship on us, a year after you and . . . and exactly as you did."

"Good heavens, yes! I know that!" cried Velchaninov, recovering himself at last. "Bagautov! Why, of course, he had a berth in your town. . . ."

"He had, he had! At the Governor's! From Petersburg. A very elegant young man, belonging to the best society!" Pavel Pavlovitch exclaimed in a positive ecstasy.

"Yes, yes, yes! What was I thinking of? Why, he, too . . ."

"He too, he too," Pavel Pavlovitch repeated in the same ecstasy, catching up the word his companion had incautiously dropped. "He too! Well, we acted *A Provincial Lady* at His Excellency's, our most hospitable Semyon Semyonovitch's private theatre—Stepan Mihalovitch was the 'count,' I was the 'husband,' and the dear departed was 'The Provincial Lady'—only they took away the 'husband's' part from me, Natalya Vassilyevna insisted on it, so that I did not act the 'husband' because I was not fitted for the part. . . ."

"How the devil could you be Stupendyev? You're pre-eminently Pavel Pavlovitch Trusotsky and not Stupendyev," said Velchaninov, speaking with coarse rudeness and almost trembling with irritation. "Only, excuse me; Bagautov's in Petersburg, I saw him myself in the spring! Why don't you go and see him too?"

"I have been every blessed day, for the last fortnight. I'm not admitted! He's ill, he can't see me! And, only fancy, I've found out from first-hand sources that he really is very dangerously ill! The friend of six years. Ach, Alexey Ivanovitch, I tell you and I repeat it, that sometimes one's feelings are such that one longs to sink into the earth; yes, really; at another moment one feels as though one could embrace any one of those who have been, so to say, witnesses and participators of the past and simply that one may weep, absolutely for nothing else but that one may weep. . . ."

"Well, anyway, I've had enough of you for to-day, haven't I?" Velchaninov brought out abruptly.

"More than enough, more!" Pavel Pavlovitch got up from his seat at once. "It's four o'clock, and, what's worse, I have so selfishly upset you. . . ."

"Listen, I will be sure to come and see you myself, and then, I hope . . . Tell me straight out, tell me frankly, you are not drunk to-day?"

"Drunk! Not a bit of it. . . ."

"Hadn't you been drinking just before you came, or earlier?"

"Do you know, Alexey Ivanovitch, you're in a regular fever."

"I'll come and see you to-morrow morning before one o'clock."

"And I've been noticing for a long time that you seem, as it were, delirious," Pavel Pavlovitch interrupted with zest, still harping on the same subject. "I feel conscience-stricken, really, that by my awkwardness . . . but I'm going, I'm going! And you lie down and get some sleep!"

"Why, you haven't told me where you're living," Velchaninov called hastily after him.

"Didn't I tell you? At the Pokrovsky Hotel."

"What Pokrovsky Hotel?"

"Why, close to the Pokrovsky Church, close by, in the side street.

I've forgotten the name of the street and I've forgotten the number, only it's close by the Pokrovsky Church."

"I shall find it!"

"You'll be very welcome."

He was by now on his way downstairs.

"Stay," Velchaninov shouted after him again; "you are not going to give me the slip?"

"How do you mean, give you the slip?" cried Pavel Pavlovitch, staring at him open-eyed and turning round to smile on the third step.

Instead of answering, Velchaninov shut the door with a loud slam, carefully locked it and fastened the hook. Returning to the room, he spat as though he had been in contact with something unclean.

After standing for some five minutes in the middle of the room, he flung himself on the bed without undressing and in one minute fell asleep. The forgotten candle burnt itself out on the table.

Chapter 4

THE WIFE, THE HUSBAND AND THE LOVER

He SLEPT very soundly and woke up at half-past nine; he remembered everything instantly, sat down on his bed and began at once thinking of "that woman's death." The shock of the sudden news of that death the night before had left a certain agitation and even pain. That pain and agitation had only for a time been smothered by a strange idea while Pavel Pavlovitch was with him.

But now, on waking up, all that had happened nine years before rose before his mind with extraordinary vividness.

This woman, this Natalya Vassilyevna, the wife of "that Trusotsky," he had once loved, and he had been her lover for the whole year that he had spent at T——, ostensibly on business of his own (that, too, was a lawsuit over a disputed inheritance), although his presence had not really been necessary for so long. The real cause of his remaining was this intrigue. The *liaison* and his love had such complete possession of him that it was as though he were in bondage to Natalya Vassilyevna, and he would probably have been ready on the spot to do anything, however monstrous and senseless, to satisfy that woman's slightest caprice.

He had never felt anything of the sort before. At the end of the year, when separation was inevitable, although it was expected to be only a brief one, Velchaninov was in such despair, as the fatal time drew near, that he proposed to Natalya Vassilyevna that she should elope with him, that he should carry her off from her husband, that they should throw up everything and that she should come abroad with him for ever. Nothing but the jibes and firm determination of the lady (who had, probably from boredom, or to amuse herself, quite approved of the project at first) could have dissuaded him and forced him to go alone. And actually, before two months had passed, he was asking himself in Petersburg the question which had always remained unanswered. Had he really loved that woman or had it been nothing but an "infatuation"? And it was not levity or the influence of some new passion that had given rise to this question: for those first two months in Petersburg he had been plunged in a sort of stupefaction and had scarcely noticed any woman, although he had at once mixed with his former acquaintances again and had seen a hundred women. At the same time he knew that if he were transported that moment to T—— he would promptly fall under the yoke of that woman's fascination again, in spite of any questions. Even five years later his conviction was unchanged. But five years later he used to admit this to himself with indignation and he even thought of "that woman" herself with hatred. He was ashamed of that year at T——; he could not even understand how such a "stupid" passion could have been possible for him, Velchaninov. All his memories of that passion had become absurd to him; and he blushed to the point of tears and was tormented by conscience-pricks at the thought of it. It is true that a few years later he had become somewhat calmer; he tried to forget it all—and almost succeeded. And now, all at once, nine years afterwards, all this had so suddenly and strangely risen up before him again, after hearing that night of the death of Natalya Vassilyevna.

Now, sitting on his bed, with confused thoughts crowding in disorder on his mind, he felt and realized clearly one thing only—that in spite of the "shock" he had felt at the news, he was nevertheless quite undisturbed by the fact of her death. "Can it be that I have no feeling for her?" he asked himself. It is true that he had now no feeling of hatred for her, and that he could criticize her more impartially, more fairly. In the course of those nine years of separation he had long since formulated the view that Natalya Vassilyevna belonged to the class of absolutely ordinary provincial ladies moving in good provincial society "and, who knows? perhaps she really was such, perhaps it was only I who idealized her so fantastically." He had always suspected, however, that there might be an error in that view; and he felt it even now. And, indeed, the facts were opposed to it; this Bagautov, too, had for several years been connected with her and apparently he, too, had been "under the yoke of her fascination." Bagautov certainly was a young man belonging to the best Petersburg society and, as he was a most "empty-headed fellow," he could only have had a successful career in Petersburg (Velchaninov used to say of him). Yet he had neglected Petersburg—that is, sacrificed his most important interests—and remained for five years in T—— solely on account of that woman! Yes, and he had finally returned to Petersburg, perhaps only because he, too, had been cast off like "an old, worn-out shoe." So there must have been in that woman something exceptional— a power of attracting, of enslaving, of dominating.

And yet one would have thought that she had not the gifts with which to attract and to enslave. She was not exactly pretty; perhaps she was actually plain. She was twenty-eight when Velchaninov first knew her. Though not altogether beautiful, her face was sometimes charmingly animated, but her eyes were not pretty: there was something like an excess of determination in them. She was very thin. On the intellectual side she had not been well educated; her keen intelligence was unmistakable, though she was one-sided in her ideas. Her manners were those of a provincial lady and at the same time, it is true, she had a great deal of tact; she had artistic taste, but showed it principally in knowing how to dress. In character she was resolute and domineering; she could never make up her mind to compromise in anything: it was all or nothing. In difficult positions her firmness and stoicism were amazing. She was capable of generosity and at the same time would be utterly unjust. To argue with that lady was impossible: "twice two makes four" meant nothing to her. She never thought herself wrong or to blame in anything. Her continual deception of her husband and the perfidies beyond number which she practised upon him did not weigh on her in the least. But, to quote Velchaninov's own comparison, she was like the "Madonna of the Flagellants," who believes implicitly herself that she is the mother of God—so Natalya Vassilyevna believed implicitly in everything she did.

She was faithful to her lover, but only as long as he did not bore her. She was fond of tormenting her lover, but she liked making up for it too. She was of a passionate, cruel and sensual type. She hated depravity and condemned it with exaggerated severity and—was herself depraved. No sort of fact could have made her recognize her own depravity. "Most likely she *genuinely* does not know it," Velchaninov thought about her even before he left T——. (We may remark, by the way, that he was the accomplice of her depravity.) "She is one of those women who are born to be unfaithful wives. Such women never become old maids; it's a law of their nature to be married to that end. The husband is the first lover, but never till after the wedding. No one gets married more adroitly and easily than this type of woman. For her first infidelity the husband is always to blame. And it is all accompanied by the most perfect sincerity: to the end they feel themselves absolutely right and, of course, entirely innocent."

Velchaninov was convinced that there really was such a type of woman; but, on the other hand, he was also convinced that there was a type of husband corresponding to that woman, whose sole vocation was to correspond with that feminine type. To his mind, the essence of such a husband lay in his being, so to say, "the eternal husband," or rather in being, all his life, a husband and nothing more. "Such a man is born and grows up only to be a husband, and, having married, is promptly transformed into a supplement of his wife, even when he happens to have unmistakable character of his own. The chief sign of such a husband is a certain decoration. He can no more escape wearing horns than the sun can help shining; he is not only unaware of the fact, but is bound by the very laws of his nature to be unaware of it." Velchaninov firmly believed in the existence of these two types and in Pavel Pavlovitch Trusotsky's being a perfect representative of one of them. The Pavel Pavlovitch of the previous night was, of course, very different from the Pavel Pavlovitch he had known at T——. He found him incredibly changed, but Velchaninov knew that he was bound to have changed and that all that was perfectly natural; Trusotsky could only as long as his wife was alive have remained all that he used to be, but, as it was, he was only a fraction of a whole, suddenly cut off and set free; that is, something wonderful and unique.

As for the Pavel Pavlovitch of the past at T——, this is how Velchaninov remembered him and recalled him now.

"Of course, at T——, Pavel Pavlovitch had been simply a husband," and nothing more. If he were, for instance, an official in the service as well, it was solely because such a position was one of the obligations of his married life; he was in the service for the sake of his wife and her social position in T——, though he was in himself zealous in his duties. He was thirty-five then and was possessed of some little fortune. He showed no special ability in his department and showed no special lack of it either. He used to mix with all the best people in the province and was said to be on an excellent footing with them. Natalya

Vassilyevna was deeply respected in T——; she did not, however, greatly appreciate that, accepting it as simply her due, but in her own house she was superb at entertaining guests, and Pavel Pavlovitch had been so well trained by her that he was able to behave with dignity even when entertaining the highest magnates of the province. Perhaps (it seemed to Velchaninov) he had intelligence too, but as Natalya Vassilyevna did not like her spouse to talk too much, his intelligence was not very noticeable. Perhaps he had many natural good qualities, as well as bad ones. But his good qualities were kept under a shade, as it were, and his evil propensities were almost completely stifled.

Velchaninov remembered, for instance, that Pavel Pavlovitch sometimes betrayed a disposition to laugh at his neighbours, but this was sternly forbidden him. He was fond, too, at times of telling anecdotes; but a watch was kept on that weakness too, and he was only allowed to tell such as were brief and of little importance. He had a weakness for a festive glass outside the house and was even capable of drinking too much with a friend; but this failing had been severely nipped in the bud. And it is noteworthy that no outside observer would have said that Pavel Pavlovitch was a hen-pecked husband; Natalya Vassilyevna seemed an absolutely obedient wife, and most likely believed herself to be one. It was possible that Pavel Pavlovitch loved Natalya Vassilyevna passionately; but no one noticed it, and, indeed, it was impossible to notice it, and this reserve was probably due to her domestic discipline. Several times during his life at T—— Velchaninov had asked himself whether the husband had any suspicion at all of his wife's intrigue. Several times he questioned Natalya Vassilyevna seriously about it, and always received the answer, uttered with a certain annoyance, that her husband knew nothing and never could know anything about it and that "it was no concern of his." Another characteristic of hers was that she never laughed at Pavel Pavlovitch and did not consider him absurd or very plain and would, indeed, have taken his part very warmly if any one had dared to show him incivility. Having no children, she was naturally bound to become a society woman, but her home life, too, was essential to her. Social pleasures never had complete sway of her, and at home she was very fond of needlework and looking after the house. Pavel Pavlovitch had recalled, that night, the evenings they had spent in reading; it happened that sometimes Velchaninov read aloud and sometimes Pavel Pavlovitch: to Velchaninov's surprise he read aloud excellently. Meanwhile, Natalya Vassilyevna did sewing as she listened, always calmly and serenely. They read a novel of Dickens, something from a Russian magazine, sometimes even something "serious." Natalya Vassilyevna highly appreciated Velchaninov's culture, but appreciated it in silence, as something final and established, of which there was no need to talk. Altogether, her attitude to everything intellectual and literary was rather one of indifference, as to something irrelevant though perhaps useful. Pavel Pavlovitch sometimes showed considerable warmth on the subject.

The *liaison* at T—— was broken suddenly when on Velchaninov's side it had reached its zenith—that is, almost the point of madness. In reality he was abruptly dismissed, though it was all so arranged that he went away without grasping that he had been cast off "like a worthless old shoe."

Six weeks before his departure, a young artillery officer who had just finished at the training college arrived in T—— and took to visiting the Trusotskys. Instead of three, they were now a party of four. Natalya Vassilyevna welcomed the boy graciously but treated him as a boy. No suspicion crossed Velchaninov's mind and indeed he had no thought to spare for it, for he had just been told that separation was inevitable. One of the hundreds of reasons urged by Natalya Vassilyevna for his leaving her as soon as possible was that she believed herself to be with child: and therefore, naturally, he must disappear at once for three or four months at least, so that it would not be so easy for her husband to feel any doubt if there were any kind of gossip afterwards. It was rather a far-fetched argument. After a stormy proposition on the part of Velchaninov that she should fly with him to Paris or America, he departed alone to Petersburg, "only for a brief moment, of course," that is, for no more than three months, or nothing would have induced him to go, in spite of any reason or argument. Exactly two months later he received in Petersburg a letter from Natalya Vassilyevna asking him never to return, as she already loved another; she informed him that she had been mistaken about her condition. This information was superfluous. It was all clear to him now: he remembered the young officer. With that it was all over for good. He chanced to hear afterwards, some years later, that Bagautov had appeared on the scene and spent five whole years there. He explained the disproportionate duration of that affair partly by the fact that Natalya Vassilyevna, by now, was a good deal older, and so more constant in her attachments.

He remained sitting on his bed for nearly an hour: at last he roused himself, rang for Mavra to bring his coffee, drank it hastily, and at eleven o'clock set out to look for the Pokrovsky Hotel. In going there he had a special idea which had only come to him in the morning. He felt somewhat ashamed of his behaviour to Pavel Pavlovitch the night before and now he wanted to efface the impression.

The whole fantastic business with the door handle, the night before, he now put down to chance, to the tipsy condition of Pavel Pavlovitch and perhaps to something else, but he did not really know, exactly, why he was going now to form new relations with the former husband, when everything had so naturally and of its own accord ended between them. Something attracted him. He had received a peculiar impression and he was attracted in consequence of it.

Chapter 5

LIZA

PAVEL PAVLOVITCH had no idea of "giving him the slip," and goodness knows why Velchaninov had asked him the question the night before; he was, indeed, at a loss to explain it himself. At his first inquiry at a little shop near the Pokrovsky Church, he was directed to the hotel in the side street a couple of paces away. At the hotel, it was explained that M. Trusotsky was staying in the lodge close by in the courtyard, in furnished rooms at Marya Sysoevna's. Going up the narrow, wet and very dirty stone stairs to the second storey, where these rooms were, he suddenly heard the sound of crying. It seemed like the crying of a child of seven or eight; the sound was distressing; he heard smothered sobs which would break out and with them the stamping of feet and shouts of fury, which were smothered, too, in a hoarse falsetto voice, evidently that of a grown-up man. This man seemed to be trying to suppress the child and to be very anxious that her crying should not be heard, but was making more noise than she was. The shouts sounded pitiless, and the child seemed to be begging forgiveness. In a small passage at the top, with doors on both sides of it, Velchaninov met a tall, stout, slovenly-looking peasant woman of forty and asked for Pavel Pavlovitch. She pointed towards the door from which the sounds were coming. There was a look of some indignation on the fat, purple face of this woman.

"You see how he amuses himself!" she said gruffly and went downstairs.

Velchaninov was just about to knock at the door, but on second thoughts he walked straight in. In a small room, roughly though amply furnished with common painted furniture, stood Pavel Pavlovitch without his coat and waistcoat. With a flushed and exasperated face he was trying, by means of shouts, gesticulations and even (Velchaninov fancied) kicks, to silence a little girl of eight, shabbily dressed in a short, black, woollen frock. She seemed to be actually in hysterics, she gasped hysterically and held out her hands to Pavel Pavlovitch as though she wanted to clutch at him, to hug him, to beseech and implore him about something. In one instant the whole scene was transformed: seeing the visitor, the child cried out and dashed away into a tiny room adjoining, and Pavel Pavlovitch, for a moment disconcerted, instantly melted into smiles, exactly as he had done the night before when Velchaninov flung open the door upon him on the stairs.

"Alexey Ivanovitch!" he cried, in genuine surprise. "I could never have expected . . . but come in, come in! Here, on the sofa, or here in the arm-chair, while I . . ."

And he rushed to put on his coat, forgetting to put on his waistcoat.

"Stay as you are, don't stand on ceremony."

Velchaninov sat down in the chair.

"No, allow me to stand on ceremony; here, now I am more respectable. But why are you sitting in the corner? Sit here in the arm-chair, by the table. . . . Well, I didn't expect you, I didn't expect you!"

He, too, sat down on the edge of a rush-bottomed chair, not beside his "unexpected" visitor, but setting his chair at an angle so as to sit more nearly facing him.

"Why didn't you expect me? Why, I told you last night that I would come at this time."

"I thought you wouldn't come; and when I reflected on all that happened yesterday, on waking this morning, I despaired of ever seeing you again."

Meanwhile Velchaninov was looking about him. The room was in disorder, the bed was not made, clothes were lying about, on the table were glasses with dregs of coffee in them, crumbs and a bottle of champagne, half full, with the cork out and a glass beside it. He stole a glance towards the next room, but there all was quiet; the child was in hiding and perfectly still.

"Surely you are not drinking that now?" said Velchaninov, indicating the champagne.

"The remains . . ." said Pavel Pavlovitch in confusion.

"Well, you have changed!"

"It's a bad habit, come upon me all at once; yes, really, since that date. I'm not lying! I can't restrain myself. Don't be uneasy, Alexey Ivanovitch. I'm not drunk now, and I'm not going to play the fool now as I did at your flat yesterday; but I'm telling the truth, it's all since then. And if any one had told me six months ago that I should break down like this, if I'd been shown myself in the looking-glass— I shouldn't have believed it."

"You were drunk last night, then?"

"I was," Pavel Pavlovitch admitted in a low voice, looking down in embarrassment. "And you see I wasn't exactly drunk then, but I had been a little before. I want to explain, because I'm always worse a little while after. If I get ever so little tipsy, it is followed by a sort of violence and foolishness, and I feel my grief more intensely too. It's because of my grief, perhaps, I drink. Then I'm capable of playing all sorts of pranks and I push myself forward quite stupidly and insult people for nothing. I must have presented myself very strangely to you yesterday?"

"Do you mean to say you don't remember?"

"Not remember! I remember it all. . . ."

"You see, Pavel Pavlovitch, that's just what I thought," Velchaninov said in a conciliatory voice. "What's more, I was myself rather irritable with you last night and . . . too impatient, I readily admit it. I don't feel quite well at times, and then your unexpected arrival last night . . ."

"Yes, at night, at night!" Pavel Pavlovitch shook his head, as though surprised and disapproving. "And what possessed me! Nothing would have induced me to come in to you if you had not opened the door yourself; I should have gone away from the door. I came to you a week ago, Alexey Ivanovitch, and you were not at home, but perhaps I should never have come again. I have some pride, too, Alexey Ivanovitch, although I do recognize the position I am in. We met in the street, too, and I kept thinking: 'Why, he must recognize me and yet he turns away; nine years are no joke,' and I couldn't make up my mind to come. And last night I had wandered from the Petersburg Side and I forgot the time. It all came from that" (he pointed to the bottle), "and from my feelings. It was stupid! Very! And if it had been any one but you—for you've come to see me even after what happened yesterday, for the sake of old times—I should have given up all hope of renewing our acquaintance!"

Velchaninov listened attentively. The man seemed to him to be speaking sincerely and even with a certain dignity; and yet he did not believe one word he had heard since he came into the room.

"Tell me, Pavel Pavlovitch, you are not alone here, then? Whose little girl is that I found with you just now?"

Pavel Pavlovitch was positively amazed and raised his eyebrows, but he looked frankly and pleasantly at Velchaninov.

"Whose little girl? Why, it's Liza!" he said, with an affable smile.

"What Liza?" muttered Velchaninov, with a sort of inward tremor. The shock was too sudden. When he came in and saw Liza, just before, he was surprised, but had absolutely no presentiment of the truth, and thought nothing particular about her.

"Yes, our Liza, our daughter Liza!" Pavel Pavlovitch smiled.

"Your daughter? Do you mean that you and Natalya . . . Natalya Vassilyevna had children?" Velchaninov asked timidly and mistrustfully, in a very low voice.

"Why, of course! But there, upon my word, how should you have heard of it? What am I thinking about! It was after you went away, God blessed us with her!"

Pavel Pavlovitch positively jumped up from his chair in some agitation, though it seemed agreeable too.

"I heard nothing about it," said Velchaninov, and he turned pale.

"To be sure, to be sure; from whom could you have heard it?" said Pavel Pavlovitch, in a voice weak with emotion. "My poor wife and I had lost all hope, as no doubt you remember, and suddenly God sent us this blessing, and what it meant to me—He only knows! Just a year after you went away, I believe. No, not a year, not nearly a year. Wait a bit; why, you left us, if my memory does not deceive me, in October or November, I believe."

"I left T—— at the beginning of September, the twelfth of September; I remember it very well."

"In September, was it? H'm! . . . what was I thinking about?" cried Pavel Pavlovitch, much surprised. "Well, if that's so, let me see: you went away on the twelfth of September, and Liza was born on the eighth of May, so—September—October—November—December—January—February—March—April—a little over eight months! And if you only knew how my poor wife . . ."

"Show me . . . call her . . ." Velchaninov faltered in a breaking voice.

"Certainly!" said Pavel Pavlovitch fussily, at once breaking off what he was saying, as though it were of no consequence. "Directly, directly, I'll introduce her!"

And he went hurriedly into the other room to Liza.

Fully three or perhaps four minutes passed; there was a hurried, rapid whispering in the room, and he just caught the sound of Liza's voice. "She's begging not to be brought in," thought Velchaninov. At last they came out.

"You see, she's all confusion," said Pavel Pavlovitch; "she's so shy, and so proud . . . the image of my poor wife!"

Liza came in, looking down and no longer tearful; her father was holding her hand. She was a tall, slim, very pretty little girl. She raised her big blue eyes to glance with curiosity at the visitor, looked at him sullenly, and dropped them again at once. Her eyes were full of that gravity one sees in children when they are left alone with a stranger and, retreating into a corner, look out solemnly and mistrustfully at the unfamiliar visitor; but she had, perhaps, some other thought, by no means childish, in her mind—so Velchaninov fancied.

Her father led her straight up to him.

"This is an uncle Mother used to know long ago; he was our friend. Don't be shy, hold out your hand."

The child bent forward a little, and timidly held out her hand.

"Natalya Vassilyevna would not have her trained to curtsey, but taught her to make a little bow, and hold out her hand in the English fashion," he added by way of explanation to Velchaninov, watching him intently.

Velchaninov knew that he was being watched, but had quite ceased to trouble himself to conceal his emotion; he sat perfectly still in his chair, held Liza's hand in his and gazed at the child. But Liza was in great anxiety about something, and, forgetting her hand in the visitor's hand, she kept her eyes fixed on her father. She listened apprehensively to all that he said. Velchaninov recognized those big blue eyes at once, but what struck him most of all was the wonderful soft whiteness of her face and the colour of her hair; these characteristics were so marked and so significant. Her features and the lines of the lips reminded him vividly of Natalya Vassilyevna. Meanwhile, Pavel Pavlovitch had for some time been telling him something, speaking, it seemed, with very great warmth and feeling, but Velchaninov did not hear him. He only caught the last sentence—

". . . so that you can't imagine our joy at this gift from the Lord, Alexey Ivanovitch! She became everything to me as soon as she came to us, so that I used to think that even if my tranquil happiness should, by God's will, be at an end, Liza would always be left me; that I reckoned upon for certain!"

"And Natalya Vassilyevna?" Velchaninov queried.

"Natalya Vassilyevna?" said Pavel Pavlovitch affectedly. "You know her way, you remember that she never cared to say a great deal, but the way she said good-bye to her on her death-bed . . . everything came out then! I said just now 'on her death-bed,' but yet only a day before her death she was upset and angry, said that they were trying to cure her with drugs, that there was nothing wrong with her but an ordinary fever, and that neither of our doctors understood it, and that as soon as Koch came back (do you remember our old friend the army doctor?) she would be up again in a fortnight! But there! five hours before her decease she remembered that in three weeks' time we must visit her aunt, Liza's godmother, on her name day . . ."

Velchaninov suddenly got up from his chair, still holding the child's hand. Among other things it struck him that there was something reproachful in the intense look the child kept fixed upon her father.

"She's not ill?" he asked hurriedly and somewhat strangely.

"I don't think so, but . . . our circumstances are here so . . ." said Pavel Pavlovitch, with mournful solicitude. "She's a strange child and nervous at all times; after her mother's death she was ill for a fortnight, hysterical. Why, what a weeping and wailing we had just before you came in . . . do you hear, Liza, do you hear? And what was it all about? All because I go out and leave her; she says it shows I don't love her any more as I used to when mother was alive—that's her complaint against me. And a child like that who ought to be playing with her toys, instead of fretting over a fantastic notion like that. Though here she has no one to play with."

"Why, how . . . you're surely not alone here?"

"Quite alone; the servant only comes in once a day."

"And you go out and leave her like this alone?"

"What else could I do? And when I went out yesterday I locked her in, into that little room there, that's what the tears have been about to-day. But what else could I do? Judge for yourself: the day before yesterday she went down when I was out, and a boy threw a stone at her in the yard and hit her on the head. Or else she begins crying and runs round to all the lodgers in the yard, asking where I've gone. And that's not nice, you know. And I'm a nice one, too; I go out for an hour and come back next morning; that's what happened yesterday. It was a nice thing, too, that while I was away the landlady let her out, sent for a locksmith to break the lock—such a disgrace—I literally feel myself a monster. All mental aberration, all mental aberration. . . ."

"Father!" the child said timidly and uneasily.

"There you are, at it again! You're at the same thing again. What did I tell you just now?"

"I won't, I won't!" Liza repeated in terror, hurriedly clasping her hands before him.

"You can't go on like this in these surroundings," Velchaninov said impatiently, in a voice of authority. "Why, you . . . why, you're a man of property; how is it you're living like this—in this lodge and in such surroundings?"

"In the lodge? But, you see, we may be going away in a week's time, and we've wasted a great deal of money already, even though I have property. . . ."

"Come, that's enough, that's enough." Velchaninov cut him short with increasing impatience, as it were expressing plainly "There's no need to talk. I know all that you have to say, and I know with what feelings you are speaking."

"Listen, I'll make a suggestion. You said just now that you'll be staying a week, maybe possibly even a fortnight. I know a household here, that is, a family where I'm quite at home—have known them twenty years. The father, Alexandr Pavlovitch Pogoryeltsev, is a Privy Councillor; he might be of use to you in your business. They are at their summer villa now. They've got a splendid villa. Klavdia Petrovna is like a sister to me or a mother. They have eight children. Let me take Liza to them at once . . . that we may lose no time. They will be delighted to take her in for the whole time you are here, and will treat her like their own child, their own child!"

He was terribly impatient and did not disguise it.

"That's scarcely possible," said Pavel Pavlovitch, with a grimace, looking, so Velchaninov fancied, slily in his face.

"Why, why impossible?"

"Why, how can I let the child go so suddenly—with such a real friend as you, of course—I don't mean, but into a house of strangers, and of such high rank, where I don't know how she'd be received either?"

"But I've told you that I'm like one of the family!" cried Velchaninov, almost wrathfully. "Klavdia Petrovna will be delighted to take her at a word from me—as though it were my child. Damn it all! Why, you know yourself that you only say all this for the sake of saying something . . . there's nothing to discuss!"

He positively stamped his foot.

"I only mean, won't it seem strange? I should have to go and see her once or twice anyway, or she would be left without a father! He—he! . . . and in such a grand household."

"But it's the simplest household, not 'grand' at all!" shouted Velchaninov. "I tell you there are a lot of children. She'll revive there, that's the whole object. . . . And I'll introduce you myself to-morrow, if you like. And of course you would have to go to thank them; we'll drive over every day, if you like."

"It's all so . . ."

"Nonsense! And, what's more, you know that yourself! Listen. Come to me this evening, and stay the night, perhaps, and we'll set off early in the morning so as to get there at twelve."

"My benefactor! And even to stay the night with you . . ." Pavel Pavlovitch agreed suddenly in a tone of fervent feeling. "You are doing me a charity literally. . . . Where is their villa?"

"Their villa is in Lyesnoe."

"Only, I say, what about her dress? For, you know, in such a distinguished household and in their summer villa, too, you know yourself . . . a father's heart . . ."

"What about her dress? She's in mourning. She couldn't be dressed differently, could she? It's the most suitable one could possibly imagine! The only thing is she ought to have clean linen . . . a clean tucker . . ."

Her tucker and what showed of her underlinen were, in fact, very dirty.

"She must change her things at once," said Pavel Pavlovitch fussily, "and we'll get together the rest of what she needs in the way of underclothes; Marya Sysoevna has got them in the wash."

"Then you should tell them to fetch a carriage," Velchaninov interposed; "and make haste if you can."

But a difficulty presented itself: Liza resolutely opposed it; she had been listening all the time in terror, and, if Velchaninov had had time to look at her attentively while he was persuading Pavel Pavlovitch, he would have seen a look of utter despair upon her little face.

"I am not going," she said firmly, in a low voice.

"There, there! You see, she's her mother over again."

"I'm not my mother over again, I'm not my mother over again!" cried Liza in despair, wringing her little hands, and as it were trying to defend herself before her father from the awful reproach of being like her mother. "Father, Father, if you leave me . . ."

She suddenly turned on Velchaninov, who was in dismay.

"If you take me I'll . . ."

But before she had time to say more, Pavel Pavlovitch clutched her by the arm and with undisguised exasperation dragged her almost by the collar into the little room. Whispering followed for some minutes; there was the sound of suppressed crying. Velchaninov was on the point of going in himself, but Pavel Pavlovitch came out and with a wry smile announced that she was coming directly. Velchaninov tried not to look at him and kept his eyes turned away.

Marya Sysoevna appeared. She was the same peasant woman that he had met just before in the passage; she began packing the linen she had brought with her in a pretty little bag belonging to Liza.

"Are you taking the little girl away then, sir?" she asked, addressing Velchaninov. "Have you a family, then? It's a good deed, sir: she's a quiet child; you are taking her from a perfect Bedlam."

"Come, come, Marya Sysoevna!" muttered Pavel Pavlovitch.

"Marya Sysoevna, indeed! That's my name, right enough. It is a Bedlam here, isn't it? Is it the proper thing for a child that can understand to see such disgraceful goings-on? They've fetched you a carriage, sir—to Lyesnoe, is it?"

"Yes, yes."

"Well, it's a blessing you came!"

Liza came out pale and, looking down, took her bag. Not one glance in Velchaninov's direction; she restrained herself and did not, as before, rush to embrace her father, even at parting; evidently she was unwilling to look at him either. Her father kissed her decorously on the head and patted it; her lips twitched as he did so and her little chin quivered, but still she did not raise her eyes to her father. Pavel Pavlovitch looked pale, and his hands were trembling—Velchaninov noticed that distinctly, though he was doing his utmost not to look at him. The one thing he longed for was to get away as quickly as possible.

"After all, it's not my fault," he thought. "It was bound to be so."

They went downstairs; there Marya Sysoevna kissed Liza good-bye, and only when she was sitting in the carriage Liza lifted her eyes to her father, flung up her hands and screamed; another minute and she would have flung herself out of the carriage to him, but the horses had started.

Chapter 6

A NEW FANCY OF AN IDLE MAN

"Are you feeling ill?" asked Velchaninov in alarm. "I will tell them to stop, I'll tell them to bring water. . . ."

She turned her eyes upon him and looked at him passionately, reproachfully.

"Where are you taking me?" she asked sharply and abruptly.

"It's a very nice family, Liza. They're in a delightful summer villa now; there are a lot of children; they'll love you; they are kind. Don't be angry with me, Liza; I only wish for your good."

How strange it would have seemed to all who knew him if any one could have seen him at that moment.

"How . . . how . . . how . . . how horrid you are!" said Liza, choking with stifled tears, glaring at him with her beautiful eyes full of anger.

"Liza, I . . ."

"You are wicked, wicked, wicked, wicked!"

She wrung her hands. Velchaninov was completely at a loss.

"Liza, darling, if you knew how despairing you make me!"

"Is it true that he will come to-morrow? Is it true?" she asked peremptorily.

"Yes, yes, I'll bring him myself; I'll take him with me and bring him."

"He'll deceive me," she whispered, looking down.

"Doesn't he love you, Liza?"

"He doesn't love me."

"Does he ill-treat you? Does he?"

Liza looked at him gloomily and was mute. She turned away from him again and sat with her eyes obstinately cast down. He began trying to coax her; he talked to her warmly, he was in a perfect fever. Liza listened with mistrust and hostility, but she did listen. Her attention delighted him extremely; he even began explaining to her what was meant by a man's drinking. He told her that he loved her himself and would look after her father. Liza lifted her eyes at last and looked at him intently. He began telling her how he used to know her mother and he saw that what he told her interested her. Little by little she began answering his questions, though cautiously and in monosyllables. She still stubbornly refused to answer his leading questions; she remained obstinately silent about everything to do with her relations with her father in the past. As he talked to her, Velchaninov took her hand in his as before and held it; she did not pull it away. The child was not silent all the time, however; she let out in her confused answers that she loved her father more than her mother, because he had always been fonder of her, and her mother had not cared so much for her, but that when her mother was dying she had kissed her and cried a great deal when every one had gone out of the room and they were left alone . . . and that now she loved her more than any one, more than any one, more than any one in the world, and every night she loved her more than any one. But the child was certainly proud. Realizing that she had spoken too freely, she suddenly shrank into herself again and glanced with positive hatred at Velchaninov, who had led her into saying so much. Towards the end of the journey her hysterical agitation almost passed off, but she sank into brooding and had the look of a wild creature, sullen and gloomily, resolutely stubborn. The fact that she was being taken to a strange family, in which she had never been before, seemed for the time being not to trouble her much. What tormented her was something else.

Velchaninov saw that; he guessed that she was ashamed before *him,* that she was ashamed of her father's having so easily let her go with him, of his having, as it were, flung her into his keeping.

"She is ill," he thought, "perhaps very ill; she's been worried to death. . . . Oh, the drunken, abject beast! I understand him now!"

He urged on the driver; he rested his hopes on the country, the fresh air, the garden, the children, and the new, unfamiliar life, and then, later on . . . But of what would come afterwards he had no doubts at all; of the future he had the fullest, brightest hopes. One thing only he knew for certain: that he had never before felt what he was experiencing now and that it would never leave him all his life.

"Here was an object, here was life!" he thought triumphantly.

A great many thoughts flashed upon his mind, but he did not dwell upon them and obstinately put away details; so long as he avoided details it all seemed clear and unassailable. His plan of action was self-evident.

"It will be possible to work upon that wretch," he mused, "by our united forces, and he will leave Liza in Petersburg at the Pogoryeltsevs', though at first only temporarily, for a certain time, and will go away alone, and Liza will be left to me; that's the whole thing. What more do I want? And ... of course, he wants that himself; or else why does he torment her?"

At last they arrived. The Pogoryeltsevs' country home really was a charming place; they were met first of all by a noisy crowd of children, flocking out into the porch. Velchaninov had not been there for a long time, and the children were in a frenzy of delight; they were fond of him. The elder ones shouted to him at once, before he got out of the carriage—

"And how about the case, how is your case getting on?"

The cry was caught up even by the smallest, and they shrieked it mirthfully in imitation of their elders. They used to tease him about the lawsuit. But, seeing Liza, they surrounded her at once and began scrutinizing her with intent, dumb, childish curiosity. Klavdia Petrovna came out, followed by her husband. She and her husband, too, began with a laughing question about the lawsuit.

Klavdia Petrovna was a lady about thirty-seven, a plump and still good-looking brunette, with a fresh, rosy face. Her husband was fifty-five, a shrewd and clever man, but above everything good-natured. Their house was in the fullest sense of the word "a home" to Velchaninov, as he had said himself. But underlying this was the special circumstance that, twenty years before, Klavdia Petrovna had been on the point of marrying Velchaninov, then a student, hardly more than a boy. It was a case of first love, ardent, ridiculous and splendid. It had ended, however, in her marrying Pogoryeltsev. Five years later they had met again, and it had all ended in a quiet, serene friendship. A certain warmth, a peculiar glow suffusing their relations, had remained for ever. All was pure and irreproachable in Velchaninov's memories of this friendship, and it was the dearer to him for being perhaps the solitary case in which this was so. Here in this family he was simple, unaffected and kind; he used to fondle the children, he admitted all his failings, confessed his shortcomings, and never gave himself airs. He swore more than once to the Pogoryeltsevs that he should before long give up the world, come and live with them and never leave them again. In his heart he thought of this project seriously.

He told them all that was necessary about Liza in some detail; but a mere request from him was enough, without any special explanations. Klavdia Petrovna kissed the "orphan" and promised for her part to do everything. The children took possession of Liza and carried her off to play in the garden.

After half an hour of lively conversation Velchaninov got up and began saying good-bye. He was so impatient that every one noticed it. They were all astonished; he had not been to see them for three weeks and now he was going in half an hour. He laughed and pledged himself to come next day. They remarked that he seemed to be in a state of great excitement; he suddenly took Klavdia Petrovna's hand and, on the pretext of having forgotten to tell her something important, drew her aside into another room.

"Do you remember what I told you—you alone—what even your husband does not know—of my year at T——?"

"I remember perfectly; you often talked of it."

"It was not talking, it was a confession, to you alone, to you alone! I never told you the surname of that woman; she was the wife of this man Trusotsky. She is dead, and Liza is her daughter—my daughter!"

"Is it certain? You are not mistaken?" Klavdia Petrovna asked with some excitement.

"It's perfectly certain, perfectly certain; I am not mistaken!" Velchaninov pronounced ecstatically.

And as briefly as he could, in haste and great excitement, he told her everything. Klavdia Petrovna already knew the whole story, but not the lady's name.

Velchaninov had always been so alarmed at the very idea that any one who knew him might ever meet Madame Trusotsky and think that *he* could *so* have loved that woman, that he had not till that day dared to reveal "that woman's" name even to Klavdia Petrovna, his one friend.

"And the father knows nothing?" asked Klavdia Petrovna, when she had heard his story.

"Y-yes, he does know. . . . It worries me that I've not got to the bottom of it yet!" Velchaninov went on eagerly. "He knows, he knows; I noticed it to-day and yesterday. But I must know how much he knows. That's why I'm in a hurry now. He is coming to me this evening. I can't imagine, though, how he can have found out—found out *everything,* I mean. He knows about Bagautov, there's no doubt of that. But about me? You know how clever women are in reassuring their husbands in such cases! If an angel came down from heaven—the husband would not believe him, but he would believe his wife! Don't shake your head and don't blame me; I blame myself and have blamed myself, for the whole affair, long ago, long ago! . . . You see, I was so certain he knew when I was there this morning that I compromised myself before him. Would you believe it, I felt so wretched and ashamed at having met him so rudely yesterday (I will tell you all about it fully afterwards). He came to me yesterday from an irresistible, malicious desire to let me know that he knew of the wrong done him, and knew who had done it; that was the whole reason of his stupid visit when he was drunk. But that was so natural on his part! He simply came to work off his resentment! I was altogether too hasty with him this morning and yesterday! Careless—stupid! I betrayed myself to him. Why did he turn up at a moment when I was upset? I tell you he's even been tormenting Liza, tormenting the child, and probably that, too, was to work off his resentment—to vent his malice if only on the child! Yes, he is spiteful—insignificant as he is, yet he is spiteful; very much so, indeed. In himself he is no more than a buffoon, though, God knows, in old days he seemed to be a very decent fellow within his limits—it's so natural that he should be going to the dogs! One must look at it from a Christian point of view! And you know, my dear, my best of friends, I want to be utterly different to him; I want to be kind to him. That would be really a 'good deed' on my part. For, you know, after all, I have wronged him! Listen, you know there's something else I must tell you. On one occasion in T—— I was in want of four thousand roubles, and he lent me the money on the spot, with no security, and showed genuine pleasure at being of use to me; and, do you know, I took it then, I took it from his hands. I borrowed money from him, do you understand, as a friend!"

"Only be more careful," Klavdia Petrovna anxiously observed, in response to all this. "And what a state of ecstasy you're in; I feel uneasy about you! Of course, Liza will be like a child of my own now. But there's so much, so much still to be settled! The great thing is that you must be more circumspect; you absolutely must be more circumspect when you are happy or so ecstatic; you're too generous when you are happy," she added, with a smile.

They all came out to see Velchaninov off. The children, who had been playing with Liza in the garden, brought her with them. They seemed to look at her with more amazement now than at first. Liza was overcome with shyness when, at parting, Velchaninov kissed her before them all, and warmly repeated his promise to come next day with her father. To the last minute she was silent and did not look at him, but then suddenly she clutched at his arm and drew him aside, fixing an imploring look on him; she wanted to tell him something. He promptly took her away into another room.

"What is it, Liza?" he asked her tenderly and reassuringly; but she, still looking about her apprehensively, drew him into the furthest corner; she wanted to be hidden from them all.

"What is it, Liza? What's the matter?"

She was dumb, she could not bring herself to speak; she gazed fixedly with her blue eyes into his face, and every feature of her little face expressed nothing but frantic terror.

"He'll . . . hang himself!" she whispered, as though in delirium.

"Who will hang himself?" asked Velchaninov in dismay.

"He, he! He tried to hang himself with a cord in the night!" the child said breathlessly. "I saw him! He tried to hang himself with a cord, he told me so, he told me so! He meant to before, he always meant to . . . I saw him in the night. . . ."

"Impossible," whispered Velchaninov in amazement.

She suddenly fell to kissing his hands; she cried, almost choking with sobs, begged and besought him, but he could make nothing of her hysterical whisperings. And the tortured face of that terror-stricken child who looked to him as her last hope remained printed on his memory for ever, haunting him awake and visiting his dreams.

"And can she, can she really love him so much?" he thought, jealously and enviously, as with feverish impatience he returned to town. "She had told me herself that morning that she loved her mother more . . . perhaps she hated him and did not love him at all! . . . And what did that mean: he will hang himself? What did she mean by that? Would the fool hang himself?" . . . He must find out, he must certainly find out! He must get to the bottom of it as soon as possible—once and for all.

Chapter 7

THE HUSBAND AND THE LOVER KISS EACH OTHER

H E WAS in terrible haste "to find out."

"This morning I was so overwhelmed. This morning I hadn't the time to realize the position," he thought, recalling his first sight of Liza, "but now I must find out." To find out more quickly he was on the point of telling the driver to take him to Trusotsky's lodging, but on second thoughts decided: "No, better let him come to me, and meanwhile I'll make haste and get this accursed legal business off my hands."

He set to work feverishly; but this time he was conscious himself that he was very absent-minded and that he was hardly capable that day of attending to business. At five o'clock, when he went out to dinner, he was struck for the first time by an absurd idea: that perhaps he really was only hindering the progress of his case, by meddling in the lawsuit himself, fussing about in the law-courts and hunting up his lawyer, who was already beginning to hide from him. He laughed gaily at his supposition. "If this idea had occurred to me yesterday, I should have been dreadfully distressed," he added, even more gaily. In spite of his gaiety, he grew more and more preoccupied and more and more impatient. He fell to musing at last; and though his restless thought clutched at one thing after another, he could arrive at nothing that would satisfy him.

"I must have that man!" he decided finally. "I must solve the riddle of that man, and then make up my mind. It's—a duel!"

Returning home at seven o'clock, he did not find Pavel Pavlovitch and was extremely surprised, then extremely wrathful, and later still extremely depressed; finally he began to be actually frightened.

"God knows, God knows how it will end!" he repeated, as he walked about the room or stretched himself on the sofa, continually looking at his watch. At last, about nine o'clock, Pavel Pavlovitch appeared. "If the fellow were trying to dupe me, he couldn't have caught me at a more favourable time—I feel so unhinged at this moment," he thought, his confidence completely restored and his spirits rising again.

To his brisk and cheerful inquiry why he was so late coming, Pavel Pavlovitch gave a wry smile, seated himself with a free and easy air, very different from his manner the night before, and carelessly threw his hat with the crape on it on another chair close by. Velchaninov at once noticed this free and easy manner and made a note of it.

Calmly, without wasting words, with none of the excitement he had shown in the morning, he told him, as though giving a report, how he had taken Liza, how kindly she had been received, how good it would be for her, and little by little, as though forgetting Liza, he imperceptibly turned the conversation entirely on the Pogoryeltsevs—what charming people they were, how long he had known them, what a splendid and influential man Pogoryeltsev was, and so on. Pavel Pavlovitch listened inattentively and from time to time glanced up from under his brows at the speaker with an ill-humoured and crafty sneer.

"You're an impulsive person," he muttered, with a particularly disagreeable smile.

"You're rather ill-humoured to-day, though," Velchaninov observed with vexation.

"And why shouldn't I be ill-humoured, like every one else!" Pavel Pavlovitch cried out suddenly, just as though he had only been waiting for that to bounce out.

"You're at liberty to please yourself," laughed Velchaninov. "I wondered if anything had happened to you."

"So it has!" the other exclaimed, as though boasting that something had happened.

"What is it?"

Pavel Pavlovitch delayed answering for a little.

"Why, our Stepan Mihalovitch has played me a trick . . . Bagautov, that elegant young Petersburg gentleman of the best society."

"Was he not at home again?"

"No, this time he was at home. For the first time I was admitted, and I gazed upon his face . . . only he was dead!"

"Wha-at! Bagautov is dead?" Velchaninov was awfully surprised, though there was no apparent reason for his being so surprised.

"Yes. For six years our true and constant friend! Only yesterday, almost at midday, he died, and I knew nothing of it! I was going maybe that very minute to inquire after his health. To-morrow there will be the service and the funeral, he's already in his coffin. The coffin is lined with crimson-coloured velvet trimmed with gold . . . he died of brain fever. I was admitted—I was admitted to gaze upon his face! I told them at the door that I was an intimate friend, that was why I was admitted. What's one to think of the way he's treated me now, my true and constant friend for six long years—I ask you that? Perhaps it was only on his account I came to Petersburg!"

"But what are you angry with him for?" laughed Velchaninov. "Why, he did not die on purpose!"

"But I speak with my heart full of regret; he was a precious friend; this was what he meant to me."

And all at once, quite unexpectedly, Pavel Pavlovitch put up his two fingers like two horns on his bald forehead and went off into a low, prolonged chuckle. He sat like that, chuckling, for a full half-minute, staring into Velchaninov's face in a frenzy of malignant insolence. The latter was petrified as though at the sight of some ghost. But his stupefaction lasted but one brief instant; a sarcastic and insolently composed smile came slowly upon his lips.

"What's the meaning of that?" he asked, carelessly drawling the words.

"The meaning of it is—horns!" Pavel Pavlovitch rapped out, taking away his fingers from his forehead at last.

"That is . . . your horns?"

"My own, generously bestowed!" Pavel Pavlovitch said with a very nasty grimace. Both were silent.

"You're a plucky fellow, I must say!" Velchaninov pronounced.

"Because I showed you my decorations? Do you know, Alexey Ivanovitch, you'd better offer me something! You know I entertained you every blessed day for a whole year at T——. Send for just one bottle, my throat is dry."

"With pleasure; you should have said so before. What will you have?"

"Why *you*? Say *we*; we'll drink together, won't we?" said Pavel Pavlovitch, gazing into his face with a challenging but at the same time strangely uneasy look.

"Champagne?"

"What else? It's not the time for vodka yet. . . ."

Velchaninov got up deliberately, rang for Mavra and gave instructions.

"To the joy of our delightful meeting after nine years' absence," said Pavel Pavlovitch, with a quite superfluous and inappropriate snigger. "Now you, and you only, are the one friend left me! Stepan Mihalovitch Bagautov is no more! As the poet says—

"'Great Patrocus is no more,
Vile Thersites still lives on!'"

And at the word "Thersites" he poked himself in the chest.

"You'd better hurry up and speak out, you swine; I don't like hints," Velchaninov thought to himself. His anger was rising and for a long time he had hardly been able to restrain himself.

"Tell me," he said in a tone of vexation, "since you accuse Stepan Mihalovitch," (he could not call him simply Bagautov now) "I should have thought you would have been glad that the man who has wronged you is dead; why are you angry about it?"

"Glad? Why glad?"

"I imagine those must be your feelings."

"He—he! You are quite mistaken about my feelings on that subject; as some wise man has said, 'A dead enemy is good, but a living one is better,' he—he!"

"But you saw him living every day for five years, I believe; you had time to get tired of the sight of him," Velchaninov observed, with spiteful impertinence.

"But you don't suppose I knew then . . . you don't suppose I knew?" Pavel Pavlovitch blurted out suddenly, just as though he had bounced out from behind a corner again, and as though he were delighted to be asked a question he had long been waiting for.

"What do you take me for, then, Alexey Ivanovitch?"

And there was a gleam in his face of something quite new and unexpected, which seemed to transform his countenance, till then full of spite and abjectly grimacing.

"Is it possible you didn't know, then?" said Velchaninov, disconcerted and completely taken by surprise.

"Is it possible I knew? Is it possible I knew? Oh, you race of Jupiters! For you a man's no more than a dog, and you judge all according to your own petty nature. I tell you that! You can swallow that!" And he banged frantically on the table with his fist, but was at once dismayed at the bang and began to look apprehensive.

Velchaninov assumed an air of dignity.

"Listen, Pavel Pavlovitch. It's absolutely nothing to me, as you can see for yourself, whether you knew, or whether you didn't. If you didn't know, it's to your credit in any case, though . . . I can't understand, however, why you've chosen to make this confidence to me?" . . .

"I didn't mean you . . . don't be angry. I didn't mean you . . ." muttered Pavel Pavlovitch, looking down.

Mavra came in with the champagne.

"Here it is!" cried Pavel Pavlovitch, evidently relieved at her entrance. "Glasses, my good girl, glasses; splendid! We ask for nothing more, my dear. And uncorked already! Honour and glory to you, charming creature! Come, you can go!"

And with renewed courage he looked impudently at Velchaninov again.

"Confess," he chuckled suddenly, "that all this is very interesting and by no means 'absolutely nothing to you,' as you were pleased to declare; so much so that you would be disappointed if I were to get up this minute and go away without explaining myself."

"I really shouldn't be disappointed."

"Oh, that's a lie!" was what Pavel Pavlovitch's smile expressed.

"Well, let's come to business!" And he filled his glass.

"Let's drink," he pronounced, taking up the glass, "to the health of our friend departed in God, Stepan Mihalovitch."

He raised his glass, and drank it.

"I'm not going to drink such a health," said Velchaninov, putting down his glass.

"Why not? It's a pleasant toast."

"I say, weren't you drunk when you came in just now?"

"I had had a little. But why?"

"Nothing particular, but I thought last night, and this morning still more, that you were genuinely grieved at the loss of Natalya Vassilyevna."

"And who told you that I'm not genuinely grieved at the loss of her now?" Pavel Pavlovitch bounced out again, exactly as though he were worked by springs.

"And I didn't mean that; but you must admit that you may be mistaken about Stepan Mihalovitch, and it is—a grave matter."

Pavel Pavlovitch smiled craftily and winked.

"And wouldn't you like to know how I found out about Stepan Mihalovitch?"

Velchaninov flushed.

"I tell you again that it's nothing to me." . . . "Hadn't I better chuck him out this minute, bottle and all?" he thought furiously, and he flushed a deeper crimson.

"That's all right!" said Pavel Pavlovitch, as though trying to encourage him, and he poured himself out another glass.

"I will explain at once how I found out all about it, and so gratify your ardent desire . . . for you are an ardent man, Alexey Ivanovitch, a terribly ardent man! He—he! Only give me a cigarette, for ever since March . . . !"

"Here's a cigarette for you."

"I have gone to the dogs since March, Alexey Ivanovitch, and I'll tell you how it's all happened—listen. Consumption, as you know yourself, my best of friends," he grew more and more familiar, "is a curious disease. Consumptives have scarcely a suspicion they may be dying to-morrow and then all in a minute they're dead. I tell you that only five hours before, Natalya Vassilyevna was planning a visit a fortnight later to her aunt, thirty miles away. You are aware, too, probably, of the practice, or rather bad habit—common in many ladies and very likely in their admirers as well—of preserving all sorts of rubbish in the way of love-letters. . . . It would be much safer to put them in the stove, wouldn't it? No, every scrap of paper is carefully stored away in a box or a *nécessaire;* even docketed in years, and in months, and in series. Whether it's a comfort to them—I don't know; but, no doubt,

it's for the sake of agreeable memories. Since only five hours before her
end she was arranging to go to visit her aunt, Natalya Vassilyevna
naturally had no thought of death to the very last hour. She was still
expecting Koch. So it happened that Natalya Vassilyevna died, and
an ebony box inlaid with mother-of-pearl and silver was left standing
on her bureau. And it was a charming box, with a lock and key, an
heirloom that had come to her from her grandmother. In that box
everything lay revealed, absolutely everything; all, without exception,
with the year and the day, everything for the last twenty years. And
as Stepan Mihalovitch had a distinct literary bent (he actually sent a
passionate love story to a journal), his contributions ran into the hundreds—to be sure they were spread out over five years. Some specimens
had been annotated in Natalya Vassilyevna's own handwriting. A
pleasant surprise for a husband. What do you think of it?"

Velchaninov reflected hurriedly and felt sure that he had never sent
Natalya Vassilyevna a single letter, not a note of any kind. Though he
had written twice from Petersburg, his letters, in accordance with a
compact between them, had been addressed to the husband as well as
the wife. To Natalya Vassilyevna's last letter, in which she had decreed
his banishment, he had never answered.

When he had ended his story, Pavel Pavlovitch paused for a full
minute with an importunate and expectant smile.

"Why do you give me no answer to my little question?" he brought
out at last, with evident anxiety.

"What little question?"

"Why, the pleasant surprise for a husband on opening that box."

"Oh! what is it to do with me!" exclaimed Velchaninov, with a
gesture of disgust, and he got up and walked about the room.

"And I bet you're thinking now, you're a swine to have shown me
your shame. He—he! You're a very fastidious man . . . you are."

"I think nothing about it. On the contrary, you are so much exasperated by the death of the man who wronged you and you've drunk
so much wine, too. I see nothing extraordinary in all this; I quite
understand why you wanted Bagautov alive, and I am ready to respect
your annoyance: but . . ."

"And what did I want Bagautov for, do you suppose?"

"That's your affair."

"I bet that you were thinking of a duel!"

"Damn it all!" cried Velchaninov, growing more and more unable
to control himself. "I imagine that a decent man . . . in such cases does
not stoop to ridiculous babble, to stupid antics, to ludicrous complaints

and disgusting insinuations, by which he only degrades himself more, but acts openly, directly, straightforwardly—like a decent man!"

"He—he! but perhaps I'm not a decent man!"

"That's your affair again . . . but in that case, what the devil did you want Bagautov alive for?"

"Why, if only to see a friend. We'd have had a bottle and drunk together."

"He wouldn't have drunk with you."

"Why not? *Noblesse oblige!* Here, you're drinking with me; in what way is he better than you?"

"I haven't drunk with you."

"Why such pride all of a sudden?"

Velchaninov suddenly broke into a nervous and irritable laugh. "Damnation! Why, you are really a 'predatory type'! I thought you were only 'the eternal husband,' and nothing more!"

"What do you mean by 'the eternal husband,' what's that?" Pavel Pavlovitch suddenly pricked up his ears.

"Oh, it's one type of husband . . . it would be a long story. You'd better clear out, it's time you were gone; I'm sick of you."

"And predatory? You said 'predatory'!"

"I said you were a 'predatory type'; I said it ironically."

"What do you mean by a 'predatory type'? Tell me, please, Alexey Ivanovitch, for God's sake, or for Christ's sake!"

"Come, that's enough, that's enough!" cried Velchaninov, suddenly growing horribly angry. "It's time you were off. Get along."

"No, it's not enough!" Pavel Pavlovitch flared up; "even though you are sick of me it's not enough, for we must drink together and clink glasses! Let us drink together, and then I'll go, but as it is it's not enough!"

"Pavel Pavlovitch! Will you go to the devil to-day or will you not?"

"I can go to the devil, but first we'll drink! You said that you would not drink *with me;* but I *want* you to drink with me!"

There was no grimacing, no sniggering about him now. He seemed all at once entirely transformed, and to have become in his whole tone and appearance so completely the opposite of the Pavel Pavlovitch of the moment before that Velchaninov was quite taken aback.

"Do let us drink, Alexey Ivanovitch! Don't refuse me," Pavel Pavlovitch persisted, gripping his hand tightly and looking strangely into his eyes.

Clearly there was more at stake than merely drinking.

"Yes, if you like," muttered Velchaninov; "but how can we? . . . There's nothing left but the dregs. . . ."

"There are just two glasses left, it's thick, but we'll drink it and clink glasses! Here, take your glass."

They clinked their glasses and emptied them.

"Since that's so—since that's so . . . Ach!"

Pavel Pavlovitch clutched his forehead in his hand and remained for some moments in that position. Velchaninov had a feeling every moment that he would speak out and utter the very *final* word. But Pavel Pavlovitch uttered nothing; he simply gazed at him and smiled again the same sly, knowing smile.

"What do you want of me, you drunken fellow! You're playing the fool with me!" Velchaninov shouted furiously, stamping.

"Don't shout, don't shout; what is there to shout for?" cried Pavel Pavlovitch, gesticulating hurriedly. "I'm not playing the fool, I'm not playing the fool! Do you know what you are to me now?"

And he suddenly seized his hand and kissed it. Velchaninov was utterly taken aback.

"That's what you mean to me now! And now—and now I'll go to the devil as soon as you please!"

"Wait a minute, stay!" cried Velchaninov, recovering himself. "I forgot to tell you. . . ."

Pavel Pavlovitch turned back from the door.

"You see," muttered Velchaninov, very quickly, flushing crimson and looking away, "you must be at the Pogoryeltsevs' to-morrow . . . to make their acquaintance and thank them; you must . . ."

"Certainly, I must. I understand that, of course!" Pavel Pavlovitch acquiesced with the utmost readiness, waving his hand quickly as though to protest that there was no need to remind him.

"And besides, Liza is very anxious to see you. I promised her . . ."

"Liza!" Pavel Pavlovitch turned back. "Liza? Do you know what Liza has meant to me and means? Has meant and still means!" he cried all at once, almost frantically. "But . . . But of that later, all that can be later. . . . But now it's not enough that we've drunk together, Alexey Ivanovitch, I must have something else to be satisfied. . . ."

He laid his hat on a chair and gazed at him, gasping for breath a little as he had done just before.

"Kiss me, Alexey Ivanovitch!" he suggested suddenly.

"You're drunk!" Velchaninov declared, stepping back.

"Yes, but kiss me all the same, Alexey Ivanovitch. Oh, kiss me! Why, I kissed your hand just now."

For some minutes Velchaninov was silent, as though stunned by a blow on the head. But suddenly he bent down to Pavel Pavlovitch, whose face was on a level with his shoulder, and kissed him on the lips, which smelt very strongly of spirits. He was not, however, perfectly certain that he had kissed him.

"Well, now, now. . . ." Pavel Pavlovitch cried again in a drunken frenzy, his drunken eyes flashing; "now I'll tell you; I thought then, What if he too? What if that one, I thought, what if he too . . . whom can I trust after that!"

Pavel Pavlovitch suddenly burst into tears.

"So you understand, you're the one friend left me now!"

And he ran with his hat out of the room. Velchaninov again stood still for some minutes in the same place, just as he had done after Pavel Pavlovitch's first visit.

"Ah! a drunken fool and nothing more!" He waved his hand, dismissing the subject.

"Absolutely nothing more," he repeated energetically as he undressed and got into bed.

Chapter 8

LIZA ILL

NEXT morning Velchaninov walked about his room expecting Pavel Pavlovitch, who had promised to arrive in good time to go to the Pogoryeltsevs. As he smoked and sipped his coffee he was conscious at every moment that he was like a man who on waking up in the morning cannot forget for one instant that he has received a slap in the face overnight. "H'm! . . . he quite understands the position and will take his revenge on me through Liza!" he thought with horror.

The charming figure of the poor child rose mournfully before him for a moment. His heart beat faster at the thought that he would soon, within two hours, see *his* Liza again. "Ah! it's no use talking about it!" he decided hotly—"It's my whole life and my whole object now! what do slaps in the face or memories of the past matter? What has my life been till now? Muddle and sadness . . . but now . . . it's all different, everything's changed!"

But in spite of his enthusiasm, he grew more and more doubtful. "He is tormenting me by means of Liza—that's clear! And he is tormenting Liza too. It's in that way he will devour me utterly in revenge for everything. H'm! ... Of course, I can't allow him to go on as he did yesterday"—he flushed crimson all at once—"and ... here it's twelve o'clock, though, he doesn't come."

He waited a long time, till half-past twelve, and his depression grew more and more acute. Pavel Pavlovitch did not appear. At last the thought that had long been stirring in his mind, that Pavel Pavlovitch had not come on purpose, simply in order to get up another scene like that of the night before, put the finishing touch to his irritation. "He knows that I depend on him, and what a state Liza will be in now. And how can I appear before her without him?"

At last he could stand it no longer, and at one o'clock he rushed off to the Pokrovsky Hotel alone. At the lodging he was told that Pavel Pavlovitch had not slept at home, but had only turned up at nine o'clock in the morning, had stayed no more than a quarter of an hour, and then gone out again. Velchaninov stood at the door of Pavel Pavlovitch's room, listening to what the servant said, and mechanically turned the handle of the locked door and pulled it backwards and forwards. Realizing what he was doing, he uttered a curse and asked the servant to take him to Marya Sysoevna. But the landlady, hearing he was there, came out readily.

She was a good-natured woman. "A woman with generous feelings," as Velchaninov said of her when he was reporting his conversation afterwards to Klavdia Petrovna. Inquiring briefly about his journey with the child the day before, Marya Sysoevna launched out into accounts of Pavel Pavlovitch's doings. In her words: "If it had not been for the child, she would have sent him about his business long ago. He was turned out of the hotel because of his disorderly behaviour. Wasn't it wicked to bring home a wench with him when there was a child here old enough to understand? He was shouting: 'She will be your mother, if I choose!' And, would you believe it? what that street wench did, she even spat in his face. 'You're not my daughter, but he's a ——!' she cried."

"Really!" Velchaninov was horrified.

"I heard it myself. Though the man was drunk till he was almost senseless, yet it was very wrong before the child; though she is but young, she broods over everything in her mind! The child cries. I can see she is worried to death. And the other day there was a terrible thing done in our building: a clerk, so folks say, took a room in the hotel overnight, and in the morning hanged himself. They say he had squandered all his money. People flocked to see. Pavel Pavlovitch was not at home, and the child was running about with no one to look after her; I looked, and there she was in the passage among the people, and peeping in behind the others: she was looking so strangely at the body. I brought her away as quickly as I could. And what do you think—she was all of a tremble, she looked quite black in the face, and as soon as I brought her in she flopped on the floor in a faint. She struggled and writhed, and it was all I could do to bring her round. It was a fit, and she's been poorly ever since that hour. He heard of it, came home, and pinched her all over—for he's not one for beating, he's more given to pinching her, and afterwards, when he came home after having a drop, he'd frighten her: 'I'll hang myself too,' he'd say; 'you'll make me hang myself; on this blind-cord here,' he'd say; and he'd make a noose before her eyes. And she'd be beside herself—she'd scream and throw her little arms round him: 'I won't!' she'd cry, 'I never will again.' It was pitiful."

Though Velchaninov had expected something strange, this story amazed him so much that he could not believe it.

Marya Sysoevna told him a great deal more; on one occasion, for instance, had it not been for Marya Sysoevna Liza might have thrown herself out of the window.

Velchaninov went out of the house reeling as though he were drunk. "I'll knock him on the head like a dog!" was the thought that floated before his mind. And for a long time he kept repeating it to himself.

He took a cab and drove to the Pogoryeltsevs. On the way the carriage was obliged to stop at the cross-roads, near the bridge on the canal, over which a long funeral procession was passing. And on both sides of the bridge there were several carriages waiting in a block; people on foot were stopped too. It was a grand funeral and there was a very long string of carriages following it, and lo and behold! in the windows of one of these carriages Velchaninov caught a passing glimpse of the face of Pavel Pavlovitch. He would not have believed his eyes if Pavel Pavlovitch had not thrust his head out and nodded to him with a smile. Evidently he was delighted at recognizing Velchaninov; he even began beckoning to him from the carriage. Velchaninov jumped out of his cab and, in spite of the crush, in spite of the police, and in spite of the fact that Pavel Pavlovitch's carriage was driving on to the bridge, he ran right up to the window. Pavel Pavlovitch was alone.

"What's the matter with you?" cried Velchaninov; "why didn't you come? How is it you are here?"

"I'm repaying a debt. Don't shout, don't shout, I am repaying a debt," sniggered Pavel Pavlovitch, screwing up his eyes, jocosely. "I'm following the mortal remains of my faithful friend, Stepan Mihalov-itch."

"That's all nonsense, you drunken, senseless man," Velchaninov shouted louder than ever, though he was taken aback for an instant. "Get out this minute and come into the cab with me."

"I can't, it's a duty. . . ."

"I'll drag you out!" Velchaninov yelled.

"And I'll scream! I'll scream!" said Pavel Pavlovitch, sniggering as jocosely as before, as though it were a game, though he did huddle into the furthest corner of the carriage. . . .

"Look out, look out! you'll be run over!" shouted a policeman.

At the further end of the bridge a carriage cutting across the procession did, in fact, cause a commotion. Velchaninov was forced to skip back; the stream of carriages and the crowd of people immediately carried him further away. With a curse he made his way back of the cab.

"No matter, I couldn't have taken a fellow like that with me, at any rate!" he thought, with a feeling of bewildered anxiety that persisted.

When he told Klavdia Petrovna Marya Sysoevna's story and described the strange meeting in the funeral procession, she grew very thoughtful.

"I feel afraid for you," she said. "You ought to break off all relations with him, and the sooner the better."

"He's a drunken fool and nothing more!" Velchaninov cried passionately; "as though I could be afraid of him! And how can I break off relations with him when there's Liza to be considered. Think of Liza!"

Liza meanwhile was lying ill; she had begun to be feverish the evening before and they were expecting a celebrated doctor, for whom they had sent an express messenger to the town in the morning. This completed Velchaninov's distress.

Klavdia Petrovna took him to the invalid.

"I watched her very carefully yesterday," she observed, stopping outside Liza's room. "She's a proud and reserved child; she is ashamed that she is here, and that her father has cast her off; that's the whole cause of her illness, to my thinking."

"How cast her off? Why do you say he's cast her off?"

"The very fact that he let her come here, among complete strangers and with a man . . . who's almost a stranger, too, or on such terms . . ."

"But it was I took her, I took her by force; I don't perceive . . ."

"Oh, my God, and even Liza, a child, perceives it! It's my belief that he simply won't come at all."

Liza was not astonished when she saw Velchaninov alone; she only smiled mournfully and turned her feverishly hot little head to the wall. She made no response to Velchaninov's timid efforts to comfort her and his fervent promises to bring her father next day without fail. On coming away from her, he suddenly burst into tears.

It was evening before the doctor came. After examining the patient, he alarmed them all from the first word, by observing that they had done wrong not to have sent for him before. When it was explained to him that the child had been taken ill only the evening before, he was at first incredulous.

"It all depends how things go on to-night," he said in conclusion. After giving various instructions, he went away, promising to come again next day as early as possible. Velchaninov would have insisted on staying the night, but Klavdia Petrovna begged him once more "to try and bring that monster."

"Try once more," Velchaninov retorted in a frenzy. "Why, this time I'll tie him hand and foot and carry him here in my arms!" The idea of tying Pavel Pavlovitch hand and foot and carrying him there took possession of him and made him violently impatient to carry it out. "I don't feel in the least guilty towards him now, not in the least!" he said to Klavdia Petrovna, as he said good-bye. "I take back all the abject, snivelling things I said here yesterday," he added indignantly.

Liza was lying with her eyes shut, apparently asleep; she seemed to be better. When Velchaninov cautiously bent over her head, to say good-bye and to kiss, if only the edge of her garment, she suddenly opened her eyes, as though she had been expecting him, and whispered to him—

"Take me away!"

It was a gentle, pitiful prayer, without a shade in it of the irritability of the previous day, but at the same time he could hear in it the conviction that he would not do what she asked. Velchaninov, in complete despair, began trying to persuade her that this was impossible.

In silence she closed her eyes and did not utter another word, as though she did not see or hear him.

On getting into Petersburg he told the driver to take him straight to Pokrovsky Hotel. It was ten o'clock; Pavel Pavlovitch was not in his lodging. Velchaninov spent a full half-hour in waiting for him and walking up and down the passage in sickening suspense. Marya Sysoevna assured him at last that Pavel Pavlovitch would not be back till early next morning. "Then I will come early in the morning," Velchaninov decided, and, beside himself, he set off for home.

But what was his astonishment when, at the door of his flat, he learned from Mavra that his yesterday's visitor had been waiting for him since ten o'clock.

"And has been pleased to drink tea here, and has sent out for wine again, and has given me a blue note to get it."

Chapter 9

AN APPARITION

PAVEL PAVLOVITCH had made himself exceedingly comfortable. He was sitting in the same chair as the day before, smoking a cigarette, and had just poured himself out the fourth and last glass from a bottle of wine. The teapot and an unfinished glass of tea were standing on a table close by. His flushed face was beaming with bliss. He had even taken off his coat, as it was warm, and was sitting in his waistcoat.

"Excuse me, most faithful of friends!" he cried, seeing Velchaninov and jumping up to put on his coat. "I took it off for the greater enjoyment of the moment. . . ."

Velchaninov went up to him menacingly.

"Are you not quite drunk yet? Is it still possible to talk to you?"

Pavel Pavlovitch was a little flustered.

"No, not quite. . . . I've been commemorating the deceased, but . . . not quite. . . ."

"Will you understand me too?"

"That's what I've come for, to understand you."

"Well, then; I begin by telling you straight out that you are a worthless scoundrel!" cried Velchaninov.

"If you begin like that, how will you end?" Pavel Pavlovitch protested, evidently cowed, but Velchaninov went on shouting without heeding him.

"Your daughter is dying, she is ill; have you abandoned her or not?"

"Can she really be dying?"

"She is ill, ill, exceedingly, dangerously ill!"

"Possibly some little fit . . ."

"Don't talk nonsense! She is ex—ceed—ing—ly, dangerously ill! You ought to have gone if only to . . ."

"To express my gratitude, my gratitude for their hospitality! I quite understand that! Alexey Ivanovitch, my precious, perfect friend" —he suddenly clutched Velchaninov's hand in both of his, and with drunken sentimentality, almost with tears, as though imploring forgiveness, he kept crying out: "Alexey Ivanovitch, don't shout, don't shout! Whether I die or fall drunk into the Neva—what does it matter in the real significance of things? We have plenty of time to go to Mr. Pogoryeltsev. . . ."

Velchaninov pulled himself together and restrained himself a little.

"You're drunk, and so I don't understand the sense of what you are saying," he observed sternly. "I am always ready to have things out with you, shall be glad to, in fact, as soon as possible. . . . I've come indeed. . . . But first of all I warn you that I shall take steps: you must stay the night here! To-morrow morning I'll take you and we'll go together. I won't let you go," he yelled again. "I'll tie you up and carry you there in my arms! . . . Would you like this sofa?" he said breathlessly, pointing to a wide, soft sofa, which stood opposite the one against the other wall, where he used to sleep himself.

"By all means, I can sleep anywhere. . . ."

"Not anywhere, but on that sofa! Here, take your sheets, your quilt, your pillow." All these Velchaninov took out of the cupboard and hurriedly flung them to Pavel Pavlovitch, who held out his arms submissively. "Make the bed at once, make it at once!"

Pavel Pavlovitch, loaded with his burden, stood in the middle of the room as though hesitating, with a broad drunken grin on his drunken face. But at a second menacing shout from Velchaninov he suddenly began bustling about at full speed; he pushed back the table and began, sighing and groaning, to unfold the sheets and make the bed. Velchaninov went to assist him; he was, to some extent, appeased by the alarm and submissiveness of his visitor.

"Finish your glass and go to bed," he ordered him again; he felt as though he could not help giving orders. "You sent for that wine yourself, didn't you?"

"Yes. . . . I knew you wouldn't send for any more, Alexey Ivanovitch."

"It was well you knew it, and there is something more you must know too. I tell you once more I've taken measures, I won't put up with any more of your antics, I won't put up with your drunken kisses as I did yesterday."

"I understand myself, Alexey Ivanovitch, that that was only possible once," sniggered Pavel Pavlovitch.

Hearing his answer, Velchaninov, who had been striding up and down the room, stopped almost solemnly before Pavel Pavlovitch.

"Pavel Pavlovitch, tell me frankly! You're a sensible man, I've recognized that again, but I assure you, you are on the wrong tack! Speak straightforwardly, act straightforwardly and I give you my word of honour I will answer any question you like."

Pavel Pavlovitch grinned his broad grin again, which was enough in itself to drive Velchaninov to fury.

"Stop!" Velchaninov shouted again. "Don't sham, I see through you! I repeat: I give you my word of honour, that I am ready to answer *anything* and you shall receive every satisfaction possible, that is every sort, even the impossible! Oh, how I wish you could understand me! . . ."

"Since you are so good"—Pavel Pavlovitch moved cautiously towards him—"I was much interested in what you said last night about a 'predatory type'! . . ."

Velchaninov, with a curse, fell to pacing about the room more rapidly than ever.

"No, Alexey Ivanovitch, don't curse, because I'm so much interested, and have come on purpose to make sure. . . . I'm not very ready with my tongue, but you must forgive me. You know of that 'predatory type,' and of that 'peaceable type' I read in a magazine, in the literary criticism. I remembered it this morning . . . only I had forgotten it, and to tell the truth I did not understand it at the time. This is what I wanted you to explain: the deceased, Stepan Mihalovitch Bagautov— was he 'predatory' or 'peaceable'? How do you classify him?"

Velchaninov still remained silent, and did not cease his pacing up and down.

"The predatory type," he began, stopping suddenly in exasperation, "is the man who would sooner have put poison in Bagautov's glass when drinking champagne with him in honour of their delightful meeting, as you drank with me yesterday, than have followed his coffin to the cemetery as you have to-day, the devil only knows from what secret, underground, loathsome impulse and distorted feeling that only degrades you! Yes, degrades you!"

"It's true that I shouldn't have gone," Pavel Pavlovitch assented; "but you do pitch into me. . . ."

"It's not the man," Velchaninov, getting hotter, went on shouting, without heeding him; "it's not the man who poses to himself as goodness knows what, who reckons up his score of right and wrong, goes over and over his grievance as though it were a lesson, frets, goes in for all sorts of antics and apishness, hangs on people's necks—and most likely he has been spending all his time at it too! Is it true that you tried to hang yourself—is it?"

"When I was drunk, I did talk wildly—I don't remember. It isn't quite seemly, Alexey Ivanovitch, to put poison in wine. Apart from the fact that I am a civil servant of good repute, you know I have money of my own, and, what's more, I may want to get married again."

"Besides, you'll be sent to the gallows."

"To be sure, that unpleasantness also, though nowadays they admit many extenuating circumstances in the law-courts. I'll tell you a killing little anecdote, Alexey Ivanovitch. I thought of it this morning in the carriage. I wanted to tell you of it then. You said just now 'hangs on people's necks.' You remember, perhaps, Semyon Petrovitch Livtsov, he used to come and see us when you were in T——; well, his younger brother, who was also a young Petersburg swell, was in attendance on the governor at V——, and he, too, was distinguished for various qualities. He had a quarrel with Golubenko, a colonel, in the presence of ladies and the lady of his heart, and considered himself insulted, but he swallowed the affront and concealed it; and, meanwhile, Golubenko cut him out with the lady of his heart and made her an offer. And what do you think? This Livtsov formed a genuine friendship with Golubenko, he quite made it up with him, and, what's more, insisted on being his best man, he held the wedding crown, and when they came from under the wedding crown, he went up to kiss and congratulate Golubenko; and in the presence of the governor and all the honourable company, with his swallow-tail coat, and his hair in curl, he sticks the bridegroom in the stomach with a knife—so that he rolled over! His own best man! What a disgrace! And, what's more, when he'd stabbed him like that, he rushed about crying: 'Ach! what have I done! Oh, what is it I've done!' with floods of tears, trembling all over, flinging himself on people's necks, even ladies. 'Ach, what have I done!' he kept saying. 'What have I done now!' He—he—he! he was killing. Though one feels sorry for Golubenko, perhaps, but after all he recovered."

"I don't see why you told me the story," observed Velchaninov, frowning sternly.

"Why, all because he stuck the knife in him, you know," Pavel Pavlovitch tittered; "you can see he was not the type, but a snivelling fellow, since he forgot all good manners in his horror and flung himself on the ladies' necks in the presence of the governor—but you see he stabbed him, he got his own back! That was all I meant."

"Go to hell!" Velchaninov yelled suddenly, in a voice not his own, as though something had exploded in him. "Go to hell with your underground vileness; you are nothing but underground vileness. You thought you'd scare me—you base man, torturing a child; you scoundrel, you scoundrel, you scoundrel!" he shouted, beside himself, gasping for breath at every word.

A complete revulsion came over Pavel Pavlovitch which actually seemed to sober him; his lips quivered.

"It is you, Alexey Ivanovitch, call me a scoundrel, *you* call *me?*"

But Velchaninov had already realized what he had done.

"I am ready to apologize," he answered, after a pause of gloomy hesitation; "but only if you will act straightforwardly at once yourself."

"In your place I would apologize without any ifs, Alexey Ivanovitch."

"Very good, so be it," said Velchaninov, after another slight pause. "I apologize to you; but you'll admit yourself, Pavel Pavlovitch, that, after all this, I need not consider that I owe you anything. I'm speaking with reference to the *whole* matter and not only to the present incident."

"That's all right, why consider?" Pavel Pavlovitch sniggered, though he kept his eyes on the ground.

"So much the better, then, so much the better! Finish your wine and go to bed, for I won't let you go, anyway. . . ."

"Oh, the wine. . . ." Pavel Pavlovitch seemed, as it were, a little disconcerted. He went to the table, however, and finished the last glass of wine he had poured out so long before.

Perhaps he had drunk a great deal before, for his hand trembled and he spilt part of the wine on the floor, and on his shirt and waistcoat. He finished it all, however, as though he could not bear to leave a drop, and respectfully replacing the empty glass on the table, he went submissively to his bed to undress.

"But wouldn't it be better for me not to stay the night?" he brought out for some reason, though he had taken off one boot and was holding it in his hand.

"No, it wouldn't," Velchaninov answered wrathfully, still pacing up and down the room without looking at him.

Pavel Pavlovitch undressed and got into bed. A quarter of an hour later Velchaninov went to bed too, and put out the candle.

He fell asleep uneasily The new element that had turned up unexpectedly and complicated the whole business more than ever worried him now, and at the same time he felt that he was for some reason ashamed of his uneasiness. He was just dozing off, but he was waked up all at once by a rustling sound. He looked round at once towards Pavel Pavlovitch's bed. The room was dark (the curtains were drawn), but Velchaninov fancied that Pavel Pavlovitch was not lying down, but was sitting on the bed.

"What's the matter?" Velchaninov called to him.

"A ghost," Pavel Pavlovitch said, scarcely audibly, after a brief pause.

"What do you mean, what sort of ghost?"

"There in that room, I seem to see a ghost in the doorway."

"Whose ghost?" Velchaninov asked again, after a pause.

"Natalya Vassilyevna's."

Velchaninov stood up on the rug, and looked across the passage, into the other room, the door of which always stood open. There were only blinds instead of curtains on the window, and so it was much lighter there.

"There's nothing in that room and you are drunk. Go to bed!" said Velchaninov. He got into bed and wrapped himself in the quilt.

Pavel Pavlovitch got into bed, too, without uttering a word.

"And have you ever seen ghosts before?" Velchaninov asked suddenly, ten minutes afterwards.

Pavel Pavlovitch, too, was silent for a while.

"I thought I saw one once," he responded faintly.

Silence followed again.

Velchaninov could not have said for certain whether he had been asleep or not, but about an hour had passed when he suddenly turned round again: whether he was roused again by a rustle, he was not sure, but felt as though in the pitch-dark something white was standing over him, not quite close, but in the middle of the room. He sat up in bed and for a full minute gazed into the darkness.

"Is that you, Pavel Pavlovitch?" he said, in a failing voice.

His own voice ringing out suddenly in the stillness and the dark seemed to him somehow strange.

No answer followed, but there could be no doubt that some one was standing there.

"Is that you . . . Pavel Pavlovitch?" he repeated, more loudly—so loudly, in fact, that if Pavel Pavlovitch had been quietly asleep in his bed he would certainly have waked up and answered.

But again no answer came, yet he fancied that the white, hardly distinguishable figure moved nearer to him. Then something strange followed: something seemed to explode within him, exactly as it had that evening, and he shouted at the top of his voice, in a most hideous, frantic voice, gasping for breath at each word:

"If you . . . drunken fool . . . dare to imagine . . . that you can . . . frighten me, I'll turn over to the wall, I'll put the bedclothes over my head, and won't turn round again all night . . . to show you how much I care . . . if you were to stand there till morning . . . like a fool . . . and I spit upon you . . ."

And he spat furiously in the direction, as he supposed, of Pavel Pavlovitch, turned over to the wall, drew the bedclothes over his head as he had said and grew numb in that position, not stirring a muscle. A deathlike silence followed. Whether the phantom was moving nearer or standing still he could not tell, but his heart was beating, beating, beating violently. Fully five minutes passed, and suddenly, two steps from him, he heard the meek and plaintive voice of Pavel Pavlovitch.

"I got up, Alexey Ivanovitch, to look for the . . ." (and he mentioned a quite indispensable domestic article). "I didn't find one there. . . . I meant to look quietly under your bed."

"Why didn't you speak when I shouted?" Velchaninov asked in a breaking voice, after an interval of half a minute.

"I was frightened, you shouted so. . . . I was frightened."

"There in the corner on the left, in the little cupboard. Light the candle. . . ."

"I can do without the candle," Pavel Pavlovitch brought out meekly, making for the corner. "Forgive me, Alexey Ivanovitch, for disturbing you so. . . . I was so bewildered . . ."

But Velchaninov made no reply. He still lay with his face to the wall, and lay so all night, without once turning over. Whether it was that he wanted to do as he had said and so show his contempt—he did not know himself what he was feeling; his nervous irritability passed at last almost into delirium, and it was a long time before he went to sleep. Waking next morning between nine and ten, he jumped up and sat up in bed, as though some one had given him a shove—but Pavel Pavlovitch was not in the room—the unmade bed stood there empty; he had crept away at dawn.

"I knew it would be so," cried Velchaninov, slapping himself on the forehead.

Chapter 10

IN THE CEMETERY

THE doctor's fears turned out to be justified; Liza was suddenly worse—worse than Velchaninov and Klavdia Petrovna had imagined possible the evening before. Velchaninov found the invalid conscious in the morning, though she was in a high fever; afterwards he declared that she had smiled and even held out her feverish little hand to him. Whether this was really so, or whether he had imagined it, in an unconscious effort to comfort himself, he had no time to make sure; by nightfall the sick child was unconscious, and she remained so till the end. Ten days after her coming to the Pogoryeltsevs she died.

It was a sorrowful time for Velchaninov; the Pogoryeltsevs were very anxious about him. He spent those bitter days for the most part with them. During the last days of Liza's illness he would sit for whole hours together in a corner apparently thinking of nothing; Klavdia Petrovna attempted to distract his mind, but he made little response, and seemed to find it a burden even to talk to her. Klavdia Petrovna had not expected that "all this would have such an effect upon him." The children succeeded best in rousing him; in their company he sometimes even laughed, but almost every hour he would get up from his chair and go on tiptoe to look at the invalid. He sometimes fancied that she recognized him. He had no hope of her recovery, nor had any one, but he could not tear himself away from the room in which she lay dying, and usually sat in the next room.

On two occasions in the course of those days, however, he showed great activity: he roused himself and rushed off to Petersburg to the doctors, called on all the most distinguished of them, and arranged for a consultation. The second and last consultation took place the evening before Liza's death. Three days before that Klavdia Petrovna urged upon Velchaninov the necessity of seeking out M. Trusotsky: pointing out that "if the worst happened, the funeral would be impossible without him." Velchaninov mumbled in reply that he would write to him. Pogoryeltsev thereupon declared that he would undertake to find him through the police. Velchaninov did finally write a note of two lines and took it to the Pokrovsky Hotel. Pavel Pavlovitch, as usual, was not at home, and he left the letter for him with Marya Sysoevna.

At last Liza died, on a beautiful summer evening at sunset, and only then Velchaninov seemed to wake up. When they dressed the dead child in a white frock that belonged to one of Klavdia Petrovna's daughters and was kept for festivals, and laid her on the table in the drawing-room with flowers in her folded hands, he went up to Klavdia Petrovna with glittering eyes, and told her that he would bring the "murderer" at once. Refusing to listen to their advice to put off going till next day, he set off for Petersburg at once.

He knew where to find Pavel Pavlovitch; he had not only been to fetch the doctors when he went to Petersburg before. He had sometimes fancied during those days that if he brought her father to Liza, and she heard his voice, she might come to herself; so he had fallen to hunting for him like one possessed. Pavel Pavlovitch was in the same lodging as before, but it was useless for him to inquire there: "He hasn't slept here for the last three nights or been near the place," Marya Sysoevna reported; "and if he does come he's bound to be drunk, and before he's been here an hour he's off again: he's going to rack and ruin." The waiter at the Pokrovsky Hotel told Velchaninov, among other things, that Pavel Pavlovitch used to visit some young women in Voznesensky Prospect. Velchaninov promptly looked up these young women. When he had treated them and made them presents these persons readily remembered their visitor, chiefly from the crape on his hat, after which, of course, they abused him roundly for not having been to see them again. One of them, Katya, undertook "to find Pavel Pavlovitch any time, because nowadays he was always with Mashka Prostakov, and he had no end of money, and she ought to have been Mashka Prohvostov (*i. e.* scoundrelly) instead of Prostakov (*i. e.* simple), and she'd been in the hospital, and if she (the speaker) liked she could pack the wench off to Siberia—she had only to say the word." Katya did not, however, look up Pavel Pavlovitch on that occasion, but she promised faithfully to do so another time. It was on her help that Velchaninov was reckoning now.

On reaching Petersburg at ten o'clock, he went at once to ask for her, paid the keeper to let her go, and set off to search with her. He did not know himself what he was going to do with Pavel Pavlovitch: whether he would kill him, or whether he was looking for him simply to tell him of his daughter's death and the necessity of his presence at the funeral. At first they were unsuccessful. It turned out that this Mashka had had a fight with Pavel Pavlovitch two days before, and that a cashier "had broken his head with a stool." In fact, for a long time the search was in vain, and it was only at two o'clock in the afternoon that Velchaninov, coming out of an "establishment," to which he had been sent as a likely place, unexpectedly hit up against him.

Pavel Pavlovitch, hopelessly drunk, was being conducted to this "establishment" by two ladies, one of whom was holding his arm and supporting him. They were followed by a tall, sturdy fellow, who was shouting at the top of his voice and threatening Pavel Pavlovitch with all sorts of horrors. He bawled among other things that "Pavel Pavlovitch was exploiting him and poisoning his existence." There seemed to have been some dispute about money; the women were much frightened and flustered. Seeing Velchaninov, Pavel Pavlovitch rushed to him with outstretched hands and screamed as though he were being murdered:

"Brother, defend me!"

At the sight of Velchaninov's athletic figure the bully promptly disappeared; Pavel Pavlovitch in triumph shook his fist after him with a yell of victory; at that point Velchaninov seized him by the shoulder in a fury, and, without knowing why he did it, shook him until his teeth chattered. Pavel Pavlovitch instantly ceased yelling and stared at his tormentor in stupid, drunken terror. Probably not knowing what to do with him next, Velchaninov folded him up and sat him on the curbstone.

"Liza is dead!" he said to him.

Pavel Pavlovitch, still staring at Velchaninov, sat on the curbstone supported by one of the ladies. He understood at last, and his face suddenly looked pinched.

"Dead . . ." he whispered strangely. Whether his face wore his loathsome, drunken grin, or whether it was contorted by some feeling, Velchaninov could not distinguish, but a moment later Pavel Pavlovitch, with an effort, lifted his trembling hand to make the sign of the cross; his trembling hand dropped again without completing it. A little while after he slowly got up from the curbstone, clutched at his lady and, leaning upon her, went on his way, as though oblivious —as though Velchaninov had not been present. But the latter seized him by the shoulder again.

"Do you understand, you drunken monster, that without you she can't be buried?" he shouted breathlessly.

Pavel Pavlovitch turned his head towards him.

"The artillery . . . the lieutenant . . . do you remember him?" he stammered.

"Wha—at!" yelled Velchaninov, with a sickening pang.

"There's her father for you! Find him—for the burial."

"You're lying," Velchaninov yelled like one distraught. "You say that from spite. . . . I knew you were preparing that for me."

Beside himself, he raised his terrible fist to strike Pavel Pavlovitch. In another minute he might have killed him at one blow; the ladies squealed and were beating a retreat, but Pavel Pavlovitch did not turn a hair. His face was contorted by a frenzy of ferocious hatred.

"Do you know," he said, much more steadily, almost as though he were sober, "our Russian . . .?" (and he uttered an absolutely unprintable term of abuse). "Well, you go to it, then!"

Then with a violent effort he tore himself out of Velchaninov's hands, stumbled and almost fell down. The ladies caught him and this time ran away, squealing and almost dragging Pavel Pavlovitch after them. Velchaninov did not follow them.

On the afternoon of the next day a very presentable-looking, middle-aged government clerk in uniform arrived at the Pogoryeltsevs' villa and politely handed Klavdia Petrovna an envelope addressed to her by Pavel Pavlovitch Trusotsky. In it was a letter enclosing three hundred roubles and the legal papers necessary for the burial. Pavel Pavlovitch wrote briefly, respectfully, and most properly. He warmly thanked Her Excellency for the kind sympathy she had shown for the little motherless girl, for which God alone could repay her. He wrote vaguely that extreme ill-health would prevent him from coming to arrange the funeral of his beloved and unhappy daughter, and he could only appeal to the angelic kindness of Her Excellency's heart. The three hundred roubles were, as he explained later in the letter, to pay for the funeral, and the expenses caused by the child's illness. If any of this money were left over he must humbly and respectfully beg that it might be spent on "a perpetual mass for the rest of the soul of the departed." The clerk who brought the letter could add nothing in explanation; it appeared, indeed, from what he said that it was only at Pavel Pavlovitch's earnest entreaty that he had undertaken to deliver the letter to Her Excellency. Pogoryeltsev was almost offended at the expression "the expenses caused by the child's illness," and after setting aside fifty roubles for the funeral—since it was impossible to prevent the father from paying for his child's burial—he proposed to send the remaining two hundred and fifty roubles back to M. Trusotsky at once. Klavdia Petrovna finally decided not to send back the two hundred and fifty roubles, but only a receipt from the cemetery church for that sum in payment for a perpetual mass for the repose of the soul of the deceased maiden Elizaveta. This receipt was afterwards given to Velchaninov to be despatched to Pavel Pavlovitch. Velchaninov posted it to his lodging.

After the funeral he left the villa. For a whole fortnight he wandered about the town aimless and alone, so lost in thought that he stumbled against people in the street. Sometimes he would lie stretched out on his sofa for days together, forgetting the commonest things of everyday life. Several times the Pogoryeltsevs went to ask him to go to them; he promised to go, but immediately forgot. Klavdia Petrovna even went herself to see him, but did not find him at home. The same thing happened to his lawyer; the lawyer had, indeed, something to tell him: his lawsuit had been very adroitly settled and his opponents had come to an amicable arrangement, agreeing to accept an insignificant fraction of the disputed inheritance. All that remained was to obtain Velchaninov's own consent. When at last he did find him at home, the lawyer was surprised at the apathy and indifference with which Velchaninov, once such a troublesome client, listened to his explanation.

The very hottest days of July had come, but Velchaninov was oblivious of time. His grief ached in his heart like a growing abscess, and he was distinctly conscious of it and every moment with agonizing acuteness. His chief suffering was the thought that, before Liza had had time to know him, she had died, not understanding with what anguish he loved her! The object in life of which he had had such a joyful glimpse had suddenly vanished into everlasting darkness. That object—he thought of it every moment now—was that Liza should be conscious of his love every day, every hour, all her life. "No one has a higher object and no one could have," he thought sometimes, with gloomy fervour. "If there are other objects none can be holier than that!" "By my love for Liza," he mused, "all my old putrid and useless life would be purified and expiated; to make up for my own idle, vicious and wasted life I would cherish and bring up that pure and exquisite creature, and for her sake everything would be forgiven me and I could forgive myself everything."

All these *conscious* thoughts always rose before his mind, together with the vivid, ever-present and ever-poignant memory of the dead child. He re-created for himself her little pale face, remembered every expression on it: he thought of her in the coffin decked with flowers, and as she had lain unconscious in fever, with fixed and open eyes. He suddenly remembered that when she was lying on the table he had noticed one of her fingers, which had somehow turned black during her illness; this had struck him so much at the time, and he had felt so sorry for that poor little finger, that for the first time he thought of seeking out Pavel Pavlovitch and killing him; until that time he had been "as though insensible." Was it wounded pride that had tortured her wounded heart, or was it those three months of suffering at the hands of her father, whose love had suddenly changed to hatred, who had insulted her with shameful words, laughing at her terror, and had abandoned her at last to strangers? All this he dwelt upon incessantly in a thousand variations. "Do you know what Liza has been to me?"—he suddenly recalled the drunkard's exclamation and felt that that exclamation was sincere, not a pose, and that there was love in it. "How could that monster be so cruel to a child whom he had loved so much, and is it credible?" But every time he made haste to dismiss that question and, as it were, brush it aside; there was something awful in that question, something he could not bear and could not solve.

One day, scarcely conscious where he was going, he wandered into the cemetery where Liza was buried and found her little grave. He had not been to the cemetery since the funeral; he had always fancied it would be too great an agony, and had been afraid to go. But, strange to say, when he had found her little grave and kissed it, his heart felt easier. It was a fine evening, the sun was setting; all round the graves the lush green grass was growing; the bees were humming in a wild rose close by; the flowers and wreaths left by the children and Klavdia Petrovna on Liza's grave were lying there with the petals half dropping. There was a gleam of something like hope in his heart after many days.

"How serene!" he thought, feeling the stillness of the cemetery, and looking at the clear, peaceful sky.

A rush of pure, calm faith flooded his soul.

"Liza has sent me this, it's Liza speaking to me," he thought.

It was quite dark when he left the cemetery and went home. Not far from the cemetery gates, in a low-pitched wooden house on the road, there was some sort of eating-house or tavern; through the windows he could see people sitting at the tables. It suddenly seemed to him that one of them close to the window was Pavel Pavlovitch, and that he saw him, too, and was staring at him inquisitively. He walked on, and soon heard some one pursuing him; Pavel Pavlovitch was, in fact, running after him; probably he had been attracted and encouraged by Velchaninov's conciliatory expression as he watched him from the window. On overtaking him he smiled timidly, but it was not his old drunken smile; he was actually not drunk.

"Good-evening," he said.
"Good-evening," answered Velchaninov.

Chapter 11

PAVEL PAVLOVITCH MEANS TO MARRY

As HE responded with this "Good-evening," he was surprised at himself. It struck him as extremely strange that he met this man now without a trace of anger, and that in his feeling for him at that moment there was something quite different, and actually, indeed, a sort of impulse towards something new.

"What an agreeable evening," observed Pavel Pavlovitch, looking into his face.

"You've not gone away yet," Velchaninov observed, not by way of a question, but simply making that reflection aloud as he walked on.

"Things have dragged on, but—I've obtained a post with an increase of salary. I shall be going away the day after to-morrow for certain."

"You've got a post?" he said this time, asking a question.

"Why shouldn't I?" Pavel Pavlovitch screwed up his face.

"Oh, I only asked . . ." Velchaninov said, disclaiming the insinuation, and, with a frown, he looked askance at Pavel Pavlovitch.

To his surprise, the attire, the hat with the crape band and the whole appearance of M. Trusotsky were incomparably more presentable than they had been a fortnight before.

"What was he sitting in that tavern for?" he kept wondering.

"I was intending, Alexey Ivanovitch, to communicate with you on a subject for rejoicing," Pavel Pavlovitch began again.

"Rejoicing?"

"I'm going to get married."

"What?"

"After sorrow comes rejoicing, so it is always in life; I should be so gratified, Alexey Ivanovitch, if . . . but—I don't know, perhaps you're in a hurry now, for you appear to be . . ."

"Yes, I am in a hurry . . . and I'm unwell too."

He felt a sudden and intense desire to get rid of him; his readiness for some new feeling had vanished in a flash.

"I should have liked . . ."

Pavel Pavlovitch did not say what he would have liked; Velchaninov was silent.

"In that case it must be later on, if only we meet again . . ."

"Yes, yes, later on," Velchaninov muttered rapidly, without stopping or looking at him.

They were both silent again for a minute; Pavel Pavlovitch went on walking beside him.

"In that case, good-bye till we meet again," Pavel Pavlovitch brought out at last.

"Good-bye; I hope . . ."

Velchaninov returned home thoroughly upset again. Contact with "that man" was too much for him. As he got into bed he asked himself again: "Why was he at the cemetery?"

Next morning he made up his mind to go to the Pogoryeltsevs. He made up his mind to go reluctantly; sympathy from any one, even from the Pogoryeltsevs, was too irksome for him now. But they were so anxious about him that he felt absolutely obliged to go. He suddenly had a foreboding that he would feel horribly ashamed at their first meeting again.

Should he go or not, he thought, as he made haste to finish his breakfast; when, to his intense amazement, Pavel Pavlovitch walked in.

In spite of their meeting the day before Velchaninov could never have conceived that the man would come to see him again, and was so taken aback that he stared at him and did not know what to say. But Pavel Pavlovitch was equal to the occasion. He greeted him, and sat down on the very same chair on which he had sat on his last visit. Velchaninov had a sudden and peculiarly vivid memory of that visit, and gazed uneasily and with repulsion at his visitor.

"You're surprised?" began Pavel Pavlovitch, interpreting Velchaninov's expression.

He seemed altogether much more free and easy than on the previous day, and at the same time it could be detected that he was more nervous than he had been then. His appearance was particularly curious. M. Trusotsky was not only presentably but quite foppishly dressed— in a light summer jacket, light-coloured trousers of a smart, close-fitting cut, a light waistcoat; gloves, a gold lorgnette, which he had suddenly adopted for some reason. His linen was irreproachable; he even smelt of scent. About his whole get-up there was something ridiculous, and at the same time strangely and unpleasantly suggestive.

"Of course, Alexey Ivanovitch," he went on, wriggling, "I'm surprising you by coming, and I'm sensible of it. But there is always, so I imagine, preserved between people, and to my mind there should be preserved, something higher, shouldn't there? Higher, I mean, than all the conditions and even unpleasantnesses that may come to pass. . . . Shouldn't there?"

"Pavel Pavlovitch, say what you have to say quickly, and without ceremony," said Velchaninov, frowning.

"In a couple of words," Pavel Pavlovitch began hastily, "I'm going to get married and I am just setting off to see my future bride. They are in a summer villa too. I should like to have the great honour to make bold to introduce you to the family, and have come to ask an unusual favour," (Pavel Pavlovitch bent his head humbly) "to beg you to accompany me. . . ."

"Accompany you, where?" Velchaninov stared with open eyes.

"To them, that is, to their villa. Forgive me, I am talking as though in a fever, and perhaps I've not been clear; but I'm so afraid of your declining."

And he looked plaintively at Velchaninov.

"Do you want me to go with you now to see your future bride?" Velchaninov repeated, scrutinizing him rapidly, unable to believe his eyes or ears.

"Yes," said Pavel Pavlovitch, extremely abashed. "Don't be angry, Alexey Ivanovitch. It's not impudence; I only beg you most humbly as a great favour. I had dreamed that you might not like, that being so, to refuse. . . ."

"To begin with, it's utterly out of the question." Velchaninov turned round uneasily.

"It is merely an intense desire on my part and nothing more," Pavel Pavlovitch went on, imploring him. "I will not conceal, either, that there are reasons for it, but I should have preferred not to have revealed them till later, and for the present to confine myself to the very earnest request. . . ."

And he positively got up from his seat to show his deference.

"But in any case it is quite impossible, you must admit that yourself. . . ."

Velchaninov, too, stood up.

"It is quite possible, Alexey Ivanovitch. I was proposing to present you as a friend; and besides, you are an acquaintance of theirs already; you see, it's to Zahlebinin's, to his villa. The civil councillor, Zahlebinin."

"What?" cried Velchaninov.

It was the civil councillor for whom he had been constantly looking for a month before, and had never found at home. He had, as it turned out, been acting in the interests of the other side.

"Yes, yes; yes, yes," said Pavel Pavlovitch, smiling and seeming to be greatly encouraged by Velchaninov's great astonishment; "the very man, you remember, whom you were walking beside, and talking to, while I stood opposite watching you; I was waiting to go up to him when you had finished. Twenty years ago we were in the same office, and that day, when I meant to go up to him after you had finished, I had no idea of the sort. It occurred to me suddenly, only a week ago."

"But, upon my word, they are quite a decent family," said Velchaninov, in naïve surprise.

"Well, what then, if they are?" Pavel Pavlovitch grimaced.

"No, of course, I didn't mean . . . only as far as I've observed when I was there . . ."

"They remember, they remember your being there," Pavel Pavlovitch put in joyfully; "only you couldn't have seen the family then; but he remembers you and has a great esteem for you. We talked of you with great respect."

"But when you've only been a widower three months?"

"But you see the wedding will not be at once; the wedding will be in nine or ten months, so that the year of mourning will be over. I assure you that everything is all right. To begin with, Fedosey Petrovitch has known me from a boy; he knew my late wife; he knows my style of living, and what people think of me, and what's more, I have property, and I'm receiving a post with increase of salary—so all that has weight."

"Why, is it his daughter?"

"I will tell you all about it." Pavel Pavlovitch wriggled ingratiatingly. "Allow me to light a cigarette. And you'll see her yourself to-day too. To begin with, such capable men as Fedosey Petrovitch are sometimes very highly thought of here in Petersburg, if they succeed in attracting notice. But you know, apart from his salary and the additional and supplementary fees, bonuses, hotel expenses, and moneys given in relief, he has nothing—that is, nothing substantial that could be called a capital. They are comfortably off, but there is no possibility of saving where there's a family. Only imagine: Fedosey Petrovitch has eight girls, and only one son, still a child. If he were to die to-morrow there would be nothing left but a niggardly pension. And eight girls! just imagine—only imagine—what it must run into simply for their shoes! Of these eight girls five are grown up, the

eldest is four-and-twenty (a most charming young lady, as you will
see) and the sixth, a girl of fifteen, is still at the high school. Of course,
husbands must be found for the five elder ones, and that ought to be
done in good time, as far as possible, so their father ought to bring
them out, and what do you suppose that will cost? And then I turn
up, the first suitor they have had in the house, and one they know all
about, that I really have property, I mean. Well, that's all."

Pavel Pavlovitch explained with fervour.

"You're engaged to the eldest?"

"N-no, I . . . no, not to the eldest; you see, I'm proposing for the
sixth, the one who is still at the high school."

"What?" said Velchaninov, with an involuntary smile. "Why, you
say she's only fifteen!"

"Fifteen now; but in nine months she'll be sixteen, she'll be sixteen
and three months, so what of it? But as it would be improper at
present, there will be no open engagement but only an understanding
with the parents. . . . I assure you that everything is all right!"

"Then it's not settled yet?"

"Yes, it is settled, it's all settled. I assure you, all is as it should be."

"And does she know?"

"Well, it's only in appearance, for the sake of propriety, that they
are not telling her; of course she knows." Pavel Pavlovitch screwed
up his eyes insinuatingly. "Well, do you congratulate me, Alexey
Ivanovitch?" Pavel Pavlovitch concluded very timidly.

"But what should I go there for? However," he added hurriedly,
"since I'm not going in any case, don't trouble to find a reason."

"Alexey Ivanovitch . . ."

"But do you expect me to get in beside you and drive off there with
you? Think of it!"

The feeling of disgust and aversion came back after the momentary
distraction of Pavel Pavlovitch's chatter about his future bride. In another minute he would have turned him out. He even felt angry with
himself for some reason.

"Do, Alexey Ivanovitch, do, and you won't regret it!" Pavel Pavlovitch implored him in a voice fraught with feeling. "No, no, no!"—
he waved his hands, catching an impatient and determined gesture
from Velchaninov. "Alexey Ivanovitch, Alexey Ivanovitch, wait a bit
before you decide! I see that you have perhaps misunderstood me. Of
course, I know only too well that you cannot be to me, nor I to you
. . . that we're not comrades; I am not so absurd as not to understand
that. And that the favour I'm asking of you will not pledge you to

anything in the future. And, indeed, I'm going away after to-morrow altogether, absolutely; just as though nothing had happened. Let this day be a solitary exception. I have come to you resting my hopes on the generosity of the special feelings of your heart, Alexey Ivanovitch —those feelings which might of late have been awakened . . . I think I'm speaking clearly, am I not?"

Pavel Pavlovitch's agitation reached an extreme point. Velchaninov looked at him strangely.

"You ask for some service from me?" he questioned, hesitatingly, "and are very insistent about it. That strikes me as suspicious; I should like to know more about it."

"The only service is that you should come with me. And afterwards, on our way back, I will unfold all to you as though at confession. Alexey Ivanovitch, believe me!"

But Velchaninov still refused, and the more stubbornly because he was conscious of an oppressive and malignant impulse. This evil impulse had been faintly stirring within him from the very beginning, ever since Pavel Pavlovitch had talked of his future bride: whether it was simply curiosity, or some other quite obscure prompting, he felt tempted to consent. And the more he felt tempted, the more he resisted. He sat with his elbow on one hand, and hesitated.

Pavel Pavlovitch beside him kept coaxing and persuading.

"Very good, I'll come," he consented all at once, uneasily and almost apprehensively, getting up from his seat.

Pavel Pavlovitch was extremely delighted.

"But, Alexey Ivanovitch, you must change your clothes now," Pavel Pavlovitch cajoled him, hanging gleefully about him; "put on your best suit."

"And why must he meddle in this, too, strange fellow?" Velchaninov thought to himself.

"This is not the only service I'm expecting of you, Alexey Ivanovitch. Since you have given your consent, please be my adviser."

"In what, for example?"

"The great question, for instance, of crape. Which would be more proper, to remove the crape, or keep it on?"

"As you prefer."

"No, I want you to decide; what would you do yourself in my place, that is, if you had crape on your hat? My own idea is that, if I retain it, it points to the constancy of my feelings, and so is a flattering recommendation."

"Take it off, of course."

"Do you really think it's a matter of course?" Pavel Pavlovitch hesitated. "No, I think I had better keep it. . . ."

"As you like."

"He doesn't trust me, that's a good thing," thought Velchaninov.

They went out; Pavel Pavlovitch gazed with satisfaction at Velchaninov's smartened appearance; his countenance seemed to betray an even greater degree of deference and of dignity! Velchaninov wondered at him and even more at himself. A very good carriage stood waiting for them at the gate.

"So you had a carriage all ready too? So you felt sure I should come?"

"I engaged the carriage for myself, but I did feel confident that you would consent to accompany me," Pavel Pavlovitch replied, with the air of a perfectly happy man.

"Ah, Pavel Pavlovitch," Velchaninov said, laughing as it were irritably when they were in the carriage and had set off, "weren't you too sure of me?"

"But it's not for you, Alexey Ivanovitch, it's not for you to tell me that I'm a fool for it," Pavel Pavlovitch responded, in a voice full of feeling.

"And Liza," thought Velchaninov, and at once hastened to dismiss the thought of her as though afraid of sacrilege. And it suddenly seemed to him that he was so petty, so insignificant at that moment; it struck him that the thought that had tempted him was a thought so small and nasty . . . and he longed again, at all costs, to fling it all up, and to get out of the carriage at once, even if he had to thrash Pavel Pavlovitch. But the latter began talking and the temptation mastered his heart again.

"Alexey Ivanovitch, do you know anything about jewels?"

"What sort of jewels?"

"Diamonds."

"Yes."

"I should like to take a little present. Advise me, should I or not?"

"I think you shouldn't."

"But I feel I should so like to," returned Pavel Pavlovitch, "only, what am I to buy? A whole set, that is, a brooch, earrings, bracelets, or simply one article?"

"How much do you want to spend?"

"About four hundred or five hundred roubles?"

"Ough!"

"Is it too much, or what?" asked Pavel Pavlovitch in a flutter.

"Buy a single bracelet for a hundred roubles."

Pavel Pavlovitch was positively mortified; he was so eager to spend more and buy a "whole set" of jewels. He persisted. They drove to a shop. It ended, however, in his only buying a bracelet, and not the one that he wanted to, but the one that Velchaninov fixed upon. Pavel Pavlovitch wanted to take both. When the jeweller, who had asked a hundred and seventy-five roubles for the bracelet, consented to take a hundred and fifty for it, Pavel Pavlovitch was positively vexed; he would have paid two hundred if that sum had been asked, he was so eager to spend more.

"It doesn't matter, does it, my being in a hurry with presents?" he gushed blissfully, when they had set off again. "They're not grand people, they are very simple. The innocent creatures are fond of little presents," he said, with a sly and good-humoured grin. "You smiled just now, Alexey Ivanovitch, when you heard she was fifteen; but that's just what bowled me over; that she was still going to school with the satchel on her arm full of copy books and pens, he—he! That satchel fascinated me! It's innocence that charms me, Alexey Ivanovitch; it's not so much beauty of face, it's that. She giggles in the corner with her school friend, and how she laughs, my goodness! And what at? It's all because the kitten jumped off the chest of drawers on to the bed and was curled up like a little ball. . . . And then there's that scent of fresh apples! Shall I take off the crape?"

"As you please."

"I will take it off."

He took off his hat, tore off the crape and flung it in the road. Velchaninov saw that his face was beaming with the brightest hopes, as he replaced his hat upon his bald head.

"Can it be that he is really like this?" he thought, feeling genuinely angry; "can it be there isn't some trick in his inviting me? Can he be really reckoning on my generosity?" he went on, almost offended at the last supposition. "What is he—a buffoon, a fool, or the 'eternal husband'—but it's impossible!"

Chapter 12

AT THE ZAHLEBININS'

THE Zahlebinins were really a "very decent family," as Velchaninov had expressed it, and Zahlebinin himself had an assured position in a government office and was well thought of by his superiors. All that Pavel Pavlovitch had said about their income was true too: "They live very comfortably, but if he dies there'll be nothing left."

Old Zahlebinin gave Velchaninov a warm and affable welcome, and his former "foe" seemed quite like a friend.

"I congratulate you, it was better so," he began at the first word, with a pleasant and dignified air. "I was in favour of settling it out of court myself and Pyotr Karlovitch (Velchaninov's lawyer) is priceless in such cases. Well, you get sixty thousand without any bother, without delay and dispute! And the case might have dragged on for three years!"

Velchaninov was at once presented to Madame Zahlebinin, an elderly lady of redundant figure, with a very simple and tired-looking face. The young ladies, too, began to sail in one after the other, or in couples. But a very great many young ladies made their appearance; by degrees they gathered to the number of ten or twelve—Velchaninov lost count of them; some came in, others went out. But among them several were girl friends from the neighbouring villas. The Zahlebinins' villa, a large wooden house, built in quaint and whimsical style, with parts added at different periods, had the advantage of a big garden; but three or four other villas looked into the garden on different sides, and it was common property, an arrangement which naturally led to friendly relations among the girls of the different households. From the first words of conversation Velchaninov observed that he was expected, and that his arrival in the character of a friend of Pavel Pavlovitch, anxious to make their acquaintance, was hailed almost triumphantly.

His keen and experienced eye quickly detected something special; from the over-cordial welcome of the parents, from a certain peculiar look about the girls and their get-up (though, indeed, it was a holiday), from all that, the suspicion dawned upon him that Pavel Pavlovitch had been scheming and, very possibly, without, of course, saying it in so many words, had been suggesting a conception of him as a bachelor

of property and of the "best society," who was suffering from ennui
and very, very likely to make up his mind to "change his state and
settle down," especially as he had just come into a fortune. The manner
and the appearance of the eldest Mademoiselle Zahlebinin, Katerina
Fedosyevna, the one who was twenty-four and who had been described
by Pavel Pavlovitch as a charming person, struck him as being in keeping with that idea. She was distinguished from her sisters by her dress
and the original way in which her luxuriant hair was done. Her sisters
and the other girls all looked as though they were firmly convinced
that Velchaninov was making their acquaintance "on Katya's account"
and had come "to have a look at her." Their glances and even some
words, dropped in the course of the day, confirmed him in this surmise. Katerina Fedosyevna was a tall blonde of generous proportions,
with an exceedingly sweet face, of a gentle, unenterprising, even torpid
character. "Strange that a girl like that should still be on hand," Velchaninov could not help thinking, watching her with pleasure. "Of
course, she has no dowry and she'll soon grow too fat, but meantime
lots of men would admire her. . . ." All the other sisters, too, were
nice-looking, and among their friends there were several amusing and
even pretty faces. It began to divert him; he had come, moreover, with
special ideas.

Nadyezhda Fedosyevna, the sixth, the schoolgirl and Pavel Pavlovitch's bride-elect, did not appear till later. Velchaninov awaited her
coming with an impatience which surprised him and made him laugh
at himself. At last she made her entrance, and not without effect,
accompanied by a lively, keen-witted girl friend, a brunette with a
comical face whose name was Marie Nikititchna, and of whom, as
was at once apparent, Pavel Pavlovitch stood in great dread. This
Marie Nikititchna, a girl of twenty-three, with a mocking tongue and
really clever, was a nursery governess in a friend's family. She had
long been accepted by the Zahlebinins as one of themselves and was
thought a great deal of by the girls. It was evident that Nadya found
her indispensable now. Velchaninov discerned at once that all the girls
were antagonistic to Pavel Pavlovitch, even the friends, and two minutes after Nadya's arrival he had made up his mind that she *detested*
him. He observed, too, that Pavel Pavlovitch either failed to notice this
or refused to.

Nadya was unquestionably the handsomest of the lot—a little brunette with a wild, untamed look and the boldness of a nihilist; a
roguish imp with blazing eyes, with a charming but often malicious
smile, with wonderful lips and teeth, slender and graceful, her face

still child-like but glowing with the dawn of thought. Her age was evident in every step she took, in every word she uttered. It appeared afterwards that Pavel Pavlovitch did see her for the first time with an American leather satchel on her arm, but this time she had not got it.

The presentation of the bracelet was a complete failure, and, indeed, made an unpleasant impression. As soon as Pavel Pavlovitch saw his "future bride" come into the room he went up to her with a smirk. He presented it as a testimony "of the agreeable gratification he had experienced on his previous visit on the occasion of the charming song sung by Nadyezhda Fedosyevna at the piano. . . ." He stammered, could not finish, and stood helpless, holding out the case with the bracelet and thrusting it into the hand of Nadyezhda Fedosyevna, who did not want to take it, and, crimson with shame and anger, drew back her hands. She turned rudely to her mother, whose face betrayed embarrassment, and said aloud:

"I don't want to take it, *maman!*"

"Take it and say thank you," said her father, with calm severity: but he, too, was displeased. "Unnecessary, quite unnecessary!" he muttered reprovingly to Pavel Pavlovitch.

Nadya, seeing there was no help for it, took the case and, dropping her eyes, curtsied, as tiny children curtsey—that is, suddenly bobbed down, and popped up again as though on springs. One of her sisters went up to look at it and Nadya handed her the case unopened, showing, for her part, that she did not care to look at it. The bracelet was taken out and passed from one to the other; but they all looked at it in silence, and some even sarcastically. Only the mother murmured that the bracelet was very charming. Pavel Pavlovitch was ready to sink into the earth.

Velchaninov came to the rescue.

He began talking, loudly and eagerly, about the first thing that occurred to him, and before five minutes were over he had gained the attention of every one in the drawing-room. He was a brilliant master of the art of small talk—that is, the art of seeming perfectly frank and at the same time appearing to consider his listeners as frank as himself. He could, with perfect naturalness, appear when necessary to be the most light-hearted and happy of men. He was very clever, too, in slipping in a witty remark, a jibe, a gay insinuation or an amusing pun, always as it were accidentally and as though unconscious of doing it— though the epigram or pun and the whole conversation, perhaps, had been prepared and rehearsed long, long before and even used on more than one previous occasion. But at the present moment nature and art were at one, he felt that he was in the mood and that something was drawing him on; he felt the most absolute confidence in himself and knew that in a few minutes all these eyes would be turned upon him, all these people would be listening only to him, talking to no one but him, and laughing only at what he said. And, in fact, the laughter soon came, by degrees the others joined in the conversation—and he was exceedingly clever in making other people talk—three or four voices could be heard at once. The bored and weary face of Madame Zahlebinin was lighted up almost with joy; it was the same with Katerina Fedosyevna, who gazed and listened as though enchanted. Nadya watched him keenly from under her brows; it was evident that she was prejudiced against him. This spurred him on the more. The "mischievous" Marie Nikititchna succeeded in getting in rather a good thrust at him; she asserted quite fictitiously that Pavel Pavlovitch had introduced him as the friend of his boyhood, so putting with obvious intent at least seven years on to his age. But even the malicious Marie Nikititchna liked him. Pavel Pavlovitch was completely nonplussed. He had, of course, some idea of his friend's abilities and at first was delighted at his success; he tittered himself and joined in the conversation; but by degrees he seemed to sink into thoughtfulness, and finally into positive dejection, which was clearly apparent in his troubled countenance.

"Well, you're a visitor who doesn't need entertaining," old Zahlebinin commented gaily, as he got up to go upstairs to his own room, where, in spite of the holiday, he had some business papers awaiting his revision; "and, only fancy, I thought of you as the most gloomy, hypochondriacal of young men. What mistakes one makes!"

They had a piano; Velchaninov asked who played, and suddenly turned to Nadya:

"I believe you sing?"

"Who told you?" Nadya snapped out.

"Pavel Pavlovitch told me just now."

"It's not true. I only sing for fun. I've no voice."

"And I've no voice either, but I sing."

"Then you'll sing to us? Well, then, I'll sing to you," said Nadya, her eyes gleaming; "only not now, but after dinner. I can't endure music," she added. "I'm sick of the piano: they're all singing and playing from morning to night here—Katya's the only one worth hearing."

Velchaninov at once took this up, and it appeared that Katerina Fedosyevna was the only one who played the piano seriously. He at once begged her to play. Every one was evidently pleased at his addressing Katya, and the mamma positively flushed crimson with gratification. Katerina Fedosyevna got up, smiling, and went to the piano, and suddenly, to her own surprise, she flushed crimson and was horribly abashed that she, such a big girl, four-and-twenty and so stout, should be blushing like a child—and all this was written clearly on her face as she sat down to play. She played something from Haydn and played it carefully though without expression, but she was shy. When she had finished Velchaninov began warmly praising to her, not her playing but Haydn, and especially the little thing which she had played, and she was evidently so pleased and listened so gratefully and happily to his praises, not of herself but of Haydn, that he could not help looking at her with more friendliness and attention: "Ah, but you are a dear!" was reflected in the gleam of his eye—and every one seemed instantly to understand that look, especially Katerina Fedosyevna herself.

"You have a delightful garden," he said, suddenly addressing the company and looking towards the glass door that led on to the balcony. "What do you say to our all going into the garden?"

"Let us, let us!" they shrieked joyfully, as though he had guessed the general wish.

They walked in the garden till dinner-time. Madame Zahlebinin, though she had been longing to have a nap, could not resist going out with them, but wisely sat down to rest on the verandah, where she at once began to doze. In the garden Velchaninov and the girls got on to still more friendly terms. He noticed that several very young men from the villas joined them; one was a student and another simply a high school boy. They promptly made a dash each for *his* girl, and it was evident that they had come on their account; the third, a very morose and dishevelled-looking youth of twenty, in huge blue spectacles, began, with a frown, whispering hurriedly with Marie Nikititchna and Nadya. He scanned Velchaninov sternly, and seemed to consider it incumbent upon himself to treat him with extraordinary contempt. Some of the girls suggested that they should play games. To Velchaninov's question, what games they played, they said all sorts of games, and catch-catch, but in the evening they would play proverbs—that is, all would sit down and one would go out, the others choose a proverb—for instance: "More haste, less speed," and when the one outside is called in, each in turn has to say one sentence to him. One, for instance, must say a sentence in which there is the word "more," the second, one in which there is the word "haste," and so on. And from their sentences he must guess the proverb.

"That must be very amusing," said Velchaninov.

"Oh, no, it's awfully boring," cried two or three voices at once.

"Or else we play at acting," Nadya observed, suddenly addressing him. "Do you see that thick tree, round which there's a seat: behind that tree is behind the scenes, and there the actors sit, say a king, a queen, a princess, a young man—just as any one likes; each one enters when he chooses and says anything that comes into his head, and that's the game."

"But that's delightful!" Velchaninov repeated again.

"Oh, no, it's awfully dull! At first it did turn out amusing, but lately it's always been senseless, for no one knows how to end it; perhaps with you, though, it will be more interesting. We did think you were a friend of Pavel Pavlovitch's, though, but it seems he was only bragging. I'm very glad you have come . . . for one thing. . . ."

She looked very earnestly and impressively at Velchaninov and at once walked away to Marie Nikititchna.

"We're going to play proverbs this evening," one of the girl friends whom Velchaninov had scarcely noticed before, and with whom he had not exchanged a word, whispered to him confidentially. "They're all going to make fun of Pavel Pavlovitch, and you will too, of course."

"Ah, how nice it is that you've come, we were all so dull," observed another girl in a friendly way. She was a red-haired girl with freckles, and a face absurdly flushed from walking and the heat. Goodness knows where she had sprung from; Velchaninov had not noticed her till then.

Pavel Pavlovitch's uneasiness grew more and more marked. In the garden Velchaninov made great friends with Nadya. She no longer looked at him from under her brows as she had at first; she seemed to have laid aside her critical attitude towards him, and laughed, skipped about, shrieked, and twice even seized him by the hand; she was extremely happy, she continued to take not the slightest notice of Pavel Pavlovitch, and behaved as though she were not aware of his existence. Velchaninov felt certain that there was an actual plot against Pavel Pavlovitch; Nadya and the crowd of girls drew Velchaninov aside, while some of the other girl friends lured Pavel Pavlovitch on various pretexts in another direction; but the latter broke away from them, and ran full speed straight to them—that is, to Velchaninov and Nadya, and suddenly thrust his bald head in between them with uneasy curiosity. He hardly attempted to restrain himself; the naïveté of his gestures and actions were sometimes amazing. He could not resist trying once more to turn Velchaninov's attention to Katerina Fedosyevna; it was clear to her now that he had not come on her account, but was much more interested in Nadya; but her expression was just as sweet and good-humoured as ever. She seemed to be happy simply at being beside them and listening to what their new visitor was saying; she, poor thing, could never keep up her share in a conversation cleverly.

"What a darling your sister Katerina Fedosyevna is!" Velchaninov said aside to Nadya.

"Katya! No one could have a kinder heart than she has. She's an angel to all of us. I adore her," the girl responded enthusiastically.

At last dinner came at five o'clock; and it was evident that the dinner, too, was not an ordinary meal, but had been prepared expressly for visitors. There were two or three very elaborate dishes, which evidently were not part of their ordinary fare, one of them so strange that no one could find a name for it. In addition to the everyday wine there was a bottle of Tokay, obviously for the benefit of the visitors; at the end of dinner champagne was brought in for some reason. Old Zahlebinin took an extra glass, became extraordinarily good-humoured and ready to laugh at anything Velchaninov said.

In the end Pavel Pavlovitch could not restrain himself. Carried away by the spirit of rivalry he suddenly attempted to make a pun too; at the end of the table, where he was sitting by Madame Zahlebinin, there was a sudden roar of loud laughter from the delighted girls.

"Papa, Papa! Pavel Pavlovitch has made a pun too," the fourth and fifth Zahlebinin girls shouted in unison. "He says we're 'damsels who dazzle all. . . .'"

"Ah, so he's punning too! Well, what was his pun?" the old man responded sedately, turning patronizingly to Pavel Pavlovitch and smiling in readiness for the expected pun.

"Why, he says we're 'damsels who dazzle all.'"

"Y-yes, well, and what then?" The old man did not understand and smiled more good-humouredly in expectation.

"Oh, Papa, how tiresome you are; you don't understand. Why, 'damsels' and then 'dazzle'; 'damsel' is like 'dazzle,' 'damsels who dazzle all. . . .'"

"A-a-ah," the old man drawled in a puzzled voice. "H'm, well, he'll make a better one next time!"

And the old man laughed good-humouredly.

"Pavel Pavlovitch, you can't have all the perfections at once," Marie

Nikititchna jerked aloud. "Oh, my goodness! he's got a bone in his throat," she exclaimed, jumping up from her chair.

There was a positive hubbub, but that was just what Marie Nikititchna wanted. Pavel Pavlovitch had simply choked over the wine which he was sipping to cover his confusion, but Marie Nikititchna vowed and declared that it was a "fish bone," that she had seen it herself and that people sometimes died of it.

"Slap him on the nape of the neck," some one shouted.

"Yes, really that's the best thing to do!" the old man approved aloud.

Eager volunteers were already at him; Marie Nikititchna and the red-haired girl (who had also been invited to dinner), and, finally, the mamma herself, greatly alarmed; every one wanted to slap Pavel Pavlovitch on the back. Jumping up from the table, Pavel Pavlovitch wriggled away and was for a full minute asseverating that he had swallowed his wine too quickly and that the cough would soon be over, while the others realized that it was all a trick of Marie Nikititchna's.

"But, really, you tease . . . !" Madame Zahlebinin tried to say sternly to Marie Nikititchna: but she broke down and laughed as she very rarely did, and that made quite a sensation of a sort.

After dinner they all went out on the verandah to drink coffee.

"And what lovely days we're having!" said the old man, looking with pleasure into the garden, and serenely admiring the beauties of nature. "If only we could have some rain. Enjoy yourselves and God bless you! And you enjoy yourself too," he added, patting Pavel Pavlovitch on the shoulder as he went out.

When they had all gone out into the garden again, Pavel Pavlovitch suddenly ran up to Velchaninov and pulled him by the sleeve.

"Just one minute," he whispered impatiently.

They turned into a lonely side path.

"No, in this case, excuse me, no, I won't give up . . ." he stuttered in a furious whisper, clutching Velchaninov's arm.

"What? what?" Velchaninov asked, opening his eyes in amazement.

Pavel Pavlovitch stared at him mutely, his lips moved, and he smiled furiously.

"Where are you going? Where are you? Everything's ready," they heard the ringing, impatient voices of the girls.

Velchaninov shrugged his shoulders and returned to the rest of the party.

Pavel Pavlovitch, too, ran after him.

"I'll bet he asked you for a handkerchief," said Marie Nikititchna; "he forgot one last time too."

"He'll always forget it!" the fifth Zahlebinin girl put in.

"He's forgotten his handkerchief, Pavel Pavlovitch has forgotten his handkerchief, Mamma, Pavel Pavlovitch has forgotten his pocket-handkerchief, Mamma, Pavel Pavlovitch has a cold in his head again!" cried voices.

"Then why doesn't he say so! You do stand on ceremony, Pavel Pavlovitch!" Madame Zahlebinin drawled in a sing-song voice. "It's dangerous to trifle with a cold; I'll send you a handkerchief directly. And why has he always got a cold in his head?" she added, as she moved away, glad of an excuse for returning home.

"I have two pocket-handkerchiefs and I haven't a cold in my head!" Pavel Pavlovitch called after her, but the lady apparently did not grasp what he said, and a minute later, when Pavel Pavlovitch was ambling after the others, keeping near Velchaninov and Nadya, a breathless maidservant overtook him and brought him a handkerchief.

"Proverbs, a game of proverbs," the girls shouted on all sides, as though they expected something wonderful from "a game of proverbs."

They fixed on a place and sat down on a seat; it fell to Marie Nikititchna's lot to guess; they insisted that she should go as far away as possible and not listen; in her absence they chose a proverb and distributed the words. Marie Nikititchna returned and guessed the proverb at once. The proverb was: "It's no use meeting troubles half-way."

Marie Nikititchna was followed by the young man with dishevelled hair and blue spectacles. They insisted on even greater precautions with him—he had to stand in the arbour and keep his face to the fence. The gloomy young man did what was required of him contemptuously, and seemed to feel morally degraded by it. When he was called he could guess nothing, he went the round of all of them and listened to what they said twice over, spent a long time in gloomy meditation, but nothing came of it. They put him to shame. The proverb was: "To pray to God and serve the Czar ne'er fail of their reward."

"And the proverb's disgusting!" the exasperated young man exclaimed indignantly, as he retreated to his place.

"Oh, how dull it is!" cried voices.

Velchaninov went out; he was hidden even further off; he, too, failed to guess.

"Oh, how dull it is!" more voices cried.

"Well, now, I'll go out," said Nadya.

"No, no, let Pavel Pavlovitch go out now, it's Pavel Pavlovitch's turn," they all shouted, growing more animated.

Pavel Pavlovitch was led away, right up to the fence in the very corner, and made to stand facing it, and that he might not look round, the red-haired girl was sent to keep watch on him. Pavel Pavlovitch, who had regained his confidence and almost his cheerfulness, was determined to do his duty properly and stood stock-still, gazing at the fence and not daring to turn round. The red-haired girl stood on guard twenty paces behind him nearer to the party in the arbour, and she exchanged signals with the girls in some excitement; it was evident that all were expecting something with trepidation; something was on foot. Suddenly the red-haired girl waved her arms as a signal to the arbour. Instantly they all jumped up and ran off at breakneck speed.

"Run, you run, too," a dozen voices whispered to Velchaninov, almost with horror at his not running.

"What's the matter? What has happened?" he asked, hurrying after them.

"Hush, don't shout! Let him stand there staring at the fence while we all run away. See, Nastya is running."

The red-haired girl (Nastya) was running at breakneck speed, waving her hands as though something extraordinary had happened. They all ran at last to the other side of the pond, the very opposite corner of the garden. When Velchaninov had got there he saw that Katerina Fedosyevna was hotly disputing with the others, especially with Nadya and Marie Nikititchna.

"Katya, darling, don't be angry!" said Nadya, kissing her.

"Very well, I won't tell Mamma, but I shall go away myself, for it's very horrid. What must he be feeling at the fence there, poor man!"

She went away—from pity—but all the others were merciless and as ruthless as before. They all insisted sternly that when Pavel Pavlovitch came back, Velchaninov should take no notice of him, as though nothing had happened.

"And let us all play catch-catch!" cried the red-haired girl ecstatically.

It was at least a quarter of an hour before Pavel Pavlovitch rejoined the party. For two-thirds of that time he had certainly been standing at the fence. The game was in full swing, and was a great success—everybody was shouting and merry. Frantic with rage, Pavel Pavlovitch went straight up to Velchaninov and pulled at his sleeve again.

"Just half a minute!"

"Good gracious, what does he want with his half-minutes!"

"He's borrowing a handkerchief again," was shouted after him once more.

"Well, this time it was you; now it's all your doing. . . ."

Pavel Pavlovitch's teeth chattered as he said this.

Velchaninov interrupted him, and mildly advised him to be livelier, or they would go on teasing him. "They tease you because you are cross when all the rest are enjoying themselves." To his surprise, these words of advice made a great impression on Pavel Pavlovitch; he subsided at once—so much so, in fact, that he went back to the party with a penitent air and submissively took his place in the game; after which they left him alone and treated him like the rest—and before half an hour had passed he had almost regained his spirits. In all the games when he had to choose a partner he picked out by preference the red-haired traitress, or one of the Zahlebinin sisters. But to his still greater surprise Velchaninov noticed that Pavel Pavlovitch did not dare try to speak to Nadya, although he continually hovered about her. At any rate he accepted his position, as an object of scorn and neglect to her, as though it were a fitting and natural thing. But towards the end they played a prank upon him again.

The game was "hide-and-seek." The one who hid, however, was allowed to run anywhere in the part of the garden allotted him. Pavel Pavlovitch, who had succeeded in concealing himself completely in some thick bushes, conceived the idea of running out and making a bolt for the house. He was seen and shouts were raised; he crept hurriedly upstairs to the first floor, knowing of a place behind a chest of drawers where he could hide. But the red-haired girl flew up after him, crept on tiptoe to the door and turned the key on him. All left off playing and ran just as they had done before to the other side of the pond, at the further end of the garden. Ten minutes later, Pavel Pavlovitch, becoming aware that no one was looking for him, peeped out of the window. There was no one to be seen. He did not dare to call out for fear of waking the parents; the maids had been sternly forbidden to answer Pavel Pavlovitch's call or go to him. Katerina Fedosyevna might have unlocked him, but, returning to her room and sitting down to dream a little, she had unexpectedly fallen asleep too. And so he stayed there about an hour. At last the girls came, as it were by chance, in twos or threes.

"Pavel Pavlovitch, why don't you come out to us? Oh, it has been fun! We've been playing at acting. Alexey Ivanovitch has been acting 'a young man.'"

"Pavel Pavlovitch, why don't you come, we want to admire you!" others observed as they passed.

"Admire what now?" they suddenly heard the voice of Madame Zahlebinin, who had only just woken up and made up her mind to come out into the garden and watch the "children's" games while waiting for tea.

"But here's Pavel Pavlovitch," they told her, pointing to the window where Pavel Pavlovitch's face, pale with anger, looked out with a wry smile.

"It's an odd fancy for a man to sit alone, when you're all enjoying yourselves!" said the mamma, shaking her head.

Meanwhile, Nadya had deigned to give Velchaninov an explanation of her words that she "was glad he had come for one reason."

The explanation took place in a secluded avenue. Marie Nikititchna purposely summoned Velchaninov, who was taking part in some game and was horribly bored, and left him alone in the avenue with Nadya.

"I am absolutely convinced," she said boldly, in a rapid patter, "that you are not such a great friend of Pavel Pavlovitch's as he boasted you were. I am reckoning on you as the one person who can do me a very great service." She took the case out of her pocket. "I humbly beg you to give this back to him at once, as I shall never speak to him again in my life. You can say so from me, and tell him not to dare to force his company and his presents on me. I'll let him know the rest through other people. Will you be so kind as to do what I want?"

"Oh, for mercy's sake, spare me!" Velchaninov almost cried out, waving his hand.

"What? Spare you?" Nadya was extraordinarily surprised at his refusal, and she gazed at him round-eyed.

The tone she had assumed for the occasion broke down immediately, and she was almost in tears.

Velchaninov laughed.

"I don't mean that. . . . I should be very glad . . . but I have my own account to settle with him. . . ."

"I knew that you were not his friend and that he was telling lies!" Nadya interrupted quickly and passionately. "I'll never marry him, I tell you! Never! I can't understand how he could presume . . . Only you must give him back his disgusting present or else what shall I do? I particularly, particularly want him to have it back to-day, the same day, so that his hopes may be crushed, and if he sneaks about it to Papa he shall see what he gets by it."

And from behind the bushes there suddenly emerged the young man in the blue spectacles.

"It's your duty to return the bracelet," he blurted out furiously, pouncing on Velchaninov. "If only from respect for the rights of women, that is—if you are capable of rising to the full significance of the question."

But before he had time to finish Nadya tugged at his sleeve with all her might, and drew him away from Velchaninov.

"My goodness, how silly you are, Predposylov!" she cried. "Go away, go away, go away, and don't dare to listen; I told you to stand a long way off!" . . . She stamped her little foot at him, and when he had crept back into the bushes she still walked up and down across the path, with her eyes flashing and her arms folded before her, as though she were beside herself with anger.

"You wouldn't believe how silly they are!" She stopped suddenly before Velchaninov. "It amuses you, but think what it means to me."

"That's not *he*, it's not *he*, is it?" laughed Velchaninov.

"Of course it isn't, and how could you imagine it!" cried Nadya, smiling and blushing. "That's only his friend. But I can't understand the friends he chooses; they all say that he's a 'future leader,' but I don't understand it. . . . Alexey Ivanovitch, I've no one I can appeal to; I ask you for the last time, will you give it back?"

"Oh, very well, I will; give it me."

"Ah, you are kind, you are good!" she cried, delighted, handing him the case. "I'll sing to you the whole evening for that, for I sing beautifully, do you know. I told you a fib when I said I didn't like music. Oh, you must come again—once at any rate; how glad I should be. I would tell you everything, everything, everything, and a great deal more besides, because you're so kind—as kind, as kind, as—as Katya!"

And when they went in to tea she did sing him two songs, in an utterly untrained and hardly mature, but pleasant and powerful voice. When they came in from the garden Pavel Pavlovitch was stolidly sitting with the parents at the tea-table, on which the big family samovar was already boiling, surrounded by cups of Sèvres china. He was probably discussing very grave matters with the old people, as two days later he was going away for nine whole months. He did not glance at the party as they came in from the garden, and particularly avoided looking at Velchaninov. It was evident, too, that he had not been sneaking and that all was serene so far.

But when Nadya began singing he put himself forward at once.

Nadya purposely ignored one direct question he addressed her, but this did not disconcert Pavel Pavlovitch, or make him hesitate. He stood behind her chair and his whole manner showed that this was his place and he was not going to give it up to any one.

"Alexey Ivanovitch sings, Mamma; Alexey Ivanovitch wants to sing, Mamma!" almost all the girls shouted at once, crowding round the piano at which Velchaninov confidently installed himself, intending to play his own accompaniment. The old people came in, and with them Katerina Fedosyevna, who had been sitting with them, pouring out the tea.

Velchaninov chose a song of Glinka's, now familiar to almost every one—

> "In the glad hour when from thy lips
> Come murmurs tender as a dove's."

He sang it, addressing himself entirely to Nadya, who was standing at his elbow nearer to him than any one. His voice had passed its prime, but what was left of it showed that it had once been a fine one. Velchaninov had, twenty years before, when he was a student, the luck to hear that song for the first time sung by Glinka himself, at the house of a friend of the composer's. It was at a literary and artistic bachelor gathering, and Glinka, growing expansive, played and sang his own favourite compositions, among them this song. He, too, had little voice left then, but Velchaninov remembered the great impression made by that song. A drawing-room singer, however skilful, would never have produced such an effect. In that song the intensity of passion rises, mounting higher and higher at every line, at every word; and, from this very intensity, the least trace of falsity, of exaggeration or unreality, such as passes muster so easily at an opera, would distort and destroy the whole value of it. To sing that slight but exceptional song it was essential to have truth, essential to have real inspiration, real passion, or a complete poetical comprehension of it. Otherwise the song would not only be a failure but might even appear unseemly and almost shameless: without them it would be impossible to express such intensity of passion without arousing repulsion, but truth and simplicity saved it. Velchaninov remembered that he had made a success with this song on some occasion. He had almost reproduced Glinka's manner of singing, but now, from the first note, from the first line, there was a gleam of inspiration in his singing which quivered in his voice.

At every word the torrent of feeling was more fervent and more boldly displayed; in the last lines the cry of passion is heard, and when, with blazing eyes, Velchaninov addressed the last words of the song to Nadya—

"Grown bolder, in thine eyes I gaze;
Draw close my lips, can hear no more,
I long to kiss thee, kiss thee, kiss thee!
I long to kiss thee, kiss thee, kiss thee!"—

she trembled almost with alarm, and even stepped back; the colour rushed into her cheeks, and at the same time Velchaninov seemed to catch a glimpse of something responsive in her abashed and almost dismayed little face. The faces of all the audience betrayed their enchantment and also their amazement: all seemed to feel that it was disgraceful and impossible to sing like that, and yet at the same time all their faces were flushed and all their eyes glowed and seemed to be expecting something more. Among those faces Velchaninov had a vision especially of the face of Katerina Fedosyevna, which looked almost beautiful.

"What a song," old Zahlebinin muttered, a little flabbergasted; "but . . . isn't it too strong? charming, but strong. . . ."

"Yes . . ." Madame Zahlebinin chimed in, but Pavel Pavlovitch would not let her go on; he dashed forward suddenly like one possessed, so far forgetting himself as to seize Nadya by the arm and pull her away from Velchaninov; he skipped up to him, gazed at him with a desperate face and quivering lips that moved without uttering a sound.

"Half a minute," he uttered faintly at last.

Velchaninov saw that in another minute the man might be guilty of something ten times as absurd; he made haste to take his arm and, regardless of the general amazement, drew him out into the verandah, and even took some steps into the garden with him, where it was now almost dark.

"Do you understand that you must go away with me this minute?" said Pavel Pavlovitch.

"No, I don't understand. . . ."

"Do you remember," Pavel Pavlovitch went on, in his frenzied whisper, "do you remember that you insisted that I should tell you everything, *everything* openly, 'the very last word . . .' do you remember? Well, the time has come to say that word . . . let us go!"

Velchaninov thought a minute, looked at Pavel Pavlovitch and agreed to go.

The sudden announcement of their departure upset the parents, and made all the girls horribly indignant.

"At least have another cup of tea," said Madame Zahlebinin plaintively.

"Come, what's upset you?" old Zahlebinin said in a tone of severity and displeasure, addressing Pavel Pavlovitch, who stood simpering and silent.

"Pavel Pavlovitch, why are you taking Alexey Ivanovitch away?" the girls began plaintively, looking at him with exasperation.

Nadya gazed at him so wrathfully that he positively squirmed, but he did not give way.

"You see, Pavel Pavlovitch has reminded me—many thanks to him for it—of a very important engagement which I might have missed," Velchaninov said, smiling, as he shook hands with Zahlebinin, and bowed to the mamma and the girls, especially distinguishing Katerina Fedosyevna in a manner apparent to all.

"We are very grateful for your visit and shall always be glad to see you," Zahlebinin said ponderously, in conclusion.

"Ah, we shall be so delighted . . ." the mamma chimed in with feeling.

"Come again, Alexey Ivanovitch, come again!" numerous voices were heard calling from the verandah, when he had already got into the carriage with Pavel Pavlovitch; there was perhaps one voice that called more softly than the others, "Come again, dear. dear Alexey Ivanovitch."

"That's the red-haired girl," thought Velchaninov.

Chapter 13

ON WHOSE SIDE MOST?

HE MIGHT think about the red-haired girl, and yet his soul was in agonies of vexation and remorse. And, indeed, during the whole of that day, which seemed on the surface so amusingly spent, a feeling of acute depression had scarcely left him. Before singing the song he did not know how to get away from it; perhaps that was why he had sung it with such fervour.

"And I could demean myself like that . . . tear myself away from everything," he began reproaching himself, but he hurriedly cut short his thoughts. Indeed, it seemed to him humiliating to lament; it was a great deal more pleasant to be angry with some one.

"Fool!" he whispered wrathfully, with a side glance at the silent figure of Pavel Pavlovitch sitting beside him in the carriage.

Pavel Pavlovitch remained obstinately silent, perhaps concentrated on preparing what he had got to say. With an impatient gesture he sometimes took off his hat and wiped his brow with his handkerchief.

"Perspiring!" Velchaninov thought spitefully.

On one occasion only Pavel Pavlovitch addressed a question to the coachman. "Is there going to be a storm?" he asked.

"Storm, indeed! Not a doubt of it; it's been brewing up all day."

The sky was indeed growing dark and there were flashes of lightning in the distance.

They reached the town about half-past ten.

"I am coming in with you, of course," Pavel Pavlovitch warned him, not far from the house.

"I understand, but I must tell you that I feel seriously unwell."

"I won't stay, I won't stay long."

When they went in at the gate, Pavel Pavlovitch ran in at the porter's lodge to find Mavra.

"What were you running off there for?" Velchaninov said sternly, as the latter overtook him and they went into the room.

"Oh . . . nothing . . . the driver . . ."

"I won't have you drink!"

No answer followed. Velchaninov lighted the candle, and Pavel Pavlovitch at once sat down on the chair. Velchaninov remained standing before him, with a frown on his face.

"I, too, promised to say my 'last' word," he began, with an inward, still suppressed irritation. "Here it is—that word: I consider on my conscience that everything between us is over, so that, in fact, there is nothing for us to talk about—do you hear?—nothing; and so wouldn't it be better for you to go away at once, and I'll close the door after you?"

"Let us settle our account, Alexey Ivanovitch," said Pavel Pavlovitch, looking in his face, however, with peculiar mildness.

"Set-tle our ac-count!" repeated Velchaninov, greatly surprised. "That's a strange thing to say! Settle what account? Bah! Isn't that perhaps that 'last word' you promised . . . to reveal to me?"

"It is."

"We've no account to settle; we settled our account long ago!" Velchaninov pronounced proudly.

"Can you really think so?" Pavel Pavlovitch brought out in a voice full of feeling, clasping his hands strangely and holding them before his breast.

Velchaninov made him no answer, but continued pacing up and down the room. "Liza! Liza!" he was moaning in his heart.

"What did you want to settle, though?" he asked him, frowning, after a rather prolonged silence.

Pavel Pavlovitch had been following him about the room with his eyes all this time, still holding his hands clasped before him.

"Don't go there again," he almost whispered in a voice of entreaty, and he suddenly got up from his chair.

"What! So that's all you are thinking about?" Velchaninov laughed spitefully. "You've surprised me all day, though!" he was beginning malignantly, but suddenly his whole face changed. "Listen," he said mournfully, with deep and sincere feeling; "I consider that I have never lowered myself as I have to-day—to begin with, by consenting to go with you, and then—by what happened there. . . . It was so paltry, so pitiful. . . . I've defiled and debased myself by mixing myself up in it . . . and forgetting . . . But there!" he cried hastily. "Listen, you attacked me to-day in an unguarded moment when I was nervous and ill . . . but there's no need to justify myself! I'm not going there again, and I assure you I take no interest in them whatever," he concluded resolutely.

"Really, really?" cried Pavel Pavlovitch, not disguising his relief and excitement.

Velchaninov looked at him contemptuously, and began pacing up and down the room again.

"You seem to have made up your mind to be happy?" he could not refrain from observing.

"Yes," Pavel Pavlovitch repeated naïvely, in a low voice.

"What is it to me," Velchaninov reflected, "that he's a buffoon and only spiteful through stupidity? I can't help hating him, though he isn't worth it!"

"I am 'the eternal husband'!" said Pavel Pavlovitch, with an abjectly submissive smile at his own expense. "I heard that expression from you, Alexey Ivanovitch, long ago, when you were staying with us in those days. I remember a great many of your sayings in that year. Last time, when you said here, 'the eternal husband,' I reflected."

Mavra came in with a bottle of champagne and two glasses.

"Forgive me, Alexey Ivanovitch; you know that I can't get on without it! Don't think it's impudence; look upon me as an outsider not on your level."

"Yes . . ." Velchaninov muttered with repugnance, "but I assure you I feel unwell. . . ."

"Directly . . . directly . . . in one minute," said Pavel Pavlovitch fussily; "just one little glass because my throat . . ."

He greedily tossed off a glassful at a gulp and sat down, looking almost tenderly at Velchaninov.

Mavra went out.

"How beastly!" Velchaninov murmured.

"It's only those girl friends," Pavel Pavlovitch said confidently, all of a sudden completely revived.

"What? Ah, yes, you are still at that. . . ."

"It's only those girl friends! And then she's so young; we have our little airs and graces! They're charming, in fact. But then—then, you know, I shall be her slave; when she's treated with deference, when she sees something of society . . . she'll be transformed."

"I shall have to give him back that bracelet, though," thought Velchaninov, scowling, as he felt the case in his pocket.

"You say that I'm resolved to be happy? I must get married, Alexey Ivanovitch," Pavel Pavlovitch went on confidentially and almost touchingly, "or what will become of me? You see for yourself!" He pointed to the bottle. "And that's only one-hundredth of my vices. I can't get on at all without marriage and—without new faith; I shall have faith and shall rise up again."

"But why on earth do you tell me this?" Velchaninov asked, almost bursting with laughter. It all struck him as wild. "But tell me," he cried, "what was your object in dragging me out there? What did you want me there for?"

"As a test . . ." Pavel Pavlovitch seemed suddenly embarrassed.

"A test of what?"

"The effect. . . . You see, Alexey Ivanovitch, it's only a week altogether . . . I've been looking round there." (Pavel Pavlovitch grew more and more confused.) "Yesterday I met you and thought: 'I've never yet seen her in outside, so to say, society, that is, in men's, except my own. . . .' A stupid idea; I feel that myself now; unnecessary. I expected too much . . . it's my horrible character. . . ."

He suddenly raised his head and flushed crimson.

"Can he be telling the whole truth?" Velchaninov was petrified with surprise.

"Well, and what then?" he asked.

Pavel Pavlovitch gave a sugary and, as it were, crafty smile.

"It's only charming childishness! It's all those girl friends! Only forgive me for my stupid behaviour before you to-day, Alexey Ivanov-itch; I never will again; and indeed it will never happen again."

"And I shan't be there again," said Velchaninov, with a smile.

"That's partly what I mean."

Velchaninov felt a little piqued.

"But I'm not the only man in the world, you know," he observed irritably.

Pavel Pavlovitch flushed again.

"It's sad for me to hear that, Alexey Ivanovitch, and, believe me, I've such a respect for Nadyezhda Fedosyevna . . ."

"Excuse me, excuse me, I didn't mean anything; it only seems a little strange to me that you have such an exaggerated idea of my attractions . . . and . . . such genuine confidence in me."

"I had such confidence just because it was after all . . . that happened in the past."

"Then if so, you look upon me even now as a most honourable man?" said Velchaninov, suddenly halting.

At another time he would have been horrified at the naïveté of his own question.

"I always thought you so," said Pavel Pavlovitch, dropping his eyes.

"Why, of course. . . . I didn't mean that; that is, not in that sense. I only meant to say that, in spite of any . . . preconceptions . . ."

"Yes, in spite of preconceptions."

"When you came to Petersburg?" Velchaninov could not resist asking, though he felt how utterly monstrous was his curiosity.

"When I came to Petersburg, too, I looked upon you as the most honourable of men. I always respected you, Alexey Ivanovitch."

Pavel Pavlovitch raised his eyes and looked candidly, without a trace of embarrassment, at his opponent. Velchaninov was suddenly panic-stricken; he was not at all anxious that anything should happen, or that anything should overstep a certain line, especially as he had provoked it.

"I loved you, Alexey Ivanovitch," Pavel Pavlovitch articulated, as though he had suddenly made up his mind to speak, "and all that year at T—— I loved you. You did not notice it," he went on, in a voice that quivered, to Velchaninov's positive horror; "I was too insignifi-cant, compared with you, to let you see it. And there was no need, indeed, perhaps. And I've thought of you all these nine years, because there has never been another year in my life like that one." (Pavel Pavlovitch's eyes began to glisten.) "I remembered many of your phrases and sayings, your thoughts. I always thought of you as a man with a passion for every noble feeling, a man of education, of the highest education and of ideas: 'Great ideas spring not so much from noble intelligence as from noble feeling.' You said that yourself; perhaps you've forgotten it, but I remembered it. I always looked on you, therefore, as a man of noble feeling . . . and therefore believed in you —in spite of anything . . ."

His chin suddenly began quivering. Velchaninov was in absolute terror; this unexpected tone must be cut short at all costs.

"That's enough, Pavel Pavlovitch, please," he muttered, flushing and irritably impatient. "And why," he screamed suddenly, "why do you fasten upon a man when he is nervous and ill, when he is almost delirious, and drag him into this darkness . . . when it's . . . when it's —nothing but delusion, mirage, and falsity, and shameful, and unnatural, and—exaggerated—and that's what's worst, that's what's most shameful—that it is so exaggerated! And it's all nonsense; we are both vicious, underground, loathsome people. . . . And if you like I'll prove that you don't like me at all, but hate me with all your might, and that you're lying, though you don't know it; you insisted on taking me there, not with the absurd object of testing your future bride (what an idea!); you saw me yesterday and felt *vindictive,* and took me there to show me and say to me, 'See what a prize! She will be mine; do your worst now!' You challenged me, perhaps you didn't know it yourself; that's how it was, for that's what you were feeling . . . and without hating me you couldn't have challenged me like that; and so you hate me!"

He rushed about the room as he shouted this. What harassed and mortified him most of all was the humiliating consciousness that he was demeaning himself so far to Pavel Pavlovitch.

"I wanted to be reconciled with you, Alexey Ivanovitch!" the other articulated suddenly, in a rapid whisper, and his chin began twitching again.

Velchaninov was overcome by furious rage, as though no one had ever insulted him so much.

"I tell you again," he yelled, "that you're fastening upon a man who's nervous and ill . . . that you're fastening upon him to extort something monstrous from him in delirium! We . . . we are men of different worlds, understand that, and . . . and . . . between us lies a grave!" he added in a furious whisper, and suddenly realized what he had done. . . .

"And how do you know"—Pavel Pavlovitch's face was suddenly pale and distorted—"how do you know what that little grave here means . . . for me!" he cried, stepping up to Velchaninov with a ridiculous but horrible gesture, pressed his fist against his heart. "I know that little grave here, and we both stand at the side of that little grave, but on my side there is more than on yours, more . . ." he whispered as though in delirium, still thumping at his heart with his fist, "more, more, more . . ."

Suddenly an extraordinarily loud ring at the door brought both of them to their senses. The bell rang so violently that it seemed as though some one had vowed to break it at the first pull.

"People don't ring like that to see me," said Velchaninov in perplexity.

"Nor to see me either," Pavel Pavlovitch whispered timidly, recovering himself too, and at once turning into the old Pavel Pavlovitch again.

Velchaninov scowled and went to open the door.

"M. Velchaninov, if I'm not mistaken?" they heard in a ringing, youthful, and exceptionally self-confident voice in the passage.

"What is it?"

"I have trustworthy information," continued the ringing voice, "that a certain Trusotsky is with you at this moment. I must see him instantly."

It would certainly have pleased Velchaninov at that moment to have given the self-confident young gentleman a vigorous kick and to have sent him flying out on the stairs; but he thought a moment, moved aside and let him in.

"Here is M. Trusotsky; come in. . . ."

Chapter 14

SASHENKA AND NADENKA

THERE walked into the room a very young man, of about nineteen, perhaps even less—to judge from the youthfulness of his handsome, self-confident, upturned face. He was fairly well dressed, or at any rate his clothes looked well on him; in height he was a little above the average; the black hair that hung in thick locks about his head, and the big, bold, dark eyes were particularly conspicuous in his face. Except that his nose was rather broad and turned up, he was a handsome fellow. He walked in solemnly.

"I believe I have the opportunity of conversing with M. Trusotsky," he pronounced in a measured tone, emphasizing with peculiar relish the word "opportunity"—giving him to understand thereby that he did not consider it either an "honour" or a "pleasure" to converse with M. Trusotsky.

Velchaninov began to grasp the position; something seemed to be dawning on Pavel Pavlovitch too. There was a look of uneasiness in his face; but he stood his ground.

"Not having the honour of your acquaintance," he answered majestically, "I imagine that you cannot have business of any sort with me."

"You had better hear me first and then give your opinion," the young man admonished him self-confidently, and, taking out a tortoiseshell lorgnette hanging on a cord, he examined through it the bottle of champagne standing on the table. When he had calmly completed his scrutiny of the bottle, he folded up the lorgnette and turned to Pavel Pavlovitch again.

"Alexandr Lobov."

"What do you mean by Alexandr Lobov?"

"That's me. Haven't you heard of me?"

"No."

"How should you, though? I've come on important business that chiefly concerns you. Allow me to sit down; I'm tired."

"Sit down," Velchaninov urged him; but the young man succeeded in sitting down before being invited to do so.

In spite of the increasing pain in his chest Velchaninov was interested in this impudent youth. In his pretty, childlike and rosy face, he fancied a remote resemblance to Nadya.

"You sit down too," the lad suggested to Pavel Pavlovitch, motioning him with a careless nod of the head to a seat opposite.

"Don't trouble; I'll stand."

"You'll be tired. You needn't go away, M. Velchaninov, if you like to stay."

"I've nowhere to go; I'm at home."

"As you please. I must confess I should prefer you to be present while I have an explanation with this gentleman. Nadyezhda Fedosyevna gave me rather a flattering account of you."

"Bah! When had she time to do that?"

"Why, just now after you left; I've just come from there, too. I've something to tell you, M. Trusotsky." He turned round to Pavel Pavlovitch, who was standing. "We—that is, Nadyezhda Fedosyevna and I," he went on, letting his words drop one by one as he lolled carelessly in the arm-chair; "we've cared for each other for ever so long, and have given each other our promise. You are in our way now; I've come to suggest that you should clear out. Will it suit you to act on my suggestion?"

Pavel Pavlovitch positively reeled; he turned pale, but a diabolical smile came on to his lips at once.

"No, it won't suit me at all," he rapped out laconically.

"You don't say so!" The young man turned round in the arm-chair and crossed one leg over the other.

"I don't know who it is I'm speaking to," added Pavel Pavlovitch. "I believe, indeed, that there's no object in continuing our conversation."

Uttering this, he too thought fit to sit down.

"I told you you would be tired," the youth observed casually. "I told you just now that my name is Alexandr Lobov, and that Nadyezhda and I are pledged to one another; consequently you can't say, as you did just now, that you don't know who it is you have to deal with; you can't imagine, either, that I have nothing more to say to you; putting myself aside, it concerns Nadyezhda Fedosyevna, whom you persist in pestering so insolently. And that alone is sufficient reason for an explanation."

All this he let drop, word by word, through his closed lips, with the air of a coxcomb who did not deign to articulate his words; he even drew out his lorgnette again and turned it upon something while he was talking.

"Excuse me, young man!" Pavel Pavlovitch exclaimed irritably; but the young man instantly snubbed him.

"At any other time I should certainly forbid your calling me 'young man,' but now you will admit that my youth is my chief advantage over you, and that you would have been jolly glad, this morning, for instance, when you presented your bracelet, to be a tiny bit younger."

"Ah, you sprat!" murmured Velchaninov.

"In any case, sir," Pavel Pavlovitch corrected himself with dignity, "I do not consider the reasons you have advanced—most unseemly and dubious reasons—sufficient to continue discussing them. I see that this is all a foolish and childish business. To-morrow I'll make inquiries of my highly respected friend, Fedosey Semyonovitch; and now I beg you to retire."

"Do you see the sort of man he is?" the youth cried at once, unable to sustain his previous tone, and turning hotly to Velchaninov. "It's not enough for him that they've put out their tongues at him to-day and kicked him out—he'll go to-morrow to tell tales of us to the old man! Won't you prove by that, you obstinate man, that you want to take the girl by force, that you want to buy her of people in their dotage who in our barbarous state of society retain authority over her? I should have thought it would have been enough for you that she's shown you how she despises you; why, she gave you back your indecent present to-day, your bracelet. What more you you want?"

"No one has returned me a bracelet, and it's utterly out of the question!" Pavel Pavlovitch said, startled.

"Out of the question? Do you mean to say M. Velchaninov has not given it you?"

"Damnation take you!" thought Velchaninov. "Nadyezhda Fedosyevna did commission me," he said, frowning, "to give you this case, Pavel Pavlovitch. I refused to take it, but she begged me . . . here it is . . . I'm annoyed. . . ."

He took out the case and, much embarrassed, laid it before Pavel Pavlovitch, who was struck dumb.

"Why didn't you give it to him before?" said the young gentleman, addressing Velchaninov severely.

"As you see, I hadn't managed to do so yet," the latter replied, frowning.

"That's queer."

"Wha-a-at?"

"You must admit it's queer, anyway. Though I am ready to allow there may be a misunderstanding."

Velchaninov felt a great inclination to get up at once and pull the saucy urchin's ears, but he could not refrain from bursting out laughing in his face; the boy promptly laughed too. It was very different with Pavel Pavlovitch; if Velchaninov could have observed the terrible look he turned upon him when Velchaninov was laughing at Lobov, he would have realized that at that instant the man was passing through a momentous crisis. . . . But though Velchaninov did not see that glance, he felt that he must stand by Pavel Pavlovitch.

"Listen, M. Lobov," he began in a friendly tone; "without entering into discussion of other reasons upon which I don't care to touch, I would only point out to you that, in paying his addresses to Nadyezhda Fedosyevna, Pavel Pavlovitch can in any case boast of certain qualifications: in the first place, the fact that everything about him is known to that estimable family; in the second place, his excellent and highly respectable position; finally, his fortune, and consequently he must naturally be surprised at the sight of a rival like you—a man, perhaps, of great merit, but so exceedingly young that he can hardly take you for a serious suitor . . . and so he is justified in asking you to retire."

"What do you mean by 'exceedingly young'? I was nineteen last month. By law I could have been married long ago. That's all I can say."

"But what father could bring himself to give you his daughter now —even if you were to be a millionaire in the future or some benefactor of mankind? At nineteen a man cannot even answer for himself, and you are ready to take the responsibility of another person's future, that is, the future of another child like yourself! Why, do you think it's quite honourable? I have ventured to speak frankly to you because you appealed to me just now as an intermediary between you and Pavel Pavlovitch."

"Ah, to be sure, his name's Pavel Pavlovitch!" observed the boy; "how is it I kept fancying that he was Vassily Petrovitch? Well," he went on, addressing Velchaninov, "you haven't surprised me in the least; I knew you were all like that! It's odd, though, that they talked of you as a man rather new in a way. But that's all nonsense, though; far from there being anything dishonourable on my part, as you so freely expressed it, it's the very opposite, as I hope to make you see: to begin with, we've pledged our word to each other, and, what's more, I've promised her, before two witnesses, that if she ever falls in love with some one else, or simply regrets having married me and wants to separate, I will at once give her a formal declaration of my infidelity —and so will support her petition for divorce. What's more, in case I should later on go back upon my word and refuse to give her that declaration, I will give her as security on our wedding-day an I O U for a hundred thousand roubles, so that if I should be perverse about the declaration she can at once change my I O U and me into the bargain! In that way everything will be secured and I shouldn't be risking anybody's future. That's the first point."

"I bet that fellow—What's-his-name?—Predposylov invented that for you!" cried Velchaninov.

"He, he, he!" chuckled Pavel Pavlovitch viciously.

"What's that gentleman sniggering about? You guessed right, it was Predposylov's idea; and you must admit it was a shrewd one. The absurd law is completely paralyzed by it. Of course, I intend to love her for ever, and she laughs tremendously; at the same time it's ingenious, and you must admit that it's honourable, and that it's not every man who would consent to do it."

"To my thinking, so far from being honourable, it's positively disgusting."

The young man shrugged his shoulders.

"Again you don't surprise me," he observed, after a brief silence. "I have given up being surprised at that sort of thing long ago. Predposylov would tell you flatly that your lack of comprehension of the most natural things is due to the corruption of your most ordinary feelings and ideas by a long life spent idly and absurdly. But possibly we don't understand one another; they spoke well of you anyway . . . you're fifty, I suppose, aren't you?"

"Kindly keep to the point."

"Excuse my indiscretion and don't be annoyed; I didn't mean anything. I will continue: I'm by no means a future millionaire, as you expressed it (and what an idea!); I have nothing but what I stand up in, but I have complete confidence in my future. I shan't be a hero or a benefactor of mankind either, but I shall keep myself and my wife. Of course, I've nothing now; I was brought up in their house, you see, from childhood. . . ."

"How was that?"

"Well, you see, I'm the son of a distant relation of Zahlebinin's wife, and when all my people died and left me at eight years old, the old man took me in and afterwards sent me to the high school. He's really a good-natured man, if you care to know. . . ."

"I know that."

"Yes; a bit antiquated in his ideas, but kind-hearted. It's a long time now, of course, since I was under his guardianship; I want to earn my own living, and to owe no one anything."

"How long have you been independent?" Velchaninov inquired.

"Why, four months."

"Oh, well, one can understand it then: you've been friends from childhood! Well, have you a situation, then?"

"Yes, a private situation, in a notary's office, for twenty-five roubles a month. Of course, only for the time, but when I made my offer I hadn't even that. I was serving on the railway then for ten roubles a month, but only for the time."

"Do you mean to say you've made an offer of marriage?"

"Yes, a formal offer, and ever so long ago—over three weeks."

"Well, and what happened?"

"The old man laughed awfully at first, and then was awfully angry, and locked her up upstairs. But Nadya held out heroically. But that was all because he was a bit crusty with me before, for throwing up the berth in his department which he had got me into four months ago, before I went to the railway. He's a capital old chap, I tell you again, simple and jolly at home, but you can't fancy what he's like as soon as he's in his office! He's like a Jove enthroned! I naturally let him know that I was not attracted by his manners there, but the chief trouble was through the head clerk's assistant: that gentleman took it into his head that I had been 'rude' to him, and all that I said to him was that he was undeveloped. I threw them all up, and now I'm at a notary's."

"And did you get much in the department?"

"Oh, I was not on the regular staff! The old man used to give me an allowance too; I tell you he's a good sort, but we shan't give in, all the same. Of course, twenty-five roubles is not enough to support a wife, but I hope soon to have a share in the management of Count Zavileysky's neglected estates, and then to rise to three thousand straight off, or else I shall become a lawyer. People are always going to law nowadays. . . . Bah! What a clap of thunder! There'll be a storm; it's a good thing I managed to get here before it; I came on foot, I ran almost all the way."

"But, excuse me, if so, when did you manage to talk things over with Nadyezhda Fedosyevna, especially if they refuse you admittance?"

"Why, one can talk over the fence! Did you notice that red-haired girl?" he laughed. "She's very active on our side, and Marie Nikititchna too; ah, she's a serpent, that Marie Nikititchna! . . . Why do you wince? Are you afraid of the thunder?"

"No, I'm unwell, very unwell. . . ."

Velchaninov, in positive agony from the pain in his chest, got up and tried to walk about the room.

"Oh, then, of course, I'm in your way. . . . Don't be uneasy, I'm just going!"

And the youth jumped up from his seat.

"You're not in the way; it's no matter," said Velchaninov courteously.

"How can it be no matter? 'When Kobylnikov had a stomach-ache' . . . do you remember in Shtchedrin? Are you fond of Shtchedrin?"

"Yes."

"So am I. Well, Vassily . . . oh, hang it, Pavel Pavlovitch, let's finish!" He turned, almost laughing, to Pavel Pavlovitch. "I will once more for your comprehension formulate the question: do you consent to make a formal withdrawal of all pretensions in regard to Nadyezhda

Fedosyevna to the old people to-morrow, in my presence?"

"I certainly do not." Pavel Pavlovitch, too, got up from his seat with an impatient and exasperated air. "And I beg you once more to spare me . . . for all this is childish and silly."

"You had better look out." The youth held up a warning finger with a supercilious smile. "Don't make a mistake in your calculations! Do you know what such a mistake leads to? I warn you that in nine months' time, when you have had all your expense and trouble, and you come back here, you'll be forced to give up Nadyezhda Fedosyevna, or if you don't give her up it will be the worse for you; that's what will be the end of it! I must warn you that you're like the dog in the manger—excuse me, it's only a comparison—getting nothing yourself and preventing others. From motives of humanity I tell you again: reflect upon it, force yourself for once in your life to reflect rationally."

"I beg you to spare me your sermonizing!" cried Pavel Pavlovitch furiously; "and as for your nasty insinuations, I shall take measures to-morrow, severe measures!"

"Nasty insinuations? What do you mean by that? You're nasty yourself, if that's what you've got in your head. However, I agree to wait till to-morrow, but if . . . Ah, thunder again! Good-bye; very glad to make your acquaintance"—he nodded to Velchaninov and ran off, apparently in haste to get back before the storm and not to get caught in the rain.

Chapter 15

THE ACCOUNT IS SETTLED

You see? You see?" Pavel Pavlovitch skipped up to Velchaninov as soon as the youth had departed.

"Yes; you've no luck!" said Velchaninov carelessly.

He would not have said those words had he not been tortured and exasperated by the pain in his chest, which was growing more and more acute.

"It was because you felt for me, you didn't give me back the bracelet, wasn't it?"

"I hadn't time. . . ."

"You felt for me from your heart, like a true friend?"

"Oh yes, I felt for you," said Velchaninov, in exasperation.

He told him briefly, however, how the bracelet had been returned to him, and how Nadyezhda Fedosyevna had almost forced him to assist in returning it. . . .

"You understand that nothing else would have induced me to take it; I've had unpleasantness enough apart from that!"

"You were fascinated and took it?" sniggered Pavel Pavlovitch.

"That's stupid on your part; however, I must excuse you. You saw for yourself just now that I'm not the leading person, that there are others in this affair."

"At the same time you were fascinated."

Pavel Pavlovitch sat down and filled up his glass.

"Do you imagine I'd give way to that wretched boy? I'll make mince-meat of him, so there! I'll go over to-morrow and polish him off. We'll smoke out that spirit from the nursery."

He emptied his glass almost at a gulp and filled it again; he began, in fact, to behave in an unusually free and easy way.

"Ah, Nadenka and Sashenka, the sweet little darlings, he-he-he!"

He was beside himself with anger. There came another louder clap of thunder, followed by a blinding flash of lightning, and the rain began streaming in bucketfuls. Pavel Pavlovitch got up and closed the open window.

"He asked you whether you were afraid of the thunder, he-he. Velchaninov afraid of thunder! Kobylnikov—what was it—Kobylnikov . . . and what about being fifty too—eh? Do you remember?" Pavel Pavlovitch sneered diabolically.

"You've established yourself here, it seems!" observed Velchaninov, hardly able to articulate the words for the pain in his chest. "I'll lie down, you can do what you like."

"Why, you couldn't turn a dog out in weather like this!" Pavel Pavlovitch retorted in an aggrieved tone, seeming almost pleased, however, at having an excuse for feeling aggrieved.

"All right, sit down, drink . . . stay the night, if you like!" muttered Velchaninov. He stretched himself on the sofa and uttered a faint groan.

"Stay the night? And you won't be afraid?"

"What of?" said Velchaninov, suddenly raising his head.

"Oh, nothing. Last time you were so frightened, or was it **my** fancy?"

"You're stupid!" Velchaninov could not help saying. He turned his head to the wall angrily.

"All right," responded Pavel Pavlovitch.

The sick man fell asleep suddenly, a minute after lying down. The unnatural strain upon him that day in the shattered state of his health had brought on a sudden crisis, and he was as weak as a child. But the pain asserted itself again and got the upper hand of sleep and weariness; an hour later he woke up and painfully got up from the sofa. The storm had subsided; the room was full of tobacco smoke, on the table stood an empty bottle, and Pavel Pavlovitch was asleep on another sofa. He was lying on his back, with his head on the sofa cushion, fully dressed and with his boots on. His lorgnette had slipped out of his pocket and was hanging down almost to the floor. His hat was lying on the ground beside it. Velchaninov looked at him morosely and did not attempt to wake him. Writhing with pain and pacing about the room, for he could no longer bear to lie down, he moaned and brooded over his agonies.

He was afraid of that pain in his chest, and not without reason. He had been liable to these attacks for a very long time, but they had only occurred at intervals of a year or two. He knew that they came from the liver. At first a dull, not acute, but irritating feeling of oppression was, as it were, concentrated at some point in the chest, under the shoulder-blade or higher up. Continually increasing, sometimes for ten hours at a stretch, the pain at last would reach such a pitch, the oppression would become so insupportable, that the sufferer began to have visions of dying. On his last attack, a year before, he was, when the pain ceased after ten hours of suffering, so weak that he could scarcely move his hands as he lay in bed, and the doctor had allowed him to take nothing for the whole day but a few teaspoonfuls of weak tea and of bread soaked in broth, like a tiny baby. The attacks were brought on by different things, but never occurred except when his nerves were out of order. It was strange, too, how the attack passed off; sometimes it was possible to arrest it at the very beginning, during the first half-hour, by simple compresses, and it would pass away completely at once; sometimes, as on his last attack, nothing was of any use, and the pain only subsided after numerous and continually recurring paroxysms of vomiting. The doctor confessed afterwards that he believed it to be a case of poisoning. It was a long time to wait till morning, and he didn't want to send for the doctor at night; besides, he didn't like doctors. At last he could not control himself and began moaning aloud. His groans waked Pavel Pavlovitch; he sat up on the sofa, and for some time listened with alarm and bewilderment, watching Velchaninov, who was almost running backwards and forwards through the two rooms. The bottle of champagne had had a great effect upon him, evidently more than usual, and it was some time before he could collect himself. At last he grasped the position and rushed to Velchaninov, who mumbled something in reply to him.

"It's the liver, I know it!" cried Pavel Pavlovitch, becoming extremely animated all at once. "Pyotr Kuzmitch Polosuhin used to suffer just the same from liver. You ought to have compresses. Pyotr Kuzmitch always had compresses. . . . One may die of it! Shall I run for Mavra?"

"No need, no need!" Velchaninov waved him off irritably. "I want nothing."

But Pavel Pavlovitch, goodness knows why, seemed beside himself, as though it were a question of saving his own son. Without heeding Velchaninov's protests, he insisted on the necessity of compresses and also of two or three cups of weak tea to be drunk on the spot, "and not simply hot, but boiling!" He ran to Mavra, without waiting for permission, with her laid a fire in the kitchen, which always stood empty, and blew up the samovar; at the same time he succeeded in getting the sick man to bed, took off his clothes, wrapped him up in a quilt, and within twenty minutes had prepared tea and compresses.

"This is a hot plate, scalding hot!" he said, almost ecstatically, applying the heated plate, wrapped up in a napkin, on Velchaninov's aching chest. "There are no other compresses, and plates, I swear on my honour, will be even better: they were laid on Pyotr Kuzmitch, I saw it with my own eyes, and did it with my own hands. One may die of it, you know. Drink your tea, swallow it; never mind about scalding yourself; life is too precious . . . for one to be squeamish."

He quite flustered Mavra, who was half asleep; the plates were changed every three or four minutes. After the third plate and the second cup of tea, swallowed at a gulp, Velchaninov felt a sudden relief.

"If once they've shifted the pain, thank God, it's a good sign!" cried Pavel Pavlovitch, and he ran joyfully to fetch a fresh plate and a fresh cup of tea.

"If only we can ease the pain. If only we can keep it under!" he kept repeating.

Half an hour later the pain was much less, but the sick man was so exhausted that in spite of Pavel Pavlovitch's entreaties he refused to "put up with just one more nice little plate." He was so weak that everything was dark before his eyes.

"Sleep, sleep," he repeated in a faint voice.

"To be sure," Pavel Pavlovitch assented.

"You'll stay the night. . . . What time is it?"

"It's nearly two o'clock, it's a quarter to."

"You'll stay the night."

"I will, I will."

A minute later the sick man called Pavel Pavlovitch again.

"You, you," he muttered, when the latter had run up and was bending over him; "you are better than I am! I understand it all, all. . . . Thank you."

"Sleep, sleep," whispered Pavel Pavlovitch, and he hastened on tiptoe to his sofa.

As he fell asleep the invalid heard Pavel Pavlovitch noiselessly making up a bed for himself and taking off his clothes. Finally, putting out the candle, and almost holding his breath for fear of waking the patient, he stretched himself on his sofa.

There is no doubt that Velchaninov did sleep and that he fell asleep very soon after the candle was put out; he remembered this clearly afterwards. But all the time he was asleep, up to the very moment that he woke up, he dreamed that he was not asleep, and that in spite of his exhaustion he could not get to sleep. At last he began to dream that he was in a sort of waking delirium, and that he could not drive away the phantoms that crowded about him, although he was fully conscious that it was only delirium and not reality. The phantoms were all familiar figures; his room seemed to be full of people; and the door into the passage stood open; people were coming in in crowds and thronging the stairs. At the table, which was set in the middle of the room, there was sitting one man—exactly as in the similar dream he had had a month before. Just as in that dream, this man sat with his elbows on the table and would not speak; but this time he was wearing a round hat with crape on it. "What! could it have been Pavel Pavlovitch that time too?" Velchaninov thought, but, glancing at the face of the silent man, he convinced himself that it was some one quite different. "Why has he got crape on?" Velchaninov wondered. The noise, the talking and the shouting of the people crowding round the table, was awful. These people seemed to be even more intensely exasperated against Velchaninov than in the previous dream; they shook their fists at him, and shouted something to him with all their might, but what it was exactly he could not make out. "But it's delirium, of course, I know it's delirium!" he thought; "I know I couldn't get to sleep and that I've got up now, because it made me too wretched to go on lying down. . . ." But the shouts, the people, their gestures were so lifelike, so real, that sometimes he was seized by doubt: "Can this be really delirium? Good heavens! What do these people want of me? But . . . if it were not an hallucination, would it be possible that such a clamour should not have waked Pavel Pavlovitch all this time? There he is asleep on the sofa!" At last something suddenly happened again, just as in that other dream; all of them made a rush for the stairs and they were closely packed in the doorway, for there was another crowd forcing its way into the room. These people were bringing something in with them, something big and heavy; he could hear how heavily the steps of those carrying it sounded on the stairs and how hurriedly their panting voices called to one another. All the people in the room shouted: "They're bringing it, they're bringing it"—all eyes were flashing and fixed on Velchaninov; all of them pointed towards the stairs, menacing and triumphant. Feeling no further doubt that it was reality and not hallucination, he stood on tiptoe so as to peep over the people's heads and find out as soon as possible what they were bringing up the stairs. His heart was beating, beating, beating, and suddenly, exactly as in that first dream, he heard three violent rings at the bell. And again it was so distinct, so real, so unmistakable a ring at the bell, that it could not be only a dream. . . .

But he did not rush to the door as he had done on awaking then. What idea guided his first movement and whether he had any idea at the moment it is impossible to say, but some one seemed to prompt him what he must do: he leapt out of bed and, with his hands stretched out before him as though to defend himself and ward off an attack, rushed straight towards the place where Pavel Pavlovitch was asleep. His hands instantly came into contact with other hands, stretched out above him, and he clutched them tight; so, some one already stood bending over him. The curtains were drawn, but it was not quite dark, for a faint light came from the other room where there were no such curtains. Suddenly, with an acute pain, something cut the palm and fingers of his left hand, and he instantly realized that he had clutched the blade of a knife or razor and was grasping it tight in his hand. . . . And at the same moment something fell heavily on the floor with a thud.

Velchaninov was perhaps three times as strong as Pavel Pavlovitch, yet the struggle between them lasted a long while, fully three minutes.

He soon got him down on the floor and bent his arms back behind him, but for some reason he felt he must tie his hands behind him. Holding the murderer with his wounded left hand, he began with his right fumbling for the cord of the window curtain and for a long time could not find it, but at last got hold of it and tore it from the window. He wondered himself afterwards at the immense effort required to do this. During those three minutes neither of them uttered a word; nothing was audible but their heavy breathing and the muffled sounds of their struggling. Having at last twisted Pavel Pavlovitch's arms behind him and tied them together, Velchaninov left him on the floor, got up, drew the curtain from the window and pulled up the blind. It was already light in the deserted street. Opening the window, he stood for some moments drawing in deep breaths of fresh air. It was a little past four. Shutting the window, he went hurriedly to the cupboard, took out a clean towel and bound it tightly round his left hand to stop the bleeding. At his feet an open razor was lying on the carpet; he picked it up, shut it, put it in the razor-case, which had been left forgotten since the morning on the little table beside Pavel Pavlovitch's sofa, and locked it up in his bureau. And, only when he had done all that, he went up to Pavel Pavlovitch and began to examine him.

Meantime, the latter had with an effort got up from the floor, and seated himself in an arm-chair. He had nothing on but his shirt, not even his boots. The back and the sleeves of his shirt were soaked with blood; but the blood was not his own, it came from Velchaninov's wounded hand. Of course it was Pavel Pavlovitch, but any one meeting him by chance might almost have failed to recognize him at the minute, so changed was his whole appearance. He was sitting awkwardly upright in the arm-chair, owing to his hands being tied behind his back, his face looked distorted, exhausted and greenish, and he quivered all over from time to time. He looked at Velchaninov fixedly, but with lustreless, unseeing eyes. All at once he smiled vacantly, and, nodding towards a bottle of water that stood on the table, he said in a meek half-whisper—

"Water, I should like some water."

Velchaninov filled a glass and began holding it for him to drink. Pavel Pavlovitch bent down greedily to the water; after three gulps he raised his head and looked intently into the face of Velchaninov, who was standing beside him with the glass in his hand, but without uttering a word he fell to drinking again. When he had finished he sighed deeply. Velchaninov took his pillow, seized his outer garments and went into the other room, locking Pavel Pavlovitch into the first room.

The pain had passed off completely, but he was conscious of extreme weakness again after the momentary effort in which he had displayed an unaccountable strength. He tried to reflect upon what had happened, but his thoughts were hardly coherent, the shock had been too great. Sometimes there was a dimness before his eyes lasting for ten minutes or so, then he would start, wake up, recollect everything, remember his smarting hand bound up in a blood-stained towel, and would fall to thinking greedily, feverishly. He came to one distinct conclusion—that is, that Pavel Pavlovitch certainly had meant to cut his throat, but that perhaps only a quarter of an hour before had not known that he would do it. The razor-case had perhaps merely caught his eye the evening before, and, without arousing any thought of it at the time, had remained in his memory. (The razors were always locked up in the bureau, and only the morning before, Velchaninov had taken them out to shave round his moustache and whiskers, as he sometimes did.)

"If he had long been intending to murder me he would have got a knife or pistol ready; he would not have reckoned on my razor, which he had never seen till yesterday evening," was one reflection he made among others.

It struck six o'clock at last; Velchaninov roused himself, dressed, and went in to Pavel Pavlovitch. Opening the door, he could not understand why he had locked Pavel Pavlovitch in, instead of turning him out of the house. To his surprise, the criminal was fully dressed; most likely he had found some way of untying his hands. He was sitting in the arm-chair, but got up at once when Velchaninov went in. His hat was already in his hand. His uneasy eyes seemed in haste to say—

"Don't begin talking; it's no use beginning; there's no need to talk."

"Go," said Velchaninov. "Take your bracelet," he added, calling after him.

Pavel Pavlovitch turned back from the door, took the case with the bracelet from the table, put it in his pocket and went out on the stairs. Velchaninov stood at the door to lock it behind him. Their eyes met for the last time; Pavel Pavlovitch stopped suddenly, for five seconds the two looked into each other's eyes—as though hesitating; finally Velchaninov waved his hand faintly.

"Well, go!" he said in a low voice, and locked the door.

Chapter 16

ANALYSIS

A FEELING of immense, extraordinary relief took possession of him; something was over, was settled; an awful weight of depression had vanished and was dissipated for ever. So it seemed to him. It had lasted for five weeks. He raised his hand, looked at the towel soaked with blood and muttered to himself: "Yes, now everything is absolutely at an end!" And all that morning, for the first time in three weeks, he scarcely thought of Liza—as though that blood from his cut fingers could "settle his account" even with that misery.

He recognized clearly that he had escaped a terrible danger. "These people," he thought, "just these people who don't know a minute beforehand whether they'll murder a man or not—as soon as they take a knife in their trembling hands and feel the hot spurt of blood on their fingers don't stick at cutting your throat, but cut off your head, 'clean off,' as convicts express it. That is so."

He could not remain at home and went out into the street, feeling convinced that he must do something, or something would happen to him at once; he walked about the streets and waited. He had an intense longing to meet some one, to talk to some one, even to a stranger, and it was only that which led him at last to think of a doctor and of the necessity of binding up his hand properly. The doctor, an old acquaintance of his, examined the wound, and inquired with interest how it could have happened. Velchaninov laughed and was on the point of telling him all about it, but restrained himself. The doctor was obliged to feel his pulse and, hearing of his attack the night before, persuaded him to take some soothing medicine he had at hand. He was reassuring about the cuts: "They could have no particularly disagreeable results." Velchaninov laughed and began to assure him that they had already had the most agreeable results. An almost irresistible desire to tell the whole story came over him twice again during that day, on one occasion to a total stranger with whom he entered into conversation at a tea-shop. He had never been able to endure entering into conversation with strangers in public places before.

He went into a shop to buy a newspaper; he went to his tailor's and ordered a suit. The idea of visiting the Pogoryeltsevs was still distasteful to him, and he did not think of them, and indeed he could not have gone to their villa: he kept expecting something here in the town. He dined with enjoyment, he talked to the waiter and to his fellow-diners, and drank half a bottle of wine. The possibility of the return of his illness of the day before did not occur to him; he was convinced that the illness had passed off completely at the moment when, after falling asleep so exhausted, he had, an hour and a half later, sprung out of bed and thrown his assailant on the floor with such strength. Towards evening he began to feel giddy, and at moments was overcome by something like the delirium he had had in his sleep. It was dusk when he returned home, and he was almost afraid of his room when he went into it. It seemed dreadful and uncanny in his flat. He walked up and down it several times, and even went into his kitchen, where he had scarcely ever been before. "Here they were heating plates yesterday," he thought. He locked the door securely and lighted the candles earlier than usual. As he locked the door he remembered, half an hour before, passing the porter's lodge, he had called Mavra and asked her whether Pavel Pavlovitch had come in his absence, as though he could possibly have come.

After locking himself in carefully, he opened the bureau, took out the razor-case and opened the razor to look at it again. On the white bone handle there were still faint traces of blood. He put the razor back in the case and locked it up in the bureau again. He felt sleepy; he felt that he must go to bed at once—or "he would not be fit for to-morrow." He pictured the next day for some reason as a momentous and "decisive" day.

But the same thoughts that had haunted him all day in the street kept incessantly and persistently crowding and jostling in his sick brain, and he kept thinking, thinking, thinking, and for a long time could not get to sleep. . . .

"If it is settled that he tried to murder me *accidentally*," he went on pondering, "had the idea ever entered his head before, if only as a dream in a vindictive moment?"

He decided that question strangely—that "Pavel Pavlovitch did want to kill him, but the thought of the murder had never entered his head." In short: "Pavel Pavlovitch wanted to kill him, but didn't know he wanted to kill him. It's senseless, but that's the truth," thought Velchaninov. "It was not to get a post and it was not on Bagautov's account he came here, though he did try to get a post here, and did run to see Bagautov and was furious when he died; he thought no more of him than a chip. He came here on my account and he came here with Liza . . .

"And did I expect that he . . . would murder me?" He decided that he did, that he had expected it from the moment when he saw him in the carriage following Bagautov's funeral. "I began, as it were, to expect something . . . but, of course, not that; but, of course, not that he would murder me! . . .

"And can it be that all that was true?" he exclaimed again, suddenly raising his head from the pillow and opening his eyes. "All that that . . . madman told me yesterday about his love for me, when his chin quivered and he thumped himself on the breast with his fist?

"It was the absolute truth," he decided, still pondering and analyzing, "that Quasimodo from T—— was quite sufficiently stupid and noble to fall in love with the lover of his wife, about whom he noticed nothing suspicious in twenty years! He had been thinking of me with respect, cherishing my memory and brooding over my utterances for nine years. Good heavens! and I had no notion of it! He could not have been lying yesterday! But did he love me yesterday when he declared his feeling and said 'Let us settle our account'? Yes, it was from hatred that he loved me; that's the strongest of all loves . . .

"Of course it may have happened, of course it must have happened that I made a tremendous impression on him at T——. Tremendous and 'gratifying' is just what it was, and it's just with a Schiller like that, in the outer form of a Quasimodo, that such a thing could happen! He magnified me a hundredfold because I impressed him too much in his philosophic solitude. . . . It would be interesting to know by what I impressed him. Perhaps by my clean gloves and my knowing how to put them on. Quasimodos are fond of all that is aesthetic. Ough! aren't they fond of it! A glove is often quite enough for a noble heart, and especially one of these 'eternal husbands.' The rest they supply themselves a thousand times, and are ready to fight for you, to satisfy your slightest wish. What an opinion he had of my powers of fascination! Perhaps it was just my powers of fascination that made the most impression on him. And his cry then, 'If that one, too . . . whom can one trust!' After that cry one may well become a wild beast! . . .

"H'm! He comes here 'to embrace me and to weep,' as he expressed it in the most abject way—that is, he came here to murder me and thought he came 'to embrace me and to weep.' . . . He brought Liza too. But, who knows? if I had wept with him, perhaps, really, he

would have forgiven me, for he had a terrible longing to forgive me!
. . . At the first shock all that was changed into drunken antics and
caricature, and into loathsome, womanish whining over his wrongs.
(Those horns! those horns he made on his forehead!) He came drunk
on purpose to speak out, though he was playing the fool; if he had
not been drunk, even he could not have done it. . . . And how he
liked playing the fool, didn't he like it! Ough! wasn't he pleased, too,
when he made me kiss him! Only he didn't know then whether he
would end by embracing me or murdering me. Of course, it's turned
out that the best thing was to do both. A most natural solution! Yes
indeed, nature dislikes monstrosities and destroys them with natural
solutions. The most monstrous monster is the monster with noble feelings; I know that by personal experience, Pavel Pavlovitch! Nature
is not a tender mother, but a stepmother to the monster. Nature gives
birth to the deformed, but instead of pitying him she punishes him,
and with good reason. Even decent people have to pay for embraces
and tears of forgiveness nowadays, to say nothing of men like you
and me, Pavel Pavlovitch!

"Yes, he was stupid enough to take me to see his future bride. Good
heavens! His future bride! Only a Quasimodo like that could have
conceived the notion of 'rising again to a new life' by means of the
innocence of Mademoiselle Zahlebinin! But it was not your fault,
Pavel Pavlovitch, it was not your fault: you're a monster, so everything
about you is bound to be monstrous, your dreams and your hopes.
But, though he was a monster, he had doubts of his dream, and that
was why he needed the high sanction of Velchaninov whom he so
revered. He wanted Velchaninov to approve, he wanted him to reassure him that the dream was not a dream, but something real. He
took me there from a devout respect for me and faith in the nobility
of my feelings, believing, perhaps, that there, under a bush, we should
embrace and shed tears near all that youthful innocence. Yes! That
'eternal husband' was obliged, sooner or later, to punish himself for
everything, and to punish himself he snatched up the razor—by accident, it is true, still he did snatch it up! 'And yet he stuck him with a
knife, and yet he ended by stabbing him in the presence of the Governor.' And, by the way, had he any idea of that sort in his mind when
he told me that anecdote about the best man? And was there really
anything that night when he got out of bed and stood in the middle
of the room? H'm! . . . No, he stood there then *as a joke*. He got up
for other reasons, and when he saw that I was frightened of him he
did not answer me for ten minutes because he was very much pleased

that I was frightened of him. . . . It was at that moment, perhaps, when he stood there in the dark, that some idea of this sort first dawned upon him. . . .

"Yet if I had not forgotten that razor on the table yesterday—maybe nothing would have happened. Is that so? Is that so? To be sure he had been avoiding me before—why, he had not been to see me for a fortnight; he had been hiding from me to *spare* me! Of course, he picked out Bagautov first, not me! Why, he rushed to heat plates for me in the night, thinking to create a diversion—from the knife to pity and tenderness! . . . He wanted to save himself and me, too—with his hot plates! . . ."

And for a long time the sick brain of this "man of the world" went on working in this way, going round and round in a circle, till he grew calmer. He woke up next morning with the same headache, but with a quite *new* and quite unexpected terror in his heart.

This new terror came from the positive conviction, which suddenly grew strong within him, that he, Velchaninov (a man of the world), would end it all that day by going of his own free will to Pavel Pavlovitch. Why? What for? He had no idea and, with repugnance, refused to know; all that he knew was that, for some reason, he would go to him.

This madness, however—he could give it no other name—did, as it developed, take a rational form and fasten upon a fairly legitimate pretext: he had even, the day before, been haunted by the idea that Pavel Pavlovitch would go back to his lodging and hang himself, like the clerk about whom Marya Sysoevna had told him. This notion of the day before had passed by degrees into an unreasoning but persistent conviction. "Why should the fool hang himself?" he kept protesting to himself every half-minute. He remembered Liza's words . . . "Yet in his place, perhaps, I should hang myself" . . . he reflected once.

It ended by his turning towards Pavel Pavlovitch instead of going to dinner. "I shall simply inquire of Marya Sysoevna," he decided. But before he had come out into the street he stopped short in the gateway. "Can it be, can it be?" he cried, turning crimson with shame. "Can it be that I'm crawling there, to 'embrace and shed tears'? That senseless abjectness was all that was needed to complete the ignominy!"

But from that "senseless abjectness" he was saved by the providence that watches over all decent and well-bred people. He had no sooner stepped into the street when he stumbled upon Alexandr Lobov. The young man was in breathless haste and excitement.

"I was coming to see you! What do you think of our friend Pavel Pavlovitch, now?"

"He's hanged himself!" Velchaninov muttered wildly.

"Who's hanged himself? What for?" cried Lobov, with wide-open eyes.

"Never mind . . . I didn't mean anything; go on."

"Tfoo! damn it all! what funny ideas you have, though. He's not hanged himself at all (why should he hang himself?). On the contrary—he's gone away. I've only just put him into the train and seen him off. Tfoo! how he drinks, I tell you! We drank three bottles, Predposylov with us—but how he drinks, how he drinks! He was singing songs in the train. He remembered you, blew kisses, sent you his greetings. But he is a scoundrel, don't you think so?"

The young man certainly was a little tipsy; his flushed face, his shining eyes and faltering tongue betrayed it unmistakably.

Velchaninov laughed loudly.

"So in the end they finished up with Brüderschaft! Ha-ha! They embraced and shed tears! Ah, you Schilleresque poets!"

"Don't call me names, please. Do you know he's given it all up over *there?* He was there yesterday, and he's been there to-day. He sneaked horribly. They locked Nadya up—she's sitting in a room upstairs. There were tears and lamentations, but we stood firm! But how he does drink, I say, doesn't he drink! And, I say, isn't he *mauvais ton,* at least not *mauvais ton* exactly, what shall I call it? . . . He kept talking of you, but there's no comparison between you! You're a gentleman anyway, and really did move in decent society at one time and have only been forced to come down now through poverty or something. . . . Goodness knows what, I couldn't quite understand him."

"Ah, so he spoke to you of me in those terms?"

"He did, he did; don't be angry. To be a good citizen is better than being in aristocratic society. I say that because in Russia nowadays one doesn't know whom to respect. You'll agree that it's a serious malady of the age, when people don't know whom to respect, isn't it?"

"It is, it is; what did he say?"

"He? Who? Ah, to be sure! Why did he keep saying 'Velchaninov fifty, but a rake,' why *but* a rake and not *and* a rake; he laughed and repeated it a thousand times over. He got into the train, sang a song and burst out crying—it was simply revolting, pitiful, in fact—from drunkenness. Oh! I don't like fools! He fell to throwing money to the beggars for the peace of the soul of Lizaveta—his wife, is that?"

"His daughter."

"What's the matter with your hand?"

"I cut it."

"Never mind, it will get better. Damn him, you know, it's a good thing he's gone, but I bet anything that he'll get married directly he arrives—he will—won't he?"

"Why, but you want to get married, too, don't you?"

"Me? That's a different matter. What a man you are, really! If you are fifty, he must be sixty: you must look at it logically, my dear sir! And do you know I used, long ago, to be a pure Slavophil by conviction, but now we look for dawn from the West. . . . But, good-bye; I'm glad I met you without going in; I won't come in, don't ask me, I've no time to spare! . . ."

And he was just running off.

"Oh, by the way," he cried, turning back; "why, he sent me to you with a letter! Here is the letter. Why didn't you come to see him off?"

Velchaninov returned home and opened the envelope addressed to him.

There was not one line from Pavel Pavlovitch in it, but there was a different letter. Velchaninov recognized the handwriting. It was an old letter, written on paper yellow with age, with ink that had changed colour. It had been written to him ten years before, two months after he had left T—— and returned to Petersburg. But the letter had never reached him; he had received a different one instead of it; this was clear from the contents of this old yellow letter. In this letter Natalya Vassilyevna took leave of him for ever, and confessed that she loved some one else, just as in the letter he had actually received; but she also did not conceal from him that she was going to have a child. On the contrary, to comfort him, she held out hopes that she might find a possibility of handing over the future child to him, declared henceforth that they had other duties—in short, there was little logic, but the object was clear: that he should no longer trouble her with his love. She even sanctioned his coming to T—— in a year's time to have a look at the child. God knows why she changed her mind and sent the other letter instead.

Velchaninov was pale as he read it, but he pictured to himself Pavel Pavlovitch finding that letter and reading it for the first time, before the opened ebony box inlaid with mother-of-pearl which was an heirloom in the family.

"He, too, must have turned pale as a corpse," he thought, catching a glimpse of his own face in the looking-glass. "He must have read it and closed his eyes, and opened them again hoping that the letter would have changed into plain white paper. . . . Most likely he had done that a second time and a third! . . ."

Chapter 17

THE ETERNAL HUSBAND

ALMOST exactly two years had passed since the incidents we have described. We meet Velchaninov again on a beautiful summer day, in the train on one of our newly opened railways. He was going to Odessa for his own pleasure, to see one of his friends, and also with a view to something else of an agreeable nature. He hoped through that friend to arrange a meeting with an extremely interesting woman whose acquaintance he had long been eager to make. Without going into details we will confine ourselves to observing that he had become entirely transformed, or rather reformed, during those two years. Of his old hypochondria scarcely a trace remained. Of the various "reminiscences" and anxiety—the result of illness which had beset him two years before in Petersburg at the time of his unsuccessful lawsuit— nothing remained but a certain secret shame at the consciousness of his faint-heartedness. What partly made up for it was the conviction that it would never happen again, and that no one would ever know of it. It was true that at that time he had given up all society, had even begun to be slovenly in his dress, had crept away out of sight of every one—and that, of course, must have been noticed by all. But he so readily acknowledged his transgressions, and at the same time with such a self-confident air of new life and vigour, that "every one" immediately forgave his momentary falling away; in fact, those whom he had given up greeting were the first to recognize him and hold out their hands, and without any tiresome questions—just as though he had been absent on his own personal affairs, which were no business of theirs, and had only just come back from a distance. The cause of all these salutary changes for the better was, of course, the winning of his lawsuit. Velchaninov gained in all sixty thousand roubles—no great sum, of course, but of extreme importance to him; to begin with, he felt himself on firm ground again, and so he felt satisfied at heart; he knew for certain now that he would not, "like a fool," squander this money, as he had squandered his first two fortunes, and that he had enough for his whole life. "However the social edifice may totter, whatever trumpet call they're sounding," he thought sometimes, as he watched and heard all the marvellous and incredible things that were being done around him and all over Russia; "whatever shape people and ideas may take, I shall always have just such a delicate, dainty dinner as I am sitting down to now, and so I'm ready to face anything." This voluptuous, comfortable thought by degrees gained complete possession of him and produced a transformation in his physical, to say nothing of his moral, nature. He looked quite a different man from the "sluggard" whom we have described two years before and to whom such unseemly incidents had befallen—he looked cheerful, serene and dignified. Even the ill-humoured wrinkles that had begun to appear under his eyes and on his forehead had almost been smoothed away; the very tint of his face had changed, his skin was whiter and ruddier.

At the moment he was sitting comfortably in a first-class carriage and a charming idea was suggesting itself to his mind. The next station was a junction and there was a new branch line going off to the right. He asked himself, "How would it be to give up the direct way for the moment and turn off to the right?" There, only two stations away, he could visit another lady of his acquaintance who had only just returned from abroad, and was now living in a provincial isolation, very tedious for her, but favourable for him; and so it would be possible to spend his time no less agreeably than at Odessa, especially as he would not miss his visit there either. But he was still hesitating and could not quite make up his mind; he was waiting for something to decide him. Meanwhile, the station was approaching and that something was not far off.

At this station the train stopped forty minutes, and the passengers had the chance of having dinner. At the entrance to the dining-room for the passengers of the first and second class there was, as there usually is, a crowd of impatient and hurried people, and as is also usual, perhaps, a scandalous scene took place. A lady from a second-class carriage, who was remarkably pretty but somewhat too gorgeously dressed for travelling, was dragging after her an Uhlan, a very young and handsome officer, who was trying to tear himself out of her hands. The youthful officer was extremely drunk, and the lady, to all appearance some elder relative, would not let him go, probably apprehending that he would make a dash for the refreshment bar. Meanwhile, in the crush, the Uhlan was jostled by a young merchant who was also disgracefully intoxicated. He had been hanging about the station for the last two days, drinking and scattering his money among the companions who surrounded him, without succeeding in getting into the train to continue his journey. A scuffle followed; the officer shouted; the merchant swore; the lady was in despair, and, trying to draw the Uhlan away from the conflict, kept exclaiming in an imploring voice, "Mitenka! Mitenka!" This seemed to strike the young merchant as too scandalous; every one laughed, indeed, but the merchant was more offended than ever at the outrage, as he conceived it, on propriety.

"Oh, I say: Mitenka!" he pronounced reproachfully, mimicking the shrill voice of the lady. "And not ashamed before folks!"

He went staggering up to the lady, who had rushed to the first chair and succeeded in making the Uhlan sit down beside her, stared at them both contemptuously and drawled in a sing-song voice—

"You're a trollop, you are, dragging your tail in the dirt!"

The lady uttered a shriek and looked about her piteously for some means of escape. She was both ashamed and frightened, and, to put the finishing touch, the officer sprang up from the chair and, with a yell, made a dash at the merchant, but, slipping, fell back into the chair with a flop. The laughter grew louder around them, and no one dreamed of helping her; but Velchaninov came to the rescue; he seized the merchant by the collar and, turning him round, thrust him five paces away from the frightened lady. And with that the scene ended; the merchant was overwhelmed by the shock and by Velchaninov's impressive figure; his companions led him away. The dignified countenance of the elegantly dressed gentleman produced a strong effect on the jeering crowd: the laughter subsided. The lady flushed and, almost in tears, was overflowing with expressions of gratitude. The Uhlan mumbled: "Fanks, fanks!" and made as though to hold out his hand to Velchaninov, but instead of doing so suddenly took it into his head to recline at full length with his feet on the chairs.

"Mitenka!" the lady moaned reproachfully, clasping her hands in horror.

Velchaninov was pleased with the adventure and with the whole situation. The lady attracted him; she was evidently a wealthy provincial, gorgeously but tastelessly dressed, and with rather ridiculous manners—in fact, she combined all the characteristics that guarantee success to a Petersburg gallant with designs on the fair sex. A conversation sprang up; the lady bitterly complained of her husband, who "had disappeared as soon as he had got out of the carriage and so was the cause of it all, for whenever he is wanted he runs off somewhere."

"Naturally," the Uhlan muttered.

"Ah, Mitenka!" She clasped her hands again.

"Well, the husband will catch it," thought Velchaninov.

"What is his name? I will go and look for him," he suggested.

"Pal Palitch," responded the Uhlan.

"Your husband's name is Pavel Pavlovitch?" Velchaninov asked, with curiosity, and suddenly a familiar bald head was thrust between him and the lady. In a flash he had a vision of the Zahlebinins' garden, the innocent games and a tiresome bald head being incessantly thrust between him and Nadyezhda Fedosyevna.

"Here you are at last!" cried his wife hysterically.

It was Pavel Pavlovitch himself; he gazed in wonder and alarm at Velchaninov, as panic-stricken at the sight of him as though he had been a ghost. His stupefaction was such that he evidently could not for some minutes take in what his offended spouse was explaining in a rapid and irritable flow of words. At last, with a start, he grasped all the horror of his position: his own guilt, and Mitenka's behaviour, "and that this monsieur" (this was how the lady for some reason described Velchaninov) "has been a saviour and guardian angel to us, while you—you are always out of the way when you are wanted. . . ."

Velchaninov suddenly burst out laughing.

"Why, we are friends, we've been friends since childhood!" he exclaimed to the astonished lady. Putting his right arm with patronizing familiarity round the shoulders of Pavel Pavlovitch, who smiled a pale smile, "Hasn't he talked to you of Velchaninov?"

"No, he never has," the lady responded, somewhat disconcerted.

"You might introduce me to your wife, you faithless friend!"

"Lipotchka . . . it really is M. Velchaninov," Pavel Pavlovitch was beginning, but he broke off abashed.

His wife turned crimson and flashed an angry look at him, probably for the "Lipotchka."

"And, only fancy, he never let me know he was married, and never invited me to the wedding, but you, Olimpiada . . ."

"Semyonovna," Pavel Pavlovitch prompted.

"Semyonovna," the Uhlan, who had dropped asleep, echoed suddenly.

"You must forgive him, Olimpiada Semyonova, for my sake, in honour of our meeting . . . he's a good husband."

And Velchaninov gave Pavel Pavlovitch a friendly slap on the shoulder.

"I was . . . I was only away for a minute, my love," Pavel Pavlovitch was beginning to say.

"And left your wife to be insulted," Lipotchka put in at once. "When you're wanted there's no finding you, when you're not wanted you're always at hand . . ."

"Where you're not wanted, where you're not wanted . . . where you're not wanted . . ." the Uhlan chimed in.

Lipotchka was almost breathless with excitement; she knew it was not seemly before Velchaninov, and flushed but could not restrain herself.

"Where you shouldn't be you are too attentive, too attentive!" she burst out.

"Under the bed . . . he looks for a lover under the bed—where he shouldn't . . . where he shouldn't . . ." muttered Mitenka, suddenly growing extremely excited.

But there was no doing anything with Mitenka by now. It all ended pleasantly, however, and they got upon quite friendly terms. Pavel Pavlovitch was sent to fetch coffee and soup. Olimpiada Semyonovna explained to Velchaninov that they were on their way from O——, where her husband had a post in the service, to spend two months at their country place, that it was not far off, only thirty miles from the station, that they had a lovely house and garden there, that they always had the house full of visitors, that they had neighbours too, and if Alexey Ivanovitch would be so good as to come and stay with them "in their rustic solitude" she would welcome him "as their guardian angel," for she could not recall without horror what would have happened, if . . . and so on, and so on—in fact, he was "her guardian angel. . . ."

"And saviour, and saviour," the Uhlan insisted, with heat.

Velchaninov thanked her politely, and replied that he was always at her service, that he was an absolutely idle man with no duties of any sort, and that Olimpiada Semyonovna's invitation was most flattering. He followed this at once with sprightly conversation, successfully introducing two or three compliments. Lipotchka blushed with pleasure, and as soon as Pavel Pavlovitch returned she told him enthusiastically that Alexey Ivanovitch had been so kind as to accept her invitation to spend a whole month with them in the country, and had promised to come in a week. Pavel Pavlovitch smiled in mute despair. Olimpiada Semyonovna shrugged her shoulders at him, and turned her eyes up to the ceiling. At last they got up; again a gush of gratitude, again the "guardian angel," again "Mitenka," and Pavel Pavlovitch at last escorted his wife and the Uhlan to their compartment. Velchaninov lighted a cigar and began pacing to and fro on the balcony in front of the station; he knew that Pavel Pavlovitch would run out again at once to talk to him till the bell rang. And so it happened. Pavel Pavlovitch promptly appeared before him with an uneasy expression in his face and whole figure. Velchaninov laughed, took him by the elbow in a friendly way, led him to the nearest bench, sat down himself, and made him sit down beside him. He remained silent; he wanted Pavel Pavlovitch to be the first to speak.

"So you are coming to us?" faltered the latter, going straight to the point.

"I knew that would be it! You haven't changed in the least!" laughed Velchaninov. "Why, do you mean to say"—he slapped him again on the shoulder—"do you mean to say you could seriously imagine for a moment that I could actually come and stay with you, and for a whole month too—ha-ha?"

Pavel Pavlovitch was all of a twitter.

"So you—are not coming!" he cried, not in the least disguising his relief.

"I'm not coming, I'm not coming!" Velchaninov laughed complacently.

He could not have said himself, however, why he felt so particularly amused, but he was more and more amused as time went on.

"Do you really . . . do you really mean it?"

And saying this, Pavel Pavlovitch actually jumped up from his seat in a flutter of suspense.

"Yes, I've told you already that I'm not coming, you queer fellow."

"If that's so, what am I to say to Olimpiada Semyonovna a week hence, when she will be expecting you and you don't come?"

"What a difficulty! Tell her I've broken my leg or something of that sort."

"She won't believe it," Pavel Pavlovitch drawled plaintively.

"And you'll catch it?" Velchaninov went on laughing. "But I observe, my poor friend, that you tremble before your delightful wife —don't you?"

Pavel Pavlovitch tried to smile, but it did not come off. That Velchaninov had refused to visit them was a good thing, of course, but that he should be over-familiar to him about his wife was disagreeable. Pavel Pavlovitch winced; Velchaninov noticed it. Meanwhile the second bell rang; they heard a shrill voice from the train anxiously calling Pavel Pavlovitch. The latter moved, fidgeted in his chair, but did not rise at the first summons, evidently expecting something more from Velchaninov, no doubt another assurance that he would not come and stay with them.

"What was your wife's maiden name?" Velchaninov inquired, as though unaware of Pavel Pavlovitch's anxiety.

"She is our priest's daughter," replied the latter in uneasy trepidation, listening and looking towards the train.

"Ah, I understand, you married her for her beauty."

Pavel Pavlovitch winced again.

"And who's this Mitenka with you?"

"Oh, he's a distant relation of ours—that is, of mine; the son of my deceased cousin. His name's Golubtchikov, he was degraded for disorderly behaviour in the army, but now he has been promoted again and we have been getting his equipment. . . . He's an unfortunate young man. . . ."

"To be sure, the regular thing; the party's complete," thought Velchaninov.

"Pavel Pavlovitch!" the call came again from the train, and by now with a marked tone of irritation in the voice.

"Pal Palitch!" they heard in another thick voice.

Pavel Pavlovitch fidgeted and moved restlessly again, but Velchaninov took him by the elbow and detained him.

"How would you like me to go this minute and tell your wife how you tried to cut my throat?"

"What, what!" Pavel Pavlovitch was terribly alarmed. "God forbid!"

"Pavel Pavlovitch! Pavel Pavlovitch!" voices were heard calling again.

"Well, be off now!" said Velchaninov, letting him go at last, and still laughing genially.

"So you won't come?" Pavel Pavlovitch whispered for the last time, almost in despair, and even put his hands before him with the palms together in his old style.

"Why, I swear I won't come! Run, there'll be trouble, you know."

And with a flourish he held out his hand to him—and was startled at the result: Pavel Pavlovitch did not take his hand, he even drew his own hand back.

The third bell rang.

In one instant something strange happened to both of them: both seemed transformed. Something, as it were, quivered and burst out in Velchaninov, who had been laughing only just before. He clutched

Pavel Pavlovitch by the shoulder and held him in a tight and furious grip.

"If I—*I* hold out this hand to you," showing the palm of his left hand, where a big scar from the cut was still distinct, "you certainly might take it!" he whispered, with pale and trembling lips.

Pavel Pavlovitch, too, turned pale, and his lips trembled too; a convulsive quiver ran over his face.

"And Liza?" he murmured in a rapid whisper, and suddenly his lips, his cheeks and his chin began to twitch and tears gushed from his eyes.

Velchaninov stood before him stupefied.

"Pavel Pavlovitch! Pavel Pavlovitch!" they heard a scream from the train as though some one were being murdered—and suddenly the whistle sounded.

Pavel Pavlovitch roused himself, flung up his hands and ran full speed to the train; the train was already in motion, but he managed to hang on somehow, and went flying to his compartment. Velchaninov remained at the station and only in the evening set off on his original route in another train. He did not turn off to the right to see his fair friend—he felt too much out of humour. And how he regretted it afterwards!

The Double

A P E T E R S B U R G P O E M

THE DOUBLE

(A PETERSBURG POEM)

Chapter 1

I T WAS a little before eight o'clock in the morning when Yakov
Petrovitch Golyadkin, a titular councillor, woke up from a long sleep.
He yawned, stretched, and at last opened his eyes completely. For
two minutes, however, he lay in his bed without moving, as though
he were not yet quite certain whether he were awake or still asleep,
whether all that was going on around him were real and actual, or the
continuation of his confused dreams. Very soon, however, Mr. Golyadkin's senses began more clearly and more distinctly to receive their
habitual and everyday impressions. The dirty green, smoke-begrimed,
dusty walls of his little room, with the mahogany chest of drawers
and chairs, the table painted red, the sofa covered with American
leather of a reddish colour with little green flowers on it, and the
clothes taken off in haste overnight and flung in a crumpled heap on
the sofa, looked at him familiarly. At last the damp autumn day,
muggy and dirty, peeped into the room through the dingy window
pane with such a hostile, sour grimace that Mr. Golyadkin could not
possibly doubt that he was not in the land of Nod, but in the city of
Petersburg, in his own flat on the fourth storey of a huge block of
buildings in Shestilavotchny Street. When he had made this important
discovery Mr. Golyadkin nervously closed his eyes, as though regretting his dream and wanting to go back to it for a moment. But a
minute later he leapt out of bed at one bound, probably all at once
grasping the idea about which his scattered and wandering thoughts
had been revolving. From his bed he ran straight to a little round
looking-glass that stood on his chest of drawers. Though the sleepy,
short-sighted countenance and rather bald head reflected in the looking-glass were of such an insignificant type that at first sight they
would certainly not have attracted particular attention in any one, yet
the owner of the countenance was satisfied with all that he saw in the
looking-glass. "What a thing it would be," said Mr. Golyadkin in an

undertone, "what a thing it would be if I were not up to the mark to-day, if something were amiss, if some intrusive pimple had made its appearance, or anything else unpleasant had happened; so far, however, there's nothing wrong, so far everything's all right."

Greatly relieved that everything was all right, Mr. Golyadkin put the looking-glass back in its place and, although he had nothing on his feet and was still in the attire in which he was accustomed to go to bed, he ran to the little window and with great interest began looking for something in the courtyard, upon which the windows of his flat looked out. Apparently what he was looking for in the yard quite satisfied him too; his face beamed with a self-satisfied smile. Then, after first peeping, however, behind the partition into his valet Petrushka's little room and making sure that Petrushka was not there, he went on tiptoe to the table, opened the drawer in it and, fumbling in the furthest corner of it, he took from under old yellow papers and all sorts of rubbish a shabby green pocket-book, opened it cautiously, and with care and relish peeped into the furthest and most hidden fold of it. Probably the roll of green, grey, blue, red and particoloured notes looked at Golyadkin, too, with approval: with a radiant face he laid the open pocket-book before him and rubbed his hands vigorously in token of the greatest satisfaction. Finally, he took it out—his comforting roll of notes—and, for the hundredth time since the previous day, counted them over, carefully smoothing out every note between his forefinger and his thumb.

"Seven hundred and fifty roubles in notes," he concluded at last, in a half-whisper. "Seven hundred and fifty roubles, a noteworthy sum! It's an agreeable sum," he went on, in a voice weak and trembling with gratification, as he pinched the roll with his fingers and smiled significantly; "it's a very agreeable sum! A sum agreeable to any one! I should like to see the man to whom that would be a trivial sum! There's no knowing what a man might not do with a sum like that. . . . What's the meaning of it, though?" thought Mr. Golyadkin; "where's Petrushka?" And still in the same attire he peeped behind the partition again. Again there was no sign of Petrushka; and the samovar standing on the floor was beside itself, fuming and raging in solitude, threatening every minute to boil over, hissing and lisping in its mysterious language, to Mr. Golyadkin something like, "Take me, good people, I'm boiling and perfectly ready."

"Damn the fellow," thought Mr. Golyadkin. "That lazy brute might really drive a man out of all patience; where's he dawdling now?"

In just indignation he went out into the hall, which consisted of a little corridor at the end of which was a door into the entry, and saw his servant surrounded by a good-sized group of lackeys of all sorts, a mixed rabble from outside as well as from the flats of the house. Petrushka was telling something, the others were listening. Apparently the subject of the conversation, or the conversation itself, did not please Mr. Golyadkin. He promptly called Petrushka and returned to his room, displeased and even upset. "That beast would sell a man for a halfpenny, and his master before any one," he thought to himself: "and he has sold me, he certainly has. I bet he has sold me for a farthing. Well?"

"They've brought the livery, sir."

"Put it on, and come here."

When he had put on his livery, Petrushka, with a stupid smile on his face, went in to his master. His costume was incredibly strange. He had on a much-worn green livery, with frayed gold braid on it, apparently made for a man a yard taller than Petrushka. In his hand he had a hat trimmed with the same gold braid and with a feather in it, and at his hip hung a footman's sword in a leather sheath. Finally, to complete the picture, Petrushka, who always liked to be in *négligé,* was barefooted. Mr. Golyadkin looked at Petrushka from all sides and was apparently satisfied. The livery had evidently been hired for some solemn occasion. It might be observed, too, that during his master's inspection Petrushka watched him with strange expectancy and with marked curiosity followed every movement he made, which extremely embarrassed Mr. Golyadkin.

"Well, and how about the carriage?"

"The carriage is here too."

"For the whole day?"

"For the whole day. Twenty-five roubles."

"And have the boots been sent?"

"Yes."

"Dolt! can't even say, 'Yes, sir.' Bring them here."

Expressing his satisfaction that the boots fitted, Mr. Golyadkin asked for his tea, and for water to wash and shave. He shaved with great care and washed as scrupulously, hurriedly sipped his tea and proceeded to the principal final process of attiring himself: he put on an almost new pair of trousers; then a shirt-front with brass studs, and a very bright and agreeably flowered waistcoat; about his neck he tied a gay, particoloured cravat, and finally drew on his coat, which was also newish and carefully brushed. As he dressed, he more than once looked lovingly at his boots, lifted up first one leg and then the other, admired their shape, kept muttering something to himself, and from time to time made expressive grimaces. Mr. Golyadkin was, however, extremely absent-minded that morning, for he scarcely noticed the little smiles and grimaces made at his expense by Petrushka, who was helping him dress. At last, having arranged everything properly and having finished dressing, Mr. Golyadkin put his pocket-book in his pocket, took a final admiring look at Petrushka, who had put on his boots and was therefore also quite ready, and, noticing that everything was done and that there was nothing left to wait for, he ran hurriedly and fussily out on to the stairs, with a slight throbbing at his heart. The light-blue hired carriage with a crest on it rolled noisily up to the steps. Petrushka, winking to the driver and some of the gaping crowd, helped his master into the carriage; and, hardly able to suppress an idiotic laugh, shouted in an unnatural voice: "Off!" jumped up on the footboard, and the whole turnout, clattering and rumbling noisily, rolled into the Nevsky Prospect. As soon as the light-blue carriage dashed out of the gate, Mr. Golyadkin rubbed his hands convulsively and went off into a slow, noiseless chuckle, like a jubilant man who has succeeded in bringing off a splendid performance and is as pleased as Punch with the performance himself. Immediately after his access of gaiety, however, laughter was replaced by a strange and anxious expression on the face of Mr. Golyadkin. Though the weather was damp and muggy, he let down both windows of the carriage and began carefully scrutinizing the passers-by to left and to right, at once assuming a decorous and sedate air when he thought any one was looking at him. At the turning from Liteyny Street into the Nevsky Prospect he was startled by a most unpleasant sensation and, frowning like some poor wretch whose corn has been accidentally trodden on, he huddled with almost panic-stricken haste into the darkest corner of his carriage.

He had seen two of his colleagues, two young clerks serving in the same government department. The young clerks were also, it seemed to Mr. Golyadkin, extremely amazed at meeting their colleague in such a way; one of them, in fact, pointed him out to the other. Mr. Golyadkin even fancied that the other had actually called his name, which, of course, was very unseemly in the street. Our hero concealed himself and did not respond. "The silly youngsters!" he began reflecting to himself. "Why, what is there strange in it? A man in a carriage, a man needs to be in a carriage, and so he hires a carriage. They're simply noodles! I know them—simply silly youngsters, who still need thrashing! They want to be paid a salary for playing pitch-farthing and dawdling about, that's all they're fit for. I'd let them all know, if only . . ."

Mr. Golyadkin broke off suddenly, petrified. A smart pair of Kazan horses, very familiar to Mr. Golyadkin, in a fashionable droshky, drove rapidly by on the right side of his carriage. The gentleman sitting in the droshky, happening to catch a glimpse of Mr. Golyadkin, who was rather incautiously poking his head out of the carriage window, also appeared to be extremely astonished at the unexpected meeting and, bending out as far as he could, looked with the greatest curiosity and interest into the corner of the carriage in which our hero made haste to conceal himself. The gentleman in the droshky was Andrey Filippovitch, the head of the office in which Mr. Golyadkin served in the capacity of assistant to the chief clerk. Mr. Golyadkin, seeing that Andrey Filippovitch recognized him, that he was looking at him open-eyed and that it was impossible to hide, blushed up to his ears.

"Bow or not? Call back or not? Recognize him or not?" our hero wondered in indescribable anguish. "Or pretend that I am not myself, but somebody else strikingly like me, and look as though nothing were the matter. Simply not I, not I—and that's all," said Mr. Golyadkin, taking off his hat to Andrey Filippovitch and keeping his eyes fixed upon him. "I'm . . . I'm all right," he whispered with an effort; "I'm . . . quite all right. It's not I, it's not I—and that is the fact of the matter."

Soon, however, the droshky passed the carriage, and the magnetism of his chief's eyes was at an end. Yet he went on blushing, smiling and muttering something to himself. . . .

"I was a fool not to call back," he thought at last. "I ought to have taken a bolder line and behaved with gentlemanly openness. I ought to have said, 'This is how it is, Andrey Filippovitch, I'm asked to the dinner too,' and that's all it is!"

Then, suddenly recalling how taken aback he had been, our hero flushed as hot as fire, frowned, and cast a terrible defiant glance at the front corner of the carriage, a glance calculated to reduce all his foes to ashes. At last, he was suddenly inspired to pull the cord attached to the driver's elbow, and stopped the carriage, telling him to drive back to Liteyny Street. The fact was, it was urgently necessary for Mr. Golyadkin, probably for the sake of his own peace of mind, to say something very interesting to his doctor, Krestyan Ivanovitch. And, though he had made Krestyan Ivanovitch's acquaintance quite recently, having, indeed, only paid him a single visit, and that one the previous week, to consult him about some symptom. But a doctor, as they say, is like a priest, and it would be stupid for him to keep out of sight, and, indeed, it was his duty to know his patients. "Will it be all right, though," our hero went on, getting out of the carriage at the door of a five-storey house in Liteyny Street, at which he had told the driver to stop the carriage: "Will it be all right? Will it be proper? Will it be appropriate? After all, though," he went on, thinking as he mounted the stairs out of breath and trying to suppress the beating of his heart, which had the habit of beating on all other people's staircases, "after all, it's on my own business and there's nothing reprehensible in it. . . . It would be stupid to keep out of sight. Why, of course, I shall behave as though I were quite all right, and have simply looked in as I passed. . . . He will see that it's all just as it should be."

Reasoning like this, Mr. Golyadkin mounted to the second storey and stopped before flat number five, on which there was a handsome brass door-plate with the inscription—

KRESTYAN IVANOVITCH RUTENSPITZ
Doctor of Medicine and Surgery

Stopping at the door, our hero made haste to assume an air of propriety, ease, and even of a certain affability, and prepared to pull the bell. As he was about to do so he promptly and rather appropriately reflected that it might be better to come to-morrow, and that it was not very pressing for the moment. But as he suddenly heard footsteps on the stairs, he immediately changed his mind again and at once rang Krestyan Ivanovitch's bell—with an air, moreover, of great determination.

Chapter 2

THE doctor of medicine and surgery, Krestyan Ivanovitch Ruten spitz, a very hale, though elderly man, with thick eyebrows and whiskers that were beginning to turn grey, eyes with an expressive gleam in them that looked capable of routing every disease, and, lastly, with orders of some distinction on his breast, was sitting in his consulting-room that morning in his comfortable arm-chair. He was drinking coffee, which his wife had brought him with her own hand, smoking a cigar and from time to time writing prescriptions for his patients. After prescribing a draught for an old man who was suffering from haemorrhoids and seeing the aged patient out by the side door, Krestyan Ivanovitch sat down to await the next visitor.

Mr. Golyadkin walked in.

Apparently Krestyan Ivanovitch did not in the least expect nor desire to see Mr. Golyadkin, for he was suddenly taken aback for a moment, and his countenance unconsciously assumed a strange and, one may almost say, a displeased expression. As Mr. Golyadkin almost always turned up inappropriately and was thrown into confusion whenever he approached any one about his own little affairs, on this occasion, too, he was desperately embarrassed. Having neglected to get ready his first sentence, which was invariably a stumbling-block for him on such occasions, he muttered something—apparently an apology—and, not knowing what to do next, took a chair and sat down, but, realizing that he had sat down without being asked to do so, he was immediately conscious of his lapse, and made haste to efface his offence against etiquette and good breeding by promptly getting up again from the seat he had taken uninvited. Then, on second thoughts, dimly perceiving that he had committed two stupid blunders at once, he immediately decided to commit a third—that is, tried to right himself, muttered something, smiled, blushed, was overcome with embarrassment, sank into expressive silence, and finally sat down for good and did not get up again. Only, to protect himself from all contingencies, he looked at the doctor with that defiant glare which had an extraordinary power of figuratively crushing Mr. Golyadkin's enemies and reducing them to ashes. This glance, moreover, expressed to the full Mr. Golyadkin's independence—that is, to speak plainly, the fact that Mr. Golyadkin was "all right," that he was "quite himself, like everybody else," and that there was "nothing wrong in his upper storey." Krestyan Ivanovitch coughed, cleared his throat, apparently in token of approval and assent to all this, and bent an inquisitorial interrogative gaze upon his visitor.

"I have come to trouble you a second time, Krestyan Ivanovitch," began Mr. Golyadkin, with a smile, "and now I venture to ask your indulgence a second time. . . ." He was obviously at a loss for words.

"H'm . . . Yes!" pronounced Krestyan Ivanovitch, puffing out a spiral of smoke and putting down his cigar on the table, "but you must follow the treatment prescribed you; I explained to you that what would be beneficial to your health is a change of habits. . . . Entertainment, for instance, and, well, friends—you should visit your acquaintances, and not be hostile to the bottle; and likewise keep cheerful company."

Mr. Golyadkin, still smiling, hastened to observe that he thought he was like every one else, that he lived by himself, that he had entertainments like every one else . . . that, of course, he might go to the theatre, for he had the means like every one else, that he spent the day at the office and the evenings at home, that he was quite all right; he even observed, in passing, that he was, so far as he could see, as good as any one, that he lived at home, and, finally, that he had Petrushka. At this point Mr. Golyadkin hesitated.

"H'm! no, that is not the order of proceeding I want; and that is not at all what I would ask you. I am interested to know, in general, are you a great lover of cheerful company? Do you take advantages of festive occasions; and, well, do you lead a melancholy or a cheerful manner of life?"

"Krestyan Ivanovitch, I . . ."

"H'm! . . . I tell you," interrupted the doctor, "that you must have a radical change of life, must, in a certain sense, break in your character." (Krestyan Ivanovitch laid special stress on the words "break in," and paused for a moment with a very significant air.) "Must not shrink from gaiety, must visit entertainments and clubs, and in any case, be not hostile to the bottle. Sitting at home is not right for you . . . sitting at home is impossible for you."

"I like quiet, Krestyan Ivanovitch," said Mr. Golyadkin, with a significant look at the doctor and evidently seeking words to express his ideas more successfully: "In my flat there's only me and Petrushka. . . . I mean my man, Krestyan Ivanovitch. I mean to say, Krestyan Ivanovitch, that I go my way, my own way, Krestyan Ivanovitch. I keep myself to myself, and so far as I can see am not dependent on any one. I go out for walks, too, Krestyan Ivanovitch."

"What? Yes! well, nowadays there's nothing agreeable in walking: the climate's extremely bad."

"Quite so, Krestyan Ivanovitch. Though I'm a peaceable man, Krestyan Ivanovitch, as I've had the honour of explaining to you already, yet my way lies apart, Krestyan Ivanovitch. The ways of life are manifold. . . . I mean . . . I mean to say, Krestyan Ivanovitch. . . . Excuse me, Krestyan Ivanovitch, I've no great gift for eloquent speaking."

"H'm . . . you say . . ."

"I say, you must excuse me, Krestyan Ivanovitch, that as far as I can see I am no great hand at eloquence in speaking," Mr. Golyadkin articulated, stammering and hesitating, in a half-aggrieved voice. "In that respect, Krestyan Ivanovitch, I'm not quite like other people," he added, with a peculiar smile, "I can't talk much, and have never learnt to embellish my speech with literary graces. On the other hand, I act, Krestyan Ivanovitch; on the other hand, I act, Krestyan Ivanovitch."

"H'm . . . How's that . . . you act?" responded Krestyan Ivanovitch.

Then silence followed for half a minute. The doctor looked somewhat strangely and mistrustfully at his visitor. Mr. Golyadkin, for his part, too, stole a rather mistrustful glance at the doctor.

"Krestyan Ivanovitch," he began, going on again in the same tone as before, somewhat irritated and puzzled by the doctor's extreme obstinacy: "I like tranquillity and not the noisy gaiety of the world. Among them, I mean, in the noisy world, Krestyan Ivanovitch, one must be able to polish the floor with one's boots . . ." (here Mr. Golyadkin made a slight scrape on the floor with his toe); "they expect it, and they expect puns too . . . one must know how to make a perfumed compliment . . . that's what they expect there. And I've not learnt to do it, Krestyan Ivanovitch, I've never learnt all those tricks, I've never had the time. I'm a simple person, and not ingenious, and I've no external polish. On that side I surrender, Krestyan Ivanovitch, I lay down my arms, speaking in that sense."

All this Mr. Golyadkin pronounced with an air which made it perfectly clear that our hero was far from regretting that he was laying down his arms in that sense and that he had not learnt these tricks; quite the contrary, indeed. As Krestyan Ivanovitch listened to him, he looked down with a very unpleasant grimace on his face, seeming to have a presentiment of something. Mr. Golyadkin's tirade was followed by a rather long and significant silence.

"You have, I think, departed a little from the subject," Krestyan Ivanovitch said at last, in a low voice: "I confess I cannot altogether understand you."

"I'm not a great hand at eloquent speaking, Krestyan Ivanovitch; I've had the honour to inform you, Krestyan Ivanovitch, already," said Mr. Golyadkin, speaking this time in a sharp and resolute tone. "H'm!" . . .

"Krestyan Ivanovitch!" began Mr. Golyadkin again in a low but more significant voice, in a somewhat solemn style and emphasizing every point: "Krestyan Ivanovitch, when I came in here I began with apologies. I repeat the same thing again, and again ask for your indulgence. There's no need for me to conceal it, Krestyan Ivanovitch. I'm an unimportant man, as you know; but, fortunately for me, I do not regret being an unimportant man. Quite the contrary, indeed, Krestyan Ivanovitch, and, to be perfectly frank, I'm proud that I'm not a great man but an unimportant man. I'm not one to intrigue and I'm proud of that too, I don't act on the sly, but openly, without cunning, and although I could do harm too, and a great deal of harm, indeed, and know to whom and how to do it, Krestyan Ivanovitch, yet I won't sully myself, and in that sense I wash my hands. In that sense, I say, I wash them, Krestyan Ivanovitch!" Mr. Golyadkin paused expressively for a moment; he spoke with mild fervour.

"I set to work, Krestyan Ivanovitch," our hero continued, "directly, openly, by no devious ways, for I disdain them, and leave them to others. I do not try to degrade those who are perhaps purer than you and I . . . that is, I mean, I and they, Krestyan Ivanovitch—I didn't mean you. I don't like insinuations; I've no taste for contemptible duplicity; I'm disgusted by slander and calumny. I only put on a mask at a masquerade, and don't wear one before people every day. I only ask you, Krestyan Ivanovitch, how you would revenge yourself upon your enemy, your most malignant enemy—the one you would consider such?" Mr. Golyadkin concluded with a challenging glance at Krestyan Ivanovitch.

Though Mr. Golyadkin pronounced this with the utmost distinctness and clearness, weighing his words with a self-confident air and reckoning on their probable effect, yet meanwhile he looked at Krestyan Ivanovitch with anxiety, with great anxiety, with extreme anxiety. Now he was all eyes, and timidly waited for the doctor's answer with irritable and agonized impatience. But to the perplexity and complete amazement of our hero, Krestyan Ivanovitch only muttered something to himself; then he moved his arm-chair up to the table, and rather drily though politely announced something to the effect that his time was precious, and that he did not quite understand; that he was ready, however, to attend to him as far as he was able, but he would not go into anything further that did not concern him. At this point he took the pen, drew a piece of paper towards him, cut out of it the usual long strip, and announced that he would immediately prescribe what was necessary.

"No, it's not necessary, Krestyan Ivanovitch! No, that's not necessary at all!" said Mr. Golyadkin, getting up from his seat, and clutching Krestyan Ivanovitch's right hand. "That isn't what's wanted, Krestyan Ivanovitch."

And, while he said this, a queer change came over him. His grey eyes gleamed strangely, his lips began to quiver, all the muscles, all the features of his face began moving and working. He was trembling all over. After stopping the doctor's hand, Mr. Golyadkin followed his first movement by standing motionless, as though he had no confidence in himself and were waiting for some inspiration for further action.

Then followed a rather strange scene.

Somewhat perplexed, Krestyan Ivanovitch seemed for a moment rooted to his chair and gazed open-eyed in bewilderment at Mr. Golyadkin, who looked at him in exactly the same way. At last Krestyan Ivanovitch stood up, gently holding the lining of Mr. Golyadkin's coat. For some seconds they both stood like that, motionless, with their eyes fixed on each other. Then, however, in an extraordinarily strange way came Mr. Golyadkin's second movement. His lips trembled, his chin began twitching, and our hero quite unexpectedly burst into tears. Sobbing, shaking his head and striking himself on the chest with his right hand, while with his left clutching the lining of the doctor's coat, he tried to say something and to make some explanation, but could not utter a word.

At last Krestyan Ivanovitch recovered from his amazement.

"Come, calm yourself!" he brought out at last, trying to make Mr. Golyadkin sit down in an arm-chair.

"I have enemies, Krestyan Ivanovitch, I have enemies; I have malignant enemies who have sworn to ruin me. . . ." Mr. Golyadkin answered in a frightened whisper.

"Come, come, why enemies? You mustn't talk about enemies! You really mustn't. Sit down, sit down," Krestyan Ivanovitch went on, getting Mr. Golyadkin once for all into the arm-chair.

Mr. Golyadkin sat down at last, still keeping his eyes fixed on the doctor. With an extremely displeased air, Krestyan Ivanovitch strode from one end of the room to another. A long silence followed.

"I'm grateful to you, Krestyan Ivanovitch, I'm very grateful, and I'm very sensible of all you've done for me now. To my dying day I shall never forget your kindness, Krestyan Ivanovitch," said Mr. Golyadkin, getting up from his seat with an offended air.

"Come, give over! I tell you, give over!" Krestyan Ivanovitch responded rather sternly to Mr. Golyadkin's outburst, making him sit down again.

"Well, what's the matter? Tell me what is unpleasant," Krestyan Ivanovitch went on, "and what enemies are you talking about? What is wrong?"

"No, Krestyan Ivanovitch, we'd better leave that now," answered Mr. Golyadkin, casting down his eyes; "let us put all that aside for the time. . . . Till another time, Krestyan Ivanovitch, till a more convenient moment, when everything will be discovered and the mask falls off certain faces, and something comes to light. But, meanwhile, now, of course, after what has passed between us . . . you will agree yourself, Krestyan Ivanovitch . . . Allow me to wish you good-morning, Krestyan Ivanovitch," said Mr. Golyadkin, getting up gravely and resolutely and taking his hat.

"Oh, well . . . as you like . . . h'm . . ." (A moment of silence followed.) "For my part, you know . . . whatever I can do . . . and I sincerely wish you well."

"I understand you, Krestyan Ivanovitch, I understand: I understand you perfectly now. . . . In any case excuse me for having troubled you, Krestyan Ivanovitch."

"H'm, no, I didn't mean that. However, as you please; go on taking the medicines as before. . . ."

"I will go on with the medicines as you say, Krestyan Ivanovitch. I will go on with them, and I will get them at the same chemist's. . . . To be a chemist nowadays, Krestyan Ivanovitch, is an important business. . . ."

"How so? In what sense do you mean?"

"In a very ordinary sense, Krestyan Ivanovitch. I mean to say that nowadays that's the way of the world. . . ."

"H'm . . ."

"And that every silly youngster, not only a chemist's boy, turns up his nose at respectable people."

"H'm. How do you understand that?"

"I'm speaking of a certain person, Krestyan Ivanovitch . . . of a common acquaintance of ours, Krestyan Ivanovitch, of Vladimir Semyonovitch. . . ."

"Ah!"

"Yes, Krestyan Ivanovitch: and I know certain people, Krestyan Ivanovitch, who don't quite keep to the general rule of telling the truth, sometimes."

"Ah! How so?"

"Why, yes, it is so: but that's neither here nor there: they sometimes manage to serve you up a fine egg in gravy."

"What? Serve up what?"

"An egg in gravy, Krestyan Ivanovitch. It's a Russian saying. They know how to congratulate some one at the right moment, for instance; there are people like that."

"Congratulate?"

"Yes, congratulate, Krestyan Ivanovitch, as some one I know very well did the other day!"

"Some one you know very well . . . Ah! how was that?" said Krestyan Ivanovitch, looking attentively at Mr. Golyadkin.

"Yes, some one I know very well indeed congratulated some one else I know very well—and, what's more, a comrade, a friend of his heart, on his promotion, on his receiving the rank of assessor. This was how it happened to come up: 'I am exceedingly glad of the opportunity to offer you, Vladimir Semyonovitch, my congratulations, my *sincere* congratulations, on your receiving the rank of assessor. And I'm the more pleased, as all the world knows that there are old women nowadays who tell fortunes.' "

At this point Mr. Golyadkin gave a sly nod, and screwing up his eyes, looked at Krestyan Ivanovitch.

"H'm. So he said that. . . ."

"He did, Krestyan Ivanovitch, he said it and glanced at once at Andrey Filippovitch, the uncle of our Prince Charming, Vladimir Semyonovitch. But what is it to me, Krestyan Ivanovitch, that he has been made an assessor? What is it to me? And he wants to get married and the milk is scarcely dry on his lips, if I may be allowed the expression. And I said as much. Vladimir Semyonovitch, said I! I've said everything now; allow me to withdraw."

"H'm . . ."

"Yes, Krestyan Ivanovitch, allow me now, I say, to withdraw. But, to kill two birds with one stone, as I twitted our young gentleman with the old women I turned to Klara Olsufyevna (it all happened the day before yesterday at Olsufy Ivanovitch's), and she had only just sung a song full of feeling, 'You've sung songs full of feeling, madame,' said I, 'but they've not been listened to with a pure heart.' And by that I hinted plainly, Krestyan Ivanovitch, hinted plainly, that they were not running after her now, but looking higher. . . ."

"Ah! And what did he say?"

"He swallowed the pill, Krestyan Ivanovitch, as the saying is."

"H'm . . ."

"Yes, Krestyan Ivanovitch. To the old man himself, too, I said, 'Olsufy Ivanovitch,' said I, 'I know how much I'm indebted to you, I appreciate to the full all the kindness you've showered upon me from my childhood up. But open your eyes, Olsufy Ivanovitch,' I said. 'Look about you. I myself do things openly and aboveboard, Olsufy Ivanovitch.' "

"Oh, really!"

"Yes, Krestyan Ivanovitch. Really. . . ."

"What did he say?"

"Yes, what, indeed, Krestyan Ivanovitch? He mumbled one thing and another, and 'I know you,' and that 'his Excellency was a benevolent man'—he rambled on. . . . But, there, you know! he's begun to be a bit shaky, as they say, with old age."

"Ah! so that's how it is now. . . ."

"Yes, Krestyan Ivanovitch. And that's how we all are! Poor old man! He looks towards the grave, breathes incense, as they say, while they concoct a piece of womanish gossip and he listens to it; without him they wouldn't . . ."

"Gossip, you say?"

"Yes, Krestyan Ivanovitch, they've concocted a womanish scandal. Our bear, too, had a finger in it, and his nephew, our Prince Charming. They've joined hands with the old women and, of course, they've concocted the affair. Would you believe it? They plotted the murder of some one! . . ."

"The murder of some one?"

"Yes, Krestyan Ivanovitch, the moral murder of some one. They spread about . . . I'm speaking of a man I know very well."

Krestyan Ivanovitch nodded.

"They spread rumours about him . . . I confess I'm ashamed to repeat them, Krestyan Ivanovitch."

"H'm" . . .

"They spread a rumour that he had signed a promise to marry though he was already engaged in another quarter . . . and would you believe it, Krestyan Ivanovitch, to whom?"

"Really?"

"To a cook, to a disreputable German woman from whom he used to get his dinners; instead of paying what he owed, he offered her his hand."

"Is that what they say?"

"Would you believe it, Krestyan Ivanovitch? A low German, a nasty shameless German, Karolina Ivanovna, if you know . . ."

"I confess, for my part . . ."

"I understand you, Krestyan Ivanovitch, I understand, and for my part I feel it. . . ."

"Tell me, please, where are you living now?"

"Where am I living now, Krestyan Ivanovitch?"

"Yes . . . I want . . . I believe, you used to live . . ."

"Yes, Krestyan Ivanovitch, I did, I used to. To be sure I lived!"

answered Mr. Golyadkin, accompanying his words with a little laugh, and somewhat disconcerting Krestyan Ivanovitch by his answer.

"No, you misunderstood me; I meant to say . . ."

"I, too, meant to say, Krestyan Ivanovitch, I meant it too," Mr. Golyadkin continued, laughing. "But I've kept you far too long, Krestyan Ivanovitch. I hope you will allow me now, to wish you good-morning."

"H'm . . ."

"Yes, Krestyan Ivanovitch, I understand you; I fully understand you now," said our hero, with a slight flourish before Krestyan Ivanovitch. "And so permit me to wish you good-morning. . . ."

At this point our hero made a scrape with the toe of his boot and walked out of the room, leaving Krestyan Ivanovitch in the utmost amazement. As he went down the doctor's stairs he smiled and rubbed his hands gleefully. On the steps, breathing the fresh air and feeling himself at liberty, he was certainly prepared to admit that he was the happiest of mortals, and thereupon to go straight to his office—when suddenly his carriage rumbled up to the door: he glanced at it and remembered everything. Petrushka was already opening the carriage door. Mr. Golyadkin was completely overwhelmed by a strong and unpleasant sensation. He blushed, as it were, for a moment. Something seemed to stab him. He was just about to raise his foot to the carriage step when he suddenly turned round and looked towards Krestyan Ivanovitch's window. Yes, it was so! Krestyan Ivanovitch was standing at the window, was stroking his whiskers with his right hand and staring with some curiosity at the hero of our story.

"That doctor is silly," thought Mr. Golyadkin, huddling out of sight in the carriage; "extremely silly. He may treat his patients all right, but still . . . he's as stupid as a post."

Mr. Golyadkin sat down, Petrushka shouted "Off!" and the carriage rolled towards Nevsky Prospect again.

Chapter 3

ALL that morning was spent by Mr. Golyadkin in a strange bustle of activity. On reaching the Nevsky Prospect our hero told the driver to stop at the bazaar. Skipping out of his carriage, he ran to the Arcade, accompanied by Petrushka, and went straight to a shop where gold and silver articles were for sale. One could see from his very air that he was overwhelmed with business and had a terrible amount to do. Arranging to purchase a complete dinner- and tea-service for fifteen hundred roubles and including in the bargain for that sum a cigar-case of ingenious form and a silver shaving-set, and finally, asking the price of some other articles, useful and agreeable in their own way, he ended by promising to come without fail next day, or to send for his purchases the same day. He took the number of the shop, listening attentively to the shopkeeper, who was very pressing for a small deposit, said that he should have it all in good time. After which he took leave of the amazed shopkeeper and, followed by a regular flock of shopmen, walked along the Arcade, continually looking round at Petrushka and diligently seeking out fresh shops. On the way he dropped into a money-changer's and changed all his big notes into small ones, and though he lost on the exchange, his pocket-book was considerably fatter, which evidently afforded him extreme satisfaction. Finally, he stopped at a shop for ladies' dress-materials. Here, too, after deciding to purchase goods for a considerable sum, Mr. Golyadkin promised to come again, took the number of the shop and, on being asked for a deposit, assured the shopkeeper that he "should have a deposit too, all in good time." Then he visited several other shops, making purchases in each of them, asked the price of various things, sometimes arguing a long time with the shopkeeper, going out of the shop and returning two or three times—in fact, he displayed exceptional activity. From the Arcade our hero went to a well-known furniture shop, where he ordered furniture for six rooms; he admired a fashionable and very ingenious toilet table for ladies' use in the latest style, and, assuring the shopkeeper that he would certainly send for all these things, walked out of the shop, as usual promising a deposit. Then he went off somewhere else and ordered something more. In short, there seemed to be no end to the business he had to get through. At last, Mr. Golyadkin seemed to grow heartily sick of it all, and he began, goodness knows why, to be tormented by the stings of conscience. Nothing would have induced him now, for instance, to meet Andrey Filippovitch, or even Krestyan Ivanovitch.

At last, the town clock struck three. When Mr. Golyadkin finally took his seat in the carriage, of all the purchases he had made that morning he had, it appeared, in reality only got a pair of gloves and a bottle of scent, that cost a rouble and a half. As it was still rather early, he ordered his coachman to stop near a well-known restaurant in Nevsky Prospect which he only knew by reputation, got out of the carriage, and hurried in to have a light lunch, to rest and to wait for the hour fixed for the dinner.

Lunching as a man lunches who has the prospect before him of going out to a sumptuous dinner, that is, taking a snack of something in order to still the pangs, as they say, and drinking one small glass of vodka, Mr. Golyadkin established himself in an arm-chair and, modestly looking about him, peacefully settled down to an emaciated nationalist paper. After reading a couple of lines he stood up and looked in the looking-glass, set himself to rights and smoothed himself down; then he went to the window and looked to see whether his carriage was there . . . then he sat down again in his place and took up the paper. It was noticeable that our hero was in great excitement. Glancing at his watch and seeing that it was only a quarter past three and that he had consequently a good time to wait and, at the same time, opining that to sit like that was unsuitable, Mr. Golyadkin ordered chocolate, though he felt no particular inclination for it at the moment. Drinking the chocolate and noticing that the time had moved on a little, he went up to pay his bill.

He turned round and saw facing him two of his colleagues, the same two he had met that morning in Liteyny Street—young men, very much his juniors both in age and in rank. Our hero's relations with them were neither one thing nor the other, neither particularly friendly nor openly hostile. Good manners were, of course, observed on both sides: there was no closer intimacy, nor could there be. The meeting at this moment was extremely distasteful to Mr. Golyadkin. He frowned a little, and was disconcerted for an instant.

"Yakov Petrovitch, Yakov Petrovitch!" chirped the two register clerks. "You here? What brings you? . . ."

"Ah, it is you, gentlemen," Mr. Golyadkin interrupted hurriedly, somewhat embarrassed and scandalized by the amazement of the clerks and by the abruptness of their address, but feeling obliged, however, to appear jaunty and free and easy. "You've deserted, gentlemen, he-he-he. . . ." Then, to keep up his dignity and to condescend to the juveniles, with whom he never overstepped certain limits, he attempted to slap one of the youths on the shoulder; but this effort at good fellowship did not succeed and, instead of being a well-bred little jest, produced quite a different effect.

"Well, and our bear, is he still at the office?"

"Who's that, Yakov Petrovitch?"

"Why, the bear. Do you mean to say you don't know whose name that is? . . ." Mr. Golyadkin laughed and turned to the cashier to take his change.

"I mean Andrey Filippovitch, gentlemen," he went on, finishing with the cashier, and turning to the clerks this time with a very serious face. The two register clerks winked at one another.

"He's still at the office and asking for you, Yakov Petrovitch," answered one of them.

"At the office, eh! In that case, let him stay, gentlemen. And asking for me, eh?"

"He was asking for you, Yakov Petrovitch; but what's up with you, scented, pomaded, and such a swell? . . ."

"Nothing, gentlemen, nothing! that's enough," answered Mr. Golyadkin, looking away with a constrained smile. Seeing that Mr. Golyadkin was smiling, the clerks laughed aloud. Mr. Golyadkin was a little offended.

"I'll tell you as friends, gentlemen," our hero said, after a brief silence, as though making up his mind (which, indeed, was the case) to reveal something to them. "You all know me, gentlemen, but hitherto you've known me only on one side. No one is to blame for that and I'm conscious that the fault has been partly my own."

Mr. Golyadkin pursed up his lips and looked significantly at the clerks. The clerks winked at one another again.

"Hitherto, gentlemen, you have not known me. To explain myself here and now would not be quite appropriate. I will only touch on it lightly in passing. There are people, gentlemen, who dislike roundabout ways and only mask themselves at masquerades. There are people who do not see man's highest avocation in polishing the floor with their boots. There are people, gentlemen, who refuse to say that they are happy and enjoying a full life when, for instance, their trousers set properly. There are people, finally, who dislike dashing and whirling about for no object, fawning, and licking the dust, and above all, gentlemen, poking their noses where they are not wanted. . . . I've told you almost everything, gentlemen; now allow me to withdraw. . . ."

Mr. Golyadkin paused. As the register clerks had now got all that they wanted, both of them with great incivility burst into shouts of laughter. Mr. Golyadkin flared up.

"Laugh away, gentlemen, laugh away for the time being! If you live long enough you will see," he said, with a feeling of offended dignity, taking his hat and retreating to the door.

"But I will say more, gentlemen," he added, turning for the last time to the register clerks, "I will say more—you are both here with me face to face. This, gentlemen, is my rule: if I fail I don't lose heart, if I succeed I persevere, and in any case I am never underhand. I'm not one to intrigue—and I'm proud of it. I've never prided myself on diplomacy. They say, too, gentlemen, that the bird flies itself to the hunter. It's true and I'm ready to admit it; but who's the hunter, and who's the bird in this case? That is still the question, gentlemen!"

Mr. Golyadkin subsided into eloquent silence, and, with a most significant air, that is, pursing up his lips and raising his eyebrows as high as possible, he bowed to the clerks and walked out, leaving them in the utmost amazement.

"What are your orders now?" Petrushka asked, rather gruffly; he was probably weary of hanging about in the cold. "What are your orders?" he asked Mr. Golyadkin, meeting the terrible, withering glance with which our hero had protected himself twice already that morning, and to which he had recourse now for the third time as he came down the steps.

"To the Ismailovsky Bridge."

"To the Ismailovsky Bridge! Off!"

"Their dinner will not begin till after four, or perhaps five o'clock," thought Mr. Golyadkin; "isn't it early now? However, I can go a little early; besides, it's only a family dinner. And so I can go *sans façons,* as they say among well-bred people. Why shouldn't I go *sans façons?* The bear told us, too, that it would all be *sans façons,* and so I will be the same. . . ." Such were Mr. Golyadkin's reflections and meanwhile his excitement grew more and more acute. It could be seen that he was preparing himself for some great enterprise, to say nothing more; he muttered to himself, gesticulated with his right hand, continually looked out of his carriage window, so that, looking at Mr. Golyadkin, no one would have said that he was on his way to a good dinner, and only a simple dinner in his family circle—*sans façons,* as they say among well-bred people. Finally, just at Ismailovsky Bridge, Mr. Golyadkin pointed out a house; and the carriage rolled up noisily and stopped at the first entrance on the right. Noticing a feminine figure at the second-storey window, Mr. Golyadkin kissed his hand to her. He had, however, not the slightest idea what he was doing, for he felt more dead than alive at the moment. He got out of the carriage pale, distracted; he mounted the steps, took off his hat, mechanically straightened himself, and though he felt a slight trembling in his knees, he went upstairs.

"Olsufy Ivanovitch?" he inquired of the man who opened the door.

"At home, sir; at least he's not at home, his honour's not at home."

"What? What do you mean, my good man? I—I've come to dinner, brother. Why, you know me?"

"To be sure I know you! I've orders not to admit you."

"You . . . you, brother . . . you must be making a mistake. It's I, my boy, I'm invited; I've come to dinner," Mr. Golyadkin announced, taking off his coat and displaying unmistakable intentions of going into the room.

"Allow me, sir, you can't, sir. I've orders not to admit you. I've orders to refuse you. That's how it is."

Mr. Golyadkin turned pale. At that very moment the door of the inner room opened and Gerasimitch, Olsufy Ivanovitch's old butler, came out.

"You see the gentleman wants to go in, Emelyan Gerasimitch, and I . . ."

"And you're a fool, Alexeitch. Go inside and send the rascal Semyonitch here. It's impossible," he said politely but firmly, addressing Mr. Golyadkin. "It's quite impossible. His honour begs you to excuse him; he can't see you."

"He said he couldn't see me?" Mr. Golyadkin asked uncertainly. "Excuse me, Gerasimitch, why is it impossible?"

"It's quite impossible. I've informed your honour; they said 'Ask him to excuse us.' They can't see you."

"Why not? How's that? Why?"

"Allow me, allow me! . . ."

"How is it, though? It's out of the question! Announce me. . . . How is it? I've come to dinner. . . ."

"Excuse me, excuse me. . . ."

"Ah, well, that's a different matter, they asked to be excused: but, allow me, Gerasimitch; how is it, Gerasimitch?"

"Excuse me, excuse me!" replied Gerasimitch, very firmly putting away Mr. Golyadkin's hand and making way for two gentlemen who walked into the entry that very instant. The gentlemen in question were Andrey Filippovitch and his nephew, Vladimir Semyonovitch. Both of them looked with amazement at Mr. Golyadkin. Andrey Filippovitch seemed about to say something, but Mr. Golyadkin had by now made up his mind; he was by now walking out of Olsufy Ivanovitch's entry, blushing and smiling, with eyes cast down and a countenance of helpless bewilderment. "I will come afterwards, Gerasimitch; I will explain myself: I hope that all this will without delay be explained in due season. . . ."

"Yakov Petrovitch, Yakov Petrovitch . . ." He heard the voice of Andrey Filippovitch following him.

Mr. Golyadkin was by that time on the first landing. He turned quickly to Andrey Filippovitch.

"What do you desire, Andrey Filippovitch?" he said in a rather resolute voice.

"What's wrong with you, Yakov Petrovitch? In what way?"

"No matter, Andrey Filippovitch. I'm on my own account here. This is my private life, Andrey Filoppovitch."

"What's that?"

"I say, Andrey Filippovitch, that this is my private life, and as for my being here, as far as I can see, there's nothing reprehensible to be found in it as regards my official relations."

"What! As regards your official . . . What's the matter with you, my good sir?"

"Nothing, Andrey Filippovitch, absolutely nothing; an impudent slut of a girl, and nothing more. . . ."

"What! What?" Andrey Filippovitch was stupefied with amazement. Mr. Golyadkin, who had up till now then looked as though he would fly into Andrey Filippovitch's face, seeing that the head of his office was laughing a little, almost unconsciously took a step forward. Andrey Filippovitch jumped back. Mr. Golyadkin went up one step and then another. Andrey Filippovitch looked about him uneasily. Mr. Golyadkin mounted the stairs rapidly. Still more rapidly Andrey Filippovitch darted into the flat and slammed the door after him. Mr. Golyadkin was left alone. Everything grew dark before his eyes. He was utterly nonplussed, and stood now in a sort of senseless hesitation, as though recalling something extremely senseless, too, that had happened quite recently. "Ech, ech!" he muttered, smiling with constraint. Meanwhile, there came the sounds of steps and voices on the stairs, probably of other guests invited by Olsufy Ivanovitch. Mr. Golyadkin recovered himself to some extent; put up his raccoon collar, concealing himself behind it as far as possible, and began going downstairs with rapid little steps, tripping and stumbling in his haste. He felt overcome by a sort of weakness and numbness. His confusion was such that, when he came out on the steps, he did not even wait for his carriage but walked across the muddy court to it. When he reached his carriage and was about to get into it, Mr. Golyadkin inwardly uttered a desire to sink into the earth, or to hide in a mouse-hole together with his carriage. It seemed to him that everything in Olsufy Ivanovitch's house was looking at him now out of every window. He knew that he would certainly die on the spot if he were to go back.

"What are you laughing at, blockhead?" he said in a rapid mutter to Petrushka, who was preparing to help him into the carriage.

"What should I laugh at? I'm not doing anything; where are we to drive now?"

"Go home, drive on. . . ."

"Home, off!" shouted Petrushka, climbing on to the footboard.

"What a crow's croak!" thought Mr. Golyadkin. Meanwhile, the carriage had driven a good distance from Ismailovsky Bridge. Suddenly our hero pulled the cord with all his might and shouted to the driver to turn back at once. The coachman turned his horses and within two minutes was driving into Olsufy Ivanovitch's yard again.

"Don't, don't, you fool, back!" shouted Mr. Golyadkin—and, as though he were expecting this order, the driver made no reply but, without stopping at the entrance, drove all round the courtyard and out into the street again.

Mr. Golyadkin did not drive home, but, after passing the Semyonovsky Bridge, told the driver to return to a side street and stop near a restaurant of rather modest appearance. Getting out of the carriage, our hero settled up with the driver and so got rid of his equipage at last. He told Petrushka to go home and await his return, while he went into the restaurant, took a private room and ordered dinner. He felt very ill and his brain was in the utmost confusion and chaos. For a long time he walked up and down the room in agitation; at last he sat down in a chair, propped his brow in his hands and began doing his very utmost to consider and settle something relating to his present position.

Chapter 4

THAT day the birthday of Klara Olsufyevna, the only daughter of the civil councillor, Berendyev, at one time Mr. Golyadkin's benefactor and patron, was being celebrated by a brilliant and sumptuous dinner-party, such as had not been seen for many a long day within the walls of the flats in the neighbourhood of Ismailovsky Bridge— a dinner more like some Balthazar's feast, with a suggestion of something Babylonian in its brilliant luxury and style, with Veuve Clicquot champagne, with oysters and fruit from Eliseyev's and Milyutin's, with all sorts of fatted calves, and all grades of the government service. This festive day was to conclude with a brilliant ball, a small birthday ball, but yet brilliant in its taste, its distinction and its style. Of course, I am willing to admit that similar balls do happen sometimes, though rarely. Such balls, more like family rejoicings than balls, can only be given in such houses as that of the civil councillor, Berendyev. I will say more: I even doubt if such balls could be given in the houses of all civil councillors. Oh, if I were a poet! such as Homer or Pushkin, I mean, of course; with any lesser talent one would not venture—I should certainly have painted all that glorious day for you, oh, my readers, with a free brush and brilliant colours! Yes, I should begin my poem with my dinner, I should lay special stress on that striking and solemn moment when the first goblet was raised to the honour of the queen of the fête. I should describe to you the guests plunged in a reverent silence and expectation, as eloquent as the rhetoric of Demosthenes; I should describe for you, then, how Andrey Filippovitch, having as the eldest of the guests some right to take precedence, adorned with his grey hairs and the orders that well befit grey hairs, got up from his seat and raised above his head the congratulatory glass of sparkling wine—brought from a distant kingdom to celebrate such occasions and more like heavenly nectar than plain wine. I would portray for you the guests and the happy parents raising their glasses, too, after Andrey Filippovitch, and fastening upon him eyes full of expectation. I would describe for you how the same Andrey Filippovitch, so often mentioned, after dropping a tear in the glass, delivered his congratulations and good wishes, proposed the toast and drank the health . . . but I confess, I freely confess, that I could not do justice to the solemn moment when the queen of the fête, Klara Olsufyevna, blushing like a rose in spring, with the glow of bliss and of modesty, was so overcome by her feelings that she sank into the arms of her tender mamma; how that tender mamma shed tears, and how the father, Olsufy Ivanovitch, a hale old man and a privy councillor, who had lost the use of his legs in his long years of service and been rewarded by destiny for his devotion with investments, a house, some small estates, and a beautiful daughter, sobbed like a little child and announced through his tears that his Excellency was a benevolent man.

I could not, I positively could not, describe the enthusiasm that followed that moment in every heart, an enthusiasm clearly evinced in the conduct of a youthful register clerk (though at that moment he was more like a civil councillor than a register clerk), who was moved to tears, too, as he listened to Andrey Filippovitch. In his turn, too,

Andrey Filippovitch was in that solemn moment quite unlike a collegiate councillor and the head of an office in the department—yes, he
was something else . . . what, exactly, I do not know, but not a
collegiate councillor. He was more exalted! Finally . . . Oh, why do
I not possess the secret of lofty, powerful language, of the sublime
style, to describe these grand and edifying moments of human life,
which seem created expressly to prove that virtue sometimes triumphs
over ingratitude, free-thinking, vice and envy! I will say nothing, but
in silence—which will be better than any eloquence—I will point to
that fortunate youth, just entering on his twenty-sixth spring—to
Vladimir Semyonovitch, Andrey Filippovitch's nephew, who in his
turn now rose from his seat, who in his turn proposed a toast, and
upon whom were fastened the tearful eyes of the parents, the proud
eyes of Andrey Filippovitch, the modest eyes of the queen of the fête,
the solemn eyes of the guests, and even the decorously envious eyes
of some of the young man's youthful colleagues. I will say nothing
of that, though I cannot refrain from observing that everything in
that young man—who was, indeed, speaking in a complimentary sense,
more like an elderly than a young man—everything, from his bloom-
ing cheeks to his assessorial rank, seemed almost to proclaim aloud the
lofty pinnacle a man can attain through morality and good principles!
I will not describe how Anton Antonovitch Syetotchkin, a little old
man as grey as a badger, the head clerk of a department, who was a
colleague of Andrey Filippovitch's and had once been also of Olsufy
Ivanovitch's, and was an old friend of the family and Klara Olsufyevna's godfather, in his turn proposed a toast, crowed like a cock, and
cracked many little jokes; how by this extremely proper breach of
propriety, if one may use such an expression, he made the whole
company laugh till they cried, and how Klara Olsufyevna, at her
parents' bidding, rewarded him for his jocularity and politeness with
a kiss. I will only say that the guests, who must have felt like kinsfolk
and brothers after such a dinner, at last rose from the table, and the
elderly and more solid guests, after a brief interval spent in friendly
conversation, interspersed with some candid, though, of course, very
polite and proper, observations, went decorously into the next room
and, without losing valuable time, promptly divided themselves up
into parties and, full of the sense of their own dignity, installed themselves at tables covered with green baize. Meanwhile, the ladies established in the drawing-room suddenly became very affable and began
talking about dress-materials. And the venerable host, who had lost
the use of his legs in the service of loyalty and religion, and had been

rewarded with all the blessings we have enumerated above, began walking about on crutches among his guests, supported by Vladimir Semyonovitch and Klara Olsufyevna, and he, too, suddenly becoming extremely affable, decided to improvise a modest little dance, regardless of expense; to that end a nimble youth (the one who was more like a civil councillor than a youth) was despatched to fetch musicians, and musicians to the number of eleven arrived, and exactly at half-past eight struck up the inviting strains of a French quadrille, followed by various other dances. . . . It is needless to say that my pen is too weak, dull, and spiritless to describe the dance that owed its inspiration to the genial hospitality of the grey-headed host. And how, I ask, can the modest chronicler of Mr. Golyadkin's adventures, extremely interesting as they are in their own way, how can I depict the choice and rare mingling of beauty, brilliance, style, gaiety, polite solidity and solid politeness, sportiveness, joy, all the mirth and playfulness of these wives and daughters of petty officials, more like fairies than ladies—in a complimentary sense—with their lily shoulders and their rosy faces, their ethereal figures, their playfully agile homeopathic— to use the exalted language appropriate—little feet? How can I describe to you, finally, the gallant officials, their partners—gay and solid youths, steady, gleeful, decorously vague, smoking a pipe in the intervals between the dancing in a little green room apart, or not smoking a pipe in the intervals between the dances, every one of them with a highly respectable surname and rank in the service—all steeped in a sense of the elegant and a sense of their own dignity; almost all speaking French to their partners, or if Russian, using only the most well-bred expressions, compliments and profound observations, and only in the smoking-room permitting themselves some genial lapses from this high tone, some phrases of cordial and friendly brevity, such, for instance, as: " 'Pon my soul, Petka, you rake, you did kick off that polka in style," or, "I say, Vasya, you dog, you did give your partner a time of it." For all this, as I've already had the honour of explaining, oh, my readers! my pen fails me, and therefore I am dumb. Let us rather return to Mr. Golyadkin, the true and only hero of my very truthful tale.

The fact is that he found himself now in a very strange position, to say the least of it. He was here also, gentlemen—that is, not at the dance, but almost at the dance; he was "all right, though; he could take care of himself," yet at this moment he was a little astray; he was standing at that moment, strange to say—on the landing of the back stairs to Olsufy Ivanovitch's flat. But it was "all right" his stand-

ing there; he was "quite well." He was standing in a corner, huddled
in a place which was not very warm, though it was dark, partly hidden
by a huge cupboard and an old screen, in the midst of rubbish, litter,
and odds and ends of all sorts, concealing himself for the time being
and watching the course of proceedings as a disinterested spectator.
He was only looking on now, gentlemen; he, too, gentlemen, might go
in, of course . . . why should he not go in? He had only to take one
step and he would go in, and would go in very adroitly. Just now,
though he had been standing nearly three hours between the cupboard
and the screen in the midst of the rubbish, litter, and odds and ends
of all sorts, he was only quoting, in his own justification, a memorable
phrase of the French minister, Villesle: "All things come in time to
him who has the strength to wait." Mr. Golyadkin had read this
sentence in some book on quite a different subject, but now very aptly
recalled it. The phrase, to begin with, was exceedingly appropriate to
his present position, and, indeed, why should it not occur to the mind
of a man who had been waiting for almost three hours in the cold
and the dark in expectation of a happy ending to his adventures? After
quoting very appropriately the phrase of the French minister, Villesle,
Mr. Golyadkin immediately thought of the Turkish vizier, Mart-
simiris, as well as of the beautiful Margravine Luise, whose story he
had read also in some book. Then it occurred to his mind that the
Jesuits made it their rule that any means were justified if only the
end were attained. Fortifying himself somewhat with this historical
fact, Mr. Golyadkin said to himself, What were the Jesuits? The
Jesuits were every one of them very great fools; that he was better than
any of them; that if only the refreshment-room would be empty for
one minute (the door of the refreshment-room opened straight into
the passage to the back stairs, where Mr. Golyadkin was in hiding
now), he would, in spite of all the Jesuits in the world, go straight in,
first from the refreshment-room into the tea-room, then into the room
where they were now playing cards, and then straight into the hall
where they were now dancing the polka, and he would go in, he would
certainly go in, in spite of anything he would go in—he would slip
through—and that would be all, no one would notice him; and once
there he would know what to do.

Well, so this is the position in which we find the hero of our perfectly true story, though, indeed, it is difficult to explain what was
passing in him at that moment. The fact is that he had made his way
to the back stairs, and to the passage, on the ground that, as he said,
"Why shouldn't he? And everyone did go that way"; but he had not

ventured to penetrate further, evidently he did not dare to do so . . .
"not because there was anything he did not dare, but just because he
did not care to, because he preferred to be in hiding"; so here he was,
waiting now for a chance to slip in, and he had been waiting for it
two hours and a half. "Why not wait? Villesle himself had waited.
But what had Villesle to do with it?" thought Mr. Golyadkin: "How
does Villesle come in? But how am I to . . . to go and walk in? . . .
Ech, you dummy!" said Mr. Golyadkin, pinching his benumbed cheek
with his benumbed fingers; "you silly fool, you silly old Golyadkin—
silly fool of a surname!" . . .

But these compliments paid to himself were only by the way and
without any apparent aim. Now he was on the point of pushing forward and slipping in; the refreshment-room was empty and no one was
in sight. Mr. Golyadkin saw all this through the little window; in
two steps he was at the door and had already opened it. "Should he
go in or not? Come, should he or not? I'll go in . . . why not? to the
bold all ways lie open!" Reassuring himself in this way, our hero
suddenly and quite unexpectedly retreated behind the screen. "No,"
he thought. "Ah, now, somebody's coming in? Yes, they've come in;
why did I dawdle when there were no people about? Even so, shall
I go and slip in? . . . No, how slip in when a man has such a temperament! Fie, what a low tendency! I'm as scared as a hen! Being scared
is our special line, that's the fact of the matter! To be abject on every
occasion is our line: no need to ask us about that. Just stand here like
a post and that's all! At home I should be having a cup of tea now.
. . . It would be pleasant, too, to have a cup of tea. If I come in later
Petrushka'll grumble, maybe. Shall I go home? Damnation take all
this! I'll go and that'll be the end of it!" Reflecting on his position
in this way, Mr. Golyadkin dashed forward as though some one had
touched a spring in him; in two steps he found himself in the refreshment-room, flung off his overcoat, took off his hat, hurriedly thrust these
things into a corner, straightened himself and smoothed himself down;
then . . . then he moved on to the tea-room, and from the tea-room
darted into the next room, slipped almost unnoticed between the card-
players, who were at the tip-top of excitement, then . . . Mr. Golyadkin
forgot everything that was going on about him, and went straight
as an arrow into the drawing-room.

As luck would have it they were not dancing. The ladies were
promenading up and down the room in picturesque groups. The
gentlemen were standing about in twos and threes or flitting about
the room engaging partners. Mr. Golyadkin noticed nothing of this.

He saw only Klara Olsufyevna, near her Andrey Filippovitch, then Vladimir Semyonovitch, two or three officers, and, finally, two or three other young men who were also very interesting and, as any one could see at once, were either very promising or had actually done something. . . . He saw some one else too. Or, rather, he saw nobody and looked at nobody . . . but, moved by the same spring which had sent him dashing into the midst of a ball to which he had not been invited, he moved forward, and then forwarder and forwarder. On the way he jostled against a councillor and trod on his foot, and incidentally stepped on a very venerable old lady's dress and tore it a little, pushed against a servant with a tray and then ran against somebody else, and, not noticing all this, or rather noticing it but at the same time looking at no one, pressing further and further forward, he suddenly found himself facing Klara Olsufyevna. There is no doubt whatever that he would, with the utmost delight, without winking an eyelid, have sunk through the earth at that moment; but what has once been done cannot be recalled . . . can never be recalled. What was he to do? "If I fail I don't lose heart, if I succeed I persevere." Mr. Golyadkin was, of course, not "one to intrigue," and "not accomplished in the art of polishing the floor with his boots." . . . And so, indeed, it proved. Besides, the Jesuits had some hand in it too . . . though Mr. Golyadkin had no thoughts to spare for them now! All the moving, noisy, talking, laughing groups were suddenly hushed as though at a signal and, little by little, crowded round Mr. Golyadkin. He, however, seemed to hear nothing, to see nothing, he could not look . . . he could not possibly look at anything; he kept his eyes on the floor and so stood, giving himself his word of honour, in passing, to shoot himself one way or another that night. Making this vow, Mr. Golyadkin inwardly said to himself, "Here goes!" and to his own great astonishment began unexpectedly to speak.

He began with congratulations and polite wishes. The congratulations went off well, but over the good wishes our hero stammered. He felt that if he stammered all would be lost at once. And so it turned out—he stammered and floundered . . . floundering, he blushed crimson; blushing, he was overcome with confusion. In his confusion he raised his eyes; raising his eyes he looked about him; looking about him—he almost swooned. . . . Every one stood still, every one was silent, every one was waiting; a little way off there was whispering; a little nearer there was laughter. Mr. Golyadkin fastened a humble, imploring look on Andrey Filippovitch. Andrey Filippovitch responded with such a look that if our hero had not been utterly crushed already he certainly would have been crushed a second time—that is, if that were possible. The silence lasted long.

"This is rather concerned with my domestic circumstances and my private life, Andrey Filippovitch," our hero, half-dead, articulated in a scarcely audible voice; "it is not an official incident, Andrey Filippovitch. . . ."

"For shame, sir, for shame!" Andrey Filippovitch pronounced in a half-whisper, with an indescribable air of indignation; he pronounced these words and, giving Klara Olsufyevna his arm, he turned away from Mr. Golyadkin.

"I've nothing to be ashamed of, Andrey Filippovitch," answered Mr. Golyadkin, also in a whisper, turning his miserable eyes about him, trying helplessly to discover in the amazed crowd something on which he could gain a footing and retrieve his social position.

"Why, it's all right, it's nothing, gentlemen! Why, what's the matter? Why, it might happen to any one," whispered Mr. Golyadkin, moving a little away and trying to escape from the crowd surrounding him.

They made way for him. Our hero passed through two rows of inquisitive and wondering spectators. Fate drew him on. He felt that himself, that fate was leading him on. He would have given a great deal, of course, for a chance to be back in the passage by the back stairs, without having committed a breach of propriety; but as that was utterly impossible he began trying to creep away into a corner and to stand there—modestly, decorously, apart, without interfering with any one, without attracting especial attention, but at the same time to win the favourable notice of his host and the company. At the same time Mr. Golyadkin felt as though the ground were giving way under him, as though he were staggering, falling. At last he made his way to a corner and stood in it, like an unconcerned, rather indifferent spectator, leaning his arms on the backs of two chairs, taking complete possession of them in that way, and trying, as far as he could, to glance confidently at Olsufy Ivanovitch's guests, grouped about him. Standing nearest him was an officer, a tall and handsome fellow, beside whom Golyadkin felt himself an insect.

"These two chairs, Lieutenant, are intended, one for Klara Olsufyevna, and the other for Princess Tchevtchehanov; I'm taking care of them for them," said Mr. Golyadkin breathlessly, turning his imploring eyes on the officer. The lieutenant said nothing, but turned away with a murderous smile. Checked in this direction, our hero was about to try his luck in another quarter, and directly addressed an important councillor with a cross of great distinction on his breast. But the councillor looked him up and down with such a frigid stare that Mr. Golyadkin felt distinctly as though a whole bucketful of cold water had been thrown over him. He subsided into silence. He made up his mind that it was better to keep quiet, not to open his lips, and to show that he was "all right," that he was "like every one else," and that his position, as far as he could see, was quite a proper one. With this object he riveted his gaze on the lining of his coat, then raised his eyes and fixed them upon a very respectable-looking gentleman. "That gentleman has a wig on," thought Mr. Golyadkin; "and if he takes off that wig he will be bald, his head will be as bare as the palm of my hand." Having made this important discovery, Mr. Golyadkin thought of the Arab emirs, whose heads are left bare and shaven if they take off the green turbans they wear as a sign of their descent from the prophet Mahomet. Then, probably from some special connection of ideas with the Turks, he thought of Turkish slippers and at once, apropos of that, recalled the fact that Andrey Filippovitch was wearing boots, and that his boots were more like slippers than boots. It was evident that Mr. Golyadkin had become to some extent reconciled to his position. "What if that chandelier," flashed through Mr. Golyadkin's mind, "were to come down from the ceiling and fall upon the company? I should rush at once to save Klara Olsufyevna. 'Save her!' I should cry. 'Don't be alarmed, madame, it's of no consequence, I will rescue you, I.' Then . . ." At that moment Mr. Golyadkin looked about in search of Klara Olsufyevna, and saw Gerasimitch, Olsufy Ivanovitch's old butler. Gerasimitch, with a most anxious and solemnly official air, was making straight for him. Mr. Golyadkin started and frowned from an unaccountable but most disagreeable sensation; he looked about him mechanically; it occurred to his mind if only he could somehow creep off somewhere, unobserved, on the sly—simply disappear, that is, behave as though he had done nothing at all, as though the matter did not concern him in the least! . . . But before our hero could make up his mind to do anything, Gerasimitch was standing before him.

"Do you see, Gerasimitch," said our hero, with a little smile, addressing Gerasimitch; "you go and tell them—do you see the candle there in the chandelier, Gerasimitch?—it will be falling down directly: so, you know, you must tell them to see to it; it really will fall down, Gerasimitch. . . ."

"The candle? No, the candle's standing straight; but somebody is asking for you, sir."

"Who is asking for me, Gerasimitch?"

"I really can't say, sir, who it is. A man with a message. 'Is Yakov Petrovitch Golyadkin here?' says he. 'Then call him out,' says he, 'on very urgent and important business . . .' you see."

"No, Gerasimitch, you are making a mistake; in that you are making a mistake, Gerasimitch."

"I doubt it, sir."

"No, Gerasimitch, it isn't doubtful; there's nothing doubtful about it, Gerasimitch. Nobody's asking for me, but I'm quite at home here— that is, in my right place, Gerasimitch."

Mr. Golyadkin took breath and looked about him. Yes! every one in the room, all had their eyes fixed upon him, and were listening in a sort of solemn expectation. The men had crowded a little nearer and were all attention. A little further away the ladies were whispering together. The master of the house made his appearance at no great distance from Mr. Golyadkin, and though it was impossible to detect from his expression that he, too, was taking a close and direct interest in Mr. Golyadkin's position, for everything was being done with delicacy, yet, nevertheless, it all made our hero feel that the decisive moment had come for him. Mr. Golyadkin saw clearly that the time had come for a bold stroke, the chance of putting his enemies to shame. Mr. Golyadkin was in great agitation. He was aware of a sort of inspiration and, in a quivering and impressive voice, he began again, addressing the waiting butler—

"No, my dear fellow, no one's calling for me. You are mistaken. I will say more: you were mistaken this morning, too, when you assured me . . . dared to assure me, I say," (he raised his voice) "that Olsufy Ivanovitch, who has been my benefactor as long as I can remember and has, in a sense, been a father to me, was shutting his door upon me at the moment of solemn family rejoicing for his paternal heart." (Mr. Golyadkin looked about him complacently, but with deep feeling. A tear glittered on his eyelash.) "I repeat, my friend," our hero concluded, "you were mistaken, you were cruelly and unpardonably mistaken. . . ."

The moment was a solemn one. Mr. Golyadkin felt that the effect was quite certain. He stood with modestly downcast eyes, expecting Olsufy Ivanovitch to embrace him. Excitement and perplexity were apparent in the guests, even the inflexible and terrible Gerasimitch faltered over the words "I doubt it . . ." when suddenly the ruthless orchestra, apropos of nothing, struck up a polka. All was lost, all was scattered to the winds. Mr. Golyadkin started; Gerasimitch stepped back; everything in the room began undulating like the sea; and Vladimir Semyonovitch led the dance with Klara Olsufyevna, while the handsome lieutenant followed with Princess Tchevtchehanov. Onlookers, curious and delighted, squeezed in to watch them dancing the polka—an interesting, fashionable new dance which every one was crazy over. Mr. Golyadkin was, for the time, forgotten. But suddenly all were thrown into excitement, confusion and bustle; the music ceased . . . a strange incident had occurred. Tired out with the dance, and almost breathless with fatigue, Klara Olsufyevna, with glowing cheeks and heaving bosom, sank into an arm-chair, completely exhausted. . . . All hearts turned to the fascinating creature, all vied with one another in complimenting her and thanking her for the pleasure conferred on them—all at once there stood before her Mr. Golyadkin. He was pale, extremely perturbed; he, too, seemed completely exhausted, he could scarcely move. He was smiling for some reason, he stretched out his hand imploringly. Klara Olsufyevna was so taken aback that she had not time to withdraw hers and mechanically got up at his invitation. Mr. Golyadkin lurched forward, first once, then a second time, then lifted his leg, then made a scrape, then gave a sort of stamp, then stumbled . . . he, too, wanted to dance with Klara Olsufyevna. Klara Olsufyevna uttered a shriek; every one rushed to release her hand from Mr. Golyadkin's, and in a moment our hero was carried almost ten paces away by the rush of crowd. A circle formed round him too. Two old ladies, whom he had almost knocked down in his retreat, raised a great shrieking and outcry. The confusion was awful; all were asking questions, every one was shouting, every one was finding fault. The orchestra was silent. Our hero whirled round in his circle and mechanically, with a semblance of a smile, muttered something to himself, such as, "Why not?" and "that the polka, so far, at least, as he could see, was a new and very interesting dance, invented for the diversion of the ladies . . . but that since things had taken this turn, he was ready to consent." But Mr. Golyadkin's consent no one apparently thought of asking. Our hero was suddenly aware that some one's hand was laid on his arm, that another hand was pressed against his back, that he was with peculiar solicitude being guided in a certain direction. At last he noticed that he was going straight to the door. Mr. Golyadkin wanted to say something, to do something. . . . But no, he no longer wanted to do anything. He only mechanically kept laughing in answer. At last he was aware that they were putting on his greatcoat, that his hat was thrust over his eyes; finally he felt that he was in the entry on the stairs in the dark and cold. At last he stumbled, he felt that he was falling down a precipice; he tried to cry out—and suddenly found himself in the courtyard. The air blew fresh on him, he stood still for a minute; at that very instant, the strains reached him of the orchestra striking up again. Mr. Golyadkin suddenly recalled it all; it seemed to him that all his flagging energies came back to him again. He had been standing as though riveted to the spot, but now he started off and rushed away headlong, anywhere, into the air, into freedom, wherever chance might take him.

Chapter 5

IT WAS striking midnight from all the clock towers in Petersburg when Mr. Golyadkin, beside himself, ran out on the Fontanka Quay, close to the Ismailovsky Bridge, fleeing from his foes, from persecution, from a hailstorm of nips and pinches aimed at him, from the shrieks of excited old ladies, from the Ohs and Ahs of women and from the murderous eyes of Andrey Filippovitch. Mr. Golyadkin was killed—killed entirely, in the full sense of the word, and if he still preserved the power of running, it was simply through some sort of miracle, a miracle in which at last he refused himself to believe. It was an awful November night—wet, foggy, rainy, snowy, teeming with colds in the head, fevers, swollen faces, quinsies, inflammations of all kinds and descriptions—teeming, in fact, with all the gifts of a Petersburg November. The wind howled in the deserted streets, lifting up the black water of the canal above the rings on the bank, and irritably brushing against the lean lamp-posts which chimed in with its howling in a thin, shrill creak, keeping up the endless squeaky, jangling concert with which every inhabitant of Petersburg is so familiar. Snow and rain were falling both at once. Lashed by the wind, the streams of rain-water spurted almost horizontally, as though from a fireman's hose, pricking and stinging the face of the luckless Mr. Golyadkin like a thousand pins and needles. In the stillness of the night, broken only by the distant rumbling of carriages, the howl of the wind and the creaking of the lamp-posts, there was the dismal sound of the splash and gurgle of water, rushing from every roof, every porch, every pipe and every cornice, on to the granite of the pavement. There was not a soul, near or far, and, indeed, it seemed there could not be at such an hour and in such weather. And so only

Mr. Golyadkin, alone with his despair, was fleeing in terror along the pavement of Fontanka, with his usual rapid little step, in haste to get home as soon as possible to his flat on the fourth storey in Shestilavotchny Street.

Though the snow, the rain, and all the nameless horrors of a raging snowstorm and fog, under a Petersburg November sky, were attacking Mr. Golyadkin, already shattered by misfortunes, were showing him no mercy, giving him no rest, drenching him to the bone, glueing up his eyelids, blowing right through him from all sides, baffling and perplexing him—though all this was hurled upon Mr. Golyadkin at once, as though conspiring and combining with all his enemies to make a grand day, evening, and night for him, in spite of all this Mr. Golyadkin was almost insensible to this final proof of the persecution of destiny: so violent had been the shock and the impression made upon him a few minutes before at the civil councillor Berendyev's! If any disinterested spectator could have glanced casually at Mr. Golyadkin's painful progress, he would instantly have grasped the awful horror of his pitiful plight and would certainly have said that Mr. Golyadkin looked as though he wanted to hide from himself, as though he were trying to run away from himself! Yes! It was really so. One may say more: Mr. Golyadkin did not want only to run away from himself, but to be obliterated, to cease to be, to return to dust. At the moment he took in nothing surrounding him, understood nothing of what was going on about him, and looked as though the miseries of the stormy night, of the long tramp, the rain, the snow, the wind, all the cruelty of the weather, did not exist for him. The golosh slipping off the boot on Mr. Golyadkin's right foot was left behind in the snow and slush on the pavement of Fontanka, and Mr. Golyadkin did not think of turning back to get it, did not, in fact, notice that he had lost it. He was so perplexed that, in spite of everything surrounding him, he stood several times stock-still in the middle of the pavement, completely possessed by the thought of his recent horrible humiliation; at that instant he was dying, disappearing; then he suddenly set off again like mad and ran and ran without looking back, as though he were pursued, as though he were fleeing from some still more awful calamity.... The position was truly awful! ... At last Mr. Golyadkin halted in exhaustion, leaned on the railing in the attitude of a man whose nose has suddenly begun to bleed, and began looking intently at the black and troubled waters of the canal. There is no knowing what length of time he spent like this. All that is known is that at that instant Mr. Golyadkin reached such a pitch of despair, was so harassed, so tortured, so exhausted, and so weakened in what feeble faculties were left him that he forgot everything, forgot the Ismailovsky Bridge, forgot Shestilavotchny Street, forgot his present plight. . . . After all, what did it matter to him? The thing was done. The decision was affirmed and ratified; what could he do? All at once . . . all at once he started and involuntarily skipped a couple of paces aside. With unaccountable uneasiness he began gazing about him; but no one was there, nothing special had happened, and yet . . . and yet he fancied that just now, that very minute, some one was standing near him, beside him, also leaning on the railing, and—marvellous to relate! —had even said something to him, said something quickly, abruptly, not quite intelligibly, but something quite private, something concerning himself.

"Why, was it my fancy?" said Mr. Golyadkin, looking round once more. "But where am I standing? . . . Ech, ech," he thought finally, shaking his head, though he began gazing with an uneasy, miserable feeling into the damp, murky distance, straining his sight and doing his utmost to pierce with his short-sighted eyes the wet darkness that stretched all round him. There was nothing new, however, nothing special caught the eye of Mr. Golyadkin. Everything seemed to be all right, as it should be, that is, the snow was falling more violently, more thickly and in larger flakes, nothing could be seen twenty paces away, the lamp-posts creaked more shrilly than ever and the wind seemed to intone its melancholy song even more tearfully, more piteously, like an importunate beggar whining for a copper to get a crust of bread. At the same time a new sensation took possession of Mr. Golyadkin's whole being: agony upon agony, terror upon terror . . . a feverish tremor ran through his veins. The moment was insufferably unpleasant! "Well, it's no matter," he said, to encourage himself. "Well, no matter; perhaps it's no matter at all, and there's no stain on any one's honour. Perhaps it's as it should be," he went on, without understanding what he was saying. "Perhaps it will all be for the best in the end, and there will be nothing to complain of, and every one will be justified."

Talking like this and comforting himself with words, Mr. Golyadkin shook himself a little, shook off the snow which had drifted in thick layers on his hat, his collar, his overcoat, his tie, his boots and everything—but his strange feeling, his strange, obscure misery he could not get rid of, could not shake off. Somewhere in the distance there was the boom of a cannon shot. "Ach, what weather!" thought our hero.

"Tchoo! Isn't there going to be a flood? It seems as though the water has risen so violently."

Mr. Golyadkin had hardly said or thought this when he saw a person coming towards him, belated, no doubt, like him, through some accident. An unimportant, casual incident, one might suppose, but for some unknown reason Mr. Golyadkin was troubled, even scared, and rather flurried. It was not that he was exactly afraid of some ill-intentioned man, but just that "perhaps . . . after all, who knows, this belated individual," flashed through Mr. Golyadkin's mind, "maybe he's that very thing, maybe he's the very principal thing in it, and isn't here for nothing, but is here with an object, crossing my path and provoking me." Possibly, however, he did not think this precisely, but only had a passing feeling of something like it—and very unpleasant. There was no time, however, for thinking and feeling. The stranger was already within two paces. Mr. Golyadkin, as he invariably did, hastened to assume a quite peculiar air, an air that expressed clearly that he, Golyadkin, kept himself to himself, that he was "all right," that the road was wide enough for all, and that he, Golyadkin, was not interfering with any one. Suddenly he stopped short as though petrified, as though struck by lightning, and quickly turned round after the figure which had only just passed him—turned as though some one had given him a tug from behind, as though the wind had turned him like a weathercock. The passer-by vanished quickly in the snowstorm. He, too, walked quickly; he was dressed like Mr. Golyadkin and, like him, too, wrapped up from head to foot, and he, too, tripped and trotted along the pavement of Fontanka with rapid little steps that suggested that he was a little scared.

"What—what is it?" whispered Mr. Golyadkin, smiling mistrustfully, though he trembled all over. An icy shiver ran down his back. Meanwhile, the stranger had vanished completely; there was no sound of his step, while Mr. Golyadkin still stood and gazed after him. At last, however, he gradually came to himself.

"Why, what's the meaning of it?" he thought with vexation. "Why, have I really gone out of my mind, or what?" He turned and went on his way, making his footsteps more rapid and frequent, and doing his best not to think of anything at all. He even closed his eyes at last with the same object. Suddenly, through the howling of the wind and the uproar of the storm, the sound of steps very close at hand reached his ears again. He started and opened his eyes. Again a rapidly approaching figure stood out black before him, some twenty paces away. This little figure was hastening, tripping along, hurrying nervously;

the distance between them grew rapidly less. Mr. Golyadkin could by now get a full view of this second belated companion. He looked full at him and cried out with amazement and horror; his legs gave way under him. It was the same individual who had passed him ten minutes before, and who now quite unexpectedly turned up facing him again. But this was not the only marvel that struck Mr. Golyadkin. He was so amazed that he stood still, cried out, tried to say something, and rushed to overtake the stranger, even shouted something to him, probably anxious to stop him as quickly as possible. The stranger did, in fact, stop ten paces from Mr. Golyadkin, so that the light from the lamp-post that stood near fell full upon his whole figure—stood still, turned to Mr. Golyadkin, and with impatient and anxious face waited to hear what he would say.

"Excuse me, possibly I'm mistaken," our hero brought out in a quavering voice.

The stranger in silence, and with an air of annoyance, turned and rapidly went on his way, as though in haste to make up for the two seconds he had wasted on Mr. Golyadkin. As for the latter, he was quivering in every nerve, his knees shook and gave way under him, and with a moan he squatted on a stone at the edge of the pavement. There really was reason, however, for his being so overwhelmed. The fact is that this stranger seemed to him now somehow familiar. That would have been nothing, though. But he recognized, almost certainly recognized this man. He had often seen him, that man, had seen him some time, and very lately too; where could it have been? Surely not yesterday? But, again, that was not the chief thing that Mr. Golyadkin had often seen him before; there was hardly anything special about the man; the man at first sight would not have aroused any special attention. He was just a man like any one else, a gentleman like all other gentlemen, of course, and perhaps he had some good qualities and very valuable ones too—in fact, he was a man who was quite himself. Mr. Golyadkin cherished no sort of hatred or enmity, not even the slightest hostility towards this man—quite the contrary, it would seem, indeed—and yet (and this was the real point) he would not for any treasure on earth have been willing to meet that man, and especially to meet him as he had done now, for instance. We may say more: Mr. Golyadkin knew that man perfectly well: he even knew what he was called, what his name was; and yet nothing would have induced him, and again, for no treasure on earth would he have consented to name him, to consent to acknowledge that he was called so-and-so, that his father's name was this and his surname was that.

Whether Mr. Golyadkin's stupefaction lasted a short time or a long time, whether he was sitting for a long time on the stone of the pavement I cannot say; but, recovering himself a little at last, he suddenly fell to running, without looking round, as fast as his legs could carry him; his mind was preoccupied, twice he stumbled and almost fell—and through this circumstance his other boot was also bereaved of its golosh. At last Mr. Golyadkin slackened his pace a little to get breath, looked hurriedly round and saw that he had already, without being aware of it, run right across Fontanka, had crossed the Anitchkov Bridge, had passed part of the Nevsky Prospect and was now standing at the turning into Liteyny Street. Mr. Golyadkin turned into Liteyny Street. His position at that instant was like that of a man standing at the edge of a fearful precipice, while the earth is bursting open under him, is already shaking, moving, rocking for the last time, falling, drawing him into the abyss, and yet the luckless wretch has not the strength, nor the resolution, to leap back, to avert his eyes from the yawning gulf below; the abyss draws him and at last he leaps into it of himself, himself hastening the moment of his destruction.

Mr. Golyadkin knew, felt and was firmly convinced that some other evil would certainly befall him on the way, that some unpleasantness would overtake him, that he would, for instance, meet his stranger once more: but—strange to say—he positively desired this meeting, considered it inevitable, and all he asked was that it might all be quickly over, that he should be relieved from his position in one way or another, but as soon as possible. And meanwhile he ran on and on, as though moved by some external force, for he felt a weakness and numbness in his whole being: he could not think of anything, though his thoughts caught at everything like brambles. A little lost dog, soaked and shivering, attached itself to Mr. Golyadkin, and ran beside him, scurrying along with tail and ears drooping, looking at him from time to time with timid comprehension. Some remote, long-forgotten idea—some memory of something that had happened long ago—came back into his mind now, kept knocking at his brain as with a hammer, vexing him and refusing to be shaken off.

"Ech, that horrid little cur!" whispered Mr. Golyadkin, not understanding himself.

At last he saw his stranger at the turning into Italyansky Street. But this time the stranger was not coming to meet him, but was going in the same direction as he was, and he, too, was running, a few steps in front. At last they turned into Shestilavotchny Street.

Mr. Golyadkin caught his breath. The stranger stopped exactly before the house in which Mr. Golyadkin lodged. He heard a ring at the bell and almost at the same time the grating of the iron bolt. The gate opened, the stranger stooped, darted in and disappeared. Almost at the same instant Mr. Golyadkin reached the spot and like an arrow flew in at the gate. Heedless of the grumbling porter, he ran, gasping for breath, into the yard, and immediately saw his interesting companion, whom he had lost sight of for a moment.

The stranger darted towards the staircase which led to Mr. Golyadkin's flat. Mr. Golyadkin rushed after him. The stairs were dark, damp and dirty. At every turning there were heaped-up masses of refuse from the flats, so that any unaccustomed stranger who found himself on the stairs in the dark was forced to travel to and fro for half an hour in danger of breaking his legs, cursing the stairs as well as the friends who lived in such an inconvenient place. But Mr. Golyadkin's companion seemed as though familiar with it, as though at home; he ran up lightly, without difficulty, showing a perfect knowledge of his surroundings. Mr. Golyadkin had almost caught him up; in fact, once or twice the stranger's coat flicked him on the nose. His heart stood still. The stranger stopped before the door of Mr. Golyadkin's flat, knocked on it, and (which would, however, have surprised Mr. Golyadkin at any other time) Petrushka, as though he had been sitting up in expectation, opened the door at once and, with a candle in his hand, followed the stranger as the latter went in. The hero of our story dashed into his lodging beside himself; without taking off his hat or coat he crossed the little passage and stood still in the doorway of his room, as though thunderstruck. All his presentiments had come true. All that he had dreaded and surmised was coming to pass in reality. His breath failed him, his head was in a whirl. The stranger, also in his coat and hat, was sitting before him on his bed, and with a faint smile, screwing up his eyes, nodded to him in a friendly way. Mr. Golyadkin wanted to scream, but could not—to protest in some way, but his strength failed him. His hair stood on end, and he almost fell down with horror. And, indeed, there was good reason. He recognized his nocturnal visitor. The nocturnal visitor was no other than himself—Mr. Golyadkin himself, another Mr. Golyadkin, but absolutely the same as himself—in fact, what is called a double in every respect. . . .

Chapter 6

AT EIGHT o'clock next morning Mr. Golyadkin woke up in his bed. At once all the extraordinary incidents of the previous day and the wild, incredible night, with all its almost impossible adventures, presented themselves to his imagination and memory with terrifying vividness. Such intense, diabolical malice on the part of his enemies, and, above all, the final proof of that malice, froze Mr. Golyadkin's heart. But at the same time it was all so strange, incomprehensible, wild, it seemed so impossible that it was really hard to credit the whole business; Mr. Golyadkin was, indeed, ready to admit himself that it was all an incredible delusion, a passing aberration of the fancy, a darkening of the mind, if he had not fortunately known by bitter experience to what lengths spite will sometimes carry any one, what a pitch of ferocity an enemy may reach when he is bent on revenging his honour and prestige. Besides, Mr. Golyadkin's exhausted limbs, his heavy head, his aching back, and the malignant cold in his head bore vivid witness to the probability of his expedition of the previous night and upheld the reality of it, and to some extent of all that had happened during that expedition. And, indeed, Mr. Golyadkin had known long, long before that something was being got up among them, that there was some one else with them. But after all, thinking it over thoroughly, he made up his mind to keep quiet, to submit and not to protest for the time.

"They are simply plotting to frighten me, perhaps, and when they see that I don't mind, that I make no protest, but keep perfectly quiet and put up with it meekly, they'll give it up, they'll give it up of themselves, give it up of their own accord."

Such, then, were the thoughts in the mind of Mr. Golyadkin as, stretching in his bed, trying to rest his exhausted limbs, he waited for Petrushka to come into his room as usual. . . . He waited for a full quarter of an hour. He heard the lazy scamp fiddling about with the samovar behind the screen, and yet he could not bring himself to call him. We may say more: Mr. Golyadkin was a litte afraid of confronting Petrushka.

"Why, goodness knows," he thought, "goodness knows how that rascal looks at it all. He keeps on saying nothing, but he has his own ideas."

At last the door creaked and Petrushka came in with a tray in his hands. Mr. Golyadkin stole a timid glance at him, impatiently waiting to see what would happen, waiting to see whether he would not say something about a certain circumstance. But Petrushka said nothing; he was, on the contrary, more silent, more glum and ill-humoured than usual; he looked askance from under his brows at everything; altogether it was evident that he was very much put out about something; he did not even once glance at his master, which, by the way, rather piqued the latter. Setting all he had brought on the table, he turned and went out of the room without a word.

"He knows, he knows, he knows all about it, the scoundrel!" Mr. Golyadkin grumbled to himself as he took his tea. Yet our hero did not address a single question to his servant, though Petrushka came into his room several times afterwards on various errands. Mr. Golyadkin was in great trepidation of spirit. He dreaded going to the office. He had a strong presentiment that there he would find something that would not be "just so."

"You may be sure," he thought, "that as soon as you go you will light upon something! Isn't it better to endure in patience? Isn't it better to wait a bit now? Let them do what they like there; but I'd better stay here a bit to-day, recover my strength, get better, and think over the whole affair more thoroughly, then afterwards I could seize the right moment, fall upon them like snow from the sky, and get off scot free myself."

Reasoning like this, Mr. Golyadkin smoked pipe after pipe; time was flying. It was already nearly half-past nine.

"Why, it's half-past nine already," thought Mr. Golyadkin; "it's late for me to make my appearance. Besides, I'm ill, of course I'm ill, I'm certainly ill; who denies it? What's the matter with me? If they send to make inquiries, let the executive clerk come; and, indeed, what is the matter with me really? My back aches, I have a cough, and a cold in my head; and, in fact, it's out of the question for me to go out, utterly out of the question in such weather. I might be taken ill and, very likely, die; nowadays especially the death-rate is so high. . . ."

With such reasoning Mr. Golyadkin succeeded at last in setting his conscience at rest, and defended himself against the reprimands he expected from Andrey Filippovitch for neglect of his duty. As a rule in such cases our hero was particularly fond of justifying himself in his own eyes with all sorts of irrefutable arguments, and so completely setting his conscience at rest. And so now, having completely soothed his conscience, he took up his pipe, filled it, and had no sooner settled down comfortably to smoke, when he jumped up quickly from the sofa, flung away the pipe, briskly washed, shaved, and brushed his hair, got into his uniform and so on, snatched up some papers, and flew off to the office.

Mr. Golyadkin went into his department timidly, in quivering expectation of something unpleasant—an expectation which was none the less disagreeable for being vague and unconscious; he sat timidly down in his invariable place next the head clerk, Anton Antonovitch Syetotchkin. Without looking at anything or allowing his attention to be distracted, he plunged into the contents of the papers that lay before him. He made up his mind and vowed to himself to avoid, as far as possible, anything provocative, anything that might compromise him, such as indiscreet questions, jests, or unseemly allusions to any incidents of the previous evening; he made up his mind also to abstain from the usual interchange of civilities with his colleagues, such as inquiries after health and such like. But evidently it was impossible, out of the question, to keep to this. Anxiety and uneasiness in regard to anything near him that was annoying always worried him far more than the annoyance itself. And that was why, in spite of his inward vows to refrain from entering into anything, whatever happened, and to keep aloof from everything. Mr. Golyadkin from time to time, on the sly, very, very quietly, raised his head and stealthily looked about him to right and to left, peeped at the countenances of his colleagues, and tried to gather whether there were not something new and particular in them referring to himself and with sinister motives concealed from him. He assumed that there must be a connection between all that had happened yesterday and all that surrounded him now. At last, in his misery, he began to long for something—goodness knows what—to happen to put an end to it—even some calamity—he did not care. At this point destiny caught Mr. Golyadkin: he had hardly felt this desire when his doubts were solved in the strangest and most unexpected manner.

The door leading from the next room suddenly gave a soft and timid creak, as though to indicate that the person about to enter was a very unimportant one, and a figure, very familiar to Mr. Golyadkin, stood shyly before the very table at which our hero was seated. The latter did not raise his head—no, he only stole a glance at him, the tiniest glance; but he knew all, he understood all, to every detail. He grew hot with shame, and buried his devoted head in his papers with precisely the same object with which the ostrich, pursued by hunters, hides his head in the burning sand. The new arrival bowed to Andrey Filippovitch, and thereupon he heard a voice speaking in the regulation tone of condescending politeness with which all persons in authority address their subordinates in public offices.

"Take a seat here," said Andrey Filippovitch, motioning the newcomer to Anton Antonovitch's table. "Here, opposite Mr. Golyadkin, and we'll soon give you something to do."

Andrey Filippovitch ended by making a rapid gesture that decorously admonished the newcomer of his duty, and then he immediately became engrossed in the study of the papers that lay in a heap before him.

Mr. Golyadkin lifted his eyes at last, and that he did not fall into a swoon was simply because he had foreseen it all from the first, that he had been forewarned from the first, guessing in his soul who the stranger was. Mr. Golyadkin's first movement was to look quickly about him, to see whether there were any whispering, any office joke being cracked on the subject, whether any one's face was agape with wonder, whether, indeed, some one had not fallen under the table from terror. But to his intense astonishment there was no sign of anything of the sort. The behaviour of his colleagues and companions surprised him. It seemed contrary to the dictates of common-sense. Mr. Golyadkin was positively scared at this extraordinary reticence. The fact spoke for itself; it was a strange, horrible, uncanny thing. It was enough to rouse any one. All this, of course, only passed rapidly through Mr. Golyadkin's mind. He felt as though he were burning in a slow fire. And, indeed, there was enough to make him. The figure that was sitting opposite Mr. Golyadkin now was his terror, was his shame, was his nightmare of the evening before; in short, was Mr. Golyadkin himself, not the Mr. Golyadkin who was sitting now in his chair with his mouth wide-open and his pen petrified in his hand, not the one who acted as assistant to his chief, not the one who liked to efface himself and slink away in the crowd, not the one whose deportment plainly said, "Don't touch me and I won't touch you," or, "Don't interfere with me, you see I'm not touching you"; no, this was another Mr. Golyadkin, quite different, yet, at the same time, exactly like the first—the same height, the same figure, the same clothes, the same baldness; in fact, nothing, absolutely nothing, was lacking to complete the likeness, so that if one were to set them side by side, nobody, absolutely nobody, could have undertaken to distinguish which was the real Golyadkin and which was the counterfeit, which was the old one and which was the new one, which was the original and which was the copy.

Our hero was—if the comparison can be made—in the position of a man upon whom some practical joker has stealthily, by way of jest, turned a burning-glass.

"What does it mean? Is it a dream?" he wondered. "Is it reality or the continuation of what happened yesterday? And besides, by what right is this all being done? Who sanctioned such a clerk, who authorized this? Am I asleep, am I in a waking dream?"

Mr. Golyadkin tried pinching himself, even tried to screw up his courage to pinch some one else. . . . No, it was not a dream, and that was all about it. Mr. Golyadkin felt that the sweat was trickling down him in big drops; he felt that what was happening to him was something incredible, unheard-of, and for that very reason was, to complete his misery, utterly unseemly, for Mr. Golyadkin realized and felt how disadvantageous it was to be the first example of such a burlesque adventure. He even began to doubt his own existence, and though he was prepared for anything and had been longing for his doubts to be settled in any way whatever, yet the actual reality was startling in its unexpectedness. His misery was poignant and overwhelming. At times he lost all power of thought and memory. Coming to himself after such a moment, he noticed that he was mechanically and unconsciously moving the pen over the paper. Mistrustful of himself, he began going over what he had written—and could make nothing of it. At last the other Mr. Golyadkin, who had been sitting discreetly and decorously at the table, got up and disappeared through the door into the other room. Mr. Golyadkin looked round—everything was quiet; he heard nothing but the scratching of pens, the rustle of turning over pages, and conversation in the corners furthest from Andrey Filippovitch's seat. Mr. Golyadkin looked at Anton Antonovitch, and as, in all probability, our hero's countenance fully reflected his real condition and harmonized with the whole position, and was consequently, from one point of view, very remarkable, good-natured Anton Antonovitch, laying aside his pen, inquired after his health with marked sympathy.

"I'm very well, thank God, Anton Antonovitch," said Mr. Golyadkin, stammering. "I am perfectly well, Anton Antonovitch. I am all right now, Anton Antonovitch," he added uncertainly, not yet fully trusting Anton Antonovitch, whose name he had mentioned so often.

"I fancied you were not quite well: though that's not to be wondered at; no, indeed! Nowadays especially there's such a lot of illness going about. Do you know . . ."

"Yes, Anton Antonovitch, I know there is such a lot of illness . . . I did not mean that, Anton Antonovitch," Mr. Golyadkin went on, looking intently at Anton Antonovitch. "You see, Anton Antonovitch, I don't even know how you, that is, I mean to say, how to approach this matter, Anton Antonovitch. . . ."

"How so? I really . . . do you know . . . I must confess I don't quite understand; you must . . . you must explain, you know, in what way you are in difficulties," said Anton Antonovitch, beginning to be in difficulties himself, seeing that there were actually tears in Mr. Golyadkin's eyes.

"Really, Anton Antonovitch . . . I . . . here . . . there's a clerk here, Anton Antonovitch . . ."

"Well! I don't understand now."

"I mean to say, Anton Antonovitch, there's a new clerk here."

"Yes, there is; a namesake of yours."

"What?" cried Mr. Golyadkin.

"I say a namesake of yours; his name's Golyadkin too. Isn't he a brother of yours?"

"No, Anton Antonovitch, I . . ."

"H'm! you don't say so! Why, I thought he must be a relation of yours. Do you know, there's a sort of family likeness."

Mr. Golyadkin was petrified with astonishment, and for the moment he could not speak. To treat so lightly such a horrible, unheard-of thing, a thing undeniably rare and curious in its way, a thing which would have amazed even an unconcerned spectator, to talk of a family resemblance when he could see himself as in a looking-glass!

"Do you know, Yakov Petrovitch, what I advise you to do?" Anton Antonovitch went on. "Go and consult a doctor. Do you know, you look somehow quite unwell. Your eyes look peculiar . . . you know, there's a peculiar expression in them."

"No, Anton Antonovitch, I feel, of course . . . that is, I keep wanting to ask about this clerk."

"Well?"

"That is, have not you noticed, Anton Antonovitch, something peculiar about him, something very marked?"

"That is . . . ?"

"That is, I mean, Anton Antonovitch, a striking likeness with somebody, for instance; with me, for instance? You spoke just now, you see, Anton Antonovitch, of a family likeness. You let slip the remark.

. . . You know there really are sometimes twins exactly alike, like two drops of water, so that they can't be told apart. Well, it's that that I mean."

"To be sure," said Anton Antonovitch, after a moment's thought, speaking as though he were struck by the fact for the first time; "yes, indeed! You are right, there is a striking likeness, and you are quite right in what you say. You really might be mistaken for one another," he went on, opening his eyes wider and wider; "and, do you know, Yakov Petrovitch, it's positively a marvellous likeness, fantastic, in fact, as the saying is; that is, just as you . . . Have you observed, Yakov Petrovitch? I wanted to ask you to explain it; yes, I must confess I didn't take particular notice at first. It's wonderful, it's really wonderful! And, you know, you are not a native of these parts, are you, Yakov Petrovitch?"

"No."

"He is not from these parts, you know, either. Perhaps he comes from the same part of the country as you do. Where, may I make bold to inquire, did your mother live for the most part?"

"You said . . . you say, Anton Antonovitch, that he is not a native of these parts?"

"No, he is not. And, indeed, how strange it is!" continued the talkative Anton Antonovitch, for whom it was a genuine treat to gossip. "It may well arouse curiosity; and yet, you know, you might often pass him by, brush against him, without noticing anything. But you mustn't be upset about it. It's a thing that does happen. Do you know, the same thing, I must tell you, happened to my aunt on my mother's side; she saw her own double before her death . . ."

"No, I—excuse my interrupting you, Anton Antonovitch—I wanted to find out, Anton Antonovitch, how that clerk . . . that is, on what footing is he here?"

"In place of Semyon Ivanovitch, to fill the vacancy left by his death; the post was vacant, so he was appointed. Do you know, I'm told poor dear Semyon Ivanovitch left three children, all tiny tots. The widow fell at the feet of his Excellency. They do say she's hiding something; she's got a bit of money, but she's hiding it."

"No, Anton Antonovitch, I was still referring to that circumstance."

"You mean . . .? To be sure! But why are you so interested in that? I tell you not to upset yourself. All this is temporary to some extent. Why, after all, you know, you have nothing to do with it. So it has been ordained by God Almighty, it's His will, and it is sinful repining. His wisdom is apparent in it. And as far as I can make out, Yakov

Petrovitch, you are not to blame in any way. There are all sorts of strange things in the world! Mother Nature is liberal with her gifts, and you are not called upon to answer for it, you won't be responsible. Here, for instance, you have heard, I expect, of those—what's their name?—oh, the Siamese twins who are joined together at the back, live and eat and sleep together. I'm told they get a lot of money."

"Allow me, Anton Antonovitch . . ."

"I understand, I understand! Yes! But what of it? It's no matter, I tell you, as far as I can see there's nothing for you to upset yourself about. After all, he's a clerk—as a clerk he seems to be a capable man. He says his name is Golyadkin, that he's not a native of this district, and that he's a titular councillor. He had a personal interview with his Excellency."

"And how did his Excellency . . . ?"

"It was all right; I am told he gave a satisfactory account of himself, gave his reasons, said, 'It's like this, your Excellency,' and that he was without means and anxious to enter the service, and would be particularly flattered to be serving under his Excellency . . . all that was proper, you know; he expressed himself neatly. He must be a sensible man. But of course he came with a recommendation; he couldn't have got in without that. . . ."

"Oh, from whom . . . that is, I mean, who is it has had a hand in this shameful business?"

"Yes, a good recommendation, I'm told; his Excellency, I'm told, laughed with Andrey Filippovitch."

"Laughed with Andrey Filippovitch?"

"Yes, he only just smiled and said that it was all right, and that he had nothing against it, so long as he did his duty. . . ."

"Well, and what more? You relieve me to some extent, Anton Antonovitch; go on, I entreat you."

"Excuse me, I must tell you again. . . . Well, then, come, it's nothing, it's a very simple matter; you mustn't upset yourself, I tell you, and there's nothing suspicious about it. . . ."

"No. I . . . that is, Anton Antonovitch, I want to ask you, didn't his Excellency say anything more . . . about me, for instance?"

"Well! To be sure! No, nothing of the sort; you can set your mind quite at rest. You know it is, of course, a rather striking circumstance, and at first . . . why, here, I, for instance, I scarcely noticed it. I really don't know why I didn't notice it till you mentioned it. But you can set your mind at rest entirely. He said nothing particular, absolutely nothing," added good-natured Anton Antonovitch, getting up from his chair.

"So then, Anton Antonovitch, I . . ."

"Oh, you must excuse me. Here I've been gossiping about these trivial matters, and I've business that is important and urgent. I must inquire about it."

"Anton Antonovitch!" Andrey Filippovitch's voice sounded, summoning him politely, "his Excellency has been asking for you."

"This minute, I'm coming this minute, Andrey Filippovitch." And Anton Antonovitch, taking a pile of papers, flew off first to Andrey Filippovitch and then into his Excellency's room.

"Then what is the meaning of it?" thought Mr. Golyadkin. "Is there some sort of game going on? So the wind's in that quarter now. . . . That's just as well; so things have taken a much pleasanter turn," our hero said to himself, rubbing his hands, and so delighted that he scarcely knew where he was. "So our position is an ordinary thing. So it turns out to be all nonsense, it comes to nothing at all. No one has done anything really, and they are not budging, the rascals, they are sitting busy over their work; that's splendid, splendid! I like the good-natured fellow, I've always liked him, and I'm always ready to respect him . . . though it must be said one doesn't know what to think; this Anton Antonovitch . . . I'm afraid to trust him; his hair's very grey, and he's so old he's getting shaky. It's an immense and glorious thing that his Excellency said nothing, and let it pass! It's a good thing! I approve! Only why does Andrey Filippovitch interfere with his grins? What's he got to do with it? The old rogue. Always on my track, always, like a black cat, on the watch to run across a man's path, always thwarting and annoying a man, always annoying and thwarting a man. . . ."

Mr. Golyadkin looked around him again, and again his hopes revived. Yet he felt that he was troubled by one remote idea, an unpleasant idea. It even occurred to him that he might try somehow to make up to the clerks, to be the first in the field even (perhaps when leaving the office or going up to them as though about his work), to drop a hint in the course of conversation, saying, "This is how it is, what a striking likeness, gentlemen, a strange circumstance, a burlesque farce!"—that is, treat it all lightly, and in this way sound the depth of the danger. "Devils breed in still waters," our hero concluded inwardly.

Mr. Golyadkin, however, only contemplated this; he thought better of it in time. He realized that this would be going too far. "That's your temperament," he said to himself, tapping himself lightly on the forehead; "as soon as you gain anything you are delighted! You're a simple soul! No, you and I had better be patient, Yakov Petrovitch; let us wait and be patient!"

Nevertheless, as we have mentioned already, Mr. Golyadkin was buoyed up with the most confident hopes, feeling as though he had risen from the dead.

"No matter," he thought, "it's as though a hundred tons had been lifted off my chest! Here is a circumstance, to be sure! The box has been opened by lifting the lid. Krylov is right, a clever chap, a rogue, that Krylov, and a great fable-writer! And as for him, let him work in the office, and good luck to him so long as he doesn't meddle or interfere with any one; let him work in the office—I consent and approve!"

Meanwhile the hours were passing, flying by, and before he noticed the time it struck four. The office was closed. Andrey Filippovitch took his hat, and all followed his example in due course. Mr. Golyadkin dawdled a little on purpose, long enough to be the last to go out when all the others had gone their several ways. Going out into the street he felt as though he were in Paradise, so that he even felt inclined to go a longer way round, and to walk along the Nevsky Prospect.

"To be sure this is destiny," thought our hero, "this unexpected turn in affairs. And the weather's more cheerful, and the frost and the little sledges. And the frost suits the Russian, the Russian gets on capitally with the frost. I like the Russian. And the dear little snow, and the first few flakes in autumn; the sportsman would say, 'It would be nice to go shooting hares in the first snow.' Well, there, it doesn't matter."

This was how Mr. Golyadkin's enthusiasm found expression. Yet something was fretting in his brain, not exactly melancholy, but at times he had such a gnawing at his heart that he did not know how to find relief.

"Let us wait for the day, though, and then we shall rejoice. And, after all, you know, what does it matter? Come, let us think it over, let us look at it. Come, let us consider it, my young friend, let us consider it. Why, a man's exactly like you in the first place, abso-lutely the same. Well, what is there in that? If there is such a man, why should I weep over it? What is it to me? I stand aside, I whistle to myself, and that's all! That's what I laid myself open to, and that's all about it! Let him work in the office! Well, it's strange and marvellous, they say, that the Siamese twins . . . But why bring in the Siamese twins? They are twins, of course, but even great men, you know, sometimes look queer creatures. In fact, we know from history that the famous Suvorov used to crow like a cock. . . . But there, he did all that with political motives; and he was a great general . . . but what are generals, after all? But I keep myself to myself, that's all, and I don't care about any one else, and, secure in my innocence, I scorn my enemies. I am not one to intrigue, and I'm proud of it. Genuine, straightforward, neat and nice, meek and mild."

All at once Mr. Golyadkin broke off, his tongue failed him and he began trembling like a leaf; he even closed his eyes for a minute. Hoping, however, that the object of his terror was only an illusion, he opened his eyes at last and stole a timid glance to the right. No, it was not an illusion! . . . His acquaintance of that morning was tripping along by his side, smiling, peeping into his face, and apparently seeking an opportunity to begin a conversation with him. The conversation was not begun, however. They both walked like this for about fifty paces. All Mr. Golyadkin's efforts were concentrated on muffling himself up, hiding himself in his coat and pulling his hat down as far as possible over his eyes. To complete his mortification, his companion's coat and hat looked as though they had been taken off Mr. Golyadkin himself.

"Sir," our hero articulated at last, trying to speak almost in a whisper, and not looking at his companion, "we are going different ways, I believe. . . . I am convinced of it, in fact," he said, after a brief pause. "I am convinced, indeed, that you quite understand me," he added, rather severely, in conclusion.

"I could have wished . . ." his companion pronounced at last, "I could have wished . . . no doubt you will be magnanimous and pardon me . . . I don't know to whom to address myself here . . . my circumstances . . . I trust you will pardon my intrusiveness. I fancied, indeed, that, moved by compassion, you showed some interest in me this morning. On my side, I felt drawn to you from the first moment. I . . ."

A this point Mr. Golyadkin inwardly wished that his companion might sink into the earth.

"If I might venture to hope that you would accord me an indulgent hearing, Yakov Petrovitch . . ."

"We—here, we—we . . . you had better come home with me," answered Mr. Golyadkin. "We will cross now to the other side of the

Nevsky Prospect, it will be more convenient for us there, and then by the little back street ... we'd better go by the back street."

"Very well, by all means let us go by the back street," our hero's meek companion responded timidly, suggesting by the tone of his reply that it was not for him to choose, and that in his position he was quite prepared to accept the back street. As for Mr. Golyadkin, he was utterly unable to grasp what was happening to him. He could not believe in himself. He could not get over his amazement.

Chapter 7

He RECOVERED himself a little on the staircase as he went up to his flat.

"Oh, I'm a sheep's-head," he railed at himself inwardly. "Where am I taking him? I am thrusting my head into the noose. What will Petrushka think, seeing us together? What will the scoundrel dare to imagine now? He's suspicious. . . ."

But it was too late to regret it. Mr. Golyadkin knocked at the door; it was opened, and Petrushka began taking off the visitor's coat as well as his master's. Mr. Golyadkin looked askance, just stealing a glance at Petrushka, trying to read his countenance and divine what he was thinking. But to his intense astonishment he saw that his servant showed no trace of surprise, but seemed, on the contrary, to be expecting something of the sort. Of course he did look morose, as it was; he kept his eyes turned away and looked as though he would like to fall upon somebody.

"Hasn't somebody bewitched them all to-day?" thought our hero. "Some devil must have got round them. There certainly must be something peculiar in the whole lot of them to-day. Damn it all, what a worry it is!"

Such were Mr. Golyadkin's thoughts and reflections as he led his visitor into his room and politely asked him to sit down. The visitor appeared to be greatly embarrassed, he was very shy, and humbly watched every movement his host made, caught his glance, and seemed trying to divine his thoughts from them. There was a down-trodden, crushed, scared look about all his gestures, so that—if the comparison may be allowed—he was at that moment rather like the man who, having lost his clothes, is dressed up in somebody else's: the sleeves work up to the elbows, the waist is almost up to his neck, and he keeps every minute pulling down the short waistcoat; he wriggles sideways and turns away, tries to hide himself, or peeps into every face, and listens whether people are talking of his position, laughing at him or putting him to shame—and he is crimson with shame and overwhelmed with confusion and wounded vanity. . . . Mr. Golyadkin put down his hat in the window, and carelessly sent it flying to the floor. The visitor darted at once to pick it up, brushed off the dust, and carefully put it back, while he laid his own on the floor near a chair, on the edge of which he meekly seated himself. This little circumstance did something to open Mr. Golyadkin's eyes; he realized that the man was in great straits, and so did not put himself out for his visitor as he had done at first, very properly leaving all that to the man himself. The visitor, for his part, did nothing either; whether he was shy, a little ashamed, or from politeness was waiting for his host to begin is not certain and would be difficult to determine. At that moment Petrushka came in; he stood still in the doorway, and fixed his eyes in the direction furthest from where the visitor and his master were seated.

"Shall I bring in dinner for two?" he said carelessly, in a husky voice.

"I—I don't know . . . you . . . yes, bring dinner for two, my boy."

Petrushka went out. Mr. Golyadkin glanced at his visitor. The latter crimsoned to his ears. Mr. Golyadkin was a kind-hearted man, and so in the kindness of his heart he at once elaborated a theory.

"The fellow's hard up," he thought. "Yes, and in his situation only one day. Most likely he's suffered in his time. Maybe his good clothes are all that he has, and nothing to get him a dinner. Ah, poor fellow, how crushed he seems! But no matter; in a way it's better so. . . . Excuse me," began Mr. Golyadkin, "allow me to ask what I may call you."

"I . . . I . . . I'm Yakov Petrovitch," his visitor almost whispered, as though conscience-stricken and ashamed, as though apologizing for being called Yakov Petrovitch too.

"Yakov Petrovitch!" repeated our hero, unable to conceal his confusion.

"Yes, just so. . . . The same name as yours," responded the meek visitor, venturing to smile and speak a little jocosely. But at once he drew back, assuming a very serious air, though a little disconcerted, noticing that his host was in no joking mood.

"You . . . allow me to ask you, to what am I indebted for the honour . . . ?"

"Knowing your generosity and your benevolence," interposed the visitor in a rapid but timid voice, half rising from his seat, "I have ventured to appeal to you and to beg for your . . . acquaintance and protection . . ." he concluded, choosing his phrases with difficulty and trying to select words not too flattering or servile, that he might not compromise his dignity and not so bold as to suggest an unseemly inequality. In fact, one may say the visitor behaved like a gentlemanly beggar with a darned waistcoat, with an honourable passport in his pocket, who has not yet learnt by practice to hold out his hand properly for alms.

"You perplex me," answered Mr. Golyadkin, gazing round at himself, his walls and his visitor. "In what could I . . . that is, I mean, in what way could I be of service to you?"

"I felt drawn to you, Yakov Petrovitch, at first sight, and, graciously forgive me, I built my hopes on you—I made bold to build my hopes on you, Yakov Petrovitch. I . . . I'm in a desperate plight here, Yakov Petrovitch; I'm poor, I've had a great deal of trouble, Yakov Petrovitch, and have only recently come here. Learning that you, with your innate goodness and excellence of heart, are of the same name . . ."

Mr. Golyadkin frowned.

"Of the same name as myself and a native of the same district, I made up my mind to appeal to you, and to make known to you my difficult position."

"Very good, very good; I really don't know what to say," Mr. Golyadkin responded in an embarrassed voice. "We'll have a talk after dinner. . . ."

The visitor bowed; dinner was brought in. Petrushka laid the table, and Mr. Golyadkin and his visitor proceeded to partake of it. The dinner did not last long, for they were both in a hurry, the host because he felt ill at ease, and was, besides, ashamed that the dinner was a poor one—he was partly ashamed because he wanted to give the visitor a good meal, and partly because he wanted to show him he did not live like a beggar. The visitor, on his side too, was in terrible confusion and extremely embarrassed. When he had finished the piece of bread he had taken, he was afraid to put out his hand to take another piece, was ashamed to help himself to the best morsels, and was continually assuring his host that he was not at all hungry, that the dinner was excellent, that he was absolutely satisfied with it, and should not forget it to his dying day. When the meal was over Mr. Golyadkin lighted his pipe, and offered a second, which was brought in, to the visitor. They sat facing each other, and the visitor began telling his adventures.

Mr. Golyadkin junior's story lasted for three or four hours. His history was, however, composed of the most trivial and wretched, if one may say so, incidents. It dealt with details of service in some law-court in the provinces, of prosecutors and presidents, of some department intrigues, of the depravity of some registration clerks, of an inspector, of the sudden appointment of a new chief in the department, of how the second Mr. Golyadkin had suffered, quite without any fault on his part; of his aged aunt, Pelagea Semyonovna; of how, through various intrigues on the part of his enemies, he had lost his situation, and had come to Petersburg on foot; of the harassing and wretched time he had spent here in Petersburg, how for a long time he had tried in vain to get a job, had spent all his money, had nothing left, had been living almost in the street, lived on a crust of bread and washed it down with his tears, slept on the bare floor, and finally how some good Christian had exerted himself on his behalf, had given him an introduction, and had nobly got him into a new berth. Mr. Golyadkin's visitor shed tears as he told his story, and wiped his eyes with a blue-check handkerchief that looked like oilcloth. He ended by making a clean breast of it to Mr. Golyadkin, and confessing that he was not only for the time without means of subsistence and money for a decent lodging, but had not even the wherewithal to fit himself out properly, so that he had not, he said in conclusion, been able to get together enough for a pair of wretched boots, and that he had had to hire a uniform for the time.

Mr. Golyadkin was melted; he was genuinely touched. Even though his visitor's story was the paltriest story, every word of it was like heavenly manna to his heart. The fact was that Mr. Golyadkin was beginning to forget his last misgivings, to surrender his soul to free-dom and rejoicing, and at last mentally dubbed himself a fool. It was all so natural! And what a thing to break his heart over, what a thing to be so distressed about! To be sure there was, there really was, one ticklish circumstance—but, after all, it was not a misfortune; it could be no disgrace to a man, it could not cast a slur on his honour or ruin his career, if he were innocent, since Nature herself was mixed up in it. Moreover, the visitor begged for protection, wept, railed at destiny, seemed such an artless, pitiful, insignificant person, with no craft or malice about him, and he seemed now to be ashamed himself, though perhaps on different grounds, of the strange resemblance of his counte-nance with that of Mr. Golyadkin's. His behaviour was absolutely unimpeachable; his one desire was to please his host, and he looked as a man looks who feels conscience-stricken and to blame in regard to some one else. If any doubtful point were touched upon, for instance, the visitor at once agreed with Mr. Golyadkin's opinion. If by mistake he advanced an opinion in opposition to Mr. Golyadkin's, and afterwards noticed that he had made a slip, he immediately corrected his mistake, explained himself and made it clear that he meant the same thing as his host, that he thought as he did and took the same view of everything as he did. In fact, the visitor made every possible effort to "make up to" Mr. Golyadkin, so that the latter made up his mind at last that his visitor must be a very amiable person in every way. Meanwhile, tea was brought in; it was nearly nine o'clock. Mr. Golyadkin felt in a very good humour, grew lively and skittish, let himself go a little, and finally plunged into a most animated and interested conversation with his visitor. In his festive moments Mr. Golyadkin was fond of telling interesting anecdotes. So now he told the visitor a great deal about Petersburg, about its entertainments and attractions, about the theatre, the clubs, about Brülov's picture, and about the two Englishmen who came from England to Petersburg on purpose to look at the iron railing of the Summer Garden, and returned at once when they had seen it; about the office; about Olsufy Ivanovitch and Andrey Filippovitch; about the way that Russia was progressing, was hour by hour progressing towards a state of perfection, so that

"Arts and letters flourish here to-day";

about an anecdote he had lately read in the *Northern Bee* concerning a boa-constrictor in India of immense strength; about Baron Brambeus, and so on. In short, Mr. Golyadkin was quite happy, first, because his mind was at rest; secondly, because, so far from being afraid of his enemies, he was quite prepared now to challenge them all to mortal combat; thirdly, because he was now in the rôle of patron and was doing a good deed. Yet he was conscious at the bottom of his heart that he was not perfectly happy, that there was still a hidden worm gnawing at his heart, though it was only a tiny one. He was extremely worried by the thought of the previous evening at Olsufy Ivanovitch's. He would have given a great deal now for nothing to have happened of what took place then.

"It's no matter, though!" our hero decided at last, and he firmly resolved in his heart to behave well in future and never to be guilty of such pranks again. As Mr. Golyadkin was now completely worked

up, and had suddenly become almost blissful, the fancy took him to
have a jovial time. Rum was brought in by Petrushka, and punch was
prepared. The visitor and his host drained a glass each, and then a
second. The visitor appeared even more amiable than before, and gave
more than one proof of his frankness and charming character; he entered keenly into Mr. Golyadkin's joy, seemed only to rejoice in his
rejoicing, and to look upon him as his one and only benefactor. Taking up a pen and a sheet of paper, he asked Mr. Golyadkin not to look
at what he was going to write, but afterwards showed his host what
he had written. It turned out to be a verse of four lines, written with
a good deal of feeling, in excellent language and handwriting, and
evidently was the composition of the amiable visitor himself. The
lines were as follows—

> "If thou forget me,
> I shall not forget thee;
> Though all things may be,
> Do not thou forget me."

With tears in his eyes Mr. Golyadkin embraced his companion, and,
completely overcome by his feelings, he began to initiate his friend into
some of his own secrets and private affairs, Andrey Filippovitch and
Klara Olsufyevna being prominent in his remarks.

"Well, you may be sure we shall get on together, Yakov Petrovitch," said our hero to his visitor. "You and I will take to each other
like fish to the water, Yakov Petrovitch; we shall be like brothers;
we'll be cunning, my dear fellow, we'll work together; we'll get up an
intrigue, too, to pay them out. To pay them out we'll get up an intrigue too. And don't you trust any of them. I know you, Yakov
Petrovitch, and I understand your character; you'll tell them everything straight out, you know, you're a guileless soul! You must hold
aloof from them all, my boy."

His companion entirely agreed with him, thanked Mr. Golyadkin,
and he, too, grew tearful at last.

"Do you know, Yasha," Mr. Golyadkin went on in a shaking voice,
weak with emotion, "you must stay with me for a time, or stay with
me for ever. We shall get on together. What do you say, brother, eh?
And don't you worry or repine because there's such a strange circumstance about us now; it's a sin to repine, brother; it's nature! And
Mother Nature is liberal with her gifts, so there, brother Yasha! It's
from love for you that I speak, from brotherly love. But we'll be cunning, Yasha; we'll lay a mine, too, and we'll make them laugh the
other side of their mouths."

They reached their third and fourth glasses of punch at last, and then Mr. Golyadkin began to be aware of two sensations: the one that he was extraordinarily happy, and the other that he could not stand upon his legs. The guest was, of course, invited to stay the night. A bed was somehow made up on two chairs. Mr. Golyadkin junior declared that under a friend's roof the bare floor would be a soft bed, that for his part he could sleep anywhere, humbly and gratefully; that he was in Paradise now, that he had been through a great deal of trouble and grief in his time; he had seen ups and downs, had all sorts of things to put up with, and—who could tell what the future would be?—maybe he would have still more to put up with. Mr. Golyadkin senior protested against this, and began to maintain that one must put one's faith in God. His guest entirely agreed, observing that there was, of course, no one like God. At this point Mr. Golyadkin senior observed that in certain respects the Turks were right in calling upon God even in their sleep. Then, though disagreeing with certain learned professors in the slanders they had promulgated against the Turkish prophet Mahomet and recognizing him as a great politician in his own line, Mr. Golyadkin passed to a very interesting description of an Algerian barber's shop which he had read in a book of miscellanies. The friends laughed heartily at the simplicity of the Turks, but paid due tribute to their fanaticism, which they ascribed to opium. . . . At last the guest began undressing, and thinking in the kindness of his heart that very likely he hadn't even a decent shirt, Mr. Golyadkin went behind the screen to avoid embarrassing a man who had suffered enough, and partly to reassure himself as far as possible about Petrushka, to sound him, to cheer him up if he could, to be kind to the fellow so that every one might be happy and that everything might be pleasant all round. It must be remarked that Petrushka still rather bothered Mr. Golyadkin.

"You go to bed now, Pyotr," Mr. Golyadkin said blandly, going into his servant's domain; "you go to bed now and wake me up at eight o'clock. Do you understand, Petrushka?"

Mr. Golyadkin spoke with exceptional softness and friendliness. But Petrushka remained mute. He was busy making his bed, and did not even turn round to face his master, which he ought to have done out of simple respect.

"Did you hear what I said, Pyotr?" Mr. Golyadkin went on. "You go to bed now and wake me to-morrow at eight o'clock; do you understand?"

"Why, I know that; what's the use of telling me?" Petrushka grumbled to himself.

"Well, that's right, Petrushka; I only mentioned it that you might be happy and at rest. Now we are all happy, so I want you, too, to be happy and satisfied. And now I wish you good-night. Sleep, Petrushka, sleep; we all have to work. . . . Don't think anything amiss, my man . . ." Mr. Golyadkin began, but stopped short. "Isn't this too much?" he thought. "Haven't I gone too far? That's how it always is; I always overdo things."

Our hero felt much dissatisfied with himself as he left Petrushka. He was, besides, rather wounded by Petrushka's grumpiness and rudeness. "One jests with the rascal, his master does him too much honour, and the rascal does not feel it," thought Mr. Golyadkin. "But there, that's the nasty way of all that sort of people!"

Somewhat shaken, he went back to his room, and, seeing that his guest had settled himself for the night, he sat down on the edge of his bed for a minute.

"Come, you must own, Yasha," he began in a whisper, wagging his head, "you're a rascal, you know; what a way you've treated me! You see, you've got my name, do you know that?" he went on, jesting in a rather familiar way with his visitor. At last, saying a friendly good-night to him, Mr. Golyadkin began preparing for the night. The visitor meanwhile began snoring. Mr. Golyadkin in his turn got into bed, laughing and whispering to himself: "You are drunk to-day, my dear fellow, Yakov Petrovitch, you rascal, you old Golyadkin—what a surname to have! Why, what are you so pleased about? You'll be crying to-morrow, you know, you sniveller; what am I to do with you?"

At this point a rather strange sensation pervaded Mr. Golyadkin's whole being, something like doubt or remorse.

"I've been over-excited and let myself go," he thought; "now I've a noise in my head and I'm drunk; I couldn't restrain myself, ass that I am! and I've been babbling bushels of nonsense, and, like a rascal, I was planning to be so sly. Of course, to forgive and forget injuries is the height of virtue; but it's a bad thing, nevertheless! Yes, that's so!"

At this point Mr. Golyadkin got up, took a candle and went on tiptoe to look once more at his sleeping guest. He stood over him for a long time, meditating deeply.

"An unpleasant picture! A burlesque, a regular burlesque, and that's the fact of the matter!"

At last Mr. Golyadkin settled down finally. There was a humming, a buzzing, a ringing in his head. He grew more and more drowsy ... tried to think about something, to remember something very interesting, to decide something very important, some delicate question— but could not. Sleep descended upon his devoted head, and he slept as people generally do sleep who are not used to drinking and have consumed five glasses of punch at some festive gathering.

Chapter 8

M R. GOLYADKIN woke up next morning at eight o'clock as usual; as soon as he was awake he recalled all the adventures of the previous evening—and frowned as he recalled them. "Ugh, I did play the fool last night!" he thought, sitting up and glancing at his visitor's bed. But what was his amazement when he saw in the room no trace, not only of his visitor, but even of the bed on which his visitor had slept!

"What does it mean?" Mr. Golyadkin almost shrieked. "What can it be? What does this new circumstance portend?"

While Mr. Golyadkin was gazing in open-mouthed bewilderment at the empty spot, the door creaked and Petrushka came in with the tea-tray.

"Where, where?" our hero said in a voice hardly audible, pointing to the place which had been occupied by his visitor the night before.

At first Petrushka made no answer and did not look at his master, but fixed his eyes upon the corner to the right till Mr. Golyadkin felt compelled to look into that corner too. After a brief silence, however, Petrushka in a rude and husky voice answered that his master was not at home.

"You idiot; why, *I'm* your master, Petrushka!" said Mr. Golyadkin in a breaking voice, looking open-eyed at his servant.

Petrushka made no reply, but he gave Mr. Golyadkin such a look that the latter crimsoned to his ears—looked at him with an insulting reproachfulness almost equivalent to open abuse. Mr. Golyadkin was utterly flabbergasted, as the saying is. At last Petrushka explained that the *other one* had gone away an hour and a half ago, and would not wait. His answer, of course, sounded truthful and probable; it was evident that Petrushka was not lying; that his insulting look and the phrase the *other one* employed by him were only the result of the disgusting circumstance with which he was already familiar, but still he understood, though dimly, that something was wrong, and that destiny had some other surprise, not altogether a pleasant one, in store for him.

"All right, we shall see," he thought to himself. "We shall see in due time; we'll get to the bottom of all this. . . . Oh, Lord, have mercy upon us!" he moaned in conclusion, in quite a different voice. "And why did I invite him, to what end did I do all that? Why, I am thrusting my head into their thievish noose myself; I am tying the noose with my own hands. Ach, you fool, you fool! You can't resist babbling like some silly boy, some chancery clerk, some wretched creature of no class at all, some rag, some rotten dishclout; you're a gossip, an old woman! . . . Oh, all ye saints! And he wrote verses, the rogue, and expressed his love for me! How could . . . How can I show him the door in a polite way if he turns up again, the rogue? Of course, there are all sorts of ways and means. I can say this is how it is, my salary being so limited . . . Or scare him off in some way saying that, taking this and that into consideration, I am forced to make clear . . . that he would have to pay an equal share of the cost of board and lodging, and pay the money in advance. H'm! No, damn it all, no! That would be degrading to me. It's not quite delicate! Couldn't I do something like this: suggest to Petrushka that he should annoy him in some way, should be disrespectful, be rude, and get rid of him in that way. Set them at each other in some way. . . . No, damn it all, no! It's dangerous and again, if one looks at it from that point of view—it's not the right thing at all! Not the right thing at all! But there, even if he doesn't come, it will be a bad look-out, too! I babbled to him last night! . . . Ach, it's a bad look-out, a bad look-out! Ach, we're in a bad way! Oh, I'm a cursed fool, a cursed fool! You can't train yourself to behave as you ought, you can't conduct yourself reasonably. Well, what if he comes, and refuses. And God grant he may come! I should be very glad if he did come. . . ."

Such were Mr. Golyadkin's reflections as he swallowed his tea and glanced continually at the clock on the wall.

"It's a quarter to nine; it's time to go. And something will happen! What will there be there? I should like to know what exactly lies hidden in this—that is, the object, the aim, and the various intrigues. It would be a good thing to find out what all these people are plotting, and what will be their first step. . . ."

Mr. Golyadkin could endure it no longer. He threw down his unfinished pipe, dressed and set off for the office, anxious to ward off the danger if possible and to reassure himself about everything by his presence in person. There was danger: he knew himself that there was danger.

"We . . . will get to the bottom of it," said Mr. Golyadkin, taking off his coat and goloshes in the entry. "We'll go into all these matters immediately."

Making up his mind to act in this way, our hero put himself to rights, assumed a correct and official air, and was just about to pass into the adjoining room, when suddenly, in the very doorway, he jostled against his acquaintance of the day before, his friend and companion. Mr. Golyadkin junior seemed not to notice Mr. Golyadkin senior, though they met almost nose to nose. Mr. Golyadkin junior seemed to be busy, to be hastening somewhere, was breathless; he had such an official, such a business-like air that it seemed as though any one could read in his face: 'Entrusted with a special commission.' . . .

"Oh, it's you, Yakov Petrovitch!" said our hero, clutching the hand of his last night's visitor.

"Presently, presently, excuse me, tell me about it afterwards," cried Mr. Golyadkin junior, dashing on.

"But, excuse me; I believe, Yakov Petrovitch, you wanted . . ."

"What is it? Make haste and explain."

At this point his visitor of the previous night halted as though reluctantly and against his will, and put his ear almost to Mr. Golyadkin's nose.

"I must tell you, Yakov Petrovitch, that I am surprised at behaviour . . . behaviour which seemingly I could not have expected at all."

"There's a proper form for everything. Go to his Excellency's secretary and then appeal in the proper way to the directors of the office. Have you got your petition?"

"You . . . I really don't know, Yakov Petrovitch! You simply amaze me, Yakov Petrovitch! You certainly don't recognize me or, with your characteristic gaiety, you are joking."

"Oh, it's you," said Mr. Golyadkin junior, seeming only now to recognize Mr. Golyadkin senior. "So it's you? Well, have you had a good night?"

Then, smiling a little—a formal and conventional smile, by no means the sort of smile that was befitting (for, after all, he owed a debt of gratitude to Mr. Golyadkin senior)—smiling this formal and conventional smile, Mr. Golyadkin junior added that he was very glad Mr. Golyadkin senior had had a good night; then he made a slight bow and shuffling a little with his feet, looked to the right, and to the left, then dropped his eyes to the floor, made for the side door and muttering in a hurried whisper that he had a special commission, dashed into the next room. He vanished like an apparition.

"Well, this is queer!" muttered our hero, petrified for a moment; "this is queer! This is a strange circumstance."

At this point Mr. Golyadkin felt as though he had pins and needles all over him.

"However," he went on to himself, as he made his way to his department, "however, I spoke long ago of such a circumstance: I had a presentiment long ago that he had a special commission. Why, I said yesterday that the man must certainly be employed on some special commission."

"Have you finished copying out the document you had yesterday, Yakov Petrovitch?" Anton Antonovitch Syetotchkin asked Mr. Golyadkin, when the latter was seated beside him. "Have you got it here?"

"Yes," murmured Mr. Golyadkin, looking at the head clerk with a rather helpless glance.

"That's right! I mention it because Andrey Filippovitch has asked for it twice. I'll be bound his Excellency wants it. . . ."

"Yes, it's finished. . . ."

"Well, that's all right then."

"I believe, Anton Antonovitch, I have always perfomed my duties properly. I'm always scrupulous over the work entrusted to me by my superiors, and I attend to it conscientiously."

"Yes. Why, what do you mean by that?"

"I mean nothing, Anton Antonovitch. I only want to explain, Anton Antonovitch, that I . . . that is, I meant to express that spite and malice sometimes spare no person whatever in their search for their daily and revolting food. . . ."

"Excuse me, I don't quite understand you. What person are you alluding to?"

"I only meant to say, Anton Antonovitch, that I'm seeking the straight path and I scorn going to work in a roundabout way. That I am not one to intrigue, and that, if I may be allowed to say so, I may very justly be proud of it. . . ."

"Yes. That's quite so, and to the best of my comprehension I thoroughly endorse your remarks; but allow me to tell you, Yakov Petrovitch, that personalities are not quite permissible in good society, that I, for instance, am ready to put up with anything behind my back— for every one's abused behind his back—but to my face, if you please, my good sir, I don't allow any one to be impudent. I've grown grey in the government service, sir, and I don't allow any one to be impudent to me in my old age. . . ."

"No, Anton Antonovitch . . . you see, Anton Antonovitch . . . you haven't quite caught my meaning. To be sure, Anton Antonovitch, I for my part could only think it an honour. . . ."

"Well, then, I ask your pardon too. We've been brought up in the old school. And it's too late for us to learn your new-fangled ways. I believe we've had understanding enough for the service of our country up to now. As you are aware, sir, I have an order of merit for twenty-five years' irreproachable service. . . ."

"I feel it, Anton Antonovitch, on my side, too, I quite feel all that. But I didn't meant that, I am speaking of a mask, Anton Antonovitch. . . ."

"A mask?"

"Again you . . . I am apprehensive that you are taking this, too, in a wrong sense, that is the sense of my remarks, as you say yourself, Anton Antonovitch. I am simply enunciating a theory, that is, I am advancing the idea, Anton Antonovitch, that persons who wear a mask have become far from uncommon, and that nowadays it is hard to recognize the man beneath the mask. . . ."

"Well, do you know, it's not altogether so hard. Sometimes it's fairly easy. Sometimes one need not go far to look for it."

"No, you know, Anton Antonovitch, I say, I say of myself, that I, for instance, do not put on a mask except when there is need of it; that is simply at carnival time or at some festive gathering, speaking in the literal sense; but that I do not wear a mask before people in daily life, speaking in another less obvious sense. That's what I meant to say, Anton Antonovitch."

"Oh, well, but we must drop all this, for now I've no time to spare," said Anton Antonovitch, getting up from his seat and collecting some papers in order to report upon them to his Excellency. "Your business, as I imagine, will be explained in due course without delay. You will see for yourself whom you should censure and whom you should blame, and thereupon I humbly beg you to spare me from further private explanations and arguments which interfere with my work. . . ."

"No, Anton Antonovitch," Mr. Golyadkin, turning a little pale, began to the retreating figure of Anton Antonovitch: "I had no thought of the kind."

"What does it mean?" our hero went on to himself, when he was left alone. "What quarter is the wind in now, and what is one to make of this new turn?"

At the very time when our bewildered and half-crushed hero was setting himself to solve this new question, there was a sound of movement and bustle in the next room, the door opened and Andrey Filippovitch, who had been on some business in his Excellency's study, appeared breathless in the doorway, and called to Mr. Golyadkin. Knowing what was wanted and anxious not to keep Andrey Filippovitch waiting, Mr. Golyadkin leapt up from his seat, and as was fitting immediately bustled for all he was worth getting the manuscript that was required finally neat and ready and preparing to follow the manuscript and Andrey Filippovitch into his Excellency's study. Suddenly, almost slipping under the arm of Andrey Filippovitch, who was standing right in the doorway, Mr. Golyadkin junior darted into the room in breathless haste and bustle, with a solemn and resolutely official air; he bounded straight up to Mr. Golyadkin senior, who was expecting nothing less than such a visitation.

"The papers, Yakov Petrovitch, the papers . . . His Excellency has been pleased to ask for them; have you got them ready?" Mr. Golyadkin senior's friend whispered in a hurried undertone. "Andrey Filippovitch is waiting for you. . . ."

"I know he is waiting without your telling me," said Mr. Golyadkin senior, also in a hurried whisper.

"No, Yakov Petrovitch, I did not mean that; I did not mean that at all, Yakov Petrovitch, not that at all; I sympathize with you, Yakov Petrovitch, and am moved by genuine interest."

"Which I most humbly beg you to spare me. Allow me, allow me . . ."

"You'll put it in an envelope, of course, Yakov Petrovitch, and you'll put a mark in the third page; allow me, Yakov Petrovitch. . . ."

"You allow me, if you please. . . ."

"But, I say, there's a blot here, Yakov Petrovitch; did you know there was a blot here? . . ."

At this point Andrey Filippovitch called Yakov Petrovitch a second time.

"One moment, Andrey Filippovitch, I'm only just . . . Do you understand Russian, sir?"

"It would be best to take it out with a penknife, Yakov Petrovitch. You had better rely upon me; you had better not touch it yourself, Yakov Petrovitch, rely upon me—I'll do it with a penknife. . . ."

Andrey Filippovitch called Mr. Golyadkin a third time.

"But, allow me, where's the blot? I don't think there's a blot at all."
"It's a huge blot. Here it is! Here, allow me, I saw it here . . .
you just let me, Yakov Petrovitch, I'll just touch it with the penknife,
I'll scratch it out with the penknife from true-hearted sympathy.
There, like this; see, it's done."

At this point, and quite unexpectedly, Mr. Golyadkin junior overpowered Mr. Golyadkin senior in the momentary struggle that had
arisen between them, and so, entirely against the latter's will, suddenly, without rhyme or reason, took possession of the document required by the authorities, and instead of scratching it out with the
penknife in true-hearted sympathy as he had perfidiously promised
Mr. Golyadkin senior, hurriedly rolled it up, put it under his arm, in
two bounds was beside Andrey Filippovitch, who noticed none of his
manoeuvres, and flew with the latter into the Director's room. Mr.
Golyadkin remained as though riveted to the spot, holding the penknife in his hand and apparently on the point of scratching something
out with it. . . .

Our hero could not yet grasp his new position. He could not at
once recover himself. He felt the blow, but thought that it was somehow all right. In terrible, indescribable misery he tore himself at last
from his seat, rushed straight to the Director's room, imploring heaven
on the way that it might somehow all be arranged satisfactorily and
so would be all right. . . . In the furthermost room, which adjoined the
Director's private room, he ran straight upon Andrey Filippovitch in
company with his namesake. Both of them were coming back; Mr.
Golyadkin moved aside. Andrey Filippovitch was talking with a
good-humoured smile, Mr. Golyadkin senior's namesake was smiling,
too, fawning upon Andrey Filippovitch and tripping about at a respectful distance from him, and was whispering something in his
ear with a delighted air, to which Andrey Filippovitch assented with
a gracious nod. In a flash our hero grasped the whole position. The
fact was that the work had surpassed his Excellency's expectations (as
he learnt afterwards), and was finished punctually by the time it was
needed. His Excellency was extremely pleased with it. It was even
said that his Excellency had said "Thank you" to Mr. Golyadkin
junior, had thanked him warmly, had said that he would remember it
on occasion and would never forget it. . . . Of course, the first thing
Mr. Golyadkin did was to protest, to protest with the utmost vigour of
which he was capable. Pale as death, and hardly knowing what he
was doing, he rushed up to Andrey Filippovitch. But the latter, hearing that Mr. Golyadkin's business was a private matter. refused to

listen, observing firmly that he had not a minute to spare even for his own affairs.

The curtness of his tone and his refusal struck Mr. Golyadkin.

"I had better, perhaps, try in another quarter. . . . I had better appeal to Anton Antonovitch."

But to his disappointment Anton Antonovitch was not available either: he, too, was busy over something somewhere!

"Ah, it was not without design that he asked me to spare him explanation and discussion!" thought our hero. "This was what the old rogue had in his mind! In that case I shall simply make bold to approach his Excellency."

Still pale and feeling that his brain was in a complete ferment, greatly perplexed as to what he ought to decide to do, Mr. Golyadkin sat down on the edge of the chair. "It would have been a great deal better if it had all been just nothing," he kept incessantly thinking to himself. "Indeed, such a mysterious business was utterly improbable. In the first place, it was nonsense, and secondly it could not happen. Most likely it was imagination, or something else happened, and not what really did happen; or perhaps I went myself . . . and somehow mistook myself for some one else . . . in short, it's an utterly impossible thing."

Mr. Golyadkin had no sooner made up his mind that it was an utterly impossible thing than Mr. Golyadkin junior flew into the room with papers in both hands as well as under his arm. Saying two or three words about business to Andrey Filippovitch as he passed, exchanging remarks with one, polite greetings with another, and familiarities with a third, Mr. Golyadkin junior, having apparently no time to waste, seemed on the point of leaving the room, but luckily for Mr. Golyadkin senior he stopped near to the door to say a few words as he passed two or three clerks who were at work there. Mr. Golyadkin senior rushed straight at him. As soon as Mr. Golyadkin junior saw Mr. Golyadkin senior's movement he began immediately, with great uneasiness, looking about him to make his escape. But our hero already held his last night's guest by the sleeve. The clerks surrounding the two titular councillors stepped back and waited with curiosity to see what would happen. The senior titular councillor realized that public opinion was not on his side, he realized that they were intriguing against him: which made it all the more necessary to hold his own now. The moment was a decisive one.

"Well!" said Mr. Golyadkin junior, looking rather impatiently at Mr. Golyadkin senior.

The latter could hardly breathe.

"I don't know," he began, "in what way to make plain to you the strangeness of your behaviour, sir."

"Well. Go on." At this point Mr. Golyadkin junior turned round and winked to the clerks standing round, as though to give them to understand that a comedy was beginning.

"The impudence and shamelessness of your manners with me, sir, in the present case, unmasks your true character . . . better than any words of mine could do. Don't rely on your trickery: it is worthless. . . ."

"Come, Yakov Petrovitch, tell me now, how did you spend the night?" answered Mr. Golyadkin junior, looking Mr. Golyadkin senior straight in the eye.

"You forget yourself, sir," said the titular councillor, completely flabbergasted, hardly able to feel the floor under his feet. "I trust that you will take a different tone. . . ."

"My darling!" exclaimed Mr. Golyadkin junior, making a rather unseemly grimace at Mr. Golyadkin senior, and suddenly, quite unexpectedly, under the pretence of caressing him, he pinched his chubby cheek with two fingers.

Our hero grew as hot as fire. . . . As soon as Mr. Golyadkin junior noticed that his opponent, quivering in every limb, speechless with rage, as red as a lobster, and exasperated beyond all endurance, might actually be driven to attack him, he promptly and in the most shameless way hastened to be beforehand with his victim. Patting him two or three times on the cheek, tickling him two or three times, playing with him for a few seconds in this way while his victim stood rigid and beside himself with fury to the no little diversion of the young men standing round, Mr. Golyadkin junior ended with a most revolting shamelessness by giving Mr. Golyadkin senior a poke in his rather prominent stomach, and with a most venomous and suggestive smile said to him: "You're mischievous, brother Yakov, you are mischievous! We'll be sly, you and I, Yakov Petrovitch, we'll be sly."

Then, and before our hero could gradually come to himself after the last attack, Mr. Golyadkin junior (with a little smile beforehand to the spectators standing round) suddenly assumed a most business-like, busy and official air, dropped his eyes to the floor and, drawing himself in, shrinking together, and pronouncing rapidly "on a special commission" he cut a caper with his short leg, and darted away into the next room. Our hero could not believe his eyes and was still unable to pull himself together. . . .

At last he roused himself. Recognizing in a flash that he was ruined, in a sense annihilated, that he had disgraced himself and sullied his reputation, that he had been turned into ridicule and treated with contempt in the presence of spectators, that he had been treacherously insulted by one whom he had looked on only the day before as his greatest and most trustworthy friend, that he had been put to utter confusion, Mr. Golyadkin senior rushed in pursuit of his enemy. At the moment he would not even think of the witnesses of his ignominy.

"They're all in a conspiracy together," he said to himself; "they stand by each other and set each other on to attack me." After taking a dozen steps, however, our hero perceived clearly that all pursuit would be vain and useless, and so he turned back. "You won't get away," he thought, "you will get caught one day; the wolf will have to pay for the sheep's tears."

With ferocious composure and the most resolute determination Mr. Golyadkin went up to his chair and sat down upon it. "You won't escape," he said again.

Now it was not a question of passive resistance: there was determination and pugnacity in the air, and any one who had seen how Mr. Golyadkin at that moment, flushed and scarcely able to restrain his excitement, stabbed his pen into the inkstand and with what fury he began scribbling on the paper, could be certain beforehand that the matter would not pass off like this, and could not end in a simple, womanish way. In the depth of his soul he formed a resolution, and in the depth of his heart swore to carry it out. To tell the truth he still did not quite know how to act, or rather did not know at all, but never mind, that did not matter!

"Imposture and shamelessness do not pay nowadays, sir. Imposture and shamelessness, sir, lead to no good, but lead to the halter. Grishka Otrepyov was the only one, sir, who gained by imposture, deceiving the blind people and even that not for long."

In spite of this last circumstance Mr. Golyadkin proposed to wait till such time as the mask should fall from certain persons and something should be made manifest. For this it was necessary, in the first place, that office hours should be over as soon as possible, and till then our hero proposed to take no step. Then, when office hours were over, he would take one step. He knew then how he must act after taking that step, how to arrange his whole plan of action, to abase the horn of arrogance and crush the snake gnawing the dust in contemptible impotence. To allow himself to be treated like a rag used for wiping dirty boots, Mr. Golyadkin could not. He could not consent to that, especially in the present case. Had it not been for that last insult, our hero might, perhaps, have brought himself to control his anger; he might, perhaps, have been silent, have submitted and not have protested too obstinately; he would just have disputed a little, have made a slight complaint, have proved that he was in the right, then he would have given way a little, then, perhaps, he would have given way a little more, then he would have come round altogether, then, especially when the opposing party solemnly admitted that he was right, perhaps, he would have overlooked it completely, would even have been a little touched, there might even, perhaps—who could tell?—spring up a new, close, warm friendship, on an even broader basis than the friendship of last night, so that this friendship might, in the end, completely eclipse the unpleasantness of the rather unseemly resemblance of the two individuals, so that both the titular councillors might be highly delighted, and might go on living till they were a hundred, and so on. To tell the whole truth, Mr. Golyadkin began to regret a little that he had stood up for himself and his rights, and had at once come in for unpleasantness in consequence.

"Should he give in," thought Mr. Golyadkin, "say he was joking, I would forgive him. I would forgive him even more if he would acknowledge it aloud. But I won't let myself be treated like a rag. And I have not allowed even persons very different from him to treat me so, still less will I permit a depraved person to attempt it. I am not a rag. I am not a rag, sir!"

In short, our hero made up his mind. "You're in fault yourself, sir!" he thought. He made up his mind to protest, and to protest with all his might to the very last. That was the sort of man he was! He could not consent to allow himself to be insulted, still less to allow himself to be treated as a rag, and, above all, to allow a thoroughly vicious man to treat him so. No quarrelling, however, no quarrelling! Possibly if some one wanted, if some one, for instance, actually insisted on turning Mr. Golyadkin into a rag, he might have done so, might have done so without opposition or punishment (Mr. Golyadkin was himself conscious of this at times), and he would have been a rag and not Golyadkin—yes, a nasty, filthy rag; but that rag would not have been a simple rag, it would have been a rag possessed of dignity, it would have been a rag possessed of feelings and sentiments, even though dignity was defenceless and feelings could not assert themselves, and lay hidden deep down in the filthy folds of the rag, still the feelings were there. . . .

The hours dragged on incredibly slowly; at last it struck four. Soon after, all got up and, following the head of the department, moved each on his homeward way. Mr. Golyadkin mingled with the crowd; he kept a vigilant look-out, and did not lose sight of the man he wanted. At last our hero saw that his friend ran up to the office attendants who handed the clerks their overcoats, and hung about near them waiting for his in his usual nasty way. The minute was a decisive one. Mr. Golyadkin forced his way somehow through the crowd and, anxious not to be left behind, he, too, began fussing about his overcoat. But Mr. Golyadkin's friend and companion was given his overcoat first because on this occasion, too, he had succeeded, as he always did, in making up to them, whispering something to them, cringing upon them and getting round them.

After putting on his overcoat, Mr. Golyadkin junior glanced ironically at Mr. Golyadkin senior, acting in this way openly and defiantly, looked about him with his characteristic insolence, finally he tripped to and fro among the other clerks—no doubt in order to leave a good impression on them—said a word to one, whispered something to another, respectfully accosted a third, directed a smile at a fourth, gave his hand to a fifth, and gaily darted downstairs. Mr. Golyadkin senior flew after him, and to his inexpressible delight overtook him on the last step, and seized him by the collar of his overcoat. It seemed as though Mr. Golyadkin junior was a little disconcerted, and he looked about him with a helpless air.

"What do you mean by this?" he whispered to Mr. Golyadkin at last, in a weak voice.

"Sir, if you are a gentleman, I trust that you remember our friendly relations yesterday," said our hero.

"Ah, yes! Well? Did you sleep well?"

Fury rendered Mr. Golyadkin senior speechless for a moment.

"I slept well, sir . . . but allow me to tell you, sir, that you are playing a very complicated game. . . ."

"Who says so? My enemies say that," answered abruptly the man who called himself Mr. Golyadkin, and saying this, he unexpectedly freed himself from the feeble hand of the real Mr. Golyadkin. As soon as he was free he rushed away from the stairs, looked around him, saw a cab, ran up to it, got in, and in one moment vanished from Mr. Golyadkin senior's sight. The despairing titular councillor, abandoned by all, gazed about him, but there was no other cab. He tried to run, but his legs gave way under him. With a look of open-mouthed astonishment on his countenance, feeling crushed and shrivelled up, he leaned helplessly against a lamp-post, and remained so for some minutes in the middle of the pavement. It seemed as though all were over for Mr. Golyadkin.

Chapter 9

EVERYTHING, apparently, and even nature itself, seemed up in arms against Mr. Golyadkin; but he was still on his legs and unconquered; he felt that he was unconquered. He was ready to struggle. He rubbed his hands with such feeling and such energy when he recovered from his first amazement that it could be deduced from his very air that he would not give in. Yet the danger was imminent; it was evident; Mr. Golyadkin felt it; but how to grapple with it, with this danger?—that was the question. The thought even flashed through Mr. Golyadkin's mind for a moment, "After all, why not leave it so, simply give it up? Why, what is it? Why, it's nothing. I'll keep apart as though it were not I," thought Mr. Golyadkin. "I'll let it all pass; it's not I, and that's all about it; he's separate too, maybe he'll give it up too; he'll hang about, the rascal, he'll hang about. He'll come back and give it up again. That's how it will be! I'll take it meekly. And, indeed, where is the danger? Come, what danger is there? I should like any one to tell me where the danger lies in this business. It is a trivial affair. An everyday affair. . . ."

At this point Mr. Golyadkin's tongue failed; the words died away on his lips; he even swore at himself for this thought; he convicted himself on the spot of abjectness, of cowardice for having this thought; things were no forwarder, however. He felt that to make up his mind to some course of action was absolutely necessary for him at the moment; he even felt that he would have given a great deal to any one who could have told him what he must decide to do. Yes, but how could he guess what? Though, indeed, he had no time to guess. In any case, that he might lose no time he took a cab and dashed home.

"Well? What are you feeling now?" he wondered; "what are you graciously pleased to be thinking of, Yakov Petrovitch? What are you doing? What are you doing now, you rogue, you rascal? You've brought yourself to this plight, and now you are weeping and whimpering!"

So Mr. Golyadkin taunted himself as he jolted along in the vehicle. To taunt himself and so to irritate his wounds was, at this time, a great satisfaction to Mr. Golyadkin, almost a voluptuous enjoyment.

"Well," he thought, "if some magician were to turn up now, or if it could come to pass in some official way and I were told: 'Give a finger of your right hand, Golyadkin—and it's a bargain with you; there shall not be the other Golyadkin, and you will be happy, only you won't have your finger'—yes, I would sacrifice my finger, I would certainly sacrifice it, I would sacrifice it without winking. . . . The devil take it all!" the despairing titular councillor cried at last. "Why, what is it all for? Well, it all had to be; yes, it absolutely had to; yes, just this had to be, as though nothing else were possible! And it was all right at first. Every one was pleased and happy. But there, it had to be! There's nothing to be gained by talking, though; you must act."

And so, almost resolved upon some action, Mr. Golyadkin reached home, and without a moment's delay snatched up his pipe and, sucking at it with all his might and puffing out clouds of smoke to right and to left, he began pacing up and down the room in a state of violent excitement. Meanwhile, Petrushka began laying the table. At last Mr. Golyadkin made up his mind completely, flung aside his pipe, put on his overcoat, said he would not dine at home and ran out of the flat. Petrushka, panting, overtook him on the stairs, bringing the hat he had forgotten. Mr. Golyadkin took his hat, wanted to say something incidentally to justify himself in Petrushka's eyes that the latter might not think anything particular, such as, "What a queer circumstance! here he forgot his hat—and so on," but as Petrushka walked away at once and would not even look at him, Mr. Golyadkin put on his hat without further explanation, ran downstairs, and repeating to himself that perhaps everything might be for the best, and that affairs would somehow be arranged, though he was conscious among other things of a cold chill right down to his heels, he went out into the street, took a cab and hastened to Andrey Filippovitch's.

"Would it not be better to-morrow, though?" thought Mr. Golyadkin, as he took hold of the bell-rope of Andrey Filippovitch's flat. "And, besides, what can I say in particular? There is nothing particular in it. It's such a wretched affair, yes, it really is wretched, paltry, yes, that is, almost a paltry affair . . . yes, that's what it all is, the incident. . . ." Suddenly Mr. Golyadkin pulled at the bell; the bell rang; footsteps were heard within. . . . Mr. Golyadkin cursed himself on the spot for his hastiness and audacity. His recent unpleasant experiences, which he had almost forgotten over his work, and his encounter with Andrey Filippovitch immediately came back into his mind. But by now it was too late to run away: the door opened. Luckily for Mr. Golyadkin he was informed that Andrey Filippovitch had not returned from the office and had not dined at home.

"I know where he dines: he dines near the Ismailovsky Bridge," thought our hero; and he was immensely relieved. To the footman's inquiry what message he would leave, he said: "It's all right, my good man, I'll look in later," and he even ran downstairs with a certain cheerful briskness. Going out into the street, he decided to dismiss the cab and paid the driver. When the man asked for something extra, saying he had been waiting in the street and had not spared his horse for his honour, he gave him five kopecks extra, and even willingly; and then walked on.

"It really is such a thing," thought Mr. Golyadkin, "that it cannot be left like that; though, if one looks at it that way, looks at it sensibly, why am I hurrying about here, in reality? Well, yes, though, I will go on discussing why I should take a lot of trouble; why I should rush about, exert myself, worry myself and wear myself out. To begin with, the thing's done and there's no recalling it . . . of course, there's no recalling it! Let us put it like this: a man turns up with a satisfactory reference, said to be a capable clerk, of good conduct, only he is a poor man and has suffered many reverses—all sorts of ups and downs— well, poverty is not a crime: so I must stand aside. Why, what nonsense it is! Well, he came; he is so made, the man is so made by nature itself, that he is as like another man as though they were two drops of water, as though he were a perfect copy of another man; how could they refuse to take him into the department on that account? If it is fate, if it is only fate, if it is only blind chance that is to blame—is he to be treated like a rag, is he to be refused a job in the office? . . . Why, what would become of justice after that? He is a poor man, hopeless, downcast; it makes one's heart ache: compassion bids one care for him! Yes! There's no denying, there would be a fine set of head officials, if they took the same view as a reprobate like me! What an addlepate I am! I have foolishness enough for a dozen! Yes, yes! They did right, and many thanks to them for being good to a poor, luckless fellow. . . . Why, let us imagine for a moment that we are twins, that we had been born twin brothers, and nothing else—there it is! Well, what of it? Why, nothing! All the clerks can get used to it. . . . And an outsider, coming into our office, would certainly find nothing unseemly or offensive in the circumstance. In fact, there is really something touching in it; to think that the divine Providence created two men exactly alike, and the heads of the department, seeing the divine handiwork, provided for two twins. It would, of course," Mr. Golyadkin went

on, drawing a breath and dropping his voice, "it would, of course . . .
it would, of course, have been better if there had been . . . if there had
been nothing of this touching kindness, and if there had been no twins
either. . . . The devil take it all! And what need was there for it? And
what was the particular necessity that admitted of no delay! My goodness! The devil has made a mess of it! Besides, he has such a character,
too, he's of such a playful, horrid disposition—he's such a scoundrel,
he's such a nimble fellow! He's such a toady! Such a lickspittle! He's
such a Golyadkin! I daresay he will misconduct himself; yes, he'll disgrace my name, the blackguard! And now I have to look after him and
wait upon him! What an infliction! But, after all, what of it? It doesn't
matter. Granted, he's a scoundrel, well, let him be a scoundrel, but to
make up for it, the other one's honest; so he will be a scoundrel and
I'll be honest, and they'll say that this Golyadkin's a rascal, don't take
any notice of him, and don't mix him up with the other; but the other
one's honest, virtuous, mild, free from malice, always to be relied upon
in the service, and worthy of promotion; that's how it is, very good
. . . but what if . . . what if they get us mixed up! . . . He is equal to
anything! Ah, Lord, have mercy upon us! . . . He will counterfeit a
man, he will counterfeit him, the rascal—he will change one man for
another as though he were a rag, and not reflect that a man is not a
rag. Ach, mercy on us! Ough, what a calamity!" . . .

Reflecting and lamenting in this way, Mr. Golyadkin ran on, regardless of where he was going. He came to his senses in Nevsky
Prospect, only owing to the chance that he ran so neatly full tilt into
a passer-by that he saw stars in his eyes. Mr. Golyadkin muttered his
excuses without raising his head, and it was only after the passer-by,
muttering something far from flattering, had walked a considerable
distance away, that he raised his nose and looked about to see where
he was and how he had got there. Noticing when he did so that he was
close to the restaurant in which he had sat for a while before the dinner-
party at Olsufy Ivanovitch's, our hero was suddenly conscious of a
pinching and nipping sensation in his stomach; he remembered that
he had not dined; he had no prospect of a dinner-party anywhere. And
so, without losing precious time, he ran upstairs into the restaurant to
have a snack of something as quickly as possible, and to avoid delay
by making all the haste he could. And though everything in the restaurant was rather dear, that little circumstance did not on this occasion
make Mr. Golyadkin pause, and, indeed, he had no time to pause over
such a trifle. In the brightly lighted room the customers were standing
in rather a crowd round the counter, upon which lay heaps of all sorts

of such edibles as are eaten by well-bred persons at lunch. The waiter scarcely had time to fill glasses, to serve, to take money and give change. Mr. Golyadkin waited for his turn and modestly stretched out his hand for a savoury patty. Retreating into a corner, turning his back on the company and eating with appetite, he went back to the attendant, put down his plate and, knowing the price, took out a ten-kopeck piece and laid the coin on the counter, catching the waiter's eye as though to say, "Look, here's the money, one pie," and so on.

"One rouble ten kopecks is your bill," the waiter filtered through his teeth.

Mr. Golyadkin was a good deal surprised.

"You are speaking to me? . . . I . . . I took one pie, I believe."

"You've had eleven," the man retorted confidently.

"You . . . so it seems to me . . . I believe, you're mistaken. . . . I really took only one pie, I think."

"I counted them; you took eleven. Since you've had them you must pay for them; we don't give anything away for nothing."

Mr. Golyadkin was petrified. "What sorcery is this, what is happening to me?" he wondered. Meanwhile, the man waited for Mr. Golyadkin to make up his mind; people crowded round Mr. Golyadkin; he was already feeling in his pocket for a silver rouble, to pay the full amount at once, to avoid further trouble. "Well, if it was eleven, it was eleven," he thought, turning as red as a lobster. "Why, what does it matter if eleven pies have been eaten? Why, a man's hungry, so he eats eleven pies; well, let him eat, and may it do him good; and there's nothing to wonder at in that, and there's nothing to laugh at. . . ."

At that moment something seemed to stab Mr. Golyadkin. He raised his eyes and—at once he guessed the riddle. He knew what the sorcery was. All his difficulties were solved. . . .

In the doorway of the next room, almost directly behind the waiter and facing Mr. Golyadkin, in the doorway which, till that moment, our hero had taken for a looking-glass, a man was standing—he was standing, Mr. Golyadkin was standing—not the original Mr. Golyadkin, the hero of our story, but the other Mr. Golyadkin, the new Mr. Golyadkin. The second Mr. Golyadkin was apparently in excellent spirits. He smiled to Mr. Golyadkin the first, nodded to him, winked, shuffled his feet a little, and looked as though in another minute he would vanish, would disappear into the next room, and then go out, maybe, by a back way out; and there it would be, and all pursuit would be in vain. In his hand he had the last morsel of the tenth pie, and before Mr. Golyadkin's very eyes he popped it into his mouth and smacked his lips.

"He has impersonated me, the scoundrel!" thought Mr. Golyadkin, flushing hot with shame. "He is not ashamed of the publicity of it! Do they see him? I fancy no one notices him. . . ."

Mr. Golyadkin threw down his rouble as though it burnt his fingers, and without noticing the waiter's insolently significant grin, a smile of triumph and serene power, he extricated himself from the crowd, and rushed away without looking round. "We must be thankful that at least he has not completely compromised any one!" thought Mr. Golyadkin senior. "We must be thankful to him, the brigand, and to fate, that everything was satisfactorily settled. The waiter was rude, that was all. But, after all, he was in the right. One rouble and ten kopecks were owing: so he was in the right. 'We don't give things away for nothing,' he said! Though he might have been more polite, the rascal. . . ."

All this Mr. Golyadkin said to himself as he went downstairs to the entrance, but on the last step he stopped suddenly, as though he had been shot, and suddenly flushed till the tears came into his eyes at the insult to his dignity. After standing stock-still for half a minute, he stamped his foot resolutely, at one bound leapt from the step into the street and, without looking round, rushed breathless and unconscious of fatigue back home to his flat in Shestilavotchny Street. When he got home, without changing his coat, though it was his habit to change into an old coat at home, without even stopping to take his pipe, he sat down on the sofa, drew the inkstand towards him, took up a pen, got a sheet of notepaper, and with a hand that trembled from inward excitement, began scribbling the following epistle.

"Dear Sir Yakov Petrovitch!

"I should not take up my pen if my circumstances, and your own action, sir, had not compelled me to that step. Believe me that nothing but necessity would have induced me to enter upon such a discussion with you, and therefore, first of all, I beg you, sir, to look upon this step of mine not as a premeditated design to insult you, but as the inevitable consequence of the circumstance that is a bond between us now."

("I think that's all right, proper, courteous, though not lacking in force and firmness. . . . I don't think there is anything for him to take offence at. Besides, I'm fully within my rights," thought Mr. Golyadkin, reading over what he had written.)

"Your strange and sudden appearance, sir, on a stormy night, after the coarse and unseemly behaviour of my enemies to me, for whom I feel too much contempt even to mention their names, was the starting-point of all the misunderstanding existing between us at the present time. Your obstinate desire to persist in your course of action, sir, and forcibly to enter the circle of my existence and all my relations in practical life, transgresses every limit imposed by the merest politeness and every rule of civilized society. I imagine there is no need, sir, for me to refer to the seizure by you of my papers, and particularly to your taking away my good name, in order to gain the favour of my superiors—favour you have not deserved. There is no need to refer here either to your intentional and insulting refusal of the necessary explanation in regard to us. Finally, to omit nothing, I will not allude here to your last strange, one may even say, your incomprehensible behaviour to me in the coffee-house. I am far from lamenting over the needless—for me—loss of a rouble; but I cannot help expressing my indignation at the recollection of your public outrage upon me, to the detriment of my honour, and what is more, in the presence of several persons of good breeding, though not belonging to my circle of acquaintance."

("Am I not going too far?" thought Mr. Golyadkin. "Isn't it too much; won't it be too insulting—that taunt about good breeding, for instance? . . . But there, it doesn't matter! I must show him the resoluteness of my character. I might, however, to soften him, flatter him, and butter him up at the end. But there, we shall see.")

"But I should not weary you with my letter, sir, if I were not firmly convinced that the nobility of your sentiments and your open, candid character would suggest to you yourself a means for retrieving all lapses and returning everything to its original position.

"With full confidence I venture to rest assured that you will not take my letter in a sense derogatory to yourself, and at the same time that you will not refuse to explain yourself expressly on this occasion by letter, sending the same by my man.

"In expectation of your reply, I have the honour, dear sir, to remain,
"Your humble servant,
"Y. GOLYADKIN."

"Well, that is quite all right. The thing's done, it has come to letter-writing. But who is to blame for that? He is to blame himself: by his own action he reduces a man to the necessity of resorting to epistolary composition. And I am within my rights. . . ."

Reading over his letter for the last time, Mr. Golyadkin folded it up, sealed it and called Petrushka. Petrushka came in looking, as usual, sleepy and cross about something.

"You will take this letter, my boy . . . do you understand?"

Petrushka did not speak.

"You will take it to the department; there you must find the secretary on duty, Vahramyev. He is the one on duty to-day. Do you understand that?"

"I understand."

" 'I understand'! He can't even say, 'I understand, sir!' You must ask for the secretary, Vahramyev, and tell him that your master desired you to send his regards, and humbly requests him to refer to the address book of our office and find out where the titular councillor, Golyadkin, is living?"

Petrushka remained mute, and, as Mr. Golyadkin fancied, smiled.

"Well, so you see, Pyotr, you have to ask him for the address, and find out where the new clerk, Golyadkin, lives."

"Yes."

"You must ask for the address and then take this letter there. Do you understand?"

"I understand."

"If there . . . where you have to take the letter, that gentleman to whom you have to give the letter, that Golyadkin . . . What are you laughing at, you blockhead?"

"What is there to laugh at? What is it to me! I wasn't doing anything, sir. It's not for the likes of us to laugh. . . ."

"Oh, well . . . if that gentleman should ask, 'How is your master, how he is?'; if he . . . well, if he should ask you anything—you hold your tongue, and answer, 'My master is all right, and begs you for an answer to his letter.' Do you understand?"

"Yes, sir."

"Well, then, say, 'My master is all right and quite well,' say, 'and is just getting ready to pay a call: and he asks you,' say, 'for an answer in writing.' Do you understand?"

"Yes."

"Well, go along, then."

"Why, what a bother I have with this blockhead too! He's laughing, and there's nothing to be done. What's he laughing at? I've lived to see trouble. Here I've lived like this to see trouble. Though perhaps it may all turn out for the best. . . . That rascal will be loitering about for the next two hours now, I expect; he'll go off somewhere else. . . .

There's no sending him anywhere. What a misery it is! . . . What misery has come upon me!"

Feeling his troubles to the full, our hero made up his mind to remain passive for two hours till Petrushka returned. For an hour of the time he walked about the room, smoked, then put aside his pipe and sat down to a book, then he lay down on the sofa, then took up his pipe again, then again began running about the room. He tried to think things over but was absolutely unable to think about anything. At last the agony of remaining passive reached the climax and Mr. Golyadkin made up his mind to take a step. "Petrushka will come in another hour," he thought. "I can give the key to the porter, and I myself can, so to speak . . . I can investigate the matter; I shall investigate the matter in my own way."

Without loss of time, in haste to investigate the matter, Mr. Golyadkin took his hat, went out of the room, locked up his flat, went in to the porter, gave him the key, together with ten kopecks—Mr. Golyadkin had become extraordinarily free-handed of late—and rushed off. Mr. Golyadkin went first on foot to the Ismailovsky Bridge. It took him half an hour to get there. When he reached the goal of his journey he went straight into the yard of the house so familiar to him, and glanced up at the windows of the civil councillor Berendyev's flat. Except for three windows hung with red curtains all the rest was dark.

"Olsufy Ivanovitch has no visitors to-day," thought Mr. Golyadkin; "they must all be staying at home to-day."

After standing for some time in the yard, our hero tried to decide on some course of action. But he was apparently not destined to reach a decision. Mr. Golyadkin changed his mind, and with a wave of his hand went back into the street.

"No, there's no need for me to go to-day. What could I do here? . . . No, I'd better, so to speak . . . I'll investigate the matter personally."

Coming to this conclusion, Mr. Golyadkin rushed off to his office. He had a long way to go. It was horribly muddy, besides, and the wet snow lay about in thick drifts. But it seemed as though difficulty did not exist for our hero at the moment. He was drenched through, it is true, and he was a good deal spattered with mud.

"But that's no matter, so long as the object is obtained."

And Mr. Golyadkin certainly was nearing his goal. The dark mass of the huge government building stood up black before his eyes.

"Stay," he thought; "where am I going, and what am I going to do here? Suppose I do find out where he lives? Meanwhile, Petrushka will certainly have come back and brought me the answer. I am only wasting my precious time, I am simply wasting my time. Though shouldn't I, perhaps, go in and see Vahramyev? But, no, I'll go later. . . . Ech! There was no need to have gone out at all. But, there, it's my temperament! I've a knack of always seizing a chance of rushing ahead of things, whether there is a need to or not. . . . H'm! . . . what time is it? It must be nine by now. Petrushka might come and not find me at home. It was pure folly on my part to go out. . . . Ech, it is really a nuisance!"

Sincerely acknowledging that he had been guilty of an act of folly, our hero ran back to Shestilavotchny Street. He arrived there, weary and exhausted. From the porter he learned that Petrushka had not dreamed of turning up yet.

"To be sure! I foresaw it would be so," thought our hero; "and meanwhile it's nine o'clock. Ech, he's such a good-for-nothing chap! He's always drinking somewhere! Mercy on us! What a day has fallen to my miserable lot!"

Reflecting in this way, Mr. Golyadkin unlocked his flat, got a light, took off his outdoor things, lighted his pipe and, tired, worn out, exhausted and hungry, lay down on the sofa and waited for Petrushka. The candle burnt dimly; the light flickered on the wall. . . . Mr. Golyadkin gazed and gazed, and thought and thought, and fell asleep at last, worn out.

It was late when he woke up. The candle had almost burnt down, was smoking and on the point of going out. Mr. Golyadkin jumped up, shook himself, and remembered it all, absolutely all. Behind the screen he heard Petrushka snoring lustily. Mr. Golyadkin rushed to the window—not a light anywhere. He opened the movable pane— all was still; the city was asleep as though it were dead: so it must have been two or three o'clock; so it proved to be, indeed; the clock behind the partition made an effort and struck two. Mr. Golyadkin rushed behind the partition.

He succeeded, somehow, though only after great exertions, in rousing Petrushka, and making him sit up in his bed. At that moment the candle went out completely. About ten minutes passed before Mr. Golyadkin succeeded in finding another candle and lighting it. In the interval Petrushka had fallen asleep again.

"You scoundrel, you worthless fellow!" said Mr. Golyadkin, shaking him up again. "Will you get up, will you wake?" After half an hour of effort Mr. Golyadkin succeeded, however, in rousing his servant thoroughly, and dragging him out from behind the partition.

Only then, our hero remarked the fact that Petrushka was what is called dead-drunk and could hardly stand on his legs.

"You good-for-nothing fellow!" cried Mr. Golyadkin; "you ruffian! You'll be the death of me! Good heavens! whatever has he done with the letter? Ach, my God! where is it? . . . And why did I write it? As though there were any need for me to have written it! I went scribbling away out of pride, like a noodle! I've got myself into this fix out of pride! That is what dignity does for you, you rascal, that is dignity! . . . Come, what have you done with the letter, you ruffian? To whom did you give it?"

"I didn't give any one any letter; and I never had any letter . . . so there!"

Mr. Golyadkin wrung his hands in despair.

"Listen, Pyotr . . . listen to me, listen to me. . . ."

"I am listening. . . ."

"Where have you been?—Answer. . . ."

"Where have I been? . . . I've been to see good people! What is it to me!"

"Oh, Lord, have mercy on us! Where did you go, to begin with? Did you go to the department? . . . Listen, Pyotr, perhaps you're drunk?"

"Me drunk! If I should be struck on the spot this minute, not a drop, not a drop—so there. . . ."

"No, no, it's no matter you're being drunk. . . . I only asked; it's all right your being drunk; I don't mind, Petrushka, I don't mind. . . . Perhaps it's only that you have forgotten, but you'll remember it all. Come, try to remember—have you been to that clerk's, to Vahramyev's; have you been to him or not?"

"I have not been, and there's no such clerk. Not if I were this minute . . ."

"No, no, Pyotr! No, Petrushka, you know I don't mind. Why, you see I don't mind. . . . Come, what happened? To be sure, it's cold and damp in the street, and so a man has a drop, and it's no matter. I am not angry. I've been drinking myself to-day, my boy. . . . Come, think and try and remember, did you go to Vahramyev?"

"Well, then, now, this is how it was, it's the truth—I did go, if this very minute . . ."

"Come, that is right, Petrushka, that is quite right that you've been. You see I'm not angry. . . . Come, come," our hero went on, coaxing his servant more and more, patting him on the shoulder and smiling to him, "come, you had a little nip, you scoundrel. . . . You had twopenn'orth of something, I suppose? You're a sly rogue! Well, that's no matter; come, you see that I'm not angry. . . . I'm not angry, my boy, I'm not angry. . . ."

"No, I'm not a sly rogue, say what you like. . . . I only went to see some good friends. I'm not a rogue, and I never have been a rogue. . . ."

"Oh, no, no, Petrushka; listen, Petrushka, you know I'm not scolding when I called you a rogue. I said that in fun, I said it in a good sense. You see, Petrushka, it is sometimes a compliment to a man when you call him a rogue, a cunning fellow, that he's a sharp chap and would not let any one take him in. Some men like it. . . . Come, come, it doesn't matter! Come, tell me, Petrushka, without keeping anything back, openly, as to a friend . . . did you go to Vahramyev's, and did he give you the address?"

"He did give me the address, he did give me the address too. He's a nice gentleman! 'Your master,' says he, 'is a nice man,' says he, 'very nice man,' says he, 'I send my regards,' says he, 'to your master, thank him and say that I like him,' says he—'how I do respect your master,' says he. 'Because,' says he, 'your master, Petrushka,' says he, 'is a good man, and you,' says he, 'Petrushka, are a good man too. . . .'"

"Ah, mercy on us! But the address, the address! You Judas!" The last word Mr. Golyadkin uttered almost in a whisper.

"And the address . . . he did give the address too."

"He did? Well, where does Golyadkin, the clerk Golyadkin, the titular councillor, live?"

"'Why,' says he, 'Golyadkin will be now at Shestilavotchny Street. When you get into Shestilavotchny Street take the stairs on the right and it's the fourth floor. And there,' says he, 'you'll find Golyadkin. . . .'"

"You scoundrel!" our hero cried, out of patience at last. "You're a ruffian! Why, that's my address; why, you are talking about me. But there's another Golyadkin; I'm talking of the other one, you scoundrel!"

"Well, that's as you please! What is it to me? Have it your own way. . . ."

"And the letter, the letter?" . . .

"What letter? There wasn't any letter, and I didn't see any letter."

"But what have you done with it, you rascal?"

"I delivered the letter, I delivered it. He sent his regards. 'Thank you,' says he, 'your master's a nice man,' says he. 'Give my regards,' says he, 'to your master. . . .'"

"But who said that? Was it Golyadkin said it?"

Petrushka said nothing for a moment, and then, with a broad grin, he stared straight into his master's face. . . .

"Listen, you scoundrel!" began Mr. Golyadkin, breathless, beside himself with fury; "listen, you rascal, what have you done to me? Tell me what you've done to me! You've destroyed me, you villain, you've cut the head off my shoulders, you Judas!"

"Well, have it your own way! I don't care," said Petrushka in a resolute voice, retreating behind the screen.

"Come here, come here, you ruffian. . . ."

"I'm not coming to you now, I'm not coming at all. What do I care, I'm going to good folks. . . . Good folks live honestly, good folks live without falsity, and they never have doubles. . . ."

Mr. Golyadkin's hands and feet went icy cold, his breath failed him. . . .

"Yes," Petrushka went on, "they never have doubles. God doesn't afflict honest folk. . . ."

"You worthless fellow, you are drunk! Go to sleep now, you ruffian! And to-morrow you'll catch it," Mr. Golyadkin added in a voice hardly audible. As for Petrushka, he muttered something more; then he could be heard getting into bed, making the bed creak. After a prolonged yawn, he stretched; and at last began snoring, and slept the sleep of the just, as they say. Mr. Golyadkin was more dead than alive. Petrushka's behaviour, his very strange hints, which were yet so remote that it was useless to be angry at them, especially as they were uttered by a drunken man, and, in short, the sinister turn taken by the affair altogether, all this shook Mr. Golyadkin to the depths of his being.

"And what possessed me to go for him in the middle of the night?" said our hero, trembling all over from a sickly sensation. "What the devil made me have anything to do with a drunken man! What could I expect from a drunken man? Whatever he says is a lie. But what was he hinting at, the ruffian? Lord, have mercy on us! And why did I write all that letter? I'm my own enemy, I'm my own murderer! As if I couldn't hold my tongue? I had to go scribbling nonsense! And what now! You are going to ruin, you are like an old rag, and yet you worry about your pride; you say, 'my honour is wounded,' you must stick up for your honour! My own murderer, that is what I am!"

Thus spoke Mr. Golyadkin and hardly dared to stir for terror. At last his eyes fastened upon an object which excited his interest to the utmost. In terror lest the object that caught his attention should prove to be an illusion, a deception of his fancy, he stretched out his hand to it with hope, with dread, with indescribable curiosity. . . . No, it was not a deception! Not a delusion! It was a letter, really a letter, undoubtedly a letter, and addressed to him. Mr. Golyadkin took the letter from the table. His heart beat terribly.

"No doubt that scoundrel brought it," he thought, "put it there, and then forgot it; no doubt that is how it happened: no doubt that is just how it happened. . . ."

The letter was from Vahramyev, a young fellow-clerk who had once been his friend. "I had a presentiment of this though," thought our hero, "and I had a presentiment of all that there will be in the letter. . . ."

The letter was as follows—

"Dear Sir Yakov Petrovitch!

"Your servant is drunk, and there is no getting any sense out of him. For that reason I prefer to reply by letter. I hasten to inform you that the commission you've entrusted to me—that is, to deliver a letter to a certain person you know, I agree to carry out carefully and exactly. That person, who is very well known to you and who has taken the place of a friend to me, whose name I will refrain from mentioning (because I do not wish unnecessarily to blacken the reputation of a perfectly innocent man), lodges with us at Karolina Ivanovna's, in the room in which, when you were among us, the infantry officer from Tambov used to be. That person, however, is always to be found in the company of honest and true-hearted persons, which is more than one can say for some people. I intend from this day to break off all connection with you; it's impossible for us to remain on friendly terms and to keep up the appearance of comradeship congruous with them. And, therefore, I beg you, my dear sir, immediately on the receipt of this candid letter from me, to send me the two roubles you owe me for the razor of foreign make which I sold you seven months ago, if you will kindly remember, when you were still living with us in the lodgings of Karolina Ivanovna, a lady whom I respect from the bottom of my heart. I am acting in this way because you, from the accounts I hear from sensible persons, have lost your dignity and reputation and have become a source of danger to the morals of the innocent and uncontaminated. For some persons are not straightforward, their words are full of falsity and their show of good intentions is suspicious. People can always be found capable of insulting Karolina

Ivanovna, who is always irreproachable in her conduct, and an honest woman, and, what's more, a maiden lady, though no longer young— though, on the other hand, of a good foreign family—and this fact I've been asked to mention in this letter by several persons, and I speak also for myself. In any case you will learn all in due time, if you haven't learnt it yet, though you've made yourself notorious from one end of the town to the other, according to the accounts I hear from sensible people, and consequently might well have received intelligence relating to you, my dear sir, in many places. In conclusion, I beg to inform you, my dear sir, that a certain person you know, whose name I will not mention here, for certain honourable reasons, is highly respected by right-thinking people, and is, moreover, of lively and agreeable disposition, and is equally successful in the service and in the society of persons of common sense, is true in word and in friendship, and does not insult behind their back those with whom he is on friendly terms to their face.

"In any case, I remain

"Your obedient servant,

"N. Vahramyev."

"P.S. You had better dismiss your man: he is a drunkard and probably gives you a great deal of trouble; you had better engage Yevstafy, who used to be in service here, and is now out of a place. Your present servant is not only a drunkard, but, what's more, he's a thief, for only last week he sold a pound of lump sugar to Karolina Ivanovna at less than cost price, which, in my opinion, he could not have done otherwise than by robbing you in a very sly way, little by little, at different times. I write this to you for your own good, although some people can do nothing but insult and deceive everybody, especially persons of honesty and good nature; what is more, they slander them behind their back and misrepresent them, simply from envy, and because they can't call themselves the same.

"V."

After reading Vahramyev's letter our hero remained for a long time sitting motionless on his sofa. A new light seemed breaking through the obscure and baffling fog which had surrounded him for the last two days. Our hero seemed to reach a partial understanding. . . . He tried to get up from the sofa to take a turn about the room, to rouse himself, to collect his scattered ideas, to fix them upon a certain subject and then to set himself to rights a little, to think over his position thoroughly. But as soon as he tried to stand up he fell back again at once, weak and helpless. "Yes, of course, I had a presentiment of all that; how he writes though, and what is the real meaning of his words? Supposing I do understand the meaning; but what is it leading to? He should have said straight out: this and that is wanted, and I would have done it. Things have taken such a turn, things have come to such an unpleasant pass! Oh, if only to-morrow would make haste and come, and I could make haste and get to work! I know now what to do. I shall say this and that, I shall agree with his arguments, I won't sell my honour, but . . . maybe; but he, that person we know of, that disagreeable person, how does he come to be mixed up in it? And why has he turned up here? Oh, if to-morrow would make haste and come! They'll slander me before then, they are intriguing, they are working to spite me! The great thing is not to lose time, and now, for instance, to write a letter, and to say this and that and that I agree to this and that. And as soon as it is daylight to-morrow send it off, before he can do anything . . . and so checkmate them, get in before them, the darlings. . . . They will ruin me by their slanders, and that's the fact of the matter!"

Mr. Golyadkin drew the paper to him, took up a pen and wrote the following missive in answer to the secretary's letter—

"Dear Sir Nestor Ignatyevitch!

"With amazement mingled with heartfelt distress I have perused your insulting letter to me, for I see clearly that you are referring to me when you speak of certain discreditable persons and false friends. I see with genuine sorrow how rapidly the calumny has spread and how deeply it has taken root, to the detriment of my prosperity, my honour and my good name. And this is the more distressing and mortifying that even honest people of a genuinely noble way of thinking and, what is even more important, of straightforward and open dispositions, abandon the interests of honourable men and with all the qualities of their hearts attach themselves to the pernicious corruption, which in our difficult and immoral age has unhappily increased and multiplied so greatly and so disloyally. In conclusion, I will say that the debt of two roubles of which you remind me I regard as a sacred duty to return to you in its entirety.

"As for your hints concerning a certain person of the female sex, concerning the intentions, calculations and various designs of that person, I can only tell you, sir, that I have but a very dim and obscure understanding of those insinuations. Permit me, sir, to preserve my honourable way of thinking and my good name undefiled, in any case. I am ready to stoop to an explanation in person, preferring a personal interview to a written explanation as more secure, and I am, moreover, ready to enter into conciliatory proposals on mutual terms, of course. To that end I beg you, my dear sir, to convey to that person my readiness for a personal arrangement and, what is more, to beg her to fix the time and place of the interview. It grieved me, sir, to read your hints of my having insulted you, having been treacherous to our original friendship and having spoken ill of you. I ascribe this misunderstanding to the abominable calumny, envy and ill-will of those whom I may justly stigmatize as my bitterest foes. But I suppose they do not know that innocence is strong through its very innocence, that the shamelessness, the insolence and the revolting familiarity of some persons, sooner or later gains the stigma of universal contempt; and that such persons come to ruin through nothing but their own worthlessness and the corruption of their own hearts. In conclusion, I beg you, sir, to convey to those persons that their strange pretensions and their dishonourable and fantastic desire to squeeze others out of the position which those others occupy, by their very existence in this world, and to take their place, are deserving of contempt, amazement, compassion and, what is more, the madhouse; moreover, such efforts are severely prohibited by law, which in my opinion is perfectly just, for every one ought to be satisfied with his own position. Every one has his fixed position, and if this is a joke it is a joke in very bad taste. I will say more: it is utterly immoral, for, I make bold to assure you, sir, my own views which I have expounded above, in regard to keeping *one's own place,* are purely moral.

"In any case I have the honour to remain

"Your humble servant,

"Y. GOLYADKIN."

Chapter 10

ALTOGETHER, we may say, the adventures of the previous day had thoroughly unnerved Mr. Golyadkin. Our hero passed a very bad night; that is, he did not get thoroughly off to sleep for five minutes: as though some practical joker had scattered bristles in his bed. He spent the whole night in a sort of half-sleeping state, tossing from side to side, from right to left, moaning and groaning, dozing off for a moment, waking up again a minute later, and all was accompanied by a strange misery, vague memories, hideous visions—in fact, everything disagreeable that can be imagined. . . .

At one moment the figure of Andrey Filippovitch appeared before him in a strange, mysterious half-light. It was a frigid, wrathful figure, with a cold, harsh eye and with stiffly polite words of blame on its lips . . . and as soon as Mr. Golyadkin began going up to Andrey Filippovitch to defend himself in some way and to prove to him that he was not at all such as his enemies represented him, that he was like this and like that, that he even possessed innate virtues of his own, superior to the average—at once a person only too well known for his discreditable behaviour appeared on the scene, and by some most revolting means instantly frustrated poor Mr. Golyadkin's efforts, on the spot, almost before the latter's eyes, blackened his reputation, trampled his dignity in the mud, and then immediately took possession of his place in the service and in society.

At another time Mr. Golyadkin's head felt sore from some sort of slight blow of late conferred and humbly accepted, received either in the course of daily life or somehow in the performance of his duty, against which blow it was difficult to protest. . . . And while Mr. Golyadkin was racking his brains over the question why it was so difficult to protest even against such a blow, this idea of a blow gradually melted away into a different form—into the form of some familiar, trifling, or rather important piece of nastiness which he had seen, heard, or even himself committed—and frequently committed, indeed, and not on nasty grounds, not from any nasty impulse, even, but just because it happened—sometimes, for instance, out of delicacy, another time owing to his absolute defencelessness—in fact, because . . . because, in fact, Mr. Golyadkin knew perfectly well *because of what!* At this point Mr. Golyadkin blushed in his sleep, and, smothering his blushes, muttered to himself that in this case he ought to be able to show the strength of his character, he ought to be able to show in this case the remarkable strength of his character, and then wound up by asking himself, "What, after all, is strength of character? Why understand it now? . . ."

But what irritated and enraged Mr. Golyadkin most of all was that invariably, at such a moment, a person well known for his undignified burlesque behaviour turned up uninvited, and, regardless of the fact that the matter was apparently settled, he, too, would begin muttering, with an unseemly little smile, "What's the use of strength of character! How could you and I, Yakov Petrovitch, have strength of character? . . ."

Then Mr. Golyadkin would dream that he was in the company of a number of persons distinguished for their wit and good breeding; that he, Mr. Golyadkin, too, was conspicuous for his wit and politeness, that everybody liked him, even some of his enemies who were present began to like him, which was very agreeable to Mr. Golyadkin; that every one gave him precedence, and that at last Mr. Golyadkin himself, with gratification, overheard the host, drawing one of the guests aside, speak in his, Mr. Golyadkin's, praise . . . and all of a sudden, apropos of nothing, there appeared again a person, notorious for his treachery and brutal impulses, in the form of Mr. Golyadkin junior, and on the spot, at once, by his very appearance on the scene, Mr. Golyadkin junior destroyed the whole triumph and glory of Mr. Golyadkin senior, eclipsed Mr. Golyadkin senior, trampled him in the mud, and, at last, proved clearly that Golyadkin senior—that is, the genuine one—was not the genuine one at all but the sham, and that he, Golyadkin junior, was the real one; that, in fact, Mr. Golyadkin senior was not at all what he appeared to be, but something very disgraceful, and that consequently he had no right to mix in the society of honourable and well-bred people. And all this was done so quickly that Mr. Golyadkin had not time to open his mouth before all of them were subjugated, body and soul, by the wicked, sham Mr. Golyadkin, and with profound contempt rejected him, the real and innocent Mr. Golyadkin. There was not one person left whose opinion the infamous Mr. Golyadkin would not have changed round. There was not left one person, even the most insignificant of the company, to whom the false and worthless Mr. Golyadkin would not make up in his blandest manner, upon whom he would not fawn in his own way, before whom he would not burn sweet and agreeable incense, so that the flattered person simply sniffed and sneezed till the tears came, in token of the intensest pleasure.

And the worst of it was that all this was done in a flash: the swiftness of movement of the false and worthless Mr. Golyadkin was marvellous! He scarcely had time, for instance, to make up to one person and win his good graces—and before one could wink an eye he was at another. He stealthily fawns on another, drops a smile of benevolence, twirls on his short, round, though rather wooden-looking leg, and already he's at a third, and is cringing upon a third, he's making up to him in a friendly way; before one has time to open one's mouth, before one has time to feel surprised, he's at a fourth, at the same manoeuvres with him—it was horrible: sorcery and nothing else! And every one was pleased with him and everybody liked him, and every one was exalting him, and all were proclaiming in chorus that his politeness and sarcastic wit were infinitely superior to the politeness and sarcastic wit of the real Mr. Golyadkin and putting the real and innocent Mr. Golyadkin to shame thereby and rejecting the veritable Mr. Golyadkin, and shoving and pushing out the loyal Mr. Golyadkin, and showering blows on the man so well known for his love towards his fellow-creatures! . . .

In misery, in terror and in fury, the cruelly treated Mr. Golyadkin ran out into the street and began trying to take a cab in order to drive straight to his Excellency's, or, at any rate, to Andrey Filippovitch's, but—horror! the cabman absolutely refused to take Mr. Golyadkin, saying, "We cannot drive two gentlemen exactly alike, sir; a good man tries to live honestly, your honour, and never has a double." Overcome with shame, the unimpeachable, honest Mr. Golyadkin looked round and did, in fact, assure himself with his own eyes that the cabman and Petrushka, who had joined them, were all quite right, for the depraved Mr. Golyadkin was actually on the spot, beside him, close at hand, and with his characteristic nastiness was again, at this critical moment, certainly preparing to do something very unseemly, and quite out of keeping with that gentlemanliness of character which is usually acquired by good breeding—that gentlemanliness of which the loathsome Mr. Golyadkin the second was always boasting on every opportunity. Beside himself with shame and despair, the utterly ruined though perfectly just Mr. Golyadkin dashed headlong away, wherever fate might lead him; but with every step he took, with every thud of his foot on the granite of the pavement, there leapt up as though out of the earth a Mr. Golyadkin precisely the same, perfectly alike, and of a revolting depravity of heart. And all these precisely similar Golyadkins set to running after one another as soon as they appeared, and stretched in a long chain like a file of geese, hobbling after the real Mr. Golyadkin, so there was nowhere to escape from these duplicates—so that Mr. Golyadkin, who was in every way deserving of compassion, was breathless with terror; so that at last a terrible multitude of duplicates had sprung into being; so that the whole town was obstructed at last by duplicate Golyadkins, and the police officer, seeing such a breach of decorum, was obliged to seize all these duplicates by the collar and to put them into the watch-house, which happened to be beside him. . . . Numb and chill with horror, our hero woke up, and numb and chill with horror felt that his waking state was hardly more cheerful. . . . It was oppressive and harrowing. . . . He was overcome by such anguish that it seemed as though some one were gnawing at his heart.

At last Mr. Golyadkin could endure it no longer. "This shall not be!" he cried, resolutely sitting up in bed, and after this exclamation he felt fully awake.

It seemed as though it were rather late in the day. It was unusually light in the room. The sunshine filtered through the frozen panes and flooded the room with light, which surprised M. Golyadkin not a little and, so far as Mr. Golyadkin could remember, at least, there had scarcely ever been such exceptions in the course of the heavenly luminary before. Our hero had hardly time to wonder at this when he heard the clock buzzing behind the partition as though it was just on the point of striking. "Now," thought Mr. Golyadkin, and he prepared to listen with painful suspense. . . .

But to complete M. Golyadkin's astonishment, the clock whirred and only struck once.

"What does this mean?" cried our hero, finally leaping out of bed. And, unable to believe his ears, he rushed behind the screen just as he was. It actually was one o'clock. Mr. Golyadkin glanced at Petrushka's bed; but the room did not even smell of Petrushka: his bed had long been made and left, his boots were nowhere to be seen either —an unmistakable sign that Petrushka was not in the house. Mr. Golyadkin rushed to the door: the door was locked. "But where is he, where is Petrushka?" he went on in a whisper, conscious of intense excitement and feeling a perceptible tremor run all over him . . . Suddenly a thought floated into his mind . . . Mr. Golyadkin rushed to the table, looked all over it, felt all round—yes, it was true, his letter of the night before to Vahramyev was not there. Petrushka was nowhere behind the screen either, the clock had just struck one, and some new points were evident to him in Vahramyev's letter, points that were obscure at first sight though now they were fully explained. Petrushka had evidently been bribed at last! "Yes, yes, that was so!"

"So this was how the chief plot was hatched!" cried Mr. Golyadkin, slapping himself on the forehead, opening his eyes wider and wider; "so in that filthy German woman's den the whole power of evil lies hidden now! So she was only making a strategic diversion in directing me to the Ismailovsky Bridge—she was putting me off the scent, confusing me (the worthless witch), and in that way laying her mines! Yes, that is so! If one only looks at the thing from that point of view, all of this is bound to be so, and the scoundrel's appearance on the scene is fully explained: it's all part and parcel of the same thing. They've kept him in reserve a long while, they had him in readiness for the evil day. This is how it has all turned out! This is what it has come to. But there, never mind. No time has been lost so far."

At this point Mr. Golyadkin recollected with horror that it was past one in the afternoon. "What if they have succeeded by now? . . ." He uttered a moan. . . . "But, no, they are lying, they've not had time— we shall see. . . ."

He dressed after a fashion, seized paper and a pen, and scribbled the following missive—

"Dear Sir Yakov Petrovitch!

"Either you or I, but both together is out of the question! And so I must inform you that your strange, absurd, and at the same time impossible desire to appear to be my twin and to give yourself out as such serves no other purpose than to bring about your complete disgrace and discomfiture. And so I beg you, for the sake of your own advantage, to step aside and make way for really honourable men of loyal aims. In the opposite case I am ready to determine upon extreme measures. I lay down my pen and await . . . However, I remain ready to oblige or to meet you with pistols.

"Y. GOLYADKIN."

Our hero rubbed his hands energetically when he had finished the letter. Then, pulling on his greatcoat and putting on his hat, he unlocked his flat with a spare key and set off for the department. He reached the office but could not make up his mind to go in—it was by now too late. It was half-past two by Mr. Golyadkin's watch. All at once a circumstance of apparently little importance settled some doubts in Mr. Golyadkin's mind: a flushed and breathless figure suddenly made its appearance from behind the screen of the department building and with a stealthy movement like a rat he darted up the steps and into the entry. It was a copying clerk called Ostafyev, a man Mr. Golyadkin knew very well, who was rather useful and ready to do anything for a trifle. Knowing Ostafyev's weak spot and surmising that after his brief, unavoidable absence he would probably be greedier than ever for tips, our hero made up his mind not to be sparing of them, and immediately darted up the steps, and then into the entry after him, called to him and, with a mysterious air, drew him aside into a convenient corner behind a huge iron stove. And having led him there, our hero began questioning him.

"Well, my dear fellow, how are things going in there . . . you under-stand me?" . . .

"Yes, your honour, I wish you good health, your honour."

"All right, my good man, all right; but I'll reward you, my good fellow. Well, you see, how are things?"

"What is your honour asking?" At this point Ostafyev held his hand as though by accident before his open mouth.

"You see, my dear fellow, this is how it is . . . but don't you imagine . . . Come, is Andrey Filippovitch here?" . . .

"Yes, he is here."

"And are the clerks here?"

"Yes, sir, they are here as usual."

"And his Excellency too?"

"And his Excellency too." Here the man held his hand before his open mouth again, and looked rather curiously and strangely at Mr. Golyadkin, so at least our hero fancied.

"And there's nothing special there, my good man?"

"No, sir, certainly not, sir."

"So there's nothing concerning me, my friend. Is there nothing going on there—that is, nothing more than . . . eh? nothing more, you understand, my friend?"

"No, sir, I've heard nothing so far, sir." Again the man put his hand before his mouth and again looked rather strangely at Mr. Golyadkin. The fact was, Mr. Golyadkin was trying to read Ostafyev's counte-nance, trying to discover whether there was not something hidden in it. And, in fact, he did look as though he were hiding something: Ostafyev seemed to grow colder and more churlish, and did not enter into Mr. Golyadkin's interests with the same sympathy as at the beginning of the conversation. "He is to some extent justified," thought Mr. Golyadkin. "After all, what am I to him? Perhaps he has already been bribed by the other side, and that's why he has just been absent. But, here, I'll try him. . . ." Mr. Golyadkin realized that the moment for kopecks had arrived.

"Here, my dear fellow. . . ."

"I'm feelingly grateful for your honour's kindness."

"I'll give you more than that."

"Yes, your honour."

"I'll give you some more directly, and when the business is over I'll give you as much again. Do you understand?"

The clerk did not speak. He stood at attention and stared fixedly at Mr. Golyadkin.

"Come, tell me now: have you heard nothing about me? . . ."

"I think, so far, I have not . . . so to say . . . nothing so far." Ostafyev, like Mr. Golyadkin, spoke deliberately and preserved a mysterious air, moving his eyebrows a little, looking at the ground, trying to fall into the suitable tone, and, in fact, doing his very utmost to earn what had been promised him, for what he had received already he reckoned as already earned.

"And you know nothing?"

"So far, nothing, sir."

"Listen . . . you know . . . maybe you will know . . ."

"Later on, of course, maybe I shall know."

"It's a poor look-out," thought our hero. "Listen: here's something more, my dear fellow."

"I am truly grateful to your honour."

"Was Vahramyev here yesterday? . . ."

"Yes, sir."

"And . . . somebody else? . . . Was he? . . . Try and remember, brother."

The man ransacked his memory for a moment, and could think of nothing appropriate.

"No, sir, there wasn't anybody else."

"H'm!" a silence followed.

"Listen, brother, here's some more; tell me all, every detail."

"Yes, sir," Ostafyev had by now become as soft as silk; which was just what Mr. Golyadkin needed.

"Explain to me now, my good man, what footing is he on?"

"All right, sir, a good one, sir," answered the man, gazing open-eyed at Mr. Golyadkin.

"How do you mean, all right?"

"Well, it's just like that, sir." Here Ostafyev twitched his eyebrows significantly. But he was utterly nonplussed and didn't know what more to say.

"It's a poor look-out," thought Mr. Golyadkin.

"And hasn't anything more happened . . . in there . . . about Vahramyev?"

"But everything is just as usual."

"Think a little."

"There is, they say . . ."

"Come, what?"

Ostafyev put his hand in front of his mouth.

"Wasn't there a letter . . . from here . . . to me?"

"Mihyeev the attendant went to Vahramyev's lodging, to their German landlady, so I'll go and ask him, if you like."

"Do me the favour, brother, for goodness' sake! . . . I only mean . . . you mustn't imagine anything, brother, I only mean . . . Yes, you question him, brother, find out whether they are not getting up something concerning me. Find out how he is acting. That is what I want; that is what you must find out, my dear fellow, and then I'll reward you, my good man. . . ."

"I will, your honour, and Ivan Semyonovitch sat in your place to-day, sir."

"Ivan Semyonovitch? Oh! really, you don't say so."

"Andrey Filippovitch told him to sit there."

"Re-al-ly! How did that happen? You must find out, brother; for God's sake find out, brother; find it all out—and I'll reward you, my dear fellow; that's what I want to know . . . and don't you imagine anything, brother. . . ."

"Just so, sir, just so; I'll go at once. And aren't you going in to-day, sir?"

"No, my friend; I only looked round, I only looked round, you know. I only came to have a look round, my friend, and I'll reward you afterwards, my friend."

"Yes, sir." The man ran rapidly and eagerly up the stairs and Mr. Golyadkin was left alone.

"It's a poor look-out!" he thought. "Ech, it's a bad business, a bad business! Ech! things are in a bad way with us now! What does it all mean? What did that drunkard's insinuations mean, for instance, and whose trickery was it? Ah! I know now whose it was. And what a thing this is. No doubt they found out and made him sit there. . . . But, after all, did they sit him there? It was Andrey Filippovitch sat him there, he sat Ivan Semyonovitch there himself; why did he make him sit there and with what object? Probably they found out . . . That is Vahramyev's work—that is, not Vahramyev, he is as stupid as an ashen post, Vahramyev is, and they are all at work on his behalf, and they egged that scoundrel on to come here for the same purpose, and the German woman brought up her grievance, the one-eyed hussy. I always suspected that this intrigue was not without an object and that in all this old-womanish gossip there must be something, and I said as much to Krestyan Ivanovitch, telling him they'd sworn to cut a man's throat—in a moral sense, of course—and they pounced upon Karolina Ivanovna. Yes, there are master hands at work in this, one can see! Yes. sir. there are master hands at work here, and not

Vahramyev's. I've said already that Vahramyev is stupid, but . . . I know who it is behind it all, it's that rascal, that impostor! It's only that he relies upon, which is partly proved by his successes in the best society. And it would certainly be desirable to know on what footing he stands now. What is he now among them? Only, why have they taken Ivan Semyonovitch? What the devil do they want with Ivan Semyonovitch? Could not they have found any one else? Though it would come to the same thing whoever it had been, and the only thing I know is that I have suspected Ivan Semyonovitch for a long time past. I noticed long ago what a nasty, horrid old man he was— they say he lends money and takes interest like any Jew. To be sure, the bear's the leading spirit in the whole affair. One can detect the bear in the whole affair. It began in this way. It began at the Ismailovsky Bridge; that's how it began. . . ."

At this point Mr. Golyadkin frowned, as though he had taken a bite out of a lemon, probably remembering something very unpleasant. "But, there, it doesn't matter," he thought. "I keep harping on my own troubles. What will Ostafyev find out? Most likely he is staying on or has been delayed somehow. It is a good thing, in a sense, that I am intriguing like this, and am laying mines on my side too. I've only to give Ostafyev ten kopecks and he's . . . so to speak, on my side. Only the point is, is he really on my side? Perhaps they've got him on their side too . . . and they are carrying on an intrigue by means of him on their side too. He looks a ruffian, the rascal, a regular ruffian; he's hiding something, the rogue. 'No, nothing,' says he, 'and I am deeply grateful to your honour,' says he. You ruffian, you!"

He heard a noise . . . Mr. Golyadkin shrank up and skipped behind the stove. Some one came down stairs and went out into the street. "Who could that be going away now?" our hero thought to himself. A minute later footsteps were audible again. . . . At this point Mr. Golyadkin could not resist poking the very tip of his nose out beyond his corner—he poked it out and instantly withdrew it again, as though some one had pricked it with a pin. This time some one he knew well was coming—that is, the scoundrel, the intriguer and the reprobate— he was approaching with his usual mean, tripping little step, prancing and shuffling with his feet as though he were going to kick some one. "The rascal," said our hero to himself.

Mr. Golyadkin could not, however, help observing that the rascal had under his arm a huge green portfolio belonging to his Excellency. "He's on a special commission again," thought Mr. Golyadkin, flushing crimson and shrinking into himself more than ever from vexation.

As soon as Mr. Golyadkin junior had slipped past Mr. Golyadkin senior without observing him in the least, footsteps were heard for the third time, and this time Mr. Golyadkin guessed that these were Ostafyev's. It was, in fact, the sleek figure of a copying clerk, Pisarenko by name. This surprised Mr. Golyadkin. Why had he mixed up other people in their secret? our hero wondered. What barbarians! nothing is sacred to them! "Well, my friend?" he brought out, addressing Pisarenko: "who sent you, my friend? . . ."

"I've come about your business. There's no news so far from any one. But should there be any we'll let you know."

"And Ostafyev?"

"It was quite impossible for him to come, your honour. His Excellency has walked through the room twice, and I've no time to stay."

"Thank you, my good man, thank you . . . only, tell me . . ."

"Upon my word, sir, I can't stay. . . . They are asking for us every minute . . . but if your honour will stay here, we'll let you know if anything happens concerning your little affair."

"No, my friend, you just tell me . . ."

"Excuse me, I've no time to stay, sir," said Pisarenko, tearing himself away from Mr. Golyadkin, who had clutched him by the lapel of his coat. "I really can't. If your honour will stay here we'll let you know."

"In a minute, my good man, in a minute! In a minute, my good fellow! I tell you what, here's a letter; and I'll reward you, my good man."

"Yes, sir."

"Try and give it to Mr. Golyadkin, my dear fellow."

"Golyadkin?"

"Yes, my man, to Mr. Golyadkin."

"Very good, sir; as soon as I get off I'll take it, and you stay here, meanwhile; no one will see you here. . . ."

"No, my good man, don't imagine . . . I'm not standing here to avoid being seen. But I'm not going to stay here now, my friend. . . . I'll be close here in the side street. There's a coffee-house near here; so I'll wait there, and if anything happens, you let me know about anything, you understand?"

"Very good, sir. Only let me go; I understand."

"And I'll reward you," Mr. Golyadkin called after Pisarenko, when he had at last released him. . . .

"The rogue seemed to be getting rather rude," our hero reflected as he stealthily emerged from behind the stove. "There's some other dodge here. That's clear. . . . At first it was one thing and another . . .

he really was in a hurry, though; perhaps there's a great deal to do in the office. And his Excellency had been through the room twice. . . . How did that happen? . . . Ough! never mind! It may mean nothing, perhaps; but now we shall see. . . ."

At this point Mr. Golyadkin was about to open the door, intending to go out into the street, when suddenly, at that very instant, his Excellency's carriage dashed up to the door. Before Mr. Golyadkin had time to recover from the shock, the door of the carriage was opened from within and a gentleman jumped out. This gentleman was no other than Mr. Golyadkin junior, who had only gone out ten minutes before. Mr. Golyadkin senior remembered that the Director's flat was only a couple of paces away.

"He has been out on a special commission," our hero thought to himself.

Meanwhile, Mr. Golyadkin junior took out of the carriage a thick green portfolio and other papers. Finally, giving some orders to the coachman, he opened the door, almost ran up against Mr. Golyadkin senior, purposely avoided noticing him, acting in this way expressly to annoy him, and mounted the office staircase at a rapid canter.

"It's a bad look-out," thought Mr. Golyadkin. "This is what it has come to now! Oh, good Lord! look at him."

For half a minute our hero remained motionless. At last he made up his mind. Without pausing to think, though he was aware of a violent palpitation of the heart and a tremor in all his limbs, he ran up the stairs after his enemy.

"Here goes; what does it matter to me? I have nothing to do with the case," he thought, taking off his hat, his greatcoat and his goloshes in the entry.

When Mr. Golyadkin walked into his office, it was already getting dusk. Neither Andrey Filippovitch nor Anton Antonovitch was in the room. Both of them were in the Director's room, handing in reports. The Director, so it was rumoured, was in haste to report to a still higher Excellency. In consequence of this, and also because twilight was coming on, and the office hours were almost over, several of the clerks, especially the younger ones, were, at the moment when our hero entered, enjoying a period of inactivity; gathered together in groups, they were talking, arguing, and laughing, and some of the most youthful—that is, belonging to the lowest grades in the service, had got up a game of pitch-farthing in a corner, by a window. Knowing what was proper, and feeling at the moment a special need to conciliate and get on with them, Mr. Golyadkin immediately approached those with whom he used to get on best, in order to wish them good-day, and so on. But his colleagues answered his greetings rather strangely. He was unpleasantly impressed by a certain coldness, even curtness, one might almost say severity, in their manner. No one shook hands with him. Some simply said, "Good-day" and walked away; others barely nodded; one simply turned away and pretended not to notice him; at last some of them—and what mortified Mr. Golyadkin most of all, some of the youngsters of the lowest grades, mere lads who, as Mr. Golyadkin justly observed about them, were capable of nothing but hanging about and playing pitch-farthing at every opportunity—little by little collected round Mr. Golyadkin, formed a group round him and almost barred his way. They all looked at him with a sort of insulting curiosity.

It was a bad sign. Mr. Golyadkin felt this, and very judiciously decided not to notice it. Suddenly a quite unexpected event completely finished him off, as they say, and utterly crushed him.

At the moment most trying to Mr. Golyadkin senior, suddenly, as though by design, there appeared in the group of fellow clerks surrounding him the figure of Mr. Golyadkin junior, gay as ever, smiling a little smile as ever, nimble, too, as ever; in short, mischievous, skipping and tripping, chuckling and fawning, with sprightly tongue and sprightly toe, as always, precisely as he had been the day before at a very unpleasant moment for Mr. Golyadkin senior, for instance.

Grinning, tripping and turning with a smile that seemed to say "good-evening," to every one, he squeezed his way into the group of clerks, shaking hands with one, slapping another on the shoulder, putting his arm round another, explaining to a fourth how he had come to be employed by his Excellency, where he had been, what he had done, what he had brought with him; to the fifth, probably his most intimate friend, he gave a resounding kiss—in fact, everything happened as it had in Mr. Golyadkin's dream. When he had skipped about to his heart's content, polished them all off in his usual way, disposed them all in his favour, whether he needed them or not, when he had lavished his blandishments to the delectation of all the clerks, Mr. Golyadkin junior suddenly, and most likely by mistake, for he had not yet had time to notice his senior, held out his hand to Mr. Golyadkin senior also. Probably also by mistake—though he had had time to observe the dishonourable Mr. Golyadkin junior thoroughly, our hero at once eagerly seized the hand so unexpectedly held out to him and pressed it in the warmest and friendliest way, pressed it with a strange, quite unexpected, inner feeling, with a tearful emotion.

Whether our hero was misled by the first movement of his worthless foe, or was taken unawares, or, without recognizing it, felt at the bottom of his heart how defenceless he was—it is difficult to say. The fact remains that Mr. Golyadkin senior, apparently knowing what he was doing, of his own free will, before witnesses, solemnly shook hands with him whom he called his mortal foe. But what was the amazement, the stupefaction and fury, what was the horror and the shame of Mr. Golyadkin senior, when his enemy and mortal foe, the dishonourable Mr. Golyadkin junior, noticing the mistake of that persecuted, innocent, perfidiously deceived man, without a trace of shame, of feeling, of compassion or of conscience, pulled his hand away with insufferable rudeness and insolence. What was worse, he shook the hand as though it had been polluted with something horrid; what is more, he spat aside with disgust, accompanying this with a most insulting gesture; worse still, he drew out his handkerchief and, in the most unseemly way, wiped all the fingers that had rested for one moment in the hand of Mr. Golyadkin senior. While he did this Mr. Golyadkin junior looked about him in his characteristic horrid way, took care that every one should see what he was doing, glanced into people's eyes and evidently tried to insinuate to every one everything that was most unpleasant in regard to Mr. Golyadkin senior. Mr. Golyadkin junior's revolting behaviour seemed to arouse general indignation among the clerks that surrounded them; even the frivolous youngsters showed their displeasure. A murmur of protest rose on all sides. Mr. Golyadkin could not but discern the general feeling; but suddenly—an appropriate witticism that bubbled from the lips of Mr. Golyadkin junior shattered, annihilated our hero's last hopes, and inclined the balance again in favour of his deadly and undeserving foe.

"He's our Russian Faublas, gentlemen; allow me to introduce the youthful Faublas," piped Mr. Golyadkin junior, with his characteristic insolence, pirouetting and threading his way among the clerks, and directing their attention to the petrified though genuine Mr. Golyadkin. "Let us kiss each other, darling," he went on with insufferable familiarity, addressing the man he had so treacherously insulted. Mr. Golyadkin junior's unworthy jest seemed to touch a responsive chord, for it contained an artful allusion to an incident with which all were apparently familiar. Our hero was painfully conscious of the hand of his enemies. But he had made up his mind by now. With glowing eyes, with pale face, with a fixed smile he tore himself somehow out of the crowd and with uneven, hurried steps made straight for his Excellency's private room. In the room next to the last he was met by Andrey Filippovitch, who had only just come out from seeing his Excellency, and although there were present in this room at the moment a good number of persons of whom Mr. Golyadkin knew nothing, yet our hero did not care to take such a fact into consideration. Boldly, resolutely, directly, almost wondering at himself and inwardly admiring his own courage, without loss of time he accosted Andrey Filoppovitch, who was a good deal surprised by this unexpected attack.

"Ah! . . . What is it . . . what do you want?" asked the head of the division, not hearing Mr. Golyadkin's hesitating words.

"Andrey Filippovitch, may . . . might I, Andrey Filippovitch, may I have a conversation with his Excellency at once and in private?" our hero said resolutely and distinctly, fixing the most determined glance on Andrey Filippovitch.

"What next! Of course not." Andrey Filippovitch scanned Mr. Golyadkin from head to foot.

"I say all this, Andrey Filippovitch, because I am surprised that no one here unmasks the impostor and scoundrel."

"Wha-a-at!"

"Scoundrel, Andrey Filippovitch!"

"Of whom are you pleased to speak in those terms?"

"Of a certain person, Andrey Filippovitch; I'm alluding, Andrey Filippovitch, to a certain person; I have the right . . . I imagine, Andrey Filippovitch, that the authorities would surely encourage such action," added Mr. Golyadkin, evidently hardly knowing what he was saying. "Andrey Filippovitch . . . but no doubt you see yourself, Andrey Filippovitch, that this honourable action is a mark of my loyalty in every way—of my looking upon my superior as a father, Andrey Filippovitch; I as much as to say look upon my benevolent superior as a father and blindly trust my fate to him. It's as much as to say . . . you see . . ." At this point Mr. Golyadkin's voice trembled and two tears ran down his eyelashes.

As Andrey Filippovitch listened to Mr. Golyadkin he was so astonished that he could not help stepping back a couple of paces. Then he looked about him uneasily. . . . It is difficult to say how the matter would have ended. But suddenly the door of his Excellency's room was opened, and he himself came out, accompanied by several officials. All the persons in his room followed in a string. His Excellency called Andrey Filippovitch and walked beside him, beginning to discuss some business details. When all had set off and gone out of the room,

Mr. Golyadkin woke up. Growing calmer, he took refuge under the wing of Anton Antonovitch, who came last in the procession and who, Mr. Golyadkin fancied, looked stern and anxious. "I've been talking nonsense, I've been making a mess of it again, but there, never mind," he thought.

"I hope, at least, that you, Anton Antonovitch, will consent to listen to me and to enter into my position," he said quietly, in a voice that still trembled a little. "Rejected by all, I appeal to you. I am still at a loss to understand what Andrey Filippovitch's words mean, Anton Antonovitch. Explain them to me if you can. . . ."

"Everything will be explained in due time," Anton Antonovitch replied sternly and emphatically, and as Mr. Golyadkin fancied with an air that gave him plainly to understand that Anton Antonovitch did not wish to continue the conversation. "You will soon know all about it. You will be officially informed about everything to-day."

"What do you mean by officially informed, Anton Antonovitch? Why officially?" our hero asked timidly.

"It is not for you and me to discuss what our superiors decide upon, Yakov Petrovitch."

"Why our superiors, Anton Antonovitch?" said our hero, still more intimidated; "why our superiors? I don't see what reason there is to trouble our superiors in the matter, Anton Antonovitch. . . . Perhaps you mean to say something about yesterday's doings, Anton Antonovitch?"

"Oh no, nothing to do with yesterday; there's something else amiss with you."

"What is there amiss, Anton Antonovitch? I believe, Anton Antonovitch, that I have done nothing amiss."

"Why, you were meaning to be sly with some one," Anton Antonovitch cut in sharply, completely flabbergasting Mr. Golyadkin.

Mr. Golyadkin started, and turned as white as a pocket-handkerchief.

"Of course, Anton Antonovitch," he said, in a voice hardly audible, "if one listens to the voice of calumny and hears one's enemies' tales, without heeding what the other side has to say in its defence, then, of course . . . then, of course, Anton Antonovitch, one must suffer innocently and for nothing."

"To be sure; but your unseemly conduct, in injuring the reputation of a virtuous young lady belonging to that benevolent, highly distinguished and well-known family who had befriended you . . ."

"What conduct do you mean, Anton Antonovitch?"

"What I say. Do you know anything about your praiseworthy conduct in regard to that other young lady who, though poor, is of honourable foreign extraction?"

"Allow me, Anton Antonovitch . . . if you would kindly listen to me, Anton Antonovitch . . ."

"And your treacherous behaviour and slander of another person, your charging another person with your own sins. Ah, what do you call that?"

"I did not send him away, Anton Antonovitch," said our hero, with a tremor; "and I've never instructed Petrushka, my man, to do anything of the sort. . . . He has eaten my bread, Anton Antonovitch, he has taken advantage of my hospitality," our hero added expressively and with deep emotion, so much so that his chin twitched a little and tears were ready to start again.

"That is only your talk, that he has eaten your bread," answered Anton Antonovitch, somewhat offended, and there was a perfidious note in his voice which sent a pang to Mr. Golyadkin's heart.

"Allow me most humbly to ask you again, Anton Antonovitch, is his Excellency aware of all this business?"

"Upon my word, you must let me go now, though. I've no time for you now. . . . You'll know everything you need to know to-day."

"Allow me, for God's sake, one minute, Anton Antonovitch."

"Tell me afterwards. . . ."

"No, Anton Antonovitch; I . . . you see, Anton Antonovitch . . . only listen . . . I am not one for free-thinking, Anton Antonovitch; I shun free-thinking; I am quite ready for my part . . . and, indeed, I've given up that idea. . . ."

"Very good, very good. I've heard that already."

"No, you have not heard it, Anton Antonovitch. It is something else, Anton Antonovitch; it's a good thing, really, a good thing and pleasant to hear. . . . As I've explained to you, Anton Antonovitch, I admit that idea, that divine Providence has created two men exactly alike, and that a benevolent government, seeing the hand of Providence, provided a berth for two twins. That is a good thing, Anton Antonovitch. You see that it is a very good thing, Anton Antonovitch, and that I am very far from free-thinking. I look upon my benevolent government as a father; I say 'yes,' by all means; you are benevolent authorities, and you, of course . . . A young man must be in the service. . . . Stand up for me, Anton Antonovitch, take my part, Anton Antonovitch. . . . I am all right . . . Anton Antonovitch, for God's sake, one little word more . . . Anton Antonovitch. . . ."

But by now Anton Antonovitch was far away from Mr. Golyadkin. . . . Our hero was so bewildered and overcome by all that had happened and all that he had heard that he did not know where he was standing, what he had heard, what he had done, what was being done to him, and what was going to be done to him.

With imploring eyes he sought for Anton Antonovitch in the crowd of clerks, that he might justify himself further in his eyes and say something to him extremely high-toned and very agreeable, and creditable to himself. . . . By degrees, however, a new light began to break upon our hero's bewildered mind, a new and awful light that revealed at once a whole perspective of hitherto unknown and utterly unsuspected cicumstances. . . . At that moment somebody gave our bewildered hero a poke in the ribs. He looked around. Pisarenko was standing before him.

"A letter, your honour."

"Ah, you've been out already, then, my good man?"

"No, it was brought at ten o'clock this morning. Sergey Mihyeev, the attendant, brought it from Mr. Vahramyev's lodging."

"Very good, very good, and I'll reward you now, my dear fellow."

Saying this, Mr. Golyadkin thrust the letter in the side pocket of his uniform and buttoned up every button of it; then he looked round him, and to his surprise, found that he was by now in the hall of the department, in a group of clerks crowding at the outer door, for office hours were over. Mr. Golyadkin had not only failed till that moment to observe this circumstance, but had no notion how he suddenly came to be wearing his greatcoat and goloshes and to be holding his hat in his hand. All the clerks were standing motionless, in reverential expectation. The fact was that his Excellency was standing at the bottom of the stairs waiting for his carriage, which was for some reason late in arriving, and was carrying on a very interesting conversation with Andrey Filippovitch and two councillors. At a little distance from Andrey Filippovitch stood Anton Antonovitch and several other clerks, who were all smiles, seeing that his Excellency was graciously making a joke. The clerks who were crowded at the top of the stairs were smiling too, in expectation of his Excellency's laughing again. The only one who was not smiling was Fedosyevitch, the corpulent hall-porter, who stood stiffly at attention, holding the handle of the door, waiting impatiently for the daily gratification that fell to his share— that is, the task of flinging one half of the door wide open with a swing of his arm, and then, with a low bow, reverentially making way for his Excellency to pass. But the one who seemed to be more delighted than any and to feel the most satisfaction of all was the worthless and ungentlemanly enemy of Mr. Golyadkin. At that instant he positively forgot all the clerks, and even gave up tripping and pirouetting in his usual odious way; he even forgot to make up to anybody. He was all eyes and ears, he even doubled himself up strangely, no doubt in the strained effort to hear, and never took his eyes off his Excellency, and only from time to time his arms, legs and head twitched with faintly perceptible tremors that betrayed the secret emotions of his soul.

"Ah, isn't he in a state!" thought our hero. "He looks like a favourite, the rascal! I should like to know how it is that he deceives society of every class. He has neither brains nor character, neither education nor feeling; he's a lucky rogue! Mercy on us! How can a man, when you think of it, come and make friends with every one so quickly! And he'll get on, I swear the fellow will get on, the rogue will make his way—he's a lucky rascal! I should like to know, too what he keeps whispering to every one—what plots he is hatching with all these people, and what secrets they are talking about. Lord, have mercy on us! If only I could . . . get on with them a little too . . . say this and that and the other. Hadn't I better ask him . . . tell him I won't do it again; say 'I'm in fault, and a young man must serve nowadays, your Excellency'? I am not in the least abashed by my obscure position—so there! I am not going to protest in any way, either; I shall bear it all with meekness and patience, so there! Is that the way to behave? . . . Though you'll never see through him, though, the rascal; you can't reach him with anything you say; you can't hammer reason into his head. . . . We'll make an effort, though. I may happen to hit on a good moment, so I'll make an effort. . . ."

Feeling in his uneasiness, his misery and his bewilderment that he couldn't leave things like this, that the critical moment had come, that he must explain himself to some one, our hero began to move a little towards the place where his worthless and undeserving enemy stood: but at that very moment his Excellency's long-expected carriage rolled up into the entrance, Fedosyevitch flung open the door and, bending double, let his Excellency pass out. All the waiting clerks streamed out towards the door, and for a moment separated Mr. Golyadkin senior from Mr. Golyadkin junior.

"You shan't get away!" said our hero, forcing his way through the crowd while he kept his eyes fixed on the man he wanted. At last the crowd dispersed. Our hero felt he was free and flew in pursuit of his enemy.

Chapter 11

Mr. GOLYADKIN'S breath failed him; he flew as though on wings after his rapidly retreating eenemy. He was conscious of immense energy. Yet in spite of this terrible energy he might confidently have said that at that moment a humble gnat—had a gnat been able to exist in Petersburg at that time of the year—could very easily have knocked him down. He felt, too, that he was utterly weak again, that he was carried along by a peculiar outside force, that it was not he himself who was running, but, on the contrary, that his legs were giving way under him, and refused to obey him. This all might turn out for the best, however.

"Whether it is for the best or not for the best," thought Mr. Golyadkin, almost breathless from running so quickly, "but that the game is lost there cannot be the slightest doubt now; that I am utterly done for is certain, definite, signed and ratified."

In spite of all this our hero felt as though he had risen from the dead, as though he had withstood a battalion, as though he had won a victory when he succeeded in clutching the overcoat of his enemy, who had already raised one foot to get into the cab he had engaged.

"My dear sir! My dear sir!" he shouted to the infamous Mr. Golyadkin junior, holding him by the button. "My dear sir, I hope that you . . ."

"No, please do not hope for anything," Mr. Golyadkin's heartless enemy answered evasively, standing with one foot on the step of the cab and vainly waving the other leg in the air, in his efforts to get in, trying to preserve his equilibrium, and at the same time trying with all his might to wrench his coat away from Mr. Golyadkin senior, while the latter held on to it with all the strength that had been vouchsafed to him by nature.

"Yakov Petrovitch, only ten minutes . . ."

"Excuse me, I've no time . . ."

"You must admit, Yakov Petrovitch . . . please, Yakov Petrovitch. . . . For God's sake, Yakov Petrovitch . . . let us have it out—in a straightforward way . . . one little second, Yakov Petrovitch . . ."

"My dear fellow, I can't stay," answered Mr. Golyadkin's dishonourable enemy, with uncivil familiarity, disguised as good-natured heartiness; "another time, believe me, with my whole soul and all my heart; but now I really can't . . ."

"Scoundrel!" thought our hero. "Yakov Petrovitch," he cried miserably. "I have never been your enemy. Spiteful people have describd me unjustly. . . . I am ready, on my side . . . Yakov Petrovitch, shall we go in here together, at once, Yakov Petrovitch? And with all my heart, as you have so justly expressed it just now, and in straightforward, honourable language, as you have expressed it just now—here into this coffee-house; there the facts will explain themselves: they will really, Yakov Petrovitch. Then everything will certainly explain itself. . . ."

"Into the coffee-house? Very good. I am not against it. Let us go into the coffee-house on one condition only, my dear, on one condition —that these things shall be cleared up. We will have it all out, darling," said Mr. Golyadkin junior, getting out of the cab and shamelessly slapping our hero on the shoulder. "You friend of my heart, for your sake, Yakov Petrovitch, I am ready to go by the back street (as you were pleased to observe so aptly on one occasion, Yakov Petrovitch). Why, what a rogue he is! Upon my word, he does just what he likes with one!" Mr. Golyadkin's false friend went on, fawning upon him and cajoling him with a little smile. The coffee-house which the two Mr. Golyadkins entered stood some distance away from the main street and was at the moment quite empty. A rather stout German woman made her appearance behind the counter. Mr. Golyadkin and his unworthy enemy went into the second room, where a puffy-looking boy with a closely shaven head was busy with a bundle of chips at the stove, trying to revive the smouldering fire. At Mr. Golyadkin junior's request chocolate was served.

"And a sweet little lady-tart," said Mr. Golyadkin junior, with a sly wink at Mr. Golyadkin senior.

Our hero blushed and was silent.

"Oh, yes, I forgot, I beg your pardon. I know your taste. We are sweet on charming little Germans, sir; you and I are sweet on charming and agreeable little Germans, aren't we, you upright soul? We take their lodgings, we seduce their morals, they win our hearts with their beer-soup and their milk-soup, and we give them notes of different sorts, that's what we do, you Faublas, you deceiver!" All this Mr. Golyadkin junior said, making an unworthy though villainously artful allusion to a certain personage of the female sex, while he fawned upon our hero, smiled at him with an amiable air, with a deceitful show of being delighted with him and pleased to have met him. Seeing that Mr. Golyadkin senior was by no means so stupid and deficient in breeding and the manners of good society as to believe in him, the infamous man resolved to change his tactics and to make a more open attack upon him. After uttering his disgusting speech, the false Mr. Golyadkin ended by slapping the real and substantial Mr. Golyadkin on the shoulder, with a revolting effrontery and familiarity. Not content with that, he began playing pranks utterly unfit for well-bred society; he took it into his head to repeat his old, nauseous trick—that is, regardless of the resistance and faint cries of the indignant Mr. Golyadkin senior, he pinched the latter on the cheek. At the spectacle of such depravity our hero boiled within, but was silent . . . only for the time, however.

"That is the talk of my enemies," he answered at last, in a trembling voice, prudently restraining himself. At the same time our hero looked round uneasily towards the door. The fact was that Mr. Golyadkin junior seemed in excellent spirits, and ready for all sorts of little jokes, unseemly in a public place, and, speaking generally, not permissible by the laws of good manners, especially in well-bred society.

"Oh, well, in that case, as you please," Mr. Golyadkin junior gravely responded to our hero's thought, setting down upon the table the empty cup which he had gulped down with unseemly greed. "Well, there's no need for me to stay long with you, however. . . . Well, how are you getting on now, Yakov Petrovitch?"

"There's only one thing I can tell you, Yakov Petrovitch," our hero answered, with sangfroid and dignity; "I've never been your enemy."

"H'm. . . . Oh, what about Petrushka? Petrushka is his name, I fancy? Yes, it is Petrushka! Well, how is he? Well? The same as ever?"

"He's the same as ever, too, Yakov Petrovitch," answered Mr. Golyadkin senior, somewhat amazed. "I don't know, Yakov Petrovitch . . . from my standpoint . . . from a candid, honourable standpoint, Yakov Petrovitch, you must admit, Yakov Petrovitch . . ."

"Yes, but you know yourself, Yakov Petrovitch," Mr. Golyadkin junior answered in a soft and expressive voice, so posing falsely as a sorrowful man overcome with remorse and deserving compassion. "You know yourself we live in difficult times. . . . I appeal to you, Yakov Petrovitch; you are an intelligent man and your reflections are just," Mr. Golyadkin junior said in conclusion, flattering Mr. Golyadkin senior in an abject way. "Life is not a game, you know yourself, Yakov Petrovitch," Mr. Golyadkin junior added, with vast significance, assuming the character of a clever and learned man, who is capable of passing judgments on lofty subjects.

"For my part, Yakov Petrovitch," our hero answered warmly, "for my part, scorning to be roundabout and speaking boldly and openly, using straightforward, honourable language and putting the whole matter on an honourable basis, I tell you I can openly and honourably assert, Yakov Petrovitch, that I am absolutely pure, and that, you know it yourself, Yakov Petrovitch, the error is mutual—it may all be the world's judgment, the opinion of the slavish crowd. . . . I speak openly, Yakov Petrovitch, everything is possible. I will say, too, Yakov Petrovitch, if you judge it in this way, if you look at the matter from a lofty, noble point of view, then I will boldly say, without false shame I will say, Yakov Petrovitch, it will positively be a pleasure to me to discover that I have been in error, it will positively be a pleasure to me to recognize it. You know yourself you are an intelligent man and, what is more, you are a gentleman. Without shame, without false shame, I am ready to recognize it," he wound up with dignity and nobility.

"It is the decree of destiny, Yakov Petrovitch . . . but let us drop all this," said Mr. Golyadkin junior. "Let us rather use the brief moment of our meeting for a more pleasant and profitable conversation, as is only suitable between two colleagues in the service. . . . Really, I have not succeeded in saying two words to you all this time. . . . I am not to blame for that, Yakov Petrovitch. . . ."

"Nor I," answered our hero warmly, "nor I, either! My heart tells me, Yakov Petrovitch, that I'm not to blame in all this matter. Let us blame fate for all this, Yakov Petrovitch," added Mr. Golyadkin senior, in a quick, conciliatory tone of voice. His voice began little by little to soften and to quaver.

"Well! How are you in health?" said the sinner in a sweet voice.

"I have a little cough," answered our hero, even more sweetly

"Take care of yourself. There is so much illness going about, you may easily get quinsy; for my part I confess I've begun to wrap myself up in flannel."

"One may, indeed, Yakov Petrovitch, very easily get quinsy," our hero pronounced after a brief silence; "Yakov Petrovitch, I see that I have made a mistake, I remember with softened feelings those happy moments which we were so fortunate as to spend together, under my poor, though I venture to say, hospitable roof . . ."

"In your letter, however, you wrote something very different," said

Mr. Golyadkin junior reproachfully, speaking on this occasion—though only on this occasion—quite justly.

"Yakov Petrovitch, I was in error. . . . I see clearly now that I was in error in my unhappy letter too. Yakov Petrovitch, I am ashamed to look at you, Yakov Petrovitch, you wouldn't believe . . . Give me that letter that I may tear it to pieces before your eyes, Yakov Petrovitch, and if that is utterly impossible I entreat you to read it the other way before—precisely the other way before—that is, expressly with a friendly intention, giving the opposite sense to the whole letter. I was in error. Forgive me, Yakov Petrovitch, I was quite . . . I was grievously in error, Yakov Petrovitch."

"You say so?" Mr. Golyadkin's perfidious friend inquired, rather casually and indifferently.

"I say that I was quite in error, Yakov Petrovitch, and that for my part, quite without false shame, I am . . ."

"Ah, well, that's all right! That's a nice thing your being in error," answered Mr. Golyadkin junior.

"I even had an idea, Yakov Petrovitch," our candid hero answered in a gentlemanly way, completely failing to observe the horrible perfidy of his deceitful enemy, "I even had an idea that here were two people created exactly alike. . . ."

"Ah, is that your idea?"

At this point the notoriously worthless Mr. Golyadkin took up his hat. Still failing to observe his treachery, Mr. Golyadkin senior, too, got up and with a noble, simple-hearted smile to his false friend, tried in his innocence to be friendly to him, to encourage him, and in that way to form a new friendship with him.

"Good-bye, your Excellency," Mr. Golyadkin junior called out suddenly. Our hero started, noticing in his enemy's face something positively Bacchanalian, and, solely to get rid of him, put two fingers into the unprincipled man's outstretched hand; but then . . . then his enemy's shamelessness passed all bounds. Seizing the two fingers of Mr. Golyadkin's hand and at first pressing them, the worthless fellow on the spot, before Mr. Golyadkin's eyes, had the effrontery to repeat the shameful joke of the afternoon. The limit of human patience was exhausted.

He had just hidden in his pocket the handkerchief with which he had wiped his fingers when Mr. Golyadkin senior recovered from the shock and dashed after him into the next room, into which his irreconcilable foe had in his usual hasty way hastened to decamp. As though perfectly innocent, he was standing at the counter eating pies, and with perfect composure, like a virtuous man, was making polite remarks to the German woman behind the counter.

"I can't go into it before ladies," thought our hero, and he, too, went up to the counter, so agitated that he hardly knew what he was doing.

"The tart is certainly not bad! What do you think?" Mr. Golyadkin junior began upon his unseemly sallies again, reckoning, no doubt, upon Mr. Golyadkin's infinite patience. The stout German, for her part, looked at both her visitors with pewtery, vacant-looking eyes, smiling affably and evidently not understanding Russian. Our hero flushed red as fire at the words of the unabashed Mr. Golyadkin junior, and, unable to control himself, rushed at him with the evident intention of tearing him to pieces and finishing him off completely, but Mr. Golyadkin junior, in his usual mean way, was already far off; he took flight, he was already on the steps. It need hardly be said that, after the first moment of stupefaction with which Mr. Golyadkin senior was naturally overcome, he recovered himself and went at full speed after his insulting enemy, who had already got into a cab, whose driver was obviously in collusion with him. But at that very instant the stout German, seeing both her customers make off, shrieked and rang her bell with all her might. Our hero was on the point of flight, but he turned back, and, without asking for change, flung her money for himself and for the shameless man who had left without paying, and although thus delayed he succeeded in catching up with his enemy. Hanging on to the side of the cab with all the force bestowed on him by nature, our hero was carried for some time along the street, clambering upon the vehicle, while Mr. Golyadkin junior did his utmost to dislodge him. Meanwhile the cabman, with whip, with reins, with kicks and with shouts urged on his exhausted nag, who quite unexpectedly dropped into a gallop, biting at the bit, and kicking with his hind legs in a horrid way. At last our hero succeeded in climbing into the cab, facing his enemy and with his back to the driver, his knees touching the knees and his right hand clutching the very shabby fur collar of his depraved and exasperated foe.

The enemies were borne along for some time in silence. Our hero could scarcely breathe. It was a bad road and he was jolted at every step and in peril of breaking his neck. Moreover, his exasperated foe still refused to acknowledge himself vanquished and was trying to shove him off into the mud. To complete the unpleasantness of his position the weather was detestable. The snow was falling in heavy flakes and doing its utmost to creep under the unfastened overcoat of the genuine Mr. Golyadkin. It was foggy and nothing could be seen.

It was difficult to tell through what street and in what direction they were being taken. . . . It seemed to Mr. Golyadkin that what was happening to him was somehow familiar. One instant he tried to remember whether he had had a presentiment of it the day before, in a dream, for instance. . . .

At last his wretchedness reached the utmost pitch of agony. Leaning upon his merciless opponent, he was beginning to cry out. But his cries died away upon his lips. . . . There was a moment when Mr. Golyadkin forgot everything, and made up his mind that all this was of no consequence and that it was all nothing, that it was happening in some inexplicable manner, and that, therefore, to protest was effort thrown away. . . . But suddenly and almost at the same instant that our hero was drawing this conclusion, an unexpected jolt gave quite a new turn to the affair. Mr. Golyadkin fell off the cab like a sack of flour and rolled on the ground, quite correctly recognizing, at the moment of his fall, that his excitement had been very inappropriate. Jumping up at last, he saw that they had arrived somewhere; the cab was standing in the middle of some courtyard, and from the first glance our hero noticed that it was the courtyard of the house in which was Olsufy Ivanovitch's flat. At the same instant he noticed that his enemy was mounting the steps, probably on his way to Olsufy Ivanovitch's. In indescribable misery he was about to pursue his enemy, but, fortunately for himself, prudently thought better of it. Not forgetting to pay the cabman, Mr. Golyadkin ran with all his might along the street, regardless of where he was going. The snow was falling heavily as before; as before it was muggy, wet, and dark. Our hero did not walk, but flew, coming into collision with every one on the way—men, women and children, and himself rebounding from every one—men, women and children. About him and after him he heard frightened voices, squeals, screams. . . . But Mr. Golyadkin seemed unconscious and would pay no heed to anything. . . . He came to himself, however, on the Semyonovsky Bridge, and then only through succeeding in tripping against and upsetting two peasant women and the wares they were selling, and tumbling over them.

"That's no matter," though Mr. Golyadkin, "that can easily be set right," and he felt in his pocket at once, intending to make up for the cakes, apples, nuts and various trifles he had scattered, with a rouble. Suddenly a new light dawned upon Mr. Golyadkin; in his pocket he felt the letter given him in the morning by the clerk. Remembering that there was a tavern he knew close by, he ran to it without a moment's delay, settled himself at a little table lighted up by a tallow candle, and, taking no notice of anything, regardless of the waiter who came to ask for his orders, broke the seal and began reading the following letter, which completely astounded him—

"You noble man, who are suffering for my sake, and will be dear to my heart for ever!

"I am suffering, I am perishing—save me! The slanderer, the intriguer, notorious for the immorality of his tendencies, has entangled me in his snares and I am undone! I am lost! But he is abhorrent to me, while you! . . . They have separated us, they have intercepted my letters to you—and all this has been the work of the vicious man who has taken advantage of his one good quality—his likeness to you. A man can always be plain in appearance, yet fascinate by his intelligence, his strong feelings and his agreeable manners. . . . I am ruined! I am being married against my will, and the chief part in this intrigue is taken by my parent, benefactor and civil councillor, Olsufy Ivanovitch, no doubt desirous of securing me a place and relations in well-bred society. . . . But I have made up my mind and I protest by all the powers bestowed on me by nature. Be waiting for me with a carriage at nine o'clock this evening at the window of Olsufy Ivanovitch's flat. We are having another ball and a handsome lieutenant is coming. I will come out and we will fly. Moreover, there are other government offices in which one can be of service to one's country. In any case, remember, my friend, that innocence is strong in its very innocence. Farewell. Wait with the carriage at the entrance. I shall throw myself into the protection of your arms at two o'clock in the night.

"Yours till death,
"KLARA OLSUFYEVNA."

After reading the letter our hero remained for some minutes as though petrified. In terrible anxiety, in terrible agitation, white as a sheet, with the letter in his hand, he walked several times up and down the room; to complete the unpleasantness of his position, though our hero failed to observe it, he was at that moment the object of the exclusive attention of every one in the room. Probably the disorder of his attire, his unrestrained excitement, his walking or rather running about the room, his gesticulating with both hands, perhaps some enigmatic words unconsciously addressed to the air, probably all this prejudiced Mr. Golyadkin in the opinion of the customers, and even the waiter began to look at him suspiciously. Coming to himself, Mr. Golyadkin noticed that he was standing in the middle of the room and was in an almost unseemly, discourteous manner staring at an old man of very respectable appearance who, having dined and said grace before the ikon, had sat down again and fixed his eyes upon Mr. Golyadkin. Our hero looked vaguely about him and noticed that every one, actually every one, was looking at him with a hostile and suspicious air. All at once a retired military man in a red collar asked loudly for the *Police News.* Mr. Golyadkin started and turned crimson: he happened to look down and saw that he was in such disorderly attire as he would not have worn even at home, much less in a public place. His boots, his trousers and the whole of his left side were covered with mud; the trouser-strap was torn off his right foot, and his coat was even torn in many places. In extreme misery our hero went up to the table at which he had read the letter, and saw that the attendant was coming up to him with a strange and impudently peremptory expression of face. Utterly disconcerted and crestfallen, our hero began to look about the table at which he was now standing. On the table stood a dirty plate, left there from somebody's dinner, a soiled table-napkin and a knife, fork and spoon that had just been used. "Who has been having dinner?" thought our hero. "Can it have been I? Anything is possible! I must have had dinner without noticing it; what am I to do?"

Raising his eyes, Mr. Golyadkin again saw beside him the waiter who was about to address him.

"How much is my bill, my lad?" our hero inquired, in a trembling voice.

A loud laugh sounded round Mr. Golyadkin, the waiter himself grinned. Mr. Golyadkin realized that he had blundered again, and had done something dreadfully stupid. He was overcome by confusion, and to avoid standing there with nothing to do he put his hand in his pocket to get out his handkerchief; but to the indescribable amazement of himself and all surrounding him, he pulled out instead of his handkerchief the bottle of medicine which Krestyan Ivanovitch had prescribed for him four days earlier. "Get the medicine at the same chemist's," floated through Mr. Golyadkin's brain. . . .

Suddenly he started and almost cried out in horror. A new light dawned. . . . The dark reddish and repulsive liquid had a sinister gleam to Mr. Golyadkin's eyes. . . . The bottle dropped from his hands and was instantly smashed. Our hero cried out and stepped back a pace to avoid the spilled medicine . . . he was trembling in every limb, and drops of sweat came out on to his brow and temples. "So my life is in danger!" Meantime there was a stir, a commotion in the room: every one surrounded Mr. Golyadkin, every one talked to

Mr. Golyadkin, some even caught hold of Mr. Golyadkin. But our hero was dumb and motionless, seeing nothing, hearing nothing, feeling nothing. . . . At last, as though tearing himself from the place, he rushed out of the tavern, pushing away all and each who tried to detain him; almost unconscious, he got into the first cab that passed him and drove to his flat.

In the entry of his flat he met Mihyeev, an attendant from the office, with an official envelope in his hand.

"I know, my good man, I know all about it," our exhausted hero answered, in a weak, miserable voice; "it's official. . . ."

The envelope did, in fact, contain instructions to Mr. Golyadkin, signed by Andrey Filippovitch, to give up the business in his hands to Ivan Semyonovitch. Taking the envelope and giving ten kopecks to the man, Mr. Golyadkin went into his flat and saw that Petrushka was collecting all his odds and ends, all his things into a heap, evidently intending to abandon Mr. Golyadkin and move to the flat of Karolina Ivanovna, who had enticed him to take the place of Yevstafy.

Chapter 12

PETRUSHKA came in swaggering, with a strangely casual manner and an air of vulgar triumph on his face. It was evident that he had some idea in his head, that he felt thoroughly within his rights, and he looked like an unconcerned spectator—that is, as though he were anybody's servant rather than Mr. Golyadkin's.

"I say, you know, my good lad," our hero began breathlessly, "what time is it?"

Without speaking, Petrushka went behind his partition, then returned, and in a rather independent tone announced that it was nearly half-past seven.

"Well, that's all right, my lad, that's all right. Come, you see, my boy . . . allow me to tell you, my good lad, that everything, I fancy, is at an end between us."

Petrushka said nothing.

"Well, now as everything is over between us, tell me openly, as a friend, where you have been."

"Where I've been? To see good people, sir."

"I know, my good lad, I know. I have always been satisfied with you, and I give you a character. . . . Well, what are you doing with them now?"

"Why, sir! You know yourself. We all know a decent man won't teach you any harm."

"I know, my dear fellow, I know. Nowadays good people are rare, my lad; prize them, my friend. Well, how are they?"

"To be sure, they . . . Only I can't serve you any longer, sir, as your honour must know."

"I know, my dear fellow, I know your zeal and devotion; I have seen it all, my lad, I've noticed it. I respect you, my friend. I respect a good and honest man, even though he's a lackey."

"Why, yes, to be sure! The likes of us, of course, as you know yourself, are as good as anybody. That's so. We all know, sir, that there's no getting on without a good man."

"Very well, very well, my boy, I feel it. . . . Come, here's your money and here's your character. Now we'll kiss and say good-bye, brother. . . . Come, now, my lad, I'll ask one service of you, one last service," said Mr. Golyadkin, in a solemn voice. "You see, my dear boy, all sorts of things happen. Sorrow is concealed in gilded palaces, and there's no escaping it. You know, my boy, I've always been kind to you, my boy."

Petrushka remained mute.

"I believe I've always been kind to you, my dear fellow. . . . Come, how much linen have we now, my dear boy?"

"Well, it's all there. Linen shirts six, three pairs of socks; four shirt-fronts; flannel vests; of underlinen two sets. You know all that yourself. I've got nothing of yours, sir. . . . I look after my master's belongings, sir. I am like that, sir . . . we all know . . . and I've . . . never been guilty of anything of the sort, sir, you know yourself, sir. . . ."

"I trust you, my lad, I trust you. I didn't mean that, my friend, I didn't mean that, you know, my lad; I tell you what . . ."

"To be sure, sir, we know that already. Why, when I used to be in service at General Stolbnyakov's . . . I lost the place through the family's going away to Saratov . . . they've an estate there. . . ."

"No; I didn't mean that, my lad, I didn't mean that; don't think anything of the sort, my dear fellow. . . ."

"To be sure. It's easy, as you know yourself, sir, to take away the character of folks like us. And I've always given satisfaction—ministers, generals, senators, counts—I've served them all. I've been at Prince Svintchatkin's, at Colonel Pereborkin's, at General Nedobarov's

—they've gone away too, they've gone to their property. As we all know . . ."

"Yes, my lad, very good, my lad, very good. And now I'm going away, my friend. . . . A different path lies before each man, no one can tell what road he may have to take. Come, my lad, put out my clothes now, lay out my uniform too . . . and my other trousers, my sheets, quilts and pillows. . . ."

"Am I to pack them all in the bag?"

"Yes, my lad, yes; the bag, please. Who knows what may happen to us? Come, my dear boy, you can go and find a carriage. . . ."

"A carriage? . . ."

"Yes, my lad, a carriage; a roomy one, and take it by the hour. And don't you imagine anything. . . ."

"And are you meaning to go far away, sir?"

"I don't know, my lad, I don't know that either. I think you had better pack my feather-bed too. What do you think, my lad? I am relying on you, my dear fellow. . . ."

"Is your honour setting off at once?"

"Yes, my friend, yes! Circumstances have turned out so . . . so it is, my dear fellow, so it is. . . ."

"To be sure, sir; when we were in the regiment the same thing happened to the lieutenant; they eloped from a country gentleman's. . . ."

"Eloped? . . . How? My dear fellow!"

"Yes, sir, eloped, and they were married in another house. Everything was got ready beforehand. There was a hue and cry after them; the late prince took their part, and so it was all settled. . . ."

"They were married, but . . . how is it, my dear fellow? . . . How did you come to know, my boy?"

"Why, to be sure! The earth is full of rumours, sir. We know, sir, we've all . . . to be sure, there's no one without sin. Only I'll tell you now, sir, let me speak plainly and vulgarly, sir; since it has come to this, I must tell you, sir; you have an enemy—you've a rival, sir, a powerful rival, so there. . . ."

"I know, my dear fellow, I know; you know yourself, my dear fellow. . . . So, you see, I'm relying upon you. What are we to do now, my friend? How do you advise me?"

"Well, sir, if you are in that way now, if you've come, so to say, to such a pass, sir, you'll have to make some purchases, sir—say some sheets, pillows, another feather-bed, a double one, a good quilt—here at the neighbours downstairs—she's a shopkeeper, sir—she has a good

fox-fur cloak, so you might look at it and buy it, you might have a
look at it at once. You'll need it now, sir; it's a good cloak, sir, satin
lined with fox. . . ."

"Very good, my lad, very good, I agree; I rely upon you, I rely upon
you entirely; a cloak by all means, if necessary. . . . Only make haste,
make haste! For God's sake make haste! I'll buy the cloak—only please
make haste! It will soon be eight o'clock. Make haste for God's sake,
my dear lad! Hurry up, my lad. . . ."

Petrushka ran to gather together a bundle of linen, pillows, quilt,
sheets, and all sorts of odds and ends, tied them up and rushed headlong out of the room. Meanwhile, Mr. Golyadkin seized the letter
once more, but he could not read it. Clutching his devoted head, he
leaned against the wall in a state of stupefaction. He could not think
of anything, he could do nothing either, and could not even tell what
was happening to him. At last, seeing that time was passing and
neither Petrushka nor the fur cloak had made an appearance, Mr.
Golyadkin made up his mind to go himself. Opening the door into
the entry, he heard below noise, talk, disputing, scuffling. . . . Several
of the women of the neighbouring flats were shouting, talking and
protesting about something—Mr. Golyadkin knew what. Petrushka's
voice was heard: then there was a sound of footsteps.

"My goodness! They'll bring all the world in here," moaned Mr.
Golyadkin, wringing his hands in despair and rushing back into his
room. Running back into his room, he fell almost senseless on the sofa
with his face in the pillow. After lying a minute in this way, he
jumped up and, without waiting for Petrushka, he put on his goloshes,
his hat and his greatcoat, snatched up his papers and ran headlong
downstairs.

"Nothing is wanted, nothing, my dear fellow! I will manage myself—everything myself. I don't need you for the time, and meantime,
things may take a better turn, perhaps," Mr. Golyadkin muttered to
Petrushka, meeting him on the stairs; then he ran out into the yard,
away from the house. There was a faintness at his heart, he had not
yet made up his mind what was his position, what he was to do, how
he was to act in the present critical position.

"Yes, how am I to act? Lord, have mercy on me! And that all this
should happen!" he cried out at last in despair, tottering along the
street at random; "that all this must needs happen! Why, but for this,
but for just this, everything would have been put right; at one stroke,
at one skilful, vigorous, firm stroke it would have been set right. I
would have my finger cut off to have it set right! And I know, indeed,

how it would have been settled. This is how it would have been managed: I'd have gone on the spot . . . said how it was . . . 'with your permission, sir, I'm neither here nor there in it . . . things aren't done like that,' I would say, 'my dear sir, things aren't done like that, there's no accepting an impostor in our office; an impostor . . . my dear sir, is a man . . . who is worthless and of no service to his country. Do you understand that? Do you understand that, my dear sir?' I should say! That's how it would be. . . . But no . . . after all, things are not like that . . . not a bit like that. . . . I am talking nonsense, like a fool! A suicidal fool! It's not like that at all, you suicidal fool. . . . This is how things are done, though, you profligate man! . . . Well, what am I to do with myself now? Well, what am I going to do with myself now? What am I fit for now? Come, what are you fit for now, for instance, you Golyadkin, you, you worthless fellow! Well, what now? I must get a carriage; 'hire a carriage and bring it here,' says she, 'we shall get our feet wet without a carriage,' says she. . . . And who could ever have thought it! Fie, fie, my young lady! Fie, fie, a young lady of virtuous behaviour! Well, well, the girl we all thought so much of! You've distinguished yourself, madame, there's no doubt of that! you've distinguished yourself! . . . And it all comes from immoral education. And now that I've looked into it and seen through it all I see that it is due to nothing else but immorality. Instead of looking after her as a child . . . and the rod at times . . . they stuff her with sweets and dainties, and the old man is always doting over her: saying 'my dear, my love, my beauty,' saying, 'we'll marry you to a count!' . . . And now she has come forward herself and shown her cards, as though to say that's her little game! Instead of keeping her at home as a child, they sent her to a boarding-school, to a French madame, an *émigrée,* a Madame Falbalas or something, and she learned all sorts of things at that Madame Falbalas', and this is how it always turns out. 'Come,' says she, 'and be happy! Be in a carriage,' she says, 'at such a time, under the windows, and sing a sentimental serenade in the Spanish style; I await you and I know you love me, and we will fly together and live in a hut.' But the fact is it's impossible; since it has come to that, madame, it's impossible, it is against the law to abduct an innocent, respectable girl from her parents' roof without their sanction! And, if you come to that, why, what for and what need is there to do it? Come, she should marry a suitable person, the man marked out by destiny, and that would be the end of it. But I'm in the government service, I might lose my berth through it: I might be arrested for it, madame! I tell you that! If you did not know it. It's that German woman's doing. She's at the bottom of it all, the witch; she cooked the whole kettle of fish. For they've slandered a man, for they've invented a bit of womanship gossip about him, a regular performance by the advice of Andrey Filippovitch, that's what it came from. Otherwise how could Petrushka be mixed up in it? What has he to do with it? What need for that rogue to be in it? No, I cannot, madame, I cannot possibly, not on any account. . . . No, madame, this time you must really excuse me. It's all your doing, madame, it's not all the German's doing, it's not the witch's doing at all, but simply yours. For the witch is a good woman, for the witch is not to blame in any way; it's your fault, madame; it's you who are to blame, let me tell you! I shall be charged with a crime through you, madame. . . . A man might be ruined . . . a man might lose sight of himself, and not be able to restrain himself—a wedding, indeed! And how is it all going to end? And how will it all be arranged? I would give a great deal to know all that! . . ."

So our hero reflected in his despair. Coming to himself suddenly, he observed that he was standing somewhere in Liteyny Street. The weather was awful: it was a thaw; snow and rain were falling—just as at that memorable time when at the dread hour of midnight all Mr. Golyadkin's troubles had begun. "This is a nice night for a journey!" thought Mr. Golyadkin, looking at the weather; "it's death all round. . . . Good Lord! Where am I to find a carriage, for instance? I believe there's something black there at the corner. We'll see, we'll investigate. . . . Lord, have mercy on us!" our hero went on, bending his weak and tottering steps in the direction in which he saw something that looked like a cab.

"No, I know what I'll do; I'll go straight and fall on my knees, if I can, and humbly beg, saying, 'I put my fate in your hands, in the hands of my superiors'; saying, 'Your Excellency, be a protector and a benefactor'; and then I'll say this and that, and explain how it is and that it is an unlawful act; 'Do not destroy me, I look upon you as my father, do not abandon me . . . save my dignity, my honour, my name, my reputation . . . and save me from a miscreant, a vicious man. . . . He's another person, your Excellency, and I'm another person too; he's apart and I am myself by myself too; I am really myself by myself, your Excellency; really myself by myself,' that's what I shall say. 'I cannot be like him. Change him, dismiss him, give orders for him to be changed and a godless, licentious impersonation to be suppressed . . . that it may not be an example to others, your Excellency. I look upon you as a father'; those in authority over us, our benefactors and protectors, are bound, of course, to encourage such impulses. . . . There's something chivalrous about it: I shall say, 'I look upon you, my bene-factor and superior, as a father, and trust my fate to you, and I will not say anything against it; I put myself in your hands, and retire from the affair myself' . . . that's what I would say."

"Well, my man, are you a cabman?"

"Yes . . ."

"I want a cab for the evening. . . ."

"And does your honour want to go far?"

"For the evening, for the evening; wherever I have to go, my man, wherever I have to go."

"Does your honour want to drive out of town?"

"Yes, my friend, out of town, perhaps. I don't quite know myself yet, I can't tell you for certain, my man. Maybe, you see, it will all be settled for the best. We all know, my friend . . ."

"Yes, sir, of course we all know. Please God it may."

"Yes, my friend, yes; thank you, my dear fellow, come, what's your fare, my good man? . . ."

"Do you want to set off at once?"

"Yes, at once, that is, no, you must wait at a certain place. . . . A little while, not long, you'll have to wait. . . ."

"Well, if you hire me for the whole time, I couldn't ask less than six roubles for weather like this. . . ."

"Oh, very well, my friend; and I thank you, my dear fellow. So, come, you can take me now, my good man."

"Get in; allow me, I'll put it straight a bit—now will your honour get in? Where shall I drive?"

"To the Ismailovsky Bridge, friend."

The driver plumped down on the box, with difficulty roused his pair of lean nags from the trough of hay, and was setting off for the Ismail-ovsky Bridge. But suddenly Mr. Golyadkin pulled the cord, stopped the cab, and besought him in an imploring voice not to drive to the Ismailovsky Bridge, but to turn back to another street. The driver turned into another street, and ten minutes later Mr. Golyadkin's newly hired equipage was standing before the house in which his Excellency had a flat. Mr. Golyadkin got out of the carriage, begged the driver to be sure to wait and with a sinking heart ran upstairs to the third storey and pulled the bell; the door was opened and our hero found himself in the entry of his Excellency's flat.

"Is his Excellency graciously pleased to be at home?" said Mr. Gol-yadkin, addressing the man who opened the door.

"What do you want?" asked the servant, scrutinizing Mr. Golyadkin from head to foot.

"I, my friend . . . I am Golyadkin, the titular councillor, Golyadkin. . . . To say . . . something or other . . . to explain . . ."

"You must wait; you cannot . . ."

"My friend, I cannot wait; my business is important, it's business that admits of no delay. . . ."

"But from whom have you come? Have you brought papers? . . ."

"No, my friend, I am on my own account. Announce me, my friend, say something or other, explain. I'll reward you, my good man. . . ."

"I cannot. His Excellency is not at home, he has visitors. Come at ten o'clock in the morning. . . ."

"Take in my name, my good man, I can't wait—it is impossible. . . . You'll have to answer for it, my good man."

"Why, go and announce him! What's the matter with you; want to save your shoe leather?" said another lackey, who was lolling on the bench and had not uttered a word till then.

"Shoe leather! I was told not to show any one up, you know; their time is the morning."

"Announce him, have you lost your tongue?"

"I'll announce him all right—I've not lost my tongue. It's not my orders; I've told you, it's not my orders. Walk inside."

Mr. Golyadkin went into the outermost room; there was a clock on the table. He glanced at it: it was half-past eight. His heart ached within him. Already he wanted to turn back, but at that very moment the footman standing at the door of the next room had already boomed out Mr. Golyadkin's name.

"Oh, what lungs," thought our hero in indescribable misery. "Why, you ought to have said: 'He has come most humbly and meekly to make an explanation . . . something . . . be graciously pleased to see him.' . . . Now the whole business is ruined; all my hopes are scattered to the winds. But . . . however . . . never mind. . . ."

There was no time to think, moreover. The lackey, returning, said, "Please walk in," and led Mr. Golyadkin into the study.

When our hero went in, he felt as though he were blinded, for he could see nothing at all. . . . But three or four figures seemed flitting before his eyes: "Oh, yes, they are the visitors," flashed through Mr. Golyadkin's mind. At last our hero could distinguish clearly the star on the black coat of his Excellency, then by degrees advanced to seeing the black coat and at last gained the power of complete vision. . . .

"What is it?" said a familiar voice above Mr. Golyadkin.

"The titular councillor, Golyadkin, your Excellency."

"Well?"

"I have come to make an explanation. . . ."

"How? . . . What?"

"Why, yes. This is how it is. I've come for an explanation, your Excellency. . . ."

"But you . . . but who are you? . . ."

"M—m—m—mist—er Golyadkin, your Excellency, a titular councillor."

"Well, what is it you want?"

"Why, this is how it is, I look upon you as a father; I retire . . . defend me from my enemy! . . ."

"What's this? . . ."

"We all know . . ."

"What do we all know?"

Mr. Golyadkin was silent: his chin began twitching a little.

"Well?"

"I thought it was chivalrous, your Excellency. . . . 'There's something chivalrous in it,' I said, 'and I look upon my superior as a father' . . . this is what I thought; 'protect me, I tear-earfully . . . b-beg and that such imp-impulses ought . . . to . . . be encouraged. . . .'"

His Excellency turned away, our hero for some minutes could distinguish nothing. There was a weight on his chest. His breathing was laboured; he did not know where he was standing. . . . He felt ashamed and sad. God knows what followed. . . . Recovering himself, our hero noticed that his Excellency was talking with his guests, and seemed to be briskly and emphatically discussing something with them. One of the visitors Mr. Golyadkin recognized at once. This was Andrey Filippovitch; he knew no one else; yet there was another person that seemed familiar—a tall, thick-set figure, middle-aged, possessed of very thick eyebrows and whiskers and a significant sharp expression. On his chest was an order and in his mouth a cigar. This gentleman was smoking and nodding significantly without taking the cigar out of his mouth, glancing from time to time at Mr. Golyadkin. Mr. Golyadkin felt awkward; he turned away his eyes and immediately saw another very strange visitor. Through a door which our hero had taken for a looking-glass, just as he had done once before—*he* made his appearance—we know who: a very intimate friend and acquaintance of Mr. Golyadkin's. Mr. Golyadkin junior had actually been till then in a little room close by, hurriedly writing something; now, apparently, he was needed—and he came in with papers under his arm, went up to his Excellency, and while waiting for exclusive attention to be paid him succeeded very adroitly in putting his spoke into the talk and consultation, taking his place a little behind Andrey Filippovitch's back and partly screening him from the gentleman smoking the cigar. Apparently Mr. Golyadkin junior took an extreme interest in the conversation, to which he was listening now in a gentlemanly way, nodding his head, fidgeting with his feet, smiling, continually looking at his Excellency—as it were beseeching him with his eyes to let him put his word in.

"The scoundrel," thought Mr. Golyadkin, and involuntarily he took a step forward. At this moment his Excellency turned round, and came rather hesitatingly towards Mr. Golyadkin.

"Well, that's all right, that's all right; well, run along, now. I'll look into your case, and give orders for you to be taken . . ."

At this point his Excellency glanced at the gentleman with the thick whiskers. The latter nodded in assent.

Mr. Golyadkin felt and distinctly understood that they were taking him for something different and not looking at him in the proper light at all.

"In one way or another I must explain myself," he thought; "I must say, 'This is how it is, your Excellency.'"

At this point in his perplexity he dropped his eyes to the floor and to his great astonishment he saw a good-sized patch of something white on his Excellency's boots.

"Can there be a hole in them?" thought Mr. Golyadkin. Mr. Golyadkin was, however, soon convinced that his Excellency's boots were not split, but were only shining brilliantly—a phenomenon fully explained by the fact that they were patent leather and highly polished.

"It is what they call *blick*," thought our hero; "the term is used particularly in artists' studios; in other places such a reflected light is called a rib of light."

At this point Mr. Golyadkin raised his eyes and saw that the time had come to speak, for things might easily end badly. . . .

Our hero took a step forward.

"I say this is how it is, your Excellency," he said, "and there's no accepting impostors nowadays."

His Excellency made no answer, but rang the bell violently. Our hero took another step forward.

"He is a vile, vicious man, your Excellency," said our hero, beside himself and faint with terror, though he still pointed boldly and resolutely at his unworthy twin, who was fidgeting about near his

Excellency. "I say this is how it is, and I am alluding to a well-known person."

There was a general sensation at Mr. Golyadkin's words. Andrey Filippovitch and the gentleman with the cigar nodded their heads; his Excellency impatiently tugged at the bell to summon the servants. At this point Mr. Golyadkin junior came forward in his turn.

"Your Excellency," he said, "I humbly beg permission to speak." There was something very resolute in Mr. Golyadkin junior's voice; everything showed that he felt himself completely in the right.

"Allow me to ask you," he began again, anticipating his Excellency's reply in his eagerness, and this time addressing Mr. Golyadkin; "allow me to ask you, in whose presence you are making this explanation? Before whom are you standing, in whose room are you? . . ."

Mr. Golyadkin junior was in a state of extraordinary excitement, flushed and glowing with wrath and indignation; there were positively tears in his eyes.

A lackey, appearing in the doorway, roared at the top of his voice the name of some new arrivals, the Bassavryukovs.

"A good aristocratic name, hailing from Little Russia," thought Mr. Golyadkin, and at that moment he felt some one lay a very friendly hand on his back, then a second hand was laid on his back. Mr. Golyadkin's infamous twin was tripping about in front leading the way; and our hero saw clearly that he was being led to the big doors of the room.

"Just as it was at Olsufy Ivanovitch's," he thought, and he found himself in the hall. Looking round, he saw beside him two of his Excellency's lackeys and his twin.

"The greatcoat, the greatcoat, the greatcoat, the greatcoat, my friend! The greatcoat of my best friend!" whispered the depraved man, snatching the coat from one of the servants, and by way of a nasty and ungentlemanly joke flinging it straight at Mr. Golyadkin's head. Extricating himself from under his coat, Mr. Golyadkin distinctly heard the two lackeys snigger. But without listening to anything, or paying attention to it, he went out of the hall and found himself on the lighted stairs. Mr. Golyadkin junior following him.

"Good-bye, your Excellency!" he shouted after Mr. Golyadkin senior.

"Scoundrel!" our hero exclaimed, beside himself.

"Well, scoundrel, then . . ."

"Depraved man! . . ."

"Well, depraved man, then . . ." answered Mr. Golyadkin's unworthy enemy, and with his characteristic baseness he looked down from the top of the stairs straight into Mr. Golyadkin's face as though begging him to go on. Our hero spat with indignation and ran out of the front door; he was so shattered, so crushed, that he had no recollection of how he got into the cab or who helped him in. Coming to himself, he found that he was being driven to Fontanka. "To the Ismailovsky Bridge, then," thought Mr. Golyadkin. At this point, Mr. Golyadkin tried to think of something else, but could not; there was something so terrible that he could not explain it. . . . "Well, never mind," our hero concluded, and he drove to the Ismailovsky Bridge.

Chapter 13

. . . IT SEEMED as though the weather meant to change for the better. The snow, which had till then been coming down in regular clouds, began growing less and less and at last almost ceased. The sky became visible and here and there tiny stars sparkled in it. It was only wet, muddy, damp and stifling, especially for Mr. Golyadkin, who could hardly breathe as it was. His greatcoat, soaked and heavy with wet, sent a sort of unpleasant warm dampness all through him and weighed down his exhausted legs. A feverish shiver sent sharp, shooting pains all over him; he was in a painful cold sweat of exhaustion, so much so that Mr. Golyadkin even forgot to repeat at every suitable occasion with his characteristic firmness and resolution his favourite phrase that "it all, maybe, most likely, indeed, might turn out for the best." "But all this does not matter for the time," our hero repeated, still staunch and not down-hearted, wiping from his face the cold drops that streamed in all directions from the brim of his round hat, which was so soaked that it could hold no more water. Adding that all this was nothing so far, our hero tried to sit on a rather thick clump of wood, which was lying near a heap of logs in Olsufy Ivanovitch's yard. Of course, it was no good thinking of Spanish serenades or silken ladders, but it was quite necessary to think of a modest corner, snug and private, if not altogether warm. He felt greatly tempted, we may mention in passing, by that corner in the back entry of Olsufy Ivanovitch's flat in which he had once, almost at the beginning of this true story, stood for more than two hours between a cupboard and an old screen among all sorts of domestic odds and ends and useless litter. The fact is that Mr. Golyadkin had been standing waiting for two whole hours on this occasion in Olsufy Ivanovitch's yard. But in re-

gard to that modest and snug little corner there were certain drawbacks which had not existed before. The first drawback was the fact
that it was probably now a marked place and that certain precautionary
measures had been taken in regard to it since the scandal at Olsufy
Ivanovitch's last ball. Secondly, he had to wait for a signal from Klara
Olsufyevna, for there was bound to be some such signal, it was always
a feature in such cases and, "it didn't begin with us and it won't end
with us."

At this point Mr. Golyadkin very appropriately remembered a novel
he had read long ago in which the heroine, in precisely similar circumstances, signalled to Alfred by tying a pink ribbon to her window.
But now, at night, in the climate of Petersburg, famous for its dampness and unreliability, a pink ribbon was hardly appropriate and, in
fact, was utterly out of the question.

"No, it's not a matter of silk ladders," thought our hero, "and I had
better stay here quietly and comfortably. . . . I had better stand here."

And he selected a place in the yard exactly opposite the window,
near a stack of firewood. Of course, many persons, grooms and
coachmen, were continually crossing the yard, and there was, besides,
the rumbling of wheels and the snorting of horses and so on; yet it
was a convenient place, whether he was observed or not; but now,
anyway, there was the advantage of being to some extent in shadow,
and no one could see Mr. Golyadkin while he himself could see
everything.

The windows were brightly lit up, there was some sort of ceremonious party at Olsufy Ivanovitch's. But he could hear no music as yet.
"So it's not a ball, but a party of some other sort," thought our hero,
somewhat aghast. "Is it to-day?" floated the doubt through him. "Have
I made a mistake in the date? Perhaps; anything is possible. . . . Yes,
to be sure, anything is possible. . . . Perhaps she wrote a letter to me
yesterday, and it didn't reach me, and perhaps it did not reach me
because Petrushka put his spoke in, the rascal! Or it was to-morrow
in the letter, that is, that I . . . should do everything to-morrow, that
is—wait with a carriage. . . ."

At this point our hero turned cold all over and felt in his pocket
for the letter, to make sure. But to his surprise the letter was not in
his pocket.

"How's this?" muttered Mr. Golyadkin, more dead than alive.
"Where did I leave it? Then I must have lost it. That is the last straw!"
he moaned at last. "Oh, if it falls into evil hands! Perhaps it has
already. Good Lord! What may it not lead to! It may lead to some-

thing such that . . . Ach, my miserable fate!" At this point Mr. Golyadkin began trembling like a leaf at the thought that perhaps his
vicious twin had thrown the greatcoat at him with the object of
stealing the letter of which he had somehow got an inkling from Mr.
Golyadkin's enemies.

"What's more, he's stealing it," thought our hero, "as evidence . . .
but why evidence! . . ."

After the first shock of horror, the blood rushed to Mr. Golyadkin's
head. Moaning and gnashing his teeth, he clutched his burning head,
sank back on his block of wood and relapsed into brooding. . . . But
he could form no coherent thoughts. Figures kept flitting through his
brain, incidents came back to his memory, now vaguely, now distinctly,
the tunes of some foolish songs kept ringing in his ears. . . . He was
in great distress, unnatural distress!

"My God, my God!" our hero thought, recovering himself a little,
and suppressing a muffled sob, "give me fortitude in the immensity of
my afflictions! That I am done for, utterly destroyed—of that there
can be no doubt, and that's all in the natural order of things, since it
cannot be otherwise. To begin with, I've lost my berth, I've certainly
lost it, I must have lost it. . . . Well, supposing things are set right
somehow. Supposing I have money enough to begin with: I must
have another lodging, furniture of some sort. . . . In the first place, I
shan't have Petrushka. I can get on without the rascal . . . somehow,
with help from the people of the house; well, that will be all right!
I can go in and out when I like, and Petrushka won't grumble
at my coming in late—yes, that is so; that's why it's a good thing to
have the people in the house. . . . Well, supposing that's all right; but
all that's nothing to do with it, all that's nothing to do with it."

At this point the thought of the real position again dawned upon Mr.
Golyadkin's memory. He looked round.

"Oh, Lord, have mercy on me, have mercy on me! What am I talking about?" he thought, growing utterly desperate and clutching his
burning head in his hands. . . .

"Won't you soon be going, sir?" a voice pronounced above Mr.
Golyadkin. Our hero started; before him stood his cabman, who was
also drenched through and shivering; growing impatient, and having
nothing to do, he had thought fit to take a look at Mr. Golyadkin
behind the woodstack.

"I am all right, my friend. . . . I am coming soon, soon, very soon;
you wait. . . ."

The cabman walked away, grumbling to himself. "What is he

grumbling about?" Mr. Golyadkin wondered through his tears. "Why, I have hired him for the evening, why, I'm . . . within my rights now . . . that's so! I've hired him for the evening, and that's the end of it. If one stands still, it's just the same. That's for me to decide. I am free to drive on or not to drive on. And my staying here by the woodstack has nothing to do with the case . . . and don't dare to say anything; think, the gentleman wants to stand behind the woodstack, and so he's standing behind it . . . and he is not disgracing any one's honour! That's the fact of the matter.

"I tell you what it is, madame, if you care to know. Nowadays, madame, nobody lives in a hut, or anything of that sort. No, indeed. And in our industrial age there's no getting on without morality, a fact of which you are a fatal example, madame. . . . You say we must get a job as a register clerk and live in a hut on the sea-shore. In the first place, madame, there are no register clerks on the sea-shore, and in the second place we can't get a job as a register clerk. For supposing, for example, I send in a petition, present myself—saying a register clerk's place or something of the sort . . . and defend me from my enemy . . . they'll tell you, madame, they'll say, to be sure . . . we've lots of register clerks, and here you are not at Madame Falbalas', where you learnt the rules of good behaviour of which you are such a fatal example. Good behaviour, madame, means staying at home, honouring your father and not thinking about suitors prematurely. Suitors will come in good time, madame, that's so! Of course, you are bound to have some accomplishments, such as playing the piano sometimes, speaking French, history, geography, scripture and arithmetic, that's the truth of it! And that's all you need. Cooking, too, cooking certainly forms part of the education of a well-behaved girl! But as it is, in the first place, my fine lady, they won't let you go, they'll raise a hue and cry after you, and then they'll lock you up in a nunnery. How will it be then, madame? What will you have me do then? Would you have me, madame, follow the example of some stupid novels, and melt into tears on a neighbouring hillock, gazing at the cold walls of your prison house, and finally die, following the example of some wretched German poets and novelists. Is that it, madame? But, to begin with, allow me to tell you, as a friend, that things are not done like that, and in the second place I would have given you and your parents, too, a good thrashing for letting you read French books; for French books teach you no good. There's a poison in them . . . a pernicious poison, madame! Or do you imagine, allow me to ask you, or do you imagine that we shall elope with impunity, or something of that sort

. . . that we shall have a hut on the shore of the sea and so on; and that we shall begin billing and cooing and talking about our feelings, and that so we shall spend our lives in happiness and content; and then there would be little ones—so then we shall . . . shall go to our father, the civil councillor, Olsufy Ivanovitch, and say, 'we've got a little one, and so, on this propitious occasion remove your curse, and bless the couple.' No, madame, I tell you again, that's not the way to do things, and for the first thing there'll be no billing and cooing, and please don't reckon on it. Nowadays, madame, the husband is the master and a good, well-brought-up wife should try and please him in every way. And endearments, madame, are not in favour, nowadays, in our industrial age; the day of Jean Jacques Rousseau is over. The husband comes home, for instance, hungry from the office, and asks, 'Isn't there something to eat, my love, a drop of vodka to drink, a bit of salt fish to eat?' So then, madame, you must have the vodka and the herring ready. Your husband will eat it with relish, and he won't so much as look at you, he'll only say 'Run into the kitchen, kitten,' he'll say, 'and look after the dinner,' and at most, once a week he'll kiss you, even then rather indifferently. . . . That's how it will be with us, my young lady! Yes, even then, indifferently. . . . That's how it will be, if one considers it, if it has come to one's looking at the thing in that way. . . . And how do I come in? Why have you mixed me up in your caprices? 'The noble man who is suffering for your sake and will be dear to your heart for ever,' and so on. But in the first place, madame, I am not suited to you, you know yourself, I'm not a great hand at compliments, I'm not fond of uttering perfumed trifles for the ladies. I'm not fond of lady-killers, and I must own I've never been a beauty to look at. You won't find any swagger or false shame in me, and I tell you so now in all sincerity. This is the fact of the matter: we can boast of nothing but a straightforward, open character and common sense; we have nothing to do with intrigues. I am not one to intrigue, I say so and I'm proud of it—that's the fact of the matter! . . . I wear no mask among straightforward people, and to tell you the whole truth . . ."

Suddenly Mr. Golyadkin started. The red and perfectly sopping beard of the cabman appeared round the woodstack again. . . .

"I am coming directly, my friend. I'm coming at once, you know," Mr. Golyadkin responded in a trembling and failing voice.

The cabman scratched his head, then stroked his beard, and moved a step forward . . . stood still and looked suspiciously at Mr. Golyadkin.

"I am coming directly, my friend; you see, my friend . . . I . . . just a little, you see, only a second! . . . more . . . here, you see, my friend. . . ."

"Aren't you coming at all?" the cabman asked at last, definitely coming up to Mr. Golyadkin.

"No, my friend, I'm coming directly. I am waiting, you see, my friend. . . ."

"So I see. . . ."

"You see, my friend, I . . . What part of the country do you come from, my friend?"

"We are under a master . . ."

"And have you a good master? . . ."

"All right. . . ."

"Yes, my friend; you stay here, my friend, you see. . . . Have you been in Petersburg long, my friend?"

"It's a year since I came. . . ."

"And are you getting on all right, my friend?"

"Middling."

"To be sure, my friend, to be sure. You must thank Providence, my friend. You must look out for straightforward people. Straightforward people are none too common nowadays, my friend; he would give you washing, food, and drink, my good fellow, a good man would. But sometimes you see tears shed for the sake of gold, my friend . . . you see a lamentable example; that's the fact of the matter, my friend. . . ."

The cabman seemed to feel sorry for Mr. Golyadkin. "Well, your honour, I'll wait. Will your honour be waiting long?"

"No, my friend, no; I . . . you know . . . I won't wait any longer, my good man. . . . What do you think, my friend? I rely upon you. I won't stay any longer."

"Aren't you going at all?"

"No, my friend, no; I'll reward you, my friend . . . that's the fact of the matter. How much ought I to give you, my dear fellow?"

"What you hired me for, please, sir. I've been waiting here a long time; don't be hard on a man, sir."

"Well, here, my good man, here."

At this point Mr. Golyadkin gave six whole roubles to the cabman, and make up his mind in earnest to waste no more time, that is, to clear off straight away, especially as the cabman was dismissed and everything was over, and so it was useless to wait longer. He rushed out of the yard, went out of the gate, turned to the left and without looking round took to his heels, breathless and rejoicing. "Perhaps it will all be for the best," he thought, "and perhaps in this way I've run away from trouble." Mr. Golyadkin suddenly became all at once light-hearted." Oh, if only it could turn out for the best!" thought our hero, though he put little faith in his own words. "I know what I'll do . . ." he thought. "No, I know, I'd better try the other tack. . . . Or wouldn't it be better to do this? . . ." In this way, hesitating and seeking for the solution of his doubts, our hero ran to the Semyonovsky Bridge; but while running to the Semyonovsky Bridge he very rationally and conclusively decided to return.

"It will be better so," he thought. "I had better try the other tack, that is . . . I will just go—I'll look on simply as an outsider, and that will be the end of it; I am simply an onlooker, an outsider—and noth-ing more, whatever happens—it's not my fault, that's the fact of the matter! That's how it shall be now."

Deciding to return, our hero actually did return, the more readily because with this happy thought he conceived of himself now as quite an outsider.

"It's the best thing; one's not responsible for anything, and one will see all that's necessary . . . that's the fact of the matter!"

It was a safe plan and that settled it. Reassured, he crept back under the peaceful shelter of his soothing and protecting woodstack, and began gazing intently at the window. This time he was not destined to gaze and wait for long. Suddenly a strange commotion became apparent at all the windows. Figures appeared, curtains were drawn back, whole groups of people were crowding to the windows at Olsufy Ivanovitch's flat. All were peeping out looking for something in the yard. From the security of his woodstack, our hero, too, began with curiosity watching the general commotion, and with interest craned forward to right and to left so far as he could within the shadow of the woodstack. Suddenly he started, held his breath and almost sat down with horror. It seemed to him—in short, he realized, that they were looking for nothing and for nobody but him, Mr. Golyadkin! Every one was looking in his direction. It was impossible to escape; they saw him. . . . In a flutter, Mr. Golyadkin huddled as closely as he could to the woodstack, and only then noticed that the treacherous shadow had betrayed him, that it did not cover him completely. Our hero would have been delighted at that moment to creep into a mouse-hole in the woodstack, and there meekly to remain, if only it had been possible. But it was absolutely impossible. In his agony he began at last staring openly and boldly at the windows, it was the best thing to do. . . . And suddenly he glowed with shame. He had been fully discovered, every one was staring at him at once, they were all waving their hands, all were nodding their heads at him, all were calling to him; then several windows creaked as they opened, several voices shouted something to him at once. . . .

"I wonder why they don't whip these naughty girls as children," our hero muttered to himself, losing his head completely. Suddenly there ran down the steps *he* (we know who), without his hat or great-coat, breathless, rubbing his hands, wriggling, capering, perfidiously displaying intense joy at seeing Mr. Golyadkin.

"Yakov Petrovitch," whispered this individual, so notorious for his worthlessness, "Yakov Petrovitch, are you here? You'll catch cold. It's chilly here, Yakov Petrovitch. Come indoors."

"Yakov Petrovitch! No, I'm all right, Yakov Petrovitch," our hero muttered in a submissive voice.

"No, this won't do, Yakov Petrovitch, I beg you, I humbly beg you to wait with us. 'Make him welcome and bring him in,' they say, 'Yakov Petrovitch.' "

"No, Yakov Petrovitch, you see, I'd better . . . I had better go home, Yakov Petrovitch . . ." said our hero, burning at a slow fire and freezing at the same time with shame and terror.

"No—no—no—no!" whispered the loathsome person. "No—no—no, on no account! Come along," he said resolutely, and he dragged Mr. Golyadkin senior to the steps. Mr. Golyadkin senior did not at all want to go, but as every one was looking at them, it would have been stupid to struggle and resist; so our hero went—though, indeed, one cannot say that he went, because he did not know in the least what was being done with him. Though, after all, it made no difference!

Before our hero had time to recover himself and come to his senses, he found himself in the drawing-room. He was pale, dishevelled, harassed; with lustreless eyes he scanned the crowd—horror! The drawing-room, all the rooms, were full to overflowing. There were masses of people, a whole galaxy of ladies; and all were crowding round Mr. Golyadkin, all were pressing towards Mr. Golyadkin, all were squeezing Mr. Golyadkin and he perceived clearly that they were all forcing him in one direction.

"Not towards the door," was the thought that floated through Mr. Golyadkin's mind.

They were, in fact, forcing him not towards the door but Olsufy Ivanovitch's easy-chair. On one side of the arm-chair stood Klara Olsufyevna, pale, languid, melancholy, but gorgeously dressed. Mr. Golyadkin was particularly struck by a little white flower which rested on her superb hair. On the other side of the arm-chair stood Vladimir Semyonovitch, clad in black, with his new order in his buttonhole. Mr. Golyadkin was led in, as we have described above, straight up to Olsufy Ivanovitch—on one side of him Mr. Golyadkin junior, who had assumed an air of great decorum and propriety, to the immense relief of our hero, while on the other side was Andrey Filippovitch, with a very solemn expression on his face.

"What can it mean?" Mr. Golyadkin wondered.

When he saw that he was being led to Olsufy Ivanovitch, an idea struck him like a flash of lightning. The thought of the intercepted letter darted through his brain. In great agony our hero stood before Olsufy Ivanovitch's chair.

"What will he say now?" he wondered to himself. "Of course, it will be all aboveboard now, that is, straightforward and, one may say, honourable; I shall say this is how it is, and so on."

But what our hero apparently feared did not happen. Olsufy Ivanovitch received Mr. Golyadkin very warmly, and though he did not hold out his hand to him, yet as he gazed at our hero, he shook his grey and venerable head—shook it with an air of solemn melancholy and yet of good-will. So, at least, it seemed to Mr. Golyadkin. He even fancied that a tear glittered in Olsufy Ivanovitch's lustreless eyes; he raised his eyes and saw that there seemed to be tears, too, on the eyelashes of Klara Olsufyevna, who was standing by—that there seemed to be something of the same sort even in the eyes of Vladimir Semyonovitch—that the unruffled and composed dignity of Andrey Filippovitch had the same significance as the general tearful sympathy—that even the young man who was so much like a civil councillor, seizing the opportunity, was sobbing bitterly. . . . Though perhaps this was only all Mr. Golyadkin's fancy, because he was so much moved himself, and distinctly felt the hot tears running down his cold cheeks. . . .

Feeling reconciled with mankind and his destiny, and filled with love at the moment, not only for Olsufy Ivanovitch, not only for the whole party collected there, but even for his noxious twin (who seemed now to be by no means noxious, and not even to be his twin at all, but a person very agreeable in himself and in no way connected with him), our hero, in a voice broken with sobs, tried to express his feelings to Olsufy Ivanovitch, but was too much overcome by all that he had gone through, and could not utter a word; he could only, with an expressive gesture, point meekly to his heart. . . .

At last, probably to spare the feelings of the old man, Andrey Filippovitch led Mr. Golyadkin a little away, though he seemed to leave him free to do as he liked. Smiling, muttering something to himself, somewhat bewildered, yet almost completely reconciled with fate and his fellow-creatures, our hero began to make his way through the crowd of guests. Every one made way for him, every one looked at him with strange curiosity and with mysterious, unaccountable sympathy. Our hero went into another room; he met with the same attention everywhere; he was vaguely conscious of the whole crowd closely following him, noting every step he took, talking in undertones among themselves of something very interesting, shaking their heads, arguing and discussing in whispers. Mr. Golyadkin wanted very much to know what they were discussing in whispers. Looking round, he saw near him Mr. Golyadkin junior. Feeling an overwhelming impulse to seize his hand and draw him aside, Mr. Golyadkin begged the other Yakov Petrovitch most particularly to co-operate with him in all his future undertakings, and not to abandon him at a critical moment. Mr. Golyadkin junior nodded his head gravely and warmly pressed the hand of Mr. Golyadkin senior. Our hero's heart was quivering with the intensity of his emotion. He was gasping for breath, however; he felt so oppressed—so oppressed; he felt that all those eyes fastened upon him were oppressing and dominating him. . . . Mr. Golyadkin caught a glimpse of the councillor who wore a wig. The latter was looking at him with a stern, searching eye, not in the least softened by the general sympathy. . . .

Our hero made up his mind to go straight up to him in order to smile at him and have an immediate explanation, but this somehow did not come off. For one instant Mr. Golyadkin became almost unconscious, almost lost all memory, all feeling.

When he came to himself again he noticed that he was the centre of a large ring formed by the rest of the party round him. Suddenly Mr. Golyadkin's name was called from the other room; the shout was at once taken up by the whole crowd. All was noise and excitement, all rushed to the door of the first room, almost carrying our hero along with them. In the crush the hard-hearted councillor in the wig was side by side with Mr. Golyadkin, and, taking our hero by the hand, he made him sit down beside him opposite Olsufy Ivanovitch, at some distance from the latter, however. Every one in the room sat down; the guests were arranged in rows round Mr. Golyadkin and Olsufy Ivanovitch. Everything was hushed; every one preserved a solemn silence; every one was watching Olsufy Ivanovitch, evidently expecting something out of the ordinary. Mr. Golyadkin noticed that beside Olsufy Ivanovitch's chair and directly facing the councillor sat Mr. Golyadkin junior, with Andrey Filippovitch. The silence was prolonged; they were evidently expecting something.

"Just as it is in a family when some one is setting off on a far journey. We've only to stand up and pray now," thought our hero.

Suddenly there was a general stir which interrupted Mr. Golyadkin's reflections. Something they had long been waiting for happened.

"He is coming, he is coming!" passed from one to another in the crowd.

"Who is it that is coming?" floated through Mr. Golyadkin's mind, and he shuddered at a strange sensation. "High time too!" said the councillor, looking intently at Andrey Filippovitch. Andrey Filippovitch, for his part, glanced at Olsufy Ivanovitch. Olsufy Ivanovitch gravely and solemnly nodded his head.

"Let us stand up," said the councillor, and he made Mr. Golyadkin get up. All rose to their feet. Then the councillor took Mr. Golyadkin senior by the hand, and Andrey Filippovitch took Mr. Golyadkin junior, and in this way these two precisely similar persons were conducted through the expectant crowd surrounding them. Our hero looked about him in perplexity; but he was at once checked and his attention was called to Mr. Golyadkin junior, who was holding out his hand to him.

"They want to reconcile us," thought our hero, and with emotion he held out his hand to Mr. Golyadkin junior; and then—then bent his head forward towards him. The other Mr. Golyadkin did the same. . . .

At this point it seemed to Mr. Golyadkin senior that his perfidious friend was smiling, that he gave a sly, hurried wink to the crowd of onlookers, and that there was something sinister in the face of the worthless Mr. Golyadkin junior, that he even made a grimace at the moment of his Judas kiss. . . .

There was a ringing in Mr. Golyadkin's ears, and a darkness before his eyes; it seemed to him that an infinite multitude, an unending series of precisely similar Golyadkins were noisily bursting in at every door of the room; but it was too late . . . the resounding, treacherous kiss was over, and . . .

Then quite an unexpected event occurred. . . . The door opened noisily, and in the doorway stood a man, the very sight of whom sent a chill to Mr. Golyadkin's heart. He stood rooted to the spot. A cry of horror died away in his choking throat. Yet Mr. Golyadkin knew it all beforehand, and had had a presentiment of something of the sort for a long time. The new arrival went up to Mr. Golyadkin gravely and solemnly. Mr. Golyadkin knew this personage very well. He had seen him before, had seen him very often, had seen him that day. . . . This personage was a tall, thick-set man in a black dress-coat with a good-sized cross on his breast, and was possesed of thick, very black whiskers; nothing was lacking but the cigar in the mouth to complete the picture. Yet this person's eyes, as we have mentioned already, sent a chill to the heart of Mr. Golyadkin. With a grave and solemn air this terrible man approached the pitiable hero of our story. . . . Our hero held out his hand to him; the stranger took his hand and drew him along with him. . . . With a crushed and desperate air our hero looked about him.

"It's . . . it's Krestyan Ivanovitch Rutenspitz, doctor of medicine and surgery; your old acquaintance, Yakov Petrovitch!" a detestable voice whispered in Mr. Golyadkin's ear. He looked round: it was Mr. Golyadkin's twin, so revolting in the despicable meanness of his soul. A malicious, indecent joy shone in his countenance; he was rubbing his hands with rapture, he was turning his head from side to side in ecstasy, he was fawning round every one in delight and seemed ready to dance with glee. At last he pranced forward, took a candle from one of the servants and walked in front, showing the way to Mr. Golyadkin and Krestyan Ivanovitch. Mr. Golyadkin heard the whole party in the drawing-room rush out after him, crowding and squeezing one another, and all beginning to repeat after Mr. Golyadkin himself, "It is all right, don't be afraid, Yakov Petrovitch; this is your old friend and acquaintance, you know, Krestyan Ivanovitch Rutenspitz. . . ."

At last they came out on the brightly lighted stairs; there was a crowd of people on the stairs too. The front door was thrown open noisily, and Mr. Golyadkin found himself on the steps, together with Krestyan Ivanovitch. At the entrance stood a carriage with four horses that were snorting with impatience. The malignant Mr. Golyadkin junior in three bounds flew down the stairs and opened the carriage door himself. Krestyan Ivanovitch, with an impressive gesture, asked Mr. Golyadkin to get in. There was no need of the impressive gesture, however; there were plenty of people to help him in. . . . Faint with horror, Mr. Golyadkin looked back. The whole of the brightly lighted staircase was crowded with people; inquisitive eyes were looking at him from all sides; Olsufy Ivanovitch himself was sitting in his easy-chair on the top landing, and watching all that took place with deep interest. Every one was waiting. A murmur of impatience passed through the crowd when Mr. Golyadkin looked back.

"I hope I have done nothing . . . nothing reprehensible . . . or that can call for severity . . . and general attention in regard to my official relations," our hero brought out in desperation. A clamour of talk rose all round him, all were shaking their heads, tears started from Mr. Golyadkin's eyes.

"In that case I'm ready. . . . I have full confidence . . . and I entrust my fate to Krestyan Ivanovitch. . . ."

No sooner had Mr. Golyadkin declared that he entrusted his fate to Krestyan Ivanovitch than a dreadful, deafening shout of joy came from all surrounding him and was repeated in a sinister echo through the whole of the waiting crowd. Then Krestyan Ivanovitch on one side and Andrey Filippovitch on the other helped Mr. Golyadkin into the carriage; his double, in his usual nasty way, was helping to get him in from behind. The unhappy Mr. Golyadkin senior took his last look on all and everything, and, shivering like a kitten that has been drenched with cold water—if the comparison may be permitted—got into the carriage. Krestyan Ivanovitch followed him in immediately. The carriage door slammed. There was a swish of the whip on the horses' backs . . . the horses started off. . . . The crowd dashed after Mr. Golyadkin. The shrill, furious shouts of his enemies pursued him by way of good wishes for his journey. For some time several persons were still running by the carriage that bore away Mr. Golyadkin; but by degrees they were left behind, till at last they had all disappeared. Mr. Golyadkin's unworthy twin kept up longer than any one. With his hands in the trouser pockets of his green uniform he ran on with a satisfied air, skipping first to one and then to the other side of the carriage, sometimes catching hold of the window-frame and hanging on by it, poking his head in at the window, and throwing farewell kisses to Mr. Golyadkin. But he began to get tired, he was less and less often to be seen, and at last vanished altogether. There was a dull ache in Mr. Golyadkin's heart; a hot rush of blood set Mr. Golyadkin's head throbbing; he felt stifled, he longed to unbutton himself—to bare his breast, to cover it with snow and pour cold water on it. He sank at last into forgetfulness. . . .

When he came to himself, he saw that the horses were taking him along an unfamiliar road. There were dark patches of copse on each side of it; it was desolate and deserted. Suddenly he almost swooned; two fiery eyes were staring at him in the darkness, and those two eyes were glittering with malignant, hellish glee. "That's not Krestyan Ivanovitch! Who is it? Or is it he? It is. It is Krestyan Ivanovitch, but not the old Krestyan Ivanovitch, it's another Krestyan Ivanovitch! It's a terrible Krestyan Ivanovitch!" . . .

"Krestyan Ivanovitch, I . . . I believe . . . I'm all right, Krestyan Ivanovitch," our hero was beginning timidly in a trembling voice, hoping by his meekness and submission to soften the terrible Krestyan Ivanovitch a little.

"You get free quarters, wood, with light, and service, the which you deserve not," Krestyan Ivanovitch's answer rang out, stern and terrible as a judge's sentence.

Our hero shrieked and clutched his head in his hands. Alas! For a long while he had been haunted by a presentiment of this.

The Friend
of the Family

THE FRIEND
OF THE FAMILY

Part 1

[1]

INTRODUCTION

—◆—

WHEN my uncle, Colonel Yegor Ilyitch Rostanev, left the army, he settled down in Stepantchikovo, which came to him by inheritance, and went on steadily living in it, as though he had been all his life a regular country gentleman who had never left his estates. There are natures that are perfectly satisfied with every one and can get used to everything; such was precisely the disposition of the retired colonel. It is hard to imagine a man more peaceable and ready to agree to anything. If by some caprice he had been gravely asked to carry some one for a couple of miles on his shoulders he would perhaps have done so. He was so good-natured that he was sometimes ready to give away everything at the first asking, and to share almost his last shirt with any one who coveted it. He was of heroic proportions; tall and well made, with ruddy cheeks, with teeth white as ivory, with a long brown moustache, with a loud ringing voice, and with a frank hearty laugh; he spoke rapidly and jerkily. He was at the time of my story about forty, and had spent his life almost from his sixteenth year in the Hussars. He had married very young and was passionately fond of his wife; but she died, leaving in his heart a noble memory that nothing could efface.

When he inherited Stepantchikovo, which increased his fortune to six hundred serfs, he left the army, and, as I have said already, settled in the country together with his children, Ilyusha a boy of eight, whose birth had cost his mother her life, and Sashenka a girl of fifteen, who had been brought up at a boarding-school in Moscow. But my uncle's house soon became a regular Noah's Ark. This was how it happened.

Just at the time when he came into the property and retired from the army, his mother, who had, sixteen years before, married a certain General Krahotkin, was left a widow. At the time of her second marriage my uncle was only a cornet, and yet he, too, was thinking of getting married. His mother had for a long time refused her blessing, had shed bitter tears, had reproached him with egoism, with ingratitude, with disrespect. She had proved to him that his estates amounting to only two hundred and fifty serfs, were, as it was, barely sufficient for the maintenance of his family (that is, for the maintenance of his mamma, with all her retinue of toadies, pug-dogs, Pomeranians, Chinese cats and so on). And, in the midst of these reproaches, protests and shrill upbraidings, she all at once quite unexpectedly got married herself before her son, though she was forty-two years of age. Even in this, however, she found an excuse for blaming my poor uncle, declaring that she was getting married solely to secure in her old age the refuge denied her by the undutiful egoist, her son, who was contemplating the unpardonable insolence of making a home of his own.

I never could find out what really induced a man apparently so reasonable as the deceased General Krahotkin to marry a widow of forty-two. It must be supposed that he suspected she had money. Other people thought that he only wanted a nurse, as he had already had a foretaste of the swarm of diseases which assailed him in his old age. One thing is certain, the general never had the faintest respect for his wife at any time during his married life, and he ridiculed her sarcastically at every favourable opportunity. He was a strange person. Half educated and extremely shrewd, he had a lively contempt for all and every one; he had no principles of any sort; laughed at everything and everybody, and in his old age, through the infirmities that were the consequence of his irregular and immoral life, he became spiteful, irritable and merciless. He had been a successful officer; yet he had been forced, through "an unpleasant incident," to resign his commission, losing his pension and only just escaping prosecution. This had completely soured his temper. Left almost without means, with no fortune but a hundred ruined serfs, he folded his hands and never during the remaining twelve years of his life troubled himself to inquire what he was living on and who was supporting him. At the same time he insisted on having all the comforts of life, kept his carriage and refused to curtail his expenses. Soon after his marriage he lost the use of his legs and spent the last ten years of his life in an invalid-chair wheeled about by two seven-foot flunkeys, who never heard anything from him but abuse of the most varied kind. The carriage, the flunkeys and the invalid-chair were paid for by the undutiful son, who sent his mother his last farthing, mortgaged and re-mortgaged his estate, denied himself necessaries, and incurred debts almost impossible for him to pay in his circumstances at the time; and yet the charge of being an egoist and an undutiful son was persistently laid at his door. But my uncle's character was such that at last he quite believed himself that he was an egoist, and therefore to punish himself and to avoid being an egoist, he kept sending them more and more money. His mother stood in awe of her husband; but what pleased her most was that he was a general, and that through him she was "Madame la Générale."

She had her own apartments in the house, where, during the whole period of her husband's semi-existence, she queened it in a society made up of toadies, lapdogs, and the gossips of the town. She was an important person in her little town. Gossip, invitations to stand godmother at christenings and to give the bride away at weddings, a halfpenny rubber, and the respect shown her in all sorts of ways as the wife of a general, fully made up to her for the drawbacks of her home life. All the magpies of the town came to her with their reports, the first place everywhere was always hers—in fact, she got out of her position all she could get out of it. The general did not meddle in all that; but before people he laughed mercilessly at his wife, asked himself, for instance, such questions as why he had married "such a dowdy," and nobody dared contradict him. Little by little all his acquaintances left him, and at the same time society was essential to him; he loved chatting, arguing; he liked to have a listener always sitting beside him. He was a free-thinker and atheist of the old school, and so liked to hold forth on lofty subjects.

But the listeners of the town of N—— had no partiality for lofty subjects, and they became fewer and fewer. They tried to get up a game of whist in the household; but as a rule the game ended in outbreaks on the part of the general, which so terrified his wife and her companions that they put up candles before the ikons, had a service sung, divined the future with beans and with cards, distributed rolls among the prisoners, and looked forward in a tremor to the after-dinner hour when they would have to take a hand at whist again and at every mistake to endure shouts, screams, oaths and almost blows. The general did not stand on ceremony with anybody when something was not to his taste; he screamed like a peasant woman, swore like a coachman, sometimes tore up the cards, threw them about the floor, drove away his partners, and even shed tears of anger and vexation— and for no more than a knave's having been played instead of a nine. At last, as his eyesight was failing, they had to get him a reader; it was then that Foma Fomitch Opiskin appeared upon the scene.

I must confess I announce this new personage with a certain solemnity. There is no denying that he is one of the principal characters in my story. How far he has a claim on the attention of the reader I will not explain; the reader can answer that question more suitably and more readily himself.

Foma Fomitch entered General Krahotkin's household as a paid companion—neither more nor less. Where he turned up from is shrouded in the mists of obscurity. I have, however, made special researches and have found out something of the past circumstances of this remarkable man. He was said in the first place to have been sometime and somewhere in the government service, and somewhere or other to have suffered, I need hardly say, "for a good cause." It was said, too, that at some time he had been engaged in literary pursuits in Moscow. There is nothing surprising in that; Foma Fomitch's crass ignorance would, of course, be no hindrance to him in a literary career. But all that is known for certain is that he did not succeed in anything, and that at last he was forced to enter the general's service in the capacity of reader and martyr. There was no ignominy which he had not to endure in return for eating the general's bread. It is true that in later years, when on the general's death he found himself a person of importance and consequence, he more than once assured us all that his consenting to be treated as a buffoon was an act of magnanimous self-sacrifice on the altar of friendship; that the general had been his benefactor; that the deceased had been a great man misunderstood, who only to him, Foma, had confided the inmost secrets of his soul; that in fact, if he, Foma, had actually at the general's urgent desire played the part of various wild beasts and posed in grotesque attitudes, this had been solely in order to entertain and distract a suffering friend shattered by disease. But Foma Fomitch's assurances and explanations on this score can only be accepted with considerable hesitation; and yet this same Foma Fomitch, even at the time when he was a buffoon, was playing a very different part in the ladies' apartments of the general's house. How he managed this, it is difficult for any one not a specialist in such matters to conceive. The general's lady cherished a sort of mysterious reverence for him—why? There is no telling. By degrees he acquired over the whole feminine half of the general's household a marvellous influence, to some extent comparable to the influence exercised by the Ivan Yakovlevitches and such-like seers and prophets, who are visited in madhouses by certain ladies, who devote themselves to the study of their ravings. He read aloud to them works of spiritual edification; held forth with eloquent tears on the Christian virtues; told stories of his life and his heroic doings; went to mass, and even to matins; at times foretold the future; had a peculiar faculty for interpreting dreams, and was a great hand at throwing blame on his neighbours. The general had a notion of what was going on in the back rooms, and tyrannized over his dependent more mercilessly than ever. But Foma's martyrdom only increased his prestige in the eyes of Madame la Générale and the other females of the household.

At last everything was transformed. The general died. His death was rather original. The former free-thinker and atheist became terror-stricken beyond all belief. He shed tears, repented, had ikons put up, sent for priests. Services were sung, and extreme unction was administered. The poor fellow screamed that he did not want to die, and even asked Foma Fomitch's forgiveness with tears. This latter circumstance was an asset of some value to Foma Fomitch later on. Just before the parting of the general's soul from the general's body, however, the following incident took place. The daughter of Madame la Générale by her first marriage, my maiden aunt, Praskovya Ilyinitchna, who always lived in the general's house, and was one of his favourite victims, quite indispensable to him during the ten years that he was bedridden, always at his beck and call, and with her meek and simple-hearted mildness the one person who could satisfy him, went up to his bedside shedding bitter tears, and would have smoothed the pillow under the head of the sufferer; but the sufferer still had strength to clutch at her hair and pull it violently three times, almost foaming at the mouth with spite. Ten minutes later he died. They had sent word to the colonel, though Madame la Générale had declared that she did not want to see him and would sooner die than set eyes on him at such a moment. There was a magnificent funeral at the expense, of course, of the undutiful son on whom the widowed mother did not wish to set her eyes.

In the ruined property of Knyazevka, which belonged to several different owners and in which the general had his hundred serfs, there stands a mausoleum of white marble, diversified with laudatory inscriptions to the glory of the intellect, talents, nobility of soul, orders of merit and rank of the deceased. Foma Fomitch took a prominent part in the composition of these eulogies. Madame la Générale persisted for a long time in keeping up her dignity and refusing to forgive her disobedient son. Sobbing and making a great outcry, surrounded by her crowd of toadies and pug-dogs, she kept declaring that she would sooner live on dry bread and I need hardly say "soak it in her tears," that she would sooner go stick in hand to beg alms under the windows than yield to the request of her "disobedient" son that she should come and live with him at Stepantchikovo, and that she would never, never set foot within his house! As a rule the word foot in this connection is uttered with peculiar effect by ladies. Madame la Générale's utterance of the word was masterly, artistic. . . . In short, the amount of eloquence that was expended was incredible. It must be observed that at the very time of these shrill protests, they were by degrees packing up to move to Stepantchikovo. The colonel knocked up all his horses driving almost every day thirty miles from Stepantchikovo to the town, and it was not till a fortnight after the general's funeral that he received permission to appear before the eyes of his aggrieved parent. Foma Fomitch was employed as go-between. During the whole of that fortnight he was reproaching the disobedient son and putting him to shame for his "inhuman" conduct, reducing him to genuine tears, almost to despair. It is from this time that the incomprehensible, inhumanly despotic domination of Foma Fomitch over my poor uncle dates. Foma perceived the kind of man he had to deal with, and felt at once that his days of playing the buffoon were over, and that in the wilds even Foma might pass for a nobleman. And he certainly made up for lost time.

"What will you feel like," said Foma, "if your own mother, the authoress, so to speak, of your days, should take a stick and leaning on it with trembling hands wasted with hunger, should actually begin to beg for alms under people's windows? Would it not be monstrous, considering her rank as a general's lady and the virtues of her character? What would you feel like if she should suddenly come, by mistake, of course—but you know it might happen—and should stretch out her hand under your windows, while you, her own son, are perhaps at that very moment nestling in a feather-bed, and . . . in fact, in luxury? It's awful, awful! But what is most awful of all—allow me to speak candidly, Colonel—what is most awful of all is the fact that you are standing before me now like an unfeeling post, with your mouth open and your eyes blinking, so that it is a positive disgrace, while you ought to be ready at the mere thought of such a thing to tear your hair out by the roots and to shed streams—what am I saying?—rivers, lakes, seas, oceans of tears. . . ."

In short, Foma in his excessive warmth grew almost incoherent. But such was the invariable outcome of his eloquence. It ended of course, in Madame la Générale together with her female dependents and lapdogs, with Foma Fomitch and with Mademoiselle Perepelitsyn, her chief favourite, at last honouring Stepantchikovo by her presence. She said that she would merely make the *experiment* of living at her son's till she had tested his dutifulness. You can imagine the colonel's position while his dutifulness was being tested! At first, as a widow recently bereaved, Madame la Générale thought it her duty two or three times a week to be overcome by despair at the thought of her general, never to return; and punctually on each occasion the colonel for some unknown reason came in for a wigging. Sometimes, especially if visitors were present, Madame la Générale would send for her grandchildren, little Ilyusha and fifteen-year-old Sashenka, and making them sit down beside her would fix upon them a prolonged, melancholy, anguished gaze, as upon children, ruined in the hands of *such a father;* she would heave deep, painful sighs, and finally melt into mute mysterious tears, for at least a full hour. Woe betide the colonel if he failed to grasp the significance of those tears! And, poor fellow, he hardly ever succeeded in grasping their significance, and in the simplicity of his heart almost always put in an appearance at such tearful moments, and whether he liked it or not came in for a severe heckling. But his filial respect in no way decreased and reached at last an extreme limit. In short, both Madame la Générale and Foma Fomitch were fully conscious that the storm which had for so many years menaced them in the presence of General Krahotkin had passed away and would never return. Madame la Générale used at times to fall on her sofa in a swoon. A great fuss and commotion arose. The colonel was crushed, and trembled like a leaf.

"Cruel son!" Madame la Générale would shriek as she came to. "You have lacerated my inmost being . . . *mes entrailles, mes entrailles!"*

"But how have I lacerated your inmost being, Mamma?" the colonel would protest timidly.

"You have lacerated it, lacerated it! He justifies himself, too. He is rude. Cruel son! I am dying! . . ."

The colonel was, of course, annihilated. But it somehow happened that Madame la Générale always revived again. Half an hour later he would be taking some one by the button-hole and saying—

"Oh, well, my dear fellow, you see she is a *grande dame,* the wife of a general. She is the kindest-hearted old lady; she is accustomed to all this refined . . . She is on a different level from a blockhead like me!

Now she is angry with me. No doubt I am to blame. My dear fellow, I don't know yet what I've done, but no doubt it's my fault. . . ."

It would happen that Mademoiselle Perepelitsyn, an old maid in a shawl, with no eyebrows, with little rapacious eyes, with lips thin as a thread, with hands washed in cucumber water, and with a spite against the whole universe, would feel it her duty to read the colonel a lecture.

"It's all through your being undutiful, sir; it's all through your being an egoist, sir; through your wounding your mamma, sir—she's not used to such treatment. She's a general's lady, and you are only a colonel, sir."

"That is Mademoiselle Perepelitsyn, my dear fellow," the colonel would observe to his listener; "an excellent lady, she stands up for my mother like a rock! A very rare person! You mustn't imagine that she is in a menial position; she is the daughter of a major herself! Yes, indeed."

But, of course, this was only the prelude. The great lady who could carry out such a variety of performances in her turn trembled like a mouse in the presence of her former dependent. Foma Fomitch had completely bewitched her. She could not make enough of him and she saw with his eyes and heard with his ears. A cousin of mine, also a retired hussar, a man still young, though he had been an incredible spendthrift, told me bluntly and simply that it was his firm conviction, after staying for a time at my uncle's, that Madame la Générale was on terms of improper intimacy with Foma Fomitch. I need hardly say that at the time I rejected this supposition with indignation as too coarse and simple. No, it was something different, and that something different I cannot explain without first explaining to the reader the character of Foma Fomitch as I understood it later.

Imagine the most insignificant, the most cowardly creature, an outcast from society, of no service to any one, utterly useless, utterly disgusting, but incredibly vain, though entirely destitute of any talent by which he might have justified his morbidly sensitive vanity. I hasten to add that Foma Fomitch was the incarnation of unbounded vanity, but that at the same time it was a special kind of vanity—that is, the vanity found in a complete nonentity, and, as is usual in such cases, a vanity mortified and oppressed by grievous failures in the past; a vanity that has begun rankling long, long ago, and ever since has given off envy and venom, at every encounter, at every success of any one else. I need hardly say that all this was seasoned with the most unseemly touchiness, the most insane suspiciousness. It may be asked, how is one to account for such vanity? How does it arise, in spite of complete insignificance, in pitiful creatures who are forced by their social position to know their place? How answer such a question? Who knows, perhaps, there are exceptions, of whom my hero is one? He certainly is an exception to the rule, as will be explained later. But allow me to ask: are you certain that those who are completely re-signed to be your buffoons, your parasites and your toadies, and consider it an honour and a happiness to be so, are you certain that they are quite devoid of vanity and envy? What of the slander and back-biting and tale-bearing and mysterious whisperings in back corners, somewhere aside and at your table? Who knows, perhaps, in some of these degraded victims of fate, your fools and buffoons, vanity far from being dispelled by humiliation is even aggravated by that very humiliation, by being a fool and buffoon, by eating the bread of dependence and being for ever forced to submission and self-suppres-sion. Who knows, maybe, this ugly exaggerated vanity is only a false fundamentally depraved sense of personal dignity, first outraged, perhaps, in childhood by oppression, poverty, filth, spat upon, perhaps, in the person of the future outcast's parents before his eyes. But I have said that Foma Fomitch was also an exception to the general rule; that is true. He had at one time been a literary man slighted and unrecognized, and literature is capable of ruining men very dif-ferent from Foma Fomitch—I mean, of course, when it is not crowned with success. I don't know, but it may be assumed that Foma Fomitch had been unsuccessful before entering on a literary career; possibly in some other calling, too, he had received more kicks than halfpence, or possibly something worse. About that, however, I cannot say; but I made inquiries later on, and I know for certain that Foma Fomitch composed, at some time in Moscow, a romance very much like those that were published every year by dozens in the 'thirties, after the style of *The Deliverance of Moscow, The Chieftains of the Tempest, Sons of Love, or the Russians in 1104*—novels which in their day afforded an agreeable butt for the wit of Baron Brambeus. That was, of course, long ago; but the serpent of literary vanity sometimes leaves a deep and incurable sting, especially in insignificant and dull-witted persons. Foma Fomitch had been disappointed from his first step in a literary career, and it was then that he was finally enrolled in the vast army of the disappointed, from which all the crazy saints, hermits and wandering pilgrims come later on. I think that his monstrous boastfulness, his thirst for praise and distinction, for admiration and homage, dates from the same period. Even when he was a buffoon he got together a group of idiots to do homage to him. Somewhere and somehow to stand first, to be an oracle, to swagger and give himself airs—that was his most urgent craving! As others did not praise him he began to praise himself. I have myself in my uncle's house at Stepantchikovo heard Foma's sayings after he had become the absolute monarch and oracle of the household. "I am not in my proper place among you," he would say sometimes with mysterious impressiveness. "I am not in my proper place here. I will look round, I will settle you all, I will show you, I will direct you, and then good-bye; to Moscow to edit a review! Thirty thousand people will assemble every month to hear my lectures. My name will be famous at last, and then—woe to my enemies."

But while waiting to become famous the genius insisted upon immediate recognition in substantial form. It is always pleasant to receive payment in advance, and in this case it was particularly so. I know that he seriously assured my uncle that some great work lay before him, Foma, in the future—a work for which he had been summoned into the world, and to the accomplishment of this work he was urged by some sort of person with wings, who visited him at night, or something of that kind. This great work was to write a book full of profound wisdom in the soul-saving line, which would set the whole world agog and stagger all Russia. And when all Russia was staggered, he, Foma, disdaining glory, would retire into a monastery, and in the catacombs of Kiev would pray day and night for the happiness of the Fatherland. All this imposed upon my uncle.

Well, now imagine what this Foma, who had been all his life oppressed and crushed, perhaps actually beaten too, who was vain and secretly lascivious, who had been disappointed in his literary ambitions, who had played the buffoon for a crust of bread, who was at heart a despot in spite of all his previous abjectness and impotence, who was a braggart, and insolent when successful, might become when he suddenly found himself in the haven he had reached after so many ups and downs, honoured and glorified, humoured and flattered, thanks to a patroness who was an idiot and a patron who was imposed upon and ready to agree to anything. I must, of course, explain my uncle's character more fully, or Foma Fomitch's success cannot be understood. But for the moment I will say that Foma was a complete illustration of the saying, "Let him sit down to the table and he will put his feet on it." He paid us out for his past! A base soul escaping from oppression becomes an oppressor. Foma had been oppressed, and he had at once a craving to oppress others; he had been the victim of whims and caprices and now he imposed his own whims and caprices on others. He had been the butt of others, and now he surrounded himself with creatures whom he could turn into derision. His boasting was ridiculous; the airs he gave himself were incredible; nothing was good enough for him; his tyranny was beyond all bounds, and it reached such a pitch that simple-hearted people who had not witnessed his manoeuvres, but only heard queer stories about him, looked upon all this as a miracle, as the work of the devil, crossed themselves and spat.

I was speaking of my uncle. Without explaining his remarkable character (I repeat) it is, of course, impossible to understand Foma Fomitch's insolent domination in another man's house; it is impossible to understand the metamorphosis of the cringing dependent into the great man. Besides being kind-hearted in the extreme, my uncle was a man of the most refined delicacy in spite of a somewhat rough exterior, of the greatest generosity and of proved courage. I boldly say of "courage"; nothing could have prevented him from fulfilling an obligation, from doing his duty—in such cases no obstacle would have dismayed him. His soul was as pure as a child's. He was a perfect child at forty, open-hearted in the extreme, always good-humoured, imagining everybody an angel, blaming himself for other people's shortcomings, and exaggerating the good qualities of others, even presupposing them where they could not possibly exist. He was one of those very generous and pure-hearted men who are positively ashamed to assume any harm of another, are always in haste to endow their neighbours with every virtue, rejoice at other people's success, and in that way always live in an ideal world, and when anything goes wrong always blame themselves first. To sacrifice themselves in the interests of others is their natural vocation. Some people would have called him cowardly, weak-willed and feeble. Of course he was weak, and indeed he was of too soft a disposition; but it was not from lack of will, but from the fear of wounding, of behaving cruelly, from excess of respect for others and for mankind in general. He was, however, weak-willed and cowardly only when nothing was at stake but his own interests, which he completely disregarded, and for this he was continually an object of derision, and often with the very people for whom he was sacrificing his own advantage. He never believed, however, that he had enemies; he had them, indeed, but he somehow failed to observe them. He dreaded fuss and disturbance in the house like fire, and immediately gave way to any one and submitted to anything. He gave in through a sort of shy good nature, from a sort of shy delicacy. "So be it," he would say, quickly brushing aside all reproaches for his indulgence and weakness; "so be it . . . that every one may be happy and contented!" I need hardly say that he was ready to submit to every honourable influence. What is more, an adroit rogue might have gained complete control over him, and even have lured him on to do wrong, of course misrepresenting the wrong action as a right one. My uncle very readily put faith in other people, and was often far from right in doing so. When, after many sufferings, he brought himself at last to believe that the man who deceived him was dishonest, he always blamed himself first—and sometimes blamed himself only. Now, imagine, suddenly queening it in his quiet home, a capricious, doting, idiot woman—inseparable from another idiot, her idol—a woman who had only feared her general, and was now afraid of nothing, and impelled by a craving to make up to herself for what she had suffered in the past; and this idiot woman my uncle thought it his duty to revere, simply because she was his mother. They began with proving to my uncle at once that he was coarse, impatient, ignorant and selfish to the utmost degree. The remarkable thing is that the idiotic old lady herself believed in what she professed. And I believe that Foma Fomitch did also, at least to some extent. They persuaded my uncle, too, that Foma had been sent from heaven by Divine Providence for the salvation of his soul and the subduing of his unbridled passions; that he was haughty, proud of his wealth, and quite capable of reproaching Foma Fomitch for eating his bread. My poor uncle was very soon convinced of the depth of his degradation, was ready to tear his hair and to beg forgiveness. . . .

"It's all my own fault, brother," he would say sometimes to one of the people he used to talk to. "It's all my fault! One ought to be doubly delicate with a man who is under obligations to one. . . . I mean that I . . . Under obligations, indeed! I am talking nonsense again! He is not under obligations to me at all: on the contrary, it is I who am under an obligation to him for living with me! And here I have reproached him for eating my bread! . . . Not that I did reproach him, but it seems I made some slip of the tongue—I often do make such slips. . . . And, after all, the man has suffered, he has done great things; for ten years in spite of insulting treatment he was tending his sick friend! And then his learning. . . . He's a writer! A highly educated man! A very lofty character; in short . . ."

The conception of the highly educated and unfortunate Foma ignominiously treated by the cruel and capricious general rent my uncle's heart with compassion and indignation. All Foma's peculiarities, all his ignoble doings my uncle at once ascribed to his sufferings, the humiliations he had endured in the past, and the bitterness left by them. . . . He at once decided in his soft and generous heart that one could not be so exacting with a man who had suffered as with an ordinary person; that one must not only forgive him, but more than that, one must, by gentle treatment, heal his wounds, restore him and reconcile him with humanity. Setting this object before him he was completely fired by it, and lost all power of perceiving that his new friend was a lascivious and capricious animal, an egoist, a sluggard, a lazy drone—and nothing more. He put implicit faith in Foma's genius and learning. I forgot to mention that my uncle had the most naïve and disinterested reverence for the words "learning" and "literature," though he had himself never studied anything. This was one of his chief and most guileless peculiarities.

"He is writing," he would whisper, walking on tiptoe, though he was two rooms away from Foma's study. "I don't know precisely what he is writing," he added, with a proud and mysterious air, "but no doubt he is brewing something, brother. . . . I mean in the best sense, of course; it would be clear to some people, but to you and me, brother, it would be just a jumble that . . . I fancy he is writing of productive forces of some sort—he said so himself. I suppose that has something to do with politics. Yes, his name will be famous! Then we shall be famous through him. He told me that himself, brother. . . ."

I know for a fact that my uncle was forced by Foma's orders to shave off his beautiful fair whiskers. Foma considered that these whiskers made my uncle look like a Frenchman, and that wearing them showed a lack of patriotism. Little by little Foma began meddling in the management of the estate, and giving sage counsels on the subject. These sage counsels were terrible. The peasants soon saw the position and understood who was their real master, and scratched their heads uneasily. Later on I overheard Foma talking to the peasants; I must confess I listened. Foma had told us before that he was fond of talking to intelligent Russian peasants. So one day he went to the threshing floor: after talking to the peasants about the farm-work, though he could not tell oats from wheat, after sweetly dwelling on the sacred obligations of the peasant to his master, after touching lightly on electricity and the division of labour, subjects of which I need hardly say he knew nothing, after explaining to his listeners how the earth went round the sun, and being at last quite touched by his own eloquence—he began talking about the ministers. I understood. Pushkin used to tell a story of a father who impressed upon his little boy of four that he, his papa, was so brave "that the Czar loves Papa. . . ." So evidently this papa needed this listener of four years old! And the peasants always listened to Foma Fomitch with cringing respect.

"And did you get a large salary from royalty, little father?" a grey-headed old man called Arhip Korotky asked suddenly from the crowd of peasants, with the evident intention of being flattering; but the question struck Foma Fomitch as familiar, and he could not endure familiarity.

"And what business is that of yours, you lout?" he answered, looking contemptuously at the poor peasant. "Why are you thrusting forward your pug-face? Do you want me to spit in it?"

Foma Fomitch always talked in that tone to the "intelligent Russian peasant."

"You are our father," another peasant interposed; "you know we are ignorant people. You may be a major or a colonel or even your Excellency, we don't know how we ought to speak to you."

"You lout!" repeated Foma Fomitch, mollified however. "There are salaries and salaries, you blockhead! One will get nothing, though he is a general—because he does nothing to deserve it, he is of no service to the Czar. But I got twenty thousand when I was serving in the Ministry, and I did not take it, I served for the honour of it. I had plenty of money of my own. I gave my salary to the cause of public enlightenment, and to aid those whose homes had been burnt in Kazan."

"I say! So it was you who rebuilt Kazan, little father?" the amazed peasant went on.

The peasants wondered at Foma Fomitch as a rule.

"Oh, well, I had my share in it," Foma answered, with a show of reluctance, as though vexed with himself for deigning to converse on *such* a subject with *such* a person.

His conversations with my uncle were of a different stamp.

"What were you in the past?" Foma would say, for instance, lolling after an ample dinner in an easy-chair, while a servant stood behind him brandishing a fresh lime branch to keep off the flies. "What were you like before I came? But now I have dropped into your soul a spark of that heavenly fire which is glowing there now. Did I drop a spark of heavenly fire into your soul or not? Answer. Did I drop a spark or did I not?"

Foma Fomitch, indeed, could not himself have said why he asked such a question. But my uncle's silence and confusion at once spurred him on. He who had been so patient and down-trodden in the past now exploded like gunpowder at the slightest provocation. My uncle's silence seemed to him insulting, and he now insisted on an answer.

"Answer: is the spark glowing in you or not?"

My uncle hesitated, shrank into himself, and did not know what line to take.

"Allow me to observe that I am waiting," said Foma in an aggrieved voice.

"Mais, répondez donc, Yegorushka," put in Madame la Générale, shrugging her shoulders.

"I am asking you, is that spark burning within you or not?" Foma repeated condescendingly, taking a sweetmeat out of a bonbon box, which always stood on a table before him by Madame la Générale's orders.

"I really don't know, Foma," my uncle answered at last with despair in his eyes. "Something of the sort, no doubt. . . . You really had better not ask or I am sure to say something wrong. . . ."

"Oh, very well! So you look upon me as so insignificant as not to deserve an answer—that's what you meant to say. But so be it; let me be a nonentity."

"Oh, no, Foma, God bless you! Why, when did I imply that?"

"Yes, that's just what you did mean to say."

"I swear I didn't."

"Oh, very well, then, I lie. So then you charge me with trying to pick a quarrel on purpose; it's another insult added to all the past, but I will put up with this too. . . ."

"Mais, mon fils!" cried Madame la Générale in alarm.

"Foma Fomitch! Mamma!" exclaimed my uncle in despair. "Upon my word it's not my fault. Perhaps I may have let slip such a thing without knowing it. . . . You mustn't mind me, Foma; I am stupid, you know; I feel I am stupid myself; I feel there is something amiss with me. . . . I know, Foma, I know! You need not say anything," he went on, waving his hand. "I have lived forty years, and until now, until I knew you, I thought I was all right . . . like every one else. And I didn't notice before that I was as sinful as a goat, an egoist of the worst description, and I've done such a lot of mischief that it is a wonder the world puts up with me."

"Yes, you certainly are an egoist," observed Foma, with conviction.

"Well, I realize myself that I am an egoist now! Yes, that's the end of it! I'll correct myself and be better!"

"God grant you may!" concluded Foma Fomitch, and sighing

piously he got up from his arm-chair to go to his room for an after-dinner nap. Foma Fomitch always dozed after dinner.

To conclude this chapter, may I be allowed to say something about my personal relations with my uncle, and to explain how I came to be face to face with Foma Fomitch, and with no thought or suspicion suddenly found myself in a vortex of the most important incidents that had ever happened in the blessed village of Stepantchikovo? With this I intend to conclude my introduction and to proceed straight with my story.

In my childhood, when I was left an orphan and alone in the world, my uncle took the place of a father to me; educated me at his expense, and did for me more than many a father does for his own child. From the first day he took me into his house I grew warmly attached to him. I was ten years old at the time, and I remember that we got on capitally, and thoroughly understood each other. We spun tops together, and together stole her cap from a very disagreeable old lady, who was a relation of both of us. I promptly tied the cap to the tail of a paper kite and sent it flying to the clouds. Many years afterwards I saw something of my uncle for a short time in Petersburg, where I was finishing my studies at his expense. During that time I became attached to him with all the warmth of youth: something generous, mild, truthful, light-hearted and naïve to the utmost degree struck me in his character and attracted every one. When I left the university I spent some time in Petersburg with nothing to do for the time, and, as is often the case with callow youths, was convinced that in a very short time I should do much that was very interesting and even great. I did not want to leave Petersburg. I wrote to my uncle at rather rare intervals and only when I wanted money, which he never refused me. Meanwhile, I heard from a house serf of my uncle's, who came to Petersburg on some business or other, that marvellous things were taking place at Stepantchikovo. These first rumours interested and surprised me. I began writing to my uncle more regularly. He always answered me somewhat obscurely and strangely, and in every letter seemed trying to talk of nothing but learned subjects, expressing great expectations of me in the future in a literary and scientific line, and pride in my future achievements. At last, after a rather long silence, I received a surprising letter from him, utterly unlike all his previous letters. It was full of such strange hints, such rambling and contradictory statements, that at first I could make nothing of it. All that one could see was that the writer was in great perturbation. One thing was clear in the letter: my uncle gravely, earnestly, almost imploringly urged me as soon as possible to marry his former ward, the daughter of a very poor provincial government clerk, called Yezhevikin. This girl had received an excellent education at a school in Moscow at my uncle's expense, and was now the governess of his children. He wrote that she was unhappy, that I might make her happy, that I should, in fact, be doing a noble action. He appealed to the generosity of my heart, and promised to give her a dowry. Of the dowry, however, he spoke somewhat mysteriously, timidly, and he concluded the letter by beseeching me to keep all this a dead secret. This letter made such an impression on me that my head began to go round. And, indeed, what raw young man would not have been affected by such a proposition, if only on its romantic side? Besides, I had heard that this young governess was extremely pretty. Yet I did not know what to decide, though I wrote to my uncle that I would set off for Stepantchikovo immediately. My uncle had sent me the money for the journey with the letter. Nevertheless, I lingered another three weeks in Petersburg, hesitating and somewhat uneasy.

All at once I happened to meet an old comrade of my uncle's, who had stayed at Stepantchikovo on his way back from the Caucasus to Petersburg. He was an elderly and judicious person, an inveterate bachelor. He told me with indignation about Foma Fomitch, and thereupon informed me of one circumstance of which I had no idea till then: namely, that Foma Fomitch and Madame la Générale had taken up a notion, and were set upon the idea of marrying my uncle to a very strange lady, not in her first youth and scarcely more than half-witted, with an extraordinary history, and almost half a million of dowry; that Madame la Générale had nearly succeeded in convincing this lady that they were relations, and so alluring her into the house; that my uncle, of course, was in despair, but would probably end by marrying the half-million of dowry; and that, finally, these two wiseacres, Madame la Générale and Foma Fomitch, were making a terrible onslaught on the poor defenceless governess, and were doing their utmost to turn her out of the house, apparently afraid that my uncle might fall in love with her, or perhaps knowing that he was already in love with her. These last words impressed me. However, to all my further questions as to whether my uncle really was or was not in love with her, my informant either could not or would not give me an exact answer, and indeed he told his whole story briefly, as it were reluctantly, and noticeably avoided detailed explanations. I thought it over; the news was so strangely contradictory of my uncle's letter and his proposition! . . . But it was useless to delay. I decided to go to Stepantchikovo, hoping not only to comfort my uncle and bring him to reason, but even to save him; that is, if possible, to turn Foma out, to prevent the hateful marriage with the old maid, and finally—as I had come to the conclusion that my uncle's love was only a spiteful invention of Foma's—to rejoice the unhappy but of course interesting young lady by the offer of my hand, and so on and so on. By degrees I so worked myself up that, being young and having nothing to do, I passed from hesitation to the opposite extreme; I began burning with the desire to perform all sorts of great and wonderful deeds as quickly as possible. I even fancied that I was displaying extraordinary generosity by nobly sacrificing myself to secure the happiness of a charming and innocent creature; in fact, I remember that I was exceedingly well satisfied with myself during the whole of my journey. It was July, the sun was shining brightly, all around me stretched a vast expanse of fields full of unripe corn. . . . I had so long sat bottled up in Petersburg, that I felt as though I were only now looking at God's world!

[II]

MR. BAHTCHEYEV

I WAS approaching my destination. Driving through the little town of B——, from which I had only eight miles further to Stepantchikovo, I was obliged to stop at the blacksmith's near the town gate, as the tyre of the front wheel of my chaise broke. To repair it in some way well enough to stand the remaining eight miles was a job that should not take very long, and so I made up my mind not to go elsewhere, but to remain at the blacksmith's while he set it right. As I got out of the chaise I saw a stout gentleman who, like me, had been compelled to stop to have his carriage repaired. He had been standing a whole hour in the insufferable heat, shouting and swearing, and with fretful impatience urging on the blacksmiths who were busy about his fine carriage. At first sight this angry gentleman struck me as extremely peevish. He was about five-and-forty, of middle height, very stout, and pock-marked; his stoutness, his double chin and his puffy, pendant cheeks testified to the blissful existence of a landowner. There was something feminine about his whole figure which at once caught the eye. He was dressed in loose, comfortable, neat clothes which were, however, quite unfashionable.

I cannot imagine why he was annoyed with me, since he saw me for the first time in his life, and had not yet spoken a single word to me. I noticed the fact from the extraordinarily furious looks he turned upon me as soon as I got out of the carriage. Yet I felt a great inclination to make his acquaintance. From the chatter of his servants, I gathered that he had just come from Stepantchikovo, from my uncle's, and so it was an opportunity for making full inquiries about many things. I was just taking off my cap and trying as agreeably as possible to observe how unpleasant these delays on the road sometimes were; but the fat gentleman, as it were reluctantly, scanned me from head to boots with a displeased and ill-humoured stare, muttered something to himself and turned heavily his full back view to me. This aspect of his person, however interesting to the observer, held out no hopes of agreeable conversation.

"Grishka! Don't grumble to yourself! I'll thrash you! . . ." he shouted suddenly to his valet, as though he had not heard what I said about delays on the journey.

This Grishka was a grey-headed, old-fashioned servant dressed in a long-skirted coat and wearing very long grey whiskers. Judging from certain signs, he too was in a very bad humour, and was grumbling morosely to himself. An explanation immediately followed between the master and the servant.

"You'll thrash me! Bawl a little louder!" muttered Grishka, as though to himself, but so loudly that everybody heard it; and with indignation he turned away to adjust something in the carriage.

"What? What did you say? 'Bawl a little louder.' . . . So you are pleased to be impudent!" shouted the fat man, turning purple.

"What on earth are you nagging at me for? One can't say a word!"

"Why nag at you? Do you hear that? He grumbles at me and I am not to nag at him!"

"Why, what should I grumble at?"

"What should you grumble at . . . you're grumbling, right enough! I know what you are grumbling about; my having come away from the dinner—that's what it is."

"What's that to me! You can have no dinner at all for all I care. I am not grumbling at you; I simply said a word to the blacksmiths."

"The blacksmiths. . . . Why grumble at the blacksmiths?"

"I did not grumble at them, I grumbled at the carriage."

"And why grumble at the carriage?"

"What did it break down for? It mustn't do it again."

"The carriage. . . . No, you are grumbling at me, and not at the carriage. It's his own fault and he swears at other people!"

"Why on earth do you keep on at me, sir? Leave off, please!"

"Why have you been sitting like an owl all the way, not saying a word to me, eh? You are ready enough to talk at other times!"

"A fly was buzzing round my mouth, that's why I didn't talk and sat like an owl. Why, am I to tell you fairy tales, or what? Take Malanya the storyteller with you if you are fond of fairy tales."

The fat man opened his mouth to reply, but apparently could think of nothing and held his peace. The servant, proud of his skill in argument and his influence over his master displayed before witnesses, turned to the workmen with redoubled dignity and began showing them something.

My efforts to make acquaintance were fruitless, and my own awkwardness did not help matters. I was assisted, however, by an unexpected incident. A sleepy, unwashed and unkempt countenance suddenly peeped out of the window of a closed carriage which had stood from time immemorial without wheels in the blacksmith's yard, daily though vainly expecting to be repaired. At the appearance of this countenance there was a general outburst of laughter from the workmen. The joke was that the man peeping out of the dismantled carriage was locked in and could not get out. Having fallen asleep in it drunk, he was now vainly begging for freedom; at last he began begging some one to run for his tool. All this immensely entertained the spectators.

There are persons who derive peculiar delight and entertainment from strange things. The antics of a drunken peasant, a man stumbling and falling down in the street, a wrangle between two women and other such incidents arouse at times in some people the most good-humoured and unaccountable delight. The fat gentleman belonged precisely to that class. Little by little his countenance from being sullen and menacing began to look pleased and good-humoured, and at last brightened up completely.

"Why, that's Vassilyev, isn't it?" he asked with interest. "How did he get here?"

"Yes, it is Vassilyev, sir!" was shouted on all sides.

"He's been on the spree, sir," added one of the workmen, a tall, lean, elderly man with a pedantically severe expression of face, who seemed disposed to take the lead; "he's been on the spree, sir. It's three days since he left his master, and he's lying hidden here; he's come and planted himself upon us! Here he is asking for a chisel. Why, what do you want a chisel for now, you addlepate? He wants to pawn his last tool."

"Ech, Arhipushka! Money's like a bird, it flies up and flies away again! Let me out, for God's sake," Vassilyev entreated in a thin cracked voice, poking his head out of the carriage.

"You stay where you are, you idol; you are lucky to be there!" Arhip answered sternly. "You have been drunk since the day before yesterday; you were hauled out of the street at daybreak this morning. You must thank God we hid you, we told Matvey Ilyitch that you were ill, that you had a convenient attack of colic."

There was a second burst of laughter.

"But where is the chisel?"

"Why, our Zuey has got it! How he keeps on about it! A drinking man, if ever there was one, Stepan Alexyevitch."

"He-he-he! Ah, the scoundrel! So that's how you work in the town; you pawn your tools!" wheezed the fat man, spluttering with glee, quite pleased and suddenly becoming extraordinarily good-humoured. "And yet it would be hard to find such a carpenter even in Moscow, but this is how he always recommends himself, the ruffian," he added, quite unexpectedly turning to me. "Let him out, Arhip, perhaps he wants something."

The gentleman was obeyed. The nail with which they had fastened up the carriage door, chiefly in order to amuse themselves at Vassilyev's expense when he should wake up, was taken out, and Vassilyev made his appearance in the light of day, muddy, dishevelled and ragged. He blinked at the sunshine, sneezed and gave a lurch; and then putting up his hand to screen his eyes, he looked round.

"What a lot of people, what a lot of people!" he said, shaking his head, "and all, seemingly, so . . . ober," he drawled, with a sort of mournful pensiveness as though reproaching himself: "Well, good-morning, brothers, good-day."

Again there was a burst of laughter.

"Good-morning! Why, see how much of the day is gone, you heedless fellow!"

"Go it, old man!"

"As we say, have your fling, if it don't last long."

"He-he-he! he has a ready tongue!" cried the fat man, rolling with laughter and again glancing genially at me. "Aren't you ashamed, Vassilyev?"

"It's sorrow drives me to it! Stepan Alexyevitch, sir, it's sorrow," Vassilyev answered gravely, with a wave of his hand, evidently glad of another opportunity to mention his sorrow.

"What sorrow, you booby?"

"A trouble such as was never heard of before. We are being made over to Foma Fomitch."

"Whom? When?" cried the fat man, all of a flutter.

I, too, took a step forward; quite unexpectedly, the question concerned me too.

"Why, all the people of Kapitonovko. Our master, the colonel—God give him health—wants to give up all our Kapitonovko, his property, to Foma Fomitch. Some seventy souls he is handing over to him. 'It's for you, Foma,' says he. 'Here, now, you've nothing of your own, one may say; you are not much of a landowner; all you have to keep you are two smelts in Lake Ladoga—that's all the serfs your father left you. For your parent,'" Vassilyev went on, with a sort of spiteful satisfaction, putting touches of venom into his story in all that related to Foma Fomitch—"'for your parent was a gentleman of ancient lineage, though from no one knows where, and no one knows who he was; he too, like you, lived with the gentry, was allowed to be in the kitchen as a charity. But now when I make over Kapitonovko to you, you will be a landowner too, and a gentleman of ancient lineage, and will have serfs of your own. You can lie on the stove and be idle as a gentleman. . . .'"

But Stepan Alexyevitch was no longer listening. The effect produced on him by Vassilyev's half-drunken story was extraordinary. The fat man was so angry that he turned positively purple; his double chin was quivering, his little eyes grew bloodshot. I thought he would have a stroke on the spot.

"That's the last straw!" he said, gasping. "That low brute Foma, the parasite, a landowner! Tfoo! Go to perdition! Damn it all! Hey, you make haste and finish! Home!"

"Allow me to ask you," I had said, stepping forward uncertainly, "you were pleased to mention the name of Foma Fomitch just now; I believe his surname, if I am not mistaken, is Opiskin. Well, you see, I should like . . . in short, I have a special reason for being interested in that personage, and I should be very glad to know on my own account, how far one may believe the words of this good man that his master, Yegor Ilyitch Rostanev, means to make Foma Fomitch a present of one of his villages. That interests me extremely, and I . . ."

"Allow me to ask you," the fat man broke in, "on what grounds are you interested in that personage, as you style him; though to my mind 'that damned low brute' is what he ought to be called, and not a personage. A fine sort of personage, the scurvy knave! He's a simple disgrace, not a personage!"

I explained that so far I was in complete ignorance in regard to this person, but that Yegor Ilyitch Rostanev was my uncle, and that I myself was Sergey Alexandrovitch So-and-so.

"The learned gentleman? My dear fellow! they are expecting you impatiently," cried the fat man, genuinely delighted. "Why, I have just come from them myself, from Stepantchikovo; I went away from dinner, I got up from the pudding, I couldn't sit it out with Foma! I quarrelled with them all there on account of that damned Foma. . . . Here's a meeting! You must excuse me, my dear fellow. I am Stepan Alexyevitch Bahtcheyev, and I remember you that high. . . . Well, who would have thought it! . . . But allow me."

And the fat man advanced to kiss me.

After the first minutes of excitement, I at once proceeded to question him: the opportunity was an excellent one.

"But who is this Foma?" I asked. "How is it he has gained the upper hand of the whole house? Why don't they kick him out of the yard? I must confess . . ."

"Kick him out? You must be mad. Why, Yegor Ilyitch tiptoes before him! Why, once Foma laid it down that Thursday was Wednesday, and so every one in the house counted Thursday Wednesday. 'I won't have it Thursday, let it be Wednesday!' So there were two Wednesdays in one week. Do you suppose I am making it up? I am not exaggerating the least little bit. Why, my dear fellow, it's simply beyond all belief."

"I have heard that, but I must confess . . ."

"I confess and I confess! The way the man keeps on! What is there to confess? No, you had better ask me what sort of jungle I have come out of. The mother of Yegor Ilyitch, I mean of the colonel, though a very worthy lady and a general's widow too, in my opinion is in her dotage; why, that damned Foma is the very apple of her eye. She is the cause of it all; it was she brought him into the house. He has talked her silly, she hasn't a word to say for herself now, though she is called her Excellency—she skipped into marriage with General Krahotkin at fifty! As for Yegor Ilyitch's sister, Praskovya Ilyinitchna, who is an old maid of forty, I don't care to speak of her. It's oh dear, and oh my, and cackling like a hen. I am sick of her— bless her! The only thing about her is that she is of the female sex;

and so I must respect her for no cause or reason, simply because she is of the female sex! Tfoo! It's not the thing for me to speak of her, she's your aunt. Alexandra Yegorovna, the colonel's daughter, though she is only a little girl—just in her sixteenth year—to my thinking is the cleverest of the lot; she doesn't respect Foma; it was fun to see her. A sweet young lady, and that's the fact! And why should she respect him? Why, Foma was a buffoon waiting on the late General Krahotkin. Why, he used to imitate all sorts of beasts to entertain the general! And it seems that in old days Jack was the man; but nowadays Jack is the master, and now the colonel, your uncle, treats this retired buffoon as though he were his own father. He has set him up in a frame, the rascal, and bows down at the feet of the man who is sponging upon him. Tfoo!"

"Poverty is not a vice, however . . . and I must confess . . . allow me to ask you, is he handsome, clever?"

"Foma? A perfect picture!" answered Bahtcheyev, with an extraordinary quiver of spite in his voice. (My questions seemed to irritate him, and he began to look at me suspiciously.) "A perfect picture! Do you hear, good people: he makes him out a beauty! Why, he is like a lot of brute beasts in one, if you want to know the whole truth, my good man. Though that wouldn't matter if he had wit; if only he had wit, the rogue—why, then I would be ready to do violence to my feelings and agree, maybe, for the sake of wit; but, you see, there's no trace of wit about him whatever! He has cast a spell on them all; he is a regular alchemist! Tfoo! I am tired of talking. One ought to curse them and say no more about it. You have upset me with your talk, my good sir! Hey, you! Are you ready or not?"

"Raven still wants shoeing," Grishka answered gloomily.

"Raven. I'll let you have a raven! . . . Yes, sir, I could tell you a story that would simply make you gape with wonder, so that you would stay with your mouth open till the Second Coming. Why, I used to feel a respect for him myself. Would you believe it? I confess it with shame, I frankly confess it, I was a fool. Why, he took me in too. He's a know-all. He knows the ins and outs of everything, he's studied all the sciences. He gave me some drops; you see, my good sir, I am a sick man, a poor creature. You may not believe it, but I am an invalid. And those drops of his almost turned me inside out. You just keep quiet and listen; go yourself and you will be amazed. Why, he will make the colonel shed tears of blood; the colonel will shed tears of blood through him, but then it will be too late. You know, the whole neighbourhood all around has dropped his acquaintance owing to this accursed Foma. No one can come to the place without being insulted by him. I don't count; even officials of high rank he doesn't spare. He lectures every one. He sets up for a teacher of morality, the scoundrel. 'I am a wise man,' says he; 'I am cleverer than all of you, you must listen to no one but me, I am a learned man.' Well, what of it? Because he is learned, must he persecute people who are not? . . . And when he begins in his learned language, he goes hammering on ta-ta-ta! Ta-ta-ta! I'll tell you his tongue is such a one to wag, that if you cut it off and throw it on the dungheap it will go on wagging there till a crow picks it up. He is as conceited and puffed out as a mouse in a sack of grain. He is trying to climb so high that he will overreach himself. Why, here, for instance, he has taken it into his head to teach the house serfs French. You can believe it or not, as you like. It will be a benefit to him, he says. To a lout, to a servant! Tfoo! A shameless fellow, damn him, that is what he is. What does a clodhopper want with French, I ask you? And indeed what do the likes of us want with French? For gallivanting with young ladies in the mazurka or dancing attendance on other men's wives? Profligacy, that's what it is, I tell you! But to my thinking, when one has drunk a bottle of vodka one can talk in any language. So that is all the respect I have for your French language! I dare say you can chatter away in French: Ta-ta-ta, the tabby has married the tom," Bahtcheyev said, looking at me in scornful indignation. "Are you a learned man, my good sir—eh? Have you gone in for some learned line?"

"Well . . . I am somewhat interested . . ."

"I suppose you have studied all the sciences, too?"

"Quite so, that is, no . . . I must own I am more interested now in observing . . . I have been staying in Petersburg, but now I am hurrying to my uncle's."

"And who is the attraction at your uncle's? You had better have stayed where you were, since you had somewhere to stay. No, my good sir, I can tell you, you won't make much way by being learned, and no uncle will be of any use to you; you'll get caught in a trap! Why, I got quite thin, staying twenty-four hours with them. Would you believe that I got thin, staying with them? No, I see you don't believe it. Oh, well, you needn't believe it if you don't want to, bless you."

"No, really I quite believe it, only I still don't understand," I answered, more and more bewildered.

"I believe it, but I don't believe you! You learned gentlemen are all fond of cutting capers! All you care about is hopping about on one leg and showing off! I am not fond of learned people, my good sir;

they give me the spleen! I have come across your Petersburgers—a worthless lot! They are all Freemasons; they spread infidelity in all directions; they are afraid of a drop of vodka, as though it would bite them—Tfoo! You have put me out of temper, sir, and I don't want to tell you anything! After all, I have not been engaged to tell you stories, and I am tired of talking. One doesn't pitch into everybody, sir, and indeed it's a sin to do it. . . . Only your learned gentleman at your uncle's has driven the footman Vidoplyasov almost out of his wits. Vidoplyasov has gone crazy all through Foma Fomitch. . . ."

"As for that fellow Vidoplyasov," put in Grishka, who had till then been following the conversation with severe decorum, "I'd give him a flogging. If I came across him, I'd thrash the German nonsense out of him. I'd give him more than you could get into two hundred."

"Be quiet!" shouted his master. "Hold your tongue; no one's talking to you."

"Vidoplyasov," I said, utterly nonplussed and not knowing what to say. "Vidoplyasov, what a queer name!"

"Why is it queer? There you are again. Ugh, you learned gentlemen, you learned gentlemen!"

I lost patience.

"Excuse me," I said, "but why are you so cross with me? What have I done? I must own I have been listening to you for half an hour, and I still don't know what it is all about. . . ."

"What are you offended about, sir?" answered the fat man. "There is no need for you to take offence! I am speaking to you for your good. You mustn't mind my being such a grumbler and shouting at my servant just now. Though he is the most natural rascal, my Grishka, I like him for it, the scoundrel. A feeling heart has been the ruin of me—I tell you frankly; and Foma is to blame for it all. He'll be the ruin of me, I'll take my oath of that. Here, thanks to him, I have been baking in the sun for two hours. I should have liked to have gone to the priest's while these fools were dawdling about over their job. The priest here is a very nice fellow. But he has so upset me, Foma has, that it has even put me off seeing the priest. What a set they all are! There isn't a decent tavern here. I tell you they are all scoundrels, every one of them. And it would be a different thing if he were some great man in the service," Bahtcheyev went on, going back again to Foma Fomitch, whom he seemed unable to shake off, "it would be pardonable perhaps for a man of of rank; but as it is he has no rank at all; I know for a fact that he hasn't. He says he has suffered in the cause of justice in the year forty something that never was, so we have to bow down to him for that! If the least thing is not to his liking—up he jumps and begins squealing: 'They are insulting me, they are insulting my poverty, they have no respect for me.' You daren't sit down to table without Foma, and yet he keeps them waiting. 'I have been slighted,' he'd say; 'I am a poor wanderer, black bread is good enough for me.' As soon as they sit down he turns up, our fiddle strikes up again, 'Why did you sit down to table without me? So no respect is shown me in anything.' In fact, your soul is not your own. I held my peace for a long time, sir, he imagined that I was going to fawn upon him, like a lapdog on its hind legs begging; 'Here, boy, here's a bit, eat it up.' No, my lad, you run in the shafts, while I sit in the cart. I served in the same regiment with Yegor Ilyitch, you know; I took my discharge with the rank of a Junker, while he came to his estate last year, a retired colonel. I said to him, '*Aïe*, you will be your own undoing, don't be too soft with Foma! You'll regret it.' 'No,' he would say, 'he is a most excellent person' (meaning Foma), 'he is a friend to me; he is teaching me a higher standard of life.' Well, thought I, there is no fighting against a higher standard; if he has set out to teach a higher standard of life, then it is all up. What do you suppose he made a to-do about to-day? To-morrow is the day of Elijah the Prophet" (Mr. Bahtcheyev crossed himself), "the patron saint of your uncle's son Ilyusha. I was thinking to spend the day with them and to dine there, and had ordered a plaything from Petersburg, a German on springs, kissing the hand of his betrothed, while she wiped away a tear with her handkerchief—a magnificent thing! (I shan't give it now, no thank you; it's lying there in my carriage and the German's nose is smashed off; I am taking it back.) Yegor Ilyitch himself would not have been disinclined to enjoy himself and be festive on such a day, but Foma won't have it. As much as to say: 'Why are you beginning to make such a fuss over Ilyusha? So now you are taking no notice of me.' Eh? What do you say to a goose like that? He is jealous of a boy of eight over his name day! 'Look here,' he says, 'it is my nameday too.' But you know it will be St. Ilya's, not St. Foma's. 'No,' he says, 'that is my name day too!' I looked on and put up with it. And what do you think? Now they are walking about on tiptoe, whispering, uncertain what to do—to reckon Ilya's day as the name day or not, to congratulate him or not. If they don't congratulate him he may be offended, if they do he may take it for scoffing. Tfoo, what a plague! We sat down to dinner. . . . But are you listening, my good sir?"

"Most certainly I am; I am listening with peculiar gratification, in

fact, because through you I have now learned . . . and . . . I must
say . . ."

"To be sure, with peculiar gratification! I know your peculiar
gratification. . . . You are not jeering at me, talking about your gratification?"

"Upon my word, how could I be jeering? On the contrary. And
indeed you express yourself with such originality that I am tempted
to note down your words."

"What's that, sir, noting down?" asked Mr. Bahtcheyev, looking
at me with suspicion and speaking with some alarm.

"Though perhaps I shall not note them down. . . . I didn't mean
anything."

"No doubt you are trying to flatter me?"

"Flatter you, what do you mean?" I asked with surprise.

"Why, yes. Here you are flattering me now; I am telling you everything like a fool, and later on you will go and write a sketch of me
somewhere."

I made haste at once to assure Mr. Bahtcheyev that I was not that
sort of person, but he still looked at me suspiciously.

"Not that sort of person! Who can tell what you are? Perhaps better still, Foma there threatened to write an account of me and to send
it to be published."

"Allow me to ask," I interrupted, partly from a desire to change
the conversation. "Is it true that my uncle wants to get married?"

"What if he does? That would not matter. Get married if you have
a mind to, that's no harm; but something else is. . . ." added Mr.
Bahtcheyev meditatively. "H'm! that question, my good sir, I cannot
answer fully. There are a lot of females mixed up in the business now,
like flies in jam; and you know there is no making out which wants
to be married. And as a friend I don't mind telling you, sir, I don't
like woman! It's only talk that she is a human being, but in reality
she is simply a disgrace and a danger to the soul's salvation. But that
your uncle is in love like a Siberian cat, that I can tell you for a fact.
I'll say no more about that now, sir, you will see for yourself; but
what's bad is that the business drags on. If you are going to get married, get married; but he is afraid to tell Foma and afraid to tell the
old lady, she will be squealing all over the place and begin kicking
up a rumpus. She takes Foma's part: 'Foma Fomitch will be hurt,'
she'd say, 'if a new mistress comes into the house, for then he won't
be able to stay two hours in it.' The bride will chuck him out by the
scruff of his neck, if she is not a fool, and in one way or another will

make such an upset that he won't be able to find a place anywhere in the neighbourhood. So now he is at his pranks, and he and the mamma are trying to foist a queer sort of bride on him. . . . But why did you interrupt me, sir? I wanted to tell you what was most important, and you interrupted me! I am older than you are, and it is not the right thing to interrupt an old man."

I apologized.

"You needn't apologize! I wanted to put before you as a learned man, how he insulted me to-day. Come, tell me what you think of it, if you are a good-hearted man. We sat down to dinner; well, he fairly bit my head off at dinner, I can tell you! I saw from the very beginning; he sat there as cross as two sticks, as though nothing were to his liking. He'd have been glad to drown me in a spoonful of water, the viper! He is a man of such vanity that his skin's not big enough for him. So he took it into his head to pick a quarrel with me, to teach me a higher standard. Asked me to tell him why I was so fat! The man kept pestering me, why was I fat and not thin? What do you think of that question? Tell me, my good sir. Do you see anything witty in it? I answered him very reasonably: 'That's as God has ordained, Foma Fomitch. One man's fat and one man's thin; and no mortal can go against the decrees of Divine Providence.' That was sensible, wasn't it? What do you say? 'No,' said he; 'you have five hundred serfs, you live at your ease and do nothing for your country; you ought to be in the service, but you sit at home and play your concertina'—and it is true when I am depressed I am fond of playing on the concertina. I answered very reasonably again: 'How should I go into the service, Foma Fomitch? What uniform could I pinch my corpulence into? If I pinched myself in and put on a uniform, and sneezed unwarily—all the buttons would fly off, and what's more, maybe before my superiors, and, God forbid! they might take it for a practical joke, and what then?' Well, tell me, what was there funny in that? But there, there was such a roar at my expense, such a ha-ha-ha and he-he-he. . . . The fact is he has no sense of decency, I tell you, and he even thought fit to slander me in the French dialect: '*cochon*,' he called me. Well, I know what *cochon* means. 'Ah, you damned philosopher,' I thought. 'Do you suppose I'm going to give in to you?' I bore it as long as I could, but I couldn't stand it. I got up from the table, and before all the honourable company I blurted out in his face: 'I have done you an injustice, Foma Fomitch, my kind benefactor.' I said, 'I thought that you were a well-bred man, and you turn out to be just as great a hog as any one of us.' I said that and I left the table, left the pudding—they were just handing the pudding round. 'Bother you and your pudding!' I thought. . . ."

"Excuse me," I said, listening to Mr. Bahtcheyev's whole story; "I am ready, of course, to agree with you completely. The point is, that so far I know nothing positive. . . . But I have got ideas of my own on the subject, you see."

"What ideas, my good sir?" Mr. Bahtcheyev asked mistrustfully.

"You see," I began, hesitating a little, "it is perhaps not the moment, but I am ready to tell it. This is what I think: perhaps we are both mistaken about Foma Fomitch, perhaps under these oddities lies hidden a peculiar, perhaps a gifted nature, who knows? Perhaps it is a nature that has been wounded, crushed by sufferings, avenging itself, so to speak, on all humanity. I have heard that in the past he was something like a buffoon; perhaps that humiliated him, mortified him, overwhelmed him. . . . Do you understand: a man of noble nature . . . perception . . . and to play the part of a buffoon! . . . And so he has become mistrustful of all mankind and . . . and perhaps if he could be reconciled to humanity . . . that is, to his fellows, perhaps he would turn out a rare nature, perhaps even a very remarkable one and . . . and . . . you know there must be something in the man. There is a reason, of course, for every one doing homage to him."

I was conscious myself that I was maundering horribly. I might have been forgiven in consideration of my youth. But Mr. Bahtcheyev did not forgive me. He looked gravely and sternly into my face and suddenly turned crimson as a turkey cock.

"Do you mean that Foma's a remarkable man?" he asked abruptly.

"Listen, I scarcely myself believe a word of what I said just now. It was merely by way of a guess. . . ."

"Allow me, sir, to be so inquisitive as to ask: have you studied philosophy?"

"In what sense?" I asked in perplexity.

"No, in no particular sense; you answer me straight out, apart from any sense, sir: have you studied philosophy or not?"

"I must own I am intending to study it, but . . ."

"There it is!" shouted Mr. Bahtcheyev, giving full rein to his indignation. "Before you opened your mouth, sir, I guessed that you were a philosopher! There is no deceiving me! No, thank you! I can scent out a philosopher two miles off! You can go and kiss your Foma Fomitch. A remarkable man, indeed! Tfoo! confound it all! I thought you were a man of good intentions too, while you . . . Here!" he shouted to the coachman, who had already clambered on the box of the carriage which by now had been put in order. "Home!"

With difficulty I succeeded somehow in soothing him; somehow or other he was mollified at last; but it was a long time before he could bring himself to lay aside his wrath and look on me with favour. Meantime he got into the carriage, assisted by Grishka and Arhip, the man who had reproved Vassilyev.

"Allow me to ask you," I said, going up to the carriage. "Are you never coming again to my uncle's?"

"To your uncle's? Curse the fellow who has told you that! Do you think that I am a consistent man, that I shall keep it up? That's just my trouble, that I am not a man, but a rag. Before a week's past, I shall fly round there again. And why? There it is, I don't know myself why, but I shall go; I shall fight with Foma again. That's just my trouble, sir! The Lord has sent that Foma to chastise me for my sins. I have as much will as an old woman, there is no consistency in me, I am a first-class coward, my good sir. . . ."

We parted friends, however; he even invited me to dine with him.

"You come, sir, you come, we will dine together; I have got some vodka brought on foot from Kiev, and my cook has been in Paris. He serves such fricassees, he makes such pasties, that you can only lick your fingers and bow down to him, the rascal. A man of culture! Only it is a long time since I thrashed him, he is getting spoilt with me. . . . It is a good thing you reminded me. . . . Do come. I'd invite you to come to-day, only somehow I am out of sorts, down in the mouth—in fact, quite knocked up. I am a sick man, you know, a poor creature. Maybe you won't believe it. . . . Well, good-bye, sir, it is time for me to set sail. And your little trap yonder is ready. And tell Foma he had better not come across me; I should give him such a sentimental greeting that he . . ."

But his last words were out of hearing; the carriage, drawn by four strong horses, vanished in clouds of dust. My chaise too was ready; I got into it and we at once drove through the little town. "Of course this gentleman is exaggerating," I thought; "he is too angry and cannot be impartial. But, again, all that he said about uncle was very remarkable. So that makes two people in the same story, that uncle is in love with that young lady. . . . H'm! Shall I get married or not?" This time I meditated in earnest.

[III]

MY UNCLE

I MUST own I was actually a little daunted. My romantic dreams suddenly seemed to me extremely queer, even rather stupid, as soon as I reached Stepantchikovo. That was about five o'clock in the afternoon. The road ran by the manor house. I saw again after long absence the immense garden in which some happy days of my childhood had been passed, and which I had often seen afterwards in my dreams, in the dormitories of the various schools which undertook my education. I jumped out of the carriage and walked across the garden to the house. I very much wanted to arrive unannounced, to inquire for my uncle, to fetch him out and to talk to him first of all. And so I did. Passing down the avenue of lime-trees hundreds of years old, I went up on to the verandah, from which one passed by a glass door into the inner rooms. The verandah was surrounded by flower-beds and adorned with pots of expensive flowers. Here I met one of the natives, old Gavrila, who had at one time looked after me and was now the honoured valet of my uncle. The old fellow was wearing spectacles, and was holding in his hand a manuscript book which he was reading with great attention. I had seen him three years before in Petersburg, where he had come with my uncle, and so he recognized me at once. With exclamations of joy he fell to kissing my hand, and as he did so the spectacles fell off his nose on to the floor. Such devotion on the part of the old man touched me very much. But disturbed by my recent conversation with Mr. Bahtcheyev, I looked first at the suspicious manuscript book which had been in Gavrila's hands.

"What's this, Gavrila? Surely they have not begun teaching you French too?" I asked the old man.

"They are teaching me in my old age, like a starling, sir," Gavrila answered mournfully.

"Does Foma himself teach you?"

"Yes, sir; a very clever man he must be."

"Not a doubt that he is clever! Does he teach you by conversations?"

"By a copy book, sir."

"Is that what you have in your hands? Ah! French words in Russian letters, a sharp dodge! You give in to such a blockhead, such an arrant fool, aren't you ashamed, Gavrila?" I cried, instantly forgetting my

ofty theories about Foma Fromitch for which I had caught it so hotly
from Mr. Bahtcheyev.

"How can he be a fool, sir," answered the old man, "if he manages
our betters as he does?"

"H'm, perhaps you are right, Gavrila," I muttered, pulled up by this
remark. "Take me to my uncle."

"My falcon! But I can't show myself, I dare not, I have begun to be
afraid even of him. I sit here in my misery and step behind the flower-
beds when he is pleased to come out."

"But why are you afraid?"

"I didn't know my lesson this morning. Foma Fomitch made me
go down on my knees, but I didn't stay on my knees. I am too old,
Sergey Alexandrovitch, for them to play such tricks with me. The
master was pleased to be vexed at my disobeying Foma Fomitch, 'he
takes trouble about your education, old grey-beard,' said he; 'he wants
to teach you the pronunciation.' So here I am walking to and fro
repeating the vocabulary. Foma Fomitch promised to examine me
again this evening."

It seemed to me that there was something obscure about this.

"There must be something connected with French," I thought,
"which the old man cannot explain."

"One question, Gavrila: what sort of man is he? Good-looking,
tall?"

"Foma Fomitch? No, sir, he's an ugly little scrub of a man."

"H'm! Wait a bit, Gavrila, perhaps it can be all set right; in fact,
I can promise you it certainly will be set right. But . . . where is my
uncle?"

"He is behind the stables seeing some peasants. The old men have
come from Kapitonovko to pay their respects to him. They had heard
that they were being made over to Foma Fomitch. They want to beg
not to be."

"But why behind the stables?"

"They are frightened, sir. . . ."

I did, in fact, find my uncle behind the stables. There he was,
standing before a group of peasants who were bowing down to the
ground and earnestly entreating him. Uncle was explaining something
to them with warmth. I went up and called to him. He turned round
and we rushed into each other's arms.

He was extremely glad to see me; his delight was almost ecstatic.
He hugged me, pressed my hands, as though his own son had returned
'o him after escaping some mortal danger, as though by my arrival

I had rescued him from some mortal danger and brought with me the solution of all his perplexities, as well as joy and lifelong happiness for him and all whom he loved. Uncle would not have consented to be happy alone. After the first outburst of delight, he got into such a fuss that at last he was quite flustered and bewildered. He showered questions upon me, wanted to take me at once to see his family. We were just going, but my uncle turned back, wishing to present me first to the peasants of Kapitonovko. Then, I remember, he suddenly began talking, apropos of I don't know what, of some Mr. Korovkin, a remarkable man whom he had met three days before, on the high road, and whom he was very impatiently expecting to pay him a visit. Then he dropped Mr. Korovkin too and spoke of something else. I looked at him with enjoyment. Answering his hurried questions, I told him that I did not want to go into the service, but to continue my studies. As soon as the subject of study was broached, my uncle at once knitted his brows and assumed an extraordinarily solemn air. Learning that of late I had been engaged on mineralogy, he raised his head and looked about him proudly, as though he had himself, alone and unaided, discovered the whole of that science and written all that was published about it. I have mentioned already that he cherished the most disinterested reverence for the word "science," the more disinterested that he himself had no scientific knowledge whatever.

"Ah, my boy, there are people in the world who know everything," he said to me once, his eyes sparkling with enthusiasm. "One sits among them, listens, and one knows one understands nothing of it all, and yet one loves it. And why? Because it is in the cause of reform, of enlightenment, of the general welfare! That I do understand. Here I now travel by train, and my Ilyusha, perhaps, may fly through the air. . . . And then trade, manufactures—those channels, so to say . . . that is, I mean, turn it which way you will, it's of service. . . . It is of service, isn't it?"

But to return to our meeting.

"But wait a bit, wait a bit, my dear," he began speaking rapidly and rubbing his hands, "you will see a man! A rare man, I tell you, a learned man, a man of science; 'he will survive his century.' It's a good saying, isn't it, 'will survive his century'? Foma explained it to me. . . . Wait a little, I will introduce you to him."

"Are you speaking of Foma Fomitch, uncle?"

"No, no, my dear, I was speaking of Korovkin, though Foma too, he too . . . but I am simply talking of Korovkin just now," he added, for some unknown reason turning crimson, and seeming embarrassed as soon as Foma's name was mentioned.

"What sciences is he studying, uncle?"

"Science, my boy, science, science in general. I can't tell you which exactly, I only know that it is science. How he speaks about railways! And, you know," my uncle added in a half-whisper, screwing up his right eye significantly, "just a little of the free-thinker. I noticed it, especially when he was speaking of marriage and the family . . . it's a pity I did not understand much of it myself (there was no time), I would have told you all about it in detail. And he is a man of the noblest qualities, too! I have invited him to visit me, I am expecting him from hour to hour."

Meanwhile the peasants were gazing at me with round eyes and open mouths as though at some marvel.

"Listen, uncle," I interrupted him; "I believe I am hindering the peasants. No doubt they have come about something urgent. What do they want? I must own I suspect something, and I should be very glad to hear . . ."

Uncle suddenly seemed nervous and flustered.

"Oh, yes! I had forgotten. Here, you see . . . what is one to do with them? They have got a notion—and I should very much like to know who first started it—they have got a notion, that I am giving them away together with the whole of Kapitonovko—do you remember Kapitonovko? We used to drive out there in the evenings with dear Katya—the whole of Kapitonovko with the sixty-eight souls in it to Foma Fomitch. 'We don't want to leave you,' they say, and that is all about it."

"So it is not true, uncle, you are not giving him Kapitonovko," I cried, almost rapturously.

"I never thought of it, it never entered my head! And from whom did you hear it? Once one drops a word, it is all over the place. And why do they so dislike Foma? Wait a little, Sergey, I will introduce you to him," he added, glancing at me timidly, as though he were aware in me, too, of hostility towards Foma Fomitch. "He is a wonderful man, my boy."

"We want no one but you, no one!" the peasants suddenly wailed in chorus. "You are our father, we are your children!"

"Listen, uncle," I said. "I have not seen Foma Fomitch yet, but . . . you see . . . I have heard something. I must confess that I met Mr. Bahtcheyev to-day. However, I have my own idea on that subject.

Anyway, uncle, finish with the peasants and let them go, and let us talk by ourselves without witnesses. I must own, that's what I have come for. . . ."

"To be sure, to be sure," my uncle assented; "to be sure. We'll dismiss the peasants and then we can have a talk, you know, a friendly, affectionate, thorough talk. Come," he went on, speaking rapidly and addressing the peasants, "you can go now, my friends. And for the future come to me whenever there is need; straight to me, and come at any time."

"You are our father, we are your children! Do not give us to Foma Fomitch for our undoing! All we, poor people, are beseeching you!" the peasants shouted once more.

"See what fools! But I am not giving you away, I tell you."

"Or he'll never leave off teaching us, your honour. He does nothing but teach the fellows here, so they say."

"Why, you don't mean to say he is teaching you French?" I cried, almost in alarm.

"No, sir, so far God has had mercy on us!" answered one of the peasants, probably a great talker, a red-haired man with a huge bald patch on the back of his head, with a long, scanty, wedge-shaped beard, which moved as he talked as though it were a separate individual. "No, sir, so far God has had mercy on us."

"But what does he teach you?"

"Well, your honour, what he teaches us, in a manner of speaking, is buying a gold casket to keep a brass farthing in."

"How do you mean, a brass farthing?"

"Seryozha, you are mistaken, it's a slander!" cried my uncle, turning crimson and looking terribly embarrassed. "The fools have misunderstood what was said to them. He merely . . . there was nothing about a brass farthing. There is no need for you to understand everything, and shout at the top of your voice," my uncle continued, addressing the peasant reproachfully. "One wants to do you good and you don't understand, and make an uproar!"

"Upon my word, uncle, teaching them French?"

"That's for the sake of pronunciation, Seryozha, simply for the pronunciation," said my uncle in an imploring voice. "He said himself that it was for the sake of the pronunciation. . . . Besides, something special happened in connection with this, which you know nothing about and so you cannot judge. You must investigate first and then blame. . . . It is easy to find fault!"

"But what are you about?" I shouted, turning impetuously to the peasants again. "You ought to speak straight out. You should say, 'This won't do, Foma Fomitch, this is how it ought to be!' You have got a tongue, haven't you?"

"Where is the mouse who will bell the cat, your honour? 'I am teaching you, clodhoppers, cleanliness and order,' he says. 'Why is your shirt not clean?' Why, one is always in a sweat, that's why it isn't clean! One can't change every day. Cleanliness won't save you and dirt won't kill you."

"And look here, the other day he came to the threshing floor," began another peasant, a tall, lean fellow all in patches and wearing wretched bark shoes, apparently one of those men who are always discontented about something and always have some vicious venomous word ready in reserve. Till then he had been hidden behind the backs of the other peasants, had been listening in gloomy silence, and had kept all the time on his face an ambiguous, bitterly subtle smile. "He came to the threshing floor. 'Do you know,' he said, 'how many miles it is to the sun?' 'Why, who can tell? Such learning is not for us but for the gentry.' 'No,' says he; 'you are a fool, a lout, you don't understand what is good for you; but I,' said he, 'am an astronomer! I know all God's planets.'"

"Well, and did he tell you how many miles it is to the sun?" my uncle put in, suddenly reviving and winking gaily to me, as though to say, "See what's coming!"

"Yes, he did tell us how many," the peasant answered reluctantly, not expecting such a question.

"Well, how many did he say, how many exactly?"

"Your honour must know best, we live in darkness."

"Oh, I know, my boy, but do you remember?"

"Why, he said it would be so many hundreds or thousands, it was a big number, he said. More than you could carry in three cartloads."

"Try and remember, brother! I dare say you thought it would be about a mile, that you could reach up to it with your hand. No, my boy; you see, the earth is like a round ball, do you understand?" my uncle went on, describing a sphere in the air with his hands.

The peasant smiled bitterly.

"Yes, like a ball, it hangs in the air of itself and moves round the sun. And the sun stands still, it only seems to you that it moves. There's a queer thing! And the man who discovered this was Captain Cook, a navigator . . . devil only knows who did discover it," he added in a half-whisper, turning to me. "I know nothing about it myself, my boy. . . . Do you know how far it is to the sun?"

"I do, uncle," I answered, looking with surprise at all this scene. "But this is what I think: of course ignorance means slovenliness; but on the other hand . . . to teach peasants astronomy . . ."

"Just so, just so, slovenliness," my uncle assented, delighted with my expression, which struck him as extremely apt. "A noble thought! Slovenliness precisely! That is what I have always said . . . that is, I never said so, but I felt it. Do you hear?" he cried to the peasants. "Ignorance is as bad as slovenliness, it's as bad as dirt. That's why Foma wanted to teach you. He wanted to teach you something good—that was all right. That's as good as serving one's country—it's as good as any official rank. So you see what science is! Well, that's enough, that's enough, my friends. Go, in God's name; and I am glad, glad. . . . Don't worry yourselves, I won't forsake you."

"Protect us, father!"

"Let us breathe freely!"

And the peasants plumped down at his feet.

"Come, come, that's nonsense. Bow down to God and your Czar, and not to me. . . . Come, go along, behave well, be deserving . . . and all that. You know," he said, turning suddenly to me as soon as the peasants had gone away, and beaming with pleasure, "the peasant loves a kind word, and a little present would do no harm. Shall I give them something, eh? What do you think? In honour of your arrival. . . . Shall I or not?"

"But you are a kind of Frol Silin, uncle, a benevolent person, I see."

"Oh, one can't help it, my boy, one can't help it; that's nothing. I have been meaning to give them a present for a long time," he said, as though excusing himself. "And as for your thinking it funny of me to give the peasants a lesson in science, I simply did that, my boy, in delight at seeing you, Seryozha. I simply wanted the peasants to hear how many miles it was to the sun and gape in wonder. It's amusing to see them gape, my dear. . . . One seems to rejoice over them. Only, my boy, don't speak in the drawing-room of my having had an interview with the peasants, you know. I met them behind the stables on purpose that we should not be seen. It was impossible to have it there, my boy: it is a delicate business, and indeed they came in secret themselves. I did it more for their sake. . . ."

"Well, here I have come, uncle," I began, changing the conversation and anxious to get to the chief point as quickly as possible. "I must own your letter so surprised me that I . . ."

"My dear, not a word of that," my uncle interrupted, as though in alarm, positively dropping his voice. "Afterwards, afterwards, all that shall be explained. I have, perhaps, acted wrongly towards you, very wrongly, perhaps. . . ."

"Acted wrongly towards me, uncle?"

"Afterwards, afterwards, my dear, afterwards! It shall all be explained. But what a fine fellow you have grown! My dear boy! How eager I have been to see you! I wanted to pour out my heart, so to speak . . . you are clever, you are my only hope . . . you and Korovkin. I must mention to you that they are all angry with you here. Mind, be careful, don't be rash."

"Angry with me?" I asked, looking at uncle in wonder, unable to understand how I could have angered people with whom I was as yet unacquainted. "Angry with me?"

"Yes, with you, my boy. It can't be helped! Foma Fomitch is a little . . . and . . . well . . . mother following his example. Be careful, respectful, don't contradict. The great thing is to be respectful. . . ."

"To Foma Fomitch, do you mean, uncle?"

"It can't be helped, my dear; you see, I don't defend him. Certainly he has his faults, perhaps, and especially just now, at this particular moment. . . . Ah, Seryozha dear, how it all worries me. And if only it could be settled comfortably, if only we could all be satisfied and happy! . . . But who has not faults? We are not perfect ourselves, are we?"

"Upon my word, uncle! Consider what he is doing. . . ."

"Oh, my dear! It's all trivial nonsense, nothing more! Here, for instance, let me tell you, he is angry with me, and what for, do you suppose? . . . Though perhaps it's my own fault. . . . I'd better tell you afterwards. . . ."

"But do you know, uncle, I have formed an idea of my own about it," I interrupted, in haste to give expression to my theory. Indeed, we both seemed nervous and hurried. "In the first place, he has been a buffoon; that has mortified him, rankled, outraged his ideal; and that has made his character embittered, morbid, resentful, so to say, against all humanity. . . . But if one could reconcile him with mankind, if one could bring him back to himself . . ."

"Just so, just so," cried my uncle, delighted; "that's just it. A generous idea! And in fact it would be shameful, ungenerous of us to blame him! Just so! . . . Oh, my dear, you understand me; you have brought me comfort! If only things could be set straight, somehow! Do you know, I am afraid to show myself. Here you have come, and I shall certainly catch it from them!"

"Uncle, if that's how it is . . ." I began, disconcerted by this confession.

"No-no-no! For nothing in the world," he cried, clutching my hands. "You are my guest and I wish it!"

"Uncle, tell me at once," I began insistently, "why did you send for me? What do you expect of me, and, above all, in what way have you been to blame towards me?"

"My dear, don't ask. Afterwards, afterwards; all that shall be explained afterwards. I have been very much to blame, perhaps, but I wanted to act like an honest man, and . . . and . . . you shall marry her! You will marry her, if there is one grain of gentlemanly feeling in you," he added, flushing all over with some sudden feeling and warmly and enthusiastically pressing my hand. "But enough, not another word, you will soon see for yourself. It will depend on you. . . . The great thing is that you should be liked, that you should make a good impression. Above all—don't be nervous."

"Come, listen, uncle. Whom have you got there? I must own I have been so little in society, that . . ."

"That you are rather frightened," put in my uncle, smiling. "Oh, that's no matter. Cheer up, they are all our own people! The great thing is to be bold and not afraid. I keep feeling anxious about you. Whom have we got there, you ask? Yes, who is there? . . . In the first place, my mother," he began hurriedly. "Do you remember mamma or not? The most kind-hearted, generous woman, no airs about her— that one can say; a little of the old school, perhaps, but that's all to the good. To be sure she sometimes takes fancies into her head, you know, will say one thing and another; she is vexed with me now, but it is my own fault, I know it is my own fault. And the fact is—you know she is what is called a *grande dame,* a general's lady . . . her husband was a most excellent man. To begin with, he was a general, a most cultivated man; he left no property, but he was covered with wounds —he was deserving of respect, in fact. Then there's Miss Perepelitsyn; well, she . . . I don't know . . . of late she has been rather . . . her character is so . . . but one mustn't find fault with every one. There, never mind her . . . you mustn't imagine she is in a menial position, she's a major's daughter herself, my boy, she is mother's confidante and favourite, my dear! Then there is my sister Praskovya Ilyinitchna. Well, there is no need to say much about her, she is simple and good-natured, a bit fussy, but what a heart! The heart is the great thing. Though she is middle-aged, yet, do you know, I really believe that queer fellow Bahtcheyev is making up to her. He wants to make a match of it. But, mind you don't say a word, it is a secret! Well, and who else is there? I won't tell you about the children, you will see for yourself. It's Ilyusha's nameday to-morrow. . . . Why there, I was almost forgetting, we have had staying with us for the last month Ivan Ivanitch Mizintchikov, your second cousin, I believe; yes, of course, he is your second cousin! He has lately given up his commission; he was a lieutenant in the Hussars; still a young man. A noble soul! But, you know, he has got through his money. I really can't think how he managed to get rid of it. Though indeed he had next to nothing, but anyway he got through it and ran into debt. . . . Now he is staying with me. I didn't know him at all till lately; he came and introduced himself. He is a dear fellow, good-humoured, quiet and respectful. No one gets a word out of him. He is always silent. Foma calls him in jest the 'silent stranger'—he doesn't mind; he isn't vexed. Foma's satisfied, he says Ivan's not very bright. And Ivan never contradicts him, but always falls in with everything he says. H'm! he seems so crushed . . . but there, God bless him, you will see for yourself. There are guests from the town, Pavel Semyonitch Obnoskin and his mother; he's young but a man of superior mind, something mature, steadfast, you know . . . only I don't know how to express it; and what's more, of the highest principles; strict morals. And lastly there is staying with us, you know, a lady called Tatyana Ivanovna; she, too, may be a distant relation. You don't know her. She is not quite young, that one must own, but . . . she is not without attractions: she is rich enough to buy Stepantchikovo twice over, she has only lately come into her money, and has had a wretched time of it till now. Please, Seryozha, my boy, be careful; she is such a nervous invalid . . . something phantasmagorial in her character, you know. Well, you are a gentleman, you will understand; she has had troubles, you know, one has to be doubly careful with a person who has had troubles! But you mustn't imagine anything, you know. Of course she has her weaknesses; sometimes she is in such a hurry, she speaks so fast, that she says the wrong thing. Not that she lies, don't imagine that . . . it all comes, my boy, from a pure and noble heart, so to say. I mean, even if she does say something false, it's simply from excess of noble-heartedness, so to say —do you understand?"

I fancied that my uncle was horribly confused.

"Listen, uncle," I began, "I am so fond of you . . . forgive the direct question: are you going to marry some one here or not?"

"Why, from whom did you hear that?" he answered, blushing like a child. "You see, my dear . . . I'll tell you all about it; in the first place,

I am not going to get married. Mamma, my sister to some extent, and most of all Foma Fomitch, whom mamma worships—and with good reason, with good reason, he has done a great deal for her—they all want me to marry that same Tatyana Ivanovna, as a sensible step for the benefit of all. Of course they desire nothing but my good—I understand that, of course; but nothing will induce me to marry—I have made up my mind about that. In spite of that I have not succeeded in giving them a decided answer, I have not said yes, or no. It always happens like that with me, my boy. They thought that I had consented and are insisting that to-morrow, in honour of the festive occasion, I should declare myself . . . and so there is such a flutter in preparation for to-morrow that I really don't know what line to take! And besides, Foma Fomitch, I don't know why, is vexed with me, and mamma is too. I must say, my boy, I have simply been reckoning on you and on Korovkin. . . . I wanted to pour out my troubles, so to say. . . ."

"But how can Korovkin be of any use in this matter, uncle?"

"He will help, he will help, my dear—he is a wonderful man; in short, a man of learning! I build upon him as on a rock; a man who would conquer anything! How he speaks of domestic happiness! I must own I have been reckoning on you too; I thought you might bring them to reason. Consider and judge . . . granted that I have been to blame, really to blame—I understand all that—I am not without feeling. But all the same I might be forgiven some day! Then how well we should get on together! Oh, my boy, how my Sashenka has grown up, she'll be thinking of getting married directly! What a fine boy my Ilyusha has become! To-morrow is his nameday. But I am afraid for my Sashenka—that's the trouble."

"Uncle! Where is my portmanteau? I will change my things and make my appearance in a minute, and then . . ."

"In the upper room, my boy, in the upper room. I gave orders beforehand that as soon as you arrived you should be taken straight up there, so that no one should see you. Yes, yes, change your things! That's capital, capital, first rate. And meanwhile I will prepare them all a little. Well, good luck to us! You know, my boy, we must be diplomatic. One is forced to become a Talleyrand. But there, never mind. They are drinking tea there now. We have tea early. Foma Fomitch likes to have his tea as soon as he wakes up; it is better, you know. Well, I'll go in, then, and you make haste and follow me, don't leave me alone; it will be awkward for me, my boy, alone. . . . But, stay! I have another favour to ask of you: don't cry out at me in there as you did out here just now—will you? If you want to make some criticism you can make it afterwards here when we are alone; till then hold yourself in and wait! You see, I have put my foot in it already with them. They are annoyed with me. . . ."

"I say, uncle, from all that I have seen and heard it seems to me that you . . ."

"That I am as soft as butter, eh? Don't mind speaking out!" he interrupted me quite unexpectedly. "There is no help for it, my boy. I know it myself. Well, so you will come? Come as quick as you can, please!"

Going upstairs, I hurriedly opened my portmanteau, remembering my uncle's instructions to come down as soon as possible. As I was dressing, I realized that I had so far learned scarcely anything I wanted to know, though I had been talking to my uncle for a full hour. That struck me. Only one thing was pretty clear to me: my uncle was still set upon my getting married; consequently, all rumours to the opposite, that is, that my uncle was in love with the same lady himself, were wide of the mark. I remember that I was much agitated. Among other things the thought occurred to me that by my coming, and by my si. lence, I had almost made a promise, given my word, bound myself for ever. "It is easy," I thought, "it is easy to say a word which will bind one, hand and foot, for ever. And I have not yet seen my proposed bride!" And again: why this antagonism towards me on the part of the whole family? Why were they bound to take a hostile attitude to my coming, as my uncle said they did? And what a strange part my uncle was playing here in his own house? What was the cause of his secretiveness? Why these worries and alarms? I must own that it all struck me suddenly as something quite senseless; and my romantic and heroic dreams took flight completely at the first contact with reality. Only now after my conversation with my uncle, I suddenly realized all the incongruity and eccentricity of his proposition, and felt that no one but my uncle would have been capable of making such a proposal and in such circumstances. I realized, too, that I was something not unlike a fool for galloping here full speed at his first word, in high delight at his suggestion. I was dressing hurriedly, absorbed in my agitating doubts, so that I did not at first notice the man who was waiting on me.

"Will your honour wear the Adelaïda coloured tie or the one with the little checks on it?" the man asked suddenly, addressing me with exceptionally mawkish obsequiousness.

I glanced at him, and it seemed to me that he, too, was worthy of attention. He was a man still young, for a flunkey well dressed, quite as well as many a provincial dandy. The brown coat, the white breeches, the straw-coloured waistcoat, the patent-leather boots and the pink tie had evidently been selected with intention. All this was bound at once to attract attention to the young dandy's refined taste. The watch-chain was undoubtedly displayed with the same object. He was pale, even greenish in face, and had a long hooked nose, thin and remarkably white, as though it were made of china. The smile on his thin lips expressed melancholy, a refined melancholy, however. His large prominent eyes, which looked as though made of glass, had an extraordinarily stupid expression, and yet there was a gleam of refinement in them. His thin soft ears were stuffed up with cotton wool— also a refinement. His long, scanty, flaxen hair was curled and pomaded. His hands were white, clean, and might have been washed in rose-water; his fingers ended in extremely long dandified pink nails. All this indicated a spoilt and idle fop. He lisped and mispronounced the letter "r" in fashionable style, raised and dropped his eyes, sighed and gave himself incredibly affected airs. He smelt of scent. He was short, feeble and flabby-looking, and moved about with knees and haunches bent, probably thinking this the height of refinement—in fact, he was saturated with refinement, subtlety and an extraordinary sense of his own dignity. This last characteristic displeased me, I don't know why, and moved me to wrath.

"So that tie is Adelaïda colour?" I asked, looking severely at the young valet.

"Yes, Adelaïda," he answered, with undisturbed refinement.

"And is there an Agrafena colour?"

"No, sir, there cannot be such a colour."

"Why not?"

"Agrafena is not a polite name, sir."

"Not polite! Why not?"

"Why, Adelaïda, we all know, is a foreign name anyway, a ladylike name, but any low peasant woman can be called Agrafena."

"Are you out of your mind?"

"No, sir, I am in my right mind, sir. Of course you are free to call me any sort of name, but many generals and even some counts in Moscow and Petersburg have been pleased with my conversation, sir."

"And what's your name?"

"Vidoplyasov."

"Ah, so you are Vidoplyasov?"

"Just so, sir."

"Well, wait a bit, my lad, and I will make your acquaintance."

"It is something like Bedlam here," I thought to myself as I went downstairs.

AT TEA

TEA was being served in the room that gave on to the verandah where I had that afternoon met Gavrila. I was much perturbed by my uncle's mysterious warnings in regard to the reception awaiting me. Youth is sometimes excessively vain, and youthful vanity is almost always cowardly. And so it was extremely unpleasant for me when immediately going in at the door and seeing the whole party round the tea-table, I stumbled over a rug, staggered, and recovering my balance, flew unexpectedly into the middle of the room. As overwhelmed with confusion as though I had at one stroke lost my career, my honour and my good name, I stood without moving, turning as red as a crab and looking with a senseless stare at the company. I mention this incident, in itself so trivial, only because of the effect it had on my state of mind during the whole of that day, and consequently my attitude to some of the personages of my story. I tried to bow, did not fully succeed, turned redder than ever, flew up to my uncle and clutched at his hand.

"How do you do, uncle?" I gasped out breathlessly, intending to say something quite different and much cleverer, but to my own surprise I said nothing but "How do you do?"

"Glad to see you, glad to see you, my boy," answered my uncle, distressed on my account. "You know, we have met already. Don't be nervous, please," he added in a whisper, "it's a thing that may happen to any one, and worse still, one sometimes falls flat! . . . And now, mother, let me introduce to you: this is our young man; he is a little overcome at the moment, but I am sure you will like him. My nephew, Sergey Alexandrovitch," he added, addressing the company.

But before going on with my story, allow me, gentle reader, to introduce to you by name the company in which I suddenly found myself. This is essential to the orderly sequence of my narrative.

The party consisted of several ladies and two men besides my uncle and me. Foma Fomitch, whom I was so eager to see, and who—even then I felt it—was absolute monarch in the house, was not there; he was conspicuous by his absence, and seemed to have taken with him all brightness from the room. They all looked gloomy and worried. One could not help noticing it from the first glance; embarrassed and upset as I was at the moment, I yet discerned that my uncle, for instance, was almost as upset as I was, though he was doing his utmost to conceal his anxiety under a show of ease. Something was lying like a heavy weight on his heart. One of the two gentlemen in the room was a young man about five-and-twenty, who turned out to be the Obnoskin my uncle had spoken of that afternoon, praising his intelligence and high principles. I did not take to this gentleman at all, everything about him savoured of vulgar *chic;* his dress, in spite of its *chic,* was shabby and common; his face looked, somehow, shabby too. His thin flaxen moustaches like a beetle's whiskers, and his unsuccessful wisps of beard, were evidently intended to show that he was a man of independent character and perhaps advanced ideas. He was continually screwing up his eyes, smiling with an affectation of malice; he threw himself into attitudes on his chair, and repeatedly stared at me through his eyeglass; but when I turned to him, he immediately dropped his eyeglass and seemed overcome with alarm. The other gentleman was young too, being about twenty-eight. He was my cousin, Mizintchikov. He certainly was extremely silent. He did not utter a single word at tea, and did not laugh when every one else laughed; but I saw in him no sign of that "crushed" condition my uncle had detected; on the contrary, the look in his light brown eyes expressed resoluteness and a certain decision of character. Mizintchikov was dark and rather good-looking, with black hair; he was very correctly dressed—at my uncle's expense, as I learned later. Of the ladies the one I noticed first of all from her spiteful anaemic face was Miss Perepelitsyn. She was sitting near Madame la Générale—of whom I will give a special account later—not beside her, but deferentially a little behind; she was continually bending down and whispering something into the ear of her patroness. Two or three elderly lady companions were sitting absolutely mute in a row by the window, gazing open-eyed at Madame la Générale and waiting respectfully for their tea. My attention was attracted also by a fat, absolutely redundant lady, of about fifty, dressed very tastelessly and gaudily, wearing rouge, I believe, though she had hardly any teeth except blackened and broken stumps; this fact did not, however, prevent her from mincing, screwing up her eyes, dressing in the height of fashion and almost making eyes. She was hung round with chains, and like Monsieur Obnoskin was continually turning her lorgnette on me. This was his mother. Praskovya Ilyinitchna, my meek aunt, was pouring out the tea. She obviously would have liked to embrace me after our long separation, and of course to have shed a few tears on the occasion, but she did not dare. Everything here was, it seemed, under rigorous control. Near her was sitting a very pretty black-eyed girl of fifteen, who looked at me intently with childish curiosity—my cousin Sashenka. Finally, and perhaps most conspicuous of all, was a very strange lady, dressed richly and extremely youthfully, though she was far from being in her first youth and must have been at least five-and-thirty. Her face was very thin, pale, and withered, but extremely animated; a bright colour was constantly appearing in her pale cheeks, almost at every movement, at every flicker of feeling; she was in continual excitement, twisting and turning in her chair, and seemed unable to sit still for a minute. She kept looking at me with a kind of greedy curiosity, and was continually bending down to whisper something into the ear of Sashenka, or of her neighbour on the other side, and immediately afterwards laughing in the most childish and simple-hearted way. But to my surprise her eccentricities seemed to pass unnoticed by the others, as though they had all agreed to pay no attention to them. I guessed that this was Tatyana Ivanovna, the lady in whom, to use my uncle's expression, "there was something phantasmagorial," whom they were trying to force upon him as a bride, and whose favour almost every one in the house was trying to court for the sake of her money. But I liked her eyes, blue and mild; and though there were already crow's-feet round the eyes, their expression was so simple-hearted, so merry and good-humoured, that it was particularly pleasant to meet them. Of Tatyana Ivanovna, one of the real "heroines" of my story, I shall speak more in detail later; her history was very remarkable. Five minutes after my entrance, a very pretty boy, my cousin Ilyusha, ran in from the garden, with his pockets full of knuckle-bones and a top in his hand. He was followed by a graceful young girl, rather pale and weary-looking, but very pretty. She scanned the company with a searching, mistrustful, and even timid glance, looked intently at me, and sat down by Tatyana Ivanovna. I remember that I could not suppress a throb at my heart; I guessed that this was the governess. . . . I remember, too, that on her entrance my uncle stole a swift glance at me and flushed crimson, then he bent down, caught up Ilyusha in his arms, and brought him up to me to be kissed. I noticed, too, that Madame Obnoskin first stared at my uncle and then with a sarcastic smile turned her lorgnette on the governess. My uncle was very much confused, and not knowing what to do, was on the point of calling to Sashenka to introduce her to me; but the girl merely rose from her seat and in silence, with grave dignity, dropped me a curtsey. I liked her doing this, however, for it suited her. At the same instant my kindly aunt, Praskovya Ilyinitchna, could hold out no longer, and abandoning the tea-tray, dashed up to embrace me; but before I had time to say a couple of words to her I heard the shrill voice of Miss Perepelitsyn hissing out that Praskovya Ilyinitchna seemed to have forgotten Madame la Générale. "That Madame has asked for her tea, and you do not pour it out, and she is waiting." And Praskovya Ilyinitchna, leaving me, flew back in all haste to her duties. Madame la Générale, the most important person of the party, in whose presence all the others were on their best behaviour, was a lean, spiteful old woman, dressed in mourning—spiteful, however, chiefly from old age and from the loss of her mental faculties (which had never been over-brilliant); even in the past, she had been a nonsensical creature. Her rank as a general's wife had made her even stupider and more arrogant. When she was in a bad humour the house became a perfect hell. She had two ways of displaying her ill-humour. The first was a silent method, when the old lady would not open her lips for days together, but maintained an obstinate silence and pushed away or even sometimes flung on the floor everything that was put before her. The other method was the exact opposite—garrulous. This would begin, as a rule, by my grandmother's—for she was my grandmother, of course—being plunged into a state of extreme despondency, and expecting the end of the world and the failure of all her undertakings, foreseeing poverty and every possible trouble in the future, being carried away by her own presentiments, reckoning on her fingers the calamities that were coming, and reaching a climax of enthusiasm and intense excitement over the enumeration. It always appeared, of course, that she had foreseen all this long before, and had said nothing only because she was forced to be silent "in this house." But if only she had been treated with respect, if only they had cared to listen to her earlier, then, etc., etc. In all this, the flock of lady companions and Miss Perepelitsyn promptly followed suit, and finally it was solemnly ratified by Foma Fomitch. At the minute when I was presented to her she was in a horrible rage, and apparently it was taking the silent form, the most terrible. Every one was watching her with apprehension. Only Tatyana Ivanovna, who was completely unconscious of it all, was in the best of spirits. My uncle purposely with a certain solemnity led me up to my grandmother; but the latter, making a wry face, pushed away her cup ill-humouredly.

"Is this that *vol-ti-geur?*" she drawled through her teeth, addressing Miss Perepelitsyn.

This foolish question completely disconcerted me. I don't understand why she called me a *voltigeur*. But such questions were easy enough to her. Miss Perepelitsyn bent down and whispered something in her ear, but the old lady waved her off angrily. I remained standing with my mouth open and looked inquiringly at my uncle. They all looked at one another and Obnoskin even grinned, which I did not like at all.

"She sometimes talks at random, my boy," my uncle, a little disconcerted himself, whispered in my ear; "but it means nothing, it's just her goodness of heart. The heart is what one must look at."

"Yes, the heart, the heart," Tatyana Ivanovna's bell-like voice rang out. She had not taken her eyes off me all this time, and seemed as though she could not sit still in her chair. I suppose the word "heart," uttered in a whisper, had reached her ear.

But she did not go on, though she was evidently longing to express herself. Whether she was overcome with confusion or some other feeling, she suddenly subsided into silence, flushed extremely red, turned quickly to the governess and whispered something in her ear, and suddenly putting her handkerchief before her mouth and sinking back in her chair, began giggling as though she were in hysterics. I looked at them all in extreme amazement; but to my surprise, every one was particularly grave and looked as though nothing exceptional had happened. I realized, of course, the kind of person Tatyana Ivanovna was. At last I was handed tea, and I recovered myself a little. I don't know why, but I suddenly felt that it was my duty to begin a polite conversation with the ladies.

"It was true what you told me, uncle," I began, "when you warned me that I might be a little abashed. I openly confess—why conceal it?" I went on, addressing Madame Obnoskin with a deprecating smile, "that I have hitherto had hardly any experience of ladies' society. And just now when I made my entry so unsuccessfully, it seemed to me that my position in the middle of the room was very ridiculous and made me look rather a simpleton, didn't it? Have you read *The Simpleton?*" I added, feeling more and more lost, blushing at my ingratiating candour, and glaring at Monsieur Obnoskin, who was still looking me up and down with a grin on his face.

"Just so, just so, just so!" my uncle cried suddenly with extreme animation, genuinely delighted that the conversation had been set going somehow and that I had recovered myself. "That's no great matter, my boy, your talking of the likelihood of your being abashed. Well, you have been, and that's the end of it. But when I first made my début, I actually told a lie, my boy, would you believe that? Yes, really, Anfisa Petrovna, I assure you, it's worth hearing. Just after I had become a Junker, I went to Moscow, and presented myself to a very important lady with a letter of introduction; that is, she was a very haughty woman, but in reality, very good-natured, in spite of what they said. I went in—I was shown up. The drawing-room was full of people, chiefly swells. I made my bow and sat down. At the second word, she asked me: 'Have you estates in the country?' And I hadn't got as much as a hen—what was I to answer? I felt crushed to the earth. Every one was looking at me (I was only a young Junker!). Why not say: no, I have nothing; and that would have been the right thing because it was the truth. But I couldn't face it! 'Yes,' I said, 'a hundred and seventeen serfs.' And why did I stick on that seventeen? If one must tell a lie, it is better to tell it with a round number, isn't it? A minute later, through my letter of introduction, it appeared that I was as poor as a church mouse, and I had told a lie into the bargain! ... Well, there was no help for it. I took myself off as fast as I could, and never set foot in the place again. In those days I had nothing, you know. All I have got now is three hundred serfs from Uncle Afanasy Matveyitch, and two hundred serfs with Kapitonovko which came to me earlier from my grandmother Akulina Panfilovna, a total of more than five hundred serfs. That's capital! But from that day I gave up lying and don't tell lies now."

"Well, I shouldn't have given it up, if I were you. There is no knowing what may happen," observed Obnoskin, smiling ironically.

"To be sure, that's true! Goodness knows what may happen," my uncle assented good-naturedly.

Obnoskin burst into loud laughter, throwing himself back in his chair; his mother smiled; Miss Perepelitsyn sniggered in a particularly disgusting way; Tatyana Ivanovna giggled too, without knowing why, and even clapped her hands; in fact, I saw distinctly that my uncle counted for nothing in his own house. Sashenka's eyes flashed angrily, and she looked steadily at Obnoskin. The governess flushed and looked down. My uncle was surprised.

"What is it? What's happened?" he repeated, looking round at us all in perplexity.

All this time my cousin Mizintchikov was sitting a little way off, saying nothing and not even smiling when every one laughed. He drank tea zealously, gazed philosophically at the whole company, and several times as though in an access of unbearable boredom broke into whistling, probably a habit of his, but pulled himself up in time. Obnoskin, who had jeered at my uncle and had attempted to attack me, seemed not to dare to glance at Mizintchikov; I noticed that. I noticed, too, that my silent cousin looked frequently at me and with evident curiosity, as though he was trying to make up his mind what sort of person I was.

"I am certain," Madame Obnoskin minced suddenly, "I am perfectly certain Monsieur Serge—that is your name I believe?—that at home, in Petersburg, you were not greatly devoted to the ladies. I know that there are many, a great many young men nowadays in Petersburg who shun the society of ladies altogether. But in my opinion they are all free-thinkers. Nothing would induce me to regard it as anything but unpardonable free-thinking. And I must say it surprises me, young man, it surprises me, simply surprises me! . . ."

"I have not been into society at all," I answered with extraordinary animation. "But that . . . I imagine at least . . . is of no consequence. I have lived, that is I have generally had lodgings . . . but that is no matter, I assure you. I shall be known one day; but hitherto I have always stayed at home. . . ."

"He is engaged in learned pursuits," observed my uncle, drawing himself up with dignity.

"Oh, uncle, still talking of your learned pursuits! . . . Only fancy," I went on with an extraordinarily free and easy air, smirking affably, and again addressing Madame Obnoskin, "my beloved uncle is so devoted to learning that he has unearthed somewhere on the high road a marvellous practical philosopher, a Mr. Korovkin; and his first word to me after all these years of separation was, that he was expecting this phenomenal prodigy with the most acute, one may say, impatience . . . from love of learning, of course. . . ."

And I sniggered, hoping to provoke a general laugh at my facetiousness.

"Who is that? Of whom is he talking?" Madame la Générale jerked out sharply, addressing Miss Perepelitsyn.

"Yegor Ilyitch has been inviting visitors, learned gentlemen; he drives along the highroads collecting them," the lady hissed out.

My uncle was completely dumbfounded.

"Oh, yes! I had forgotten," he cried, turning upon me a glance that expressed reproach. "I am expecting Korovkin. A man of learning, a man who will survive his century. . . ."

He broke off and relapsed into silence. Madame la Générale waved her arm, and this time so successfully that she knocked over a cup, which flew off the table and was smashed. General excitement followed.

"She always does that when she is angry; she throws things on the floor," my uncle whispered in confusion. "But she only does it when she is angry. . . . Don't stare, my boy, don't take any notice, look the other way. . . . What made you speak of Korovkin? . . ."

But I was looking away already; at that moment I met the eyes of the governess, and it seemed to me that in their expression there was something reproachful, even contemptuous; a flush of indignation glowed upon her pale cheeks. I understood the look in her face, and guessed that by my mean and disgusting desire to make my uncle ridiculous in order to make myself a little less so, I had not gained much in that young lady's estimation. I cannot express how ashamed I felt!

"I must go on about Petersburg with you," Anfisa Petrovna gushed again, when the commotion caused by the breaking of the cup had subsided. "I recall with such enjoyment, I may say, our life in that charming city. . . . We were very intimately acquainted with a family— do you remember, Pavel, General Polovitsin. . . . Oh, what a fascinating, fas-ci-na-ting creature his wife was! You know that aristocratic distinction, *beau monde! . . .* Tell me, you have most likely met her? . . . I must own I have been looking forward to your being here with impatience; I have been hoping to hear a great deal, a very great deal about our friends in Petersburg. . . ."

"I am very sorry that I cannot . . . excuse me. . . . As I have said already, I have rarely been into society, and I don't know General Polovitsin; I have never even heard of him," I answered impatiently, my affability being suddenly succeeded by a mood of extreme annoyance and irritability.

"He is studying mineralogy," my incorrigible uncle put in with pride. "Is that investigating all sorts of stones, mineralogy, my boy?"

"Yes, uncle, stones. . . ."

"H'm. . . . There are a great many sciences and they are all of use! And do you know, my boy, to tell you the truth, I did not know what mineralogy meant! It's all Greek to me. In other things I am so-so, but at learned subjects I am stupid—I frankly confess it!"

"You frankly confess!" Obnoskin caught him up with a snigger.

"Papa!" cried Sashenka, looking reproachfully at her father.

"What is it, darling? Oh, dear, I keep interrupting you, Anfisa Petrovna," my uncle caught himself up suddenly, not understanding Sashenka's exclamation. "Please forgive me."

"Oh, don't distress yourself," Anfisa Petrovna answered with a sour smile. "Though I have said everything already to your nephew, and will finish perhaps, Monsieur Serge—that is right, isn't it?—by telling you that you really must reform. I believe that the sciences, the arts . . . sculpture, for instance . . . all those lofty ideas, in fact, have their fas-ci-na-ting side, but they do not take the place of ladies! . . . Women, women would form you, young man, and so to do without them is impossible, young man, impossible, im-poss-ible!"

"Impossible, impossible," Tatyana Ivanovna's rather shrill voice rang out again. "Listen," she began, speaking with a sort of childish haste and flushing crimson, of course, "listen, I want to ask you something. . . ."

"Pray do," I answered, looking at her attentively.

"I wanted to ask you whether you have come to stay long or not?"

"I really don't know, that's as my affairs . . ."

"Affairs! What sort of affairs can he have? Oh, the mad fellow! . . ."

And Tatyana Ivanovna, blushing perfectly crimson and hiding behind her fan, bent down to the governess and at once began whispering something to her. Then she suddenly laughed and clapped her hands.

"Stay! stay!" she cried, breaking away from her confidante and again addressing me in a great hurry as though afraid I were going away. "Listen, do you know what I am going to tell you? You are awfully, awfully like a young man, a fas-ci-na-ting young man! Sashenka, Nastenka, do you remember? He is awfully like that madman—do you remember, Sashenka? We were out driving when we met him . . . on horseback in a white waistcoat . . . he put up his eyeglass at me, too, the shameless fellow! Do you remember, I hid myself in my veil, too, but I couldn't resist putting my head out of the carriage window and shouting to him: 'You shameless fellow!' and then I threw my bunch of flowers on the road? . . . Do you remember, Nastenka?"

And the lady, half-crazy over eligible young men, hid her face in her hands, all excitement; then suddenly leaped up from her seat, darted to the window, snatched a rose from a bowl, threw it on the floor near me and ran out of the room. She was gone in a flash! This time a certain embarrassment was apparent, though Madame la Générale was again completely unmoved. Anfisa Petrovna, for instance, showed no surprise, but seemed suddenly a little troubled and looked with anxiety at her son; the young ladies blushed, while Pavel Obnoskin, with a look of vexation which at the time I did not understand, got up from his chair and went to the window. My uncle was beginning to make signs to me, but at that instant another person walked into the room and drew the attention of all.

"Ah, here is Yevgraf Larionitch! Talk of angels!" cried my uncle, genuinely delighted. "Well, brother, have you come from the town?"

"Queer set of creatures! They seem to have been collected here on purpose!" I thought to myself, not yet understanding fully what was passing before my eyes, and not suspecting either that I was probably adding another to the collection of queer creatures by appearing among them.

[v]

YEZHEVIKIN

THERE walked or rather squeezed himself into the room (though the doors were very wide ones) a little figure which even in the doorway began wriggling, bowing and smirking, looking with extraordinary curiosity at all the persons present. It was a little pock-marked old man with quick and furtive eyes, with a bald patch at the top of his head and another at the back, with a look of undefined subtle mockery on his rather thick lips. He was wearing a very shabby dress-coat which looked as though it were second-hand. One button was hanging by a thread; two or three were completely missing. His high boots full of holes, and his greasy cap, were in keeping with his pitiful attire; he had a very dirty check pocket-handkerchief in his hand, with which he wiped the sweat from his brow and temples. I noticed that the governess blushed slightly and looked rapidly at me. I fancied, too, that there was something proud and challenging in this glance.

"Straight from the town, benefactor! Straight from there, my kind protector! I will tell you everything, only first let me pay my respects," said the old man. And he made straight for Madame la Générale, but stopped half-way and again addressed my uncle.

"You know my leading characteristic, benefactor—a sly rogue, a regular sly rogue! You know that as soon as I walk in I make for the chief person of the house, I turn my toes in her direction first of all, so as from the first step to win favour and protection. A sly rogue, my good sir, a sly rogue, benefactor. Allow me, my dear lady, allow me, your Excellency, to kiss your dress, or I might sully with my lips your hand of gold, of general's rank."

Madame la Générale to my surprise gave him her hand to kiss rather graciously.

"And my respects to you, our beauty," he went on, "Miss Perepelitsyn. There is no help for it, madame, I am a sly rogue. As long ago as 1841 it was settled that I was a rogue, when I was dismissed from the service just at the time when Valentin Ignatyevitch Tihontsev became 'your honour.' He was made an assessor; he was made an assessor and I was made a rogue. And, you know, I am so open by nature that I make no secret of it. It can't be helped. I have tried living honestly, I have tried it, but now I must try something else. Alexandra Yegorovna, our little apple in syrup," he went on, going round the table and making his way up to Sashenka, "let me kiss your dress; there is a smell of apples and all sorts of nice things about you, young lady. Our respects to the hero of the day; I have brought you a bow and arrow, my little sir. I was a whole morning making it, my lads helped me; we will shoot with it presently. And when you grow up you will be an officer and cut off a Turk's head. Tatyana Ivanovna . . . but oh, she is not here, my benefactress! Or I would have kissed her dress too. Praskovya Ilyinitchna, my kindest friend, I can't get near you or I would kiss your foot as well as your hand, so there! Anfisa Petrovna, I protest my profound respect for you. I prayed for you only to-day, benefactress, on my knees with tears I prayed for you and for your son also that God might send him honours of all sorts—and talents too, talents especially! And by the way, our humblest duty to Ivan Ivanitch Mizintchikov. May God send you all that you desire for yourself, for you will never make out, sir, what you do want for yourself: such a silent gentleman. . . . Good-day, Nastya! All my small fry send their love to you, they talk of you every day. And now a deep bow to my host. I come from the town, your honour, straight off from the town. And this, no doubt, is your nephew who is being trained in a learned faculty? My humble duty, sir; let me have your hand."

There was laughter. One could see that the old man played the part of an amateur clown. His arrival livened the party up. Many did not even understand his sarcasms, and yet he had made slight digs at them all. Only the governess, whom to my surprise he called simply Nastya, blushed and frowned. I was pulling back my hand, but I believe that was just what the horrid old man wanted.

"But I only asked to shake it, sir, if you will allow me; not to kiss it. And you thought I meant to kiss it? No, my dear sir, for the time being I will only shake it. I suppose you took me for the clown of the establishment, kind sir?" he said, looking at me mockingly.

"N-no, really, I . . ."

"To be sure, sir! If I am a fool, then some one else here is one too. Treat me with respect; I am not such a rogue yet as you imagine. Though maybe I am a clown too. I am a slave, my wife is a slave, and so there is nothing for it but flattery. That's how it is! You get something by it anyway, if only to make sop for the children. Sugar, scatter as much sugar as you can in everything, that will make things more wholesome for you. I tell you this in secret, sir; maybe you will have need of it. Fortune has been hard on me, that is why I am a clown."

"He-he-he! The old man is a comical fellow! He always makes us laugh!" piped Anfisa Petrovna.

"My dear madame and benefactress, a fool has a better time of it in this world! If I had only known that, I would have enlisted among the fools in early childhood, and I dare say by now I might have been a wise man. But as it is, I wanted to be a clever man at first, so now I am a fool in my old age."

"Tell me, please," interposed Obnoskin (he probably was not pleased by the remark about *talents*), lolling in a particularly free and easy way in his arm-chair and staring at the old man through his eyeglass as though at an insect, "tell me, please . . . I always forget your surname . . . what the deuce is it? . . ."

"Oh, my dear sir! Why, my surname, if it please you, is Yezhevikin; but what does that matter? Here I have been sitting without a job these nine years, I just go on living in accordance with the laws of nature. And my children, my children are simply a family of Holmskys. As the proverb goes, 'The rich man has calves, the poor man has kids.'"

"Oh, yes . . . calves . . . but that's beside the point. Come, listen, I have been wanting to ask you a long time: why is it that when you come in, you look back at once? It's very funny."

"Why do I look back? Why, I am always fancying, sir, that some one behind me wants to slap me on the back and squash me like a fly. That is why I look round. I have become a monomaniac, sir."

Again there was laughter. The governess got up from her seat as though she would go away, but sank back in her chair again. There was a look of pain and suffering on her face in spite of the colour that flooded her cheeks.

"You know who it is, my boy?" my uncle whispered. "It's *her* father, you know!"

I stared at my uncle open-eyed. The name of Yezhevikin had completely slipped out of my mind. I had been playing the hero, had been dreaming all the journey of my proposed bride, had been building magnificent plans for her benefit, and had utterly forgotten her name, or rather had taken no notice of it from the first.

"What, her father?" I answered, also in a whisper. "Why, I thought she was an orphan."

"It's her father, my boy, her father. And do you know, a most honest, a most honourable man and he does not even drink, but only plays at being a fool; fearfully poor, my boy, eight children! They live on Nastya's salary. He was turned out of the service through his tongue. He comes here every week. He is such a proud fellow—nothing will induce him to take help. I have offered it, many times I have offered it—he won't take it. An embittered man."

"Well, Yevgraf Larionitch, what news have you?" uncle asked, and slapped him warmly on the shoulder, noticing that the suspicious old man was already listening to our conversation.

"What news, benefactor? Valentin Ignatyitch made a statement about Trishin's case yesterday. The flour under his charge turned out to be short weight. It is that Trishin, madame, who looks at you and puffs like a samovar. Perhaps you graciously remember him? So Valentin Ignatyitch writes of Trishin: 'If,' said he, 'the often-mentioned Trishin could not guard his own niece's honour'—she eloped with an officer last year—'how,' said he, 'should he take care of government property?' He stuck that into his report, by God, I am not lying."

"Fie! What stories you tell!" cried Anfisa Petrovna.

"Just so, just so, just so! You've overshot the mark, friend Yevgraf," my uncle chimed in. "*Aïe!* your tongue will be your ruin. You are a straightforward man, honourable and upright, I can say that, but you have a venomous tongue! And I can't understand how it is you can't get on with them. They seem good-natured people, simple . . ."

"Kind friend and benefactor! But it's just the simple man that I am afraid of," cried the old man with peculiar fervour.

I liked the answer. I went rapidly up to Yezhevikin and warmly pressed his hand. The truth is, I wanted in some way to protest against the general tone and to show my sympathy for the old man openly. And perhaps, who knows? perhaps I wanted to raise myself in the opinion of Nastasya Yevgrafovna! But my movement led to no good.

"Allow me to ask you," I said, blushing and flustered as usual, "have you heard of the Jesuits?"

"No, my good sir, I haven't; well, maybe something . . . though how should we! But why?"

"Oh . . . I meant to tell you something apropos. . . . But remind me some other time. But now let me assure you, I understand you and . . . know how to appreciate . . ."

And utterly confused, I gripped his hand again.

"Certainly, I will remind you, sir, certainly. I will write it in golden letters. If you will allow me, I'll tie a knot in my handkerchief."

And he actually looked for a dry corner in his dirty, snuffy handkerchief, and tied a knot in it.

"Yevgraf Larionitch, take your tea," said Praskovya Ilyinitchna.

"Immediately, my beautiful lady; immediately, my princess, I mean, not my lady! That's in return for your tea. I met Stepan Alexyevitch Bahtcheyev on the road, madame. He was so festive, that I didn't know what to make of it! I began to wonder whether he wasn't going to get married. Flatter away, flatter away!" he said in a half-whisper, winking at me and screwing up his eyes as he carried his cup by me. "And how is it that my benefactor, my chief one, Foma Fomitch, is not to be seen? Isn't he coming to tea?"

My uncle started as though he had been stung, and glanced timidly at his mother.

"I really don't know," he answered uncertainly, with a strange perturbation. "We sent for him, but he . . . I don't know really, perhaps he is indisposed. I have already sent Vidoplyasov and . . . Perhaps I ought to go myself, though?"

"I went in to him myself just now," Yezhevikin brought out mysteriously.

"Is it possible!" cried out my uncle in alarm. "Well, how was it?"

"I went in to him, first of all, I paid him my respects. His honour said he should drink his tea in solitude, and then added that a crust of dry bread would be enough for him, yes."

These words seemed to strike absolute terror into my uncle.

"But you should have explained to him, Yevgraf Larionitch; you should have told him" . . . my uncle said at last, looking at the old man with distress and reproach.

"I did, I did."

"Well?"

"For a long time he did not deign to answer me. He was sitting over some mathematical problem, he was working out something; one could see it was a brain-racking problem. He drew the breeches of Pythagoras, while I was there, I saw him myself. I repeated it three times, only at the fourth he raised his head and seemed to see me for the first time. 'I am not coming,' he said; 'a *learned* gentleman has arrived here now, so I should be out of place beside a luminary like that!' He made use of that expression 'beside a luminary.' "

And the horrid old man stole a sly glance at me.

"That is just what I expected," cried my uncle, clasping his hands. "That's how I thought it would be. He says that about you, Sergey, that you are a 'learned gentlemen.' Well, what's to be done now?"

"I must confess, uncle," I answered with dignity, shrugging my shoulders, "it seems to me such an absurd refusal that it is not worth noticing, and I really wonder at your being troubled by it. . . . ."

"Oh, my boy, you know nothing about it!" he cried, with a vigorous wave of his hand.

"It's no use grieving now, sir," Miss Perepelitsyn put in suddenly, "since all the wicked causes of it have come from you in the first place, Yegor Ilyitch. If you take off your head you don't weep for your hair. You should have listened to your mamma, sir, and you would have had no cause for tears now."

"Why, how am I to blame, Anna Nilovna? Have some fear of God!" said my uncle in an imploring voice, as though begging for an explanation.

"I do fear God, Yegor Ilyitch; but it all comes from your being an egoist, sir, and not loving your mother," Miss Perepelitsyn answered with dignity. "Why didn't you respect her wishes in the first place? She is your mother, sir. And I am not likely to tell you a lie, sir. I am a major's daughter myself, and not just anybody, sir."

It seemed to me that Miss Perepelitsyn had intervened in the conversation with the sole object of informing us all, and me in particular as a newcomer, that she was a major's daughter and not just anybody.

"It's because he ill-treats his own mother," Madame la Générale herself brought out at last in a menacing voice.

"Mamma, have mercy on us! How am I ill-treating you?"

"It is because you are a black-hearted egoist, Yegorushka," Madame la Générale went on, growing more and more animated.

"Mamma, mamma! in what way am I a black-hearted egoist?" cried my uncle, almost in despair. "For five days, for five whole days you have been angry with me and will not speak to me. And what for? what for? Let them judge me, let the whole world judge me! But let them hear my defence too. I have long kept silent, mamma, you would not hear me; let these people hear me now. Anfisa Petrovna! Pavel Semyonitch, generous Pavel Semyonitch! Sergey, my dear! You are an

678The Short Novels of Dostoevsky

outsider, you are, so to speak, a spectator. You can judge impartially. . . ."

"Calm yourself, Yegor Ilyitch, calm yourself," cried Anfisa Petrovna, "don't kill your mamma."

"I am not killing my mamma, Anfisa Petrovna; but here I lay bare my heart, you can strike at it!" my uncle went on, worked up to the utmost pitch as people of weak character sometimes are when they are driven out of all patience, though their heat is like the fire of burning straws. "I want to say, Anfisa Petrovna, that I am not ill-treating any one. I start with saying that Foma Fomitch is the noblest and the most honourable of men, and a man of superior qualities too, but . . . but he has been unjust to me in this case."

"H'm!" grunted Obnoskin, as though he wanted to irritate my uncle still more.

"Pavel Semyonitch, noble-hearted Pavel Semyonitch! Can you really think that I am, so to speak, an unfeeling stone? Why, I see, I understand—with tears in my heart, I may say I understand—that all this misunderstanding comes from the excess of *his* affection for me. But, say what you like, he really is unjust in this case. I will tell you all about it. I want to tell the whole story, Anfisa Petrovna, clearly and in full detail, that you may see from what the thing started, and whether mamma is right in being angry with me for not satisfying Foma Fomitch. And you listen too, Seryozha," he added, addressing me, which he did, indeed, during the rest of his story, as though he were afraid of his other listeners and doubtful of their sympathy; "you, too, listen and decide whether I am right or wrong. You will see what the whole business arose from. A week ago—yes, not more than a week— my old chief, General Rusapetov, was passing through our town with his wife and stepdaughter, and broke the journey there. I was overwhelmed. I hastened to seize the opportunity, I flew over, presented myself and invited them to dinner. He promised to come if it were possible. He is a very fine man, I assure you; he is conspicuous for his virtues and is a man of the highest rank into the bargain! He has been a benefactor to his stepdaughter; he married an orphan girl to an admirable young man (now a lawyer at Malinova; still a young man, but with, one may say, an all-round education); in short, he is a general of generals. Well, of course there was a tremendous fuss and bustle in the house—cooks, fricassees—I sent for an orchestra. I was delighted, of course, and looked festive; Foma Fomitch did not like my being delighted and looking festive! He sat down to the table—I remember, too, he was handed his favourite jelly and cream—he sat on and on without saying a word, then all at once jumped up. 'I am being insulted, insulted!' 'But why, in what way are you being insulted, Foma Fomitch?' 'You despise me now,' he said; 'you are taken up with generals now, you think more of generals now than of me.' Well, of course I am making a long story short, so to say, I am only giving you the pith of it; but if only you knew what he said besides . . . in a word, he stirred me to my inmost depths. What was I to do? I was depressed by it, of course; it was a blow to me, I may say. I went about like a cock drenched with rain. The festive day arrived. The general sent to say he couldn't come, he apologized—so he was not coming. I went to Foma. 'Come, Foma,' I said, 'set your mind at rest, he is not coming.' And would you believe it, he wouldn't forgive me, and that was the end of it. 'I have been insulted,' he said, 'and that is all about it!' I said this and that. 'No,' he said. 'You can go to your generals; you think more of generals than of me, you have broken our bonds of friendship,' he said. Of course, my dear, I understand what he was angry over, I am not a block, I am not a sheep, I am not a perfect post. It was, of course, from the excess of his affection for me, from jealousy—he says that himself—he is jealous of the general on my account, he is afraid of losing my affection, he is testing me, he wants to see how much I am ready to sacrifice for him. 'No,' he said, 'I am just as good as the general for you, I am myself "your Excellency" for you! I will be reconciled to you when you prove your respect for me.' 'In what way am I to prove my respect for you, Foma Fomitch?' 'Call me for a whole day "your Excellency,"' says he, 'then you will prove your respect.' I felt as though I were dropping from the clouds; you can picture my amazement. 'That will serve you,' said he, 'as a lesson not to be in ecstasies at the sight of generals when there are other people, perhaps, superior to all your generals.' Well, at that point I lost patience, I confess it! I confess it openly. 'Foma Fomitch,' I said, 'is such a thing possible? Can I take it upon myself to do it? Can I, have I the right to promote you to be a general? Think who it is bestows the rank of a general! How can I address you as, "your Excellency"? Why, it is infringing the decrees of Providence! Why, the general is an honour to his country; the general has faced the enemy, he has shed his blood on the field of honour. How am I to call you, "your Excellency"?' He would not give way, there was no doing anything. 'Whatever you want, Foma,' I said, 'I will do anything for you. Here you told me to shave off my whiskers because they were not patriotic enough—I shaved them off; I frowned, but I did shave them. What is more, I will do anything you like, only do give up the rank of a general!' 'No,'

said he, 'I won't be reconciled till you call me "your Excellency";
that,' said he, 'will be good for your moral character, it will humble
your spirit!' said he. And so now for a week, a whole week, he won't
speak to me; he is cross to every one that comes; he heard about you,
that you were learned—that was my fault; I got warm and said too
much—so he said he would not set foot in the house if you came into
it. 'So I am not learned enough for you now,' said he. So there will be
trouble when he hears now about Korovkin! Come now, please, tell
me in what way have I been to blame? Was I to take on myself to call
him 'your Excellency'? Why, it is impossible to live in such a position!
What did he drive poor Bahtcheyev away from the table to-day for?
Supposing Bahtcheyev is not a great astronomer, why, I am not a great
astronomer, and you are not a great astronomer. . . . Why is it? Why
is it?"

"Because you are envious, Yegorushka," mumbled Madame la
Générale again.

"Mamma," cried my uncle in despair, "you will drive me out of my
mind! . . . Those are not your words, you are repeating what others
say, mamma! I am, in fact, made out a stone, a block, a lamp-post and
not your son."

"I heard, uncle," I interposed, utterly amazed by his story—"I heard
from Bahtcheyev, I don't know whether it was true or not—that Foma
Fomitch was jealous of Ilyusha's nameday, and declares that to-morrow
is his nameday too. I must own that this characteristic touch so
astounded me that I . . ."

"His birthday, my dear, his birthday!" my uncle interrupted me,
speaking rapidly. "He only made a mistake in the word, but he is right;
to-morrow is his birthday. Truth, my boy, before everything. . . ."

"It's not his birthday at all!" cried Sashenka.

"Not his birthday!" cried my uncle, in a fluster.

"It's not his birthday, papa. You simply say what isn't true to deceive
yourself and to satisfy Foma Fomitch. His birthday was in March.
Don't you remember, too, we went on a pilgrimage to the monastery
just before, and he wouldn't let any one sit in peace in the carriage?
He kept crying out that the cushion was *crushing* his side, and pinching us; he pinched auntie twice in his ill-humour. 'I am fond of
camellias,' he said, 'for I have the taste of the most refined society,
and you grudge picking me any from the conservatory.' And all day
long he sulked and grizzled and would not talk to us. . . ."

I fancy that if a bomb had fallen in the middle of the room it would
not have astounded and alarmed them all as much as this open

mutiny—and of whom?—of a little girl who was not even permitted to speak aloud in her grandmother's presence. Madame la Générale, dumb with amazement and fury, rose from her seat, stood erect and stared at her insolent grandchild, unable to believe her eyes. My uncle was paralyzed with horror.

"She is allowed to do just as she likes, she wants to be the death of her grandmother!" cried Miss Perepelitsyn.

"Sasha, Sasha, think what you are saying! What's the matter with you, Sasha?" cried my uncle, rushing from one to the other, from his mother to Sashenka to stop her.

"I won't hold my tongue, papa!" cried Sashenka, leaping up from her chair with flashing eyes and stamping with her feet. "I won't hold my tongue! We have all suffered too long from Foma Fomitch, from your nasty, horrid Foma Fomitch! Foma Fomitch will be the ruin of us all, for people keep on telling him that he is so clever, generous, noble, learned, a mix-up of all the virtues, a sort of potpourri, and like an idiot Foma Fomitch believes it all. So many nice things are offered to him that any one else would be ashamed; but Foma Fomitch gobbles up all that is put before him and asks for more. You'll see, he will be the ruin of us all, and it's all papa's fault! Horrid, horrid Foma Fomitch! I speak straight out, I am not afraid of any one! He is stupid, ill-tempered, dirty, ungentlemanly, cruel-hearted, a bully, a mischief-maker, a liar. . . . Oh, I'd turn him out of the house this minute, I would, but papa adores him, papa is crazy over him!"

"Oh!" shrieked her grandmother, and she fell in a swoon on the sofa.

"Agafya Timofyevna, my angel," cried Anfisa Petrovna, "take my smelling-salts! Water, make haste, water!"

"Water, water!" shouted my uncle. "Mamma, mamma, calm yourself! I beg you on my knees to calm yourself! . . ."

"You ought to be kept on bread and water and shut up in a dark room . . . you're a murderess!" Miss Perepelitsyn, shaking with spite, hissed at Sashenka.

"I will be kept on bread and water, I am not afraid of anything!" cried Sashenka, moved to frenzy in her turn. "I will defend papa because he can't defend himself. Who is he, who is your Foma Fomitch compared with papa? He eats papa's bread and insults papa, the ungrateful creature. I would tear him to pieces, your Foma Fomitch! I'd challenge him to a duel and shoot him on the spot with with two pistols! . . ."

"Sasha, Sasha," cried my uncle in despair. "Another word and I am ruined, hopelessly ruined."

"Papa," cried Sashenka, flinging herself headlong at her father, dissolving into tears and hugging him in her arms, "papa, how can you ruin yourself like this, you so kind, and good, and merry and clever? How can you give in to that horrid ungrateful man, be his plaything and let him turn you into ridicule? Papa, my precious papa! . . ."

She burst into sobs, covered her face with her hands and ran out of the room.

A fearful hubbub followed. Madame la Générale lay in a swoon. My uncle was kneeling beside her kissing her hands. Miss Perepelitsyn was wriggling about them and casting spiteful but triumphant glances at us. Anfisa Petrovna was moistening the old lady's temples and applying her smelling-salts. Praskovya Ilyinitchna was shedding tears and trembling, Yezhevikin was looking for a corner to seek refuge in, while the governess stood pale and completely overwhelmed with terror. Mizintchikov was the only one who remained unchanged. He got up, went to the window and began looking out of it, resolutely declining to pay attention to the scene around him.

All at once Madame la Générale sat up, drew herself up and scanned me with a menacing eye.

"Go away!" she shouted, stamping her foot at me.

I must confess that this I had not in the least expected.

"Go away! Go out of the house! What has he come for? Don't let me see a trace of him!"

"Mamma, mamma, what do you mean? Why, this is Seryozha," my uncle muttered, shaking all over with terror. "Why, he has come to pay us a visit, mamma."

"What Seryozha? Nonsense. I won't hear a word. Go away! It's Korovkin. I am convinced it is Korovkin. My presentiments never deceive me. He has come to turn Foma Fomitch out; he has been sent for with that very object. I have a presentiment in my heart. . . . Go away, you scoundrel!"

"Uncle, if this is how it is," I said, spluttering with honest indignation, "then excuse me, I'll . . ." And I reached after my hat.

"Sergey, Sergey, what are you about? . . . Well, this really is . . . Mamma, this is Seryozha! . . . Sergey, upon my word!" he cried, racing after me and trying to take away my hat. "You are my visitor; you'll stay, I wish it! She doesn't mean it," he went on in a whisper; "she only goes on like this when she is angry. . . . You only keep out of her sight just at first . . . keep out of the way and it will all pass over. She will forgive you, I assure you! She is good-natured, only she works herself up. You hear she takes you for Korovkin, but afterwards she will forgive you, I assure you. . . . What do you want?" he cried to Gavrila, who came into the room trembling with fear.

Gavrila came in not alone; with him was a very pretty peasant boy of sixteen who had been taken as a house serf, on account of his good looks as I heard afterwards. His name was Falaley. He was wearing a peculiar costume, a red silk shirt with embroidery at the neck and a belt of gold braid, full black velveteen breeches, and goatskin boots turned over with red. This costume was designed by Madame la Générale herself. The boy was sobbing bitterly, and tears rolled one after another from his big blue eyes.

"What's this now?" cried my uncle. "What has happened? Speak, you ruffian!"

"Foma Fomitch told us to come here; he is coming after us himself," answered the despondent Gavrila. "Me for an examination, while he . . ."

"He?"

"He has been dancing, sir," answered Gavrila in a tearful voice.

"Dancing!" cried my uncle in horror.

"Dancing," blubbered Falaley with a sob.

"The Komarinsky!"

"Yes, the Kom-a-rin-sky."

"And Foma Fomitch found him?"

"Ye-es, he found me."

"You'll be the death of me!" cried my uncle. "I am done for!" And he clutched his head in both hands.

"Foma Fomitch!" Vidoplyasov announced, entering the room.

The door opened, and Foma Fomitch in his own person stood facing the perplexed company.

[VI]

OF THE WHITE BULL AND THE KOMARINSKY PEASANT

BEFORE I have the honour of presenting the reader with Foma Fomitch in person, I think it is absolutely essential to say a few words about Falaley and to explain what there was terrible in the fact of his dancing the Komarinsky and Foma Fomitch's finding him engaged in that light-hearted diversion. Falaley was a house serf boy, an orphan from the cradle, and a godson of my uncle's late wife. My uncle was very fond of him. That fact alone was quite sufficient to make Foma Fomitch, after he had settled at Stepantchikovo and gained complete domination over my uncle, take a dislike to the latter's favourite, Falaley. But Madame la Générale took a particular fancy to the boy, who, in spite of Foma Fomitch's wrath, remained upstairs in attendance on the family. Madame la Générale herself insisted upon it, and Foma gave way, storing up the injury—he looked on everything as an injury—in his heart and revenging it on every favourable occasion on my uncle, who was in no way responsible. Falaley was wonderfully good-looking. He had a girlish face, the face of a beautiful peasant girl. Madame la Générale petted and spoiled him, prized him as though he were a rare and pretty toy, and there was no saying which she loved best, her little curly black dog Ami or Falaley. We have already referred to his costume, which was her idea. The young ladies gave him pomatum, and it was the duty of the barber Kuzma to curl his hair on holidays. This boy was a strange creature. He could not be called a perfect idiot or imbecile, but he was so naïve, so truthful and simple-hearted, that he might sometimes be certainly taken for a fool. If he had a dream, he would go at once to tell it to his master or mistress. He joined in the conversation of the gentlefolk without caring whether he was interrupting them. He would tell them things quite impossible to tell gentlefolks. He would dissolve into the most genuine tears when his mistress fell into a swoon or when his master was too severely scolded. He sympathized with every sort of distress. He would sometimes go up to Madame la Générale, kiss her hands, and beg her not to be cross—and the old lady would magnanimously forgive him these audacities. He was sensitive in the extreme, kind-hearted, as free from malice as a lamb and as gay as a happy child. They gave him dainties from the dinner-table.

He always stood behind Madame la Générale's chair and was awfully fond of sugar. When he was given a lump of sugar he would nibble at it with his strong milk-white teeth, and a gleam of indescribable pleasure shone in his merry blue eyes and all over his pretty little face.

For a long time Foma Fomitch raged; but reflecting at last that he would get nothing by anger, he suddenly made up his mind to be Falaley's benefactor. After first pitching into my uncle for doing nothing for the education of his house serfs, he determined at once to set about training the poor boy in morals, good manners and French.

"What!" he would say in defence of his absurd idea (an idea not confined to Foma Fomitch, as the writer of these lines can testify), "what! he is always upstairs waiting on his mistress; one day, forgetting that he does not know French, she will say to him, for instance: 'Donnay mooah mon mooshooar'—he ought to be equal to the occasion and able to do his duty even then!"

But it appeared not only that it was impossible to teach Falaley French, but that the cook Andron, the boy's uncle, who had disinterestedly tried to teach him to read Russian, had long ago given it up in despair and put the alphabet away on the shelf. Falaley was so dull at book-learning that he could understand absolutely nothing. Moreover, this led to further trouble. The house serfs began calling Falaley, in derision, a Frenchman, and old Gavrila, my uncle's valet, openly ventured to deny the usefulness of learning French. This reached Foma Fomitch's ears, and bursting with wrath, he made his opponent, Gavrila, himself learn French as a punishment. This was the origin of the whole business of teaching the servants French which so exasperated Mr. Bahtcheyev. It was still worse in regard to manners. Foma was absolutely unable to train Falaley to suit his ideas, and in spite of his prohibition, the boy would go in to tell him his dreams in the morning, which Foma Fomitch considered extremely ill-mannered and familiar. But Falaley obstinately remained Falaley. My uncle was, of course, the first to suffer for all this.

"Do you know, do you know what he has done to-day?" Foma would exclaim, selecting a moment when all were gathered together in order to produce a greater sensation. "Do you know what your systematic spoiling is coming to? To-day he gobbled up a piece of pie given him at the table; and do you know what he said of it? Come here, come here, silly fool; come here, idiot; come here, red face. . . ."

Falaley would come up weeping and rubbing his eyes with both hands.

"What did you say when you greedily ate up your pie? Repeat it before every one!"

Falaley would dissolve in bitter tears and make no answer.

"Then I'll speak for you, if that's how it is. You said, slapping yourself on your stuffed and vulgar stomach: 'I've gobbled up the pie as Martin did the soap!' Upon my word, Colonel, can expressions like that be used in educated society, still more in aristocratic society? Did you say it or not? Speak!"

"I di-id . . ." Falaley would assent, sobbing.

"Well, then, tell me now, does Martin eat soap? Where have you seen a Martin who eats soap? Tell me, give me an idea of this phenomenal Martin!"

Silence.

"I am asking you," Foma would persist, "who is this Martin? I want to see him, I want to make his acquaintance. Well, what is he? A registry clerk, an astronomer, a provincial, a poet, an army captain, a serving man—he must have been something. Answer!"

"A ser-er-ving ma-an," Falaley would answer at last, still weeping.

"Whose? Who is his master?"

But Falaley was utterly unable to say who was his master. It would end, of course, in Foma Fomitch's rushing out of the room in a passion, crying out that he had been insulted; Madame la Générale would show symptoms of an attack, while my uncle would curse the hour of his birth, beg everybody's pardon, and for the rest of the day walk about on tiptoe in his own rooms.

As ill-luck would have it, on the day after the trouble over Martin and the soap, Falaley, who had succeeded in completely forgetting about Martin and all his woes of the previous day, informed Foma Fomitch as he took in his tea in the morning, that he had had a dream about a white bull. This was the last straw! Foma Fomitch was moved to indescribable indignation, he promptly summoned my uncle and began upbraiding him for the vulgarity of the dream dreamed by his Falaley. This time severe steps were taken: Falaley was punished, he had to kneel down in the corner. He was sternly forbidden to dream of such coarse rustic subjects.

"What I am angry at," said Foma, "apart from the fact that he really ought not to dare to think of blurting out his dreams to me, especially a dream of a white bull—apart from that—you must agree, Colonel—what is the white bull but a proof of coarseness, ignorance and loutishness in your unkempt Falaley? As the thoughts are, so will the dreams be. Did I not tell you before that you would never make anything of him, and that he ought not to remain upstairs waiting upon the family? You will never, never develop that senseless peasant soul into anything lofty or poetical. Can't you manage," he went on, addressing Falaley, "can't you manage to dream of something elegant, refined, genteel, some scene from good society, such as gentlemen playing cards or ladies walking in a lovely garden?"

Falaley promised he would be sure to dream next night of gentlemen or ladies walking in a lovely garden.

As he went to bed, Falaley prayed tearfully on the subject and wondered for a long time what he could do so as not to dream of the accursed white bull. But deceitful are the hopes of man. On waking up next morning, he remembered with horror that he had again been dreaming all night of the hateful white bull, and had not dreamed of even one lady walking in a lovely garden. This time the consequences were singular. Foma Fomitch positively declared that he did not believe in the possibility of such a coincidence, the possibilty of such a repetition of a dream, and that Falaley was prompted to say this by some one of the household, perhaps even by the colonel himself on purpose to annoy Foma Fomitch. There was no end of an uproar, tears and reproaches. Madame la Générale was taken ill towards the evening, the whole household wore a dejected air. There was still a faint hope that the following, that is, the third night, Falaley would be sure to have some dream of refined society. What was the universal indignation when for a whole week, every blessed night, Falaley went on dreaming of the white bull and nothing but the white bull. It was no use even to think of refined society.

But the most interesting point was that Falaley was utterly incapable of thinking of lying, of simply saying that he had dreamed not of the white bull, but of a carriage, for instance, full of ladies and Foma Fomitch. This was all the more strange since lying indeed would not have been so very sinful in so extreme a case. But Falaley was so truthful that he positively could not tell a lie even if he wanted to. It was, indeed, not even suggested to him by any one. They all knew that he would betray himself at the first moment, and Foma Fomitch would immediately detect him in lying. What was to be done? My uncle's position was becoming intolerable. Falaley was absolutely incorrigible. The poor boy was positively growing thinner from worry.

The housekeeper Malanya declared that he was bewitched, and sprinkled him with magic water. She was assisted in this compassionate and salutary operation by the tender-hearted Praskovya Ilyinitchna, but even that was no use. Nothing was of use!

"The deuce take the damned thing!" Falaley said. "The same dream every night! Every evening I pray, 'Don't let me dream of the white bull, don't let me dream of the white bull!' and there it is, there it is, the damned beast facing me, huge, with horns and such thick lips, oo-oo-oo!"

My uncle was in despair, but luckily Foma Fomitch seemed all at once to have forgotten about the white bull. Of course no one believed that Foma Fomitch could forget a circumstance so important. Every one assumed with terror that he was keeping the white bull in reserve, and would bring it out on the first suitable occasion. It appeared later on that Foma Fomitch had no thoughts to spare for the white bull at that moment. He had other business in hand, other cares. Other plans were maturing in his beneficent and fertile brain. That is why he let Falaley breathe in peace, and every one else too had a respite. The boy grew gay again, and even began to forget what had happened; even the white bull began to visit him less and less frequently, though it still at times reminded him of its fantastic existence. In fact, everything would have gone well if there had been no such thing as the Komarinsky.

It must be noted that Falaley was an excellent dancer. Dancing was his chief accomplishment, even something like his vocation. He danced with vigour, with inexhaustible gaiety, and he was particularly fond of dancing the Koraminsky Peasant. Not that he was so much attracted by the frivolous and in any case inexplicable steps of that volatile peasant—no, he liked dancing the Koraminsky solely because to hear the Komarinsky and not dance to the tune was utterly beyond him. Sometimes in the evenings two or three of the footmen, the coachmen, the gardener who played the fiddle, and even some of the ladies of the servants' hall would gather together in a circle in some back yard as far away as possible from Foma Fomitch. Music and dances would begin, and finally the Komarinsky would triumphantly come into its own. The orchestra consisted of two balalaikas, a guitar, a fiddle, and a tambourine, with which the postillion Mityushka was a capital hand. Falaley's condition was worth watching at such times: he would dance to complete oblivion of himself, to utter exhaustion, encouraged by the shouts and laughter of his audience. He would squeal, shout, laugh, clap his hands. He danced as though carried away by some intangible outside force with which he could not cope, and he struggled persistently to keep up with the continually increasing pace of the reckless tune as he tapped on the ground with his heels. These were minutes of real delight to him; and everything would have gone happily and merrily if rumours of the Komarinsky had not at last reached Foma Fomitch.

Foma Fomitch was petrified, and sent at once for the colonel.

"There is only one thing I wish to learn from you," Foma began, "have you positively sworn to be the ruin of that luckless idiot or not? In the first case I will stand aside at once; if not, then I . . ."

"But what is the matter? What has happened?" cried my uncle, alarmed.

"You ask what has happened? Do you know that he is dancing the Komarinsky?"

"Well . . . well, what of it?"

"Well, what of it!" shrieked Foma. "And you say that—you, their master, standing in a sense in the place of their father! But have you then a true idea of what the Komarinsky is? Do you know that that song describes a debauched peasant, attempting in a state of drunkenness the most immoral action? Do you know what sacrilege it is that vicious little Russian is committing? He is trampling upon the most precious bonds and, so to say, stamping them under his big loutish boots, accustomed to tread only the floor of the village inn. And do you realize that you have wounded my moral feelings by your answer? Do you realize that you have insulted me personally by your answer? Do you understand that or not?"

"But, Foma; why, it's only a song, Foma. . . ."

"You say only a song! And you are not ashamed that you own to me that you know that song—you, a member of honourable society, the father of honourable, innocent children and a colonel into the bargain! Only a song! But I am certain that the song is drawn from real life. Only a song! But what decent man can without a blush of shame admit that he knows that song, that he has ever heard that song? What man could?"

"Well, but, you see, you know it yourself, Foma, since you ask about it," my disconcerted uncle answered in the simplicity of his heart.

"What, I know it, I . . . I? You have insulted me," Foma Fomitch cried at once, leaping up from his chair and spluttering with fury.

He had never expected such a crushing answer.

I will not undertake to describe the wrath of Foma Fomitch. The colonel was ignominiously driven from the presence of the guardian of morality for the ill manners and tactlessness of his reply. But from that hour Foma Fomitch vowed to catch Falaley in the act of dancing the Komarinsky. In the evening, when every one supposed he was busy at work, he stole out into the garden, went the round of the kitchen garden, and threaded his way into the hemp patch, from which there was a view in the distance of the back yard in which the dances took place. He stalked poor Falaley as a sportsman stalks a bird, picturing with relish the wigging he would, if he succeeded, give the whole household and the colonel in particular. His unwearying efforts were at last crowned with success. He had come upon the Komarinsky! It will be understood now why my uncle tore his hair when he saw Falaley weeping and heard Vidoplyasov announce Foma Fomitch, who so unexpectedly and at such a moment of perturbation was standing before us in person.

[VII]

FOMA FOMITCH

I SCRUTINIZED this gentleman with intense curiosity. Gavrila had been right in saying that he was an ugly little man. Foma was short, with light eyebrows and eyelashes and grizzled hair, with a hooked nose, and with little wrinkles all over his face. On his chin there was a big wart. He was about fifty. He came in softly with measured steps, with his eyes cast down. But yet the most insolent self-confidence was expressed in his face, and in the whole of his pedantic figure. To my astonishment, he made his appearance in a dressing-gown—of a foreign cut it is true, but still a dressing-gown—and he wore slippers too. The collar of his shirt unadorned by any cravat was a lay-down one *à l'enfant;* this gave Foma Fomitch an extremely foolish look. He went up to an empty arm-chair, moved it to the table, and sat down in it without saying a word to any one. All the hubbub, all the excitement that had been raging a minute before, vanished instantaneously. There was such a hush that one could have heard a pin drop. Madame la Générale became as meek as a lamb. The cringing infatuation of this poor imbecile for Foma Fomitch was apparent now. She fixed her eyes upon her idol as though gloating over the sight of him. Miss Perepelitsyn rubbed her hands with a simper, and poor Praskovya Ilyinitchna was visibly trembling with alarm. My uncle began bustling about at once.

"Tea, tea, sister! Only plenty of sugar in it, sister; Foma Fomitch likes plenty of sugar in his tea after his nap. You do like plenty of sugar, don't you, Foma?"

"I don't care for any tea just now!" Foma pronounced deliberately and with dignity, waving him off with a careworn air. "You always keep on about plenty of sugar."

These words and Foma's entrance, so incredibly ludicrous in its pedantic dignity, interested me extremely. I was curious to find out to what point, to what disregard of decency, the insolence of this upstart little gentleman would go.

"Foma," cried my uncle. "Let me introduce my nephew Sergey Alexandrovitch! He has just arrived."

Foma Fomitch looked him up and down.

"I am surprised that you always seem to take pleasure in systematically interrupting me, Colonel," he said after a significant silence, taking absolutely no notice of me. "One talks to you of something serious, and you . . . *discourse* . . . of goodness knows what. . . . Have you seen Falaley?"

"I have, Foma. . . ."

"Ah, you have seen him. Well, I will show you him again though you have seen him; you can admire your handiwork . . . in a moral sense. Come here, you idiot! come here, you Dutch-faced fool! Well, come along! Don't be afraid!"

Falaley went up to him with his mouth open, sobbing and gulping back his tears. Foma Fomitch looked at him with relish.

"I called him a Dutch-faced fool with intention, Pavel Semyonitch," he observed, lolling at his ease in his low chair and turning slightly towards Obnoskin, who was sitting next him. "And speaking generally, you know, I see no necessity for softening my expressions in any case. The truth should be the truth. And however you cover up filth it will still remain filth. Why trouble to soften it? It's deceiving oneself and others. Only a silly worldly numskull can feel the need of such senseless conventions. Tell me—I submit it to your judgment—do you find anything lovely in that face? I mean, of course, anything noble, lovely, exalted, not just vulgar red cheeks."

Foma Fomitch spoke quietly, evenly, and with a kind of majestic nonchalance.

"Anything lovely in him?" answered Obnoskin, with insolent carelessness. "I think that he is simply a good piece of roast beef—and nothing else."

"Went up to the looking-glass and looked into it to-day," Foma continued, pompously omitting the pronoun *I*. "I am far from considering myself a beauty, but I could not help coming to the conclusion that there is something in these grey eyes which distinguished me from any Falaley. There is thought, there is life, there is intelligence in these eyes. It is not myself I am praising. I am speaking generally of our class. Now what do you think, can there be a scrap, a grain, of soul in that living beefsteak? Yes, indeed, take note, Pavel Semyonitch, how these people, utterly devoid of thought and ideal, and living by meat alone, always have revoltingly fresh complexions, coarsely and stupidly fresh! Would you like to know the level of his intellectual faculties? Hey, you image! Come nearer, let us admire you. Why are you gaping? Do you want to swallow a whale? Are you hand-some? Answer, are you handsome?"

"I a-am!" answered Falaley, with smothered sobs.

Obnoskin roared with laughter. I felt that I was beginning to tremble with anger.

"Do you hear?" Foma went on, turning to Obnoskin in triumph. "Would you like to hear something more? I have come to put him through an examination. You see, Pavel Semyonitch, there are people who are desirous of corrupting and ruining this poor idiot. Perhaps I am too severe in my judgment, perhaps I am mistaken; but I speak from love of humanity. He was just now dancing the most improper of dances. That is of no concern to any one here. But now hear for yourself. . . . Answer: what were you doing just now? Answer, answer immediately—do you hear?"

"I was da-ancing," said Falaley, mastering his sobs.

"What were you dancing? What dance? Speak!"

"The Komarinsky. . . ."

"The Komarinsky! And who was that Komarinsky? What was the Komarinsky? Do you suppose I can understand anything from that answer? Come, give us an idea. Who was your Komarinsky?"

"A pea-easant. . . ."

"A peasant, only a peasant! I am surprised! A remarkable peasant, then! Then was it some celebrated peasant, if poems and dances are made about him? Come, answer!"

Foma could not exist without tormenting people, he played with his victim like a cat with a mouse; but Falaley remained mute, whim-pering and unable to understand the question.

"Answer," Foma persisted. "You are asked what sort of peasant was it? Speak! . . . Was he a seignorial peasant, a crown peasant, free, bond, industrial? There are ever so many sorts of peasants. . . ."

"In-dus-tri-al. . . ."

"Ah, industrial! Do you hear, Pavel Semyonitch? A new historical fact: the Komarinsky peasant was industrial. H'm. . . . Well, what did that industrial peasant do? For what exploits is he celebrated in song . . . and dance?"

The question was a delicate one, and since it was put to Falaley, a risky one too.

"Come . . . Though . . ." Obnoskin began, glancing towards his mamma, who was beginning to wriggle on the sofa in a peculiar way.

But what was to be done? Foma Fomitch's whims were respected as law.

"Upon my word, uncle, if you don't suppress that fool he'll . . . you see what he is working up to—Falaley will blurt out some nonsense, I assure you," I whispered to my uncle, who was utterly distracted and did not know what line to take.

"You had really better, Foma . . ." he began. "Here, I want to introduce to you, Foma, my nephew, a young man who is studying mineralogy."

"I beg you, Colonel, not to interrupt me with your mineralogy, a subject of which, as far as I am aware, you know nothing, and *others* perhaps little more. I am not a baby. He will answer me that this peasant, instead of working for the welfare of his family, has been drinking till he is tipsy, has sold his coat for drink, and is running about the street in an inebriated condition. That is, as is well known, the subject of the poem that sings the praises of drink. Don't be uneasy, he knows *now* what he has to answer. Come, answer: what did that peasant do? Come, I have prompted you, I have put the words into your mouth. What I want is to hear it from you yourself, what he did, for what he was famous, how he gained the immortal glory of being sung by the troubadours. Well?"

The luckless Falaley looked round him in misery, and not knowing what to say, opened and shut his mouth like a carp, hauled out of the water on to the sand.

"I am ashamed to sa-ay!" he bellowed at last in utter despair.

"Ah, ashamed to say!" bellowed Foma in triumph. "See, that's the answer I have wrung out of him, Colonel! Ashamed to say, but not ashamed to do. That's the morality which you have sown, which has sprung up and which you are now . . . watering; but it is useless to waste words! Go to the kitchen now, Falaley. I'll say nothing to you now, out of regard for my audience, but to-day, to-day you will be severely and rigorously punished. If not, if this time they put you before me, you may stay here and entertain your betters with the Komarinsky while I will leave this house to-day! That's enough. I have spoken, you can go!"

"Come, I think you really are severe . . ." mumbled Obnoskin.

"Just so, just so, just so," my uncle began crying out, but he broke off and subsided. Foma looked gloomily askance at him.

"I wonder, Pavel Semyonitch," he went on, "what all our contemporary writers, poets, learned men and thinkers are about? How is it they pay no attention to what songs are being sung by the Russian people and to what songs they are dancing? What have the Pushkins, the Lermontovs, the Borozdins been about all this time? I wonder at

them. The people dance the Komarinsky, the apotheosis of drunkenness, while they sing of forget-me-nots! Why don't they write poems
of a more moral tone for popular use, why don't they fling aside their
forget-me-nots? It's a social question. Let them depict a peasant, but
a peasant made genteel, so to say, a villager and not a peasant; let them
paint me the village sage in his simplicity, maybe even in his bark
shoes—I don't object even to that—but brimming over with the virtues
which—I make bold to say—some over-lauded Alexander of Macedon
may envy. I know Russia and Russia knows me, that is why I say this.
Let them portray that peasant, weighed down maybe with a family
and grey hair, in a stuffy hut, hungry, too, maybe, but contented; not
repining, but blessing his poverty, and indifferent to the rich man's
gold. Let the rich man at last with softened heart bring him his gold;
let, indeed, in this the virtues of the peasant be united with the virtues
of his master, perhaps a grand gentleman. The villager and the grand
gentleman so widely separated in social grade are made one at last in
virtue—that is an exalted thought! But what do we see? On one side
forget-me-nots, and on the other the peasant dashing out of the pot-
house and running about the street in a dishevelled condition! What is
there poetic in that? Tell me, pray, what is there to admire in that?
Where is the wit? Where is the grace? Where is the morality? I am
amazed at it!"

"I am ready to pay you a hundred roubles for such words," said
Yezhevikin, with an enthusiastic air. "And you know the bald devil
will try and get it out of me," he whispered on the sly. "Flatter away,
flatter away!"

"H'm, yes . . . you've put that very well," Obnoskin pronounced.

"Exactly so, exactly so," cried my uncle, who had been listening with
the deepest attention and looking at me with triumph. "What a subject has come up!" he whispered, rubbing his hands. "A topic of many
aspects, dash it all! Foma Fomitch, here is my nephew," he added,
in the overflow of his feelings. "He is engaged in literary pursuits
too, let me introduce him."

As before, Foma Fomitch paid not the slightest attention to my
uncle's introduction.

"For God's sake, don't introduce me any more! I entreat you in
earnest," I whispered to my uncle, with a resolute air.

"Ivan Ivanitch!" Foma began, suddenly addressing Mizintchikov
and looking intently at him, "we have just been talking. What is your
opinion?"

"Mine? You are asking me?" Mizintchikov responded in surprise, looking as though he had only just woken up.

"Yes, you. I am asking you because I value the opinion of really clever people, and not the problematic wiseacres who are only clever because they are being continually introduced as clever people, as learned people, and are sometimes sent for expressly to be made a show of or something of the sort."

This thrust was aimed directly at me. And yet there was no doubt that though Foma Fomitch took no notice whatever of me, he had begun this whole conversation concerning literature entirely for my benefit, to dazzle, to annihilate, to crush at the first step the clever and learned young man from Petersburg. I at any rate had no doubt of it.

"If you want to know my opinion, I . . . I agree with your opinion," answered Mizintchikov listlessly and reluctantly.

"You always agree with me! It's positively wearisome," replied Foma. "I tell you frankly, Pavel Semyonitch," he went on, after a brief silence again addressing Obnoskin, "if I respect the immortal Karamzin it is not for his history, not for *Marfa Posadnitsa,* not for *Old and New Russia,* but just for having written *Frol Silin;* it is a noble epic! It is a purely national product, and will live for ages and ages! a most lofty epic!"

"Just so, just so! a lofty *epoch!* Frol Silin, a benevolent man! I remember, I have read it. He bought the freedom of two girls, too, and then looked towards heaven and wept. A very lofty trait," my uncle chimed in, beaming with satisfaction.

My poor uncle! he never could resist taking part in an *intellectual* conversation. Foma gave a malicious smile, but he remained silent.

"They write very interestingly, though, even now," Anfisa Petrovna intervened discreetly. "*The Mysteries of Brussels,* for instance."

"I should not say so," observed Foma, as it were regretfully. "I was lately reading one of the poems . . . not up to much! 'Forget-me-nots.' Of contemporary writers, if you will, the one I like best of all is 'Scribbler,' a light pen!"

" 'Scribbler!' " cried Anfisa Petrovna. "Is that the man who writes letters in the magazine? Ah, how enchanting it is, what playing with words!"

"Precisely, playing with words; he, so to speak, plays with his pen. An extraordinary lightness of style."

"Yes, but he is a pedant!" Obnoskin observed carelessly.

"Yes, a pedant he is, I don't dispute it; but a charming pedant, a graceful pedant! Of course, not one of his ideas would stand serious criticism, but one is carried away by his lightness! A babbler, I agree, but a charming babbler, a graceful babbler. Do you remember, for instance, in one of his articles, he mentions that he has his own estates?"

"Estates!" my uncle caught up. "That's good! In what province?"

Foma stopped, looked fixedly at my uncle, and went on in the same tone—

"Tell me in the name of common sense, of what interest is it to me, the reader, to know that he has his own estates? If he has—I congratulate him on it! But how charmingly, how jestingly, it is described! He sparkles with wit, he splashes with wit, he boils over! He is a Narzan of wit! Yes, that is the way to write! I fancy I should write just like that, if I were to consent to write for magazines. . . ."

"Perhaps you would do even better," Yezhevikin observed respectfully.

"There is positively something musical in the language," my uncle put in.

Foma Fomitch lost patience at last.

"Colonel," he said, "is it not possible to ask you—with all conceivable delicacy of course—not to interfere with us, but to allow us to finish our conversation in peace. You cannot offer an opinion in our conversation! You cannot. Don't disturb our agreeable literary chat. Look after your land, drink your tea, but . . . leave literature alone. It will lose nothing by it, I assure you—I assure you!"

This was surpassing the utmost limit of impudence! I did not know what to think.

"Why, you yourself, Foma, said it was musical," my uncle brought out in confusion and distress.

"Quite so, but I spoke with a knowledge of the subject, I spoke appropriately; while you . . ."

"To be sure, but we spoke with intellect," put in Yezhevikin, wriggling round Foma Fomitch. "We have just a little intelligence, though we may have to borrow some; just enough to run a couple of government departments and we might manage a third, if need be—that's all we can boast of!"

"So it seems I have been talking nonsense again," said my uncle in conclusion, and he smiled his good-natured smile.

"You admit it, anyway," observed Foma.

"It's all right, it's all right, Foma. I am not angry. I know that you pull me up like a friend, like a relation, like a brother. I have myself allowed you to do it, begged you to, indeed. It's a good thing. It's for my benefit. I thank you for it and will profit by it."

My patience was exhausted. All that I had hitherto heard about Foma Fomitch had seemed to me somewhat exaggerated. Now when I saw it all for myself, my astonishment was beyond all bounds. I could not believe my senses; I could not understand such impudence, such insolent domineering on one side and such voluntary slavery, such credulous good-nature on the other. Though, indeed, my uncle himself was confused by such impudence. That was evident. . . . I was burning with desire to come to grips with Foma, to do battle with him, to be rude to him in some way, in as startling a fashion as possible —and then let come what may! This idea excited me. I looked for an opportunity, and completely ruined the brim of my hat while I waited for it. But the opportunity did not present itself. Foma absolutely refused to notice me.

"You are right, perfectly right, Foma," my uncle went on, doing his utmost to recover himself, and to smooth over the unpleasantness of what had been said before. "What you say is true, Foma. I thank you for it. One must know the subject before one discusses it. I am sorry! It is not the first time I have been in the same predicament. Only fancy, Sergey, on one occasion I was an examiner . . . you laugh! But there it is! I really was an examiner, and that was all about it. I was invited to an institution, to be present at an examination, and they set me down together with the examiners, as a sign of respect, there was an empty seat. So, I will own to you, I was frightened, I was positively alarmed, I do not know a single science. What was I to do? I thought that in another minute they would drag me myself to the blackboard! Well, what then? Nothing happened, it went off all right, I even asked questions myself; who was Noah? On the whole they answered splendidly; then we had lunch and toasted enlightenment in champagne. It was a fine school!"

Foma Fomitch and Obnoskin burst into roars of laughter.

"Indeed, I laughed myself afterwards," cried my uncle, laughing in a most good-natured way and delighted that general cheerfulness was restored. "Yes, Foma, here goes! I will amuse you all telling you how I put my foot in it once. . . . Only fancy, Sergey, we were staying at Krasnogorsk . . ."

"Allow me to inquire, Colonel, will you be long in telling your story?" Foma interposed.

"Oh, Foma! Why, it is the most delightful story, enough to make one split with laughter; you only listen, it is good, it really is good. I'll tell you how I put my foot in it."

"I always listen with pleasure to your stories when they are of that sort," Obnoskin pronounced, yawning.

"There is no help for it, we must listen," Foma decided.

"But upon my word it is good, Foma, it really is. I want to tell you how I put my foot into it on one occasion, Anfisa Petrovna. You listen too, Sergey, it is an edifying story indeed. We were staying at Krasnogorsk," my uncle began, beaming with pleasure, talking with nervous haste, and falling into innumerable parentheses as he always did when he was beginning to tell some story for the pleasure of his audience. "As soon as we arrived, the same evening we went to the theatre. There was a first-rate actress, Kuropatkina; she afterwards ran away with the cavalry captain Zvyerkov and did not finish the play she was acting: so they let down the curtain. . . . This Zvyerkov was a beast, both for drinking and playing cards, and not that he was a drunkard, but simply ready to join his comrades at festive moments. But when he did get really drunk then he forgot everything, where he lived, in what country, and what his name was. Absolutely everything, in fact— but he was a very fine fellow really. . . . Well, I was sitting in the theatre. In the interval I got up, and I ran across a comrade called Kornouhov. . . . A unique fellow, I assure you. We had not seen each other for six years, it is true. Well, he had stayed in the company and was covered with crosses. I have heard lately—he's an actual civil councillor; he transferred to the civil service and worked his way up to a high grade. . . . Well, of course, we were delighted. One thing and another. In the box next to us were three ladies; the one on the left was the ugliest woman in the world. . . . Afterwards I found out that she was a splendid woman, the mother of a family, and the happiness of her husband. . . . Well, so I like a fool blurt out to Kornouhov: 'I say, old man, can you tell me who that scarecrow is?' 'Who do you mean?' 'Why, that one.' 'That's my cousin.' Tfoo, the devil! judge of my position! To put myself right: 'Not that one,' I said. 'What eyes you've got! I mean the one who is sitting there, who is that?' 'That's my sister.' Tfoo, plague take it all! And his sister, as luck would have it, was a regular rosebud, a sweet little thing; dressed up like anything —brooches, gloves, bracelets; in fact, a perfect cherub. Afterwards she married a very fine fellow called Pyhtin; she eloped with him, it was a runaway match; but now it is all right, and they are very well off; their parents are only too delighted! Well, so I cried out, 'Oh, no!' not knowing how to get out of it, 'not that one, the one in the middle, who is she?' 'In the middle? Well, my boy, that's my wife.' . . . And she, between ourselves, was a perfect sugarplum. I felt that I could have eaten her up at one mouthful, I was so delighted with her. . . . 'Well,' I said, 'have you ever seen a fool? Here is one facing you, and here's his head; cut it off, don't spare it!' He laughed. Afterwards he introduced them to me and must have told them, the rascal. They were in fits of laughter over something! And I must say I never spent an evening more merrily. So you see, Foma, old man, how one can put one's foot in it! Ha-ha-ha-ha!"

But it was no use my poor uncle laughing; in vain he looked round the company with his kind and good-humoured eyes; a dead silence was the response that greeted his light-hearted story. Foma Fomitch sat in gloomy dumbness and all the others followed his example; only Obnoskin gave a faint smile, foreseeing the baiting my uncle would get. My uncle was embarrassed and flushed crimson. This was what Foma desired.

"Have you finished?" he asked at last, turning with dignity to the embarrassed storyteller.

"Yes, Foma."

"And are you satisfied?"

"How do you mean, satisfied?" asked my poor uncle miserably.

"Are you happier now? Are you pleased at having broken up the pleasant literary conversation of your friends by interrupting them and so satisfying your petty vanity?"

"Oh, come, Foma, I wanted to amuse you all, and you . . ."

"Amuse!" cried Foma, suddenly becoming extraordinarily heated; "but you are only able to depress us, not amuse us. Amuse! but do know that your story was almost immoral. I say nothing of its impropriety, that is self-evident. . . . You informed us just now with rare coarseness of feeling that you laughed at innocence, at an honourable lady, simply because she had not the honour to please you, and you wanted to make us, *us* laugh, that is, applaud you, that is, applaud a coarse and improper action, and all because you are the master of this house! You can do as you like, Colonel, you can seek out toadies, flatterers, sycophants, you can even send for them from distant parts and so increase your retinue to the detriment of straightforwardness and frank nobility of soul, but never will Foma Opiskin be your toady, your flatterer, your sycophant! I can assure you of that, if of any thing. . . ."

"Oh, Foma! You misunderstand me, Foma."

"No, Colonel; I have seen through you for a long time, I know you through and through. You are devoured by boundless vanity. You have pretensions to an incomparable keenness of wit, and forget that wit is blunted by pretension. You . . ."

"Oh, stop, Foma, for God's sake! Have some shame, if only before people!"

"It's sad, you know, to see all this, Colonel, and it's impossible to be silent when one sees it. I am poor, I am living at the expense of your mother. It may be expected, perhaps, that I should flatter you by my silence, and I don't care for any milksop to take me for your toady! Possibly when I came into this room just now I intentionally accentuated my truthful candour, was forced to be intentionally rude, just because you yourself put me into such a position. You are too haughty with me, Colonel, I may be taken for your slave, your toady. Your pleasure is to humiliate me before *strangers,* while I am really your equal—your equal in every respect. Perhaps *I* am doing you a favour in living with you, and not *you* doing me one. I am insulted, so I am forced to sing my own praises—that's natural! I cannot help speaking, I must speak, I am bound at once to protest, and that is why I tell you straight out that you are phenomenally envious. You see, for instance, some one in a simple friendly conversation unconsciously reveals his knowledge, his reading, his taste, and so you are annoyed, you can't sit still. 'Let me display my knowledge and my taste,' you think! And what taste have you, if you will allow me to ask? You know as much about art—if you will excuse my saying so, Colonel—as a bull about beef! That's harsh and rude, I admit; anyway it is straightforward and just. You won't hear that from your flatterers, Colonel."

"Oh, Foma! . . ."

"It is 'Oh, Foma,' to be sure. The truth is not a feather-bed, it seems. Very well, then, we will speak later about this, but now let me entertain the company a little. You can't be the only one to distinguish yourself all the time. Pavel Semyonitch, have you seen this sea monster in human form? I have been observing him for a long time. Look well at him; why, he would like to devour me whole, at one gulp."

He was speaking of Gavrila. The old servant was standing at the door, and certainly was looking on with distress at the scolding of his master.

"I want to entertain you, too, with a performance, Pavel Semyonitch. Come here, you scarecrow, come here. Condescend to approach us a little nearer, Gavrila Ignatitch! Here you see, Pavel Semyonitch, is Gavrila; as a punishment for rudeness he is studying the French dialect. Like Orpheus, I soften the manners of these parts not only with songs but with the French dialect. Come, Mossoo Frenchy—he can't bear to be called Mossoo—do you know your lesson?"

"I have learnt it," said Gavrila, hanging his head.

"Well, Parlay—voo—fransay?"

"Vee, moossyu, zhe—le—parl—on—peu. . . ."

I don't know whether it was Gavril's mournful face as he uttered the French phrase, or whether they were all aware of Foma's desire that they should laugh, but anyway they all burst into a roar of laughter as soon as Gavrila opened his lips. Even Madame la Générale deigned to be amused. Anfisa Petrovna, sinking back on the sofa, shrieked, hiding her face behind her fan. What seemed most ludicrous was that Gavrila, seeing what his examination was being turned into, could not restrain himself from spitting and commenting reproachfully: "To think of having lived to such disgrace in my old age!"

Foma Fomitch was startled.

"What? What did you say? So you think fit to be rude?"

"No, Foma Fomitch," Gavrila replied with dignity. "My words were no rudeness, and it's not for me, a serf, to be rude to you, a gentleman born. But every man bears the image of God upon him, His image and semblance. I am sixty-three years old. My father remembers Pugatchev, the monster, and my grandfather helped his master, Matvey Nikititch—God grant him the kingdom of heaven!—to hang Pugatchev on an aspen tree, for which my father was honoured beyond all others by our late master, Afanasy Matveyitch: he was his valet, and ended his life as butler. As for me, Foma Fomitch, sir, though I am my master's bondman, I have never known such a shame done me from my birth upward till now."

And at the last word Gavrila spread out his hands and hung his head. My uncle was watching him uneasily.

"Come, that's enough, Gavrila," he cried. "No need to say more, that's enough!"

"Never mind, never mind," said Foma, turning a little pale and giving a forced smile. "Let him speak, these are the fruits of your . . . "

"I will tell you everything," said Gavrila with extraordinary fervour, "I will conceal nothing! You may bind the hands, but there is no binding the tongue. Though I may seem beside you, Foma Fomitch, a low man, in fact, a slave, yet I can feel insulted! Service and obedience I am always bound to give you, because I am born a slave and must do my duty in fear and trembling. You sit writing a book, it's my duty not to let you be interrupted—that is my real duty. Any service that is needed I am pleased to do. But in my old age to bleat in some outlandish way and be put to shame before folk! Why, I can't go into the servants' room now: 'You are a Frenchy!' they say, 'a Frenchy!' No. Foma Fomitch, sir, it's not only a fool like me, but all good folks have begun to say the same: that you have become now a wicked man and that our master is nothing but a little child before you, that though you are a gentleman by birth and a general's son, and yourself may be near being a general too, yet you are as wicked as a real fury must be."

Gavrila had finished. I was beside myself with delight. Foma Fomitch sat pale with rage in the midst of the general discomfiture and seemed unable to recover from Gavrila's sudden attack upon him; he seemed at that moment to be deliberating how far his wrath should carry him. At last the outburst followed.

"What, he dares be rude to me—me! but this is mutiny!" shrieked Foma, and he leapt up from his chair.

Madame la Générale followed his example, clasping her hands. There was a general commotion, my uncle rushed to turn the culprit out.

"Put him in fetters, put him in fetters!" cried Madame la Générale. "Take him to the town at once and send him for a soldier, Yegorushka, or you shall not have any blessing. Fix the fetters on him at once, and send him for a soldier."

"What!" cried Foma. "Slave! Lout! Hamlet! He dares to be rude to me! He, he, a rag to wipe my boots! He dares to call me a fury!"

I slipped forward with unusual determination.

"I must confess that in this affair I am completely of Gavrila's opinion," I said, looking Foma Fomitch straight in the face and trembling with excitement.

He was so taken aback by this onslaught that for the first minute he seemed unable to believe his ears.

"What's this, now?" he cried out at last, pouncing upon me in a frenzy, and fixing his little bloodshot eyes upon me. "Why, who are you?"

"Foma Fomitch . . ." my uncle, utterly distracted, began, "this is Seryozha, my nephew. . . ."

"The learned gentleman!" yelled Foma. "So he's the learned gentleman! *Liberté—égalité—fraternité. Journal des Débats!* No, my friend, you won't take me in! I am not such a fool. This isn't Petersburg, you won't impose upon us. And I spit on your *des Débats.* You have your *des Débats,* but to us that's all fiddlesticks, young man! Learned.

You know as much as I have forgotten seven times over. So much for your learning!"

If they had not held him back I believe he would have fallen upon me with his fists.

"Why, he is drunk," I said, looking about me in bewilderment.

"Who, I?" cried Foma, in a voice unlike his own.

"Yes, you!"

"Drunk?"

"Yes, drunk."

This was more than Foma could endure. He uttered a screech as though he were being murdered and rushed out of the room. Madame la Générale seemed desirous of falling into a swoon, but reflected that it would be better to run after Foma Fomitch. She was followed by all the others, and last of all by my uncle. When I recovered myself and looked round I saw in the room no one but Yezhevikin. He was smiling and rubbing his hands.

"You promised just now to tell me about the Jesuits," he said in an insinuating voice.

"What?" I asked, not understanding what he was talking about.

"About the Jesuits, you promised just now to tell me . . . some little anecdote. . . ."

I ran out into the verandah and from there into the garden. My head was going round. . . .

[VIII]

A DECLARATION OF LOVE

I WANDERED about the garden for about a quarter of an hour, feeling irritated and extremely dissatisfied with myself, and deliberating what I should do now. The sun was setting. Suddenly at a turning into a dark avenue I met Nastenka face to face. She had tears in her eyes, in her hand a handkerchief with which she was wiping them.

"I was looking for you," she said.

"And I for you," I answered. "Tell me, am I in a madhouse?"

"Certainly not in a madhouse," she answered resentfully, with an intent glance at me.

"Well, if that's so, what's the meaning of it all? For Christ's sake give me some advice. Where has my uncle gone now? Can I go to him? I am very glad that I have met you; perhaps you will be able to suggest what I ought to do."

"No, better not go to him. I have just come away from them."

"Why, where are they?"

"Who knows? Perhaps by now they have run into the kitchen garden again," she said irritably.

"Into the kitchen garden!"

"Why, last week, Foma Fomitch began shouting that he wouldn't stay in the house, and all at once he ran into the kitchen garden, found a spade in the shed and began digging the beds. We were all amazed, and wondered whether he hadn't gone out of his mind. 'That I may not be reproached for doing nothing for my keep,' said he, 'here I will dig and pay for the bread I have eaten, and then I will go away. That's what you have driven me to.' And then they all began crying and almost falling on their knees before him; they took the spade away from him; but he would go on digging; he dug up all the turnips, that was all he did. They humoured him once, he may do it again. That would be just like him."

"And you . . . you tell that with such coolness!" I cried out, with intense indignation.

She looked at me with flashing eyes.

"Forgive me, I really don't know what I am saying! Listen! do you know what I've come here for?"

"N-no," she answered, flushing crimson, and some painful feeling was reflected in her charming face.

"You must excuse me," I went on. "I am upset, I feel that this is not how I ought to have begun speaking of this . . . especially with you. . . . But never mind! To my thinking, openness in such matters is best. I confess . . . that is, I meant to say . . . you know my uncle's design? He has told me to ask for your hand. . . ."

"Oh, what nonsense! don't speak of it, please," she said hurriedly interrupting me and flushing crimson.

I was disconcerted.

"How nonsense? But he wrote to me, you see."

"So he wrote to you?" she asked eagerly. "Oh, what a man! How he promised that he would not write! What nonsense! Good heavens, what nonsense!"

"Forgive me," I muttered, not knowing what to say. "Perhaps I have acted incautiously, crudely . . . but, you see, it's such a moment! Only think, goodness knows what's going on around us. . . ."

"Oh. for God's sake don't apologize! Believe me that it is painful for me to hear this apart from that, and yet, do you know, I wanted to speak to you myself, to find out something. . . . Oh, how vexatious! So he really wrote to you? That's what I was most afraid of! My God, what a man he is! And you believed him and galloped here full speed? Well, that's the last straw!"

She did not conceal her annoyance. My position was not an attractive one.

"I must confess I did not expect . . ." I blurted out in the utmost confusion, "such a turn . . . I expected, on the contrary . . ."

"Ah, so that's what you expected? . . ." she brought out with light irony, biting her lip. "And do you know, you must show me the letter he wrote."

"Very good."

"And please don't be angry with me, don't be offended; I have trouble enough without that!" she said in an imploring voice, though a mocking smile faintly gleamed on her pretty lips.

"Oh, please don't take me for a fool," I cried hotly. "But perhaps you are prejudiced against me, perhaps some one has spoken against me? Perhaps you say this because I put my foot in it just now? But that is nothing, I assure you. I know what a fool I must look to you now. Don't laugh at me, please! I don't know what I am saying, and it is all because I am twenty-two, damn it."

"Oh, mercy on us, why?"

"You ask why? Any one who is twenty-two, you know, has it written in his face; as I had, for instance, when I bounced out just now in the middle of the room, or as when I stand before you now. . . . It's a damnable age!"

"Oh, no, no!" answered Nastenka, hardly able to restrain her laughter. "I am sure that you are kind and nice and clever, and I say that sincerely, I do really! But . . . you are only very vain. You may get over that in time."

"I fancy I am only as vain as I ought to be."

"Oh, no. Think how embarrassed you were just now, and what for? Because you stumbled as you came in! . . . What right had you to turn into ridicule your good generous uncle who has done you so much kindness? Why did you try to turn the laugh against him when you were laughable yourself? That was horrid, shameful! It does not do you credit, and I must own I disliked you very much at that minute, so there!"

"That's true! I was a blockhead! more than that—I did a mean thing! You noticed it, and that is my punishment. Abuse me, laugh at me, but listen; perhaps you will change your opinion of me in the end," I added, carried away by a strange feeling. "You know so little of me as yet; afterwards when you know more of me, then . . . perhaps . . ."

"For God's sake let us stop this conversation!" cried Nastenka, with visible impatience.

"Very well, very well, let us stop! But . . . where can I see you?"

"Where can you see me?"

"Why, you know, this cannot be the last word we have to say to each other, Nastasya Yevgrafovna! For God's sake, let me meet you again to-day, for instance. But it's already getting dark. So if it is anyhow possible let it be to-morrow early; I will ask to be called earlier on purpose. You know there's an arbour over there by the pond. You see, I remember it, I know the way. I used to stay here when I was little."

"Meet you! What for? Why, we are talking now."

"But I know nothing yet, Nastasya Yevgrafovna, I will first find out everything from my uncle. Why, he is bound to tell me everything now. And then, perhaps, I shall have something very important to tell you. . . ."

"No, no! You mustn't, you mustn't!" cried Nastenka. "Let us end it all at once now, so that we may never think of it again. And don't go to that arbour for nothing; I assure you I shall not go. And please put all this nonsense out of your head—I beg you in earnest. . . ."

"So then uncle has behaved like a madman to me!" I cried, in an excess of insufferable vexation. "Why did he send for me? But listen, what is that noise?"

We were close to the house; from the open windows came the sounds of shrieking and extraordinary outcries.

"My God!" she said, turning pale, "again! I foresaw it would be so!"

"You foresaw it? Nastasya Yevgrafovna, one more question. Of course I have not the least right to do so, but I venture to put this last question to you for the good of us all. Tell me—and I will keep it secret to the grave—tell me frankly: is my uncle in love with you or not?"

"Oh! Please, please put that nonsense out of your head once for all," she cried, flushing crimson with anger. "And you, too! If he were in love with me, he wouldn't have wanted to have married me to you," she added with a bitter smile. "And what put that idea into your head? Don't you know what the trouble's about? Do you hear those shouts?"

"But . . . It's Foma Fomitch. . . ."

"Yes, of course it is Foma Fomitch; but now the trouble is over me because they are saying the same thing as you, the same senseless thing; they, too, suspect that he is in love with me. And as I am poor and of no consequence, and as it costs nothing to throw dirt on me and they want to marry him to some one else, they are insisting that he should send me home to my father to make things sure. And when they talk to him of that he flies into a rage at once; he's ready to tear Foma Fomitch to pieces even. They are quarrelling about that now; I feel that it is about that."

"So that's the truth! So he really is going to marry that Tatyana, then."

"Yes, that silly fool!"

"Not a silly fool at all! She is good; you have no right to talk like that! She has a noble heart, nobler than many other people. It's not her fault that she is unfortunate."

"Forgive me. Supposing you are quite right about that, yet aren't you mistaken about the chief point? Tell me, how is it, then, that they make your father welcome, as I noticed? Why, if they were so set against you as you say and were turning you out, they would be angry with him too, and would give him a cold welcome."

"Why, don't you see what my father is doing for my sake? He is playing the fool before them! He is received just because he has succeeded in ingratiating himself with Foma Fomitch; and as Foma Fomitch was a buffoon himself, you see it flatters him to have buffoons about him now. For whose sake do you suppose my father does it? He does it for me, only for me. He wants nothing; he wouldn't bow down to any one for himself. He may be very absurd in some people's eyes, but he is a noble man, the noblest of men! He thinks—goodness knows why, and certainly not because I get a good salary here, I assure you—he thinks that it is best for me to stay here in this house; but now I have quite brought him round. I wrote to him firmly. He has come on purpose to take me; and if it comes to extremes, to-morrow. For things have got beyond everything; they are ready to tear me to pieces, and I am certain that they are quarrelling about me now. They are at *him,* on my account, they will be the death of *him!* And he is like a father to me—do you hear? more even than my own father. I won't stay to see it. I know more than other people. To-morrow, to-morrow I am going! Who knows: perhaps that will make them put off, if only for a time, his marriage to Tatyana Ivanovna. . . . Here I have told you all about it now. Tell him this, because I

:an't speak to him now; we are watched, especially by that Perepelitsyn woman. Tell him not to worry about me, tell him I would rather eat black bread and live in my father's hut than be the cause of his sufferings here. I am a poor girl, and I ought to live like a poor girl. But, my God, what an uproar! What shouting! What is happening? Yes, come what may I shall go in! I will tell them all this straight to their faces myself, whatever happens! I ought to do it! Good-bye."

She ran away. I remained standing on the same spot, fully conscious of the absurdity of the part it had just been my lot to play, and completely puzzled to think how it would all be settled. I was sorry for the poor girl, and I was afraid for my uncle. All at once I found Gavrila at my side; he was still holding the exercise book in his hand.

"Please come to your uncle," he said in a dejected voice.

I pulled myself together.

"To my uncle? Where is he? What's happening to him now?"

"In the tea-room. Where your honour had tea this afternoon."

"Who is with him?"

"His honour's alone. He is waiting."

"For whom? For me?"

"He has sent for Foma Fomitch. Happy days have come for us," he added, with a deep sigh.

"Foma Fomitch? H'm! Where are the others? Where's your mistress?"

"In her own apartments. Her honour's fallen into a swoon, and now she is lying unconscious and crying."

Conversing in this way, we reached the verandah. It was almost completely dark outside. My uncle really was alone in the very room in which my encounter with Foma Fomitch had taken place, and he was striding up and down it. There were lighted candles on the tables. Seeing me, he rushed up to me and warmly pressed my hands. He was pale and breathing hard; his hands were trembling, and from time to time a nervous shudder ran over his whole frame.

[ix]

YOUR EXCELLENCY

MY DEAR boy, it's all over, it's all settled," he pronounced in a tragic half-whisper.

"Uncle," I said, "I heard shouts and uproar."

"Yes, my boy, shouts there were; shouts of all sorts! Mamma is in a swoon, and everything is upside down now. But I have made up my mind, and shall insist on my own way. I am afraid of no one now, Seryozha. I want to show them that I, too, have a will of my own, and I will show them! And so I have sent for you on purpose that you may help me show them. . . . My heart is broken, Seryozha . . . but I ought, I am bound to act with severity. Justice is inexorable."

"But whatever has happened, uncle?"

"I am parting with Foma," my uncle pronounced in a resolute voice.

"Uncle," I cried, delighted, "you could have thought of nothing better! And if I can assist in any way to carry out your decision . . . make use of me now and always."

"Thank you, my boy, thank you! But now it is all settled. I am waiting for Foma, I have already sent for him. Either he or I! We must part. Either Foma leaves this house to-morrow or I swear I'll throw up everything and go into the Hussars again. They will take me and give me a division. Away with all this bobbery! A fresh start in every way now. What have you got that French exercise book for?" he cried furiously, addressing Gavrila. "Away with it! Burn it, stamp on it, tear it to pieces! *I* am your master, and *I* order you not to learn French. You can't disobey me, you dare not, for *I* am your master, and not Foma Fomitch!"

"I thank Thee, O Lord!" Gavrila muttered to himself.

Evidently things had got beyond a joke.

"My dear," my uncle went on, with deep feeling, "they are asking me the impossible. You shall decide; you stand between me and them now as an impartial judge. You don't know what they have insisted on my doing, you don't know, and at last they have formally demanded it, they have spoken out. But it's repugnant of humanity, to decent feeling, to honour. . . . I will tell you all about it, but first . . ."

"I know about it already, uncle!" I cried, interrupting him. "I can guess . . . I have just been talking to Nastasya Yevgrafovna."

"My dear, not a word, not a word of that now!" he interrupted me hurriedly, as though he were frightened. "I will explain about it later on, but meanwhile. . . . Well?" he cried to Vidoplyasov, who walked in. "Where is Foma Fomitch?"

Vidoplyasov entered with the information "that Foma Fomitch did not wish to come, and considered that the insistence on his doing so was rude to the point of impertinence, so that his honour, Foma Fomitch, was greatly offended by it."

"Bring him! Drag him! Fetch him here! Drag him here by force!" cried my uncle, stamping.

Vidoplyasov, who had never seen his master in such a rage, retreated in alarm. I was surprised.

"Something very important must have happened," I thought, "if a man of his character is capable of being moved to such wrath and such determination."

For some moments my uncle walked up and down the room as though struggling with himself.

"Don't tear up your exercise book though," he said to Gavrila at last. "Wait a little and stay here. You may perhaps be wanted. My dear," he went on, turning to me, "I think I was too noisy just now. Everything must be done with dignity and manliness, but without shouting and insulting people. Do you know what, Seryozha; wouldn't it be better if you were to go out? It will be just the same to you. I will tell you all about it later on—eh? What do you think? Do that for my sake, please."

"Are you frightened, uncle? Are you repenting?" I said, looking at him intently.

"No, no, my dear boy, I am not repenting," cried my uncle, with redoubled earnestness. "I am afraid of nothing now. I have taken decisive steps, the most decisive! You don't know, you can't imagine what they have demanded of me! Ought I to consent? No, I will show them. I have made a stand against them and I will show them. I was bound to show them sooner or later! But you know, my dear boy, I am sorry I sent for you; it will be very hard, perhaps, for Foma if you are here, so to say, the witness of his humiliation. You see, I want to turn him out of the house in a gentlemanly way, without humiliating him at all. Though, indeed, it is only a form of words to say, without humiliation. The position is such, my boy, that however honeyed one's speech is it will still be insulting. I am coarse, uneducated perhaps, I may do something in my foolishness that I may regret later. Anyway he has done a great deal for me. . . . Go away, my dear. . . . Here, they are bringing him! Seryozha, I entreat you, go away; I will tell you all about it afterwards. For Christ's sake go away!"

And uncle led me out on to the verandah at the very moment when Foma walked into the room. But I must confess I did not go away; I made up my mind to stay on the verandah where it was very dark, and so it was difficult to see me from within. I made up my mind to play the eavesdropper! I do not justify my action, but I can boldly sav that I consider I performed an heroic feat in standing that whole half-hour on the verandah without losing patience.

From my position I could not only hear well, but could even see well; the doors were of glass. I now beg the reader to imagine Foma Fomitch after he had been *commanded* to come, and threatened with force if he refused.

"Can my ears have heard that threat aright, Colonel?" cried Foma, entering the room. "Was that your message?"

"Yes, Foma, yes; calm yourself," my uncle answered valiantly. "Sit down; we must have a little serious friendly talk like brothers. Sit down, Foma."

Foma Fomitch majestically sat down on a low chair. My uncle walked about the room with rapid and uneven steps, evidently puzzled how to begin.

"Like brothers, precisely," he repeated. "You understand me, Foma; you are not a boy, I am not a boy either—in fact, we are both getting on. . . . H'm! You see, Foma, we don't get on together on certain points . . . yes, on certain points precisely, and so, Foma, would it not be better to part? I am convinced that you are a generous man, that you wish me well, and so . . . But why prolong the discussion? Foma, I am your friend now and always, and I swear that by all the saints! Here are fifteen thousand roubles in silver; it's all I have to bless myself with. I have scraped together every farthing, I have robbed my own children. Take it boldly! I ought—it is my duty—to secure your future. It's almost all in banknotes and very little in cash. Take it boldly; you owe me nothing, for I shall never be able to repay you for all you have done for me. Yes, yes, precisely, I feel that, though now we are in disagreement over the most important point. To-morrow or the day after, or when you like, let us part. Drive to our little town, Foma, it is not eight miles away; there behind the church in the first side street there is a little house with green shutters, a charming little house belonging to the widow of a priest, that looks as though it had been built for you. She is selling it, and I will buy it for you in addition to this money. Settle there near us. Work at literature, study science, you will win fame. . . . The officials there are gentlemanly, agreeable, disinterested men; the head priest is learned. You shall come and stay with us for the holidays—and we shall all live as in paradise. Will you?"

"So these are the terms on which Foma is to be kicked out!" I thought. "Uncle did not say a word to me about money."

For a long time a profound silence reigned. Foma sat in his easy-chair as though struck dumb, gazing fixedly at my uncle, who was evidently becoming uncomfortable from that silence and that stare.

"The money!" Foma articulated at last in an affectedly faint voice. "Where is it? Where is that money? Give it me, give it here at once!"

"Here it is, Foma, everything I have to the last farthing, just fifteen thousand. Here are notes and securities; you can see for yourself . . . here!"

"Gavrila, take that money," Foma said mildly, "it may be of use to you, old man. But no!" he cried all at once, raising his voice to an extraordinary squeal and leaping up from his chair; "no, give me that money first, Gavrila! Give it me. Give it me. Give me those millions that I may trample them under foot; give them to me that I may tear them to pieces, spit on them, fling them away, spurn them, scorn them! . . . They offer money to me—to me! They try to buy me to leave this house! Have I heard that? Have I lived to see this last ignominy? Here they are, here are your millions! Look! there, there, there, there. That is how Foma Opiskin behaves if you did not know it before, Colonel!"

And Foma threw the whole roll of notes about the room. It was noticeable that he did not tear or spit on one of the notes as he had boasted of doing; he only crumpled them a little, and even that rather carefully. Gavrila flew to pick up the notes from the floor, and later on, after Foma's departure, he carefully restored them to his master.

Foma's action produced an overwhelming impression upon my uncle. In his turn, he now stood facing him, immovably, senselessly, openmouthed. Foma meanwhile had replaced himself in his arm-chair and was panting as though from unutterable agitation.

"You are a man of lofty feelings, Foma!" my uncle cried out at last, recovering himself. "You are the noblest of men!"

"I know it," Foma answered in a faint voice, but with ineffable dignity.

"Foma, forgive me! I have been a mean wretch to you, Foma!"

"Yes, to me," Foma assented.

"Foma, it is not your disinterestedness that I marvel at," my uncle went on enthusiastically, "but that I could have been so coarse, blind and mean as to offer you money in such circumstances. But, Foma, you are mistaken about one thing; I was not bribing you, I was not paying you for leaving this house, but just simply I wanted you to have money that you might not be in straits when you leave me. I swear that! On my knees, on my knees I am ready to beg your forgiveness, Foma; and if you like, I am ready to go down on my knees before you this moment . . . if you wish me to. . . ."

"I don't want your kneeling, Colonel."

"But, my God! Foma, consider: you know I was carried away, overwhelmed, I was not myself. . . . But do tell me, do say in what way I can, in what way I may be able to efface this insult! Instruct me, admonish me. . . ."

"In no way, in no way, Colonel! And rest assured that to-morrow morning I shall shake the dust from off my boots on the threshold of this house."

And Foma began to get up from his chair. My uncle rushed in horror to make him sit down again.

"No, Foma, you will not go away, I assure you!" cried my uncle. "It is no use talking about dust and boots, Foma! You are not going away, or I will follow you to the utmost ends of the earth, and I will follow you till such time as you forgive me. . . . I swear it, Foma, and I will do it!"

"Forgive you? You are to blame?" said Foma. "But do you yet understand the wrong you have done me? Do you understand that even the fact that you have given me a piece of bread here has become a wrong to me now? Do you understand that now in one minute you have poisoned every morsel I have tasted in your house? You reproached me just now with those morsels, with every mouthful of the bread I have eaten; you have shown me now that I have been living like a slave in your house, like a flunkey, like a rag to wipe your polished boots! And yet I, in the purity of my heart, imagined up to now that I was residing in your house as a friend and a brother! Did you not, did you not yourself in your snake-like speeches assure me a thousand times of that brotherly relation? Why did you mysteriously weave for me the snare, in which I have been caught like a fool? Why have you dug in the darkness this wolf-pit into which you have yourself thrust me now? Why did you not strike me down with one blow before? Why did you not wring my neck at the very beginning like a cock, because he . . . well, for instance, simply because he doesn't lay eggs? Yes, that's just it! I stick to that comparison, Colonel, though it is taken from rustic life and recalls the trivial tone of modern literature; I stick to it, because one sees in it all the senselessness of your accusation; for I am as much in fault as this supposititious cock who displeases his frivolous owner by not laying eggs! Upon my word, Colonel! Does one pay a friend, a brother, with money—and what for? That's the point, what for? 'Here, my beloved brother, I am indebted to you; you have even saved my life; here are a few of Judas's silver pieces for you, only get away out of my sight!' How naïve! How crudely you have behaved to me! You thought that I was thirsting for your gold, while I was cherishing only the heavenly feeling of securing your welfare. Oh, how you have broken my heart! You have played with my finest feelings like some wretched boy with a ninepin! Long, long ago, Colonel, I foresaw all this—that is why I have long choked over your bread, I have been suffocated by your bread! That is why your feather-beds have stifled me, they have stifled me instead of lulling me to slumber! That is why your sugar, your sweetmeats have been cayenne pepper to me and not sweetmeats! No, Colonel! live alone, prosper alone, and let Foma go his sorrowful way with a wallet on his back. So it shall be, Colonel!"

"No, Foma, no! It shall not be so, it cannot be so!" moaned my uncle, utterly crushed.

"Yes, Colonel, yes! So it shall be, for so it must be. To-morrow I shall depart from you. Scatter your millions, strew all my way, all the high road to Moscow with your banknotes—and I will walk proudly and scornfully over your notes; this very foot, Colonel, will trample your notes into the mud and crush them; for Foma Opiskin the nobility of his own soul will be enough! I have said it and I have shown it! Farewell, Colonel, fa-re-we-ell!"

And Foma began again getting up from his chair.

"Forgive me, forgive me, Foma; forget it! . . ." repeated my uncle, in an imploring voice.

"Forgive you! Why, what use will my forgiveness be to you? Why, supposing I do forgive you: I am a Christian; I cannot refuse to forgive; I have almost forgiven you already. But consider yourself: is it in the least consistent with common sense and gentlemanly feeling for me to stay one minute longer in your house? Why, you have turned me out of it!"

"It is consistent, it is consistent, Foma! I assure you that it is consistent!"

"It is? But are we equals now? Don't you understand that I have, so to speak, crushed you by my generosity, and you have crushed yourself by your degrading action? You are crushed and I am uplifted. Where is the equality? Is friendship possible without equality? I say this, uttering a cry of lamentation from my heart, and not triumphing, not exalting myself over you, as you perhaps imagine."

"But I am uttering a cry of lamentation from my heart too, Foma, I assure you."

"And this is the man," Foma went on, changing his severe tone for a sanctimonious one, "this is the man for whom I so often kept vigil at night! How many times on my sleepless nights have I arisen from my bed, have lighted a candle and said to myself, 'Now he is sleeping peacefully, trusting in you. Do not you, Foma, sleep, be valiant for him; maybe you will think of something more for the welfare of that man.' That is what Foma thought on his sleepless nights, Colonel! And this is how that colonel has repaid him! But enough, enough . . .'"

"But I will deserve your friendship again, Foma; I will deserve it, I swear to you."

"You will deserve it? Where is the guarantee? As a Christian I will forgive you, and even love you; but as a man and a gentleman I shall not be able to help despising you. I must, I am bound to, in the name of morality, because—I repeat it—you have disgraced yourself, while my action has been most high-minded. Why, who out of *your set* would perform such an action? Would any one of them refuse an immense sum of money which poor destitute Foma, despised by all, has refused from devotion to true greatness? No, Colonel; to be on a level with me you must perform now a regular series of heroic deeds. And what are you capable of when you cannot even address me as your equal, but call me Foma like a servant. . . ."

"Foma! but I call you so from affection!" wailed my uncle. "I did not know you disliked it. My God! if I had only known! . . ."

"You," Foma pursued, "you who could not, or rather, would not, grant the most insignificant, the most trivial request when I asked you to address me like a general as 'your Excellency' . . ."

"But, Foma, you know that is really, so to say, high treason, Foma."

"High treason! You have learnt some phrase out of a book and repeat it like a parrot! But, do you know, you put me to shame, covered me with ignominy by your refusal to call me 'your Excellency'; you covered me with ignominy because without understanding my reasons you made me look a capricious fool worthy of a madhouse. Why, do you suppose I don't understand that I should have been ridiculous if I had wanted to be styled 'Excellency'—I who despise all these ranks and earthly grandeurs, insignificant in themselves if they are not lighted up by virtue? For a million I would not accept the rank of general, without virtue. And meanwhile you looked upon me as a madman! It was for your benefit I sacrificed my pride and allowed you, *you* to be able to look upon me as a madman, you and your learned gentlemen! It was solely in order to enlighten your mind, to develop your morals, and to shed upon you the light of new ideas that I made up my mind to demand from you a general's title. I wanted you for the future not to regard generals as the highest luminaries on this earthly sphere; I wanted to show you that rank is nothing without greatness of soul, and that there is no need to rejoice at the arrival of your general when there are, perhaps, standing at your side, people made illustrious by virtue! But you have so constantly prided yourself before me on your rank of colonel that it was hard for you to say to me: 'your Excellency.' That was the root of it! That was where one must look for the reason, and not in any breach of the decrees of Providence! The whole reason is, that you are a colonel and I am simply Foma. . . ."

"No, Foma; no, I assure you that it is not so. You are a learned man . . . you are not simply Foma. . . . I respect you. . . ."

"You respect me! Good! Then tell me, since you respect me, what is your opinion, am I worthy of the rank of a general or am I not? Answer at once and straightforwardly, am I or not? I want to see your intelligence, your development."

"For honesty, for disinterestedness, for intelligence, for lofty nobility of soul you are worthy of it," my uncle brought out with pride.

"Well, if I am worthy of it, why will you not say 'your Excellency' to me?"

"Foma, I will, perhaps."

"But, I insist! And I insist now, Colonel, I require it and insist. I see how hard it is for you, that is why I insist. That sacrifice on your side will be the first step in your moral victory, for—don't forget it— you will have to gain a series of moral victories to be on a level with me; you must conquer yourself, and only then I shall feel certain of your sincerity. . . ."

"To-morrow, then, I will call you 'your Excellency,' Foma."

"No, not to-morrow, Colonel, to-morrow can take care of itself. I insist that you now at once address me as 'your Excellency.' "

"Certainly, Foma, I am ready; only what do you mean by 'at once,' Foma?"

"Why not at once, or are you ashamed? That's an insult to me if you are ashamed."

"Oh, well, if you like, Foma. I am ready . . . I am proud to do so, indeed; only it's queer, Foma, apropos of nothing, 'Good-day, your Excellency.' You see, one can't."

"No, not 'Good-day, your Excellency.' That's an offensive tone, it is like a joke, a farce. I do not permit such jokes with me. You forget yourself, Colonel, you forget yourself. Change your tone!"

"And you are not joking, Foma?"

"In the first place, I am not Foma, Yegor Ilyitch, and don't you forget it. I am Foma Fomitch."

"Oh, Foma Fomitch, I am delighted, really, I am altogether delighted, only what am I to say?"

"You are puzzled what to add to the phrase 'your Excellency.' That I understand. You should have explained yourself long ago. It is excusable indeed, especially if a man is not a *literary character,* to put it politely. Well, I will help you, since you are not a literary character. Repeat after me, 'Your Excellency!' . . ."

"Well, your Excellency . . ."

"No, not 'Well, your Excellency,' but simply 'your Excellency!' I tell you, Colonel, you must change your tone. I hope, too, that you will not be offended if I suggest that you should make a slight bow. And at the same time bend forward, expressing in that way respectfulness and readiness, so to say, to fly on his errands. I have been in the society of generals myself, and I know all that, so then 'your Excellency.' "

"Your Excellency . . ."

"How inexpressibly delighted I am that I have at last an opportunity of asking your forgiveness for not having recognized from the first moment your Excellency's soul. I make bold to assure you that I will not for the future spare my poor efforts for the public welfare. . . . Well, that's enough!"

Poor uncle! He had to repeat all this rigmarole phrase by phrase, word by word. I stood and blushed as though I were guilty. I was choking with rage.

"Well, don't you feel now," the torturer went on, "that your heart is suddenly lighter, as though an angel had flown into your soul? . . . Do you feel the presence of that angel? Answer."

"Yes, Foma, I certainly feel more at ease," answered my uncle.

"As though after you have conquered yourself your heart were, so to say, steeped in holy oil?"

"Yes, Foma; certainly it all seems as it were in butter."

"As it were in butter? H'm, I wasn't talking of butter, though. . . . Well, never mind! You see, Colonel, the value of a duty performed! Conquer yourself. You are vain, immensely vain!"

"I see I am, Foma," my uncle answered, with a sigh.

"You are an egoist, and indeed a gloomy egoist. . . ."

"An egoist I am, it is true, Foma, and I see it; ever since I have come to know you, I have learned to know that too."

"I am speaking to you now like a father, like a tender mother. . . . You repel people and forget that a friendly calf sucks two mothers."

"That is true too, Foma!"

"You are coarse. You jar so coarsely upon the human heart, you so egoistically insist upon attention, that a decent man is ready to run from you to the utmost ends of the earth."

My uncle heaved another deep sigh.

"Be softer, more attentive, more loving to others; forget yourself for the sake of others, then they will think of you. Live and let others live—that is my rule! Suffer, labour, pray and hope—those are the truths which I would like to instil into all mankind at once! Model yourself on them and then I shall be the first to open my heart to you, I shall weep on your bosom . . . if need be. . . . As it is, it is always 'I' and 'I' and 'my gracious self' with you. But, you know, one may get sick at last of your gracious self, if you will allow me to say so."

"A sweet-tongued gentleman," Gavrila brought out, awestruck.

"That's true, Foma, I feel all that," my uncle assented, deeply touched. "But I am not altogether to blame, Foma. I've been brought up like this, I have lived with soldiers; but I swear, Foma, I have not been without feeling. When I said good-bye to the regiment, all the hussars, all my division, simply shed tears and said they would never get another like me. I thought at the time that I too was not altogether a lost soul."

"Again a piece of egoism! Again I catch you in vanity. You are boasting and at the same time reproaching me with the hussars' tears. Why don't I boast of any one's tears? And yet there may have been grounds, there may have been grounds for doing so."

"I meant nothing, Foma, it was a slip of the tongue. I couldn't help remembering those old happy times."

"Happy times do not fall from heaven, we make them ourselves; it lies in our hearts, Yegor Ilyitch. That is why I am always happy and, in spite of my sufferings, contented, tranquil in spirit, and am not a burden to any one unless it is to fools, upstarts and *learned gentlemen,* on whom I have no mercy and don't care to have. I don't like fools! And what are these learned gentlemen? 'A man of learning'; and his learning turns out to be nothing but a hoaxing trick, and not learning. Why, what did *he* say just now? Let him come here! Let all these men of learning come here! I can refute them all; I can refute all their propositions! I say nothing of greatness of soul . . ."

"Of course, Foma. Who doubts it?"

"This afternoon, for instance, I showed intelligence, talent, colossal erudition, knowledge of the human heart, knowledge of contemporary literature; I showed and displayed in a brilliant fashion how some wretched Komarinsky may furnish a lofty topic of conversation for a man of talent. And did any one of them appreciate me as I deserved? No, they turned away! Why, I am certain he has told you already that I know nothing, and yet perhaps Macchiavelli himself or some Mercadante was sitting before him and only to blame for being poor and in obscurity. . . . That does not penetrate to them! . . . I hear of Korovkin too. What sort of queer fish is he?"

"He is a clever man, Foma, a man of learning. . . . I am expecting him. He will certainly be a nice man, Foma."

"H'm, I doubt it. Most likely some modern ass laden with books; there is no soul in them, Colonel, no heart in them! And what is learning without virtue?"

"No, Foma, no. How he talked of family happiness! The heart feels it of itself, Foma."

"H'm! We will have a look at him; we will examine Korovkin too. But enough," Foma concluded, getting up from his easy-chair. "I cannot altogether forgive you yet, Colonel; the insult was too deadly; but I will pray, and perhaps God will shed peace on the wounded heart. We will speak further of this to-morrow, but now permit me to withdraw. I am tired and exhausted. . . ."

"Oh, Foma!" cried my uncle in a fluster, "why, of course you are tired! I say, won't you have something to support you, a snack of something? I will order something at once."

"A snack! Ha-ha-ha!" answered Foma, with a contemptuous laugh. "First they offer you a drink of poison, and then they ask you if you won't have a snack of something. They want to heal the wounds of the heart with stewed mushrooms or pickled apples! What a pitiful materialist you are, Colonel!"

"Oh, Foma, I spoke in all simplicity . . ."

"Oh, very well. Enough of that. I will withdraw, and you go at once to your mother; fall on your knees, sob, weep, but beg for her forgiveness, that is your duty, that is a moral obligation."

"Oh, Foma, I have been thinking of nothing but that all the time; even now while I have been talking to you I have been thinking of it. I am ready to implore her on my knees till dawn. But only think, Foma, what they are expecting of me. Why, you know it's unjust, Foma, it's cruel. Be entirely magnanimous, make me completely happy, think a little, decide, and then . . . then . . . I swear! . . ."

"No, Yegor Ilyitch, no, it's no business of mine," answered Foma. "You know that I do not meddle in the slightest degree in all that;

you may be persuaded that I am at the bottom of it all, but I assure you that from the very beginning I have held entirely aloof from this affair. It is solely the desire of your mother, and she, of course, wishes for nothing but your good. . . . Go to her, make haste, fly and rectify the position by your obedience . . . and let not the sun go down upon your wrath; while I . . . I shall be all night long praying for you. I have known no sleep for many a night, Yegor Ilyitch. Good-night! I forgive you too, old man," he said, turning to Gavrila. "I know you did not do it of yourself. You forgive me too if I have offended you. . . . Good-night, good-night all, and may the Lord bless you."

Foma went out. I rushed at once into the room.

"You've been listening!" cried my uncle.

"Yes, uncle, I have been listening! And you, you could call him 'your Excellency'?"

"What could I do, brother? Indeed, I am proud of it. . . . That was no great act of sacrifice. But what a noble, what a disinterested, what a great man! Sergey, why, you heard yourself . . . and how I could, how I could thrust that money on him, I simply don't understand! My dear, I was carried away, I was in a rage. I did not understand him; I suspected him, I accused him. . . . But no, he could not be antagonistic to me—I see that now . . . and do you remember what a noble expression there was on his face when he was refusing the money?"

"Very well, uncle, you can be as proud as you like, but I am going; my patience is at an end. For the last time I say it, tell me what you want of me? Why did you send for me, and what do you expect? And if it is all over and I am of no use to you, then I am going. I can't endure such exhibitions! I am going this very day."

"My dear!" My uncle was in a fluster as usual. "Only wait two minutes; I am going now, dear boy, to mamma, to settle there . . . a grave, important, immense question! . . . And you meanwhile go to your room. Here, Gavrila will take you to the summer lodge. You know the summer lodge, it is in the garden. I have given orders, and your trunk has been taken there; and I am going in to beg forgiveness and settle one question—I know now what to do—and then I will be with you in a flash, and then I'll tell you everything, I'll open my whole soul to you and . . . and . . . happy days will come for us too, some time! Two minutes, only two minutes, Sergey!"

He pressed my hand and hurriedly went out. There was nothing to be done, I had to go off with Gavrila again.

[x]

MIZINTCHIKOV

THE lodge to which Gavrila conducted me was called "the new lodge" only from old habit, because it was built long ago in the time of the former owners. It was a pretty little wooden house, standing in the garden a few paces from the old house. It was surrounded on three sides by tall old lime-trees which touched the roof with their branches. All the four rooms of this little house were kept ready for visitors, and were not badly furnished. Going into the room assigned me, to which my portmanteau had been already taken, I saw on a little table before the bedstead a sheet of notepaper, covered with magnificent handwriting in various styles framed in garlands and flourishes. The capital letters and the garlands were illuminated in various colours. The whole made a very pretty specimen of calligraphy. From the first words I read I saw that it was a begging letter addressed to me, and that in it I was styled "Enlightened benefactor." It was headed "The Plaints of Vidoplyasov." Though I tried with strained attention to make out something of what was written, my efforts were all in vain; it was the most inflated nonsense, written in a high-flown flunkey lingo. I could only surmise that Vidoplyasov was in trouble of some sort, was begging for my assistance, was building great hopes upon me, "by reason of my enlightenment," and in conclusion begged me to interest myself on his behalf with my uncle and to work upon him with "my machinery," as he expressed it at the end of this epistle. I was still reading it when the door opened and Mizintchikov walked in.

"I hope you will allow me to make your acquaintance," he said in a free and easy way, though with extreme courtesy, offering me his hand. "I could not say two words to you this afternoon, and yet from the first glance I felt a desire to know you better."

I answered at once that I was delighted and so on, though I was, in fact, in an extremely bad temper. We sat down.

"What have you got here?" he said, glancing at the sheet of paper which I was still holding in my hand. "Not 'The Plaints of Vidoplyasov'? That's what it is. I was certain that Vidoplyasov was attacking you too. He presented me with just such a document with the same complaints; and he has been expecting you a long time and most likely got ready beforehand. You need not be surprised: there's a great deal that's queer here, and really there is plenty to laugh at."

"Only to laugh at?"

"Oh, well, surely not to cry over. If you like I will give you Vidoplyasov's history, and I am certain that you will laugh."

"I confess I am not interested in Vidoplyasov just now," I answered with vexation.

It was evident to me that Mr. Mizintchikov's friendliness and his polite conversation were all assumed by him with some object, and that he was simply trying to get something out of me. He had sat scowling and serious in the afternoon; now he was good-humoured, smiling, and ready to tell me long stories. It was evident from the first glance that the man was perfectly self-possessed, and he seemed to understand human nature.

"That cursed Foma!" I said, banging my fist on the table with fury. "I am positive that he is at the bottom of every sort of mischief here and mixed up in it all! Cursed brute!"

"I think your anger is excessive," Mizintchikov observed.

"My anger excessive," I cried, instantly firing up. "I let myself go too far this afternoon, of course, and so gave every one a right to blame me. I know very well that I plunged in and put my foot in it on every point, and I think there is no need to tell me that! ... I know, too, that that's not the way to behave in decent society; but how could I help letting myself go? tell me that. Why, this is a madhouse, if you care to know! And ... and ... in fact ... I am simply going away, so there."

"Do you smoke?" Mizintchikov asked calmly.

"Yes."

"Then you will probably allow me to smoke? They won't let me in there, and I am wretched without it. I agree," he went on, as he lighted a cigarette, "that all this is like a madhouse; but believe me, I do not venture to criticize you, just because in your place I should perhaps be three times as excited and violent as you."

"And why were you not violent if you really were angry too? I remember you very cool, on the contrary, and, I confess, I even thought it strange that you did not stand up for my poor uncle, who is ready to befriend ... all and every one!"

"You are right: he has befriended many people; but I consider it perfectly useless to stand up for him: in the first place it would be useless and even derogatory for him in a way; and in the second I should be kicked out to-morrow. And I tell you frankly my circumstances are such that to be a guest here is a great advantage for me."

"But I do not make the slightest claim on your frankness in regard to your circumstances. . . . I should, however, have liked to ask, since you have been here a month . . ."

"Please, do, ask anything: I am at your service," Mizintchikov answered, hurriedly moving up a chair.

"Well, explain this, for instance: Foma Fomitch has just refused fifteen thousand roubles which were in his hands—I saw it with my own eyes."

"What? Impossible!" cried Mizintchikov. "Tell me, please."

I told him, saying nothing about "your Excellency." Mizintchikov listened with greedy curiosity. He positively changed countenance when the fifteen thousand were mentioned.

"That's smart!" he said, when he heard my story. "I really did not expect it of Foma."

"He did refuse the money, though! How do you explain that? Surely not by the nobility of his soul?"

"He refused fifteen thousand to take thirty later. Though, do you know," he added after a moment's thought, "I doubt whether Foma had any mercenary design in it. He is not a practical man; he is a sort of a poet, too, in his own way. Fifteen thousand . . . h'm. He would have taken the money, do you see, but he couldn't resist the temptation to strike an attitude and give himself airs. I tell you he's a sentimental mush, and the sloppiest old sniveller and all that, with the most unbounded vanity!"

Mizintchikov was positively roused to anger. It was evident that he was very much annoyed and even envious. I looked at him with curiosity.

"H'm! We may expect great changes," he added, musing. "Now Yegor Ilyitch is ready to worship Foma. I shouldn't wonder if he does get married now that his heart is softened," he muttered through his teeth.

"So you think that this abominable, unnatural marriage with that crazy fool really will come off?"

Mizintchikov looked at me searchingly.

"The scoundrels!" I cried emphatically.

"There is a fairly sound idea at the back of it, though. They maintain that he ought to do something for his family."

"As though he hadn't done enough for them," I cried indignantly. "And you, you talk of there being a sound idea in marrying a vulgar fool!"

"Of course I agree with you that she is a fool. . . . H'm! It's a good thing that you are so fond of your uncle; I sympathize with him myself . . . though he could round off his estate finely with her fortune! They have other reasons, though; they are afraid that Yegor Ilyitch may marry that governess . . . do you remember, an attractive girl?"

"But is that likely to be true? . . ." I asked in agitation. "It seems to me that it's spiteful gossip. Tell me, for goodness' sake, it interests me extremely. . . ."

"Oh, he is head over ears in love with her! Only, of course, he conceals it."

"He conceals it? You think that he is concealing it? And she? Does she love him?"

"It is very likely she does. It is all to her advantage to marry him, though; she is very poor."

"But what grounds have you for your supposition that they love each other?"

"Oh, you know, you can't help seeing it; besides, I believe they meet in secret. They do say that she has illicit relations with him, in fact. Only, please, don't repeat that. I tell you as a secret."

"Is it possible to believe that?" I cried. "And you, you acknowledge that you believe it?"

"Of course I do not fully believe it, I wasn't there. But it's very possible, though."

"Very possible? Think of my uncle's sense of honour, his noble character."

"I agree; but one may be carried away, with a conviction that one is going to make it right with matrimony afterwards. People often are. But, I repeat, I don't insist on the absolute certainty of the facts, especially as they have blackened her character in all sorts of ways here; they even say that she had an intrigue with Vidoplyasov."

"There, you see," I cried, "with Vidoplyasov. Why, as though it were possible! Isn't it revolting even to listen to such a thing? Surely you can't believe it?"

"I tell you that I do not quite believe it," answered Mizintchikov calmly, "but it might happen. Anything may happen in this world. I was not there, and besides, I consider it not my business. But as I see you take great interest in all this, I feel I ought to add that I really don't put much faith in the story about Vidoplyasov. It's all the invention of Anna Nilovna, that Miss Perepelitsyn; it's she who has set those rumours going here out of envy because she dreamed in the past of marrying Yegor Ilyitch herself—yes, by Jove, on the ground that she is a major's daughter. Now she is disappointed and awfully furious. But I believe I have told you all about that business now, and I confess I greatly dislike gossip, especially as we are losing precious time. I have come to ask you a trifling favour, you see."

"A favour? Certainly; any way in which I can be of use to you."

"I understand, and indeed I hope to interest you, for I see you love your uncle and take great interest in his fate in the matrimonial line; but before I ask you that favour I will ask you another, a preliminary one."

"What is that?"

"I'll tell you; perhaps you will consent to grant my chief request, and perhaps not; but in any case, before telling it you I will humbly ask you to grant one great favour, to give me your word of honour as a nobleman and a gentleman that all you hear from me shall remain a dead secret, and that you will not betray the secret in any case or for the sake of any person, and will not take advantage for your own benefit of the idea which I now find it necessary to communicate to you. Do you agree or not?"

It was a solemn introduction. I gave my assent.

"Well?" . . . I said.

"It is really a very simple matter," Mizintchikov began. "I want to elope with Tatyana Ivanovna and to marry her; in short, there is to be something in the Gretna Green style, do you understand?"

I stared Mizintchikov straight in the face, and for some time I could not utter a word.

"I confess I don't understand at all," I brought out at last; "and what's more," I went on, "expecting that I had to do with a sensible man, I did not in the least expect . . ."

"Expecting you did not expect," interrupted Mizintchikov; "which may be translated, that I and my project are stupid—that's so, isn't it?"

"Oh, not at all . . . but . . ."

"Oh, please, don't mind speaking plainly! Don't be uneasy; you will do me a great pleasure by plain speaking, in fact, for so we shall get nearer our object. I agree with you, though, that all this must seem somewhat strange at the first glance. But I venture to assure you that so far from being foolish, my project is extremely sensible; and if you will be so good as to listen to all the circumstances . . ."

"Oh, certainly! I am listening eagerly."

"There is scarcely anything to tell, though. You see, I am in debt and haven't a farthing. I have, besides, a sister, a girl of nineteen, fatherless and motherless, living in a family and entirely without means, you know. For that I am partly to blame. We inherited a property of forty serfs. Just at that time I was promoted to be a cornet. Well, at first, of course, I mortgaged, and then I squandered our money in other ways too. I lived like a fool, set the fashion, gave myself airs, gambled, drank—it was idiotic, in fact, and I am ashamed to remember it. Now I have come to my senses and want to change my manner of life completely. But to do so it is absolutely essential to have a hundred thousand roubles. As I shall never get anything in the service, since I am not qualified for anything and have scarcely any education, there are, of course, only two resources left me: to steal or to marry a rich wife. I came here almost without boots to my feet, I walked, I could not drive. My sister gave me her last three roubles when I set off from Moscow. Here I saw Tatyana Ivanovna, and at once the idea dawned upon me. I immediately resolved to sacrifice myself and marry her. You will agree that all that is nothing but good sense. Besides, I am doing it more for my sister's sake . . . though, of course, for my own too."

"But allow me to ask, do you mean to make a formal proposal to Tatyana Ivanovna? . . ."

"God forbid, they would kick me out at once; but if I suggest an elopement, a runaway match, she will marry me at once. That's the whole point, that there should be something romantic and sensational about it. Of course it would all immediately end in legal matrimony. If only I can allure her away from here!"

"But why are you so sure that she will elope with you?"

"Oh, don't trouble about that! I am perfectly sure of that. The whole plan rests on the idea that Tatyana Ivanovna is ready to carry on an intrigue with any one she meets, with any one, in fact, to whom it occurs to respond to her. That is why I first asked you to give me your word of honour that you would not take advantage of the idea. You will understand, of course, that it would be positively wicked of me not to take advantage of such an opportunity, especially in my circumstances."

"So then she is quite mad. . . . Oh, I beg your pardon," I added, catching myself up. "Since you now have intentions . . ."

"Please don't mind speaking out, as I have asked you already. You ask, is she quite mad? What shall I tell you? Of course she is not mad, since she is not yet in a madhouse; besides, I really don't see anything particularly mad in this mania for love affairs. She is a respectable girl in spite of everything. You see, till a year ago she was horribly poor, and from her birth up has lived in bondage to the ladies who befriended her. Her heart is exceptionally susceptible; no one has asked her in marriage. . . . Well, you understand: dreams, desires, hopes, the fervour of feelings which she has always had to conceal, perpetual agonies at the hands of the ladies who befriended her—all that of course might well drive a sensitive character to derangement. And all at once she comes in for a fortune; you'll allow that is enough to upset any one. Well, now of course people make up to her and hang about her, and all her hopes have risen up. She told us this afternoon about a dandy in a white waistcoat; that's a fact which happened literally as she described. From that fact you can judge of the rest. With sighs, notes, verses you can inveigle her at once; and if with all that you hint at a silken rope ladder, a Spanish serenade and all that nonsense, you can do what you like with her. I have put it to the test, and at once obtained a secret interview. But meanwhile I have put it off till the right moment. But I must carry her off within four days. The evening before I shall begin to make tender speeches, to sigh: I can sing and play the guitar pretty well. At night there will be a meeting in the arbour, and at dawn the coach will be in readiness; I shall entice her away, we shall get into the coach and drive off. You understand that there is no risk about it whatever; she is of age, and what's more, completely her own mistress. And if once she ran away with me she would, of course, be bound to me. I should take her to a poor but respectable family, thirty miles away, who would look after her, and not let any one come near her till the wedding; and meanwhile I shan't lose time, we'll get married within three days—it can be done. Of course, first of all, money is needed; but I have reckoned that I shall not need more than five hundred roubles for the whole business, and for that I rely on Yegor Ilyitch. He will give it, of course, without knowing what is up. Do you understand now?"

"I do," I answered, taking it all in fully. "But tell me, in what way can I be of use to you?"

"Oh, in a great deal, I assure you, or I would not have asked you. I told you that I had in view a poor but very respectable family. You can help me both here and there, and as a witness. I must own that without your help I should be at a loss."

"Another question, why have you done me the honour to select me to receive your confidence, though you know nothing of me, since I have only been here a few hours?"

"Your question," Mizintchikov answered with the most polite smile, "your question, I frankly confess, gives me great satisfaction, because it affords me an opportunity of expressing my special regard for you."

"Oh, you do me too much honour!"

"No; you see, I have been studying you a little this afternoon. Admitting you are both hasty and . . . and . . . well, young, I tell you what I am thoroughly certain of: when you have given me your word that you will tell no one you will certainly keep it. You are not Obnoskin—that's the first point. Secondly, you are honest and will not take advantage of my idea—for yourself, of course, I mean—unless you would like to enter into a friendly compact with me. In that case I will perhaps agree to yield to you my idea—that is, Tatyana Ivanovna—and be ready to help you zealously in the elopement, only on condition of receiving from you a month after your marriage fifty thousand roubles, for which you would of course give me security beforehand in the shape of an I O U."

"What!" I cried out. "So now you are offering her to me?"

"Naturally, I can give it up to you if on reflection you wish it. I should of course be a loser, but . . . the idea belongs to me, and you know one is paid for one's ideas. Thirdly and lastly I asked you because I had no choice. And taking into consideration the position here, it was impossible to delay long; besides which it will soon be the fast of the Assumption, and they won't celebrate weddings. I hope you fully understand me now?"

"Perfectly. And once more, I feel bound to keep your secret quite sacred; but I cannot be your accomplice in the business, and I think it my duty to tell you so at once."

"Why so?"

"You ask, why so?" I cried, giving the rein to my pent-up feelings at last. "Why, surely you must understand that such an act is positively dishonourable. Supposing you were quite correct in your calculations, reckoning on the lady's weakness of mind and unhappy mania, why, it's that very thing which ought to restrain you as an honourable man! You say yourself that she is worthy of respect in spite of being ridiculous, and you are taking advantage of her misfortune to rob her of a hundred thousand. You will not, of course, be a real husband to her, carrying out your obligations: you will certainly leave her . . . it's so dishonourable that, excuse me, I can't even understand how you could bring yourself to ask me to assist you."

"Ough! my goodness! how romantic!" cried Mizintchikov, looking at me with unfeigned surprise. "Though, indeed, it's not that it's romantic, but simply I believe that you don't understand the position.

You say that it's dishonourable, and yet all the advantages are not on my side, but hers . . . only consider . . ."

"Of course, if one looks at it from your point of view I dare say it will appear that you will be doing something most magnanimous in marrying Tatyana Ivanovna," I answered, with a sarcastic smile.

"Well, what else? Just so, it is something most magnanimous," cried Mizintchikov, growing hot in his turn. "Only consider: in the first place, I am sacrificing myself in consenting to be her husband. Is not that some sacrifice? In the second place, although she has certainly a hundred thousand in silver roubles I shall only take a hundred thousand in paper, and I have sworn that I won't take another farthing from her all my life, though I could; that's some sacrifice again. Lastly, look into it more deeply. Could she anyway lead a peaceful life? For her to live in peace one would have to take her money from her and put her in a madhouse, for one may expect any minute that some worthless fellow, some scheming rogue, some adventurer, will turn up with a moustache and an imperial, with a guitar and serenades, some one in the style of Obnoskin, who will inveigle her, marry her and strip her completely, and then turn her out into the gutter. This, for instance, is a most respectable household, and yet they are only keeping her here because they are speculating on her fortune. From such risks she must be saved, rescued. Well, you see, as soon as she marries me such risks are over, it will be my duty to see that no trouble comes near her. In the first place, I shall settle her at once in Moscow, in a poor but honourable family—not the one I have spoken of to you, but another; my sister will be constantly with her; they will look after her and pay her every attention. She will have two hundred and fifty thousand, possibly three hundred, in paper left, one can do well on that, you know! Every pleasure will be provided for her, all sorts of entertainment, balls, masquerades and concerts. She may even dream of love affairs, only of course I shall look after that. She may dream as much as she likes, but not so in reality! Now, for instance, any one can ill-treat her, but no one will be able to then; she will be my wife, she will be a Mizintchikov, and I won't allow my name to be insulted! That alone is worth something, isn't it? Naturally I am not going to live with her. She will live in Moscow, and I shall live somewhere in Petersburg. I admit that, because I am doing things straightforwardly with you. But what if we do live apart? Look at her character and just consider, is she fit to be a wife and live with a husband? Is it possible to go on living with her continually? Why, she is the most light-headed creature in the world. She must have incessant change;

she is capable next day of forgetting that she was married yesterday and made a lawful wife. Why, I should make her wretched in the end if I were to live with her and insist on her strictly performing her duties. Naturally I shall go and see her once a year or oftener, and not to get money, I assure you. I have told you that I am not going to take more than a hundred thousand in paper from her, and I shan't either! On the money side I shall treat her in the most honourable way. If I come to see her for two or three days, my visit will actually be a pleasure to her and not a bore; I shall laugh with her, tell her stories, take her to a ball, make love to her, give her little souvenirs, sing songs to her, make her a present of a lapdog, have a romantic parting from her, and keep up an exchange of love letters. Why, she will be in ecstasies over such a romantic, devoted, and amusing husband. To my thinking, that is the rational way to proceed; that's how all husbands ought to behave. Husbands are only precious to their wives when they are absent, and following my system, I shall engage Tatyana Ivanovna's heart in the most honeyed way for the whole of her life. What more can she want? tell me that. Why, it is paradise, not life!"

I listened in silence and with wonder; I realized that it was impossible to turn Mr. Mizintchikov from his plan. He was fanatically persuaded of the rectitude and even the greatness of his project, and spoke of it with the enthusiasm of an inventor. But there was still one rather delicate question which was essential to clear up.

"Have you reflected," I said, "that she is almost betrothed to my uncle? It will be a great insult to him if you elope with her; you will be carrying her off almost on the eve of her wedding, and what's more, will borrow from him to carry out your exploit."

"That is just where I have you!" Mizintchikov cried out with heat. "You needn't trouble, I foresaw your objection. But first and foremost, your uncle has not yet made her an offer, consequently there is no need for me to know that they are intending her for a match for him; moreover, I beg you to note that I thought of this enterprise three weeks ago, when I knew nothing of their intentions, so I am perfectly justified from the moral point of view as regards them. And in fact, strictly speaking, it is rather he who is carrying off my betrothed than I his, whom, take note, I have already met in secret at night in the arbour. And lastly, allow me to ask, were not you yourself in a perfect frenzy at your uncle's being forced to marry Tatyana Ivanovna? And now you are all at once standing up for the marriage, and talking of honour, of some insult to the family! Why, on the contrary, I am doing your uncle the greatest service, I am saving him—you ought to understand that. He looks on the match with aversion, and what's more, is in love with another young lady! Why, what sort of wife would Tatyana Ivanovna be to him? And she would be wretched with him too because, say what you like, she would then have to be restrained from throwing roses at young men. And you know if I elope with her in the night, then no Madame la Générale, no Foma Fomitch, will be able to do anything. To bring back a bride who has run away from the wedding would be too discreditable. Isn't that a service, isn't it a benefit to Yegor Ilyitch?"

I must own this last argument had a great effect on me.

"But what if he makes her an offer to-morrow?" I said. "You see, it would be rather too late then; she will be formally betrothed to him."

"To be sure it will be, but that is just why we must work to prevent it. What am I asking you to help me for? It's hard for me alone, but the two of us together can arrange things and prevent Yegor Ilyitch from making a proposal. We must do everything we can to prevent it, even if it comes to thrashing Foma Fomitch and so distracting the general attention from all thoughts of the match. Of course that is only in the last extremity, I only give that for the sake of example. This is what I am relying on you for."

"One more last question: have you told no one but me of your scheme?"

Mizintchikov scratched the back of his head and made a very wry face.

"I must confess that question is worse than the bitterest pill for me. That's just the trouble, that I have given away the idea . . . in fact, I have been the most awful fool! And to whom, do you suppose? To Obnoskin! I can scarcely believe it myself. I don't know how it happened! He is always about the place, I did not know him so well, and when this inspiration dawned upon me I was, of course, greatly excited; and as I realized even then that I should need some one to help me, I appealed to Obnoskin . . . it was unpardonable, unpardonable!"

"Well, and what did Obnoskin say?"

"He agreed with enthusiasm, but next day early in the morning he disappeared. Three days later he turned up again with his mamma. He doesn't say a word to me, and in fact avoids me as though he were afraid of me. I saw at once what was up. And his mother is a regular shark, she's been in tight places before now. I used to know her in the past. Of course he has told her all about it. I am waiting and keeping

quiet; they are spying on me, and things are in rather a strained
position . . . that's why I am in a hurry."

"What is it exactly you fear from them?"

"They can't do a great deal, of course, but that they will do something nasty—that is certain. They will insist on having money for
keeping quiet and helping, that I expect. . . . Only I can't give them
a great deal, and I am not going to. I have made up my mind about
that. I can't give more than three thousand paper roubles. Judge for
yourself: three thousand to them, five hundred in silver for the wedding, for I must pay your uncle back in full; then my old debts; then
at least something for my sister, something at least. There won't be
much left out of a hundred thousand, will there? Why, it will be
ruin! . . . The Obnoskins have gone away, though."

"Gone away?" I asked with curiosity.

"Just after tea, damn them! but they will turn up again to-morrow,
you will see. Well, how is it to be, then? Do you agree?"

"I must own," I answered, shrugging, "I really don't know what to
say. It's a delicate matter. . . . Of course I will keep it all secret, I am
not Obnoskin; but . . . I think it's no use your building hopes on me."

"I see," said Mizintchikov, getting up from his chair, "that you are
not yet sick of Foma Fomitch and your grandmother; and though you
do care for your kind and generous uncle, you have not yet sufficiently
realized how he is being tormented. You are new to the place. . . . But
patience! You will be here to-morrow, look about you, and by evening
you'll consent. Your uncle is lost if you don't, do you understand?
They will certainly force him to marry her. Don't forget that to-morrow he may perhaps make her an offer. It will be too late, we must
settle things to-day."

"Really, I wish you every success, but as for helping you . . . I don't
know in what way."

"We know! But let us wait till to-morrow," said Mizintchikov,
smiling ironically. *"La nuit porte conseil.* Good-bye for the present.
I will come to you early in the morning, and you think things
over. . . ."

He turned and went out whistling.

I almost followed him out, to get a breath of fresh air. The moon
had not yet risen; it was a dark night, warm and stifling. The leaves
on the trees did not stir. In spite of being terribly tired, I wanted to
walk to distract my mind, collect my thoughts; but I had not gone
above ten paces when I suddenly heard my uncle's voice. He was
mounting the steps of the lodge in company with some one, and speak-

ing with great animation. I turned back and called to him. My uncle
was with Vidoplyasov.

[xi]

THE EXTREME OF PERPLEXITY

Uncle," I said, "at last I have got you."

"My dear boy, I was rushing to you myself. Here, I will just finish
with Vidoplyasov, and then we can talk to our hearts' content. I have
a great deal to tell you."

"What, Vidoplyasov now! Oh, get rid of him, uncle."

"Only another five or ten minutes, Sergey, and I shall be entirely
at your disposal. You see, it's important."

"Oh, no doubt, it is his foolishness," I said, with vexation.

"What can I say to you, my dear? The man has certainly found a
time to worry me with his nonsense! Yes, my good Grigory, couldn't
you find some other time for your complaints? Why, what can I do
for you? You might have compassion even on me, my good boy. Why,
I am, so to say, worn out by you all, devoured alive, body and soul!
They are too much for me, Sergey!" And my uncle made a gesture
of the profoundest misery with both hands.

"But what business can be so important that you can't leave it? And,
uncle, I do so want . . ."

"Oh, my dear boy, as it is they keep crying out that I take no trouble
over my servants' morals! Very likely he will complain of me to-
morrow that I wouldn't listen to him, and then . . ." and my uncle
waved his hand in despair again.

"Well, then make haste and finish with him! Perhaps I can help you;
let us go up the steps. What is it? What does he want?" I said as we
went into the room.

"Well, you see, my dear, he doesn't like his own surname, and asks
leave to change it. What do you think of that?"

"His surname! What do you mean? . . . Well, uncle, before I hear
what he has to say himself, allow me to remark that it is only in your
household such queer things can happen," I said, flinging up my hands
in amazement.

"Oh, my dear boy, I might fling up my hands like you, but that's no
good," my uncle said with vexation. "Come, talk to him yourself, you
have a try. He has been worrying me for two months past. . . "

"It's not a respectable surname," Vidoplyasov observed.

"But why is it not respectable?" I asked him in surprise.

"Oh, because it suggests all sorts of abomination."

"But why abomination? And how can you change it? Does any one change his surname?"

"Well, really, sir, do other people have such surnames?"

"I agree that your surname is a somewhat strange one," I went on, in complete bewilderment; "but there is no help for it now, you know. Your father had the same surname, I suppose, didn't he?"

"That is precisely so, that through my parent I have in that way had to suffer all my life, inasmuch as I am destined by my name to accept many jeers and to endure many sorrows," answered Vidoplyasov.

"I bet, uncle, that Foma Fomitch has a hand in this!" I cried with vexation.

"Oh no, my boy; oh no, you are mistaken. Foma certainly has befriended him. He has taken him to be his secretary, that's the whole of his duty. Well, of course he has developed him, has filled him with noble sentiments, so that he is even in some ways cultivated. . . . You see, I will tell you all about it. . . ."

"That is true," Vidoplyasov interrupted, "that Foma Fomitch is my true benefactor, and being a true benefactor to me, he has brought me to understand my insignificance, what a worm I am upon the earth, so that through his honour I have for the first time learned to comprehend my destiny."

"There you see, Seryozha, there you see what it all means," my uncle went on, growing flustered as he always did. "He lived at first in Moscow, almost from childhood, in the service of a teacher of calligraphy. You should see how he has learned to write from him, and he illuminates in colours and gold with cupids round, you know—in fact, he is an artist, you know. Ilyusha has lessons from him; I pay him a rouble and a half a lesson. Foma himself fixed on a rouble and a half. He goes to three gentlemen's houses in the neighbourhood; they pay him too. You see how he is dressed! What's more, he writes poetry."

"Poetry! That's the last straw!"

"Poetry, my dear boy, poetry. And don't imagine I am joking; real poetry, so to say, versifications, and so well composed, you know, on all sorts of subjects. He'll describe any subject you like in a poem. It's a real talent! On mamma's nameday he concocted such a harangue that we listened with our mouths open; there was something from mythology in it, and the Muses flying about, so that indeed, you know, one could see the . . . what do you call it? . . . polish of form—in fact, it was perfectly in rhyme. Foma corrected it. Well, I have nothing against that, and indeed I am quite pleased. Let him compose, as long as he doesn't get into mischief. You see, Grigory, my boy, I speak to you like a father. Foma heard of it, looked at his poetry, encouraged him, and chose him as his reader and copyist—in fact, he has educated him. It is true, as he says, that Foma has been a benefactor to him. Well, and so, you know, he has begun to have gentlemanly and romantic sentiments, and a feeling of independence—Foma explained it all to me, but I have really forgotten; only I must own that I wanted, apart from Foma, to give him his freedom. I feel somehow ashamed, you know! . . . but Foma opposes that and says that he finds him useful, that he likes him; and what's more he says: 'It's a great honour to me, as his master, to have poets among my own servants; that that's how some barons somewhere used to live, and that it is living *en grand*.' Well, *en grand* so be it, then! I have begun to respect him, my boy— you understand. . . . Only goodness knows how he is behaving! The worst of it is that since he has taken to poetry he has become so stuck-up with the rest of the servants that he won't speak to them. Don't you take offence, Grigory, I am speaking to you like a father. Last winter, he promised to marry a serf girl here, Matryona, and a very nice girl she is, honest, hard-working and merry. But now it is 'No, I won't.' That's all about it, he has given her up. Whether it is that he has grown conceited, or has planned first to make a name and then to seek a match in some other place."

"More through the advice of Foma Fomitch," observed Vidoplyasov, "seeing that his honour is my true well-wisher."

"Oh, of course Foma Fomitch has a hand in everything," I could not help exclaiming.

"Ough, my dear boy, that's not it!" my uncle interrupted me hurriedly. "Only, you see, now he has no peace. She's a bold, quarrelsome girl, she has set them all against him, they mimic him, bait him, even the serf boys look upon him as a buffoon. . . ."

"It's chiefly owing to Matryona," observed Vidoplyasov; "for Matryona's a real fool, and being a real fool, she's a woman of unbridled character. Through her I have come in this manner to endure such prolonged sufferings."

"Ough, Grigory, my boy, I have talked to you already," my uncle went on, looking reproachfully at Vidoplyasov. "You see, Sergey, they have made up some horrid rhyme on his surname. He comes to me and complains, asks whether he cannot somehow change his surname, says that he has long been upset at its ugly sound. . . ."

"It's an undignified name," Vidoplyasov put in.

"Come, you be quiet, Grigory! Foma approved of it too . . . that is, he did not approve exactly, but, you see, this was his idea; that in case he were to publish his poems—and Foma has a project of his doing so—such a surname perhaps might be a drawback, mightn't it?"

"So he wants to publish his verses, uncle?"

"Yes, my boy. It's settled already—at my expense, and on the title-page will be put, 'the serf of so-and-so,' and in the preface, the author's thanks to Foma for his education. It's dedicated to Foma. Foma is writing the preface himself. Well, so just fancy if on the title-page there stands, 'The Poems of Vidoplyasov.' "

"The Plaints of Vidoplyasov," Vidoplyasov corrected.

"There, you see, plaints too! Well, Vidoplyasov is no use for a surname, it positively revolts the delicacy of one's feelings, so Foma says. And all these critics, they say, are such fellows for picking holes and jeering; Brambeus, for instance. . . . They don't stick at anything, you know! They will make a laughingstock of him for his surname alone; they'll tickle your sides for you till you can do nothing but scratch them, won't they? What I say is, put any surname you like on your poems—a pseudonym it's called, isn't it? I don't remember; some word ending in *nym*. 'But no,' he says; 'give the order to the whole servants' hall to call me by a new name hereafter, for ever, so that I may have a genteel surname to suit my talent.' "

"I bet that you consented, uncle. . . ."

"I did, Seryozha, my boy, to avoid quarrelling with them; let them do as they like. You see, at that time there was a misunderstanding between Foma and me. So since then it has come to a new surname every week, and he keeps choosing such dainty ones as Oleandrov, Tulipov. . . . Only think, Grigory, at first you asked to be called 'Vyerny' (*i. e.* true, faithful)—'Grigory Vyerny'; afterwards you didn't like the name yourself because some simpleton found a rhyme to it, 'skverny' (*i. e.* nasty, horrid). You complained, and the fellow was punished. You were a fortnight thinking of a new name—what a selection you had!—at last you made up your mind and came to be asked to be called 'Ulanov.' Come, tell me, my boy, could anything be sillier than 'Ulanov'? I agreed to that too, and gave instructions a second time about changing your surname to Ulanov. It was simply to get rid of him," added my uncle, turning to me. "You spoilt all the walls, all the window-sills in the arbour, scribbling 'Ulanov' in pencil; they have had to paint it since. You wasted a whole quire of good paper on signing your name 'Ulanov.' At last that was a failure too, they found a rhyme for you: 'Bolvanov' (*i. e.* fool, blockhead). He didn't want to be a blockhead, so the name must be changed again! What did you choose next? I have forgotten."

"Tantsev," answered Vidoplyasov. "If I am destined through my surname to be connected with dancing, it would be more dignified in the foreign form: 'Tantsev.'"

"Oh, yes; 'Tantsev.' I agreed to that too, Sergey. Only they found a rhyme to that which I don't like to repeat. To-day he comes forward again, he has thought of something new. I bet he has got some new surname. Have you, Grigory? Confess!"

"I have truly been meaning for a long time to lay at your feet a new name, a genteel one."

"What is it?"

"Essbouquetov."

"Aren't you ashamed, really ashamed, Grigory? A surname off a pomatum pot! And you call yourself a clever man. How many days he must have been thinking about it! Why, that's what is written on scent-bottles."

"Upon my word, uncle," I said in a half-whisper, "why, he is simply a fool, a perfect fool."

"It can't be helped," my uncle answered, also in a whisper. "They declare all round that he is clever, and that all this is due to the working of noble qualities. . . ."

"But for goodness' sake, get rid of him!"

"Listen, Grigory! I have really no time, my boy," my uncle began in something of an imploring tone, as though he were afraid even of Vidoplyasov. "Come, judge for yourself, how can I attend to your complaints now? You say that they have insulted you in some way again. Come, I give you my word that to-morrow I will go into it all; and now go, and God be with you. . . . Stay! What is Foma Fomitch doing?"

"He has lain down to rest. He told me that if I was asked about him, I was to say, that he is at prayer, that he intends to be praying a long time to-night."

"H'm! Well, you can go, you can go, my boy! You see, Seryozha, he is always with Foma, so that I am actually afraid of him. And that's why the servants don't like him, because he is always telling tales to Foma. Now he has gone away, and very likely to-morrow he will have spun some fine yarn about something! I've made it all right, my boy, and feel at peace now. . . . I was in haste to get to you. Now at last I am with you again," he brought out with feeling, pressing my hand.

"And you know I thought, my dear, that you were desperately angry with me, and would be sure to slip off. I sent them to keep an eye on you. But now, thank God! And this afternoon, Gavrila, what a to-do; and Falaley, and you, and one thing after another! Well, thank God! thank God! At last we can talk to our hearts' content. I will open my heart to you. You mustn't go away, Seryozha; you are all I have, you and Korovkin. . . ."

"But excuse me, uncle, how have you put things right, and what have I to expect here after what has happened? I must own my head's going round."

"And do you suppose that mine isn't? It has been waltzing round for the last six months, my head has, my boy! But, thank God, everything is settled now. In the first place, they have forgiven me, completely forgiven me, on certain conditions of course; but now I am scarcely afraid of anything. Sashenka has been forgiven too. Ah, Sasha, Sasha, this afternoon . . . a passionate little heart! She went a little too far, but she has a heart of gold! I am proud of that girl, Seryozha. May the blessing of God be with her for ever. You too have been forgiven, and even—do you know—you can do just what you like; you can go all over the house and into the garden, and even among the guests. In fact, you can do just as you like; but only on one condition, that you will say nothing to-morrow in the presence of mamma or Foma—that's an absolute condition, that is, literally not half a word, I have promised for you already—but will only listen to what your elders . . . that is, I mean what others may say. They say that you are young. Don't you be offended, Seryozha; you know you really are young. . . . That's what Anna Nilovna says. . . ."

Of course I was very young, and showed it at once by boiling over with indignation at such insulting conditions.

"Listen, uncle," I cried, almost breathless. "Tell me one thing and set my mind at rest: am I really in a madhouse or not?"

"There you are, my boy, criticizing at once! You can't be patient," my uncle answered, in distress. "It's not a madhouse at all, it's nothing but over-hastiness on both sides. But you must consider, my boy, how you have behaved yourself. You remember what a sousing you gave him—a man, so to say, of venerable years?"

"Such men have no venerable years, uncle."

"Oh, there, my boy, you go too far! That's really free-thinking. I have nothing against rational free-thinking myself, my boy, but really that is beyond the mark; you really surprise me, Sergey."

"Don't be angry, uncle. I beg pardon, but I only beg your pardon. As for your Foma Fomitch . . ."

"There, now, it is *your!* Oh, Sergey, my boy, don't judge him too harshly; he is a misanthropical man and nothing more, morbid! You mustn't judge him too severely. But he is a high-minded man; in fact, he is simply the most high-minded of men! Why, you saw it yourself just now; he was simply glorious. And as for the tricks he plays sometimes, it is no use noticing it. Why, it happens to every one."

"On the contrary, uncle, it happens to nobody."

"Ough, he keeps on at the same thing! There is not much good nature in you, Seryozha; you don't know how to forgive."

"Oh, all right, uncle, all right! Let us leave that. Tell me, have you seen Nastasya Yevgrafovna?"

"Oh, my dear, the whole bother has been about her. I tell you what, Seryozha, and first, what is most important: we've all decided to congratulate him to-morrow on his birthday—Foma, I mean—for to-morrow really is his birthday. Sashenka is a good girl, but she is mistaken; so we will go, the whole tribe of us, rather early, before mass. Ilyusha will recite some verses to him which will be like oil on his heart—in fact, it will flatter him. Oh, if only you, Seryozha, would congratulate him with us! He would perhaps forgive you altogether. How splendid it would be if you were reconciled! Forget your wrongs, Seryozha; you insulted him too, you know . . . he is a most worthy man. . . ."

"Uncle! uncle!" I cried, losing all patience, "I want to talk of what is important, and you . . . Do you know, I say again, what is happening to Nastasya Yevgrafovna?"

"Why, what is the matter, my boy? Why are you shouting? All the trouble has arisen over her, though indeed it arose some time ago. I did not want to tell you about it before, so as not to frighten you, for they wanted simply to turn her out, and they insisted on my sending her away too. You can imagine my position. . . . Oh, well, thank God, all that is set right now. They thought, you see—I will confess it all to you—that I was in love with her myself, and wanted to marry her; that I was, in short, rushing to ruin, for that really would be rushing to my ruin, they have explained it so to me. And so, to save me, they meant to turn her out. It was mamma's doing, and most of all Anna Nilovna's. Foma says nothing so far. But now I have convinced them all that they are wrong; and I must confess I have told them already, that you are making Nastenka a formal proposal and that is what you have come for. Well, that has pacified them to some extent, and now she will remain, though not altogether; that is, so far only on probation. Still, she will remain. And indeed you have risen in general esteem since I told them you were courting her. Anyway, mamma seems pacified. Only Anna Nilovna goes on grumbling! I really don't know what to think of to satisfy her. And what is it she really wants, Anna Nilovna?"

"Uncle, you are greatly in error! Why, do you know that Nastasya Yevgrafovna is going away to-morrow if she has not gone away already? Do you know that her father came to-day on purpose to take her away? That it's all a settled thing, that she told me of it to-day herself, and in conclusion asked me to give you her greetings? Do you know that or not?"

My uncle stood blankly facing me with his mouth open. I fancied that he shuddered, and a moan broke from his lips.

Without loss of time I hastened to describe to him all my conversation with Nastenka; my attempt to pay her my addresses, her resolute refusal, her anger with my uncle for having summoned me. I explained that she was hoping by her departure to save him from marrying Tatyana Ivanovna. In fact, I concealed nothing from him; indeed, I purposely exaggerated everything that was unpleasant in my story. I wanted to impress my uncle so as to wring some resolute step out of him, and I really did impress him. He cried out and clutched at his head.

"Where is she, don't you know? Where is she now?" he brought out at last, turning pale with alarm. "And I, like a fool, came here quite easy in my mind, I thought everything had been set right," he added in despair.

"I don't know where she is now; only when the uproar was beginning she went to you: she meant to proclaim all this aloud, before them all. Most likely they would not let her go in."

"No, indeed! What might she not have done! Ah, the hot-headed proud little thing! And what is she going to? What is she going to? And you, you are a pretty fellow. Why, what did she refuse you for? It's nonsense! You ought to have made her like you. Why doesn't she like you? For God's sake, answer, why are you standing there?"

"Have mercy on me, uncle! How can you ask such questions?"

"But you know this is impossible! You must marry her, you must. What did I bring you from Petersburg for? You must make her happy! Now they will drive her away, but when she is your wife, my own niece, they won't drive her away. If not, what has she to go to?

What will become of her? To be a governess. Why, that is simply senseless nonsense, being a governess. While she is looking for a place, what is she going to live upon at home? Her old father has got nine to keep; they go hungry themselves. She won't take a farthing from me, you know, if she goes away through this disgusting gossip; she won't, nor will her father. And to go away like this—it is awful! It will cause a scandal—I know. And her salary has been paid for a long time in advance for necessities at home; you know she is their breadwinner. Why, supposing I do recommend her as a governess, and find an honest and honourable family . . . But where the devil is one to find them, honourable, really honourable people? Well, granting that there are many—indeed it's blasphemy to doubt it, but, my dear boy, you see it's risky—can one rely on people? Besides, any one poor is suspicious, and apt to fancy he is being forced to pay for food and kindness with humiliation! They will insult her; she is proud, and then . . . and what then? And what if some scoundrelly seducer turns up? She would spurn him, I know she would, but yet he would insult her, the scoundrel! And some discredit, some slur, some suspicion may be cast upon her all the same, and then . . . My head is going round! Ah, my God!"

"Uncle, forgive me for one question," I said solemnly. "Don't be angry with me; understand that your answer to this question may decide much. Indeed, I have a right in a way to demand an answer from you, uncle!"

"What, what is it? What question?"

"Tell me as in God's presence, openly and directly; don't you feel that you are a little in love with Nastasya Yevgrafovna yourself and would like to marry her? Just think; that is why she is being turned away from here."

My uncle made a vigorous gesture of the most violent impatience.

"I? In love? With her? Why, they have all gone off their heads, or are in a conspiracy against me. And why did I write to you to come if not to prove to them that they were all off their heads? Why am I making a match for her with you? I? In love? With her? They are all crazy, that's all about it!"

"But if it is so, uncle, do allow me to speak freely. I declare to you solemnly that I see absolutely nothing against the suggestion. On the contrary, you would make her happy, if only you love her and—and—God grant it may be so! And God give you love and good counsel!"

"But upon my word, what are you talking about?" cried my uncle, almost with horror. "I wonder how you can say such a thing coolly

... and ... you are altogether, my boy, in too great a hurry, I notice that characteristic in you! Why, aren't you talking nonsense? How, pray, am I to marry her when I look upon her as a daughter and nothing else? It would be shameful for me, indeed, to look upon her in any other light; it would be a sin, in fact! I am an old man, while she is a flower! Indeed, Foma made that clear to me in those very words. My heart glows with a father's love for her, and here you talk of marriage! Maybe out of gratitude she would not refuse me, but you know she would despise me afterwards for taking advantage of her gratitude. I should spoil her life, I should lose her affection! And I would give my soul for her, she is my beloved child! I love her just as I do Sasha, even more, I must own. Sasha is my daughter by right, by law, but this one I have made my daughter by love. I took her out of poverty, I have brought her up. Katya, my lost angel, loved her; she left her to me as a daughter. I have given her a good education: she speaks French and plays the piano, she has read books and everything. . . . Such a sweet smile she has! Have you noticed it, Seryozha? As though she were laughing at one, but yet she is not laughing, but on the contrary, loving one. . . . You see I thought that you would come and make her an offer; they would be convinced that I had no intentions in regard to her, and would give over spreading these disgusting stories. She would remain with us then in peace, in comfort, and how happy we should be! You are both my children, both almost orphans, you have both grown up under my guardianship . . . I should have loved you so! I would have devoted my life to you; I would not part from you; I would follow you anywhere! Oh, how happy we might have been! And why are these people always so cross, always so angry, why do they hate each other? If only I could explain it all to them! If only I could make them see the whole truth! Ah, my God!"

"Yes, uncle, yes, that is all so; but, you see, she has refused me."

"Refused you! H'm. . . . Do you know, I had a sort of presentiment that she would refuse you," he said, musing. "But no!" he cried. "I don't believe it. It's impossible. In that case, all our plans are upset! But you must have begun injudiciously somehow, even offended her perhaps. Perhaps you tried your hand at paying compliments. . . . Tell me how it was again, Sergey."

I repeated the whole story in full detail again. When I came to Nastenka's hoping by her departure to save my uncle from Tatyana Ivanovna, he gave a bitter smile.

"Save me!" he said. "Save me till to-morrow morning. . . ."

"But you don't mean to say that you are going to marry Tatyana Ivanovna!" I cried in alarm.

"How else could I have paid for Nastasya's not being sent away to-morrow? To-morrow I make the offer—the formal proposal."

"And you have made up your mind to it, uncle?"

"What could I do, my boy, what could I do? It rends my heart, but I have made up my mind to it. The proposal will be to-morrow; they suggest that the wedding should be a quiet one, at home; it would certainly be better at home. You will perhaps be best man. I have already dropped a hint about you, so they won't drive you away before then. There is no help for it, my boy. They say, 'It's a fortune for your children!' Of course one would do anything for one's children. One would turn head over heels, especially as really, perhaps, what they say is right. You know I really ought to do something for my family. One can't sit an idle drone for ever!"

"But, uncle, she is mad, you know!" I cried, forgetting myself, and there was a sickly pang at my heart.

"Oh, mad, is she now? She is not mad at all; it's only, you know, that she has had trouble.... There is no help for it, my boy. Of course I should have been glad of one with sense.... Though, after all, some who have sense are no better! If only you knew what a kind-hearted creature she is, noble-hearted!"

"But, my God! he is resigning himself to the thought of it already," I said in despair.

"And what else is there to do? You know they are doing their utmost for my benefit, and, indeed, I felt beforehand that sooner or later they would force me to marry, that there is no getting out of it. So better now than make more quarrelling about it. I am telling you everything quite openly, Seryozha. In a way I am actually glad. I have made up my mind, anyway, and it's a load off my back—I am more at ease, somehow. Why, I came here with my mind almost at ease. It seems, it's my fate. And the great thing to make up for it was that Nastenka would stay on. You know I agreed on that condition. And now she wants to run away of herself! But that shall not be!" my uncle cried, stamping. "Listen, Sergey," he added with a determined air; "wait for me here, don't go away. I will come back to you in an instant."

"Where are you off to, uncle?"

"Perhaps I shall see her, Sergey; it will all be cleared up, believe me that it will all be cleared up, and ... and ... you shall marry her I give you my word of honour!"

My uncle went quickly out of the room, and turned not towards the house, but into the garden. I watched him from the window.

[XII]

THE CATASTROPHE

I WAS left alone. My position was insufferable; I had been rejected, and my uncle meant to marry me almost by force. I was perplexed and lost in a tangle of ideas. Mizintchikov and his proposition were not absent from my mind for an instant. At all costs uncle must be saved! I even thought of going to look for Mizintchikov and telling him all about it. But where had my uncle gone, though? He had said himself that he was going to look for Nastenka, but had turned in the direction of the garden. The thought of secret meetings flashed through my mind, and a very unpleasant feeling clutched at my heart. I remembered what Mizintchikov had said of a secret liaison. After a moment's thought I rejected my suspicions with indignation. My uncle was incapable of deceit: that was obvious. My uneasiness grew greater every moment. Unconsciously I went out on to the steps, and walked into the garden down the very avenue into which my uncle had disappeared. The moon was beginning to rise. I knew that garden through and through, and was not afraid of losing myself. As I drew near the old arbour which stood in solitude on the bank of the neglected scum-covered pond, I suddenly stood rooted to the spot; I heard voices in the arbour. I cannot describe the strange feeling of annoyance that took possession of me. I felt convinced that my uncle and Nastenka were there, and went on going nearer, appeasing my conscience by thinking that I was walking at the same pace as before and not trying to approach stealthily. Suddenly there was the distinct sound of a kiss, then stifled exclamations, and immediately afterwards a shrill feminine shriek. At that instant a woman in a white dress ran out of the arbour and flashed by me like a swallow. It even seemed to me that she hid her face in her hands that she might not be recognized: probably I had been noticed from the arbour. But what was my amazement when in the swain who emerged after the flying lady I recognized—Obnoskin, Obnoskin, who, according to Mizintchikov's words, had gone away some hours before. Obnoskin on his side was greatly confused when he saw me; all his impudence vanished instantly.

"Excuse me, but . . . I did not in the least expect to meet you," he brought out, smiling and hesitating.

"Nor I you," I answered ironically, "especially as I heard you had already gone away."

"No. . . . It was just . . . I went a little on the way with my mother. But may I appeal to you as an absolutely honourable man?"

"What about?"

"There are cases—and you will agree yourself that it is so—when a truly honourable man is forced to appeal to the highest sense of honour of another truly honourable man. . . . I hope you understand me. . . ."

"Do not hope, I understand absolutely nothing. . . ."

"You saw the lady who was here with me in the arbour?"

"I saw her, but I did not recognize her."

"Ah, you did not recognize her. . . . That lady I shall shortly call my wife."

"I congratulate you. But in what way can I be of use to you?"

"Only in one way, by keeping it a dead secret that you have seen me with that lady."

Who can she be? I wondered. Surely not . . .

"I really don't know," I answered Obnoskin. "I hope that you will excuse me for not being able to promise."

"Yes, please, for God's sake," Obnoskin besought me. "Understand my position, it's a secret. You may be betrothed too: then I . . ."

"Sh! some one is coming!"

"Where?"

We did indeed catch a glimpse thirty paces away of the shadow of some one passing.

"It . . . it must be Foma Fomitch!" Obnoskin whispered, trembling all over. "I know him from his walk. My God! And steps again from the other direction! Do you hear? . . . Good-bye! I thank you . . . and I entreat you . . ."

Obnoskin vanished. A minute later, as though he had sprung out of the earth, my uncle was before me.

"Is it you?" he greeted me. "It is all over, Seryozha, it is all over!" I noticed, too, that he was trembling from head to foot.

"What is all over, uncle?"

"Come along!" he said, gasping for breath, and clutching my hand tightly, he drew me after him. He did not utter a word all the way to the lodge, nor did he let me speak. I was expecting something mon·strous, and my expectations were almost realized.

When we went indoors he was overcome with giddiness, he was

deathly pale. I promptly sprinkled him with water. "Something very awful must have happened," I thought, "for a man like this to faint."

"Uncle, what is the matter with you?" I asked him at last.

"All is over, Seryozha! Foma found me in the garden with Nastenka, at the very moment when I was kissing her."

"Kissing her! In the garden!" I cried, looking at my uncle in amazement.

"In the garden, my boy. The Lord confounded me! I went there to be sure of seeing her. I wanted to speak openly to her to make her see reason—about you, I mean. And she had been waiting for me a whole hour, on the broken seat, beyond the pond. . . . She often goes there when she wants to speak to me."

"Often, uncle?"

"Yes, often, my boy! Of late we have been meeting almost every night. Only they must have watched us—in fact, I know that they watched us and that it was Anna Nilovna's doing. We gave it up for a time. The last four days we have not met; but to-day it was necessary again. You saw yourself how necessary it was; how else could I have said anything to her? I went in the hope of finding her, and she had been sitting there a whole hour, waiting for me: she, too, wanted to tell me something. . . ."

"Good heavens, how incautious! Why, you knew that you were being watched!"

"But, you see, it was a critical matter, Seryozha; there was a great deal we had to discuss together. I don't dare to look at her in the day-time. She looks in one corner and I look in another, as though she did not exist. But towards night we meet and have a talk. . . ."

"Well, what happened, uncle?"

"Before I could utter a couple of words, you know, my heart began throbbing and the tears gushed from my eyes. I began trying to persuade her to marry you, and she answered me: 'You certainly don't love me—you must be blind.' And all of a sudden she flings herself on my neck, throws her arms round me, and begins crying and sobbing! 'I love no one but you,' she said, 'and won't marry any one. I have loved you for ever so long, but I will never marry you. And to-morrow I am going away and going into a nunnery.'"

"My goodness! Did she really say that? Well, what then, uncle, what then?"

"I looked up and there was Foma facing us! And where had he sprung from? Could he have been sitting behind a bush, and waiting for some such lapse?"

"The scoundrel!"

"I was petrified, Nastenka ran away, while Foma Fomitch passed by without a word and held up his finger at me. Sergey, do you understand what a hubbub there will be to-morrow?"

"I should think I do!"

"Do you understand?" he cried in despair, leaping up from his seat. "Do you understand that they will try to ruin her, to disgrace her, to dishonour her; they are looking for a pretext to accuse her of something disgraceful, and now the pretext is found. You know they will say that she is carrying on an abominable intrigue with me! You know, the scoundrels made out that she had an intrigue with Vidoplyasov! It's all Anna Nilovna's tales. What will happen now? What will happen to-morrow? Will Foma really tell them?"

"He'll certainly tell them, uncle."

"If he does, if he really does tell . . ." he brought out, biting his lips and clenching his fists. "But no, I don't believe it! He won't tell, he will understand . . . he is a man of the loftiest character! He will spare her. . . ."

"Whether he spares her or whether he doesn't," I answered resolutely, "it is your duty in any case to make Nastasya Yevgrafovna an offer to-morrow."

My uncle looked fixedly at me.

"Do you understand, uncle, that you have ruined the girl's reputation if this story gets about? Do you understand that you ought to prevent that calamity as quickly as possible; that you ought to look them all in the face boldly and proudly, ought to offer her your hand publicly, to spurn their arguments and pound Foma to a jelly if he hints a word against her?"

"My dear boy," cried my uncle, "I thought of that as I came along here!"

"And did you make up your mind?"

"Yes, and finally! I had made up my mind before I began speaking to you."

"Bravo, uncle!"

And I rushed to embrace him.

We talked for a long time. I put before him all the arguments, all the absolute necessity for marrying Nastenka, which, indeed, he understood far better than I did. But my eloquence was aroused. I was delighted on my uncle's account. He was impelled by a sense of duty or he would never have taken a stand. He had the deepest reverence for duty, for obligation. But in spite of that I was quite unable to imagine how things would be settled. I knew and blindly believed that nothing would induce my uncle to fall short of what he had once recognized as his duty; but yet I could not believe that he would have the strength to stand out against his household. And so I did my utmost to incite him and urge him on, and set to work with all the fervour of youth.

"The more so," I said, "as now everything is settled and your last doubts have vanished! What you did not expect, though in reality every one else saw it, and every one noticed it before you did, has happened; Nastasya Yevgrafovna loves you! Surely," I cried, "you will not let that pure love be turned into shame and disgrace for her?"

"Never! But, my dear boy, can I really be going to be so happy?" cried my uncle, throwing himself on my neck. "And how is it she loves me, and what for? What for? It seems to me there is nothing in me likely to . . . I am an old man compared to her; I certainly did not expect it! My angel, my angel! . . Listen, Seryozha! you asked me this evening whether I were not in love with her: had you any idea?"

"All I saw, uncle, was that you love her as much as any one can love: you love her and at the same time you don't know it yourself. Upon my word! You invite me, you want to marry me to her solely in order that she may become your niece, and so you may have her always with you. . . ."

"But you . . . you do forgive me, Sergey?"

"Oh, uncle. . . ."

And he embraced me again.

"Mind, uncle, they will all be against you: you must stand up for yourself and resist them, and no later than to-morrow!"

"Yes . . . yes, to-morrow . . ." he repeated somewhat pensively. "And you know we must attack the business with manliness, with true nobility of soul, with strength of will. . . . Yes, with strength of will!"

"Don't be frightened, uncle."

"I am not frightened, Seryozha! There's one thing, I don't know how to begin, how to proceed."

"Don't think about it, uncle. To-morrow will settle everything. Set your mind at rest for to-day. The more you think the worse it will be. And if Foma begins—kick him out of the house at once and pound him to a jelly."

"And can't we avoid kicking him out? What I have decided, my boy, is this. To-morrow I shall go to him early, at dawn, I shall tell him all about it, just as I have told you here. Surely he cannot but understand me, he is a high-minded man, the most high-minded of men. But I tell you what does worry me: what if mamma speaks to Tatyana Ivanovna to-day of the offer to be made to her to-morrow? That would be unlucky, won't it?"

"Don't worry yourself about Tatyana Ivanovna, uncle."

And I told him about the scene in the arbour with Obnoskin. My uncle was extremely surprised. I did not say a word about Mizintchikov.

"A fantastical person. A really fantastical person!" he cried. "Poor thing! They ingratiate themselves with her and try to take advantage of her simplicity. Was it really Obnoskin? But you know he has gone away. . . . Strange, awfully strange! I am astonished, Seryozha. . . . We must look into it to-morrow and take steps. . . . But are you perfectly certain that it was Tatyana Ivanovna?"

I answered that I had not seen her face, but for certain reasons I was positive that it was Tatyana Ivanovna.

"H'm. Wasn't it a little intrigue with one of the servant girls and you fancied it was Tatyana Ivanovna? Wasn't it Dasha, the gardener's daughter? A sly hussy! She has been remarked upon, that's why I say so. Anna Nilovna caught her! . . . But it wasn't she, though! He said he meant to marry her. Strange, strange!"

At last we parted. I embraced my uncle and gave him my blessing.

"To-morrow, to-morrow," he repeated, "it will all be settled; before you are up it will be settled. I shall go to Foma and take a chivalrous line, I will speak frankly as I would to my own brother, I will lay bare the inmost recesses of my heart. Good-bye, Seryozha. You go to bed, you are tired; but I am sure I shan't shut my eyes all night."

He went away. I went to bed at once, tired out and utterly exhausted. It had been a hard day. My nerves were overwrought, and before I fell really asleep, I kept starting and waking up again. But strange as my impressions were on going off to sleep, the strangeness of them was as nothing beside the queerness of my awakening next morning.

Part 2

[I]

THE PURSUIT

I SLEPT soundly without dreaming. Suddenly I felt as though a load of some hundredweights was lying on my feet. I cried out and woke up. It was daylight; the sun was peeping brightly into the room. On my bed, or rather on my feet, was sitting Mr. Bahtcheyev. It was impossible to doubt that it was he. Managing somehow to release my legs, I sat up in bed and looked at him with the blank amazement of a man just awake.

"And now he is looking about him," cried the fat man. "Why are you staring at me? Get up, sir, get up. I have been waking you for the last half-hour; rub away at your eyes!"

"Why, what has happened? What's the time?"

"It's still early by the clock, but our Fevronya did not wait for dawn, but has given us the slip. Get up, we are going in pursuit!"

"What Fevronya?"

"Why, our young lady, the crazy one! She has given us the slip! She was off before dawn. I came to you, sir, only for a minute, to wake you, and here I have been busy with you a couple of hours. Get up, your uncle's waiting for you. They waited for the festive day!" he added, with a malignant quiver in his voice.

"But whom and what are you talking about?" I asked impatiently, though I was beginning to guess. "Surely not Tatyana Ivanovna?"

"To be sure. She it is. I said so, I foretold it; they wouldn't listen to me. A nice treat she has given us for the festive day now! She is mad on *amour,* and has *amour* on the brain. Tfoo! And that fellow, what do you say to that fellow? With his little beard, eh?"

"Can you mean Mizintchikov?"

"Tfoo, plague take it! Why, my dear sir, you had better rub your eyes and pull yourself together—if only for the great holy festive day. You must have had a great deal too much at supper last night, if you are still hazy this morning! With Mizintchikov! It's with Obnoskin, not Mizintchikov. Ivan Ivanovitch Mizintchikov is a moral young man and he is coming with us in pursuit."

"What are you saying?" I cried, jumping up in bed. "Is it really with Obnoskin?"

"Tfoo, you annoying person!" answered the fat man, leaping up from his seat. "I come to him as to a man of culture to inform him of what has happened, and he still doubts it. Well, sir, if you want to come with us, get up, shoot into your breeches. It's no good my spending more words on you; I've wasted golden time on you as it is."

And he went out in extreme indignation.

Amazed by the news, I jumped out of bed, hurriedly dressed, and ran downstairs. Thinking to find my uncle in the house, where every one still seemed asleep and knowing nothing of what had happened, I cautiously mounted the front steps, and in the hall I met Nastenka. She seemed to have dressed hurriedly in some sort of *peignoir* or *schlafrock*. Her hair was in disorder; it was evident that she had only just jumped out of bed, and she seemed to be waiting for some one in the hall.

"Tell me, is it true that Tatyana Ivanovna has run away with Obnoskin?" she asked hurriedly in a breaking voice, looking pale and frightened.

"I am told it is true. I am looking for my uncle, we want to go after them."

"Oh, bring her back, make haste and bring her back. She will be ruined if you don't fetch her back."

"But where is uncle?"

"Most likely in the stable; they are getting the carriage out. I have been waiting for him here. Listen: tell him from me that I must go home to-day; I have quite made up my mind. My father will take me; I shall go at once if I can. Everything is hopeless now. All is lost!"

Saying this, she looked at me as though she were utterly lost, and suddenly dissolved into tears. I think she began to be hysterical.

"Calm yourself," I besought her. "Why, it's all for the best—you will see. What is the matter with you, Nastasya Yevgrafovna?"

"I . . . I don't know . . . what is the matter with me," she said, sighing and unconsciously squeezing my hands. "Tell him . . ."

At that instant there was a sound from the other side of the door on the right.

She let go of my hand and, panic-stricken, ran away upstairs without finishing her sentence.

I found the whole party—that is, my uncle, Bahtcheyev, and Mizintchikov—in the back yard by the stable. Fresh horses had been harnessed in Bahtcheyev's carriage. Everything was ready for setting off; they were only waiting for me.

"Here he is!" cried my uncle on my appearance. "Have you heard, my boy?" he asked, with a peculiar expression on his face.

Alarm, perplexity, and at the same time, hope were expressed in his looks, in his voice and in his movements. He was conscious that a momentous crisis had come in his life.

I was immediately initiated into all the details of the case. Mr. Bahtcheyev, who had spent a very bad night, left his house at dawn to reach the monastery five miles away in time for early mass. Just at the turning from the high road to the monastery he suddenly saw a chaise dashing along at full trot, and in the chaise Tatyana Ivanovna and Obnoskin. Tatyana Ivanovna with a tear-stained, and as it seemed frightened face, uttered a shriek and stretched out her hands to Mr. Bahtcheyev as though imploring his protection—so at least it appeared from his story; "while he, the scoundrel, with the little beard," he went on, "sits more dead than alive and tries to hide himself. But you are wrong there, my fine fellow, you can't hide yourself." Without stopping, Stepan Alexyevitch turned back to the road and galloped to Stepantchikovo and woke my uncle, Mizintchikov, and finally me. They decided to set off at once in pursuit.

"Obnoskin, Obnoskin," said my uncle, looking intently at me, looking at me as though he would like to say something else as well. "Who would have thought it!"

"Any dirty trick might have been expected of that low fellow!" cried Mizintchikov with the most vigorous indignation, and at once turned away to avoid my eye.

"What are we going to do, go or not? Or are we going to stand here till night babbling!" interposed Mr. Bahtcheyev as he clambered into the carriage.

"We are going, we are going," cried my uncle.

"It's all for the best, uncle," I whispered to him. "You see how splendidly it has all turned out?"

"Hush, my boy, don't be sinful. . . . Ah, my dear! They will simply drive *her* away now, to punish her for their failure, you understand. It's fearful, the prospect I see before me!"

"Well, Yegor Ilyitch, are you going on whispering or starting?" Mr. Bahtcheyev cried out a second time. "Or shall we unharness the horses and have a snack of something? What do you say; shall we have a drink of vodka?"

These words were uttered with such furious sarcasm that it was impossible not to satisfy Bahtcheyev at once. We all promptly got into the carriage, and the horses set off at a gallop.

For some time we were all silent. My uncle kept looking at me significantly, but did not care to speak to me before the others. He often sank into thought; then as though waking up, started and looked about him in agitation, Mizintchikov was apparently calm, he smoked a cigar, and his looks expressed the indignation of an unjustly treated man. But Bahtcheyev had excitement enough for all of us. He grumbled to himself, looked at every one and everything with absolute indignation, flushed crimson, fumed, continually spat aside, and could not recover himself.

"Are you sure, Stepan Alexyevitch, that they have gone to Mishino?" my uncle asked suddenly. "It's fifteen miles from here, my boy," he added, addressing me. "It's a little village of thirty souls, lately purchased from the former owners by a provincial official. The most pettifogging fellow in the world. So at least they say about him, perhaps, mistakenly. Stepan Alexyevitch declares that that is where Obnoskin has gone, and that that official will be helping him now."

"To be sure," cried Bahtcheyev, starting. "I tell you, it is Mishino. Only by now maybe there is no trace of him left at Mishino. I should think not, we have wasted three hours chattering in the yard!"

"Don't be uneasy," observed Mizintchikov. "We shall find them."

"Find them, indeed! I dare say he will wait for you. The treasure is in his hands. You may be sure we have seen the last of him!"

"Calm yourself, Stepan Alexyevitch, calm yourself, we shall overtake them," said my uncle. "They have not had time to take any steps yet, you will see that is so."

"Not had time!" Mr. Bahtcheyev brought out angrily. "She's had time for any mischief, for all she's such a quiet one! 'She's a quiet one,' they say, 'a quiet one,' he added in a mincing voice, as though he were mimicking some one. 'She has had troubles.' Well, now, she has shown us her heels, for all her troubles. Now you have to chase after her along the high roads with your tongue out before you can see where you are going! They won't let a man go to church for the holy saint's day. Tfoo!"

"But she is not under age," I observed; "she is not under guardianship. We can't bring her back if she doesn't want to come. What are we going to do?"

"Of course," answered my uncle; "but she will want to—I assure you. What she is doing now means nothing. As soon as she sees us she will want to come back—I'll answer for it. We can't leave her like this, my boy, at the mercy of fate, to be sacrificed; it's a duty, so to say. . . ."

"She's not under guardianship!" cried Bahtcheyev, pouncing on me at once. "She is a fool, my dear sir, a perfect fool—it's not a case of her being under guardianship. I didn't care to talk to you about her yesterday, but the other day I went by mistake into her room and what did I see, there she was before the looking-glass with her arms akimbo dancing a schottische! And dressed up to the nines: a fashion-plate, a regular fashion-plate! I simply spat in disgust and walked away. Then I foresaw all this, as clear as though it were written in a book!"

"Why abuse her so?" I observed with some timidity. "We know that Tatyana Ivanovna . . . is not in perfect health . . . or rather she has a mania. . . . It seems to me that Obnoskin is the one to blame, not she."

"Not in perfect health! Come, you get along," put in the fat man, turning crimson with wrath. "Why, he has taken an oath to drive a man to fury! Since yesterday he has taken an oath to! She is a fool, my dear sir, I tell you, an absolute fool. It's not that she's not in perfect health; from early youth she has been mad on Cupid. And now Cupid has brought her to this pass. As for that fellow with the beard, it's no use talking about him. I dare say by now he is racing off double quick with the money in his pocket and a grin on his face."

"Do you really think, then, that he'll cast her off at once?"

"What else should he do? Is he going to drag such a treasure about with him? And what good is she to him? He'll fleece her of everything and then sit her down somewhere under a bush on the high-road—and make off. While she can sit there under the bush and sniff the flowers."

"Well, you are too hasty there, Stepan, it won't be like that!" cried my uncle. "But why are you so cross? I wonder at you, Stepan. What's the matter with you?"

"Why, am I a man or not? It does make one cross, though it's no business of mine. Why, I am saying it perhaps in kindness to her. . . . Ech, damnation take it all! Why, what have I come here for? Why, what did I turn back for? What is it to do with me? What is it to do with me?"

So grumbled Mr. Bahtcheyev, but I left off listening to him and mused on the woman whom we were now in pursuit of—Tatyana Ivanovna. Here is a brief biography of her which I gathered later on from the most trustworthy sources, and which is essential to the explanation of her adventures.

A poor orphan child who grew up in a strange unfriendly house, then a poor girl, then a poor young woman, and at last a poor old maid, Tatyana Ivanovna in the course of her poor life had drained the overfull cup of sorrow, friendlessness, humiliation and reproach, and had tasted to the full the bitterness of the bread of others. Naturally of a gay, highly susceptible and frivolous temperament, she had at first endured her bitter lot in one way or another and had even been capable at times of the gayest careless laughter; but with years destiny at last got the upper hand of her. Little by little Tatyana Ivanovna grew thin and sallow, became irritable and morbidly susceptible, and sank into the most unrestrained, unbounded dreaminess, often interrupted by hysterical tears and convulsive sobbing. The fewer earthly blessings real life left to her lot, the more she comforted and deluded herself in imagination. The more certainly, the more irretrievably her last hopes in real life were passing and at last were lost, the more seductive grew her dreams, never to be realized. Fabulous wealth, unheard-of beauty, rich, elegant, distinguished suitors, always princes and sons of generals, who for her sake had kept their hearts in virginal purity and were dying at her feet from infinite love; and finally, *he—he,* the ideal of beauty combining in himself every possible perfection, passionate and loving, an artist, a poet, the son of a general—all at once or all by turns—began to appear to her not only in her dreams but almost in reality. Her reason was already beginning to fail, unable to stand the strain of this opiate of secret incessant dreaming. . . . And all at once destiny played a last fatal jest at her expense. Living in the last extreme of humiliation, in melancholy surroundings that crushed the heart, a companion to a toothless old lady, the most peevish in the world, scolded for everything, reproached for every crust she ate, for every threadbare rag she wore, insulted with impunity by any one, protected by no one, worn out by her miserable existence and secretly plunged in the luxury of the maddest and most fervid dreams—she suddenly heard the news of the death of a distant relation, all of whose family had died long before (though she in her frivolous way had never taken the trouble to ascertain the fact); he was a strange man, a phrenologist and a money-lender, who led a solitary, morose, unnoticed life, in seclusion somewhere very remote in the wilds. And now all at once immense wealth fell as though by miracle from heaven and scattered gold at Tatyana Ivanovna's feet; she turned out to be the sole legitimate heiress of the dead money-lender. A hundred thousand silver roubles came to her at once. This jest of destiny was the last straw. Indeed, how could a mind already tottering doubt the truth of dreams when they were actually beginning to come true? And so the poor thing took leave of her last remaining grain of common-sense. Swooning with bliss, she soared away beyond recall into her enchanted world of impossible imagination and seductive fancies. Away with all reflection, all doubt, all the checks of real life, all its laws clear and inevitable as twice two make four. Thirty-five years and dreams of dazzling beauty, the sad chill of autumn and the luxuriance of the infinite bliss of love—all blended in her without discord. Her dreams had once already been realized in life; why should not all the rest come true? Why should not *he* appear? Tatyana Ivanovna did not reason, but she had faith. But while waiting for *him,* the ideal—suitors and knights of various orders and simple gentlemen, officers and civilians, infantry men and cavalry men, grand noblemen and simply poets who had been in Paris or had been only in Moscow, with beards and without beards, with imperials and without imperials, Spaniards and not Spaniards (but Spaniards, by preference), began appearing before her day and night in horrifying numbers that awakened grave apprehensions in onlookers; she was but a step from the madhouse. All these lovely phantoms thronged about her in a dazzling, infatuated procession. In reality, in actual life, everything went the same fantastic way: any one she looked at was in love with her; any one who passed by was a Spaniard; if any one died it must be for love of her. As ill-luck would have it, all this was confirmed in her eyes by the fact that men such as Obnoskin, Mizintchikov, and dozens of others with the same motives began running after her. Every one began suddenly trying to please her, spoiling her, flattering her. Poor Tatyana Ivanovna refused to suspect that all this was for the sake of her money. She was fully convinced that, as though at some signal, people had suddenly reformed, and all, every one of them, grown gay and kind, friendly and good. *He* had not appeared himself in person; but though there could be no doubt that *he* would appear, her daily life as it was was so agreeable, so alluring, so full of all sorts of distractions and diversions, that she could wait. Tatyana Ivanovna ate sweetmeats, culled the flowers of pleasure, and read novels. The novels heated her imagination and were usually flung aside at the second page; she could not read longer, but was carried to dreamland by the very first lines, by the most trivial hint at love, sometimes simply by the description of scenery, of a room, of a toilette. New finery, lace, hats, hair ornaments, ribbons, samples, paper patterns, designs, sweetmeats, flowers, lapdogs were being continually sent her. Three girls spent whole days sewing for her in the maid's room, while their lady was trying on bodices and flounces, and twisting and turning before the looking-glass from morning to night, and even in the night. She actually seemed younger and prettier on coming into her fortune. To this day I don't know what was her relationship to the late General Krahotkin. I have always been persuaded that it was the invention of Madame la Générale, who wanted to get possession of Tatyana Ivanovna and at all costs to marry her to my uncle for her money. Mr. Bahtcheyev was right when he spoke of its being Cupid that had brought Tatyana Ivanovna to the last point; and my uncle's idea on hearing of her elopement with Obnoskin—to run after her and bring her back even by force—was the most rational one. The poor creature was not fit to live without a guardian, and would have come to grief at once if she had fallen into evil hands.

It was past nine when we reached Mishino. It was a poor little village, lying in a hole two miles from the high road. Six or seven peasants' huts, begrimed with smoke, slanting on one side and barely covered with blackened thatch, looked dejectedly and inhospitably at the traveller. There was not a garden, not a bush, to be seen for a quarter of a mile round. Only an old willow hung drowsily over the greenish pool that passed for a pond. Such a new abode could hardly make a cheering impression on Tatyana Ivanovna. The manor house consisted of a new long, narrow, wooden building with six windows in a row, and had been roughly thatched. The owner, the official, had only lately taken possession. The yard was not even fenced, and only on one side a new hurdle had been begun from which the dry leaves of the nut branches had not yet dropped. Obnoskin's chaise was standing by the hurdle. We had fallen on the fugitives like snow on the head. From an open window came the sound of cries and weeping.

The barefoot boy who met us dashed away at breakneck speed. In the first room Tatyana Ivanovna with a tear-stained face was seated on a long chintz-covered sofa without a back. On seeing us she uttered a shriek and hid her face in her hands. Beside her stood Obnoskin, frightened and pitifully confused. He was so distraught that he flew to shake hands with us, as though overjoyed at our arrival. From the door that opened into the other room we had a peep of some lady's dress; some one was listening and looking through a crack imperceptible to us. The people of the house did not put in an appearance;

it seemed as though they were not in the house; they were all in hiding somewhere.

"Here she is, the traveller! Hiding her face in her hands too!" cried Mr. Bahtcheyev, lumbering after us into the room.

"Restrain your transports, Stepan Alexyevitch! They are quite unseemly. No one has a right to speak now but Yegor Ilyitch; we have nothing to do here!" Mizintchikov observed sharply.

My uncle, casting a stern glance at Mr. Bahtcheyev, and seeming not to observe the existence of Obnoskin, who had rushed to shake hands with him, went up to Tatyana Ivanovna, whose face was still hidden in her hands, and in the softest voice, with the most unaffected sympathy, said to her—

"Tatyana Ivanovna, we all so love and respect you, that we have come ourselves to learn your intentions. Would you care to drive back with us to Stepantchikovo? It is Ilyusha's nameday, mamma is expecting you impatiently, while Sasha and Nastenka have no doubt been crying over you all the morning. . . ."

Tatyana Ivanovna raised her head timidly, looked at him through her fingers, and suddenly bursting into tears, flung herself on his neck.

"Oh, take me away, make haste and take me away from here!" she said, sobbing. "Make haste, as much haste as you can!"

"She's gone off on the spree and made an ass of herself!" hissed Mr. Bahtcheyev, nudging my arm.

"Everything is at an end, then," said my uncle, turning drily to Obnoskin and scarcely looking at him. "Tatyana Ivanovna, please give me your arm. Let us go!"

There was a rustle the other side of the door; the door creaked and opened wider.

"If you look at it from another point of view though," Obnoskin observed uneasily, looking at the open door, "you will see yourself, Yegor Ilyitch . . . your action in my house . . . and in fact I was bowing to you, and you would not even bow to me, Yegor Ilyitch. . . ."

"Your action in *my* house, sir, was a low action," said my uncle, looking sternly at Obnoskin, "and this house is not yours. You have heard: Tatyana Ivanovna does not wish to remain here a minute. What more do you want? Not a word—do you hear? not another word, I beg! I am extremely desirous of avoiding further explanations, and indeed it would be more to your interest to do so."

But at this point Obnoskin was so utterly crestfallen that he began uttering the most unexpected drivel.

"Don't despise me, Yegor Ilyitch," he began in a half-whisper, almost crying with shame and continually glancing towards the door, probably from fear of being overheard. "It's not my doing, but my mother's. I didn't do it from mercenary motives, Yegor Ilyitch; I didn't mean anything; I did, of course, do it from interested motives, Yegor Ilyitch . . . but I did it with a noble object, Yegor Ilyitch. I should have used the money usefully . . . I should have helped the poor. I wanted to support the movement for enlightenment, too, and even dreamed of endowing a university scholarship. . . . That was what I wanted to turn my wealth to, Yegor Ilyitch; and not to use it just for anything, Yegor Ilyitch."

We all felt horribly ashamed. Even Mizintchikov reddened and turned away, and my uncle was so confused that he did not know what to say.

"Come, come, that's enough," he said at last. "Calm yourself, Pavel Semyonitch. It can't be helped! It might happen to any one. . . . If you like, come to dinner . . . and I shall be delighted."

But Mr. Bahtcheyev behaved quite differently.

"Endow a scholarship!" he bawled furiously. "You are not the sort to endow a scholarship! I bet you'd be ready to fleece any one you come across. . . . Not a pair of breeches of his own, and here he is bragging of scholarships! Oh, you rag-and-bone man! So you've made a conquest of a soft heart, have you? And where is she, the parent? Hiding, is she? I bet she is sitting somewhere behind a screen, or has crept under the bed in a fright. . . ."

"Stepan, Stepan!" cried my uncle.

Obnoskin flushed and was on the point of protesting; but before he had time to open his mouth the door was flung open and Anfisa Petrovna herself, violently irritated, with flashing eyes, crimson with wrath, flew into the room.

"What's this?" she shouted. "What's this going on here? You break into a respectable house with your rabble, Yegor Ilyitch, frighten ladies, give orders! . . . What's the meaning of it? I have not taken leave of my senses yet, Yegor Ilyitch! And you, you booby," she went on yelling, pouncing upon her son, "you are snivelling before them already. Your mother is insulted in her own house, and you stand gaping. Do you call yourself a gentlemanly young man after that? You are a rag, and not a young man, after that."

Not a trace of the mincing airs and fashionable graces of the day before, not a trace of the lorgnette even was to be seen about Anfisa Petrovna now. She was a regular fury, a fury without a mask.

As soon as my uncle saw her he made haste to take Tatyana

Ivanovna on his arm, and would have rushed out of the room, but Anfisa Petrovna at once barred the way.

"You are not going away like that, Yegor Ilyitch," she clamoured again. "By what right are you taking Tatyana Ivanovna away by force? You are annoyed that she has escaped the abominable snares you had caught her in, you and your mamma and your imbecile Foma Fomitch; you would have liked to marry her yourself for the sake of filthy lucre. I beg your pardon, but our ideas here are not so low! Tatyana Ivanovna, seeing that you were plotting against her, that you were bringing her to ruin, confided in Pavlusha of herself. She herself begged him to save her from your snares, so to say; she was forced to run away from you by night—that's a pretty thing! That's what you have driven her to, isn't it, Tatyana Ivanovna? And since that's so, how dare you burst, a whole gang of you, into a respectable gentleman's house and carry off a young lady by force in spite of her tears and protests? I will not permit it! I will not permit it! I have not taken leave of my senses! Tatyana Ivanovna will remain because she wishes it! Come, Tatyana Ivanovna, it is useless to listen to them, they are your enemies, not your friends! Come along, don't be frightened! I'll see them all out directly! . . ."

"No, no!" cried Tatyana Ivanovna, terrified. "I don't want to, I don't want to! He is no husband for me. I don't want to marry your son! He's no husband for me!"

"You don't want to!" shouted Anfisa Petrovna, breathless with rage. "You don't want to! You have come and you don't want to! Then how dared you deceive us like this? Then how dared you give him your promise? You ran away with him by night, you forced yourself upon him, and have led us into embarrassment and expense. My son has perhaps lost an excellent match through you! He may have lost a dowry of ten thousand through you! . . . No! you must pay for it, you ought to pay for it; we have proofs; you ran away at night. . . ."

But we did not hear this tirade to the end. All at once, grouping ourselves round my uncle, we moved forward straight upon Anfisa Petrovna and went out on to the steps. The carriage was at hand at once.

"None but dishonourable people, none but scoundrels, behave like that," cried Anfisa Petrovna from the steps, in an absolute frenzy. "I will lodge a petition, you shall pay for it . . . you are going to a disreputable house, Tatyana Ivanovna. You cannot marry Yegor

Ilyitch; under your very nose he is keeping his governess as his mistress."

My uncle shuddered, turned pale, bit his lip and rushed to assist Tatyana Ivanovna into the carriage. I went round to the other side of the carriage, and was waiting for my turn to get in, when I suddenly found Obnoskin by my side, clutching at my hand.

"Allow me at least to seek your friendship!" he said warmly, squeezing my hand, with an expression of despair on his face.

"What's that, friendship?" I said, lifting my foot to the carriage step.

"Yes! I recognized in you yesterday a man of culture; do not condemn me. . . . My mother led me on, I had nothing to do with it. My inclinations are rather for literature—I assure you; this was all my mother. . . ."

"I believe you, I believe you," I said. "Good-bye!"

We got in and the horses set off at a gallop. The shouts and curses of Anfisa Petrovna resounded for a long way after us, and unknown faces suddenly poked out of all the windows of the house and stared after us with wild curiosity.

There were five of us now in the carriage, but Mizintchikov got on to the box, giving up his former seat to Mr. Bahtcheyev, who had now to sit directly facing Tatyana Ivanovna. The latter was greatly relieved that we had taken her away, but she was still crying. My uncle consoled her as best he could. He was himself sad and brooding; it was evident that Anfisa Petrovna's frantic words about Nastenka were echoing painfully and bitterly in his heart. Our return journey would, however, have ended without any disturbance if only Mr. Bahtcheyev had not been with us.

Sitting opposite Tatyana Ivanovna, he seemed not himself, he could not look indifferent, he shifted in his seat, turned as red as a crab, and rolled his eyes fearfully, particularly when my uncle began trying to console Tatyana Ivanovna. The fat man was absolutely beside himself, and grumbled like a bulldog when it is teased. My uncle looked at him apprehensively. At last Tatyana Ivanovna, noticing the extraordinary state of mind of her *vis-à-vis,* began watching him intently; then she looked at us, smiled, and all at once picking up her parasol, gracefully gave Mr. Bahtcheyev a light tap on the shoulder.

"Crazy fellow!" she said with a most enchanting playfulness, and at once hid her face in her fan.

This sally was the last straw.

"Wha-a-at?" roared the fat man. "What's that, madame? So you are after me now!"

"Crazy fellow! crazy fellow!" repeated Tatyana Ivanovna, and she suddenly burst out laughing and clapped her hands.

"Stop!" cried Bahtcheyev to the coachman, "stop!"

We stopped. Bahtcheyev opened the door, and hurriedly began clambering out of the carriage.

"Why, what is the matter, Stepan Alexyevitch? Where are you off to?" cried my uncle in astonishment.

"No, I have had enough of it," answered the fat man, trembling with indignation. "Deuce take it all! I am too old, madame, to be besieged with amours. I would rather die on the highroad! Good-bye, madame. *Comment vous portez-vous?*"

And he actually began walking on foot. The carriage followed him at a walking pace.

"Stepan Alexyevitch!" cried my uncle, losing all patience at last. "Don't play the fool, come, get in! Why, it's time we were home."

"Bother you!" Stepan Alexyevitch brought out, breathless with walking, for owing to his corpulence he had quite lost the habit of exercise.

"Drive on full speed," Mizintchikov shouted to the coachman.

"What are you doing? Stop!" my uncle cried out as the carriage dashed on.

Mizintchikov was not out in his reckoning, the desired result followed at once.

"Stop! Stop!" we heard a despairing wail behind us. "Stop, you ruffian! Stop, you cut-throat. . . ."

The fat man came into sight at last, half-dead with exhaustion, with drops of sweat on his brow, untying his cravat and taking off his cap. Silently and gloomily he got into the carriage, and this time I gave him my seat; he was not anyway sitting directly opposite Tatyana Ivanovna, who all through this scene had been gushing with laughter and clapping her hands. She could not look gravely at Stepan Alexyevitch all the rest of the journey. He for his part sat without uttering a single word all the way home, staring intently at the hind wheel of the carriage.

It was midday when we got back to Stepantchikovo. I went straight to my lodge, where Gavrila immediately made his appearance with tea. I flew to question the old man, but my uncle walked in almost on his heels and promptly sent him away.

[II]

NEW DEVELOPMENTS

I HAVE come to you for a minute, dear boy," he began, "I was in haste to tell you. . . . I have heard all about everything. None of them have even been to mass to-day, except Ilyusha, Sasha and Nastenka. They tell me mamma has been in convulsions. They have been rubbing her, it was all they could do to bring her to by rubbing. Now it has been settled for us all to go together to Foma, and I have been summoned. Only I don't know whether to congratulate Foma on the nameday or not—it's an important point! And in fact how are they going to take this whole episode? It's awful, Seryozha, I foresee it. . . ."

"On the contrary, uncle," I hastened in my return to reply, "everything is settling itself splendidly. You see you can't marry Tatyana Ivanovna now—that's a great deal in itself. I wanted to make that clear to you on our way."

"Oh, yes, my dear boy. But that's not the point; there is the hand of Providence in it no doubt, as you say, but I wasn't thinking of that. . . . Poor Tatyana Ivanovna! What adventures happen to her, though! . . . Obnoskin's a scoundrel, a scoundrel! Though why do I call him 'a scoundrel'? Shouldn't I have been doing the same if I married her? . . . But that, again, is not what I have come about. . . . Did you hear what that wretch Anfisa Petrovna shouted about Nastenka this morning?"

"Yes, uncle. Haven't you realized now that you must make haste?"

"Certainly, at all costs!" answered my uncle. "It is a solemn moment. Only there is one thing, dear boy, which we did not think of, but I was thinking of it afterwards all night. Will she marry me, that's the point?"

"Mercy on us, uncle! After she told you herself that she loves you . . ."

"But, my dear boy, you know she also said at once that nothing would induce her to marry me."

"Oh, uncle, that's only words; besides, circumstances are different to-day."

"Do you think so? No, Sergey, my boy, it's a delicate business, dreadfully delicate! H'm. . . . But do you know, though I was worrying, yet my heart was somehow aching with happiness all night. Well, good-bye, I must fly. They are waiting for me; I am late as it is. I only ran in to have a word with you. Oh, my God!" he cried, coming back, "I have forgotten what is most important! Do you know what? I have written to him, to Foma!"

"When?"

"In the night, and in the morning, at daybreak, I sent the letter by Vidoplyasov. I put it all before him on two sheets of paper, I told him everything truthfully and frankly, in short that I ought, that is, absolutely must—do you understand?—make Nastenka an offer. I besought him not to say a word about our meeting in the garden, and I have appealed to all the generosity of his heart to help me with mamma. I wrote a poor letter, of course, my boy, but I wrote it from my heart, and so to say, watered it with my tears. . . ."

"Well? No answer?"

"So far no; only this morning when we were getting ready to set off, I met him in the hall in night attire, in slippers and nightcap—he sleeps in a nightcap—he had come out of his room. He didn't say a word, he didn't even glance at me. I peeped up into his face, not a sign."

"Uncle, don't rely on him; he'll play you some dirty trick."

"No, no, my boy, don't say so!" cried my uncle, gesticulating. "I am sure of him. Besides, you know, it's my last hope. He will understand, he'll appreciate it. He's peevish, he's capricious, I don't deny it; but when it comes to a question of true nobility, then he shines out like a pearl. . . . Yes, like a pearl. You think all that, Sergey, because you have never seen him yet, when he is most noble . . . but my God! if he really does spread abroad my secret of yesterday, then . . . I don't know what will happen then, Sergey! What will be left me in the world that I can believe in? But no, he cannot be such a scoundrel. I am not worth the sole of his shoe. Don't shake your head, my boy; it's true—I am not."

"Yegor Ilyitch! Your mamma is anxious about you." We hear from below the unpleasant voice of Miss Perepelitsyn, who had probably succeeded in hearing the whole of our conversation from the open window. "They are looking for you all over the house, and cannot find you."

"Oh, dear, I am late! How dreadful," cried my uncle in a fluster. "My dear boy, for goodness' sake dress and come too. Why, it was just for that I ran in, so that we might go together. . . . I fly, I fly! Anna Nilovna, I fly!"

When I was left alone, I recalled my meeting with Nastenka that morning and was very glad I had not told my uncle of it; I should have upset him even more. I foresaw a great storm, and could not imagine how my uncle would arrange his plans and make an offer to Nastenka. I repeat: in spite of my faith in his honour, I could not help feeling doubtful of his success.

However, I had to make haste. I considered myself bound to assist him, and at once began dressing; but as I wanted to be as well dressed as possible, I was not very quick in spite of my haste. Mizintchikov walked in.

"I have come for you," he said. "Yegor Ilyitch begs you to come at once."

"Let us go!"

I was quite ready, we set off.

"What news there?" I asked on the way.

"They are all in Foma's room, the whole party," answered Mizintchikov. "Foma is not in bad humour, but he is somewhat pensive and doesn't say much, just mutters through his teeth. He even kissed Ilyusha, which of course delighted Yegor Ilyitch. He announced beforehand through Miss Perepelitsyn that they were not to congratulate him on the nameday, and that he had only wanted to test them. . . . Though the old lady keeps sniffing her smelling-salts, she is calm because Foma is calm. Of our adventure no one drops a hint, it is as though it had never happened; they hold their tongues because Foma holds his. He hasn't let any one in all the morning, though. While we were away the old lady implored him by all the saints to come that she might consult him, and indeed she hobbled down to the door herself; but he locked himself in and answered that he was praying for the human race, or something of the sort. He has got something up his sleeve, one can see that from his face. But as Yegor Ilyitch is incapable of seeing anything from any one's face, he is highly delighted now with Foma's mildness; he is a regular baby! Ilyusha has prepared some verses, and they have sent me to fetch you."

"And Tatyana Ivanovna?"

"What about Tatyana Ivanovna?"

"Is she there? With them?"

"No; she is in her own room," Mizintchikov answered drily. "She is resting and crying. Perhaps she is ashamed too. I believe that . . . governess is with her now. I say! surely it is not a storm coming on? Look at the sky!"

"I believe it is a storm," I answered, glancing at a storm-cloud that looked black on the horizon.

At that moment we went up to the terrace.

"Tell me, what do you think of Obnoskin, eh?" I went on, not able to refrain from probing Mizintchikov on that point.

"Don't speak to me of him! Don't remind me of that blackguard," he cried, suddenly stopping, flushing red and stamping. "The fool! the fool! to ruin such a splendid plan, such a brilliant idea! Listen: I am an ass, of course, for not having detected what a rogue he is!—I admit that solemnly, and perhaps that admission is just what you want. But I swear if he had known how to carry it through properly, I should perhaps have forgiven him. The fool! the fool! And how can such people be allowed in society, how can they be endured! How is it they are not sent to Siberia, into exile, into prison! But that's all nonsense, they won't get over me! Now I have experience anyway, and we shall see who gets the best of it. I am thinking over a new idea now. . . . You must admit one can't lose one's object simply because some outside fool has stolen one's idea and not known how to set about it. Why, it's unjust! And, in fact, this Tatyana will inevitably be married, that's her predestined fate. And if no one has put her into a madhouse up to now, it was just because it is still possible to marry her. I will tell you my new idea. . . ."

"But afterwards, I suppose," I interrupted him, "for here we are."

"Very well, very well, afterwards," Mizintchikov answered, twisting his lips into a spasmodic smile. "And now . . . But where are you going? I tell you, straight to Foma Fomitch's room! Follow me; you have not been there yet. You will see another farce. . . . For it has really come to a farce."

[III]

ILYUSHA'S NAMEDAY

FOMA occupied two large and excellent rooms; they were even better decorated than any other of the rooms in the house. The great man was surrounded by perfect comfort. The fresh and handsome wall-paper, the particoloured silk curtains on the windows, the rugs, the pier-glass, the fireplace, the softly upholstered elegant furniture— all testified to the tender solicitude of the family for Foma's comfort. Pots of flowers stood in the windows and on little marble tables in front of the windows. In the middle of the study stood a large table covered with a red cloth and littered with books and manuscripts. A handsome bronze inkstand and a bunch of pens which Vidoplyasov had to look after—all this was to testify to the severe intellectual labours of Foma Fomitch. I will mention here by the way that though Foma had sat at that table for nearly eight years, he had composed absolutely nothing that was any good. Later on, when he had departed to a better world, we went through his manuscripts; they all turned out to be extraordinary trash. We found, for instance, the beginning of an historical novel, the scene of which was laid in Novgorod, in the seventh century; then a monstrous poem, "An Anchorite in the Churchyard," written in blank verse; then a meaningless meditation on the significance and characteristics of the Russian peasant, and how he should be treated; and finally "The Countess Vlonsky," a novel of aristocratic life, also unfinished. There was nothing else. And yet Foma Fomitch had made my uncle spend large sums every year on books and journals. But many of them were actually found uncut. Later on, I caught Foma Fomitch more than once reading Paul de Kock, but he always slipped the book out of sight when people came in. In the further wall of the study there was a glass door which led to the courtyard of the house.

They were waiting for us. Foma Fomitch was sitting in a comfortable arm-chair, wearing some sort of long coat that reached to his heels, but yet he wore no cravat. He certainly was silent and thoughtful. When we went in he raised his eyebrows slightly and bent a searching glance on me. I bowed; he responded with a slight bow, a fairly polite one, however. Grandmother, seeing that Foma Fomitch was behaving graciously to me, gave me a nod and a smile. The poor woman had not expected in the morning that her paragon would take the news of Tatyana Ivanovna's "escapade" so calmly, and so she was now in the best of spirits, though she really had been in convulsions and fainting fits earlier in the day. Behind her chair, as usual, stood Miss Perepelitsyn, compressing her lips till they looked like a thread, smiling sourly and spitefully and rubbing her bony hands one against the other. Two always mute lady companions were installed beside Madame la Générale. There was also a nun of sorts who had strayed in that morning, and an elderly lady, a neighbour who had come in after mass to congratulate Madame la Générale on the nameday and who also sat mute. Aunt Praskovya Ilyinitchna was keeping in the background somewhere in a corner, and was looking with anxiety at Foma Fomitch and her mother. My uncle was sitting in an easy-chair, and his face was beaming with a look of exceptional joy. Facing him stood Ilyusha in his red holiday shirt, with his hair in curls, looking like a little angel. Sasha and Nastenka had in secret from every one taught him some verses to rejoice his father on this auspicious day by his progress in learning. My uncle was almost weeping with delight. Foma's unexpected mildness, Madame la Générale's good humour, Ilyusha's nameday, the verses, all moved him to real enthusiasm, and with a solemnity worthy of the occasion he had asked them to send for me that I might hasten to share the general happiness and listen to the verses. Sasha and Nastenka, who had come in just after us, were standing near Ilyusha. Sasha was continually laughing, and at that moment was as happy as a little child. Nastenka, looking at her, also began smiling, though she had come into the room a moment before pale and depressed. She alone had welcomed Tatyana Ivanovna on her return from her excursion, and until then had been sitting upstairs with her. The rogue Ilyusha seemed, too, as though he could not keep from laughing as he looked at his instructresses. It seemed as though the three of them had prepared a very amusing joke which they meant to play now. . . . I had forgotten Bahtcheyev. He was sitting on a chair at a little distance, still cross and red in the face; holding his tongue, sulking, blowing his nose and altogether playing a very gloomy part at the family festivity. Near him Yezhevikin was fidgeting about; he was fidgeting about everywhere, however, kissing the hands of Madame la Générale and of the visitors, whispering something to Miss Perepelitsyn, showing attention to Foma Fomitch, in fact he was all over the place. He, too, was awaiting Ilyusha's verses with great interest, and at my entrance flew to greet me with bows as a mark of the deepest respect and devotion. Altogether there was nothing to show that he had come to protect his daughter, and to take her from Stepantchikovo for ever.

"Here he is!" cried my uncle gleefully on seeing me. "Ilyusha has got a poem for us, that's something unexpected, a real surprise! I am overpowered, my boy, and sent for you on purpose, and have put off the verses till you came. . . . Sit down beside me! Let us listen. Foma Fomitch, confess now, it must have been you who put them all up to it to please an old fellow like me. I'll wager that is how it is!"

Since my uncle was talking in such a tone and voice in Foma's room one would have thought that all must be well. But unluckily my uncle was, as Mizintchikov expressed it, incapable of reading any man's face. Glancing at Foma's face, I could not help admitting that

Mizintchikov was right and that something was certainly going to happen. . . .

"Don't trouble about me, Colonel," Foma answered in a faint voice, the voice of a man forgiving his enemies. "I approve of the surprise, of course; it shows the sensibility and good principles of your children. . . . Poetry is of use, too, even for the pronunciation. . . . But I have not been busy over verses this morning, Yegor Ilyitch; I have been praying . . . you know that. . . . I am ready to listen to the verses, however."

Meanwhile I had congratulated Ilyusha and kissed him.

"Quite so, Foma, I beg your pardon. I had forgotten . . . though I am sure of your affection, Foma! Kiss him once more, Seryozha! Look what a fine big boy! Come, begin, Ilyusha! What is it about? I suppose it is something solemn from Lomonosov?"

And my uncle drew himself up with a dignified air. He could scarcely sit still in his seat for impatience and delight.

"No, papa, not from Lomonosov," said Sashenka, hardly able to suppress her laughter; "but as you have been a soldier and fought the enemy, Ilyusha has learnt a poem about warfare. . . . The siege of Pamba, papa!"

"The siege of Pamba! I don't remember it. . . . What is this Pamba, do you know, Ilyusha? Something heroic, I suppose."

And my uncle drew himself up again.

"Begin, Ilyusha!" Sasha gave the word of command.

Ilyusha began in a little, clear, even voice, without stops or commas, as small children generally recite verses they have learned by heart—

> "Nine long years Don Pedro Gomez
> Has besieged the fort of Pamba,
> On a diet of milk supported.
> And Don Pedro's gallant warriors,
> Brave Castilians, full nine thousand,
> All to keep the vow they've taken
> Taste no bread nor other victuals,
> Milk they drink and milk alone."

"What? What's that about milk?" cried my uncle, looking at me in perplexity.

"Go on reciting, Ilyusha!" cried Sashenka.

> "Every day Don Pedro Gomez,
> In his Spanish cloak enveloped,
> Bitterly his lot bewails.
> Lo, the tenth year is approaching;

> Still the fierce Moors are triumphant;
> And of all Don Pedro's army
> Only nineteen men are left. . . ."

"Why, it's a regular string of nonsense!" cried my uncle uneasily. "Come, that's impossible. Only nineteen men left out of a whole army, when there was a very considerable corps before? What is the meaning of it, my boy?"

But at that point Sasha could not contain herself, and went off into the most open and childish laughter; and though there was nothing very funny, it was impossible not to laugh too as one looked at her.

"They are funny verses, papa," she cried, highly delighted with her childish prank. "The author made them like that on purpose to amuse everybody."

"Oh! Funny!" cried my uncle, with a beaming face. "Comic, you mean! That's just what I thought. . . . Just so, just so, funny! And very amusing, extremely amusing: he starved all his army on milk owing to some vow. What possessed them to take such a vow? Very witty, isn't it, Foma? You see, mamma, these are jesting verses, such as authors sometimes do write, don't they, Sergey? Extremely amusing. Well, well, Ilyusha, what next?"

> "Only nineteen men are left!
> Them Don Pedro doth assemble
> And says to them: 'Noble Nineteen!
> Let us raise aloft our standards!
> Let us blow on our loud trumpets!
> And with clashing of our cymbals
> Let us from Pamba retreat!
> Through the fort we have not taken,
> Yet with honour still untarnished
> We can swear on faith and conscience
> That our vow we have not broken;
> Nine long years we have not eaten,
> Not a morsel have we eaten,
> Milk we've drunk and milk alone!' "

"What a noodle! What comfort was it for him that he had drunk milk for nine years?" my uncle broke in again. "What is there virtuous in it? He would have done better to have eaten a whole sheep, and not have been the death of people! Excellent! capital! I see, I see now: it is a satire on . . . what do they call it? an allegory, isn't it? And perhaps aimed at some foreign general," my uncle added, addressing me, knitting his brows significantly, and screwing up his eyes, "eh? What do you think? But of course a harmless, good, refined satire that injures nobody! Excellent! excellent! and what matters most, it is refined. Well, Ilyusha, go on. Ah, you rogues, you rogues!" he added with feeling, looking at Sasha and stealthily also at Nastenka, who blushed and smiled.

> "And emboldened by that saying,
> Those nineteen Castilian warriors,
> Each one swaying in his saddle,
> Feebly shouted all together:
> 'Sant' Iago Compostello!
> Fame and glory to Don Pedro!
> Glory to the Lion of Castile!'
> And his chaplain, one Diego,
> Through his teeth was heard to mutter:
> 'But if I had been commander,
> I'd have vowed to eat meat only,
> Drinking good red wine alone.' "

"There! Didn't I tell you so?" cried my uncle, extremely delighted. "Only one sensible man was found in the whole army, and he was some sort of a chaplain. And what is that, Sergey: a captain among them, or what?"

"A monk, an ecclesiastical person, uncle."

"Oh, yes, yes. Chaplain? I know, I remember. I have read of it in Radcliffe's novels. They have all sorts of orders, don't they. . . . Benedictines, I believe? . . . There are Benedictines, aren't there?"

"Yes, uncle."

"H'm! . . . I thought so. Well, Ilyusha, what next? Excellent! capital!"

> "And Don Pedro overhearing,
> With loud laughter gave the order:
> 'Fetch a sheep and give it to him!
> He has jested gallantly!' "

"What a time to laugh! What a fool! Even he saw it was funny at last! A sheep! So they had sheep; why did he not eat some himself! Well, Ilyusha, go on. Excellent! capital! Extraordinarily cutting!"

"But that's the end, papa!"

"Oh, the end. Indeed there wasn't much left to be done—was there, Sergey? Capital, Ilyusha! Wonderfully nice. Kiss me, darling. Ah, my precious! Who was it thought of it: you, Sasha?"

"No, it was Nastenka. We read it the other day. She read it and said: 'What ridiculous verses! It will soon be Ilyusha's nameday, let us make him learn them and recite them. It will make them laugh!' "

"Oh, it was Nastenka? Well, thank you, thank you," my uncle

muttered, suddenly flushing like a child. "Kiss me again, Ilyusha. You kiss me too, you rogue," he said, embracing Sashenka and looking into her face with feeling. "You wait a bit, Sashenka, it will be your name-day soon," he added, as though he did not know what to say to express his pleasure.

I turned to Nastenka and asked whose verses they were.

"Yes, yes, whose are the verses?" my uncle hurriedly chimed in. "It must have been a clever poet who wrote them, mustn't it, Foma?"

"H'm . . ." Foma grunted to himself.

A biting sarcastic smile had not left his face during the whole time of the recitation of the verses.

"I have really forgotten," said Nastenka, looking timidly at Foma Fomitch.

"It's Mr. Kuzma Prutkov wrote it, papa; it was published in the *Contemporary*," Sashenka broke in.

"Kuzma Prutkov! I don't know his name," said my uncle. "Pushkin I know! . . . But one can see he is a gifted poet—isn't he, Sergey? And what's more, a man of refined qualities, that's as clear as twice two! Perhaps, indeed, he is an officer. . . . I approve of him. And the *Contemporary* is a first-rate magazine. We certainly must take it in if poets like that are among the contributors. . . . I like poets! They are fine fellows! They picture everything in verse. Do you know, Sergey, I met a literary man at your rooms in Petersburg. He had rather a peculiar nose, too . . . really! . . . What did you say, Foma?"

Foma Fomitch, who was getting more and more worked up, gave a loud snigger.

"No, I said nothing . . ." he said, as though hardly able to suppress his laughter. "Go on, Yegor Ilyitch, go on! I will say my word later. . . . Stepan Alexyevitch is delighted to hear how you made the acquaintance of literary men in Petersburg."

Stepan Alexyevitch, who had been sitting apart all the time lost in thought, suddenly raised his head, reddened, and turned in his chair with exasperation.

"Don't you provoke me, Foma, but leave me in peace," he said, looking wrathfully at Foma with his little bloodshot eyes. "What is your literature to me? May God only give me good health," he muttered to himself, "and plague take them all . . . and their authors too. . . . Voltairians, that's what they are!"

"Authors are Voltairians?" said Yezhevikin immediately at his side. "Perfectly true what you have been pleased to remark, Stepan Alexyev-itch. Valentin Ignatyitch was pleased to express the same sentiments the other day. He actually called me a Voltairian, upon my soul he did! And yet, as you all know, I have written very little so far. . . . If a bowl of milk goes sour—it's all Voltaire's fault! That's how it is with everything here."

"Well, no," observed my uncle with dignity, "that's an error, you know! Voltaire was nothing but a witty writer; he laughed at superstitions; and he never was a Voltairian! It was his enemies spread that rumour about him. Why were they all against him, really, poor fellow? . . ."

Again the malignant snigger of Foma Fomitch was audible. My uncle looked at him uneasily and was perceptibly embarrassed.

"Yes, Foma, I am thinking about the magazine, you see," he said in confusion, trying to put himself right somehow. "You were perfectly right, my dear Foma, when you said the other day that we ought to subscribe to one. I think we ought to, myself. H'm . . . after all, they do assist in the diffusion of enlightenment; one would be a very poor patriot if one did not support them. Wouldn't one, Sergey? H'm. . . . Yes. . . . The *Contemporary,* for instance. But, do you know, Seryozha, the most instruction, to my thinking, is to be found in that thick magazine—what's its name?—in a yellow cover . . ."

"*Notes of the Fatherland,* papa."

"Oh, yes, *Notes of the Fatherland,* and a capital title, Sergey, isn't it? It is, so to say, the whole Fatherland sitting writing notes. . . . A very fine object. A most edifying magazine. And what a thick one! What a job to publish such an omnibus! And the information in it almost makes one's eyes start out of one's head. I came in the other day, the volume was lying here, I took it up and from curiosity opened it and reeled off three pages at a go. It made me simply gape, my dear! And, you know, there is information about everything; what is meant, for instance, by a broom, a spade, a ladle, an ovenrake. To my thinking, a broom is a broom and an ovenrake an ovenrake! No, my boy, wait a bit. According to the learned, an ovenrake turns out not an ovenrake, but an emblem or something mythological; I don't remember exactly, but something of the sort. . . . So that's how it is! They have gone into everything!"

I don't know what precisely Foma was preparing to do after this fresh outburst from my uncle, but at that moment Gavrila appeared and stood with bowed head in the doorway.

Foma Fomitch glanced at him significantly.

"Ready, Gavrila?" he asked in a faint but resolute voice.

"Yes, sir," Gavrila answered mournfully, and heaved a sigh.

"And have you put my bundle on the cart?"

"Yes, sir."

"Well, then, I am ready too!" said Foma, and he deliberately got up from his easy-chair. My uncle looked at him in amazement. Madame la Générale jumped up from her seat and looked about her uneasily.

"Allow me, Colonel," Foma began with dignity, "to ask you to leave for a moment the interesting subject of literary ovenrakes; you can continue it after I am gone. As I am *taking leave of you for ever,* I should like to say a few last words to you. . . ."

Every listener was spellbound with alarm and amazement.

"Foma! Foma! but what is the matter with you? Where are you going?" my uncle cried at last.

"I am about to leave your house, Colonel," Foma brought out in a perfectly composed voice. "I have made up my mind to go where fortune takes me, and so I have hired at my own expense a humble peasant's cart. My bundle is lying in it already, it is of no great dimensions: a few favourite books, two changes of linen—that is all! I am a poor man, Yegor Ilyitch, but nothing in the world would induce me now to take your gold, which I refused even yesterday!"

"But for God's sake, Foma, what is the meaning of it?" cried my uncle, turning as white as a sheet.

Madame la Générale uttered a shriek and looked in despair at Foma Fomitch, stretching out her hands to him. Miss Perepelitsyn flew to support her. The lady companions sat petrified in their chairs. Mr. Bahtcheyev got up heavily from his seat.

"Well, here's a pretty to-do!" Mizintchikov whispered beside me.

At that moment a distant rumble of thunder was heard; a storm was coming on.

[IV]

THE EXPULSION

Y OU ask me, I believe, Colonel, what is the meaning of this?" Foma brought out with solemn dignity, as though enjoying the general consternation. "I am surprised at the question! Will you on your side explain how it is *you* can bring yourself to look me in the face now? Explain to me this last psychological problem in human shamelessness, and then I shall depart, the richer for new knowledge of the depravity of the human race."

But my uncle was not equal to answering him. With open mouth and staring eyes he gazed at Foma, alarmed and annihilated.

"Merciful heavens! What passions!" hissed Miss Perepelitsyn.

"Do you understand, Colonel," Foma went on, "that you had better let me go now, simply without asking questions? In your house even I, a man of years and understanding, begin to feel the purity of my morals gravely endangered. Believe me, that your questions can lead to nothing but putting you to shame."

"Foma! Foma!" cried my uncle, and a cold perspiration came out on his forehead.

"And so allow me without further explanation to say a few farewell words at parting, my last words in your house, Yegor Ilyitch. The thing is done and there is no undoing it! I hope that you understand to what I am referring. But I implore you on my knees: if one spark of moral feeling is left in your heart, curb your unbridled passions! And if the noxious poison has not yet caught the whole edifice, then, as far as possible, extinguish the fire!"

"Foma, I assure you that you are in error!" cried my uncle, recovering himself little by little and foreseeing with horror the climax.

"Moderate your passions," Foma continued in the same solemn voice, as though he had not heard my uncle's exclamation, "conquer yourself. 'If thou would'st conquer all the world—conquer thyself.' That is my invariable rule. You are a landowner; you ought to shine like a diamond in your estate, and what a vile example of unbridled passion you set your inferiors! I have been praying for you the whole night, and trembled as I sought for your happiness. I did not find it, for happiness lies in virtue. . . ."

"But this is impossible, Foma!" my uncle interrupted him again. "You have misunderstood and what you say is quite wrong."

"And so remember you are a landowner," Foma went on, still regardless of my uncle's exclamations. "Do not imagine that repose and sensuality are the destined vocation of the landowning class. Fatal thought! Not repose, but zealous work, zealous towards God, towards your sovereign, and towards your country! Hard work, hard work is the duty of the landowner, he should work as hard as the poorest of his peasants!"

"What, am I to plough for the peasant, or what?" growled Bahtcheyev. "Why, I am a landowner, too. . . ."

"I turn to you now, servants of the house," Foma went on, addressing Gavrila and Falaley, who had appeared in the doorway. "Love your master and his family, and obey them humbly and meekly, and they will reward you with their love. And you, Colonel, be just and compassionate to them. A fellow-man—the image of God—like a child of tender years, so to say, is entrusted to you by your sovereign and your country. Great is the duty, but great also is the merit."

"Foma Fomitch, my dear man, what notion is this?" cried Madame la Générale in despair, almost swooning with horror.

"Well, that is enough, I think," Foma concluded, paying no attention even to Madame la Générale. "Now to lesser things; they may be small, but they are essential, Yegor Ilyitch. Your hay on the Harinsky waste has not been cut yet. Do not be too late with it: mow it and mow it quickly. That is my advice. . . ."

"But, Foma . . ."

"You meant to cut down the Zyryanovsky copse, I know; don't cut it—that's a second piece of advice. Preserve forest land, for trees retain humidity on the surface of the earth. It is a pity that you have sown the spring corn so late; it's amazing how late you have been in sowing the spring corn! . . ."

"But, Foma . . ."

"But enough! One cannot convey everything, and indeed there is not time. I will send you written instructions in a special book. Well, good-bye, good-bye all, God be with you, and the Lord bless you. I bless you too, my child," he went on, turning to Ilyusha; "and may God keep you from the noxious poison of your passions. I bless you too, Falaley; forget the Komarinsky! . . . And all of you. . . . Remember Foma. . . . Well, let us go, Gavrila! Come and help me in, old man."

And Foma turned towards the door. Madame la Générale gave a piercing shriek and flew after him.

"No, Foma, I will not let you go like this," cried my uncle, and overtaking him, he seized him by the hand.

"So you mean to have resort to force?" Foma asked haughtily.

"Yes, Foma . . . even to force," answered my uncle, quivering with emotion. "You have said too much, and must explain your words! You have misunderstood my letter, Foma! . . ."

"Your letter!" squealed Foma, instantly flaring up as though he had been awaiting that minute for an explosion; "your letter! Here it is, your letter! Here it is. I tear this letter, I spit upon it! I trample your letter under my foot, and in doing so fulfil the most sacred duty of humanity. That is what I will do if you compel me by force to an explanation! Look! Look! Look! . . ."

And scraps of paper flew about the room.

"I repeat, Foma, you have misunderstood it," cried my uncle, turning paler and paler. "I am making an offer of marriage, Foma, I am seeking my happiness."

"Marriage! You have seduced this young girl, and are trying to deceive me by offering her marriage, for I saw you with her last night in the garden, under the bushes."

Madame la Générale uttered a scream and fell fainting into an armchair. A fearful hubbub arose. Poor Nastenka sat deathly pale. Sasha, frightened, clutched Ilyusha and trembled as though she were in a fever.

"Foma!" cried my uncle in a frenzy, "if you divulge that secret you are guilty of the meanest action on earth!"

"I do divulge that secret," squealed Foma, "and I am performing the most honourable action! I am sent by God Himself to unmask your villainies to all the world. I am ready to clamber on some peasant's thatched roof and from there to proclaim your vile conduct to all the gentlemen of the neighbourhood and all the passers-by. . . . Yes, let me tell you all, all of you, that yesterday in the night I found him in the garden, under the bushes with this young girl whose appearance is so innocent. . . ."

"Oh, what a disgrace!" piped Miss Perepelitsyn.

"Foma! Don't be your own destruction!" cried my uncle, with clenched fists and flashing eyes.

"He," squealed Foma, "he, alarmed at my having seen him, had the audacity to try with a lying letter to persuade me into conniving at his crime—yes, crime! . . . for you have turned a hitherto innocent young girl into a . . ."

"Another word insulting to her and I will kill you, Foma, I swear! . . ."

"I say that word, since you have succeeded in turning the most innocent young girl into a most depraved girl."

Foma had hardly uttered this last word when my uncle seized him by the shoulder, turned him round like a straw, and flung him violently at the glass door, which led from the study into the courtyard. The shock was so violent that the closed door burst open, and Foma, flying head over heels down the stone steps, fell full length in the yard. Bits of broken glass were scattered tinkling about the steps.

"Gavrila, pick him up!" cried my uncle, as pale as a corpse. "Put him in the cart, and within two minutes let there be no trace of him in Stepantchikovo!"

Whatever Foma's design may have been, he certainly had not expected such a climax.

I will not undertake to describe what happened for the first minutes after this episode. The heart-rending wail of Madame la Générale as she rolled from side to side in an arm-chair; the stupefaction of Miss Perepelitsyn at this unexpected behaviour of my hitherto submissive uncle; the sighs and groans of the lady companions; Nastenka almost fainting with fright while her father hovered over her; Sashenka terror-stricken; my uncle in indescribable excitement pacing up and down the room waiting for his mother to come to herself; and lastly, the loud weeping of Falaley in lamentation over the troubles of his betters—all this made up an indescribable picture. I must add, too, that at this moment a violent storm broke over us; peals of thunder were more and more frequent, and big drops of rain began pattering on the window.

"Here's a nice holiday!" muttered Mr. Bahtcheyev, bowing his head and flinging wide his arms.

"It's a bad business," I whispered to him, beside myself with excitement too. "But anyway they have turned Foma out, and he won't come back again."

"Mamma! Are you conscious? Are you better? Can you listen to me at last?" asked my uncle, stopping before the old lady's arm-chair.

She raised her head, clasped her hands, and looked with imploring eyes at her son, whom she had never in her life before seen moved to such wrath.

"Mamma," he went on, "it was the last straw, you have seen for yourself. It was not like this that I meant to approach this subject, but the hour has come, and it is useless to put it off. You have heard the calumny, hear my defence. Mamma, I love this noble and high-minded girl, I have loved her a long while, and I shall never cease to love her. She will make the happiness of my children, and will be a dutiful daughter to you. And so now, before you, and in the presence of my friends and my family, I solemnly plead at her feet, and beseech her to do me infinite honour by consenting to be my wife."

Nastenka started, then flushed crimson all over and got up from her seat. Madame la Générale stared some time at her son as though she did not understand what he was saying to her, and all at once with a piercing wail flung herself on her knees.

"Yegorushka, my darling, bring Foma Fomitch back," she cried. "Bring him back at once, or without him I shall die before night."

My uncle was petrified at the sight of his self-willed and capricious old mother kneeling before him. His painful distress was reflected in his face. At last, recovering himself, he flew to raise her up and put her back in her chair.

"Bring Foma Fomitch back, Yegorushka," the old lady went on wailing. "Bring him back, darling! I cannot live without him!"

"Mamma," my uncle cried sorrowfully, "have you heard nothing of what I have just said to you? I cannot bring Foma back—understand that. I cannot and I have not the right to after his low and scoundrelly slander on this angel of honour and virtue. Do you understand, mamma, that it is my duty, that my honour compels me now to defend virtue? You have heard: I am asking this young lady to be my wife, and I beg you to bless our union."

Madame la Générale got up from her seat again and fell on her knees before Nastenka.

"My dear girl!" she wailed, "do not marry him. Do not marry him, but entreat him, my dear, to fetch back Foma Fomitch. Nastasya Yevgrafovna, darling! I will give up everything, I will sacrifice everything if only you will not marry him. Old as I am, I have not spent everything, I had a little left me when my poor husband died. It's all yours, my dear, I will give you everything, and Yegorushka will give you something too, but do not lay me living in my grave, beg him to bring back Foma Fomitch."

And the old woman would have gone on wailing and drivelling if Miss Perepelitsyn and all the lady companions had not, with shrieks and moans, rushed to lift her up, indignant that she should be on her knees before a hired governess. Nastenka was so frightened that she could hardly stand, while Miss Perepelitsyn positively shed tears of fury.

"You will be the death of your mamma," she screamed at my uncle. "You will be the death of her. And you, Nastasya Yevgrafovna, ought not to make dissension between mother and son; the Lord has forbidden it. . . ."

"Anna Nilovna, hold your tongue!" cried my uncle. "I have put up with enough!"

"Yes, and I have had enough to put up with from you too. Why do you reproach me with my friendless position? It is easy to insult the friendless. I am not your slave yet. I am the daughter of a major myself. You won't see me long in your house, this very day . . . I shall be gone. . . ."

But my uncle did not hear; he went up to Nastenka and with reverence took her by the hand.

"Nastasya Yevgrafovna! You have heard my offer?" he said, looking at her with anguish, almost with despair.

"No, Yegor Ilyitch, no! We had better give it up," said Nastenka, utterly dejected too. "It is all nonsense," she said, pressing his hand and bursting into tears. "You only say this because of yesterday . . . but it cannot be. You see that yourself. We have made a mistake, Yegor Ilyitch. . . . But I shall always think of you as my benefactor and . . . I shall pray for you, always, always! . . ."

At this point tears choked her. My poor uncle had evidently foreseen this answer; he did not even think of protesting, of insisting. He listened, bending down to her, still holding her hand, crushed and speechless. There were tears in his eyes.

"I told you yesterday," Nastya went on, "that I could not be your wife. You see that I am not wanted here . . . and I foresaw all this long ago; your mamma will not give you her blessing . . . *others* too. Though you would not regret it afterwards, because you are the most generous of men, yet you would be made miserable through me . . . with your soft-heartedness . . ."

"Just because of your *soft-heartedness!* Just because you are so *soft-hearted!* That's it, Nastenka, that's it!" chimed in her old father, who was standing on the other side of her chair. "That's just it, that's just the right word."

"I don't want to bring dissension into your house on my account," Nastenka went on. "And don't be uneasy about me, Yegor Ilyitch; no one will interfere with me, no one will insult me . . . I am going to my father's . . . this very day. . . . We had better say good-bye, Yegor Ilyitch. . . ."

And poor Nastenka dissolved into tears again.

"Nastasya Yevgrafovna! Surely this is not your final answer?" said my uncle, looking at her in unutterable despair. "Say only one word and I will sacrifice everything for you! . . ."

"It is final, it is final, Yegor Ilyitch . . ." Yezhevikin put in again, "and she has explained it all very well to you, as I must own I did not expect her to. You are a very soft-hearted man, Yegor Ilyitch, yes, very soft-hearted, and you have graciously done us a great honour! A great honour, a great honour! . . . But all the same we are not a match for you, Yegor Ilyitch. You ought to have a bride, Yegor Ilyitch, who would be wealthy and of high rank, and a great beauty and with a voice too, who would walk about your rooms all in diamonds and ostrich feathers. . . . Then perhaps Foma Fomitch would make a little concession and give his blessing! And you will bring Foma Fomitch back! It was no use, no use your insulting him. It was from virtue, you know, from excess of fervour that he said too much, you know. You will say yourself that it was through his virtue—you will see! A most worthy man. And here he is getting wet through now. It would be better to fetch him back now. . . . For you will have to fetch him back, you know. . . ."

"Fetch him back, fetch him back!" shrieked Madame la Générale. "What he says is right, my dear! . . ."

"Yes," Yezhevikin went on. "Here your illustrious parent has upset herself about nothing. . . . Fetch him back! And Nastya and I meanwhile will be on the march. . . ."

"Wait a minute, Yevgraf Larionitch!" cried my uncle, "I entreat you. There is one thing more must be said, Yevgraf, one thing only. . . ."

Saying this, he walked away, sat down in an arm-chair in the corner, bowed his head, and put his hands over his eyes as though he were thinking over something.

At that moment a violent clap of thunder sounded almost directly over the house. The whole building shook. Madame la Générale gave a scream, Miss Perepelitsyn did the same, the lady companions, and with them Mr. Bahtcheyev, all stupefied with terror, crossed themselves.

"Holy saint, Elijah the prophet!" five or six voices murmured at once.

The thunder was followed by such a downpour that it seemed as though a whole lake were suddenly being emptied upon Stepantchikovo.

"And Foma Fomitch, what will become of him now out in the fields?" piped Miss Perepelitsyn.

"Yegorushka, fetch him back!" Madame la Générale cried in a voice of despair, and she rushed to the door as though crazy. Her attendant ladies held her back; they surrounded her, comforted her, whimpered, squealed. It was a perfect Bedlam!

"He went off with nothing over his coat. If he had only taken an overcoat with him!" Miss Perepelitsyn went on. "He did not take an umbrella either. He will be struck by lightning! . . ."

"He will certainly be struck!" Bahtcheyev chimed in. "And he will be soaked with rain afterwards, too."

"You might hold your tongue!" I whispered to him.

"Why, he is a man, I suppose, or isn't he?" Bahtcheyev answered wrathfully. "He is not a dog. I bet you wouldn't go out of doors yourself. Come, go and have a bath for your *plaisir.*"

Foreseeing how it might end and dreading the possibility, I went up to my uncle, who sat as though chained to his chair.

"Uncle," I said, bending down to his ear, "surely you won't consent to bring Foma Fomitch back? Do understand that that would be the height of unseemliness, at any rate as long as Nastasya Yevgrafovna is here."

"My dear," answered my uncle, raising his head and looking at me resolutely, "I have been judging myself at this moment and I know what I ought to do. Don't be uneasy, there shall be no offence to Nastenka, I will see to that. . . ."

He got up from his seat and went to his mother.

"Mamma," he said, "don't worry yourself, I will bring Foma Fomitch back, I will overtake him; he cannot have gone far yet. But I swear he shall come back only on one condition, that here publicly in the presence of all who were witnesses of the insult he should acknowledge how wrong he has been, and solemnly beg the forgiveness of this noble young lady. I will secure that, I will make him do it! He shall not cross the threshold of this house without it! I swear, too, mamma, solemnly, that if he consents to this of his own free will, I shall be ready to fall at his feet, and will give him anything, anything I can, without injustice to my children. I myself will renounce everything from this very day. The star of my happiness has set. I shall leave Stepantchikovo. You must all live here calmly and happily. I am going back to my regiment, and in the turmoil of war, on the field of battle, I will end my despairing days. . . . Enough! I am going!"

At that moment the door opened, and Gavrila, soaked through and incredibly muddy, stood facing the agitated company.

"What's the matter? Where have you come from? Where is Foma?" cried my uncle, rushing up to Gavrila.

Every one followed him, and with eager curiosity crowded round the old man, from whom dirty water was literally trickling in streams. Shrieks, sighs, exclamations accompanied every word Gavrila uttered.

"I left him at the birch copse, a mile away," he began in a tearful voice. "The horse took fright at the lightning and bolted into the ditch."

"Well? . . ." cried my uncle.

"The cart was upset. . . ."

"Well? . . . and Foma?"

"He fell into the ditch."

"And then? Tell us, you tantalizing old man!"

"He bruised his side and began crying. I unharnessed the horse, got on him and rode here to tell you."

"And Foma remained there?"

"He got up and went on with his stick," Gavrila concluded; then he heaved a sigh and bowed his head.

The tears and sobs of the tender sex were indescribable.

"Polkan!" cried my uncle, and he flew out of the room. Polkan was brought, my uncle leapt on him barebacked, and a minute later the thud of the horse's hoofs told us that the pursuit of Foma Fomitch had begun. My uncle had actually galloped off without his cap.

The ladies ran to the windows. Among the sighs and groans were heard words of advice. There was talk of a hot bath, of Foma Fomitch being rubbed with spirits, of some soothing drink, of the fact that Foma Fomitch "had not had a crumb of bread between his lips all day and that he is wet through on an empty stomach." Miss Perepelitsyn found his forgotten spectacles in their case, and the find produced an extraordinary effect: Madame la Générale pounced on them with tears and lamentations, and still keeping them in her hand, pressed up to the window again to watch the road. The suspense reached the utmost pitch of intensity at last. In another corner Sashenka was trying to comfort Nastya; they were weeping in each other's arms. Nastenka was holding Ilyusha's hand and kissing him from time to time. Ilyusha was in floods of tears, though he did not yet know why. Yezhevikin and Mizintchikov were talking of something aside. I fancied that Bahtcheyev was looking at the girls as though he were ready to blubber himself. I went up to him.

"No, my good sir," he said to me, "Foma Fomitch may leave here one day perhaps, but the time for that has not yet come; they haven't got gold-horned bulls for his chariot yet. Don't worry yourself, sir, he'll drive the owners out of the house and stay there himself!"

The storm was over, and Mr. Bahtcheyev had evidently changed his views.

All at once there was an outcry: "They are bringing him, they are bringing him," and the ladies ran shrieking to the door. Hardly ten minutes had passed since my uncle set off; one would have thought it would have been impossible to bring Foma Fomitch back so quickly; but the enigma was very simply explained later on. When Foma Fomitch had let Gavrila go he really had "set off walking with his stick," but finding himself in complete solitude in the midst of the storm, the thunder, and the pouring rain, he was ignominiously panic-stricken, turned back towards Stepantchikovo and ran after Gavrila. He was already in the village when my uncle came upon him. A passing cart was stopped at once; some peasants ran up and put the unresisting Foma Fomitch into it. So they conveyed him straight to the open arms of Madame la Générale, who was almost beside herself with horror when she saw the condition he was in. He was even muddier and wetter than Gavrila. There was a terrific flurry and bustle, they wanted at once to drag him upstairs to change his linen; there was an outcry for elder-flower tea and other invigorating beverages, they scurried in all directions without doing anything sensible; they all talked at once. . . . But Foma seemed to notice nobody and nothing. He was led in, supported under the arms. On reaching his easy-chair, he sank heavily into it and closed his eyes. Some one cried out that he was dying; a terrible howl was raised, and Falaley was the loudest of all, trying to squeeze through the crowd of ladies up to Foma Fomitch to kiss his hand at once. . . .

[v]

FOMA FOMITCH MAKES EVERY ONE HAPPY

W HERE have they brought me?" Foma articulated at last, in the voice of a man dying in a righteous cause.

"Damnable humbug!" Mizintchikov whispered beside me. "As though he didn't see where he had been brought! Now he will give us a fine exhibition!"

"You are among us, Foma, you are in your own circle!" cried my uncle. "Don't give way, calm yourself! And really, Foma, you had better change your things, or you will be ill. . . . And won't you take something to restore you, eh? Just something . . . a little glass of something to warm you. . . ."

"I could drink a little Malaga," Foma moaned, closing his eyes again.

"Malaga? I am not sure there is any," my uncle said, anxiously looking towards Praskovya Ilyinitchna.

"To be sure there is!" the latter answered. "There are four whole bottles left." And jingling her keys she ran to fetch the Malaga, followed by exclamations of the ladies, who were clinging to Foma like flies round jam. On the other hand, Mr. Bahtcheyev was indignant in the extreme.

"He wants Malaga!" he grumbled almost aloud. "And asks for a wine that no one drinks. Who drinks Malaga nowadays but rascals like him? Tfoo, you confounded fellow! What am I standing here for? What am I waiting for?"

"Foma," my uncle began, stumbling over every word, "you see now

... when you are rested and are with us again ... that is, I meant to say, Foma, that I understand how accusing, so to say, the most innocent of beings ..."

"Where is it, my innocence, where?" Foma interrupted, as though he were feverish and in delirium. "Where are my golden days? Where art thou, my golden childhood, when innocent and lovely I ran about the fields chasing the spring butterflies? Where are those days? Give me back my innocence, give it me back! ..."

And Foma, flinging wide his arms, turned to each one of us in succession as though his innocence were in somebody's pocket. Bahtcheyev was ready to explode with wrath.

"Ech, so that's what he wants!" he muttered in a fury. "Give him his innocence! Does he want to kiss it, or what? Most likely he was as great a villain when he was a boy as he is now! I'll take my oath he was."

"Foma!" ... my uncle was beginning again.

"Where, where are they, those days when I still had faith in love and loved mankind?" cried Foma; "when I embraced man and wept upon his bosom? But now where am I? Where am I?"

"You are with us, Foma, calm yourself," cried my uncle. "This is what I wanted to say to you, Foma. ..."

"You might at least keep silent now," hissed Miss Perepelitsyn, with a spiteful gleam in her viperish eyes.

"Where am I?" Foma went on. "Who are about me? They are bulls and buffaloes turning their horns against me. Life, what art thou? If one lives one is dishonoured, disgraced, humbled, crushed; and when the earth is scattered on one's coffin, only then men will remember one and pile a monument on one's poor bones!"

"Holy saints, he is talking about monuments!" whispered Yezhevikin, clasping his hands.

"Oh, do not put up a monument to me," cried Foma, "do not! I don't need monuments. Raise up a monument to me in your hearts, I want nothing more, nothing, nothing more!"

"Foma," my uncle interposed, "enough, calm yourself! There is no need to talk about monuments. Only listen. You see, Foma, I understand that you were perhaps, so to say, inspired with righteous fervour when you reproached me, but you were carried away, Foma, beyond the limit of righteousness—I assure you you were mistaken, Foma. ..."

"Oh, will you give over?" hissed Miss Perepelitsyn again. "Do you want to murder the poor man because he is in your hands? ..."

After Miss Perepelitsyn, Madame la Générale made a stir, and all her suite followed her example; they all waved their hands at my uncle to stop him.

"Anna Nilovna, be silent yourself, I know what I am saying!" my uncle answered firmly. "This is a sacred matter! A question of honour and justice. Foma! you are a sensible man, you must at once ask the forgiveness of the virtuous young lady whom you have insulted."

"What young lady? What young lady have I insulted?" Foma articulated in amazement, staring round at every one as though he had entirely forgotten everything that had happened, and did not know what was the matter.

"Yes, Foma; and if now of your own accord you frankly acknowledge you have done wrong, I swear, Foma, I will fall at your feet and then . . ."

"Whom have I insulted?" wailed Foma. "What young lady? Where is she? Where is the young lady? Recall to me something about the young lady! . . ."

At that instant, Nastenka, confused and frightened, went up to Yegor Ilyitch and pulled him by his sleeve.

"No. Yegor Ilyitch, leave him alone, there is no need of an apology. What is the object of it all?" she said in an imploring voice. "Give it up!"

"Ah, now I begin to remember," cried Foma. "My God, I understand. Oh, help me, help me to remember!" he implored, apparently in great excitement. "Tell me, is it true that I was turned out of this house, like the mangiest of curs? Is it true that I was struck by lightning? Is it true that I was kicked down the steps? Is it true? Is it true?"

The weeping and wailing of the fair sex were the most eloquent reply to Foma Fomitch.

"Yes, yes," he repeated, "I remember . . . I remember now that after the lightning and my fall I was running here, pursued by the thunder, to do my duty and then vanish for ever! Raise me up! Weak as I may be now, I must do my duty."

He was at once helped up from his chair. Foma stood in the attitude of an orator and stretched out his hands.

"Colonel," he cried, "now I have quite recovered. The thunder has not extinguished my intellectual capacities; it has left, it is true, a deafness in my right ear, due perhaps not so much to the thunder as to my fall down the steps, but what of that? And what does any one care about Foma's right ear!"

Foma threw such a wealth of mournful irony into these last words, and accompanied them with such a pathetic smile, that the groans of the deeply moved ladies resounded again. They all looked with reproach, and some also with fury, at my uncle, who was beginning to be crushed by so unanimous an expression of public opinion. Mizintchikov, with a curse, walked away to the window. Bahtcheyev kept prodding me more and more violently with his elbow; he could hardly stand still.

"Now listen to my whole confession!" yelled Foma, turning upon all a proud and determined gaze, "and at the same time decide the fate of poor Opiskin! Yegor Ilyitch, for a long time past I have been watching over you, watching over you with a tremor at my heart, and I have seen everything, everything, while you were not suspecting that I was watching over you. Colonel! Perhaps I was mistaken, but I knew your egoism, your boundless vanity, your phenomenal sensuality, and who would blame me for trembling for the honour of an innocent young person?"

"Foma, Foma! . . . you need not enlarge on it, Foma," cried my uncle, looking uneasily at Nastenka's suffering face.

"What troubled me was not so much the innocence and trustfulness of the person in question as her inexperience," Foma went on, as though he had not heard my uncle's warning. "I saw that a tender feeling was blossoming in her heart, like a rose in spring and I could not help recalling Petrarch's saying, 'Innocence is often but a hair's breadth from ruin.' I sighed, I groaned, and though I was ready to shed the last drop of my blood to safeguard that pure pearl of maidenhood, who could answer to me for you, Yegor Ilyitch? I know the unbridled violence of your passions, and knowing that you are ready to sacrifice everything for their momentary gratification, I was plunged in the depths of alarm and apprehension for the fate of the noblest of girls. . . ."

"Foma! Could you really imagine such a thing?" cried my uncle.

"With a shudder at my heart I watched over you. And if you want to know what I have been suffering, go to Shakespeare: in his *Hamlet* he describes the state of my soul. I became suspicious and terrible. In my anxiety, in indignation, I saw everything in the blackest colour and that not the 'black colour' sung of in the well-known song— I can assure you. That was the cause of the desire you saw in me to remove *her* far away from this house: I wanted to save her; that was why you have seen me of late irritable and bitter against the whole human race. Oh! who will reconcile me with humanity? I feel that I was perhaps over-exacting and unjust to your guests, to your nephew, to Mr. Bahtcheyev, when I expected from him a knowledge of astronomy; but who will blame me for my state of mind at the time? Going to Shakespeare again, I may say that the future looked to my imagination like a gloomy gulf of unfathomed depth with a crocodile lying at the bottom. I felt that it was my duty to prevent disaster, that I was destined, appointed for that purpose—and what happened? You did not understand the generous impulse of my heart, and have been repaying me all this time with anger, with ingratitude, with jeers, with slights . . ."

"Foma! If that is so . . . of course I feel . . ." cried my uncle, in extreme agitation.

"If you really do feel it, Colonel, be so kind as to listen and not interrupt me. I will continue. My whole fault lay in the fact, therefore, that I was too much troubled over the fate and the happiness of this child; for compared with you she is a child. It was the truest love for humanity that turned me all this time into a fiend of wrath and suspicion. I was ready to fall on people and tear them to pieces. And you know, Yegor Ilyitch, all your actions as though of design, made me more suspicious every hour, and confirmed my fears. You know, Yegor Ilyitch, when you showered your gold upon me yesterday to drive me from you, I thought: 'He is driving away in my person his conscience, so as more easily to perpetrate this wickedness. . . .'"

"Foma, Foma, can you have thought that yesterday?" my uncle cried out with horror. "Merciful heavens! and I hadn't the faintest suspicion . . ."

"Heaven itself inspired those suspicions," Foma went on. "And judge for yourself: what could I suppose when chance led me that very evening to that fatal seat in the garden? What were my feelings at that moment—oh, my God!—when I saw with my own eyes that all my suspicions were justified in the most flagrant manner? But I had still one hope left, a faint one indeed, but still it was a hope, and—this morning you shattered it into dust and ashes! You sent me your letter, you alleged your intention to marry; you besought me not to make it public. . . . 'But why?' I wondered. 'Why did he write now after I have found him out and not before? Why did he not run to me before, happy and comely—for love adorns the countenance—why did he not fly to my embrace, why did he not weep upon my bosom tears of infinite bliss and tell me all about it, all about it?' Or am I a crocodile who would have devoured you instead of giving you good advice? Or am I some loathsome beetle who would only have bitten you and not assisted your happiness? 'Am I his friend or the most repulsive of insects?' that was the question I asked myself this morning. 'With what object,' I asked myself, 'with what object did he invite his nephew from Petersburg and try to betroth him to this girl, if not to deceive us and his *frivolous* nephew, and meanwhile in secret to persist in his criminal designs?' Yes, Colonel, if any one confirmed in me the thought that your mutual love was criminal, it was you yourself and you only! What is more, you have behaved like a criminal to this young girl; for through your tactlessness and selfish mistrustfulness you have exposed her, a modest and high-principled girl, to slander and odious suspicions."

My uncle stood silent with bowed head, Foma's eloquence was evidently getting the better of his convictions, and he was beginning to regard himself as a complete criminal. Madame la Générale and her followers were listening to Foma in awestruck silence, while Miss Perepelitsyn looked with spiteful triumph at poor Nastenka.

"Overwhelmed, nervously exhausted and shattered," Foma went on, "I locked myself in this morning and prayed, and the Lord showed me the right path. At last I decided: for the last time and publicly to put you to the test. I may have gone about it with too much fervour, I may have given way too much to my indignation; but for my well-meaning effort, you flung me out of the window! As I fell out of the window I thought to myself: 'This is how virtue is rewarded all the world over.' Then I struck the earth, and I scarcely remember what happened to me afterwards."

Shrieks and groans interrupted Foma Fomitch at this tragic recollection. Madame la Générale made a dash at him with a bottle of Malaga in her hand, which she had just snatched from Praskovya Ilyinitchna, but Foma majestically waved aside the hand and the Malaga and Madame la Générale herself.

"Let me alone," he shouted; "I must finish. What happened after my fall—I don't know. I know one thing only, that now, wet through and on the verge of fever, I am standing here to secure your mutual happiness. Colonel! From many signs which I do not wish now to particularize, I am convinced at last that your love was pure and even exalted, though at the same time criminally distrustful. Beaten, humiliated, suspected of insulting a young lady in defence of whose honour I am ready like a mediaeval knight to shed the last drop of my blood I have made up my mind to show you how Foma Opiskin revenges an injury. Give me your hand, Colonel!"

"With pleasure, Foma!" cried my uncle. "And since you have now fully cleared the honour of this young lady from every aspersion, why ... of course ... here is my hand, Foma, together with my regrets. ..."

And my uncle gave him his hand warmly, not yet suspecting what was to come of it.

"Give me your hand too," went on Foma in a faint voice, parting the crowd of ladies who were pressing round him and appealing to Nastenka.

Nastenka was taken aback and confused, she looked timidly at Foma.

"Approach, approach, my sweet child! It is essential for your happiness," Foma added caressingly, still holding my uncle's hand in his.

"What's he up to now?" said Mizintchikov.

Nastenka, frightened and trembling, went slowly up to Foma and timidly held out her hand.

Foma took her hand and put it in my uncle's.

"I join your hands and bless you," he pronounced in the most solemn voice. "And if the blessing of a poor sorrow-stricken sufferer may avail you, be happy. This is how Foma Opiskin takes his revenge! Hurrah!"

The amazement of every one was immense. The conclusion was so unexpected that every one was struck dumb. Madame la Générale stood rooted to the spot, with her mouth open and the bottle of Malaga in her hand. Miss Perepelitsyn turned pale and trembled with fury. The lady companions clasped their hands and sat petrified in their seats. My uncle trembled and tried to say something, but could not. Nastya turned deathly pale and timidly murmured that "it could not be" . . . but it was too late. Bahtcheyev was the first—we must do him that credit—to second Foma's hurrah. I followed suit, and after me Sashenka shouted at the top of her ringing voice as she flew to embrace her father; then Ilyusha joined in, then Yezhevikin, and last of all Mizintchikov.

"Hurrah!" Foma cried once more; "hurrah! And on your knees, children of my heart, on your knees before the tenderest of mothers! Ask her blessing, and if need be I will kneel before her by your side. . . ."

My uncle and Nastya, not looking at each other, and seeming not to understand what was being done to them, fell on their knees before Madame la Générale, the whole company flocked round them; but the old lady seemed to be stupefied, not knowing what to do. Foma came to the rescue at this juncture too; he plumped down himself before his patroness. This at once dispelled all her hesitation. Dissolving into tears, she said at last that she consented. My uncle jumped up and clasped Foma in his arms.

"Foma, Foma! . . ." he began, but his voice broke and he could not go on.

"Champagne!" bawled Mr. Bahtcheyev. "Hurrah!"

"No, sir, not champagne," Miss Perepelitsyn caught him up. She had by now recovered herself, and realized the position and at the same time its consequences. "Put up a candle to God, pray to the holy image and bless with the holy image, as is done by all godly people. . . ."

At once all flew to carry out the sage suggestion; a fearful bustle followed. They had to light the candle. Mr. Bahtcheyev drew up a chair and got up on it to put the candle before the holy image, but immediately broke the chair and came down heavily on the floor— still on his feet, however. Not in the least irritated by this, he at once respectfully made way for Miss Perepelitsyn. The slender Miss Perepelitsyn had done the job in a flash: the candle was lighted. The nun and the lady companions began crossing themselves and bowing down to the ground. They took down the image of the Saviour and carried it to Madame la Générale. My uncle and Nastya went down on their knees again and the ceremony was carried out under the pious instructions of Miss Perepelitsyn, who was saying every minute: "Bow down to her feet, kiss the image, kiss your mamma's hand." Mr. Bahtcheyev thought himself bound to kiss the image after the betrothed couple, and at the same time he kissed the hand of Madame la Générale.

"Hurrah!" he shouted again. "Come, now, we will have some champagne."

Every one, however, was delighted. Madame la Générale was weeping, but it was now with tears of joy. Foma's blessing had at once made the union sanctified and suitable, and what mattered most to her was that Foma Fomitch had distinguished himself and that now he would remain with her for ever. All the lady companions, in appearance at least, shared the general satisfaction. My uncle at one moment was on his knees kissing his mother's hands, at the next was flying to embrace me, Bahtcheyev, Mizintchikov and Yezhevikin. Ilyusha he almost smothered in his embraces. Sasha ran to hug and kiss Nastenka. Praskovya Ilyinitchna dissolved into tears. Bahtcheyev, noticing this, went up to kiss her hand. Poor old Yezhevikin was completely overcome, he was weeping in a corner and was wiping his eyes with the same check handkerchief. In another corner Gavrila was whimpering and gazing reverently at Foma Fomitch, and Falaley was sobbing loudly and going up to each of the company in turn, kissing his hand. All were overwhelmed with feeling; no one yet had begun to talk, or explain things; it seemed as though everything had been said; nothing was heard but joyful exclamations. No one understood yet how all this had been so quickly arranged. They knew one thing only, that it had all been arranged by Foma Fomitch, and that this was a solid fact which could not be changed.

But not five minutes had passed after the general rejoicing when suddenly Tatyana Ivanovna made her appearance among us. In what way, by what intuition, could she, sitting in her own room upstairs, have so quickly divined love and marriage below? She fluttered in with a radiant face, with tears of joy in her eyes, in a fascinating and elegant get-up (she had had time to change her dress before coming down), and flew straight to embrace Nastenka with loud exclamations.

"Nastenka, Nastenka! You loved him and I did not know!" she cried. "Goodness! They loved each other, they suffered in silence! They have been persecuted. What a romance! Nastya, darling, tell me the whole truth: do you really love this crazy fellow?"

By way of reply Nastya hugged and kissed her.

"My goodness, what a fascinating romance!" And Tatyana Ivanovna clapped her hands in delight. "Nastya, listen, my angel: all these men, all, every one, are ungrateful wretches, monsters, and not worthy of our love. But perhaps he is the best of them. Come to me, you crazy fellow!" she cried, addressing my uncle and clutching him by the arm. "Are you really in love? Are you really capable of loving? Look at me, I want to look into your eyes, I want to see whether those eyes are lying or not? No, no, they are not lying; there is the light of love in them. Oh, how happy I am! Nastenka, my dear, you are not rich— I shall make you a present of thirty thousand roubles. Take it, for God's sake. I don't want it, I don't want it; I shall have plenty left. No, no, no," she cried, waving her hand as she saw Nastenka was meaning to refuse. "Don't you speak, Yegor Ilyitch, it is not your affair. No, Nastya, I had made up my mind already to give you the money; I have been wanting to make you a present for a long time, and was only waiting for you to be in love. . . . I shall see your happiness. You will wound me if you don't take it; I shall cry, Nastya. No, no, no and no!"

Tatyana Ivanovna was so overjoyed that for the moment at least it was impossible, it would have been a pity indeed, to cross her. They could not bring themselves to do it, but put it off. She flew to kiss Madame la Générale, Miss Perepelitsyn and all of us. Mr. Bahtcheyev squeezed his way up to her very respectfully and asked to kiss her hand.

"My dear, good girl! Forgive an old fool like me for what happened this morning. I didn't know what a heart of gold you had."

"Crazy fellow! I know you," Tatyana Ivanovna lisped with gleeful playfulness. She gave Mr. Bahtcheyev a flick on the nose with her glove, and swishing against him with her gorgeous skirts, fluttered away like a zephyr.

The fat man stepped aside respectfully.

"A very worthy young lady!" he said with feeling. "They have stuck a nose on to the German! You know!" he whispered to me confidentially, looking at me joyfully.

"What nose? What German?" I asked in surprise.

"Why, the one I ordered, the German kissing his lady's hand while she is wiping away a tear with her handkerchief. Only yesterday my Yevdokem mended it; and when we came back from our expedition this morning I sent a man on horseback to fetch it. . . . They will soon be bringing it. A superb thing."

"Foma!" cried my uncle in a frenzy of delight. "It is you who have made our happiness. How can I reward you?"

"Nohow, Colonel," replied Foma, with a sanctimonious air. *"Continue to pay no attention to me* and be happy without Foma."

He was evidently piqued; in the general rejoicing he seemed, as it were, forgotten.

"It is all due to our joy, Foma," cried my uncle. "I don't know whether I am on my head or my feet. Listen, Foma, I have insulted you. My whole blood is not enough to atone for my wrong to you, and that is why I say nothing and do not even beg your pardon. But if ever you have need of my head, my life, if you ever want some one to throw himself over a precipice for your sake, call upon me, and you shall see. . . . I will say nothing more, Foma."

And my uncle waved his hand, fully recognizing the impossibility of adding anything that could more strongly express his feeling. He only gazed at Foma with grateful eyes full of tears.

"See what an angel he is!" Miss Perepelitsyn piped in her turn in adulation of Foma.

"Yes, yes," Sashenka put in. "I did not know you were such a good man, Foma Fomitch, and I was disrespectful to you. But forgive me, Foma Fomitch, and you may be sure I will love you with all my heart. If you knew how much I respect you now!"

"Yes, Foma," Bahtcheyev chimed in. "Forgive an old fool like me too. I didn't know you, I didn't know you. You are not merely a learned man, Foma, but also—simply a hero. My whole house is at your service. But there, the best of all would be, if you would come to me the day after to-morrow, old man, with Madame la Générale too, and the betrothed couple—the whole company, in fact. And we will have a dinner, I tell you. I won't praise it beforehand, but one thing I can say, you will find everything you want unless it is bird's milk. I give you my word of honour."

In the midst of these demonstrations, Nastenka, too, went up to Foma Fomitch and without further words warmly embraced him and kissed him.

"Foma Fomitch," she said, "you have been a true friend to us, you have done so much for us, that I don't know how to repay you for it all; but I only know that I will be for you a most tender and respectful sister. . . ."

She could say no more, she was choked by tears. Foma kissed her on the head and grew tearful.

"My children, the children of my heart," he said. "Live and prosper, and in moments of happiness think sometimes of the poor exile. For myself, I will only say that misfortune is perhaps the mother of virtue. That, I believe, is said by Gogol, a frivolous writer; but from whom one may sometimes glean fruitful thoughts. Exile is a misfortune. I shall wander like a pilgrim with my staff over the face of the earth, and who knows?—perchance my troubles will make me more righteous yet! That thought is the one consolation left me!"

"But . . . where are you going, Foma?" my uncle asked in alarm.

All were startled, and pressed round Foma.

"Why, do you suppose I can remain in your house after your behaviour this morning?" Foma inquired with extraordinary dignity.

But he was not allowed to finish, outcries from all the company smothered his voice. They made him sit down in an easy-chair, they besought him, they shed tears over him, and I don't know what they didn't do. Of course he hadn't the faintest intention of leaving "this house," just as he had not earlier that morning, nor the day before, nor on the occasion when he had taken to digging in the garden. He knew now that they would reverently detain him, would clutch at him, especially since he had made them all happy, since they all had faith in him again and were ready to carry him on their shoulders and to consider it an honour and a happiness to do so. But most likely his cowardly return, when he was frightened by the storm, was rankling in his mind and egging him on to play the hero in some way. And above all, there was such a temptation to give himself airs; the opportunity of talking, of using fine phrases and laying it on thick, of blowing his own trumpet, was too good for any possibility of resisting the temptation. He did not resist it; he tore himself out of the grasp of those who held him. He asked for his staff, besought them to let him have his freedom, to let him wander out into the wide, wide world, declared that in *that house* he had been dishonoured, beaten, that he had only come back to make every one happy, and, he asked, could he remain in this "house of ingratitude and eat soup, sustaining, perhaps, but seasoned with blows"? At last he left off struggling. He was reseated in his chair, but his eloquence was not arrested.

"Have I not been insulted here?" he cried. "Have I not been taunted? Haven't you, you yourself, Colonel, have you not every hour pointed the finger of scorn and made the long nose of derision at me, like the ignorant children of the working-class in the streets of the town? Yes, Colonel, I insist on that comparison, because if you have not done so physically it has yet been a moral long nose, and in some cases a moral long nose is more insulting than a physical one. I say nothing of blows. . . ."

"Foma, Foma," cried my uncle, "do not crush me with these recollections. I have told you already that all my blood is not enough to wash out the insults. Be magnanimous! Forgive, forget, and remain to contemplate our happiness! Your work, Foma . . ."

"I want to love my fellow-man, to love him," cried Foma, "and they won't give me him, they forbid me to love him, they take him from me. Give me, give me my fellow-man that I may love him! Where is that fellow-man? Where is he hidden? Like Diogenes with his candle, I have been looking for him all my life and cannot find him; and I can love no one, to this day I cannot find the man. Woe to him who has made me a hater of mankind! I cry: Give me my fellow-man that I may love him, and they thrust Falaley upon me! Am I to love Falaley? Do I want to love Falaley? Could I love Falaley, even if I wanted to? No. Why not? Because he is Falaley. Why do I not love humanity? Because all on earth are Falaleys or like Falaley. I don't want Falaley, I hate Falaley, I spit on Falaley, I trample Falaley under my feet. And if I had to choose I would rather love Asmodeus than Falaley. Come here, come here, my everlasting torment, come here," he cried, suddenly addressing Falaley, who was in the most innocent way standing on tiptoe, looking over the crowd that was surrounding Foma Fomitch.

"Come here. I will show you, Colonel," cried Foma, drawing towards him Falaley, who was almost unconscious with terror, "I will show you the truth of my words about the everlasting long nose and finger of scorn! Tell me, Falaley, and tell the truth: what did you dream about last night? Come, Colonel, you will see your handiwork! Come, Falaley, tell us!"

The poor boy, shaking with terror, turned despairing eyes about him, looking for some one to rescue him; but every one was in a tremor waiting for his answer.

"Come, Falaley, I am waiting."

Instead of answering, Falaley screwed up his face, opened his mouth wide, and began bellowing like a calf.

"Colonel! Do you see this stubbornness? Do you mean to tell me it's natural? For the last time I ask you, Falaley, tell me: what did you dream of last night?"

"O-of . . ."

"Say you dreamed of me," said Bahtcheyev.

"Of your virtue, sir," Yezhevikin prompted in his other ear.

Falaley merely looked about him.

"O-of . . . of your vir . . . of a white bu-ull," he roared at last, and burst into scalding tears.

Every one groaned. But Foma Fomitch was in a paroxysm of extraordinary magnanimity.

"Anyway, I see your sincerity, Falaley," he said. "A sincerity I do not observe in others. God bless you! If you are purposely mocking at me with that dream at the instigation of others, God will repay you and those others. If not, I respect your truthfulness; for even in the lowest of creatures like you it is my habit to discern the image and semblance of God. . . . I forgive you, Falaley. Embrace me, my children. I will remain with you."

"He will remain!" they all cried in delight.

"I will remain and I will forgive. Colonel, reward Falaley with some sugar, do not let him cry on such a day of happiness for all."

I need hardly say that such magnanimity was thought astounding. To take *so much* thought at *such* a moment and for whom? For Falaley. My uncle flew to carry out his instruction in regard to the sugar. Immediately a silver sugar-basin—I don't know where it came from—appeared in the hands of Praskovya Ilyinitchna. My uncle was about to take out two pieces with a trembling hand, then three, then he dropped them, at last, seeing he was incapable of doing anything from excitement.

"Ah!" he cried, "for a day like this! Hold out your coat, Falaley," and he poured into his coat all the contents of the sugar-basin. "That's for your truthfulness," he said, by way of edification.

"Mr. Korovkin!" Vidoplyasov announced, suddenly appearing in the doorway.

A slight flutter of consternation followed—Korovkin's visit was obviously ill-timed. They all looked inquiringly at my uncle.

"Korovkin!" cried my uncle, in some embarrassment. "Of course I am delighted . . ." he added, glancing timidly towards Foma; "but really I don't know whether to ask him in at such a moment. What do you think, Foma?"

"Oh, yes, why not," said Foma amicably. "Invite Korovkin too; let him, too, share in the general rejoicing."

In short, Foma Fomitch was in an angelic frame of mind.

"I most respectfully make bold to inform you," observed Vidoplyasov, "that the gentleman is not quite himself."

"Not quite himself? How? What nonsense are you talking?" cried my uncle.

"It is so, indeed; he is not quite in a sober condition."

But before my uncle had time to open his mouth, flush red, and show his alarm and extreme embarrassment, the mystery was explained. Korovkin appeared in the doorway, pushed Vidoplyasov aside and confronted the astonished company. He was a short, thickset gentleman of forty, with dark hair touched with grey and closely cropped, with a round purple face and little bloodshot eyes, wearing a high horsehair cravat, fastened at the back with a buckle, an extraordinarily threadbare swallow-tail coat covered with fluff and hay and disclosing a bad rent under the arm, and unspeakable trousers, and carrying an incredibly greasy cap which he was holding out at arm's length. This gentleman was completely drunk. Advancing into the middle of the room, he stood still, staggering, nodding his head as though he were pecking at something with his nose in drunken hesitation; then he slowly grinned from ear to ear.

"Excuse me, ladies and gentlemen," he began, "I . . . er . . ." (here he gave a tug at his collar) "got 'em!"

Madame la Générale immediately assumed an air of offended dignity. Foma, sitting in his easy-chair, ironically looked the eccentric visitor up and down. Bahtcheyev stared at him in perplexity, through which some sympathy was, however, apparent. My uncle's embarrassment was incredible; he was deeply distressed on Korovkin's account.

"Korovkin," he began. "Listen."

"*Attendez!*" Korovkin interrupted him. "Let me introduce myself: a child of nature. . . . But what do I see? There are ladies here. . . . Why didn't you tell me, you rascal, that you had ladies here?" he added with a roguish smile. "Never mind! Don't be shy. Let us be presented to the fair sex. Charming ladies," he began, articulating with difficulty and stumbling over every word, "you see a luckless mortal ... who ... and so on. ... The rest must remain unsaid. ... Musicians! A polka!"

"Wouldn't you like a nap?" asked Mizintchikov, quietly going up to Korovkin.

"A nap? You say that to insult me?"

"Not at all. You know a little sleep is a good thing after a journey. ..."

"Never!" Korovkin answered with indignation. "Do you think I am drunk?—not a bit. But where do they sleep here?"

"Come along, I'll take you at once."

"Where? In the coach-house? No, my lad, you won't take me in! I have spent a night there already. ... Lead the way, though. Why not go along with a good fellow. ... I don't want a pillow. A military man does not want a pillow. ... But you produce a sofa for me, old man ... a sofa. And, I say," he added, stopping, "I see you are a jolly fellow; produce something else for me ... you know? A bit of the rummy, enough to drown a fly in, only enough for that, only one little glass, I mean."

"Very well, very well!" answered Mizintchikov.

"Very well. But you wait a bit, I must say good-bye. *Adieu, mesdames* and *mesdemoiselles*. You have, so to speak, smitten ... But there, never mind! We will talk about that afterwards ... only do wake me when it begins ... or even five minutes before it begins ... don't begin without me! Do you hear. Don't begin! ..."

And the merry gentleman vanished behind Mizintchikov.

Every one was silent. The company had not got over their astonishment. At last Foma without a word began noiselessly chuckling, his laughter grew into a guffaw. Seeing that, Madame la Générale, too, was amused, though the expression of insulted dignity still remained on her face. Irrepressible laughter arose on all sides. My uncle stood as though paralyzed, flushing almost to tears, and was for some time incapable of uttering a word.

"Merciful heavens!" he brought out at last. "Who could have known this? But you know ... you know it might happen to any one. Foma, I assure you that he is a most straightforward, honourable man, and an extremely well-read man too, Foma ... you will see! ..."

"I do see, I do see," cried Foma, shaking with laughter; "extraordinarily well-read. Well-read is just the word."

"How he can talk about railways!" Yezhevikin observed in an undertone.

"Foma," my uncle was beginning, but the laughter of all the company drowned his words. Foma Fomitch was simply in fits, and looking at him, my uncle began laughing too.

"Well, what does it matter?" he said enthusiastically. "You are magnanimous, Foma, you have a great heart; you have made me happy . . . you forgive Korovkin too."

Nastenka was the only one who did not laugh. She looked with eyes full of love at her future husband, and looked as though she would say—

"How splendid, how kind you are, the most generous of men. and how I love you!"

[VI]

CONCLUSION

FOMA'S triumph was complete and beyond attack. Certainly without him nothing would have been settled, and the accomplished fact stifled all doubts and objections. The gratitude of those he had made happy was beyond all bounds. My uncle and Nastya waved me off when I attempted to drop a faint hint at the process by which Foma's consent to their marriage had been obtained. Sashenka cried: "Good, kind Foma Fomitch; I will embroider him a cushion in wool-work!" and even reproached me for my hard-heartedness. I believe that Bahtcheyev in the fervour of his conversion would have strangled me if I had ventured to say anything disrespectful about Foma Fomitch. He followed Foma about like a little dog, gazed at him with devout reverence, and at every word the latter uttered he would exclaim: "You are a noble man, Foma. You are a learned man, Foma." As for Yezhevikin, he was highly delighted. The old man had for a long time past seen that Nastenka had turned Yegor Ilyitch's head, and from that time forward his one dream, waking and sleeping, was to bring about this marriage. He had clung to the idea to the last, and had only given it up when it had been impossible not to do so. Foma had changed the aspect of the affair. I need hardly say that in spite of his delight the old man saw through Foma; in short, it was clear that Foma Fomitch would be supreme in that household for ever, and that there would be no limit to his despotism. We all know that even the most unpleasant and ill-humoured people are softened, if only for a time, when their desires are gratified. Foma Fomitch, on the contrary, seemed to grow stupider when he was successful, and held his nose higher in the air than ever. Just before dinner, having changed all his clothes, he settled down in an arm-chair, summoned my uncle, and in the presence of the whole family began giving him another lecture.

"Colonel," he began, "you are about to enter upon holy matrimony. Do you realize the obligation . . ."

And so on and so on. Imagine ten pages of the size of the *Journal des Débats,* of the smallest print, filled with the wildest nonsense, in which there was absolutely nothing dealing with the duties of marriage, but only the most shameful eulogies of the intellect, mildness, magnanimity, manliness and disinterestedness of himself, Foma Fomitch. Every one was hungry, they all wanted their dinners; but in spite of that no one dared to protest, and every one heard the twaddle reverently to the end. Even Bahtcheyev, in spite of his ravenous appetite, sat without stirring, absolutely respectful. Gratified by his own eloquence, Foma Fomitch grew livelier, and even drank rather heavily at dinner, proposing the most extraordinary toasts. He proceeded to display his wit by being jocose, at the expense of the happy pair, of course. Everybody laughed and applauded. But some of the jokes were so gross and suggestive that even Bahtcheyev was embarrassed by them. At last Nastenka jumped up from the table and ran away, to the indescribable delight of Foma Fomitch, but he immediately pulled himself up. Briefly but in strong terms he dwelt upon Nastenka's virtues, and proposed a toast to the health of the absent one. My uncle, who a minute before had been embarrassed and unhappy, was ready to hug Foma Fomitch again. Altogether the betrothed pair seemed somewhat ashamed of each other and their happiness—and I noticed that they had not said one word to each other from the time of the blessing, they even seemed to avoid looking at one another. When they got up from dinner, my uncle vanished, I don't know where. I strolled out on to the terrace to look for him. There I found Foma sitting in an easy-chair, drinking coffee and holding forth, extremely exhilarated. Only Yezhevikin, Bahtcheyev and Mizintchikov were by him. I stopped to listen.

"Why," asked Foma, "am I ready at this moment to go through fire for my convictions? And why is it that none of you are capable of going through fire? Why is it? Why is it?"

"Well, but it's unnecessary, Foma Fomitch, to go through fire," Yezhevikin said banteringly. "Why, what's the sense of it? In the first place it would hurt, and in the second it would burn—what would be left?"

"What would be left? Noble ashes would be left. But how should you understand, how should you appreciate me? To you, no great men exist but perhaps some Caesar or Alexander of Macedon. And what did your Caesars do? Whom did they make happy? What did your vaunted Alexander of Macedon do? He conquered the whole earth? But give me such a phalanx and I could be a conqueror too, and so could you, and so could he. . . . On the other hand, he killed the virtuous Clitus, but I have not killed the virtuous Clitus. . . . A puppy, a scoundrel! He ought to have had a thrashing, and not to have been glorified in universal history . . . and Caesar with him!"

"You might spare Caesar, anyway, Foma Fomitch!"

"I won't spare the fool!" cried Foma.

"No, don't spare him!" Bahtcheyev, who had also been drinking, backed him up. "There is no need to spare them, they are all flighty fellows, they care for nothing but pirouetting on one leg! Sausage-eaters! Here, one of them was wanting to found a scholarship just now —and what is a scholarship? The devil only knows what it means! I bet it's some new villainy! And here is another who in honourable society is staggering about and asking for rum. I have no objection to drinking. But one should drink and drink and then take a rest, and afterwards, maybe, drink again. It's no good sparing them! They are all scoundrels. You are the only enlightened one among them, Foma!"

If Bahtcheyev surrendered to any one he surrendered unconditionally and absolutely without criticism.

I looked for my uncle in the garden, by the pond in the most secluded spot. He was with Nastenka. Seeing me, Nastenka shot into the bushes as though she were in fault. My uncle came to meet me with a beaming face; there were tears of happiness in his eyes. He took both my hands and warmly pressed them.

"My dear," he said, "I still cannot believe in my happiness. . . . Nastya feels the same. We only marvel and glorify the Almighty. She was crying just now. Would you believe it, I hardly know what I am doing yet, I am still utterly beside myself, and don't know whether to believe it or not! And why has this come to me? Why? What have I done? How have I deserved it?"

"If any one deserves anything, it is you, uncle," I said with conviction. "I have never seen such an honest, such a fine, such a kind-hearted man as you."

"No, Seryozha, no, it is too much," he answered, as it were with

regret. "What is bad, is that we are kind (I am talking only about
myself really) when we are happy; but when we are unhappy it is
best not to come near us! Nastenka and I were only just talking of
that. Though I was dazzled by Foma, up to this very day perhaps,
would you believe it, I did not quite believe in him, though I did
assure you of his perfection; even yesterday I did not believe in him
when he refused such a present! To my shame I say it. My heart
shudders at the memory of this morning, but I could not control myself. . . . When he spoke of Nastya something seemed to stab me to
the very heart. I did not understand and behaved like a tiger. . . ."

"Well, uncle, perhaps that was only natural."

My uncle waved away the idea.

"No, no, my boy, don't say so. The fact of it is, all this comes from
the depravity of my nature, from my being a gloomy and sensual
egoist and abandoning myself to my passions without restraint. That's
what Foma says." (What could one answer to that?) "You don't know,
Seryozha," he went on with deep feeling, "how often I have been
irritable, unfeeling, unjust, haughty, and not only to Foma. Now it
has all come back to my mind, and I feel ashamed that I have done
nothing hitherto to deserve such happiness. Nastya has just said the
same thing, though I really don't know what sins she has, as she is an
angel, not a human being! She has just been saying that we owe a
terrible debt of gratitude to God; that we must try now to be better
and always be doing good deeds. . . . And if only you had heard how
fervently, how beautifully she said all that! My God, what a wonderful girl!"

He stopped in agitation. A minute later he went on.

"We resolved, my dear boy, to cherish Foma in particular, mamma
and Tatyana Ivanovna. Tatyana Ivanovna! What a generous-hearted
creature! Oh, how much I have been to blame towards all of them!
I have behaved badly to you too. . . . But if any one should dare to
insult Tatyana Ivanovna now, oh! then . . . Oh, well, never mind!
. . . We must do something for Mizintchikov too."

"Yes, uncle, I have changed my opinion of Tatyana Ivanovna now,
One cannot help respecting her and feeling for her."

"Just so, just so," my uncle assented warmly. "One can't help respecting her! Now Korovkin, for instance, no doubt you laugh at him,"
he added, glancing at me timidly, "and we all laughed at him this
afternoon. And yet, you know, that was perhaps unpardonable. . . .
You know, he may be an excellent, good-hearted man, but fate . . . he

has had misfortunes. . . . You don't believe it, but perhaps it really is so."

"No, uncle, why shouldn't I believe it?"

And I began fervently declaring that even in the creature who has fallen lowest there may still survive the finest human feelings; that the depths of the human soul are unfathomable; that we must not despise the fallen, but on the contrary ought to seek them out and raise them up; that the commonly accepted standard of goodness and morality was not infallible, and so on, and so on; in fact, I warmed up to the subject, and even began talking about the realist school. In conclusion I even repeated the verses: 'When from dark error's subjugation.' . . ."

My uncle was extraordinarily delighted.

"My dear, my dear," he said, much touched, "you understand me fully, and have said much better than I could what I wanted to express. Yes, yes! Good heavens! Why is it man is wicked? Why is it I am so often wicked when it is so splendid, so fine to be good? Nastya was saying the same thing just now. . . . But look, though, what a glorious place this is," he added, looking round him. "What scenery! What a picture! What a tree! Look: you could hardly get your arms round it. What sap! What foliage! What sunshine! How gay everything is, washed clean after the storm! . . . One would think that even the trees understand something, have feeling and enjoyment of life. . . . Is that out of the question—eh? What do you think?"

"It's very likely they do, uncle, in their own way, of course. . . ."

"Oh, yes, in their own way, of course. . . . Marvellous, marvellous is the Creator! You must remember all this garden very well, Seryozha; how you used to race about and play in it when you were little! I remember, you know, when you were little," he added, looking at me with an indescribable expression of love and happiness. "You were not allowed to go to the pond alone. But do you remember one evening dear Katya called you to her and began fondling you. . . . You had been running in the garden just before, and were flushed; your hair was so fair and curly. . . . She kept playing with it, and said: 'It is a good thing that you have taken the little orphan to live with us!' Do you remember?"

"Faintly, uncle."

"It was evening, and you were both bathed in the glow of sunset, I was sitting in a corner smoking a pipe and watching you. . . . I drive in to the town every month to her grave . . ." he added, dropping his voice, which quivered with suppressed tears. "I was just speaking to Nastya about it; she said we would go together. . . ."

My uncle paused, trying to control his emotion. At that instant Vidoplyasov came up to us.

"Vidoplyasov!" said my uncle, starting. "Have you come from Foma Fomitch?"

"No, I have come more on my own affairs."

"Oh, well, that's capital. Now we shall hear about Korovkin. I wanted to inquire. . . . I told him to look after him—Korovkin, I mean. What's the matter, Vidoplyasov?"

"I make bold to remind you," said Vidoplyasov, "that yesterday you were graciously pleased to refer to my petition and to promise me your noble protection from the daily insults I receive."

"Surely you are not harping on your surname again?" cried my uncle in alarm.

"What can I do? Hourly insults . . ."

"Oh, Vidoplyasov, Vidoplyasov! What am I to do with you?" said my uncle in distress. "Why, what insults can you have to put up with? You will simply go out of your mind. You will end your days in a madhouse!"

"I believe I am in my right mind . . ." Vidoplyasov was beginning.

"Oh, of course, of course," my uncle interposed. "I did not say that to offend you, my boy, but for your good. Why, what sort of insults do you complain of? I am ready to bet that it is only some nonsense."

"They won't let me pass."

"Who interferes with you?"

"They all do, and chiefly owing to Matryona. My life is a misery through her. It is well known that all discriminating people who have seen me from my childhood up have said that I am exactly like a foreigner, especially in the features of the face. Well, sir, now they won't let me pass on account of it. As soon as I go by, they all shout all sorts of bad words after me; even the little children, who ought to be whipped, shout after me. . . . As I came along here now they shouted. . . . I can't stand it. Defend me, sir, with your protection!"

"Oh, Vidoplyasov! Well, what did they shout? No doubt it was some foolishness, that you ought not to notice."

"It would not be proper to repeat."

"Why, what was it?"

"It's a disgusting thing to say."

"Well, say it!"

"Grishka the dandy has eaten the candy."

"Tfoo, what a man! I thought it was something serious! You should spit, and pass by."

"I did spit, they shouted all the more."

"But listen, uncle," I said. "You see he complains that he can't get on in this house, send him to Moscow for a time, to that calligrapher. You told me that he was trained by a calligrapher."

"Well, my dear, that man, too, came to a tragic end."

"Why, what happened to him?"

"He had the misfortune," Vidoplyasov replied, "to appropriate the property of another, for which in spite of his talent he was put in prison, where he is ruined irrevocably."

"Very well, Vidoplyasov, calm yourself now, and I will go into it all and set it right," said my uncle, "I promise! Well, what news of Korovkin? Is he asleep?"

"No, sir, his honour has just gone away. I came to tell you."

"What? Gone away! What do you mean? How could you let him go?" cried my uncle.

"Through the kindness of my heart, sir, it was pitiful to see him, sir. When he came to himself and remembered all the proceedings, he struck himself on the forehead and shouted at the top of his voice. . . ."

"At the top of his voice! . . ."

"It would be more respectful to express it, he gave utterance to many varied lamentations. He cried out: how could he present himself now to the fair sex? And then added: 'I am unworthy to be a man!' and he kept talking so pitifully in choice language."

"A man of refined feeling! I told you, Sergey. . . . But how could you let him go, Vidoplyasov, when I told you particularly to look after him? Oh, dear! oh, dear!"

"It was through the pity of my heart. He begged me not to tell you. His cabman fed the horses and harnessed them. And for the sum lent him three days ago, he begged me to thank you most respectfully and say that he would send the money by one of the first posts."

"What money is that, uncle?"

"He mentioned twenty-five silver roubles," answered Vidoplyasov.

"I lent it him at the station, my dear; he hadn't enough with him. Of course he will send it by the first post. . . . Oh, dear, how sorry I am! Shouldn't we send some one to overtake him, Seryozha?"

"No, uncle, better not send."

"I think so too. You see, Seryozha, I am not a philosopher of course, but I believe there is much more good in every man than appears on the surface. Korovkin now: he couldn't face the shame of it. . . . But let us go to Foma! We have lingered here a long time; he may be wounded by our ingratitude, and neglect. . . . Let us go. Oh, Korovkin, Korovkin!"

My story is ended. The lovers were united, and their good genius in the form of Foma Fomitch held undisputed sway. I might at this point make very many befitting observations; but in reality all such observations are now completely superfluous. Such, anyway, is my opinion. I will instead say a few words about the subsequent fortunes of all the heroes of my tale. As is well known, no story is finished without this, and indeed it is prescribed by the rules.

The wedding of the couple who had been so graciously "made happy" took place six weeks after the events I have described. It was a quiet family affair, without much display or superfluous guests. I was Nastenka's best man, Mizintchikov was my uncle's. There were some visitors, however. But the foremost, the leading figure, was of course Foma Fomitch. He was made much of; he was carried on their shoulders. But it somehow happened that on this one occasion he was overcome by champagne. A scene followed, with all the accompaniment of reproaches, lamentations and outcries. Foma ran off to his room, locked himself in, cried that he was held in contempt, that now "new people had come into the family and that he was therefore nothing, not more than a bit of rubbish that must be thrown away." My uncle was in despair; Nastenka wept; Madame la Générale, as usual, had an attack of hysterics. . . . The wedding festival was like a funeral. And seven years of living like that with their benefactor, Foma Fomitch, fell to the lot of my poor uncle and poor Nastenka. Up to the time of his death (Foma Fomitch died a year ago), he was sulky, gave himself airs, was ill-humoured and quarrelsome; but the reverence for him of the couple he had "made happy," far from diminishing, actually increased every day with his caprices. Yegor Ilyitch and Nastenka were so happy with each other that they were actually afraid of their happiness, and thought that God had given them too much; that they were not worthy of such blessings and were inclined to expect that their latter days would be spent in hardship and suffering to atone for them. It will be readily understood that in this meek household, Foma Fomitch could do anything that took his fancy. And what did he not do in those seven years! One could never imagine to what unbridled absurdities his pampered, idle soul led him in inventing the most perverse, morally Sybaritic caprices. My grandmother died three years after my uncle's marriage. Foma was stricken with despair at his bereavement. His condition at the time is described with horror in my uncle's household to this day. When they were throwing earth into the grave, he leapt into it, shouting that he would be buried in it too. For a whole month they would not give him a knife or fork; and on one occasion four of them forced open his mouth and took out of it a pin which he was trying to swallow. An outsider who witnessed the conflict, observed that Foma Fomitch might have swallowed the pin a thousand times over during the struggle, but did not, however, do so. But every one heard this criticism with positive indignation, and at once charged the critic with hard-heartedness and bad manners. Only Nastenka held her peace and gave a faint smile, while my uncle looked at her with some uneasiness. It must be observed that though Foma gave himself airs, and indulged his whims in my uncle's house as before, yet the insolent and despotic presumption with which he used to rail at my uncle was now a thing of the past. Foma complained, wept, blamed, reproached, cried shame, but did not scold as he had done—there was never another scene like the one concerned with "your Excellency," and this, I think, was due to Nastenka. Almost imperceptibly she compelled Foma to yield some points and to recognize some limits. She would not see her husband humiliated, and insisted on her wishes being respected. Foma perceived clearly that she almost understood him. I say *almost,* for Nastenka, too, humoured Foma and even seconded her husband whenever he sang the praises of his mentor. She tried to make other people, too, respect everything in her husband, and so publicly justified his devotion to Foma Fomitch. But I am sure that Nastenka's pure heart had forgiven all the insults of the past; she forgave Foma everything when he brought about her marriage. And what is more, I believe she seriously with all her heart entered into my uncle's idea that too much must not be expected from a "victim" who had once been a buffoon, but on the contrary, balm must be poured on his wounded heart. Poor Nastenka had herself been one of the *humiliated,* she had suffered and she remembered it. A month after the death of his old patroness, Foma became quieter, even mild and friendly; but on the other hand, he began to have quite sudden attacks of a different sort—he would fall into a sort of magnetic trance, which alarmed every one extremely. Suddenly, for instance, the sufferer, while saying something, or even laughing, would in one instant become unconscious and rigid, and rigid in the very position he happened to be in a moment before the attack. If, for instance, he was laughing, he would remain with a smile on his lips; if he were holding something, a fork for instance, the fork would remain in his raised hand. Later on, of course, the hand would drop, but Foma Fomitch felt nothing and knew nothing of its dropping. He would sit, stare, even blink, but would say nothing, hear nothing, and understand nothing. This would last sometimes for a whole hour. Of course every one in the house nearly died of fright, held their breath, walked about on tiptoe and shed tears. At last Foma would wake up feeling terribly exhausted, and would declare that he had seen and heard absolutely nothing all that time. The man must have been so perverse, so eager to show off, that he endured whole hours of voluntary agony, solely in order to say afterwards: "Look at me, I even feel more intensely than you." Finally Foma cursed my uncle for the "hourly slights and insults" he received from him, and went to stay with Mr. Bahtcheyev. The latter, who had quarrelled with Foma Fomitch many times since my uncle's marriage, but always ended by begging his pardon, on this occasion took the matter up with extraordinary warmth; he welcomed Foma with enthusiasm, stuffed him with good things, and at once resolved on a formal breach with my uncle, and even on lodging a complaint against him. There was a bit of land in dispute between them, though they never disputed about it, for my uncle had yielded all claim to it and had freely given it to Mr. Bahtcheyev. Without saying a word to any one, Mr. Bahtcheyev ordered out his carriage, drove off to the town, there scribbled off a petition and handed it in, appealing to the court to adjudge him the land formally with compensation for loss and damage and so to punish contumacy and robbery. Meanwhile next day Foma Fomitch, getting bored at Mr. Bahtcheyev's, forgave my uncle, who came to apologize, and went back to Stepantchikovo. The wrath of Mr. Bahtcheyev when he returned from the town and did not find Foma was terrible; but three days later, he turned up at Stepantchikovo to apologize, begged my uncle's pardon with tears in his eyes, and quashed his petition. My uncle made the peace between him and Foma Fomitch the same day, and Bahtcheyev followed Foma Fomitch about like a little dog, and again said at every word: "You are a clever fellow, Foma! You are a learned man, Foma!"

Foma Fomitch is now lying in his grave near his old patroness; over him stands an expensive monument of white marble covered with lamentations and eulogistic inscriptions. Yegor Ilyitch and Nastenka sometimes go for a walk to the cemetery to pay reverent homage to his memory. They cannot even now speak of him without great feeling; they recall all his sayings, what he ate, what he liked. His things have been preserved as priceless treasures. Feeling so bereaved, my uncle and Nastya grew even more attached to each other. God has not granted them children; they grieve over this, but dare not repine. Sashenka has long been married to an excellent young man. Ilyusha is studying in Moscow. And so my uncle and Nastya are alone together, and are devoted to each other. Their anxiety over each other is almost morbid. Nastya prays unceasingly. If one of them dies first, I think the other will not survive a week. But God grant them long life. They receive every one with a most cordial welcome, and are ready to share all they have with any one who is unfortunate. Nastenka is fond of reading the lives of the saints, and says with compunction that to do ordinary good work is not enough, that one ought to give everything to the poor and be happy in poverty. But for his concern for Ilyusha and Sashenka, my uncle would have done this long ago, for he always agrees with his wife in everything. Praskovya Ilyinitchna lives with them, and enjoys looking after their comfort; she superintends the management of the place. Mr. Bahtcheyev made her an offer of marriage very soon after my uncle's wedding, but she refused him point-blank. It was concluded from that that she would go into a nunnery, but that did not come off either. There is one striking peculiarity about Praskovya Ilyinitchna's character: the craving to obliterate herself completely for the sake of those she loves, to efface herself continually for them, to watch for their every inclination, to humour all their caprices, to wait upon them and serve them. Now, on the death of her mother, she considers it her duty not to leave her brother, and to take care of Nastenka in every way. Old Yezhevikin is still living, and has taken to visiting his daughter more and more frequently of late. At first he drove my uncle to despair by absenting himself from Stepantchikovo almost entirely and also keeping away his "small fry" (as he called his children). All my uncle's invitations were in vain; he was not so much proud as sensitive and touchy. His over-sensitive amour-propre sometimes approached morbidity. The idea that he, a poor man, should be entertained in a wealthy house from kindness, that he might be regarded as an intrusive and unwelcome guest, was too much for him; he sometimes even declined Nastenka's help, and only accepted what was absolutely essential. From my uncle he would take absolutely nothing. Nastenka was quite mistaken when she told me that time in the garden that her father played the fool for *her sake*. It was true that he was extremely eager at that time to marry Nastenka to Yegor Ilyitch; but he acted as he did simply through an inner craving to give vent to his accumulated malice. The impulse to jeer and mock was in his blood. He posed as the most abject, grovelling flatterer, but at the same time made it perfectly clear that he was only doing this for show; and the more cringing his flattery, the more malignantly and openly apparent was the mockery behind it. It was his way. All his children were successfully placed in the best scholastic establishments in Moscow and Petersburg. But this was only after Nastenka had made it perfectly clear to him that it was being paid for out of her own pocket, that is, out of the thirty thousand given her by Tatyana Ivanovna. That thirty thousand she had actually never taken from Tatyana Ivanovna; but not to grieve and mortify her, they appeased her by promising to appeal to her at any sudden emergency. What they did was this: to satisfy her, considerable sums were borrowed from her on two occasions. But Tatyana Ivanovna died three years ago, and Nastya received her thirty thousand all the same. The death of poor Tatyana Ivanovna was sudden. The whole family were getting ready for a ball given by a neighbour, and she had hardly decked herself out in her ball-dress and put on a fascinating wreath of white roses, when she suddenly felt giddy, sat down in an easy-chair and died. They buried her in the wreath. Nastya was in despair. Tatyana Ivanovna had been cherished and looked after like a little child in the house. She astonished every one by the good sense of her will. Apart from Nastenka's thirty thousand, her whole fortune of three hundred thousand was devoted to the education of poor orphan girls and the provision of a sum of money for each on leaving the institution. In the year that she died Miss Perepelitsyn was married; on the death of Madame la Générale she had remained in the family in the hope of ingratiating herself with Tatyana Ivanovna. Meanwhile the petty official who had bought Mishino, the little village in which our scene with Obnoskin and his mother over Tatyana Ivanovna took place, was left a widower. This individual was terribly fond of going to law, and had six children. Supposing that Miss Perepelitsyn had money, he began making proposals to her through a third person and she promptly accepted them. But Miss Perepelitsyn was as poor as a hen, her whole fortune was three hundred silver roubles, and that was given her by Nastenka on her wedding day. Now the husband and wife are quarrelling from morning till night. She pulls his children's hair, and boxes their ears; as for him, she scratches his face (so people say), and is constantly throwing her superior station as a major's daughter in his face. Mizintchikov has also established himself. He very sensibly gave up all his hopes of Tatyana Ivanovna, and began little by little to learn farming. My uncle recommended him to a wealthy count, who had an estate of three thousand serfs, sixty miles from Stepantchikovo, and who occasionally visited his property. Ob-